The Navigator's Children

DAW Books Presents
The Finest in Imaginative Fiction by
TAD WILLIAMS

MEMORY, SORROW AND THORN
THE DRAGONBONE CHAIR
STONE OF FAREWELL
TO GREEN ANGEL TOWER

THE LAST KING OF OSTEN ARD
THE WITCHWOOD CROWN
EMPIRE OF GRASS
INTO THE NARROWDARK
THE NAVIGATOR'S CHILDREN

THE HEART OF WHAT WAS LOST
BROTHERS OF THE WIND

* * *

THE BOBBY DOLLAR NOVELS
THE DIRTY STREETS OF HEAVEN
HAPPY HOUR IN HELL
SLEEPING LATE ON JUDGEMENT DAY

SHADOWMARCH
SHADOWMARCH
SHADOWPLAY
SHADOWRISE
SHADOWHEART

OTHERLAND
CITY OF GOLDEN SHADOW
RIVER OF BLUE FIRE
MOUNTAIN OF BLACK GLASS
SEA OF SILVER LIGHT

TAILCHASER'S SONG

THE WAR OF THE FLOWERS

TAD WILLIAMS

THE NAVIGATOR'S CHILDREN

The Last King of Osten Ard

DAW BOOKS
New York

Jacket illustration and design by Jim Tierney

Maps by Isaac Stewart

Edited by Betsy Wollheim and Sheila E. Gilbert

DAW Book Collectors No. 1969

DAW Books
An imprint of Astra Publishing House
dawbooks.com
DAW Books and its logo are registered trademarks of Astra Publishing House

Printed in the United States of America

Library of Congress Cataloging-in-Publication Data

Names: Williams, Tad, author.
Title: The navigator's children / Tad Williams.
Description: New York : DAW Books, 2024. |
Series: The Last King of Osten Ard ; book 4
Identifiers: LCCN 2024032181 (print) | LCCN 2024032182 (ebook) |
ISBN 9780756418557 (hardcover) | ISBN 9780756418564 (ebook)
Subjects: LCGFT: Fantasy fiction. | Novels.
Classification: LCC PS3573.I45563 N38 2024 (print) |
LCC PS3573.I45563 (ebook) | DDC 813/.54--dc23/eng/20240712
LC record available at https://lccn.loc.gov/2024032181
LC ebook record available at https://lccn.loc.gov/2024032182

First edition: November 2024
10 9 8 7 6 5 4 3 2 1

Dedication

All four volumes of The Last King of Osten Ard are dedicated to my American editors/publishers, Betsy Wollheim and Sheila Gilbert, and to my wife and partner, Deborah Beale.

Acknowledgments

A book (and story) this long requires the help of many people, and I have been very lucky in all my helpers.

Ylva von Loehneysen, Ron Hyde, Angela Welchel, and Jeremy Erman, as Official Canoneers, have steered the creation of these stories and kept me as true to Osten Ard as possible.

Deborah Beale (wife, editor, and Official Beloved), my publishers Betsy Wollheim and Sheila Gilbert, along with Josh Starr and super-clever copy editor Marylou Capes-Platt, have all contributed mightily to this and previous volumes Making Sense and Being Spelled Correctly. My wonderful agent, Matt Bialer, as always helps me to make things work and (more importantly) helps me stay out of trouble.

Isaac Stewart (with research help from Ron Hyde) again made the beautiful maps, for which I cannot thank him enough.

And along the way I have received moral support from many, many people, including Lisa Tveit and the folks on tadwilliams.com, my German and British publishers (and my other publishers, too, of course), our Sunday Reading Crowd scattered across many different countries, as well as my social media friends on several different platforms. Welcome to the Wicked Tribe Worldwide, all of you! Hail the WTW! You are the wind beneath my wobbly, weary wings.

Synopsis of The Witchwood Crown

More than thirty years have passed in Osten Ard since the end of the Storm King's deadly, magical war—a war that nearly doomed mankind. *King Simon* and *Queen Miriamele*, scarcely more than children when the Storm King was defeated, now rule over the human nations from the High Throne, but they have lost touch with their onetime allies, the immortal *Sithi* folk. Then *Tanahaya*, the first Sithi envoy since the end of the war, is ambushed on her way to the Hayholt, the ancient castle that is the seat of the High Throne.

While *Tiamak*, scholar and close friend of the king and queen, works with his wife *Thelía* to save Tanahaya's life, Queen Miriamele and King Simon are away from the castle on a royal progress. Currently they are visiting the neighboring country of Hernystir and its *King Hugh* as part of a royal progress to the north, where Simon and Miriamele are troubled by the behavior of Hugh and his new love, the mysterious *Lady Tylleth*. Dowager queen *Inahwen* warns the royal couple's advisor *Count Eolair* that King Hugh and Tylleth have revived worship of the *Morriga*, an ancient, dark, and bloodstained Hernystiri goddess.

Even while accompanying the royal family on their progress, *Prince Morgan*, the seventeen-year-old grandson of Simon and Miriamele, spends his days drinking and womanizing with his knightly companions *Astrian*, *Olveris* and old *Porto*. Morgan's father, *Prince John Josua*—the only child of Simon and Miriamele—died of a strange illness some years earlier, leaving his wife *Idela* a widow, Morgan and his younger sister *Lillia* fatherless, and the king and queen, John Josua's royal parents, still grieving.

When not nursing the poisoned Sithi envoy, royal counselor Tiamak is collecting books for a library to commemorate the late John Josua, but when his helper *Brother Etan* investigates some of the dead prince's possessions, he discovers a banned and dangerous volume, *A Treatise on the Aetheric Whispers*. Tiamak is filled with foreboding, because the *Treatise* once belonged to the wizard *Pryrates*, now dead, who collaborated with the *Storm King Ineluki* to destroy humanity, though they ultimately failed.

The threats to Simon's and Miriamele's peaceful reign are increasing. In the icy north, in the cavern city of Nakkiga beneath the mountain Stormspike, the ageless ruler of the Norns, *Queen Utuk'ku*, has awakened from a years-long magical slumber. Her chief servant, the magician *Akhenabi*, summons the High Magister of Builders *Viyeki* to an audience with the queen, who declares her intention to attack the mortal lands again. The queen leads a strange ceremony that resurrects *Ommu*, one of the chief servants of the Storm King, though Ommu was thought to have perished forever during the Norns' failed attempt to destroy the Hayholt and the mortal kingdoms.

In Elvritshalla, the capital of Rimmersgard, King Simon and Queen Miriamele are reunited with their old ally *Sludig* and his wife *Alva*, as well as their dear Qanuc friends *Binabik* and his wife *Sisqi*. They also meet the trolls' daughter *Qina* and her betrothed, *Little Snenneq*.

The royal progress reaches Elvritshalla just in time to say farewell to *Duke Isgrimnur*, who dies shortly after their arrival. His last request to Simon and Miriamele is that they renew their search for *Prince Josua* (Miriamele's uncle, Simon's mentor, and John Josua's namesake) and his twin children, *Derra* and *Deornoth*, who mysteriously vanished twenty years earlier. Later Little Snenneq, who is Binabik's apprentice, meets Prince Morgan and predicts that he will become as important to Morgan as Binabik became to Morgan's grandfather, King Simon.

In a castle in southern Rimmersgard where the royal party is guesting on their way home, Simon realizes he has not dreamed in many days. He consults Binabik, who creates a talisman to help him. That very night, Simon dreams of his dead son and the voice of the child *Leleth*, who had once whispered to him in dreams three decades earlier. Leleth tells him "the children are coming back." After Simon frightens the whole household while sleepwalking, Miriamele destroys the talisman, and Simon again loses the ability to dream.

In the still more distant north, the half-blood Sacrifice *Nezeru*, daughter of Norn noble Viyeki and human woman *Tzoja*, is sent as part of a "Talon" of Norn warriors to retrieve the bones of *Hakatri*, brother of Ineluki, the defeated Storm King. Nezeru and her fellows, commanded by their chieftain *Makho*, find the bones being venerated by mortals, but Makho and the Norns take them and escape from the angry islanders. During the escape, Nezeru fails to kill one of their enemies (a child) and is severely punished for it by Makho.

However, before the Talon can return to Nakkiga with Hakatri's remains, they are met by the Norn Queen's arch-magician Akhenabi, who takes the bones and sends the Talon on a new quest to Mount Urmsheim to collect the blood of a living dragon. To aid in this dangerous feat, he sends with them an enslaved giant named *Goh Gam Gar*.

While traveling eastward towards Mount Urmsheim, the Norn Talon encounters a mortal man named *Jarnulf*, a former slave in Nakkiga who has vowed to destroy the Norns and their undying queen, Utuk'ku. Because the Talon has lost its Echo—their trained communicator—Jarnulf, hoping to further his own private aims, convinces the Norns to take him on as a guide. They all travel eastward towards the mountain, last known home of dragons, and on the way Jarnulf overhears the Norns discussing their queen's great plan to defeat the mortals by recovering something called "The Witchwood Crown."

In central Rimmersgard, the Talon encounters the royal party, and Jarnulf is able to get a secret message to Queen Miriamele and King Simon that the

Norn Queen is looking for something called the Witchwood Crown. Simon, Miriamele, and their advisors are alarmed, and they have seen enough signs of renewed hostility from the Norns that they take Jarnulf's message seriously, though this is the first they have heard of him.

In the City of Nabban, a Wrannawoman named *Jesa* cares for *Serasina*, the infant daughter of *Duke Saluceris* and *Duchess Canthia*, Simon's and Miriamele's allies. Tensions in Nabban are rising: *Count Dallo Ingadaris* has allied with Saluceris's brother *Earl Drusis* to fan fears of the nomadic Thrithings-men whose lands border on Nabban. Drusis accuses Saluceris of being too cowardly to properly punish the barbarians and drive them back into the grasslands.

Meanwhile, on the plains of the Thrithings, gray-eyed *Unver*, an adopted member of the Crane Clan, and his companion *Fremur*, participate in a raid on a Nabbanai settlement. As they escape, Unver saves Fremur's life, perhaps in part because Unver hopes to marry Fremur's sister, *Kulva*.

Sir Aelin catches up with the royal party, bringing messages for his great-uncle, Count Eolair. *Lord Pasevalles*, Eolair's temporary replacement at the Hayholt, sends his worries about Nabban, and Queen Inahwen of Hernystir sends news that King Hugh and Lady Tylleth are growing ever more open in their worship of terrible old gods. Eolair sends Aelin with this bad news to a trustworthy ally, *Earl Murdo*. But while seeking shelter from a passing storm, Aelin and his men spend the night in a border castle with *Baron Curudan*, leader of King Hugh's private, elite troops. During a storm that night, Aelin sees the dim shapes of a vast Norn army outside the fort, and then watches Curudan meet with humankind's deadliest enemies. But before Aelin and his men can escape with the news of this treachery, they are captured and imprisoned by Curudan's Silver Stags.

In the Norn city of Nakkiga, Viyeki is sent by Lord Akhenabi on a secret mission to the mortal lands with his Builders, but he is accompanied by a small army of Norn soldiers as well. Tzoja discovers that with Viyeki gone, her life is threatened by her lover's wife, *Lady Khimabu*, who hates Tzoja for giving Viyeki a child, Nezeru, when Khimabu could not. Tzoja knows she must escape if she wishes to live.

As Tzoja thinks of her past with the Astaline sisters in Rimmersgard and her childhood in Kwanitupul, it becomes clear Tzoja is actually Derra, one of the lost twins of Prince Josua and his Thrithings wife *Vorzheva*. Tzoja flees to Viyeki's empty lake-house in a cavern deep beneath the city.

Their royal progress finally returned to the Hayholt, Simon and Miriamele ask Tiamak to honor Isgrimnur's dying request with a new search for Prince Josua. Tiamak sends his assistant Brother Etan south to try to discover what happened to Josua when he disappeared twenty years earlier.

Meanwhile, challenged by Little Snenneq, Morgan climbs Hjeldin's Tower, the Hayholt's most infamous spot, and is almost killed. He believes he saw long-dead Pryrates while he was atop the tower, and swears Little Snenneq to secrecy.

With evidence of the Norn resurgence everywhere, Simon and Miriamele realize these ancient and magical foes are too powerful to face alone. They decide to try to contact the Sithi, especially their old allies *Jiriki* and *Aditu*. At Simon's urging, Miriamele reluctantly agrees to send their grandson Prince Morgan with Eolair and a host of soldiers to Aldheorte Forest to find the Sithi and return their poisoned messenger Tanahaya for more healing.

Viyeki travels south from Nakkiga toward mortal lands, accompanied by an army of Norns who plan to attack the mortal fortress of Naglimund. Viyeki is told that he and his Builders are going to excavate the tomb beneath the fortress of the legendary Tinukeda'ya *Ruyan Vé*, called "the Navigator," and salvage his magical armor, though Viyeki does not understand how this can happen without causing a war with the mortals. *Tinukeda'ya*, also called "Changelings," came to Osten Ard with the Sithi and Norn, though they are not the same as these other immortals. In Osten Ard, the Tinukeda'ya have taken on many shapes and roles.

Prince Morgan and Count Eolair finally contact the Sithi at the edge of Aldheorte Forest. The immortals have abandoned their settlement of Jao é-Tinukai'i and their matriarch Likimeya was attacked by humans and has fallen into a deep, magical sleep. *Khendraja'aro*, of the ruling Sithi Year-Dancing House, has declared himself Protector of their people and refuses to help the mortals in any way, causing friction with Likimeya's children, Jiriki and Aditu. Aditu is pregnant, a rarity among the Sithi. The father is Yeja'aro, nephew and militant supporter of Khendraja'aro.

In the Thrithings, Unver challenges and kills his rival for Fremur's sister Kulva. But Kulva's brother, *Thane Odrig*, does not want to give his sister to an outsider and slits her throat instead. Unver kills Odrig and flees the Crane Clane to return to the Stallion Clan of his mother Vorzheva. Unver, we learn, is actually Deornoth, the other of Josua and Vorzheva's twins. When Unver demands his mother tell him why he was sent away and where his sister has gone, Vorzheva says he was sent away by order of her father, *Thane Fikolmij*, and that Derra ran away shortly after.

Thane Gurdig, husband to Vorzheva's sister *Hyara* and Fikolmij's successor, comes to attack Unver, and in the confusion Vorzheva kills her now old and infirm father, Fikolmij. A giant flock of crows appears out of nowhere to attack Gurdig and his allies, causing many Thrithings-folk to declare that Unver may be the new Shan, the universal monarch of the Thrithings. Unver kills Gurdig, and is then declared the new thane of the Stallion Clan.

Far to the northeast, the Talon and Jarnulf manage to capture a small, young dragon, but then the mother dragon appears. During the struggle Chieftain Makho is badly burned by dragon blood and one of the other Talon members is killed, but the rest manage to escape and begin dragging the captive young dragon down the mountain.

Eolair and Morgan are returning from their embassy to the Sithi to their camp beside Aldheorte Forest, but discover that their party has been attacked and all the soldiers wiped out by Thrithings-men, some of whom are still there, looking for victims and pillage. Eolair and Morgan become separated and the prince ends up lost back in ancient Aldheorte.

Back in the Hayholt, Queen Miriamele and King Simon are invited to attend an important wedding in populous and troubled Nabban. Hoping the presence of the High Throne will help solve the problems between Duke Saluceris and his brother Earl Drusis, Simon and Miriamele accept the invitation. With the increased threat of the Norns and disturbing news from Hernystir they cannot both go to Nabban, so they decide Miriamele will attend the wedding while Simon stays in the Hayholt.

Royal counselor Lord Pasevalles meets his secret lover Princess Idela, John Josua's widow. When she gives him a letter from Nabban he had dropped, Pasevalles sees the seal is broken and fears she has read the letter. He pushes Idela down a flight of stairs and when the fall does not kill her, he breaks her neck with his boot.

In Aldheorte Forest the onetime Sithi envoy Tanahaya at last awakes from her terrible illness and is reunited with Jiriki and Aditu. Despite her recovery, the future seems dark. It is clear that the Norn Queen Utuk'ku intends war on both the Sithi and the human world.

Synopsis of Empire of Grass

Osten Ard has fallen into confusion and struggle after years of peace. And at a time when *King Simon* and *Queen Miriamele* most need each other, they are far apart.

While Simon remains in their castle home, the Hayholt in *Erkynland*, Miriamele is at sea, headed for *Nabban* to attend the wedding that will unite two powerful families. *Drusis*, feuding brother of *Duke Saluceris*, is marrying young *Turia Ingadaris*, whose family are the duke's greatest rivals. But before Miriamele can even begin to worry about Nabbanai politics, she gets the terrible news of a death back home, her daughter-in-law, *Princess Idela*, who (although everyone thinks it an accident) was murdered by the Lord Chancellor, *Pasevalles*.

At the Hayholt, Simon has to deal with not only the death of his daughter-in-law, but the disappearance of grandson *Prince Morgan*, the heir to the throne. Morgan and *Count Eolair*, after a mission to meet with *Jiriki* and *Khendraja'aro* of the *Sithi* people, have been attacked by *Thrithings-Men* on the broad grasslands west of Erkynland. Eolair has been captured and Morgan has disappeared into the vast Aldheorte Forest. While the old knight *Sir Porto*, and the four trolls—*Binabik*, *Sisqi*, their daughter *Qina*, and her betrothed *Little Snenneq*—hunt for Morgan, the lost prince is in real danger of starving in the forest until he saves a squirrel-like animal he calls *ReeRee* and nurses her back to health. Living in the trees with ReeRee and her troop of creatures that he names *Chikri*, he learns to survive in the unfamiliar environment.

Count Eolair is taken by his bandit captors to the Thanemoot, where all the Thrithing-folks gather at mid-summer every year. This year the most powerful thane, *Rudur Redbeard*, has heard reports about *Unver* (born "Deornoth," one of *Josua*'s and *Vorzheva*'s twin children) who many of the grasslanders think might be the *Shan*, a great leader foretold in legend. Jealous Rudur captures Unver and sentences him to torture and then exposure, but after being brutally flogged, Unver survives being chained to a pole overnight, and there are signs that wild wolves have come to bow before him—or that is the story that his friend *Fremur* and Unver's mother Vorzheva make sure the other Thrithings-folk hear. Now in a difficult position, Rudur tries to poison Unver, but somehow the shaman *Volfrag* gives Rudur the wrong cup and Redbeard himself drinks the poison. With Rudur dead, Unver is freed and is acclaimed the Shan of the Thrithings people.

While all this is happening, *Queen Utuk'ku* of the *Norns*—the Sithi's equally immortal kin—seems to have designs on mortal territory, even planning to renew outright conflict with the mortals despite their disastrous loss in the Storm King's War. The Norns make a bargain with *King Hugh*, the mortal king of Hernystir, who allows them to cross his lands in secret, but this betrayal of humankind is discovered by *Sir Aelin*, Count Eolair's young relation. Hugh's soldiers try to imprison Aelin and his men, but they escape, meaning to warn others of Hugh's treachery and the approaching Norn army.

Meanwhile, High Magister *Viyeki*, an important Norn leader, is beginning to have real concerns about what Queen Utuk'ku plans—he does not think another war with the mortals is a good idea after the terrible defeat the Norns suffered in the last one. But he is one of the few with doubts, and it soon becomes clear that the Norns are going to attack the mortals' important fort, *Naglimund*.

Sir Aelin and his men race to Naglimund to warn the defenders, but on the same evening they arrive, the Norn armies also show up. The battle is brutal but swift, with the Norns throwing down Naglimund's walls and killing most of its defenders. The only mortal survivors are those Viyeki claims he must have as laborers to fulfill his given task of opening the grave of *Ruyan the Navigator*, hero of the Tinukeda'ya people (or "Vao"), a changeling folk who came to Osten Ard with the Sithi and Norns thousands of years earlier on the *Eight Ships* when their shared homeland, the *Garden*, was destroyed by a deadly, unstoppable force called *Unbeing*.

Viyeki's mortal concubine *Tzoja* was born "Derra," and is Josua's and Vorzheva's other lost twin. After Viyeki has left Nakkiga on his mission for the queen, Tzoja faces retribution from Viyeki's murderous wife, *Khimabu*, but escapes and goes into hiding in the depths of Nakkiga, where she meets a strange, deformed group called *The Hidden*. Tzoja is eventually captured, but to her surprise, instead of being given to a vengeful Khimabu, she is instead assigned as a healer to Queen Utuk'ku because of Tzoja's previous experiences with the Astaline sect. Utuk'ku, the only living being who saw the Garden, is suffering both from sheer age and the loss of the *Witchwood Trees*, whose fruits have extended her life for thousands of years. And when Queen Utuk'ku leaves Nakkiga for the first time in memory, headed for captured Naglimund, she takes not just Tzoja but hundreds of Norn nobles with her into mortal lands.

Back in the Hayholt in Erkynland, King Simon and others have learned of the destruction of their embassy to the Sithi by Thrithings raiders, as well as the disappearance of Count Eolair and the royal heir, Prince Morgan. Since he thinks the new Shan of the grasslands, Unver, may be holding Morgan hostage, Simon sends out an army under Morgan's other grandfather, *Duke Osric*, to negotiate with Unver for Morgan's return. Meanwhile, Unver Shan has purchased Count Eolair from the bandits who captured him, intending to use the Hernystirman as an envoy to negotiate between himself and the High Throne of Erkynland. But instead Eolair is rescued by *Sir Astrian* and *Sir Oliveris*. As they escape Unver's camp, Eolair tries to convince Vorzheva to come with them, since Simon and Miriamele have been hunting for her and her missing husband, Prince Josua, for years. But Vorzheva refuses and attacks Eolair with a knife. She accidentally stabs her own sister *Hyara*, then blames Eolair, who escapes. Unver and the rest of the Thrithings leaders consider this an act of treachery by King Simon, and when a battle is provoked between Duke Osric and the grasslanders, Unver decides he must invade Erkynland to avenge what he sees as King Simon's double-dealing.

In Nabban, far to the south, Queen Miriamele meets with the elders of the *Niskies* and is told that they (and other descendants of the Tinukeda'ya or Changeling race, who came from the lost Garden with the Sithi and Norns) are having powerful dreams in which they are called to go north. But Miriamele has greater worries, and soon finds herself in the middle of a deadly rivalry between Duke Saluceris and powerful House Ingadaris (into which the duke's brother, Drusis, has just married) that threatens to turn into a civil war. While mobs of the two houses' supporters clash in the streets of the ancient city, and as Miriamele discovers lies and treachery even within the duke's own household, Drusis is murdered and Saluceris is naturally blamed for it. The dead man's widow, child-bride Turia Ingadaris, tells Miriamele that she should leave Nabban, because violence is coming. It is more of a threat than a friendly warning.

In Aldheorte forest, where Prince Morgan has been living with little ReeRee and her tree-dwelling troop of Chikri creatures, he is separated from his small allies when they climb the steep hills into a mysterious valley full of fog and odd creatures. Before Morgan can follow them along the valley floor, a gigantic, monstrous ogre chases him through the mist and he only survives because he is saved by *Tanahaya*, the Sithi envoy sent to the Hayholt in *The Witchwood Crown*, who was attacked on her way to the castle and almost died. Morgan's own mission with Count Eolair returned her to her people, who have cured her, and on her way back to Erkynland she has stumbled onto Morgan's trail and decided to investigate. But she is not the only one. A group of Norn soldiers are tracking Morgan as well, but he and Tanahaya escape and flee the valley. She leads him to what should be a place of safety, the hillside home of her mentor, *Master Himano*, but they discover that the Norns have been there first and have murdered her old teacher. Tanahaya finds a parchment on Himano's body that suggests the Norns are seeking witchwood seeds that were buried under the Hayholt long ago, back when it was the Sithi stronghold called *Asu'a*. Tanahaya is desperate to get this information to Jiriki and *Aditu*, her two close Sithi allies, but she has no Witness—a magical device for communication—and so leads Morgan toward the ancient Sithi city of *Da'ai Chikiza*, hoping to find a Witness there. But they are captured by the current inhabitants, a breakaway Sithi sect called *The Pure*, and because Morgan is a mortal, he is threatened with execution. But when Tanahaya tells the Pure of Himano's death and the parchment, they reluctantly allow her to use a Witness to inform Jiriki about the witchwood seeds that may be hidden beneath the Hayholt. She has time only to tell him that it seems likely Utuk'ku will try to conquer the Hayholt, then they are interrupted by a force of Norn soldiers attacking Da'ai Chikiza. In the ensuing fight, Tanahaya manages to bring down the ceiling of the chamber, killing many Norns, but she and Morgan and all the others are buried under collapsing stone.

Not far away, Aelin and his few remaining men escape Naglimund only to be captured in Aldheorte. But they are fortunate: their captors are Sithi, not Norns.

Back in the Hayholt, Simon and *Tiamak* and Tiamak's wife *Thelía* are struggling with many problems. Tiamak's helper *Brother Etan* is away in the south searching for news of Prince Josua, missing for many years, but *Bishop Boez* informs them that he has discovered many thousands of gold pieces are missing from the royal treasury. All the news seems bad—Simon has just heard of the civil war flaring in Nabban, and is frightened for Miriamele, who is still there.

And in fact, things have gone from bad to worse in Nabban. Angry citizens, enflamed by several mysterious murders and the propaganda of House Ingadaris, now storm the ducal palace. Duke Saluceris is killed by the mob, but Queen Miriamele helps the duke's wife, *Duchess Canthia*, to escape with her two children and *Jesa*, the children's Wrannawoman nurse. Miriamele gives Canthia her wedding ring so that Simon will know the message the duchess carries is truly from her, but then Miriamele herself barely escapes the mob and the destruction of the palace. Miriamele must ride north alone, through wild country, in a desperate attempt to get back to Erkynland and safety. But she is attacked by bandits, and though she escapes, her horse is killed and Miriamele falls down the hillside and is struck senseless. Canthia and Jesa are even less lucky. Their carriage is chased by Thrithings mercenaries and set on fire. The duchess and her little son are killed, with Canthia burning to death in the wagon after it is hit with flaming arrows. Canthia's friend Jesa manages to escape the carriage with infant *Serasina*, but the two of them are now stranded in an unfamiliar land and still being mercilessly hunted.

In Aldheorte forest, Binabik and the other trolls are searching for Prince Morgan, but the Norn invasion of Da'ai Chikiza prevents them from finding him. They have also discovered that many people and creatures—humans, ghants, even kilpa—are moving north as if drawn by some invisible force. They decide to split up, Binabik and Sisqi to take news of what is happening south to the Hayholt, their daughter Qina and her betrothed Little Snenneq to continue searching the forest for Morgan.

Inside the conquered fortress of Naglimund, Queen Utuk'ku herself has arrived—the first time she has left her mountain city of Nakkiga in living memory. Viyeki, his Builders Order, and his conscripted mortal slaves open the ancient tomb of Ruyan the Navigator and find the Tinukeda'ya lord's fabled armor. In a strange ceremony, Utuk'ku's Order of Song sorcerers put the bones of the Storm King's brother *Hakatri*, burned by dragon's blood and in terrible pain until his death, into Ruyan's armor. (The bones had been found and retrieved earlier by Nezeru and her Norn companions.) Then the dragon that Nezeru and the rest captured on Urmsheim is sacrificed and the blood is poured into armor as Queen Utuk'ku invokes a terrible spell. *Jarnulf,* a mortal who insinuated himself into the Urmsheim expedition but then left afterward, is hoping to have a chance to kill the Norn queen with an arrow from a high spot overlooking the ceremony, but the forces Utuk'ku unleashes are so terrible that Jarnulf is overcome with terror and flees. Even Viyeki, who had already seen the resurrection ceremony that brought *Ommu the Whisperer* back to the world, is sickened when Ruyan's armor comes to life, inhabited now by Hakatri's tormented spirit. The resurrected Sitha lets out a cry of horror so dreadful that it kills birds flying overhead.

In the Hayholt, and already overwhelmed by terrible news—the Norn attack on Naglimund in the north, Unver's grasslanders invading over the western border—Simon and his closest advisors learn that a corpse has been found in the ashes of a carriage on the border between Nabban and Erkynland. The body inside was burned beyond recognition, but it wears Miriamele's wedding ring. Simon is devastated, and all Erkynland is plunged into mourning for their beloved queen.

Synopsis of
Into the Narrowdark

At the end of the previous volume, *Empire of Grass,* King Simon, ruling alone from the Hayholt in Erkynland after his beloved wife Miriamele had gone south to the troubled capital of Nabban, and with his grandson (and heir) Prince Morgan lost somewhere in the great Aldheorte Forest, Simon then received news (and seeming proof) that Queen Miriamele had died trying to escape a political uprising. Simon was, and remains, absolutely devastated, but he is the monarch and must go on for the sake of his people.

In truth, though, Miriamele has survived and escaped Nabban, though she is alone, lost, and on foot, trying to make her way north to the Hayholt. Along the way, she is attacked and almost drowned by a river creature called a *Kallipuk* but saved by a fisherman named *Agga.* However, she quickly realizes she has been made a chained hostage by this unstable stranger, who has visions of a near-future event to which he has been "called." He plans to make Miriamele his wife in the coming new world he imagines.

Prince Morgan, lost in the ancient Sithi city of Da'ai Chikiza, has been captured by a mysterious *Hikeda'ya* (Norn) soldier. His captor is Nezeru, the half-mortal daughter of Viyeki and Tzoja. She has been unfairly proclaimed a deserter by her own Norn military order and has been caught between them and her other enemies, the city's Sithi defenders, as the Norns attack Da'ai Chikiza. She is determined to use Morgan as a shield to help her escape, but along the way, Morgan is impressed by Nezeru's fighting skills and the enmity between them thaws a bit.

Tanahaya, the Sithi woman who had been accompanying Morgan, survives the fighting in Da'ai Chikiza despite being buried under a fallen roof. After strange, symbolic dreams and a fight to escape the wreckage, Tanahaya realizes that she is pregnant.

Back at the Hayholt, Simon and his chief advisor Tiamak learn of some very disturbing problems with the royal accounts—much gold has secretly been stolen from the treasury. There are only a few people who could be responsible: Simon himself, Tiamak, Duke Osric, and the acting Hand of the Throne, Pasevalles. Simon's other trusted advisor, Count Eolair, decides to return to his home country of Hernystir because of the growing strangeness of Hernystir's King Hugh, and rumors that Hugh is dabbling in old, dark magics. But when he reaches his home in Hernystir, Eolair is arrested by King Hugh's soldiers and taken away.

King Simon also learns that a battle against the Thrithings-men in the east of Erkynland has gone badly, and that Duke Osric and many Erkynlandish troops are under siege by the Thrithings leader Unver Shan in a castle called *Winstowe.* Simon and his advisors decide an army must be sent to relieve them. Much against Tiamak's counsel, Simon (not much in love with life after Miri's apparent death) insists on leading the army to Winstowe.

But after Simon and the others ride out from the Hayholt toward Winstowe, the chancellor who revealed the thefts of the crown's money dies from poisoning before the thief can be discovered, and things at the Hayholt very quickly go from bad to worse. Pasevalles, who is the thief of the royal exchequer and the murderer of Simon's and Miriamele's daughter-in-law, Idela, tries to arrest Tiamak and his wife Thelía so he can blame his crimes on them, but they have escaped just before he arrives at their chambers, and nobody knows where they have gone.

In Aldheorte forest, after a narrow escape from the Norn conquest of the Erkynlandish stronghold of Naglimund, Count Eolair's young relative Aelin is rescued from the Norns by Jiriki and Aditu. Aditu is traveling to *Anvi'janya* to lead a crucial year's-end ceremony, while Jiriki is trying to help the Sithi fighters in the distant Narrowdark Valley. *Ayaminu* of Anvi'janya and Yeja'aro, the father of Aditu's unborn child, are with them. Jiriki wants to send Aelin and his men back to Hernystir because of the troubles there and sets Yeja'aro the task. Yeja'aro is angry at being given the job, but even though he had earlier (mistakenly) tried to strangle Aelin, he and the mortals set off together.

Viyeki, the head of the Norn Builders' Order, has been sent by the impossibly ancient Norn Queen, Utuk'ku, to ride north along with her royal descendant, *Prince-Templar Pratiki*, to perform an important task, and though Viyeki still is not told what exactly that task is, he finds himself getting along with Pratiki and even admiring him a little.

In the Aldheorte Forest, Simon's troll friend Binabik and Binabik's wife Sisqi find themselves separated from their daughter, Qina, and her betrothed, Little Snenneq. Binabik is bitten by a snake, and he and Sisqi cannot search for the younger trolls until he recovers. Meanwhile, in another part of the forest, Qina and Snenneq are seeing creatures like kilpa and ghants that do not belong so far north, but seemingly summoned toward some unknown goal. The two trolls also meet an odd pair of Tinukeda'ya, *Kuyu-Kun* and *Tih-Rumi*. Kuyu-Kun calls himself the "Voice of the Dreaming Sea"—the keeper of Tinukeda'ya lore and history—and claims that he has seen in prophetic dreams that everything is coming to an end. This news does not cheer anyone.

Jesa, the onetime friend and child-nurse to the Duchess of Nabban, survives the Duchess's murder by Thrithings mercenaries during their escape from Nabban and is able to rescue her friend's child, infant Serasina. Together, Jesa and the baby try to make their way north through southern Erkynland, hoping to reach the Hayholt, where Jesa knows that Miriamele, who she much admires, is queen. On the way, she is found by a seeming ally, *Viscount Matreu*, whom she knows from Nabban, but Jesa realizes that Matreu must have been complicit in the Duchess's murder, and tricks him into falling into a ghant nest where he finds an unpleasant end.

Back at the Hayholt, Princess Lillia, Simon and Miriamele's younger grandchild, secretly follows Pasevalles and discovers a hidden door leading down into the undercroft of the Hayholt, but when she enters to explore, the door shuts on her and she is trapped there.

Simon and his allies ride to Winstowe, where they help to push back the Thrithings-men, and Simon challenges the younger Thrithings leader, Unver Shan, to single combat. At a critical moment, with the appearance of Unver's mother, Vorzheva, Simon suddenly realizes that Unver Shan is the son of his old ally Prince Josua, Miriamele's uncle—Josua and his entire family have been missing for decades. After declaring that he cannot fight against Josua's son, Simon bares his breast to Unver; a moment later, believing he has been stabbed through the heart, Simon falls down, insensible.

The Sitha Hakatri, the long-dead brother of Ineluki the Storm King, has been brought back to life by the spells of Queen Utuk'ku, who sets out to convince him of the lie that mortals destroyed his family in order to use him for her own purposes. Hakatri, confused by his resurrection and the return of the terrible pain that had ruined the last years of his living existence—he was badly burned by the blood of a dragon trying to save his brother Ineluki—is willing to do almost anything to return to oblivion and escape the dreadful pain that has gripped him once more. He exists only as a sort of spirit, kept contained in the armor of Ruyan the Navigator. Ruyan was the most famous of all Tinukeda'ya, and helped conceive, build, and captain the Eight Great Ships that brought the Tinukeda'ya, *Zida'ya* (Sithi), and Hikeda'ya to Osten Ard after Norn philosophers had created and unleashed a terrible something called Unbeing on the Garden where they all lived, which swallowed up and eventually destroyed their ancient home.

Tanahaya escapes from Da'ai Chikiza and spends several days searching for Prince Morgan, because she feels responsible for bringing the young mortal there, but when she cannot find him, she begins to head north, hoping to reach the city of Anvi'janya, where she knows her closest friend Aditu will be going to preside over the Year-Dancing Ceremony, a sacred gathering that occurs only once every sixty or so mortal years. She finds Aditu and Ayaminu—the semi-ruler of Anvi'janya—on their way there and joins them. She begs for news about Jiriki, Aditu's brother (and Tanahaya's lover), and is told he has gone north to fight with the Sithi against Utuk'ku's armies at the mysterious place called *Tanakirú*, deep in Aldheorte Forest at the northernmost end of the Narrowdark River valley.

As for King Simon, thought dead by many, after a series of dreams in which he meets and apparently speaks with Jiriki's and Aditu's mother, Likimeya—who in the real world remains in a deathlike sleep—Simon discovers that he is not dead at all, but instead has suffered an apoplexy, and now finds himself a prisoner deep under the Hayholt, with the traitor Pasevalles his jailer. Pasevalles taunts Simon with the true story of how he has waited a long time to bring down Simon's and Miriamele's kingdom, and of his murder of Idela and various other terrible crimes. Simon, chained and helpless to fight back, has no choice but to hear the traitor gloat.

In the southern part of Erkynland, Jesa of the Wran, with little Serasina, has discovered Miriamele and helped her escape from her kidnapping. Chased by a furious Agga, they lead him to his death at the webbed hands of the Kallipuk Agga was keeping alive until he was ready to skin it. They then make their way toward the Hayholt, but do not tell anyone who they are, because Miriamele learned of Pasevalles' treachery back in Nabban, and she does not know who truly rules the Hayholt now. Along the way, they hear news of Simon's supposed death fighting at Winstowe. Miriamele is stunned and heartbroken, but she is still the queen and must continue on to the Hayholt for the sake of her people.

The mortal Jarnulf, once Nezeru's companion after he joined her group of Norn soldiers, has left that company to pursue his real goal—the death of Utuk'ku—but fails when his arrow seems to pass right through her as she leads a mighty army of Norn Sacrifice soldiers south toward the Hayholt. Jarnulf is captured and is about to be interrogated by the Norn magician Akhenabi, but he avoids giving away all the secrets he knows by using the old, dried dragon's blood he had found while helping the Norns capture a living dragon (later used to raise Hakatri in a magical ceremony). By plunging his finger into a pot of the blood, he suffers such pain that Akhenabi cannot read his thoughts. When Jarnulf is sent back to his cell, which he shares with the giant Goh Gam Gar, he discovers the blood has burnt off the tip of his finger.

Jiriki has reached the Narrowdark Valley, where he meets with his uncle Khendraja'aro, but Jiriki has now learned of Utuk'ku's march southward into mortal lands and tries to get his uncle's help to defend the mortal castle, the Hayholt, against her attack. Khendraja'aro at first refuses, because they are fighting the rest of the Norn army there, but at last lets Jiriki recruit a few other Sithi to go south with him to help Jiriki's mortal friends. (Jiriki does not know anything of what has happened to Simon and Miriamele.) This small force then sets out to travel the long road to Erkynland and the Hayholt.

Nezeru's mother, Tzoja, who we have learned was one of the twin children of Josua and Vorzheva, so long missing, has been recruited for her mortal healing knowledge to work directly for Queen Utuk'ku until the Norn Queen leaves captured Naglimund, supposedly to lead the Norn army south to the Hayholt. Tzoja and her fellow slave, *Vordis*, aid Jarnulf, who has escaped from his Norn captors, but though they help Jarnulf stay away from the soldiers, they are all still prisoners of the Norn army, and are forced with the other slaves and Norn nobles to leave Naglimund and march north in a great group toward the Narrowdark Valley, with no idea of why this is being done to them.

Morgan and Nezeru, mortal and Hikeda'ya warrior, have wandered into a strange relationship, and have even become lovers, though insists nothing more than convenience is behind it, though Morgan is more than a bit smitten with her. They make their way into the Narrowdark Valley, because she wants nothing to do with either side—she is hunted by her own people her people's enemy, the Sithi—but soon find that the Norns are beginning to make their way into the Narrowdark in force.

When she and Morgan finally reach the valley, they encounter the much-rumored *uro'eni*, a monstrously huge ogre tall as a church steeple, though they can see little of it in the darkness in which it always appears. They barely escape being crushed and Morgan saves Nezeru at the last moment, which complicates their already odd relationship, since previously it has generally been her saving him

In a cell under the Hayholt, Simon thinks he has been rescued when Jiriki's relative, the Sitha Yeja'aro, arrives to give him a message, but the message is of no use to Simon in his current predicament and Yeja'aro, willing to do only exactly what Jiriki told him to do, refuses to help Simon escape, but leaves him a Sithi witchwood knife to kill himself if he chooses. Simon is not pleased but does his best to use the knife to get free from his shackles, but only manages to remove one.

Meanwhile, also beneath the Hayholt, but even deeper, Simon's young granddaughter Lillia has been struggling to survive, staying alive by eating the food put out to trap her by the *Red Thing*, a mysterious and deadly being who has set snares, flung nooses, and set out poisoned nails all over the undercroft of the castle, and can somehow manipulate the passageways by moving walls around. Lillia survives a physical attack by the creature and, while fleeing, finds an upward route and follows it, desperate to find safety.

South of the Hayholt, Jesa and Queen Miriamele have reached the loyal Erkynlandish city of Meremund. Miriamele makes plans to take a small army to the Hayholt to defeat Pasevalles, whom she now blames for Simon's apparent death as well as other crimes. Jesa insists on going with her and bringing the baby, and Miriamele reluctantly agrees.

Tanahaya, Aditu, and Lady Ayaminu reach Anvi'janya, a Sithi city set in a great cavern in a mountain, and Tanahaya tells Aditu that she is carrying Jiriki's baby. Aditu is pregnant too, but much farther along, and Aditu makes a prophesy about Tanahaya's coming child. But Tanahaya is upset with both her dear friends Aditu and Jiriki when she learns the secret behind the struggle for Tanakirú in the far-away Narrowdark Valley, a place forbidden to all Sithi centuries ago by Amerasu Ship-Born, greatest of the Sithi matriarchs, who died during the Storm King's War. But Tanahaya loves her friends, and does her best to forgive, though it is hard to have lived with a lie for so long. The secret of Tanakirú is not revealed to the rest of us at this point, though.

A messenger comes to Anvi'janya to report that the Sithi fortress in the Narrowdark has been overwhelmed by a Norn army led by an undead warrior—Nezeru's former chief, Makho—and that Aditu's and Jiriki's uncle Khendraja'aro has been killed. The few remaining Sithi have retreated to the northernmost end of Tanakirú at the head of the valley in a last-ditch stand against Utuk'ku's forces, though even those who know the valley's secret still do not understand why the Norn Queen wants to possess Tanakirú so badly.

In the Hayholt, the monk Brother Etan—after returning with the news of what happened in Winstowe (Simon's apparent death) and discovering that Tiamak and Thelía have fled Pasevalles' clutches and disappeared—has been made a prisoner as their accomplice. Pasevalles has left the Hayholt, supposedly to bargain with Queen Utuk'ku, but shortly after that an astonishingly large Norn army appears at the Hayholt, overcomes the meager defenses, and Norn soldiers rush in and begin to set the Hayholt on fire. Etan manages to escape, then does his best to help others in danger from the apparently unstoppable Norn attack.

At the same time, as the castle begins to burn, little Lillia finds her way up out of the undercroft and into the dungeon, where she finds her grandfather Simon, who has won a fight to the death against one of Pasevalles' henchmen despite having one arm still shackled, using the knife Yeja'aro had left. She unlocks his remaining shackle and together they climb up out of the dungeons only to discover the castle in flames and a vast Norn force surrounding it. Simon encounters Jiriki, who has led his Sithi followers to the Hayholt but has been overwhelmed by Norn Sacrifice soldiers. Almost as soon as they are reunited though, Simon and Jiriki are both astonished to discover that the thousands of Norns who surrounded the castle gate have abruptly disappeared, along with Queen Utuk'ku, as if by magic. Only a few Norn corpses remain, though the burning of the castle is very real.

A bizarre, supernatural figure wrapped in burning bandages stumbles toward them. This is Ommu the Whisperer, another creature resurrected from death by Utuk'ku, and as the terrifying thing approaches them, it collapses. A moment later Simon's granddaughter cries out that something is inside her. Ommu's spirit has leaped from the dying, burning body into Lillia.

And in the far distant northern mountains around the Narrowdark Valley and Tanakirú, Magister Viyeki, who has been given the immense task of having his builders tunnel down through a stony peak into the valley below so the Norn Queen's soldiers can attack the Sithi defenders from behind, discovers that the undead Sitha Hakatri, the spirit confined in Ruyan the Navigator's ancient armor, has escaped his sarcophagus and is wandering through the heights. Viyeki (and Prince-Templar Pratiki) still do not know what purpose the revenant Sithi is to serve, but they know they must recover him or they will be executed by Utuk'ku, so they take several soldiers and pursue him. They find him sitting on the edge of a precipice high on the mountain, staring down into the misty valley of Tanakirú and listening to something they cannot hear, but which clearly fascinates the resurrected Hakatri. They bring him back to the camp, the escape thwarted but the mystery still unsolved.

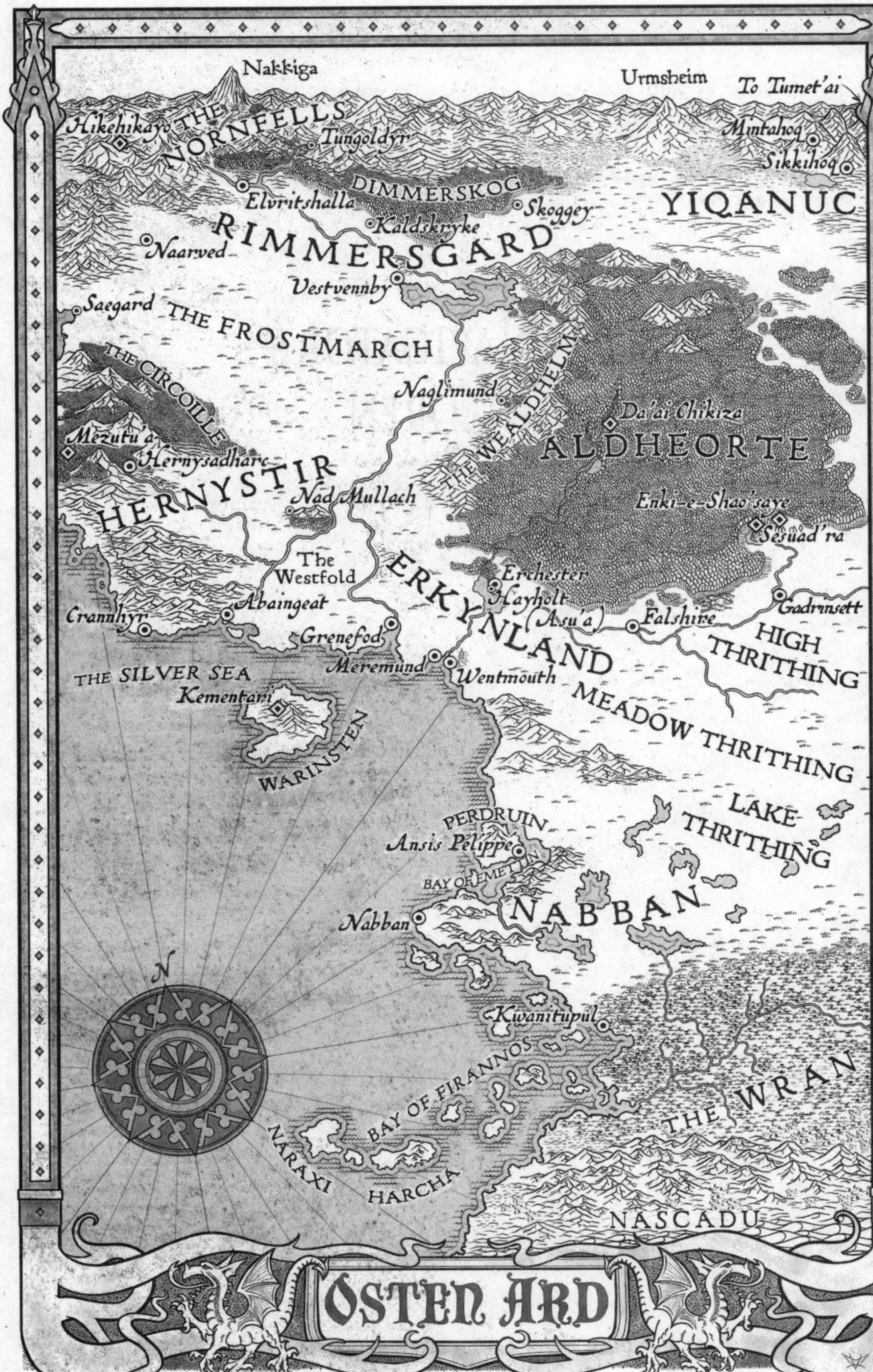
OSTEN ARD
Nakkiga
Urmsheim
To Tumet'ai
Hikehikayo
THE NORNFELLS
Tungoldyr
Mintahoq
Sikkihoq
DIMMERSKOG
Elvritshalla
Skoggey
YIQANUC
Kaldskryke
RIMMERSGARD
Naarved
Vestvennby
Saegard
THE FROSTMARCH
THE CIRCOILLE
Naglimund
THE WEALDHELM
Da'ai Chikiza
ALDHEORTE
Mezutu'a
Hernysadharc
HERNYSTIR
Nad Mullach
Enki-e-Shao'saye
Sesuad'ra
The Westfold
ERKYNLAND
Erchester
Hayholt
(Asu'a)
Gadrinsett
Falshire
Crannhyr
Abaingeat
HIGH THRITHING
Grenefod
Meremund
Wentmouth
THE SILVER SEA
Kementari
WARINSTEN
MEADOW THRITHING
LAKE THRITHING
PERDRUIN
Ansis Pelippe
BAY OF EMETTIN
Nabban
NABBAN
N
Kwanitupul
BAY OF FIRANNOS
THE WRAN
NARAXI
HARCHA
NASCADU

THE NAVIGATOR'S CHILDREN

Foreword

Hakatri

Why did you call me *back into this world?* he asked when he was drawn out of the dark into wakefulness again. Though he had no body of flesh, he still was beset by pain he thought he had left behind with life itself, and also tormented by thoughts that would not leave him. *Why did you pull me out of blessed unknowing? And how do you wield such might, to break the bonds of death itself?*

Ask no questions, Hakatri of the Year-Dancing, the Voice of Three told him, *You have been summoned because only you can do what must be done. You alone of our kind have truly been touched by the blood of the dragon. It burned you, but it also changed you. Only you can create the bridge to the power that I need. You alone of our people can compel that power to serve my great need—that is,* our *great need.*

Many have felt great need since Jenjiyana the Nightingale led us out of the Garden and into the new lands. Hakatri felt a wave of displeasure from the Voice at his mention of Jenjiyana, which puzzled him. *But few of our folk have ever had the craft to drag the dead back from their rest. How is it that I live again—if this can be called life?*

You wallow in your own suffering, said the Voice of Three, and he felt the sting of its scorn. *Do you not see that you have been honored beyond all other Gardenfolk, Hakatri? I convened the Three Who Are One, the mightiest spell that has ever been sung in these lands, just to bring you back. And I must draw continuously on that strength to keep you in the world of the living, though each moment the song goes on, it costs me greatly. But I do it for our people, to save us from the mortal vermin who destroyed our kind and murdered your family. Will you not do all you can?*

It was meant to shame him—even in his dreamlike confusion he could sense that—but instead it struck a spark of resistance. *And which One are you, who speaks for all the Three?*

That is not your concern. The thought-voice softened. *It is very hard for you, as only I, of all who live, truly know. Because I too have traveled in the realms beyond the Veil and know how different things there can be. You are weary at being pulled back into existence, wracked with pain you thought left behind, and confused by both memories and things that seem like memories, but are only dreams. Trust none of them. Hear only my Voice.*

These words put doubt in his mind. Could it be true? Might some of the recollections that had come swarming back to him be phantoms, things that never happened? If so, then what was real? He knew he was Hakatri of the Zida'ya, and he knew he had died after years of suffering, but everything beyond that now seemed doubtful.

Sleep again, prince of Year-Dancing, said the Voice of Three, and he felt a power beyond the words take hold of him. *A great task lies before you, but it is not yet time. Sleep and rest. You have been awakened for a great purpose—one that will bring your people glory and a lasting peace, a purpose that you alone can accomplish.*

The questions that still troubled him began to fray and drift away, like mist dispersed by a fresh breeze. The Voice spoke truly, he decided: too much thought only brought woe. Exhausted, he once more surrendered to emptiness.

Again, he drifted up into waking, but this time he could not discern what had roused him: the Voice of Three had not spoken, but something had reached him in the void as he drifted, neither dead nor alive, neither completely asleep nor truly awake, a mote of suffering in a great and indistinguishable void.

Is it time? he wondered. *Am I to perform the great task the Voice of Three spoke of, and then be released into blessed, blessed oblivion once more?*

Because something had summoned him up from sleepy darkness; he knew, though he could not say how or why he knew it. He tried to search outside himself for what had reached him, but the senses that fed him in life were now being starved. In the darkness of his sarcophagus, sight meant nothing, and the heavy Navigator's helmet of bronze, crystal, and golden wires denied him sound and scent as well. But even in death, he could remember what it was like to feel. Even during the agonizing misery of his life's final days, as his ship sailed pointlessly on and he writhed helplessly in his berth, he had still been able to smell rock roses, rosemary, and the sweet tang of sea buckthorn drifting to him from the nearby coast. Consumed by his pain then, he had barely noticed their scents, but now that he was sealed away in the Navigator's armor like a tomb offering in an ancient, stoppered jar, he remembered and yearned to feed his senses once more.

But *something* had awakened him, he knew, and though anything but insensibility brought him back to terrible pain, suffering was Hakatri's old and familiar companion, and it could not keep him from wanting to feel.

So, deep in his dark prison, he struggled now to learn what had awakened him. After a period of throbbing silence, he found it again at last—a faint but ordered throbbing, something he knew he had never felt before, though it also seemed oddly familiar. Rising then falling, it had the form and cadence of music.

Music? Could the dead hear music?

Hakatri had grown used to floating in darkness and silence except for the occasional intrusion of the Voice of Three. In the brief moments that the Voice had brought him out into the world of the living, he had perceived what lay beyond his prisoning armor as a madness of unrecognizable forms and dim flashes. But now, his attention was caught and Hakatri felt himself truly awake for the first time since he had been dragged back into this strange afterlife. And something in him resonated to the music's distant strains, even longed to join with it. But in his prisoning sarcophagus, it seemed he could only yearn toward it, as a man dying of thirst might ache at the sound of falling water he could not reach.

What is out there, beyond my prison? I want to know. This was an entirely new thought. *Where does that music come from? Am I the only one who can feel its call?*

Driven by an urge he had not felt in so long he could not identify it, he reached out in search of life and movement beyond his unbodied self. As he narrowed his thought, he could even begin to separate these presences into individual clusters. Each one, he realized, must represent some kind of living thing. Many such presences were gathered around him, some moving, some still.

Excited by this new freedom, Hakatri let his thoughts continue drifting outward, out beyond the living creatures clustered around him. As his awareness expanded, he began to sense little eddies of thought from these shades, but the thoughts were small, little more than the rote performances of life among the living.

Could such small, insignificant things as these have brought me back? No, their presences are too small. They must be the living servants of the Voice of Three.

But something other than these shadows had caught at him, had sparked his dreamy interest, and now that he had sensed it, he clutched at it—at first only dimly, as he might once have walked toward a river for some time before recognizing its murmur. But as he fixed his attention on the distant, inexplicable music, he could sense it was something more powerful than anything else around him, even the Voice of Three.

And it sang. Separate and unique from anything else in the dark obscurity of Hakatri's surroundings, it sang. And in some way, the song found a resonance in Hakatri himself, as if the armor that held him captive somehow also heard the song and even rang in sympathy with its slow, complicated music, in matching, chiming tones—an unexpected resonance he could feel in his very being. For the first time, the sheath of crystal and gold in which he was prisoned was bringing something to him instead of merely sealing him away. As he fixed his thoughts on the music, he could hear the inexplicable song more and more clearly. He could *feel* the song. And it called to him.

Hakatri summoned his strength, determined to follow the mysterious song. It was not the play of muscles and bone he fought to accomplish, but a thing much stranger—the pure hardening of will to be used in place of living flesh. Moving his nerveless, fleshless limbs, and thus moving his casing of armor, was a matter of cold calculation, of decision after complicated decision. He lifted the gauntlets that should have had hands inside and tried to remember how his living hands had felt, how they had moved. When the gloves' empty fingers finally spread, he pushed upward on the sarcophagus lid with the force that a body would have given him. At first nothing happened, and Hakatri despaired—he could not even be certain whether his hands and arms had moved at all. He tried again, ignoring the pain that nearly always tormented him even though he had no body to be tormented, as if the dragon's blood had burned not just his skin and bone but his very spirit. Then he narrowed his will until he became nothing except an upward force, and at last the lid tilted and an angled beam of light played across the scratched crystal of his helmet's eyeholes. The weak glow was only the shadowed interior of his wagon, but it felt as redemptive as sunrise.

He could not have guessed how long it took him to struggle out from the massive witchwood box. His armored movements were grotesquely slow and difficult, but the lure of the mysterious song had now supplanted all else. It promised to return everything he had lost—senses, understanding, even his freedom. It called, and slowly, agonizingly, he clambered out of the wagon and into the blindingly bright starlit night to answer that call.

He was ascending now, following the song, although directions like up and down were only important to him because he needed to keep the Navigator's armor upright. Some steps were harder than others, some angles more difficult, but though he often had to stop and consider how to proceed, he continued to climb. The mysterious song grew more and more powerful—a wild, many-voiced music unlike anything he had ever heard. Unlike the Voice of Three, he could hear no individual parts in the song, only a magnificent swelling chorus that strengthened as he clambered upward into the heights, until he could think of scarcely anything else.

But at last he found he could go no farther. Though the lure of the song remained as compelling as ever, a great chasm, a darkness, now gaped before him. The music was so alluring that he almost tried to continue toward it across the naked air, but he knew that though he no longer had a physical body, the armor in which he was prisoned was real and that he could not exist without it. He folded himself into an awkward seated position beside the edge of the cliff and listened to the sublime singing, for a while forgetting everything else.

But it was not long before the strands of another kind of song began to insinuate themselves into the glorious, seamless chorale. This new music seemed out of rhythm with the throbbing perfection that had drawn him here, but it had a power of its own. Desperate to keep his connection to the first, greater music, he tried to shut out the new song but could not. Instead, the interloping melody grew and slid its tendrils into the song that had brought him until he could no longer separate one from the other. He could sense living beings nearby, faint, moving spots of heat, breath, and spirit, and knew that the minions of the Voice of Three had come to take him back into confinement.

But Hakatri did not want to go. He did not want to hear the new song, a paean to surrender, a sluggish stream of ideas and tones that deadened his will and slowly numbed him to everything except the control it sought to impose on him. The glorious and greater music was now gradually but inexorably eclipsed, until finally he could hear it no longer. He felt those living figures surround him and urge him to his feet, then he was guided back downward, though a part of him yearned to stay near the source of the strange, beautiful music forever.

It is unlike anything I have ever known, he thought—*a power beyond all others.*

A new idea came to him then, even as he stumbled in near-blindness—a frightening, exciting idea. *A power like that could be a weapon if I can learn how to wield it. A weapon against the mortals who have destroyed my family and my people. A weapon that will destroy our enemies and avenge us.*

And then I can rest again. The pain will be gone, and so will I.

PART ONE

Dance of Sacrifice

My son is dead, killed by one who shared his blood.
The queen's son died, but lives still in stone;
I see his face everywhere and every day.
The grief felt by our Mother of All is shared by all her people. Bells toll her sadness with each hour,
But my son's search for the Garden is a secret to all but me.

—FROM THE DAYBOOK OF
LADY MIGA SEYT-JINNATA

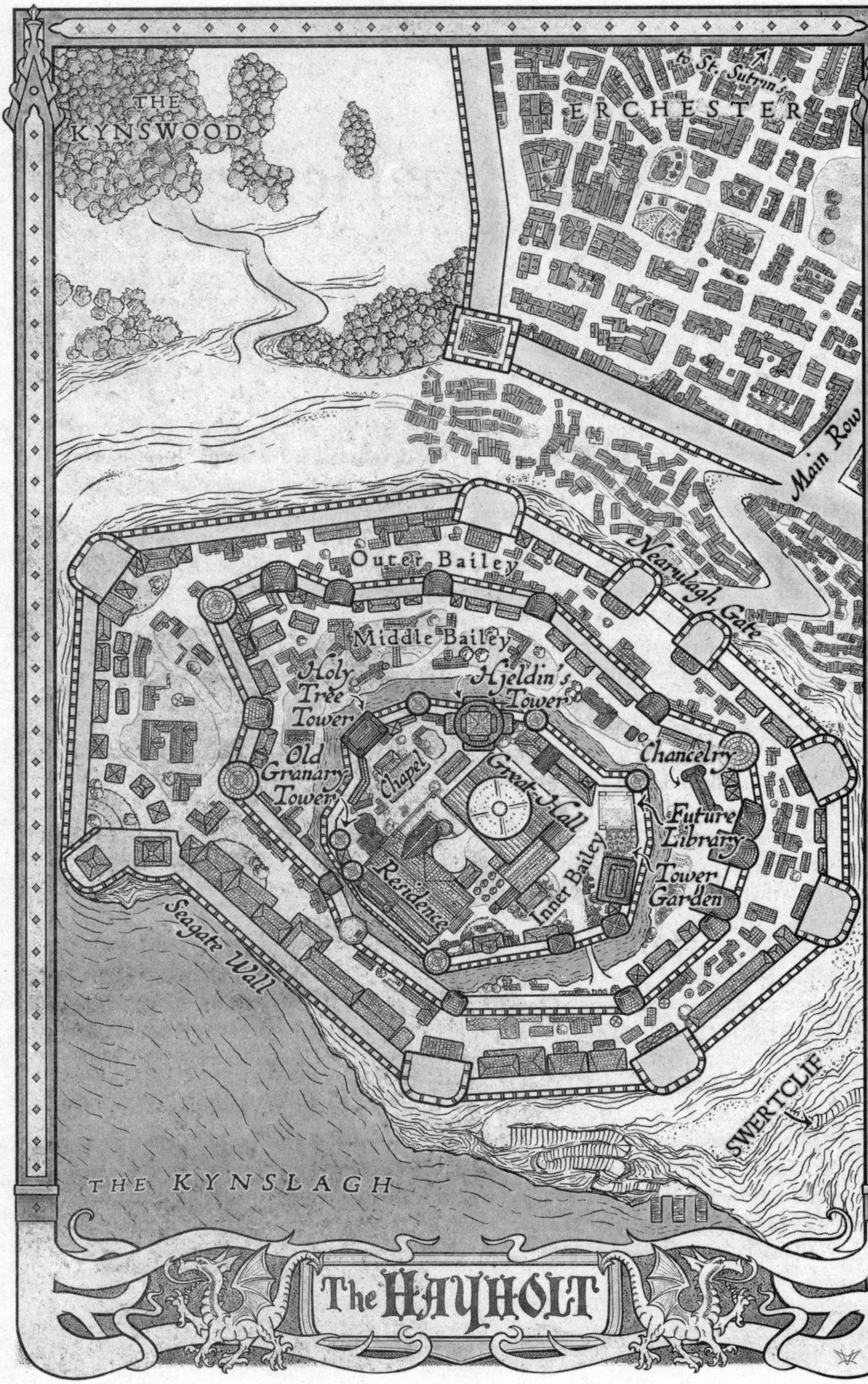
THE KYNSWOOD
to St. Sutryn's
ERCHESTER
Main Row
Outer Bailey
Nearulagh Gate
Middle Bailey
Holy Tree Tower
Hjeldin's Tower
Old Granary Tower
Chapel
Great Hall
Chancelry
Future Library
Residence
Inner Bailey
Tower Garden
Seagate Wall
SWERTCLIF
THE KYNSLAGH
The HAYHOLT

1

They Bite Fierce

Fincher, the captain of the *Elysiamansa* was a thick, bewhiskered man with a maimed left hand. He spoke surprisingly softly most of the time, except to his crew, at whom he bellowed like a madman about what seemed to Jesa the most mundane shipboard matters.

"Three bells!" he would howl so loudly that Jesa had to move away from him. "'Ware that bar!" And when she would try to make her way from one end of the pitching ship to the other, he would sometimes shout "Wet deck, m'lady!" so loudly from right behind her that she could have sworn he had crept up on her just to do it.

For someone who had spent much of her life in and around boats, Jesa was finding it difficult to enjoy the voyage. The cog on which she and the queen sailed—along with quite a few fighting men and almost as many sailors who seemed always up in the ropes, whistling like birds and swinging like monkeys—rose up in the front and the back so far that it almost dizzied Jesa to look over the bow rail at the churning river below. In her childhood the boats had all been flat things, usually poled or rowed by one person, and so low that the younger Jesa could even trail her hand in the green Wran waters, at least until her father or uncles reminded her about the crocodiles.

On the second day, Jesa joined Queen Miriamele and Captain Fincher on the high castle-shaped structure at the rear of the ship—which end, she had learned, was called *the stern*. Since she had Duchess Canthia's little Serasina in her arms, Jesa kept her feet planted solidly on the deck and well away from the ship's rail. "Why are they rowing when yesterday the sail was up?" she asked the captain. "I can feel wind and it seems no less strong."

"Ah, there is a good question, m'lady," said Fincher in a gentle, serious voice. "The answer is simple enough. Yesterday, we set sail with the sea tide under us. Today we must row upriver because the Gleniwent is against us. Hoy!" he suddenly shouted, making Jesa jump. "Beshrew me, what are you about there? Mind that yard!" He saw her put her hand to her pounding heart and was all apologies. "So sorry, m'lady. Meant no harm. Just those be-damned skiving sailors." He made a fretful face. "Sorry for the cursing, Y'r Majesty. It's not often we have the tender ears of royalty on board. 'Fact, it's never happened before."

"Do not worry, Captain. You should hear my husband when he is in a rage. Once Archbishop Gervis fainted dead away at one of Simon's outbursts—" Her smile faltered.

Jesa quickly said to Captain Fincher: "If I am not impolite to ask, sir, what happened to your hand?"

Fincher looked at the extremity in question for a moment, as if he had forgotten it. The two smaller fingers were gone, puckered lumps of flesh all that remained. "Ah, that. Well, m'lady, it were a rope. They bite fierce, 'specially when they're tied to a sinking anchor. Begging y'r pardons and hoping that weren't too unpleasant to speak about."

"She asked, Captain," said Miriamele. "No need to apologize."

He nodded and thanked her, then made his excuses, bowed low to the queen, and clattered down the stairs to upbraid the oarsmen in a voice like a war-horn.

Miriamele was silent for a while, but before Jesa could summon up a subject of conversation to distract her from her sorrows, the queen said, "And how is the little one? Is she feeding well?"

"Yes, Majesty. Many people in Meremund told me sea air improves the appetite, and it seems true for her . . . but not for me." She shook her head. Jesa had been sick several times the day before, and the only reason the pitching voyage had not sent her to the rail again was that her stomach was empty.

"It's not sea air, though," said the queen. "It's river air here, since we're on the river. I don't know if that works the same way." She sighed. "It is so slow, traveling against the current! It will be dark long before we reach Storm Cove."

Jesa did not know anything about either Storm Cove or the broad Kynslagh Bay itself, of which the cove was just a nick in the shoreline, but she knew that was the place Miriamele planned to leave the ship before advancing on the castle with soldiers. She had wondered why they would not simply berth at one of the castle docks until she realized that Miriamele did not expect a friendly welcome.

How strange, Jesa thought. *For a queen to come home after most of a year and expect, not a welcome from her admiring subjects, but an attack by those left to protect the place.*

Miriamele was stroking Serasina's small head where the blanket exposed it. "I must have been mad to let you talk me into this arrangement," she said, then gave Jesa a shrewd look. "I know you would not leave the baby unless you had to—but why were you so bent on coming with me?"

Jesa thought for a moment before answering. "Because I trust no one else."

The queen was surprised. "What do you mean? Lady Dorret would have treated you well, as would many others, especially with you under my protection. And did you not trust Duchess Canthia and others in Nabban?"

Jesa was concerned that she had confused the queen, but she was not entirely certain she understood it herself, so she did her best to order her thoughts before replying. "I trusted them not to hurt me, Majesty. I trusted Canthia because I was her friend since we were children—though she forgot that sometimes." At the thought of her friend and mistress, tears came to her eyes. Holding Serasina with both arms she could not wipe them. A moment later, to Jesa's astonishment, the queen reached out and gently rubbed the tears away with the back of her finger.

"You loved the duchess, didn't you?"

"Of course. She was a good person. She did not deserve—" And then the tears came again, this time in floods. At last she handed the baby to Miriamele so she could wipe her eyes properly. "I am sorry, Majesty."

"Nothing to apologize for. But you still haven't answered my question. Why do you trust me more than anyone else? Because queens—rulers in general—are notoriously bad risks for trust. For one thing, we seldom see people as individuals because we are always thinking of them as subjects, as a nation."

"But that is it," Jesa said. "You are not that way. Everyone in Nabban saw me as a servant, or as Canthia's childhood friend, or as a woman of the Wran. Not one of them ever looked at me and saw *me*."

Miriamele looked skeptical. "If you are saying I saw the truth of who you really are, Jesa, I'm afraid you're mistaken. Only in the time we have spent together have I come to know how clever and brave you are."

"But you did not make a mask for me to wear."

"I don't understand."

Jesa was frustrated. She had set out to tell the queen how much she respected her but had made a muddle of things. "It is what we say in the Wran—or at least on Red Pig Lagoon—when someone thinks they know a person before they do. That you never did, Majesty. When you met me, you did not see just another servant, just a dark-skinned girl from the swamp. What you did not know at first you waited to find out. That is . . . rare."

The queen looked at her for a long time. "And to think Westerling is your second tongue. You astonish me, Jesa. And you shame me, too. I would like to believe I am the person you think I am—I would admire such a person too—but I am afraid I am far more flawed than that."

Jesa laughed. "Which is just what such a person always says when others praise them."

"Do you see what I mean?" said Miriamele, and now she was smiling too. "Too clever by half." She started to hand back Serasina, then stopped long enough to plant a kiss on the child's half-exposed forehead. "Look at her. On a ship, in a country she's never been in, and she's just sleeping like . . . like . . ."

"Like a crocodile," said Jesa.

Miriamele laughed, startled. "I was going to say, 'like a baby', but it seemed too obvious. Do crocodiles sleep a lot?"

"They pretend. It looks like they are asleep, but truly they are watching."

"I don't think Serasina is pretending to be asleep."

"I know." Jesa smelled the baby, whispered a few words to her before turning to the queen again. "And anyway, she will not bite. No teeth yet."

Miri sighed. "It's hard to wait. I want to see my home again. I want to see my . . . my people again." She shook her head as if to clear away cobwebs. "Enough of that. How do you fare? Do you think you could eat something?"

Jesa shuddered. "Not yet. But the baby will be hungry soon."

"I could use a little something myself," said the queen. "Let's go see what Captain Fincher has to offer us."

"Husband," said Lady Thelía, speaking quietly, "you know I am not a fainthearted woman. That is correct, is it not?"

"I have never found you anything but courageous and firm."

"I am pleased to hear that. Then perhaps you will understand that it is not a mere lack of courage that prompts me to say that I am most uncomfortable with this pursuit."

"I do not like it either," said Tiamak. "But the fact remains that something in front of us is bleeding." He lowered his torch. Drops of blood gleamed with reflected light. "Since there is a good chance that whatever is bleeding is the same thing that has tried several times to kill us, I want to find it while it is wounded. These dark places under the castle are perilous enough without us being hunted by an unknown enemy, too."

"You see, that is just my point." She was still whispering, but Tiamak could tell she was on the verge of getting louder, so he stopped and waited. "We are following something that has tried several times to throttle us," she continued. "You have said several times that you think whatever it is may also be responsible for the numerous traps we have so far evaded—mostly by luck."

"And by bundling ourselves up like Qanuc trolls," he said. "That has been much help, at least with the poisoned needles littered about the place."

"This is no beast," she said. "We know that. It has made traps, and it also seems to be using levers and winches to change the paths here beneath the Hayholt. This is a thinking creature."

"I cannot argue with that. In fact, I think I was the one who first suggested it."

She let out a long, exasperated breath. "I want to go back to the safe hiding place we found, Tiamak. I am tired and frightened. I do not want to come upon that thing if it is wounded, whatever it is, madman or clever beast . . . or something worse."

"Neither do I. Still, if we can find where its lair is, we can at least avoid that spot. And if we find it dying—well, then we can perhaps finish it off."

"You think it was caught on one of its own envenomed spikes?"

"I don't know. I thought I saw something else, just before the light blinded me. Another person, but small, like one of Simon's troll friends."

"There are no trolls left in the castle!" she said, just remembering to keep her voice low. "And treacherous Pasevalles would be searching for us if he knew we were down here. Why risk revealing ourselves to anyone?"

Tiamak lowered the torch again. "Ah. Luck appears to have deserted us," he said sadly. "See, the drops are getting smaller. It was a minor wound, it seems." He took another few steps, bending low to the ground. "And now they have stopped altogether."

"Then let us go back."

Tiamak raised the torch and peered at a vast wall of close-packed dirt- and soot-covered stones. "I think we must be close to the base of Hjeldin's Tower," he said. "See, there is what looks like the great foundations of the Inner Bailey wall. We must be somewhere under the southern gatehouse."

"Hjeldin's Tower!" Thelía was horrified. "That cursed spot! That is the last place we should seek. The red wizard's old haunts. And we seem to be chasing his ghost." She made the sign of the Tree.

"I am not superstitious in that way, my dear," he said. "But neither am I completely without fear. That is why I have my knife and torch, and you have that heavy piece of wood that you have been clutching so tightly for so long."

"Do not tease me, Tiamak. I am not in the mood. We have followed this bleeding phantom for what must be hours. Do you still know how to find our way back to our camp?"

"It is not much of a camp," he pointed out. "Everything we brought down we still carry on our backs or in our purses."

"It is a place where we were untroubled by the terrible thing that lives down here," she said flatly. "Tiamak, come back! Where are you going?"

"Just a little farther, my dear. I see an opening in the wall at the end of the corridor."

"Oh, you man!" She hurried to catch up to him. "Just because I left the church and my order to marry you does not mean I cannot divorce you. I do not accept Mother Church's authority to yoke me forever to a madman."

He stopped, gesturing for her to come close. "Dear Thelía," he said in a whisper. "If I lead you astray, you will likely not need to divorce me, because one or both of us will be dead. Now, please just stay silent while we explore this chamber, or whatever it is, then afterward I promise I will be led by you—back to our previous camp or anywhere else."

She gave him a furious look that could have set the contents of an alchemical flask boiling, but then lifted the piece of wood back onto her shoulder and followed him along the corridor.

At the opening—a broken stone arch that had collapsed halfway, leaving a space at the bottom big enough to crawl beneath—Tiamak handed her the torch, then got down on his knees and first listened, then sniffed the opening. "If there was anything in here, it has been dead for a long time." He made a face. "It smells dreadful."

"Husband . . ."

"Hand me back the torch." And so, holding it before him, doing his best not to singe his own eyebrows, he crawled through. On the other side he rose to his feet and held up the torch as he turned slowly in a circle. "By the cold, cold hand of She Who Waits," he murmured after a moment of silent shock. "I have never seen anything so terrible."

In mere moments, Thelía had crawled beneath the broken arch and stood beside him. Tiamak heard her gasp. "What hellish place is this?"

At first, crawling, he had been only able to see the bones and filth that littered the floor, like the offal of some fierce carnivore's den. But with the torch held high, the whole chamber was revealed. At the center of the room a square basin was cut into the stone floor, as large as a royal bathtub, with pillars at each corner. The basin was covered with a crusty brown and black stain, but it was what hung above it that held the eye. Two ropes crisscrossed the space over the basin, and from those ropes hung a dozen or more animal corpses, each hanging upside down by tail or hind legs—rats, squirrels, cats, and even a larger, headless torso that looked like it might once have been a hunting hound. But at the very center where the ropes overlapped was the unmistakable shape of a naked human body. It had been a woman, and the throat had been ripped out by something that had left a ragged red wound. The rest of the body, though, was as white as snow under the light of Tiamak's torch.

"Sweet Elysia, Mother of our Redeemer," Thelía moaned. "What devil's work is this?" She stared at the upside-down corpse. "Is it one of the Norns? It is so pale!"

Tiamak took a few steps closer, holding his nose with the fingers of one hand against the awful stench of putrefaction. He lifted the torch close to the dead face. "I think not. By the bits of clothing still hanging from the legs, I would guess it was one of the castle's serving maids."

"But so white!"

"Someone has drained out her blood. I suspect—" He had to pause as his gorge rose, then settled again. "I suspect that is what filled the basin."

"I want to get out of here," Thelía said, in a tone that admitted of no argument. "We must leave. This stinks of sorcery."

"I agree, and we will leave, yes. I want only to—"

Tiamak did not finish.his sentence because something abruptly dropped on him from above, enfolding him like the wings of a huge bat, and he was driven to the ground by the force of it. Before he could begin to understand what had happened, he felt rough claws tear savagely at his neck and face, then his head was rammed again and again into the hard floor, scattering his thoughts and filling his skull with black stars. Then he felt a blow like a blacksmith's hammer, and though it did not strike him anywhere that he could feel it, it reverberated through him. A heartbeat later, the strangling thing slid off him.

When Tiamak could again understand where he was, his wife had hold of his arm and was trying to drag him onto his feet. "Do not pull my arm out of my shoulder," he said in a complaining tone, still not quite certain what was happening.

"Dear God, your eye!" She sounded terrified. "What has that thing done to you?"

He reached up to his brow and felt torn flesh and a pain that was just beginning to throb. His fingers came back wet. "I think I can still see out of it, but I am bleeding badly." He staggered to his feet, and only then became aware of the red thing lying before him. The torch, which had tumbled from his hand, lay on the floor so that the unmoving shape was half lit, half in shadow.

"I hit it as hard as I could," Thelía said. "I smashed its head in. I think I killed it."

"I hope so. If not for the heavy cloth around my neck, it would have torn out my throat. But I am bleeding there, too."

Still groggy and unsure, Tiamak almost fell over before he managed to retrieve the torch, then stood swaying over the ragged red thing that had attacked him. His wounded eye had now swollen closed, and blood from his face and throat spattered on the ground.

"Oh! Husband, you are badly hurt!" He had never heard Thelía sound so close to utter panic. "We must go!"

"Not until I see what this is." He reached out his foot and shoved the thing over onto its back. It was lighter than he had expected, certainly after feeling the strength of those choking fingers, and despite his earlier words against superstition, Tiamak was all too ready to discover that his wife had knocked down some demon. He leaned over and flicked the hood of the ragged garment out of the way, then lowered the torch so he could see, revealing a grotesque face smeared in red and brown and a sagging mouth with only a few teeth, but those few had each been scraped or filed into points. It was horrible, but it appeared to be human. "By They Who Breathe Darkness," Tiamak said in soft astonishment, "I think it is a woman."

"A woman? Who is she?"

"How would I know, wife? She is covered all over in dried blood—I think she bathed in it." His gaze flicked back to the basin and the string of corpses hanging over it. "Oh, gods of my people," he said, "this is a terrible place. And all this time, we were living only a few steps above it all. All this time!"

"We have to leave this place," she said. "And do not even think of hauling that stinking corpse back to our camp so you can examine it, though I do not doubt you would like to."

Tiamak was kneeling beside the body now, turning the head from side to side so that even with only one eye working, he could see the profile, the prominent nose and chin. When the thing's hood fell back, he saw that the scalp was shaved. "Who could it be?" he wondered aloud. "It almost looks as though she imitated the red priest himself. But it is not Pryrates—" Again he stopped, this time because an idea had seized him. "I think I know who this was," he said.

"Tell me after we have left," his wife said. "Your wounds must be foul—they need cleaning. And this place sickens me. I do not want to stay another moment."

But Tiamak was deep in thought and continued speaking as though he had not heard her. "When Pryrates came to the Hayholt, he brought a servant with him, a woman named Munshazou. She is listed in the household accounts once or twice. She lived in Hjeldin's Tower and, I presume, acted as cook and maid for him. She was never seen or heard of again after the Storm King's War and the fall of Green Angel Tower. It was assumed she had died in those last hours, as so many did, but her body was never found."

A tremor shook the walls around them. A scattering of dust and a few small stones fell from above.

"Husband—!"

"It is just an earth-shake," he said, looking down at the motionless, rag-draped body, curled against itself like the shell of a dead spider. "I suspect that this is what has been living down here," he said. "The she-thing that has killed so many animals . . . and people . . . and has bathed in their blood as well." He stared at the gaunt, red-smeared features. "And she was likely responsible for the traps and poison nails down here as well, and thus most likely the murderer of poor Prince John Josua." He shook his head, overwhelmed with a sense of futility. "No monster—at least, not a ghost or demon—except this horrible woman, Pryrates' servant."

"Husband, I thought I saw her breathe—"

An instant later, the seemingly dead creature grabbed him, her terrible nails clawing for him once more. Tiamak let out a cry of disgust and fear.

"Not servant!" the thing shrieked in a raw voice that sounded as if it had been long out of use. "Not servant! *MOTHER!*"

He kicked at it, trying to push himself backward, but the red thing clung to his legs. "Get out of the way," cried Thelía. "I will hit her!"

"You all kill my son," the red-painted horror screeched, her few teeth showing against the dark of her throat like the standing stones on Thisterborg. Tiamak managed to snatch up the torch, which had fallen. "My lovely Pryrat. But soon I bring him back. Soon I bring him back!"

Even as she spoke, she tried to pull Tiamak down to the floor, long, scrawny fingers clawing at him. Without thinking, he struck her with the torch. The pitch caught in the tatters of her clothing; a moment later, she was ablaze. Screaming in a way that sounded like nothing human, the thing he had named Munshazou straightened, batting at the fires with her hands, but the fire only strengthened as it blazed up her rotting clothes. Still screeching, the red thing turned and staggered toward the far corner of the collapsed chamber. In that fearful, expanding moment Tiamak assumed she was mad with pain from the flames and would batter herself against the far wall like a trapped fly, but an instant later she tumbled over an invisible edge and vanished. Tiamak and Thelía both hurried forward and found what had obviously once been a well, though the cover had long since fallen to pieces.

Tiamak got down on his knees and cautiously stretched his head over the hole, ignoring the blood that ran down his face and dripped from his chin. He could smell damp below him, but even holding out the torch he could see no water below and heard no sound of a splash, only darkness and silence.

"She has escaped!" Thelía cried. "She is free again. Tiamak, we must leave!"

"I do not think she has escaped anything," he said. "She was burning alive, and the well is deep. She could not survive such—"

Again the earth trembled, and this time the shaking was so strong that the broken arch through which they had entered scraped and shuddered. The stones settled so that the opening became half the size, and in the torchlight Tiamak could see showers of stone fragments and cracks running jaggedly through the stonework.

"Out," he said, but his wife was already crawling out through the now smaller opening, and Tiamak did not hesitate to follow her.

On the other side they stood in the corridor for a moment, but stones and dust were falling here too, and some of the pieces shaken loose from the shadows above were as big as a child's head. "You are badly hurt. We must go back to our camp," Thelía said. "Oh, husband, hurry!"

"No." Tiamak shook his head. "We cannot go back down. Do you not smell the burning?"

"It's your torch," she said, but he shook his head again.

"No, it is more than that. See?" He held the burning brand high. At the upper edge of its light, trails of smoke seeped down through the cracks in the vaulted ceiling. Already the air was thick with it. "We cannot go down. Somewhere above a fire must have broken out—a bad one, hot enough to crack the very stones. We must go up if we want to live."

"But Tiamak, Pasevalles and his soldiers will seize us if we reveal ourselves."

"Place that danger against all those thousandweight of stone falling on us." He grabbed her arm to get her moving back down the way they came. The rocky groaning grew louder, as did new and frightening percussive noises like the clapping of giant hands. "We must get out before more walls come down."

Even as he spoke, another crash sounded behind them and a great gust of smoke and tumbling debris flew out of the archway from the chamber they had just quitted, stopping all conversation. Tiamak yanked his wife's scarf up over her nose and mouth, then did the same with his own. Hand in hand inside a small sphere of torchlight, surrounded by darkness and smoke, they ran along the shuddering passageway.

Miriamele did not know what hour of the clock it was, only that she had been asleep. She struggled upright, tatters of dream falling away. Someone knocked again.

"Who . . . ?" asked Jesa, rolling over and pulling the baby to her.

Still muzzy with sleep, Miriamele reached for the knife she kept close, then put her bare feet on the floor. "Come in, then," she called.

The sailor in the doorway was holding a hooded lantern. Miri lifted her hand to shield her eyes from the glare. "Begging pardon, Your Majesty," he said. "Captain Fincher and Lord Norvel ask you to join them on the foredeck."

She wiped her eyes. "What time is it?"

"An hour left of the early watch, Majesty. Sun's just coming up." He hesitated. "Captain asks you to put this on, if you please, Ma'am." He held out what looked like a heavy bundle.

"What is happening, Majesty?" asked Jesa from the bed.

"Nothing. Go back to sleep." Miriamele took the offered garment, thinking it was a heavy thick cloak against the cold weather, but the weight of it surpassed any cloak she had ever lifted: she almost dropped it in surprise. "This is armor!"

"Yes, Your Majesty. Captain says please put it on, then come to the foredeck."

"I do not know how to do it," she said. "Help me."

If it had not been the middle of the night, and if she had not been worried about why the captain had summoned her, the following moments would have been rare comedy. Though Miriamele wore a night-dress and had pulled a shawl around her shoulders, the lieutenant kept averting his eyes as though she were naked, which meant he was more of a hindrance than a help with the sagging, overlarge shirt of chain mail.

"Let us hope that I do not have to run away from anything," she said as the sailor tried blindly to fasten the catch on the back of the armor. At last he found it and stepped away, still looking tactfully in any direction except where she stood. Miriamele felt weighed down already, as if she had worn one of her court dresses into the bath.

"Lead on," she said. "No, walk behind me until we are on deck, please, in case I fall backward down the stairs."

At first all she could see was black water and an eastern horizon delicately washed with the pink and orange of early dawn. She followed the lieutenant up to the raised forecastle where the captain and Baron Norvel were waiting for her. When they saw her, the baron bent a knee and the captain bowed.

"It is early, Captain Fincher," she said. "I did not expect to be awakened yet, and I think you might have found me something more comfortable than this to wear." She lifted an arm weighted with a wide, armored sleeve.

"My apologies, Majesty," he said. "But I did not want to take chances."

"Y'do look a bit like St. Ebbe, drowned in a barrel," said Norvel.

"Thank you, Baron. That makes me feel holier, if not warmer." She turned back to the captain. "May I ask why you called for me?"

Fincher was staring over the side at the black water. The rosy glow on the horizon tipped the waves with light. "Look, Majesty. Do you see that?"

Miri advanced to the rail of the forecastle and looked down. A confusion of slippery, gleaming shapes fell and rose among the swells. She thought they must be dolphins. "Yes. And—?"

"Those be kilpa, Majesty. At the mouth of the Kynslagh."

She stared as one of the shapes rolled in the water, revealing the gleam of eyes and the black hole of a mouth before slipping beneath the waves again. She felt a moment of disgust and unease but was not badly frightened: half a dozen kilpa were not much danger to a ship carrying two hundred armed soldiers. "I have seen kilpa before, Captain. And though it disturbs me to see them so far north of their usual haunts, I have already heard many tales of this. Was it truly necessary to call me from my bed—apologies, *your* bed, since we have taken your cabin—to see it?"

"I did not call you out in the cold to see kilpa, Majesty," said Fincher.

For the first time, she noticed the tremor in his voice and her heart sank a little. "Then what?"

"You will see in a moment, when the Gleniwent bends again at the inlet and we pass the headland."

As the captain spoke, Baron Norvel moved closer as if to shield her. For the first time since the knock on the cabin door Miriamele's heart began to race.

She did not have long to wonder. Within a few moments they slid past the great black cliff that had been blocking their view and the *Elysiamansa* entered the Kynslagh.

"Mother of God," she said in a hushed, choked voice. "Mother of God, what is that? What has happened?" The horizon had not been turned orange by the light of dawn, she now saw, but by flames mounting to the sky from the far shore.

"I fear it is the Hayholt, Majesty," said Norvel, his voice empty of his usual cheer. "It is on fire."

Miri stared at the flames whose towering heights almost seemed to scorch the low clouds, an inferno that stretched from high Swertclif all the way to the seawall edging the Kynswood. "God save us," was all she could say.

2

The Thing Inside

Simon stood by the ruins of the Hayholt's Nearulagh Gate and held his granddaughter by her shoulders, afraid to pull her near. He felt as if his heart was being ripped in two. The smoldering, bandaged demon that had come with the Norns had somehow left its own failing body and leaped into this precious child, and it was all he could do not to try to shake it out of her.

"Lillia," he said. "Grandfather's here."

"Something is gravely wrong," said Jiriki. The Sitha was striped with cuts and smears of blood but seemed more or less whole.

"I know that! That horrible burning thing has got into Lillia, somehow!" Simon was frantic. "Get the demon out of her!"

"Grandfather, make it stop! I don't like this," the child said in her natural voice, that of a frightened child only seven years old. She squirmed in his grip, eyes full of tears. "I don't like it!"

Jiriki came and kneeled beside her. He laid his hands on her temples and she quieted. "You are right, Seoman," he said. "I can feel another presence, but it is like nothing I know. Perhaps the wisest healers among my people can help her, but none of them are here."

"Yes, Jiriki, something is gravely wrong," said a voice that was not Lillia's, though it issued from her throat, her mouth. *"I cannot see all of Utuk'ku's intentions—the queen of Nakkiga has removed herself from me, doubtless thinking me exhausted and useless now that I have done her bidding here—but I can sense that she is full of triumph."*

"What are you?" Simon demanded. "Get out of my granddaughter, you foul thing! I would rather see her dead than possessed by you, hell-creature."

To his astonishment, the raw voice laughed—not a laugh of exulting villainy, or even of contempt, but the sad sound of something disappointed. *"Have you forgotten me so completely, Simon Snowlock?"*

"Who are you? *What* are you?" he demanded, near tears himself.

"You know me well, Simon. You met me first in my hut beside the lake, you and little Binabik, when you were driven out of the Hayholt in your youth."

A bizarre, impossible idea floated into his head. Something in the voice had been familiar, but his terror had kept him from hearing it. "It cannot be. It cannot be." He took a long, shaky breath. "Geloë? Is that truly you?"

"Ah." His granddaughter's head nodded in calm acknowledgement. *"So I am not forgotten after all."*

Startled, Simon set his granddaughter down—she stood stiffly where he put her—and took a step back, heart pounding, sick in his stomach. "No!" he said, holding up his hands as if to ward off an attack. "It can't be. You're *dead*!"

The startlingly cold eyes followed him. *"Death is not as simple as you have been taught."*

To Simon's astonishment, Jiriki dropped to one knee. "Geloë—Ruyan's own, last of the line. Can I hope that you offer us help? Or has the queen of Nakkiga made a slave of you?"

"She did, for a little while. But now I am my own once more—at least while I have the strength to keep my true self hidden from her." She lifted her hands—Lillia's small hands. *"This is hard for me and uncomfortable for Simon's granddaughter. I will try to explain quickly, because time is a luxury we no longer have."*

"Get out of her!" Simon pleaded. "If it's you, Geloë, I can't believe you want to hurt a child this way—frighten her out of her wits. Come out of my granddaughter!"

"Do not be foolish, Simon." The rough voice seemed flat, almost empty of human feeling. *"I cannot leave her or I will cease. There is nowhere else for me to go, and I have worked too long and too hard—and kept myself secret through a thousand horrors—to give up now, when I am most needed."*

"Then whatever you've done, do it to me instead," he said. "You're hurting her. Come into me."

Again, the preternaturally calm expression, a single shake of the head. *"I would not have entered a child if I had any other choice. I did not. Only Lillia has a heart and mind that will still stretch to hold me, that can survive this intrusion without tipping into madness. Please, do not beg me anymore. It is difficult enough for me to do what must be done. It is difficult enough for me to live with what I have already done at Utuk'ku's bidding."*

Jiriki, still kneeling before her, looked up. Simon heard approaching riders, but he was still fixed on his granddaughter and the thing—a thing he still did not understand—that lived inside her now.

"But you were dead," he said helplessly.

"Yes, my body died, or at least I left it behind. But as I told you, it is all more complicated than you can know." She turned toward the approaching riders. *"I can explain all, but now we must hasten north as swiftly as we can."*

"North?" Jiriki said. "I heard you say we had been tricked. Part of that is obvious now—where ten thousand Hikeda'ya Sacrifices stood is now empty air. Was that your doing, Geloë?"

"Yes, and I used up nearly all my strength fashioning that illusion. Utuk'ku sent me here with the few hundred real Sacrifices she was willing to throw away. They are the

ones who burned the castle, and they are the ones who, like Marshal Muyare, were killed when your people came to break the siege."

"But why would the Norn Queen do all that?" asked Simon.

"In part, to divide our forces. Perhaps also for revenge." The childish shape shrugged. *"That may be why they came prepared to burn the Hayholt. Utuk'ku is the oldest, and her ways are hard to fathom. But her greater motive Jiriki knows, though he likely did not recognize it until now."*

Simon turned. The Sitha's golden face had gone pale. "Tanakirú?" Jiriki asked. "The Vale of Mists?"

"Yes. She has decided that she must have it," Geloë said. *"But she tried to make it seem she meant to strike at the Hayholt. She wanted you to bring a sizable portion of your warriors here to defend it."*

"I brought all I could," said Jiriki. "It seems I must be grateful for my people's reluctance to aid the mortals, because if I had got my way, I would have brought many more."

"Counting is foolishness now," Geloë said. *"Every Zida'ya is needed in Tanakirú. Utuk'ku is moving against it in haste and with great force. It may be only days before she has taken the valley and everything in it."*

"I will tell my people here to make ready," said Jiriki, and swung himself back onto his horse, calling to the other Sithi with words like low birdsong as he gathered them together.

"But why?" demanded Simon, still struggling to understand. "Why did you do all this, Geloë? How are you here—alive again? And why were you serving the Norn Queen?"

"Questions I will not try to answer until we are riding north," she said. *"Find a horse. Mount up. I will ride on the saddle before you."*

"But I have only just escaped from Pasevalles' cell! My people don't even know I'm alive." Another, darker thought struck him. "Are you saying there's a war in the north . . . a war against the White Foxes . . . and that you want me to take Lillia there?"

"I do not dare to leave her body, Simon. And without me, even if Jiriki's people were ten times as many, defeat would still be inevitable. You cannot conceive the dreadful price Utuk'ku might exact if she wins."

"But I can't take Lillia there!"

"You can and you must, I fear. There is no other hope for men or Sithi, and the stakes for my own folk might be even higher."

"Your own folk?" Simon felt battered, as if he had been struck in the head over and over, until the world spun around him. "What does that mean?"

"The Tinukeda'ya," she said. *"Though we call ourselves Vao—the changeling folk. I am the last of the Navigator's line, Simon. Ruyan Vé was my many-times-great grandfather, but he is long gone into shadow. All my people's hopes—and all your peoples' hopes, too, both Sithi and mortals—now rest on me . . . and I am weary. So weary that I can barely hold myself together. We must ride now. There is no other choice."*

With the help of the cook Brannan and several soldiers, Brother Etan finally managed to get Aengas down the slippery steps beside the seagate, where other survivors were already gathered, many of them soldiers who had fought to save the castle and failed. As Brannan held a cup of water to his master's lips, weary Etan stared up at the smoke-wreathed spike that was Holy Tree Tower and at the blazing roofs of the throne hall and the royal residence. The monk was full of a curious numbness, though his thoughts were all hopelessness and loss.

All the treasures collected here in this castle, all the history—gone in a single night! It was a catastrophe so huge it would not fit into his thoughts except in pieces. *Oh, merciful God, and the people who lived here!* He looked around the seagate dock and made a rough count. Four dozen souls, five dozen at the most, huddled together as flecks of ash drifted and danced. *Is this all that survived? And have we survived in truth, or will the Norns come now to finish us off?*

"I swear it was the king's ghost come back," he heard one of the soldiers say to a comrade. "I saw him! He was mad—furious!"

And so begin the stories, Etan thought. *We need them to make sense of terrible things. One day, the destruction of this place and the angry ghost of King Simon will be in a book, with no witness still alive to say otherwise.* A new idea came to him with a shock like a body blow. *God preserve us, Lord Tiamak's books are burned, too! He worked so hard to gather that library for so many years, the wisdom of so many minds and so many hands. Now they are all gone.* For some reason this realization finally broke through the monk's numbness and he wept.

Someone patted him on the shoulder. He looked up to see one of the Erkynguard. "Don't cry, Father," the soldier said. "God has gathered them all to Heaven." But the man's own ash-blackened face showed the tracks of tear stains.

Perhaps he has lost his family, Etan thought. *He has surely lost comrades. And yet he consoles me while I weep over books.* But he knew it was not just the books he was mourning, nor even the lost wisdom contained in them, but the loss of an entire world. Just a year ago the king and queen had both been alive and the Norns merely frightening old stories from a bygone time. Now the king and queen were dead and everything was ruined, everything burning, the life Etan had known vanished into swirling smoke and a drizzle of filthy rain.

St. Sutrin's! It struck him like another blow. *Is the great church gone too? Usires our Ransomer, preserve us from such evil! Have the cursed Norns burned down Erchester as well?*

Etan nodded to the soldier who had tried to comfort him, made the sign of the Tree in the air, then began to climb the steps back up to the castle.

"Where do you go, Father?" asked the guardsman in alarm. "It is all burning there."

"It may not be burning everywhere," he called over his shoulder. "I go to find out."

"Godspeed, Father."

"Brother," he said, but quietly. "I am no one's father, but I am meant to be everyone's brother."

Etan returned to the Inner Bailey and climbed a section of the wall that still stood. To his immense relief, he could see that Erchester still seemed to be standing and whole, its buildings red-lit by the castle's rippling flames. Best of all, he could make out St. Sutrin's tall spire still looming above the other structures, limned in scarlet. But other than the glare from the burning castle, no other lights showed anywhere in the city's dark spread. *Have all the people of Erchester run off?* he wondered. *Or are they hiding? But why didn't the White Foxes burn the city too?*

As he tried to make sense of this, he was distracted by movement below him in the westernmost part of the otherwise deserted Middle Bailey, and he saw two small figures holding onto each other as they staggered toward the Kynslagh side of the castle. He wondered briefly whether they were survivors or Norn soldiers, but then his attention was seized by the sloping defensive earthwork that only a short time earlier had been covered with thousands of Norn soldiers. Now they were all gone, the slope empty but for a few dark, fallen shapes.

Etan was thunderstruck. How could such a thing be? How could even the mysterious Norns appear in such numbers and then suddenly vanish? And why? It made no sense at all, and for a moment he could only wonder if he was dreaming—if everything that had happened might have only been a nightmare.

But then his attention was caught once more by the figures struggling across the narrow part of the Middle Bailey. One of them had now fallen to the ground, and the other was crouching beside it, as if praying or trying to shake the other awake.

God reminds me, Etan thought. *I must leave the great matters to others and look to the small.* He looked out across the slope beneath the ruined outwall one more time, wondering if the Norn army were only hiding until survivors showed themselves, but the grassy slope was always kept short: there was no place for even a small company to hide, let alone the massive army that he had seen with his own eyes. It almost seemed as if the Norns had sprouted wings and then, like a monstrous flock of birds, flown away.

As Etan reached the bottom of the staircase, he could see that a battle had taken place at the foot of the stairs—a battle that would never be sung about. Many bodies lay on the ground, most of them ordinary castle-folk, though he saw armored Erkynguards and a few dead Norns as well. The castle people, unarmed men and women, seemed to have been chased toward the stairs by the invaders, then the guardsmen had come down to help them. He made the Tree and said a shortened version of the *Mansa sea Cuelossan* over them all, victims, defenders, and even attackers, not because he could forgive the Norns, but because he was in a hurry to find the survivors he had seen. But as he made his way back out through the Inner Bailey he encountered so many more bodies that he gave up trying to bless them all.

The air was becoming harder to breathe because of the dust from the collapsed tower and the smoke pouring from the blazing residence, but despite burning eyes from the soot, he at last spotted a kneeling figure and hurried toward it. When the hooded shape looked up at his approach with a face full of terror, he was so surprised that he missed his footing, stumbled, and almost fell.

"Lady Thelía?" he cried. "Can it truly be you? Oh, praise Usires, I thought you dead." A new shock followed the first. "And, God's mercy, is that Lord Tiamak there?" He hurried forward to kneel beside her. "Is he badly hurt?"

"I do not know." Thelía's face was pale in those few spots where she was free of dirt and bloody scratches. "He was attacked. The creature who did it is dead, I think, but my poor husband bleeds so much, and he has been getting steadily weaker. Help me, Etan! I am so frightened for him!"

Etan turned Tiamak over. He seemed insensible, and though it was hard to tell through the thick cloth that wrapped him from neck to ankle, Etan could see Tiamak's chest moving up and down. His face and neck were deeply gouged and covered in blood, especially the area around his left eye; so much so that Etan could not be certain the eye was still whole. He did his best to clean the wounds but had nothing to work with except the sleeve of his shirt, which he used to wipe away the worst of the blood. "I think he will live," he told Lady Thelía, "but we must pour some strong wine on those cuts, especially on his face. Let us take him down to the seagate where the other survivors are waiting."

Suddenly Tiamak's good eye opened. "Etan? Is that you? Do not waste time worrying about me—I am only scraped and scratched."

"It is a bit worse than that," he began, trying to keep his voice calm. "You are bleeding badly—"

"Doesn't matter. I need you." He grimaced. "Ah, I wish I did not. I hate myself for this . . . we are all so weary . . ." Tiamak closed his eye again.

"Husband, save your strength," said Thelía.

Etan squatted beside the Wrannaman. "I should be able to carry you to safety."

Tiamak's eye open again. "No! Not yet. Thelía and I will find our way to the seagate, now that you have told us. But I fear I must ask you to do something else for me—oh, forgive me, Brother, because it is something difficult and terribly dangerous."

Etan felt a tightness in his gut, as if a snake had coiled around his innards and squeezed. "What do you mean? And where have you two been all this time?"

"Underneath the castle," said Thelía breathlessly. "When we learned that Pasevalles would arrest us, we took the things we had put aside for such a time, then hid in the ruins beneath the Hayholt. It is another world down there, Brother Etan—a strange and dreadful place."

Tiamak suddenly began to writhe on the ground. For a frightening moment Etan thought he was suffering some fit, but then realized that he was only trying to shrug off the peddler's pack on his back. By the time Tiamak finished his face was bleeding afresh and he was breathing hard beneath his thick clothing. "First, Brother, tell me," he gasped, "did you get my letter to the king at Winstowe?"

So many things had happened, it took a moment for Etan to remember. "The letter. I took it to Winstowe, yes," he said. "But the king did not read it."

"Why not?" Tiamak struggled to sit up. His wife did not seem able to decide whether to help him or force him to lie down again.

"Because, although the king was not wounded, he collapsed during the fighting there. He died shortly afterward."

Thelía let out a sudden cry of grief. Tiamak stared at Etan as though he did not believe him. "The king?" he said. "King Simon . . . is dead?"

"I fear it is so."

"Did you see his body?"

"No, my lord. Pasevalles had me locked up, saying I must have been a party to your treason. But others told me they saw the king's body go to the funerary priests."

Tiamak slowly shook his head. "No. I cannot believe it—but perhaps I only want not to believe it. Pasevalles is a monster. You know that, Etan, do you not? He has been behind many of our troubles, and perhaps was the author of the queen's death as well. Is he with the survivors?"

Etan shook his head. "Pasevalles is gone. Reports say that he rode out with his own guards a sennight ago to try to parley with the Norns."

"To join them, most likely." Tiamak dabbed at his bloody face with his padded forearm, wincing. "If this dreadful news is true, I will mourn Simon when there is time. A most bitter loss—He Who Steps on Sand, forgive me! I should have seen all this much sooner!"

"Husband, you cannot blame yourself," said Thelía. "Pasevalles fooled everyone."

"He had help." Tiamak seemed to find a little new strength. "Our greater enemy Utuk'ku directed him somehow, I feel sure. Now I must make my request, Brother." He paused, slowly turning his head from side to side. "I am so dizzy! Oh, Etan, if I could think of any other way to do this, I would not put this burden on you—"

"What burden? What do you want of me?" Etan was overwhelmed. Trying to tell Tiamak and Thelía what had happened in their absence had only made him more aware of how bad things truly were. "Pasevalles is gone—you can reveal yourself now. There are many waiting down at the seagate dock who will be joyful to know you survive."

"Not all, I'll wager," said Tiamak with a small, grim smile. "But we will make our way there soon enough. First, though, I must pass my burden on to you. Did you know the Sithi were here?"

"Is that who drove the Norns away? Because there were thousands of Norns outside the walls, but they all vanished in a moment, as if they had melted into the air." A moment later the whole of what Tiamak said struck him. "Hold—the Sithi? They were here?"

"It's true," Thelía said. "We saw them from the top of the Granary Tower. When we came out of the tunnels and saw the flames and the dead, we climbed up to better understand what had happened, and where might be safe to go. The Sithi came riding and fell on the Norns."

"They were few," Tiamak said, "but they came on so bravely that for a moment I felt hope, despite the enemy's numbers."

"The Sithi . . ." Etan shook his head. "I saw nothing of this. It must have happened while I was helping Aengas and the others to the seagate."

"My friend Aengas lives? May your God bless you for that, Brother." Tiamak shook his head and tried to rise, but his wife's slender hand kept him down. "But our time grows short."

"What do you mean, time grows short? The Norns are gone now, whatever the reasons. The castle is ruined, but Erchester seems to be largely unharmed."

"You do not understand," Tiamak said. "The world will burn, and Utuk'ku will be the one who puts fire to it. This has only been part of a larger plan, and I do not think even the Sithi can see all her design. That is why the thing I carry must go to them. They must know what I have found."

"Must go to the Sithi? What must? What are you saying?"

Tiamak reached into his pack and pulled out a small wooden chest covered in painted scenes that even the burning buildings were not bright enough to illuminate. "In this box is something that the Sithi must see. It might be enough to end the fighting, or at least to help the Sithi guess at the Norn queen's strategy. It must be given to Jiriki or his sister Aditu—they will know what to do with it."

"What is in it?" A new chill moved through him. "Is it Bishop Fortis's terrible book?"

"No, not that. Something stranger than anything men have made. But it must reach the Sithi."

"You keep saying that, my lord, and it frightens me. Do you mean *I* must take it to them?"

Tiamak looked at him for a long moment. "Do you believe your God watches over you, Brother?"

Etan was caught by surprise. "Of course!"

"I am glad. I am not always so certain of my own gods, but I find myself reluctant to doubt them just now—and we will need all the aid that both your Heaven and mine can provide. Yes, I need you to ride after the Sithi. I do not know where they go, but I can hope they will leave more trace than they usually do, because they will be in terrible haste."

Etan was beginning to feel angry. After everything he had gone through, he was being asked to do still more—and it was something that sounded utterly mad. "Ride after the Sithi? The fastest riders in the world, with horses swifter than even the best the Thrithings breed, while I have no mount at all? And somehow find them when I cannot even know where they are headed? How am I supposed to do such a thing, my lord?"

"Please forgive me, Brother." Tiamak's bloody face twisted in unhappiness. "I would not ask it if there was any other way. I would take it myself if I could."

"You cannot even sit up," said Thelía. "And you may still lose your eye, husband. You are going nowhere."

Tiamak stared at her, but Etan saw no anger, only desperation and fear. Then Tiamak reached past the shredded and bloodied collar of his tunic and fumbled out something that Etan could not quite see except for a length of chain. As Tiamak pulled it over his head he grunted in pain, but he waved away his wife's hands when she bent to help him. "Here, Brother," he said. "This is overdue, I fear, but better late than not at all." He thrust his hand toward Etan.

"What is it?" But even in the dim light, he recognized the golden thing a moment later. "Your League of the Scroll medallion?"

"No—not mine. It is yours now." Tiamak sighed and dragged himself up into a sitting position. A new dribble of blood started down his cheek.

Etan shook his head. "I do not understand. I have seen it many times. It is yours."

"I have wanted to make you a member of our league, Brother. Now I do so—if you will accept it." Tiamak was panting from the exertion of raising himself.

"But this is your badge—!"

"It came to me from another Scrollbearer. If we live to happier days, I can have another made for myself. But you have earned this with your fidelity and your courage. Do you accept it, Etan?"

For a moment he felt his mind sway, as if he stood balanced on a dangerous spot. He looked from the pendant to the small wooden chest. "You wish me to chase the Sithi and give them this box, and then I will be part of your Scroll League?"

Tiamak waved a bloody hand. "No, no, if you accept this, you will be a Scrollbearer no matter what, Brother. Whether to seek after Jiriki and his immortals, that is up to you. I would not force you into such great danger against your will—how could I?"

"But I don't understand any of this." Etan felt short of breath. He was being compelled to a decision that would have been difficult even with a long time to consider. "What is in the box? And how will I ever find the Sithi?"

"I cannot answer the second question, I fear. But you must believe me when I say that time is growing ever shorter and that the errand is vital." Tiamak had clearly used most of his available strength: Etan had to bend close to hear him. "As for what is in the box, you may look for yourself, but you should not do it now. Time is short." He took a ragged breath. "We are all at the end of our powers, dear Etan. But if we stop fighting, our defeat—and worse—is assured."

Etan took the scroll pendant from Tiamak's hand and stared at it. The gold parchment and quill made him miserable, reminding him of all the irreplaceable books that had been destroyed in the Norn attack, but he could not bear to tell Tiamak and Thelía of that loss—they would learn soon enough. "Yes, then. I will take the box to Jiriki—or at least do my best to catch up to them, though I have no idea how I will do it."

"May your God bless you," said Tiamak, and finally lowered his trembling hand. "And may my own gods watch over you, too."

"There are survivors at the seagate," Etan told Thelía. "You can get help there."

She made the sign of the Tree, then helped her husband to his feet. If Etan had not reached out a hand to steady him, Tiamak would have fallen, even with his wife holding his arm.

"Go with God, Brother," Lady Thelía told Etan. "May our Lord watch over you." She looked scarcely better than her husband. Etan could not imagine what had happened to them under the castle but did not have the strength to inquire.

Tiamak was unsteady, holding onto his wife with one hand. He shook his head, his good eye now spilling tears. "Ah, is the king really dead? Is Simon truly gone, or did I imagine that?"

"I wish I could tell you otherwise," said Etan. "By the time I returned from Winstowe, our good king had died from an apoplexy."

Tears were running freely down the Wrannaman's face now. "Even if we survive, we have lost so much!" He reached out and squeezed Etan's hand. "Go now, Brother. Haste is your best chance to find the Sithi before all trace of them is gone. Take the box to Jiriki or his sister—or to whoever now leads the Sithi—and know I that would never have asked you if I saw any other choice. Take care. I cannot bear to welcome another Scrollbearer only to lose him."

The last Brother Etan saw the pair, Lady Thelía was supporting her husband as they both trudged across the Middle Bailey, headed toward the seagate.

Simon still found it hard to believe that Geloë had survived her long-ago death, but here she was, hiding in the body of his granddaughter like a cuckoo's egg in the nest of another bird, though she seemed to have retreated again. He clutched Lillia's sleeping form to his chest and stumbled after Jiriki down the slope below the gate, heading toward Erchester.

"Good God," said Simon. "I don't see anyone in the city at all. Where have the people gone?"

"Fled, or at least many of them have," Jiriki told him. "We saw hundreds upon hundreds crossing the graveyard and filling the roads."

"I understand none of this." A sudden memory surfaced. "Your servant, that Sithi fellow—you sent him to me."

"So Yeja'aro reached you. I am glad. But he is not my servant. He is the father of my sister's child."

Simon had been about to complain about that strangely unhelpful messenger, but a moment later he realized what Jiriki had said. "Your sis . . . do you mean Aditu? Aditu has a child?"

"Not yet. But soon—perhaps even at this moment it is coming."

"Is she here somewhere?" Simon asked, craning his neck to search among the Sithi, who were now gathering on the empty slope where the great army of Norns had stood only a short time before. "It would be good to see her."

Jiriki shook his head. "She has gone to the high city of Anvi'janya to perform the Year-Dancing ceremony, but we will not go there. Our destination is northeast of that place, in a valley called Tanakirú—the Vale of Mists where the Narrowdark River runs—"

Just then, one of Jiriki's fellow Sithi rode up and called to him in the Sithi tongue, a swift, liquid flow of words. Jiriki replied in kind, and for a long moment Simon could only wait.

"I must go look for my kinsman, Ki'ushapo," Jiriki said when the other Sitha had ridden away. "He is missing, and he is not among the fallen. Even his horse is gone."

"I think I know that name," said Simon.

"You do. He met you when you were young. He went to Urmsheim with us, where the dragon's blood scarred you."

"I hope he has not been hurt."

Jiriki's face was even more grim than it had been. "As do I. I cannot leave without trying to find him, but we will have to ride north soon, no matter what. Wait for me here, Seoman."

"I'll go with you. I should discover how many of my people have survived the Norns' attack. They will need me."

Jiriki surveyed him with a doubtful eye. "The castle is still on fire and stones are still falling. It will be dangerous enough for us without having to protect you and the child, too. Also, you look to me as though you are exhausted and very sore."

All too true, Simon realized. The need of the last hours had let him ignore the worst effects of his long captivity by Pasevalles, and even to fight, but that borrowed strength was flowing out of him fast. In fact, by the time he could think of another argument for him to accompany Jiriki, the Sitha and his fellows had already gone.

Simon awoke to Jiriki bending over him. He had fallen asleep sitting up, with a silent Lillia still cradled in his arms.

"I have a horse for you and your granddaughter, Seoman. Mount up."

It was hard to piece the world back together again. "Did you find your friend?"

Jiriki's face was composed, but Simon thought he saw pain, even desperation, in his eyes. "No. We cannot find him on the field or in the outer ring of the castle, and farther in, it is still mostly aflame. But we cannot wait any longer."

"I'm sorry." He remembered now who Ki'ushapo was, a handsome Sitha with pale golden hair, but the thirty years since then had rubbed away almost all the other memories. "But I still don't understand what's happening. Not where we're going, or even why. I should stay with my people. They haven't seen me—they may not even know I'm alive. They are without homes, the castle is on fire . . . and you want to take my granddaughter with you—!"

"Seoman, you are my friend," Jiriki told him. "I would not compel you, and even in this terrible hour I will not steal the child out of your arms. We can talk more of everything that is happening as we ride, but on the living memory of the Garden, I swear that if you do not heed Geloë's words, you may doom us all."

Simon could only shake his head. He knew Jiriki was telling the truth, and despite how unbelievable it all was, he could not doubt that the woman who had died so long ago was now somehow alive in his granddaughter. But it still seemed an impossible choice.

The childish form in front of him stirred. "Grandfather . . . ?"

He pulled her closer. "Lillia? Is that truly you? Oh, thank the Lord!"

"What happened?" She freed one hand from his enveloping embrace and rubbed her eyes. "My head hurts. It feels like I'm ill. I don't want to be ill."

"Bless you, child," he said.

Lillia turned to look up at him. "Why do you sound so strange, Grandfather? And why are you crying?"

"Nothing, nothing. I've just lost too many people that I love."

"I will let you and your grandchild speak to each other," Jiriki said. "But a few moments only. Then we must leave—with you or without you, as we must also do with my kinsman Ki'ushapo."

Simon could not remember having seen Jiriki so cold, so hard-faced, though the Sitha's expression softened as he turned to the child on Simon's lap.

"And I give greetings to you, young Princess Lillia," Jiriki said in a gentler tone. "You have not met me before, but my mother named me Jiriki. I hope to speak to you again."

"Who was that man?" she asked as Jiriki spurred his horse back to his people, who had swiftly buried their dead and were helping their wounded onto horses. "He was funny—his hair was the color of lavender flowers. And his eyes looked funny, too."

"Jiriki is a Sitha," said her grandfather. "And one of my oldest friends."

"A Sither? Really?" She looked after Jiriki, wide-eyed. "I thought fairies were little."

"Only in stories," Simon said and draped his arm around her once more. "I think we are going to travel with them for a while. But for now, you rest. Later you must tell me how you came to be under the castle."

"Am I in trouble?"

"No, child. I promise you are not."

Lillia settled back against his chest, already having taken in several things that would have rattled the wits of any adult. "I'm glad I found you, Grandfather. I was scared, but now we can be brave together!"

He did not reply, but only hugged her more tightly.

They might not have been riding at their fastest pace, but the Sithi horses were swift and smooth, and the first glimmer of dawn had only just touched the sky when they reached the Stanshire Gap, many leagues north of Erchester. The meadowed hills, brown and sere with winter, flowed past Simon on either side, and he found himself nodding, but the knowledge of the precious child clutched against his chest kept bringing him up out of his drowse with a start.

So tired. What have I done? He had deserted his people in their hour of greatest need, the castle burning, the citizens of Erchester scattering into the wild; and only God knew what had happened to those still inside the castle.

But Jiriki says we must go north this moment, and I can't leave Lillia. I can't let anyone take her away from me now. If my dear Miri is watching from Heaven, she would never forgive me.

And Geloë—how could she still be alive, thirty years and more since her death? Alive and without a body, nesting in his granddaughter. He had known since he first met the wise woman, in those long-ago days when he had also first met Binabik—and Miriamele too, though he had not realized it at the time—that Geloë was not like others, that she had knowledge and perhaps even powers that were hers alone. But nothing he had known of her could prepare him for this.

Thirty years dead. He had a moment of true fear as he thought of it. *How can Lillia stand it? What will it do to her?*

But one thing had not changed. Geloë had always been slow to explain things, but he ached to understand what had happened—and what would happen.

They rode on, the Sithi around him in a great, shining horde, as the first light warmed the sky. Some of them were singing. It might have been a war song or a love song—Simon could not tell—but the unfamiliar words and strange melodies wound around him as he rode, as though he moved in a dream.

But I don't dream, he thought. *That has been taken from me.*

3

Everything and the End

It was cold—bitter cold. Snow powdered the peaks far above them, and the icy air in Morgan's throat (as well as the streaming nose which he had to keep wiping on his sleeve) told that winter was upon them.

"What month is it?" he called to Nezeru.

"Month? I do not know how you call your months or days. I am a soldier, not a celebrant."

"You know enough to point out all the things *I* don't know. What do your people call this time of year?"

"The Wolf Moon must almost be upon us," she said. "A good time not to shout on hillsides. Later, when we fight in practice, I will tell you more."

Nezeru had decided that Morgan must have more training if they were to continue traveling together through the perilous valley of the Narrowdark—much to his shame, since he had spent his youth being taught by the best swordsmen the Hayholt had to offer. So far, it seemed that the main lesson was how to take a beating. Nezeru was almost unbelievably quick, and she seemed to know each thing he would do next, despite his best efforts to fool her.

"You are too slow," she said every time. "I can almost hear you thinking."

Ah, well, he thought. *I like the other sort of training better—the lovemaking lessons, where I can be the teacher. But she is learning those faster than I am learning mine.*

Morgan was aware of having grown even colder during the night, so in his drowsy, still-sleeping way, he reached out for Nezeru to pull her close but did not find her. Alarmed, he sat up and discovered her crouching beside their makeshift bed, pulling her armor back on.

His alarm receding, he watched the muscles of her milky back rippling like stones beneath a river's surface. Nezeru was strong—startlingly strong. She could likely break his neck should the need arise, but he could not watch her pulling on her arming shirt without a rush of longing so powerful that he had to hide it by pretending to wake up.

"Are you going somewhere?" he said.

She did not jump or otherwise seem startled, but he could tell by the tightening of the muscles in her waist that she had been caught by surprise. "Out to hunt. Somewhere in this valley there must be something wholesome to eat. We have eaten almost all the *pu'ja*—only crumbs remain." She looked over her shoulder. "Sleep a little more if you wish. We will be walking again soon."

He stretched out his hand to her bare back just before it disappeared beneath the arming shirt and stroked her cool skin with his fingertips, confirming that she was real, that he was not alone in this strange, deadly place. "Come back," he said. "The sun is not even up."

"The sun has been up for hours." She slid her armored chest plate over her head and began doing up the cords. "We are in a valley, but Mother Sun is not."

A sudden memory of Lillia and her rhyme about the sun swam up from the depths like a bright fish, bringing with it a homesickness that he had long been holding at bay. "Don't go."

"I must. You are hungry. I am hungry too, and that is a bad sign. We must have some food."

"No salamanders," he said, withdrawing his hand in defeat. "Nothing with too many legs—or no legs when they should have some, for that matter."

"Certainly, your Royal Highness. We of the Order of Sacrifice live only to make certain you do not eat anything that fails to delight you." She gave him a look, half-fond, half-annoyed. "If I find anything at all I deem worth eating, mortal man, you will eat it too or go without. We cannot afford a prince's particulars."

"That's not what I meant and you know it. You said it yourself—'wholesome'. But nothing in this valley seems wholesome. Everything is strange and wrong. I'm just asking you to bring back something I can swallow and then keep down."

Her look became something less human. He marveled at how she could flush all expression from her face in an instant, like water down a culvert. "Perhaps I was unfair, Prince Morgan. I did not mean to cause offense."

"Sweet Usires, you are the most difficult creature!" he said. "I wasn't offended, I was just explaining. But you knew that, didn't you?"

"This difficult creature is going out in search of food," she said, her expression now a defensive outwall not easily breached. "When I bring it back—if I find something to bring—we may discuss what is wholesome and what is not." She stood then, picked up the bow she had taken from one of the dead Norns in Da'ai Chikiza, and checked the two knives thrust through her belt. She had pulled her white hair into a tight horsetail, and with the long witchwood sword dangling at her hip, Morgan thought she looked like a war goddess out of some pagan temple. He was filled with a mixture of lust and surprise that what had begun with a knife at his throat had become something so complicated, so unexpected.

"Go carefully, then," he said. "I . . . I care for you."

Again a look that he could not unpick. "And I care about you, mortal prince. You have been a brave companion, though I did not expect it. Stay here and stay safe. I will return soon." She slipped through a crevice in the pile of boulders under which they had sheltered and was gone.

* * *

For a long time he stayed hidden among the rocks that had collected at the bottom of a ravine as though they were the discarded toys of some monstrously huge child. He wrapped his cloak tight around him and tried to think of anything but home, but that was a feat beyond his strength.

What must they all think? he wondered. *Mother will be furious, of course, that I have been gone so long. She might even be a bit worried, like Grandmother Miriamele will be. And Lillia . . .* A cloud of guilt and sorrow engulfed him at the thought. *My little sister will be miserable with me gone so long. And Grandfather Simon may be worried too, but he will cover it with bluster.* That set him thinking of something. *Grandfather blusters when he is afraid to show things. Is that why he was always angry with me when I made a fool of myself? Because it frightened him, not just angered him?*

It was a strange thought, one that he could not give his full attention. His bladder was full to bursting, and he was famished. He could not do much about the latter until Nezeru returned, but he could attend to the former.

Standing outside the pile of massive stones, each one almost as big as a farm wagon but a hundred times heavier, he wondered how they had ended up piled at the bottom of a ravine. Had they just rolled? Or had the thunderous steps of the ogre shaken them loose? The ogre they had never seen, despite almost being killed by it?

Or did it throw them? he wondered, looking up in sudden concern. But the upper edges of the ravine were empty of anything except the growing light of morning. Morgan was suddenly filled with a keen desire to feel a little sun, even if it was veiled behind the perpetual mists of the valley. He clambered up to the edge of the ridge that ran down from the valley's high walls and realized that he would have to climb much higher to see the sun.

But if I wait, it will rise past the highest peaks. He settled himself to wait for whatever meager sunlight the valley might grant him.

His stomach rumbled, but he did not want to climb slipping and sliding down to the place they had slept just to look for the last dry crumbs of *pu'ja* bread. He ignored the ache—nothing new, after all—and watched the valley's mists eddy with the wind, drifting like unhomed ghosts. He could dimly see the high hills of the valley's western side, great lumps of stone that stretched toward the sky as though they meant to drink the sun's rays.

Far away from home. The thought kept running through his head like a familiar melody. *Far away from home. Far away from everything and everyone I knew.*

As he crouched in the lee of a large stone to stay out of the morning winds, he saw something that suddenly drove all other thoughts from his head. Down at the bottom of the vale, where the ravine widened to become part of the valley floor, he thought he could see movement in the mist. Norn soldiers? They certainly seemed upright, though their shapes were strange. Startled and fearful, he began to make his way awkwardly down the slope, hoping that Nezeru would not stumble onto these interlopers unawares. The thought of losing her filled him with horror—to be alone in this weird place!—but to his surprise, it brought another kind of anguish as well.

What if I never see her again? Morgan had done his best to keep his growing feelings for the Norn girl at a distance. She was like something wild, and he sensed that to try to capture her or even just hold her would only make her pull away, maybe leave him entirely. But it was growing harder by the day to stay silent, to treat their lovemaking as nothing more than two people thrown together making the best of things.

What if I lose her?

He reached the pile of boulders and climbed it, using the bulk of it to shield him while raising his head to look downward. The fogs were swirling, and for long moments he saw no sign of the moving shapes that had so alarmed him. But then he glimpsed them again, two shadowy figures mounting upward side by side, but they puzzled him: no Norn ever looked so squat, whether on horseback or on foot.

And then a breeze swept the mist away for a moment. Another heartbeat later and Morgan was scrambling down the rocks.

As he ran down the slope, Morgan waved his hands over his head. He almost shouted before realizing that he did not know why the two figures were climbing up the ravine toward the valley wall—something might be pursuing them. Still, he kept waving his arms as he hurried down the widening ravine, until at last they seemed to see him.

"Snenneq!" he called as he approached. "Qina! It is me, Morgan!"

They stopped, stared, and before Morgan reached them the larger of the two leaped down off the ram he'd been riding and began to trot up the slope, moving faster than his short, thick legs would suggest.

"It *is* Morgan!" Little Snenneq cried, his round face stretched in a broad smile. "Qina, come and see!"

A moment later Morgan and Snenneq met. The troll hugged Morgan's belly so hard that the air huffed out of him.

"Morgan Prince!" Qina said, laughing as she slid off her ram. "I told! I told! Morgan Prince—I found!"

"Qina swore to me that she was following your track," Snenneq said, his short but steely arms still wrapped around Morgan's hips, his face against Morgan's belly. "I expressed doubt, but she was certain."

"Doubt?" said Qina, trotting up the slope. "You said wrong! You said no Morgan, Qina is fallish."

"Foolish, not fallish. But I do not think I said it that way."

Qina wrapped her arms around Morgan's leg. He could barely stand upright and feared that any moment, the trolls would tip him over and they would all roll down the slope into the rams, who were watching the two-legged creatures with mild irritation. "Hold on, you two, you'll knock me down."

The embraces finally loosened and Morgan was able to take a step back. "What are you doing here?" he asked.

"Follow you!" said Qina, grinning again. She was clearly very proud of herself. "Your . . . trick."

"Track," said Snenneq. "We followed your track."

"First little, then gone," said Qina. "Then little again. Then gone. But I find!"

Before Morgan could ask anything else, he felt a momentary snap of wind, then a second later a black arrow was shivering in the ground between him and the trolls. He turned to see a slender figure stepping out of a copse of stubby birches and moving toward them at a swift but graceful trot—even more impressive because the figure already had another arrow nocked and aimed at them.

"Nezeru!" he said, lifting his hands high in the air. "All is well! These are—"

The second arrow buzzed past him and pierced the knotted trunk of a pine tree a few steps away. Morgan left his hands in the air. Had he made a terrible mistake? Was this some other Sacrifice?

As the figure came closer, he was relieved to have his first impression confirmed. "Truly, Nezeru—" he said, but got no further.

"Step away," she said in a quiet but steely tone, and now her arrow was clearly aimed at the two trolls, who had taken a few steps back down the slope, eyes wide. Snenneq merely seemed puzzled, but Qina looked skittish as a rock-rabbit, a sudden noise or movement away from out and out flight. "Who are you," Nezeru asked, "and what do you want with my mortal?"

My mortal. Morgan was tickled that she would think of him that way, though she might have said the same of a hound or a horse.

"And this is my Norn," he told the trolls. "She is a friend. More or less." He turned to Nezeru, whose white face was still a stern mask, as if she had kept the same expression since she had left him. "And these are friends too, Nezeru. This is Qina, and this is Little Snenneq. They are trolls from Qanuc."

"From Yiqanuc. The Qanuc are us," said Snenneq.

Nezeru eased the bowstring and then slipped her arrow back into the quiver, never taking her eyes off the two trolls. "How did they find us?"

"We can talk, if you permit us," said Snenneq, then went on as if the permission had been granted. "We are Morgan's friends, and we have been following him for weeks through the valley of the Coolblood River, all along the outskirts of the ruined city Da'ai Chikiza, then across the hills to this place—"

"Tell," said Qina, frowning. "Not 'we'. Me. I found."

"—And it was, of course, the tracking skills of my beloved *nukapik* that helped us find you."

Snenneq did not notice the look of keen interest that flitted across Nezeru's face at the word "tracking," but Morgan did.

"Although it could also be said that my own large knowing of these wild places was very useful as well." Snenneq smiled, relieved that he had been able to mention his own part. "So here we are. Well met in the wilderness, friend Morgan! And well met to you as well, new friend Nezeru of the Hikeda'ya." But despite his cheerful words, he watched the Norn with a slightly worried eye.

"You said you know these wilds." Nezeru was retrieving her arrows, and barely looked at the newcomers. "Do you know much of this valley? Of what lies ahead?" She glanced quickly up and down the ravine. "We should go back to the shelter of the rocks. Someone—or something—might see us. If you swear these are your friends, Morgan, I will trust them."

He was sourly amused. What did she think—that these little troll-folk might have threatened him, demanding he pretend to know them? Had she managed to miss the embraces that followed the unexpected reunion? But a secret part of him was glad for her concern and glad that she had been watching over him. "Very well," he said, then turned back to the trolls. "But I warn you two, I have a thousand questions!"

"As do we," said Snenneq cheerfully. "And a fire and a meal will help to push the cold hunger from my belly and make me a better conversationalist!"

"We have no—" Morgan began, but Nezeru, still stone-faced, produced a dangling bundle of fur from her bag and held it before him as they walked. He took it, his mouth salivating at the prospect of roasted meat—of any meat—but as he looked closer, he felt a moment of horror and disgust. The creature was too big to be an ordinary rodent, and in the limpness of death, looked almost exactly like one of the Chikri.

"What is it?" he asked.

"Squirrel," Nezeru told him. "Big, but otherwise like any squirrel. I have smelled it. It is wholesome."

He was relieved and suddenly extremely hungry. "Then let's make a fire and cook it," he said. "Hang the smoke. Nobody will see it through all this God-cursed fog."

They had an excellent supper of roast squirrel, while the two rams wandered the ravine outside the sheltering pile of boulders, searching for vegetation. Even Qina, whose command of Westerling was elementary, could not stop talking as they shared stories of their adventures. Morgan's only worry was Nezeru. Even as he marveled and shuddered at the trolls' description of ghants and kilpa far from their northern homes, and as he regaled them in turn with his memories of the Sithi and the deadly fight in the ruins of Da'ai Chikiza, Nezeru remained aloof, listening but not commenting, her face like the wall of a castle turret, meant to turn away all who came.

Is she jealous that I have found my friends? he wondered. *Or does she still not trust them?* He had never been good at deciphering her moods, and this one seemed to be new. It also seemed to be one he might have to get used to: not even Snenneq's most boastful declarations nor Qina's brief but pointed commentaries brought any emotion to her face. But when they mentioned the hordes of Hikeda'ya soldiers they had seen traveling from the Coolblood Valley into the Narrowdark, some animation came back to her features.

"How many?" she asked abruptly, interrupting Snenneq.

"How many Norn soldiers?" He frowned. "We saw them marching several times, though it is not marching as the men of the flatlands do it—"

"How many?"

Snenneq gave her a slightly hurt look. "I could not say—we were not counting. But it could not be less than a few thousand, all told."

"But *why*?" she said. "I do not ask this of you, troll. I ask myself why my people are here. I have been in the Order of Sacrifice since I could first stand and walk, but I never heard anything of the forts I saw west of here, nor any reason my order should care about this valley, so far from everything."

"Perhaps they are seeking a way to attack the Sithi from a different side," Morgan suggested. "You said there was a fort north of here where the pass leads through from Coolblood Valley into this one."

"But that still does not tell me why," she said.

The trolls watched, clearly made uneasy by Nezeru's anger and frustration. *It's a good thing they never saw her kill things,* Morgan thought, *or they wouldn't have dared to speak a word tonight.* He had a sudden thought. "Snenneq, could you find your way back across, to the farther valley?"

"I think it is possible," said Snenneq.

"I find here the trail," Qina said. "I can find back."

Morgan felt Nezeru's eyes on him. She knew he was thinking about leaving her to go with Snenneq and Qina, and he knew almost as certainly that she would not prevent him, nor likely even protest. It made his heart ache.

"Do you have anything to drink?" he asked Snenneq, who nodded cheerfully.

"Our two water bags are full. We found a snowmelt stream yesterday and filled them."

"That wasn't what I meant, but I'll take some." Morgan took a long swig from Snenneq's skin bag. "It may be a while until we find more clean water. You don't want to drink out of the river—but you probably decided that already."

"The Narrowdark is befouled in a way I do not understand," said Nezeru suddenly. "This whole valley is a mystery that we have not come close to solving."

She will go on without me, Morgan thought. *Perhaps it's for the best. It's not as if we could stay together. How could I bring one of the White Foxes home to my mother and grandparents? "Here is the woman I love. Please don't think about how her people are trying to slaughter us."*

"Mystery mean secret?" said Qina suddenly. "Then I ask mystery. What is big very big giant? We see it from away far, at night." She shivered. "Very scaring."

"We don't know the answer to that either." Morgan was unwilling to look too closely at Nezeru. "It's always hidden in the mist—even in daylight. It makes tracks like nothing on earth. But it's real enough to kill us in a heartbeat."

"The *uro'eni*—the ogre—also comes from the north," said Nezeru. "The far end of the valley, beyond the Zida'ya fort. And that is where I must go to find the truth."

Morgan did not reply. He still did not entirely understand his own feelings.

Nezeru was adrift in unfamiliar waters. The arrival of Morgan's troll friends offered the mortal youth a chance to find his way back home without her. Her responsibility for him was over, but her need to have her questions answered had not changed. In truth, every day that passed in the valley seemed to bring more puzzles. Why were Queen Utuk'ku and the Zida'ya fighting over this obscure valley? Why had the Hikeda'ya armies—an entire Northeastern Host whose existence she had never known—built underground forts in mortal lands?

I have been deceived by my order, Nezeru thought as the others slept that night. *All those secret forts—we have been waging a quiet war in this part of the world for a long time. And I must know the reason.*

Morgan had given her a hopeful look while bedding down, lifting his arm so that she might lay herself down next to him, but she had been too full of anger and confusion to show that kind of neediness. Now he would leave with the trolls, she thought, and she would be alone again.

Alone! She almost laughed. *When have I ever not been alone? And it is even more pathetic to suppose that I dislike losing the company of a mortal boy.*

No, be honest, Nezeru of the Enduya. You fear it. You fear being alone once more because you do not know anymore what you are.

It made for a long, bitter time of darkness, but she sat silently with her thoughts, though they brought neither comfort nor clarity, until the sun finally rose behind the ever-present mists.

When Nezeru came back from a morning scouting expedition, she discovered the newcomers and Morgan awake and sitting around the ashes of the fire. They had a look she could recognize even on mortals—an argument just finished, but without any satisfying resolution.

"I want to talk with you," Morgan told her.

She knew her expression was perfect: showing her thoughts had been slapped and beaten out of her by Sacrifice officers in her earliest years. She answered him without a trace of outward emotion, "So then?" But inside she was full of raw feeling, emotions so unfamiliar she could not even name them. "What do you wish to say?" But she knew full well what was coming.

"I want to stay with you for at least a while longer," Morgan said, which astonished her. "My friends are not so sure. They think it would be better for me to go back."

"Not better," said Snenneq, picking at the remains of the cooked squirrel, taking a bite, chewing. "Safer. We are having a responsibility to Qina's parents and to your grandparents, Morgan-friend."

Nezeru had been expecting the opposite, and for a moment could not summon words. "I do not understand," she said at last.

Morgan smiled. "You have saved me many times. How could I just leave you? And remember, I saved you at least once, too."

"I remember." Her heart seemed to ache and swell inside her. Mortals! How could you hope to understand them? Because what he was saying made no sense to her. The risks were so much greater for him in going forward with her, while bringing no advantage to him at all. What could possibly make him want to do such a thing?

Morgan turned to the trolls. "She probably doesn't want to talk about it, but when we first came here, I pulled her out from under the ogre—the 'big very big giant'," he added for Qina's sake.

"It is not that," Nezeru said, but then the mortal tongue failed her again. "You all will go with me?"

"I hope you stop somewhere before we're all killed," Morgan said. "But yes. For a while, at least. Until you learn what you need to learn. We will go together."

Nezeru only nodded, then left the shelter once more, although she had no reason to do so except to avoid sitting any longer with these confusing, short-lived creatures. She also did not understand Morgan's strange and troubling certainty that, somehow, she needed him too.

There were advantages to traveling up the valley with Morgan's trolls, she soon discovered. Their rams could find safe paths in hilly places where even a trained Sacrifice had difficulty, and they seemed almost as unmoved by privation and cold as was Nezeru herself.

Morgan was a bit less hardy, though he was at least becoming more skilled with his blade each time they worked together. He had been well-muscled for a mortal when she met him, but days upon days of scant rations and hard climbing had made him almost as lean and strong as a soldier of her Sacrifice Order, though nothing would ever give him the same quickness or sharpness of senses.

They stayed mainly on the highest slopes along the valley's eastern wall, at the upper edges of the ocean of mist; at times, when a favorable wind blew, they could make out the highest crests and even the distant, gray winter sky. But the going was arduous—sometimes both Nezeru and the rams were balked and could not find a way forward for hours. Increasingly, she began to wonder what lay ahead of them, toward what strange, unforeseeable fate she was leading them all, and why she felt so compelled to do so. But the trolls and Morgan did not complain, only followed her as she led them on, ever northward. The trolls, at first hesitant around a Hikeda'ya soldier, did not precisely warm to her, but as days passed, they all grew used to each other. Each night they talked quietly in whatever shelter they had found until it was time for the mortals to sleep.

Morgan clearly wanted to lie with her, to make love and share the warmth of their bodies, but Nezeru could not bring herself to do it. Sacrifices were almost never alone and learned to do everything—even coupling—in the presence of order-mates, so it was not shyness that held her back; rather, it was the feeling that she had lost a part of herself, something valuable that she could not name but whose absence she could feel. She feared that if she surrendered to the animal comfort of being with Morgan, she would lose that part of herself forever, like a dream that vanished on awaking.

And what would I be then? she wondered. *Not me. Not Nezeru.*

Morgan was pained by her reticence, she could tell, but she could not afford to let his hurt affect her. She was fighting for her very existence, or so it sometimes seemed.

Several days' suns had risen behind the eastern peaks and sunk behind the fogs in the west when they finally saw the Zida'ya fortress called the Hornet's Nest. It had only ever been a name to her when she had studied in the order-house, just another stronghold of the hated Zida'ya, another thing for the traitors to use against her own folk instead of against the true enemy of all Keida'ya, the mortals. But when she climbed to a high promontory only a few hundred steps below the top of the valley and looked down on the fort's shadowy bulk through the swirling gray, she was struck suddenly by the realization that a Zida'ya fort in such an out-of-the-way spot was almost as strange as a secret fifth Sacrifice host she had never heard about, or a monstrous, invisible ogre. Why would the Zida'ya craft such a broad, strong redoubt so far from what she had been taught were their nearest settlements?

Morgan struggled up and stood beside Nezeru, panting with exertion. His glance moved over the dark, seemingly deserted Zida'ya fortress without interest, then he turned to look back over the lands they had crossed to reach the Narrowdark Valley. "Why is there so much mist here but nowhere else?" he asked.

She turned to follow his gaze and saw that he was right—only the valley beneath them was filled with swirling white. The valley of the Narrowdark was only one wrinkle in what looked like a vast, crumpled blanket of hills that stretched almost as far as the eye could see. The lines of those hills converged toward the north, as if some great hand there had pinched the rifts together, forming a delta of valleys. And in any sane place, Nezeru knew, the fogs that filled the valley just beneath them should have been present in the nearby vales as well, but that was not the case: the Narrowdark and its hidden river were sunk in a fog that was absent from the surrounding valleys.

What is different about this valley? she wondered. *And why should both my people and the Zida'ya want it enough to wage war here?*

"I am going to go take a closer look at the fort," she told Morgan. "You and your friends stay here. I will not be long."

He argued—he did not want her to go alone—but she only shook her head. "I can go more quietly and more swiftly by myself."

Nezeru made her way along the steep eastern wall of the valley, drawing closer with each treacherous step to the connecting gorge she dimly remembered was called Serpent Pass or Snake Pass, a deep ravine that sliced across from the Coolblood Valley in the west to the Narrowdark. At last she reached a point on the cliffs above the pass where she could get no closer without descending the sheer and dangerous valley walls. The fort was close now, close enough for her to hear a faint sound drift across the gorge, like fingernails scratching at a door, but whatever caused it was invisible to her behind a curtain of billowing fog.

Nezeru was just about to turn back when the wind freshened and the streamers of mist began to flee westward, dragged across the face of the promontory on which the fort stood, and she could make out the windows of the tower, empty as the eyes of skulls. A moment later the mists were swept from the cliff top, and she saw the shapes of many armored Zida'ya scattered along the path that led to the fort—all dead, sprawled where they had fallen. Ravens hopped from corpse to corpse and perched in the eye-socket windows of the fortress; their hoarse voices, muffled by distance, were the fingernail-scrapes she had heard. But to her astonishment, the Zida'ya were not the only meals that had been left for the birds: a portion of the corpses wore Hikeda'ya armor. If the Sacrifices had won here, they had retreated again without the bodies of their fallen, an incomprehensible dereliction of the order's ancient, sacred duty.

Shaken in a way she could not define, Nezeru returned to the others, but did not answer any of their questions about what she had seen. She was clearly showing more of her feelings than she wanted to, and since she did not understand them herself, displaying them for mortals felt like a failure.

"Enough," was all she said. "We go on."

Nezeru had been mostly silent since her scouting trip—not just with her usual reserve, but a deeper quiet that had lasted several days. She seemed more troubled than Morgan had ever seen her. He had spent enough time with her to know she would not take kindly to being questioned, so he pretended not to notice. When he could summon the breath, he talked with the trolls instead, but the air of the high places where they traveled was so thin that most of the time he did not have much strength for conversation.

"We are almost out of water again," pronounced Snenneq when Morgan handed him back the skin bag. "We must find another snowmelt stream soon."

"If I smell any," Nezeru said, "I will tell you."

Those were her first words since they had set out that morning, and Morgan hoped it meant that she was beginning to thaw once more, but in truth she had been strange since the trolls arrived, and he missed the companionship he had found with her when it had been just the two of them. There were times when he could almost believe he had imagined it.

Surely this is the most foolish thing I have ever done or could ever do, he thought. *Mooning after a woman of the White Foxes, someone as unlike me as a cat to a dog. And why? Because we had a few moments of happiness—or what I thought was happiness? Think how many girls must have thought the same of me after a night of disordering the bedsheets, only to find me gone in the morning. It is truly wretched being on the other end of that uneven bargain. If I am not careful, I might learn something I didn't want to know.*

Because of cold wind and treacherous footing, they had moved a good distance lower down the slope, so that they once more traveled in perpetual fog. In what might have been afternoon—at least in a world where the sun was something other than a faint white smear in the mists above them—Nezeru stopped, her nostrils flaring.

"I smell water," she said, but she looked as if she could not quite believe her own senses. "Ahead."

Soon they heard the cheerful sound of splashing water. Farther on, they saw the dark line of a gully that had worn away the soil and stone on its journey downslope, and Morgan and the trolls hurried toward it. The stream had been flowing here for some time, it was plain to see from the depth of the furrow it had cut. But the water moved swiftly and, unlike the Narrowdark, looked clean and clear. Snenneq made his way down the side of the gully to fill his skin bag, but Nezeru called to him. "No. Do not touch that water. Something is wrong."

Snenneq looked up at her in disbelief and maybe even a little annoyance. "It is fast-moving and clean," he said. "See, it must be melting snow from above."

Nezeru shook her head. "My nose tells me otherwise."

Qina looked down at the rushing stream, then at Nezeru. "It will sick us?"

"I cannot tell yet." She clambered over the edge and made her way down the gully until she stood beside Snenneq at the bottom. "Something is wrong with it."

The troll was still holding his water skin out like a child with a broken toy. "But we need water," he said.

Nezeru bent down, sniffing, then took a stone and dipped it into the water where it eddied at the stream's edge. She shook her head again and straightened up before turning to Qina, who had joined them. "You have the best nose of any of you mortals. Can you not sense it?"

Qina frowned, not in dismay but in concentration, as Nezeru dipped the stone again and lifted it up for Qina to smell. "Not know. Perhaps. Something . . ."

"Wait here," Nezeru said. "All of you. I want to find out where this comes from. And do not drink until I come back!"

Morgan had learned to trust her senses, which were amazingly sharp. "We won't. But I'll come with you—"

"No. Again, I can go more quietly and swiftly by myself."

Morgan could not keep himself from scowling. "You're going to sneak up on a stream?"

She did not dignify the remark with a reply but turned and clambered up out of the gully, then set off upslope, following the gurgling rill. In moments she had vanished in the mist.

"I cannot help worrying for you, friend Morgan," said Little Snenneq. "How well do you know this Hikeda'ya woman? I know she saved you, and that was a good thing for which she deserves thanks. But I still do not understand why we travel with her when we could take you back instead to your home and family."

"Fallish man!" said Qina suddenly, giving her betrothed's arm a light slap, as one might discipline an over-eager puppy. "His heart is with her."

Snenneq's eyes went wide. "Truly, Morgan? You have love-feelings for this Norn woman?"

Qina made a sputtering noise of disgust. "Mens," was all she said.

It was agonizing to sit beside the noisy streamlet while they were all thirsty; and hard to keep the rams away from it as well. A long time seemed to pass—longer for Morgan, because he was beginning to worry about Nezeru's safety. Had she climbed to the very crest of the hills? Perhaps she had encountered some of the Norn soldiers that Qina and Snenneq had seen on their way into the valley. He was on the verge of setting out himself to find her when he heard her voice from the hillside above.

"Morgan! Trolls! Do not drink there. Come up instead. You must see this!"

Qina and her betrothed climbed back onto their mounts, and with Morgan they followed the winding course of the gully upward. Tendrils of mists still writhed around them, and Morgan could not help wondering if they had been tricked, if it might not have been Nezeru they had heard but some phantom of the heights luring them to destruction.

At last they climbed past the thickest of the valley fogs and, to Morgan's relief, found Nezeru waiting. "Come," she said before they had reached her. "Follow. I must show you something."

They climbed beside the winding stream, which continued to tease them with its wet, ringing nearness. A few more furlongs up the slope, as the top of the hill they were on finally became visible through the thinning mists, Morgan saw a dark, angular smear against the hillside—the mouth of a cavern. The stream they had been following issued from it in a small but actively splashing cataract where it had worn away the stone at the entrance.

"Come inside," Nezeru said. "Come see what I have found." The entrance to the cavern was high enough that she didn't have to bend. Then something flashed in her hand and filled the chamber with light. Morgan had seen the sphere before, and knew that Nezeru used it only sparingly, since her vision was sharp enough that she seldom needed it.

The cave's interior seemed nothing unusual to Morgan's eyes, a deep fissure in the rocky hilltop, much broader than it was tall. The stream they had been warned not to drink from issued from the darkness at the back. Nezeru walked along it, following the water toward what Morgan presumed was its source, some spring in the rocks of the hill. But as they trailed behind her, ducking under low points in the ceiling when necessary, he was surprised at how far back the cavern extended.

"What is this?" he asked. "Has someone been here before us? Did you find—"

She turned and gave him a hard look, then put a finger to her lips. Chastened, he did not ask any more questions.

Morgan did not have to stay silent long. Another few turns and the cavern suddenly widened out into an echoing natural chamber, and beyond that he could even see another cavern beyond it through a wide opening in the back wall. But what he saw in the light from Nezeru's glowing sphere struck him like a blow.

The farther cavern was made of jewels.

No, he saw a moment later, not jewels but huge crystals, hard-edged blocks of translucent stone bigger than any crystals he had ever seen. They filled the whole of the cavern beyond the one in which they stood, growing out of the walls and ceiling at all angles, flashing back the sphere's light from a thousand different facets, sparking rainbows of color in their depths. He stood, staring, overwhelmed by the strangeness and beauty.

"My God," said Morgan. "Look at it!"

"It is interesting, yes," Nezeru said. "And that is where the water comes from, which makes me trust it even less. But that is not what I wanted you to see."

He could barely tear his eyes from that monstrous jewel-box. "What?"

"That," she said, pointing a little way behind him as her light swept away from crystal cavern and fell on a part of the outer cave he had not so far noticed because he had been arrested by the spectacle beyond. A pair of shapes—manlike shapes—were huddled on the ground near the cavern wall.

"Kuyu-Kun!" said Snenneq, staring at the smaller, thinner of the two figures. The troll hurried forward and squatted beside this person, then lifted the limp shape. The hood fell back, revealing a wrinkled face, large eyes, and a head as hairless as a chicken's egg. "Are you hurt?" Snenneq asked. "Where are the rest of your comrades?"

The figure in his arms groaned and the large, heavy-lidded eyes opened. "All gone. Fled. Who can blame them? Only my acolyte Tih-Rumi and I remain, and we can go no farther." The heavy-lidded eyes shifted to the glittering chamber as Nezeru's light swept across it again. "Beyond lies my death—no, the death of all our people. It is too much for me. It gnaws the life from me. But how can I go back, after coming so far?"

"You know this person?" Morgan asked Snenneq.

"This is Kuyu-Kun. We met him and his fellows before, when first we traveled to this valley. Kuyu-Kun is Tinukeda'ya. He is called the Voice of the Dreaming Sea."

"What does that mean?" asked Morgan.

"It means he is Tinukeda'ya," said Nezeru, but the tone of her words was strange. "And for some reason, he has been drawn to this place."

"Drawn but unable to go farther," gasped Kuyu-Kun. "I fear my heart will stop." Beside the hairless figure, the other dark-robed shape now sat up, revealing similar Tinukeda'ya features but in a younger face.

"But we must go on, Master," said Tih-Rumi in a raw, cracked voice. "You always say it yourself—the Dreaming Sea has no shore."

"No," said Kuyu-Kun. "I thought I had the courage, but I do not. What lies beyond is too terrible."

"What lies beyond?" Morgan asked. "I don't understand any of this. Do you mean beyond the chamber of crystals?"

"What lies beyond?" Kuyu-Kun shuddered, his wrinkled head protruding from the dark robe like a tortoise's, but the Tinukeda'ya's fear was palpable even to Morgan. "Everything. And the end of everything, too."

4

Favor and Fate

"Tzoja!" said Vordis in a frightened whisper. "Wake up! Something is scratching at the door."

Startled out of sleep, Tzoja rolled over on the hard floor and lifted her head to listen. The storeroom was a poor substitute for the wagon from which they had been evicted. It had only one cot. Tonight was Vordis's turn on it, and Tzoja ached all over. "What? It's just rain. I don't hear anything—"

Skritch. Soft as the rattle of dry leaves, quiet as the whisper of a snake's belly against the earth. Vordis reached down and squeezed Tzoja's arm so hard her friend almost cried out in surprise. For a long moment they both sat frozen, hearts speeding.

Skritch, skritch, skritch.

"What could it be?" Vordis whispered, on the edge of terror. "The Queen's Teeth? Did they find out you gave water to that prisoner?"

"Hush." Tzoja crawled across the rammed-earth floor and stopped in front of the doorway, listening. Why should anyone who wanted to harm them bother to scratch at the door? It was not as if they could lock it. Anyone who wanted to come in had only to lift the latch and enter.

"It must be an animal," she whispered, but Vordis only shook her head in confusion, unable to hear Tzoja's quiet words. Tzoja leaned closer just as the noise came another time, softer than before—*skritch.* She had no idea what to do. If it was a beast, some creature from the hills that surrounded the mortal fortress, it might hurt them. But the last scratch had sounded so weak, as if whatever waited outside was ill or even dying.

She forced herself to be brave and leaned heavily against the door to keep it from flying open. Then she asked, in a very quiet voice, "Is someone there?"

After a moment a reply came, a single soft word in the Hikeda'ya tongue. *"Help."*

Tzoja looked at her friend, but Vordis hadn't heard and was staring at nothing in the disconcerting way of the blind. Tzoja steeled herself and quietly pulled the door open a little way so she could peer out. She could hear rain hissing down, splashing on the muddy ground, but it was so dark that she did not at first see the man-sized shape huddled in front of the door. When she did, she let out a gasp.

"What is it?" Vordis asked. "You're frightening me!"

"Quiet. Come and help me." Tzoja prodded the dark shape with her foot but elicited only a faint groan.

Vordis came to join her. "Who is it?" she asked.

"It does not matter. Someone who needs our help. Now grab hold where I put your hands and help me pull."

It took a moment to get a good grip—the stranger's clothes were ragged to the point of falling apart, and slimy with mud and rainwater—but at last they managed to drag the heavy shape inside. Tzoja did not like being unable to see this unknown person who might only be feigning injury, so she fumbled for the candle, then for the flint and steel, and managed after a few tense moments to strike a light.

The stranger lay on the floor in a spreading puddle. Tzoja took a deep breath, then turned the body over. She breathed again, a swift, startled out-and-in: it was the man who had been imprisoned with the giant in the storeroom next door.

"What is it?" Vordis demanded. "Who is he?"

"The man I took water to, before the soldiers moved him and that giant."

The stranger groaned and curled into a ball. "They will be looking for me," he said in a breathless murmur.

"By Usires and all the gods," said Tzoja, "you are bleeding! What happened to you?"

The stranger lifted his hand, wet and red. "The sentries. I tried to go over the wall. One of them shot me, but I pulled the arrow out. There were other sentries coming, so I hid until they were all scattered again, then doubled back."

"Vordis, bring me my healer's bag," Tzoja said, less terrified now that she could fix her attention on something practical. "And several lengths of linen bandage."

"Don't bother," the bleeding man said. "They will come looking for me soon. I just need to rest for a moment . . ."

"You will leave a trail of blood everywhere you go," she said as she began pulling jars and small bags out of the sack Vordis had handed her. She managed to tug off his tattered tunic and gasped at the deep hole in his side. A fresh rill of blood came with the removal of the shirt, and she used up much of the first roll of linen cleaning his skin. She peered at the wound and was grateful to see that the arrowhead did not appear to have been barbed.

"Vordis, if we have any of the *kei-mi* liquor left, give it to me."

"It must be empty," she said. "We drank it all, I think, the day they took our wagon."

"If the cork is still in it, there may be a little at the bottom. Just bring it."

A few drops remained. After blotting away the blood again, Tzoja was able to dribble a thimble's worth into the man's wound, though she and Vordis had to hold him down as he squirmed in agony. She then stuffed more linen into the arrow-wound and covered it with a poultice made of honey and Harchan ginger before wrapping two more bandages around his waist to hold the poultice in place.

Vordis was feeling the stranger's face. "Poor man, he must hurt so! But he seems very handsome."

He lifted a hand and pushed her fingers away. "Good lady," he said through pain-clenched teeth, "this is not the time. The soldiers are after me and this is one of the first places they will look."

"We know," Tzoja said. "You were prisoned beside us and I brought you water."

"I thought so. It is why I came here." He sat up, still favoring his side, where the blood had already seeped out and made a red flower on his bandage. "I thank you for the water, and for tending my wound, but I have put you in enough danger already. I must go."

"You speak very well for a slave," said Tzoja. "Who are you?"

"Even if the guards have given up on finding me, there might not be time for that story. But you can call me Jarnulf. Now, help me up and I will—"

The sentence was not finished because at that moment someone hammered at the door. The two women both jumped. The wounded man only sighed. "Is there a weapon in this place?" he asked in a whisper. "Tell them I held you as prisoners."

"We are slaves too—we have no weapons," Tzoja whispered back, trying desperately to think. "Vordis, your cloak." She snatched her friend's long wrap and threw it over the man called Jarnulf, covering his head. "Under the bed," she told him. He rolled under the cot and pressed himself against the wall even as the door sprang open.

Two Hamakha guards stood in the doorway, streaming with rain. The eyes in the slots of their serpentine helms gleamed in the candlelight—cold black dots, like those of dead sharks Tzoja had seen in the Kwanitupul markets as a child. Vordis could not see the soldiers' eyes, but she seemed to feel their cold anger, and she let out a small gasp of fear.

The first guard through the door wrinkled his nose in distaste. "The stink of mortals is strong in here." He looked down at Vordis where she sat hunched on the floor. "Why did you make that noise, slave?" he said. "Have you something to hide? Stand up. There are two of you living here, yes?"

"Please do not force her to stand," said Tzoja. "She is having her monthlies and is in pain. What do you want?"

The guard lifted a gloved fist as if to strike her. "Watch your insolence. Another dead slave will not trouble our commander."

The other Hamakha soldier was glancing around the dark room. It was lit only by the guttering candle, but Tzoja knew the Hikeda'ya did not need much light to see. "Why are you here when it is time for sleeping?" she asked hurriedly. "Why do you disturb us?" Despite her pounding heart, she stood and moved toward the soldiers, trying to hold their attention. "We are not just any slaves, we are Anchoresses of the queen herself."

"That does not matter," said the first, but his tone became fractionally more civil. "The queen has ordered that all in this mortal fortress must be removed. Gather whatever you would carry with you."

"Carry with us? Removed to where?"

"You have one bell to prepare yourself to leave this place." He spoke with flat finality. "Then you will join the other slaves outside and all will leave Ujin together."

"But the queen is not even here," said Tzoja. "She went away south with the army."

"A slave questions the orders of the Mother of All?" His hand dropped to the hilt of his sword.

His companion had stopped beside the bed. "The stink of mortals is strong in here. Something is strange."

Before the first guard could reply, a horrifying, rumbling roar came rolling through the night from outside, so loud that for an instant Tzoja thought it a sudden thunderstrike, terrifyingly close. Something crashed and then crashed again, as though only a few yards away, a great gate was being smashed by a battering ram.

"By Drukhi the White Prince!" said the second guard, startled. "What is that?"

The door flew open again. A third Hamakha guard stood there, streaming rainwater, and the dreadful roaring rolled past him. "It is the cursed giant!" he cried to the first two. "The beast is trying to break free. Hurry!"

The two guards raced after him, leaving the door swinging and rain blowing in. Tzoja quickly pushed it closed again, but nothing could keep out the earth-shaking bellows of the giant.

Jarnulf rolled out from under the cot and flung off Vordis' cloak. "While they are occupied with Goh Gam Gar, we must slip away."

"The giant has a name?" Tzoja was utterly bewildered, and it took her a moment to remember what the guard had said. "The queen has left this place. Why would she order us out? And where are we to go?"

"I did not mean to involve you," said Jarnulf. "But now it has happened. If they can subdue the giant, they will be certain I am not there. They will remember the scent of a sweating mortal here and come back."

"But if you are no longer with us—!"

"They will still punish you," he said. "There is no fairness in them, woman. They think us animals. I cannot force you, but I would not see you go needlessly to the Cold, Slow Halls."

"Do you mean us to escape?"

He shook his head. "With all the Sacrifices alerted? No. We must join the other slaves and hope to blend in."

Tzoja, head spinning, began gathering up her things. She could not let herself be hurried, for fear of leaving the stopper out of a jar of something she would not be able to gather or find again. "But where are they taking us?"

"It does not matter. Hurry, both of you."

"We must go to the other Anchoresses," said Tzoja. "They will know what is going on and where we are being sent. We can travel with them."

"No, we cannot, unless you have saved me only to send me to suffering and death." Jarnulf moved in front of the door. "The Queen's Anchoresses are all blind, like your friend here, but they are still Hikeda'ya. They will smell a man—a mortal man at that—just as the guards did, and they will have no hesitation denouncing me, and you with me. If I am to live through the night, it must be hidden among the other mortal slaves. Will you help me to reach them? Because if not, I might as well tear off these bandages and get on with the business of bleeding to death."

Vordis had stopped gathering up her belongings and stood listening, her face full of worry.

I owe this man nothing, Tzoja thought. *Vordis and I are in danger ourselves, simply by being mortal, even if we are the queen's own chosen slaves. I cannot afford to let pity endanger us both.*

But it was not pity that had the strongest grip on her, she realized, but anger. She was angry with her cruel, immortal masters, angry with the Hamakha guards who had so abruptly delivered the news that they were to be uprooted yet again, with no explanation of why or where they were going. In truth, she was angry with the entire Hikeda'ya race, who had controlled every moment of her life for most of two decades.

"Well, then," she said at last. "We will help you hide among the rest of the mortal slaves." She found it hard to ignore the surprised, frightened look on her friend's face. "But if your presence puts us at risk, be warned—I will denounce you to the guards and tell them you held us hostage."

"More than fair," said Jarnulf with a harsh laugh. "More than fair."

"High Magister Viyeki," said the Hamakha guard. "His Highness the Prince-Templar wishes to speak to you. Are you free to come with me?"

Viyeki looked up from the map of the hills. "Of course. I will come at once."

He followed the soldier out through the winding tunnels toward the surface, passing shivering mortal slaves carting away rubble from the newest excavations, hurried along with curses and blows from Hikeda'ya guards. For a moment he thought he saw among the harried slaves the simple-minded mortal whose name he could not remember, but whose round, childlike face he could not forget, and he felt a pang of unfamiliar guilt.

Poor creature, he thought. *What have I saved him from only to deliver him to this? Would it not have been more merciful to let one of my foremen give him a quick death?*

He pushed the thought from his mind. That kind of weakness and sentiment could bring his own death, either directly for treason or by the loss of his position, which was all that separated him from the scorn and hatred of the Order of Sacrifice.

General Kikiti would happily see me dead. I do not wish to give him that satisfaction.

Pratiki was waiting in his tent, a structure a great deal larger and more comfortable than Viyeki's own. Two Hamakha guards looked the magister over before letting him enter; he wondered if he imagined the look of contempt in their eyes. *The only one who seems able to stand me is Pratiki himself,* he thought. *I must take the closest care of that connection.*

The prince-templar waved him to a stool, then handed him a goblet of dark purple wine. "How goes your digging, Magister?"

"As well as can be expected under the circumstances, Serenity." He did not want to sound defeatist, but he knew Pratiki valued honesty. "We are too few to make fast progress, and we have already had several collapses which have robbed us of time and slaves."

"Unfortunate." Pratiki sat back and sipped from his cup. "Because the queen is on her way. She will not be happy with any delays."

The news struck Viyeki like a thunderbolt. For a moment he could not catch his breath. "The queen is coming *here*?" he said at last, hoping his voice did not sound as strangled and squeaking as it seemed to him. "But the queen went south with the army—how could she—?"

"Nevertheless, she is on her way and will arrive shortly," said the prince-templar in a harsh tone chosen to direct Viyeki back onto the correct path. "She will want to know how long until the tunnel into the Vale of Mists is finished." He gave Viyeki a look that seemed to contain a warning. "So, High Magister—how long?"

His heart was beating very swiftly. "By the Garden, I . . . it will not . . ." He carefully folded his hands together to keep them from trembling. "As things stand at the present time, Serenity, it will be at least another month before the passage can be used."

"Impossible—and the queen will not be patient," said Pratiki with cold precision. "I strongly suggest you establish an earlier date for the completion of your task, High Magister."

Viyeki felt as if all his limbs had turned to wet sand. He could barely remember to keep his head up in the preferred posture of a confident underling, but he knew that Pratiki, of all people, would not be fooled. "Do you have any suggestions for me, Serenity?"

To Viyeki's astonishment, Pratiki smiled. "As it happens, High Magister, I do. Are you free to accompany me on a brief walk?"

"Of course, Highness." He was stunned. Was the prince-templar offering him a lifeline or simply leading him out to be killed? Certainly, he reflected, any sensible servant of the queen who must present her with bad news would want to be able to tell her the guilty parties had already been executed.

It did not make him feel any better when the two Hamakha guards followed them out of the tent, though he knew they accompanied Pratiki almost everywhere.

Pratiki led him across the plateau to a well-guarded stockade made of rough-cut timbers lashed together with ropes. He could see many shapes inside it, but few were moving. *He has brought me more slaves,* Viyeki thought. *It is better than having my head removed, I suppose, but a few dozen beaten, exhausted mortal slaves will make little difference. We will still be weeks and weeks lengthening the tunnel.* He also knew he had stretched the truth—finishing the task would take at least two moons, perhaps twice that.

It is time to stop this pointless fight for my life, he thought. *It is clear I will not succeed. Better to confess my failure now and kill myself. Perhaps then the queen will have mercy on my daughter and my family. Enduya Clan, I have failed you.*

"Still so glum," said Pratiki, smiling again in contravention of all sense, unless the prince-templar enjoyed seeing Viyeki suffer. "Why do you not inspect your newest workers?"

He nodded, though it was all he could do not to fall on his knees and admit defeat. The Norn nobility had a long history of honorable self-slaughter. Perhaps Pratiki would defend him if he wrote a letter accepting all blame and made a swift end of himself. As if in a dream, Viyeki walked past the guards at the stockade gate with the prince-templar just behind, then entered in among the slaves that were being given to him.

They were not mortals. Nor were they Hikeda'ya or even Zida'ya. The eyes that regarded him from flatly expressionless faces were huge, the bodies—what he could make out beneath their ragged garb, at least—long and achingly thin. The hands that reached out to him seemed impossibly wide, with flattened fingers like those of cave frogs.

"By the Eight Ships," Viyeki said, almost breathless. "These are—"

"Delvers, yes," said Pratiki. "Tinukeda'ya. Thirty-seven of them to be precise, brought from their work building the forts of the Northwestern Host. With those hands they can find a fracture no Hikeda'ya could see and shape hard stone like clay. Will that help you to complete the queen's passage down to the valley?"

Viyeki was stunned. "Of course!" *But I must not be too optimistic. It is still a nearly impossible task.* "I mean, of course it will make things better—faster. But we must see how they work." He moved close to the prince-templar. "Remember, Serenity," he said quietly, "you warned me the Tinukeda'ya were not to be trusted. That we should not use the carry-men at the mortal fortress of Ujin because the Tinukeda'ya folk had become restless and unpredictable."

"And they are," Pratiki agreed. "But those Tinukeda'ya were monstrous brutes who could tear apart an armored Sacrifice the way you or I would dress a rock rabbit. These are peaceable creatures—cowardly, in my experience. You will have to be stern with them, but they will not fight back." Pratiki raised his arms. Thirty-seven huge pairs of eyes turned to fix on him. "This is your new master, High Magister Viyeki," he told them. "If you work well for him, you will be rewarded. If you resist him or hinder the effort in any way, your ends will be terrible. Do you understand?"

One of the Delvers spoke. "We understand."

"That is Min-Senya," said Pratiki. "He is their leader, or so it seems. He is almost civilized, so do not hesitate to give your orders for the rest through him."

Min-Senya nodded, but Viyeki thought he saw a flash of something hard in the Delver's eyes before he bowed his head again. Pratiki saw it too and smiled, sharing the secret with Viyeki. "The clever ones are always the most dangerous," Pratiki said. "Now, I will leave you to decide how best to use your new workers."

"Thank you, Serenity. This will be a great help."

Pratiki put a hand on his shoulder. "Remember, High Magister, this is a high and important task, vital to our queen's plans. Use what I have given you well."

When the prince-templar and his guards had left, Viyeki was alone in the stockade with the Delvers. They remained as wide-eyed and seemingly incurious as a pond full of overfed fish, but he thought he sensed something else, some shared understanding between the gathered Tinukeda'ya, and it made the hairs on the back of his neck rise. "Min-Senya, if I have your name right," he said, "have your people eaten recently?"

The Delver gave him a curious look. "Not since yesterday, Master."

"Then that is the first thing you must do. I will have someone bring food." He looked up at the sky. "When the sun touches the top of that peak, I will return and we will begin. Do you understand?"

Min-Senya nodded once. "Yes, Master." But he seemed to want to say more.

"Have you a question?"

The Delver shook his head. "No, Master, no question. We will work hard for you. We will sing and mold the stone into the shapes you wish. We will find the hidden seams. But we will not work long."

"I don't understand."

"We will not work long because a day is coming that will change everything, for us—and for our masters as well. It has been promised to us and it comes soon. Prepare yourself, for many will die and many will be changed forever."

Viyeki tried to get the strange creature to explain what he meant, but Min-Senya had said all he wished to say. Viyeki might have had him beaten into speaking more—the guards outside the stockade would have been glad of the distraction—but he did not have the stomach for it.

Has Pratiki of the Hamakha given me a gift—my salvation? he wondered as he made his way back across the cold, windy clifftop. *Or has he handed me a poisoned cup?*

Head down, trying to appear as small and unimportant as possible, Tzoja slipped through the crowd of whispering nobles. The rainy, ruined courtyard of the mortals' Naglimund fortress was full of Hikeda'ya, most of them members of the nobility who had accompanied the queen from Nakkiga. There was little order: even the Sacrifice soldiers seemed confused by having to herd their own leaders. After several heart-pounding moments, Tzoja and her companions finally reached the comparative safety of the crowding mortal slaves, most of whom had been taken from their Hikeda'ya owners' wagons and forced to wait in the open, suffering in the cold rain and sleet. They moaned and some even wept, confused and frightened by the sudden change.

"The rumors say we are being marched into the hills," Tzoja told Vordis and Jarnulf. "The guards claim it is by the queen's orders, but everyone knows the queen is not here! She left for the south in the last moon!"

"The Hikeda'ya do not need to send letters to converse," said Jarnulf in a whisper. "You know they have Witnesses. Why are you surprised?"

How could she explain? Tzoja had thought Queen Utuk'ku valued her knowledge—a terrible mistake, but an idea she still did not want to believe had been entirely wrong. "Where do you think they will take us? Do they mean to execute us all?"

Jarnulf pulled his hood farther down over his eyes though, since it was Vordis's spare cloak and too small for him, the lowered hood raised the hem of the garment higher, exposing the back of his muscular legs. "If they want us dead, why not simply execute us here?" he asked. "No, something else must be happening." He looked around slowly. "There are more Hikeda'ya in this throng than our own kind. Many of them look to be the queen's most important nobles. And is that not Lord Zuniyabe? I know that frowning mask—who doesn't? There stands the queen's chief celebrant, shivering like a wet hound. No, something strange is going on, but what it might be, I cannot guess." He laughed, loud enough to make Tzoja flinch. "Utuk'ku is known as the Queen of Cruel Games for a reason."

Until a few hours ago Tzoja had felt . . . not safe, but as though she could rest for a little while after many moons of terror. The Mother of All had thought she had value as a healer, and that had been enough to keep her alive. It had almost made her grateful to the immortal witch-queen. Now everything had changed in a moment. And if someone caught her in the company of an escaped prisoner, Tzoja did not think her role as one of the queen's healers would save either her or Vordis.

With a skirl of horns as plaintive and ominous as the cries of night birds, the whole vast crowd of immortals and mortals now began to move, urged on by the soldiers surrounding them. Tzoja and her companions fell in with the other slaves and followed the train of nobles through the burned and broken remnants of the mortal stronghold. All were driven toward Ujin's eastern wall and the looming hills.

Viyeki, she thought, *I pray you are still alive. Nezeru, my child, I pray that you too still live, and still hold the queen's favor.* But as she trudged through the mud, sleet hard as gravel blowing into her face, she found it increasingly difficult to believe that anything good awaited her or her family.

Thank you, O Lord my God, for keeping me safe. Thank you for hiding me among the slaves and womenfolk. Jarnulf did not wish to be ungrateful—anything was better than falling into the warlock Akhenabi's corpse-colored hands again—but he still feared an ignoble death. How much better it would be to die on his feet, killing his godless enemies! Instead, he was hiding himself like a coward. He had no sword, no weapon at all but his bare hands. It was a disturbing, unfamiliar feeling and Jarnulf did not like it.

I would give much to have my long killing knife back. He contemplated the still agonizing pain of his mutilated finger, which had not eased in the days since he burned it to confuse Akhenabi's questioning. *If I cannot kill the queen, I would settle for shoving a length of sharp steel into the Lord of Song.*

The sighted woman, whose name he still did not know, stumbled, then caught at his elbow to keep from falling, interrupting his doom-laden thoughts. *And what now?* he wondered. *This pair saved me and hid me from the guards. Must I now be their champion as well? How can I even think of it? I have done badly at avenging poor Father and his murdered family—how can I take on two more endangered souls?*

He had been given two chances at the witch-queen but neither arrow had even drawn Utuk'ku's attention, much less harmed her. How could he consider himself anyone's champion? *But God would surely not give me any burden beyond my power,* he told himself. *The Book of the Aedon says, "And if you harvest only bitter grasses, eat of them and praise your God for His goodness and your faith will be rewarded."*

As they made their way over the ruins of the inner keep wall and into the muddy, rain-spattered wasteland of collapsed stone—all that was left of Naglimund's outer keep—Jarnulf wondered what the Norns planned. Was the war going so badly that the Hikeda'ya were going to force their nobles, many of whom had never fought in any kind of conflict, into the ranks of the Sacrifice Order? But the throng being marched across Naglimund included women and children. No matter how he turned it in his mind, Jarnulf could make no sense of it.

The hand of the woman beside him tightened on his arm again. This time it was no sudden clutch to keep from falling, but a fierce, almost painful grip. "What?" he whispered. "Why do you pull at me—?"

"Don't look up." Her voice quivered with fear. "I need to get on the other side of you. I will tell you later."

He paused, sliding a little in the mud, and let her cross to his other side so that she walked half behind him, with the blind woman in front of her. He let his gaze roam around the crowd but could see nothing that might have alarmed her.

The guards kept them moving forward with shouts and the points of their spears as the unhappy company made its way through a notch in the walls, past the empty shell of a huge borer buried under fallen bricks. Jarnulf saw a spear sticking out between two of the creature's huge back plates and silently cheered to see that some of the castle's mortal defenders, at least, had fought back.

We will not be destroyed, Utuk'ku, he thought, and for a moment felt a swelling of hope and even a little pride. *We men will not be disposed of so easily.*

The vast throng was herded along the narrow track that crisscrossed the hill behind Naglimund, mounting ever upward toward the heights. Forced to go two abreast by the narrow path, Jarnulf walked beside the blind woman while his other companion stayed a step behind him. At last, after they had climbed perhaps halfway up the slope, he felt her hand on his arm again. "All is well," she said softly. "I can no longer see her. She is far ahead."

"She? Who is this she?" he asked. Was this all because of some foolish feud between a pair of pampered court slaves?

"The wife of my master. I never dreamed she would be here. She hates me, and has several times tried to have me killed."

Jarnulf cocked an eyebrow. "Are you surprised to find her here? The cream of the Hikeda'ya court has been brought from Nakkiga. Queen Utuk'ku has gathered all her nobles, for some reason—even I can see that."

"We have not gone out among them unless we had to. We—Vordis and I—had our own wagon for a long time. I did not lie to those guards when I said we were Anchoresses of the Queen herself."

Jarnulf felt himself bristle but did his best not to show it. So, these were no ordinary mortal slaves—not helpless wretches but pampered pets of the cursed Mother of All herself. "Then you are the lucky ones here," he said.

"Lucky?" She shook her head angrily but kept her voice low. "You cannot imagine how untrue that is."

Jarnulf wondered what kind of small disappointments such a fortunate creature might consider bad luck. Still, the woman had saved him, and he did his best to swallow his contempt. *Protect me, O Lord, from the false contentment of comfortable sinners.*

They reached the top as the rising sun appeared for a moment from behind the veil of clouds. The hills of the Wealdhelm stretched away on either side, but below them, at the base of the eastern slopes, lay the vast green tangle of Aldheorte Forest. "Where are we?" said the blind one. "The wind feels different, and I can hear strange echoes."

"We have reached the hilltop," her companion told her. "It seems they are taking us into the great woods."

"But why?"

"Who can guess what is in the minds of the Hikeda'ya?"

"Or their queen," said Jarnulf quietly, staring down on the broad expanse of green and gray, speckled with a few lingering autumn leaves and wisps of mists that clung to the treetops like river moss. *I may be able to find a place to get away from the Hikeda'ya here,* he thought. *And there is no doubt these two will be safer without me. That would be a suitable repayment of my debt to them. They can go back to living their protected lives as body-servants to the Queen of Death, whatever that brings to them.*

"I do not want to go into the forest," said the blind one.

"We have no choice," said her companion. "But I will be with you, dear friend. Have no fear. I will keep you safe."

Jarnulf thought it one of the most foolish, presumptuous promises he had ever heard. It did not occur to him that the woman who made it might know that just as well as he did.

Viyeki had returned to the tunnel to consider how best to use the Delver slaves the prince-templar had presented to him. His experience working with Tinukeda'ya earth-shapers was limited, since their numbers had dwindled to almost nothing in Nakkiga's latter age. The few times he had done so, however, he had learned a good deal about the strange creatures, how they thought and how they worked. Viyeki's Order of Builders venerated the past, like most Hikeda'ya institutions, ergo his training as a Builder magister had been full of old lessons about working with Delvers. In the earliest days of Nakkiga, Delvers had been everywhere, shaping the mountain city the way they had shaped so many other creations of both Hikeda'ya and Zida'ya.

As he stood watching mortal slaves trudge past with heavy sacks of rubble on their backs, and others wheeling even heavier loads on carts, Viyeki heard a commotion—the sound of angry voices. Curious, and irritated at the thought of any delay, he made his way down the tunnel past the flow of mortal slaves, all of whom were doing their best to avoid his eye and pretend they didn't hear the shouting behind them. He followed the noise into a side-passage where he stumbled upon a group of mortal slaves shouting at and kicking a figure who lay huddled on the floor of the tunnel. The outliers looked up at his approach; their eyes went wide with fright, and many of them scuttled past him, some stumbling and falling and then crawling past him in their hurry to escape the anger of a Hikeda'ya High Magister. The four who were still pummeling and kicking the figure on the ground did not notice him until he was standing beside them.

"Step away, slaves," Viyeki said in Westerling, his voice so full of anger that the attackers stopped and staggered back as one. When they recognized him their red mortal faces went as pale as Viyeki's, and all four fell to their knees before him. *"Why are you beating that one?"* he demanded.

One of the attackers looked up, blinking hard, as if Viyeki's anger cast a blinding light. *"Don't kill us, High Magister, I beg you!"* he cried. *"This one, he gets us all in trouble. He never stops talking and it's all foolishness. He doesn't work when he should, and he upsets everyone with his talk of angels."*

Viyeki was distracted. The pitiful figure on the ground, bleeding from the nose and above his eye, was the simple-minded creature Viyeki saved, the mortal who called himself . . . what did he call himself? *"I know you, boy,"* he said. "*Speak."*

"Cuff don't mean to make them angry." The creature was bleeding from the mouth, too, which made him even harder to understand. *"Only tell them what I know—what I dream."* He burst into tears. *"Please, make them stop kicking me. I want to be good! I try!"*

A part of Viyeki could barely stand to look at him. The boy was ugly even for a mortal, and his tongue was too big for his mouth, which made him hard to understand, especially in a language Viyeki had hardly spoken in years. The slave's face was covered in dirt and blood. *He seems more animal than human,* Viyeki thought. *Why do I keep protecting him?*

"You are a good man, Master," the bloody creature said. *"Good man. Good and kind."*

No, I am not, Viyeki thought. *I cannot afford to be.* But the other slaves were staring at him and he had already wasted enough time on this scuffle. *"You savages,"* he snapped at them. "*Get up. Go back to work. If I hear or see you abusing another worker, I will have you destroyed. There is much to be done and if it is not finished, we will all be killed, and in a much less pleasant way than you had planned for this poor fool."*

Looking as if they could not believe their luck, the four rose from their knees and, with many bows and protestations of gratitude, fled back up the side-corridor to join the rest of the slaves. Viyeki looked down at the huddled, bloody figure at his feet.

"Get up," he said. *"You are a problem that must be solved."*

Despite his other deficits, Cuff the Scaler was nimble and surprisingly strong, as Viyeki now recalled, but it still took the poor creature several long moments to get to his feet. One of his legs was bleeding, doubtless from being kicked over and over, and he could barely stand.

"Follow me," Viyeki told him, but when the creature hopped a few steps after him and then collapsed again, the magister took a deep breath and waited. *"You must make it on your own,"* he said. "*I cannot help you."* To be seen carrying a slave—seen by Kikiti and his Sacrifices or even by his own Builders—just the thought made the magister's blood run cold. *"Get up and follow me, mortal, if you want to live."*

Cuff struggled to his feet once more and this time managed to keep hopping after Viyeki. When they left the cavern, Viyeki sped his pace a little, enough to put a suitable distance between them, but then slowed himself several times to avoid leaving the sad creature behind completely.

At the Delver stockade, he waved to the guard to open the gate, then stood until Cuff had stumbled past into the enclosure and followed him in. He gestured for Cuff to sit down, which the slave did with evident gratitude, eyes wet with tears. Several of the silent Delvers came forward and gathered around the mortal, observing both the bloodied newcomer and Viyeki with a sort of insolent indifference, as if they saw no difference between a beaten slave and the queen's High Magister of Builders.

"Min-Senya?" Viyeki could not tell the Delvers apart. Their strange, slender necks and staring, saucer-like eyes made them as indistinguishable to him as a field of sunflowers.

One of them stepped forward. "You wish to speak to me, High Magister?"

"That's why I called your name, yes. I came to ask you a favor."

Min-Senya showed what might have been the mildest sort of surprise. "A favor, High Magister?"

"Yes. You do know the word, don't you?"

"Of course. But we seldom hear it from the lips of your people."

Viyeki had little doubt he was being mocked, and at another time would have been furious, but now he only wanted to solve a nagging problem. "This mortal is being mistreated by others. He is too different, and if I leave him among them, they will kill him."

Min-Senya looked from Cuff's bloody, tear-streaked face and back to Viyeki. The Delver was as devoid of expression as the most veteran Nakkiga courtier. "You want us to take him—to keep him with us—so that his fellow slaves will not kill him?"

"Yes, yes." Viyeki was impatient now and not in the mood for this game of making him say everything twice. "That is what I am asking."

"But a favor is a bargain," said Min-Senya. "What will you give us in return?"

For a moment it was all Viyeki could do to restrain his temper. *They are slaves,* he reminded himself. *They have been driven here to work just as I have—and in far worse conditions. Why shouldn't they try to haggle for what they can get?* "I will leave that up to you. Talk among yourselves and tell me what you want—more food? More space? But if you ask for something unreasonable or impossible, you will lose the return of favor, and things may go worse for you. Do you understand?"

"Of course, High Magister." Min-Senya pressed his broad, flat hands together in front of his chest and bowed low, just like a Hikeda'ya noble abasing himself before a member of the ruling family.

This jibe was not lost on Viyeki, but he had spent long enough trying to solve this small irritation and wanted only to be gone. He had larger matters to occupy him, including the never-ending problem of preserving his own life in the snake-pit that was the world of the Hamakha Clan.

"Very well," he said. "I thank you, Min-Senya, and your people. Let no harm come to the young mortal."

"We will protect him from everything . . . except his fate."

Viyeki was weary of cryptic pronouncements and did not reply. In fact, he had been weary for a long, long time, he now realized, but there was no rest for him in sight. He called to the guard to let him out of the stockade.

5

The Duchess

On the *Elysiamansa,* Miri had to call on all her queenly powers to overcome the cautiousness of Baron Norvel and Captain Fincher. Both men wanted to anchor the vessel in Storm Cove, a safe distance from the burning castle, but she insisted that they dock at the Hayholt's seagate instead. Unable to talk her out of what they considered folly, the two men begged her at least to go below until the ship's soldiers had a chance to discover what exactly was happening in the devastated castle. Miri would not bend for this either, though she did agree to wear a helmet with her chain mail shirt. Then she sent Jesa to the captain's cabin with orders to stay there and protect the infant Serasina.

As they approached the seagate, Miri could only stare in amazement and horror at the extent of the destruction. The air was full of smoke, and the light of the flames revealed more of the low clouds overhead than of the castle itself, but what she could see was heartbreaking. Holy Tree Tower was wreathed in flame, though it still stood, and the roof of the great hall had collapsed, though fire still licked the walls.

As the dawn finally began to outshine the false sunrise of the flames, Miri could make out scores of figures waiting on the dock, but the numbers were so pitiful compared to the castle's usual population that she could not bear to think about how many must have been killed. But early reports suggested that the city of Erchester itself was largely unharmed. What had happened here? she wondered. Had treacherous Pasevalles recognized that his days were numbered and set fire to the castle to cover his escape? Or had the Norns finally returned to the Hayholt, bent on revenge?

She watched as the soldiers who had filled the first landing boat got out at the seagate dock and a dozen or more anxious survivors quickly boarded. As the oarsmen came about and began to beat back across the Kynslagh toward the queen's ship, Baron Norvel stuck his head above the top of the *Elysiamansa's* stern castle stairs.

"You must go into your cabin now, Majesty," he said. "The dock looks safe, but there is no telling yet who might be on the walls."

"Nonsense," she said. "I need to talk to the folk being brought back. I need to know what happened here."

"All well and good, Majesty," he said. "But there was no time to look closely at who's coming—they just loaded them on and shoved off. Who can say there might not be an assassin or two among 'em?"

She was about to argue further, but decided that the baron was right, and not just about the possibility of a disguised assassin. *If Pasevalles is somewhere nearby, I would prefer he not know I am alive. I want him overconfident, certain he has triumphed.* Still seething with fury at the destruction of her home, she allowed Norvel to escort her back to the captain's cabin, where Jesa was waiting wide-eyed and fretful, the baby in her arms.

"Majesty! Will we go to war here?" the young woman asked.

"I think it is over, but nothing is certain yet," Miri said. "We will know more soon. Survivors waiting on the castle docks are being brought back to the ship."

A short while later, the door opened to reveal one of Norvel's retainers. "His Lordship says there are some of the survivors asking to see you," he said.

"What? How could they know to ask?" she demanded. "Nobody even knows I still live."

The guard shrugged, then tried to turn it into a bow, with indifferent success. "Sorry I am, Your Majesty, but I couldn't tell you. But the baron said that Your Majesty'd want to see them."

Miriamele told the soldier to bring the survivors in one at a time, but also to bring two more guards to the cabin. She reached for her knife and held it in her lap, hidden in a heavy fold of the mail shirt she still wore.

She did not recognize the first person through the door behind the three soldiers because the rescued woman's face was blackened by ash and streaked with drying blood. The newcomer stared wide-eyed at Miriamele for a moment as if at a ghost, then fell to her knees, eyes wet with tears.

"How can this be?" the woman asked in a ragged voice. "How can it be? I saw . . . I saw . . . ?"

The voice gave her away. "Lady Thelía?" Miriamele stood and extended her hands. "God bless you! And Tiamak, where is he? Is he . . . ?"

"He lives," Thelía said. "He is aboard, having his wounds cleaned and bound, Majesty. But how is this possible? How do you live?" She could only stare. "I saw your body . . . Tiamak did too!" She came forward, swaying, but, superstitiously, would not take Miriamele's hand.

"I know you did. But it was not me."

"Then this is a miracle!" Thelía said. "God has given us a true miracle!" She made the sign of the Tree, then bowed low.

"Don't do that, good lady, I beg you," Miriamele told her. "It makes me feel like something unreal."

"But this *is* unreal!" Thelía said, looking up at her. "How can it be? We saw your burned body, Miriamele—Majesty. How do you live?"

"That was not me, but Duchess Canthia of Nabban. She was attacked by Thrithings men as we all fled Nabban." She extended her hands. "Please, rise and come sit beside me. I feared for you and Tiamak so much. You say he is alive? That is a blessing. I have so much to tell you, but first I must learn what happened here."

Thelía wiped her eyes again, and for a long moment did not speak. "Oh, Majesty," she said finally, "I had never thought to have to say these words, but . . . do you know about the king? About Simon?" She took a breath. "His Majesty is dead."

Miri did her best to keep her face calm, as befitted a queen. "Do not torture yourself, Thelía. I already know what happened to my beloved. And someone will pay for that, too, as they will pay for the Hayholt. Do you know who has burned our home?"

"The Norns," Thelía said. "We saw them. But how and why and where they went afterward—there seem as many stories as there are survivors, Majesty."

Baron Norvel appeared in the doorway with a bemused look on his face. "The other woman waiting is demanding to see Duchess Nelda," he said. "Who she seems to think is here and in charge. She is most demanding, and she also said something quite impressive about taking Murhagh's lost arm and beating me about the head with it if I did not bring her to—"

The baron did not get a chance to finish, because a figure pushed in behind him, ineffectually restrained by one of the guards, while the soldiers in the cabin lowered their pikes to protect the queen, leaving almost no room for anyone to move in the small space.

"I *will* speak to her. Duchess Nelda knows me well—!" The woman who had burst in stopped and her face, which had been contorted in anger and frustration, went slack, as she saw the queen. "How can this be?" she finally asked in a breathy voice that had lost most of its strength.

"Rhona?" Miri said. "Sweet Elysia, God's good mother, is that you?" She rose and spread her arms. "Come here!"

If Miri was surprised, Lady Rhona was astounded. For a moment the countess of Nad Glehs did not move, only stared back at her. "Is that truly you, Miriamele?" she asked at last in a halting voice. "Am I alive, or are we all in Dunn's shadow-kingdom now?"

Miriamele laughed but could not hide the pain in it. "You and I are both alive, though only by great fortune. Come, give me your arms and you will feel how real I am."

Rhona almost flew toward her, and for a long moment Miri reveled in the embrace of one of her oldest and dearest friends. When they finally leaned apart, both faces were wet with tears. "But how can this be?" Rhona asked.

"I will tell the whole dreadful story again, as many times as there are friends to tell it to," said Miriamele, but then something occurred to her, a sudden coldness in her belly. "But first, dearest, where is Lillia?"

Rhona only looked at her, mouth open and eyes brimming. "Majesty . . . Miriamele . . ."

"Just tell me, and quickly!" The cold feeling crawled all through her body, threatening to turn her to living ice. "Quickly! Where is my granddaughter?"

Rhona sagged and almost fell, but Norvel stepped forward and caught her. "I do not know!" she said. "May all the gods protect her, I do not know! But she was not anywhere among the fallen, nor on the dock—I looked and looked." She could not look Miriamele in the eye. "She vanished just after your husband rode out. Pasevalles claimed that Lord Tiamak and his lady had taken her."

"Never!" said Thelía. "Another of his wicked lies. We did not take her, although I sorely wish we had—may He Who Always Steps On Sand protect her life. But I think Tiamak and I may have seen her."

"Where?" demanded Miriamele. It was all she could do not to shout. "Where do you think you saw her? Was she alone?"

"We think we saw her in the tunnels under the castle, where we hid from Pasevalles." Thelía's face was full of woe. "There was no one else with her, but we never came close enough to know for certain it was Lillia." Gulping for breath, she could not force out the next words for the span of several heartbeats—time enough for Miri's heart to race until it felt as if it might burst. When she finally spoke, Thelía was close to tears. "A-and then the c-castle caught fire."

Brother Etan looked around at the hellish wasteland that only hours before had been the familiar Hayholt. Flames still capered among the collapsed roof beams and the low, smoky clouds threw back their sullen red glow.

Tiamak had asked him to follow the supernaturally swift Sithi, to catch up to them and their leader Jiriki—no, the Wrannaman had all but demanded it of him, a task that would have been nearly impossible even at the best of times. With no idea what to do next, he stood just inside the fallen Nearulagh Gate, an exhausted, shivering wreckage of a monk who had used all but the last reserves of his strength to save as many people as he could from the fires and the brutal, dead-faced Norns. *Do the impossible or be the cause of some terrible, unspecified doom,* he thought. Etan felt tears running down his cheeks and wiped them away, then stared at his hand, streaked with muddy ash.

They say God gives us no task we cannot fulfill if we keep our faith in Him. Etan believed it to the core of his being, but at that moment he simply could not feel it.

He needed a horse, that was the first thing. Even if Scand, Tiamak's donkey, had survived this storm of fire and blood and dark magicks, Etan knew that the slow, selfish beast was no mount for someone trying to catch a troop of Sithi riders. He wondered whether the Hayholt's stables had survived the Norn attack, and if any of the horses could still be there. But what would the poor creatures be like after such a night of fire and blood? Etan had become a seasoned rider during his long journey through the south in search of news about long-vanished Prince Josua, but he did not for a moment think he was up to calming a maddened horse. Still, what choice did he have? He had given Tiamak and Thelía his word, although that promise now hung around his neck, heavy as a harbor chain.

As he made his way between the smoldering ruins of the close-packed houses and warehouses that had once lined the Outer Bailey, Etan saw something unexpected through the smoke and swirling night-mist—a vision, or so it seemed in that first moment. A huge shadow leaped across an open space between two rows of tumbled, fire-blackened buildings a hundred paces ahead of him, then disappeared a moment later—a great horse. Etan wondered if it was the product of exhaustion, madness, or a sign from God only a fool could miss.

Despite his weary, trembling legs, he hurried ahead, leaping over burning timbers, fighting to catch another glimpse of what was already beginning to seem like a trick of light and smoke. When he reached the end of the alley he saw no sign of the beast and decided his eyes had deceived him.

But when he turned back and again began walking toward the stables he saw movement ahead of him once more, a four-legged, high-headed shadow, slipping in and out of the inconstant firelight, and this time he could not dismiss it. It almost seemed that the creature—or holy messenger—was trying to lead him. Fully immersed now in the night's unreason, Etan did his best to follow.

Not far from the Nearulagh Gate he came upon a collapsed section of the outwall that blocked most of the narrow street, but it was not what made him stop—fallen walls were everywhere, as if some angry monster had picked up the burning city and then dropped it to the ground a moment later. What made this huge pile of rubble notable was the trio of white-skinned Norn corpses on the ground, two of them smashed beneath stones, the third simply lying dead in a puddle of blood that flickered with reflected flames. Even as Etan stared, wondering what had happened here, he sensed a presence behind him and turned.

It was the shadow-horse, now fully revealed in the firelight. Its coat was shiny black, and it stood almost as tall at the withers as the top of Etan's head. The beast was kitted in battle armor, and as he stared, it lowered its head as though inviting him to come nearer. Had God answered his prayer? For surely this magnificent steed would be a Heavenly gift for a man sent to chase the Sithi. With only a brief glance to make sure the three Norns were as dead as they looked, Etan took a step toward the black horse, but as he stretched out his hand the beast reared, hooves thrashing, dangerous as blacksmiths' hammers.

As he skipped backward, almost falling, he barely missed stepping into a hole where the front of a shop had collapsed down into its cellar. As he caught himself at the edge, he glimpsed something pale in the depths—another dead Norn, he thought at first, but dressed in colorful armor instead of the black plate that the others wore. As he stared, he realized that this corpse did not have the bloodless pale face of a Norn, but something warmer in hue.

Then the corpse stirred and its eyes opened. Startled, Etan jumped back, but when he heard only a groan from the hole, he crept cautiously back to the edge.

This, he now felt almost certain, was not a Norn attacker, but one of the Sithi that Tiamak and Thelía said had come to the castle's defense.

"Are you badly hurt?" he called.

The Sitha did not move, but his eyes followed Etan. "I will know when I try to get up," the stranger said in creditable Westerling. "But I do not think I can climb out just yet. You are one of the castle-folk? Do you see any of my fellow Zida'ya? Can you call them for me?"

"If they were here, they are gone," said Etan. "There are only mortal survivors and three dead Norns left."

"Then I will need your help."

Etan had a moment of misgiving. Could he be certain this was truly one of the Sithi and not a Norn who could speak the Westerling tongue? "Who are you? Do you know Jiriki?"

"Know him? Jiriki i-Sa'onserei is my kinsman and one of my oldest friends. But how do you know him, mortal?"

Etan thought it had the sound of truth. "It doesn't matter now. How can I help you?"

"Do you have a rope?"

"No. But if there is something I can do, tell me quickly. There is a horse here who keeps trying to kick me."

"A black horse? Yes? My excellent Shadowswift! I knew she would not desert me." A low whistle issued from the hole. The black horse walked to the edge of the pit, then the Sitha spoke to her in his own fluid tongue. "She will not harm you now," he called. "Reach into the saddlebag and you will find a length of cord."

Etan cautiously approached the huge animal, who stood stock-still and let him rummage in the bag until he found the length of smooth, slippery rope. He tied one end around a chunk of fallen masonry and tossed the other into the pit. A moment later, a figure with golden skin mostly smeared with blood and ash clambered up out of the hole, then slumped to the cobbled ground. "I am very sore," he said. "But I think nothing is broken. My mother named me Ki'ushapo. I thank you for your help."

Etan had not seen a living immortal so close, except for the poisoned female Sitha that Pasevalles had brought into the castle, and he caught himself staring at the stranger's odd, birdlike movements as Ki'ushapo put his arms around his mare's neck and spoke softly into her ear before turning back to Etan. "I chased those Hikeda'ya soldiers," he said, gesturing to the dead Norns, "but the ground collapsed beneath me." He looked around the narrow, deserted street. "Where are the rest of them? There were thousands outside the gates."

Etan shook his head. "I can't tell you anything for certain, except that they're all gone. In the middle of the attack, they simply . . . vanished. Hundreds were on the hill—thousands—then in an instant they were all gone."

The Sitha stared at him. "Strange. Almost impossible, or so it seems—the might that such trickery would require! But my kin—you said they had gone, too."

"I did not see them ride away after the Norns disappeared, but I trust the ones who told me."

Ki'ushapo swung onto his saddle with surprising ease. "Then I must go now. If my people have already left this place so quickly after we rode so long to get here, there must be a pressing reason. I must catch up to them."

"Wait, please, Sir Sitha." Etan had put Tiamak's wooden box down to tie the rope for Ki'ushapo's escape, but now he picked it up again. "You told me Jiriki is your friend—that you are kin."

"Both things are true," the immortal said. "It seems strange you know of him."

"Because I have been sent to find him. I have something here I must give him. I swore an oath to do so. Can you help me?"

For the first time, the Sitha really looked at him. To Etan, the eyes in the dirt-smeared face seemed as fierce as a hawk's. "And who exactly are you?"

"Brother Etan. I am a man of God, if that means anything to you."

"Something—though not much, in all truth. But what do you want with Jiriki?"

"I may not say—I made a promise—but I swear on my faith I mean him no harm. My lord Tiamak, the king's counselor, tasked me to bring Jiriki this," he displayed the decorated wooden box. "Tiamak said it was important—more important than anything, he said."

"Can you tell me what is in it?"

"I cannot, mostly because I don't know—I haven't yet looked in the box. Tiamak told me I must give it to Jiriki." *Or whoever leads the Sithi, he said,* Etan remembered. So here was a chance to escape this terrible duty. *Perhaps I could give it to this kinsman of his—he is more likely to bring it to Jiriki safely than I could ever be.* Still, for form's sake, he asked, "Can you tell me how to find him?"

"Find him?" The Sitha laughed, astonishing Etan. "You would head north in search of Jiriki? Do you think this night just past was frightening?" He waved a hand at the smoking ruins around them. "If Jiriki and whoever survived this have started off already, then they are hurrying toward something far grimmer, far more deadly than anything you have seen here—or anything you can imagine." He shook his head. Etan thought the line of his long jaw made the Sitha look young, even beneath the smears of ash, but his golden eyes seemed much older. "Give your prize to me, mortal. I will do what I can to see that it reaches Jiriki."

And there it was—the perfect opportunity to pass along the bitter cup. Instead, Etan heard himself say, "I thank you, but I cannot." He took a breath. "I swore I would give it to Jiriki myself—if he still lived."

"Then it seems you must come with me." Again, the Sitha shook his head, this time in something like wonderment. "You will ride with me on Shadowswift. We will have to travel swiftly indeed, though, if we want to catch Jiriki of the Year-Dancing. And we do not have much time."

"Where are we going?"

"North to Tanakirú," said the Sitha, extending his arm down to help Etan struggle up onto the saddle behind him. "Far from here. And the journey will be dangerous."

"Yes. I guessed that."

"My men are hungry," said Pasevalles. "It is not a good idea to starve them. They will take it badly."

"But, my lord, we are doing all we can! We do not have the supplies to keep feeding so many for so long."

He regarded the castellan with a patient expression. "Sir Rawlie, I fear you do not understand me. The answer is not, 'We cannot do it,' the answer is, 'I will find a way, sire.' You do know who I am, do you not?"

"Yes, lord."

"With Duke Osric dead in the Hayholt fires, I am the only power left in Erkynland, the only one keeping the Norns at bay and holding the country together. Or do you think otherwise?"

"Of course not, my lord, of course not, but—"

Stilling him with a raised hand, Pasevalles shook his head. "*But,* he says. That is another word I do not like. Hulgar, this fellow keeps saying things I do not want to hear. What should I do?"

The huge and almost impossibly ugly Thrithings-man, whose shaggy, braided beard hung down to his waist and was not even close to the most impressive thing about him, looked up from where he was sharpening a war-ax. "Take off his head. Find someone who can do better."

Sir Rawlie fell to his knees and then onto his belly. "No, my lord, please! I will find a way to feed them all."

"And your own people here, too," said Pasevalles. "You see, I am not an unreasonable man. We are surrounded by farms and estates. The barns are doubtless groaning with what they have put aside for the winter. Take a company from your household and inform the neighboring landowners that until the Hayholt is rebuilt, I am making this castle the seat of the High Throne."

"As you say, my lord!" The castellan was still clinging to the floor as though it were the deck of a pitching ship. "I will go at once."

"Send a few clansmen with him, Hulgar," Pasevalles said. "To make certain he does not get ideas."

"I would never get an idea, my lord!" Sir Rawlie shrilled as Hulgar curled a huge fist in the neck of Rawlie's velvet robe and jerked him up onto his feet. When he could breathe again, the castellan backed out of the hall sputtering grateful apologies. "I will go this moment!" he called from the doorway.

"It would have been faster to take his head off and send my clansmen out instead," said Hulgar.

"Yes, and they would burn down every cottage and manor for leagues." Pasevalles rose. "Then the local people would turn against us, and instead of keeping their larders open for us when we need them, they would flee west, and sooner than later, we would starve." He patted the huge Thrithings-man on the shoulder as if he were a monstrous pet. "I chose this place as a safe refuge and intend to keep it that way as long as I need it."

Hulgar grunted. "Where is my brother? He should have joined us by now."

"Zhadu was left with a simple task to perform. He is either on his way to us, or he has fallen afoul of Queen Utuk'ku, somehow."

"The whitefaces better not have killed him," said Hulgar. "He owes me twenty gold pieces."

Pasevalles curled his lip. "I knew I could not trust the Norns. That ancient bitch of a queen has betrayed everyone she ever dealt with. I confess I did not think she was so petty as to burn the Hayholt, though. That will make it all the harder for me to take charge of the High Ward. I too hope your brother arrives soon. There will be more than enough killing to keep both of you satisfied."

Hulgar looked up, grinning his broken grin. "I like the sound of that."

Pasevalles shook his head. "I might as well be talking to a mastiff. All you truly care about is the smell of blood and meat, eh?"

The grasslander glanced up, teeth like ruined tombstones in a desecrated graveyard. "Would you want me any other way?"

"Please," begged the mistress of the castle. "I do not know anything of a vault. Please, let me see my son!"

Pasevalles sighed. "Madam, like so many else in this backwater shire, you misunderstand your position. Your late husband, as is well known, was a famously greedy man. And I am inconveniently separated from my own funds. His gold—and doubtless other fine things he hoarded—must be hidden somewhere here in the castle. All you must do is tell me where, and your son will be free to join you again."

"But I hear him crying! He says over and over that he is hungry!" She was trembling all over but trying not to weep, her fine-boned face blue beneath the eyes from lack of sleep.

"Ah, well. At that age they are always hungry." Pasevalles reached out and cupped her chin in his hand. "You are a high nobleman's widow, lady, and not uncomely. I would think that you would be anxious to please a guest like me—a guest who will almost certainly be the next king of Erkynland. But instead, you continue to frustrate me." He gave her chin enough of a squeeze to make her wince, then released her. "Perhaps I should look to your daughter instead."

She looked at him in astonishment. "But she is far too young to marry! Surely you do not think—!"

"Did I say anything about marrying her?" Pasevalles sighed again. "I never believed what was said at court about you nobles of the Erkynlandish countryside, but now I am beginning to believe that the unpleasant gossip was right—you are not, as a group, very clever." He leaned toward her. "I have had a very trying month, my lady. The Hayholt was burned to the ground. The old king, his queen, and Duke Osric are all dead. Their heir, so-called, has vanished and is almost certainly dead, and his younger sister, the last of the royal grandchildren, is also gone, stolen away by traitors." He turned to survey the ladies-in-waiting, who had shrunk back to the walls of the retiring room at his entrance. "Do you fear my tame Thrithings-men? Then think of this, my lady. I am the only thing that stands between your little castle and ten times ten thousand grasslanders who will soon descend on Erkynland in search of pillage and rape. I am the only thing that stands between you and utter destruction between the hammer of the immortal Norns and the anvil of those grassland barbarians. All I ask is access to your husband's hoarded gold so that we may fight off these threats. And yet you continue to defy me, as if I were some peasant, some . . . upstart."

"No, my lord, no . . . !"

"Yes, my lady, yes. And so I think it is time for your daughter to join your son. Perhaps sharing each other's company will comfort them as the pangs of hunger increase. And in the end, if you continue to defy me, it may be that one of them will at the last provide a meal for the other."

She stared at him wide-eyed for a moment, then her cheeks and forehead suddenly grew as pale as a Norn's face, and she crumpled to the floor in a faint. The other women rushed toward her, but kept glancing at Pasevalles, as if he might forbid them helping her. It made him angry, and though he had long ago decided to execute the castle's owners and their courtiers when they were no longer useful, he decided now to give all of them to his clansmen first.

Arms crossed, face somber, he told the women, "When your mistress awakes, tell her she has until midnight tolls to tell me what I wish to know. She knows what will happen if she doesn't. I am a patient man, but I will not be trifled with when the fate of all our land is in jeopardy. Is that understood?"

The women all nodded. A few openly wept.

"I am glad to hear it." He turned and went out. His clansmen locked the door behind him.

So many self-defeating fools, he thought. *Ruling these people is a wearisome responsibility, and the challenges are hardly worth the time spent on them.* He had thought power without restraint would be more satisfying, somehow. *There may be a larger lesson here,* he decided. *I will go listen to the boy crying in his chamber for a time while I consider it.*

Three days had passed since the Hayholt had burned, and Miriamele was growing weary of being confined on the *Elysiamansa* when there was so much to do on land, so a visit from Tiamak and Thelía was a welcome distraction. Tiamak was leaning heavily on his wife's arm, and his head was bandaged, but he took the trouble to bow before her, although it made him wince.

"It is still hard to see you and not believe it a dream, Majesty," he told her.

Miriamele smiled sadly. "The world we knew is gone, old friend. I think it is the past that is the dream now. How is your eye?"

"He is a most difficult patient," said Thelía in disgust. "I ordered him to stay in bed, yet here you see him."

Miriamele smiled again. "And how is Duke Osric?"

"Doing as well as can be hoped," Thelía told her. "But he is no easier to care for than my husband. His Grace took in a great deal of smoke before he was brought out of the castle, and he is not breathing well, although his other wounds are healing. I think the worst may be past."

"Thank God for that. We have lost too many of our loved ones in this cursed year. I will continue to pray for him." She gave her visitors a searching look. "And you two? From what your wife has told me, Tiamak, you both had a terrifying time beneath the castle, hiding from Pasevalles."

"Terrifying, yes, but also instructive," he said. "As to our health, we are both well enough, though my wife is correct—I have been up and about more than she would wish. So many here are in need of care."

"Yes, but I cannot risk losing either one of you. You both must rest, Tiamak."

"We will, once the worst is over." He gave her a look. "And as the castle physician, more or less, I would recommend the same for you."

Miriamele shook her head. "I fear we will be arguing over this many times in the days to come, since both of us have so many tasks that will not wait." She poured them each a cup of wine. "Do we know any better what happened here?"

"From talking to the surviving Erkynguards, and to Sir Porto, we know much of what happened, but little of why or how," said Tiamak. "What seemed like thousands of Norns surrounded the castle. Some entered and began setting fires. But when the Sithi arrived, most of the Norns vanished. I suspect that most of them were never here—that the great majority were only illusion, some trick of the Norn Queen, though I cannot imagine how it was accomplished."

"Hold, hold," said Miriamele. "Sithi? This is the first I have heard of this. Are you telling me they were here?"

"The Perdruinese knight Sir Porto and several others swear it is so. A few hundred of their folk came and fought against the Norns, but after the Norns disappeared, the Sithi quickly rode away."

"Are you sure it was them?"

"Porto saw them. And we discovered something near the Nearulagh Gate." Tiamak gestured to his wife, and Lady Thelía took out an object wrapped in cloth and unfolded the covering.

"A knife," said Miriamele.

"A witchwood knife," said Tiamak. "Only the immortals carry them. But do you see the runes on the blade? They are Sithi, not Norn."

"So the Sithi did come, but then left again? Why?"

"That is one of many things we still cannot answer," Tiamak said. "Perhaps the attack was a diversion. That would explain why Utuk'ku expended so much power on a mere trick. When they realized what had happened, the Sithi might have understood that they had been drawn away from something more important."

"I am more and more confused," said Miriamele. "Drawn away from what? From where?"

"We do not know that either, Majesty," said Thelía.

Miri took a long sip of her wine and sat back. "Riddles and more riddles. Pasevalles has the Hayholt under his control but then he bolts. The Norns come and burn the castle but, if what you have said is true, they send only a few real soldiers and leave the city outside the walls untouched." She shook her head. "Still, such mysteries aside, it is Pasevalles I most want. He killed Idela, my daughter-in-law, and I am sure he had something to do with Simon's death, too." She paused until she had found her composure again. "So where is he?"

Tiamak raised his hands—still crisscrossed with deep scratches—and spread them in a gesture of helplessness. "Something else we do not know. Yet. But I have a favor to ask, and it could help answer that question."

"Whatever will help find Pasevalles, the murdering dog. I cannot rest until that traitor is in shackles," she said. "Other things such as this struggle between Norns and Sithi may be beyond our reach, but I pray that Pasevalles is not."

"Then give me leave to take a few strong soldiers to begin searching in the ruins of the castle," said Tiamak. "I am particularly interested in the Chancelry, which does not seem to have been as badly burned as other parts of the castle. That was where Pasevalles kept his private papers, and though I much doubt he would have left anything behind that might help to tell us where he has gone, it is possible he might have left some traces that even he himself did not notice."

"Of course." She took a sip of wine. "Tell me, do you have any knowledge of what happened to my husband's body?"

Tiamak shook his head. "We were gone when Simon was brought back from Winstowe, but I have heard that his coffin was in the chapel. The castle burned before a funeral could be held, of course. The chapel is nothing now but ashes and a few standing stones, and the Throne Hall is an utter ruin, too."

"The only thing that survived," said Thelía, "besides Holy Tree Tower, are the blackened bones of the Dragonbone Chair."

Miriamele laughed, but her eyes were brimming with tears. "Oh, sweet Elysia, what a dreadful jest! Simon hated that thing so much. I never understood why, not really. Now he is gone—yet the chair remains!"

"He hated it because he hated lies, Miriamele," Tiamak said gently. "To him, it meant that the founding tale of the kingdom was a trick—that King John did not truly kill the dragon, the feat for which he was so celebrated, the thing that made John king. Your husband hated lies so much that he raged against even the hero-stories that were told about himself and the Storm King's War, though most of them barely exaggerated all that Simon did—and all that you did."

Miriamele did not wipe away the tears this time, but let them run down her cheeks. "There will never be anyone like him—not for me, not for Erkynland. He drove me mad at times with his impatience, and even with his honesty. But how could I not love him for being that way?" She paused, struggling for breath. "How can I live without him?"

The two of them waited until she had composed herself. "That I cannot answer, Majesty—Miriamele, my friend," said Tiamak. "But when someone has made our lives richer by their presence, we should not only mourn but also be thankful."

"Ah! Go away now, and take your good sense with you," she said, laughing through her tears. "All I know is that if the High Ward did not need me so desperately, I would be tempted to join him."

"Do not say that!" Thelía put down her goblet. "We already lost you once, Majesty, or so we thought."

"My wife is right. They Who Watch and Shape have given us a great gift by bringing you back to us against all reason," Tiamak told her. "We need you, my queen. We need you now more than ever."

"And that is my curse, I suppose." She lifted her glass to salute them. "Go then, Tiamak. Take soldiers and dig in the embers for some trace of the criminal Pasevalles."

As they rose to go, Miriamele abruptly lifted her hand. "Wait! I almost forgot. I have decided that for all who do not know the truth, I must remain dead. Neither the word 'queen' nor my name should pass anyone's lips, and we are swearing those who already know to secrecy."

"But if we are asked, who is in authority here?" wondered Lady Thelía.

"I do not care. Say Baron Norvel is. No, better, say that it is 'the Duchess' who rules now. Most will think it means Nelda rules in her husband Osric's place."

"That will not frighten our enemies at all."

"All the better," said Miriamele.

After they left, she finished her wine and then looked around the small cabin and decided to pour herself another.

6

A Fold in the Veil

"Where are we, Grandfather? I fell asleep."

It pained Simon's heart to hear Lillia's voice again after it had been silent so long, but it also filled him with relief. "We are riding with the Sithi-folk, dear one—our friends. Do you remember?"

She yawned and looked at the brightly clad riders all around them. "The fairies are our friends?"

"Some of them. The best of them."

"Where are we going?"

"I'll explain later." The sun was just rising, but the morning was bitterly cold. The empty, winter-yellow fields sped past like a bumpy carpet beneath the ceiling of gray sky. "You're going to sleep again soon, but don't fear. I'll take care of you, little cub."

"I don't want to sleep. I want to be with you."

"You will be with me, I promise." Speaking the words, so close to a lie without being one, made Simon's heart ache. "I love you very much, my Lillia. You know that, don't you?"

"Of course!" She yawned. "But I just woke up. I don't think I'll go to sleep again for a long time."

"Perhaps not." Except he knew better. Geloë had surfaced a short time before, from some unknowable place inside his granddaughter, to tell him that soon she would need to command the child's body for a substantial length of time. But Simon did not want to yield his granddaughter, even in the face of the great catastrophe about which Geloë and Jiriki kept hinting but had so far not explained.

"Will we stop soon? I'm hungry. Is it Aedonmansa already? I keep thinking about the pudding I like—the one with raisins and apples."

"Aedonmansa," said Simon. "Hmmm." In truth, he no longer had any idea what month it was, let alone the day. He had spent so long in the darkness of the cell beneath the castle, and lost in his own mind before that, that he could not even guess.

Winstowe Castle, he thought. *The battle with the Thrithings-men. That would have been just before Harrow's Eve, wouldn't it? The day I fought Josua's son—when I thought he killed me.* But that was the last date fixed in his head. *And the rest of the things I remember?* he wondered. *Likimeya, the old Hayholt, when it was Asu'a—all those visions. Were they even real?*

"Here is a promise, little beast," he said. "When I've done with all this, with the fairy-folk and all the other things I have to do, I'll make certain you get your pudding and even a gift, whether it's Aedonmansa or not."

"That would be good," she said, squirming with pleasure in his arms. "And can I light the candles this year?"

"Of course," he said, struggling with sorrow and shame. "You can light them all. I'll hold you up for the high ones."

"Good. I love . . . when all the candles . . . are lit . . ."

Despite her protestations, Lillia was nodding in his lap even as their horse thundered along with the rest of the shining Sithi. He pulled her closer and whispered in her ear. "You had a very bad dream, I know. Have good dreams now, child. I'm here."

She did not reply, and for long moments he could only clutch her against his chest. Then she stirred a little, raising his hopes.

"I am sorry to have to take her down so far," said the familiar, harsh voice—a rasp that should never have issued from a child's throat. "It is not out of callousness but raw need. The deeper she sleeps, the less she will be troubled by what I must say and do while I share her body."

"Oh, dear Lord. Is she safe?"

"She is as safe as her body is, for now, Simon—as is true for all mortals."

As if he had heard Geloë's quiet voice, or sensed her renewed presence in some other way, Jiriki reined up where he rode at the vanguard and waited until Simon and his small passenger caught up, then guided his horse into a matching pace beside them.

"It is good you have returned, Sa-Ruyan Geloë," he said with a formality that made the odd moment even stranger.

"Did you know?" Simon asked him. Suddenly, almost everything else he thought he knew had proved false, and he was even finding it hard to trust his Sitha friend. "Jiriki, did you know that Geloë was still alive—that she would take my granddaughter's body for a hiding place when that Norn-thing burned up?"

"I did not. I was as surprised as you, Seoman. But when she revealed herself, certain things began to make sense to me—things I had wondered about. But I will leave it to our wise woman to complete our understanding."

Geloë snorted in sour amusement. "Wise is as wise does. There are still a few things you do not know, Likimeya's son." Simon was reminded that Geloë had never liked ceremony or flowery speech. "In truth, there are still many things I do not know, either. But I will tell you what I can."

Simon's anger had dissipated. "Be careful," was all he said. "Please, Geloë, be careful with this precious, precious child."

Again the voice was flat as roof slate. "It hurts me more than you can know to have to do this, but I have little choice. Now listen, both of you, and I will tell you all I can: You both know that in the closing days of our war with the Storm King, I was attacked by Hikeda'ya assassins. It was a sign, I suppose, that Utuk'ku feared me, or at least feared what I knew, but it was still a bitter defeat, and I went down into death with a violent curse for her on my lips. And now we come to the place where words cannot explain all the truth.

"I awoke, or came back, or was again aware, to find myself on the far side of the Veil of Death. But do not mistake me—the Veil is not a thing, not a curtain or a wall. Neither is it a place. It is simply another part of the greater truth, a moment that does not end. What lies beyond it might be Simon's Heaven or Jiriki's Garden or something quite unlike either. But even though that moment is without time of its own, the world you think of as real still spins on and the hours still march past beyond the Veil, and that passage is perceived by those on the far side of the Veil, though it touches them in no other way. A moment behind the Veil can be a fraction of an instant so small you could not measure it, or it can seem a century. Time does not flow there, it eddies, it pools, it falls like rain or leaps up like a fountain."

Simon was mystified, and it must have been obvious on his face.

"Do not frown," she said. "I can only speak in such confusing terms, because there can be only approximations, and those are so unlike truth that, by comparison, you might as well describe the sun as something shiny.

"It took me a while to understand that I was dead," she continued, "or at least that my mortal form had died but the part of me I will call my spirit had not. But even as I reached that first understanding, I also realized that I was not alone in that place beyond death. I floated in a dark ocean, surrounded by other . . . presences, for lack of a better word. Not all of them were like me. Huge and powerful things also swam there, things I could sense but never quite see. One seemed more powerful and dangerous than the others—a hot mass of rage and writhing darkness. If I had known in those early moments that Ineluki had been defeated, I would have guessed it to be him, but I would have been wrong. Because Ineluki Storm King, as far as I can tell, has finally let go of his strange existence after his first death and passed on to whatever is truly next.

"Instead, I came to understand that the seething, angry presence was Ommu the Whisperer, the last survivor of the Red Hand, the Storm King's resurrected followers. Like their master, four of those Hikeda'ya mystics had vanished into the final mystery at the end of the Storm King's War. But Ommu's hatred of humankind and the Zida'ya must have been too great for her to free herself from life, and her essence had survived—like mine. I could feel her terrible heat, like standing too close to a forge-fire. Nothing was left of the person the Whisperer had once been but a mad lust for revenge. And like me, she was trapped in that between-place—or so I thought. But I was wrong. Because someone else soon passed through the Veil. Someone who wanted to set Ommu free.

"The Whisperer and I had never been truly alone in that place beyond death, of course. Many small spirits, mortal and Keida'ya both, were trapped there with us, captured by their own hatred or loss or grief, or even just confusion. These spirits shone like tiny, distant stars, but they were almost invisible against the great sun of hatred that was Ommu. Then I perceived the coming of another burning power—Utuk'ku, the queen of the Hikeda'ya.

"Utuk'ku was not dead, though. After expending so much of her power in the Storm King's failed scheme, the Norn Queen had only survived by falling into the long, deep sleep called the *keta-yi'indra*. But if her living body slept, her mind did not, and it was fixed like a nail on undoing her defeat. I was fortunate, though. Because I had lost my own body, I was hard for Utuk'ku to perceive, and she never knew that I watched her. Her hatred burned as fiercely as Ommu's, but Utuk'ku had an advantage that neither the Whisperer nor I had—she still lived. She, at least, would eventually return to the world, rested and restored, her terrible goal unchanged.

"Even in that foggy, confusing netherworld, Utuk'ku and Ommu soon found each other. They did not speak as I am speaking now—not in that place—but the heedless strength of those two was such that I could glean much of their shared thought, so I hid myself in a fold in the Veil and tried to discover what Utuk'ku was planning. It soon became clear to me that she intended to bring back Ommu from death's antechamber, then with her help, sing up the Three Who Are One—a great and terrible magic."

"The Three Who Are One has not been sung or even contemplated since the last days of the Garden," said Jiriki in surprise. "Not since my people struggled to hold back Unbeing."

"Just so," said Geloë. "It is a rare and terrible magick, dangerous both to those who make it and to the innocents around them. It was frightful even to know they were considering it. And the death of the first innocent was not far away."

"At last, Utuk'ku ended her healing sleep and returned to her body. If she was to bring the Whisperer back to the world, a sacrifice had to be made—an earthly body prepared for Ommu to inhabit." Geloë paused, then was silent for no little while. "I do not want to speak of that," she said at last. "A living being, an innocent child, lost her life without a choice. It was the last of that poor child's mortal form that burned away outside the Hayholt a day ago, forcing me to enter your granddaughter, Simon."

A sudden terror swept through Simon. "What do you mean, burned away? Is that going to happen to Lillia? You can't do that! You must leave her!"

"Calm yourself," said Geloë. "I was in that poor, stolen body for many moons, and as part of the Three Who Are One, I wielded powers that have never been known in this world. You saw how I sang up the appearance of ten thousand Hikeda'ya soldiers and made that illusion last, day and night, for an agonizing length of time. No mortal form could last forever under such effort. It will be different with Lillia—"

"I don't care. It's too dangerous!"

"Hear me out, Simon. I have prepared a place for my spirit to go to when it must, and even if that fails, I will not stay in your granddaughter long enough to harm her. This I promise, Simon of the Fisher People, and the dead cannot lie."

He shuddered to hear those words coming out of the frail form of his beloved grandchild. "Please, Geloë. She is all I have left. Miri, Morgan, everyone . . ."

"I know something of what has happened to you. Calm your heart. I promise you that at this moment, the child you hold is experiencing nothing more frightening than a deep sleep, healing and dreamless."

He did not like the sound of it—his own dreamlessness had brought him only unhappiness—but now Jiriki spoke. "Let her say what she must, Seoman. She has given you her word not to harm the child."

He nodded, jaw clenched, not trusting himself to speak.

"The hour of Ommu's resurrection came," Geloë continued. "In a ceremony deep in Nakkiga, Utuk'ku opened a doorway, for lack of a better word—or it might be said she tore an opening in the Veil itself, then exerted her strength to hold it open. On my side of the Veil, I felt Ommu move toward that opening like a leviathan of the depths, so close to freedom and a return to life that she was blind to everything around her, to all but the beckoning escape. And that was the moment I struck. Be certain that I could never have overcome Ommu without the advantage of surprise. Those like the Whisperer and Utuk'ku Silvermask are not omnipotent, but they have given away so much of themselves for power that they cannot easily be overcome. I also knew that if I failed in that moment, Ommu would return to the mortal world in search of revenge, so I held nothing back.

"We fought. I cannot tell you for how long, since time runs so differently there. Ommu had no shape. She was like a storm of hatred, a blazing star of pure rage. She did not know me, but she could feel what I was—Tinukeda'ya, one of the slave race that Ommu and her kind had treated like animals for so long. This knowledge enraged her even more, so that her fury blinded her to all strategy. At the last moment, just as Utuk'ku's ceremony beneath the mountain was reaching its culmination—and with my very last strength—I managed to pull myself free from Ommu and pass through the Veil in her place. I had won, but the victory was terrible, because I had been delivered into the shameful gift of an innocent sacrifice, a vessel meant to hold a great power, and I could feel the poor Hikeda'ya child's horror as I flowed into her. And as the gap in the Veil closed, I felt Ommu's burning, desperate wrath at being cheated of her return, but I had no sense of victory, because I had caused the death of an innocent." She was breathing hard, overwhelmed by the memory.

"You cannot blame yourself for that," said Jiriki. "That Hikeda'ya child would have been doomed in any case if Ommu had passed over instead of you. At least her sacrifice was not wasted."

"Tell that to the young Hikeda'ya girl I felt dying in horror," said Geloë bitterly. "Her name was Yu-Jalamu, and her only crime was suiting Utuk'ku's wicked purpose. I sent her to sleep—not like I have done with your grandchild, Simon, do not fear. I used just a touch of the strength of the Three to push poor Yu-Jalamu into an unknowing so deep that when she lost her grip on life, she was not in fright or pain." Lillia's body took a deep, shuddering breath. "Forgive me. I must rest for a while. Remembering that terrible hour has left me exhausted."

"If you are done for now, will you bring Lillia back to me?" Simon asked.

"No. She is resting peacefully. It would only confuse her and unsettle her to draw her up to the light again. I have much more to say when I have regained some strength."

The small, flaxen head tipped forward and Geloë's voice fell silent.

Tanahaya of Shisae'ron made her way up the three hundred and seventy-seven steps of Virayu's Tower, pausing from time to time to admire the carvings that lined the walls, great swirls filled with smaller, more intricate patterns as ornate and yet apparently random as ivy. She was not ascending slowly because the climb wearied her but because she was struggling with an emotion so unusual that she did not quite know what to do with it. Tanahaya was unhappy, even angry. Though neither of these feelings were foreign to her, the object of her unhappiness was unprecedented—her closest friend and sister-of-the-heart, Aditu.

She had not slept since Lady Ayaminu, mistress of Anvi'janya, had revealed the truth about Tanakirú's secret. It was not the revelation itself that had so disturbed her—though disturbing it certainly was—but the fact that her friend Aditu and her lover Jiriki had both kept it from her.

They had been sworn to secrecy by our beloved Amerasu, she reminded herself. But when unhappiness rushed over her once more like a wave breaking across the deck of a ship, she could do nothing but wait for it to seep away again. It was hard, though; she had never thought such a thing could happen between her and the two Sa'onserei.

At last, she reached the top, the only part of the tall, slender tower with windows. The spire had been built long ago for Virayu herself, the companion of Tululiko and co-founder of the city. As Anvi'janya had grown, old tales related, Virayu had become increasingly weary of the bustle, talk, and commerce, and had asked for a place she could go where her thoughts would not be interrupted by the presence of others. Some of the tales suggested that in her old age Virayu never left the tower at all, but had her meals brought by a few trusted, silent servants. There were moments when Tanahaya thought she could see the attraction of such a life, and this was one of them.

One of the oddities of Virayu's Tower was that it had no doors, only open arches: as she reached the topmost step, Tanahaya was already in the highest chamber. Aditu sat at the center of the room, eyes closed, arms around her jutting belly as if to protect it, though Tanahaya could not imagine anyone or anything in Anvi'janya that would be a risk to Aditu's child. Birth was already rare among the Zida'ya, so the birth of a child to the Year-Dancing Clan's next Sa'onsera was something extraordinary.

"My sense of smell is so strong since this child started to grow that I scented you when you had only just begun to climb," said Aditu, eyes still closed. Her black hair swirled in the breeze that danced through the room. She wore only a simple white gown, with a pendant of creamy, sea-green stone around her neck. By the light from the single broad window, her skin seemed to glow like sun shining through the leaves of an autumn poplar. Tanahaya had always thought Aditu extraordinarily beautiful, so lovely that it was even hard to stay angry with her; still, she was determined to hold onto her discontent, at least for the moment. "In fact," Aditu said, "I can even smell your mood, dear Spark. What troubles you?"

Tahanaya looked around, not wanting to answer until she had her emotions in harness. The tower top had a wide window that looked out over the city, the cavern's broad entrance framing the shapely towers and meandering streets. Tanahaya could not help admiring the simple and graceful lines of Anvi'janya's buildings, the way each seemed to echo the others without mere imitation. Even the stone of the buildings seemed to have been chosen for the effect it gave from this one window: most of them were white, but others had been faced in pale blue, tan, and rose pink, and had been so carefully created that the city seemed something small and precious, as if it were only a miniature.

"Did the Tinukeda'ya build this place?" she asked.

Aditu stirred. "Of course. All of the cities built by the Landborn when they first came into this land were made with the help of Tinukeda'ya miners and stonemasons."

"What we did to them was terrible." She turned to see that Aditu was watching her, her eyes full of kindness and concern. "A sin, as the mortals would say."

"Yes. It was." Aditu raised her arms above her head, stretching. "My brother has spoken of it for as long as I can remember, as bitterly as if he had been alive himself when they were made slaves."

"As we all should feel, I think." Tanahaya knew she was avoiding the thing that, at least in this hour, troubled her most.

"But remember that we Zida'ya came to see that it was wrong. The Hikeda'ya still have not."

"I do not think it is enough to point to others who have behaved worse than ourselves," said Tanahaya. "There will always be such. If not the Hikeda'ya, then the worst of the mortals."

"I agree, Spark," said Aditu. "I merely meant that as long as Utuk'ku lives and rules over our kin, the changeling Tinukeda'ya will not have justice, no matter what we may believe." She smiled, but there was little cheer in it. "Now, tell me what troubles you so. I know your concern for the Tinukeda'ya folk is sincere, but I can tell it is not the true object of your visit."

Tanahaya shook her head. "Now that I am here, I do not feel right troubling you with my concerns. You are sitting your vigil before the Year-Dancing ceremony—your first ceremony as the Sa'onsera. I should not have disturbed you."

"I have been preparing for this ceremony half a Great Year, at least," her friend said. "Since Utuk'ku killed my father and my mother went to war. I knew this day would come." Her smile had long since gone. "Nor is a Sa'onsera some exalted thing, set above the concerns of friends and family. To believe so would be a misunderstanding of everything the first Sa'onsera was, and why the ancient Keida'ya clans split between her and her husband."

"Ah, yes," said Tanahaya. "Do tell me about old days, Rabbit. We scholars have so little chance to learn about them."

Aditu gave her an amused look. "Do not be sharp with me, mistress. Of course, you scholars know everything about the past, about our history—except for the things you do not."

That stung more than a little, and now Tanahaya had to struggle to keep her voice even. "I do not think it is fair to tease me over a secret you and your family kept from me—kept from most of our people."

"So now we come to the heart of it," Aditu said. "I suspected this was your concern. But if the message you take from Ayaminu's tale is only that we of Year-Dancing House kept secrets, you have missed much that was important, Spark."

"Please, Rabbit. Please, my dear Aditu. Don't say such things to me. I know I am not of the Sa'onserei. I was not raised in the bustle of the Sithi home, Jao é-Tinukai'i, let alone in the stone halls of old Asu'a, but I can understand as well as anyone why you kept this secret. And it is possible that if I had been one of the leaders of your clan, I would have done the same. But I was not, and it is bitter to me. It feels as though our friendship—the most important thing in my life for many years—was something less than I thought it was."

Aditu was silent for a long time. "I understand," she said finally. "And I am sorry. You are my beloved friend, Tanahaya. I have never wanted to keep secrets from you, least of all such a great one as this, but it was First Grandmother Amerasu's choice that we should tell no one not directly involved in protecting Tanakirú and the Vale of Mists. In truth, I am relieved that you finally know."

"But it is *still* a secret, even if I am now one of the few who shares it," said Tanahaya. "The rest of our people still do not know."

"They will know soon enough. The end of secrecy is coming . . . the end of many things." She looked down at her belly for a moment. "I know I cannot truly make it up to you, my dear one. And I suspect you must one day have this same frustrating conversation with my brother. But now that you are here, may we put this difference aside for just a little time? I need you. I need my friend."

Tanahaya was still unhappy, but the words touched her. "What can I do?"

Aditu rose with surprising ease. "You told me that the mortal lad, Prince Morgan, said he had dreamed about my mother, Likimeya, and that he had spoken to her that way several times. Were it anyone else I might think it just an errant breeze off the Road of Dreams, but since she spoke to him once before in my presence, in the sacred Yásira at H'ran Go-jao, it must mean something—perhaps something important." She leaned forward. "And you told me yourself you thought you heard Likimeya speak to you in a dream, though what you saw was your own mother."

Tanahaya nodded. "All true, but I have no idea what it means. Why do you find it so troubling?"

"Because I have felt nothing of my mother except that one time in H'ran Go-jao—she does not speak to me in my dreams. Year-Dancing is upon us, and Utuk'ku threatens everything we care for, and though my mother seems to speak to others, even to a mortal youth, she does not come to me. That troubles me. No, it frightens me, Spark."

Tanahaya understood. "I was near death in Da'ai Chikiza when I thought she spoke to me. Perhaps that had something to do with it."

"Was young Morgan also in such a state?"

"He did not say so. He said Likimeya spoke to him in his sleep." She shook her head. "I am sorry I cannot offer you more. He told me a little of what she said, but we were in danger at the time and his words were hurried and confusing."

Aditu sighed. "It is hard not to feel something is hidden here, something fateful. My mother is not one for idle speech at the best of times, let alone when she has sunk into the depths of the *keta-yi'indra*, the life-saving sleep." She shook her head as if to drive off troubling thoughts. "Enough of dreams and dreaming. Tell me something of yourself, dear one. What about the child *you* carry? Can you feel it moving?"

"Sometimes I think so. At other times, I think I am fooling myself."

"That is not unusual among our kind. It is common to feel such a fear."

"Perhaps. Yet I am still fearful." She reached out and took Aditu's hand. "You have always had a gift. Can you tell me anything of what is inside me? Is the child healthy?"

"My friend, you truly are frightened." Aditu was clearly hesitating. "But some doors should remain closed until they *must* be opened."

"Now you are making me even more fearful," said Tanahaya.

"I say it only out of caution. I am sometimes given hints and glimpses, but that is all they are, not strong foundations for making choices."

"Then give me a glimpse, at least. I only want to know the child lives, that my dreams were true."

"Very well. Sit beside me." When they were both seated, Aditu reached out her hand to touch Tanahaya's belly, then closed her eyes. Tanahaya thought her friend's hand felt almost unnaturally warm.

"Ah!" Aditu's eyes suddenly opened.

"What?" Tanahaya realized her heart was pounding. "By the Lost Garden, tell me what you feel."

"Calm yourself." She closed her eyes again, and for long moments only sat in silence, her hand still spread against Tanahaya's middle. After a moment, she took a deep breath and lifted her hand, then turned to her friend, reluctance clear on her face.

"Tell me the truth, whatever it is," said Tanahaya. "The tale is bad, I can tell."

"Oh, Spark, you see confusion, not grief. I have never felt anything quite like it. But your daughter is hale and strong."

"Daughter?" The swoop from despair to relief was dizzying. "Truly?" In an instant, she could suddenly feel herself a link in a chain that stretched back through her mother and grandmother to the Garden itself. She swayed a little. She had to put both hands on the floor to steady herself. "You are certain it is a girl child?"

Aditu laughed, but something was still held in reserve. "I cannot doubt it. But there is a strength in her, even with birth so far away, that I have not sensed before. I wish I could tell you more, but I must think about what I have felt. Then I would like to try again, to see what else I can feel of her. You will stay in Anvi'janya for the Year-Dancing Ceremony, I hope?"

"Of course."

"Then we have time."

Tanahaya was holding her own belly now, as if in imitation of Aditu. "Between my journey to the mortal castle and the poisoning that almost took my life, we have not had much of that. It will be good to spend some together." But the secret that Aditu and Jiriki had kept from her still gnawed, casting a shadow over everything. "Who knows when we will have such a chance again?"

Aditu heard the meaning in Tanahaya's words. "Who knows indeed?"

"I would ask you another question."

Her friend's smile was less than wholehearted. "I sensed you might. Is it about Tanakirú?"

"Oh, I have many questions about that, but I will save them for our next counsel with Mistress Ayaminu. No, I would ask you a more delicate question."

Aditu laughed, catching Tanahaya by surprise. "At last! I have felt you wanting to ask it since I first told you of the child inside me. You wonder why I chose Yeja'aro to be the father."

Tanahaya blinked. "Are my thoughts so obvious?"

"No, dear Spark, no. It is a question I see in the eyes of everyone. Except for Jiriki. Only my brother has never doubted me."

"I do not doubt you. I only wonder. I know you must have your reasons."

Aditu nodded and made the two-handed sign for *beginning again*. "And I did not mean to place you with the doubters. I have already handled our friendship roughly with the secret Jiriki and I were forced to keep, and I regret that." She let her hands drop to her swollen belly again. "The truth is, I do not know all the reasons."

Tanahaya did not know what to say.

"I know that has the sound almost of madness, but I promise you it is not, or else everything I learned from my mother the Sa'onsera was madness." She frowned. "It is hard to put into words. I had a sense that the strength in Yeja'aro's blood was needed—needed for our people, not for myself. If anyone has been cheated, it is poor Yeja'aro, who loves me." She laughed again, but this time it was clearly mixed with sadness. "He is young and angry and shaped by the wrong lessons, but there is more in him than anyone can see, a core as strong as finely worked witchwood. I say that not as someone lovestruck, but as the daughter of House Sa'onserei. And do not doubt that our people will be gravely tested in days yet to come. We will need such strength."

"But surely the danger in Tanakirú will have to be met long before your child is of an age—"

Aditu shook her head. "I do not speak of the time just ahead. It is all too possible we have no future beyond this threat. Utuk'ku has waited and planned for this moment, and there are strands to the web she has woven that we have not even glimpsed. No, it is both the past and the future of the Garden's children that the Sa'onsera must guard, and if we somehow survive this terrible moment in our history, there will still be dreadful challenges ahead. It is for this uncertain future—a future that may not even come to be—that I chose Yeja'aro as the father of my child. I made the choice for our people, not myself."

For a moment Tanahaya could only sit in silence. "Yours is not an easy road," she said at last.

"Life is not an easy road." Aditu smiled again, but Tanahaya felt it was meant mostly to reassure her.

Tanahaya rose. Her anger had cooled, but she was still troubled, not least by the changes she saw in her friend, once so carefree. "I wish to consider all the things you have told me today, so I will leave you now." She bowed her head. "I am sorry for my unhappiness about Tanakirú, dear Rabbit, even if the hurt is not completely healed. I understand that you felt you could not go against Amerasu's decision to keep the secret. We all loved First Grandmother, but she meant even more to you and Jiriki."

Aditu tried but failed to summon another smile. "She was in some ways more a mother to me than my Likimeya, my true mother."

"Amerasu had time to think—many more Great Years than Likimeya. Given time, I do not doubt your mother would have been the same."

"But she did not get that time. Perhaps none of us will." Aditu appeared to push the dark thoughts away. "And you, Spark—will you stay for the ceremony?"

"Of course! I have never been part of Year-Dancing. I am sure you will be perfect as the Sa'onsera."

"My mother once told me that I would only become the Sa'onsera when I understood the sacrifice. But how can I perform the ceremony if she will not speak to me, though she visits the dreams of mortals? I have always tried to be a dutiful daughter, but it seems even in her dying hours Likimeya does not think I am good enough to follow her path."

Suddenly moved, Tanahaya crouched beside her friend and wrapped her arms around her, setting her face against the dark hair as she held her close. "Do not be so quick to suspect disapproval," she said quietly. "Your mother can be hard, but she is also wise, and you should never doubt she loves you."

"I am sorry I had to keep a secret from you, Spark." Aditu laid her head in the hollow of her friend's neck. "How is it we can hurt the ones we love and be hurt by them so easily in turn?"

Tanahaya thought of the many wounds, both given and received, that troubled her own memories. "Because to love is to make ourselves vulnerable, I think. It means we have opened the door and invited someone in. We have given them the freedom of our house, so when something they do troubles us, we are naked and defenseless."

Aditu did not reply, but she pulled Tanahaya close once more before letting her go.

The Sithi finally stopped at twilight to water and feed their horses. Simon and his granddaughter were given a meal of bread and dried fruit. Lillia had awakened enough to chew and swallow, though she did not speak, but only murmured wordlessly before slipping back down again. Simon was sore, cold, and weak from his ordeal, and knew that his grandchild had suffered too, so at his request, the Sithi built a fire, and Simon sat close to it with Lillia asleep in his arms. The cold was intense, though there was little wind. Powdery snow flurries sparkled against the sky in the dying light.

"Here," said Jiriki, handing Simon his cloak. "Wrap this around her. It is made of fine stuff and should protect her from all but the most severe storms. I am sorry I did not think of it earlier."

Simon took it gratefully, covering all his granddaughter except for her small, pale face. It reminded him painfully, so painfully, of the helplessness he had felt during John Josua's last days. "But will you not be cold?" he asked Jiriki.

The Sitha smiled. "Have you forgotten so much about me in the years that passed, my friend? Compared to mortals, my folk are like the otters that swim in half-frozen streams. Although even that may change for us now that the witchwood is no more."

"Do you think that's what all this is about?" Simon asked. "Utuk'ku wanting to find more witchwood? We kept hearing about "the Witchwood Crown," but I never learned what it meant."

Swift as a blink, a look of discomfort passed over Jiriki's fine-boned face. "Some of this, Geloë will no doubt answer," he said. "She knows more of the tale than me, and I will wait to hear how she tells it. But I still do not know the meaning of the Witchwood Crown, though for a while I thought it an actual thing, a relic of Hamakho Dragonslayer carried out of the Lost Garden. That is what brought me and all these brave Zida'ya to the Hayholt."

As Jiriki explained, Simon could not help marveling at the strangeness of all he described. "You say Tanahaya told you this? Do I know that name?" he asked.

A subtler expression touched Jiriki's features, something Simon could not immediately name. "You saw her, though she did not see you. Aditu and I sent her to you as an envoy, but she was attacked and almost killed."

"The Sitha woman—yes!" Simon unbent his legs and set his cold feet nearer the fire. "I am glad to hear she survived. And it sounds as if she helped to keep Morgan alive. For that alone, she would be my friend forever."

"But that was the last I heard from her," Jiriki said grimly. "Just after she told me of Hamakho's crown, the queen of Nakkiga somehow found a way to silence the Witnesses. At the time when the Zida'ya most need to be able to speak to one another, we are blind, deaf, and mute."

"I pray that Tanahaya and Morgan are still alive," Simon said. "But you seem so sad, Jiriki. It is not like you. Then again, we haven't seen each other for a very long time."

Jiriki smiled, but it did not make him seem any less distracted. "Much of that is simply the way of my people, Seoman—we do not make a show of our feelings. But the danger we are facing is not the only reason for my sadness. Nothing troubles us so deeply as a threat to those we love. A victory in which we lose a beloved one is no victory at all."

"A beloved one? Is Aditu in danger?" Simon asked.

"Of course, but just now she is quite safe, I think." Jiriki lowered himself to sit beside Simon, his movements as swift and smooth as a bird settling onto a branch. "No, it is Tanahaya I fear for. As well as your grandson Morgan, of course, if they are still together."

"Is Tanahaya one of your relatives—?" Simon began, then suddenly understood. "Brave Saint Rhiap," he said, "I think that you love her! She is your sweetheart! Is that true?"

Jiriki nodded. "It is. By your mortal measure, Simon, I have lived a very long time, though by my people's count I am only a short while out of my youth. Tanahaya is younger than I am, but even when I first met her, as my sister's friend, she shone like a flame. So full of life! So full of wonder! Wanting to understand the all and everything of a cosmos that not even the Sa'onsera can hope to comprehend in its fullness. I named her 'Spark,' and she brought a light into my life I did not know I was missing." He fell silent for a time. "You only knew her as someone on the brink of death, my friend. I wish you had truly met her. I hope you have the chance."

A chill passed up Simon's spine. He wrapped his arms more tightly around Lillia so that he could feel her narrow chest move in and out. "Do not say that! She will survive, and so will Morgan. I have to believe that."

"I did not mean it that way," Jiriki said. "Only that because of the length of our lives, we Zida'ya travel through wider circles than mortals do. In fact, it is for that reason I must apologize to you. What was a terrible long time for you not hearing from me seemed to pass for me like a comet in the night sky. My people were in terrible disarray. We abandoned Jao é-Tinukai'i—the place of your confinement, as I am sure you remember—and then my mother Likimeya was badly wounded at the hands of mortals."

"Mortals? My people?"

"I suspect it might have been part of some larger scheme of Utuk'ku's—but yes. Those who dealt my mother several near-deadly wounds were of your own folk."

He felt queasy just hearing it. "I knew nothing of this, but I am sorry, Jiriki. More than I can say."

He put a hand on Simon's shoulder. "I know that. And though some of my people blamed all mortals for it, Aditu and I—and Tanahaya, too—never believed you had anything to do with it. But a tempest blew through the lives of all my folk, and many of them turned against us for consorting with your people—for defending mortals—and before I knew it, years had passed without us speaking. It is a poor justification, without doubt, but I cannot change what happened. Know at least that I am sorry."

"Terrible things have happened, and keep happening," said Simon. "When you talk about the queen of the Norns, I have to wonder if she had something to do with Pasevalles turning traitor. So many wretched things came from that . . ." He had not wanted to think of Miriamele, but she was never far from his thoughts, and for long moments he could do nothing except sit, hugging his granddaughter and holding back tears.

"Utuk'ku weaves webs that span many leagues and many years," Jiriki said. "And she may well have prompted this treacherous minister of yours. But there are still many things to learn and understand."

"Do you think she took away my dreams, too?" Simon asked. "I stopped dreaming, and it wasn't caused by anything natural. I have not dreamed since the spring—except when I thought I was dead, and that seemed much different than ordinary dreams." He thought of how he had spoken to Likimeya, or imagined that he had, and wondered if he should tell Jiriki, but was distracted when Lillia began to move restlessly in his lap.

"That was my fault." Geloë's rough voice startled him. "I stole your dreams, Simon Snowlock. And I will tell you why, because it is a part of my tale that neither of you know in full—a tale of oaths and lies and monstrous crimes. A tale of the Garden's death, and of this world, and perhaps of this world's ending."

"I am listening," said Simon, though his heart felt like stone. "Speak."

"Then know first that I had no choice. It was only a small misdeed set against the greater need, but I am sorry for it, nonetheless. I had to take away your dreams, Simon, because you are not entirely of mortal blood."

7

Through Jeweled Halls

"I believe I must follow the stream deeper into the mountain," Nezeru declared. "There is something very strange about it—and not just the crystals. I want to know what made them, but also where the water comes from."

Morgan did not know what to say. This cavern in the rocky cliffside of the Narrowdark Valley had proved full of surprises. Not just the glimmering passage from the inner chamber that led deeper into the hills, but also the two Tinukeda'ya travelers who had collapsed beside the passage's opening. These two were strangers to both Nezeru and Morgan, but the trolls had met them earlier, and Snenneq explained that the old one was Kuyu-Kun, called the Voice of the Dreaming Sea, and the younger Tinukeda'ya was Kuyu-Kun's acolyte, Tih-Rumi. But it was the jewel-like tunnel extending back into the hill's roots that troubled Morgan the most, a passage lined with inexplicable, gemlike shapes, some as large as the columns of St. Sutrin's Cathedral. Morgan did not want Nezeru to leave them behind and continue on her own, but the bizarre tunnel, at first marvelous, now had begun to fill him with an unease bordering on terror. *I don't want Nezeru go in there without me,* he told himself. *But if I follow her, will I ever see Erchester or the Hayholt again?* Fate seemed to be leading him ever farther from his home and into the frightening unknown.

The two Tinukeda'ya still had not found the strength to stand. "We should do what we can to help them," Morgan said, hoping to put off any arguments about where to go next.

Nezeru only shrugged at this. Snenneq gave Kuyu-Kun a drink from his waterskin and then gave some to his companion as well. "We have some small amount of food left," the troll announced. "But that is almost the end of our water. Do you still think the water of the stream so untrustworthy, Nezeru?"

"You can drink from it yourself if you wish," said Nezeru. "But I suspect you will not live long afterward."

"Isn't it just water from melting snow?" Morgan asked.

"Consider this question," she said. "Did the crystals make the stream, or did the stream make the crystals? Either way, I smell a perilous strangeness in that water."

"I think," said Qina in her halting Westerling, "we get water somewhere not from cave."

Nezeru nodded. "I am glad to see that one of you at least has some sense. Which reminds me—as I climbed, I thought I scented better water nearby, untainted by whatever makes this stream smell so untrustworthy."

The travelers gave the two exhausted Tinukeda'ya the last drops from Snenneq's water skin and left them with a few mouthfuls of dried fish from the trolls' store, then went back out of the cavern into the mist-shrouded noon sun. Morgan and the trolls followed Nezeru along the hillside for no small distance until they found a rivulet that gurgled down from the invisible upper reaches of the fog-shrouded hill. It was ice-cold and as inviting as the sight of a campfire on a stormy night, but Morgan and the trolls dutifully waited until Nezeru had bent down and taken a long, deep sniff. She then plunged her hand into the water and licked a little off her fingers.

"I think it is good," she said, but had barely finished before Morgan was kneeling beside her, scooping it up in handfuls, feeling something like pure joy as it ran down his throat in great, chilly swallows.

Water skins filled, they made their way back to the cave, moving more carefully this time as the light was fading and the mists had risen even higher. If Nezeru had not stopped to wait for them several times, Morgan thought even the trolls might have become lost.

When they reached the cavern, they let the Tinukeda'ya drink again. Nezeru, her glowing sphere now casting a dimmer but still generous light, sat down beside them and questioned them in her own Hikeda'ya tongue, sentences full of liquid sibilances and small, harsh clicks. Kuyu-Kun responded only tersely, as if it pained him to do so, but Tih-Rumi seemed quite content to speak Hikeda'ya, and he and Nezeru talked together for no little time.

"It is agreed," she announced at last. "This Tinukeda'ya, Tih-Rumi, will accompany me to the end of the valley."

"Agreed?" Morgan was angry. "By whom? And what about the rest of us?"

"It is simple, I think." Nezeru's face was so devoid of emotion that Morgan thought she must be hiding something from him. "The time has come for us to part ways."

"I don't understand. I already said I was going with you. So did my friends."

She scowled. "Must I say it outright, Morgan? Then I will. I do not want to take you any further into this danger. I do not want to see you die for something that does not concern you. I have become . . . fond of you."

"Fond?" Morgan had spent many hours pondering his astonishingly strong feelings for Nezeru and he wished she would have offered something more solid to characterize her own feelings toward him, but he did his best to hide his hurt. "As you wish then, my lady," he said stiffly. "I would not force my company on you." He saw that she maintained her look of unconcern, and so he turned to the trolls. "You heard Nezeru. We are not wanted. We should prepare to go back."

To his surprise though, Snenneq spoke up. "I do not agree."

For a moment, Morgan felt the old resentment rise at having his wishes disputed. What good was it to be a prince if everyone was allowed to contradict you? But even the briefest reflection reminded him that whatever his birth might mean back home, it meant nothing here. He took a breath. "Why, Snenneq?"

The trolls shared a brief look. Qina nodded. "Tell Morgan Prince reason," she said.

"Because the way back is also full of danger, my friend, not least of which is the great ogre. There are Norn soldiers everywhere in the valley, and unlike your kindly friend Nezeru, those Norns will not hesitate to kill us. Qina and I think that at least if we follow this cavern, we will be safe from both those things."

"But Nezeru doesn't want us along," he said. "She has made that clear."

Snenneq almost smiled, which Morgan found annoying, as if the troll knew something that he did not—something obvious. "Nevertheless, Qina and myself are thinking that the best plan is to go forward. If we travel far enough this way, the mountains end and we climb down at last to the White Waste. north of the great forest. We trolls know that territory well. Cold, yes, but no giants and no Norns. And when you finally turn toward home, it will be much easier to skirt the northern end of the Wealdhelm and then take the roads south toward your family and castle."

Morgan was caught by surprise, and for a moment could only stand, mouth working. Nezeru's face remained unreadable.

The silence was interrupted by Kuyu-Kun, the ancient Tinukeda'ya, struggling upright. "I, too, will go," he said. "I have considered, and I see now that I cannot turn back, however painful or dangerous the way has become. As Voice of the Dreaming Sea, I am sworn to my people's service and the conservation of our history. I was called to come here for a reason. Without knowing that reason, I would die in failure."

"I will help you, of course, Master," said Tih-Rumi. "Together we will discover the truth."

Morgan looked at them, then at the trolls. It was clear that he had been defeated by some kind of quiet conspiracy, but he could not guess the nature of it. He could turn back by himself, or try to argue Snenneq and Qina into accompanying him, but he had already experienced the stubbornness of trolls, both Snenneq's wordy version and Qina's quieter but equally implacable variety. And as hurt as he was by Nezeru's indifference, he did not truly want to leave her to face alone whatever dangers were doubtless waiting.

He tried to show some grace in defeat. "If you are all decided to go on, then you must convince Nezeru, since I will not force myself on her against her will."

To his even greater surprise, Nezeru only shook her head gently and told the trolls, "You do not know what dangers we may face."

"Neither do you, I think," said Snenneq.

"True," she said with a shrug, and that was the end of the discussion.

"So we prepare," said Snenneq. "I think we should wear our ice shoes to walk on such slipping crystals, yes?"

"I lost one of mine," said Morgan, still trying to grasp what had just happened. "It fell off in the trees."

"I hope you kept the other," said Snenneq, rummaging in his bag. "Because here is the one you lost."

Morgan stared at it in astonishment, recognizing every nick and scrape on the leather straps. "You found it?"

"I told you once, we are fated to have great adventures together." Snenneq wore a huge grin. "Do you need any further sign?"

The trolls did not want to take their rams into the crystal tunnels, with no idea of what obstacles lay ahead.

"We will let them stay here and roam free," said Little Snenneq. "My Falku is afraid of nothing, not soldiers or wild animals—see his proud horns! Our rams will feed and protect themselves until we return."

"*If* we return," Morgan heard Nezeru murmur, but he knew all had likely thought the same thing.

Nezeru had decided they should rest one night in the outer cavern before moving on into the crystal tunnel. Morgan found it hard to sleep, his thoughts turning back again and again to the day just passed. Why had the trolls resisted his decision to go home? What secret were they sharing between them?

As sleep finally began to tug at him, the huffing night-sounds of the rams as soothing as the murmur of a distant ocean, it suddenly came to him. *The trolls think Nezeru and I are in love!*

Anger and scorn and a deep scrape of pain accompanied the realization. *Can't they see what is obvious? I have feelings for her, yes, but she has none to speak of for me. She has made that as plain as can be. And even if it were true, what a mad idea for Snenneq and Qina, risking death for someone else's love.*

Trolls are fools, he thought fuzzily as sleep closed in. *They are so small, but they think they know everything.*

The jostling throng of slaves and nobles became a long, straggling line as Jarnulf, the two women, and all the rest of the slaves and nobles were marched out of the ruined fortress through its shattered eastern wall, then shepherded up into the hills behind the castle. The Hamakha Guard did not treat the Nakkiga nobles with much more kindness than they did the mortal slaves; when one of either group fell, the soldiers prodded them to their feet with the butts of their spears and set them back on the muddy path again.

"Why are they doing this?" Tzoja asked him. "Where are they leading us?"

"It is beyond me," he admitted. "Except I do not think the hilltop is our final destination."

"Then where?"

"The greatest forest in the world lies on the far side—Aldheorte, as the mortals call it."

"You say that as though you were not mortal yourself."

Tzoja's friend Vordis stumbled. Jarnulf moved closer and helped both women over a slippery fallen trunk. As he did, Tzoja finally saw his wounded left hand, which he had been hiding in his sleeve. She stared at the blackened flesh and the raw, red ooze at the end of his pointing finger. "Oh, your hand!" she said. "What happened?"

He was reluctant to discuss it. "Burned."

"When we stop for the night—if we do—you must let me tend it for you," she said. "I think I have some oils that will help. But I have never seen an injury quite like it."

Jarnulf gave her a warning look. "Remember, we are speaking the language of our masters—our enslavers," he said. "I think you know what I mean. Do you speak Westerling?"

"Of course," she said with a spark of annoyance. "I was not always a slave."

"Good. I learned that tongue after I left Nakkiga," he said. "Let us use it instead."

Tzoja asked Vordis how she would feel about that, but her friend only waved a weary hand. "*Very well, then,*" said Tzoja, changing to Westerling. "Though I admit it is strange after so long."

"Long for me, too."

"You say you traveled outside Nakkiga. If you were born a slave, how did that come to be?"

Still cautious, he looked around, but the other marchers were distant and preoccupied by climbing the muddy hillside road. "It is a long tale," he said.

"What else do we have to do?"

"As you say." He told her of his birth into slavery in the White Snail Castle household, of his stolen lessons with the famed weapons master Xoka, and his eventual escape. He did not talk much of his time with Father, though the priest had been his companion and mentor for many months. He was still hurt by the way Father had simply left him behind one night, so he dwelt instead on the other things he had experienced while traveling in mortal lands, then finished the tale with an abbreviated explanation of how he had sacrificed the tip of his finger to thwart Akhenabi. The injured finger throbbed agonizingly as he spoke but he did his best to ignore it. He did not want to show his suffering to people he had known so briefly, though he was not entirely certain why.

"You have had many adventures," Tzoja said when he had finished. "And suffered many hardships. My story is different, but in many ways the same."

"Tell me, then," he said as he helped Vordis over a slick, half-buried stone that was blocking the track; Tzoja stood on Vordis' other side and helped her friend find her footing. *This Tzoja woman is kind,* he thought. *And I do not doubt she has fought hard to stay alive. Slaves of the Hikeda'ya who survive must be either very clever, very strong, or both. This woman is no cowed, beaten creature. I may have underestimated her.* "You must have tales of your own," he said.

But before Tzoja could reply, one of the guards moved toward them and jabbed the butt of his spear into Jarnulf's side, making him cry out in surprise and pain.

"Do not speak," the serpent-helmed soldier snarled in Hikeda'yasao. *"Walk and be silent."*

Jarnulf would have liked nothing more than to smash the guard's cruel, death-pale face into a bloody ruin, but he forced himself instead to turn away and keep moving. The guards were hurrying them all toward some unknown destination, not sparing even their Hikeda'ya masters. *The Queen's soldiers treat even their own people like slaves—what a monstrous race they are! Forgive me, my Lord God. I have failed You at every turn. But I will not give up hope so long as You are with me.*

The early winter dark fell, but the vast crowd of Hikeda'ya nobles and mostly mortal slaves trudged on, finally cresting the great hill that loomed behind Naglimund where their march halted for the night with the waxing moon already high and fat in the sky. Several slaves, and even one of the Hikeda'ya nobles who had fallen on the way, had been left behind to die in the cold night. As he stared down the steep slope that still lay before them, Jarnulf could make out little of the sea of trees, an immense blackness stretching below, and his heart suddenly stirred.

I could lose myself there. I will have to be ready for any moment of confusion, then I will vanish among the trees. I spent years in the wilderness—even the best Sacrifice trackers will have a hard time finding me.

He did feel a twinge of shame at the prospect of deserting Tzoja and Vordis, but he pushed it aside. *What do the lives of two women mean set against the chance to finally kill the Queen of the Hikeda'ya, the wicked Mother of All?* But it felt a little like an excuse. *You have tried already,* a bitter, cynical part of him declared. *You have tried and failed. Now you make excuses so that you can run away, so that you will be free even if others will not.*

There was no resolving such an argument, especially against himself. He helped Tzoja and Vordis to a fallen log so that they could sit, then gathered up the driest deadfall he could find to build a fire. Only when he had finished his pyramid of branches did he remember that he had neither flint nor steel.

Even my pot of dragon's blood is gone. No sword, no knife, no bow or arrows. How long can even I survive in the wild with none of those things? He shook off the dreary thought and went toward the nearest fire to light a brand. The slaves there stared at him with dislike, perhaps because he looked stronger and healthier than they did, but they said nothing as he held his torch in the fire until it caught, then trudged back along the hill.

As he neared the spot where he had left his companions, he saw that they had been joined by someone new. The stranger was Hikeda'ya, and it was equally clear that she was of the nobility: her clothing, though mud-stained, was of exquisite workmanship. Even in the dying evening light, Jarnulf could not help being impressed by the noblewoman's beauty: the paleness of her skin and perfection of her features made her look like the moon's daughter sent down to earth.

He did not immediately approach but moved quietly until he stood a short distance behind the stranger.

"I knew I had seen you, little Tzoja." The Norn's voice was like water hissing on a hot stone. "I do not know how you survived the queen's vengeance, but you will not survive mine, mortal sow." Still, for all the rage in her voice, the woman did not advance on Tzoja, so Jarnulf still waited, watching and listening.

"You mistake what happened, Lady Khimabu." Tzoja's voice trembled, but only a little, and there was anger in it, too. Jarnulf guessed that the hatred between them was something old and deep. "I was not taken from you as a mere prisoner, but to be a healer to the queen herself."

"Liar!"

"No." Tzoja's voice strengthened. "No, you may ask the queen's Anchoresses if you doubt me. My friend here is also one."

"Only a slave would think I could believe such a thing. The Mother of All taking mortals into her closest company? Impossible." The noblewoman was furious, but not entirely certain that what Tzoja said was a lie. "I will call the guards and they will make short work of you. And I will watch and laugh."

Jarnulf moved a little closer.

Tzoja sounded weary, as if her defiance was sapping her strength. "Do as you wish, Khimabu. I no longer much care. But I can promise you, when the Mother of All returns, she will ask for me. Whatever happened to me—and whoever ordered it—will feel the weight of the queen's unhappiness."

"Who is this, Tzoja?" asked Vordis in a worried voice. "Why does she threaten us?"

The one named Khimabu swayed just a little, still murderous but plainly uncertain: nothing in the Hikeda'ya world was as dangerous as angering Queen Utuk'ku. Still, Jarnulf could see in Khimabu's dim silhouette that she had tensed herself as if to strike, and at that moment he also saw what looked like a long knife in her white hand, concealed against her side.

Jarnulf considered killing the interloper on the spot but decided that only bad things could come from attacking a Nakkiga noblewoman, even in such circumstances; he would have to flee immediately afterward, leaving Tzoja and Vordis to face the consequences. He set down the burning brand, fumbled on the ground until he found a broken branch with a sharp point, then slipped out of the trees and moved silently forward until he was just behind the intruder. He grabbed her so that her arm was pinned against her side and pressed the pointed stick against her neck. If he acted quickly, he felt sure she would think it was a knife.

"Do not move," he said in the Hikeda'ya tongue, tightening his grip. "Let the knife fall or you will die here and now."

To her credit, Khimabu fought to get free, but Jarnulf pressed the sharp point harder against the side of her throat until she gasped in pain. "Are you mad?" she snarled. "Who are you? Do you know who I am?"

"I do not know—and I do not care. More importantly, though, you do not know who *I* am. And if any harm comes to Tzoja, if she is bothered by guards or I see you near her again, I will certainly kill you."

"Fool!" she said, but now her rage had a crack of fear running through it. "I am the wife of one of the queen's highest officials!"

"I would not care if you were the queen herself," Jarnulf said quietly. So far, none of the nearby slaves seemed to have noticed the struggle. Most were so exhausted they were already fast asleep. "But you have made a great mistake. You have threatened folk who have nothing to lose. I would rather die after gutting you like a cave fish than live and let you harm Tzoja in any way. Do you understand?" Khimabu did not reply, so he lifted her off the ground and pushed the sharp stick into her neck until it pierced the skin and she gasped. "They say you Hikeda'ya do not feel pain," he said in her ear. "I would like to find out if that is true. The choice is yours. Drop the knife."

After another moment, though her heels still kicked against his shins, she opened her hand and Jarnulf heard the knife fall to the ground. He kept the stick against her throat as he bent and snatched up the dagger. He could tell just by the feel of it that it was witchwood, a thing of fine workmanship, well-balanced and extremely sharp. He quietly tossed away the stick and lifted the witchwood knife to her cheek just below her eye.

"Now I will let you go," he said. "If you wish to keep your life, walk away and do not look back. You have not seen my face so you will never know when I am near. But if you turn and try to look back at me, I will kill you here and now and hide your body so that no one will ever find you." For a moment he considered doing it in any case, but decided it was too great a risk with so many Hamakha Guards within shouting distance. He was grateful that in her blind pride and the self-assurance of one born into high nobility, this Lady Khimabu had chosen to confront Tzoja in the middle of the slave camp by herself.

He let her arm go and tugged down the hood of his borrowed robe in case she decided to test his bluff. But the Norn woman only pulled herself free, then walked stiffly along the slope without looking back, holding up her long skirts to avoid brushing against any of the slaves. He followed her at a distance for a little way to make certain she did not run straight to the guards, but she seemed to be following his instructions, so he turned back.

When he had reached Tzoja and Vordis again, he slipped the knife into the waist of his tattered breeks, grateful to have a proper weapon again, then gestured for the two women to stay silent. They both looked pale and frightened. He took his torch from where he had dropped it, then gathered up the unlit firewood and led them away.

"We must find a new spot to sleep, in case she comes back with armed men," he said. "We are lucky there are so many of us slaves here."

"Thank you," said Tzoja in a ragged whisper. "Thank you. But Lady Khimabu is hateful and dangerous. I pray you have not doomed yourself."

"As do I," he said, and hoped that God was listening.

In all the time since they had descended from Urmsheim, the dragon-mountain, Nezeru had never found answers to the mortal Jarnulf's disturbing questions, and those questions troubled her still. Why *had* a very young Sacrifice like herself been chosen as part of the Talon sent to retrieve the bones of Hakatri and then to capture a living dragon? And why did the queen want those two tasks done at all?

Now she was traveling with three mortals and two Tinukeda'ya, and she was even more troubled by doubts. Her distrust and dislike of mortals had diminished so much that she had to admit, at least to herself, that she felt strong ties to the youth Morgan—a connection dangerous to both of them, and thus one she knew she had to sever, though she had cravenly failed to do so when she might have.

As she led the small company through the depths of the crystal-walled cave and over the continuous confusion of huge, gemlike stones, she was also troubled by a new worry: What compelled her to keep traveling north toward the end of the valley? It was obviously a place of dire conflict between her own Hikeda'ya folk and the Zida'ya—if the number of Sacrifice troops in the previously empty valley hadn't made that clear, the ruthless but hurried destruction of the Sithi fortress in the pass had more than done so.

What does the queen want here? Why have we built so many forts in mortal lands—huge, secret, underground forts full of Sacrifices, all from legions I have never heard of before?

And now her need to understand had brought Nezeru and her companions into this twisting cavern and its strange waters, a stream that smelled wrong in ways she could not even describe—not of poison, but of something alive and potent and unknown, perhaps unknowable.

She spoke none of this, but only sloshed on upstream against the current, trying to find a safe place where they could clamber back out onto the tumbled crystals of the tunnel floor.

"Remember, keep your heads high," she reminded them for the third or fourth time. "If you get the water on your hands do not touch your mouth."

"We know, Nezeru" said Morgan wearily. The mortal prince had been quiet too. *He is angry with me, that is obvious, though he tries not to show it. But the faces of mortals are like clear pools—it is not hard to see what goes on beneath. I do not doubt he thinks me as foolish as I fear that I am, going forward into unknown dangers when I said before that I wanted to find a place safe from both sides in this war . . .*

A war the Mother of All has been preparing a long time, she suddenly realized. *Since before I was born. But why fight over this valley in the middle of nowhere? I cannot help it—I need to know. If everything else I have been taught is a lie, then I need to learn what the truth is, even if I do not survive the learning.*

They had climbed out of the suspect stream at last onto the damp, treacherous crystal slabs that lined the cavern tunnel. Nezeru had seen ice caves in and around Nakkiga that looked a little like this place, but these oblong shapes were hard, translucent stone: the light of her *ni'yo* sphere sometimes turned them into prisms, making the cavern walls seem to sparkle. The jumbled crystal blocks were beautiful to look at, but their hard, sharp surfaces were slick and difficult to walk on and the company's progress was achingly slow. Still, at least they were safe here from the ogre: the unbelievable, immense monstrosity could not even reach an arm into such narrow, spiky passages.

As they paused to rest, Nezeru scouted ahead up the torturous passage. She thought the air might be a little cooler in front of them, which she hoped meant a source from outside.

"We don't mind sitting in the dark," said Morgan when she returned, "but a little warning would not go amiss."

Nezeru realized that she had walked off with the *ni'yo*. "You could have made a fire. There is enough air that it would not be a risk."

Morgan stretched out his hands. "With what? I don't think these crystals will burn."

Nezeru's first impulse was to stay silent—it rankled to be corrected—but she knew it must have been unpleasant to wait in the utter blackness of the cavernous tunnel, not knowing when she would return. "I am sorry," she said, and was surprised to discover the words were not as painful as she had feared. "I went to see what might lie before us. I think the air smells a little sweeter ahead."

"It does not matter," said ancient Kuyu-Kun. "What will come will come. The end of all is waiting for us, I feel certain. It is only a matter of time until we reach it—or it reaches us."

"Now I know why we brought you along," said Morgan with a sour laugh. "For the good cheer you spread."

"I will not apologize for my master," Tih-Rumi said. "He is the Sa-Vao. He feels things the rest of us cannot—not even Nezeru, daughter of Nakkiga. But he does not lie or stretch the truth. What he feels is unbearable."

"We don't have much food," Morgan said later, as the trolls and Nezeru shared out a tiny meal of *pu'ja* bread and dried fish. "And our water won't last forever."

Nezeru nodded, suddenly ashamed of her own obstinate selfishness. *What will it prove if I drag these companions to their deaths to satisfy a yearning I cannot entirely name. Unless it is death I yearn for . . .*

The thought of dying did not frighten her—such weakness had been scourged from her in the order-house long ago—but the thought that she might be dragging others down with her in such a joyless quest did.

They have all been good to me in their way. Certainly, the trolls deserve better. And Morgan . . . Her thoughts became confused again.

"Nezeru, we need to hear from you," Morgan said. "You are leading us. What will we do when—"

"We will talk of these things later," she said abruptly, and stood. "Now that you have rested, let us see if I have rightly sensed better air ahead."

She thought Morgan gave her an odd, inquiring look, but she was careful not to meet his eyes.

They struggled on, up the shining corridor, stopping two times to sleep. Sometimes the ceiling of the twisting watercourse tunnel rose far above their heads, so that they seemed to walk through elegant, jeweled halls; at other times it leaned so close they had to keep their heads lowered to avoid scraping against the sharp crystals. Water and food were both nearly gone, and with such meager provisions, she knew they had come too far to return the same way. They could only continue forward, searching for someplace they could climb out into the upper air. Nezeru had stopped eating anything so that there would be more for the others, but she was beginning to feel a strong, painful hunger too. The waft of fresher air had brought them hope, but as they clambered across the great crystals there was no other sign of change until Nezeru finally noticed a low rumbling noise. Every time she stopped to listen it was there, a hushed roar like the noise of the ocean, but without rise or fall.

"Nezeru, please," Morgan said when she had stopped again to listen. "We cannot go on this way. The old Tinukeda'ya fellow, Kuyu-Kun—I think he's dying."

She held up her hand to silence him, ignoring his look of frustration and anger. "I hear something ahead," she said at last. "A rushing noise. Perhaps it is the wind moaning in a crevice to the outside."

"And Tih-Rumi has to carry his master, but he's getting weaker and weaker too. We will lose them both soon."

"One last march," she said. "Then we will rest and talk about these things."

"But—"

"One last march. I ask you this, Morgan." She hated having to put herself in debt to anyone, most of all this strange youth who so muddled her feelings, but her heart had sped at the strange sound that seemed so close and she did not want to give up yet.

And what good would it do us anyway? If nothing changes for the better, they will starve soon. May the Garden forgive me, I have made a terrible mistake.

Morgan rallied the rest of the exhausted, hungry company to follow Nezeru forward one last time. Qina, the smallest, was also dangerously weak now, sometimes so much so that she could not climb the higher crystal outcrops and Snenneq had to carry her over them.

The noise finally became loud enough for the others to hear it too.

"What is that?" Snenneq asked. "Is it some great beast?"

"Not unless it has lungs the size of the mountain itself," Nezeru said. "The sound does not stop—listen. I think it is wind or falling water."

The new sound kindled a little hope in the company, or at least dulled their hopelessness. As they clambered on over the slippery crystals, the noise grew and grew until Nezeru could identify it.

"It is a cataract, or rapids," she said. "Water moving with great force."

"Rapids?" asked Morgan breathlessly, struggling to catch up to her. "What good will that do us?"

"I do not know," she told him. "Hurry, please. I do not want to leave you behind."

"You're going to have to soon," he said, but struggled on.

Nezeru was the first to see the crystal-studded tunnel open before her into a cavern far larger than the eroded watercourse through which they had been climbing. After days of relative quiet, the roar of falling water battered her ears, but she waited as patiently as she could until the rest of the company caught up and stood beside her on the lip of the great expanse.

She let the light of her *ni'yo* shine out. Her companions gasped; Nezeru was surprised too. Before them lay a great stone chamber as large as the widest streets of Nakkiga, curtained at one end by an immense waterfall pouring down from a great, dark crevice in the cavern ceiling. The cataract plunged into a broad lake edged with crystals like those of the tunnel, but the rest of the cavern's vast interior was only naked stone. A small outlet at the near end of the great underground pool appeared to be the source of the stream they had been following for days. But Nezeru's attention had been caught by something at the edge of the water—something moving. She aimed the light of her sphere, and several pairs of gleaming red eyes suddenly kindled in the dark water.

"God's Bloody Tree, what are *those*?" asked Morgan in an unsteady whisper.

Before Nezeru could even guess, more dark shapes erupted from the lake at the nearest edge and began moving toward them, but she could not immediately make sense of what she saw. Some crouched, some went on all fours, but most of them seemed to walk upright.

"Kilpa!" said Little Snenneq, startled. "Those are kilpa. We saw them before, in the Coolblood Valley."

"They do not look like any kilpa I have heard of," said Nezeru. At least one of the creatures shuffling slowly toward them had more than two arms, and many were covered in spines and other growths. The dripping shapes were climbing up the slope toward them, letting out muffled hoots and deep chugging noises like the croaking of monstrous frogs.

"Trust my words," said Snenneq in an urgent voice. For some reason Nezeru didn't understand, he was pulling the walking stick he always carried into pieces. "Those are kilpa, and if they have been living down here, they are no doubt hungry—and thinking that we look like a tasty meal."

"Do not move," said Kuyu-Kun. The old changeling could barely stand, and Tih-Rumi raced to support him as he stepped forward. The Voice of the Dreaming Sea pulled back the hood of his robe and raised his thin arms as if to bless the advancing creatures. "I know all the speech of our Tinukeda'ya kind." He began to call out to the kilpa in strange hoots and low, dyspeptic belches, but though a few of the creatures hesitated, the rest continued to make their way forward, even speeding into a shambling trot, feet slapping wetly on stone.

"It is no good." Kuyu-Kun lowered his arm. He sounded more sad than frightened. "They are too changed—too far gone."

"Then we must fight," Nezeru said. She dropped her *ni'yo* to the ground so that its light, still shining, spread across the stony chamber, then she drew Cold Root from its scabbard with a ringing scrape that quickly died beneath the thunder of the cataract. "Behind me, all of you. If you cannot fight, stay out of the way of those who can."

8

A Very Slender Reed

After many, many days of captivity, Eolair still wore the traveling clothes he had worn while riding to Nad Mullach. He would have given much to be able to wash himself and put on something clean, even if only to face death, but he doubted King Hugh would provide such amenities. *He will want to execute a traitor who looks like a traitor. He will want to drag me to the scaffold looking like the villain he will paint me.*

It was a very rough and ready cell that Hugh had provided for him, Eolair could not help noting—a small cubicle cut into the mountain stone, with a pallet on the cold floor, a bucket for a chamber pot, and a single candle for light—but it was not the worst lodging he had ever suffered.

No ewer, no basin, no stool to sit upon. A few cups of water and two sparse meals a day. Still, he admitted, *I suppose it is a shade better than when I was the trussed prisoner of Thrithings bandits. But it is a sad place to spend the last days of one's life, by any measure.*

He did not much fear death, but hoped he would not shame himself during the public execution, or the torture that would doubtless come before it. *At least I know in my heart that I did nothing against my beloved country. It is only against Hugh that I have sinned, and he earned that and much more when he turned against the High Ward—and against humankind as well. By bargaining with the Norns, he has lost any sympathy I might have felt for him.*

Eolair paced a few more times back and forth beneath the low ceiling of the starkly empty rock chamber. *What was this place when the Sithi lived here?* he wondered. *Before Hugh put a heavy door on it and made it a dungeon?* Considering the ancient past was better than what he had been thinking about. *Something simple, like a storage room? Or perhaps something more exalted? A changing room for an immortal lady, or a shrine to whatever it is that the Fair Ones worship? They speak sometimes of a Lost Garden. Do they light candles to that garden, as we do to Mircha or Brynioch?* He tried to imagine what the small place might have looked like when the Sithi were there, but he was sad and weary and found it hard to summon up a picture. *This has been too long a haunted place—a dead place. Even the Dwarrows we found here could hardly remember the days when the Sithi made it their home. The Dwarrows lived in shadow and regret, and in fear of dangers that were long past.*

Or were they right? he suddenly wondered. *They feared the queen of the Norns, and she is all too alive at this very moment. The people of Naglimund found that out, to their sorrow.*

He had stopped pacing, and in that moment of silence the click of the door latch sounded as loud as a hand clap. Eolair started, wondering whether he had miscounted the days until he was to be executed. For a moment, everything seemed to turn upside down, and he realized how terrified he was of what was to come, and how he had tried to coax himself through it, like a child being put on a surgeon's table, parents telling him, "Do not fear, do not fear. It will not hurt," when everyone present knew it would hurt and hurt terribly.

The door slowly swung open, and Eolair tensed. Should he fight? Hugh would never allow him the chance to escape, so any struggle would end in defeat, but did he want to go quietly, like a beast led to sacrifice?

A helmeted head appeared in the open door, sweeping the room with a glance, then a soldier wearing the emblem of Hugh's Silver Stags stepped in and carefully pulled the door closed behind him.

"If you have come to take my head," said Eolair, struggling to keep his voice even, "you should call for another guard to hold me down. We would not want a ragged cut to spoil King Hugh's trophy."

"Quiet, please, Count." The soldier stood beside the door for a moment, listening. "I have two more men standing in the corridor, but they are not here to hold you down." He took his helmet off and held it in one hand. "I am Glinn of Shanross, and I bear a message for you."

Eolair was surprised. "Do not hold it in, then, man. Tell it me."

"It is not that sort." He reached into his helmet and took out a folded piece of parchment. "It is a letter, from Her Majesty, Queen Inahwen."

He did not know what to make of this. It seemed strange that one of Hugh's own Silver Stags, his elite guards, would be carrying a message from the dowager queen, who was prisoner elsewhere in the deserted Sithi city. But if it was some sort of trap, Eolair could see no sense to it. Hugh did not need any new pretense to have them executed. "Why are you here?" he asked at last.

"I told you—"

"No, I mean why are *you* here. A member of the king's guard."

Glinn of Shanross, a large, strong man, could not meet Eolair's eye. "Not all of us are happy with what Hugh has done," he admitted. "And it seems particularly cruel to prevent two old friends from writing to each other in their last days."

Eolair was interested. "Quite a risk to take. Hugh would not look kindly on this."

"He would have me killed, my lord. But my friends and I are willing to risk it, for the sake of doing what is right."

"Would you consider doing more?"

Glinn shook his head. "To my shame, no. It is not possible, my lord. There are forty more Stags between you and freedom, and most of them do not feel as I do. But I have brought more parchment for you—and this." He reached into the cloak he wore over his armor and pulled out a parcel. "Ink and a quill, so that you may reply to Her Majesty if you so please. I will be back in an hour, the rotations of the guards permitting, to take it from you and deliver it to her. May the gods speed you, Count Eolair, and Brynioch of the Skies cover you both in glory. We are praying for you." And with that, he handed over the bundle and the loose parchment and quickly made his way out again.

Eolair waited a few moments after the door was latched, in case it turned out to be only some trick of Hugh's, but at last, he sat down beneath the candle and opened Inahwen's letter.

My dearest Count,

it began.

I hope you still remember the time all those years ago when we took shelter together from the cruelties of fate, me trying to forget the death of my husband King Lluth, and you the death of your love, his daughter Maegwin. We always spoke of our shared time as a brief respite before we returned to the duties that weighed so heavily on both of us, mine the throne of Hernystir, you the great work of building a more peaceful world under the High Ward.

Those days weigh heavy upon me now, as the end of my life nears, because I must confess that I lied to you when I sent you away then, telling you we could no longer be lovers. The truth is, dear Eolair, I never stopped loving you. You captured my heart even before I was widowed, though of course I would never have dreamed of acting on it. And even when we found each other at last in the ruins of a terrible war, it was often hard for me, a flesh and blood woman with all the faults and shortcomings of a living person, to live up to the ghost that lived in your heart, the phantom of Maegwin.

In the days after the war, in our grief, you and I fell into each other's arms, and we comforted each other. But I had always cared deeply for you, and in my youthful foolishness I thought that everything would follow from the two of us coming together at last. But it was not to be, whether because you simply did not care as much for me as I did for you, or because the tasks before us outweighed any happiness we might have given each other. It no longer matters. All that matters now is telling truth.

Here is that truth. I still care for you, Eolair, and I will take my love for you to Heaven. A terrible fate lies ahead of us, but I am devout enough to believe that beyond the burning pyre there may be a place where we can be together. If that is so, I wish you to know that I would gladly spend all the time the gods will give us in your company, because I love you still.

I am not a clever woman, and it could be I have upset you with such a bold admission. I was largely unlettered until I married the king, and even after, I could do little more than write my name until the war forced me to master the tools of ruling an entire people. I still think like the country girl I was, and so I will speak a blunt truth—I would rather go to a hundred funeral pyres, one after the other, than to risk losing you in eternity as well as in life.

Do not feel you must write back. If I do not hear from you again, I can at least pretend that you never received this letter, and that I have not lowered myself by such a shameless declaration. Whatever happens, I treasure our hours together, and will spend my last days thinking of little else.

She had signed it, *"she whose true name you may still remember."*

Eolair stared down at the parchment. For a moment he thought that the circular stains that blurred the edges of some letters were Inahwen's, until he realized the tears were his own.

Elu, I used to call her, he remembered. *Swan. Long ago—that was so very long ago . . .*

He wiped his eyes with his dirty sleeve, then spread the blank parchment Glinn had brought him against the stone floor, cleared the wax stopper from the jar of ink, and began to write a letter of his own.

Since he had first entered knighthood, in a ceremony conducted by his great-uncle Eolair and the priests of Murhagh, Sir Aelin had dreamed of one day being part of a war council, of sitting as an equal with the highest nobles of Hernystir. Now he was doing just that. He had not dreamed it would be his own king the council was preparing to fight, and he had never in his wildest imaginings foreseen that a goat would be chewing on the sleeve of his shirt.

"Ah, is that my little Keeva?" asked Tace Odhran. "Is she being wicked again? Just give her a swat on the rump and she'll go away."

Odhran, a beaming, kindly man of some seventy summers or more, was the master of the hall, with its carved and decorated wooden pillars holding up the high ceiling. Earl Murdo had insisted that Odhran send all his people except his son off to other parts of the settlement, so that the unhappy nobles could speak openly about what King Hugh was doing. Even the goats and sheep, who seemed to regard the hall as their own, had been driven out, but by the time the conclave was underway, many of the animals had wandered back in, led by Keeva the goat. She was apparently Odhran's favorite, and as a result almost immune to threats and oblivious of the courtesy due to guests.

"Father," said Odhran's wife, Lady Fionola, a stout, handsome woman, "if you will not send that creature out—see, she is nosing the poor fellow's lap!—then I will see she is served up for the Embolg feast. With onions and carrots."

The tace—an old word for "chieftain"—looked at his wife in alarm. "Don't say such things, Mother. She'll hear you!" But he got off his bench and moved swiftly, at least for a man his age, to chase the goat out through the great hall's door.

Aelin thought Odhran seemed a bit foolish, but the tace's family had been kings in the ancient days when Hernystir had several such rulers constantly at war against each other. His seat, Carn Buic, sat in a splendid, easily defended position in the foothills of the Grianspog Mountains, only a few leagues from Hernysadharc itself. In truth, the old man was only a baron, but his family's history was long and glorious, which was why everybody called him "Tace," a title which carried far more weight than any more recent mark of nobility.

At least a dozen other Hernystiri nobles, barons and viscounts and counts, had come to join Aelin and Murdo at Odhran's rustic table, and those nobles had not taken long to make clear that they were as angry—and fearful—about King Hugh's plans as Aelin and Murdo.

"This is news I had not heard," said Colum, Viscount of Dor Drumm. "It turns my stomach. Are you certain of it, Aelin?"

"He tells the truth to you as he told it to me," said Murdo. "And I believe him." Murdo was a man all of them held in high regard, and Aelin was grateful to have his backing. "In any case," the earl continued, "what more proof do we need? The White Foxes crossed our lands. The king's Silver Stags and their captain, Curudan, met with the immortals as if they were old neighbors. Then the whitefaces marched into Erkynland and threw down Naglimund. The truth is no longer in question. Hugh has no shame about what he has done."

"Nor any shame about the rites they practice these days in the hills, and even in the royal Taig itself!" said one of the barons. "That she-wolf Tylleth is behind it all, as Heaven is my witness."

"Lady Tylleth may have led Hugh astray," said Aelin carefully, "but Hugh was riding in that direction anyway. You all know how he insulted our dowager queen, and even King Simon and Queen Miriamele themselves during their visit. I suspect his ambition had swollen beyond our borders even before he met Tylleth. I doubt that she changed him. Rather, I believe she offered him a way to make new allies with her spells and rituals—immortal allies."

"And now he will execute poor Queen Inahwen," said Odhran sadly. "That angers me."

Aelin was astonished, and felt his stomach roil. "What? Execute Queen Inahwen? I have heard nothing of that!"

Murdo too seemed shocked. "How do you know this, Tace?"

Odhran looked surprised. "The news has raced from county to county in the last weeks. There are rumors Hugh plans to do the same for your great-uncle Eolair, too. He has even declared it a festival day."

Aelin felt a rush of panic and rage. It was all he could do not to leap to his feet and call for his horse. "Mircha clothed in rain," he swore, "this cannot happen!"

"A festival?" said Murdo gravely. "No, Hugh brings back the *Pauh Morriga*—the Cook-Pit of the Crow Mother." He turned to Aelin, his face pale. "In the old days, the evil days, her priests burned sacrifices in her name—men, women, and children."

"By all the gods," said Aelin. "That must be what Hugh intends—to sacrifice Inahwen and my uncle to the Morriga in front of his subjects. He has truly gone mad!"

"That may be," said Colum. "But he still has his Silver Stags, and because he has them, he has the palace guard and many other warriors to protect him. He is not so moon-touched as to leave himself vulnerable to a rebellion."

"But we must stop him," Aelin said. "If he succeeds, only Heaven knows what will follow. He and his doxy are practicing ancient, evil magicks, rites that have been banned for centuries!"

"I think we all here agree that Hugh has lost his right to sit the Throne of Hern," said serious, thin-faced Torin of the Meadows, a canny war chieftain who had fought beside King Simon in the Thrithings. "But it is the cold iron of his soldiers we must defeat. The people do not know all he has done. They will not rise against a handsome young king simply because of a few accusations."

"If they will stand by while their queen is burned," said Murdo in fury, "then they are not men of Hernystir but sheep and deserve being fleeced and slaughtered."

"You are making Keeva very anxious," said Odhran mildly. The goat had snuck back in and laid her head across his lap, where she watched the nobles with slot-eyed distrust. "She is not a sheep, but goats and sheep are brothers, after all. The word 'slaughter' troubles her as well."

"Father, you are talking nonsense again," said his wife.

"Your pardon, Mother."

Aelin was seething, and it felt to him as though the sharp edge of outrage he had sensed only moments earlier was becoming blunted. "Enough!" he said loudly, ignoring the shocked look from Tace Odhran and his horned companion. "This monstrous festival must not happen. We all owe Count Eolair our lives several times over, and Queen Inahwen as well. The two of them held this land together after the Storm King and Skali Sharp-Nose reduced us to homeless tribes, and we have known nothing but peace and plenty under Inahwen's rule since King Lluth died."

"It took a while," said Odhran sadly. "I did not taste an apple for almost two years after the Rimmersmen burned down the orchards."

"Sir Aelin is right," said Murdo, laying his broad hand flat upon the table. "And we have until this Morriga-festival to save the two of them—and our beloved country."

"But how?" demanded Viscount Colum. "Even with all the men we here can muster, I make our count less than a thousand. The king has twice that number, as well as the Silver Stags, many of whom are mighty warriors. And the walls of the city are old and strong, though long untested. Even if we mount a siege against it, they could hold out for months. Small use that would be in trying to keep the old queen alive—or your uncle, Sir Aelin."

They all began to argue. Aelin, full of frustrated rage, did not have the strength or patience to join any of them: he felt as though he was likely to strike someone, and all of these folk were allies, or potential allies. As he thought of the kindness his great-uncle Eolair had always shown him, the knowledge of what was going to happen to him was like a spear-point prodding Aelin's heart, and it was all he could do to hold in the pain.

And Queen Inahwen, he thought. *That good old woman. I cannot count the kindnesses she has done for me. When I was little, she would take me on her knee and tell me stories, as if I were her own child.*

That memory brought an idea, but as the idea began to kindle into something bright and foolish and just barely possible, he heard a scuffle and shouting outside the hall. The doors burst open, and a tall man with a guard wrapped around each of his arms stood there, face bright red.

"For the love of Mircha, Odhran, get your lackeys off me or I will hurt them."

"Count Nial!" Odhran rose from his bench, arms outstretched, and the goat Keeva waddled off in annoyance. "Let him be, you fools," he told his men. "Do you not know Count Nial of Nad Glehs?"

As soon as the soldiers let go of his arms, Nial stomped forward into the hall. "No time for greetings or even courtesy—they both must wait because I have news. The White Foxes have moved into the south of Erkynland and are on their way to attack the Hayholt."

"Oh, dear," said Odhran amid the clamor this aroused. "Are you quite sure?"

"It is hard to mistake an army of thousands of Norns," said Nial.

He quickly described the stories he had heard of the vast force of immortals marching through Erkynland beneath a storm of their own making, led by the terrifying Norn Queen herself. "We must throw down our false king," he cried as he finished. "This cannot be!"

"But we cannot take the city of Hernysadharc by siege in time," said Colum. "Not even if we had ten times the men."

Aelin's idea had continued to grow. Now he stood, waiting until the tumult had died down and the nobles began to look in his direction.

"Queen Inahwen used to tell me stories," he said. "My favorites were her stories of Flann Coilleoir—Flann the Woodsman, whom the Erkynlanders call Jack Mundwode."

"What is this in service of, Sir Aelin?" asked Nial.

"I always liked those tales," said Odhran, and settled himself in his chair. "Did she tell you the one about the priest's donkey?"

Aelin would not be distracted. "There is a story that a baron, one of Tethtain's chief supporters, wished to draw Flann and his men out of the woods so they could be captured. He announced a tournament, saying that the winner would receive a bag of gold. Flann and his men knew it was a trap, so they came to Hernysadharc in disguise. Flann won handily, and by that his enemies knew it was him, so they surrounded him. But of a sudden, his men shed their disguises and saved him, killing a score of the baron's men before escaping."

"What are these old tales?" asked one of the nobles, and others catcalled at Aelin and his childhood memories.

"Be quiet," said Murdo. So admired was the earl of Carn Inbarh that the hall quickly fell silent. "I begin to see where this may lead."

Aelin nodded. "We know we could not besiege the city, not in time to save the queen and my great-uncle. But with all the people who will come into Hernysadharc for Hugh's festival—Hugh's abomination, in truth—we can bring many of our men, perhaps all our men, into the city in disguise during the days before. The weather will be such that everyone will wear cloaks and hats, making it easier to go without being recognized."

"But they will search for weapons at the gates," said Count Nial. "Hugh and Curudan are not fools."

"And neither are we," said Aelin. "We will find a way to get the weapons inside Hernysadharc's walls first, long before the festival, and leave them in places where we can recover them quickly. Then we will bring in our men, unarmed. When we are ready, they will take up those bows and swords from their hiding spots, and with the weapons concealed beneath their cloaks, they will join the crowds in the marketplace. They will seem as innocent as sheep until we give the signal for them to rise against the king's soldiers. Then Hugh will learn that the sheep he despises are wolves after all."

More argument followed, but Aelin's idea had caught the nobles' attention, and most of the discussion—as well as the occasional fights, not uncommon among Hernystirmen trying to find agreement—were not about whether to do it, but how to make it work.

Earl Murdo found Aelin off to one side, where the young knight, pleased at the reception of his plan, had refilled his goblet with good Carn Buic mead. "It is a very thin reed, this plan," Murdo told him. "But I suppose you do not need me to tell you that."

"To help my Uncle Eolair—and the queen," said Aelin, "I would grasp at any reed, no matter how slender."

"Well, then, let us take up your reed and see if we can't poke out Hugh's eye with it." Murdo clapped him on the back with a heavy hand, spilling half a cup of Aelin's mead.

Dearest Elu,

One of the most terrible things about growing old is having to remember. Not because life is dreadful, but because we take so long to become ourselves, while everyone who met us during our journey knows only the person that we were then. All our errors, foolish mistakes, and unthinking cruelties are still alive to be recollected and often regretted, but the gods seldom give us another chance to be the better person we wish now we could have been.

When I read your words, I was filled with sadness. Not because of the kindness and love you have always offered me—and did again in your letter. No, it is my own life I question, and my own worth. Your letter, sent in love and friendship, only makes those questions harder to answer.

The gods know that I owe you an apology, my gentle friend, but the person who truly owes it to you is no more. That was another Eolair, one who perished in those years after the war against Skali, mad King Elias, and the White Foxes, poisoned by his own certainties. I cannot mourn him. For he was the victim of yet an earlier Eolair, one who felt that nothing was more important than bringing his skills and wit to the task of making the world safe. But the world cannot be made safe. The gods have chosen to give us only short, fragile lives. Most of us travel through those lives, certain that only a few things will bring us true happiness and determined to do whatever we can to gain them. And yet those very prizes eventually become a source of pain, even terror. If we do not reach those prizes, we feel our lives were useless. If we do, we must then protect them, and this also changes us, until the reason we wanted them is forgotten in the constant struggle to keep them.

Such are goals, such are prizes. And such is the foolishness of mortal men like me, that we start out to say one thing and realize we have written countless words about something completely different.

Of all the lessons I have most painfully learned, here is the deepest and most subtle.

When we look too fixedly at either the past or the future, we fail to use the most important gift the gods gave us—the reason they made us mortal, the reason they made our bodies weak and then filled the world with dangers. The gods want us to see that each moment we live is a gift.

When you and I had our brief time together, I did not truly understand that splendid gift or my own good fortune. Always I was thinking of what I had to do next for the world and for our people—for all people. Though your affection and kindness gave me great comfort, in those days I put the simple things behind me as soon as possible, thinking that they were distractions from the great and important matters still before me, the debt I owed to my fellow man and the great deeds that I would show to the gods as proof they made me wisely. The gods did make me wisely—but they did not make me wise. That was my own responsibility, and it has taken a long time. In fact, that task will now never be finished, but I think I have at least learned some useful things.

All these words, and still Eolair keeps the truth at bay, trying to make it do what he wants it to do! The curse of supposedly clever men is that we have great difficulty seeing and understanding simple things.

I know now that we mortals must live each day in the present moment. We must see what is before our eyes and feel everything our hearts can feel. You offered me love, but I could see only one important thing at a time then, and in honoring my memory of Maegwin, I slighted you even as you stood, living, beside me.

Please forgive me. If I go to my death thinking that you at least understand my mistake, and know that I regret it deeply, then I will count all my other sorrows as nothing, and my soul will weigh no more than a feather when it floats up to Heaven.

Farewell, dearest Elu. If there is no time for us to write again, remember me on the day that is coming and know that at the end, I will be thinking of you. And if we reach eternity, I will look for you first of all.

Your servant, now and forever,
Eolair, Count of Nad Mullach, Hand of the High Throne

9

An Unknown City

"What madness is this, Geloë?" Simon could make no sense of what he had just heard. "Me, one of the immortals? Don't you see with my granddaughter's eyes as well as speak with her voice? I am old! My beard is going gray, and my skin is wrinkled!"

"You have certainly aged," she said, "but in other ways you have changed little. For one thing, you still do not listen very well. I did not say you were immortal, I said you were *not entirely mortal.* Now, do you wish to know why you have not dreamt for more than half a year?"

"You may have died, but you haven't changed much either," he grumbled. "Everything always needs a long explanation."

They were still riding north, the Sithi horses deceptively swift, the land sliding smoothly past them. Simon held his granddaughter on his lap but Lillia was absent, Geloë still speaking from the child's body.

"The sooner started, the sooner finished," she said. "So be silent and listen, Simon. In long-ago days, the Keida'ya—the ancestors of both Zida'ya and Hikeda'ya—lived in the land called the Garden, surrounded by the waters of the Dreaming Sea, and thought they were alone. They did not understand that the Dreaming Sea, too, was alive, that in its own way, it could feel and think."

"I am sorry to interrupt again," Simon said carefully, "but I truly do not understand what you mean. The sea could think?"

"This time I will not fault you, because it is not easy to explain or to grasp. Something in those waters—perhaps even the water itself—was alive. But it was not a living thing as you know living things, nor did it have a single way of seeing. It was many, but all were one. I can put it no more clearly than that."

Simon made a face but said nothing.

"As the Keida'ya multiplied," Geloë went on, "they began to change the Garden to suit themselves. They tamed the witchwood trees and other things to their uses and built ever larger settlements, at last raising a great city called *Tzo* upon the shore. The Dreaming Sea began to fear them, and it fought back, as will anything menaced by what it does not understand. The sea made monsters—dragons and other, even stranger beasts—which came out of its waters and attacked the two-legged creatures who had spread across the land. The Keida'ya in turn became ever more warlike to protect themselves, and for a long time these two very different enemies struggled against each other—both sides fearful, neither understanding the other.

"But as it saw more of the Keida'ya, the Dreaming Sea realized that these strange new creatures could also think and feel. It began to hope they might be reasoned with, made to understand that the Garden was meant to be shared, not given over to one race to use and use up.

"So, after a long age of monsters, the first of my folk, the Tinukeda'ya—or *Vao*, as we called ourselves—came out of the Dreaming Sea to make peace. This time they took forms much like the Keida'ya themselves. The Keida'ya did not trust them at first, and some never would, but the Vao taught those who would listen much about the Garden. For a time, it seemed there might be true peace, that both races would prosper together."

Jiriki had slowed to ride near them. "If only it had happened that way," he said.

Geloë gave him a stern look. "Yes—if only. But the nature of my people, like water itself, is to shape ourselves to fit whatever place we find, so even dispersed into individual bodies, my kind still did not fully understand the Keida'ya. The idea of one individual gaining while another lost was so foreign that the Vao did not suspect that our yielding nature would ultimately betray us."

"Betray you?" asked Simon.

"Yes, sadly. Over long, long years, separation into individual bodies and minds led my ancestors to forget what it felt like to be part of the Dreaming Sea that had birthed us. Some Vao even lost all memory of their origins, becoming little more than beasts, helpless thralls without history or understanding. Eventually, only a small number of our kind remembered who and what they truly were. My ancestor Ruyan Vé and his clan decided that for the Vao to survive, they had to escape from the Garden and their Keida'ya masters. Thus, they began secretly to build a great witchwood ship, one that could carry them far away from those who had enslaved them.

"What Ruyan and his folk did not know, however, was that some of the Keida'ya had never trusted my people—especially the followers of Hamakho the Dragonslayer, who would later become the Hikeda'ya. Hamakho tasked a Hikeda'ya philosopher, Nerudade by name, to search for a weapon that could be used against the Dreaming Sea if our two races should ever war against each other again. And after much study, Nerudade found such a weapon, a dire force that swallowed up whatever it touched, leaving nothing behind, not even memory of what had been. The jubilant philosopher declared that its endless hunger could even swallow the Dreaming Sea itself. That scourge is what we name Unbeing."

Jiriki made a strange sign with his hands. "Nerudade's Curse," he said in a voice heavy with sorrow.

"Indeed," said Geloë. "In the end, it would destroy its discoverer—and much, much more beside.

"But once it had been brought into the world, Unbeing could not be unmade, so Hamakho and his people hid their weapon away in a deep place far from Tzo, keeping its very existence secret from the rest of their folk. But the power of Unbeing remained as potent as the first moment in which Nerudade had summoned or created it. And eventually, it escaped."

"How could they let that happen?" Simon asked in horror.

"No one knows," she said. "All who were present were devoured by Unbeing's empty blackness, and the story was lost with them."

Simon could not help shivering as Geloë described how Unbeing, once free, continued to spread. It did not move swiftly but devoured all, leaving nothing behind, not even light; where it conquered, only black emptiness remained. Where it touched the Dreaming Sea, Unbeing's destruction was hindered but never completely halted, and nothing else could even slow its attack on the Garden lands. It devoured mountains, ate forests, and chewed holes in the sky. Every attempt to defeat or destroy it proved futile. The Garden was doomed.

"Thus, the Hamakha's ghastly mistake was revealed, but the ship the Vao had been building to escape the Garden was still unknown. The rest of Ruyan Vé's folk urged him to finish it, so that our folk could flee the dying land, though it would mean leaving the Keida'ya behind. But Ruyan would not permit such intentional cruelty, and he went instead to Hamakho, leader of the Keida'ya, and told him that the Vao knew how to craft ships that would enable all to escape—though he kept secret the first ship that his folk had already begun."

As Simon listened, Geloë told of how with Keida'ya and Tinukeda'ya working together, the famous Eight Ships were built at great speed in the Garden's final days. Witchwood could not be shaped fast enough, so they used silverwood instead. One by one as they were finished, the ships—*Singing Fire, Time of Gathering* and the rest, all led by Ruyan's flagship, *Lantern Bearer*—sailed out onto the Dreaming Sea, leaving the Garden behind. After a voyage whose span and course are still debated among the wise, they landed here in Osten Ard, a land empty of any creatures like themselves.

"Then it was your people who saved Jiriki's folk and brought them here?" Simon asked.

"Yes, and those who would become the Norn people as well, including Utuk'ku herself. But things were no better for us in these lands—most Vao remained little more than slaves to Keida'ya masters. In the years that followed, many of my folk fled from the Keida'ya, hiding in the wilds of the new country, being shaped by the places they settled and the ways that they kept themselves alive. Many sought protection by living near or even among the first mortals who found their way into Osten Ard, and such was the strange, inconstant nature of the Dreaming Sea and its creations that our kind could mate even with those mortals. Thus did the Niskies come to be, along with other cross-bred folk of countless shapes and sizes."

"The Tinukeda'ya mated with my kind?" Simon could not hide his surprise.

"With mortal men and women, yes. Are you truly listening?" Geloë sighed and Simon felt it through Lillia's small body. "I feel myself growing weary now," Geloë said. "Telling these tales is more difficult than you can guess—it takes much of my strength just to keep Utuk'ku from discovering who I am and what I have done."

Simon's heart sank. "But you said you would tell me what you meant when you said I wasn't mortal."

Her laugh was harsh. "*Not entirely mortal* is what I said, fool of a boy."

"Please, just tell me what you can before you sleep, if it will not threaten my granddaughter's safety."

She sighed again. "Very well. But it will be short and swift, and the questions it will no doubt inspire must go unanswered for now." She paused. "When I first met you all those years ago, Simon, I puzzled about why you should be so close to the Road of Dreams—do you remember?"

"Of course. I have always had strong, strange dreams, until they were taken away. Until *you* took them away, or so you tell me."

"Just so. And that is why I did it. I have been playing a long game against Utuk'ku. She is old—far, far older than I am—and fiercely cunning. I could allow no inkling of my scheme to come to her."

After another long pause, he finally began, "I still don't—"

"I have called my people north," she said. "Those of us with Tinukeda'ya blood still share a bond that others do not, because to carry the blood is to share a little of the Dreaming Sea, where all were one, where all voices were heard. I have called them because I can take strength from that bond, and I will need all the strength I can muster to fight Utuk'ku. The moment I passed through the Veil and back into this world, I began to summon as many of my people as could come to my side. Not just the pure Vao, but all who carry our blood. But I could not risk that Utuk'ku should learn of it, and because I knew you would hear this dream-call, Simon, and because I sensed that Utuk'ku had found a traitor somewhere close to you, I decided I must weave a sort of spell around you to keep you from dreaming. A song of power."

"That still doesn't explain much," Simon said. "Why did you know I'd hear that call? Why do I have such powerful, prophetic dreams in the first place?"

Her weariness had grown. "Have you not seen the truth yet, old man who is yet a young fool? You dream such dreams because you have Tinukeda'ya blood in you—the blood of the Vao. You are a mortal, but in your veins flows a bit of . . . the Dreaming Sea."

And so saying, she slid back into sleep once more and Lillia's body sagged in his lap.

The old Tinukeda'ya, Kuyu-Kun, had tried to speak to the kilpa of the cavern pool but the creatures either did not understand him or did not care; they continued to shamble up the rocky slope, rounded heads swinging aimlessly from side to side, apparently finding their way by organs other than their milk-white eyes. Nezeru had already drawn her witchwood sword and charged toward them as if battle were some sweet thing she had been denied too long.

I have to protect her, was Morgan's first thought, dissolved an instant later by the realization that he had never met anyone less in need of his protection. Still, he could not stand by and leave her to fight alone, so although the horrible, round-mouthed things terrified him, he drew Snakesplitter and ran after her.

Nezeru suddenly plunged to the floor, frightening Morgan badly until he realized that she had not fallen, but thrown herself down to slide across the wet, smooth stone between the two nearest kilpa. As she skidded past, she disemboweled one with a stroke of Cold Root so swift that Morgan barely saw it, then brought her blade around to hamstring the other creature before turning and springing up to finish it off, splitting its ridged skull with a single blow. A heartbeat later she was cutting her way through the next group of dripping monstrosities like a worker mowing hay. One caught her leg even as she skewered it, then clung to her as it died, and several more closed in around her.

As he hurried toward Nezeru, Morgan heard Little Snenneq shout behind him: a kilpa had veered off from the others and was closing on Morgan. Long, clawed hands lashed at his face, passing so near he could feel the air move. This beast was thinner and more strangely shaped than the kilpa he had seen during journeys to the south, with lumpy growths on all its limbs, but its face had the same look of idiot malice that had chilled him from the deck of his grandparents' ship. He drove his sword at the attacking kilpa's midsection but it writhed out of the way and Morgan only scraped its rough, wet skin, then he had to duck beneath another sweeping blow of its talons. He was desperately trying to remember the tricks and feints Nezeru had taught him, but they had mostly been for fighting against an enemy with a weapon.

He swiped at the oncoming creature's face to make it lean back, then tried another stab at its gut. He managed to get the tip of his blade deep into the thick, rough skin; the creature gurgled in pain but did not fall. As his enemy staggered back, another kilpa came up behind him, then a wet, squeezing claw snatched at his sword-arm. Morgan struggled to free himself, but now the first kilpa returned to the fight, and he was caught between them.

A memory of one of Nezeru's maneuvers came to him then, like a whisper from Heaven. He passed his sword hilt from one hand to the other, then stabbed backward at the second attacker and felt Snakesplitter shove through the horny skin and into meat. The creature loosed its grip, making a strange chunking sound with its round mouth, even as he freed his blade, then he gripped Snakesplitter in both hands and swung at its neck, splitting the kilpa's head from its body.

But Morgan's first attacker, though bleeding down its belly, was now close enough to grab at him. He ducked, so instead of shredding his face, the webbed, clawed fingers only closed on the top of his head, but the thing's other arm now wrapped around his chest. He felt its claws digging into the spaces between the plates of his Hikeda'ya armor, then he was yanked off his feet. Before he had time to think, the bleeding creature dragged him to the edge of the roiling pool and then pulled him underneath the surface.

Within a few heartbeats, Morgan's chest was burning—he had not had a chance to take a breath. Fighting to free himself, he opened his eyes but could see nothing except frothing water and the dim form of his attacker. He still had his sword in his hand but the kilpa was wrapping itself around him like some terrible serpent, and he was terrified that the empty eyes and gaping mouth might be the last thing he would ever see. He grabbed the hilt with both hands and rammed the pommel upward as hard as he could, hoping to smash the thing's underslung jaw. He struck something hard, and the kilpa lost its hold. As he wriggled free of it, lungs on fire, Morgan saw that both he and the creature were wreathed in dark tendrils of blood. Then the thing swam toward him once more, swift as any ocean predator—water was its element, but not Morgan's, and it grasped him in its claws again. The expressionless face loomed before his own.

His sword was too long for this kind of fight, too hard to swing under water. Morgan dropped it so he could use both hands to push the thing's twisting, mobile mouth away from his throat. Something pale, almost like a beak, gnashed behind its lips. In desperation, he took one hand away long enough to reach down to his belt. He pulled out one of his climbing-irons, then drove its spiked end into the kilpa's eye as hard as he could.

The thing roared, or at least he felt a vibration and saw a cluster of bubbles spring from the kilpa's mouth as it fell back, eye shedding streamers of black like smoke from a chimney. It turned and swam toward the far side of the pond, dipping lower and lower as it went, until it stopped moving and sank to the bottom.

Morgan touched the bottom, then shoved himself upward until his head broke the surface and he could take a deep, rattling breath. By the light of Nezeru's dropped sphere, he saw that she and Snenneq were both surrounded by flapping shapes, but he saw no sign of Qina or the two Tinukeda'ya. His climbing-iron was still in his hand, dribbling dark blood. He tucked it back into his belt, then remembered he had dropped his sword in the waterfall pool.

No kilpa were near him, but more were sloshing across the pond toward the shallows, enough to double the number of enemies Nezeru and the troll were facing. Morgan took a deep breath, then dropped to his knees and lowered his face into the shallow water and began feeling for the blade. When he could not immediately find it, he opened his eyes and began searching down the incline, half floating, half crawling. As his air was beginning to grow scarce, he finally spotted it, but as relief surged through him and his hand closed on its hilt, he saw a vast shadow moving slowly along the bottom of the wide pool. It looked so large, and thus seemed so close, that for an instant he thought one of the kilpa had snuck up on him, but then realized he was seeing something larger than any of the creatures they had been fighting, and it was coming toward them from the deepest, darkest part of the underground pool.

This time he breached the surface shouting and coughing. "'Ware! There's . . . something under the water! Something big!"

Nezeru was beset by several kilpa, although at least that many lay dead in a ragged, oozing circle around her, and Little Snenneq was surrounded by his own substantial pile of gray-skinned corpses. It had been so long since the night in Elvritshalla that Morgan had forgotten how skilled the troll was in a fight.

Snenneq saw Morgan splashing his way out of the pool and called, "Friend, what did you say?" His words were barely audible over the rush of falling water.

"Something is coming—!"

His warning remained not just unfinished but unnecessary. Loud smacking sounds echoed through the cavern, and an instant later a massive wave rolled past him as he stumbled up onto the stony slope at the edge of the pool.

He turned to see something rise out of the water, which ran off it in great sheets. For the first heartbeat or two, as he stared in stunned terror at the hideous thing, he thought he was finally seeing the true face of the ogre of Misty Vale—even crouching on all fours, this monster loomed high above the kilpa and everyone else in the cavern. But even as his heart turned cold with despair, he realized that for all its size, it was still too small to be the giant that stalked the mists.

The thing was like a kilpa, though it seemed to go on all fours as it sloshed through the now choppy waters toward the bank. Its head was like theirs, though it had a crest that ran from the front of its skull down its back, but it also looked a little like a gigantic toad or even a spider. Then it stood on its hind legs, water drizzling off its bumpy skin, and he saw that its bulging, swaying belly was wider than the rest of it, a great translucent sac of flesh filled with round lumps pressing against the skin as it moved.

Eggs, he thought. *It's full of eggs.*

All thought of fighting evaporated in an instant—the mother-beast would crush them like ants. He scrambled up onto the cavern's stony floor where Nezeru was still fighting for her life against the kilpa who had already left the pool. He started toward her, determined that she would not die alone.

"Morgan!" someone called. "Here!"

He turned and for the first time saw that there was another opening in the far side of the cavern wall, half-hidden by the great cataract pouring down from above. It was Qina's voice that had called him from there, he felt sure, but he could not see her or the two Tinukeda'ya.

"Nezeru!" he cried "Follow me! There is something coming too big to fight!" He turned to the opening under the waterfall that he now felt sure was the continuation of the tunnel that had brought them, but as he neared it, he saw that the crystals grew even more thickly in it, choking it so thoroughly that not even the trolls would make it through. His heart sank.

As he turned back toward Nezeru, something smacked him painfully in the face. He whirled, lifting his sword, but saw no kilpa there. Then a second rock cracked against the cavern floor at his feet and he finally looked up.

"Morgan! Here!" It was Qina, standing high above him on what looked like a sheer wall of rock beside the waterfall. Even more unbelievable, he could see Snenneq below her, and he seemed to be climbing directly up the smooth stone wall like a fly.

"Get Nezeru!" Qina shouted. "Here way!"

Morgan stared in gape-jawed astonishment for a moment, then heard a dreadful rasping sound and turned to see the great she-kilpa dragging her immense bulk out onto the pool's stony edge. Morgan turned and ran to Nezeru. The smaller kilpa surrounding her seemed determined to seize this lively but interesting meal before the big one could reach it, and they did not retreat even when Morgan fell upon them from behind, Snakesplitter flailing.

Now Nezeru finally saw the kilpa mother. She did not say a word, but her eyes widened even as she hacked off one of her attackers' claws with Cold Root, then stabbed another in the throat and sent it stumbling backward, gouting black blood.

"We can't fight something that big," Morgan cried. "Qina and the others have found a way out. This way!"

A gurgling bellow, deep and loud as thunder, pummeled Morgan's ears. The giant kilpa's head loomed over them now, eyeless but seemingly intent; Morgan grabbed Nezeru's arm and pulled her away from the remaining attackers, then the two of them turned and sprinted along the edge of the pool.

As they drew closer to their companions, Morgan saw that Snenneq had not been climbing with only his hands: a length of rope dangled down from the high rock shelf where Qina and the Tinukeda'ya stood waiting, shouting at them to hurry. Morgan knew he could not climb as fast as Nezeru, so he pushed her toward the rope, then followed behind as swiftly as he could. The immense, sag-bellied creature had turned and was squelching toward them, and as Morgan finally got both feet on the rope, it reached for him with a dripping claw bigger than a hay rake. He struggled upward, but he knew he was too slow, and he braced for the moment that the shambling horror would pluck him like a plum and swallow him whole.

Then he was rising into the air without any effort of his own. The great claw swung so close he could smell its stink, but it missed and clutched at empty air. Snenneq, Qina, and now Nezeru were all pulling hard on the rope, drawing him upward, and before the monster could grab for Morgan again, he had been lifted out of its reach. He was dripping wet, and when he tried to grasp the lip of stone on which his companions stood, he slid off again to dangle helplessly for a moment before they finally managed to drag him up to safety.

"Here way," Qina said urgently. "I find. Go this!" Morgan, panting, took a last look down into the waterfall cavern. Smaller kilpa were now gathered at the base of the wall, staring up with unsatisfied hunger, their eyes empty as those of fish laid out in the market. But the great she-kilpa was already laboring its way back into the water.

Qina led them along the rocky shelf and into another tunnel just above the cataract. She had found another passage, this one also cut by a stream, which tumbled over the edge to join the water of the catract falling into the pool, but no crystals lined the walls of this tunnel, only ordinary stone. Morgan tried to stumble deeper into the tunnel, but his strength was gone. "I have to lie down," he called, then turned a bend and saw that his friends had slumped against the walls in exhaustion. Morgan let himself sag to the stony floor, then rolled onto his back and dropped into a shivering doze.

He drifted back to wakefulness to find Nezeru standing over him. "The air smells different here," she announced before climbing down to the pebbled riverbank and crouching beside the water. To Morgan's surprise she dipped her finger into it, sniffed, then touched it to her tongue.

"What are you doing?" he cried. "You said it was foul—poison!"

"This is not like the water down in the crystal tunnel. This is only clean snowmelt."

Qina joined Nezeru, bending low to take in the scent. "Good smell," she said, nodding; then, despite Snenneq's worried look, she scooped up a handful and lifted it to her lips. "Good taste." She was smiling now. "Good water!" She took her skin bag and began to fill it.

Kuyu-kun sat up, assisted by his young acolyte. "Perhaps I have misunderstood the dream I had of our people's ending," he said, solemn and sad. "Could it be that what I foresaw as the ending of our life here was not a vision of our race's sudden destruction, but instead our descent into bestial ignorance?"

"Do not torment yourself, Master," Tih-Rumi told him.

"What should we do now?" asked Morgan. "We can't go back past those kilpa. We may have clean water to drink now, but we still have no food."

"Ah," said Snenneq, "but in water that is clean there may be fish to catch!"

"A lovely idea." Morgan let his weary eyes fall closed once more. "I'll believe it when you catch one."

They traveled onward up the new tunnel for what must have been several days, following the course of the underground river as it twisted and turned through the mountain darkness, until Morgan wondered if the tunnel might have doubled back on itself, and they were heading back in the direction they had come. They did manage to catch a few fish to eat, which lifted everyone's spirits, but as hours and days passed and they continued to plod on in near darkness, the company fell into silence but for the murmur of the water and the echoes of their footfalls.

At the end of yet another long march, while the rest were arranging themselves for sleep on the unforgiving stones, Nezeru called softly for Morgan.

"I was a chosen Sacrifice," she said when he joined her. "A warrior of the queen. But now I am nothing."

He took her hand in his. "You were scouting ahead much of last night, and you've been leading us all day. You're tired. Even if you don't need to sleep, you still need to rest sometimes."

She shook her head. "It is not that. I feel as if I have lost everything that made me. And more shameful still, I examine my feelings—Hah! As if a Sacrifice were allowed feelings!—and it becomes more and more plain to me what much of my misery is about. Day after day we travel in dark tunnels, far beneath the ground, hidden from the sky. But in darkness, under stone is how I lived most of my life before I left Nakkiga as one of the Queen's Talons, and I should revel in it. But all it makes me do is miss my true home."

"I am homesick too," he said. "That is natural."

"No, it is not! Or it should not be. I miss my father, of course. He is a good, upright man who has always done what is honorable, even among others who think of nothing but their own advancement. But I miss my mother even more. All those years I thought her weak, a mere human, full of mortal fears and mortal failings. But she is half of me! And what I miss most of all is the love she always gave to me, no matter what I did, though I mocked her for it in my thoughts and sometimes to her face."

"You can torture yourself, Nezeru, but it does no good."

She shook her head in frustration. "I need to understand why things have happened as they have. But tonight I have no more strength." She lifted her other hand to his face and touched him in a rare display of tenderness. Her eyes, even in the dim light of the *ni'yo*, were bright as if with tears, though he doubted they could be. "Stay with me for this sleeping-time, Morgan. We will find someplace away from the others where we can lie together. Make love with me, as you mortals say. I need that kindness, and if it is a weakness of my mortal half, so be it."

Morgan rose and they walked together along the river, over shifting, current-smoothed stones, looking for a place where they could be alone for a little while.

The company had only been traveling up the new tunnel for a little while when Nezeru suddenly waved them to a halt. "Something is strange just ahead," she said, then swung her light upward and narrowed its beam. The stone of the corridor wall had peeled away like the broken shell of a boiled egg, revealing a smooth gray wall just behind it. The uncovered surface looked distinctly different from anything Morgan knew, glossy, concentric swirls of black and gray.

"What is it?" Morgan asked.

"A seam of some kind of stone I do not know," Nezeru said, but he thought she sounded uneasy.

As they continued up the water-cut passage, they found many more places the outer stone had fallen away to display more of the strange surface. Morgan thought it almost looked as though someone had polished it.

"I swear that is no stone I have seen before," said Snenneq, echoing Morgan's thoughts.

"Wait for Kuyu-Kun," Morgan suggested. "Don't his people know about things like that?"

Tih-Rumi and the aged Voice of the Dreaming Sea finally caught up with the rest. Kuyu-Kun studied the glossy, unknown surface. "It cannot be," he said quietly. Beside him, Tih-Rumi looked anxious and confused.

"Speak up," demanded Nezeru. "What cannot be?"

Kuyu-Kun wore an expression Morgan had never seen before, a combination of excitement and agitation that seemed close to terror. "This is not stone. It is very, very old witchwood."

"Witchwood? Impossible." Nezeru swept the light of the *ni'yo* across the inner wall. "Do you claim this is a single tree growing here? A tree as big as the mountain . . . *inside* the mountain?"

Kuyu-Kun still looked fearful, as though he were only a single sudden loud noise away from fleeing, but he shook his head. "No, not a tree, or at least it did not grow like this. See? The grain goes side to side. This is worked witchwood, shaped and fitted without nails, as was the Tinukeda'ya custom. This wall has been built by my own folk, or I have never seen the work of our people before."

"A wall of witchwood?" said Nezeru doubtfully. "So gigantic? Then the city it surrounds must be vast indeed."

Morgan's heart was beating fast. *A city that should not be . . . in a place no one has ever visited.* "Are you telling me someone built a city here inside the mountain? But that nobody has heard of it?" He turned to Kuyu-Kun. "You said you carry the history of your people. There must be some story about it, some legend."

Kuyu-Kun shook his hairless head. "If there is, young one, I did not learn it from my predecessors or discover it in any chronicle. This is a mystery to me, too."

"We keep on, then," said Nezeru flatly. "Keep on until we find some answer to this *mystery.*" Her emphasis made it sound as though she thought Kuyu-Kun must be lying. The aged Tinukeda'ya only shrugged and hobbled after her, followed by the rest of the company.

Qina was wide eyed as they left the main tunnel behind them and began to walk in file once more. "Do not like," she said.

"I see something ahead of us," Nezeru announced. They had been walking for some time—Morgan guessed it must have been the best part of an hour—and the featureless wall, occasionally exposed beside them, had remained just that—featureless.

"I see it too!" said Snenneq. "It is a gate or door, I think."

They drew up as Nezeru played the light of her *ni'yo* across the smooth inner surface. Morgan stared for long moments before he could discern what Nezeru and the troll had already spotted in the complicated grain of the wall—a curving line that stretched four or five ells high, forming a shallowly pointed arch like a bird's wishbone. The sudden appearance of this clearly unnatural outline made Morgan's stomach sink. It was old, he could feel it somehow—old and dangerous.

"Can you open it, Nezeru?" Snenneq asked, as though that were the most reasonable thing to do.

"No. I do not think it is the work of my people. Better to ask the old changeling."

"Speak of the Sa'Vao with respect," said Tih-Rumi. He would not look directly at Nezeru, but Morgan still admired his bravery. "He is the memory of our people."

"Fairly spoken," Nezeru said, but she gave him a hard stare. "Does the memory of your people recall how to open your people's door so that we may learn something of this city that has sprouted inside a mountain?"

Kuyu-Kun tottered forward. As Nezeru held the *ni'yo* close, he examined the door, then set his long-fingered hand against it and murmured a few words that Morgan could not hear. Nothing happened. He tried again, and again nothing changed. Then Tih-Rumi leaned forward and whispered into his master's ear. One more time Kuyu-Kun set his hand against the interior of the arched opening—if that was what it was—and spoke a few words. A low rumble began to fill the cavern, as if some vast ancient beast was stirring from sleep. Qina gave a squeak of dismay, and even Nezeru took a step back. Then the rumble ceased and the great door slid silently upward, exposing blackness beyond.

Morgan made the Sign of the Tree.

"What song did you sing?" Nezeru asked the Sa'Vao.

"No song—not as you mean it." Kuyu-Kun's expression was strange and his voice trembled. "I only used the tongue our people spoke when we still lived in the Garden. I asked it to open, and it opened."

They were fortunate that Nezeru and her bright *ni'yo* led them, because the floor beyond the walls was several times Morgan's height below the tunnel, so anyone entering without light would have fallen and likely broken their limbs or their skulls or both.

As Nezeru tied a rope to a limestone outcrop and slid down into the dark interior, the light dwindling with her, Morgan wondered at the unusual thickness of the wall around the arched doorway. The thick barrier was partially hollow, a web of witchwood fibers resembling the inside of an old, split bone, but when touched it felt hard as rock. It was also wider than the great curtain wall of the Hayholt. If it truly was the outer wall of a city, he decided, it was meant to resist the fiercest sieges imaginable.

Nezeru's light finally reappeared below them, and she called for Morgan and the rest to follow her. When they had all descended, they found themselves in an open space, a passage between two curving walls that stretched away in opposite directions. The passageway that led back along the direction they had come was blocked by a fallen witchwood buttress, but the other stretched forward until it disappeared into darkness. With Nezeru in the lead they began to follow this direction. At first, they took each step cautiously, fearful of another drop, but the floor of the passage was smoooth and level, and as they continued on, they quickened their pace.

"By Blessed Rhiap, how big is this city?" Morgan asked after they had been following the featureless witchwood corridor a good, long while. "And what is this road that seems to run for miles along the edge of it?"

"Is it a city?" asked Nezeru.

"It is a story," Kuyu-Kun said softly, but when Little Snenneq asked him what he meant, the Sa'Vao did not explain.

At last, they came to a widening of the passage and discovered a staircase, also made of polished witchwood, that spiraled up into the darkness.

"Your people made this too?" Nezeru asked Kuyu-Kun with an odd catch in her voice.

"No one else," he said.

She led them up the stairs, footsteps echoing softly, and Morgan realized it had been a long time since he had heard the sound of the stream they had been following outside, before they entered this strange place.

"This must certainly be a city," said Snenneq in wonder. "But how was it built here, inside a mountain?"

"Magic," suggested Morgan.

Nezeru shook her head. "That is a word that means only, 'I do not understand'."

"But I don't. That's why I said it."

They discovered several wider places along the endless corridor, and occasionally one had marks that looked like another door, but Kuyu-Kun could not open any of these, though he tried a variety of Tinukeda'ya words and phrases. At last they reached a landing where a wide, twisting stairwell led up to other levels.

"We should go back," said Morgan as he stared mistrustfully at the stairway, uneasy with the brooding silence of the place and how deep into it they had ventured. "We should at least return to the stream and fill our water skins if we're going to explore in here for very long."

"You may do as you wish," Kuyu-Kun told him with surprising firmness. "This is the work of my Vao people and I must see it all."

"But we will need water, Master," said Tih-Rumi.

"I trust to the Garden," declared the Voice of the Dreaming Sea, full of calm certainty. "I was meant to be here."

Morgan thought Kuyu-Kun quite changed from the defeated creature he had seemed only hours earlier. "I thought you Tinukeda'ya built lots of cities for the Sithi." He was suddenly very weary. "Why are you so interested in this one?"

"Because this is one that no story tells of—" began the old Tinukeda'ya, but then was interrupted by a cry of surprise from Nezeru, who had climbed a distance up the stairs. The others immediately rushed after her to the next landing. Nezeru stood bathed in light, but it did not come from the sphere in her hand.

"Look," she said.

Morgan had never seen her so wide-eyed, so shaken. The light came from something he first took for a vast glowing panel, like the luminous tiles that had lit the depths of Da'ai Chikiza, but far, far larger, long and high as the wall around the Inner Bailey back in the Hayholt. As he stepped closer, he realized he could see through the impossibly thick crystal panel to a distorted glimpse of mist and sky: Nezeru had not discovered a piece of glowing stone, but an immense window. Outside, Morgan could make out the rocky walls of the valley, though its bottom was hidden in a blanket of thick, swirling mists. Breathless at this sudden glimpse of the world after so long traveling in darkness, Morgan leaned forward so he could look down, though staring through the thick window made his eyes hurt. "Merciful God," he said in awe. "We are halfway up a mountain!"

"Look here, to the other side." Nezeru's voice was hushed, almost haunted.

As he turned to follow her pointing hand, he could see the witchwood outer wall of the great structure they had been exploring as it stretched away along the cliff face, a convex span that he thought must extend for a league or more. "It truly is huge," he said slowly. "God our Redeemer! It's almost as big as that other ruined city where we met." It was all strange, all of it. "Where you took me prisoner."

"No, Morgan, it isn't like Da'ai Chikiza at all," Nezeru said as the others pushed in beside them, murmuring in awe. "Because this is no city." She sounded almost hopeless, as if instead of this wooden marvel of fantastic, almost unbelievable size, she had just seen a glimpse of her own ending. "It is a ship."

10

Hymn to the Torch

The Sithi halted so infrequently during their swift ride north that Simon was doing most of his slumbering in the saddle. He even bound Lillia's small body to his own with his wide sword belt to be certain she did not fall away as he slept.

He was startled awake by his horse's jerking to a sudden halt, lifting him in the saddle so that he was almost flung from it. Heart racing, he clutched the horse's side with his legs. The sky was gray, the late afternoon fading, but the tops of the hills still glowed with the day's last light. All the other Sithi had reined up as well, as colorful but composed as a branch full of sleeping birds.

"We have reached the southern edge of the hills you call Wealdhelm," Jiriki told him. "We will water the horses here before we strike east into the forest."

Simon could feel Lillia's chest rise and fall beneath his arm. It hurt his heart to have his grandchild so close but always sleeping, as if sunk in a deep and mortal fever. Now she stirred.

"I feel a little stronger." The rough tone was Geloë's. "But it will not last long. Soon Utuk'ku will realize how I have tricked her and bring her strength to bear on finding and destroying me. We must not stay long in any one place, Jiriki, if I am to give this child back hale and unscathed."

"You said her life was not at risk!" Simon wanted to shake Geloë but knew he would only be shaking his own helpless granddaughter. "You promised!"

"You know I do not do this by choice, Simon, but out of direst necessity."

Perhaps to calm him, Jiriki interrupted. "Now we will follow the old Heartwood Road north toward Da'ai Chikiza—the ancient track is overgrown but still our fastest way. Then we turn west again, through Wormscale Gorge and east into the valley of the Narrowdark, then on to Tanakirú at its northern end."

"These are just names," Simon said. "Da'ai Chikiza I know, but the rest mean nothing to me."

Geloë made a noise of irritation. "Again I tell you—peace! You will learn much more about this part of the world before the sun rises again, that I promise."

To Simon's eyes, the dark forest seemed an ocean in which entire mortal armies might founder and drown. *But these are the Sithi's woods,* he reminded himself, thinking of the time he had lived among them, so long ago. *They kept summer in Jao é-Tinukai'i when all the rest of the world was freezing beneath the Storm King's snows.*

The shape in his lap stirred. "Jiriki!" Geloë called. "I am awake once more. Come and ride with us again—remember, some of the next part of this tale is yours to tell."

As he reined up and waited to join them, Simon said, "You told me that I have Tinukeda'ya blood, Geloë—but what does that mean? God's Bloody Tree, I can barely pronounce it!"

"What it means is that among your ancestors—as with many more of your kind than you would suspect—was at least one who bore the blood of *my* kin. Your strange and often prescient dreams are likely owed to that tie. My own people have always been connected to each other, and the Road of Dreams is a place where such things happen."

"One of my ancestors was one of your people? Who?"

"I do not know, Simon. No more questions for now. I need you to listen to the rest of the tale so you will understand why we must hurry to Tanakirú."

"The Vao and the Keida'ya together built the famed Eight Ships which brought them here, but Ruyan the Navigator never disclosed the first ship he had begun, the great witchwood craft meant to carry his people out of slavery. And sometime during the Garden's final days, that ninth ship was also launched, though it was empty but for Ruyan's chosen captain. The Navigator intended that once all had reached the new land, his own folk would take the secret ninth ship and sail away again, escaping slavery. But that ninth ship never came. Ruyan had wagered my people's safety, but lost his wager. In the years to come, the Tinukeda'ya were trapped, still thralls to their Keida'ya masters."

"Not so much to the Zida'ya," said Jiriki. "We at least came to understand that we had treated your people badly. That was what led at last to the Parting of the two tribes, Zida'ya and Hikeda'ya."

"Ah, yes, the fabled Parting," said Geloë harshly. "Both tribes of the Keida'ya, Zida'ya and Hikeda'ya, mourn that separation, but we Tinukeda'ya have a greater reason to regret it. The Parting condemned a great part of our people—those still enslaved by the Norns of Nakkiga—to hopeless bondage. And that is the greatest crime of *your* people, Jiriki." Geloë's voice was cold now. "That in that moment, Amerasu and the other leaders of your Zida'ya tribe never considered what the Parting would mean for my own folk." She suddenly broke off. When she spoke again, much of the fury had drained from her voice. "I have said enough about that. The past is gone and cannot be remade. In any case, Jiriki i-Sa'onserei, I think it is time for you to tell your people's part of the story."

Simon's friend did not immediately speak, but rode for a while in silence beside him, their mounts' smooth gaits and quiet hoofbeats belied by how swiftly the trees rushed past. The Sithi steeds seemed to know the old road so well they could have followed it blind, sweeping around the trees and brambles as easily as the wind, leaving only a few shuddering leaves to show that they had passed.

Like ghosts, Simon thought. *But we are the ghosts of days yet to come.*

"I often wonder," Jiriki said suddenly, "which is better—the innocence of true ignorance, when all you know seems part of some benign universal order, or the unhappiness of knowledge. When I rode this track in my youth, full of the tales of my people's great history, I was happy. But when I grew and learned, it became clear to me that when some are free, it is often because others are not." He made a delicate hand sign. "Alas, I have never tasted that innocent happiness since! I would not trade my greater understanding for that glad ignorance, I think, but I cannot help mourning it."

"But ignorance is never better." Simon realized with some surprise that he had spoken aloud. "My Miri is gone, and my heart is broken—I feel as if I will never be truly happy again. But would it be better if I wrongly believed I would find her waiting for me when I return?" He shook his head. "I don't think so, Jiriki, though I don't have the philosophy or learning to explain. Isn't it better to know the truth, however bad, however painful? Because wanting to be ignorant is like . . . like wanting to be dead just to avoid the pain of being alive." He stopped, a little shamed at saying such things in front of beings so much older and wiser than himself. He could feel himself coloring, his cheeks warm against the brisk, chill wind. "That's all I wanted to say."

"I do not know why anyone ever called you 'Mooncalf,'" Jiriki said. "Even if it was once true, Seoman King, you have grown to be a very wise mortal indeed." He smiled. It was a sad smile. "And just as ignorance is a flimsy shelter, so is hesitation, at least in this case. So it seems I must now explain the rest of the story.

"You of all mortals, friend Seoman, know of what befell my people half a thousand of your years ago, of the siege of Asu'a by the Rimmersmen and the downfall of its protector, Ineluki. My grandfather Hakatri might have been a better protector of our home, but he was gone, burned by dragon's blood, his suffering so great that he left his people behind to seek a cure. His brother fell out with their father and, in an act that is still hard to understand, slew his own sire. My grandmother and many of the other Zida'ya fled the Hayholt then, and Ineluki was left behind to defend Asu'a with little help beyond Utuk'ku's Red Hand magicians. He failed and died, and the northern mortals took Asu'a. But you know all this, Seoman, so I will move swiftly to what you do not.

"In the years after Asu'a fell, those who had escaped retreated to Jao é-Tinukai'i in the deeps of the Oldheart, but many still lived in other cities, especially Da'ai Chikiza. Then, one day, the Zida'ya of that city felt a great grinding in the earth. They were frightened but told themselves it was only an earth-shake, the world turning beneath them in its uneasy sleep as it sometimes did. Then the river stopped flowing.

"Yes, T'si Suhyasei, the Coolblood River, suddenly went dry—not over weeks or months, but in a matter of days. It ceased to flow and then the city began to die. There was no longer enough water to slake the thirst of the people, and the boats that had traveled to other settlements for trade and fellowship sank into what had become a winding track of mud. They could discover no cause for this catastrophe anywhere near the city, no fall of rocks or shifting of the earth, so they sent to Amerasu and the Year-Dancing Clan for help. A company led by of the wisest of Amerasu's advisors was sent north, to the source of the river, to see what might be discovered there. But that company never returned.

"Others were sent after them, but they also vanished, though one expedition sent back word through a Witness that they had almost reached the end of the mountains, a place where the Coolblood and Narrowdark valleys met. Then they too were heard from no more."

Jiriki ducked beneath a low-hanging branch. Simon felt it whisk past him, felt a spray of needles slap his shoulder, but he was intent on Jiriki, trying to understand. "And then?"

"More missions were sent north in separate companies so that Amerasu and her allies could better understand why their people were disappearing in the valley's ever-present mists. Each party carried a Witness, and one by one they went silent. But one company made it far enough into the valley to discover what had caused the waters of the Coolblood to stop flowing. The source of both the Narrowdark and Coolblood lay at the valley's far end, in Tanakirú. To their astonishment, they found that a great ship, much like one of the renowned vessels that carried our people out of the Garden, had somehow gone aground at Tanakirú, causing a fall of stones that blocked the Coolblood River from its source in the high mountains."

"A *ship*? Like one of the Eight Ships from the Lost Garden?" Simon asked. "Was it the other ship—the one that was started first?"

"Likely, but we have never known for certain. That company of explorers did not reach it, and we had only one last message from them before they too were silenced. Their last communication was that they had encountered something else in the Narrowdark Valley, a giant far bigger than anything seen before. The terrified report claimed it was taller than trees, stronger and more fearsome than the direst storm. *Uro'eni,* they named it—*ogre.* But it walked only by night, and the heavy mists of the valley hid its appearance, so the creature's true nature was a mystery—and still is.

"After the loss of this final party of searchers, First Grandmother Amerasu decided that the ship and the valley of Tanakirú should be forbidden to all our Zida'ya folk, and the Hikeda'ya must be kept away too—even then it was clear that Utuk'ku was not to be trusted. We built forts in what became known as the Forbidden Hills, north of the great forest, and a stronghold called the Hornet's Nest above Wormscale Gorge. But the secret was too big to keep. Utuk'ku learned of the ship and claimed an equal right to it, but after a few Hikeda'ya companies were also destroyed by the valley's mysterious guardian, both sides dug in to wait until things might change."

"But why did Utuk'ku want the ship?"

"I could not begin to guess," Jiriki said. "Her scheming, like her malice, is unfathomable. But getting it is still her goal, which is why we are hurrying back to my people there. Perhaps you can suggest a reason, Geloë."

The small shape in Simon's lap took a long, deep breath, as if about to leap from a high place. "My ancestor, Ruyan the Navigator, was long dead by the time this last ship was discovered, but Utuk'ku's soldiers rounded up as many of his descendants as they could find and demanded to know the purpose of this ninth ship that had arrived so many hundreds of Great Years after the first eight. The prisoners were tortured in ways both crude and subtle, until my father, Sa-Ruyan Mardae, finally gave up the secret."

"Your father?"

"Did you think I was hatched from an egg, Simon?"

But he thought he could hear some deep pain in her voice.

"Yes," she continued. "Some say Mardae did it to protect the rest of his people. Others say it was to save his own life. We can never know, but at the hands of the queen's Order of Song, he told them what he knew about the ninth ship. Launched after the others, it had somehow become lost on the way until its appearance in Tanakirú."

"But why?" It was too much for Simon to take in. "I still don't understand why the Norn Queen should take such interest in a ship. Couldn't she build any ship she wanted?"

"Not like those that sailed out of the Garden and across the Ocean Indefinite and Eternal, in flight from Unbeing." Geloë spoke with flat assurance. "Those were created with the guidance of the Dreaming Sea itself, which was swallowed into nothingness when the Garden was devoured by Unbeing. As to why Utuk'ku wants this last ship badly enough to go to war, who can say? She may believe it contains some weapon that will let her avenge the failures of the Storm King's War."

"A weapon on a Tinukeda'ya ship?" Jiriki shook his head. "Is that not unlikely? Your people have always been peaceful, Geloë."

"Yes, and we have suffered much because of it. But even when Utuk'ku thought I was her ally, Ommu the Whisperer, there were things about Mardae's trial that the undying queen kept hidden from me. And not only about what Mardae revealed in his torment, but things about your grandfather Hakatri as well, Jiriki of the Year-Dancing."

"My grandfather? Why have I not heard anything about it before this moment, Geloë?" he demanded. Simon was not used to hearing such anger in his friend's voice.

"Because I still do not know what those things are!" She seemed to have little patience left. "I shared a connection with Utuk'ku—I still do, in some small way—but do not mistake that for equality. Because Utuk'ku had sung up the power of the Three Who Are One, she always held the whip-hand, and she hid far more from me than I have managed to hide from her."

"So neither of you can guess why the Norn Queen wants this ship," Simon said. "But you still intend to drag my granddaughter into the middle of it all."

"What Utuk'ku wants is to triumph over all her enemies and . . . and to see them destroyed, Simon," Geloë told him, exhaustion now plain in her voice.

"You cannot stop her without me, and for now, this is the only host in which I can survive."

"But why my granddaughter? Just because she was nearby when your other body died?"

"If you are wondering whether I could have chosen some other vessel, no. It had to be someone young, a child—and also, Lillia has your blood in her. The blood of the Vao."

They fell silent for a time as the horses rushed along the ancient Sithi road. "And that is why you took away my dreams," he said at last.

It took her a little while to respond. "I hid your dreams from you to be certain no knowledge of my survival would reach Utuk'ku after I began summoning my people to Tanakirú. Because soon I will have to face the Norn Queen, and without the living remnants of the Dreaming Sea around me, my failing strength would be like a candle flame set against a howling gale. As it is, even that small hope is almost certainly futile, but it is the only hope we have." Lillia's small hand lifted in a trembling gesture of defeat. "I have no more strength left. Let me sleep again."

In the Repository of Anvi'janya, in the depths of the Clanhold, Tanahaya was studying an old scroll written by one of the few Zida'ya observers present at the Nakkiga trial of Sa-Ruyan Mardae and half a dozen other Tinukeda'ya prisoners, a trial instigated by the self-styled Queen Utuk'ku after the discovery of the Tanakirú ship. Because the Hikeda'ya and their Zida'ya kin had parted ways many Great Years earlier, Utuk'ku could ignore the objections of Amerasu and rest of the Zida'ya. Like all such intentional spectacles, it was not so much an attempt to discover truth as a chance to link a despised group—the changelings of Ruyan the Navigator's clan—to Utuk'ku's enemies, Tanahaya's own Zida'ya folk.

But there had been at least one way that actual truth had been pursued at Mardae's trial, and that was in the matter of the ninth ship itself. Nakkiga's most infamous philosopher, Yedade, son of Nerudade, the discoverer of Unbeing, asked the prisoner many questions about the ship's history, and Tanahaya thought his persistence seemed to go far beyond mere philosophical curiosity. The nameless observer reported that, again and again, Yedade threatened the prisoners with torture and even execution if they did not give him the answers he sought, though the few Zida'ya allowed to be present had murmured their displeasure at such threats. Judging by the questions he asked, Tanahaya thought that Yedade must have already made a detailed study of the records and remnants of the other Great Ships: as he interrogated poor, tormented Mardae, Yedade spoke of things like "the division of the seven aethers" and "the opposition of motive forces," although Tanahaya could make little sense of either his questions or the prisoner Mardae's halting answers.

But something about the phrase 'motive forces' caught at her, and as she stared at the notes of the trial, she finally remembered. It was nothing about Yedade or the Garden ships or even about Ruyan and his people, but rather words in an ancient poem by Fololi Unshoon of Hikehikayo that she had encountered her first day in the Repository.

After a lengthy and unpleasantly dusty shuffle through all the tracts piled on her table, she decided she must have set the poem back in its alcove and went to look for it. A long stretch of the afternoon passed before she found the scroll again: to her shame, she had replaced it in the wrong alcove, something that she could only thank the Garden that the archive master had not noticed.

A few moments later, as if summoned, Dineke himself walked into the Repository, staring around with a frown as though he had heard the scuttling of parchment-eating rats.

"Ah. There you are." He sounded as if he was not entirely pleased to have found her. "Ayaminu summons you, scholar—the ceremony is about to begin." He stared unhappily at the pile Tanahaya had made on the table, now even more disordered after her search for Fololi's verses. "I suppose since you are off to Year-Dancing, it will fall to me to put all these back in place."

"Please do not, Archive Master—not yet. I have not finished with them." She turned to him, a little surprised. "But are you not going to the ceremony?"

"I have attended many of them," he said flatly. "And in better days as well, when the *kei-t'si* elixir was real and our people still had hope."

"But that is what the ceremony is for—to give us hope. To remind us that we still survive!"

"You are very young."

She thought he might add something to it, but Dineke seemed to believe he had said all he needed to say.

"So, then," he said a moment later. "I will leave this offensive clutter where it is, but it scrapes at my heart to see it. I trust that you will come back as soon as the first day's events are over and complete your work, then put all this away so that I might know where things are when I need them."

"I will, I promise." She climbed down from the wall-alcove. The archive master had already turned his back on her and was scowling around the Repository as though her mere presence had disordered the whole thing in some invisible but terrible way. Tanahaya was in such a hurry to escape his disapproval that she did not realize until many moments later, when she had mounted the stairs to the Clanhold's entry hall, that she was still holding the scroll that contained Fololi Unshoon's poem.

As she passed through the front doors and onto the wide stairway, she was surprised to encounter a crowd moving in what seemed to be the wrong direction. As she stood puzzling, a voice at her shoulder said, "You seem to be deep in thought."

It was Ayaminu, and she had neither entourage nor guards. Tanahaya was shamed to be still holding a scroll taken from the Repository, and hurriedly slipped it into her tunic. "You surprised me, *S'huesa,*" she said. "It was not deep thought you saw but mere confusion. If all these people are going to the Year-Dancing Ceremony, as I guess, why do they go that way? Is it not to be celebrated at the Pavilion?"

Ayaminu smiled a small, dry smile. "The structure my son calls the False Yásira? No, the ceremony will take place beneath the sky so that we can see the Year-Torch." Ayaminu made the sign for *changes, good or bad*. "Our people are gathering in the Sunset Fields. Come, I will show you the way."

"You are by yourself?"

"Present company excepted, I prefer it that way," said Ayaminu.

They followed the quiet crowd down the stairs and along a corridor until they emerged at last into a hollow in the mountain's side, open to the sky and the surrounding hills. The afternoon sun had dropped behind the tallest peaks, but its rosy light lay smeared across the horizon. Tanahaya realized to her shock she had spent almost a full night and day in the archives.

They followed the rest of the Anvi'janyans out of the cavern and onto a broad, grassy plateau. The only structure before them was a ring of stone pillars in the center of the close-cropped meadow. Aditu stood in the middle of the ring, head bowed, dressed in a belted robe the color of new spring grass. Tanahaya could not help feeling a thrill of awe to see her friend taking up the sacred role of the Sa'onsera.

Ayaminu was not so opposed to the privileges of rank that she settled for a place at the rear of the throng. As her people made way for her, she and Tanahaya moved to the front row of the great semi-circle of watchers.

A skirl of music floated through the evening air, though Tanahaya could see no source and decided that the musicians must be part of the crowd. Aditu looked up slowly, as if awakened from a dream, then glanced at the rapidly darkening sky before lowering her eyes to the waiting crowd, which numbered many hundreds.

"Welcome, Children of the Garden." Her voice echoed back from the cavern behind the crowd. "Children of the Witchwood, welcome. Let me say first what you all are thinking. This is a strange Year-Dancing and surely it will birth a Great Year unlike any other."

Though no one in the gathered throng spoke, Tanahaya could sense the ripple of unease that passed through the people of Anvi'janya to hear such frank talk during this moment of high and ritual solemnity. But she thought that she also saw curiosity and even approval on some faces, as though they were pleased that the obvious had not been ignored, even at such a time.

"In that, you are correct," Aditu continued. "But that which is strange is not always evil. When Jakoya first taught us to gather the fruits of the Garden, to plant its seeds so that what we took for ourselves could be renewed, some thought it wrong simply because it was new to them. When the first of the Ocean Children, the Tinukeda'ya, came among us, many thought that although they looked much like us, they could only be enemies. But if they had not come among us, we would have perished with our lost Garden." Another stir went through the listeners like wind in the grass. Tanahaya thought it likely no one had ever spoken of the Tinukeda'ya at such a time before. *I pray you know what you do, Aditu, my better-than-sister.*

"And when the One stood hidden in darkness before Time began," she continued, "and felt itself to be alone, what if the One had feared to change? It would never have become the primal Three, and everything would still be wrapped in darkness and cold—no life, no song, no hearts to rise and rejoice at the turning of another year.

"Now I must share a hard truth," she said. "My mother Likimeya is dying. You all know that. When last we gathered the clans to dance the end of a Great Year, she led the ceremony in Jao é-Tinukai'i. Now that refuge is gone, and only a few of our people's places of safety remain. And I am not the true Sa'onsera. My mother's voice is silent—she has not taught me how to properly, respectfully sing all the songs of change. But I am her daughter, and no matter what, I have come here today to honor the ending of one year and the beginning of another. We cannot choose which paths will be offered us—we can only pick the one we think best. And I choose to accept this path with eyes open, and to go forward into what the new year will bring.

"Look now, my kin," she suddenly cried. "Look up into the sky and take heart! For no matter how some things change, not all things do. The promise of another Great Year is above us—look to the Year-Torch!"

And like a field of flowers yearning toward the sun, the gathered Zida'ya turned as one to gaze into the darkest part of the evening sky. There, high above the horizon, a bright spot had become visible, a fog of light trailing behind it like the smoke from a burning brand.

"Surely that is a promise to us all," said Aditu. "Thirteen days will it ride the skies above us, and when it is gone again, the old Great Year will vanish with it and the new one will begin. No, the Sa'onserei have never danced the new year in Anvi'janya before, but we have danced in many other places! We danced in the witchwood groves of Jao é-Tinukai'i, in great Asu'a and Enki-e-Shao'saye and ancient Tumet'ai, long covered by ice. Before that, we danced in the Garden itself. Do not hide from that glorious ancient promise simply because things will not be just as they were. Rejoice! Another year is promised to us! Rejoice! The Zida'ya still live! Rejoice!"

And then Aditu began to sing the Hymn of the Torch, and before more than a few words of the song had left her lips, other voices joined in. Tanahaya had been taught the song at her mother's knee, in what she always thought of as the distant days of her childhood, but as she sang, she was reminded that her own life was but a single tiny bubble floating on the immeasurable river of time.

A yew tree will grow by the Gatherer's cairn,

they sang, Aditu's voice floating above them all,

We live again!
We live again!
Death hangs on its branches, but so does eternity
Hear now our song!
Hear now our song!

A stake of white spearwood makes the spinning world safe
Fear not the shadow
Fear not the shadow
Brings health to the wounded and fire to the darkness
Hear now our song!
Hear now our song!

The larks gather thick on the silverwood's branches
They smell the sea
They smell the sea
The tree will be crafted into our vessel's keel
Hear now our song!
Hear now our song!

Yew wood and silverwood and spearwood together
Bound in a bundle, thus the One made a torch
Cast it up to the heavens to mark out the year's turn
A light that would outshine the bravest of stars!

"Thirteen nights we will sing and dance," Aditu declared when the song had ended.

The Year-Torch had climbed higher in the sky: it was now almost as bright as Dásaku, the Winter-Lantern.

"The potent *kei-t'si* elixir is gone, as all know," she continued, "but we still have some of the lesser *kei-mi* liquor. We will share that among us, even if it is only a drop for each, because the witchwood that has always bound us is more than just its wood, its bark, its fruit, its sap. And we will share the old stories and welcome the changes that this Great Year will bring us, because our lives are a gift. The One made the Three, and the Three made us, so that the infinite would not be lonely on the long road of Time, so that silence could speak to itself, so that Memory would have things to recall and dream about when night came again. Rejoice—!"

Then a strange thing happened: Aditu suddenly fell silent. Her eyes closed and her chin sank to her chest, almost as if she had fallen asleep standing. She remained that way for so long Tanahaya heard worried murmurs from the watching crowd, and she was about to hurry forward when Aditu looked up again—almost in surprise, as though she had forgotten the ceremony entirely. With a slightly hurried air, she then began the Hymn to the Three. When that was finished, Aditu ended the ceremony and bade the assembled multitude return to their homes until the following night.

As the citizens dispersed, many still unsettled by the last moments of the ritual, Tanahaya hastened to Aditu. Ayaminu went with her.

"Are you well, Rabbit?" she asked. "You frightened me, going so quiet for so long. Was it something to do with the child you carry?"

"No, it was something else," said Ayaminu. "I felt it myself, though only barely. Someone spoke to you, Aditu, is that not true? Someone only you could hear."

"Yes. Someone did." Aditu was paler than usual, and she leaned on Tanahaya's arm as though she needed the help to stay upright. "It was a child—a little mortal girl, of all things. But she spoke with my mother's voice."

"Your mother!" said Tanahaya. "After we only just talked of it!"

Aditu nodded. "But I did not like what she had to say."

"What do you mean?"

"She—they—told me that you must go to Tanakirú, Spark."

"What? Me?" Tanahaya turned to Ayaminu, but the mistress of Anvi'janya was still watching Aditu. "Why?"

"I was not told, dear friend. But my mother's voice said you must go now. You must leave with the morning sun."

Tanahaya was swept by a cold wave of fear. "How do we know this is not some trick of Utuk'ku's? A false message?"

"Did it feel false?" Ayaminu asked Aditu.

Tanahaya was leery. "How would she know?"

"She is the next Sa'onsera," Ayaminu said. "She would know if anyone would."

"It was not my mother's voice—but it was." Aditu sagged, letting her head rest on Tanahaya's shoulder. "I am so sorry, dear one. I would give anything to have you stay with me here, but I felt my mother's fear and it was very real."

"But you said it wasn't your mother—it was some mortal child!"

"It was both," said Aditu. "I cannot explain." She let go of Tanahaya and reached into the neck of her tunic. "Utuk'ku has somehow cast a pall over all the Witnesses, as you know, but I will give you this." She withdrew the green stone on a chain she had been wearing. "It is called the Seastone, made from the same substance that formed the Mist Lamp of Tumet'ai. If the Witnesses can ever be brought back to life, it may help you. Even if they do not, though, it is a thing the women of Year-Dancing have worn when they are with child—an omen of good fortune. It is appropriate you should wear it now, I think."

Ayaminu said, "If you are to ride out, Tanahaya, then arrangements must be made."

"So you think what Aditu heard is a true message? That the voice really was Sa'onsera Likimeya's?"

"I do not know," said Ayaminu. "But I know it would be foolish, perhaps even perilous, to ignore such a summons in this dark hour."

"I am sorry, Spark," Aditu told her. "Truly sorry to burden you with this."

Tanahaya tried to find words. "What must be must be," she said at last.

11

Frogs and Mice

Viyeki was again summoned to the prince-templar's tent. He did not dare offend Pratiki by refusing, but every moment away from the tunnel work was nightmarish. He had slept only a few moments at a stretch for more days than he could remember and felt as though he was crumbling into fragments.

My master Yaarike taught me to look for the seam of good news, but what would that be? he thought miserably. *That perhaps fear will stop my heart before the queen has a chance to order my execution?*

Pratiki was seated at his table with a jug and two goblets in front of him. "Come in, High Magister," he said. "I have momentous news. An outrider has come to say that the Mother of All and her company have reached Kushiba and are only an hour away. Let us have a drink to celebrate."

Viyeki began to reach out for the goblet, but his hand was shaking so badly that he quickly withdrew it into his sleeve. "I think I should keep my wits about me, in case Her Majesty wishes to question me."

Pratiki gave him an odd look, but quickly changed it to a small but amiable smile. "Nonsense, Magister. I know how hard you have been working and I know how much you have been worrying. But our queen is merciful to those who serve her well. You have done all that any loyal Hikeda'ya could do."

Viyeki still kept his hands out of sight below the edge of the table, though he felt sure that if his limbs were trembling so obviously, he must wear his terror on his face as well. "Forgive me, Serenity. I would never speak ill of the Mother of the People, but you know that she wanted this tunnel to be finished before she arrived. I do not think she will care much that I did my best. And if that is to be my epitaph—well, it was not the one I would have chosen."

Pratiki nodded in sympathy. "Of course. But I will speak for you with my esteemed ancestor, so do not despair! *I* know how valuable you are, Magister, and I will do my best to make the queen understand it as well. Now, take this and drink up."

There was no way to continue resisting the prince-templar's invitation without open rudeness, so Viyeki reached out and accepted the goblet with both unsteady hands. The wine was the color of violets at midnight.

"To the Mother of All," said Pratiki, lifting his own cup. "May her name live forever, and the story of her brave leadership inspire the Hikeda'ya for as long as our race exists!"

Viyeki took a sip, then another. The wine was strong and complex, with tastes he did not recognize, but it brought a tingle to the back of his tongue and his throat, reminding him of the cloudberry wine infused with *kei-mi* that Pratiki had shared with him on Drukhi's Day. "It strikes me as very rich," he said. "May I ask what it is?"

The prince-templar waved his hand. "Nothing special. Just Firecap from one of the royal caves—you can taste the ash wood it grows on, I'm sure."

Can I? Viyeki wondered. *Can one like me, from a middling clan and unexceptional parents, discern such things?* Of course, he did not share these sour thoughts. The prince-templar was likely his lone ally among the nobles, generals, and members of the Order of Song gathered here to wait for the queen.

Pratiki urged him to drain his goblet, then poured him another. As Viyeki sipped the second cup, the prince-templar asked questions about the progress of the digging, and listened with what seemed like real sympathy as Viyeki talked about the many complications slowing progress as they dug down toward the bottom of the gorge.

"But it sounds as though your workers have done wondrously well under these unfortunate conditions," Pratiki said, lifting the jug to refill Viyeki's cup for a third time.

"Mostly thanks to the Delvers you found for me." Viyeki was becoming aware of a certain fuzziness at the edges of his perception, but it seemed like something stranger than mere drunkenness. The thought of meeting with the queen reasserted itself, setting his heart racing, and he covered his goblet with his hand. "No more, Prince Templar. I have enjoyed it, but I fear that I will not be at my best to speak with our . . . with your honored ancestor."

"Just a bit," urged Pratiki. "Half a cup. As the poets say, 'When blood is thin, wine will thicken it,' and that is what you need—thicker blood, to carry you through this time of fretfulness and concern."

It seemed quite an understatement to call the very real fear about his very likely execution 'fretfulness', but Viyeki was beginning to feel that none of it made much difference anyway. He allowed Pratiki to pour him a little more. Utuk'ku would discover that he had failed whether he was drunk or sober; perhaps with enough wine in his stomach he would not care so much about the terrible thing that was about to happen. *But it is not my own pain I fear,* he told himself. *That will end at some point, as it does for everything that lives. But it is the pain that will come to those I care about—that is the true horror.* He upended the cup and downed the contents.

A Hamakha guard stepped through the doorway of the tent and stood silently, eyes downcast. Pratiki took another long drink from his own cup, then turned to the guard. "What is it? Speak up."

"The Mother of All has arrived with her wagons. She has requested Prince Templar Pratiki's presence in one bell." He bowed his head. "And I also bear a message for High Magister Viyeki of the Builders Order. He is called to join the queen at the bell after that, Serenity. The high magister is to bring all his plans and writings."

So that she can give them to whoever replaces me after I am dead, Viyeki felt sure, but the fog of wine obscured a little of the horror. He had been running from this beast so long that knowing it was about to pounce was almost a relief.

"Tell Her Majesty's messenger that we will both be there at our assigned times." Pratiki turned to Viyeki and smiled again. "And so the dice roll, and how they land nobody knows—not even our queen." And with those cryptic words the prince-templar bade Viyeki farewell for the moment and called for his servants to come in and help him dress for his audience with the Mother of the People.

With all his experience, Viyeki still could not imagine how the queen's huge wagons and those of her advisors had been dragged all the way to this high, desolate place. In other circumstances he would have questioned the Sacrifice engineers about it, but not today. Today was for discovering whether he would live until the end of the Wolf Moon.

Somewhere, a stone bell tolled and the door to the inner chamber of the huge wagon opened. In the doorway stood a celebrant whose unmasked face Viyeki did not recognize. He had half hoped to see venerable Zuniyabe, one of the few high nobles who treated him well, but even Zuniyabe himself would not be able to save his life if the queen decided otherwise. Viyeki got to his feet and shuffled into the queen's reception chamber, but it was beyond his strength of will to look directly at Queen Utuk'ku. He felt that if he met those glittering midnight eyes, he would instantly begin to beg for mercy.

"High Magister Viyeki," said the celebrant by the door. "You are summoned to the inner ring."

As Viyeki crawled forward toward where the highest nobles crouched at the foot of the queen's throne, he glimpsed Pratiki, who covertly signaled him to take the open place beside him. The other nobles were delivering all the ancient, expected salutations to the queen, and Viyeki mumbled along with them, though in his Firecap haze he could barely remember the words. As he reached Pratiki's side the prince-templar gave him a look that seemed meant to be encouraging, but even a sign of friendship from such an important noble brought Viyeki little hope. His drunkenness had not receded, and now, in fact, seemed more profound than when he had left the prince-templar's tent. He could only barely remember Nonao dressing him in his robes of office, and the walk with his guards to the queen's wagons was as vague as a fading dream.

The ritual salutations over, the chamber fell silent. Viyeki stared intently at the richly decorated carpet.

I have come to finish what I promised to my people. The intrusion of the queen's thoughts into his mind was as startling as ever, like unexpectedly feeling the touch of someone else's hand in the dark. But through the swirl of disorder that beset him, half fear, half drunkenness, he felt something else as well: Utuk'ku's words seemed more muted than usual, as if the Mother of All had lost some of her strength. *And that is the destruction of our enemies,* she continued. *Already we have won a great victory. The place where Ineluki Storm King died twice, both times at the hands of mortal vermin, has been destroyed. Hikeda'ya warriors have burned the mortal castle that stood atop Great Asu'a's bones.*

"Hail the queen!" some of the nobles cried. *"The Mother of the People!"* cried others, and, *"Death to her enemies!"*

But although we lost very few of our people in the destruction of the mortal stronghold, we did suffer one sad passing. High Marshal Muyare sey-Iyora was killed at the gates of that upstart fortress, leading a brave charge against not only the mortals, but their Zida'ya allies, those traitors to the Garden and to our shared blood. Hail to Muyare, who gave everything for his people!

"Hail!" cried the assembled nobles and officers. *"Hail Muyare!"*

And so, the Hamakho Baton, symbol of his command, passes now to General Kikiti sey-Sanga, she said. *General, step forward.*

As Kikiti, in silvered ceremonial witchwood armor, approached the dais and knelt at Utuk'ku's feet, Viyeki finally found the courage to look at the queen and those who stood beside her. Utuk'ku sat on a high throne of ornately carved, milky chalcedony so immense that it must have arrived on a wagon of its own. With the white walls behind her and her snowy robes of mourning, the queen's silver mask seemed almost to float in empty air. At her right hand stood Akhenabi, Lord of Song, watching silently from behind his wrinkled, translucent flesh-mask. A bulky shape in a hooded robe sat on the queen's right. Viyeki could see nothing of the face inside the low-hanging hood, and the figure sat so still that he could almost believe it only a statue, though that made no sense. Who was it? Who had been given such a position of honor?

When Kikiti retreated to the first row, the marshal's baton firmly clutched in his fist, another hush fell over the hall. Utuk'ku raised one white-gloved hand, and Viyeki wondered if he was the only one who detected a slight tremor in her movements.

We are close to victory, my people, she declared. *Our day of freedom will soon come, when our enemies will be made nothing, when you will see what our power can accomplish. Your loyalty to the Hamakha will be rewarded beyond your dreams. Even as we speak, our splendid Sacrifices, led by General Ensume, are pushing back the remnants of the Zida'ya warriors, a small, desperate company who are all that remains between us and our prize in the valley below. When we reach that prize, we will finally put an end to all strife. Rejoice, Hikeda'ya! But remember also that our work is not yet finished. Many of our bravest spirits will fall before the end, but never doubt that final victory will be ours, and that you will witness it with me.*

Now you may all go. The war is almost won. Give all that you have to give!

But even as the other nobles began to inch backward toward the door of the hall, Viyeki's thoughts were pierced by the very words he had dreaded: *High Magister Viyeki, you are to stay behind.*

A weight of dull hopelessness descended on him.

Prince-Templar Pratiki had also been kept back, but Viyeki was less reassured to see that Singer Sogeyu and the new High Marshal, Kikiti, remained as well. He wondered if Kikiti had pleaded with the queen to let him enact Viyeki's sentence with his own hand.

"Courage," Pratiki told him when the closing of the hall's doors gave him a moment to whisper without being overheard. "Think of what you love most."

High Magister Viyeki, of the Order of Builders. The queen's voice pierced his disordered thoughts like a spear-thrust. *I am told that you have failed to prepare the way for Kikiti's soldiers to enter the valley. Kneel before me.*

On hands and knees, shaky as a newborn foal, Viyeki crawled to the foot of the dais.

Pratiki claims you have worked miracles in the time you were given. But I do not care about miracles, only success.

He could not meet her stare and waited numbly for the pronouncement of his death. Then he felt Utuk'ku reach into his thoughts, and for a moment he was consumed with blind panic at what she might find there. Death was one thing, but treason would send him to the Cold, Slow Halls and spell destruction for his family and clan.

Think of what you love, Pratiki had told him. Desperate, feeling the queen's intrusion already like hot pincers in his head, he tried to summon his feelings of loyalty to the Hamakha and the Hikeda'ya, but he could not concentrate, and in any case those feelings were overlain with others, more recent, that would surely send him straight to Akhenabi's torturers. He thought of his pointless, mediocre Enduya clan, which meant much to him but little to anyone else, but that was too formless to hold in his mind. His home, his family—he could not even remember Khimabu's face! And he knew that his next thought would be of Tzoja, and then his fate would be sealed.

Nezeru. She came to him suddenly, and with such a powerful flood of feeling, he grasped the thought of her as though she were there, seizing it as though it were a rock he clung to amid the waves of an angry sea. The queen had loved her son Drukhi almost beyond reason, after all—many said she had never gotten over losing him. How could she fault him for loving his daughter, his proud, brave daughter? Nezeru had wanted so much to be a Sacrifice, to prove her love and loyalty—not to him, not to her father, but to the Mother of All!

But even as he strove desperately to keep Nezeru in his mind, to fix his thoughts on his pride at her accomplishments and his hopes for her future, he could also feel something strange. He had experienced the queen's clawing through his thoughts before in a time when he had much less to hide, but this time her grip seemed weaker, almost enfeebled. He did not dare think about it too much, terrified the queen would sense any thought of her own weakness as treachery, but the way that she fumbled at his memories, and even seemed to slide away from things she had easily grasped the last time, filled him with confusion.

The mushroom wine? he suddenly wondered, then realized that memory would lead him to thoughts that would not only endanger himself but Prince-Templar Pratiki as well.

Nezeru, he reminded himself. Nezeru, raised to the high honor of a Queen's Talon. Nezeru, whose favorite response when he said something properly fatherly to her, was "I hear the queen in your voice." Nezeru, who had been so loyal she had even made Viyeki himself feel ashamed sometimes.

I miss her so. I pray she is safe—

And then, so abruptly that it felt like something torn out of him, the queen released her control. He dropped to the stone floor as if boneless and the world spun around and around.

Pratiki also says that you found Delver slaves and put them to work to speed the task you were given. Utuk'ku's thoughts echoed in his head, as calmly as if she had not just tried to tear him apart from the inside. *I feel your concern for your daughter, Nezeru seyt-Enduya—but do not fear for her. She does my bidding precisely, and I have no complaint. Her role in all this is greater than you can guess.*

A small breeze of relief blew through his fevered thoughts at the queen's words. He thought he could stand anything, even the stretching agony of the Cold, Slow Halls, if his fall did not bring disgrace on his daughter.

Sit up, High Magister. Sit up and look at me.

"Yes, my queen." He did his best to rise to a sitting position, though he felt as though he had been beaten and left for dead in one of Nakkiga's lower-level alleys. Now the sentence would come, the words that would end his time in the light. *O, Garden, receive me. I am coming to you. I will walk where my ancestors walked.*

Many of our Sacrifice fighters are still marching to join us, the queen declared, *but the war in the valley goes well. Soon almost two thousand of our warriors will descend through your tunnel and take our Zida'ya enemies from the rear. The Sunset Children will suffer an utter and final destruction.* A tendril of her thought grabbed him again, seizing control of his body and dragging him up straight like hooked fish. *Know that your daughter's valued role in this war will not save you again, High Magister. You have a sennight to see that the passage down to the valley is complete, so that my Sacrifice legions can descend through it and take our enemies by surprise. But fail me again and I will destroy not only you, Magister Viyeki. Your entire clan will cease to exist.*

He realized she was waiting for him to say something, but in his astonishment at the reprieve he could barely make his mouth work. "Th-thank you, great queen," he managed to stutter out. "I will not fail Your Majesty. Hail to the Hamakha."

Beside him, Pratiki rose, perhaps at some unheard order from Utuk'ku, then helped Viyeki to his feet. Unable to do more than stagger, he let the prince-templar lead him toward the door of the hall but realized that he was breaking protocol by turning his back on the queen, so he disengaged Pratiki's grasp to turn around and bow. But already the queen, Akhenabi, the Singer Sogeyu, and even his nemesis, the newly minted Marshal Kikiti, had lost interest in him. Instead, they were all watching the robed and hooded shape on the squat black chair as two of Akhenabi's hooded minions stepped forward and lifted the figure's hood and threw it back.

For a startled instant Viyeki could not make sense of what he was seeing—an oversized face with two round, empty eyes and a circular hole of a mouth. But of course, he realized, it was Hakatri in the armor of the dead Navigator, Ruyan. Viyeki had not expected to see the undead thing sitting with the queen like a member of her inner circle. Even as he stared, the grotesque helmet slowly turned, and Viyeki's heart jounced hard in his breast. Out of all the Hikeda'ya gathered there, the revenant was looking straight at him. He half expected it to speak, to denounce him or utter some cryptic prophesy, but it only stared until Viyeki shuddered and turned away.

For long moments after Pratiki helped him through the door and out of the antechamber, he could not speak. All he had seen in the eyeholes of the helmet had been naked flame.

The prince-templar's guards followed them at a discreet distance. When they had reached the stone-studded field where the tents waited, Viyeki finally found his voice again.

"What will it do? Why did she bring that dead thing back?"

Pratiki only shook his head. "Do not seek to know too much of my ancestor's plans, especially about such dark things. You have troubles enough, Magister."

"Ah, true. I thought I would certainly die today. I thought my last hour had come." His hands were trembling, and his legs felt as flimsy as reeds. "But you saved me, Prince-Templar. There are not enough words in our tongue to tell you of my gratitude."

Pratiki gave him a calm look. "Saved you? I think not, Magister. I did nothing."

"You told the queen that it was I who brought the Delvers in—but it was you."

"Oh, that." Pratiki had reached his own tent. He directed his guards to open the door for him. "It was the least I could do."

"You did not have to do anything for me, Prince-Templar."

Pratiki smiled. "As a poet said, 'When the serpent is hunting, the frog and the mouse must share a burrow.' Is that not right?" And with a salute of one hand, the prince ducked through his tent-flap even as Viyeki was still bobbing up and down, bowing.

As he walked slowly and unsteadily back to his own tent, Pratiki's words cut through even the terror and threats he had just experienced, filling him once more with confusion. *He must know I know what poet he was quoting—Shun'y'asu, he of the verses forbidden by Hamakha law.* But was there more? Pratiki had said, 'When the serpent is hunting,' which could only mean the queen, since the snake was the Hamakha Clan symbol, but Pratiki was Hamakha too, so what had he meant? The frog—that was Viyeki's own Enduya Clan totem. But the mouse?

The mouse, he suddenly remembered. Shun'y'asu the disgraced poet had been born into Nakkiga's impoverished Mouse Clan and had frequently used mice as a symbol of his own smallness and unimportance.

There seemed to be a message there, something of desperate importance, but Viyeki's head felt like a cracked bell. *And he gave me something in that wine. Something to make my thoughts harder for the queen to grasp. Was that to protect me, or just himself?*

He could think no longer. He gave orders to his secretary Nonao to make certain that work in the cavern was continuing according to plan, then he collapsed onto his cot, his head full of thoughts both fantastic and terrifying.

Tzoja had accompanied Vordis to the part of the ancient city where the guards were giving out the evening's meal. She was distracted by the crumbling ruins, and even more by the unburied bodies made faceless and abstract by a powdering of snow. *Tree of the Singing Wind, they called this place—Da'ai Chikiza.* She wondered what it had been like during the city's life, and who the bodies that now littered the ruins had been. She had very little doubt who had done the killing.

So long apart from my own people, she thought. *Most of the time now I think in Hikeda'yasao. Would even my mother recognize me? Would my father, if he had lived?*

Thinking of her shattered family in that melancholy place was a bad idea, she decided. In fact, thinking about much of anything on this march to nowhere was pointless. Who could guess why the Hamakha Guard and a legion of Sacrifices were marching them through this wilderness? It was hard to imagine anything good waited for them at the end of it.

"Tzoja! Where are you?"

The sound of Vordis' voice startled her, and she hurried to where her friend stood, weighted down by bowls and a jug of small beer. Tzoja took the jug from her, then guided her back to their place among the slaves. "This is heavy—and look how much food they gave you!"

"I know the slave who is giving it out," said Vordis. "I asked for a little more than usual. She said she would be in trouble if the guards saw, so don't shout about it."

As Tzoja had expected, by the time they found their spot again, Jarnulf was pacing. The man was like a caged animal, she thought—always ready to do something, anything, strung tight like a bow. "I feared you had happened upon your old mistress," he told her. "I was going to come looking for the two of you."

"There were many waiting for food," said Vordis. "We got some for you, too."

"You didn't need to," he said. "I can catch my own."

"You can't hunt and also watch over us," said Tzoja. "So just thank Vordis for thinking of you instead of only herself."

Now it was Jarnulf who looked uncomfortable. "Of course. Forgive me. I thank you, Anchoress Vordis."

Tzoja was equally amused and annoyed with him. "Was that so very difficult? Now, come and eat, then let me tend to your burned finger."

The meal had little taste, a pottage of grain and beans with a few sticks of dry *pu'ja* bread, but at least it was filling. As Tzoja carefully and gently rubbed an ointment of elm rind and lily roots onto his disfigured hand, Vordis whispered something to her and Tzoja laughed.

"My friend says she does not know what you look like," she told Jarnulf. "Since you have become our companion and protector, she is curious."

"I do not know how to remedy that," he said. He was a little hard to understand because his jaws were clenched against the pain of her ministrations. "Does she expect me to describe myself? I am a mortal man, unexceptional in all ways. My people are Black Rimmersmen, as they call us in the world outside the Norn territories, so I suppose I have the Rimmersgard look. Make of it what you will."

"She doesn't want you to describe yourself," said Tzoja, entertained by his discomfiture. "She wants to touch your face with her hands. That is how she sees."

"What is the point?" Jarnulf seemed almost ready to get up and stalk away. "What do such things matter?"

"They don't. But she has risked just as much as me to help you stay free. It seems a small indulgence."

He glared at her, clearly unhappy, though she could not guess why. Vordis might be blind, but Jarnulf was not, and her face and form were both very pleasing. Could her blindness alone put him off so badly?

"Go ahead, Vordis," Tzoja said, letting go of his newly bandaged hand "You can see his face now. His Majesty approves."

Vordis kneeled beside Jarnulf and put her slender fingers on his neck, then moved them delicately over his face, tracing every feature. The light was fading, but Tzoja could see that Vordis was blushing, and she had a moment of misgiving. *Do not give your heart to this one, dear girl*, she thought. *He seems like one who carries his own doom with him.*

Finished, Vordis made her way back to sit beside Tzoja, her cheeks still blooming. "He is very pretty," she told Tzoja. "No—handsome. Like a knight from some old story."

Tzoja could only agree, but she did not want to encourage anything that might lead her friend to heartbreak. "But could you not feel the expression on his face? He thinks we are foolish."

Jarnulf made a quiet noise of disgust. "I do not think that. I admit though, that I do not understand women's ways. There is danger all around us, and not just from the armed guards and your lover's wife, and yet the two of you giggle like children about how I look."

"I don't think it is just the ways of women you don't understand," Tzoja said. "I think it is the ways of people—most people. Yes, there is danger all around us. What are we to do about it? Fight the guards? Run away into the forest, where even if we escape we will starve, or be eaten by bears, or dragons, or . . . or God knows what?"

"Be careful when you call on the Lord," Jarnulf said seriously. "Because God *does* know, although that knowledge is too much for mere mortals like us."

Tzoja laughed with sour amusement. "We are fortunate to have you, friend Jarnulf. Without your example, we might have all shared a pleasant moment, which clearly God would not countenance."

"You do not understand," he said, but then sank into silence.

"I understand that we will have to walk all day when the light returns," she said. "I am going to try to sleep."

Days passed, some merely cold, others so bitterly chill that Tzoja's fingers and face lost feeling. The great caravan of Hikeda'ya nobles and slaves were herded north along the length of the Coolblood River Valley until they reached a canyon that crossed over into the Narrowdark Valley, a place the Hikeda'ya called Wormscale Gorge. The slaves at the back of the company, long used to hardship, did their best to avoid the attention of the soldiers, but the Hikeda'ya nobles were unused to such treatment; when the great company stopped to sleep, Tzoja heard them talking in hushed, indignant voices about the terrible suffering that had been forced upon them. Many of the nobles seemed to think it must all be a mistake, that the Order of Sacrifice had misunderstood the queen's order. Many spoke ominously about how the overzealous soldiers would be punished for inflicting such indignities on the cream of the Nakkiga court.

As they began the climb into the hills, many of the marchers began to slow or even to fall by the wayside, unable to get up. Though the soldiers treated the fallen nobles with much greater forbearance than the fallen slaves, they did not allow any to remain behind. Those who could still walk were pulled to their feet and forced to keep going. Those who could not continue on their own were piled into goat-drawn wagons so crowded that Tzoja did not think it could be much improvement on trudging up the snowy hills. But fallen slaves who could not rise and had no kin to carry them were simply executed on the spot, providing an example to the others that was hard to ignore.

The more Tzoja traveled with the man Jarnulf, the less certain she felt about him. Not his loyalty or his bravery—those had already been proved—but she had glimpsed dark corners in him, especially when he was angry, that left her puzzled and a little afraid. Sometimes a great coldness swept over him, as if he had taken a step back out of the world of the living. And he talked about God as if He was a person that Jarnulf knew personally.

I cannot guess what he has seen and done, or what has made him what he is, but he was a slave, and that I can understand. Still, he does not trust anyone. He must have led a very lonely life.

But every time she thought he was merely distant from the rest of humanity, Jarnulf would do something that caught her by surprise, helping Tzoja and Vordis to climb a treacherous slope while the other slaves around them were slipping and crawling in mud, as though the two of them were members of his own family. And he seemed to have none of the coarseness Tzoja had seen in soldiers both mortal and Hikeda'ya, though in most ways he was much like a soldier. The sight of his strong calves and sinewy legs beneath his too-short robe reminded her often that he was strong and very fit. But at other times he seemed far too disdainful of the other mortals around them—almost prim, like a priest. When she or Vordis squatted to urinate by the side of the track, Jarnulf would turn away as though it embarrassed him. He had mentioned a mother and a sister, but in such a way that it seemed clear they were both dead. Had he avoided women since then? Could he even be a virgin? She thought that unlikely, especially for a slave who had freedom as a Queen's Huntsman, but once the idea came to her it was hard to shed it. A virgin . . . or perhaps one of the sort who did not lie with women at all, but preferred other men?

He was a puzzle to her, and with so much in her life that was frighteningly unknown, she spent more time thinking about his quirks than she otherwise would have.

She thought, *They have taken both my protector and my daughter from me. I do not know if they even still live. What do I have left? My blind friend and this strange, dangerous man.*

Jarnulf was struggling to rein in his frustration and anger. He reminded himself that though he traveled among his enemies, he was himself a wanted man, and nothing was more likely to cause notice than a troublemaker. It was hard enough simply putting up with the nightly squeezing and oiling of his wounded finger by Tzoja, though her intent at least was kind. He had also been forced into several fights with other slaves who had tried to steal the women's food, or push them out of a favored sleeping spot, and each time he had made himself back off because he knew that even bare-handed, he could easily take the lives of those who had angered him. And every day he was shouted at or threatened by their Hikeda'ya masters as well. Jarnulf had been trained by great Xoka himself and he knew that even most Sacrifice soldiers would not stand a chance against him in a fight, but he was now bound to these two women. If he was discovered to be Akhenabi's escaped prisoner, he might kill several guards and escape, but enough people had seen him traveling with Tzoja and Vordis that the women would be immediately seized and questioned—perhaps even by the Lord of Song himself. Jarnulf still thought little of anyone who would accept slavery as willingly as the two women seemed to have done, trading freedom to serve the silver-masked queen, the living personification of the Adversary's evil, but he did not want them tortured for his sake. He forced himself each day to act like the other slaves, who went where they were directed, like cattle, even if they were being led to slaughter.

It is only killing the witch-queen that matters, he reminded himself in the moments when his restraint began to fray. *Only that. All else are the things of earthly struggle—"immaterial as clouds" St. Hoderund told us in the Rebuke to a Proud King. I have God's plan to enact. I pray that He will give me the strength to resist all things which would distract me or hinder me.*

For Jarnulf, the most frustrating part of the days that followed were the women's nightly excursions to get food and water. He hoped the threats he had made to the Hikeda'ya noblewoman, Khimabu, might keep her from searching for their nightly camps, but he had no such certainty that if she saw the two women alone, she might not try to harm them. But he also knew that Tzoja was right when she told him that roving through the makeshift camps was more of a risk for him. He did not recognize most of the Sacrifice legion badges he saw, but he might stumble on a soldier who would recognize him from the border outposts where he had returned slaves during his White Hand days. He had occasionally roused suspicion then, having only ever brought back slaves of Hikeda'ya blood. What the fort Sacrifices had not known was what mercy he showed by capturing and returning them: any other Hikeda'ya he had encountered in the wilderness, especially Sacrifice soldiers, he had killed without hesitation. But the few mortal slaves he had encountered must have thought themselves blessed that a sharp-eyed Queen's Huntsman had somehow not seen them, no matter how poor their hiding places.

Tzoja and Vordis returned. The older woman put down the stew-bucket so they could all share it, but Jarnulf let the women eat first.

I do not foresee any good end to this trek, he thought. *I must be ready for whatever God sends me.*

12

A Glimpse of Forever

Lillia was alone in a strange place. She was looking for her grandfather, but she couldn't find him. What was even stranger was that she couldn't find anybody. She was somewhere she had never been, she was lost, and she didn't know why.

She stood on the shore of a great span of water that looked bigger than the Kynslagh—so big that she could not see the farthest edge of it. She was on top of a sand dune, surrounded by waving grasses that tickled her stomach as she made her way through them, but the grasses were not green, or at least no shade of green that she recognized; in fact, they were nearly black. And the sand under her feet was purple.

At least the sky seemed the right color, a rich, pale blue like the kind that stretched above her home in the Hayholt on a midsummer day, the kind of day where she begged Auntie Rhoner or the nurses to take her outside, the kind of sky that should always be seen from beneath, stretching across the world like a beautiful blanket. But though the sky should have made her feel happy, it did not, and part of that was because Lillia didn't know where she was. The other part was the sun. It was too small. It seemed barely larger than her thumbnail, though it was still so bright she could not look at it for more than an instant.

Why had the sun shrunk?

She had not been frightened before, not truly, but now she felt a helpless shiver travel through her. She called for her grandfather as loudly as she could. Her voice seemed to go only a little way and then fall, like the rocks she had tried to throw into the middle of the moat one day with Morgan. His had flown through the air in a great, swooping curve, to drop—*klunk*!—in the center of the mossy water, making a hole in the greenery and spreading ripples toward the embankment, smaller and smaller until they were gone. Her own rocks had hardly flown at all, tumbling into the water only a few paces away, and Morgan had laughed at her.

She wondered where Morgan was now. Grandfather had told her, but she could not remember. She could not remember almost anything about where she had been, and nothing about how she had come to this place. First she had been in the dark, where things had tried to catch her. Then she had been above the ground, but with flames all around and people shouting. Then she had been on a horse with Grandfather King Simon. But if this was a place they had stopped, where was he? Where were the horses and the Sithers, the fairy-folk?

Fairy-folk. When she woke up with her grandfather, they had been all around her. She could even remember what they looked like, beautiful and frightening, with golden-yellow skin and eyes like cats. But that was all she could remember—that, and the safety she had felt in the king's strong arms despite the strangeness of their companions.

Lillia looked around, and realized for the first time that it was not just the sun and the sand beneath her that seemed different. She had never been anywhere that smelled like this place, either. As she stood, breathing in, she could smell the tang that came from the wide water, but there were other scents too, some as familiar as the castle kitchens, like cinnamon and nutmeg, but others she could not put a name to, both sweet perfumes and sharp, sour odors. With some, she could not even decide what *kind* of smells they were, sweet or foul, and she was all but certain she had never smelled them before.

A sound from nearby, high-pitched and mournful, made her jump. It sounded a little like a seabird, but also a little like a lost kitten, and though it made her heart turn over with worry for whatever could make such a sad sound, it also reminded her that she was by herself in a place she did not know. The wind whispered through the dark grasses, and suddenly Lillia felt very exposed, as if things she couldn't see might be watching her; she wondered whether she should find some place to wait for her grandfather to find her. She looked back, but the grassy dunes rose for a long way to a few stubby trees lining the top of the farthest hillock. The tops of those dunes looked like a long way to walk and she did not know what might be on the far side—a forest, perhaps, full of bears and other animals, some of which might eat little girls. She turned back toward the great expanse of water and began walking down the dunes toward the sands, which seemed almost as dark as the wind-stirred grasses slapping at her legs.

The beach was made of black sand, although she was not entirely certain of the color because the sun, already small, had descended farther toward the horizon, and now seemed only the width of her finger from setting. She thought of what it would be like to be by herself beside a dark ocean and shivered again. She called out for her grandfather again, then for Morgan, and even for Auntie Rhoner, but still had no reply except the wind moving through the dunes and the dim, dim sound of the waves touching lightly on the shore.

Birds she didn't recognize dropped to the surface of the wide water and then leaped up again with wriggling prizes in their beaks. The beach meandered between high, violet dunes and the shallow waves that took the sparkle from the sands wherever they rolled in and then slid out. As she walked, the sun dipped even lower. She worried about whether she should have stayed in the place she had first been, as her grandparents had several times told her to do if she ever became separated from whoever was watching over her. But she could not have borne the loneliness of the dunes any longer, and the sound of the ocean lapping at the shore was, along with the sky, the only truly familiar thing here. She let it surround her and cover her like a blanket and tried not to think about all the things that did not make sense.

The sun finally disappeared into a small flat sunset, a bare smear of red along the flat surface of the sea. Lillia made her way around a rocky promontory that stretched close to the water, but though she had several times waded in the Kynslagh at home, she felt a superstitious unwillingness to let this ocean touch her and carefully stayed on dry sand. As she passed the great thrust of weathered stone the beach widened again before her; Lillia stopped, startled.

A fire was burning on the beach ahead of her, at the base of the purple dunes, which had lost their color with the sun's departure and loomed dark gray in the twilight. She stared, frightened yet fascinated, because someone in a hooded cloak was sitting beside the fire, the flames dancing in the wind like a bright, living curtain.

Lillia shrank back against the promontory and tried not to move. If she could not say where she was, she had even less idea who might be sitting beside the fire, but she was certain that her grandparents would not want her to talk to a stranger—especially not here, in this deserted place. But the wind was rising as the darkness came on, beating the tops of the waves into froth, and although she did not feel cold, she thought that very soon she might.

I'll go a little closer, so I can see better, she thought. *Maybe it's Grandfather. Maybe I got lost and he's been waiting for me.*

Then another, stranger idea came to her. *Maybe it's Mama, and I'm in Heaven. But if I'm in Heaven, maybe I died.*

This was so unexpected and so upsetting that for long moments she could not move, as if the wind from the sea had turned her to stone. Then the figure turned toward her and lifted a hand.

"There you are," said the voice—an old person's voice, but one Lillia did not recognize. It sounded strong and calm, neither menacing nor unpleasantly sweet. It sounded as if it would tell nothing but the simple truth. "Come, child," the stranger said. "Come, Lillia. I have been waiting for you."

She looked around, but nothing in the unfamiliar landscape could tell her what to do, and she was tired of being alone. Whoever this was, they knew her name. If they were someone bad, how could they know who she was?

She walked slowly. As she drew closer, the figure rose and beckoned. The sky was almost completely dark now, and the fire began to seem as though it was at the end of a tunnel of darkness, as if it were something more than just a campfire. She hardly realized she had reached it until the crackle of the flames was loud in her ears and the tongues of fire stretched higher than her head, tossing off little handfuls of sparks that flickered upward and then went out.

"Sit," said the cloaked figure. The voice was deep and rough, but it was a woman's voice. "You are safe here. Sit. Warm yourself." And as if to demonstrate that Lillia was in no danger, the hooded stranger sat back down on a wide rock.

Lillia carefully chose a place on the far side of the fire, so that if the cloaked figure tried to grab her, she would be able to jump up and run away. But the stranger only folded work-worn hands in her lap and contemplated Lillia for a moment, then pushed back her hood. Her face was reassuringly ordinary, aged but not sunken-cheeked or toothless. The stranger's face was very wrinkled, but they looked like the kind that came from sun, wind, and weather, like the fishermen Lillia had often seen in Market Square, selling their catch from the backs of wagons. The woman's hair was cropped short, its dark color shot through with so much gray that Lillia could not have said whether there was more pale than dark or dark than pale. She looked like someone who had led a long life of hard work, but that work had not beaten her down but made her strong.

"Who are you?" Lillia asked.

The stranger looked at her without saying anything at first. As their eyes met, Lillia jumped to her feet, startled. The woman's eyes were no ordinary color, but yellow—yellow as the glare of an owl or a hunting falcon. "Names are dangerous now," the woman said, "but do not fear me, little one. I am an old friend of your grandfather's."

"Where is he? Is he here?"

The woman shook her head. "No, I am afraid he is not, child. And to be honest, this is not truly a place."

"What do you mean? Where am I?" She had never had to ask that question before and it frightened her.

"It is a dream, of sorts. A memory. It is hard to explain. Come, sit down and I will tell you what I can."

"Do you have anything to eat?" The fire was warm and its light reassuring, though it did not stretch very far in either direction up the beach and did not touch the murmuring sea at all.

"No. But if you think about it, you will realize you are not hungry."

That seemed a strange thing to say, but after a moment's consideration Lillia realized that the strange woman was correct. "How did you know?"

"Because I brought you here, to this place—this memory. We are in a dream of the Lost Garden." She extended an arm, her sleeve rippling in the wind. "That is the Dreaming Sea. It is not part of the Garden, but the Garden is part of it. Do you see how this only becomes more confusing when I try to explain?"

"Perhaps you're not good at explaining."

Her laugh was like the bark of a startled dog. "Perhaps not, young one. All you need to know is that you are safe here. No one can find this place but me."

"What about my grandfather?"

"He is close, I promise you. You are still riding with him—and the Sithi—even as you dream." The woman got to her feet again—slowly, as if she ached all over. "I have to leave you now, but with one warning. Do not go in the water."

"The water? You mean the ocean?" She looked out into the dark emptiness beyond the beach and shuddered. It looked like a hole as big as the world, a hole with no bottom.

"Yes. The Dreaming Sea. It is not only the memory of the living ocean that birthed us, but also a memory of what we were like when we were all one. It would be too much for you, child. Do not enter it—not even to wet your toes."

Lillia felt as if she could not get a deep breath. "You're going to leave me here? By myself?"

The woman held out her hand. Although she had not reached into her shapeless robes, a long feather now lay across her palm, trembling a little in the breeze from the ocean. "Keep this," she said. "If you are very frightened, call me with it and I will come. But please, only if you truly, truly need my help."

"But I don't know your name."

"As I said, names are dangerous now. But I promise that if you hold the feather, think of me as you see me now, and ask me to return, I will."

Lillia hesitated, then reached out and took the feather. It felt quite ordinary—the striped wing feather of some large bird.

"Now, farewell until we see each other again," the woman said. "If you are frightened, remember that you are only sleeping, and that you are safe in your grandfather's arms." She turned, the wind plucking at the hem of her cloak, and began to walk away up the beach, but before she had taken half a dozen steps, she grew dim and began to fade until there was nothing left of her.

Lillia slipped the feather into her torn dress so it would not be lost, then cried for a little while, mostly because she had nothing else to do. She had always liked being on her own, but that had been because she knew that people were waiting for her, or even looking for her. This was different and she didn't like it very much at all. Then her attention strayed, and for a moment she forgot to be sad.

The stars—she had not noticed the stars before, but the sky was darker now. The shapes of the stars seemed strange, but it was their brightness that drew her. They did not look like the stars she knew, tiny white flecks, but like little balls of white fire instead, like pinholes in a black curtain with the light of Heaven blazing brilliantly behind it—a glimpse of forever.

And then Lillia saw movement on top of the bluff above her, and for a moment real terror seized her: her grandfather's friend had said no one else could find this place, but what was that? It looked like a person dressed in windblown white, with a face that gleamed and shone, as if one of the stars had fallen to earth. The figure was looking out at the ocean, and Lillia bent down as low as she could before realizing that it did not matter what she did because the campfire could be seen from a great distance away. The thing on top of the bluff must have noticed it; it would only be a moment until it would turn that shining face toward her and then descend. Lillia tensed, ready to run, but a moment later the white shape seemed to fly into pieces, as though the wind had caught it and torn it apart. Then it was gone and she was alone again beside the black ocean, beneath the blazing, unfamiliar stars.

"Will we stop at Da'ai Chikiza?" Simon asked. "I have not seen the place since I was young."

"It has not changed much," said the dry voice. "It is still a ruin."

Despite all the times it had happened, the grown woman's words coming from his grandchild's body still startled him. "So, you are back, Geloë."

"Yes. And I have been with your granddaughter. She is safe, and she misses you."

Before he could ask what that meant, Jiriki slowed his horse to let them catch up.

"In answer to your question, Seoman," he called, "no, we will not venture near Da'ai Chikiza. We are dearly needed in the north or Utuk'ku would never have gone to such lengths to separate us from the rest of our people in the north. Geloë has said that it took a great deal of the strength she and Utuk'ku shared, the mighty song of the Three That Are One, to create the illusion of a great Hikeda'ya army." Jiriki paused for a moment as if startled, then slapped his thigh. "Of course, now I see! When she was in Da'ai Chikiza with Prince Morgan, Tanahaya had time only to tell me of the document she found on Himano's body before the Witnesses were silenced and the attack began. Utuk'ku and her advisors were only waiting for me to hear the false information about witchwood seeds buried beneath the Hayholt, and then made sure Tanahaya would not tell me of any second thoughts." He shook his head, that birdlike movement of his neck Simon knew so well. "Utuk'ku has planned for this carefully."

"Her hatred is cold, not hot," said Geloë. "She has been pondering revenge upon her enemies for age upon age. Such ploys are only the latest additions to ancient schemes."

"Why didn't *you* tell Jiriki about what was happening, Geloë?" Simon's anger had not subsided, and he was tired of being an ignorant pawn for others. "Or me, for that matter? You took away my dreams, but what if you had sent me a dream instead to explain what was happening? Many of my people would still be alive, and Jiriki and his folk would not have been tricked into leaving the rest of the Sithi behind."

"Do not mistake me for your God, Simon," she told him. "My strength is limited, even when I was still able to use the strength of the Three Who Are One. I had to employ that power in the best ways I could, for the greatest good of the greatest number of people—yours, Jiriki's, *and* my own—while keeping my identity secret from Utuk'ku. It was the hardest thing I have ever done—so far."

Simon did not know what to say at first. "What is this Three Who Are One you keep talking about? How could you share power with the Norn Queen? You said she corrupts everything she touches. How do you know she isn't still using you as well?"

"She would if she could, which is why I struggle so hard to keep myself secret from her, Simon. She still controls the great song of power, but it must trouble her that part of the triad is now beyond her reach. I am hoping she will decide that Ommu faded out of this world from the effort of making it seem an army of thousands was descending on the Hayholt."

"But you keep saying how clever the Norn Queen is. How could she not know something like this might happen?"

"Because though she has crossed the Veil, she has not died. The difference between the dead and the living—like Utuk'ku, old as she is—is impossible to explain, but I guess that she cannot completely know the mind of one who has passed over. And never forget, Utuk'ku is one of the Keida'ya, while I am of the Tinukeda'ya. There are parts of my people's thoughts she cannot understand. I hope she cannot touch them, either, because that is how I have hidden from her. But she likely suspects now that she has been tricked, and that will enflame her beyond words."

"But how can we hope to defeat her?" Simon asked.

"Her greatest weakness is she cannot understand anything that thinks differently than she does," said Geloë. "She is selfishness personified. She cannot fully comprehend the mind of someone who would put others before themselves."

"All the Hikeda'ya cannot be as cruelly greedy as she is," said Jiriki. "I do not believe our two tribes are so different."

"We may test the truth of that before this war is over," said Geloë.

"The Three Who Are One," said Simon, shaking his head. "I still don't understand it."

The spirit inside his granddaughter's body was silent for a while as Simon's horse and Jiriki's Cloudfoot sped smoothly on through the trees, side by side, with the rest of the Sithi ranged around them. At last, Geloë said, "It may not be possible to explain it in a way that you can grasp, Simon—and that is no criticism of your wits. I have been in strange places a long time, and I often struggle just to speak like a person. You cannot imagine what I have seen and done since I was with you as a living being. Very little of it can even be put into your words—but I will try. The Three Who Are One is an old song of power—one of the very oldest, discovered in the Garden in the legendary days of Jakoya the Gatherer, before my people had left the sea and met Jiriki's folk. It can only be created by those who are already wise and powerful, and for this ancient song to succeed—this *spell*, mortals would call it—one of the participants must be on the far side of the Veil. In other words, at least one of the dead is required."

Simon shuddered. "And that one is you?"

His granddaughter's shiny, golden hair bobbed in a solemn nod. "Yes. And the second must be one of the living. That is Utuk'ku, ancient but—so far—deathless. The third must be someone who straddles both worlds, someone hovering at the edge of the Veil between life and death. And Jiriki will know who that is."

The Sitha made a sound that Simon had never heard from him, a sigh of such deep pain that he might have suffered a mortal wound. "My mother, Likimeya, of course. I should have seen it—should have guessed! She does not die, but she does not recover, caught in an unending sleep, though after all these seasons she should either have awakened or passed over into death. But she would never willingly help the witch of Nakkiga. Is it Utuk'ku's hand that keeps my mother trapped between life and death? Is that another cruelty to lay at the she-monster's feet?"

"Perhaps," said Geloë. "But do not underestimate your mother, Jiriki. She and I could not speak to each other because Utuk'ku would have sensed it, but Sa'onsera Likimeya is strong, brave, and wise. I suspect that, in her own way, she fights against the shackles of the Three Who Are One just as I did, striving to keep herself whole and sane."

Jiriki fell silent, looking so bleak that Simon did not have the heart to ask more questions. For a long while they simply rode in silence.

"And if against all likelihood we defeat Utuk'ku?" Jiriki asked at last. "Will my mother return to us? Will she make her way back from the Veil?"

"I truly do not know, Jiriki i-Sa'onserei," she said. "Utuk'ku's plans, your mother's plans, and my own desperate machinations are all whirling at the same time, like a juggler's trick—no, I think it is more like the wooden tops that children wind with a thread and then spin. The tops may crash together and then all will fail at once. Or they may all twirl on, slower and slower, until only one remains upright."

13

Saint Sutrin's

St. Sutrin's cathedral was huge and cold, but it was home—at least for the moment. Tiamak was one of its new residents, although he was anxious to find another place to sleep. The cold that made even the smallest chambers feel icy in the mornings was hard on his sore leg, memento of a long-ago fight with a Wran crocodile.

Still, it is better to be alive and in a little pain, he told himself. *And it is far better to be shivering in St. Sutrin's than trapped in the poisoned catacombs beneath the Hayholt.* And it was not as though he did not have ample distractions as the acting Hand of the Throne. The dead had to be buried, displaced castle residents had to be housed and fed, wounded Duke Osric nursed back to health, along with a thousand other small but important tasks he needed to oversee.

Tiamak and his countrywoman Jesa were waiting for Queen Miriamele on a bench in the cathedral's cloisters beside the open-air garden, both Wran exiles happy to get a little sun during chilly Novander. The need to wait for the queen had become familiar. Miriamele not only had all the duties of a monarch whose capital and home had been destroyed by war but also had to do it without letting her enemies discover she was still alive.

A clever trick if we can manage it. Tiamak knew that the queen's concerns were, sadly, justified: Pasevalles seemed to have undermined the High Throne for a long, long time, and had employed agents both inside and outside the castle. To his surprise and disgust, Tiamak had found a letter in the scorched ruins of the Chancelry that suggested the traitor had been helped by King Simon's longtime friend, Lord Chamberlain Jeremias. Tiamak desperately wished he could question Jeremias, but like many others who had been living in the castle, the chamberlain was missing, and because of the terrible fires it was hard to guess what had happened to him. He might have been one of the hundreds who had died in the Norn attack, or—if his treachery had been intentional—might have fled with Pasevalles.

Ah, warmth, Tiamak thought, lifting his chin to enjoy the sun on his face. *That is at least one thing I miss from my old home. I was never cold there.*

When he opened his eyes again, he saw that young Jesa was watching him closely. She held the rescued baby of Nabban's duke and duchess in her lap as such disagreements with this tall sister. And it was obvious to me that here was a woman who thought for herself, who put kindness ahead of propriety. I was fascinated by her. But of course, the lady was in religious service, so I did not think of trying to know her better.

"Some weeks later, I met Thelía again, this time at one of Nabban's spice markets. I thought she might be the abbey's cook, but the things she was buying had little to do with food and more to do with healing. I gathered the courage to talk to her, and discovered a mind interested in all things. We spent no little time walking up and down the market, telling each other about our lives. At first it was but a friendship between two like-minded sorts, but my admiration for her was already strong. Just before I left Nabban to return to the Hayholt, I received a letter from her saying she had decided to leave her order, and that her family was angry and disgusted, thinking it would bring shame on them. I spoke with King Simon and Queen Miriamele, telling them that she would be a fine healer to replace me, since I was spending more and more of my time acting as counselor to the throne. And they agreed, although they may have seen that my interest in her was something beyond merely finding another skilled healer. And if so, they were right, because a year after she came to Nabban, we were married. I have never had the slightest cause to regret it—rather the reverse. I am amazed every day that she found good favor in me."

"I have met your wife, Lady Thelía," said Jesa, "and it is plain to see that she is a very admirable woman. She has barely rested, though I hear both you and she suffered a great deal even before the fire, and I have seen her taking care of both Duke Osric and the poorest of the castle servants, treating them all with equal kindness. I have nothing at all against her. I was just puzzled by you taking a spouse so different from yourself in a place already so different from where we were raised."

Tiamak nodded. "Then let me ask you a question in turn. That baby that you hold so closely and carefully—why do you devote yourself to her? Little Serasina is a drylander child, and one who can never truly belong to you because her blood makes her part of the game of kings and queens. And yet you care for her as though she were your own. Why is that?"

Jesa looked down at the infant. "Because I love her, of course. Without me, she would have died. I don't care for the feuding of nobles. Whether she becomes a duchess or a servant, I will still love her."

Tiamak nodded. "And there we agree. Love, I think, is like fire. We do not know where it comes from, or why it gives us light, but it is what we use to hold back the darkness." He stood.

She was still looking at him, but a tiny smile pulled at the corner of her mouth. "You are a man who is clever with words, Lord Tiamak."

"They are my only tools," he said. "Words and ideas. And speaking of those, I have some important things to show the queen, and I think she has probably finished with her other duties. Please, come with me."

She shook her head. "I have no place in such things."

"I disagree. I have watched you, Jesa of Red Pig Lagoon. Despite having to speak someone else's tongue here, you always make yourself understood. You have wit and you have good sense—those two do not always walk together—and in the days ahead, Queen Miriamele will have great need of both. She trusts you. And I think she still trusts me. So come—we will go together. And bring little Serasina. It is always good to remind a busy ruler of the things that really matter."

Jesa was silent as she got up to follow him, but Tiamak could tell she was thinking over what he said.

He Who Always Steps On Sand, thank you for bringing me this far. Guide me just a little while longer—that is all I ask.

Because I am tired, so tired.

"Duke Osric must be dead." Pasevalles was unhappy, even worried, but kept his voice flat and uninterested. "If he still lived, even too crippled to ride out with the troops, they would be trumpeting his well-known name up and down the south of Erkynland. No, our enemies are likely only a few minor nobles who have banded together, with Osric's wife, Duchess Nelda, as their figurehead in a bid to capture the crown."

"But my lord," said the castellan, Gar Cockerel, "what will we do about them?"

"Do about them? Wait for them to fall out with each other, or for one to step forward to claim kingship."

"But everyone says they have raised an army in Erchester! That they will march out soon and crush all rebellion!"

Pasevalles looked at the courtier, barely hiding his disgust. Cockerel had been the first of the captured stronghold's residents to switch allegiances to Pasevalles, but such opportunism did not inspire trust. "I am no rebel," Pasevalles began. "I am the High Throne's trusted steward. And, in any case, look around you. Where are we, you fool? In a castle which was built to withstand sieges, and if necessary, that is what we will do. Or do you think we should simply surrender to these interlopers, these . . . opportunists? To men without patience, without a plan, and without loyalty, while I struggle to hold our kingdom together?"

"Surrender to them, my lord? No, I did not mean any such thing!" Cockerel immediately lowered himself to one knee. "But it might be a good idea to send an emissary to them—to parley—"

"Parley? Parley with thieves?" It was all Pasevalles could do not to kick him in the head. "Get up, you lackwit. Send in Hulgar. I wish to speak to a less civilized man—someone who doesn't breathe cowardice with every word."

As the castellan scuttled out, Pasevalles reflected on his own bad temper. It was not the resistance of the so-called duchess and the ragtags who were gathering in Duchess Nelda's name that worried him. He had not expected to keep the throne of Erkynland without opposition. But he had hoped that with winter upon the country, he would have at least until full spring, or even the summer campaigning season, before the opposition would be able to organize itself. He had also hoped there would be several nobles in competition, so he could safely wait in in his captured stronghold while they killed each other, or at least greatly weakened each other's forces. But apparently the mere mention of the duchess's name was enough to bluff most of them into caution.

As if that old cow has any claim to the throne. The king and queen are dead, their heirs dead or lost. Simon's entire wretched bloodline is all but ended, and the Commoner King himself is now either the Norn Queen's prisoner or a scatter of cooling ashes in the ruins of the Hayholt. And when I crush this new threat, the other nobles will see quickly enough which way the wind blows. Most of them care less for seizing a throne than they do for protecting their own comfort, and I will be strong enough to give them that protection. Still, it did not do to be too confident. Many who had thought their position unassailable had learned otherwise without making any provision for failure. Pasevalles was not that type of fool.

"Hulgar," he called. "Go and fetch the Gemmian."

The ugly clansman made a disgusted face, but after a moment he heaved his bulky body off the divan where he had been sitting. He slid the long knife he had been sharpening back into its sheath. "If you say so. But I don't trust him."

"Did I ask you?" Pasevalles was amused. He suspected it was less that Hulgar found the other man untrustworthy as that he was a little afraid of him—a very unusual situation for the massive Thrithings mercenary. "Just fetch him. And then find something else to do, so I don't have to watch you glaring at us like a chained mastiff."

Hulgar did not reply, his broken mouth still set in a sullen expression.

A deadly, murderous child, Pasevalles thought. *A child who could kill a bullock with his bare hands. But I have methods to keep him sweet.* "What do you wait for?" he said out loud. "Get on with you."

Fecca entered the room as he always did, like a young swain entering a lovely lady's bower in full expectation of coming delights.

"What are you grinning at?" asked Pasevalles. "An army is being raised to destroy us even as we speak. Does that please you?"

"Nothing pleases me except your happiness, my lord Pasevalles," said Fecca.

"Then stop smiling, because happy is the one thing I am not."

Despite his short-cropped, salt and pepper whiskers and his tan, wrinkled skin, the man called Fecca the Gemmian carried himself like a carefree youth, but that was far from the truth. He came from an old and extremely distressed noble family on Warinsten, the island once called Gemmia; he was even, some whispered, distantly related to the family of old King John, founder of the High Ward. The relationship was very, very distant, however, or Pasevalles might have considered him a potential rival instead of a trusted helper. He had been very useful during Pasevalles's years of planning: Fecca spoke both Westerling and Nabbanai fluently. Also, as Pasevalles had been delighted to discover, Fecca had no scruples whatsoever. No crime daunted him, from simple bribery to murder, and best of all, he seemed to consider gold ample return for the things he did.

If I thought he had an ounce of power lust in him, I would have had to kill him years ago.

Fecca dropped onto the steps of the dais at Pasevalles's feet, lazy and nimble as a stripling. The grin was back. "Hulgar looked like he'd bitten into a beehive. Did you scold him again?"

"What I say to Hulgar is of no importance to you." That was Fecca's greatest shortcoming as far as Pasevalles was concerned—he was far too familiar.

Fecca made a face of mock surprise. "Ah. So old Duchess Nelda has you worried, does she?"

Pasevalles would not let himself be goaded. "You heard, eh? It is time to send out the boy, I think. I leave that to you. After that, I have another little chore for you. I suspect you will like that one even better."

"Ah? You arouse my curiosity, Lord Pasevalles." Fecca's narrow, mobile face shifted through several expressions in an instant before settling into a well-crafted imitation of patient attention. "Speak, so I may know your will, my lord."

"I have little fear that Nelda, or whoever uses her name, will be able to cause us any harm while we are protected behind our walls, but only a fool says *never* and believes it. If, somehow, enough of the other barons fell in behind her banner, we would be in danger." He allowed himself a moment of anger. "Curse the Norn Queen. I should never have made compact with that ancient witch. Because of her, we have lost the Hayholt, which would have been our assurance of keeping the throne. And what did we receive from her in return? Not much, and certainly very little I could not have accomplished for myself."

"Oh, aye, my lord," Fecca began. "That's true, right enough—"

"Don't humor me, you scarecrow." He cast a disdainful eye over Fecca's unprepossessing garb and grizzled chin. "But we have one boon because of Utuk'ku, and I aim to make use of it." He reached into his sleeve and withdrew an object wrapped in fine cloth. He unfolded it with a snap of his hand, revealing a round, shiny object the width of his palm, set in a frame of dark wood.

Fecca did not say anything for a moment, but one eyebrow crept upward. "Is that what I think it is, my lord?"

"Yes. It is a wormscale Witness."

"The Norn Queen gave it to you?"

"Indirectly. When the men you hired hunted down the Sithi envoy to the Hayholt and filled her with poisoned arrows, this was found in her saddlebag. The she-fairy didn't die, as you know." Pasevalles had already spoken many hard words to Fecca about the Sithi envoy's survival, and it took all his restraint not to revisit the subject. "But I wound up with this little prize, so I still had the best of the bargain."

The Gemmian sat back, stretching his long, thin legs. "So why do you show it to me, my lord? Are you going to use it to call the Norn Queen a few well-deserved names?"

"Your wit is as sharp as ever, Fecca—which is to say, not very. No, I am going to send this trinket to Turia Ingadaris in Nabban. I can promise you that even on her wedding day, she never received a gift like this."

For the first time since he entered, Fecca seemed at a loss. "Turia? Widow of Drusis? Why send such a fine, rare thing to that child?" He grinned. "Are you sweet on her?"

"Idiot. Because with my help, that child is going to rule Nabban—in truth, she largely does, though Sallin—her lackwit cousin—has tried to keep her isolated from any allies. I wonder how long she will let him live in ignorance, thinking he is calling the tune." He wrapped the mirror back in its cloth. "And if the worst happens and we are driven out of this refuge, then we must have a safe harbor ready for us. Unless you want to wind up beside me on the gibbet."

"And how would we get out of here?" For the first time, Fecca's long face was intent. "I assumed with all the men we have brought in and the work on the walls, we were planning to last out a siege."

"That would be the best circumstance," Pasevalles admitted. "But only a fool makes no provision for failure. If I were that sort of fool, I would be a lump of smoking meat in the Hayholt's throne hall this moment."

"Very sensible, my lord. Very wise. So, I repeat my question—how will we get out of here if it comes to that unfortunate happenstance?"

Pasevalles laughed without mirth. "I said I am not that sort of fool. Neither am I the sort who will give away all his secrets before he has to—even to a trusted ally like you."

Fecca made a mocking bow, but his eyes were cold. "As I said—very sensible, my lord. When do you want me to depart for House Ingadaris with this . . . gift?"

"No later than tomorrow—but as I said, send the boy out before you leave. That will give me time to write a letter for Lady Turia." He paused, giving Fecca another long look. "Not that I doubt your loyalty, but I advise you not to meddle with the Witness, although I am sure you will be tempted. The Queen of the Norns has bespelled all of them into dark silence, and even if that spell ended, you could use it only to speak to the sorcerers of Nakkiga. Trust me—that would not make for either a pleasant experience or a happy partnership. I did everything they asked, and yet I still had to flee for my life and the castle they promised me is a charred ruin."

Fecca gave him a jaunty salute and sprang to his feet. "I thank you for your concern and advice, Lord Pasevalles. I will go and make ready for my pilgrimage to the south."

"The boy first, remember. Better to get some use out of him."

"As you say."

Pasevalles watched him saunter out. *The clever ones*, he thought, *are the most useful. But also the least trustworthy. If things go wrong and I must escape this place, I think I might prefer to leave Fecca to the vengeance of Erkynland.*

Brother Etan thought that in better times Jiriki's Sitha kinsman Ki'ushapo might have been good company. But these were not such times.

Perched on the back of the great black horse's saddle, clinging desperately to Ki'ushapo's narrow waist as they thundered across the snow-sprinkled fields north of Erchester, Etan wondered whether Ki'ushapo would even notice if he fell off. The immortal seemed almost to have forgotten he was there, and the horse ran for hours upon hours without stopping. Ki'ushapo did not speak—it would have been hard to hear him in any case over the drumroll of Shadowswift's hooves—and Etan was beginning to wonder if they would ever stop, or just race on to the end of the world, when they finally halted beside a creek to let the horse drink. They had reached the hill country of northern Erkynland, the nearest end of the Wealdhelm Hills a pale scrape on the horizon, barely visible against gray winter skies, and Etan realized with a shudder that he was once more on his way to places he had never seen before, this time without even the slender protection of a royal commission.

After a moment watching the big horse drink, Etan turned to Ki'ushapo. "You said that Jiriki was riding fast."

"Yes. And we are following him, but I doubt we can catch him—even my faithful Shadowswift will struggle a little carrying the weight of two riders."

Etan didn't know if he was supposed to feel bad about that—the Sitha had invited him, after all. "But where is Jiriki going? Where are *we* going? You said a name—Tankaroo or something like—"

"Tanakirú. The end of the Vale of Mists, at the headwaters of the Narrowdark River, far into the northern reaches of the Oldheart Forest."

Etan had guessed they might be traveling through the great wood, but hearing it confirmed was still disheartening. "Why?"

"Shadowswift has quenched her thirst. Mount up and I will tell you as we ride."

"A ship?" Etan could not make sense of it. "Why is there a ship up in the mountains?"

"I wish I could say," Ki'ushapo said. "Some of the Eight Ships from the Garden arrived in strange places, but that was many, many, *many* years ago. The ship in Tanakirú seems to have arrived only a few short centuries gone, as mortals count them, so I have no answer for you. My people did not even guess this ship existed until the Coolblood River flooded Da'ai Chikiza, and since then, as I told you, we have been kept busy defending the valley from the Hikeda'ya. And there is the ogre. Did I tell you of the ogre?"

By the time Ki'ushapo had finished telling of the monstrous creature that made it so difficult to learn anything about the valley and the ship, Etan was shivering with fear.

"But why would Jiriki go there?" he asked.

"We have been there for a long time, trying to keep Utuk'ku out of the valley. Brave warriors of the Zida'ya folk have protected Tanakirú for longer than you have been alive, my mortal friend. But in the last few turns of seasons, Utuk'ku has sent thousands of her Sacrifice soldiers to the Narrowdark Valley, determined to sweep away all who would keep her from the ship." His voice was somber. "I cannot even promise that there will still be defenders if we make our way there."

"But you said that Jiriki's ahead of us with his warriors. When he gets there, that will help, won't it?"

"Scarcely two hundred of our folk came with us to defend the mortal Hayholt, and even fewer of us are now returning to Tanakirú. But Jiriki will find a way to use even such small numbers. He has a rare mind and a great heart. Do not give up hope yet."

Outnumbered and surrounded, Etan thought. *And I'll be with them.* The sky above seemed to grow a shade darker. *Into another war as Tiamak's messenger, but this time I don't think anyone's going to let me walk across the battlefield unharmed.* "So Jiriki is your kin," he said aloud. "I hear admiration in your voice when you speak of him."

"We have known each other since we were children. That was not very long ago by my people's reckoning, but quite a few years for yours."

"How many?"

Ki'ushapo shook his head. "Hard to say—I do not know mortal things as well as Jiriki and his sister do. Two or three hundred of your years, I believe. But Jiriki has always had the wisdom of one much older. When I still thought only of hunting and riding, he was trying to understand the needs of our people—our mistakes, but also our shared hopes."

Shadowswift rushed on across the winter meadows. Etan was struggling with the knowledge that this slender being to whom he clung was centuries old. People called them immortals, and he had always known they were long-lived, but it felt different to meet such a one in the flesh.

"I hear great love for Jiriki in your words, Ki'ushapo."

"As I said, he is kinsman and friend, but he has always been more. Despite his youth he, not S'hue Khendraja'aro, should have been the Protector of our people in a desperate hour like this. We have already seen the old ways fail, and Utuk'ku will never accept anything but the utter triumph of her own designs." He looked back over his shoulder as easily as an owl might, catching and holding the monk's eye with his golden stare. "If there is any hope for my people, it rests with Jiriki and his sister Aditu."

"Then I thank God that He led me to you. If anyone can help me fulfill my task, Ki'ushapo,"—Etan struggled with pronouncing the strange name—"you are that one." He felt a convulsive movement in the Sitha's chest and a hot flush of shame ran through him. "Are you laughing at my faith?"

"No, no!" said the other. "I beg you to believe me, I meant no insult. It was just the way you said my name. I know our tongue is difficult for *Sudhoda'ya*—for mortals." After a moment's silence, he said, "In truth, it was Jiriki who gave me that name."

"What do you mean?"

"My mother did not name me Ki'ushapo, but Kisha'atu." Etan could not see the Sitha's face, but something in his voice suggested he was probing a painful memory. "When we were both young, Jiriki used to tease me for always speaking up without considering the consequences. 'Never play *Shent*,' he would tell me. 'Because I can see your every thought.' I would argue, telling him, 'You cannot guess how deep I am!' One day I again made that claim, and Jiriki gently mocked me, saying, 'Deep you may be, kinsman, layer upon layer like an onion—but also like an onion, every layer is quite easy to see through.' That was the day he began calling me Ki'ushapo—Onion Skin. At first I did not much like it, but after a while, it came to seem more my name than the one my mother had given me."

As a small stocky child, Etan had withstood insults from other children and could not help remembering how it felt. "Were you angry at him?"

"How could I be?" Ki'ushapo seemed to have regained his good cheer. "He was right. I am as deep as any of my folk, but there is no mystery to me at all."

As she walked across St. Sutrin's Square with a small company of guards, Miriamele avoided looking back at the castle hill, where the ruined Hayholt still smoldered. Wisps of smoke from the hottest parts bled into the gray sky, then were frayed by the wind. The weather was mild today, but the cold still bit through her garments; she shivered a little as she reached the great cathedral doors and a soldier sprang forward to open them for her.

Archbishop Gervis had decamped to his country estate, leaving behind only a small contingent of priests to oversee St. Sutrin's. Miriamele had made it the center of the High Throne's business, since it was the largest building still standing outside the ruined castle, but she was still surprised to be greeted in the cathedral's nave by only Tiamak and Jesa.

"How are your accommodations, Majesty?" Tiamak asked, bowing.

Miriamele gave Jesa a smile and a nod. "More than adequate, old friend, but I cannot stay long in my chambers. There is far too much to do. And you? Is your lady wife also comfortable?"

"The monks of the cloister have been generous enough to prepare the old abbot's house for us, so we are well settled, but Thelía is like you—she cannot abide staying in our chamber when there are so many who need her help."

"She has been doing magnificent work with the burned, the wounded, and the sick," said Miri. "I hear she has even brought Osric back to health—if not to good temper." She turned to Jesa. "And you, my dear. It is very good to see you and too long since we talked. Where is little Serasina?"

"I left her with the wetnurse, my queen." Jesa spoke hurriedly, as though concerned Miriamele might think her careless. "The milk does her good, though she is eating other food too. But she has grown fatter and smiles often."

"I'm glad to hear it. Bring her to me later, will you? I long to pinch those little pink cheeks."

"Of course, Majesty."

"So, Lord Tiamak," the queen continued, "I hear you have something to show me here. Lead on—there is much to do, so much. Erchester may not have burned, but the people of the city are hungry and cold, and traders are taking cruel advantage of our need for provisions and wood."

"There is a line of petitioners waiting for you at the cathedral gates." Tiamak sounded apologetic. "Or rather, waiting for 'the Duchess.' You cannot show yourself to them, of course—not if we wish to keep your survival secret a while longer—but I will make certain that any legitimate requests are sifted out and brought to you later."

"All well, but is that what you wished me to know? Anxious subjects are not exactly hard to find."

He smiled and bowed. "I promise you, Miriamele—Majesty—I would not have asked you here for such an ordinary thing. Follow me, please."

Miri left all but a pair of her guards in the nave and followed Tiamak through the cathedral and out to the old abbot's chambers, which he had chosen for his offices. The sumptuously tiled ground floor of the abbot's house was all but invisible now beneath several tables covered with stacks of records, and with more piles of documents waiting on the floor.

"However can you find anything?" Miriamele asked. "So many parchments!"

"I have help from the counting priests who fled the fire," Tiamak confessed. "Many of them already lived in the cloisters, so they were easy enough to find, and over time we will bring this chaos to better order. But this is not what I wished to show you, Majesty. Follow me to the abbot's library. He had a pleasant but small collection of books—several dozen in all—but clearly planned to acquire more. And he had a very fine set of cases built to keep them in."

"I never knew him well," Miri said. "But he seemed a good fellow, and Gervis considered him very clever."

"I am grateful to him for his planning, I confess," said Tiamak, and opened a door at the far end of the room, then led Miri and Jesa into a room bathed in light by high, colorful windows. So many candles and lamps burned there that

Miriamele was almost dazzled; she did not truly see the room's contents for some moments.

"I thought you said a few dozen books!" She looked around in astonishment. Almost every wall of the library room was covered in shelves, and every shelf was packed from end to end with books and scrolls. Even more volumes were stacked on the floor in front of the bookcases, and a dozen or more earthenware jars stood among them, each filled to the brim and above with scrolls and loosely rolled sheets of parchment. "There must be hundreds here—thousands!"

"So many," said Jesa, shaking her head. "I did not know there were so many books in the world!"

Tiamak's smile was broad now. "The night I first saw you on the ship, Majesty—the night the castle burned—you were kind enough to lament the loss of my books. But you must know, Miriamele, my queen and my friend, that I never considered them *my* books. Knowledge is for everyone, and the greatest minds of our past and present ages live in these pages. I had gathered them all in readiness to move them to John Josua's library when it was finished, but with rumors of a possible attack by the Norns—rumors which proved dreadfully true—I feared to leave them vulnerable."

Miriamele was surprised. "You worried more about the fate of books than the people in the castle?"

Tiamak was offended, though he seemed to be doing his best not to show it. "Majesty, it is my duty to worry about *everything.* I could not empty the castle of people, though I argued often for more defensive work to be done to the walls and towers, but I could at least make certain these books, which had no other defender but myself, were safe. As I said, the thoughts held in these volumes do not belong to me, but to all men and women of learning. They are our gift to the generations that will come after us."

Miriamele was almost amused by his indignation. "Of course, Tiamak. I did not mean to accuse you of dereliction. I was just surprised to see all these here. How did you manage? Did Pasevalles never know you were doing it?"

His look softened, the momentary hurt supplanted by a flush of pride. "I had to keep it secret, of course. At the time I did not fully suspect Pasevalles of anything, though I wondered. But I trusted no one. We thought you dead, of course, and King Simon had gone away to war, so I had to disguise the outgoing wagons I sent to St. Sutrin's as household goods, which required some help from Jeremias, the Lord Chamberlain."

"Jeremias!" Miriamele was startled. "I have heard nothing of him since I returned. Did he survive the fire?"

Tiamak seemed to hesitate, but at last shook his head. "I do not know, but I have found no trace of him since the fire. There was much I missed during the fortnight or so that Thelía and I were hiding beneath the castle—"

Miriamele sighed. She had sometimes found Jeremias exhausting in the pursuit of his duties, but he had been one of Simon's oldest friends. "If he is gone, may his soul find rest," she said, making the Sign of the Tree. "Well, I am glad to see this, Tiamak. You have done well to save the books, and you are right—the generations that follow us will thank you for taking such good care of them all."

"Ah, but there are a few I have not found," said Tiamak. "And *that* is why I have asked you to come here."

"I don't understand your meaning."

"Come." He led Miriamele and Jesa to one of the bookshelves, which—unlike the others, all close-packed—showed a gap more than a cubit wide. "All the books I assembled before Duke Osric's campaign in the Fingerdale Valley should be here. You will see that the volumes about Fellmere, the first castle besieged by the Thrithings-men, are here on one side." He pointed to a group of ledgers. "And there is more. Tenant rolls, plans of the castle, everything you might wish to know about several castles in the Fingerdales, all here. I gave these to Osric and the rest when they were planning their assault on Shan's grasslanders."

"I am still unclear—"

"Pardon me if I seem mysterious, Majesty. I merely wish you to understand what led me to my conclusions. I assembled a great number of such records while Duke Osric prepared to ride out against the Thrithings-men. Then, when I was preparing to send our library to safety here in St. Sutrin's, I took those volumes back—all of them. Osric was long departed, after all, and the battle-planning was finished. But sometime between my gathering up all my loaned volumes and the moving of the books here, someone came and took back several volumes—they belong in this gap on the shelf you see here—which I thought at first were lost in the castle's burning."

"I can understand that would upset you . . ." Miriamele began.

"Forgive me," Tiamak said. "The books I loaned to Duke Osric, then took back after he rode out, detailed many things about the Fingerdale, its towns and settlements and tax records and such. But the *missing* books all had a single subject—the castle at Winstowe and what was around it, its defenses, and all the secret ways in and out. I think you will see now, my queen, what seems plain to me."

"Winstowe—the place where Simon fought the Thrithings-men?" She pondered what he had told her. "And these books were taken even after the campaign had begun?" Miriamele suddenly felt she understood. "Then you think—?"

Tiamak nodded. "I think this has all been planned since before I fled arrest at Pasevalles's hand. We have had no word from Winstowe Castle since the battle where Simon fought and fell, despite there being much to discuss with Winstowe's lord, Count Aglaf, after the fighting. That does not seem entirely innocent to me."

"And you think it was Pasevalles," she said. "Our traitor. You think he took the books for his own purposes."

"Yes, I think it was our unlamented Lord Chancellor," Tiamak agreed. "I think the murderer was searching for a bolt hole, a place he could hide in safety until the Norn attack was over or use as a base for his own ambitions if the Norns refused to leave. Winstowe is a good place to withstand a siege, and with so many tunnels and ancient mine shafts, it would also be an easy place to escape if he wished to disappear into the wilds of the High Thrithings." He took a deep, shuddering breath, surprising Miriamele a little with his emotion, which seemed almost to match hers. "And, yes, I think there is every chance Pasevalles is still there, holding Winstowe Castle for his own."

14

Climbing to Heaven

Since leaving the Hayholt only a few short months ago, Morgan had traveled to meet the Sithi, had lived in forest treetops with the Chikri creatures, and had been captured in a net in the ruins of Da'ai Chikiza as he traveled with Tanahaya, one of the immortals. He had struggled for his life against monsters and Norn soldiers on more occasions than he could count. He had even taken one of the Norns as his lover. Or had been taken—he was not quite sure which. But he had never seen anything as strange and unbelievable as this ship, nor did he think he ever would again.

Their small company followed the long, largely featureless corridor until they reached a cross-passage that led back across the middle of the ship. Various large chambers opened off it, so they were able to continue their journey toward the far end of the ship—if it truly *was* a ship: Morgan was still finding it hard to believe one could be so large. These new chambers ranged in size from huge to almost unbelievable, some as big as the inside of St. Sutrin's great dome-topped nave. The ceilings were crisscrossed with beams that, though made of witchwood, were curved, smoothed, and intertwined, so that they almost looked like parts of a living body. Here and there they found stairwells or hatches with ladders that led down to lower levels, but each time they reached one and listened there, they heard sounds beneath them—the gurgling and splashing of what might have been kilpa, or other strange, unidentified noises, reverberating bangs and scrapes that sounded like something very large indeed moving around in the depths.

"It is clear that we are not the only living things in this place," said Little Snenneq. "I do not want to meet those kilpa again, or perhaps something worse. We should return to smaller corridors."

"Why are we trudging through this thing anyway?" Morgan demanded. "If it's a city, who would live here? If it's a ship, who is it for?"

"I am certain it is a ship." Nezeru was staring up into the heights of the large chamber, shining her *ni'yo* among the bracing beams.

"I want to know more of how big this place is," said Snenneq.

"Too big," offered Qina.

"Not only how big," her betrothed said, "but it would be good to learn more of what this thing is, through which we are so slowly walking. If it is a city, there must be rooftops. If it is a ship, there must be a deck. We should go higher."

"But we haven't seen any stairs leading up," Morgan said. "Only down."

"I think Little Snenneq the troll is correct," said Nezeru. "And I would also like a better look at this thing. We must find a way to climb upward. And if there are kilpa or other unpleasant things in the bowels of this place, then the higher we go, the better."

Kuyu-Kun trailed scrawny fingers across the surface of a ceiling pillar as they made their way around it. "Witchwood," he said in a wondering tone. "Everything is witchwood and all beautifully worked. This was made in the Garden."

"It could have been made nowhere else," said Nezeru. "There has never been so much witchwood in all these lands." Morgan thought her words hid a deep unease. They were all frightened by how little they understood. Even the younger Tinukeda'ya, Tih-Rumi, looked around with wide, unbelieving eyes.

"But the tales tell that the Eight Ships were mostly built from silverwood," said Tih-Rumi. "Is that not so, Sa-Vao? Our ancestors did not have enough time to grow and harvest so much witchwood under the threat of Unbeing."

"It seems unlikely," agreed the old Tinukeda'ya.

"Then this ship was made first," Nezeru said. "Or at least begun before the other eight."

Kuyu-Kun seemed about to argue, but then fell silent, considering. "Perhaps," was all he said.

Their long, tiresome march was suddenly halted as they passed beneath another vast arch and found themselves in an open place larger than any they had entered yet.

"What is *that* thing?" asked Morgan, almost in a whisper.

Nezeru had no answer. She too could only stare at it.

At the center of the massive space that now stretched before them, dominating the vast, cavernous interior like a mountain towering over rolling hills, stood a single massive cylinder of multicolored witchwood, cut, fitted, and polished with the same apparent loving care they had seen in even the smallest details. It stretched upward, high above their heads, its upper end invisible in the shadows far above them. Nezeru could see a chaos of different shapes clinging to the pillar's outer surface and piled high around its base; shapes that even Nezeru's keen eyes only slowly deciphered as a mix of makeshift structures and thickly growing trees and brush—a miniature forest inside the high-ceilinged chamber, lit from above by some dim, unseen source of light. "What are those clumps around it?" asked Morgan. "They look like nests."

"Creatures have made their homes there," said Nezeru. "But I see nothing living now. Remember, we have no idea how long this has been here."

"But even if they're gone, why were they here?" Morgan asked. "And what is that great . . . *pole*? A beam? But we haven't seen anything like it anywhere else."

Kuyu-Kun turned to him. "It must be the ship's mast, reaching all the way to the highest part of the ship, as with the famous Eight and their sails of silver and golden light. The opening through which this great thing passes must allow rainwater and sunlight to fall from above. Any creatures who found their way here would choose that spot first to make their homes."

Now that it had been spoken, Nezeru saw that it must be true. A cold thrill of almost superstitious dread climbed her spine.

Morgan seemed less certain. He stared, open-mouthed, at the monstrous wooden shape. "A mast? It's as big around as a cathedral. It can't be a mast."

"I think it is." Kuyu-Kun nodded his bald head. "The stories tell that all the Vao's great ships were built with a single tree like that as the mast, trimmed and shaped."

Nezeru finally spoke. "I believe this ship—and seeing the mast, what else could it be?—is what draws the queen and my people to this valley. This is why Hikeda'ya and Zida'ya are killing each other. Something in this ship—or the ship itself—must be the prize."

"I have a thought," said Little Snenneq as they all stared at the massive wooden cylinder. "If that is truly a mast, then it likely stretches all the way up and out past the deck of the ship. It is my proposal that we use it to climb up to the higher reaches."

"We can't!" Morgan protested. "It's a mast—scraped and smoothed! How can we climb it?"

"I think it only looks smooth because we are far away," said Little Snenneq. "And see, it is wound around with vines and other growing things, which will likely make for useful handholds. Only think, friend Morgan! We have not seen any other way to escape this level and go upward—until now." He turned to the ancient Tinukeda'ya. "Kuyu-Kun, is this ship like the other ships we know? Is there a deck at the top, open to the sky, where we may see more of the ship and what is around us?"

Kuyu-Kun shook his head. "I cannot say. I have heard many tales about the Eight Ships, especially *Lantern Bearer,* which carried my ancestors to this land, but little is told about the making of the ships themselves. If this is truly a Ninth Ship, and built out of witchwood, not silverwood, how can I be sure it is like the others?"

"Too much talk," said Nezeru, trying to quiet her heart's swift beating. "I am ready to continue."

"As am I," Snenneq said. "And as Nezeru mentioned earlier, I think the chances are good that we will at least meet no more kilpa if we can find a main deck. They gather in the water, as we saw. The higher we go, I am guessing, the fewer places there will be for them to live."

Nezeru suddenly understood something that had eluded her until this moment. "The water," she said. "I have heard the Eight Ships were ballasted with water from the Dreaming Sea."

"So the stories say," agreed Kuyu-Kun.

"Then that may explain the strangeness of the water in the crystal tunnels," she said. "Water running out from this ship's hold has run into some of the mountain's underground streams and the Narrowdark itself, making the whole valley an abode of monsters. Another reason to climb toward the deck—if there is one."

Kuyu-Kun nodded slowly. "I think you must be right. I wish now I had tasted it. What a glory, to swallow a little of the Dreaming Sea itself—!"

"You saw the monstrous things that live in it," said Nezeru. "And were perhaps even *made* by it. You would have been a fool to drink that poison."

"Poison?" Kuyu-Kun's hairless head trembled with emotion. "You may descend from the Garden, but I am *part* of that Dreaming Sea." He turned to Tih-Rumi. "But in one thing the Hikeda'ya is right—you should mount up as high as you can, using the great mast as the ladder, until the ship's deck is found."

"But, Master," said Tih-Rumi, "surely you cannot climb such a distance."

Kuyu-Kun nodded and turned to the others. "Sadly, he is correct. I am old and my strength is all but gone. You will have to leave me here."

"Hah! No, we will make a sling for you," said Snenneq with his usual cheerful confidence. "That way all of us who are stronger can take turns helping bear you up. I will help. Morgan will help." He smiled at Morgan, then turned to Nezeru. "And unless I miss my guess, you will help too."

Nezeru was not quite certain why, but she was irritated with the old Tinukeda'ya. "If I must," she said.

"But you have forgotten me!" said Tih-Rumi. "I am the Sa-Vao's acolyte. If anyone should have the task of helping him, I should."

"We will do it together," declared Snenneq. "In turns. Do you still have your boot-irons, Morgan—my extremely clever invention for ice or tree-climbing?" Beside him, Qina rolled her eyes.

"Of course, since you brought the lost one back to me."

"Then let those who have them put them on," declared Snenneq. "And up the mast we will go!"

"Wait a bit before putting on any climbing gear," said Nezeru. "We are not as close to the tree as you think—distances are deceptive with something that large. It will take us a good hour or so to reach it."

"Daughter of the Mountains!" said Snenneq. "What an adventure."

"Don't like adventure," said Qina in a small, serious voice. "Like home more."

It took even longer to reach the gigantic wooden pillar than Nezeru had supposed. The closer they got, the more astonishing its size became, until it bulked so hugely before them that they might have been standing at the base of a mountain, and Morgan thought he might take a while to ride around it even on a fast horse.

The wood looked shiny as metal in some places, with an oily sheen, but in others was not much different than that of an ordinary tree. It was smooth and straight as the trunk of a spruce—if spruces grew high enough to touch the clouds—but the very size of the mast and the centuries of vines and moss that had grown on it meant that Snenneq's prediction seemed correct: They would be able to climb it without too much trouble if they could work out Kuyu-Kun's sling. So they all got to work.

Nezeru still carried her own length of silky cord, light but strong, and both trolls had a long coil of their own woven sheep's-hide rope. Using lengths of them all, the company constructed a cloth basket that could hold the spindly weight of the old Tinukeda'ya and be carried by two climbers, but which could be quickly remade so that slender, aged Kuyu-Kun could ride on the back of only one climber if necessary. Neither Nezeru nor Tih-Rumi had climbing irons, but Nezeru made it clear that she needed no such help, so Snenneq fashioned a makeshift pair for Tih-Rumi, tying a knife to each of his feet, though it meant both Tinukeda'ya would now have to go weaponless.

"It is well I did not plan to have a knife fight while climbing," Tih-Rumi said as the troll secured the blades to his boots—either a bit of forced humor, or simply a statement of truth.

Their preparations done, the little company settled a safe distance from the hole around the massive trunk to rest before beginning their climb. The trolls curled up together and quickly fell asleep while Nezeru paced the great tree's circumference, searching for deadfall. She returned with a handful of small branches and began to make a fire.

"Witchwood will not burn," Tih-Rumi told her. "Not once it has been worked into its final shape."

"I know that." Nezeru could not keep a touch of frost out of her voice. "These are other woody plants that have grown and died here. A great mass of them cling to the far side of the trunk, so that is where we should start our climb. I pulled hard and only these small pieces came loose." She used flint and steel over a handful of dried moss; within a few moments the tinder caught, and soon a yellow glow brought the dimming faces of the companions back into view.

"If this thing truly was the ship's mast, the sail must have been even bigger," said Morgan after a while. "As big as the Kynslagh Bay."

"But made of light," said Kuyu-Kun. "That is what the tales tell."

"How could such a thing be?" Nezeru thumped her hand against the deck beneath her. "See! This is made of wood from the Garden—strange, but solid and real. I cannot believe in sails made of light."

Kuyu-Kun gave her a stiff look. "You believed the tales your own people taught you, Sacrifice. But you doubt the words of the Sa-Vao, even when the proof of my people's stories lies all around you. Utuk'ku has trained you well."

A cold hardness crept through her, and for a moment Nezeru had to fight against the urge to strike him. When she had mastered herself, she said, "What does that mean?" Sensing something of her anger, Morgan put a hand on her arm, but she shook it off. "Are you saying I am the queen's tool?"

"Until you recognize the deceit that created you, you cannot help it," the old one said. "Those lies shaped every part of your life before now."

Nezeru stood, upset and angry. "Why would you say such a thing?" she demanded. "Why would you call me a fool and my people liars?"

"I did not do either of those things," said Kuyu-Kun, voice high and tense. "But you Hikeda'ya have never known another ruler than Utuk'ku, and she . . . by the Garden that spawned us all, she is the *queen* of lies. The things you have learned in your short life are only what she wished you to learn, and her cruel, selfish will has shaped your people for countless years—much to the sorrow of the rest of us. So be careful of what you decide to believe and not to believe, warrior."

"No," said Nezeru. "Enough. It is one thing when you mock me, but I will not sit here and listen as you insult my queen and my entire race." She turned and walked away from the shadowy mast, her startled companions, and the light of the small fire.

"Soon we will enter the Narrowdark Valley and head northward, where Tanakirú waits," Jiriki told Simon. "Ki'ushapo is my lieutenant as well as my kinsman, and I miss him sorely. His absence will mean I must spend more time with my people as we approach the fighting. But I do not like leaving you to ride alone." He fell silent, and Simon thought he saw signs of age in his friend for the first time. Jiriki's face was as unlined as ever, but weariness shadowed his features, as well as traces of worry that Simon had never seen even in the worst times.

"Rukayu!" Jiriki suddenly called.

One of the female Sithi looked up from where she was cleaning her horse's hooves. As she came toward them, she said something in the Zida'ya language, but Jiriki shook his head.

"You must use the mortal tongue, at least when you are with my friend. Your grandfather said you speak it."

"I do, Prince Jiriki," she said in careful Westerling. "I do not know how well, though."

"Well enough, it seems." He turned to Simon. "This is Rukayu Crow's Claw of the Redstart Clan. She will ride with you and keep watch on you and your granddaughter—and thus on Geloë as well." Jiriki rattled off a series of what sounded like instructions in the Zida'ya tongue, pointing first at Simon, then at sleeping Lillia, then he walked off to attend to other matters.

"He has chosen me as your defender, King Seoman," said Rukayu. "I know the importance of your child, both for who she is and whose spirit she carries."

Simon looked down at Lillia's head, her dirty and disarrayed hair, and felt a sharp jab of fear. He did not worry much for himself—he had already been dead once, and he could only hope the next time would reunite him with Miriamele—but he was mortally afraid for his granddaughter. "She is all that is left of our family," he said, shamed by the ragged sound of his own voice. "All that is left."

"I will guard her—and you—as though you were my own kin," Rukayu assured him. "I know of you, King Seoman. You were Protector Jiriki's *Hikka Staja*—his Arrow Bearer—and that is a great honor indeed. You are one of the few mortals our people have called friend. It is a . . ." She paused, trying to find the word, then called to Jiriki in their shared tongue. He called back an answer. "A sacred trust," she finished.

"Thank you." Simon felt the lost years and lost chances sorely, all the times mortals and Sithi could have overcome their differences and made a more peaceful world. Now he was old, his castle had been razed, and the queen of the Norns was about to triumph. The chance for a better world seemed to have slipped away.

The Sithi company climbed into the eastern heights of the Coolblood Valley, where even their nimble steeds found the going hard and slow. As they neared the crest, Jiriki waited on his horse, Cloudfoot, until Simon reached him. They had not spoken for more than a day, and Rukayu courteously kept her distance.

"The race is near its end," Jiriki said. "We will have to go swiftly up the valley to reach Tanakirú with any time left for Geloë to act."

"Time left?" Simon had assumed from the grim attitude of the Sithi that defeat was inevitable. "You think we still have time to do something? A couple of hundred of you against all the queen's armies?"

"I do not believe it is mere happenstance that we are in the midst of the Year-Dancing celebration and welcoming a new Great Year," Jiriki said. "The turning of the Great Year is a time of great meaning for our entire race—that is one reason. And because it is a time when things become thin at the edges, as we say. When the forces that act on this world from outside sometimes seep through and can even be summoned."

The small form in Simon's lap stirred as if about to wake, but he doubted it was his granddaughter who would be joining their talk. He asked Jiriki, "If this new year is so important, isn't it too late for us to do anything? You told me that the ceremony has already started."

"As I said, it lasts thirteen days. We have eleven left, and we must hope that what Utuk'ku plans cannot be accomplished until the moment the year changes."

"You're riding all this way and you're going to fight the Norns with the few of your people you have left—but you only *hope* you can be in time? It might already be too late?"

"Of course," Jiriki said. "As is true of all great and terrible times. We cannot know the ends that await us. We can only do what we think is best and hope it is enough."

* * *

Once they had reached the upper reaches of the Coolblood Valley, leaving the river itself far behind, the Sithi company turned north, headed toward a fort that Jiriki said overlooked a spot called Wormscale Gorge.

Simon could not easily interpret Sithi expressions or posture, but it was plain that Jiriki's folk were downhearted, not only because of the terrible threat they faced, and the knowledge that their trip south had been the result of a ruse, but also because they had lost many of their already shrunken numbers for no real reason.

But Jiriki would not let them flag. The Sithi had reserves of strength that Simon could barely believe. They would ride through both night and day without stopping when it suited them, but Simon wondered if they would have set such a merciless pace without Jiriki driving them on. He spoke little, though at times he sang loudly, stirring martial songs that the rest would pick up until their voices rang through the dells and across the hills. When he did speak, it was to individual Sithi, riding beside them, saying things that would sometimes make them sit straighter in their saddles long after he had left them.

Rukayu rode beside Simon, her skills as a rider so assured that she always held her bow in one hand, no matter how difficult the terrain, with an arrow nocked and ready on the string. She also watched Jiriki with clear admiration, the same way Simon himself had once watched King John's knights ride out in their martial finery.

"Where do you come from?" he asked her one morning, when they paused to water their horses.

"Peja'ura," she said. "Deep in the Oldheart—it is one of the older forest settlements. But I fear my people there have grown soft. Many of them do not even want to fight, though they know that Utuk'ku means to destroy us all."

"Because they're afraid?"

She shrugged. "That is not our way—at least not how you mean it, I think. They were . . ." Again she hesitated, searching for a word. "What is it called in your tongue? When someone no longer cares?"

Simon puzzled. "Hopeless?" he offered at last. "Resigned?"

"Resigned—that sounds to have the right shape. They are resigned to their fate and wish only to enjoy what days they have left." Rukayu's narrow face showed more than most of her peers' did: Simon thought he could see anger in the tight muscles around her mouth. "They have made their peace with eventual destruction."

"But you haven't."

"No more than any hunted animal, who will turn at the last and claw and bite as many of its enemies as it can before it dies." She said it with perfect calm.

"I wish you could have met my wife." Pride and pain were almost balanced. "You and Miriamele would have understood each other well. She was fierce, too."

"I know she was one of Jiriki's few mortal friends," Rukayu said. "By that alone, I am certain I would have been proud to know her."

By the end of the following day their company reached Wormscale Gorge, a steep ravine surrounded by high cliffs connecting the Coolblood and Narrowdark Valleys. Jiriki reined up, pointing to a stone structure barely visible through the trees on the crest of the gorge's far side. "That is our fortress, the Hornet's Nest," he told Simon. "But seeing it so quiet, I have a sudden fear we will find no rest or help there. We must have been visible as we approached, but no one has hailed us by sounding a horn or showing a lantern." As the sun dipped beneath the distant western hills, Jiriki sent a small company of scouts into the deep valley to make their way up to the fortress, then the whole company removed themselves to the trees to wait. Simon would have liked a fire—he worried about Lillia, even though she was wrapped in the cloak Jiriki had given him—but he understood that they were in dangerous lands now and Hikeda'ya soldiers might be anywhere, so he shivered in the cold wind that found him even among the trees as he ate his sparse meal of bread and dried fruit. He even got Lillia to rise close enough to waking to take a few mouthfuls of bread and drink some water.

It was near midnight by the stars when the Sithi scouting party returned. They huddled with Jiriki, who sat for some time after they had left him. Simon did not think he had ever seen his friend look so grim—"haunted" was the only word that seemed to fit. He passed his sleeping granddaughter to Rukayu, who looked a little startled but did not complain, then he went to join Jiriki, who he found sitting on a rock, staring at the ground.

"The news is not good, I take it," Simon said.

Jiriki gestured to the stone and Simon sat beside him. "The dead—our dead—were everywhere in the fortress," Jiriki said at last. "None of the defenders seem to have survived. Most were our folk from the Forbidden Hills, who have long held this place. My mother's brother, Protector Khendraja'aro, was one of the fallen." His expression was grim. "But only his body. The Hikeda'ya took his head for a trophy."

Simon remembered Khendraja'aro well, although not with much fondness. The older Sitha had never liked or trusted mortals and had made that abundantly clear, over and over, but Simon was still taken aback. "I'm very sorry."

"It seems I am my clan's protector now," said Jiriki. "Khendraja'aro and I agreed about very little, but the Garden knows I never wanted this."

"What do we do now?"

"What we were already doing—hastening on without delay to whatever waits us in Tanakirú. It seems clear Queen Utuk'ku must be ready to finish her game, whatever its purpose may be."

"Why?"

"It was not only Zida'ya dead that littered the fortress, Seoman. Hikeda'ya died there too, although in smaller numbers. But the victorious Sacrifices did not carry away their dead or bury them where they fell. That goes against all their traditions, and the Order of the Sacrifice is nothing if not tradition-bound. Utuk'ku must have called them to hurry back for her final assault on Tanakirú, even if it meant leaving their comrades unmourned and unburied."

"All this for . . . for a ship?"

Jiriki shook his head. "I do not think it is the ship itself that is her object," he said. "Even Sa-Ruyan Geloë cannot guess what Utuk'ku plans, but I doubt she would employ such mighty songs, would summon not only Ommu the Whisperer back from death but my own ancestor Hakatri as well, if her scheme was only to get her hands on the Ninth Ship."

"But what else could she want?"

"I do not know, my friend. I have not spent a near-endless lifetime thinking dark thoughts of revenge as Utuk'ku seyt-Hamakha has done, but I have no doubt she means some great strike that will clear the board of her enemies, once and for all."

"Mortals, too." It was not a question.

"Mortals, too," said Jiriki. "The depth of Utuk'ku's hatred for those who have resisted her is something we can scarcely imagine." He got to his feet as slowly as an exhausted, aching mortal—a sign of frailty which frightened Simon as badly as anything else that night. "I fear we must ride again," the new protector said. "Take your granddaughter and mount up."

The moss that grew on the mast was tough as leather, and clung to the wood like something with sharp, strong claws. Nezeru found it so easy to climb that it was difficult to stay close to the others laboring after her. Light had begun to filter down from an unknown source high above—enough that Nezeru could have made her way without the *ni'yo.* For the rest of the company, however, it was the only reliable source and had to stay lit. She kept stopping to look below her, so that she did not climb too far and leave Morgan and the others in darkness.

But that was just what she often wished she could do. She was still full of anger at what old Kuyu-Kun had said about Queen Utuk'ku, though Nezeru thought she had tamed her unwanted feelings in the way she had been taught to do. *Unbridled anger is confusion,* she reminded herself—one of the chief tenets of the Order of Sacrifice. *If it is not narrowed and directed, then like a flood it will overspill its banks.*

But the troubling thoughts would not go away. Over the past year she had allowed herself to believe that the nobles of Nakkiga's court, and perhaps even the officers of her own order, could act in ways that were selfish or foolish. Sometimes the rules of Hikeda'ya society even seemed to encourage it. But she had never known a moment of life without Queen Utuk'ku enthroned at the very summit of order. Even her father, Viyeki, who prided himself on independent thought, had never said or even hinted at feeling anything but complete loyalty to the Mother of All. And through everything, Nezeru had clung to a hope that after all the current chaos had ended, the queen would learn the truth about her loyal subject Nezeru being wrongly accused and would make things right. Kuyu-Kun might as well have told her, *"You are doomed to lose your people, your heritage, and your memories, and you will receive nothing in return."*

As she stopped and looked down once more, she saw that Morgan and Snenneq were struggling with the sling carrying Kuyu-Kun; she nearly wished for the ropes to snap and the wizened, wretched creature to fall, but aimed the sphere in her hand downward and held it steady until they had found surer handholds. Morgan was having trouble with the climb. He was used to being able to loop a length of rope around the small trunks of the forest trees, but the mighty witchwood was far, far too large: even if they tied together every piece of rope they had, it would not have begun to encompass the immense girth of the mast.

What was it that her father had once said? He had quoted the words of a poet to her, words that had sounded suspicious even to her child's ear. *"Freedom is not freedom when its cost is silence."* Later, after her return to the order-house, she had made the mistake of saying it to one of her fellow Sacrifice trainees, who had reacted with horror and demanded to know where she had heard such a foul, seditious sentiment. Nezeru had not divulged the source, of course, claiming she had heard it from a stranger, but she had been terrified for months afterward that her comrade would report it and the Order of Song would seize her. She had nightmares about being interrogated in the Cold, Slow Halls, subject of so many dreadful rumors.

Could my father be something other than entirely loyal? she wondered now. *Did he only pretend to whole-heartedly venerate the Mother of All?* It was a startling, fearful thought, but as she considered it and remembered other odd moments, little things Viyeki had said and done that almost seemed to mock the queen's most loyal nobles, she also felt a strange sense of relief. Perhaps she was not the only one in the family whose loyalty was flawed. This was a new thought. Perhaps this unwelcome questioning was in her father's blood as well, and was not simply because of Nezeru's having an inferior, mortal mother.

The possibility did not ease isolation or her present unhappiness, or even blunt much of the anger she felt, but it was worth considering.

After half a day of exhausting climb, as the deck from which they had begun dropped increasingly and terrifyingly farther below them, they finally reached the top of the massive space, which was also the deck of the space above. Up close, with the light of the *ni'yo* splashing on it, Nezeru could see that boards between the huge beams had been carved in the stylized form of ocean waves. It was not a single unending pattern, but a masterful evocation of an actual sea. The waves were of different sizes, and where they met another surface, they had been shaped to seem as though they splashed around carved rocks in delicate traceries of foam. It looked so perfect that Nezeru began to feel as though she was looking at a real ocean, which meant she was hanging upside down, a dizzying and dangerous illusion. She turned her attention back to her companions a short way beneath her who, for some reason, had stopped.

Nezeru climbed back down, prepared to help them past an obstacle, but then a voice lifted in wordless song, a melody she had never heard but which felt somehow familiar.

It was Kuyu-Kun singing, and as she looked on, his song grew louder, a mournful wail that echoed through the impossibly large chamber. He was still suspended in his sling between Morgan and Tih-Rumi, but as Nezeru watched in bafflement, she saw both Tinukeda'ya running their hands over the mast in a way that looked almost reverent. The old, hairless Tinukeda'ya was weeping.

She knew the next deck was only a short way above them and would be a good place to rest—and likely a better spot for Kuyu-Kun to perform his strange devotions—but she tried to curb her impatience. At last, when the singing had ended for a while without resuming, her patience failed. "Why do we wait?" she called. "We have almost reached the top. Come and climb out to the next deck!"

Kuyu-Kun looked up at her as though seeing her for the first time ever. "This mast came from the largest witchwood tree I have ever seen or even heard of. Nothing so great has ever grown in this land, nor ever will."

"We know that already. Is that a reason to halt here in such a dangerous place and pray to it?" Nezeru realized she had not conquered her anger as completely as she had thought.

"We are the Vao," said Kuyu-Kun in a deep, mournful voice. "We *are* the witchwood, as we are part of everything that came from the Garden and the Dreaming Sea. I can feel its living story beneath my fingers, to the moment where that story ends when it was felled and worked. But it must have been one of the Garden's greatest glories." His wrinkled cheek was wet with tears.

"Climb a little farther, Voice of the Dreaming Sea," she said with a hard edge to her words. "Let the ones carrying you have their rest."

The gap between the gigantic mast and the edge of the deck was more than wide enough for the company to climb through it. When they reached the deck above, they discovered it was much like the one they had left behind, a cavernous space pierced from bottom to top by the great mast, though the next ceiling looked a little nearer. As each of Nezeru's comrades found their way over the edge of the mast hole and onto the horizontal solidity of the deck, they slumped where they stopped and lay like dead things.

Several more days passed as they climbed, differentiated only by the length of mast they had to scale and the unpredictable, spiraling patterns of the patches of moss, which sometimes led them almost as far sideways as upward. Several times, a patch that looked well fixed came loose, leaving one of the climbers dangling until the others could help. Once, Tih-Rumi came untied from his end of Kuyu-Kun's sling, and only a timely grab from Little Snenneq kept the aged Voice of the Dreaming Sea from falling. Each time that they reached a higher deck and clambered out, they were more silent than the day before, overwhelmed by the magnitude of the climb they had undertaken, and each time they immediately collapsed into exhausted sleep. Nezeru, who needed little rest compared to her companions, used these long waits to explore, though nothing she found did much to ease her troubled thoughts.

But with every new deck they reached, more light came streaming in around the edges of the mast, and eventually, Nezeru no longer needed her *ni'yo*, so she gave it to Morgan. She could feel cold moving air and knew they must finally be near some sort of opening to the outside world, though they had not seen one yet in the chambers they had climbed. But after all the days of the climb, Nezeru only had more questions about the ship, the valley, and her queen's plans.

At last, near the end of a slightly shorter day, owing to the comparative closeness of the great ribbed roof, Nezeru saw something that filled her with weary satisfaction. Above her, in an arc around the huge circumference of the mast, she could see gray, cloud-filled sky.

"Just a little farther," she called down to the others. "We have reached the top. I see the world again."

Someone below her, probably Qina, made a little sound of joy.

Nezeru redoubled her own efforts. When she reached the underside of the deck above, she discovered that it was more thickly braced than any of the lower decks, and as she pulled herself upward, the gray light of a late winter afternoon surrounded her.

Standing at last in open air, she could see little but fog, as though she stood atop a cloud; the naked mast stretched upward until it vanished in the swirling white. Where she could glimpse the sky through breaks in the mist, it seemed impossibly wide after so many days journeying through the caverns and climbing through the bowels of the ship. For a dizzy moment it even seemed as if its immensity was about to fall on her, and she had to look down at her feet until the dizziness passed. What she could see of the ship's deck through the thick mist was as cluttered with structures as the interior sections, but these were almost completely overgrown by trees and other plants, all well-nourished by sunshine and the misty mountain air. It almost seemed as though she stood in the middle of a great settlement swallowed by a forest, and for a moment she wondered whether Morgan might have been right. Was this truly a great ship, or some impossibly strange, long-forgotten city?

Morgan and the rest now clambered out onto the deck, panting. Once Nezeru saw that they were all safe, she began picking her way through the tangled forest that grew across the deck, which included trees that anywhere else would have been ancient giants. As she got farther from the mast she could see more of their surroundings, though she could make out nothing below the looming cliffs above them except the mourning-white mist that also filled the valley below. The wind was refreshing. She picked her way through the branches and fronds of the deck-forest until she reached a walled edge and looked out. She sighed in amazement.

Morgan had followed her and stood at her elbow. For a long moment neither of them spoke.

Nezeru could no longer doubt what they had found, the vast structure they had climbed through like souls trying to reach Heaven. She leaned outward, looking left and right. The immense, sweeping curve of the ship's witchwood hull stretched away on either side, so vast that from where they stood, both bow and stern were lost in the fog, though the curve of the hull suggested where they must be. And though the ship's draft was immensely deep—as they already knew, having just climbed up through a large part of it—the ship itself was far, far longer than that, shaped a little like a curved leaf that might float on a stream.

"Mother of God," Morgan said in a strangled voice. "Mother of our Holy God. I cannot believe it. How could such a thing be? How could it be so big? And how did it get here?"

"That does not matter," Nezeru said. "It exists. And it has been waiting all these years for someone to find it."

"Mother of God," said Morgan again.

15

True Choices

Tanahaya came upon Dunao the Rider in the Clanhold's stables as he prepared his dishearteningly small band of warriors for departure. When he heard her approach, Dunao turned on Tanahaya with a critical eye.

"I have no need of a scholar," he said, "nor do any of the others who are fighting so bravely against cursed Utuk'ku's Sacrifices in Tanakirú. I cannot stop you from accompanying us, but neither will we wait for you. If you cannot keep up, we will simply leave you behind."

"No, Dunao, you will not," said a new voice. Tanahaya turned to see the mistress of Anvi'janya standing in the doorway of the stable block. "Because I am also coming on this journey," Ayaminu said, "and I will decide how fast we ride."

Dunao looked as surprised as Tanahaya felt. "*You* are riding east? Why?"

"Because I wish to. I am needed there, and the time has come."

Dunao made an irritated hand-sign—*contested*—that swooped like a bird's wing and then curled like a claw. "Perhaps. That still does not mean you can order me as you choose. I am the lawful protector of my own clan and a battle-chieftain of the Zida'ya—"

"All true," she said, interrupting him, "but until you reach the actual place of battle these folk are still part of my clan, and I am their protector. You may do as you like, Lord Dunao—I have no claim over you—but I will decide how fast the rest of us ride."

As the riders made their way across the swaying rope bridge, Silken Span, and down the long, winding trail around the mountain, Tanahaya was still wondering about Ayaminu's presence. "Why would you leave your own city before the Year-Dancing Ceremony is ended, *S'huesa*?" she asked.

"Year-Dancing celebrates our history here in these lands and our history in the Garden—you of all folk must know that, scholar. But I fear that if we do not stop the self-styled Queen of Nakkiga this time, we may have no more history to celebrate."

It was hard for Tanahaya not to flinch at Ayaminu's grim words. "Truly?"

"I fear so. We have often misjudged the depth of Utuk'ku's malice. When my father Kuroyi was alive, he did not fear her as I do, though after Amerasu's murder he believed Utuk'ku should be overthrown and forced to face justice. But he died in the depths of ruined Asu'a at the end of the Storm King's War because he underestimated the powers with which Utuk'ku had made compact."

"Powers?"

"Call them what you like. There are things outside our world that do not understand life, Scholar Tanahaya, and do not like it, except as something to despoil and devour. Our enemy has strengthened herself by alliance with some of those presences, those . . . malevolent spirits, for lack of a better name."

"Is that why Amerasu declared that the Ninth Ship and the valley was forbidden? Not to keep it away from her own people, but from Utuk'ku?"

"Of course," said Ayaminu.

They rode on in silence for some time. Ayaminu had deliberately started out a short distance ahead of Dunao and his conscripts, so she and Tanahaya had nothing before them but the track down from the heights of the mountain known as the Step. Tanahaya could see a long distance ahead of her, but the place they were bound, the distant valley of Tanakirú, was hidden by clouds and darkness as if a storm hung over it.

"May I talk to you about something else, Mistress?" Tanahaya asked as they reached the bottom of the mountain track.

Ayaminu nodded. "Speak, young one."

"Like all our people, I revere Amerasu's memory. Her wisdom kept our people together and gave shape to what we are now—fragmented and frail, perhaps, but still the Zida'ya, still children of the Garden." She hesitated. "So it is hard for me to say this . . . but I think she was wrong."

"Wrong in what way?"

"In the matter of the Ninth Ship. In restricting knowledge of its existence to a few clan leaders and keeping it secret from the rest of our folk."

"Ah." Ayaminu nodded. "And what would you have done in Amerasu's place?"

Tanahaya let out a breath. "My lifelong calling has been to find out the truth, or whatever best approximation can be culled from the raw materials of history. But most of the secrets I hunt are secret only because of failing memories, or because the true nature of the issue was not understood at the time, not because the facts were purposefully hidden. To me, the worst enemy of scholarship is deliberate distortion of the truth for some other purpose, however much that purpose is meant to be for the good of our people."

"Then you think it is wrong to hide things from those who might be affected."

"I cannot think anything else. Otherwise, we make our own people into children, protecting them not just from actual danger but from dangerous ideas."

Ayaminu nodded as if she considered this. "And you think there is a difference between 'actual danger' and 'dangerous ideas'?"

"It troubles me that a small group of Zida'ya decided to keep secret such an astounding thing—the existence of a Ninth Ship! The unknown truth of our people's greatest story—a secret held by a privileged few."

Ayaminu nodded again. "Would it shock you to learn that I too objected to that decision?"

Tanahaya stared at her. "A bit, I confess."

"I also did not agree with Amerasu's decision. But I trusted the Sa'onsera beyond any other of our people. She was the oldest Zida'ya, of course, but age alone does not ensure either wisdom or kindness, or Utuk'ku would not be threatening us all. I trusted Amerasu because her heart was great, but her thoughts were even greater. She truly loved her people, and unlike the mistress of Nakkiga, she did not let the untimely death of her loved ones turn her against life. It is too bad you did not meet her, Tanahaya. I think even Jenjiyana the Nightingale—no, even Jakoya the Gatherer herself in her sublime wisdom—would have acknowledged Amerasu's greatness. We have suffered no greater loss since the Garden itself than her death at Utuk'ku's hand."

Tanahaya smiled, which seemed to surprise Ayaminu. "But I did meet her," she said. "It was more than half a Great Year ago, when I first came to Jao é-Tinukai'i. I sought to study under Master Himano, who was living there at that time. During that visit I met Aditu—and her brother, of course." A twinge of regret and a sudden, fierce pang of missing Jiriki made it hard to breathe for a moment.

"One day," she went on, "as we were walking to a gathering at the Yásira, Aditu said to me, 'Oh, here is someone I would like you to know,' as if it were only another of her cousins. I turned to find Amerasu Ship-born herself standing behind me, leaning on Jiriki's arm." Tanahaya could see it again as if it had happened only yesterday, the small, slender figure of Amerasu and the obvious pride of her young descendant. Jiriki's fierce loyalty to the one he and Aditu called First Grandmother had been one of the things that had attracted Tanahaya to him. "She greeted me before I had a chance to make any of the appropriate salutes, as though they meant little to her."

"You are right," said Ayaminu, smiling more easily now. "They meant little to her."

"And then she asked me whether I had met Himano yet. I had not, because he was gathering herbs in the forest and had been gone for many days. Amerasu promised that he would see me when he returned, and that she would make sure of it. 'Aditu and Jiriki have told me much about you, young one,' she said. Her voice was soft, but it had a strength in it I had never heard before in anyone else. 'I can see that they were right—you do indeed have the calling of a scholar, or I miss my guess. You will do rare things. Go in joy.' And with that she let Jiriki lead her away. I left Jao é-Tinukai'i not long after, traveling to the Flowering Hills with Himano as his student. By the time I returned, Amerasu was dead, and the Zida'ya had begun to scatter. Jao é-Tinukai'i was a city of phantoms, the remains of the silken houses now rags, the created summer departed and the real world of wind and weather returned. But I have never forgotten that moment of meeting her—nor will I, until death takes my memories away."

"We never know what lies beyond this life," said Ayaminu, nodding. "But

I can tell you understood something of her greatness even from that one meeting. And I will tell you something else that may not have been so apparent. Utuk'ku has lived since the days of the Garden. Amerasu lived less than half that long. And yet the deeper thoughts, the more sublime understanding, was all Amerasu's."

Another silence followed. Tanahaya looked back. Dunao and the Zida'ya troop traveled so quietly that she had almost forgotten they were so close. *No battle songs,* she could not help thinking. *They ride as though to inevitable death, quiet and thoughtful.*

"I thank you for honoring me with your attention," Tanahaya said at last. "But I still think that Amerasu Ship-born made the wrong decision."

Ayaminu made a non-committal hand sign, *water finds its level.* "Perhaps she did. It would certainly be a good thing if all of life's questions had straightforward answers, but in my experience, almost nothing is simple. Sometimes, right and wrong are not even the true choices."

Days passed as Etan and the Sitha, Ki'ushapo followed a winding course through Aldheorte Forest—invisible trackways that the great black horse Shadowswift seemed to know well, though Etan could see only endless forest and winter mist. Most of the trees were bare, and the skeletal branches of birch and oak clutched at them as they rode. Coupled with their nearly colorless surroundings, it made Etan feel that they rode through a country of grasping phantoms.

"I miss the sun," he said, shivering as he watched the black warhorse drinking deeply from a hillside stream, ankle-deep in the water. "How long will we be under these trees?"

"Until we are not," said Ki'ushapo unhelpfully, but saw the look on Etan's face and relented a little. "We will reach the pass at Wormscale Gorge soon and find allies waiting at the Hornet's Nest, the fortress above the pass—if we still hold it."

"Is that where the ship is?"

The Sitha shook his head, a movement that looked almost human. "No. On the far side of that pass lies the Narrowdark Valley, and the place we call Tanakirú is at the valley's northern end. That is where the ship was discovered, and where the last and bitterest part of the fighting will be." Shadowswift had finished drinking and was making her way back up the stream bank. "Come," Ki'ushapo said. "Let us ride once more, Brother. With luck, we will reach the pass by the time the sun rises. That may be the last time we see it for a while."

Etan felt a chill that was more than just the winter wind. "What do you mean?"

"The valley of the Narrowdark is always covered with fog, a place of perpetual gray where it is hard to see very far, and the sun is usually only a white spot overhead. That is what Tanakirú means—Valley of Mists—because it is where the murk is thickest."

The chill now poked at Etan with icy fingers. "And that's . . . you said there was an ogre—?"

"I should not have told you that much. We know very little about the creature, precisely because of the thick and constant mist. It only seems to come out at night."

"Have you seen it?"

"I have not—I fought with Protector Khendraja'aro to hold the pass we will reach tomorrow, but I did not travel to the far end of the valley. But I heard many fearful stories from those who had been to the valley's end, and I cannot doubt them. The *uro'eni* is like nothing seen since the days of the great worms."

"But what *is* it?"

"Mount up." Ki'ushapo easily swung himself onto the saddle, then stretched his hand down to Etan. "I have told you what I know. Not one seeker who saw it closely has returned to enlighten the rest of us, so it remains a mystery."

None of this eased the cold clutch on Etan's heart, not even a little.

Etan woke abruptly and found he was sliding backward off the saddle. Ki'ushapo reached back to keep him from falling. It was impossible to be certain in the fastness of the wood, but twilight seemed to have come while he slept.

"Hold fast now, mortal," the Sitha said. "Shadowswift has found her stride. You do not want to tumble off."

"Are we almost at the pass?" he asked, still feeling as though he had not entirely returned to the world. They were on high ground now, he saw, traveling across a ridge that loomed above the forest around it. A shadow-spine of mountains loomed against the dimming, purple and pink sky of day's end.

"Not so far now," Ki'ushapo said over his shoulder. "And just to the west of us—there, among those peaks—lies High Anvi'janya."

"Are we stopping there?"

"No, though I wish we could. Much that is dear to me—and to all our folk—is to be found there. But our road leads to the pass instead, and on into the Narrowdark."

Etan did not want to think about that place. "I am very hungry, I fear. Do you have any more of the bread you gave me before?"

Ki'ushapo fished a leaf-wrapped bundle out of one of his saddlebags. "Eat this. It will hold you until the next time we stop. Near midnight we must let Shadowswift drink again."

The bread tasted of flower petals and herbs. It was light and airy, and to someone like Etan used to biscuit baked so hard that eating it felt like chewing his own teeth, it seemed as though it could not be filling, but it was only the third portion he had eaten during the several days they had been riding, so clearly it was.

"Tell me about Anvi'janya," Etan said.

"Are you a child who must be entertained?" asked Ki'ushapo, but he sounded more amused than annoyed. "It is a city built in a great cavern in a mountain—the last of our old cities we still use. The walls are of white stone so bright they can be seen for miles, sparkling like adamant in the afternoon sun. The people are confident and cheerful, unlike my own folk, exiled so long from our old home of Hekhasor that they have lost nearly all their joy." Though he spoke calmly, the monk heard something deeply mournful in Ki'ushapo's words. "But it is Anvi'janya you asked about. Just now, many will be gathering there for Year-Dancing, the ceremony that marks the turn of a Great Year. Jiriki's sister Aditu will lead the ritual, because her mother, the Sa'onsera, has fallen into a long, terrible sleep."

Etan did not know what this meant, but he recognized a name. "This Aditu—I've heard my lord Tiamak speak of her."

"And I met your Tiamak when Ineluki Storm King was defeated—a young man from the southern marshes, as I remember. I am glad to hear he still lives."

Hearing Tiamak described as a young man reminded Etan that he was talking to someone who might be hundreds of years old. He had forgotten, because Ki'ushapo was surprisingly easy to speak with—Etan had not expected it of one of the legendary Sithi. "And I am glad to hear that Aditu still lives," he said. "Tiamak will be pleased—he was very taken by her, all those years ago."

Ki'ushapo laughed. "Yes, not even mortals are immune to her charms! I remember your king, Seoman Snowlock, who was then little more than a child, used to moon after her like a lamb trailing its shepherdess."

Now it was Etan's turn to be amused. "Is she truly so fair, this Aditu?"

The rider was silent for a little while as they rushed on through the snowbound forest. "She is," he said at last. "But not just in the outward way that I think your Westerling words signify. She is certainly comely, but there is far more to her than simply the face she shows the world. I pray she is still safe."

Despite his recent travels, Brother Etan was not a worldly man, but he heard something in the Sitha's words that made him wonder. "You think a great deal of her," he suggested.

Ki'ushapo gave him a swift backward glance. "If you met her, you would know why, and you would think the same. She is altogether admirable." But there was a heaviness to his words that did not seem to fit what he said.

Etan could not help thinking of Lady Faiera, still yearning for Prince Josua in her hut in the Perdruinese hills. *I may not know anything about the fairy-folk, but I think I know the sound of someone who loves deeply but without hope.*

Days later, with most of that time spent in the saddle, they crossed the Coolblood River where it spread across a series of marshy fords, then they turned east toward the gorge through the hills where the Sithi fortress crouched.

"We must go quietly now," Ki'ushapo warned him. "Even before Jiriki and

I rode through here in the last moon, the hills were full of Sacrifice troops. With luck, we should reach the Hornet's Nest tomorrow."

Etan did not much like the stronghold's name—it suggested something sinister, no mere castle or fortress but a place of darkness and inhuman creatures. But however disturbing the name, he thought it would be good to have strong walls around himself once more, and perhaps even something softer to sleep on than the ground and something to eat besides fairy-bread.

As they skirted the base of the eastern hills, snow flying from Shadowswift's hooves, Etan saw for the first time the blocky, shadowed patch lying between two of the high, snowbound peaks not far ahead of them.

The wind was fierce. He had to raise his voice. "Is that the pass ahead?"

Ki'ushapo's head twisted through another disconcertingly owlish turn, but this time he was looking back over Etan's shoulder and did not answer the question.

"Is that the pass?" Etan called, even more loudly.

Ki'ushapo still did not answer, but instead bent low over Shadowswift's neck. "Put your head down!" he cried, his voice muffled by the snapping tendrils of the horse's black mane.

Startled, Etan looked back. For a moment it seemed that they were being overtaken by an avalanche, a moving, seething mass of snow; an instant later he realized it was not snow but a half dozen riders dressed in bulky white armor, riding horses of the same hue, racing along the hillside just behind them, as noiseless as phantoms.

"God protect us, who is that?"

"Hikeda'ya," Ki'ushapo cried, still bending low in the saddle. "Sacrifice troops! Lower your head!"

Etan pressed himself against the Sitha's back. He could see nothing, and for long moments could only feel the horse flowing beneath them, bones and muscles churning flat out, eating up the ground. *We are faster than they are—we must be! They're wearing armor!* he thought with more hope than certainty. But he and Ki'ushapo were two on a horse and had been riding all day. Could even tireless Shadowswift outrun so many enemies and get them to safety?

He had his answer a moment later. As though struck by a heavy hand, Ki'ushapo shuddered in front of him then straightened in the saddle. Another stride or two and Etan could feel him slump sideways. He grabbed Ki'ushapo as hard as he could with both arms but the Sitha's motion nearly unseated them both—Etan had to cling to Shadowswift's chest by pressing his knees together as hard as he could. Ki'ushapo, though not heavy compared to a mortal of his size, had gone utterly limp, and it was all Etan could do to push him even farther forward against Shadowswift's neck. As he fumbled for the reins in rising terror, view blocked by Ki'ushapo's slumped body, he saw a single black arrow wagging in the Sitha's side.

He finally found the reins and grabbed them in one hand, but Ki'ushapo was sliding again, and it was all Etan could do to hold on and keep him in the saddle. Even with the reins gripped tightly in his hand, he could do nothing to steer Shadowswift or get a better grip on either Ki'ushapo or the horse. And now he could hear the voices of their pursuers, excited, keening cries like hunting hawks, as they grew closer and closer.

Viyeki badly needed to talk to Pratiki, but since the queen's arrival, the Prince-Templar had been perpetually dancing attendance on her, and he was doing so now. Viyeki could only wait outside the queen's immense black wagon in a milling crowd of other nobles, all of them looking tense and fearful but doing their best to hide it by dutifully following the ancient ceremony of the court. Utuk'ku's newly-arrived company had quickly turned the hilly redoubt and tunnel site into a small version of Nakkiga—a hundred slaves or more, mostly brutish Tinukeda'ya carry-men, had wrestled her train of carriages halfway up Kushiba's peak to accomplish the transformation. Nor was it only the wagons that now made the place feel uncomfortably like home: many court functionaries had traveled with the queen's company, and more arrived every day, to the point where Viyeki began to wonder where they were all coming from.

Were all these nobles at Ujin? She seems to have brought the leading lights of the court with her. He could only guess that Utuk'ku expected such a total victory over her enemies that she wanted a large audience to witness her triumph. *But surely that is no way to fight a war,* he thought, *even if it is the wish of the Mother of All. And how are we housing and feeding them all? Such a vast expedition must be emptying even the Maze Palace's deep coffers. What is worth such a gamble?*

Viyeki moved closer to the steps of the largest wagon, a black-lacquered palace on wheels, a cubit wide and as tall as the high magister himself. As he approached, the Queen's Teeth guards on either side of the door watched him, silent and deadly as sunning serpents.

"His Serene Highness Pratiki asked me to wait for him inside," Viyeki announced.

The white-helmeted pair did not look at each other, or show any sign of even having heard him, but simultaneously raised their poleaxes to let him pass. A few of the other waiting nobles stared at him as he climbed the steps, only years of court training keeping their envy hidden. *If they only knew!* Viyeki was taking a dangerous risk because he had not been invited to the queen's wagon today, but he desperately needed to speak with the Prince-Templar. The members of his Builders Order were already in great turmoil—a disorder Viyeki had spent the last few hours doing his best to suppress, and he did not want any more attention drawn to him than absolutely necessary. Tongues had been set wagging in Nakkiga over far less, and this wild place had now become a smaller and even more insular version of the great city and the Maze Palace.

To his relief, he found he was not the only one in the wide antechamber of the queen's wagon. Several celebrants were talking so earnestly (if quietly) among themselves that they acknowledged Viyeki's presence with only the barest formality before returning to their conversations. Many servants also moved busily about the room, some cleaning things that were already spotless, others carrying trays of food and drink into the queen's private chamber beyond the inner door guarded by silent Queen's Teeth.

Then the inner door swung open. Viyeki had a sudden, dire premonition, and stepped into the shadows in an out-of-the-way corner, doing his best to look as though he was admiring the exquisite witchwood paneling of the antechamber walls. The carvings portrayed scenes from the life of the queen's son, Drukhi, and would have been touching, especially the scene of her mourning over his dead body, had he not seen others just like them on nearly every state building in Nakkiga.

Viyeki's cautious urge proved to have been well-founded: Marshal Kikiti came out of the inner chamber like a thunderhead, all in black, silent but ominous. His lieutenant Hezidri was at his elbow, and neither of them looked happy. Kikiti was so agitated that he broke silence before he and Hezidri had left the antechamber; and from his hiding place, Viyeki could hear the marshal's whispered words clearly.

"I honor the Hamakha, of course I do. The bloodline of the Dragonslayer is our people's greatest treasure. But this—this is outrageous!"

"Of course, High Marshal. But the queen is always—"

"Of course, of course." But Kikiti seemed to have trouble heeding his subordinate's cautious words. *"But descendant or no, that mad creature should never have been brought here. Is he a pet? Because I would not allow even my wife's stoat so much freedom—!"*

With senses honed from years in a dangerous court, Viyeki felt a stir of interest run through the celebrants in the antechamber at the high marshal's obvious agitation, although he did not think anyone but himself could hear Kikiti's actual words. The marshal must have sensed the attention too because a moment later he fell silent and strode purposefully out the door of the wagon with Hezidri hurrying beside him.

What did he mean? Viyeki wondered. *Mad creature—a Hamakha descendant? Surely that must mean the queen's relative, Jijibo. But what could that one have done to make Kikiti so furious?*

Then he heard someone else speak—but this voice did not reach him through his ears.

Do not misunderstand me, Akhenabi—I am not pleased! But he is of royal blood, however adulterated by mischance and bad choices.

For a moment, Viyeki was stunned into panic. That was the queen's voice—but how could he hear her? Was there a hole in the wall somewhere near him? He quickly looked out at the others in the antechamber, but with Kikiti gone, the celebrants had returned to their previous quiet intercourse. He could not believe any of them could have heard the queen's voice issuing from her private chamber yet show no sign of it.

I do not care, she said now. *He is not to be harmed and that is final. I will deal with him myself when he is found. And as I told Kikiti, I now tell you—he will not be questioned by Sacrifice inquisitors, nor will he be subjected to the mercies of your order, either. Is that understood?*

The words were in his head. The queen was speaking in thought to her chief mage, Akhenabi, but somehow Viyeki could hear it too, which both amazed and terrified him. And if he did not tell anyone that he had heard the queen's private conference, but then was found out . . . well, that was surely the sort of thing that led to an unmarked grave in the Fields of the Nameless.

But why could he hear her when the others waiting could not? Perhaps—and he hardly dared think it, even in his own secret thoughts—the queen's strength was failing. Perhaps, like Viyeki's own grandsire, who had lived for many sad years beyond his wits, the Mother of All was slowly losing her faculties.

It was a terrifying thought. Viyeki had now lost his nerve: he could not force himself to wait inside the royal wagon any longer. Slowly, and with as much ceremony as was appropriate, he exchanged bows with the milling celebrants and went out again, but his heart was beating so swiftly that he swayed on the steps and had to pause to find his balance.

No little time passed before Pratiki appeared in the wagon's doorway. The prince-templar ignored the nobles trying to get his attention, and although he saw Viyeki, looked as though he wished to avoid him as well—but Viyeki could not afford to let him.

"Greetings, Serenity," he said, stepping forward as the prince-templar walked away from the wagon, his clerics trotting after him like goslings behind their mother. "It is good to see you. I trust your audience with the Mother of All went well."

"Ah. High Magister." The prince-templar gave him a look Viyeki had not seen from him before, the impenetrable stare of a high noble being annoyed by some lesser being. It left him chilled. "Is there something I can do to help you?"

"Actually, I had hoped to have a moment with you, Serenity—in privacy," he added, indicating the two clerics with his eyes.

"So." The prince-templar regarded him for a stretching moment, then gestured for the clerics to stay where they were before stepping a few paces out of the flow of passers-by. "Would here be convenient?" He did not sound as if he cared much one way or another.

Viyeki described in an urgent whisper what had happened in the deepest section of the tunnels only an hour or two earlier. "Nine killed, Serenity. Part of the tunnel roof has collapsed. I fear it will take hours to clear, even if I take the slaves away from every other task."

Pratiki was hiding his anger but did not bother to do it well. "This is a disaster, Magister Viyeki. You are already on borrowed time."

"Nobody knows that better than I do, Serenity."

"You must put the Delvers to work there," Pratiki told him. "They have skills your mortal workers and Builders do not."

"But we agreed to keep them away from the most vital parts of the tunnels," Viyeki said. "Because of their . . . untrustworthiness."

"You have no choice. As it is, we are both in terrible danger, because I have spoken up for you many times. In truth, I cannot understand why the queen has not punished you. Other nobles would have gone to the Fields of the Nameless long ago."

Viyeki let out a strangled sound midway between a moan of pain and a bitter laugh. "In truth, I cannot understand it either, Serenity. But I am doing the best I can with what I have been given."

"Do you not understand? The Mother of All does not care about the trials and setbacks of any of her subjects. She cares only that what she has ordered comes to pass. If I tell her of this setback, she will destroy us both. Just an hour ago Kikiti was telling her that his Sacrifice engineers would have been long done by now."

Terror and fury clashed in Viyeki's breast. "It is the mess that Kikiti's engineers made before my Builders arrived that is the main cause of our problems. They dug without any care, and because of their slipshod work, dozens of my workers died in the first fortnight. We have spent as much time hauling out bodies as we have with rubble."

Pratiki now showed him the hardening glance of a Hikeda'ya noble who was just about to sacrifice one of his peers to save himself. "Whatever you must do, do it now," he said in an urgent whisper. "Work the Delvers until they die on their feet if you must. Do anything you can. By two days from now, Kikiti must be able to march his Sacrifices down through the mountain and into the valley below, no matter the cost. The queen wants her prize, and she will destroy any noble who fails her in her desire to reach it."

"I do not even know what the prize is," said Viyeki, and immediately regretted speaking the thought.

"Nor do you need to!" Pratiki was as close to losing his temper as Viyeki had ever seen him. "You have slaves, you have your Builders Order, you have those cursedly insolent Delvers. I can do nothing more for you, Magister Viyeki. My own life hangs on this, and because of that, so does—" He stopped himself abruptly, leaving Viyeki to wonder what would have come next. "Enough." The prince-templar once more assumed his mask of imperturbability. "We all must suffer to fulfill the queen's commands. Your suffering does not make you different, High Magister, and it certainly will not save you. I recommend that you remember that in the coming hours."

For long moments after Pratiki and his guards left, Viyeki could only stand in silence, stunned, disheartened, and trembling.

My family, he thought. *My clan. Nezeru, my daughter, and poor, dear Tzoja. I cannot give up now without risking them as well.*

He walked out into the night with the feeling that he had already reached the Fields of the Nameless, that instead of drifting snow and mud he waded through charred bones and ashes.

"Where are we now?" Tanahaya asked. "I do not know these northern lands. There is a great difference between seeing a map and traveling through the actual country."

"A telling admission, scholar," said Ayaminu, but Tanahaya thought she might be jesting. The older Sitha was, as always, wrapped in her own secrets and gave little away. *How old is she?* Tanahaya wondered, looking at the mistress of Anvi'janya's placid features. *I do not recall seeing it recorded.* Ayaminu's father, Kuroyi, had been one of the so-called Landborn, the earliest generation raised in the new land. "Your father was a mighty leader and warrior," she said.

"What made you think of him?" asked Ayaminu.

"Nothing of importance. But having seen Da'ai Chikiza and met the Pure—may the Garden welcome their spirits—and after visiting Anvi'janya, I cannot help reflecting on how the histories I have studied are now all around me."

"And do they match your expectations? Or, like the maps, does the truth seem different?"

Tanahaya smiled. This time she knew she was being teased. "That is far too large a question to have a single answer, Mistress. Each thing is different—and each in different ways—from what I expected. So I wondered what your famous father was like."

"You are persistent," said Ayaminu, "a mark of your calling. Before I tell you of my father—and my mother, no less admirable—tell me what you discovered in our Repository. When you came to the Year-Dancing Celebration you had the flushed look of someone with a secret to tell."

"Ah." This caught Tanahaya by surprise. Her initial excitement at her find had cooled as she realized how little it advanced their knowledge. "I found the records of Sa-Ruyan Mardae's trial after Utuk'ku had him seized when the Ninth Ship was revealed. And I saw that of all those who questioned him—some fiercely, others with what seemed like obvious reluctance—Utuk'ku's minion, Yedade, was by far the most zealous." And she had found something else of interest in the Repository, she remembered now. But what had it been?

"Amerasu did not want that trial," said Ayaminu. "In truth, all the Zida'ya opposed it. But Utuk'ku was determined to learn everything she could about why the last ship took so long to appear and what its condition might be. But how did Yedade's actions catch your interest?"

"His questions were not about the *whys* of the Ninth Ship—he seemed little interested in why the Tinukeda'ya made it or hid its existence, which was the supposed purpose of the trial. He was much more interested in how it was built."

"Yedade was the greatest mind of the Hikeda'ya—perhaps in some ways the greatest mind of all those who came from the Garden—but his was a cursed, labyrinthine wit that observed no limits." Ayaminu frowned. "No surprise there. It was Yedade's father who first unleashed Unbeing on our Garden. It killed him, of course—Nerudade and his helpers were the first to be devoured by it—but it did not kill the unwholesome curiosity his son inherited. But Yedade met an ugly fate as well, though it was not curiosity but pride that doomed him."

"I have not heard this tale."

"That does not surprise me. It is written in no account, and even among the Hikeda'ya themselves it is spoken of only in whispers. Despite his father's end and what came with it, Yedade was high among Utuk'ku's counselors—so high that another clever schemer envied his place in the queen's trust. That one's name, as you might guess, was Akhenabi, called the Lord of Song."

A chill swept over Tanahaya, so strong and sudden that she looked back to be certain nothing was creeping up on them. "I know him—and not only by name and dark reputation, Mistress. I believe it was his voice that taunted me in Da'ai Chikiza when I spoke to Jiriki, before the use of the Witness was twisted away from me. I have never felt such coldness and cruelty on the other side of a Witness. I hope I never do again."

"You are not the only one to regret meeting the Lord of Song—be grateful that it was only through a dragon-scale Witness. And have you heard the name some call him, 'Akhenabi of the Stolen Face'?"

"Yes. I know it is because of his mask, which is made of flesh."

"It is. Made from Yedade's flesh."

Tanahaya felt a moment of dizziness. "Truly?"

"They had long feuded. At last, in a rage at what he considered an upstart's provocations, Yedade challenged Akhenabi to what is called a Singers' Duel. Such contests have no set beginning or agreed-upon end—rather, it is a lifelong pledge to try to bring about the other's death or surrender. Yedade lost." Ayaminu shook her head. "It did not happen quickly—Yedade was himself very powerful and full of knowledge otherwise lost to time and the escape from the Garden. But over the years, as their struggle played out, Yedade began to falter and grow weaker. It happened when I lived in Hikehikayo, though it took place in far-off Nakkiga. At the end, he had no more strength to resist whatever curses and foul songs that Akhenabi employed, and he withered away and died in terrible agony. Akhenabi took his face for a trophy and had it made into a mask like those all the oldest Hikeda'ya wear."

"How dreadful." Tanahaya felt more than a little ill. "How could these people be our kin? None among us are so savage, so . . . murderous."

"Do not be too quick to assume the Hikeda'ya are entirely different from us, scholar. They have merely lived separately a long time, and Utuk'ku has always been there to guide them. She is more than a little mad, I think—not like her great-great-great-great-grand-nephew Jijibo the Dreamer, but in a different way, like a crack deep inside an otherwise brilliant gem—a flaw that never shows until it is too late to save it from shattering."

"Will she shatter then, someday?" Tanahaya felt as though she tempted fate even to ask such a question.

Ayaminu made a considering face. "I doubt it. The so-called queen of the Hikeda'ya has lived all her astonishingly long life with this flaw, and the main results of such a defect are suspicion, rage, and the desire to bend everything to her own will. I suspect she will destroy us all before it ever harms her."

16

The Unliving Thing

"We are about to cross into the Narrowdark Valley," Jiriki told the gathered Sithi as Rukayu translated for Simon. "We ride into lands that few have entered, and from which even fewer have returned." Simon saw no fear on any Sitha face but felt certain it must be in some of their hearts—it was certainly in his own. He did not much fear death, not after all he had been through and all he had lost, but the thought of carrying Lillia into such a perilous place made his heart ache.

"Tanakirú is almost unknown to us, despite all the years we have defended it against the Hikeda'ya," Jiriki continued. "Mists shroud it both day and night and we will not be able to see each other well, so we must take great care not to be separated. Listen for the horns. If you are confused by the mist or simply lost, ride toward them!"

"What of the *uro'eni*—the ogre?" asked one of the Sithi captains.

"Nobody has ever seen the monster except dimly," Jiriki said, "but it has killed more than a few of our folk. That is why Amerasu Ship-born forbade all Zida'ya from coming here. But now we have no choice." He looked over the company, who stared back at him with eyes as golden as his own.

Like falcons on their perches, Simon thought. *No, these Zida'ya have never been tamed. They have the eyes of free, wild things.*

"Now," Jiriki continued. "I will tell you what very few have heard before—also by the Sa'onsera Amerasu's order. We have long held this place against Utuk'ku's soldiers and spies. We defend it because one of the Garden ships appeared here in the Narrowdark less than ten Great Years ago. Yes, a new ship, one never before seen or told of—a Ninth Ship. It came from the Garden like the others, but somehow went astray, and was not seen again until it landed here in the years just after Asu'a fell to the mortal Northmen."

Even the usually stone-faced Sithi could not hide their surprise at this revelation. Simon had never seen so many emotions from the immortals at one time, except on the terrible night when First Grandmother Amerasu was murdered. "Who was on this ship?" one of Jiriki's followers asked.

"We do not know," he said. "Nobody has been able to get past the ogre to reach it. We think the Tinukeda'ya built it in secret, and that it fled the Garden just before or after the Eight Ships. But as all know, the Ocean Indefinite and Eternal took a toll of years from the passengers of those vessels, and the Ninth Ship traveled for even longer through those bleak, unknowable reaches. Nobody knows what is on it, or what happened to those who traveled in it. But we know it finally came to rest in Tanakirú, and we also know that Utuk'ku wants it. Even now the last of Khendraja'aro's defenders are protecting it with their blood and flesh."

"We must ride to them!" cried one of the other Sithi.

"That is just what we shall do," Jiriki said. "Do not fear the *uro'eni*—it comes only after dark." He lifted his sword Indreju high over his head. "Follow me, Zida'ya! We ride now to the aid of our sisters and brothers!" He urged his horse onto the descending path and the other riders followed him in file.

They descended past Wormscale Lake along a frighteningly narrow path. After peering into the dizzying depths below him, Simon decided it was not really meant for mortal riders and that he should stop looking down. Still, his Sithi mount seemed comfortable even on the steepest and narrowest sections, and though at times Simon clutched sleeping Lillia so tightly against himself that he feared he might be hurting her, he could not resist an occasional glance down at Wormscale Lake, a wide blue oval that covered most of the bottom of the gorge. He was a little puzzled by its name until he remembered that many of the Sithi's Witnesses were made from the scales of dragons, and it did resemble such a mirror. But he did not dare look down on it for long. Every lurch of his saddle made him fear he might reach it faster than he wished, especially because it was hard to keep Lillia's limp weight upright with only one arm, so he was constantly leaning this way or that.

As they neared the end of the pass, the mists swallowed the Sithi company in a single gulp. One moment they were riding toward a pale, wavering curtain of white, the next moment it was all around them—even Rukayu, riding close to Simon, all but disappeared. He had not dreamed it would be like this, the mist so thick it seemed to inhale everything, both light and noise, so that they seemed to be riding through some netherworld between life and death.

They continued northward through heavy fogs for most of the next two days. The only constant was the gurgle of the muddy Narrowdark River, which Simon could barely see through the mists, and the weird shape of the thick, strange things that grew around it and in it. Sometimes the river ran wide and flat; other times the valley narrowed into rocky canyons and they had to ride along its very brink. Jiriki warned them all not to drink from the river, and Simon had no trouble obeying him. Every time he could see the Narrowdark clearly, it looked foul and strange, and the plants and animals around it were as disturbing as the water.

Simon had never ridden so fast for so long, not even during his youth in the days of the Storm King's War, and he was feeling every one of his five decades and more. Hour after hour passed in a blur of billowing mist, livened only by the occasional cries of animals and birds, none of which he could comfortably identify.

"Your eye is healing well, my lord."

"Thank you, Lord Captain," said Tiamak, "my wife provides excellent physick and the swelling is almost gone. The scar, though, I think will last. But I doubt the state of my wound is the reason you asked to speak to me."

"You are right." Zakiel bent close to Tiamak's ear. "Someone is outside the camp begging to speak to the duchess," he whispered.

Tiamak shrugged. "As are all those other poor folk waiting here. That is why I have come to listen to their complaints and fears." The army that Queen Miriamele and Baron Norvel had assembled had covered the hilltops around the ruins of the burned castle with their tents. Many of the local people had camped there too, preferring the safety of an armed camp.

"He is most insistent, my lord," said Zakiel the new-minted Lord Captain. "He weeps. He is just a young fellow, perhaps twelve or thirteen summers."

"Is he mad?" Tiamak thought Captain Zakiel had lost some of his sharpness of speech after being wounded in the attack on the Hayholt, but, luckily, no sharpness of wit. "My apologies, Lord Captain, but I do not understand what exactly you want of me. It has already been a long morning. Bring him here and he can join the rest."

"He claims he can only talk to the duchess, and that it must be in private. I would not have bothered you, my lord, but the boy gave me this."

Tiamak stared at the thing Zakiel held. It was a signet ring made of good gold, with an odd beast engraved on its bezel—half fish, half animal. "This is Aglaf's Lionfish." He looked around to make sure none of the waiting townsfolk could see it. "Does that mean this youth is from Winstowe?"

"It certainly seems that way."

"And he wants to speak to the duchess, face to face? Well, that will not happen—not even if he were Aglaf himself. But I suppose we must give him a private audience. Calm him down and bring him to my tent when the noon bell rings. We will try to discover what is so important."

Tiamak looked at the stark furnishings of his field office—a pair of stools, a table with several candles, and a chest that held most of the written matter he needed to fulfill his role as Hand of the Throne. He was not looking forward to the hardships of traveling again, and even less to being part of a siege. *My work will be almost as makeshift as when I lived in Village Grove, in my tiny, tiny little house in the depths of the Wran.* But he suddenly found himself missing the simplicity of his early life, when the only thing he cared about was checking his traps so he could eat, and the occasional missive from Doctor Morgenes at the

Hayholt. *Still, I must admit that even this simple tent is a great improvement over the ruined catacombs under the Hayholt.* He sighed, then realized a soldier in a green Erkynguard tabard was standing in the doorway.

The guardsman bobbed his head. "Captain Zakiel sent me, my lord, with two more guardsmen. He said, and please do not blame me for the words are his, 'The Hand of the Throne will do anything for the kingdom except protect himself properly.' So, we are to stay with you."

Tiamak hid a smile. "As long as you wait near the door and do not loom over the young man. We do not want to frighten our visitor into silence." He did his best to make himself comfortable. Soon, two more soldiers arrived—both woefully young, Tiamak could not help noticing—leading an even younger-looking figure. The supposed emissary seemed as frightened as a prisoner climbing to the gibbet.

Tiamak gestured to the other stool. "Sit, young man, I pray you. You have nothing to fear from me or these soldiers."

The youth, dressed in clothes that might have been costly once, but were now torn and travel-stained, only stood and stared, eyes wide and face pale. "Who are you?"

"I am Lord Tiamak, the Hand of the Throne. I speak for the duchess. And who are you, young fellow? You look like you have had a hard journey." The boy was just edging into manhood, but he seemed as fearful as a much younger child in a loud thunderstorm.

The youth's eyes darted from side to side. "No. No! Where is the duchess? I must speak to the duchess! I've been—" He lowered his head. Tears glistened on his cheeks.

Tiamak was trying hard to be patient. "Calm yourself, lad. As I said, no one here will hurt you. Tell me your name and why you have Count Aglaf's signet ring." He held it up. "Did he give it to you? Or did someone else? Were you sent with a message?" But if so, Tiamak wondered, who would choose such a terrified, weeping messenger? "Come, sit. I will have someone bring you something to eat and drink."

The youth finally sat on the stool opposite Tiamak. He held his arms close to his body and kept looking around the little tent as though fearing he might be attacked. His hands trembled in his lap. "I need to speak to the duchess," he said. "Only the duchess!"

"Yes, you said that, but I am sorry to tell you that will not happen." Tiamak felt a twinge of annoyance. Did this shivering child think he could take all day before telling his story? "You likely do not know it by my garb, but I am a fairly important fellow here. If there is something you need, or words you wish to have passed along to the duchess, I am your man. In truth, there are a hundred people or more waiting at the base of the hill for me, doubtless angry that you have been given the first chance." He heard the edge in his own voice and did his best to sweeten his words. "So, come, fellow—do not make me beg you. Tell me your name and your business with the duchess and I will—"

The youth's attack was so sudden that Tiamak did not even realize what had happened until he had been knocked off his stool and onto the ground and was grappling for his life. He shouted in surprise and began to fight back when he felt the cold edge of a blade against his neck. He instantly stopped struggling.

"Please!" the youth said, his voice ragged. He was weeping again. "I only want to see the duchess! I must! I must!"

Three guards crashed into the tent, nearly ripping loose the door flap.

"No!" cried the boy. "I will kill him if you come near! Take me to the duchess!" He waved the knife at them as he spoke—he had Tiamak firmly collared around the neck, unable to break away. At the sight of the blade, Tiamak's heart turned to cold stone. Its tip had been daubed with something black and sticky.

"Stay back," he told the soldiers. "Well back. The dagger is poisoned."

His captor brought the blade back against his neck. "The duchess—!"

"I hear you," Tiamak said as calmly as he could. "But the duchess is not here. She is back in Erchester. Even if you murder me, she is far away."

The boy looked down at him in agonized disbelief, like an infant dropped from a parent's arms, betrayed by life itself. "No. You are lying!"

"Look at me, child—yes, look in my eyes. It *is* the truth. There is no duchess here. Now tell me what you want and I will try to help you. But be careful with that knife!"

"I can't! They will kill them!"

"Kill who? Easy, lad. Who is 'they', and who is in danger?"

The boy stared at him wide-eyed, then at the soldiers. A heartbeat later he shoved Tiamak away and bolted for the back wall of the tent, slashing it with a vertical swipe of the blade, but he had not made the hole big enough and he was snagged part way through.

"'Ware that blade!" Tiamak cried as the soldiers leaped forward. Even as Tiamak scrambled out of the way, they yanked the youth back through the hole into the tent. To Tiamak's great relief, the knife had fallen from his hand.

"Find that cursed weapon. Do not touch the blade," he said. "And beware of any of the poison it may have left on the cloth of the tent." Two of the soldiers knelt on the thrashing, weeping boy as the other went outside to retrieve the knife. "And search him for other weapons." Tiamak was furious that Zakiel and the guards had let the young man get so far without the knife being discovered, but he had other concerns. "And when we have a moment," he added, "I think I would like to have my things carried to another tent." He looked sourly at the gaping hole in the wool canvas. "I suspect it is going to be uncomfortably cold in here tonight."

"I would advise you not to speak to him, Majesty," Tiamak told the queen. "He is Count Aglaf's son, Averel, and he is terrified that Pasevalles and his barbarians are going to murder his mother and sister."

"Because he failed to murder me."

Tiamak sighed. "He did not know you are 'the duchess'—and still doesn't, which is why I think you should stay away from him, in case he has a way to communicate with whoever sent him."

"He doesn't have one of those Sithi mirrors, does he?" the queen asked.

"No, only the envenomed knife. He was sent to kill, and there was enough poison on that blade to do it with just a glancing cut, I suspect. But it shows that we were right—our enemy is at Winstowe."

"I suppose I am shocked to know that one of my own subjects, the child of an old and firm ally, should have come to kill me," she said.

"He was starved, and who knows what other dreadful things were done to him?"

Miri paused. "Do you think Pasevalles will truly murder his mother and daughter now? Aglaf's wife, Countess Marah, is a good woman. I have met her many times."

"The traitor has already killed Count Aglaf, from what the young man says." Tiamak shook his head. "Still, they failed to harm you, Majesty. Despite Pasevalles' best effort, nothing has changed."

"No, one thing has changed. I will not leave Jesa and the baby behind now, in case the monster sends more killers."

"As you wish," he said. "I will arrange it."

Miriamele stood. "And tell Captain Zakiel that we march out as soon as the muster is complete. By Heaven, Pasevalles must pay for his crimes."

"That day will come." Tiamak did his best to put strength and reassurance into his voice. "And it will come soon."

"God grant you are right," the queen said.

Simon was ashamed by how grateful he was to have a night out of the saddle. As he sat beside the small fire he had been allowed to build, Jiriki came to join him.

"Where is your granddaughter?" Jiriki asked. "Or is it only Geloë just now?"

Simon frowned. "At risk of sounding ungrateful, I am glad to say that Lillia woke up this evening, not Geloë. She is with Rukayu just now, washing and then getting something to eat. I would have gone with them, but I confess that I am so weary I asked them to bring something back for me while I rest."

Jiriki shook his head. "Do not blame yourself, Seoman. You have been part of a heroic ride. My people are weary too, they just do not show it."

"I did not think you would ever let us stop."

"We no longer have the freedom to ride during the night as well as the day. We are in the lands the *uro'eni* haunts now, and the dark is its time."

"Does it never come out in the day?"

Jiriki shrugged like a snake sloughing an old skin. "We have only the words of those who have survived meeting it, and there were few of those. I hope not.

But it is not the worst of our problems. I begin to fear we will have to fight all the way to Tanakirú." The last few days had seen several skirmishes with Norn Sacrifices, although none of them had been severe enough to force Simon into risking Lillia's safety by joining the battle. "Fight all the way? We seem to be encountering only the Norn Queen's stragglers."

Jiriki shook his head. "I do not think so. Several days in a row we have met them, and though each time their numbers were small, they were organized and commanded like any other Sacrifice troops. Whether it is Utuk'ku's own strategy or General Ensume's, if they truly hoped to stop us, it would make more sense for them to have found a single narrow spot and put all their soldiers there. Instead, it is like digging in dry sand—every time we push through one Sacrifice defense, another comes in behind it."

"What does it mean?" Simon asked, but then answered himself. "They know they can't stop us without a major battle. They're trying to slow us."

The Sitha nodded. "Just so. For whatever reason, Utuk'ku and her officers seem more intent on delaying us than on defeating us. Which suggests either the fighting at the valley's head is much fiercer than I deem likely with our numbers there so small, or Utuk'ku has her eyes not just on the battlefield, but on the calendar, the weather, or something I cannot even imagine. No matter which it is, I am worried."

They suffered through several more days of intermittent Sacrifice ambushes, and though the Sithi broke through the resisting Sacrifices each time, the Hikeda'ya soldiers fought to the death, so that with each struggle, Jiriki's company lost casualties they could not afford. The last struggle had been so fierce that they had been forced to battle long past sunset, but Jiriki was desperate and implored them to hurry onward. After briefly tending to their wounded, they set out again an hour before dawn despite the risk of traveling the valley in darkness.

Drowsing in his saddle sometime later with Lillia in his lap, Simon woke when his horse suddenly changed direction and began to climb up the slope, away from the valley floor. He could hear quiet communications between the nearby Sithi, birdlike trills and whistles, but he had no idea what was happening. The sky was thinly smeared with light, and streaks of gray fog hung in the trees like melted pearls, but at first he could not remember whether day was dawning or ending.

Rukayu was suddenly beside him, leaning forward in her saddle as her horse scaled the slope. The thickest part of the mist now fell away behind them; Simon could see that her jaw was clenched, her wide golden eyes intent.

"Up!" she said. "Keep going up! Jiriki has heard something and bids us hide ourselves."

Simon rode up the slope holding Lillia tightly, swiveling between boulders that loomed from the mist like exposed, long-buried bones. He and Rukayu found a great shelf of rock jutting from the hillside, and with some two dozen of the Sithi, took refuge beneath it.

"What did Jiriki hear?" Simon asked.

"I do not know." Rukayu had her bow in her hands, arrow already on the string, as usual. "But now we must be silent."

Simon's horse and the others were crowded together beneath the outcrop, nearly touching each other. He could heard only the breathing and occasional sputtering of the horses, then a booming impact made the ground shudder beneath them. A long moment later came another, just as loud. A few small stones rolled away and down the slope.

"Good God," Simon said in a choked gasp. "What is that?"

Rukayu gestured for silence, but leaned close and whispered, "The *uro'eni*—the ogre. Do not speak, do not move."

Though his heart pounded in fright, Simon could not help wondering at the discipline of the Sithi and their horses: they waited, almost uniformly still and silent, even as the thunderous footsteps increased in ground-shaking force, growing steadily closer. A few of the horses danced in place, full of nervous excitement, but other than that the row of riders stood as motionless as Simon's Erkynguard in formal ceremony.

Just when it seemed that they must finally see whatever moved so ponderously below them, the footsteps halted. For an instant, Simon thought he saw a huge shadow in the mist down beside the Narrowdark, an immense, confusing shape that seemed far too large to belong to any living thing. Then the steps again shook the hillside. Simon seized his sword-hilt, heart beating painfully fast, but the sounds slowly diminished. Whatever it was had turned back upstream.

When the valley grew quiet again, Rukayu lowered her drawn bow, then Simon heard Jiriki call out from somewhere nearby. The Sithi began to ride back down the slope, gathering as they went, until the whole company had assembled near the river once more.

Jiriki stood in his stirrups and said a few brief but forceful words.

"He thinks that dawn has driven the creature back to its lair," Rukayu translated for Simon. "But he says that is only a guess, and since too much confidence might have fatal consequences, we must go carefully."

Unnerved by a single glimpse of the shadowy ogre, Simon could only shake his head. "Too much confidence?" he asked quietly. It seemed less a warning than a grim sort of jest.

The deeper they rode into the Narrowdark Valley, the thicker the murk became, until even the swift, sure-footed horses and their keen-eyed riders had to slow to little more than a trot. The lower part of the valley was full of twisted trees, ash, poplar, and willow, their limbs curling and thrusting out at strange angles like tormented figures struggling for escape. As night fell, they heard (and felt) the sound of monstrous footsteps again and rode hurriedly up into the hills to hide.

This time the ogre walked past them down the valley, and as they watched from their high place it was clear from its bulky shadow that this monstrosity was far taller and larger than any giant Simon had ever seen; as tall as half a dozen Frostmarch giants standing on each other's shoulders. At times, the monstrous shape seemed to have bent forward onto all fours, like an island ape, other times it stood almost like a man, slouching but erect. But even those glimpses through the mist just confused Simon more, because its silhouette seemed shaggy or even spiny, and its limbs appeared weirdly crooked.

"What do you think it is?" he asked Jiriki after the thing had passed, the thunder of its footsteps diminishing as it vanished downstream in the fog. "Some demon?"

"I cannot even guess," Jiriki replied. For once he was in no hurry and had announced they would not ride again until the thing had turned back to the headwaters of the river at the northern end of the valley, as it always seemed to do. "Nothing in our history, not even the greatest of dragons, was ever shaped thusly. Perhaps it is something that has grown so large because of the strangeness of this valley."

Simon nodded. "I've seen some of the other creatures here. They aren't like their kin outside the valley, that's certain. Some I have never seen before."

"Nor have I." Jiriki made a sign Simon didn't recognize, bringing his hands together and interlacing the fingers. "It is possible we will find the answer at the end of our ride. But it is also possible we may never know what that thing is. We could kill an ordinary giant, even a very large one, but I doubt we have enough arrows and spears in all our company to bring that monster down—or even to discomfort it, I fear."

The ogre only ever appeared after darkness fell on the fogbound valley but seemed to roam almost every night, so the Sithi continued riding only in daylight. Simon could see that Jiriki was agonized by the slow pace, and he was growing increasingly uneasy himself about keeping Lillia safe in such a strange and dangerous situation. Geloë often remained submerged within the child for hours at a stretch, but Lillia never reclaimed her body, so Simon had to continue holding his granddaughter upright, though it felt as though life had fled her body completely. *Where is she?* he wondered miserably. *Does she dream in this magical sleep? I told her that the bad dream was over and her dreams would be safe and happy.* He could only pray it was true.

He longed to ask Geloë, but she had not surfaced since the previous day. In his darkest moments he wondered if Lillia would ever truly come back. Sometimes he even wept a little, though his pride made him quickly wipe away the tears before anyone saw them. The immortals did not often weep, and his own weakness made him feel ashamed.

On they rode, along steep, fogbound slopes and through silent, murky forest—a shadow-world of grotesque shapes that appeared from the mist and then swiftly vanished again. Even vegetation and stone took on the appearance of menace: Simon often felt that the whole valley was watching them with malicious eyes. He could even imagine sometimes, when he dared a look back, that the trees had closed the track behind them after they had passed.

Midway through their third day in the Narrowdark, as the sun began to ease down into the west, Jiriki brought the company to a halt again. They were high on a hillside in a grove of evergreens, and Rukayu told Simon they were to wait while scouts rode ahead.

Time passed slowly. Simon had been struggling during the ride north with his own troubled conscience, and his worries kept coming back. How could he have failed to see what Pasevalles was doing? And how could he make sure such a thing never happened again? How could he keep power out of the hands of determined liars and outright monsters? After all, a throne was a sort of weapon—perhaps the most dangerous weapon of all—and when someone untrustworthy or even just mad could use its power, no one was safe. The dreadful, deathless Norn Queen was only the most terrible example, but Simon could think of many.

Such grim thoughts were not a very pleasant distraction from waiting. He turned to Rukayu, who was displaying the usual maddening Sithi patience.

"Is this the first time we have sent out scouts?" he asked.

She looked amused. "Of course not. But it is the first time we have sent them to look at the Hikeda'ya."

A chill stole up Simon's spine. "Does that mean the Norns are near?"

"Jiriki and some of the others believe they can hear the fighting now, not far ahead of us—perhaps only a league away."

Simon could only marvel at being able to hear quiet enemies a league distant.

"Shen'de the Bowman is your great-grandfather, is that right?" he asked.

She nodded. "He has fought at Jiriki's side before. My father would have fought too, but he fell a long distance when he was a child and his legs were badly broken, so that he cannot stand long or walk for more than a few steps. He became a bow-maker instead."

"Is that how you learned to use a bow so well?"

Now Rukayu laughed a little. "It has more to do with my great-grandfather, who is famous for it. Most of our people can wield a bow. Shen'de is the only one in all our clan who is called 'the Bowman'."

"And you," Simon said, forgetting his worries for a happy moment. "Why are you called Crow's-Claw? Was your other grandfather a bird?"

It was difficult to know whether her look was mocking or aggrieved, but Rukayu pulled the leather gauntlet from her left hand. That hand, when exposed, showed much more red than golden, and the skin looked as though it had melted and then hardened again, like candlewax. Simon could not help a sharp intake of breath. "By our Lord!" he said. "How did that happen?"

"When I was young," Rukayu said. "A Great Year and more has passed since then. I told you that my father was a bowyer. A boiling pot of glue spilled on my hand. The healers worked hard to give me back what little command of it they could." Now, surprisingly, she smiled. "But my grandfather told them, 'Do not let it heal without curling it around the grip of her bow. She is my best pupil. She can still hold steady, and nothing is wrong with her eye or her other hand.' What else could I do, but honor that faith in me? I practiced even more in the years ahead than I ever had."

"And they called you Crow's Claw?" he said. "I did not think the Sithi so cruel."

Her smile widened. "I gave myself that name, King Seoman. Does it not look just like the claw of a bird?" She held up her crabbed left hand. "I have always admired crows and ravens. They are the cleverest of all flying things, and it is said that of all birds, only the crow, the owl, and the nightingale can travel to the world beyond the Veil." But even as she spoke, she tilted her head to one side as though listening, then began to pull her gauntlet back on.

"What is it?"

"The first scouts are back." Her wide eyes were bright. "Soon we will learn what we do next, and when we will fight."

As the woman who had left her beside the ocean had promised, the campfire did not go out. At first Lillia had wandered a short way along the heather-hued sand in search of more wood, but each time she returned she found that the sticks burning in the fire had not diminished.

It's just a magic place, she decided. That made sense to her because nothing else did. *She said it was the Garden, but it's not a garden at all. It's a beach, like beside the Kynslagh at home.*

The ocean, green and active, seemed to cover most of the world, at least from where Lillia sat watching it, but the sky seemed no different from what she knew, except for the small, blazing dot of the sun. She did not like to see the sun so distant—it reminded her that she was far away from what she knew, her home, her family.

The woman had told her to wait, so wait Lillia did, but it was fearfully hard. She had no toys, no dolls, no books. Nobody was around to tell her what to do, and that at first seemed like a good thing, but after hours and hours sitting by herself, or walking up and down the beach—though never beyond sight of the fire—she began to wish someone *would* tell her what to do, so at least she could tell them that she didn't want to.

As she endured the seemingly endless boredom of the day, enlivened only by a few stilt-legged birds wading along the strand, leaning to dart their beaks into the shallow water as they hunted small things, Lillia began to wonder whether she should use the owl feather the woman had given her to summon her back.

She said to do it if I needed her. She certainly felt that she needed someone or something. The woman had told her she would not need food, and it was true that she did not feel anything like the ordinary pangs of hunger, but though she did not *need* to eat, she missed the routine of eating, the excitement or disappointment when she found out what she was being served, the pleasure she felt after she had run around the Hayholt all day and could sit down and fill her empty stomach. In fact, in this place that seemed to have no other human inhabitants but herself, she was missing almost everything about her ordinary life.

I even would let Aedonita bring her little sister—even though Elyweld is a terrible blower and a cry-baby—just so I would have someone to play with.

She had an idea, and as the small and distant sun began to settle behind the horizon, painting a single wavy line of fire across the placid sea, she walked a little way along the beach and up the dunes to where she had first awakened in the patch of swaying black grass. The woman had told her not to leave the fire, but how could she expect Lillia to stay in one place for what already felt like days and days (though she was seeing only her first sunset)? Still, she did not want to stay away from it for long, and although its flickering flames were still bright and easy to see, the distance between her and it made her feel anxious. She hurriedly picked grass until she had a bulging handful, but when she finished and stood up, she again saw a shape on the top of the dunes, closer this time than before. The specter's cloak or dress billowed in the breeze, but slowly, like plants beneath the surface of a stream, and Lillia's heart lurched. Frightened, she turned and staggered down the uneven dunes, then hurried along the beach to return to her fire.

When she was seated by the flames again, she looked back at where she had been, but saw no trace of the rippling, ghostly form.

I scared myself, she decided. *There's nothing there.* But her swiftly beating heart seemed to feel otherwise.

She picked up a stick and began to knot some of the grass around it. Her idea had been to make a doll for herself out of sticks and grass, but for some reason every time she thought she was making progress, something went wrong. The grass was still wet and would not hold its shape when she tried to wrap it around the stick, and the head she made from a grass-wrapped stone kept coming apart. It was all she could manage not to throw the whole misbegotten thing into the fire. The sun disappeared, but she labored on. She managed to get the head wrapped but could not tie it successfully to the grass-wound stick that was meant to be its body—it kept falling off. At last, frustrated and wanting to cry, she set down her doll makings and looked out at the ocean.

The pale figure was standing on the other side of the fire, just at the edge of the circle of firelight. Framed by the gauzy, wafting hood, the face around the black eyes seemed made of rippling flames.

Startled and terrified, Lillia pushed herself back from the campfire, leaving a gouge in the sand.

Do not be afraid, mortal child. The voice was in her head, not just her ears. It sounded like an old woman's voice, older even than her grandmother or Great-Aunt Nelda, but sweeter than either, and far more soothing than the rasp of the woman who had left her here.

"I'm . . . I'm not afraid," Lillia said, though it was a terrible lie. "Who are you?"

A friend. The shape moved closer to the fire, and Lillia saw that she seemed to have no body beneath the blowing garments. The only thing that seemed solid was the floating face, which Lillia saw now was an oval mask of reflecting silver.

"Who are you?" Lillia asked, her voice shaking.

Did the one who left you here give her name to you? I think not. But that is strange, is it not? That she pretended to be your friend, but did not tell you who she was?

"You're not my friend." Lillia felt certain about that. Every part of her wanted to get up and run away, but she could not forget how the first woman had told her not to leave the fire.

Ah, but I am. Because I will tell you the truth, child—all the things that the other would not. But first, call her here so she can answer your questions. Who is she? Why did she leave you here, alone and friendless? Where are the people who care for you?

The voice was sweetly convincing, and Lillia found herself wishing she could believe it. Where was her grandfather? Why had she been left here all alone?

The drifting shape moved a little closer. The glinting mask tipped down, looking at the place where Lillia had sat and the things she had dropped. *Do you make yourself a doll? How sweet. I never had a girl child, but I would have liked one. I had a son, but he is gone now. Watch. I shall make your plaything better.* The sleeve lifted and moved, as if an invisible arm gestured within it. The bits of Lillia's unfinished doll moved a little, as if in a stiff breeze, then slowly began to draw together in an intricate dance. Bits of grass waved in the air, then found other bits, and gradually the parts pulled together into the shape of a person, body, legs, and faceless head. *See! Is that not better?*

Lillia looked at the doll where it lay in the sand. She wanted to lift it up to look at it more closely, but also did not want to touch it.

Call the one who brought you. Bring her here. The shining mask was now looking straight at her. *Demand her name. She owes you that, at least.*

Lillia's hand touched the owl-feather thrust through the belt of her tunic. She did not know what was happening, but she did not like it. The masked woman was right—the other had not told her anything useful, and then had left her alone. If the feather worked as she had said it would, Lillia had only to call the woman and she would come. The two of them, the yellow-eyed woman and the silver-masked phantom, could work it out between themselves.

Because it's not fair, Lillia thought, frightened and angry. *I didn't want any of this.*

I feel you hesitating, child. Why? I mean you no harm. I do not even mean harm to the one who left you here. I only want to see her, to meet her and talk with her. We have many things to discuss—grown-up things that would bore you. Call her, and when she comes, we will leave you alone to play with your new doll.

The eyes in the shiny mask were only holes, black emptiness, but Lillia could still feel the invisible stare, holding her in place. Her hand touched the frothy end of the owl feather. *Just call,* she told herself. *Just call the campfire woman. This one doesn't want* you, *she wants* her.

But at the final moment, her hand dropped away, and her fingers curled into a fist.

"No," she said. "She told me not to. Not unless I was scared. And I'm not scared of you."

What a sweet little falsehood. You are a brave girl. The wispy garments, insubstantial as fog, snapped and streamed in the rising wind. *But you are right not to fear me. Soon, you will come to understand that I am your friend.* The mask glittered with fiery reflections. *I will leave you now to think. And when I come back to you again, I am certain that you will understand what you need to do.* Suddenly the cloud of pale garments twisted against the darkness, swirling like a spiral of dust, then a sudden blast of chilly air made the flames dance and lean sideways as the ghostly shape vanished into the darkness.

Alone and comfortless, Lillia held herself and cried.

"*S'hue* Jiriki is speaking with our scouts," said Rukayu when she returned to Simon, who was sitting on a rock, cradling his sleeping granddaughter. "That means we will ride soon, and at the end of the ride there will be fighting."

Simon took a deep breath and pulled Lillia's body close to his own. *She is all I have left.* His heart sped until he could feel blood throb in his temples. *I will do anything I can to protect her.*

Jiriki left the scouts and approached him. "Seoman King," he said, "we will soon meet the Hikeda'ya enemy. They stand between us and what is left of my people, so we must get past them or the defense of Tanakirú fails."

"Past them? How? I don't understand."

Jiriki squatted beside him. "I will try to explain, but we have only a little time. Watch closely." He leaned forward and traced an upside-down "V" shape in the frosty soil with his finger. "At the end of this valley, two lines of hills come together." He drew a rough, angular line of peaks along each side of the V. "They are high and sheer on the eastern side, but much less so on the western slopes, where we are. The eastern cliffs drop straight down to the river, and there is no way down them. Now, see, here is the Narrowdark River, like a snake with a large head." He traced a shape, roughly round where the two sides of the V came together near the valley's end, with the snake's body trailing away down toward the bottom of the V. "And the rest of the snake is the river itself. It is created by the cataracts which tumble down from the mountainous heights at the valley's end, and those waters have dug a deep gorge—that is the snake's head."

"I think I see," said Simon, squinting.

"Here is the most important thing to understand. Not all the end of the valley is the deep, splashing gorge. At the base of the cliffs, here just beside the snake's head," he said, pointing to the northwestern end of the valley, "there remains a rocky plateau. The gorge separates it from the rest of the valley. That small, flat piece of stone beneath the cliffs is what my people defend, protected by the deep waters pounding in the gorge as they rush away down the valley." Jiriki marked out the slender strip just beyond the northwestern edge of the river gorge. "The Hikeda'ya are here." He marked a series of positions blocking the bottom of the valley's western slope.

Simon quickly saw the problem. "But if we are here on the western slopes south of the gorge," he said, "then the headwaters separate us from your people."

"They do," said Jiriki. "There was a bridge across the gorge, when all this valley was under our control, between a promontory here"—he stroked a short line from the western slope out over the gorge, "—and the plateau. When the Hornet's Nest fell, our folk retreated across the gorge and threw down the bridge behind them, keeping our enemies out, but also trapping themselves on the plateau beneath steep cliffs. The Hikeda'ya have tried several times to force their way across that gap, but so far we have kept them from succeeding."

Simon was puzzled. "Is that true? You said your Witnesses don't work, so how can you know?"

Jiriki smiled, but there was not a fleck of mirth in it. "Because our scouts have seen the fighting, and I can hear it even from here. My folk are still holding the end of the valley—somehow."

Trying to make sense of this, Simon's eyes strayed back to the makeshift map Jiriki had drawn. "And we are going down into that?" Almost without realizing it, he squeezed Lillia's silent form again. "But you said there is no bridge. How will we cross the gorge? You said that their numbers are much larger than ours."

"They are. And because you are my friend, I will tell you honestly that for us to survive and reach our allies, we must be very fortunate. Much will depend on good luck."

Anger flared inside Simon. "That is not what I want to hear, Jiriki. This is my granddaughter. Geloë, who says she is our only hope, is inside her. How can I protect them when I don't understand what you're planning?"

"I cannot anticipate everything that will happen. Neither can I tell you every possibility." Even Jiriki now seemed short of temper. "Stay in the middle of our troop with Rukayu. Stay away from the fighting as best you can. As you say, your task is only to protect the child—and Geloë." He looked up as if someone had called him, though Simon had heard nothing. "I must go now. Prepare yourself. Pray to your God, friend Seoman."

Jiriki rose and returned to his scouts.

"I will not leave you and your granddaughter," promised Rukayu. But she, too, seemed to be listening to something Simon could not hear.

A short while after Simon had mounted his horse once more and taken Lillia on his lap, the Sithi company silently began to move northward along the forested slope. As Jiriki had suggested, he and Rukayu took a place in the middle of the troop, but toward the rear. The horses trotted into the obscuring mist, then gradually increased their pace until ghostly white willows and thickets of alders, slender trunks like upright spears, swept past in a blur. The Narrowdark bent and then bent again, and soon even Simon could hear the dim sounds of strife ahead—shouts, cries, and the ominous booming of war-drums.

Another message from Jiriki was passed down from one Sitha to another until it reached Rukayu and Simon at the rear.

"We are almost at the head of the valley, but it will be hard to see what is happening through the mist. Stay together and do not attack until you hear Ti-Tuno's call."

The Sithi, who had been carrying their helmets on their saddle horns, now donned them, and archers set arrows on bowstrings. Closely following the twisting track of the river, the company increased its speed until it seemed the entire valley must hear the thunder of their hooves, Simon doing his best to stay with them despite his extra burden. A part of him was filled with dread, but another part ached to do something at last, to finally strike a blow at the Norn Queen's soldiers who had burned down his home.

But my task here is not to kill enemies, he reminded himself. *My only trust sits right here before me. But how can I protect her when I do not understand Jiriki's battle plan? Does even Jiriki know what he will do?*

He could sense a difference in the noise now, louder than the purr of the river, a growing rush and roar that rose even above the hoofbeats of the Sithi horses. The gorge seemed to widen suddenly before him, and for the first time he saw the end of the valley, massive raw limestone cliffs that echoed with the thunder of falling water. He could see sky as well, and after so long in the perpetual evening beneath the trees, he was surprised to discover it was still afternoon. A moment later his horse plunged into the mist and cliffs and sky were hidden again. The mist closed in all around him, dancing in milky streaks, pulled up by the wind into a froth like beaten egg whites.

They were now high on the wooded western slope of the valley, and when the mist parted again, Simon could see down to the great watercourse on the valley floor. Dark shapes—Norn soldiers, Simon realized—scuttled along the slope far below them like ants flowing toward a pile of crumbs, and for a moment Simon felt a grip of dread at how many more they looked than the minuscule Sithi company, which did not number much beyond six or seven score.

Even as he thought this, Jiriki's troop reached a stand of pines that covered a broad expanse of the slope. At Jiriki's signal they reined up, so that the trees hid them from the Hikeda'ya army below. Jiriki gestured again and a troop of some two or three dozen riders separated themselves from the others and galloped out of the thicket—not down toward the Norns but along the upper slope of the valley instead.

"Where are they going?" Simon asked.

"Jiriki has set them to their work," whispered Rukayu, squinting at the distant Protector, who was making broad hand-signals. "I do not know what that work is, but he tells the rest of us to be vigilant—the Hikeda'ya likely already know we are here. When the time comes, we must ride at Jiriki's command through the enemy, as fast as we can. I cannot lie, you may need to use your blade, but I will do my best to lead you and your granddaughter through the battle to safety."

If it had been hard for Simon to carry his silent, sleeping granddaughter into such a strange place, it was harder still to wait with her at the edge of a battle, knowing that any moment bloody fighting might suddenly reach them. He tested the belt that held her against his chest to make sure it was still in place, then did his best simply to breathe.

The wind blew, cold as betrayal, and the mists from the river billowed and streamed, often leaving Simon blind in a wilderness of empty white. Many, many years had passed since he had fought in a battle where he had not been one of the leaders, where his words had not carried great weight. This felt like the days when he had fought for Prince Josua as an inexperienced youth—he was just another defender again, just another sword.

And this time, I should not even swing that sword except to protect Lillia.

The winds rose again, sharp and bitter, and the mist was torn as if by a giant hand, again revealing the headlands of the valley.

Simon had never seen anything quite like Tanakirú. The high cliffs came together at the end of the valley like a row of bottom teeth, but a great jumble of stone had fallen away from the granite cliffs and filled the plateau at the valley's end with huge broken blocks, as if a mason had tipped all his remnants into a pile. At least half a dozen waterfalls plunged down the sheer rock and into the deep gorge at the base of the cliffs. Water splashing against the base had gnawed away the stone until the cliffs on the eastern side loomed outward above the headwaters of the Narrowdark like the upper stories of Erchester's oldest houses. The valley floor rose on the slope beneath them, ending in a tongue of land—Jiriki's "promontory"—that extended over the booming, splashing outflow of the Narrowdark. In one spot the wide spur of stone jutted so far above the crashing water of the river gorge that only a stone's throw of empty air separated it from the plateau on the far side. Foaming waves crashed against this protruding spit of stone and flew into the air as spray, but that was not what now caught Simon's eye. The promontory swarmed with Norn Sacrifices and armored giants, working together to move vast, wheeled war-engines up the spit of stone that stretched partway out over the gorge. Across from it, at the edge of the plateau, the defending Sithi had built a high, deep wall of dry stone where the bridge that Jiriki had said they demolished during their retreat to the stony shelf must have connected them to the rest of the valley. At the bottom of the wall was a sally-gate made of large, rough logs. Through the tatters of mist, Simon could see that a few Sithi archers were crouched atop the wall, but even though Norn arrows fell around them, the defenders did not let fly in return.

The leading siege engine being laboriously edged up the promontory was massive, a broad tower several times a man's height. Its huge siege-bridge stuck out at the rear of the engine but was clearly meant to be swiveled forward across the narrowest part of the gorge once the wheeled engine had reached the tip of the promontory. Four shaggy giants pushed it from behind while a squadron of Sacrifice engineers pulled at it with heavy ropes, slowly dragging it up the slope, followed closely by the other two engines and their own straining crews.

Even as Simon watched, one of the larger giants on the first engine was struck by a sudden flurry of Sithi arrows from atop the defensive wall, but the missiles did little damage: the giant howled and brushed the shafts away as if they were no more than clinging burrs, then staggered back into place and began pushing once more.

Simon could see no way for his own company to cross the gorge, but the Norn engines would soon allow Utuk'ku's soldiers to reach the plateau. A huge number of Sacrifice soldiers were crouching at the base of the promontory, waiting to clamber over the bridge as soon as it swung into place.

"We can't just sit here watching," he said, holding Lillia tightly against his belly. "The defenders are going to be overrun!"

"Jiriki has made his plan," said Rukayu. "We must wait for his signal." But Simon thought he heard a worrying uncertainty in her voice.

Simon had led his horse forward as far as Rukayu would let him, so he could look down on the valley. His arm was aching, but he did not dare set down Lillia's ragdoll form for even an instant. A ripple of new noise moved across the misty hillside, and he heard shouts of alarm from the Norn soldiers below and in front of him.

"What is happening?" he cried.

"I cannot see either," said Rukayu. "But we must wait."

"But Jiriki's blown the horn twice now! And that is the Sithi singing and the sound of their horses—they must be attacking!" Even as he said it, he could hear the first ringing noises of blade on blade and the cries of wounded fighters rising from below him.

"We wait for Jiriki's third call," Rukayu said firmly, staring into the murk. "He made that very plain to me. Be patient, King Seoman."

Lillia began to writhe in his arms, increasing the ache. Simon was terrified she would wake up to this nightmare of fog and blood. "Lillia," he whispered as loudly as he dared. "Stop that! I cannot hold you if you do that—"

"I do not want you to hold me." It was Geloë's rough tone—she was awake and staring at Simon. "Lift me up so I can learn what is happening."

"There is nothing to see, Sa-Ruyan Geloë," said Rukayu. "At the moment, the mist has settled in over us again."

"I do not see only with my eyes, child of the cedar wood." And as if to prove it, when Simon raised her higher, his granddaughter's eyes once more fell closed. "The raiding party is rushing down on the Norn logging camp," she announced, "and our hammer-wielders are hurrying into place." She paused. "Now Jiriki and his company have thrown themselves into the side of the Norn legion that is rushing uphill to protect the great felled trees."

"Trees?" Simon asked. "Are they witchwood, is that why Jiriki wants them? And how can you know all this?"

"So many questions, Seoman Snowlock," said Geloë. Even in the middle of such chaos, she almost sounded amused. "No, the trees are only pine and spruce, but Utuk'ku's General Ensume is no fool. He has grasped Jiriki's plan."

"What plan? I don't understand!"

"Trust Jiriki," the aged voice told him. "He has waited long for this moment. And he has something that neither Ensume nor his cruel monarch has."

"What is that?"

"Something worth fighting for—the survival of his people."

Jiriki's sword Indreju had already been many times bloodied, and Cloudfoot's witchwood armor was studded with black Norn arrows, but none of the barbs hissing past had yet found the flesh of either the horse or its rider. He tugged the reins and his horse spun in a swift circle, nimble as a dancer, through a swarm of Spider Legion Sacrifices. "Strike and keep moving!" he called to his nearest allies. "They outnumber us—we must not be surrounded!"

He looked up the hill and saw his three *m'yon rashi* creeping along, bent low to the ground as they moved into position at the front of the largest stack of felled timbers. Some of the huge logs were as wide as a wagon track and forty or fifty cubits long. Several of the strikers' fellow Sithi, having finished off the few guards left to watch over the logging camp, had moved in front of the wood-rick with shields held high to protect the strikers from the arrows of the Hikeda'ya Sacrifices who were racing up the slope toward them, slowed only by Jiriki's own small force. The rest of the Sithi raiding party now hurried down from the upper slopes to join the others, making a wall of bronze and witchwood between the charging Hikeda'ya and the trio of hammer-wielding *m'yon rashi,* who were hurriedly inspecting the posts that held the massive logs in place. If the rest of the Sithi could just hold the Hikeda'ya at bay a short while longer, Jiriki knew there was still a chance of success.

But even as he turned back to the fierce, bloody fighting that surrounded him, Jiriki's eye was caught by something strange. A dark figure, man-shaped and man-sized but moving with the long, loping gait of something out of a nightmare, came rushing up the slope through the Hikeda'ya troops, dispatching any Sithi it met with an almost invisibly swift blow of its long, hooked sword. A moment later, as if overcome by impatience, the weird dark shape leaped onto the backs of the nearest Sacrifice soldiers and began vaulting through the thick of the battle, springing from one living step-stone to the next, nimble as a southern ape.

Everything about the thing stank of wicked sorcery. Jiriki spurred his horse up the slope, trying to catch up and head it off, but it paused at each landing only long enough to kill any of Jiriki's people it could reach.

"What are you, foul creature?" Jiriki cried. "Have the courage to face me!"

The man-shape turned to look at him, even as blades rose and fell all around. Jiriki saw only a gray blur of a face and an empty hole where one eye should be, but it was enough to confirm that the attacker was nothing natural—an unliving thing somehow raised to a mockery of life.

"Stay!" Jiriki cried. "Stay for me and I will send you back to whatever cold hell birthed you!"

But the foul thing had remembered its task, turning from Jiriki to continue its inhumanly swift progress up the slope, as swift and unpredictable in its great leaps as a black frog. Jiriki knew he could never catch it before it reached the top and slaughtered the defenders there, and the vital hammer-wielders with them. He raised Ti-Tuno to his lips and blew it for the third time, a long, echoing blast that must have been heard all over the valley.

At the log-rick, the Sithi hammer-wielders now lifted their crystal-headed weapons and swung them against the great posts driven deep into the hillside to keep the trimmed trunks in place. Jiriki's own company, hearing Ti-Tuno's mighty call, broke away from the Hikeda'ya enemy and urged their horses back down the slope, toward the side nearest the deep gorge. Above them, the hammer-wielders, their work done, hurried out of the way, quickly followed by the surviving members of the Sithi raiding party. The *m'yon-rashi* vaulted up behind their mounted fellows, then they all sped out of the way even as the posts shivered, then collapsed, and the first of the great logs came tumbling out of the rick and began to roll down the slope.

Jiriki saw the leaders of the Hikeda'ya charge look up, eyes wide and startled in their helmets, a heartbeat before the first massive log reached them, crushing Sacrifices by the dozens as it skidded and bounced over them. Half a dozen more of the great trunks followed, smashing General Ensume's Spider-soldiers flat, gathering speed as they careened down the slope toward the gorge.

"Did you not hear me?" Jiriki cried, though all his people had, and his enemies as well. "Ride, Zida'ya, ride! To the Narrowdark!"

As Ti-Tuno's echoes were still reverberating, Simon and Rukayu's horses sprang forward across the slope, following Jiriki and the rest downward into the mist, toward the great gorge at the head of the valley. Simon could barely see anything, but Geloë urged him to ride on. "We must make haste," she told him. "There are only moments left."

The sun had almost set, and with the end of its light the wind began to move over the valley, pulling the mist into shreds, so that for the first time Simon could get some idea of what was happening. Jiriki and his riders seemed to have retreated from their fight with the Hikeda'ya who had been coming up the slope, but instead of returning to the place their attack began, the Sithi were galloping toward toward the northern end of the valley. Then, even as Simon watched, they turned as one and began to pelt down the slope toward the thundering waters of the wide gorge.

"This way," called Rukayu, waving her arm to show him that she was following the path of Jiriki and the others.

"But we'll go straight into the Norn army!" he cried, clutching his granddaughter's body tightly, struggling to keep his seat as they jounced across the uneven ground. "Or into the river!" The gorge, loud, wide, and terrifying, grew nearer with each moment as they raced downward.

Rukayu was too busy to answer, standing in her stirrups, loosing arrow after arrow. Simon saw two or three dark-armored Norns fall in their tracks, pierced by shafts fletched with feathers the color of fire. Despite these kills, the Sithi were still greatly outnumbered, but Simon was now more worried about the wide gorge than he was about even the Norn soldiers.

Another loud sound, almost a twin to the roar of the cataracts, reached his ears. Its source seemed to be above him. He looked up to an astonishing sight—a monstrous tree-trunk, stripped of its branches, was tumbling down the hill, crushing Sacrifice soldiers the way Judith the old Hayholt cook had once flattened pastry with a rolling pin. The few of the White Foxes who avoided the massive log were almost immediately smashed by more rolling, sliding trunks, which came down in a complicated mass, some momentarily catching and stopping others before more great logs tumbled down from above and knocked them all free once more.

"Stop staring," cried Geloë, less sanguine than before. "Ride, boy, ride!"

She was right, he realized—they were in the path of the log avalanche, and arrows from the Norn soldiers below were snapping past. He bent low over his horse's back and did his best to cover Lillia's small body with his own.

They escaped the path of the plunging logs with only an arm's length to spare—the last of the great trunks nearly caught the back of his mount's legs but did no more than scrape her flank as she leaped forward. Simon looked back to make certain no more were on the way and saw a single slender figure standing at the top of the slope where the logs had come from, arms outstretched, swaying.

Singing, he thought. *It's one of the Sithi, and she's singing!*

But a moment later a dark figure scrambled up the devastated slope and with a single, horrifying swipe, beheaded the singer. The dark thing then turned to look down, and for a moment its gaze seemed to meet Simon's. He had only a momentary impression, but even that chilled him—either the thing wore a mask, or its face was the color of something dead and decaying.

"Follow Jiriki!" said Geloë. "Head for the spur of rock!"

Rukayu was already galloping downslope toward the place where the promontory stood out over the deep gorge. The Norns there had abandoned their siege engines, which stood like confused animals strayed from their pen. And as Simon drew nearer by the instant to the chasm and the surging water, the first of the tumbling logs reached the promontory, crushing even the Hikeda'ya's heavy engines as if they were dead leaves and sweeping two of the structures right over the edge and into the gorge.

"But—!" was all Simon had time to cry out, then they reached the bottom and were sprinting toward the promontory, Rukayu barely a length in front of him, Jiriki and the rest of his company only a short distance ahead. Three of the trimmed trunks had rolled to a stop spanning the gorge, but as they approached, one of them rolled back and disappeared over the edge and into the angry waters. Through the rags of mist, Simon saw Jiriki leading his troop, many dozens strong, up onto one of the logs. It had been a huge tree, but was still barely wider than the Sithi horses now galloping across it in single file, nose to tail, a feat of balance Simon could only gape at.

Then he and Rukayu were racing up the promontory as well. His horse seemed to need no guidance from him at all: it leaped high off the stony point and landed on the great trunk, slipping a little so that Simon almost lost his grip on Lillia's small form before the beast righted itself. Simon could not bear to look, and clung to the horse with his legs, his head pushed against his granddaughter's back and his fingers wrapped so tightly in the horse's bridle that he did not think he would ever be able to let go. He felt the entire log shudder beneath their mounts' hooves, heard cracking and groaning from the wood, and commended his soul to God.

I will be with you soon, Miri.

They leaped again, with nothing beneath them but air, and for an instant he thought his heart would stop. A moment later his mount's hooves came down hard on solid stone, still racing. Startled, Simon looked up and saw that they had made it to the other side of the gorge. The massive gate in the drystone wall had been opened, and as Jiriki's riders went flooding in, armored Sithi came rushing out, shields held high to keep off the enemy's arrows. Simon guessed they meant to throw down the bridging logs so the Norns could not follow.

Just before he reached the gate and was carried in past the wall, a last beam of dying afternoon sunlight fell on the cliff face that stretched high above the defended plateau. Eyes drawn upward, Simon saw a curious thing, one that he could make no sense at first. Halfway up the cliff, several hundred cubits above his head, a huge shape protruded directly from the rocky face, like a bravo's knife stuck in a tavern wall. But this weird object, Simon saw, was sunk into the mountain's very stone and looked as big as all Erchester.

It's the Ninth Ship, he realized as his mount raced through the gate. An instant later he lost sight of it once more. *Merciful God, it truly is real. It's the biggest thing I've ever seen.*

17

Rabbits and Rumors

Fremur walked down from the keep in a series of long, irregular curves. He held a jug in his hand to provide an explanation for his meandering progress, but Fremur was utterly sober, and his heart was beating as swiftly as it ever had during a midnight raid on a Nabbanai settlement.

As he passed by the clansmen at the gate, Fremur avoided meeting their eyes, doing his best to seem just another drunkard, and he succeeded well enough that a few shouted jests as he passed.

"You're going the wrong way!" bellowed one. "They keep the boys upstairs. In fact, that bare chin of yours is so pretty, it's giving *me* the horn."

Fremur turned to see Broga, a bulky, pale-bearded man, grabbing at his own loins and laughing so uproariously that he sprayed the air with spit. Like most of the Thrithings-men in Winstowe, Broga wore no clan insignia on his jacket, but Fremur could see the ends of the pale threads where he had cut it away, a ghostly shape of a head with spreading horns. *So you're a Great-horn Bull,* he thought. *I'll remember you.*

The thick man didn't like being stared at. "Get on with you, sweetheart," he growled, face darkening. "Don't look for something you don't want. I'll gut you so fast you'll walk for an hour before you know you're dead."

I've killed a few men myself, Fremur thought, not without pride. *And if the chance comes, Broga, you gape-mouthed lump of suet, I'll gladly kill you too.* But he said nothing, only shook his head and stumbled on. He didn't want a fight now. He knew Unver had seen him, which was all that mattered.

Fremur wandered away from Broga and the others, continuing to lurch from side to side, until he reached the shuttered chapel, a black bulk built against one side of the keep. He took refuge on the shadowed side where even the moonlight didn't reach, then watched his breath float up into the cold sky as he waited.

At last, a tall, silent shape appeared beside him. Unver Shan was carrying a spear and wearing one of the conical helmets from Count Aglaf's armory.

"Pasevalles doesn't trust you," Fremur told him in a low voice. "I heard him talking to his ugly watchdog, Hulgar."

Unver shook his head. "I have done nothing to make him suspect me."

"Didn't need to—he can smell you." Faced with the Shan's cold look, he tried to explain. "Not with his nose. I mean he knows you are watching him but he doesn't know why. People *see* you, Unver Shan. They didn't use to—not like I always could—but now you don't hide yourself." He tried to smile but felt his lips twist into a frown of worry. "Not even when you should."

"I am no fool, Fremur. I will not give us away."

"It has nothing to do with being a fool, Unver." But he did not have the words to explain. "In any case, I came to tell you that after Pasevalles finishes his meat, he is going to send for you. Have your lies ready."

Unver grunted. Fremur thought that was the only reply he would get and had already turned away when the Shan suddenly said, "Thank you, Fremur of the Cranes. You have been a good friend."

Fremur did not know what to say. He bobbed his head and set out on his mock-drunken path back to the keep.

Fremur sat at the far end of the high table and drank slowly, more cautious than on other nights because he knew what was to come. Around him the rest of the mercenary clansmen guzzled and boasted, happy to sit in a stolen castle and drink someone else's ale. At the far end, two of the drunkest were arm wrestling; the tabletop between them was slick with sweat. The court's few remaining courtiers cowered in the hall's dark alcoves or hid in their chambers, letting the beleaguered servants take the brunt of the grasslanders' bad behavior.

The current master of Winstowe sat in Count Aglaf's ornamented chair, watching the room like a vulture waiting for something to finish dying. Pasevalles had strong, regular features and wore his sandy hair in the short style set by the Erkynlandish court, but Fremur thought his hooded eyes and carefully expressionless face gave away his real nature. This was a man who never rested, who never let himself be distracted by the ordinary things of life, bad or good.

He is a different kind of animal from the rest of them, Fremur decided. *Like a cat among slobbering dogs.*

Fremur heard the hall doors open and looked up to see Unver being ushered in by a pair of guards. Like the gatekeepers, they wore Count Aglaf's mail and tunics bearing the Lionfish of Winstowe, but their tattoos and ornamented beards showed they too were Thrithings mercenaries. Most of Aglaf's soldiers who had survived the battle with Unver Shan had been sent away on false errands and had discovered on returning that they could not get back into Winstowe. The few who remained had either been locked in the castle's dungeon or had died resisting the castle's change of ownership.

Pasevalles signaled for Unver to join him at the high table. Fremur turned slowly and, he hoped, discreetly on his bench so he could better overhear their conversation.

Unver reached the table and bowed his head. "You called for me, my lord?"

Pasevalles looked him up and down. "A tall fellow indeed. You are Sanver of the Lake Thrithings, am I right?"

"Yes, my lord."

"What clan were you?"

"Kestrels, lord."

"Ah, yes. So I was told. I had forgotten."

A lie, thought Fremur. *That cold creature is testing, always testing. Does it mean he suspects Unver is not what he seems? Or is he this way with all strangers?*

Pasevalles leisurely examined the Shan. "You look a mighty man, at least in size," he said at last. "I would think you could make your way in any clan on the grassland. Why are you without one of your own, Sanver. Why did the Kestrels expel you?"

"A woman," said Unver. "I wanted her. Another man claimed her. I fought with him fairly and killed him, but his friends said that I set on him in ambush. For that I was driven out."

Pasevalles shook his head in mock-sympathy. "A woman. Is that not the cause of half our woes in this world—or more?" His smile was wide, but his eyes stayed fixed on Unver. "I believe I see some wit behind that stony face of yours, Sanver. And more than a little anger. Have you led men in battle?"

Unver shrugged. "I rode at the front of many raiding parties against the stone-dwellers—the cursed Nabbanai. I have killed my share."

Pasevalles showed his teeth, but this time it was not meant to be taken for a smile. "I guessed as much. Would you like that chance again?"

Unver took a moment before replying. "I do not understand you, my lord."

"Would you like to use your blade against the southerners again? Make your enemies pay for the lands they have stolen from you?"

Unver nodded slowly. "Of course."

"Then stick by me. Hulgar and Broga Broomstraw are my war thanes, but I have plans and will need more officers. One day you may be able to put some of those Nabbanai cities to the flame—after taking your pick of their women and gold, of course. Would that please you?"

"Nothing would please me more, my lord. The stone-dwellers deserve death for what they have done to my people," said Unver, with such cold finality in his voice that it almost made Fremur shiver.

"Good! Good. Then we understand each other." Pasevalles leaned back in his chair and took a long swallow from his cup, then wiped his chin with a careless flick of his hand. "Just do as I tell you, Sanver of the Kestrels, even if you do not always see the reason, and you will get what you want."

"I hope so," Unver said. "My lord."

Pasevalles waved a negligent hand to let him know he was dismissed. Unver picked up someone's neglected cup from a nearby table and swallowed down what was left, then nodded his head—a gesture just short of a bow—and made his way out of the hall. No look passed between him and Fremur, but a short while later Fremur stood up, still wearing a guise of unsteadiness, and made his way out into the antechamber. Unver was there, staring at a painting of one of Count Aglaf's ancestors with what looked like real interest, so much so that Fremur only went and stood silently next to him. Aglaf's forebear had been portrayed in full armor, holding his sword upside-down to emphasize the shape of the Erkynlanders' Holy Tree formed by the weapon's hilt.

"I know him," Unver said quietly, and at first Fremur thought he meant the armored knight in the picture. "Pasevalles. I have his measure."

"What do you mean?"

"He sees no one but himself. Everyone around him is only a reflection. Some he thinks are like him, some he thinks are too weak to matter."

"He does not think you are weak," Fremur warned. "He picked you out as soon as we came. That is why he seeks to buy you with promises of a war against Nabban."

"And that is another way in which he sees only what he wants, though he never stops watching. He thinks everyone except the stupid and sentimental can be bought." Unver looked around to make certain they were still alone. The sounds of drunken merriment were loud on the far side of the great doors. "He bought Rudur Redbeard. He thinks he can buy me, too. But he will find me a poor bargain."

Fremur's fears returned as he saw the icy look on Unver's face. "You have faced him now, as you wished, and learned what kind of man this Pasevalles is. It is time for us to go now, Unver. He may say he wishes to reward you, but I promise that he is thinking about how and when to kill you if you do not serve as he wants."

"As does any leader of strong men," said Unver.

For a long moment Fremur could not speak. "*You* are a leader," he whispered at last. "Do you mean you are no different than Pasevalles? That you already plan to murder your friends if they become inconvenient? Even Odobreg? Even *me*?"

Unver shook his head. "Do not put words in my mouth, Fremur. There is a wide, wide ditch between thinking and doing. That man in there would kill anyone to further his own ambitions. As for me, yes, I would kill even you if I had to—*if I had to*—but not because I am ambitious."

"Then why, by the holy Sky-Piercer? Why?"

Unver turned his hard gray eyes on him. "Because I love my people, and I am sworn to protect them. I did not ask to be Shan but Heaven arranged it so. That is the only thing you must understand about me, Thane Fremur—the only thing that anyone needs to know." His voice, though low, was flat and surprisingly harsh. "I would do anything—yes, even kill my only friends—to protect my people and to lift them up out of savagery into the place they belong."

After so many words, more than he generally spoke in a whole day, Unver surprised Fremur further by reaching out to grab his shoulder, then gave him an awkward squeeze of fellowship before turning to leave the antechamber.

Tzoja was squatting by the fire, cleaning a brace of rabbits for the pot, but her thoughts were elsewhere. Vordis sat nearby, choosing herbs for the stew.

What would we do without that man? Tzoja wondered. *And what will we do when he eventually leaves us, as I feel certain he will?*

Jarnulf had fashioned himself a small bow and some arrows from deadfall branches, and though he said sourly that "they wouldn't make it through a Sacrifice's cloak, let alone armor," the missiles had proved entirely adequate for shooting rabbits and squirrels and the occasional bird. He was doing quite a bit of hunting during this part of the journey, in part because food stores were growing scant, and in part because of an unspoken agreement with the Sacrifice guards watching over the slaves: Jarnulf made sure the guards got a large share of the meat he brought back, and they turned a blind eye to his roving the hills.

Still, we survived without him, Tzoja told herself. *I have always managed on my own.* But she also knew that things were different now, especially since Viyeki's wife Khimabu had discovered her. *She has always wanted me dead. Only Viyeki kept me safe. I would be a fool to think she will leave me alone just because Jarnulf threatened her.*

As if her thoughts had been a magical summoning, she looked up and saw Khimabu staring at her from only a few paces away. Tzoja gasped and almost fell over, but though she was startled and fearful, the knife in her hand gave her a little confidence. She noted that somehow, even in the middle of the wilderness, Khimabu had managed to arrange her hair in complicated braids, and her face had been put on as if by a court painter. Still, Khimabu's muddy boots and the stained, ragged hem of her dress showed that all was not quite as ordinary these days as she might wish.

"Do not gawk at me with your mouth open like a fish," Khimabu said in a mocking tone. "Where is your man—the savage who defends you? Has he left you already?"

"He's close." Tzoja gripped the hilt of the knife, the naked rabbit in her other hand forgotten for the moment. "He will be back soon. You had better hurry back to your own kind."

Khimabu waved a slender hand. "I go where I please, slave. And you need not clutch that knife so bravely. I need only raise my voice and the guards will come." She took a step closer. "Besides, if I had come to kill you, would I come alone and unarmed?" She raised her hands to show them empty. Tzoja saw dirt beneath the long nails that had once been without blemish but now were cracked and ragged; it gave her an almost childish pleasure.

"If you want nothing, then go away," she said, but did not take her eyes off Khimabu.

"I only thought to share some news with you, about something that I know matters to you—your daughter."

"Your husband's daughter, I think you mean."

"Yes, my husband's mongrel daughter." Khimabu smiled thinly. "The news has swept like wildfire through all the nobles and their households on this march. Your Nezeru has deserted the Sacrifices."

It felt like a fist had struck her in the stomach. She waited a moment until she was certain she could answer without her voice quavering. "Lies."

"Oh, I do not think so. Lady Gan'ua heard it from her husband, the lieutenant commander of the Owl Legion. Nezeru ran away from her Hand, was arrested, and then killed several guards and fled."

"I do not believe you." But it sounded so unlikely that it had a ring of truth, and Tzoja could not easily push it away. Already it was festering in her like a deep wound. "Get away and spread your poison elsewhere."

Khimabu smiled again, showing teeth this time, as if she had just taken a small but vicious bite of something. "It is only what my husband deserves, I fear—fathering a child on a thing like you! I hope his reputation can survive it when Nezeru is finally captured and executed."

"Shut your mouth, you witch." Tzoja got clumsily to her feet, cursing the sudden weakness of her legs. Even at the best of times, being around Viyeki's wife had always made her feel awkward, malformed. She brandished the knife, still slick with rabbit blood. "Get away, or no matter how many guards you summon, I will gut you before they can stop me."

Khimabu raised her hands in distaste. "You show the truth of your race's nature, mortal. When we leave you behind, no doubt those who remain will quickly fall back into the savagery in which we found you."

Her words surprised Tzoja, blurring her anger a little. "What do you mean, leave me behind?"

"Oh, but it is not for you to worry about such things, little mortal mother of a traitor," Khimabu said. "I doubt you will survive our departure in any case." Then she turned, and without a look back, made her way through the crowd of exhausted slaves as if picking her way across a pasture full of animal turds.

"Wh-what did she mean?" asked Vordis.

Tzoja jumped; she had forgotten that her friend was there. "I don't know. Pay her no mind. She is as full of venom as a cross adder. She knows she cannot harm my flesh without Jarnulf taking revenge, so she seeks to ruin my peace instead." Tzoja sat back down, but her hands were trembling. "Let us get the stew onto the fire. I will not let her poison words sicken me. I will not."

As Vordis went back to work sifting herbs into the heating water, Tzoja could already feel the corruption of doubt and fear working its way into every corner of her mind. *Oh, Nezeru, my only child, may all the gods protect you. What have you done?*

♛

Viyeki's could barely keep his thoughts coherent; anger and fear about this latest disaster threatened to stop his breath. The crudely cut stairway beneath the place where the collapse had happened was still littered with bits of rubble, which forced him to go carefully. By the time he reached the end of the tunnel, still some hundred paces of solid rock from being finished, he had achieved a little more control of himself.

One of the slaves carrying rubble up the tunnel looked up and recognized him. The slave dropped his basket and hurried toward him, grinning widely. Even as Viyeki recognized Cuff, the simple-minded mortal he had placed with the Delvers, the youth threw himself down at Viyeki's feet, bumping his forehead against the raw stone of the passage.

"Welcome, Father!" he said in Westerling, the mortal tongue. *"Thank you, Father!"*

Viyeki could only stare, caught by surprise.

"I am happy, so happy," said the mortal youth. *"The Vao people are so kind to me. And they know about the Angel Made of Stars who is coming for us! Thank you, Father!"*

Viyeki looked down at the kneeling mortal, caught between a confusion of tongues and a reflexive distaste for the over-exuberant greeting. *"I am not your father,"* he said at last.

"You are as good as any of the Fathers," Cuff insisted.

"Get up, young one. Enough of this. You must have work to do."

"Cuff likes to work," the youth said as he got back on his feet. Impulsively, he grabbed Viyeki's hand and kissed it before the magister could pull it back. *"You are a good man!"* He turned and went back to his basket, then set off up the tunnel under the heavy load, taking a hand from his burden to wave as he passed.

Viyeki could only shake his head and look at the smear of dirt the kiss had left behind. He wiped his hand on his opposite sleeve. "Why does he call me Father?" he said aloud, though he spoke mostly to himself.

One of the slender Tinukeda'ya who was watching over the slaves slid out of the shadows of the lamplit tunnel and moved toward him. Viyeki recognized Min-Senya, the apparent leader of the Delvers Pratiki had given him. "He does not mean you are his father of birth," said Min-Senya. "He was raised by mortal priests, who are all called 'Father.' It is his highest praise."

Viyeki waved it away. "I have been looking for you, Delver." He took a moment to calm himself again—already desperate fury was bubbling up inside him once more. "I have been to the site of the collapse."

"It is almost entirely cleared. We will have it properly restored by today's sunset."

"That is not the point I wished to raise, though every delay brings you and me closer to a very unpleasant fate." Viyeki's hands were shaking. He hid them in his sleeves. "The work was shoddy. It was almost inevitable that the tunnel should come down."

Min-Senya gave what might have been a shrug. "We are working at great speed, under threats and whippings from your overseers, High Magister. Mistakes happen in such situations."

His calmness further infuriated Viyeki. "We cannot *have* mistakes," he said through clenched teeth. "In only a matter of days, our queen intends to lead her army down this tunnel into the valley below to finish the war against our Zida'ya enemies. You cannot even imagine what will happen if the work is not finished."

"I think I can imagine, High Magister. You would be surprised how many of our people have become unwilling guests in the Cold, Slow Halls."

"You may not fear such a fate, but I do!" Viyeki again fought for calm. "Step away from the tunnel face. I would have private words with you."

"As you wish, High Magister." Min-Senya pointed to a spur tunnel off the main passage. "We can find privacy there."

Once they were alone in the rough-cut spur, a space not quite high enough for either of them to stand completely upright, Viyeki said, "We have more serious matters to speak of, you and I."

The huge eyes of the Delver blinked. "Yes, my lord?"

"I have worked with your kind before. And I have treated them well. I have seen what your people can do, the art you bring to shifting and cutting stone. And I have just examined the whole of the tunnel section that collapsed."

Another blink, slow and innocent as the stare of a sleepy child. "I am sure that with all your training and experience, you missed nothing, High Magister."

Viyeki could not escape the feeling that he was being mocked somehow. "Yes. And I have come to a conclusion that you will not like." He clenched his hidden hands into fists. "That collapse was no accident."

"That seems a strange thing to say, my lord," Min-Senya said slowly, but this time he held Viyeki's gaze with his own. "Do you think my people were responsible? But our lives are even more at risk than yours. As you say, if we fail here our punishment will be terrible. Why would we cause the collapse of our own tunnel?"

"I don't know. Out of some misguided sense of fighting back against the Hikeda'ya for enslaving you or mistreating you, perhaps. They say you Tinukeda'ya do not think of yourselves as individuals so much as a single creature made of many parts. Perhaps you are willing to sacrifice a few of your folk for what you see as a greater good." He was breathing hard now. He had the distinct sensation that he was losing an argument, which—under the circumstances—seemed preposterous but did not change what he felt. "Whatever the case, though, if you are intent on delaying or even destroying this tunnel, I will make certain your martyrdom begins this moment!"

Min-Senya regarded him for a few more heartbeats before speaking. "The young one called Cuff the Scaler called you a good person. Is he correct, High Magister?"

"What madness is this? We are speaking of the tunnel collapse."

"I ask only that you consider the question and answer it as best you can, Magister. Then I will know better how to give you my own answer in turn." He fixed Viyeki with his stare. "Are you a good person?"

"I could have you killed this moment!"

"Is that your answer?"

Viyeki had seldom in his life wanted so badly to hit someone, to do something violent with his own hands, but he resisted the impulse. "If I play your game, will you answer my questions and give me honest answers? Because I am desperate, Min-Senya. I do not fear for my own life so much, but I will not bring ruin on my clan and my household without a struggle!"

Min-Senya nodded. "Answer me, then I will happily tell you what you need to know."

Viyeki let out his breath in a gust. "So. As to your foolish, impudent question, I suppose the answer is yes. I think I am a good person. I do my duty to my queen. I try to show mercy when I can and protect those who need my protection. If that makes a person good, then I am good. Does that satisfy you?"

"What do your slaves think of you?"

"What? How should I know?"

"You said you try to protect those who need your protection. That is obviously your family, but what about your slaves? You are a high noble, the leader of your clan. You are lord over many slaves, both in Nakkiga and here. Do they think you are good?"

"I have always tried to treat them well—or at least with fairness."

"Do they eat well? Do have they have warm, comfortable places to sleep? Do you reward them when their labor brings you benefit?" Min-Senya spread a long-fingered hand. "Peace, High Magister, I do not mean you to answer all those questions this moment. I ask them only so that when our talk is finished, you may reflect on them later."

The insolence of this creature was making Viyeki more enraged by the moment, but he could not ignore the small ember of shame the Tinukeda'ya's words had kindled inside him. "I am mystified by everything you say, Delver. I seek only an answer. Why was the tunnel brought down, when its failure threatens all our lives—me, my Builders, and you and your fellow Tinukeda'ya as well."

"Vao," said Min-Senya calmly. "We call ourselves Vao. Tinukeda'ya is your people's name for us, not our own." He nodded. "Let me say something else now and I ask you to consider it carefully. Can you still your anger and listen, High Magister? It might be very important."

Viyeki's jaw was clenched so tight it made his head hurt, but he nodded.

"You said you have been told our race are like bees in a hive. That we are not separate creatures, but only parts of a single thing. That is one of the better understandings of us I have heard from your people, but it is still wrong. The answer is much more complicated than that—peace, Magister, peace! Hear me out, please." He spread his long fingers again. "We Vao who are fortunate enough to be aware of our race's story are different than the rest of our kind, different from those who have been changed by slave-breeding into near-beasts. But even those unlucky ones are still Vao. And those of us who are, let us say, more mindful, know that as long as one of our number lives a life of brutish suffering, those of us who have been given greater gifts must also suffer, because we are all one. One member of our race is *all* of our race. In learning that, you have learned at least a little bit of truth about the Vao." He smiled sadly, his solemn face for a moment taking on a very different aspect. "Yes, I see your impatience, High Magister. This is much to think about at a time when you have so many worries, so many fears, so let me tell you what you most want to know. Heed me well." He took a step closer, and for a moment Viyeki feared some kind of assault, but the Delver only lowered his voice. "When the moment comes for your queen and her armies to march down to the valley, we will have finished carving out this tunnel. And on the day they march, we of the Vao will all have been removed from these works, because your Hikeda'ya folk are careful. They will want us all penned together in case they decide we have earned the execution you spoke of."

"I am glad you say the tunnel will be finished—" Viyeki began.

The hand lifted again. "Wait, High Magister Viyeki—I have almost finished. On that day, in that hour when the queen's Sacrifices are about to set off, I ask you to come back to this place. Unlike my own folk, you will not be under restraint, and as leader of the Order of Builders and the chief of these works, you will be able to go where you please. I ask you to come back to this very spot—here, where we now stand."

"For the love of the Garden, why?" He felt as if his head might burst like a seedpod.

"I cannot tell you now, but when you come here, you will understand my request. And if you have thought about what I have been saying, you will recognize the choice that stands before you. Then you will decide once and for all what it truly means to be a good person, and whether you can think of yourself in that way." Finished, Min-Senya bowed deeply—something that surprised Viyeki as much as anything else the Delver had said or done—then turned and made his way out of the spur tunnel, back to the larger corridor where his kin, and Builder overseers, and dozens of mortal slaves were still working.

What madness is this? Viyeki wondered, his anger momentarily subdued by utter confusion. *Why would I come back here? What could he mean?* But he could find no answers, could only stand, swaying a little, as if he had been slapped in the face.

Jarnulf knew that the guards would not have wanted him to stray so far from the great camp in the snow-patched meadow, but he was not willing to stop yet. He had been tracking a herd of mountain sheep, driven on by an occasional glimpse of them in the heights above him, and even more by the thought of mutton to roast or put in the stew pot. But the winter sun was sliding swiftly down the sky, and he did not want to be caught so far up the hills if the weather changed.

He reached a scree of boulders just below the top of the nearest ridge. He could see plenty of tracks around him, even in the newest snow. It seemed to be a place many animals frequented: the prints were everywhere, with no single direction. He stared up at the ridge, then began to climb through the deep snow toward the top of the saddleback. He went slowly, since he had no idea how deep the snow was, and his life on Nakkiga and the high Nornfells had taught him that what seemed solidly packed could turn into nothingness beneath a traveler's boots in a heartbeat.

After only a few stumbles, none of them serious, he reached the ridge and found a rock that stretched above the snow, then climbed it to get a better view. As he surveyed the ridge, he saw no sign of the animals he had been tracking, only the confusion of hoofprints, and his stomach gurgled in sad protest. From this vantage point he could discern that their company's forced march had almost reached the spot where three ridges of high hills came together in a shape like a pair of arches pressed together, side by side. The far end of the valley, the place the guards called Tanakirú, was invisible beneath a thick mass of fog.

Some of the guards had let slip that their queen was waiting for them now at the northern end of the valley. Jarnulf, who only days earlier had witnessed Utuk'ku on her wagon heading south—had even tried to kill her with an arrow—found that hard to believe, but he had no doubt that if he and the others were truly being herded to Tanakirú, then the end of the valley must be the queen's ultimate destination as well. Was there some stronghold there? Did they plan a last stand against the Zida'ya forces whom he had heard were also in the valley? But Jarnulf could make no sense of that, either. Why would Queen Utuk'ku have left Nakkiga to fight in such a distant place? What possible advantage could there be here in the wasteland that was not doubly true of Nakkiga, a fortress in a mountain that no one had ever overthrown?

Jarnulf shook his head and pulled his hood up against the bitter wind. Loose snow drifted into the air, for a moment obscuring his vision completely.

When he turned his back on mysterious Tanakirú he saw his own footprints where he had climbed the slope, a solitary trail of shadowed holes leading all the way back down the hills. No guards or any of the Hikeda'ya were anywhere in sight, and a word suddenly leaped into his head.

Freedom.

And why not? Even if the Hikeda'ya soldiers decided to come looking for him, Jarnulf knew he could cross into the empty lands to the west before they ever reached the part of the road he could see. He had spent years living by his own wits and sinews in some of the coldest places in all the world while killing dozens of Hikeda'ya and leaving their corpses marked with the White Hand. Why should he continue as a prisoner of the Hikeda'ya when he could break from this spot and run free—when he could go anywhere he wanted?

The first thought that pushed back against this sudden excitement was of the two women he had left behind in the camp, Tzoja and Vordis. *How can I leave them to their fate? They are not bad people.* A brief and strange imagining took hold, of him saving the two women and them all living together as a sort of family. He could even marry one of them. Tzoja was older than he was, but only by a few years. She was comely enough, and he had spent enough time with her to know she had wit and more than a little courage.

But the thought would not take hold. He did not feel drawn to either Tzoja or her blind friend, handsome as they both were, and grateful to him as well. It was the face of a third female that filled his thoughts now, one to whom he owed far more than he did to a pair of mortal slaves.

Utuk'ku, the queen of death. The eternal monster who stole my mother and my sister away and let my brother die like an animal, whose followers penned me and beat me and starved me. God has given me a task—a holy task—and I cannot rest until she is dead. I have even given up my own name for revenge. No one called me by my true name again after my mother was taken away—never Gilhedur, but only "slave" and "you there." Even Weapons-Master Xoka never bothered to learn my name or even ask if I had one, but only called me San'nakuno—Sad Little Dog.

His anger had grown until he felt as though the snowflakes that touched his skin might melt into hissing steam. But another voice was in him too, quieter but just as compelling. *And how are you any less Utuk'ku's slave than you ever were?* it demanded. *You may think you are the master of your destiny, but if she is all you can think of, if you cannot rest while she lives, then your life is hers.*

No. He struggled to silence the cursed thought. *God wants me to do what I have sworn to do. That is not slavery to the witch, it is fealty to God.*

But all through his empty-handed trudge back down the snowy hillside to the road, he felt as if he was at war with himself—a war where neither side could hope to win a clear victory.

He presented Tzoja with the rabbit and a black grouse he had startled from its snow-hole on his way back. The grouse was large and excellently fat, and normally he would have been very pleased to bring it back, but his mood was so dark that he barely greeted Vordis, who was stirring the pot.

He did not at first notice how silent Tzoja was, how bereft of her usual good humor, as she began to pluck the grouse's feathers. When he finally saw it, he was ashamed of his own self-absorption. After all, these women were God's creatures too, just as he was. "You look grim," he told Tzoja as he wiped grouse blood from his hands onto his breeks.

"I am sorry for that," she said. "Thank you for bringing back more meat."

"I did not mean you owed me any words or apologies," he said carefully. He was still sometimes unsure about speaking with people who did not spend as much time alone as he did. "But you have a look on your face I do not like. Has something bad happened?"

She frowned but did not look up. "Khimabu was here."

"The woman who threatened you before—your master's wife?" In a moment he was rising to his feet. "Did she try to harm you? Have you been hurt?"

"No, no. It was nothing like that. She did not even come close to me. But she brought me bad news, and I cannot stop thinking about what she said. I do not want to believe it, but I think I do." She resolutely kept her eyes on the grouse she was denuding, but Jarnulf could see a shimmer of tears just below the lashes. "I am angry because I know it is what she wants—to anger me, to frighten me."

He sat down again. "What did she say?"

"She told me that my daughter had been disgraced. That rumors were being passed among the Hikeda'ya nobles that she had deserted her troop of Queen's Talons—that she was a traitor."

"Lies. It is only meant to trouble you. If you brood on it, if you let it pain you, she will have accomplished her purpose."

"I know. But the thing is, it could be true. My daughter was always headstrong. Even when she was small, she would scold me for my softness—for my mortal foolishness, as she called it, though she was half-mortal herself. She would even scold her father, who is high among the Hikeda'ya nobles."

Something caught at Jarnulf's thoughts, something he wanted to ignore but could not. "Tell me about your daughter," he said.

"She is my only child—doubtless the only child I will ever have." Tzoja tried to smile but did not manage it. "And though she may never think of me at all, I think always of her. I did not want Nezeru to be a Sacrifice, but her father said that the decision of Yedade's Box was law . . ." She had finally noticed. "Why are you staring like that?"

"Nothing." But his earlier moment of peace, the decision that had brought him back to the camp, was shattered. He stood up.

"Where are you going?"

"To relieve myself." He did his best to scrub the emotion from his words. "I will return."

He marched out across the camp. What he truly wanted was to be alone, but he knew that the guards would not let him cross their lines again now that dark had fallen. His hackles were up. He felt like an animal hearing the hunters close in.

Is this a trap? Have I fallen into some cruel Hikeda'ya device, like a rabbit stepping into a springe? Every instinct told him to run, to get away, to put distance between himself and Tzoja. *Nezeru, who went with me to Urmsheim, is this woman's daughter! How could that be mere happenstance?*

As he paced between the slaves huddled around numerous small fires over the snow-spattered meadow, Jarnulf gradually regained control. It could be sheer chance. And if it was not, what was different now than it had been? If Tzoja was part of some plot against him, why would she throw out Nezeru's name so easily, without even looking up to see how it struck him? The more he thought about it, the more he became convinced that it was truly pure chance. In fact, he decided, if he looked at it a certain way, it could even be a sign that God was watching over him, that all his trials, seemingly so separate, were but one great trial.

Another moment's thought and he suddenly realized something he should have grasped immediately—that it was his own kidnapping of Nezeru that had made her an outcast, a seeming traitor to her own kind, though she had not wanted that at all.

When he returned to the fire at last, he let Vordis fill his bowl with soup and sat down, but he did not taste anything he put in his mouth.

"Are you well?" Tzoja asked.

"I have thought about what the woman Khimabu told you of your daughter," he said as evenly as he could. "Even if it is true—and I do not say it is—I think you should put it in God's hands. Let Him guide you. It is all part of His plan."

"I wish I could believe that." She had not touched the supper she had made.

"You must!" he said and heard desperation in his own words. "You must. Without God's plan, Tzoja, all is meaningless."

18

The Last Navigator

"This makes no sense," Nezeru said.

The immense ship stretched away in either direction, both bow and stern disappearing into the valley mist. Above them, the mast's upper end was hidden by more roiling white fog. Still overwhelmed by the vessel's sheer, staggering size, Morgan could think of nothing worth saying.

"No sense," she said again. "By the gifts of the Garden, how did such an immense thing get here?"

"Perhaps it sailed here when the whole valley was full of water," Morgan offered.

"No," she said. "Even at its highest flow, the Narrowdark would barely have been a ribbon compared to this hull. And how could the ship have run against the cliff hard enough to embed itself without breaking apart? It is all beyond understanding."

Morgan looked down at the mists billowing around the monstrous ship, as if the vessel floated through a bank of clouds. "Perhaps it flew."

Nezeru gave him a sour look. "No one—not even the famous Navigator, Ruyan Vé—could make such an impossible thing happen." She called, "Kuyu-Kun! Come here!"

Morgan thought it sounded as if she summoned an underling, though he doubted Nezeru herself even recognized it.

Kuyu-Kun, the Voice of the Dreaming Sea, threaded his slow way through the miniature forest that had taken root atop the overgrown deck; his acolyte, Tih-Rumi followed close behind.

"I want to know how this monstrous ship got here," Nezeru said when he reached them. "What do your people's stories tell you?"

"Very little," Kuyu-Kun admitted. "There are many tales about the Eight Ships, but none about this one, and none describe how any of them were built. All history tells is that it was a great labor, with almost all my people engaged in it, and many of the Keida'ya as well."

"You tell me everything except what I want to know." Nezeru seemed oddly distraught, though Morgan could not guess why. "How could such a vast thing find its way into this narrow valley and then lodge in these cliffs?"

Again, Kuyu-Kun shook his head. "I cannot tell you, Nezeru of Nakkiga. It is well known that the Eight Ships sailed out into the Ocean Indefinite and Eternal, that after years they at last found this land and came to rest here. Nothing I have ever heard described the details of landfall. 'The ships at last came to rest in such fit places as they found,' are the words I recall."

"Useless," scoffed Nezeru.

Tih-Rumi stirred. "The story of our people is not meant for you, Hikeda'ya soldier. It is for the Vao. It is not meant to teach us how to build the Great Ships again, but how to live our lives and find the Garden once more."

"The Garden is gone."

"*Our* Garden is gone," said Tih-Rumi. "No one can argue with that." But the look on his face suggested that if he had wanted to, he could have.

"Other friends!" Qina shouted from the other side of the broad mast. "Waving and calling to us is Snenneq!" She pointed to where Snenneq had climbed twenty cubits or so up the mast in a quest for a better view, and was now climbing back down—carefully, but with a certain haste that filled Morgan with unease.

"What does he see?" He hurried toward the place where Qina waited.

"Friend Morgan!" Little Snenneq shouted as he neared the deck. "On the far side of the mast there is a building bigger than the others—much bigger. A temple, perhaps, or a palace!"

Nezeru and the others had joined Morgan, and together they waited for Snenneq. "It is like nothing else we have seen on the ship," he said when he had dropped the last, short distance onto the deck. "We must go and see it."

They quickly gathered up the odds and ends of their camp and followed Snenneq. They could not at first make out what he had discovered through the trees and other vegetation that grew around the mast. "You will see it soon," Snenneq assured them. He was so pleased he could barely contain himself. "It is large, though nowhere near so high as the mast."

And then suddenly they saw the top of the structure, a great wooden curve like an overturned bowl. As they approached, Morgan could see that Snenneq's find was indeed a very large structure—a dome that seemed to grow directly out of the witchwood deck. It was much flatter than the domes Morgan knew from cathedrals like St. Sutrin's or St. Tankred's, which were shaped like cups set upside down on top of the cathedral nave. If this great, rounded thing was a section of a sphere, the sphere itself would have been wider than even the immense ship. The dome was made of giant ribs of witchwood, wider at the bottom than where they joined at the top, with vast panes of clear crystal stretched between the curved ribs. A few of the panes were cracked, and the one nearest to them had a chunk of its upper edge missing.

Morgan was so absorbed by this strange sight that Little Snenneq's quiet voice startled him. "I could not see it before against the mist from the valley, but I swear that is smoke." The troll pointed to where a gray darker than the valley haze trailed from the broken pane, drifting clear of the dome for a little way before being shredded and dispersed by the wind. "Someone is alive in there," he said.

"Someone—or something." Nezeru's voice was tight. "Remember the kilpa. We approach without noise, weapons out. I will lead."

As they neared the wide, low dome, Morgan guessed it to be as big around as the wall of the Hayholt's Inner Bailey; like that wall, its top stretched far above their heads. Led by Nezeru, they snaked their way through the last patches of deck-forest until only naked witchwood lay between them and the dome.

"I will go first," Nezeru whispered. "I will go to the broken part and look in. Do not come forward unless I give you a sign."

Morgan had learned to throttle his chivalrous impulses. Of all their company, Nezeru was the best at such things: she knew it and he knew it too. "Be careful," was all he said.

"I could go with you—" began Snenneq, but Nezeru curtly shook her head before starting across the deck. She moved swiftly to the edge of the dome, then eased herself along just below the bottom of the crystal windows until she had reached the damaged pane. She crouched below it for a moment, listening, then slowly rose to peer through the place where the pane was broken. She did not move for a frustratingly long time, but at last she turned and waved the rest of the company forward until all had reached her and were crouching below the bottom of the great window.

"There are living folk in there," she whispered. "Snenneq, you were right—they have a fire. I cannot tell what manner of beings they are, but they do not look like either Hikeda'ya or Zida'ya—perhaps they are mortals, or more of Kuyu-Kun's Vao. But we must go cautiously." She turned to the old Tinukeda'ya. "You speak many of your people's tongues. Are you strong enough to go with me?"

"No!" said Tih-Rumi, "don't take my master. I know almost as many kinds of speech as he does, and I am not as important. Let me go with you."

"Well enough," she said. "But do not make even a sound unless in need. It may yet come down to a fight and we would be foolish to give up surprise."

As Morgan and the others watched, she led Tih-Rumi around the dome and out of their sight. After long, silent moments had passed, Morgan pulled himself up to peer over the sill of the huge, broken crystal pane, and immediately saw the fire burning on a bed of stone on the floor of the dome, a few fathoms below him, as well as several figures seated or lying near it. It seemed Nezeru had found an entrance on the far side because, as Morgan watched, he saw her appear in a doorway at the top of a stairwell inside the dome. A moment later, with Tih-Rumi cautiously following, she made her way down the long staircase, Cold Root in her hand. Morgan's heart beat a little faster as he saw some of the reclining figures notice her, but they did not seem hostile; none of them even rose as she and Tih-Rumi descended.

"What are you seeing?" Snenneq demanded. "Should I climb up beside you?"

"No. Stay where you are." Morgan knew he was being a little unfair, but he did not want to be distracted from Nezeru's safety by the talkative troll.

Some moments later Nezeru had climbed back up the stairs again. She turned and gestured broadly toward the very place Morgan was crouching, as if she could see him. *She knew I'd be watching out for her,* he thought, and felt a moment of pride. She was beckoning.

"She says to come ahead," Morgan reported as he lowered himself from the broken window.

"Are there living creatures there?" asked Kuyu-Kun. "Are they of our Vao people?"

"I can't tell. But there are definitely people of some kind."

As they made their way around the dome, they could finally see the rest of the way to the bow of the ship—*at least,* Morgan thought, *if that's which end that is.* As with what they could see of the other end, it seemed to maintain its wide curve, which made it broader than the prow of any other ship he had seen.

On the dome's far side they found stairs leading down to an elaborately carved entrance sunk below the level of the deck. The entrance to the dome was halfway open, and the door seemed built to slide into the wall of the dome instead of swinging on hinges; Morgan had never seen or heard of anything like it. As he led the others down the stairs, his own sword Snakesplitter now drawn and gripped tightly in his hand, his surprise and unease only grew deeper.

Although the fire they had seen burned merrily in its stone fire pit on the floor of the dome, the large, shadowed chamber was largely free of smoke, which seemed to be drawn up and out through the broken panes by the mountain winds outside. As Morgan's eyes grew used to the dark interior, he saw that the two dozen or so figures sitting or lying around the fire represented a range of different kinds of folk, dressed in a variety of ragged garments that suggested they might have come from anywhere in Osten Ard. A few had the pop-eyed faces and large hands common to Dwarrows, and others had the appearance of Niskies, long-armed and rough-skinned; but at least half looked to be the sort of workaday mortal folk Morgan might have met in Erchester's Main Row. All of them, Tinukeda'ya and ordinary mortals alike, were now watching the newcomers, but though Morgan thought he saw alarm on a few of the faces, none of them made any show of hostility.

But as Morgan's gaze moved up from the fire-circle, he saw something he had not noticed until that moment. "Blessed Saint Rhiappa," he said. "What in the name of our Lord is that thing?" He squinted. "And why in the name of God's Bloody Tree is Tih-Rumi on his knees, bowing to it?"

Nezeru mounted the last few stairs and put out an arm to keep the rest of the company from descending any farther. "Something is strange here," she declared.

Morgan, still staring, thought that went without saying.

At the base of the dome, opposite what must be the great ship's distant bow, stood a bizarre structure. At first glance it seemed a sort of shrine constructed of blocks of the same thick, transparent crystal as the windows overhead. In the middle of this shrine, behind a broad, flat table of some kind, sat a nightmare shape. All Morgan could see of the seated figure was its weird head—no, not a head at all but a bulbous helmet with staring circular eye holes and an equally round mouth that seemed frozen in an "oh!" of surprise. Tih-Rumi was prostrate on the deck before it, his arms stretched out in front of him in an attitude of worship.

Before Morgan could gather his wits and speak, old Kuyu-Kun pushed past him with surprising strength, hobbled down the stairs, then hurried across the intervening floor toward Tih-Rumi. The dome's inhabitants around the fire watched him pass, then turned their gazes back to the newcomers on the stair.

"What is that thing?" Morgan asked. "And who are these people?"

"Come," said Nezeru, leading them down toward the apparent shrine.

"Are you come in peace?" one of the dome-people asked Morgan in the Westerling tongue. He had a ragged gray beard and sleepy eyes. "Are you one of the dreamers too?"

Morgan felt neither inclined to answer, nor capable of stringing the words together to say so.

Kuyu-Kun had fallen to his knees beside his acolyte, and as the rest approached, Morgan could hear the two Tinukeda'ya murmuring and guessed they were praying. Up close, the motionless figure in the shrine seemed bigger than an ordinary person, but Morgan thought that was likely the armor the seated shape wore, a strange suit made mostly of rectangular crystal tiles held together by thin golden wires that must have taken innumerable hours to pound and stretch to such a fine degree. The crystalline blocks that made up the shrine itself also had golden traces in them that stretched through the crystal itself like minute golden veins. The gauntleted hands of the enshrined figure lay flat on the table, as if at any moment it might push back from it and stand. The table itself was a single slightly curved expanse of what almost looked like mother-of-pearl, a shiny, semi-translucent substance that seemed to throw back the light from the dome in all the colors of the rainbow.

"What is that? Is it a statue, or is it a dead person?" Morgan asked, but the others seemed just as baffled. He reached toward the polished tabletop, fascinated that stone could look so liquid, so changeable, but Kuyu-Kun suddenly and harshly said, "Do not touch it, Sudhoda'ya! It is sacred. This is both a treasure and a tomb." The old one climbed awkwardly to his feet; after a moment, Tih-Rumi also rose, but they did not take their eyes from the armored shape.

"Treasure?" said Nezeru. "Tomb? What do you two know of this? Tell us."

Morgan saw that several of the dome's other inhabitants had shuffled closer as if to listen, and though he did not see menace on any of the faces, their nearness still worried him. He stepped between Nezeru and the onlookers, his hand on Snakesplitter's hilt.

Kuyu-Kun raised his thin arms toward the shrine as if in invocation. "This is the armor—and within it, the body—of one the greatest of all the Vao, the

Navigator's beloved eldest daughter. She gave her life for our people and has waited here all these years without proper ceremony, without thanks, without any of the glory she deserved."

"She? How can you tell?" Morgan asked.

"Because it is a famous story whose ending was never known—until now," said Kuyu-Kun, turning preternaturally bright eyes on them. He was breathing hard, as though he had just run a great distance. "She disappeared from our history after the ships fled the Garden. Some said that she must have died during the journey to this land, but no tale of the escape contains her death, and the wisest of the Vao have long argued over what might have happened to her. Look—do you see the crest?" He pointed to a fin on top of the figure's helmet, carved from crystal and pierced by more of the tiny golden wires. "That is the symbol of the First Wave, and we know it was the sign of Ruyan the Navigator's clan. This can only be her, the lost one—Ruyan Ká, the last navigator. We have found her after all these years!"

"What do you think you have found?" Nezeru sounded angry. She pointed to one of the figure's gauntleted hands where the crystal-tiled sleeve had pulled away from the gold-threaded glove, revealing a finger's breadth of naked brown bone. "You have found a dead thing."

"She is not dead," said Kuyu-Kun calmly. "She is all around us. I can feel her."

Nezeru shook her head. "Old stories and lies—things that cannot be. Why does nobody speak about things that are real, that we can see? Below us in the valley this moment, my people and the Zida'ya are slaughtering each other for reasons no one can explain to me. And we stand inside something that has remained a secret across many mortal centuries—ten Great Years of silence! But all you offer me are fables about living corpses. Does that . . . thing . . . look alive to you?" She turned to Morgan, and he thought he saw a deep disappointment lurking behind the unfeeling, Sacrifice-trained mask. "I am going on the deck to breathe air that may not be so tainted with madness and pointless belief," she said.

Morgan watched her go, as did several of the dome's other inhabitants. He wanted to hurry after her, but it was clear that she did not want company.

Nezeru eventually came back but remained silent for the rest of the long evening. The two Tinukeda'ya, Kuyu-Kun and Tih-Rumi, seemed uninterested in anything but the armored cadaver they had named Ruyan Ká, but the trolls and Morgan found seats for themselves beside the fire and, at the invitation of the dome's other residents, shared a meal of fish.

"One of the waterfalls comes down the cliffs on the far side of the ship," said a mortal who looked to be at least part Niskie, a man of middling age who called himself Yek Fisher. "Beneath it there is a pool that cannot be seen that eventually spills down into the gorge. With a long enough line, we can reach it, and it has given us fresh water for a long time. We fish in it every day for our food, too. There are almost two score of us living here."

"Is that all?" asked Little Snenneq. "In all this great ship?"

"Oh, no," said Yek. "Most who were summoned are afraid of the Navigator—" he nodded respectfully toward the mummy of Ruyan Ká—"and have made their homes on the deck below this one."

"How were you summoned?" said Morgan. "Why are you living here, so far from your homes—from everything?"

"Because of the dream," Yek explained. "We have all had the dream. It brought us here. We are needed, and so she called us."

"Who is call you?" asked Qina.

"The angel made of lights, as some name her. The Mother, as others say. But we all know her, and we have all heard her call."

"Do you speak for the others here, Yek the Fisher?" Snenneq asked. "Are you their chief?"

"We have no chief. But I came the farthest," he said proudly. "In Bayun Risa of the southern islands, I heard the call. Six nights in a row I had the dream. My wife could not hear the calling—my children could not hear it either." For a moment his expression grew troubled, even mournful. "I had to leave them behind. It was hard, so hard, but they could not hear what I heard. They did not believe me. But I knew. And I was right."

"Right about what?" asked Nezeru. "Squatting beside a fire in an empty ship? Is this what you dreamed of?"

The bearded man who had earlier spoken to Morgan now leaned forward. "The hour has not yet come. We do not know when it will, but when it does, we will be remade. The Garden will bloom again."

"The Garden is lost," said Nezeru, looking out of the dome at the sky they had been denied so long. The mist had retreated with the sun, at least from above the great ship, and she stared up at the twinkling evening stars as though they alone made some kind of sense.

"I am Little Snenneq of Mintahoq," the troll told them. "And this is Qina, my betrothed, as well as Morgan of Erchester and Nezeru of Nakkiga. We did not come because of the dream, but because our path led us here."

"Just because you did not know the dream was in you," said Yek with a tiny smile, "does not mean the dream did not bring you. You should meet the others now, since I have already told you my name. This bearded fellow is Halwende. Beside him sit Daffn and Conn, sister and brother out of old Crannhyr on the Hernystir coast. Those over there are all members of the Suru clan, Gen-Suru, Je-Suru, and Shim-Suru. They come from Perdruin and call themselves Niskies." He went on to introduce several more of the dome's inhabitants, until Morgan had completely lost track of who was who. "And lurking over there behind them," Yek finished, "not with us but not going away, as is his wont, is our friar."

Morgan inspected the thin-faced man. "Is he truly an Aedonite monk?"

"Nobody is certain," said Halwende. "He seldom speaks, but when he does it is mostly with words from Aedon's holy book."

"*As Crexis descended into madness,*" the friar suddenly intoned, "*Zinovia his wife called all the scryers to Nabban to learn why the gods had cursed the Imperator in that cruel way.*"

"As you see," said Yek Fisher with a chuckle.

"Are there any other people on this ship?" Morgan asked.

Yek gave him a look of surprise. "Any other people? There are hundreds on this ship, and that is only those who look like us. Most of them do not come here, though. As I said, they are frightened of—" he gestured toward the corpse of the navigator—"that. But countless creatures live on the ship, and I warn you that some of them are dangerous. A clan of giants lives at the stern end, in the depths of the hull. They sometimes leave the ship to hunt . . . but sometimes they don't." He shook his head. "That is why we stay here, and why a fire is always burning. The giants do not like this part of the ship."

"And what are you all waiting for, all you people and beasts?" asked Little Snenneq.

"The end of the dream to be revealed," said Halwende. "The Garden to be born again. That was promised to us."

"But promised to you by whom?" Snneneq prodded. "Who spoke in your dreams?"

"We told you—an angel made of light," said Yek Fisher. "Now, if you are truly friends and peaceful folk, you may share our sleeping place."

They thanked him and began to make places for themselves to lie down on the floor of the domed chamber. Morgan was exhausted and craved sleep, but for a long time he could not stop thinking about hungry giants in the ship's dark depths.

In his dream, Morgan was again clambering in the crystalline tunnel through the mountains, but this time something seemed different. A light shone upon them—though he had no idea of its source—and the angled facets reflected it in a thousand different colors. But this time the colors came not from the crystals themselves, but from countless butterflies locked inside them, frozen like fish in a winter stream.

Come to me, a voice said—one he had heard before. *I beg you. I am not strong enough to reach any farther.*

He moved forward, surrounded by glittering wings, all motionless as chips of stained glass. As he moved deeper, he could see that not all the butterflies were trapped in crystal: a few crouched in the open, wings moving so slowly he had to stop and stare to see that they lived. The farther into the passage he went, the more butterflies he saw, but the free ones seemed barely more alive than those entombed in the crystal walls.

At last, he came to a place where the walls narrowed and came together. A figure stood waiting there, wrapped in pale strands like a corpse in a winding sheet. He could see nothing of what lay beneath the shroud of silken threads except the eyes, which gleamed through the strands like molten gold.

May the Garden bless you, said a female voice. *You have come.*

I know you, I think. His own voice, like hers, seemed to issue not from his mouth, but from his thoughts. *You spoke to me before.*

Yes. Somehow, I can speak to you but not to any of my own blood, and I am growing desperate. Come closer, child. I am weary beyond telling.

He took a step forward. *What do you want? And why have you chosen me to hear you?*

Because no one else can. Her words were full of frustration and regret. *No, that is not true. One other can hear me, and I have told her everything that I could—all that I could see of what lies ahead.*

About what lies ahead? Even in his dreamy, detached state, Morgan felt a chill of fear. *I don't think I want to know.*

You must. Those I love are deaf to me because of the One Who Will Not Cross Over and her grip on the Three, but we may yet thwart her—somehow.

All those words and ideas were mysterious to him, swirling through his head like windblown leaves, like floating ash. *I don't understand any of that.*

Such things are not for you to understand, young one, but I have a boon to beg of you. You must find my son and tell him not to despair, and not to abandon the fight until he has received the mortal's gift.

Your son? For a moment Morgan was confused again, then he realized who this ghostly presence must be. *Do you mean Jiriki?*

Yes, my son. He is our people's protector now, but he must fight alone. His sister has her own battle, one that has not finished yet.

But why me?

I told you—because I can choose no one else. Her frustration buffeted his thoughts. *No more questions, mortal, I beg you! My strength is fading, and the Queen of Deceit pulls her web ever tighter. Her attention is elsewhere, but that will last only a moment, and I have one more thing to tell you while I can, mortal—though you will not like to hear it.*

The tunnel and the crystal-captured butterflies had faded into darkness. All he saw was the shrouded face and the smoldering golden eyes. *Then don't tell me,* he thought. *I'm frightened enough. I didn't ask to be here. I want nothing to do with the Norns or their witch-queen.*

Please, mortal youth! I am fading back into my prison again, but I must warn you. For a moment the eyes seemed to grow before him, blazing like twin suns. *You cannot imagine what I can see from where I am—the meandering lines of past and present, of might and might-not, cryptic as the aimless burrowing of beetles in a piece of wood. But one who travels with you is at the center of more lines than any other, a web of possibility and doom the like of which I have never seen or even dreamed of. But what makes me truly fearful is that at every step of the journey, she has been under the watchful eye of her queen. In the shadow-realm of possibility, she is the city at the end of every road, every track. And she is under some sort of protection from the silver-masked one herself.*

Do you mean Nezeru? How can that be? She protected me—fought against her own people!

The silk-wound specter continued as if he had not spoken. *I cannot see the ends of these tracks, only their existence. But I have a cold, grim feeling, and your companion is at the heart of it. She has been chosen as the carrier of some great doom, and it is a doom that Utuk'ku herself does not fear. The queen has protected this one's path again and again.*

I don't believe it. Nezeru can't—she wouldn't.

Give my warning to my son, I beg you. And beware of your Hikeda'ya warrior. Something about her is not right . . . not right . . .

Morgan woke in darkness but for the red glow of the fire's coals. He sat up, heart hammering. Had the dream been real? Had he truly just been told that Nezeru could not be trusted?

He looked around the domed chamber. All the others were sleeping, but there was no sign of Nezeru.

She doesn't sleep like we do, he told himself. *Why should she stay here with the rest of us through hours of silence?* He looked up through the dome to the bright points in the sky, gleaming through the wisps of fog. *She's probably just out looking at the stars.* But it took him a long time to get back to sleep again.

19

Taxing Red Pig Lagoon

They had ridden far ahead of the rest of their company when Ayaminu suddenly fell silent. "I smell horses," she said after a few moments. "And armor."

"As do I," said Tanahaya. "But surely it is only Dunao and the others."

"I do not think—" Ayaminu began, then a black arrow suddenly appeared, quivering, in the base of her saddle next to her thigh. Tanahaya had only an instant to gape as several more arrows snapped past, then Ayaminu drove her war-horse sideways into Tanahaya's mount and together they crashed off the track and into the trees. In the flimsy shelter of trunks and intertwined branches they slid from their saddles and tried to put the widest trees between themselves and their enemies. Tanahaya was not even certain where the arrows had come from. Ayaminu already had her bow drawn, and immediately let fly—one, two, three arrows in a matter of moments. Tanahaya had her own bow now, and when Ayaminu had loosed her last bolt, Tanahaya leaned out and sent several shafts speeding after Ayaminu's, toward a copse on the far side of the road a small distance uphill from where they had been riding.

"Curse me for talking so much and so loudly without paying proper attention!" Ayaminu was a little breathless but seemed otherwise composed. "Those are Hikeda'ya arrows, as you must have noticed. We have walked into a trap."

More arrows buzzed through the foliage, one passing so close to Tanahaya that it flew between her bow and bowstring. "What can we do?" she whispered.

"This," said Ayaminu, then raised her voice. "Soldiers of Nakkiga, do you know what you do? Do you have any idea who you attack?"

"We do not care, Little Mother," called a voice from the distant trees. "We will learn who you are as we pluck our arrows out of your body."

To Tanahaya's utter astonishment, Ayaminu dropped her bow to the ground and walked around her horse toward the road. Tanahaya tried to grab her arm as she passed but Ayaminu shook her off and stepped out onto the track; her arms were raised, and she looked more like someone welcoming strangers than surrendering. "Come out," she called, "unless you fear me, brave Sacrifices."

"We are more than mere Sacrifices," the voice replied. "We are Queen's Talons, and we are your death."

"Ah. So, you truly do not know me." Standing in the center of the track, Ayaminu looked small and very vulnerable. Tanahaya wanted to run and drag her to safety, but something in the strangely calm way Ayaminu waited held her back. "You do not know me, but you will. I am Ayaminu of High Anvi'janya. If your masters have not taught you about your greatest enemies, then I pity you. If you are frightened, I will allow you to flee now. But if you have courage, step out and face me. I am old, but the blood of mighty ancestors is in my veins. Tall Kuroyi was my father, who slew the Snowdrake in the heights of the mountain. My mother was Minasennu of the Pool, great in lore. Come out and face me, little Nakkiga cave-crickets. Or is attacking from the shadows your only skill? Who were your ancestors, that you shame them so?"

Astonishingly, the arrows stopped flying. And though Tanahaya was stunned by the risk Ayaminu was taking, she was also becoming aware of a rhythm in her words: she spoke at carefully chosen intervals, as if declaiming a poem. And with each word spoken, even Tanahaya found it harder to do anything but listen.

"Come out, scuttling minions of the northern tyrant," Ayaminu continued. "Utuk'ku has told you that the Zida'ya are soft and decadent, too weak to defend themselves or their lands. So why do you fear? Step out of the shadows—step out! Show your courage to the light. Unless you fear one who has cast her arms away and stands before you with empty hands."

"You will not defeat us with words, witch!" shouted the one who had spoken before, but this time the voice had lost some of its certainty.

"I do not seek to defeat you. I seek only to know who has brought me my death. After all, I have lived long and I fear nothing. But I feel sorry for those who must kill from in hiding. In the days of our greatness, no Keida'ya warrior fought without challenge. Even those who dared to face the great worms did not strike from hiding but rode out to face those beasts in clean daylight. Who are you? Were your ancestors slaves, that you hang back?"

A male Hikeda'ya strode out of the trees and onto the track, black-armored, arrow drawn and pointing at Ayaminu's heart. No more than a dozen paces separated them. "I am no coward," he cried. "I was chosen by the Mother of All herself!"

"Ah," said Ayaminu as if in disappointment, "only one brave spirit out of a whole Talon? The greatness of Nakkiga has been lost, it seems—how sad! When I lived in ancient Hikehikayo, I knew many high ones of your folk. They would be ashamed to see you cower and strike from ambush. The Tearfall must have become a flood at seeing its children so shamed by a single Zida'ya. Pity, pity, pity."

Even as it took on a weird, subtle music, Ayaminu's voice kept growing louder; it now had the relentless, pounding feel of an ocean beating on the shore, a rhythm that Tanahaya could feel echoed by her heart, as if the mistress of Anvi'janya's words had reached into her and taken command of her body. Where a moment earlier she had decided that leaving her hiding place in the copse was foolishness, it was now all she could do not to walk out of the trees. Then a second dark-armored Talon came down toward the road. A moment later two more emerged, but haltingly, as if their legs forced them to do what their hearts resisted.

"Your song is sour," said the first Talon, but his arrow now sat on a slackened bowstring. "It is old and middling strong, but the queen has given us our own Singer, and soon she will make a song that will leave you weeping in the mud."

"Let her come out and sing, then," said Ayaminu. "I do not fear Nakkiga's Order of Song. All those of my blood are born with that song inside them. We do not have to be taught, like children, how to weave the stuff of the unseen world." The oceanic rhythms still moved beneath her words, but now Tanahaya thought she heard a real sound, a rumble like the crash of the tide, and this roar did not fade and return, but only grew. "Come out of hiding, little Singer," Ayaminu called. "Let me hear your pretty voice. Let us sing together and we will see who owns the melody when the song is ended."

A female Hikeda'ya appeared from the copse, chanting loudly, fingers splayed in a gesture Tanahaya had never seen. Ayaminu raised her voice but did not counter with any gesture of her own. A moment later the Singer stumbled and sank to one knee.

"White Bear Song," said Ayaminu, bemused, "—and she tried to use it against a Proficient!"

The other Hikeda'ya were beginning to shake off the power of Ayaminu's words, so the Mistress of Anvi'janya lifted her voice again.

"There is no shame in weariness," she called, her voice compelling even to Tanahaya, who felt herself sway a little. "No shame. Sleep comes, strength fades, body craves for rest—"

Even as she chanted, the roaring noise continued to grow louder, and suddenly it burst upon the road like an arriving thunderstorm: Dunao and the rest of the Zida'ya company had appeared at the top of the rise in a cloud of rainbow colors and glinting blades. Before the Hikeda'ya soldiers could dive off the path, a flurry of arrows sped toward them and smacked into witchwood armor with a noise like a hailstorm on a slate roof. Within moments three of the enemy were down, including the Singer, and another was crawling for the shelter of the undergrowth. The fifth, who had somehow evaded the arrow storm, turned and began to run. An instant later several arrows struck him in the back and he fell heavily and did not move.

"Have you lost your wits, Lady?" Dunao cried as the Zida'ya moved forward to examine the fallen bodies. "Why would you ride off without us? You know that these lands are now the haunt of Utuk'ku's soldiers."

"Spare me your scorn, Rider," said Ayaminu. "I see one of our enemies still lives. I wish to question him."

"As well might we question a fish or a bird," said Dunao angrily.

Tanahaya could see something moving where the Hikeda'ya had waited in ambush, so she signaled for a few of the Anvi'janyan conscripts to accompany her and climbed toward the copse with an arrow ready on her bowstring. There were always five of Utuk'ku's dedicated minions in any Talon, but that did not mean there might not be slaves or other servants waiting there.

The Talon's mounts had been tied deep in the trees, out of sight of the road. Tanahaya found six horses in all, but one of them looked very different than the others: a struggling figure was hanging upside down over the black mare's saddle—perhaps a captured Zida'ya prisoner. Tanahaya moved closer and saw to her great surprise that it was a mortal.

"Please, do not kill me," he said in Westerling. *"I am not one of them. I was taken."*

"I have no intention of killing you—especially if what you say is true," she replied in the mortal tongue. *"Calm yourself."* She examined him and saw that his arms were bound with cruel knots, so that it looked as if twin black snakes had entwined around them.

"My mother named me Tanahaya, and I am here to help. Hold still, and I will free you," she said, then set down her bow and cut through the rope that still bound him to the saddle. The mortal fell to the ground.

"Peace!" he said, groaning. *"My head is broken, I think. You said you would not harm me."*

"*I said I would not kill you,"* she replied. *"But I suggest you do not move now, or you may find yourself less a finger or two."* She cut through his bonds with a single flick of her sharp blade.

"Oh, Sweet Elysia, Mother of Mercy," he moaned, rubbing his hands together as though to clean them of some invisible stain. *"The blood is out of them and my fingers feel like they are on fire!"* He looked around suddenly. *"Ki'ushapo!"*

Tanahaya was startled. *"Why do you speak that name?"*

"I was traveling with him. The Norns attacked us. He is here somewhere."

"Alive?"

"He was when I last saw him."

She left the mortal rubbing his arms and grimacing, and with the help of the other Zida'ya, began to search the grove. They quickly discovered Ki'ushapo propped against a trunk, bound and insensible but still breathing: the Hikeda'ya had likely been questioning him when she and Ayaminu came down the road. Finding one of Jiriki's closest companions here in the clutch of their enemies frightened Tanahaya greatly. Was Ki'ushapo the only survivor of some battle? Was that what had happened to Jiriki? She called for Ayaminu, who looked him over carefully, touching his forehead and chest. "He will live, scholar," she announced, "but we should make camp here until we know how badly he is hurt." Her eyes narrowed. "And I will have questions for your mortal prisoner."

When they had begun to build a fire, Tanahaya settled the mortal and brought him a water-skin.

"How is Ki'ushapo?" he asked.

"Alive," Tanahaya told him. "He is being tended now."

As she watched him drink, she could hear Ayaminu and Dunao speaking sharply to each other. Fearful they might have heard some news about Jiriki, she went to find them. But instead of wounded Ki'ushapo, the pair stood over a dark-armored figure, the only member of the Queen's Talon who had survived the Zida'ya attack.

"I will tell you nothing," the Hikeda'ya soldier said, his white face drawn with pain from the arrow in his upper chest. "You know I will not betray the Mother of All. You may put me to any torture you wish but you will get nothing from me but silence. Scum of the Garden, you can take my legs, take my arms, take all my limbs, it will not loosen my tongue."

"Tie him," said Ayaminu, but the words were scarcely out of her mouth when the Talon kicked out at her and tried to roll away. Without a word, Dunao leaped forward and hacked through the Hikeda'ya's neck with a single stroke of his long witchwood sword. The head fell and rolled a step to one side where it stopped, face upward. Like molten metal cooling, the dark eyes hardened into their final stare.

"Dunao, you are a fool." Ayaminu's disgust was plain. "There was no need to kill this creature. We could have learned from him."

"Do not name me so!" Dunao said in a low, furious voice. "You know that a Talon cannot be made to speak. They are trained to ignore even the greatest pain. This one would have stayed silent no matter what we did."

"Do you tip over the shent board when you are losing, instead of trying to learn from your opponent's strategy?" she demanded. "A good questioner can pull secrets even from one who refuses to speak. There is much to be learned from silence."

Dunao only looked at her, then turned away. "In truth," he said over his shoulder, sounding a little sullen, "I am a very good shent player, my lady."

"We will tend Ki'ushapo here tonight," Ayaminu declared. "And we will bury these dead Hikeda'ya before we ride again. They are our kin, remember."

"Your *kin* would have murdered you if we had not arrived to save you," snarled Dunao.

"Even the highest and oldest families have their disagreements," was all she said.

Jesa was relieved to see so many others gathered in the queen's tent at the center of the camp that had been set up outside Erchester. Miriamele had sent for her with no explanation, and even as Jesa handed Serasina over to the nurse, she had been wracking her memory, trying to imagine what she might have done to make the queen angry. The wind on the hilltop was bitterly cold; she walked as fast as she dared without breaking into a run.

The queen looked up at Jesa's entrance and waved her to one of the few empty seats along the trestle table. The wind strummed at the walls, making the candles flicker and dance. There were no servants to wait on those gathered, only soldiers in Erkynguard green tabards.

Jesa seated herself as unobtrusively as she could at one end of the bench, next to Lord Tiamak and Lady Thelía—not the most comfortable spot after her marriage conversation with Tiamak. But Thelía nodded to her and smiled, which brought Jesa a little ease. Countess Rhona, the queen's close friend and confidante, sat on the other side of the table, engaged in quiet conversation with Baron Snell, who had been at Winstowe with the queen's husband, King Simon. Beside him sat Lord Norvel, who had come on the ship with Jesa and the queen from Meremund, and now watched the proceedings from behind half-shut lids.

Or perhaps he is napping, thought Jesa, and did not know whether to be amused or worried.

Nearly a dozen others had gathered around the board, including Lord Captain Zakiel and the old knight Porto. Zakiel, who had suffered badly during the attack on the Hayholt, looked like a man bravely hiding a great deal of discomfort. When the queen gave the order to prepare the army to leave Erchester, Zakiel had begged Miriamele to let him lead the Erkynguard contingent because of the hatred he had developed for the traitor Pasevalles. Sir Porto, though, looked as though he wasn't entirely certain why he had been included.

"We will set out for Winstowe with tomorrow's morning light," the queen said. "Is all prepared, both to lay the siege and to protect what we leave behind?"

Zakiel stirred and got to his feet. The wounds on his head had healed, but scars still showed beneath his dark hair. "Captain Kenrick says the soldiers we are leaving behind are not happy with being forced into double-duty—"

"We are at war," said Miriamele flatly. "We will find a way to repay our brave subjects for their labors when the criminal Pasevalles has been captured and the threat ended. Until then, every Erkynlander must do his share. Thank you for your report, Lord Captain."

"But they are also having to guard the royal granaries both night and day," Zakiel said. "The people are restless and frightened, and many are hoarding food."

"I would be surprised if they did not. But that is why we are leaving Captain Kenrick and a sizeable force to watch over the city in Duke Osric's name. Kenrick has plenty of soldiers—almost as many as we do, but we must bring down a defended castle. Again, I thank you, Lord Captain."

Zakiel nodded and sat down, keeping his eyes fixed on the table.

The queen surveyed the gathered counselors. "We all know what Pasevalles has done to this kingdom," she said. "To all the kingdoms of the High Ward. He has murdered our loved ones and betrayed our trust. In a very few days we will be outside his hiding place at Winstowe."

"Are we so certain that Pasevalles is there?" asked Baron Snell. "If we are wrong, it could give him time to make his way out of Erkynland—"

"He sent Count Aglaf's son to kill me—or to kill the duchess, at least."

Miriamele's expression was as cold as the hilltop wind. "I think that is proof enough that Lord Tiamak was right in his guess, my lord."

"But a siege is a very complicated thing," said Norvel, still looking half-asleep. Jesa suspected the old nobleman might have drunk a bit too much the night before.

"Norvel is right," said Snell. "Even when we arrive, Majesty, we will have to look over the land, see what defenses have been added to Winstowe, and so on."

"We will do what needs to be done, and we will do it swiftly," she said flatly. The queen and Baron Snell had differed on a few issues in the past days, and Miriamele had been short with him more than once. "We cannot rebuild the kingdom while the traitor remains free."

"But perhaps Lord Snell is right, Majesty," Tiamak offered. "Perhaps we should not be in too much of a hurry. Of course, we all want Pasevalles captured . . . or dead. But as I told you, we have no maps of the mine tunnels that surround Winstowe Castle—those are among the books Pasevalles took with him—and as things stand, we cannot put enough men into the field to cut off all the traitor's possible avenues of escape. The Winwood is several leagues across, and the forest is not the only spot there are likely to be abandoned tunnels. But the coming year will bring us more help, soldiers from other parts of Erkynland and the High Ward. King Hugh of Hernystir—well, he is not only no longer an ally, but a problem we must eventually deal with, so there will be no help from that quarter. But surely Grimbrand in Rimmersgard would be willing to send us some of his own warriors."

"Grimbrand has enough problems with Hugh gnawing at his southern border, not to mention the encroaching Norns, I think," said Miriamele. "He will not be helping us soon, though it is still worth asking."

"This is new to me," Snell declared. "What problems does Grimbrand have with the Norns?"

"From our best knowledge," Miriamele told him, "after burning the Hayholt, the Norn Queen Utuk'ku has not retreated to Nakkiga in the Nornfells but is continuing her campaign at the north end of the Wealdhelm near the Rimmersgard border."

"She campaigns? In the White Waste?" said Snell. "But why? There is nothing there!"

"Nothing we know about, at least, Baron," said Miriamele. "But as our current situation makes only too clear, ignorance is not the same as safety. At the moment, though, we can do nothing about Utuk'ku except to be grateful her armies are far away." She spread her hands flat on the tabletop. "What Lord Tiamak says makes sense, but I do not choose to accept it. The longer we wait, the greater likelihood Pasevalles builds his power in Winstowe, perhaps kidnapping the kinfolk of local lords, as he has done with Aglaf's family, to force them to join him. Or if he sees his fortunes fading in Erkynland, he might escape through the mines, and we will have to find him all over again, while in the meantime he creates more mischief."

"Still, is there any way to keep him bottled up with the scant resources we have?" asked Tiamak. "As I said before, Majesty, my lords, we have no idea how many old tunnels there might be or where they open outside of the castle, and the land around Winstowe is full of steep crags and deep dells. How can we hope to find every bolt hole the traitor might use?"

Jesa waited for someone else to say something, but a grim silence had fallen over the council table. She finally spoke up, with the feeling of one who dives from an uncomfortable height. "I . . . I think I see a way."

All the faces at the table turned toward her, some with obvious looks of skepticism.

"Do you?" But Miriamele's voice was not sharp, only inquiring. "For those who do not yet know her, this is Jesa, Tiamak's countrywoman from the Wran. She saved Duchess Canthia's only surviving child from grassland mercenaries, then helped me escape from a madman and make my way back to Erkynland. Without her bravery and wit, we would not be gathered here today. So, what are your thoughts, Jesa?"

Jesa almost wished the queen had not praised her, because now everyone was watching and waiting for her to speak. She rose and stood on unsteady legs. "When I was a child in Red Pig Lagoon, they sent a tax collector from Kwanitupul because the governors there thought we were giving too little. Several village elders came to our house to talk about it, and I remember them laughing. 'Once again,' one of them said, 'they send someone to find our wealth and take it from us. Do they not know how many hiding places there are? And yet they send this person, this Wrannaman who is in truth no real Wrannaman, who has never lived anywhere but the governor's palace in Kwanitupul, to find out our secrets.' And, of course, the tax collector came, but went away cursing at his meager harvest from Red Pig Lagoon—a few skinny old pigs and a few bags of rice. When he was gone, the elders of the village brought all their food and beer back out again and we had a festival."

The faces around her continued to stare.

"I'm not following," said Baron Snell, breaking a long moment's silence. "Can someone explain what the girl means? Tax collectors? Pigs?"

"She has just said what she means." Miriamele looked weary, but also a little angry. "If you want explanations, ask her. Jesa, they do not understand—but I think I do. Tell them how this speaks to our problem today."

Jesa had thought she was ready for the doubtful looks the others had given her simply for daring to speak in such august company, but she was a little shaken. "What I mean is, the people—the people who live in a place, whether it is Red Pig Lagoon or . . ." she turned to Miriamele. "What is the name of the valley where we are going, Majesty? Where the traitor hides?"

"The Fingerdale," said the queen.

"Whether it is Red Pig Lagoon or this Fingerdale," Jesa continued, "the people who know things are the people who live there. Like my folk, they have no maps. I do not think there is a single map in all of the Wran, but the people of my village knew where to hide things and where to find them again when the tax collector was gone."

"I am glad someone is finally speaking some sense," said Countess Rhona loudly. "I was about to say something myself. Nad Glehs—*my* home—is also full of old, half-forgotten places, barrows, mines, and ruins. But the people who live on the land know them and have names for all, and stories about them."

"May God strike me blind if I understand any of this!" said Snell. "Perhaps I am losing my wits. Can no one speak clearly?"

"I doubt you are losing your wits, my lord," said Miriamele. "The idea is that if we want to find out where the tunnels are, we must ask the common people who live around Winstowe. We must rely on them to show them to us. Even if they do not go into them, they will know where they are."

"Ah!" said Snell. "Yes, I see it now. Ha. There is good reason in that." He turned to Norvel. "You must listen more carefully."

"Me?" said Norvel, startled for the first time into opening his eyes all the way.

"So instead of having to surround all of the Fingerdale with soldiers to keep Pasevalles imprisoned in Winstowe," Miriamele continued "—an amount of soldiers we obviously do not have—we need only let the folk who live there point out the tunnels these rats might use to flee the castle. Sir Porto, you were with Duke Isgrimnur during the siege of Nakkiga after the Storm King's War, were you not?"

The old knight looked surprised to be addressed. "Yes! Yes, I was, Your Majesty."

"If I remember rightly, Isgrimnur laid siege to Nakkiga itself in the last month of the fighting, and you were one of those who searched the mountainside for all the Norns' paths in and out. True?"

"I am astonished that you remember so much, Majesty," said Porto. "Yes, I served with Aerling Surefoot and his scouts—"

The queen cut across his explanation. "Good. Then I put you in charge of doing the same around Winstowe. Treat the folk of the Fingerdale with restraint but convince them to tell you of any secret ways they know, in or out of the castle, even old tales. Only remember—it is 'the duchess' who asks their help, not me. I am not ready yet to let the traitor know he failed to kill me."

"I remember one such hidden path already, Majesty," said Snell abruptly. "Yes! Aglaf sent a message when we came with King . . ." He suddenly seemed reluctant to speak Simon's name, perhaps because of the flicker of pain on the queen's face. "Count Aglaf sent messengers from inside the castle, by hidden paths."

"That is a good start." Miriamele turned to Zakiel. "Give Sir Porto enough men that he can set guards at the places he finds. And then we will squeeze Winstowe like a nut until it cracks and Pasevalles and his grassland mercenaries come spilling out, right into our hands."

"It will take no little time to starve them out," warned Baron Snell.

"There is nothing more important than this," said the queen. "Pasevalles has killed members of my family, stolen from the crown, and made compact with our direst enemies. He connived at my husband's death too—I am certain of it—and for that alone I would spend the rest of my life hunting him down like the mad dog he is—"

Jesa watched the queen pause and take a deep breath to recover her composure.

"But if we try to starve them out, what about Count Aglaf and his family?" asked Zakiel.

"His son said that Aglaf is already dead," Miriamele said. "The whole of the High Ward and the throne of Erkynland cannot be held hostage to the safety of one lord's family and retainers, though I mourn for them as I do for the traitor's other victims." She suddenly stood. "We start for the Fingerdale tomorrow at first light. We must strike as swiftly and as hard as we can, since the thieving wretch has left our exchequer in ruins and we can ill afford a long siege. But as I have already told you, there is nothing more important than this. Nothing."

She swept out, and it seemed as though a strong wind had passed through the tent, leaving everything ruffled and confused.

"You did well," said Countess Rhona, patting Jesa's shoulder as they followed the others out of the great tent and into the camp. "Never be afraid to speak up, at least as long as that woman is our queen."

Brother Etan ached in his hams and buttocks. His back felt as if someone had been pounding on it with a blacksmith's hammer.

How do knights go for days in the saddle? he wondered, rubbing at his sore backside through his cassock as he limped to the edge of the clearing, for the moment not even caring what the graceful Sithi must think of him. He relieved himself, then wandered back to the others, who were waiting as their horses drank.

At least half the animals had not yet descended the narrow path down to the stream, but that was just as well: Etan was in no hurry to mount up again. As the Norns' prisoner, he had been trussed like a stuffed goose and ignominiously draped over a saddle. Then, after a night spent taking care of wounded Ki'ushapo, the Sithi had set Etan behind Tanahaya on her horse, and he could not guess how long they rode after that, because he had slipped in and out of exhausted sleep.

The saving grace of his rescuers' desire to hurry north was that no one had examined the saddlebags of Ki'ushapo's horse Shadowswift, so Tiamak's box must still be there, Etan thought, and still safe. But the more he considered, the less certain he felt. He had looked inside the box only once since leaving the Hayholt, but had found only a collection of old oddments, some broken, some whole. It was hard to believe even Jiriki would find them useful or even interesting, but Etan had made a promise to Lord Tiamak and Lady Thelía. The more he thought about the ornamented box, the more he wanted to make certain it was still where he had left it.

None of the Sithi seemed to be paying much attention to him, so he wandered to where Shadowswift stood in the line leading down to the stream. He reached into the saddlebag and was greatly relieved to find that the box Tiamak had given him had survived and seemed to be in good condition. He looked around to make certain no one was watching, then slipped it out and carried it away.

Etan was pleased that he did not seem to be a prisoner, but he knew almost nothing about the immortals and was not certain how far he could trust them. He trusted Ki'ushapo, but Ki'ushapo was still insensible after losing so much blood from his arrow-wound. Tiamak had told Etan to trust only Jiriki or his sister, Aditu, and he could not guess what rivalries might divide even friendly immortals.

He was relieved that everything in the box still seemed the same as when Tiamak had given it to him. As he closed the lid, he felt rather than saw or heard something and looked up, startled. The Sitha-woman Tanahaya had slipped up behind him as silently as a shadow. He pulled the box close against his belly and beneath a fold of his cassock, hoping she had not seen it.

"Greetings. Ki'ushapo says you are called Brother Etan."

"Is he better? I'm glad he can speak again. He was kind to me."

"He is kind to many, although not to our enemies." She leavened the words with a half-smile. "He will live and, I think, recover all his strength, though only time will tell the full tale. The wound does not seem to be poisoned. That was my greatest fear."

The heaviness of what she said made him wonder for a moment if this Tanahaya was a relative or even Ki'ushapo's lover. "I am glad to hear it."

"I must ask what errand brought you, a mortal—and not a mortal warrior, but a priest—into the great forest at such a time?"

"I was traveling with Ki'ushapo. But then the Norns caught us—"

"You evade my question, Brother, and not particularly well." She spoke very good Westerling, Etan realized with a sinking feeling. "I know *who* brought you. I ask *what* brought you. Did you not know there was war here in Oldheart—that the soldiers of Queen Utuk'ku are everywhere?"

He stared at her for a long moment, trying to think of an answer. Something about her seemed familiar, and he had a swift, very strange desire to trust her, but he knew from many tales that the fairy-folk were said to carry a glamor that could bespell mortal men. But he also knew that he had to make a choice. "I was sent on a mission," he admitted. "By Lord Tiamak of the Hayholt."

Her eyes widened. "I know that name. He and his wife helped save me when I was dying."

For a few heartbeats Etan could make no sense of her words, then it struck him like a blow. "By Elysia, our Holy Mother!" he cried, making the Sign of the Tree on his breast. "I know you! You're the one who was brought into the castle! You had been shot by poison arrows!"

Now it was Tanahaya's turn to look surprised. "Yes, that was me. I was sent to the Hayholt as an envoy by Jiriki and Aditu of House Sa'onserei, but I was ambushed."

"Jiriki!" His heart was racing. "That is who Tiamak sent me to find!"

The Sitha's golden eyes narrowed. "This seems a strange coincidence. But, as Ayaminu says, the boundaries between things have grown very thin as the year ends, and perhaps may grow thinner still. How do you know me? I do not recognize you."

"I am Brother Etan of St. Sutrin's," he said. "I was one of those who tried to keep you alive. I am truly glad to see you recovered, noble lady."

"I am no one's noblewoman," she said. "Even among my own people I am nothing so high. But why did Tiamak send you to seek Jiriki, and how did Ki'ushapo become involved? Do either of you know where Jiriki is now? Because I have heard nothing from him for more than two moons."

Etan was overwhelmed. "I don't know what to say to all this. Please, let me think." The decision he had to make was momentous, but he knew so little about the risks. "Do you really know Jiriki? You are his friend?"

She gave him a strange look, something he could not possibly put mortal emotions to. "We seek to join the rest of our people. We also hope to find Jiriki somewhere on our journey or get some news of him. As to whether I truly know him—yes. He is my lover. And I carry his child."

Etan was more than a little surprised by this last, but for some reason it made up his mind. "Then I will show you what I carry. But please, if there is something you can swear by, promise me you will tell no one else."

She looked at him with what seemed true sympathy but shook her head. "I cannot promise that to you, Etan of St. Sutrin's. The stakes are too high in this game, and one of the wisest of our people, Ayaminu of Anvi'janya, is here with me. If what your master Tiamak gave you is important to our people, I cannot keep it from her. But I trust nobody more than Ayaminu, except for Jiriki himself and his sister."

It was too late for Etan to turn back now. He reached up to his throat, touched the Scroll League pendant Tiamak had given him. *Please, Heavenly Father,* he prayed, *twice I have given my word to my friend the royal counselor, and I am about to break that word for the second time. Please let me not fail him and the folk in Erchester, for my heart tells me to speak truth to this Sitha.* "Then look here," he said. "See what I carry." He passed her the box with as much reverence as if it contained a holy relic. "It is a jumble of things that mean little to me. Perhaps you will see more in it."

As if some of his own caution had rubbed off on her, Tanahaya looked around, but the other Sithi seemed engaged in everything except watching them. She opened the lid and peered in, then quickly snapped it shut again. He could not read the expression on her face, but it was one he had not seen before.

"May I take this?" she asked, her voice suddenly hushed. "I promise you only Ayaminu will see it—but she must. She *must*."

"Take it?" He felt as if he had betrayed Tiamak's trust. "Can I not take it to her with you?"

"It will cause less notice among our people if I speak to her alone. Also, we will have to speak in our own tongue about it." She reached out and touched his arm. "Will you trust me, Brother Etan? I swear on the precious child growing in my belly I will not betray you or your master, Tiamak." She seemed so grim it frightened him. "No one else will see it until we find Jiriki."

He took a single steadying breath. "Then take it. I put my honor and perhaps much else in your hands, Tanahaya—and in God's."

She nodded. "I think your people say, 'Bless you,' in such moments, yes? Bless you, then, Brother Etan, for bringing this so far. I will protect it with my all my strength."

Ayaminu shut the box and handed it back to Tanahaya. Her expression was no more revealing than the closed lid. "What else did he say?"

She explained what the mortal had told her about the attack on the Hayholt and the arrival of a Sithi company, then their subsequent departure. "But what of the box?" she asked Ayaminu. "Will it change anything? Will it end this terrible struggle?" Tanahaya asked.

"Who can say? It depends on what Utuk'ku hopes to accomplish. In days past, when both sides sought to avoid open conflict, it might have meant much. Whatever the case, though, we must keep it safe and secret until we can speak with Jiriki and the others in Tanakirú."

"Do you think he is there?" Tanahaya asked.

"The mortal said they left in haste, and there is no more important place for our people just now," Ayaminu replied. "It seems likely."

Tanahaya sighed. "By our Garden, why has that ancient ship become the most important thing in all the world?"

"Because it is important to Utuk'ku, scholar. The rest of us only guard it so carefully—so expensively—to keep it from her."

"How many of our people have known about it?"

"In Amerasu's time or now?" Ayaminu looked weary. "I do not know the answer to the first, but in these later days, the number is small indeed. The Sa'onsera Likimeya and her children know, of course. My father, Kuroyi, who shared the secret with me before he went to war against the Storm King. A few other clan protectors—Dunao, Enazashi Blackspear of the Silverhome, and Blackspear's son, Yizashi. And Khendraja'aro and Cheka'iso, of course, who have defended the Narrowdark Valley for years." Ayaminu climbed into her saddle. "Less than a dozen of us altogether, I think. We called it the Mushroom Circle because we remained quiet and close to the ground." She shrugged. "We did our best to honor Amerasu's decree to keep the ship and valley secret, though we did not always like what we were bound to do."

The rest of Dunao's troops had remounted, but the mortal was struggling to get back onto Tanahaya's tall Hikeda'ya horse. She went to him and helped steady his foot in the stirrups as he clambered back into the high saddle.

"Thanks to you," he said. "May I have my box back now? I swore an oath."

She took a breath and did her best to put her fears aside. The mortal deserved consideration too. "It will be safer with me, but I promise I will stay close to you." She could see in his face that this upset him, and quickly added, "You have done well, Brother Etan. I would even say you have fulfilled your promise to Lord Tiamak, because I swear that on the Garden itself that I will do everything possible to put the box in Jiriki's hands. Please, trust me to keep it safe." *And now I too am holding back a great secret*, she realized. *How easy it is to keep things from those we think we are protecting!*

"In truth, you need not come the rest of the way," she told him gently. "You have risked your life coming this far. If we could, we would send an escort to accompany you back home, but I fear we cannot afford to lose any of our number—not with battle so close."

Etan hesitated, then at last nodded his head. "No, you may carry it—I will trust you. And I promised Tiamak I would see it into Jiriki's hands, so I will go on with you, though this all terrifies me."

20

At Tanakirú

It was a dream. Simon knew that, but even while caught in its confusing folds, he was surprised that he was dreaming at all.

It was not a good dream. He was high above a long, twilit beach, its farther ends in both directions invisible because of the mist drifting in from the ocean. He knew it was a dream because though he could clearly see what lay below him, he could make out nothing of what supported him so far above the ground. But such illogic meant nothing to him, because he could see his granddaughter Lillia down below, and she was being chased across the odd, dark sand.

The thing pursuing her seemed barely a thing at all, only a flying scrap of cloth or a swirl of mist or sea foam, but he could feel that Lillia was badly frightened by it, and though he was too far away to do anything, he was desperate to help. As his little granddaughter turned first this way and that, as she pelted across the sand, he could see that in her terrified flight from the ragged wisp, Lillia was drawing closer and closer to the water itself. The sea was calm, but for some reason he felt fearfully certain that if she went into it, his granddaughter would never come out again.

He tried to call to her, to warn her of the danger, but could not make the words. The ragged, pursuing shape was drawing nearer with every step the child took, and Lillia's irregular path veered ever closer to the waiting ocean. Even as he despaired, the world suddenly darkened. The bruised-looking sky seemed to contract toward the horizon, threatening to obliterate everything but restless, rolling sea. Lillia turned one last time to look back as she pounded through the dark, wet sand toward the water. He thought he could hear her calling, but the sound was thin and distant and might have been only the cry of a seabird.

And then he woke up.

Long moments passed before Simon felt sure he was indeed awake. He shivered—the dream had been so strong, so frighteningly real, and he had not dreamed at all for so long! He reached out in the darkness for his granddaughter, to pull her close and reassure her, and to reassure himself. But Lillia was gone.

His heart rattled inside his chest like a fast march on a battle drum. "Lillia!" he called. "Where are you?" He felt uneven stone beneath him and remembered where he was—the Sithi caverns at Tanakirú, the refuge they had finally reached after a battle with the Norns and a breakneck gallop over the deadly gorge. "Lillia!" he cried again. He clambered to his feet, looking around for her in the near darkness. His muscles were woefully sore, but that was nothing compared to his growing terror. "Lillia, where did you go?"

"Peace, King Seoman," said a voice. "The child is cared for and safe. I will take you to her."

He turned to see Rukayu Crow's Claw standing in the entrance which admitted the cavern's only light. She still wore the same blood-spattered armor he had last seen her in, and he realized with some shame that unlike him, she had probably not slept at all since they had all staggered in. "Where is she?"

"I will take you there—it is not far. But recover yourself a little first. I could feel you struggling on the Dream-Road all the way across the cavern."

He looked at her, unsure what this meant. "I . . . have not dreamed at all in a very long time. That was Geloë's doing, so I suppose she released me. In any case, yes—take me to my granddaughter, please, I beg you. I do not doubt you, but my heart will not stop pounding until I see that she is whole and well."

Rukayu smiled a little. "Of course. Come."

The section of cavern where he had fallen asleep—in truth, little more than a tunnel with a sealed end—was deserted, although there were signs that other Sithi had been there. "I dimly remember us both being brought here. Why did someone take Lillia from me?"

"It did not quite happen that way," said Rukayu gently. "After we arrived, you were very weary, so we found you a place to sleep. Geloë fell back into a deep slumber, and although Lillia herself did not emerge with Geloë's absence, the child seemed uncomfortable with your thrashing."

"I was thrashing?"

"Yes, you were. But as you said, you have only just begun to walk the Dream Road again." She extended a gloved hand. "I will take you to your granddaughter."

Simon had been too exhausted to observe his surroundings the previous night, but it was quickly clear to him that the caverns beneath the cliffs were extensive. They passed a few other Sithi, but the camp seemed very sparsely inhabited.

"Where is everyone?" he asked. "Surely this isn't all that are left, is it?"

"Most are already out, preparing to defend the wall. It will be light soon. When night ends, the threat of the ogre is gone and the threat of Hikeda'ya attack returns." Rukayu shook her head. "But we still make a small number—so small that even my great-grandfather Shen'de was surprised. There can only be a few hundred defenders left here all told."

Simon's heart was heavy. "Truly?"

"Remember, King Seoman, it is not the numbers," she said, "but the courage of those being counted that matters."

But for the first time, he thought Rukayu herself did not sound entirely convinced.

She led him out of the wide cavern they were in and down a branching tunnel; Simon had to duck because the ceiling was low and jagged. Most of the caverns seemed entirely natural, and in the other parts, like this corridor, the work seemed hurried, at least by Sithi standards. The chisel-work on the passage was crude and had not been dressed at all.

"Here," Rukayu said as she stepped to one side and gestured.

The tunnel now opened into another natural chamber, this one quite small, lit by a single torch pushed into a crevice in the far wall. In one corner was a pool, fed by water splashing unevenly out of a crack in the ceiling. Several shapes, most of which seemed to be sleeping, lay scattered around the chamber on blankets as two Sithi healers ministered to them.

"Where—?" he began, but Rukayu pointed to the far corner, where he saw Lillia asleep on a blanket of her own, with a small figure crouching beside her. Simon hurried across the uneven floor and let himself down, bending to look closely at his granddaughter's sleeping face. Lillia looked healthy but finding her gone had frightened him badly and he could not forget his dream. He looked back to Rukayu. "Is she—?"

"She is very well," piped up the small figure beside him, speaking Westerling almost as well as Rukayu did. "I have been watching over the little one since she was brought here."

"This is Xila," said Rukayu as she joined them. "She has kindly made herself your granddaughter's caretaker."

Xila laughed, a sound so cheery Simon could hardly believe he was hearing it in this place. "I have little else to do. It is my dark curse to be a child."

Simon looked at her more closely. He had thought her just a particularly small Sitha, in the same way that his friend Tiamak was a small mortal. He had not seen any Sithi children on the ride north and very few of them even during the long months he had lived in Jao é-Tinukai'i during the Storm King's War. Now that he examined the youthful roundness of her features, he could see his error.

"Forgive me," he said, relieved to feel that Lillia's forehead was cool and that her sleep seemed peaceful, even if he knew it was not entirely natural. "I have met so few young ones of your folk."

Xila laughed again, a little ruefully this time. "Because we are so few, I know. And that is why they wanted to send me away from here after my mother died. But I would not go!"

"You need not sound so proud," said Rukayu, but gently.

"What, and take more fighters away from here just to escort me to safety? It is bad enough that Cheka'iso and the rest will not let me bear arms."

"You and King Seoman can talk more later," said Rukayu. "But now, I need to take him to Jiriki and the others."

"You need to take me too," said another voice. Simon's granddaughter's body stretched its arms and then sat up. "We have many things to decide, and time is short."

Even though she had been sleeping, Simon had felt connected to his granddaughter. With Geloë's return that tie felt severed, and he could not help resenting it. "You are still keeping my granddaughter hidden away."

"Not hidden from you, fretful Simon," she said. "Although, unhappily, that is what it comes to. I am hiding her from our enemies, remember. Now, help me up. It always takes me a little while to remember how to use this body properly."

"I'm coming with you," announced Xila. "Let Cheka'iso try to send me away. I'll tell him I'm doing my part by watching over this little one."

The Sithi clan leaders were gathered in a large cavern deep in the warren of tunnels and dreamlike chambers, as strange and fantastical in shape as if made of melted wax; Rukayu named it the "Flower Hall." Misshapen columns stretched between the uneven floor and the bumpy cavern ceiling; in other spots, spikes of creamy stone had grown up from the floor or stretched down from the ceiling, as if trying to make themselves into pillars, but not quite able to stretch the full distance.

The unlikely choice of name for a spot so deep within the mountain's roots quickly became clearer as Simon moved farther into the cavern: its walls were festooned with what Simon at first took for actual blooms, but as he neared them, he realized they were in fact composed of pale, threadlike crystals. Most of these formations had the petaled shape of blossoms, but he saw other shapes too, curling branches like unfolding ferns and spirals like sleeping snakes. The majority, though, did look much like flowers, and the glowing crystal globes the Sithi called *ni'yo*, the only lights in the dark cavern but for a single, small fire at the center, made the place seem even stranger and more unworldly.

Simon recognized only a few of the gathered Sithi—Jiriki and the others he had come here with, like Shen'de the Bowman. The Sithi fell silent, though none of them looked up as he and his three companions approached. He had seen the immortals' councils before, but he did not think he had ever seen them wear such grim faces except in the days after First Grandmother Amerasu's death all those years ago. Sithi emotions were usually too subtle for Simon's mortal eyes, but the group sitting around the fire looked almost haunted, and it chilled him.

They do not believe they will survive this place, this war. Which means my granddaughter and I will not escape either. Merciful God, what have I done in bringing her here?

He watched Geloë join them, seating the small, borrowed body atop a stone. Jiriki looked up and said something to her in his own liquid tongue. Someone else spoke—golden-haired Cheka'iso, one of the few others whose name Simon recognized—and the conversation continued.

"Can you tell me what they're saying?" he asked Rukayu.

She shook her head. "Not now," she whispered. "It is too much all at once. Let me listen and make sense out of all the different speech."

Simon sat and stared at what should have been his granddaughter, occupied and animated now by a ghost. He had come a long way, it seemed, only to become once more the mortal tag-along he had been as a youth.

"I am sorry you had to wait, Seoman." Jiriki had left the fire to come join him while the other Sithi continued their quiet conversation. Simon had noticed that none of them seemed to interrupt any of the others, but talk moved quickly and smoothly between them, like a stream rushing downhill through many channels, joining and separating and then joining again.

"*S'hue* Jiriki has been in council since we rode in last night," said Rukayu.

"There was much to learn about what has happened since I had the last news at the Hornet's Nest, when my mother's brother Khendraja'aro still lived," he said. "Before the Norns' walking corpse-thing murdered him."

"Jiriki is protector of his clan now," Rukayu said. "And not just of Year-Dancing Clan, but all the clans who lived under the wisdom of Amerasu Ship-born."

Simon's immortal friend did not have the strength even to smile, though he gave Rukayu a fond look. "You have worked as hard in the last days as I have, young warrior," he told her. "While I tell Simon what I have learned, you should rest and eat."

"First I will bring King Seoman and his granddaughter something for their bellies," she said. "Then, with thanks, I will take my leave for a little while."

She returned soon with half a loaf of bread and a bowl of water. "Do not fear," she said, setting it down before him. "This water is clean. I made sure. But do not drink here without asking one of our people first."

"What does that mean?" Simon asked as he pulled the bread apart. "Is the water bad here?"

"It is to do with the presence of the Ninth Ship—but Jiriki will no doubt explain." After Simon had drunk, she took the rest of the bread and the water to Geloë, who was conversing with the Sithi in their own musical language. As Jiriki began to talk, Simon watched Lillia's fingers clumsily lift a piece of bread and fold it into her mouth, as though she were a baby again. If Geloë's control over her was that imperfect, he wondered, how could she be sure she could keep the child safe?

"Do you need to rest again?" Jiriki asked.

"I beg your pardon. Please, go on. You said something about that . . . corpse-thing."

"Yes. As if we did not have enough to struggle against, the Hikeda'ya have summoned or made a terrible creature—an unliving thing that yet seems to live. Another of Utuk'ku's abomination."

"I saw it, too!" said Simon with a shudder. "The thing with gray skin? It was horrible. I have never seen anything quite like it!"

"Nor I," said Jiriki, but did not dwell on it. Instead, he explained how the Hornet's Nest survivors had fought their way through a long retreat to join Cheka'iso and the rest, here in Tanakirú, at the end of the Narrowdark Valley.

"So our numbers are a little better than I had feared," Jiriki said, "but still meager."

"And that huge shape high on the cliff wall—that's the ship?" Simon asked. "The Ninth Ship? It's so big!"

"It is. And it was hard enough keeping the Hikeda'ya away from it before our Hornet's Nest fortress was overthrown, when we could hold most of them out of the Narrowdark Valley. But now things here have become even worse. I have learned that our garrison atop Kushiba has been destroyed by another Sacrifice force."

More bad news, clearly, although Simon did not recognize the name. "What is Kushiba?"

"The peak above us. We are hiding inside its roots at this moment." Jiriki got up and took a stick with a burnt end from the council-fire, then returned to Simon and began to draw on a smooth expanse of stone, making a jagged line—like ocean waves, but far steeper. "Here are the mountains at this end of the valley. This tall one is Kushiba, and we are under it, although if you dig down far enough, I suppose they all share the same rocky foundations, like the towers on a city wall. In any case, you have seen that our greatest protection for ourselves and the ship is the violent river formed by the cataract that plunges down from above and keeps the Hikeda'ya on the far side of the gorge. Our trick with the Hikeda'ya's own cut timbers worked to get us across it, but General Ensume and his Sacrifice troops will keep trying to bridge it from their side, so we must continue to prevent it. Only that deep plunge down to wild water has kept us from being overrun long ago."

"But I saw your people roll the logs away after we crossed. That means we can't get out, either—it truly is a siege. How are we being supplied?"

Jiriki's face looked wearier than Simon had ever seen it. "That is the other foul news I have learned. We used to have our supplies—food, arrows, healing herbs—lowered down to us by the Zida'ya fighters who held the flanks of Kushiba above. But now they are gone—slaughtered, every single one—and Utuk'ku's Sacrifices hold that high ground. The Zida'ya here had to listen to the destruction of our kin, helpless to do anything. We will receive no help from Kushiba's slope anymore."

"It's hopeless, then."

"It became hopeless when the Hornet's Nest fell and the Hikeda'ya could come swarming into the valley in force. Almost all of it is theirs now. The only reason they have not won is the width and fury of the Narrowdark, here where it forms—the riverhead is our moat. But our scouts have heard tunneling in the mountain above us and felt it in some of the deep places here as well. If the Hikeda'ya can break into the caverns and descend through Kushiba, they will be able to pour Sacrifice soldiers down into our end of the valley from above. They will catch us between those troops and the river gorge, which will then no longer be our shield but instead the other half of a trap."

"And you made me bring my granddaughter here! Into this trap." At that moment he could almost convince himself simply to take Lillia and try to escape the valley, leaving the Sithi and Norns to kill each other.

"If I believed your people and mine had any other choice, Seoman, I would not have done it. But Geloë and her knowledge are our last and only hope."

"I don't care about any of this! I only have one of my family left, and she's been possessed by a dead woman. And now she's going to be murdered by your wretched demon-kin." He waved his hands. "Go away, Jiriki. I know you did not mean this to happen, but . . ." He could only gesture again, helpless. "Leave me alone. Please."

Jiriki arose without another word and walked back to the circle of his people around the fire. Simon looked at Geloë, who wore his granddaughter's stolen body as if it were no more than a cloak, and utter hopelessness rushed through him like a flood, carrying all before it, leaving him shaking and near to weeping.

Miriamele, he thought. *My lost beloved. Oh, Miri, I'm so sorry. I have done a terrible, foolish thing. If I cannot save our granddaughter, I pray that we two will see you soon. And I hope you and God can forgive me.*

There were only so many times, Viyeki reflected bitterly, that he could prepare himself for death. As he pulled on his boots, the two Queen's Teeth guards stood in the doorway, stiff and silent as stalagmites. Nonao, Viyeki's secretary, hurried in with a roll of plans, pointedly not looking at the white-helmed soldiers as he passed them. They had not announced themselves or their mission—the Teeth never did—but it was impossible to misunderstand their presence. High Magister Viyeki was summoned to attend the queen once more.

This audience had not been limited to Viyeki alone, he saw as he entered the royal presence. Akhenabi was there, and newly elevated Marshal Kikiti, along with Prince-Templar Pratiki, High Celebrant Zuniyabe, and a few others. Viyeki got down and crawled to the foot of the throne. Utuk'ku acknowledged his presence with the slightest of nods, but her eyes never touched him. He moved to a place beside the Prince-Templar before sitting up, his emotions a mixture of momentary relief, fear, and confusion.

The queen seemed to be in the middle of a conversation with Kikiti over the progress of the battle in the valley below, and she either could not or did not bother to keep it private.

I am not impressed with General Ensume's effort. Viyeki thought Utuk'ku's voice seemed even weaker than the last time, and though she sat as erect as ever, she kept her gloved hands on the arms of her throne as though she needed something to hold. *I have given him eight entire Sacrifice legions,* she said, *but the pitiful remnants of the Zida'ya still hold him off from our prize.*

So there is something here in Tanakirú that she wants more than simply defeating the Zida'ya, Viyeki realized, but then hurriedly tried to make his mind empty again. If he had not been told the reason for the war, it was unwise to speculate here, where the queen might perceive his thoughts.

To Viyeki's surprise, Marshal Kikiti, perhaps buoyed by his recent promotion, took Ensume's side, although he did so very carefully. "The Dawn Children do what I would do in their place, Great Majesty. They are trapped and helplessly outnumbered, so they avoid open battle where they can. They send their best fighters out on the cusp of dawn and dusk to harry our positions. They kill our warriors from hiding, then retreat before the ogre finds them out of their caves. We used tactics like these ourselves against the Northmen during their siege of Nakkiga."

The queen was silent for a long, uncomfortable time. *Do you suppose I need instruction on our history, Marshal?* she finally said. *I, who had already ruled our people for a hundred Great Years when those bloody-handed mortal vermin came across the sea with their ships and iron weapons?*

"Of course not, Majesty. I only meant—"

I know what you meant to do, Marshal. I know that you in the Order of Sacrifice are loyal to other Sacrifices. But are you more loyal to General Ensume than you are to your queen?

This thought, full of barely cloaked rage, struck not just the high marshal but all of those present like a thunderclap; Viyeki felt as though the bones of his skull had tightened until they began to crack. Even Kikiti, the embodiment of his order, let out a muffled gasp of shock and almost fell over. "Never, Majesty!" he said in a strangled voice.

I am pleased to hear that, Marshal. She turned to stare at the other supplicants, light and shadow playing across the shiny surface of her mask, wavering like the ripples from a cast stone. Her cold, dark eyes stopped on Viyeki. *Well, High Magister? Have you earned yourself more days of life? Tell me of your tunnel.*

So it's my *tunnel now,* he thought bitterly, then was terrified the queen would perceive this disrespect. This time there had been no Pratiki, no wine, nothing to prepare him. If she chose to, Viyeki knew, Utuk'ku could enter his head and he would be as nakedly defenseless as a cave-borer rolled on its back. His head still throbbing with the queen's anger, he did his best to sift the jumble of frightened thoughts to form a reply.

"The passage . . . the passage is finished, Majesty," he said. "Many died in its building—especially in the last—"

So. Utuk'ku's flat response made it clear she did not care about the fate of a few slaves and Builders. *That is what I wanted to hear—and all I wanted to hear. High Marshal Kikiti, you will make your troops ready to descend through the tunnels to the plateau tomorrow at sunrise.*

"They could set out immediately, Majesty," Kikiti said. "If you wish it so, my queen."

No. The queen lifted her hand in the sign for silence, and Viyeki thought all present must be able to see the trembling of her gloved fingers. *I do not rely solely on the Order of Builders or even the Order of Sacrifice, Marshal,* she said. *I also watch with the eyes of outer darkness. The firmament speaks, but only I understand it.* She paused. *I perceive that you wish to ask me a question, Kikiti.*

"It is about your august clansman, Lord Jijibo," he said slowly. "He is missing, along with several soldiers of his household guard—"

I am aware. Your question?

"Ah." For a moment Kikiti seemed unsure of whether to continue. "Is he—is it with your permission, then, Great Mother?"

It is not. And I am displeased—my descendant, though often useful to me, has always been too full of his own ideas. If you happen to find him, bring him back to me—but he must not be harmed. He is of the pure Hamakha blood, and only I can decide his fate. As for his household guard . . . I care little whether they live or die. But Jijibo must be kept alive.

It was clear even to Viyeki that Kikiti was not happy with these orders, but he had not reached the highest rank in his order without knowing when to swallow his objections. "It will be as you say, Majesty, of course," he said, bowing his head. "As for the attack on Tanakirú, I will assemble my Sacrifices and have them ready to march into the tunnels. At the instant you order it, I will lead them to victory for the glory of Nakkiga, Clan Hamakha—and, of course, the Mother of All."

No, Kikiti, she said. *I will lead them. But you will be at my side, which should be honor enough for you.*

Despite himself, Kikiti stared in surprise. "You will lead them, Majesty?"

Viyeki could feel the air tightening as Utuk'ku regarded her greatest general. *Yes, High Marshal,* she said at last. *Or do you object?*

"Never, Majesty. The queen knows what her people need. I am and always will be your servant."

Yes, she said, and though her words still seemed weaker than usual, the final one stung in a way even Viyeki could feel. *You will. Always.*

Tzoja had never been anyone's wife, and she didn't think that was likely to change. She certainly had no intention of becoming Jarnulf's little woman, so when he finally appeared at the camp, her resentment spilled out. "The food is cold. We have been waiting for you since dark, not knowing if you even lived. Have you no care for our worries?"

Jarnulf was clearly distracted, his eyes darting about the forested hillside where they were camped among the rest of the Hikeda'ya slaves. "Quickly, gather your things," he said in a whisper. "We must go."

"What? What things? What do you mean?"

For a moment Tzoja thought he might hit her. "Your *things*—your medicaments, your herbs, if they are important to you. We must leave here this moment."

Vordis had heard the urgency in his voice too. She came forward, hands outstretched to feel her way, as though even the trees and stones might have changed positions. "What are you saying?"

"Have I not made it clear enough?" Jarnulf was struggling to keep his voice low. "Gather everything you have. Guards will be here soon looking for me. The other slaves will tell them you are my companions. You must come with me as quickly as you can. Haste!"

Tzoja swallowed her questions. She had faced sudden danger enough times in her life to know when to stop wondering and start moving, though she was far from content. She began throwing the few things she had brought out for cooking into the chest with her healer's tools and powders. "What of the food?" she asked.

"Leave it," he said. "There is no time."

She disobeyed him, taking time to dump out the food so she could keep the bowls, something she could not imagine being able to replace in this wilderness. Just a short time ago, she thought as she and Vordis swiftly bundled up their few possessions, things had been ordinary. Not ordinary compared to most people's lives, perhaps, but for Tzoja a time of comparative quiet, of marches, making camp, and a fixed daily routine, however exhausting. Now Jarnulf had thrown everything into chaos, and she had no idea why.

He led them out of the camp, passing as far from the lights of other fires as possible. The noise of the Narrowdark River was distant, but Tzoja hoped it would help hide their escape. They bent low, not just out of worry about the other slaves noticing, but because they all knew of the sharp eyes of their Hikeda'ya masters. Jarnulf guided them up the slope, away from the road they had traveled for so many days; and though he no longer spoke, the hard, impatient hand that guided them over the most difficult spots, gripping first Vordis's arm then her own, conveyed all that needed to be said.

As they reached a greater height, he led them through a field of rocky boulders that had been carved into odd shapes by wind and water, then through a wood of spruces and pines powdered with snow before turning upslope once more.

"Where are we going?" Tzoja finally asked when she could find the breath.

"Stay silent," he whispered. "Remember, this is the Narrowdark Valley. There are things here beside the Norns, and we want none of them to hear us."

She did her best to help Vordis make her way over the uneven, rock-strewn slope. In what seemed less than an hour they reached a wide shelf of pale stone mostly hidden by trees. It jutted from the hillside like a duck's bill, and Jarnulf led them quickly across the top of it, then swung down over the far edge, waiting to help first Vordis climb down, then Tzoja. Once their feet were on the ground, he ducked beneath the overhang and beckoned them to follow him. There they discovered a cave, its entrance concealed beneath the stone shelf. "No noise," he hissed as they settled into the low-ceilinged hole.

After listening for no little time, Jarnulf appeared satisfied. "You can speak now. But quietly!"

"How did you find this place?" Tzoja asked him.

"I have wandered far while hunting. That is what got me into trouble. A few sentries stopped me as I was returning. I did not know them—they were not those who had turned a blind eye on my way out. I tried to bribe them with the game I had caught, but they were stubborn and suspicious and would not let me go. So I dealt with the guards as quickly as I could and then made a run for it."

"You . . . dealt with them?"

"I did not kill them—but that will make no difference if we are caught. Now that I have told you what happened, we need to be quiet again."

It was grim to hide in a damp, cold, cobwebby hole in the hillside that she had never seen in the light. Tzoja found a few sticks of *pu'ja* bread among her things, but they made a poor replacement for the freshly prepared meal she had been forced to leave behind. She was frightened, but she was angry, too. If not for Jarnulf's insistence on roaming far from the rest of the marchers, they would have had a dinner and a fire. It was unfair. *He* was the fugitive. She and Vordis were, at least in theory, servants of the queen herself, but now he had made them fugitives as well.

Jarnulf abruptly held up his hand. She looked a question at him, but it was impossible to make out his face in the dark.

"Something is coming," he whispered. "Do not move and make no noise."

Her anger vanished in a heartbeat, replaced by terror, as though she had been thrown into a freezing river. Jarnulf sat silent and as alert as a pointing hound, staring out into the trees and the darkness.

She heard it then. *Scrape. Scruff. Scrape. Scruff.* Something was crawling up the hillside toward them, something large. She heard branches breaking beneath its weight, cracking sounds like knots bursting in a cookfire; whatever it was seemed utterly unconcerned with stealth. Tzoja prayed that it was only some forest creature, a bear or a very large boar, anything natural, but the closer the sound came, the less she could make herself believe it. Jarnulf had his bow in his hand and an arrow on the string, so Tzoja tried to find something she could use to defend herself, settling at last on a shard of rock longer than her hand.

As they waited in silence, a choking scent rose to them, animal musk and dried blood and other things she could not identify. Then a massive shadow filled the space at the bottom of the stone promontory, and the rock dropped from her suddenly clumsy fingers. The intruding shape was huge, much bigger than any Hikeda'ya soldier, and it made grunting noises like an animal.

The light was completely blocked. Like cornered rats, she and Vordis scrambled away from the cave opening in terror until their backs were pressed against stone.

A rumbling groan shook her bones and punished her ears, so close that it seemed as loud as thunder, then a harsh, deep voice said, "I have . . . found you. I could smell you . . . from far away."

"Goh Gam Gar?" said Jarnulf. Tzoja, heart rattling, almost unable to breathe, had no idea what the words meant.

"I am dying," the thing rumbled, the gasping words still so reverberant that little bits of dirt and stone shook loose and fell on Tzoja's head. It was clear the giant shape could not rise. "The queen's yoke . . . killing me." The great beast groaned once more and then was silent, though its massive torso still heaved as it struggled for breath.

At first Simon did not recognize the male Sitha who came and squatted beside him. Then he realized it was Shen'de, Rukayu's great-grandfather. Not that he looked old: Simon wished he still looked so lean and strong himself. The only telltales were the net of fine wrinkles around the bowman's eyes and how tightly his skin lay stretched over his bones.

At the center of the Hall of Flowers, Geloë was still using Lillia's body, speaking in low, urgent tones with Jiriki. Simon was no longer angry but he felt empty, used up, as though nothing was left inside him but memories and regrets.

"I see a story in your face," said Shen'de in slow, careful Westerling. "You look full of fear. But that is not the story I hear of you from Jiriki."

"Jiriki may think more of me than I do of myself. But I'm not frightened for me."

The old Sitha considered this for a moment, then followed Simon's gaze toward the firepit at the center of the cavern. "Ah. It is the child."

"Yes, it is the child. I carried her here, but only to die, it seems."

"Where would you wish her to die?"

Simon peered sideways at Shen'de, uncertain whether the problem was unfamiliarity with the mortal tongue or the cruelty of a harsh jest, but Shen'de's face showed no sign of joking or taunting. "I would wish her to die at home, as an old woman," Simon said. "An old, happy woman with lots of children and grandchildren."

"If that is what your granddaughter would wish, then I wish it for her too," Shen'de said. "But wishes are only hopes. I had no wish to see my own great-granddaughter here. You know her—Rukayu. But she chose to come."

"My granddaughter didn't have that choice." Simon tried to hold back his bitterness, not altogether successfully. "She was carried like a sack of barley. She was scarcely even awake for most of the journey."

"That is sad, yes." Shen'de nodded his head slowly, as one who acknowledges the world's great failings. "But would she choose to leave you if she could?"

Simon thought of Lillia's missing brother and dead mother and all the other dear ones the child had lost. "No," he admitted. "I think she would want to be with me no matter what."

Shen'de touched his arm, a fleeting gesture like a bird alighting and then immediately taking flight again. "Then it is the working of the Garden in her life that has brought her here, not you. You have no need to blame yourself."

"I'm not a Sitha. I don't believe in the Garden."

"Ah." Shen'de nodded slowly. "Yes, you believe in a king who lives in the sky called God. We Zida'ya are here for the very reason that we know the Garden existed, and part of it landed here. But if I say 'Garden,' you can say 'God.'" Shen'de rose. "No matter. For the sake of the child, you can only be the brave one she knows. That is all any of us can do."

Without another word or gesture, he rose, turned, and walked away, leaving Simon to feel he might have learned something, but not certain it made any difference.

PART TWO

Sacred Seed

I met the Gatherer as I slept and wandered.
She held out her hands to show me what she held:
A seed as bright as sunlight on snow.
"Open it, you shall find another," she said;
"And inside that another still—smaller and smaller
Until they can no longer be seen.
Only a dream can hold that much life."

—FROM THE DAYBOOK OF
LADY MIGA SEYT-JINNATA

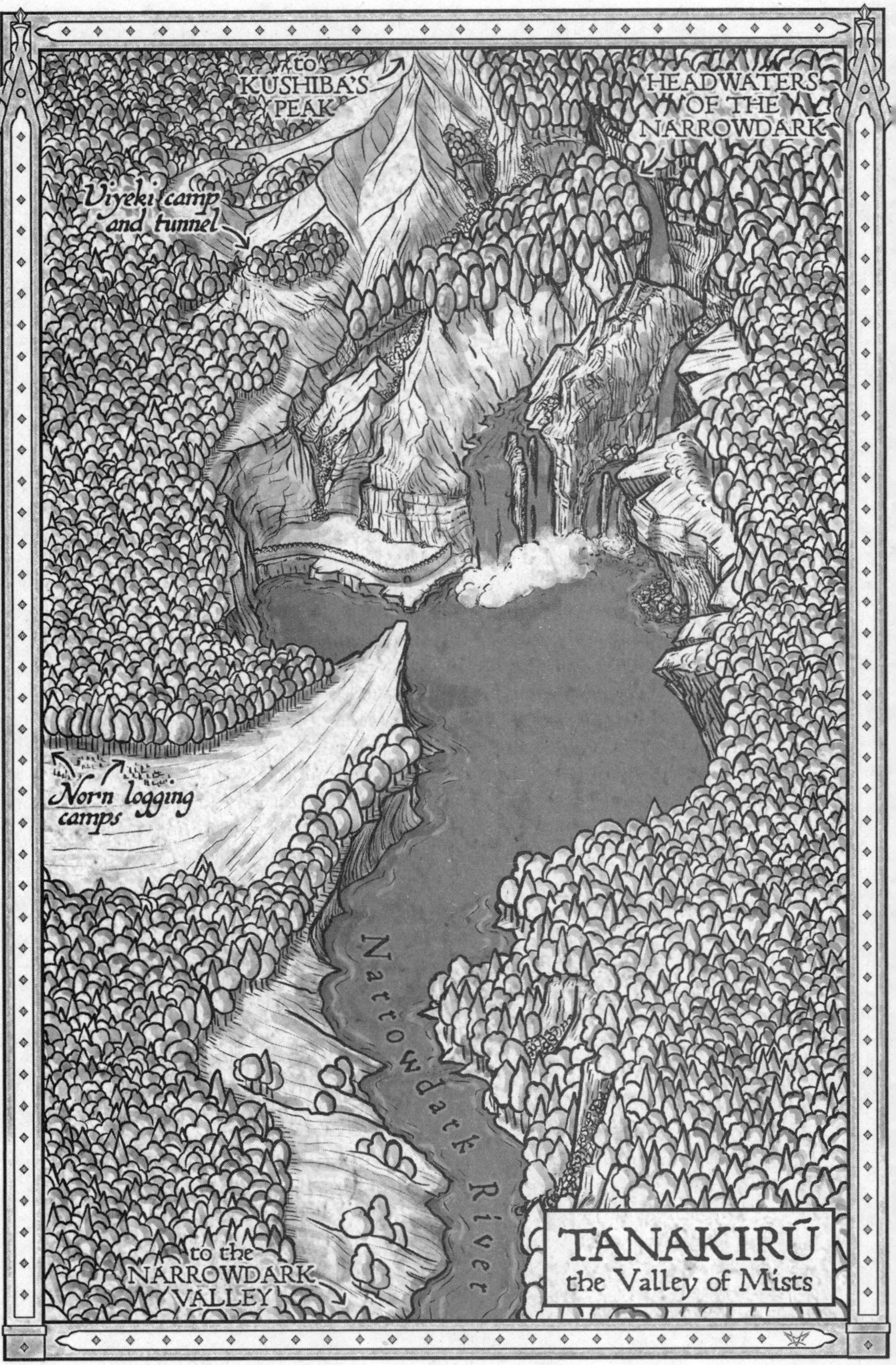
to
KUSHIBA'S
PEAK
HEADWATERS
OF THE
NARROWDARK
Viyeki camp
and tunnel
Norn logging
camps
Narrowdark River
to the
NARROWDARK
VALLEY
TANAKIRŪ
the Valley of Mists

21

A Confession

Morgan awoke, this time as the shivering light of dawn gave the mists outside the dome a little color and form. He could hear sounds of sleep around him, murmurs and quiet snoring from Yek Fisher and the others, but again Nezeru was nowhere to be seen. This time Morgan did not think he could sleep again. He climbed to his feet and stepped carefully over Snenneq and Qina, who were huddled together like bear cubs in a den, then made his way out of the chamber and up to the deck.

After a brief search, he found her standing by the rail near the great mast, staring down over the side into the fog-shrouded valley. Morgan did not think he had made any noise, but before he got within thirty paces, she whirled to face him, drawing her sword Cold Root so quickly and smoothly that it seemed to have sprouted from her hand like a huge blade of grass.

"You," was all she said as she sheathed it again.

It did not, Morgan had to admit, sound much like a lover's glad cry at the approach of her heart's desire. "I just came out to see that you were safe," he said, then immediately regretted it: there was no quicker way to make Nezeru angry than to suggest she might need help of any kind. "That is, I wondered where you were."

She gave him a long and somewhat strange look before turning back to the rail once more.

"The Year-Torch has appeared in the sky for several nights. That means my people's year-end celebrations have begun," she said at last. "The Queen's Rule Festival, we call it in Nakkiga. And I am troubled, Morgan."

"Troubled?" He could not help thinking of Likimeya's dream-warning not to trust Nezeru, but did his best to push it aside. "Why wouldn't you be? Look where we are! Look what is all around us! I'm troubled too—although in my case I would call it 'terrified'."

She did not smile. "Have you heard what happens in the valley below? All day yesterday it was in my ears."

"The fighting? Yes, I heard it, though I could make little of it but for an occasional horn. But you hear more than I do."

She shook her head. "I wish I did not. Down there, Hikeda'ya and Zida'ya are killing each other. It is war." She turned toward him and even a mortal could see the anguish on her face. "I was bred and raised for war! And yet while the fate of my people is being decided, I am trapped here, unable to do anything."

"Do you . . . do you wish you could fight?"

"Of course!" She turned back to the railing, gripping it so hard he could see her knuckles bulge. "That is what I was made for. In truth, it is all I know."

He hesitated, then asked, "For which side?"

She kept her eyes on the billowing white below. "That is the problem. I do not know. I no longer know any of the things I once knew with certainty."

He stepped up beside her but did not speak, and for long moments they stood together in silence.

"My first day in the Order of Sacrifice, the other children and I were taught our catechism," she said abruptly. "The first thing we learned was, 'The queen is the Hikeda'ya race. The Hikeda'ya race is the queen. The two cannot be separated—they are one and the same." She let out a small, bitter laugh. "Our first instructor in combat told us, 'There is no such thing as a wrong order. Discipline must be unthinking, obedience instantaneous. Any command comes down from the queen herself, through her ministers and the officers of the Sacrifice Order. Any command is the queen's voice speaking to you.' And that is what I always believed, until this cursed journey. Until I was cast out of my order and named a traitor, through no fault of my own."

He could hear the pain in her words but could also sense she wanted to talk, not to hear soothing words. He stared at the mists below as they rose into twisting, swirling peaks, like dancing wraiths, then parted again.

"I have often wondered," she said slowly, "if things had gone differently—if our Talon had not made compact with that cursed mortal Jarnulf, or if I had been a proper Sacrifice and ignored his impudent questions—whether I would still be an unquestioning servant of the throne. I think that I would. And I would be at peace."

At last Morgan felt compelled to say something. "Would that truly have been better? To be ignorant but at peace?"

"How could it be worse than this?" Her words were like something thrown down and broken, all sharp edges. "How could it be worse than standing here, knowing the Sacrifice brothers and sisters I trained with are fighting for their lives below? And while I do not help them, but instead do exactly what I was trained never to do—question the great truths of our people?"

"Asking questions can never be wrong," asserted Morgan. "Else God would not have made us able to do it."

"You think so? Try questioning the leaders of your mortal faith, of your mortal kingdoms," she said bitterly. "See how they welcome your doubts."

He wanted to tell her that not all leaders demanded such unswerving obedience, but he could only think of his own grandparents as examples and did not think she would believe him. "Questioning a queen is not the same as questioning God," he said.

She shook her head. "You cannot understand. You were raised in another world entirely. Our queen *is* our god. She has been our monarch since we came to these sad lands. There is not one of our people but the queen herself who can remember a time without her on the throne. Our entire lives are spent working for her, believing that her every word is the veriest truth."

She was trembling a little. Morgan did not think it was from cold, though he himself was feeling quite chilled. He wanted to put an arm around her but feared to break the spell of her revelatory mood, especially with Likimeya's dream-warning still rattling in his thoughts. "But you know now that isn't true."

"I do not know *what* I know, Morgan. I have learned that many secrets were kept from us. That my people have fought a secret war against the Zida'ya since before I was born. That a Great Ship nobody ever told us about has been hidden here in the mountains since Asu'a fell. What else was kept from us?"

"No ruler shares all secrets with their people," Morgan said, uncomfortably aware that he was close to defending the enemy of all humankind. "My grandparents—"

"Your grandparents have not sent thousands of their people to die for an abandoned ship."

He could think of nothing to say to that.

Nezeru straightened up. "You do not need to stand over me, Morgan. I am not a child, I am a soldier. I may not know where my duty lies, but I have not become a coward. I will not take my own life."

The thought had not occurred to him. "I only came to find you—"

She interrupted him again. "Because you are kind. I know that. It is one of the things that has long troubled me. I was told your people were brutal killers, that they wanted only to see our race destroyed. I was also told that the Zida'ya were cowardly traitors who sided with mortals because they hated us, their kin. I do not think I believe either of those things any longer, but I have not found any other belief to fill their places." She put her hand on his arm and gave him a light shove. "Go back to sleep. I know you need it. I wish to be alone now."

An unfamiliar bird call drifted up from the billowing whiteness. Morgan wanted to believe in her, and desperately wanted something from her she might not be able to give him, but he was also frightened that the weight of her training might be too much for her, that Likimeya's warnings might prove right.

"I think I understand," he said at last. "But is there anything else troubling you? Even before we found this ship, you turned away from me. I'm not talking about lovemaking," he said hurriedly, "although I've missed that too. But it seems as though you can no longer bear to look at me for long. Even now, as we stand here face to face, you gaze at everything else instead. What are you hiding from me, Nezeru? Disgust? Regret?"

His heart beat a dozen times, two dozen, as the silence stretched.

"You are right," she said at last, eyes still fixed on the brightening mists. "I have hidden my deepest thoughts from you. I told you that confusion has overtaken me—regret, too, yes. But it is because I fear you, not because I hate you."

"Fear me?"

"Fear what I feel for you. I do not know who I am, I do not know what I was made for, but I feel . . . I feel an attachment."

He almost laughed. He felt frightened and jubilant at the same time. "An *attachment*?"

"What do you wish to hear, Morgan? That word, 'love'? I do not know what it means. I once loved the queen and my order. I loved my father and mother, but I mistreated one and now I have shamed the other. So here is the truth—I care for you as I have never cared for one of my own people. That shakes me to my center, because even if we survive the destruction all around us, what future could we have? To even consider it is the ripest madness."

"You care for me." That was the only part he had truly heard. "You care for me. And I care for you too. By Heaven, Nezeru, I think of almost nothing else but you."

"Quiet," she said, and met his eyes again. She reached out a pale finger and touched his lips. "I know you think it a joyful thing, this . . . love you feel, but to me it is a wound that will not mend. Please, as you say you care for me, do not speak of it again—unless you wish to torment me."

"But—"

Nezeru suddenly went rigid. "*Quiet*!" she said, her whisper surprisingly harsh. She was staring over his shoulder, her attention fixed like a hunting hound's. He slowly turned to follow her gaze but saw nothing.

"What . . . ?" he said.

"Be silent." She spoke so softly he could barely make out her words. *"I hear something. I smell something, too—the scent of the oil used on Sacrifice armor. There are Hikeda'ya on this ship."*

♛

Nezeru let the damp air wash over her. She could smell several soldiers—a Queen's Hand, at least—but also an odor she could not immediately identify. Was it . . . perfume?

"Stay here," she said. "I think they are near. I will go to see what they are and how many."

"No. We'll go together. I can't fight as well as you, but I can guard your back."

She took his hand and felt that it was steady, not shaking. She squeezed it and let go. "As you wish," she said at last. "But stay behind me."

"Gladly."

They made their way from one hiding place to another as they crossed the deck, headed back toward the dome but staying out of view of its windows.

Nezeru was doing her best to be patient but to her ears the mortal youth seemed to bump against every possible obstacle. She might feel uncomfortably attached to him, she might be struggling with strong feelings she didn't come close to understanding, but at this moment Nezeru would have been happier with a couple of well-trained Sacrifices instead, not least because she wouldn't have to worry as much about leading them into danger.

As they drew closer, the unusual, sweet scent she had detected became stronger than the others, a mixture of powerful floral odors not quite masking other, less pleasant smells like dried blood and putrefied flesh. They reached the great dome and crept to the windows to peer inside. Nezeru felt a clutch in her guts as she counted at least half a dozen Sacrifices on the stairs leading down to the interior.

How did they get onto the ship? And why so few? No self-respecting officer would try to take a target this large with just a handful of soldiers. Were others hiding on the deck or moving in on her even now? She tilted her head and slowly turned, but she heard nothing else moving on the deck except the wind keening around the monstrous mast. The invaders' numbers seemed bafflingly small, but there were still more Hikeda'ya warriors here than she could hope to deal with herself, even with Morgan and the trolls to help her. She pulled the mortal prince down beneath the edge of the dome.

"Sacrifices have come," she whispered. "No more talk. We are going to move around to the door so that we can hear."

"But our friends—!"

She held up her hand, then beckoned him to follow. They made their way around the dome on hands and knees; when they reached the door, she signaled Morgan to remain silent. The strange combination of scents was even stronger now, flower petals and heavy perfume not quite masking the odor of decaying mortality.

"*Take up the boards here,*" said a voice in Nezeru's native tongue, but it was too high-pitched and excitable to be a Sacrifice officer. She risked leaning a little way out into the open doorway for a better look and got a surprise. At the center of a squadron of Sacrifices stood Lord Jijibo, the infamous noble they called The Dreamer. Utuk'ku's strangest descendant wore a mismatched assortment of clothing and armor, as if he had simply donned battle dress over his sleeping robe. His white hair was pulled into a high, wagging topknot like the crest of a bird, and he seemed unable to stand still for even a moment. He whirled in place to stare at the dome's inhabitants, who had all pushed themselves back against the walls and were watching the invaders with unhidden fear. "Look at these!" Jijibo said. "Wild hybrids as strange as anything I have created myself! I would love to have them all."

"My lord—" said a Sacrifice officer. "Take up the boards, you said. Where?"

"There," said Jijibo, pointing at the plinth on which the great crystal shrine held the body of Ruyan Ká. "Under the corpse. Start at the front. I wish I could take all these creatures with me," he added, as if it were the same thought. "Oh, but the Dreaming Sea is potent! I could spend a hundred lifetimes and not begin to understand it. Take them apart! That is the only way. Bend them and stretch them and cut them to pieces."

"My lord?"

"Why do you stand there staring?" cried Jijibo, suddenly stern.

"Do you mean we should take apart . . . that throne? The dead thing, too?"

Jijibo shook his head, topknot swaying. "No, you execrable fool. What we seek is beneath it."

Nezeru felt Morgan lean forward, wanting to know what was happening, but she gently pushed him back. Was *this* what the entire war had been about—as well as the last seasons of her own life? Years of struggle, secret forts, secret armies, the bones of dead Zida'ya and the blood of dragons, all so mad Jijibo could retrieve some magical trinket or ancient weapon? And what would happen when it fell into Queen Utuk'ku's hands?

The only one of the dome's inhabitants who had not shrunk back from the invading Hikeda'ya was Kuyu-Kun, but an instant later another dark-robed figure darted forward and grabbed him—the acolyte, Tih-Rumi, who dragged the protesting, struggling Voice of the Dreaming Sea out of the path of the Hikeda'ya soldiers.

"Let me go!" Kuyu-Kun shouted, but he was weeping. "They will profane the last navigator's body! They do not know—!"

Tih-Rumi clapped a hand over his master's mouth and dragged him back toward the wall.

The Hikeda'ya soldiers had brought long witchwood bars which they now applied to the deck around the base of the crystal shrine, gouging and prying at the witchwood planks. *Why did they not bring a hammer-wielder?* Nezeru wondered. *A stroke of the hammer-crystal would collapse that floor in moments. There must be something under the deck they fear they might damage. Or do they fear the noise and what it might bring?* She looked out at the sky beyond the valley. A smear of light painted the eastern horizon, but morning had not truly arrived.

The Hikeda'ya paid little attention to those who had been living in the dome, intent instead on the widening hole at the base of the crystal shrine. When enough boards had been yanked free, Jijibo gestured to one of the Sacrifice soldiers, who shrugged a bulky pack off her back and produced from it a box the size of a newborn's coffin. From the casual way she handled it, Nezeru felt certain it was empty. Jijibo took it from her, then clambered down into the hole, clumsy as a newborn deer compared to the nimbleness of his soldiers.

Now Jijibo called for help. Three more Sacrifices broke away from the ring of defenders and slipped into the hole. Above them, the sightless eyes of Ruyan Ká's grotesque helmet stared out at nothing as her ship was plundered, but Nezeru could feel a tightening of the air—a growing pressure against her ears as if a storm was descending on the great ship—and her skin began to prickle.

Could Kuyu-Kun be right? she wondered. *Is that desiccated thing still alive some-*

how? If not, why do I feel as though we are being watched—as though something hovers over us? Something . . . angry?

Now the Sacrifice soldiers made their way up from the hole once more, followed by Lord Jijibo. The casket he carried was now heavy enough that he had to pass it up one of the soldiers before he could climb out. When he reached the deck again, Jijibo snatched back the chest as though he could not bear to be parted from it.

"The ship's spirit is ours," he said quietly, as if to himself; Nezeru had to strain to hear. "The queen will praise me to the skies—yes, she will be pleased and praise me! But before I give it to her, I will play with it first. I will learn its secrets. But we must hurry back."

"What about these changelings?" the Sacrifice officer asked.

Jijibo's topknot swung like a horse's tail as he turned to examine the wide-eyed watchers cowering against the walls. "These? I would love to take all these mongrels back with us—what secrets I might learn about how they all came to be! But this is too important, so other pleasures must be put aside." He shrugged. "I suppose you might as well kill them—your men deserve a little recreation after their hard work. But do it swiftly and quietly. Danger grows with each instant we stay here—"

Nezeru had anticipated him, if only by an instant or two, and already had one of her throwing knives in her hand; even as the Hikeda'ya officer opened his mouth to give the order, she let it fly. She aimed for his eye and did not miss by much: the weighted dagger flew into his open mouth and the Sacrifice commander fell backward, gurgling blood as he tried to scream.

Nezeru did not have time to warn Morgan to stay back. She could hear him following her as she leaped through the doorway and onto the stairs, but she could not spare him more attention—already three Sacrifices were moving to intercept her attack. She very much disliked the current odds, and though only halfway down the stairs, she suddenly leaped downward, smashing her boot into the knee of the nearest Sacrifice with a satisfying crunch of bone and sinew, then rolled back onto her feet in time to catch the second soldier's swinging attack on Cold Root's hilt and twist it away. She could only hope Kuyu-Kun and the others would stay out of the fighting. She did not need any additional distractions from clumsy, untrained mortals.

Nezeru tried to empty her mind of everything but the ancient Warrior's Way, following the precise movements she had practiced for so many years, struggling to improve even after the most zealous of others in her order house had finally gone to eat and rest. She ducked now beneath a stab at her face, raised Cold Root to catch the other soldier's thrust—witchwood clashed dully against witchwood—then bent backward to avoid an attack by his comrade, who had slid behind her and now tried to take off her head with a swinging stroke. Still leaning so far backward that she was almost upside-down, she drove her sword into the stomach of the Sacrifice behind her. Cold Root punched through his armor, then she let herself fall onto her back to avoid the blade of the remaining Sacrifice. She hacked at his leg, finding meat and bone with her blade; then, as her enemy stumbled, she finished him with a long, stretching thrust under his chin and into his unprotected throat. She rose, but before she could do more than glance around, she saw another Sacrifice raise a long, slender reed to his lips.

Kei-vishaa! she thought. If he discharged the poisonous witchwood pollen she would be overwhelmed or killed outright, as would many others in the small, roofed chamber, but she could not reach him with an attack before he spewed out the powder. She threw herself into a roll and came up a step and a half short of her enemy, then swung her blade toward his face, giving it a quarter-turn as she did, so that the flat of her blade hit the end of the pipe and forced it deep into his throat. He fell back, plucking haplessly at the reed, but already a froth of sunset orange was spilling out of his mouth on either side of the embedded pipe. She turned her back on him, then heard him fall to the floor, thrashing and choking before he fell silent.

Morgan had quickly been separated from Nezeru, but had no time to think about it, because a black-eyed Sacrifice soldier was now doing his best to cut Morgan into pieces. It was all he could do to block the blows with Snakesplitter, even while being forced back up the stairs that Nezeru had already descended. Most of the rest of the Norns in the domed chamber were ranged in a circle around the hole they had made beneath the withered corpse of Ruyan Ká. The strange Norn who seemed to command them was shrieking for the Sacrifices to kill everyone. After many encounters with silent, seemingly emotionless Norn warriors, it was a shock to see this shrieking creature commanding the attack.

If Morgan had hoped the rest of the hostages would spring forward to help, he was disappointed. As he desperately blocked several lightning-swift blows from his white-faced enemy, Morgan knew he could not last more than a few moments against warriors like these, but none of the rest of the dome's residents seemed to be doing anything except watching in goggle-eyed fear as Nezeru and Morgan fought for them.

Not fighting so much as trying not to die, Morgan thought in a terrified moment as the Sacrifice barely missed with a sword-stab that scored his armored midsection but did not reach flesh. He was deeply grateful that the invaders did not seem to have bows, but it only meant his ultimate death would take a little longer.

What could be in the box—the thing they came here after? a part of him wondered, even as he strove desperately to keep the Norn soldier at bay. His attacker was systematically breaking down his defenses; Morgan could not even risk looking to see if Nezeru was still alive.

Morgan's enemy suddenly lunged, cutting at his legs and catching Morgan's shin with the edge of his blade hard enough to slice through his breeks and draw blood. He almost dropped his sword at the shock of it and would likely have died within moments if something had not whirled through the air and struck his Norn enemy in the neck. It was only as the Sacrifice tugged the weapon loose and Morgan saw the dangling leather thongs that he realized it was one of the trolls' climbing irons. An instant later the Norn soldier stumbled and fell onto the stairs, grabbing at his leg.

Little Snenneq had followed up the thrown climbing iron by jabbing his knife into the Sacrifice's calf, and though it did not seem to have gone very deep, it had certainly distracted him. The Norn struck Snenneq across the head with a heavy backhand blow of his gauntleted fist, which knocked Snenneq from the stairway all the way to the floor where he landed like a dropped grain sack and did not move again. But Morgan now had his chance: he brought Snakesplitter down as hard as he could on the Norn's wrist, half-separating it from the rest of the sword arm; then, as his enemy let out a hissing cry of surprise and pain, Morgan stabbed through the unprotected throat. The Sacrifice soldier folded backward and tumbled down to lie near Snenneq, neck a bubbling red ruin.

Morgan was finally able to look around the domed chamber, but his momentary victory seemed to mean little. At the bottom of the stairs, where the floorboards had been torn loose, Nezeru was surrounded by several of her once-peers. They had recognized her skill, and instead of fighting her singly, were now moving in on her together with swords and short spears. But even as they began to tighten the circle of sharpened bronze and witchwood, something blocked the light from above and the chamber suddenly fell into shadow.

Several voices, both Norn and mortal, shouted in terror. Morgan looked up to see a monstrous, dark shape leaning over the dome, vast enough to block all the sky. Then, with a thunderous noise like the world ending, something huge smashed down through the dome, shattering the wooden ribs and crystal windows into a cascade of deadly, knifelike edges.

For an instant, Morgan's mind refused to believe what his eyes were seeing—a great descending hand or claw, almost as big as the dome itself. The stunned Sacrifices had no time to move and, as the claw closed, it crushed most of them like a plow going through loose soil—but they were not its main object. Instead, the monstrous claw plunged down to the deck, then rose again with the Norn's scrawny leader gripped tightly, still clutching his precious box, his mouth a red hole in his face as he screamed and screamed. Then the monstrous, misshapen hand withdrew up and out of the shattered dome, lifting away a great handful of bloody and broken bodies. More daggers of broken crystal fell clattering to the ground. A wooden spar groaned, teetered, and then crashed to the floor. Then silence fell.

"By the Lord's Bloody Tree!" said Morgan. "What . . . how . . . ?" He turned to where Nezeru had been, but he saw no sign of her or the Sacrifices she had been fighting. "Aedon's mercy, the ogre took Nezeru!" he cried. "It took Nezeru!"

With all the Norns now either snatched away or lying dead, Qina hurried out from where she had been hiding to crouch over Little Snenneq. She patted his face and called to him urgently in their Qanuc tongue, but her betrothed was not responding. Morgan was overwhelmed by the need to chase after Nezeru but hurried down the blood-slippery stairs to the trolls.

"Hurt!" Qina said, looking up at him with imploring eyes. "Help, Morgan Prince!"

He kneeled beside Snenneq and did what he had seen Tiamak do so many times, feeling the pulse in the troll's neck and lifting his eyelids. As he did, Snenneq began to move a little and groaned.

"Hit his head, that's all," Morgan said. "He's not bleeding, Qina. Take care of him. I have to find Nezeru. That giant thing took her!"

Snenneq's eyes blinked open, although he could not immediately fix them on anything. "No, Morgan-friend," he said. "Do not go without us. We will come along to help you."

"You can't even sit up yet," Morgan said, patting Snenneq's chest. "Qina, take care of him. The Tinukeda'ya may know how to help. I must go after her."

Even as a bleary Snenneq reached out, trying to hold him back, Morgan turned and mounted the stairs, his own wounds forgotten in his desperation to catch up to Nezeru before the ogre killed her.

"Do not chase the *uro'eni,*" cried Kuyu-Kun, the Voice of the Dreaming Sea. "It is living vengeance. You will throw your own life away for nothing!"

Morgan did not waste breath replying.

As he emerged onto the deck, he blinked in the angled morning light. Something about the bright day puzzled him but he could not waste time trying to understand. He sprinted along the trail of broken and toppled structures that showed where the ogre had gone. It was only as the dome disappeared in the low-lying mist behind him that he realized what had seemed so strange. It was morning, with the sun well into the sky, but before now the ogre had only appeared at night. Why had the Norns' attack called the great thing out of its daytime hiding place?

As he hurried toward the bow end of the seemingly endless deck, he came across fewer and fewer signs of the creature's passage, as if it had slowed to a more careful retreat, and Morgan began to fear that soon he would no longer be able to mark its path at all. *God save us, what if it climbed down over the edge of the ship?* he wondered. He had no idea if the monstrous thing was nimble enough for that, but he also knew he would never be able to follow if it did.

Soon he had reached a section of the ship that he had never visited, a long way beyond the dome. He was trying to find his way in the murk when the deck abruptly slanted down. He was standing at the top of a long and extremely wide ramp that led down to a lower level. He guessed it might have been used for bringing supplies up to the deck, but the place where it finally disappeared into the dark interior looked much too low to allow the massive ogre to pass, its height not much above the ceiling of one of the guild halls of Erchester. As he drew closer, an irregular dark spot as wide as a hay wain caught his attention, color splashed unevenly along the lintel of the opening to the lower deck. It was irregular, and gleamed wetly, as if something had smashed a jar of preserved berries across the lintel and then dragged a gigantic hand through it. A few steps closer and he could make out the barely recognizable shape of crushed Norn bodies lying on the deck beneath it, wiped on the lintel by the ogre's monstrous, huge hand.

He stared in shock and horror, then forced himself closer, praying that he would not see Nezeru's remains in the ghastly smear of destruction and wondering if he would even be able to tell. But the heads he could see all wore helmets—or the crushed remains of helmets—and Morgan did his best to convince himself that none of them could be Nezeru.

She's clever. She'll get free somehow, he told himself, trying hard to believe it. *She'll get free and escape, but she'll need help.*

He looked away from the grotesque mincemeat smears as he passed beneath them.

Where did that thing go? Where did it take her? Morgan was now several levels beneath the upper deck. He slowed to a walk and lifted the *ni'yo* to illuminate the nearest end of the town-sized forward hold. Then he saw the nest.

And what in the name of the Lord God and our Redeemer is that?

It was no ordinary nest of sticks and feathers nor a burrow in which a mother badger might birth her cubs. In truth, his first thought was that the immense spread of spars covering much of the deck here must be the result of whatever catastrophe had driven the great ship into the mountainside. But as he picked his way across the tumbled wreckage, following the obvious signs that something vast had recently passed by, it became clear to him that the ruination was too ordered to have been caused by a sudden shipwreck against a rocky cliff.

He did not have to worry that the thing he was following was waiting for him—nothing that big could hide even in a space as vast as this—but he had no idea what else might be lurking in the unexplored hold. As Morgan wove his way in and out among the monstrous timbers, some broken, some as pristine as if they had been lifted out of the hull by skilled craftsmen, he might have been walking through an ancient cemetery, and the mist that drifted in even here, so far below the deck, only added to the uncomfortable, dreamlike feeling of lurking doom.

But he had to go on. Nezeru was in danger, might be hurt—might even, he admitted to himself, be dead, though he could not make himself truly consider that possibility.

No, it can't be true. Not after she finally admitted . . . whatever it was she admitted.

As he left the nest behind and the obstacles became fewer, he sped his pace to a near-run, though he still had no idea what he would do when he found his quarry. The ogre of the Narrowdark was an impossible, undefeatable thing—it had smashed through the ceiling and stolen Nezeru right before his eyes, snatched her up like he might pluck a dove out of a dovecote.

I'll find her. I'll find her. And then . . . and then . . .

But he could not imagine what would come next.

Even though he ran more than he walked, it still took him a long time to cross the forward hold. When he finally reached the far end, he discovered why there was so much mist, almost stumbling over the edge of a monstrous hole in the ship's hull before he caught himself.

More spars and timbers lay piled around the tower-tall opening, but it was what he saw beyond the hole in the hull that made him stop and stare, heart beating painfully fast. Great piles of stone rubble lay among the wrack of timbers, great uneven chunks of limestone that seemed to have been torn out of the mountain's hide. And beyond these treetop-tall piles of stone and wood he could see a vast crevice leading into the mountain, big enough for even the ogre to crawl through.

Morgan lifted the *ni'yo* and made his way forward. A huge cavern opened beyond the hole, which looked as if it might have been dug out by the same massive claws that had smashed through the dome. He stood, dumbstruck, wondering if he should wait for Little Snenneq and Qina and the rest to catch up, but he could not bear the thought of letting the huge horror carry Nezeru even farther away. With their tracking skills the trolls would have no trouble finding where he had gone—a man with his head in a sack could follow the ogre's progress across the ship. Meanwhile, Nezeru was in terrible danger.

If she still lives.

He silenced that wretched thought as he scrambled over the rubble and into the cavern. Nezeru must still be alive. He was overwhelmed by how important she had become to him, how swiftly and completely it had happened. Only a few moons had passed since he had been her prisoner, held with a knife at his throat. Now he was ready to risk his life—and almost certainly lose it—to try to steal her back from something more terrifying than the most fearful dragon that ever lived.

Mad ideas about rescuing her had been fluttering through his thoughts as he chased the ogre, things that would have been difficult even for legendary knights like Camaris or Tallistro, and though he had never seen the monster clearly, he had seen enough of it to know that there was absolutely nothing he could do to harm a creature that size or even to inconvenience it.

But I would have liked to see my family again, he thought as he passed into the dark depths. *Just to tell them I did my best.*

22

Fatwood Fire

"I fear it is a mistake," Sisqi told her husband. "I do not want you to go up that hill. What if you are taken for an enemy and killed by our own lowlander friends? They do not always recognize us Qanuc-folk at first meeting."

"Unless I am very, very mistaken," Binabik said, "the soldiers I saw on the hilltop have nothing to do with the Erkynlanders camped in the valley—nothing good, at least." He was clearly worried. "But we need to know who they are for certain, and how many they are."

"We have only just arrived. We are not even certain those are Simon's countrymen down below that your hilltop spies are watching. This might all be some battle between rivals we have never heard of."

"That is the flag of the High Throne, flying over the Erkynlandish camp," he said. "Even if we have lost both Miriamele and Simon, we must do what we can to help keep their kingdom alive, whoever now leads it. But make no mistake—I am fearful of the risk too, my love."

"Then let us go together. I do not want to wait here, wondering if you are dead. And what if a roving patrol stumbles upon this spot?"

"Vaqana will stay with you."

She shook her head firmly. "No. Either we go together or stay here together. I will not be left behind like an unwanted burden."

"You are the very opposite of an unwanted burden, dearest wife," he said. "May Qinkipa of the Snows desert me if I ever forget that." He began pulling apart his stick, handling the leaf-wrapped poison darts with great care. "So. You are right. I am wrong. Let us go together and see what we can see."

"I count at least a score of grasslanders camped on the top," she whispered. "They have lit no fires. All are armed for battle. Why are they here, so far from the Thrithings?"

Binabik shook his head. "The question for me is, why are they so few?" he said into her ear. "You do not attack an army with a couple of dozen warriors."

"What else would they be doing? Scouting?"

"Perhaps, but they look too heavily armored for stealth." He frowned and motioned for her to follow him back down the hillside. Vaqana obediently trotted after them. When they had reached a place of better concealment, Binabik crouched and stroked the wolf's head. "You were right, Sisqi. We face a difficult choice now, and it would be harder if we were separated."

"What choice do you see?"

"We could try to go down and warn the Erkynlanders, but we might be mistaken for enemies. And even if we survived that confusion, it would certainly cause alarm and warn the spying grasslanders to keep away."

"But that would be good!"

"It would only solve the problem for one night. And if we were killed by the sentries, the Erkynlanders would never know they were being watched by armed Thrithings-men."

"Could we send a message to those camped below?"

"I cannot see how—" he began, then fell silent.

"What is it, husband?"

"A moment, please. I have the beginning of an idea." He rose from a crouch and made his way quietly through the undergrowth to a stand of pines with Sisqi following closely. "Pray that there have been recent windstorms," he whispered.

"Why?"

"I need broken trees—especially exposed stumps. Because I dare not make noise trying to fell even a small tree."

"I am still not understanding, but there is a large stump over here, and I feel its sharp edges, as if the tree recently came down." She scrabbled briefly in the undergrowth. "Yes, here is the fallen tree itself. The wood smells fresh, as if it has only recently come down."

Binabik hurried back across the open ground, then bent low. By the cloud-curtained moonlight, he might have been a badger or some other scuttling animal. He squatted beside her and felt the top of the exposed stump. "This is an excellent start!" he said. "I will take my knife and start digging it out. See if you can find me more like it. We will need quite a large amount."

"I have no idea what you are planning," she said, but there was as much fondness as worry in her tone. "Find more of what?"

"Fatwood," he said. "Wonderful, wonderful fatwood."

"How many more are you going to set out?" she asked, her mouth against his ear. They were only a short distance from the hillcrest now, but the sky had cleared and they could see the occasional silhouette of a sentry passing in front of the distant stars. "It will be dawn before very long."

"Yes, and I suspect the grasslanders plan to strike soon. An hour before sunrise seems the most likely time to surprise an enemy. But we are almost done. This is the last—we have made a ring around the hilltop."

"Did you have enough of the fire-starting powder?"

"It has taken all I had left, but I have saved this last bit so we can move back down the slope a little way. Follow me." He turned and hissed to get Vaqana's attention. So close to the hilltop, the wolf was distracted by the smell of the men above, and it took a moment. "*Ninit*!" he said. With evident reluctance, she got up and followed them downward, sniffing at the trail of powder that Binabik trickled from the sack.

The waning moon had sunk below the horizon at least an hour earlier. It had taken them no little while to carefully arrange so many unlit bonfires around the hillcrest, with each connected to those on either side by a train of Binabik's fire-starting powder. At the heart of each rick of dry deadfall sticks sat a pile of fatwood, the resinous heartwood he had dug out the pine stumps. Fatwood burned fiercely and would not be doused even if the clouds returned and brought rain.

"We cannot wait any longer," Binabik said. "The men on the hill may be launching their attack any moment. Gather up everything and be ready to flee."

"Flee where, husband?"

"Ah. A good question. We do not want to flee into surprised and angry warriors coming either down from the top or up from the valley."

"Let us head for that great pile of boulders that we passed on our way to building the second fire. That should be far enough out of the middle to be safe."

"Good. Do you have everything? Keep a grip on Vaqana—this may surprise her." He struck together the two stones he was holding, knocking a few tiny sparks into the mound of fire powder. He hit the stones together once more, and this time one of the sparks stuck and flared. The growing flame quickly set the sticks burning, then branched out to either side, following the lines of fire powder Binabik had laid out that linked the waiting bonfires. The leading edges of the fiery stream quickly vanished into the underbrush, but a few moments later they saw a sudden blaze to their left; then, only a couple of heartbeats later, another fire bloomed on their right.

"It begins," said Binabik, scrambling to his feet. "Let us move to someplace safer, wife."

"I hear you." She followed him along the hillside, one fist gripping Vaqana's hackles. The wolf shook her head at the sudden and acrid smell of smoke but allowed herself to be guided toward the relative safety of the rocks.

♛

Pasevalles paced atop the walls for a short time before he gave up and descended the stairs again, his dark cloak spattered with snowflakes and flapping in the wind. Winstowe's current master was restless. He did not do his best thinking when he was restless, he knew. He wanted to walk the castle's high places, but with so many Erkynlandish soldiers camped at the base of the walls, it was too dangerous to linger out in the open.

Yes, that would be both tragic and comical—to risk so much and succeed, only to have some dung-footed peasant put an arrow in me. He made a noise of irritation. *It is my own fault. I should have planned to take the throne from the beginning. Yes, I should have killed Simon while he was grieving his wife. With Eolair gone and Osric gone, with the boy Morgan vanished God knows where, and the girl-princess under my control, it would have been much simpler. Then I would not be penned in a backwater castle, surrounded by some other usurper's troops.*

"You look sour." Hulgar was sharpening a knife almost as long as his master's forearm.

"Truly? I cannot imagine why that would be. Perhaps because a thousand soldiers and more are outside our walls?"

"And busy making war wagons, too, from the looks of things. They have cut down half the forest."

"Not war wagons, you bearded fool—siege engines, to knock down our walls. You will learn the difference soon enough if we do not solve this problem."

The mercenary gave him a calculating look, lips pursed over his shattered teeth. "You do not have so many allies these days that you should insult me, my lord."

"Are you threatening me?" Pasevalles was doing his best to hold down his temper, but with limited success. "That would be a mistake."

Hulgar showed a jagged grin. "The price on my head means I stand or fall with you. But why do we not slip out of this trap? This pile of stone has a rat's nest of tunnels under it, yet here you sit, watching your enemies build their . . . siege engines."

"Because like most men, you think only of today, not tomorrow and the days after. Let me teach you a bit of statecraft, Hulgar. Come with me."

As he led the hulking grasslander across the courtyard, the other mercenaries touched their foreheads in salute. Pasevalles wondered which of them Hulgar had already convinced to betray him to their enemies if things went badly. "Oh, and not that I do not trust you, my friend," he said. "Your loyalty has been a great source of strength for me in these trying days. But I think I should explain something."

Hulgar appeared to be only half-listening, his eyes taking in every detail of the castle defenders' expressions and postures. "And what is that, castle-thane?"

"Do you remember that excellent cask of spiced Perdruinese from the count's cellar that we opened last night?"

"Just tasted like wine to me. What of it?"

"It was poisoned."

Hulgar stopped. His eyes widened. "Do you jest, Pasevalles?" He reached out and curled his thick fingers in his master's collar, lifting him up onto tiptoes. The large knife was in his hand already. "Speak quickly."

Pasevalles expression of mild amusement did not change. "I will speak as slowly as I wish. It is not I who drank the poisoned cup, and it is not I who will die in terrible pain without the remedy. Surely you do not want to harm—or even anger—the one person in the world who can give that remedy to you."

Hulgar let go of the neck of Pasevalles' costly silken blouse. His sullen expression was that of a huge, malformed child. "But why? I have been faithful to you."

"Yes, you have. And I value your loyalty. But we are come on hard times now, and other ideas might occur to you and some of your underlings. So I put a pinch of Norn venom—one of the cursed queen's few gifts that has been of any use—in your cup. The tincture has no taste or odor but do not doubt me—it is inside you already."

Hulgar looked around to see if anyone was watching, then set the point of his knife against Pasevalles's belly just below the ribs. "You will die too," he growled. "I will gut you right here."

"Hulgar, Hulgar. I thought you were a smarter man than that or I would never have hired you."

The big man's face was decidedly pale, but he was thinking now. "Is there truly a remedy?"

"Oh, yes. I have several dozen little glass bottles among my effects, as you doubtless already know. None of them are marked. Most of them are poisons, but one of them is the cure for what you drank." Pasevalles smiled in perverse satisfaction. Another grassland mercenary might have killed him in a rage already, but he had long known Hulgar was a different sort of monster. "Is it clear to you now?"

"You . . . you will cure me?"

"Oh, it is not quite that simple. The cure takes a long time—you must take the remedy for several months, in very small portions. But I promise you that as long as I am alive and satisfied with your service, you will stay alive too. And one day I will reward you with a full cure. So, do we understand each other?"

Hulgar stared at him for a long time. "You have a vulture's eyes, Pasevalles," he said slowly. "There is no life in them."

"As long as there is life in the rest of me. But you did not answer my question."

"You live, I live. Is that what you are saying?" Hulgar slid his knife back into his belt. "When do I receive this remedy?"

"You will have your first taste tonight, I promise. After we finish this next little bit of business with our late host's widow."

Count Aglaf's corpse had been laid out on a board in a small, cold room that had once been a bedchamber for several of Winstowe's servants. His wife, Countess Marah, looked up as Pasevalles and his pet clansman entered. Tears shone on her cheeks, but when she saw who it was, her face twisted in a grimace of disgust and rage.

"What have you done to his poor hand, you monster?" she demanded. "Where is my husband's finger?"

"You should be praying for his soul, Lady, not worrying about bits and pieces," Pasevalles said. "Still, if it is troubling you . . ." He reached into his tunic and produced a bundle wrapped in bloodstained linen and tossed it into her lap. Hands trembling, she unwrapped it to reveal a single white finger. She gasped, and her eyes spilled over once more.

"You are a monster," she said.

Pasevalles sat down on the edge of the board. His nose wrinkling, he thought better of it and stood once more. Even in cold winter weather, the count was beginning to spoil. "I needed his signet ring and it would come off no other way. Be reasonable, woman. It was not as if he was using it—"

"Devil! Monster!" she cried, and dove at him, but Hulgar caught her arm and yanked her to her feet as easily as a man might lift a cat by the scruff of its neck.

Pasevalles looked her over as she struggled uselessly in the clansman's grasp. *Trim and handsome for her age,* he thought, *and she has spirit.* That was good. He needed her to understand him. "Now listen to me, Countess Marah, and listen carefully."

"Listen to you? You are an animal! You killed my husband and my son—"

He longed to strike her, but forced himself to remain calm, to keep the regretful smile fixed on his face. "No, no, I have done nothing to your son. He was sent on a mission to parley with this pretender who calls herself—or himself, for all I know—'the Duchess.' I told you that already, my lady. As to your husband—well, he was clearly not well, to collapse under a little questioning. If he had only shared what I want to know, he would doubtless be with you now."

"Liar."

He sighed, though in truth he was moments away from simply killing her to end her insolence. Having power was only enjoyable when you could employ it as you wished, but it made being balked at even more annoying. "Tell me, Countess, have you already forgotten your poor daughter Aedra?"

"Never. But I have not seen her in days, so I must assume you have murdered her too."

"You think so? Then perhaps you would be interested to hear how loud the dead can scream. No, she lives, but as I told you, her continued health depends on you helping me. If you continue to frustrate me, I will have no choice but to give her to my men."

"You inhuman devil! She is only a child!"

"The men do not think so. They have been dicing with each other to see who will get her if I do not want her—which I do not. You yourself, my lady, are considered a less valuable prize, I am sad to say, but are still the subject of some rivalry."

The countess burst into tears. "I have told you over and over again—I have no notion of this gold you say my husband hid! If Aglaf did such a thing, I did not know of it. Or of any secret tunnel."

He took a breath to calm himself, then another. The Thrithings mercenaries had to be paid: their loyalty would last no longer than their wages, and he was almost running out of the treasure he had so carefully filched from the royal treasury during his years in the Chancelry. Unpaid mercenaries were worse than no mercenaries at all—and he had no wish to be locked up in Winstowe Castle with a group of aggrieved, armed barbarians.

"Your loyalty to your late husband is admirable, my lady—but foolish, and very, very dangerous. I need to know where Aglaf's gold is hidden, and I need to find the entrance to the tunnel. I know it is in the castle somewhere because that map was torn out of the castle plans. If your husband truly did not share these secrets with you, then you must blame him for what happens next—for what happens to your young daughter—not me."

"I will blame you and you alone until my dying breath, you beast—you traitorous beast!" Countess Marah struggled fruitlessly in Hulgar's grasp, face pale, eyes red-rimmed. "And after that I will denounce you in Heaven, to God Himself."

Again, Pasevalles fought to keep his anger pent, though he could feel his fingers trembling to encircle her throat and silence her priggish nonsense. "I am certain that knowledge will be a great solace to your daughter when I give her to my barbarians."

The countess burst into tears again and sagged. Hulgar, with artful timing, let go of her so that she tumbled to the floor.

"Remember, my lady," said Pasevalles, "time is running out. I want the gold and I want to know the way out of this backwater place. My men grow restless, and I must give them something soon—something sweet that they will enjoy. And you will watch it all. You see, Countess, I am a famously patient man, but now I am done with patience."

♛

The Shan, ruler of all the Thrithings, was at least half drunk.

Fremur had not seen Unver drink so much since the terrible day of Kulva's wedding, and it made him uneasy. Three people had died that day, Fremur's sister Kulva, his brother, Odrig, and his sister's betrothed, the last two killed by Unver himself, and the Shan seemed determined to match that dreadful occasion: he was already finishing his second jug of the weak ale that Pasevalles doled out to the castle's defenders.

"Do you know what day this is?" Unver said abruptly.

Fremur shrugged. "Day? I do not know what stone-dwellers call it. The last Red Moon is two days on the wane."

Unver shook his head. "In Kwanitupul, where I grew up, this is a sacred night—Asak's Eve. Tomorrow is the first day of the old New Year, as the Varnfolk call it. The Aedonites call it Saint Asak's day, but everyone in Kwanitupul, even the stone-dwellers, know that it used to mark the start of the new year long before the Nabbanai changed the calendar and put their names on everything."

After this unusual and surprisingly long speech, Unver fell silent once more, staring at his empty jug as though it was a friend who had disappointed him. Fremur's confusion and fear had been growing ever since the first reports of the approaching army. Now, seeing Unver so careless about what was happening—and also the quantity of beer he had drunk—made him speak up.

"We should have left here when we had the chance, Shan," he said. "Before the stone-dwellers came to lay siege. What will we do now?"

"Wait to see what happens," Unver said carelessly. "What else should we do?"

"There are ways out of this trap—" Fremur began.

"The ways out of the castle are all guarded," Unver said. "By Pasevalles's gold-bought soldiers on the inside, but likely on the outside as well . . . if the Erkynlanders have any wit." He fell silent. "Tell me, Fremur, what lies west of the stone-dweller lands?"

"West? The sea."

Unver nodded. "And what lies to the east of the grasslands?"

Fremur could make no sense of these questions. "Nothing. Nascadu and the Eastern Wastes."

The Shan nodded again. "Let me tell you something of the stone-dwellers, Fremur." Deep in drink, he spoke with exaggerated precision. "I grew up among them. They build their great fortresses of stone, like this castle, and live in them always. Even their cities have walls. Why do you think that is?"

Fremur spat on the ground. "To keep us out. Because they are afraid of free men."

Unver shook his head. "No. They fear us, that is true. But they fear their own kind more. They build stone walls and high towers to protect themselves from each other."

Another stretch of time passed in silence. Fremur could not understand the meaning behind the Shan's words.

"Why are our people always dreaming of taking back the lands the stone-dwellers hold?" Unver said. "Because they can think only of what is in those places—gold, jewels, livestock. But if we did that, what would we do with the people who live there?"

"Kill them?"

Unver laughed. "Spoken like a true son of the grasslands. Do you really think we could kill all the stone-dwellers? They outnumber us—just those living in Nabban are as many as the blades of grass on the Meadow Thrithing. Eventually we would give up, sickened by blood. No, if we somehow conquered them, we would become their rulers, take their women for wives, fight among ourselves for the best castles. After a time, we would take on their ways as well, because when you live in stone cities, you soon take on civilized things. *We* would become the stone-dwellers." He shook his head. "If we want to remain free—if we want to keep the lives the spirits of Heaven have granted us—we must find another way."

"Another way?" Fremur was now completely muddled. "Are you saying we should let the Nabbanai steal our land and do nothing?"

Unver snorted. "Fool." But he said it with affection. "Fear not, we will punish the Nabbanai for everything they have done. But in the years ahead, we must think about the lands to the east and south."

Fremur was astonished. "Nascadu is a burning desert! The Eastern Wastes are a frozen emptiness in the winter and dry as bone the rest of the year! Only savages and madmen live in those places!" He shook his head. "I do not understand you, Unver."

"I know."

Before Fremur could ask more questions, Broga, the bulky clansman with the long flaxen beard, appeared from the far side of the chapel. The Great-horn Bull Clan renegade looked as though he might have had more than his share of Pasevalles' beer himself: his face was the color of a rooster's comb.

"Sanver of the Cranes," he growled, stopping to stand over them. "I should have known I would find you with your Lakeland sweetheart."

"Go away, Broga Broomstraw," Unver said. "I am celebrating my holy day."

"What nonsense do you speak?" Broga demanded. "This is no holy day." He was a little shorter than the Shan, but huge across the shoulders and chest, the strongest of the mercenaries after only the monstrous Hulgar. "The stone-dwellers sit outside the gates with their armies, and where is Sanver? Not watching the gatehouse. Not where he should be."

"Do not push things too far, Broomstraw," Unver said quietly, and for a moment he seemed almost sober. "This is exactly the time when the gate needs no guarding. Do you hear the sounds of axes and hammers? The stone-dwellers are building engines to attack the castle walls. They will not throw away any of their troops before they are ready to attack in earnest. So leave me alone, fool."

The one he called Broomstraw turned a darker shade of red. "I do not care who you are—you should not speak to me that way."

An instant later, Unver had hooked his foot behind Broomstraw's knee and tripped him up. A heartbeat more and Unver was straddling the larger man's chest, holding a knife—which had appeared as suddenly as a mole popping out of a hole—against Broga's throat. Fremur's heart was speeding. Nothing good would happen if Unver killed Broomstraw, but the wild look on the Shan's face kept him silent.

Sky-piercer, he prayed, *Lord of the Skies, I beg you, calm Unver's heart!*

Instead of the bloody conclusion that Fremur feared, however, Unver slowly leaned forward, almost as if he would kiss wide-eyed Broga, and then whispered something in his ear. The ruddy hue ran out of Broomstraw's face like wine thinned with too much water. A moment later, Unver stood, but Broga lay still for long moments, then heaved his bulk up off the ground and trudged away without another word.

"What . . . what did you say to him?" Fremur asked.

Unver seemed distracted. "Eh?"

"I thought you were going to kill him. What did you tell him to send him off with his tail between his legs that way?"

"Oh, just . . ." He gestured loosely. "I told him that where I came from, my holy day was always celebrated by killing and eating a fat man."

Fremur could not guess either from Unver's tone or his odd expression whether he was jesting.

As Binabik and Sisqi had hoped, the sudden ring of bonfires around the mercenaries' hilltop camp roused not only the clansmen, whom they could hear shouting and beating the undergrowth in their haste to extinguish the fires, but also the large company of soldiers camped below. As the trolls listened, the widely separated sounds of alarm drew together as Erkynlandish soldiers climbed the hill to see what was going on, then met the desperate Thrithings-men in the flickering light of the blazes the clansmen had not been able to put out in time.

The tumult of battle grew louder, only a bowshot away from the trolls' hiding-place—the shouts of alarmed men and the screams of the newly wounded. Lying in the undergrowth beside them, Vaqana whined softly, restrained only by Binabik's urgent, whispered commands. Sisqi took her husband's hand.

"Do not rush out to help," she told him.

"You need not fear," he said softly. "As my master used to say, 'Coneys stay in their burrows when the dragons are dancing,' I have no urge to be mistaken for either a small Erkynlander or an undersized clansman. We will wait here until the fighting ends."

But at least a little of the fighting came to them instead: at one point, a Thrithings mercenary with an arrow in his leg staggered into their hiding spot and nearly stepped on them. Vaqana could no longer be restrained, and as she dragged the grasslander down, her teeth in his arm, as the suddenly terrified mercenary shrieked at this unexpected attack, Binabik pushed himself back a few paces and blew into the pipe-end of his walking stick, putting a poisoned dart into the thrashing clansman's neck. Only a few moments passed, a dozen racing heartbeats, before the Thrithings-man stopped fighting. Vaqana did not release her toothy grip on his arm immediately, but when she did, he tumbled into the bracken and was still.

Whether because of the fierceness of the mercenaries' resistance or simply the confusion of the night and the fires, the trolls had to wait a long time for the sounds of conflict to end. When they could hear only Erkynlandish soldiers calling to each other along the hillside, Binabik beckoned to Sisqi, and they came out of hiding. Binabik kept Vaqana at his side so that she would not be the victim of a startled archer.

"Ho!" he cried in Westerling as they emerged onto the open hillside, showing their hands. *"We are friends! We are peaceful friends of the High Throne!"*

They were quickly surrounded by Erkynlandish soldiers, many with their armor incompletely assembled, some even without their helmets—evidence of how the encamped Erkynlanders had been surprised by the fires. The bearded corpses of so many clansmen, most looking just as unprepared for a deadly fight, showed that the grasslanders had also been caught by surprise.

"Hmmm," Binabik said to his wife. "Perhaps they were not planning an attack this night after all."

"I do not think they chose that spot for the view," she said. "An attack was coming."

The trolls offered no resistance as their captors marched them across the hillside. Binabik kept a tight grip on Vaqana's fur, but the wolf seemed to understand her master's mood and remained quiet, only reacting a little when one of the soldiers waved a spear at Binabik to get him to walk faster.

"*Shummuk*, Vaqana!" the troll said in a low voice as the wolf bared her fangs. "*Da muqang.*"

They were led to a trio of Erkynlandish men-at-arms, one of whom wore a constable's chevron on his tunic. As the trolls were brought before him, the one with the chevron dismissed the other two, sending them for one more sweep of the hilltop to make certain none of the mercenaries had survived.

"Greetings, your lordship constable," said Binabik in Westerling. "You saw the fires and that is a good thing. We are the ones who set them, hoping to persuade your coming."

"You are trolls," said the officer slowly. "Is that wolf tame?"

"No more than are we," said Binabik. "But she will not harm anything that does not mean harm to my wife or myself. There is one more dead clansman in the woods where your men were finding us. I killed him myself with more silence than Vaqana would have done, because we were not wanting to give away our place of hiding."

The officer was now staring, open-mouthed. "Blessed Elysia, Mother of God, I know you! Or at least I have seen you before, I think. Were you not friends of the king and queen?"

Binabik nodded. "We were, and still we are friends of Erkynland, though we mourn both Simon and Miriamele."

"We did all to help only," said Sisqi. She had not spoken the lowland tongue for some time and had never been comfortable with it. "Fires to call you. Only help."

Suddenly, and to the surprise of both Qanuc, the Erkynlandish constable laughed. "Well, this has been a strange night and no mistake. But you must come with me, both of you. I will trust the wolf if you swear you will keep him tame, but I do not want him biting any of my men."

"Vaqana is a she-wolf," said Binabik with admirable dignity. "And she will do what I tell her—as long as no soldier is poking at her or us with a spear. But where do you take us?"

"To the duchess, of course." He laughed again, but it had a weary sound. "Yes, the duchess will certainly want to see you two."

23

A Maul and Three Beams

The massive, motionless form of Goh Gam Gar still lay face down in the entrance of their hiding-spot when Jarnulf returned from exploring their surroundings. Tzoja was washing one of the blind woman Vordis's legs.

"That dreadful thing is still alive," she told him with unhidden bitterness. "Every time it wakes, it growls and thrashes. See—it raked poor Vordis all down her leg with its filthy claws!" She pointed at the furrows on her friend's shin, already brimming with blood again after being wiped. "How could you leave us with that creature? What if I had not been able to pull Vordis away? She would be dead."

"I am sorry, but I had to go and see if he was being followed." Jarnulf rested his hand on the monster's bristly back, felt the slow thumping of its heart and the rise and fall of its torso. "If there were queen's soldiers after him, he evaded them. I searched for signs of them for a long distance from this spot."

"I fear that monster more than I do Sacrifice soldiers."

"Then you are foolish. I owe my life to that monster."

She stared at him for long moments, then went back to tending Vordis.

Goh Gam Gar let out a deep, rumbling groan, then the giant's eyes opened and turned toward Jarnulf. "I cannot feel the rod they use to punish me anymore," he growled. "The pain grows less—I have escaped those sent after me, at least for now." His eyes fluttered closed once more. "Let me rest a little. Then old Gam will get on with his work."

"I do not know what work you mean," said Jarnulf. "But first I must tell you there are other mortals here with me and they are under my protection. Promise you will not harm them."

"Mortals?" The giant lifted its head a little, peering into the darkness at the back of the cave where the two women huddled. Tzoja felt her heart speed as the creature's gleaming eyes fixed on her, green as marsh fire. "I care nothing for mortals," the giant rumbled. "My enemies are *Higdaja* who put that collar on me, and the wretched white queen. Let me sleep, then I do what I have long wanted to do—kill as many *Higdaja* as I can before I die."

* * *

When daylight came, Goh Gam Gar finally began to stir. He tried to sit up, but could not rise inside the low, shallow cavern, so as Tzoja watched with speeding heart, the monster backed his way out. As he slowly lifted himself onto his huge, shaking legs, she was astonished by his size, a full head taller than any giant she had ever seen.

He said he does not care about mortals. If he lied, he can tear us to pieces in an instant.

But the creature did not even glance back at the women in the cavern. "They tried to kill me with the burning pain of the yoke, but they could not get close enough," he growled, so low and harsh it churned Tzoja's innards. "They will pay for what they did to old Gam." The great head swiveled until the deep-sunk eyes lit on Jarnulf. "Now I go to crush as many white-skins as I can find." The immense creature began to make his way down the hillside.

"Wait!" Jarnulf shouted. "I will come with you!" But the giant did not look back.

Jarnulf had sheathed the Norn blade and was hastily collecting the bow and quiver of arrows he had set down at the cave entrance.

"You can't leave us," Tzoja said. "What will we do?"

"Stay here," he said. "Stay hidden."

"You will truly leave us behind?"

"I owe that giant my life."

"You owe us your life, too." She could barely contain her fury. "I brought you water when you were dying. We hid you and nursed you when you were wounded."

"You do not understand," he said, almost pleading. "God gave me a task, and to do His will I must follow Goh Gam Gar against the Hikeda'ya. But the battlefield will be no place for you. Stay here and take care of your blind friend." He turned and began to make his way down the hillside. The giant's path was plain: the monster had made his way around the largest trees, but simply smashed through the smaller ones, so that the hillside was studded with broken and uprooted trunks.

Tzoja ran after him and caught at Jarnulf's ragged cloak. "If you run off, we will follow you. I will not be left in a strange place—a foggy valley full of Hikeda'ya soldiers and only Heaven knows what other monsters besides your giant."

Jarnulf turned, his face contorted with frustration and anger. "If you follow us into battle, you will die for no purpose, woman. What of your daughter? Would you leave her orphaned out of stubbornness? Let go of me."

Tzoja still clung to his cloak. "Stubborn? Who is stubborn here? I think it is the man who believes God has singled him out for some holy mission."

For a moment his anger seemed hot enough that Tzoja feared he would strike her, but instead a look of desperation transfixed his features. "Please, do not do this. I cannot fight the Norns if I am lumbered with protecting you two, but fighting the Norn Queen is what God wants of me." A look of calculation passed over his face. "Hear me now, Tzoja—I make you a promise. Stay here, stay alive, and stay hidden. If you do, not only will I come back to you, I'll tell you all I know of your daughter Nezeru."

She was so surprised she let go of his cloak. "What does that mean? What do you know of my daughter? Are you lying, or have you been hiding this from me?"

"Peace. I did not speak before because of shame. I traveled with her a long time. It was my fault that she was driven from the Sacrifices, not her own. Just wait here, and if I survive, I promise I will tell you all." And even as Tzoja stood, stunned and staring, he turned away and began trotting down the hillside.

A rage such as she could not remember ever feeling suddenly welled inside her. "How dare you hide that from me!" she cried, but Jarnulf did not look back. "I was wrong!" she shouted, forgetting in her desperation that enemies might be all around. "*You* are the monster—*you*!"

Viyeki had not slept, nor even tried, though he felt as weary as he could ever remember. Long before dawn he made his way down into the tunnels, to be certain all was in readiness. At sunrise Queen Utuk'ku, High Marshal Kikiti, and hundreds upon hundreds of Sacrifice soldiers would be making their way down to the valley, and too much had gone wrong in the past days for Viyeki to feel any sort of confidence.

The guards at the cavern entrance recognized him and lifted their pikes to let him pass. Inside, the cave that served as the tunnel's antechamber was deserted, lit only by a few oil lanterns.

One of the many things that had slowed the digging of the tunnel through the rocky cliff had been Kikiti's insistence that the passages should be wide and high. When Viyeki had tried to argue that would take precious time they could not afford, Kikiti had said only, "The queen does not *stoop*. And her Teeth do not go in single file when they are protecting the Mother of All." Because of the marshal's order, the ceiling of the corridor through which Viyeki was now descending, and all others connecting the caverns, stretched two hands'-breadth above his head, and the walls were far enough apart for several soldiers to march abreast.

How many died so that the queen will not have to bend her neck? How many slaves? How many of my own faithful Builders? He was not used to being so angry, especially with the Mother of All and her officials. It felt like heresy. It terrified him, but his anger would not go away.

All the passages were deserted now but for an occasional lantern flame dancing fitfully in the ebb and flow of the underground air. The Delvers had been herded out as soon as their work was finished, then returned to their pens under guard, but the words of Min-Senya, their leader, still echoed in Viyeki's memory.

"I ask you to come back to this very place—this place, here, where we stand. When you come here, you will understand my request. And if you have thought about what I say now, you will know the choice that stands before you."

That place was the site of the collapse that had almost doomed the entire task, and with it Viyeki and all his tunnel workers, including Min-Senya and his comrades—the "Vao," as they called themselves. Viyeki still could not entirely understand what their strange conversation had been about but he was approaching the place where the ceiling had fallen.

As he descended the slope, he examined the ceiling carefully for any sign that another collapse could happen. Massive wooden pillars had been brought in to shore up the passage, and the top of the cavern had been carefully netted with heavy rope cables, each as wide as Viyeki's arm. He could see no sign of danger, though he tapped the walls and pillars in several places and even pulled at the thick ropes to make certain they were tight and firm. He could see no reason that Min-Senya had made such a point of directing him back here. *They must all be mad,* he thought in disgust. *Min-Senya and that simple-minded mortal too, all their talk of angels and beehives—just mad babble.* He was relieved. Trying to understand Min-Senya's talk of a choice that he would face had haunted him through all the hours since, even as he fought to get the tunnel finished on time.

His mind easier now, Viyeki descended the passage, angling back and forth through the belly of Kushiba. They had dug carefully around most of the caves, avoiding running water and the uncertainty it created. And though the race to finish had been terrifying, Viyeki was relieved and even a little proud to see what a commendable job his Builders had done under dreadful conditions. It was painful to see the crude hack marks left in the walls of the passage because they had not been given time to finish properly, but what did it matter? The Sacrifice soldiers would not be admiring the walls but marching to war. Even without smoothing the stone, the amount of work completed in just the last few days was astounding.

Does that tell you whether I am good or not, Min-Senya? he thought bitterly. *My Builders have worked harder for me than they would have for a magister who beat them bloody and killed those who dug too slowly.*

At last, after a long descent, he came around the last bend of the tunnel to the flat rock face at the end—all that remained between the passage and the floor of the valley. The stone had been chiseled away, leaving only a thin shell, so that with a single blow or two the last of the stone would shatter and Kikiti's Sacrifices would appear almost as if by magic behind the Zida'ya's defensive lines.

A pair of Sacrifice hammer-wielders stood at rigid attention on either side of the rough, flat stone wall, their weapons on their shoulders. Viyeki wondered if they had been at attention the entire time or had merely risen when they heard him coming.

The two soldiers saluted him. "Pay no mind to me," Viyeki said. "I am just checking to make certain all is in readiness for the queen's passage."

The guards looked a little surprised, as if they could not conceive of being less than ready for the Mother of All and their high marshal, Kikiti. *Perhaps they truly have been standing there at attention all night.* He glanced at the hammer on the nearest soldier's shoulder, a hardened witchwood branch or root that had grown around the hammer head, an oblong chunk of crystal. One or two of the crystal hammer heads was lost each time they were used; few of the ancient war-tools remained, and without living witchwood, no more could be made.

So many things we have lost, Viyeki thought mournfully. *So many things we once took for granted. What would our ancestors in the Garden think if they saw us now? What would they think of my halfblood daughter?*

Such musings seemed pointless and saddening. He nodded to the waiting hammer-wielders and then retreated up the passage, headed back toward the top of the cliff.

As he approached the place where the tunnel had fallen and been repaired, this time from the other direction, he saw something he had missed on his way down—a small spur tunnel cut into the stone, hidden by a rocky outcrop. He guessed it must have been created to allow the Delvers to make repairs after the ceiling collapsed, but they had forgotten to seal it again in the haste to finish. He was about to continue, but again remembered Min-Senya's words and the strange, solemn way the Delver had stared at him as he spoke.

"I ask you to come back to this place. When you come here, you will understand my request."

A chill plucked at him as he stared at the recess, as though the freezing mountain air had rolled down the passage like the long-ago river that had carved its way through this part of the mountain. Even the anger that had burned so hot only moments earlier was extinguished by his sudden fear. *Walk away,* the voice of caution warned him. *This can mean only trouble.* It would be dawn soon—even now High Marshal Kikiti must be forming up his Sacrifices on the top of the cliff, waiting to follow the Mother of All down to the valley.

But for some reason that Viyeki himself did not fully understand, he took a lantern from an alcove cut in the stone wall and carried it into the spur tunnel. He had to get down on his hands and knees to see inside but could make out little other than rubble. Then, just as he was about to rise once more, he saw something strange deep inside the hole—a large wooden beam standing on end.

The chill clutched at him once more. He thrust the lantern even farther into the hole, then climbed in after it. Once inside, he discovered that the space was much larger than he had guessed, not a tunnel but a wide opening set at an angle off the main tunnel. He could also see now that there was not just one standing beam in its depths, but three, spaced a few paces apart, each as long as Viyeki was tall, all three beams wedged under a great outcropping of naked stone that hung like a goiter off what must be the back side of the main tunnel.

"By my clanhold." Viyeki was so astounded that he did not even realize he was talking out loud. "By all my Enduya ancestors, what is this?"

He lifted the lantern high and looked at the place where the beams propped the bulging stone. It was a single boulder, but the bottom showed countless chisel marks, while the rest of the massive stone seemed untouched. As he moved down the length of it, he discovered something leaning against the farthest wooden beam—a heavy maul with a huge bronze head. Without thinking, he set down the lantern and lifted the hammer. It was not easy, but he could get it up onto his shoulder, and because the spur tunnel was so much bigger than it looked from the outside, he could even find room to swing it.

To swing it. To knock these props away.

Even as he thought it, he understood what would happen then—what Min-Senya and his Vao had contrived. The weakened boulder would fall out of the wall and the wall would collapse. The fallen section of the ceiling above the passage, which looked so well repaired that it had even passed Viyeki's own inspection, would fall again. Anyone under it would be killed and the tunnel would be sealed. Those behind the collapse might survive, but they would not reach the valley.

Viyeki lowered the hammer and stood it against the beam once more. He felt as if he himself had been turned to stone.

Why have they left this ridiculous choice to me? he wondered. *Do they truly think I would help their plan? They must know I am a faithful servant of my queen, that I have everything to lose and nothing to gain by collapsing my own tunnel.* Another thought nagged at him. *And why would the Tinukeda'ya go to such trouble to weaken the tunnel but not bring it down themselves? Did they really think I would help them with such treason?* His head ached from trying to understand the Vao-folk's madness, but even in the turbulence of disgust and fear, he could not stop trying to understand. *And why did Min-Senya keep asking me if I thought of myself as good?*

As he stood with the ponderous hammer in his hands, Viyeki heard a skirl of distant war trumpets echo down the passage, and he recognized the notes of The Queen's March of Glory. The sound acted on him like a bitter tonic, straightening his spine and making him regret even looking at what the Vao had planned.

My people are about to set out, he thought. *Soon, the queen, Kikiti, and our brave Sacrifices will come marching down this passage. I must hurry and join them. Show that I am loyal. They must know nothing of this.*

He set the hammer down with sudden distaste, as though even handling it might be seen as a crime against the throne. After all, if the tunnel came down and blocked the passage of the queen and her army, the Zida'ya might win. Worse, the queen herself might be killed. Even without dwelling on the horrors that Viyeki and his family would suffer if his part was discovered afterward, he knew that chaos would envelop Nakkiga and the entire Hikeda'ya race if something happened to Utuk'ku. How could his people go on without the monarch who had ruled them since they had fled the Garden?

Chastened, shaking at how close he had come to being drawn into some fatal and irreversible crime, he hastened out of the spur tunnel.

Viyeki had only climbed a short way back toward the entrance when he heard the muffled footfalls of an approaching host, as well as something else he had not expected and did not understand—a strange music, familiar but oddly formless. As it grew louder, and the approaching footfalls grew louder too, he recognized the tune as more of the Queen's March, but instead of being played on war-horns, the melody came from instruments he had never heard before, a flaccid murmur like pipes winded in their lowest register. As the noise of the approaching marchers grew, he shrank back into a shallow recess in the cavern wall, not to hide, but to avoid being trampled in the narrow corridor. The odd music grew louder, its sound not martial but solemn and funereal.

The first of the Queen's Teeth guards rounded the corner of the tunnel above him and marched into view, their conical white helmets glinting in the light of their torches like the fangs of a hungry beast. As they came toward him four abreast, and began to march past, shields on their backs and pikes on their shoulders, the melody grew louder. The mouths of the Teeth soldiers were moving behind the vertical slits of their helms, and he realized that the odd music was coming from the queen's guards themselves. The Teeth were singing or humming the royal war-march—it was hard to tell which, so strange was the noise they made—and Viyeki realized then that the old rumors were true: all the Queen's Teeth had been robbed of speech.

The idea of those tongueless mouths serenading the immortal queen who had made them tongueless brought a sickened dizziness sweeping over him, so that he had to feel for the stone behind him to keep from falling.

At least two dozen rows of white-helmeted guards marched past, all still wordlessly chewing their way through the royal battle song. They were followed by the queen herself, supported in her litter not by Tinukeda'ya carrymen, but by eight more of her Teeth. Even after Kikiti's directions to make the tunnels high, the ornamented roof of the litter had to be lowered a little in spots to allow it to pass without scraping—Viyeki did not want to imagine what the queen must think about *that*—but despite a certain unevenness to her progress, the queen only sat and stared out over the heads of her guards, her shiny mask as unbending as her posture. Oddly, the Mother of All wore regalia that Viyeki did not think he had never seen before, a voluminous white dress with wide skirts and a high, veiled crown that shadowed but did not hide her silver mask. Then he realized he had seen these clothes before, on a tapestry in the Maze Palace. It was the gown Utuk'ku had worn during her long-ago wedding to Ekimeniso.

Viyeki could not help staring, but as the queen reached him, he lowered his head. She did not turn to look at her high magister as she was carried past, but he could feel her thoughts trail across him and then withdraw in disinterest, intent on greater things.

As he stood watching her pass, overwhelmed and grateful she had not squeezed his recent memories out of him, a second litter approached. This one was also borne by a foursome of white helmeted guards in the front and another in the back, but the only thing on it was a great witchwood sarcophagus, a casket so ornamented he could not see a single part not covered in carved runes. The dizzy feeling and the sickness in his stomach suddenly increased.

Hakatri, he thought. *The Zida'ya prince that the queen brought back from death to serve her.* Memories flooded through him of the terrible day in the mortal fortress when Utuk'ku had raised the dead Zida'ya, how the Storm King's resurrected brother had screamed as if in unspeakable pain, killing the very birds in the sky. And with it came the recollection of another terrible hour, when he had met the floating, burning thing called Ommu the Whisperer and she had prophesied to him. Deep below Nakkiga, she had told him, "*To save what you love, you will be forced to kill that which you love even more. If you fail, all will fall to pieces.*"

Viyeki had pushed those strange and disturbing words from his mind and had tried not to think about them since. What the dead told the living could surely never be good, that had seemed plain to him. But now, with the remembered feel of the great maul still in his hands, and the mutilated song of the Queen's Teeth sounding in his ears, it all seemed to close on him like the jaws of a trap.

The dead are our masters. He did not know what his sudden thought meant, or why it brought him such despair, but he suddenly felt as though he were choking.

An equal number of Queen's Teeth followed the two litters, and as the last of them passed, Viyeki saw Kikiti and a small group of Sacrifices, the high marshal's personal guard, coming next. Behind them marched two rows of high Hikeda'ya nobles, dressed in finery that looked to have seen better days: even the most elevated of the queen's relatives had tattered clothes and mud splashed on hems of their garments.

Why has she brought unarmed nobles with her to a battlefield? he wondered.

There came Prince-Templar Pratiki, in full religious regalia of hooded robes and witchwood circlet, his eyes carefully trained on the vanguard of the column, the queen and her Teeth. Viyeki stepped out of his alcove and slipped into the procession next to Pratiki. He could not help noticing that although a few more rows of Nakkiga nobles were behind them, after those important folk came nothing—none of the thousands of Sacrifice legionaries that had been ready to invade the valley floor. The tunnel was empty.

Viyeki was astounded. *Where is the queen's army?*

The prince-templar did not look at Viyeki—his eyes were still fixed on the queen's litter leading the procession—but he whispered sharply, "What are you doing here, Magister? You cannot walk with me here! These are all Hamakha nobles, the queen's own family."

"But Serenity—"

Pratiki interrupted him. "No." For the first time, Viyeki heard raw fear in the Prince-Templar's voice. "Her Majesty's rage is already smoldering about the slave rebellion. If she finds you walking with the Hamakha Clan, only the Garden knows what will happen." He spoke from the side of his mouth. "Fall back! Walk with the others, I beg you!"

Surprised by the heat of this rejection and puzzled by talk of a rebellion, Viyeki stepped out to the side and let the column of the queen's relatives pass, each lord or lady as solemn as Pratiki, each prominently displaying the Hamakha serpent-crest, then he stepped back into the last row of nobles when he recognized Luk'kaya, High Magister of the Gatherers.

"What are you doing here, Magister Viyeki?" she whispered.

"Inspecting the queen's route," he whispered back. "But where are all the Sacrifice soldiers? I thought we marched to war."

Like Pratiki, Luk'kaya did not turn her head as she spoke, but stared ahead. "Just after the trumpets blew, a number of the Tinukeda'ya slaves escaped their pen and began to riot," she whispered. "Most of Kikiti's soldiers are still struggling with the rest. The queen refused to wait in the cold wind for the revolt to be crushed. She ordered the Sacrifices to kill or capture the rebel slaves, then to hurry and catch up with us at the bottom of the cavern tunnels."

This news struck Viyeki like a blow. *So that is what Pratiki meant. Did the Tinukeda'ya stage their revolt because they guessed I would not be willing to risk the queen's life?* he wondered. *Min-Senya and his so-called Vao have sacrificed themselves*—that particular word, *sacrifice,* did not escape his own ironic notice—*to hold up the queen's soldiers. By rising up and keeping the rest of the soldiers at the entrance, they have created a gap between the Mother of All and the army she plans to use against the Zida'ya.*

But surely there is no reason for me to care about any of that, he told himself. He had followed his monarch's orders: the tunnel down to the valley floor had been completed. What advantage for him could there be in carrying out the rest of the Tinukeda'ya's absurd plot? What possible reason could Viyeki have to bring down the tunnel and separate Utuk'ku from the greatest part of her army?

He looked at Magister Luk'kaya, wondering what she would think if she knew his inner turmoil, and saw the tightness of her jaw and the way she stared resolutely ahead, posture and expression he recognized all too well. A sudden realization swept over him. *Terrified. Luk'kaya is terrified. They all are—even Pratiki. Terrified of our deathless queen, of what she might do, of what will happen next. Why did Min-Senya task me so harshly over how I treat my slaves? Because we are all slaves here.*

And with that understanding came something stronger, something deep and painful.

The queen is on her way to destroy our enemies. But they are not our enemies. Is Tzoja my enemy? Because if the queen succeeds in whatever she plans, I cannot pretend she will settle for destroying just the hated Zida'ya. The Mother of All does not settle. She will not be content to resume the long standoff between herself and the mortals. She will burn their cities and slaughter them all.

For a moment he indulged himself with a brief, fantastic idea, that the defeat of the mortal kingdoms might bring such a surfeit of new slaves that he would be able to make something better of Tzoja, give her a security that merely being his concubine could never provide. But that glad daydream only lasted an instant, until he looked back and saw the faces of the lesser nobles behind him, each one trying desperately to hide any emotion other than placid loyalty. And in every fearful face he saw himself, saw the ways he had continually abased himself to crawl before the queen and Akhenabi and the rest of the tyrant Hamakha.

This moment of self-understanding struck Viyeki so powerfully that, dizzied with contempt for his own cowardly choices, he nearly lost his balance. He knew that in a short while Kikiti and his armies would finish subduing the rebellious Vao at the camp up on Kushiba, and then would proceed down this tunnel to rejoin the queen. Once assembled, they would burst out of the tunnel that Viyeki had built and sweep over the enemy, destroying the last Zida'ya defenders and giving Utuk'ku her final victory. And after that? The heavy, murderous hand of the Hamakha and their undying queen would spread over all the lands, and the fear Viyeki saw on the faces around him would be eternal. Utuk'ku would rule on and on, until the sun fell from the sky, and perhaps beyond that.

He tottered out of the line of nobles and fell against the wall before sinking down to the tunnel's stone floor. He thought he saw Luk'kaya's face briefly turn back toward him, but neither she nor any of the other nobles returned to help him. But someone had noticed his actions.

Let him fall. Leave him. Utuk'ku's voice was inside his head, but Viyeki knew he was not the only one hearing her. *The magister and his bloodline have done all that was needed. He is no longer important. If he is too craven or too weak to witness my final triumph, he shall feel its results soon enough.*

And with the queen's harsh words echoing in all their heads, the nobles marched on, vanishing around a bend in the descending tunnel.

Viyeki sat for only a moment, feeling as though he were a visitor in someone else's body, and wondering what the owner of that body might decide to do. He watched with detached interest as this other Viyeki rose to his feet and began following the trail of the Hikeda'ya nobles and their queen. But he was not trying to catch up to them.

A moment later he had again found the wide place where the roof had fallen, the net of heavy cords stretched above his head like an immense spiderweb. He ducked into the spur tunnel; a few moments later, he was standing before the three heavy beams.

He could not think, there was such a clamor of voices in his thoughts, alarmed voices, angry voices, voices of utter confusion, an almost maddening din. He could only watch himself pick up the massive hammer and heft it. Then he felt its thick wooden handle and knew for certain that it was he, Viyeki sey-Enduya and none other, who stood in this small place and who held the fate of countless of his own folk and others in his hand. He had no idea what would come of anything he might do, only a single burning thought.

Enough. Enough of being frightened.

He pulled back the heavy maul, then swung it against the outermost pillar as hard as he could. The post splintered but did not fall, so he swung again, even harder. The pillar slipped out from beneath the bulge of stone and fell, splintered in the middle. Viyeki moved to the second pillar and hammered until it too fell. He could hear a sound now, and for a panicky moment thought it was the irregular marching of the Sacrifices hurrying to catch up to the queen, but then he realized it was something deeper, something less ordinary, a rumble that came up through his feet and bones as though the mountain was waking from an uneasy sleep.

Viyeki knocked away the last pillar. For a long, long moment nothing happened. Then the great boulder began to slide downward from the place it had been held. Suddenly remembering his own peril, he dropped the hammer and ran out into the passage, then sprinted downward toward the valley and the queen's planned triumph.

He did not get very far before the mountain, or at least a very substantial part of it, fell in. The rush of air and rock dust flung Viyeki down the tunnel so that he bounced and rolled, limbs flailing helplessly. Long before he stopped tumbling, his thoughts escaped him and fled into darkness.

24

The Battle at the Leap

Jiriki climbed the last ladder and joined the three Sithi captains on top of the wall. The Year-Torch was still in the sky but dim as the bow lantern of a distant ship. "Hail, brothers and sisters," he said quietly. "Blessings of the Garden on all houses. I wish you favor for the new year."

Cheka'iso grimaced. "Today is only its eve. It might be rash to assume we will even be here tomorrow to celebrate the Great Year's true arrival."

"All the more reason to wish you well now," Jiriki told him.

"Yes. The Garden will endure." Red Okajata of the Firethorn Clan, helmet the color of fresh blood tucked under her arm, stared out into the mist. "Whether we do or not."

"The *uro'eni* has just retreated ahead of the dawn," said Yizashi Grayspear, protector of the Skyglass Lake Clan. Like Cheka'iso, he had fought beside Jiriki in the final hours of the Storm King's War. "We heard the monstrous creature's retreating steps as we came from the caverns. But it will be back when darkness falls again. Do you see the bodies it left behind?"

"I see them." Jiriki looked to the gorge's far rim, where only half a day earlier, hundreds of Hikeda'ya warriors had swarmed. Now the stony ground held only the crushed, almost unrecognizable remains of a few Sacrifice soldiers. "What a wretched way to die. Where do Ensume's troops retreat to when the day ends and the ogre comes out?"

"The cliffs are full of caves on the far side, just as on this one," said Yizashi. "We and our Hikeda'ya cousins are like squabbling mice who come out of their holes to contend with each other, except that we only emerge in daylight. And the ogre is the cat, who hates all rodents."

Jiriki nodded. "But I have heard that many Tinukeda'ya have come to this valley, too, summoned by Sa-Ruyan Geloë. Did they find caves of their own where they can evade the ogre?"

"It seems they must have, but it is a strange thing," Cheka'iso said. "Some of our people have seen the monster walk right past groups of Tinukeda'ya foolish or unlucky enough to be caught outside when night fell."

Jiriki nodded. "Perhaps the creature is blind, or at least short-sighted."

"That does not explain why it has been able to reach into caves like a bear plucking a honeycomb from a tree trunk and pull out Zida'ya and Hikeda'ya who did not shelter deep enough. We have found the crushed and discarded corpses of some our folk that had reached the caverns. How could the ogre know where they were hiding, yet walk past cringing Tinukeda'ya without noticing them?"

Jiriki shook his head. "This valley is as thick with mysteries as it is with mist."

"The longer I am here," said Okajata, "the more I hate this place." She gestured to the high valley walls just visible through the mist. "Even the cliffs seem to watch us—and to hate our presence. Amerasu was right to proscribe it. Only a mad creature like Utuk'ku would insist on coming here. I curse her for making us defend it."

"That is the least of things we should curse her for," said Yizashi.

"Let us not talk of that undying creature," said Cheka'iso. "We captured a Sacrifice spy not long ago who bragged Utuk'ku was coming to the valley soon to see our ending. It was hard enough to keep Ensume and his Spiders at bay without her dreadful presence to inspire them."

"Let us talk only of what we must do," suggested Yizashi. "Your trick did us more good than you knew, Jiriki. See!" He pointed to a slope on the western side of the valley. "The rolling timbers not only destroyed the siege engines they were bringing against us but flattened a grove of trees that they had used to shield their catapults, though the devices themselves were not there when the logs smashed their way through. Still, they cannot set them up again without our being able to see them and put our archers to work."

"Archers without arrows are small threat to stone-throwing engines," said Okajata. "But your arrival and heroic ride has put heart back into our defenders."

"I wish I could claim to have foreseen all the results of our stratagem," Jiriki said. "But I confess it was spawned by desperation. There was no other way for us to cross the water and join you."

"Still, it was a clever idea to use the very trees the Hikeda'ya had felled to make your war instruments," said Cheka'iso. "In any other time, your company's astonishing ride over the gorge would be the stuff of songs and legends—" He suddenly went silent.

"But it is unlikely anyone outside this place will ever know of it," Jiriki finished for him. "I know, old friend. We all came here knowing this valley would likely be the place we would leave our bones."

"Only the Garden is eternal," said Okajata. "No one could see Tanakirú without recognizing it as a place to lose a hard-fought battle, not to win one."

"Quiet!" said Cheka'iso. "Can you hear that?"

They all fell silent, staring down into the swirling white fogs. "The sound of wheels carrying something heavy," Jiriki said. "It seems we did not destroy all their siege engines. Or they have repaired them."

Cheka'iso Amber-Locks shouted down to a kinsman at the base of the wall.

"Sound the call! General Ensume is on our doorstep once more, seeking entry, and we must show him again that he is not welcome here."

Liquid Sithi voices raised in alarm lured Simon up from a fitful sleep and into confusion. He thought he might still be in a dream—for a moment he thought he was deep beneath the Hayholt during his first youthful escape, lost in the endless, dark tunnels once more and surrounded by the moaning phantoms of the castle's ancient, bloody past. But one ghost had a grip on him and would not let go.

"No," he murmured, struggling. "Unhand me—!"

"Seoman King, rouse yourself!" It was not a ghost, he realized, but Rukayu tugging at his arm. He sat up, heart racing. She had put her war armor back on, and had her long bow gripped in her cramped left hand.

"What? What is happening?" He started to pull on his boots.

"The Hikeda'ya. They have rebuilt two of their siege engines, and they are trying to bridge the gorge again."

"Where is my granddaughter?"

"She is safe, sleeping in the healers' cavern. Young Xila is with her."

"Safe? How could she be safe? If the Norns cross—"

"If Ensume's Sacrifices cross the gorge, and we cannot hold them at the wall, we are all dead. Will you stay here with her, or will you fight?"

He clambered to his feet. His thoughts were still slow, as if the acres of stone in the mountain above him weighed them down. "And Jiriki?"

"He is already on the wall."

He took a long breath. "Then I'll come. I'll fight."

"Follow me. I will take you to find some armor, although I fear nothing of ours will fit one as tall as you."

He clambered to his feet and followed her across the cavern. She was right, of course: if the Norns won out and made their crossing, there would be nothing he could do for Lillia except die with her. He could only pray that when the end came, she would still be deep in whatever unnatural slumber Geloë had sunk her. As they made their way along the tunnels between caverns, he dragged his fingers through the matted tangle of his whiskers. "If only I had cut off this beard when I came here. I suppose I will have to die looking twice my age."

Rukayu turned to him and smiled, though it was quick and less than happy. "There is the brave King Seoman I have heard about."

Simon guessed his new armor must be colorfully painted in the Sithi manner, but it was almost impossible to tell in a cavern lit only by a single glowing sphere. The chest piece had belonged to a tall immortal, that at least was clear, although perhaps not quite as tall as Simon himself: it only reached a little below his waist, and he had to wear an added kilt of chain to protect his lower regions. The chest piece was something like a brigandine, made not out of witchwood like Jiriki's plate armor, but from plates of hammered bronze carefully riveted to thick but supple leather.

"Here—try this," said Rukayu, passing him a helmet. He was surprised by how light it was. Unlike the armor coat, this was made of true witchwood: he could feel its fine grain beneath his fingers. It had long cheek pieces and stylized wings that rose from either side of the crown.

"Wings," Rukayu said. "But they are the wrong color."

Simon squinted, trying to understand. In the dim light, the artfully hammered ornaments looked white, or at least very pale. "Why wrong?"

"Because I prefer them black—like a crow's."

Her face was still grim, but Simon knew she was trying to return his own weakly offered jest. He nodded, but he had been distracted by the pile of weapons, some still smirched with dried blood. He selected a long, slender blade, its guard shaped like a flower with widespread petals. He tried not to think too much about the Sitha who must have carried it, and who was almost certainly now dead. "Are there spears as well?" he said as he buckled the scabbard's belt around his hips.

"Many—too many. There, against the wall. Sadly, we have lost more of our folk than we have defenders left."

With the spear Simon chose a shield. It had scalloped edges and an enameled, semicircular design that reminded him of the Sithi cord-art.

"It bears the sigil of Sunrise House," said Rukayu. "One of Cheka'iso's followers carried it."

And now must be dead. Simon could not bear to be among these bleak remnants any longer. "May I see my granddaughter one last time? Bid her farewell?"

"We will pass the healers' room."

Lillia, or at least her small form, still lay sleeping. Simon knelt and embraced her, then kissed her cheek and smooth forehead, praying that this would not be the last time.

"Do not fear," said the Sitha child Xila, who sat cross-legged next to Lillia. "I will protect her and the other wounded here to my last breath. There are not many left to protect, though—all who could walk and carry a weapon have gone to the wall with Jiriki." She showed Simon her slim dagger. "I am not grown enough to swing a proper sword, but if any Sacrifices enter here, I promise that they will leave some of their blood behind. I am small, but I am Zida'ya, too."

"Bless you," said Simon, then kissed his granddaughter's brow one last time. "And . . . bless this child. Please keep her safe." He feared that if he tried to say more, he would begin to weep.

"The Garden watch over both of you—and all who rest here," added Rukayu.

"And you," Xila replied. "Now go kill as many of the Hikeda'ya as you can. Kill them all. Hack them to pieces."

"It is their mad queen who is the true enemy," Rukayu said gently. "The

Hikeda'ya are her slaves. We must hold them off, but remember, they are still our kin."

"They are no kin of mine," said Xila. "They killed my mother."

Simon kept his sword sheathed because he thought any fighting on the wall was more likely to be spear-work, at least at first. As he followed Rukayu through the maze of caverns and out into the dim, directionless light of the valley morning, he lifted his salvaged shield high above his head against incoming arrows. Fewer shafts came from the Norn side of the gorge than he had expected, but one did strike the shield and bounce away as he and Rukayu ran toward the high wall and the crowd of Sithi defending it. The high peaks along the edge of the valley were covered in winter snow, but here at the bottom the air was thick with moisture and almost warm. He glanced back and up, taking one last look at the astoundingly large shape that jutted from the cliff above him.

Such an impossible thing. But how could it be worth killing so many?

It didn't matter. Everything had come down to this narrow plateau between stony cliffs and a deep, deadly river gorge. He would fight to protect it until he died. He and these few brave Sithi were all that stood between Utuk'ku's White Fox army and her prize—the Ninth Ship. Simon could not make himself care much for the ship, however huge and strange; but he and the other defenders were also all that stood between a thousand white-faced murderers and his grandchild.

The clouds streamed past. The waves of the Dreaming Sea broke on the strand, then slid away again. The strangely distant sun slid across the sky for what seemed like hours, then vanished. Hours later, it returned once more to drive away the dark night. But still no one came for her.

Lillia had waited so long that she felt sure even her grandfather had forgotten her. Days and days had passed, bringing nothing but the calls of strange birds and the unending rush and crash of the waves. She had not eaten. She was not hungry, as the woman had promised, but her heart was hungry and felt as if it would never be full again.

For perhaps the hundredth time she took out the owl feather, held it up to the light of the always-burning campfire to see its bands of gray and brown. *The first lady—the good lady—said I could call her with this, but only if I was too scared to stay by myself any longer. Would she come if I called her?* Lillia desperately wanted to see and speak to someone. The woman with the shining face, the one that frightened her, had returned several times, but after the first appearance had not spoken, only stared at Lillia before vanishing again. She lifted the feather against the darkening sky. What if she called now? What if she asked the woman to bring her grandfather to her, or take her back to him?

So that is the summoner, said a cold voice behind her, making Lillia's heart jump inside her chest. *I should have known. Trust a changeling to leave a changeling token.*

Frightened, Lillia spun so that the fire was at her back, then looked out across the deepening shadows. The shining-faced apparition had appeared once more in the dunes, standing deep in the purple grass, her pale garments swirling around her. "Go away!" Lillia cried.

The figure only drifted slowly toward her. *The time has come, child,* said the voice. For the first time Lillia heard something in it that spoke of weakness, a beseeching quaver that might have been real and might have been artifice. *Tell me of anything you desire. I will give you gifts beyond price in return for that one sad, small thing you hold, the false promise of someone who has already forgotten about you. What would you ask? Your mother alive again?* The shape drifted nearer, billowing like a scarf. Lillia thought she could see eyes in the heart of the glare that was its face, tiny holes into a black much darker than the twilit sky. *I could bring her back. Your father, too? Do you wish you had known him? He would have loved you very much. I can summon him for you. Just give me that single bedraggled token in your hand.*

Lillia thought it was a lie—but what if it wasn't? What if her mother and her father were waiting at the gates of Heaven to come back, and this drifting, gleaming thing could bring them to her?

"You can't do it," she said. "You're lying."

Ah, child, you have no idea what I can do. I have brought people back through the veil of death before. I can give them both to you—and riches, too. More than you can imagine. Mountains of gems, piles of gold!

"I'm a princess," she said stubbornly. "I don't need any riches. My grandparents have a whole castle."

They did, said the fluttering thing, very close now. *But it is no more. It has burned to the foundations. But I can build it for you again, just as it was.* Lillia thought she could see the wiry stalks of the dune grasses through the figure. *And you and your father and mother can live there together, happy and safe, forever.*

"What about Morgan?" she asked.

For a moment the voice seemed angry, but the momentary harshness quickly subsided. *What about him? I can bring him back to you too. I had a son once, you know. I loved him very much, just like your parents loved you. But he was taken from me. Do you see? I understand you, child, and I want to give you what you want. In return, I only want one little thing—*

"If your son died, why didn't you bring *him* back?"

For a moment the phantom shape did not speak, did not move, only hung over the lowest dunes, flapping like clothes drying on a line. Then it seemed to grow larger, so that it stretched far on either side of her and high above her.

You are very insolent, child. I offer you life and happiness, but be certain, I can also take both away. I can send you from here to my home in the heart of the mountain, where you will cry and cry forever, but no one will hear you. Would you prefer that? Give me the feather!

The icy anger that beat out from the phantom was so strong and so painful that Lillia lowered her face into her hands as tears sprang to her eyes. Her heart raced until she was certain it would burst inside her. The feather was still in her hand, but it was growing hotter by the moment, hot as the fire: she was certain she could feel it burning the tender skin of her fingers.

"Come and take it from the fire, if you want it so much!" said Lillia, then held out the feather as though to toss it into the flames.

The winds abruptly rose and the billowing, masked figure grew, as if the suddenly violent air had filled it like a sail. For a moment the shining face swung down toward her, and she saw it was a mask of something hard and shiny, with eyes empty as an abandoned well and a mouth that howled with the wind. *How dare you! I will pull you into pieces!*

It felt as though the great flapping thing would swoop down, cover and smother her. Before Lillia even realized what she was doing, she was on her feet and running away from the fire, the feather still clutched in her fist, digging down the sloping beach toward the ocean as she fled the raging phantom.

The shape rose and came after her, snapping and fluttering in the growing wind, the holes that were its mouth and eyes widening until they were all Lillia could see. She did not look back again, but raced on toward the water, which frothed with white chop as the rushing air scraped at it. She felt it first wet beneath her feet, then around her ankles, but she splashed on until it had risen past her knees. When it touched her waist, she could feel it all around her, surging and tugging, but it was warmer than she had expected. She turned to look back once more and saw that the phantom shape had stopped at the edge of the shore, apparently unwilling to touch the Dreaming Sea.

I curse your mistress for her meddling, and you, child, for your stubbornness, the voice cried, all pretense of sweetness gone. *I curse you both!* A moment later, in a sudden, whistling blast of cold air, it swirled, thinned, and vanished.

Panting, Lillia stared at the place where the apparition had floated, but it seemed truly gone. The wind calmed and the waves around her subsided to a low swell, losing their pale caps. Once more the steady roll of the tide against the beach was all she could hear.

Welcome, something said, startling her badly. Like the silver-masked apparition, it seemed to speak only in her thoughts, not her ears. It felt like many voices speaking as one, or as one voice with the breathiness of an entire host. In a sudden panic, Lillia tried to wade back toward the sand, but she could not make her limbs do what she wanted. *Do not be afraid*, the voice-of-many said, and Lillia felt the words moving gently through her, quieting her heart and comforting her shivering limbs.

You have no cause to fear us, child, it said—all the voices said. *We do not come to harm you, but to welcome you back.*

As Simon followed Rukayu across the open plateau between the caves and the defensive wall, he kept his eyes on the sky, watching for arrows. When he lowered his gaze, he saw that at least a hundred Sithi had already climbed into defensive positions along the wall, and that others had taken up places in protected spots around the stony cliff porch, whence they aimed and loosed arrows across the gorge as carefully as if each shaft was precious. Which they were, of course: Simon knew that after a fortnight or more of daily attacks by the superior Norn forces, the Sithi were not only down to a few hundred defenders, but almost out of arrows as well. Their surviving fletchers had been working as swiftly as they could with wood salvaged from the last bedraggled pines growing on the cliffs, but their efforts were nothing like enough. The only new supply would be whatever the Norns shot at them, and the Norns were being very penurious in responding to the Sithi's flights—the Sacrifice officers knew that time and numbers were on their side.

All around the immortals called warnings and exhortations to each other. Simon could not understand more than an occasional word, but it was clear from their tone that the defenders were at a pitch of determination and desperation.

If this is the final hour, he thought, *it cannot be helped.* His heart felt like a stone in his breast, heavy and cold, squeezing his breath. He recited the *Cansim Felis* as he climbed a ladder to the top of the wall, where Jiriki and several others were crouched, peering out across the gorge. On the far side of the chasm, flanked by Norn soldiers with shields held over their heads so that they looked like swarming beetles, a quartet of growling giants were dragging one of the great bridge-engines up the promontory toward the edge that stretched out above the gorge. Several of the armored giants had Sithi arrow-shafts wagging in their shaggy legs and arms, and a few arrows had even pierced the heavy leather armor they wore over their chests and bellies, but the giants seemed oblivious.

Something flew over Simon's head. He ducked, but the hurtling stone passed high above him, then struck and skidded to the base of the cliff, fortunately striking none of the defenders hurrying to join their comrades on the wall. On the far side of the roaring river, on the slope where Jiriki's scouts and hammer-wielders had sent the trimmed trunks rolling downhill, the Norns had rebuilt one of their catapults. As Simon watched, something bright arched up from the engine, a burning streak that rippled its way across the gray dawn sky, then flew over the wall and struck behind him. Simon heard a terrible shriek: the burning missile had found at least one victim. Simon climbed faster.

"They will not beat us with fire," called Rukayu from above him. She had reached the walk that ran behind the high battlement the Sithi had built. The bulk of the defenders huddled along it, watching the approach of the giants and the massive siege-bridge. "This wall is good stone that flame cannot touch," Rukayu called, "and the wood of the gate was soaked with wet cloths overnight. No fire will catch there."

It was the approaching engine that truly worried Simon. Another blazing missile sped toward them but this time fell short, spattering flame against the wall's base. The Norn war-drums were beating now as their siege-engine was hauled to the edge of the promontory; a huge counterweight at the weapon's back end slowed the giants' progress, but they still forced the wheeled engine steadily upward. The rhythm of the drums seemed as doomful and inescapable as the ground-shaking footsteps of the ogre. Simon shuddered. *God grant that we don't have to face that monstrosity as well.*

He climbed onto the walk and found himself in a row of Sithi archers, two or three crowded around each ragged arrow slit in the drystone wall, all with arrows pent on bowstrings, waiting for a signal from their leaders. Jiriki had gone all the way down to the far end of the wooden walk and was now moving lightly but swiftly back toward Simon, exhorting his fellow Sithi in their own tongue.

"Seoman! What are you doing here?" Jiriki asked when he saw him. "I thought you would be with your grandchild."

"She's safe for now," he said. "But if we fail here, it won't matter, will it?"

Jiriki put a hand on Simon's shoulder. "You are indeed my brave *Hikka Staja*—I never doubted that. But I would not see you lost in the first flurry. Stay down. I see you carry only a spear."

"And a sword."

"There will be use for both, but not yet. I doubt we can drive them off Izuka's Leap—we have not enough arrows."

"Izuka's Leap . . . ?"

"The spur of stone that we rode up, where the Hikeda'ya now drag their war engine into place. Only a moon ago, Izuka of the Snowdrop Clan and several of her kinfolk held it against many times their number as the survivors of the Hornet's Nest made their way across the old bridge to safety. Izuka was the last one living, but she held the Sacrifices at bay until her kin destroyed the bridge behind her. She refused General Ensume's offer of surrender and threw herself into the gorge instead. Even if we die here today, we will honor it with her name to the end."

Suddenly, as if he had heard something, Jiriki turned away from Simon and spread his arms. He called sharply to the waiting defenders, and his meaning seemed clear: *Be ready. It is almost time.* Simon peered out through the slit, over the shoulders of two of the archers, and saw that the armored giants, all a-prick with arrows, had pushed the creaking engine to the very end of the of the Leap.

"Jiriki says to ignore the giants," Rukayu said, leaning close to his ear to be heard over the tumult. "They are only burden-beasts, and their work is done—arrows scarcely harm them, anyway. Instead, he tells the archers to wait until the Sacrifices mount the bridge."

Norn engineers now scrambled up the Leap and began to turn a windlass on the bridge-engine. A massive bronze-bound plank as wide as a wagon slid out from the front of the engine like the tongue of some massive serpent testing the air and, as it did, the counterweight in the back crept out in the other direction on its own huge plank, holding the engine firmly in place as the bridge extended over the booming waters of the gorge, moving steadily toward the Sithi wall.

Jiriki called out a single word and dozens of arrows leaped across the chasm. As always, the Sithi shot well, and several of the Norn engineers fell, but the rest only redoubled their efforts, cranking on the great windlass. When Jiriki called for another flight and a few more of the engineers staggered or fell where they stood, the Norn commanders brought the giants up to turn the windlass, and the great bronze-bound plank continued to stretch toward the wall.

Now Simon heard Cheka'iso Amber-Locks shouting from somewhere else along the wall, and suddenly more Sithi came scrambling up the ladders from the ground, each one bearing a heavy branch, some which had been cut into shapes like huge hayforks. The archers moved aside; the branch-wielders replaced them on the battlement, crouching out of reach of Norn arrows as they waited. The Sacrifice catapults were still flinging missiles across the gorge. Most of the stones and balls of burning pitch hit the thick wall and fell harmlessly away, but one flaming projectile landed and burst near the top of the battlement, showering two Sithi defenders with blazing fragments. They did not utter a word, though they were clearly in horrible pain. When no one could extinguish the flames, the unlucky pair turned and flung themselves off the back of the wall to protect their fellows, plummeting to the stony ground below where they lay broken, still burning.

In that moment of distraction, the extended bridge of bronze-armored wood reached the near edge of the gorge. The Norn's giants were driven with whips and curses by their masters into a new position on the engine, then they began cranking another windlass, lifting the end of the massive bridge toward the battlement. Now the newest crop of Sithi defenders scrambled onto the very top of the wall, even as the Norns across the gorge sent a volley of arrows toward them. Some of the defenders were immediately struck and tumbled to their deaths, but the rest lifted their forked sticks and long branches and tried to push the tongue of the bridge away from the battlement.

The Sithi fought hard to keep the bridge from finding purchase, but they were fighting against the giants' mighty thews cranking the windlass. Jiriki and the other commanders ordered the archers to take places around the stick-wielders, but the Hunën on the far side of the gorge barely seemed to feel the darts. The Norn soldiers stayed behind their shields, waiting for the bridge to reach the battlement. One of the giants bellowed, stumbled, and fell with an arrow in its eye, but this small victory came too late: despite the defenders' efforts to shove it away, the bridge reached the top of the defensive wall and the huge metal hooks on its end slid over the top of the wall and anchored it in place so it could not easily be pushed loose again.

Rukayu had been sending an occasional arrow toward the Norn siege engineers but had seemed reluctant to waste shafts at such a distance. Now she turned to Simon, her face fearful but determined. "I think it is almost time for you to use your spear, King Seoman."

His mouth was so dry he could not immediately speak, but he wiped his hands and gripped the haft, ready to do his part.

Jiriki called something, then lifted his voice in a snatch of song.

"He says that three Queen's Talons are coming over the bridge first. He also says the Hikeda'ya must imagine they are playing a pageant for the Year's End if they think that is enough. And he sings the Hymn to the Torch, to honor the day."

Simon did not know what most of that meant and did not care. His heart was pounding, but a quiet voice inside his head was telling him oddly calming things. *There are worse ways to die than fighting the witch-queen. I pray that God will see I did my best for my friends and family, even if I failed more often than I succeeded.*

And then the first of the armored Norn Sacrifices came rushing up the bridge over the chasm, three abreast and loosing arrows so swiftly as they came that most of the Sithi defenders had to duck back behind the battlements or be skewered where they stood. As the attackers crossed the bridge and reached the wall, Simon leaned between Sithi defenders to jab at the Norn warriors with his spear. Cries like the keening of shorebirds lifted to the sky, soured by screams of pain. Simon had had lost track of where Rukayu or Jiriki were. He could see only the dark armor and pale faces of the oncoming Norns and did not dare to look away. Fighters on both sides tumbled from the wall, shoved or stabbed, and fell to their deaths on the stony ground below. For a while, Simon forgot himself, even forgot Lillia and his lost beloved, Miri, caught up in the swift-flowing madness of war.

Several waves of Norn fighters had scrambled over the bridge to throw themselves against the defenders but had so far failed to get a real foothold on the wall, inflicting terrible casualties on the Sithi but suffering greater losses of their own. Still, Simon knew Jiriki's folk could not hope to outlast the much larger Hikeda'ya army.

Cheka'iso took an arrow to the thigh and toppled backwards from the wall but was kept from a death-plunge by the grasping hands of comrades. A Sithi healer now braved the rain of arrows to bandage his wound, and Simon could hear Cheka'iso shouting to his fellows at the top of the wall, doubtless telling them to stay strong, that he would soon return. Red Okajata had also nearly died, struck by a stone flung by a bellowing giant, who had come out onto the bridge until its weight had bowed the span so gravely that the huge beast had been forced to retreat. Okajata's scarlet helmet was ruined, and blood ran down her forehead and cheek, but she seemed to have suffered no great damage and had already returned to the fighting without her helm. Her snow-white hair, shocked loose from its binding by the impact of the missile, streamed in the breeze like a torn spiderweb.

But after the Norns' last failure, during which Simon and several spear-wielding Sithi managed to hold back the swarming Sacrifices, a horn blew from the heart of the Norn army and more black-armored troops began to form around the base of the bridge. As Simon stared, wondering what devilry would follow, Rukayu shouldered her way up beside him. She had slashes on her padded sleeves and a deep cut on the back of her right hand but seemed otherwise hale.

"The general is angry," she said, watching the far side of the gorge as she wiped blood onto her breeks. "He has called up his personal guard."

Simon was exhausted. He dropped to one knee, gasping. "What general?" he asked at last.

"Ensume, the leader of these Hikeda'ya. One of the mightiest of all Utuk'ku's warriors. There—do you see him?"

A tall Norn in gray witchwood armor swung down from his saddle and stepped onto the far end of the siege-bridge. A few Sithi archers let fly at him, but Ensume raised a wide shield, black with a white spider ensign, and warded off the arrows as easily as if they were twigs thrown in a children's game. A company of Norns with spider badges arrayed themselves around him, then Ensume cupped his hands before his mouth and shouted across the gorge in the harsh Norn version of the Garden tongue.

"He asks who commands here—he calls us a rabble of traitors." Rukayu's face was as hard, her expression sharp as chipped flint.

After a moment, Jiriki climbed up onto the battlement. Several Norns lifted their bows, but Ensume thrust out his hand and they lowered them again. The general took off his helmet, revealing white hair in knotted war-braids. He had a broad face and haughty posture, Simon thought, but could make out little else from such a distance.

As first Ensume spoke, then Jiriki, Rukayu whispered a translation.

"This valley and all in it belong to Utuk'ku, Queen of Nakkiga," the general declared. *"If you are the protector here, whoever you are, you have been led astray by your masters—and by the lies of the ancient traitor, Amerasu of Asu'a."*

After a moment, Jiriki called back. *"I am Jiriki i-Sa'onserei, as you doubtless already know—you may remember me, since I rode straight through your army only yesterday—and it is you and your soldiers who trespass here. Do not pretend after months of warfare that there is anything left to dispute, Ensume. If you want the valley and what is in it, come ahead and take it. You have many soldiers, and you seem eager to throw lives away. We are not so many, but we are enough to supply your Sacrifices with the deaths they crave."*

General Ensume flicked his hand as at a remark of no significance. *"If you surrender, the Mother of All will be generous."*

"I know all about the generosity of your mistress," Jiriki said as Rukayu translated. *"I saw how she made peace with Amerasu, and I have seen the mercy she showed at the Hornet's Nest—bones of both our clans left behind to rot, unburied and unburnt. No, I think something hurries you—whether it is the impatience of your so-called queen, or something else—and you hope to save time. If you want what we guard, I repeat—come and take it. I will wait for you eagerly."* He turned then and called something over his shoulder to Okajata and Yizashi.

"Jiriki says that the bridge is narrow—that the three of them should try to hold it," Rukayu translated. "The rest of our folk should stay close behind until he or one of his companions falls, then we must step up to take their places."

"But Jiriki has been fighting for hours!" Simon protested. "He must be exhausted!"

"He is also subtle," Rukayu said. "You must trust him, King Seoman. We all must trust the Protector now."

Simon bit his lip and said no more.

General Ensume did not bother with a reply but vaulted easily onto the engine at the base of the siege-bridge, ducked as a single Sithi arrow whistled past him, then leaped onto the bridge and began to walk across the gorge, shield held high, a great ax gripped in his gauntleted fist. Dozens of armored Sacrifices swarmed after him.

The afternoon sun had now sunk behind the high valley walls, bringing early twilight, and mist drifted up from the depths of the river canyon to drift across the bridge. As Simon waited, still fighting to get his breath back, Rukayu began to sing in a quiet, clear voice—the same distantly familiar melody that Jiriki had been singing a short time earlier.

Ai-Ereb Irigú
Ka'ai shikisi aruya'a
Shishei, shishei burusa'eya!
Pikuuru n'dai-tu.

Simon turned toward her and saw that her eyes were full of tears.

25

Woolyard Market

When he heard the clink of mail and the shuffling of booted feet in the stone passageway outside his cell, he quickly stoppered the jar of ink, then rolled it and the quill into the sheepskin parchment on which he had been writing and hid the bundle beneath the scratchy horsehair pallet that was his prison bed. Imprisoned by King Hugh in a cell in the ruins of a long-deserted Sithi city under a mountain, Eolair had been making his will, though he knew there was scant chance that anyone beside Hugh and his minions would ever see it. He feared what would happen to his demesne, Nad Mullach, and his sister Elatha more than he feared his own death. His family would almost certainly be one of Hugh's next targets. Tyrants did not allow the kinfolk of executed enemies to prosper, and Hugh had become a tyrant.

The key turned in the lock with a sound like something being dropped, heavy and final. The door swung open and half a dozen guards shouldered into his rocky cell.

"So many to deal with an old man?" Eolair asked.

The leader, a hawk-nosed, muscular soldier wearing the badge of Hugh's Silver Stags, seemed to be in a good mood. "We are here to celebrate!" he said with a mocking grin. "Tomorrow is to be a holy day, so today we are taking a traitor down to Hernysadharc for execution."

Eolair felt a coldness in his guts that swiftly spread through his body. So, the time had come. "I remember you now," he told the chieftain. "You are Samreas, Baron Curudan's hunting dog."

"Call me what you will—better a living dog than a dead traitor. Come, stand up."

Eolair looked at the row of guards, but none would meet his eye. "Where is your comrade, Glinn?" he asked. "I wanted to thank him for his courtesy to me during my imprisonment."

"He was a little *too* courteous," said the Stag captain, grinning. "He is under arrest for disloyalty to His Majesty."

The cold in Eolair's middle seemed to squeeze his heart. "He did nothing wrong. Is it disloyal to show kindness to a condemned prisoner?"

"A condemned prisoner who conspired to overthrow the rightful king of

Hernystir?" He laughed. "Do not worry, Hand of the High Throne. Glinn of Shanross will receive a fair hearing from his fellow Stags before we cut off his head."

Bile rose in Eolair's throat. "Like the fair hearing Hugh gave me?"

"Why should you receive a trial? Traitors cannot be trusted, so nothing you might say needs to be heard."

A vast, hopeless weariness settled over Eolair. "We waste time talking, Samreas. You are not just a dog, you are a dog that has been taught to bark human words—although you do not understand them."

For a moment a bright light of rage kindled in the soldier's eyes and his hand lifted. "No," he said, and lowered it again. "I will not deliver you with bruises that might make the foolish crowd pity you." He turned to the other soldiers. "Bind him."

Eolair did not bother to struggle but stood passively as his hands were tied. He balked only when someone stepped behind him and tied a cloth across his eyes. "This is not necessary. It is a long ride down to Hernysadharc. Can you not let me see the land of my birth one last time before I die?"

"Gag him, too," said Samreas.

From the smell, a mixture of dung and hay and animal musk, Eolair could tell that the vehicle they had chosen for his last ride was a farm wagon. As he was roughly shoved into it, the wagon began to move, wheels squeaking plaintively as the driver whipped the animals forward. His gag tasted of someone else's sweat, and Eolair wondered what poor soul had been tied with it before him.

Better days will come after this—after I am gone. I must believe it. He prayed to Brynioch, who was always watching, or at least so the priests said. *Sky-lord, my end is come, but do not forget the others who have kept your name in their hearts. They say you do not interfere in the affairs of mortal men, but surely no one, not even the gods, can stand by and let a tyrant murder his own people. If you honor the prayers of your worshippers, hear mine! As you once cast down Tethtain for his tyranny, throw down this mad king, I beg you.*

The wagon bumped slowly down the winding track. Eolair could tell it was morning by the sounds of the birds in the trees above him, bravely chirping in the chill winter air. As he listened, their songs were overtaken by a nearer noise, a ringing scrape from close by that went on and on—*skring, skring, skring.*

"Take the blindfolds off," said Samreas.

The knot at the back of Eolair's head was loosened and the cloth lifted away. Light rushed in, blinding him for an instant. The first thing he could make out was Inahwen at the front of the wagon, dressed in the ragged remnants of what had once been a costly gown, but now was torn and stained. Her head was bent sharply backward by one of the Silver Stags and her pale neck exposed, which made Eolair's heart leap in anger and fear. But even as he tried to struggle to his feet, the soldier who had removed his blindfold shoved him back down. The other guard finished removing Inahwen's blindfold and let go of her hair. For a moment her head hung as if the soldier had broken her neck, but at last she looked up.

All Eolair could do was lock eyes with her, since they were both still gagged. Inahwen's eyes, he was relieved to see, were clear and almost calm: she would not let what was coming steal her dignity. He put everything he could into his silent stare. *I will not desert you, even in death,* he tried to make his eyes say. *I will not leave this time without you.* Behind her he could see the top of the Taig in the distance, its roof tiles glinting in pale sunshine, though a few snowflakes whirled down from the sky.

"You spoke earlier of courtesy," said Samreas. The ringing scrape resumed, *skring, skring.* The stag chieftain had a long, bright sword across his lap and was whetting the edge of the blade with oil and a sharpening stone. "Now you know *true* courtesy, Count Eolair. I have ordered your blindfolds taken off so that you and the dowager queen may look out over the city one last time before you meet the Withy Crow tomorrow. You may thank me if you wish." He smiled. "Oh, I forgot, you cannot speak. Ah, well."

Eolair stared at him with as much contempt as he could muster.

The wagon, which was even more decrepit than he had imagined, trundled on down the wide hill road. Eolair could see the walls of Hernysadharc now behind Inahwen's shoulders, the massive, ancient stones at the bottom topped by rows of sharpened, outward-leaning stakes that Eolair had never seen before. Perhaps, he thought hopefully, King Hugh was not as certain of his invulnerability as he would like to be.

Eolair knew he was a drowning man grabbing at flotsam that could not buoy him. It would take a great deal to bring down a king, and even if it happened, he would not be around to see it. He caught Inahwen's eyes again, willing her peace and courage, and once more began to pray.

Eolair's grandnephew Aelin thought he saw something from the corner of his eye—a flicker of movement above him—but when he stopped and looked up, nothing but chimneys and gables were visible along the roof-crests of wide Tethtain's Way.

To look as though you are afraid of being followed will suggest to anyone watching that you have reason to fear, Aelin chided himself. *Uncle Eolair would not startle at every shadow like an untrained horse. These are only phantoms of your worry. Do not make your ancestors ashamed.* But, of course, he had every reason to fear.

He pulled his hood lower as he approached torchlit Woolyard Market in the heart of the city, nestled at the base of the Taig's rocky hill. He did not expect anyone in the narrow streets to recognize a young knight from a distant county who had been largely absent from the Hernysadharc court, but it was a bad idea to be careless.

Though it was the middle of the night, the streets around the market square were far from empty: many of the city's inhabitants had already assembled in rough camps on the cobbles of the square, wanting to be certain of a good seat for the next day's execution. Aelin trailed after a group of drunken apprentices, but at the last moment decided that entering the square itself might be stretching his luck. He had already surveyed it several times during the day, planning where he thought would be the best places to distribute their rebels once they had collected weapons from their hiding spots. Beside the gibbet and the ghastly, spread-winged structure that had been built atop it, workmen had also erected a viewing stand on the other side of the square, from which King Hugh and Lady Tylleth would watch the proceedings. As Aelin watched from a street that opened into the square, the last remaining workers were covering the royal stand with bunting. The elaborate preparations, as if for some glad celebration, sickened him. Aelin turned away.

Tomorrow, he thought. *Tomorrow we must win or we die.* Such simplicity felt both terrifying and liberating. *May Brynioch and Heaven preserve us.* He tried to ignore the knot of sick fear in his gut. *One way or another, we will be free—*

Another moving shadow, this one at the end of a side street, momentarily caught his eye, then was gone. *Someone hurrying home, no doubt,* he told himself. But he could not rid himself of the feeling that the night was alive with malign presences and watching eyes.

After his latest scouting expedition, undertaken more to ease his anxious nerves than out of real need, Aelin crossed back through the district known as Little Erkyn, then across wide Temple Way into the neighborhood of Anvil Row, perched on a spur of the stony hill just inside the city walls. As he approached the farrier's house, he could hear hammering from a few of the nearby smithies even at this late hour, which was a relief, because he knew there would be much noise coming from their own forge, where men were laboring through the night to craft arrows for the next day.

The large, silent men guarding the street door recognized him and let him pass. He nodded to the half-dozen sweating smiths in the firelit shop as he headed to the stairs, but few bothered to look up, too busy pounding and shaping iron barbs for the fletchers at work in the next room. There was often noise at night in Anvil Row, but seldom this much, and he could only pray that the clangor would not draw the attention of the city watch.

Still, we have had no trouble in these last days. Hugh must think himself unassailable because of the hundreds of soldiers he has brought into Hernysadharc to keep the people cowed tomorrow. May Heaven grant that he is wrong!

At the top of the stairs two more men were waiting. He recognized one of them as Tace Odhran's large, fair-haired son Orin, and nodded a greeting, receiving a nod in return as he passed through to the shop's living quarters. Nobody in the house seemed to want to speak—Aelin thought it strange, when the men downstairs were making such a clatter.

Maccus and Evan greeted him with relief—they had clearly worried at his being out so late—then followed him into the main room.

Earl Murdo was sitting with Tace Odhran and a few other leaders of the conspiracy. The old noble Odhran looked up for a moment before recognizing Aelin, who was half-surprised that Odhran had not brought his beloved goat to town with him.

"Well, young fellow? Have you any news?" asked Odhran. "What does Lady Ethna say?"

Aelin seated himself. "Before I speak of that, has anyone beside me said anything of spies on the housetops?"

Earl Murdo sat forward. "What did you see?"

Aelin quickly described the odd shadows and his sensation of being watched.

"I think it is only the worry we all feel," Murdo said when he had finished. "As long as you are certain you were not followed."

"I chose a way in thick shadow, but where anyone behind me would have to cross through torchlight. I saw no one."

"Then your concern is likely just worry, but we will also keep our eyes open," said Murdo. "Now, tell us of Lady Ethna. Will she be with us? We will need all the support we can find inside the city, and she is trusted by the other nobles. Things will be very pressing in the first hour. If we cannot quickly dispatch Curudan and arrest the king, there will be battle through all the streets of Hernysadharc." He shook his head. "I do not like our chances well if it comes to that."

"Not to speak of how many innocents would suffer—Hugh will not hesitate to make it a slaughter." Aelin had to stop and take a calming breath; it was hard to keep his hatred of the king harnessed. "Lady Ethna said she has not lost any of her anger at the king for what he's done to her husband." Baron Gilmor was currently imprisoned in the same mountain fastness as Eolair and Queen Inahwen, dragged out of his own house in chains for complaining about the influence of Lady Tylleth. Gilmor been held for over a year without a trial and was reputedly now in failing health. "But her lands in the east are surrounded by some of Hugh's staunchest supporters, which is why she moved here to her city house."

"Yes, and where she keeps several score armed retainers who could be a great help to us. What will she do?" demanded Tace Odhran in an aggrieved voice. "Goodness, this is like talking to your great-uncle Eolair—so much explanation!"

Aelin smiled despite himself. "I know you do not mean that as an insult, my lord Tace, and I do not take it that way. Like him, I am trying to tell all the truth that is needed." He took another deep breath. "If it comes to a fight in the streets, Ethna will support us with her household guard, and with sanctuary in her great house . . . but not if we fail in our original strike and the king remains free. She says that much as she hates Hugh and Tylleth, she is too old to become a fugitive from an angry king."

"Gods curse it!" said Murdo, dropping both hands on his knees. "Will none of these cowardly nobles stand up for the people? Will they all sit by and watch as Hugh hands our kingdom over to the white witch and her Norns?"

"It only means that we must be disciplined, I think," Aelin said. "We are all pledged to stop Hugh executing the dowager queen and my great-uncle, no matter the cost. If we risk our lives and those of our supporters for that goal, then King Hugh's life cannot be sacred, either."

Odhran seemed shocked by this. "We swore we would arrest him, young Aelin, but that we would then give him fair trial as the Edicts of Cormach dictate. Would you simply assassinate Lluth's grandson? Whatever it is claimed Hugh has done, he is the rightful monarch until his crimes are proved."

"No," said Aelin loudly, and realized that not just his own men but all the lords in the room were looking at him now with expressions ranging from surprise to actual alarm. "No, my lord Tace. Much as I hate him, I do not think we should kill Hugh—*if* we can capture him instead. If we do that, then Curudan, his Silver Stags, and the soldiers will fall or flee. But if the king escapes arrest, he will eventually overpower us. Then we are *all* dead, and neither swiftly nor painlessly. So, I for one will rule out nothing." He tried to make his voice even firmer: he knew some of the older nobles had doubts about letting a young knight like himself take such a strong part in the planning. "Hugh has declared tomorrow a festival of in honor of the Morriga—the Crow Mother. This execution of Inahwen and my uncle is not just a royal murder, it is meant to be a sacrifice to that horrid, shunned goddess—do you see? Hugh has made compact with the foulest enemies of mankind, and the reports say that he has also moved many soldiers out of the Frostmarch forts that used to protect us from the Norn demons, sending them to the Erkynlandish borders instead." He looked around the gathering. "You all know as well as I do that he has not done this to protect Hernystir, but in preparation for a push into Erkynland because of the deaths of Simon and Miriamele. If that was all that our so-called king planned, some of you might even honor him as a new Tethtain, thinking he wanted only to expand Hernystiri power . . . but those of you who have been at court in the Taig know better, I think." Aelin did his best to slow his heart, to keep his voice strong but reasonable. Old Odhran of Carn Buic still looked dubious but was at least listening. "They say Hugh even goes about these days wearing the armor of a Norn lord, and it is well known that he consorts by night with envoys from the White Queen of the North herself. And he has brought back the worship of the most dreadful of the old gods, the Morriga . . . though he and his doxy call her 'Talamh' to soothe the superstitious peasants. Remember, it is not just the queen and Eolair who will be his victims, my lords! Hugh imprisons and executes all who show the least resistance. If we do not stop him, he will come for all of us, sooner or later. He took Count Eolair out of his own house!"

Aelin still saw doubt in some eyes. *Brynioch and brave Rhynn*, he prayed, *send me strength to convince these careful men!* "The time for debate is gone, my lords," he insisted. "And half-measures like Lady Ethna offers are of no use to us. Such timidity will only bring more death, and the strangling of our freedom. No, we must force Lady Ethna's hand—force the hand of every good-hearted noble left in Hernystir. Hugh must not leave Woolyard Square as a free man, and I will gladly give my own life to ensure that. I swear this on Brynioch Sky-Father and all of Heaven." He let his last words hang in the air for a long moment before asking, "Now what of the rest of you?"

Much discussion followed, of course—many of the gathered lords still seemed troubled by what they had put into train—but after Murdo and several others returned to their city manors for the night, and Aelin finally made his way up the stairs of the farrier's house in search of a bed and a few hours' sleep, he thought he had felt a difference in the way they spoke, a more pointed and practical understanding of what was before them, and perhaps even a greater resolve in several of them who had wavered before. He hoped so.

Aelin awoke to find a dark figure leaning over him. For a moment, still tangled in sleep, he thought it was the Sitha Yeja'aro again, come back to finish strangling him, but before he could defend himself, the shadow spoke in an urgent whisper. "My lord, it is me—Evan!"

"Mircha's Tears, what are you doing, man? What if I had stabbed you?"

"The girl, Sir Aelin. The girl is here and she demands to see you."

"Girl?"

"Murdo's daughter. The one we met—"

"Lady Isleen?" He looked to the window, but the shutters were down. "What hour of the clock is it? Where is Maccus?"

"Still an hour of darkness left," said Evan. "And I have not seen Maccus since the knocking woke me. Come. The girl is full of upset."

Aelin pulled on his trews, picked up his sword, and followed Evan down the stairs to the bottom floor. The workshop was silent now, all the workmen asleep near the fire, which had burned down to a few coals. Isleen wore a heavy winter cloak, but she had thrown back the hood and the look on her startlingly pale face made Aelin's heart stutter. "My lady, what is it?" He only just remembered to keep his voice low.

"Disaster," she said. "They have arrested my father."

"What?" His heart seemed to drop like a stone. "What do you mean? Arrested? How? By whom?"

"The king's men, curse them all! They came to the house with a royal warrant, only an hour ago and our treacherous castellan had the gates opened to let them in. The Silver Stags took my father away in chains."

"We have been betrayed." It seemed too small a word to compass the evil that had been done. "One of the lords who were here last night must have gone to Hugh and given us all up in return for his own skin. We must—" But before he could finish, someone began pounding with a mailed fist at the farrier's front door.

"Open up in the name of King Hugh," a voice shouted.

"Gods curse it, they're here," said Aelin, drawing his sword. "Then we must take a few Stags with us, at least. We should not die cheaply." But even his brave words sounded hollow, as if he could not quite force out enough air to give them the needed strength.

The door sagged inward as the latch broke. A company of armed, scarlet-clad men shoved their way in, many bearing torches that threw long, antic shadows around the workshop. Several of the farriers and apprentices awakened at the noise, and some of them reached for hammers or other weapons, but they were already surrounded by soldiers with poleaxes.

"And here we have young Sir Aelin," said a voice from the doorway. "It has been some time since we last met." The hawk-nosed man stepped into the room and came toward them, almost strutting, like the only cock in a barnyard. "What was it you boasted on that day? That you would meet my lord, Count Curudan, face to face? That you will. And that will not be your only meeting. You will also be reunited with your uncle—at least for a little while."

"God will punish you, Samreas," said Evan, making the Sign of the Tree.

"And this must be the little Aedonite who convinced Fintan to turn against his brother Stags," said the chief Stag. "Never fear, I will collect Fintan soon enough, when we root the rest of the traitors out of Carn Inbarh—my lord Curudan has said I may take my revenge privily on him. You, though, Sir Aelin—you will be questioned in the presence of the king himself, and then join your uncle in a traitor's death. I brought old Eolair here earlier today, along with the king's treacherous stepmother. The Withy Crow awaits them both."

Though surrounded, not all the farriers had dropped their hammers. "Are we simply to surrender?" cried one of them. "Let us die like men!"

"Aye!" shouted another of the workers, only half-dressed, but holding a heavy pair of iron tongs in his hands.

"Put those away," said Aelin dully. "What of Lady Isleen? Would you doom her, too?"

"Do not give yourself up for me," she said. "I would rather die here beside you."

Samreas shook his head as if in sadness. "Even if these fools think to make a brave show, I am bound to take you alive, Lady Isleen. The king wants you as assurance that your father's liegemen do not make trouble. But if your friends here insist on a fight, I cannot guarantee your safety. Make your choice."

The soldiers surrounding Aelin and his companions lowered their poleaxes and thrust them forward, making a ring of sharpened steel around them. Aelin looked at Isleen's frightened, determined face and found he could not bear to see her harmed. His own struggle might have failed, but that did not mean all struggles would fail. Still, it was bitter. So much for the noble death in battle he had once imagined.

Aelin raised his hands. "We surrender. But know that the gods will judge you harshly, Samreas, as well as your master Curudan. When Dunn of the Deep Roots reaches out for you, it will not be to take you into Heaven."

Samreas shook his head, smiling. "Feeble gods, feeble ideas. Our King Hugh has found a more ancient power, a stronger ally than any of your tired, weakling gods."

"You blaspheme so easily," said Aelin in disgust. "Your king has not found a goddess, he has made himself a slave to the Queen of the Norns. But I promise a day will come when he has his eyes opened—you all will—and most cruelly."

"This talk has been most enjoyable," said Samreas. "But dawn is coming soon, and the day ahead promises even greater pleasures. So, if you have decided to come without trouble—"

"Aelin, no!" said Isleen.

"We must," Aelin told her. "While we live, there is always hope."

They were marched out in a line, Aelin, Evan, and Isleen, as the rest of Samreas' soldiers rounded up the other rebels in the farrier's house. Aelin's protests that the workmen had done nothing wrong were ignored.

Outside, a few of the other conspirators had been caught trying to flee and had been rounded up by Silver Stags. Aelin did not see Maccus among them. But Tace Odhran and his large son Orin stood to one side, unguarded, watching with carefully expressionless faces as Aelin and the others were marched into the street.

"Was it you?" Aelin shouted at the old baron. "Did you betray us?"

He at least had the decency to look ashamed. "It was a foolish, treacherous plan that would never have succeeded," Odhran said. "The king is too strong. I was led astray by you and Murdo. When I understood what you meant to do, of course I could not allow it."

"Tace Odhran had the good sense to send his son to beg King Hugh's forgiveness," said Samreas, grinning. "I'll wager you wish you had thought of it first."

"No fiery pit in Cuamh's earthy deeps is wretched enough for you and yours, Odhran," Aelin said, and spat on the floor. "To think that my great-uncle Eolair once called you friend."

Odhran had no reply, but his son put a large hand on the old man's shoulder. "Do not waste time arguing with dead men, Father," he said. "Let us thank our good King Hugh for his mercy and then go home." He led the ancient lord away as Aelin and Evan were shackled and dragged toward a waiting wagon.

26

The Poison of Despair

Jiriki, Yizashi Grayspear, and Red Okajata crouched at the northernmost end of the siege-bridge, waiting as General Ensume and his Sacrifices swarmed toward them over the narrow span. Simon and the rest of the Sithi defenders waited behind them on the wall, the last obstacle between the Hikeda'ya and possession of Tanakirú and the Ninth Ship.

How much longer can we hold them back? Simon felt the creeping poison of despair. *And what can I do? All these damnable Norns are faster and stronger than I am.* He was only taking up a place better filled by one of the Sithi defenders. But every spear counted against the oncoming horde of black-armored immortals, and that was all that mattered.

But Lillia . . . That single thought—just an image, in truth—came to him like the illuminated world of a lightning flash. *If I fall, who will protect her and take her home?*

As he hesitated, several of Jiriki's folk pushed by him onto the base of the bridge; he had to lift his long spear to let them pass. For the moment, at least, his decision had been made. At least a dozen Sithi climbed onto the bridge, crowding in behind Jiriki and the other two stalwarts, awaiting Ensume's charge with astonishing calm.

Rukayu had appeared beside him once more. "If Jiriki and the others cannot hold the Hikeda'ya back, we must step up in their stead."

Simon moved along the wall, nearer to the bridge, steeling himself to oppose any Norns who might make it past Jiriki and the first knot of defenders.

"Courage, King Seoman," Rukayu said. "We can die but once."

Simon was no longer so sure about the finality of death. He only nodded.

Because of the rising mists and the constrained area of fighting on the narrow span, he could no longer see Jiriki, but he could guess from the small number of straggling Norns who reached the wall that the Sithi must still be keeping most of the Sacrifices at bay. But even as he watched, two Norn soldiers clambered up from beneath the siege-bridge and onto the span behind Jiriki and his companions. They had somehow swung along the underside of the bridge, under the main struggle. These breakthrough attackers would have fallen on the Sithi's leading defenders from behind, but even before Simon could shout a warning, one of the Sacrifices was immediately pierced by an arrow and went flailing over the edge into the gorge. Yizashi, fighting at Jiriki's side, turned and transfixed the second Norn with his long spear. Simon could not help himself: he let out a ragged cry of relief.

But Yizashi's momentary distraction allowed several more Norns to scramble past him. While several surrounded Yizashi, the rest hurried toward the top of the wall. Changed from observer to desperate participant in an instant, Simon had to struggle against a Norn soldier who, though he had two arrows jutting from his chest plate, was doing his best to twist Simon's spear out of his hands. The Norn shoved hard on the shaft, almost forcing him off the walkway, but in a moment of exhausted inspiration, Simon took a sudden step back and yanked hard; the white-faced soldier, already leaning forward, was dragged face-first into the battlement with a satisfying *crunch* of facial bones. A moment later the stunned Sacrifice was gone, stabbed by two of the other defenders and then shoved from the wall, where he bounced from the edge of the gorge, down into the foaming depths. Already exhausted, though the battle had scarcely begun, Simon set his shoulder against the nearest Sithi defender and struggled to get back his breath.

I cannot fight like this all day. It is not in me anymore. His limbs were already trembling, and his long spear felt heavy as a tree trunk.

A mere instant of rest was all he had, then the next wave of fighting broke over him, and it was all leaning, ducking, and jabbing as the Norns who had slipped past Jiriki and the other vanguard defenders fought desperately to take the wall. Sweat stung Simon's eyes so that he could barely see, and the swarming Norns just kept coming, uncountable as raindrops. The mist began to sweep back in. Soon anything more than a few paces in front of him had become a mystery of cries and tumbling shadows, and the nightmare went on and on.

General Ensume had led the first charge, but then dropped back. Jiriki and his companions fought wave after wave of Hikeda'ya who seemed as silent and relentless as ants, and almost as numerous. Jiriki could feel his defenders flagging.

"Where is the great coward Ensume?" he suddenly shouted, loud enough to be heard even over the tumult of battle. *"Has he fled the field?"*

"What are you doing?" cried Yizashi. "Ensume is one of their greatest warriors. You will bring him against us, too."

"I hope so." Jiriki caught a sword-swipe with the chipped edge of his shield, then gutted the attacker with a swift, deadly thrust of his sword Indreju before raising his voice again. "General Ensume, Master of the Spiders! If you are not afraid to face me, come out of your hiding hole!"

A tall shape heaved into view at mid-span, pushing its way forward between Sacrifice fighters—Ensume in his unmistakable war-helm with its bars like spider legs. The general shoved his way toward the front of the battle, knocking at least one of his own soldiers off the bridge in his angry haste.

"May the Garden preserve us," said Yizashi. "You called him. Now he is coming."

"Good."

The Sacrifices in front of Ensume had already shrunk back to make room for their commander. Jiriki strode out beyond his companions, gesturing for Yizashi and Okajata to stay behind him. He had hoped for just this: if he could turn the conflict into a grudge-fight between the general and himself, it would give his beleaguered comrades a chance to catch their breath—assuming he could hold off the powerful Ensume long enough.

"So, Spider-chieftain, there you are!" Jiriki called as the general approached. A cleared space had appeared on the bridge between the two sides. "You have crept out from under your rock at last. I thought you might hide until it was time to retreat, as you did at Ma'asha!"

As the general pushed his way past the last of his Sacrifices and out onto the open span, he spun his heavy, double-bladed ax in one hand as easily as if it were a wooden toy. Ensume was half a head taller than Jiriki and broad-shouldered for one of the Gardenfolk. His black witchwood shield was almost as tall as he was.

"One of Amerasu's cubs, are you? Well, I hope she taught you . . . how to die." Ensume's words had only been meant to distract as he aimed a whistling swing of his ax at Jiriki's head. Jiriki ducked it and then jabbed back with Indreju, but Ensume caught the thrust harmlessly on his huge shield, then followed with another bludgeoning attack that Jiriki had to leap back to avoid. The end of the swaying siege-bridge and the defended wall lay only a half-dozen paces behind him, leaving precious little room for retreat.

"Not enough strength to talk while you fight?" demanded Ensume. "Just as well—what would a Zida'ya weakling have to say in any case?" Even as he threw out this jibe, the general hacked at Jiriki's shield, further splintering its edge, then whirled smoothly and swiftly into a new attack. Jiriki managed to ward off the general's first blow, but a few more such impacts and he knew his shield would break. He could not beat the Sacrifice lord with force alone, not in his already weary state, but he hoped he could find some way to drive Ensume from the field, if only to dishearten the Spider legionaries watching their general fight, their eyes keen in the slits of their helmets.

The day's outcome was balanced on this slender bridge, Jiriki knew: the Sithi would win either a small, temporary victory or suffer a final defeat. Jiriki increased his efforts, teeth clenched with exertion as he tried to carry the fight to the general, but Ensume was one of the Hikeda'ya's best and had not already been laboring against terrible odds as Jiriki had. Ensume absorbed Jiriki's attempted strikes with little effort, barely using his shield at all, catching many of them on the head of his war ax instead and simply turning them aside with a disdainful flick.

"Make him lower his shield!" someone shouted from the wall behind Jiriki, though in the frenzy of the moment, he did not recognize the voice. "Draw his shield down!"

Yet another deflected attack left Jiriki momentarily off-balance. Taking advantage, Ensume swung his tall shield and clipped Jiriki's helmet hard enough to make him stumble backward and nearly fall from the bridge into the roaring waters below. Only Okajata's swift, red-gauntleted grab kept him from falling. Trying to defend Jiriki's momentarily unprotected back, Yizashi sprang forward and thrust his spear at Ensume's visor, but the general caught the thrust with his shield and directed it over his shoulder. Still, Yizashi had put enough force behind his attack that Ensume had to take a few steps back against the front of his own line to keep his balance. Several of his Sacrifice warriors moved forward into his place, but Ensume, regaining his balance, roared at them to get out of his way.

This time Ensume came on more slowly, having seen his victory would not be as quick as he had supposed, but the general was still the stronger of the two and he seemed relentless; Jiriki had all he could manage just to avoid being beaten down by his enemy's strength and heavy weapon. After a series of battering attacks, Ensume managed to sink his ax deep into the edge of Jiriki's shield, then nearly ripped it away, brutally twisting Jiriki's arm in its socket. Jiriki only barely managed to keep the shield but found he could not lift that arm without excruciating pain in his shoulder. Ensume stepped forward, ax swinging high. In his dark, plated armor, the general looked more like a war-engine than a living creature.

Yizashi Grayspear, on Jiriki's left side, now flung himself forward and lunged with his long spear at Ensume's exposed legs, stabbing again and again like a striking snake, so that the general had to step back out of Yizashi's reach.

"So, you admit you cannot fight me by yourself, little Year-Dancer!" Ensume crowed.

Jiriki fought for breath. "I admit . . . that I have been on this bridge all day. While you . . . watched from safety."

Ensume emitted a single derisive bark of laughter. "I am a leader of many thousands! You are a rebel whose clan has dwindled and failed. You cannot shame me."

"That was clear long before now," said Jiriki.

The insult was not lost on Ensume. He leaped forward with a snarl, and Jiriki had to employ both Indreju and his battered shield simply to preserve his life against the savage attack. Ensume scented victory now: his attacks forced Jiriki backward, and with each retreating step, the Norn fighters pressed forward behind their leader.

"His shield!" the voice from the wall shouted again, and this time Jiriki recognized it. "Make him lower it!"

"I need your spear," Jiriki called to Yizashi.

"But you cannot use it without giving up sword or shield!"

"I know! Trust me."

Yizashi hesitated for but a moment as Jiriki, with a surge of strength that he knew would not last long, forced Ensume onto his back foot with an aggressive rain of sword-blows, all of which the general caught on his shield; in that moment's lull, Yizashi took a step back and tossed his spear to Jiriki, then drew a long knife from his belt as he hurried to aid Cheka'iso, who was struggling with several more Sacrifices who had crept in along the underside of the bridge and were trying to climb onto the wall. The Hikeda'ya clung like cats and could only be dislodged by hacking them loose.

Jiriki dropped his shield, then caught and momentarily steadied Yizashi's gray spear in his hand before he whirled and flung it at Ensume's head as hard as he could. The general was unsurprised, and raised his shield in time to block it, but the force of Jiriki's throw pierced the shield so that the shaft hung, wagging. Ensume was unharmed, though the additional weight did not seem to bother him at all.

"Weak," the general said. "You would not survive Sacrifice training, little golden-skin."

"Jiriki, what have you done?" Yizashi turned and shouted for someone to find him another weapon, but Jiriki had already leaped toward Ensume once more. Indreju clashed hard against the edge of Ensume's shield. The general had his feet set. He barely moved, but nearly took off Jiriki's head with a scything backhanded swing of his battle ax.

As Yizashi watched his treasured spear wagging in Ensume's shield, hopelessly out of reach, Cheka'iso and Okajata, both wounded but still fighting, struggled to keep the resurgent Sacrifices from reaching the wall. Jiriki attacked the general again and again, though it was plain to see that his strength was fading. If he had hoped the weight of the heavy spear would make it harder for Ensume to use his shield, that hope seemed to have been in vain: Ensume did not even try to dislodge the long shaft but instead swung shield and spear together in a broad arc and would have knocked Jiriki off the bridge if he had not dropped beneath the blow.

"As you said, Year-Dancer," Ensume gloated. "You have fought for hours. But I am strong, still strong!"

Jiriki did not waste breath on a reply but ducked just beneath another deadly swing of the war-ax and threw himself at the general's feet. As he stabbed at Ensume's boots, the general tried to swing the bottom edge of the shield down on Jiriki's head and nearly succeeded. If the heavy shield had struck fairly, it would have smashed Jiriki's skull even through his helmet, but he managed to evade it by a finger's-breadth and the witchwood shield thumped harmlessly against the bridge. In that instant, Jiriki let go of Indreju, reached up, and caught the wagging shaft of Yizashi's spear with both hands, then threw his weight upon it. Surprised, but seeing a chance to end the fight, Ensume ignored

Jiriki's downward pull on his shield and lifted his ax for a killing blow. An instant later the general halted, as if puzzled by something. The great ax dropped from his suddenly nerveless hand, then Ensume fell backward with an arrow shaft throbbing in the visor of his helmet.

"Peja'ura!" a triumphant voice shouted from the wall—the voice of Shen'de, the Bowman. "Death to the enemies of the Zida'ya!"

A sudden murmur of shock rose from the Sacrifices as Ensume fell. For a moment they seemed to lose heart, and those nearest the general caught his body and began to retreat down the bridge.

Yizashi now rushed forward, looking first to make certain Jiriki was not badly hurt, then wrenched his spear out of Ensume's fallen shield.

"Well aimed, Bowman!" Jiriki called to Shen'de as Yizashi helped him to his feet. He staggered a little until he found his balance.

"They are falling back." Okajata's red war-gear hid the worst of her injuries, but a substantial rivulet of blood drizzled from her leg and splashed on the bridge, as if her armor was turning to liquid.

"Not . . . for long, I fear," said Jiriki, panting. Around him, several Sithi hurried forward to gather up stray arrows and dropped weapons. "I am glad to see you that you three still live, though," he told Yizashi, Cheka'iso, and Okajata. "Where is the mortal Seoman?"

"I am here," called Simon from the wall. "Do not worry for me."

"By our ancestors, that was nobly fought!" Cheka'iso said. Already the remaining Sacrifices behind them had begun to reform their line atop the wall, readying for the next Hikeda'ya attack. "Now step back and rest, Protector, and I will hold your place until you find your breath."

"Even if Ensume is dead, his captains will not give up," Jiriki said. "They know we cannot hold them off forever."

"We do not need to hold them off so long." Yizashi Grayspear cleaned blood off his spear, though his own armor was thoroughly spattered with it. "Only until sunset, when the ogre will drive us all back into our caves."

"Sunset is far, far away," said Jiriki, looking to the western sky. "This is the only rest we shall have, so breathe deeply. They still are fifty to one against us."

"Only fifty to one?" said Cheka'iso, grinning with blood on his teeth. "And to think I feared the odds were against us. We will make short work of them."

Jiriki did not have the strength even to smile. "See, already they form up to attack again," he said. "I swear by the Grove of my first Year-Dance, I have never been so weary. Let us fall back to our wall this time, so our archers can have better effect with their few remaining shafts."

Hakatri was only dimly aware that his body—or at least the shell that contained his spirit, like ashes contained in a funeral jar—was being carried down through the mountain tunnels by silent Queen's Teeth guards. Most of his thoughts were somewhere else entirely, roaming through the stony heights far above, searching once more for the music and for the ship that sang it.

For that was what waited, he now knew, although his thoughts were not words or even complete ideas. A ship made that music, like the Garden ships but somehow different. It sang so that only he could hear, and it recognized him, not only by the Navigator's armor that housed his essence, but because of the burning blood that had destroyed his life, the black essence of the dragon Hidohebhi. Because of this blood, Hakatri's essence throbbed with the music of the Dreaming Sea, with all that it promised, and because of that, the ship did not fear him.

This is what the Voice of Three wanted. For me to feel this power and to harness it, then use it to punish the thrice-cursed mortals for what they have done. This was the reason he had been summoned back from blissful nothingness and plunged anew into the suffering that had ruined his long life—to punish the creatures who had killed his brother, father, and wife, the mortal vermin who had attacked his daughter Likimeya and sent her beyond his reach to the edge of death.

For a moment, as he thought of his child, Hakatri's anger swelled until it seemed it might burst even the shell of armor that contained him, that he might flare up and then collapse like a blazing bonfire falling in on itself. In that moment of rage, a voice spoke in his thoughts. It was not the Voice of Three, but something that seemed small and frightened.

Father?

Hakatri tried to reach out to this new presence, but the timorous voice was already gone, vanished back into the continuous swirl of ship-music running through his strange, muddled thoughts.

Could it have been Likimeya? Who else would call him Father? But his daughter's last accusatory words to him before he sailed away into the west still echoed in his memory, burning as painfully as the dragon's caustic blood: *"My real father would never leave us."*

But if it was not his daughter's voice he had just heard, then who had called out?

No, he told himself. *I must not let myself be distracted by phantoms. I must trust the Voice of Three. I have been brought back for only two things—destruction and then oblivion. I must create one to give myself the other. Nothing else matters.*

Simon had watched his friend's battle against the Norn general in almost unendurable fear. He knew Jiriki's prowess, but he had never seen him in such extremity.

Now the brief rest following Ensume's fall was over. Even without their formidable general to lead them, the Norns were once more trying to force their way across the bridge by sheer strength of numbers. Rukayu and Shen'de and the other bow-wielders on the wall were able to pick out individual targets and let fly with deadly results, but they were almost out of arrows, and very few came back from the Norns on the other side of the gorge. Rukayu had already emptied one of her two quivers and had less than half a dozen shafts in the other.

A few more Norn soldiers wriggled past the knot of defenders around Jiriki and clambered onto the wall. The nearest of them picked out Simon and rushed toward him, blade already drawn back for the first blow. Simon knew he would not be able to free his own sword from its scabbard before the Sacrifice was on him—it would be his spear or nothing—and threw himself to his left side, away from the Norn's shield with its white spider-blazon. His foot slipped from under him and he fell heavily on his side, but that saved his life: his attacker could not stop himself and tumbled onto Simon, tangling them together so they both rolled down onto the broad wooden walkway beneath the battlement. All the Sitha around them were engaged in deadly struggles of their own, and Simon had no hope of using the long spear when his enemy was already bending for his sword, so he kicked out and managed to knock the Norn's blade away. The Sacrifice climbed on top of him, death-white hands grasping for his throat. Simon tried to reach his dagger, but he was lying on the sheath. He struggled to draw breath, blood pounding behind his eyes and in his ears.

An instant later his enemy's clutch weakened. He broke the Norn's grip, gasping for air even as he struggled to throw his attacker off his chest, but before Simon could free himself the Sacrifice slumped forward, then tumbled limply off him. An arrow jutted from the Norn's neck just below the rim of his helmet. Rukayu stood behind the fallen Sacrifice, panting. As Simon stared in amazement, she leaned forward and set her booted foot against the corpse's back, then pulled her arrow free in a freshet of blood.

"It is my last," she explained. "And I still may wish to use it for something other than stabbing Hikeda'ya."

Simon could not yet reply. As he crouched, fighting for breath through a throat that felt crushed, a strange sound rose above the clamor on the bridge. Drums—drums and voices. The Norns on the far side of the gorge were shouting what sounded like three words, over and over.

"Ur-Ma-Ko! Ur-Ma-Ko! Ur-Ma-Ko!" Their voices grew louder and louder.

Simon finally got air back into his lungs. "What are they saying?"

"I am not sure," said Rukayu, peering into the misty distance. "*Ur-Makho*—Makho-That-Was—is what it sounds like. But I do not know who or what this Makho could be."

Groaning, Simon struggled onto his feet again and followed Rukayu back to the top of the wall. He was heartened to see Jiriki and several of the Sithi captains still up and fighting, and for a moment was even more relieved to see that the Norn soldiers had drawn back a short distance once more. Then he saw something climbing over the Norns at the base of the bridge, a manlike shape making its way swiftly across the backs of the Sacrifices like a crab scuttling over seaside stones, and his blood went cold in his veins.

God's Bloody Tree! It's the thing I saw when we came to Tanakirú—the gray, dead thing.

The newcomer sprang quickly from one Sacrifice to another, using the crush of Sacrifices as a living staircase to reach the bridge. In size and shape it seemed little different from the Norn soldiers, but it moved like nothing Simon had ever seen. In the first moments of its appearance it had been half-hidden by mist, but as it leaped off the last of the Norns and landed on the bridge, Simon saw it whole for the first time. The creature's face was a leathery, desiccated gray, and one of its eyes was just a black hole in its skull; the other ghastly orange orb stared unblinkingly at the defenders.

"Ur-Makho! Ur-Makho!" The voices of the shouting Norns rose in triumph.

"I saw that thing before as we rode in." Simon felt sick. "In the name of God the Father, what is it?"

"I cannot imagine," said Rukayu in a ragged voice. "It must be the spawn of some dreadful dark song of Utuk'ku's. See! It is dead . . . but it lives."

Even as she spoke, the lifeless thing abruptly sprang across the remaining length of the bridge like a black frog and landed before the first row of Sithi, already whirling and striking with its hooked blade. Several of the first defenders to face it were knocked from the bridge by the sheer force of its blows, flung down so swiftly that Simon did not even see who fell.

The following moments were a terrible blur. Even as Simon was pushed forward by the Sithi behind him, rallying to aid their captains against this new and fearsome threat, the gray thing scythed its way through all who came against it. Each time the hooked gray blade lifted and fell it seemed to leave a bleeding, fallen body behind.

Simon saw Rukayu on her hands and knees at the base of the bridge, but he was too hemmed in by other Sithi to help her. He prayed she had not been badly wounded, but when he stole a glance a moment later, he saw that she was searching for Norn arrows.

He turned back in time to see Cheka'iso, one of the Sithi's most feared warriors, reel away from the undead, gray thing, a huge gash in his armored shoulder bubbling blood. Several of his comrades caught at Cheka'iso as he stumbled. The Sitha warrior was insensible, and pale as a Sacrifice.

Strangely, the Norns did not surge forward behind the Ur-Makho's attack, as though even its allies found the creature frightening. Instead, they hung back at the midpoint of the siege bridge, eyes fierce with anticipation, as Jiriki stepped past his retreating companions and back onto the span to confront the gray thing. Simon felt sickly certain that his friend was far too weary to hold off such a foe. The leathery thing was stronger and swifter than any Hikeda'ya warrior, and Jiriki had barely survived his struggle with the general.

"Let me through!" Simon cried. "We have to help him." But he could not get past the thicket of Sithi spears, shields, and swords to reach the bridge.

Some dim part of whatever the dead gray thing had once been seemed to recognize its opponent: it stopped, flung aside a limp Sitha it had caught by the neck, then lifted its strange blade toward Jiriki in something like a salute. A heartbeat later it leaped forward, covering the distance between them in a blink, aiming a sudden swipe at Jiriki's head, but Jiriki, moving more swiftly than Simon could have guessed, flung himself to one side. Makho's hooked blade crashed down into the bridge so hard that splinters flew into the air and the entire wooden span trembled.

"Don't, Jiriki!" Simon shouted. "Fall back!"

But Jiriki was on his feet again, and he and the gray shape moved back and forth in half-circles as they measured each other's reach, both confined by the narrow span. "No, Seoman!" cried Jiriki. "Retreat to the wall. Try to knock their bridge loose while I keep the *hageloi* at bay." He shouted the command once more in his own tongue.

"No!" cried Simon. The Sithi around him were moving back toward the wall now, and after long moments struggling to get free of the crush, Simon abruptly found himself alone at the near edge of the siege bridge.

Jiriki and the undead thing were still cautiously circling each other, as if they traced the steps of some strange, slow dance. Then, as if in silent agreement, they suddenly closed. Blade clashed loudly on blade, again and again in swift succession.

Simon felt as though he was caught in a bad dream. The Ur-Makho seemed to pulse with hideous strength, while Jiriki was clearly trying to exert himself as little as possible to save his waning vigor. As the pair traded attacks, several Sithi arrows snapped out from the wall and struck the gray thing, staggering it a little, but even with two shafts now sunk deep in its chest and another transfixing its left arm so that the arrowhead showed on the far side, the terrible creature seemed not to notice. It continued to stalk Jiriki like a cat with a cornered mouse, unhurried, merciless. Its hooked blade seemed light as a willow wand in its withered hand, its slashing attacks so swift and effortless that it seemed to be continuing the stately movements of the first instant—but this was no dance: Jiriki managed to turn aside several blows of the creature's weapon, any of which would have ended the struggle immediately if it had fallen. Simon could see that his friend was exhausted, and that the fight could have only one end, but the combatants and their swinging blades were leaping too swiftly back and forth across the narrow siege bridge for anyone to step up and help, and arrows had already proved useless.

As Jiriki retreated from yet another whirlwind assault he slipped in a smear of wet blood and his foot went out from under him. He fell to his knees, losing his sword, which skittered to the edge of the bridge and hung there, teetering. The Ur-Makho saw the opening and lifted its hooked sword with both hands, sinews straining beneath leathery gray flesh. The rigid mouth twitched as if trying to grin, and its single eye widened in anticipation of triumph. But as the butcher blade swung down, Jiriki was able to shove himself backward; the blow missed him by scarcely a hands-breadth, cleaving the siege-bridge with such force that it dug a deep gouge into the wood. Jiriki struggled up onto one knee, exhaustion plain in his every movement as the Ur-Makho fought to yank its weapon free. Jiriki's sword was out of his reach, and the undead creature blocked his way to it.

"Here!" Simon cried, flinging his spear toward Jiriki. For a long instant his friend did not look up, and Simon was sickeningly certain Jiriki had not heard him, that his spear would sail past and into the gorge, but Jiriki turned just enough to snatch it out of the air, though the weight of it almost knocked him off balance once more. The gray thing finally tore the hooked blade loose from the bridge in a fountain of chips and splinters, then heaved it up again for the delayed killing blow. More swiftly than Simon would have thought possible, Jiriki spun the spear into place and, with both hands gripping the shaft, slammed it through the gray thing's breastplate with such force that it came bloodlessly out at the back, tearing loose a chunk of armor. A moment of stunned silence fell over the bridge—for the length of a heartbeat the whole of the valley seemed to go utterly still—then Simon heard a ragged cheer rise from the Sithi defenders behind him. But the celebration ended quickly: the Makho-thing would not fall. Even with a Sithi spear driven through its body from ribs to backbone and beyond, it was still trying to land another blow with its weird, wide blade as Jiriki struggled to grip the spear and hold the deathless thing at bay.

Simon ran forward, his own sword in his hand.

"No, Seoman!" Jiriki cried. "This is beyond you—stay back!" Even as he warned Simon off, Jiriki leaned forward, shoving with the spear to force the Ur-Makho off the bridge. For a moment, he even seemed to have succeeded: the lifeless thing, unbalanced by one of its own swinging blows, had to take a stumbling step backward to keep its feet, which gave Jiriki a chance to move closer to where his had fallen. But before he could reach down and snatch up Indreju, his gray-skinned enemy regained its footing and began to push forward against the weapon piercing its chest, single eye blazing as it shoved its way up the spear shaft toward Jiriki like a dying boar determined to kill its hunter. But this thing was not dying—it was already dead, and it seemed nothing could stop it.

The chanting from the Norns' end of the bridge began again—"Ur-Makho! Ur-Makho!"

The gray thing had pushed halfway up the spear-shaft now, its own weapon still in its hands. Showing no sign of pain or discomfort, it raised the hooked blade again, but before it could bring it down Jiriki gave the spear a last shove, then ducked down to snatch up Indreju. In a single smooth motion, he rose from his crouch, swinging Indreju with both hands like a woodsman felling a tree. The sword's blade struck between the revenant's breastplate and helmet, hacking through the neck with the dry, percussive sound of someone chopping wood. Makho's head fell to the bridge, bounced once, then stopped, the eye still glaring.

A shout of joy welled up in Simon's throat. Then the headless body, still standing, brought its upraised sword down with terrible strength, smashing the hooked end into Jiriki's chest and through his armor.

A shocked cry went up from the watching Sithi. Simon could only stare in cold horror as the Ur-Makho turned from where Jiriki lay in a pool of spreading blood, then bent to pick up its own head. It shook off the helm as though shelling a nut, then curled its gray fingers in the pale, braided hair and lifted the head like a night-watchman's lantern. Calmly, as if it had not just been decapitated, it began walking up the bridge toward Simon and the wall, bloody, hooked blade held effortlessly in one hand, its head dangling from the other.

A rage like nothing he had ever known blazed through Simon. He drew his sword and ran toward the ghastly thing, unable to think of anything except chopping the murderous creature into pieces, but his sword blow met the lifted Hikeda'ya blade and Simon's borrowed Sithi sword shattered into pieces. Numb from wrist to neck, he fell to his hands and knees, helpless and resigned to death, but the gray thing walked past him as if he was not there.

Indreju lay a short distance away, beside Jiriki's outflung hand. Crawling on his hands and knees like a child, Simon caught it up, then rose and staggered after the Ur-Makho. His right arm was so numb from the gray thing's blow he could barely feel it: he had to clutch Jiriki's sword in his left hand.

The dead creature's ears still seemed to work, despite its head no longer being attached: as Simon raced after it, it swiveled slowly to face him. Simon tried to hack at its leg—the thing could live without a head, but how would it walk without legs?—but using the wrong arm betrayed him, and his blow only glanced off the gray thing's armored thigh. The single flame-red eye in its dangling face regarded him for several of Simon's racing heartbeats, then the headless body turned away again, toward the wall and the stunned defenders.

"No!" Simon ran after it and swung Indreju again, but this time he did not aim at the gray thing's leg, but at something easier to cut. Jiriki's witchwood blade slashed through thing's braided hair and the head fell to the bridge with a thump. Before the creature could stop him, Simon shouted in rage and disgust and kicked the dreadful thing off the bridge and into the chasm.

This time the lifeless body did not stand impassively, but turned, arms suddenly thrashing as if it could no longer find its balance. It took a clumsy step in the direction the head had gone, then another, then the Ur-Makho plunged off the bridge and vanished into the crashing white froth of the Narrowdark.

Simon got back to Jiriki even before his swift Sithi comrades could reach him. The Norn soldiers, shocked by what had happened to their undead champion, hung back at the base of the bridge, but Simon felt sure it would not be long before some Sacrifice officer spurred them to attack again.

Jiriki's eyes were open, but he could not fix them on anything. His chest plate was dinted inward, with a terrible hole in the center below the breastbone, and that hole welled with blood. Simon began to weep.

"Hurry!" he shouted to the approaching Sithi. "Help him!"

"Is it finished?" Jiriki asked in a ragged whisper. "The *hageloi*?"

"Only God knows," Simon said. "But it is gone. Fallen from the bridge and swept away."

Jiriki nodded. Through the blur of his tears, Simon saw something appear beside him and looked up to see bare-headed Okajata in her scarlet armor. She bent down and touched Jiriki's brow with her fingertip, then called out in their shared tongue. Other Sithi surrounded Jiriki and together they carefully lifted him onto a cloak to carry him back to the wall.

As he followed the Sithi, Simon heard a strange wailing noise rise from the direction of the cliffs at the valley's near end. In the first moment he thought it might be something to do with the great ship, and the startled behavior of the Sithi suggested the noise surprised them as much as it did him. Then the wailing call sounded again, louder, and he could hear that it was not one noise but many, a discordant and growing shrill of war-horns.

"Ai!" cried a voice beside him, a hopeless wail. It was Rukayu, he realized, and she was terrified. "It is her! *It is her!"*

Simon looked past the wall to the plateau and saw that the few Sithi who had not already joined them were now running away from the cliffs, but he could barely make out what was happening, so he reached up to wipe the tears from his eyes with a grimy, gloved hand. A host of white shapes were boiling out of the cliffside caverns behind the Sithi defenders as if they were being hatched like maggots—dozens of them, no, hundreds, tall, corpse-skinned Norn soldiers in pointed white helmets and gleaming white armor. And behind these soldiers, born aloft on a litter so that she seemed to float through the air, came a figure also dressed in white, but this one's face shone like a sun-splashed mirror—her silver mask, Simon realized with a sinking heart.

"Utuk'ku has come." Rukayu's voice was flat and utterly without hope. "We are trapped between her Queen's Teeth and the Sacrifice army, King Seoman. It is time to choose where we will die."

27

An Ogre's Nest

At first it was easy for Morgan to follow the *uro'eni*'s trail. Each time the ogre passed from one cavern to another it scraped stone debris from the edges of the opening. Some of these passages seemed bafflingly small for a creature of such immense bulk, but Morgan could tell by the piles of freshly broken stone that the monstrous thing was still ahead of him. The caverns and passages through which it traveled seemed to go on and on, as if the mountain that looked so solid from the ship's deck was little more than a vast rabbit warren of limestone chambers and tunnels.

Water drizzled down the walls or ran across the floor in many places; Morgan's boots were soaking before he had gone far. In some spots the cavern walls were studded with lumps of crystal like those in the river-etched tunnels that led them to the great ship in the first place. With every step deeper into the tunnel, the more it seemed he had left behind the world he knew.

Idiot, he chided himself. *You have been living in a magical Sithi ship. The half-immortal you're trying to find was stolen by an ogre as big as a church steeple. And Nezeru herself is one of the Norn Queen's soldiers. The world you knew is long gone.*

And the me that I used to know, too, he realized suddenly. *I will never be that Morgan again.*

As he continued doggedly after his quarry, Morgan could not help wondering if the monster itself hadn't dug out much of the mountain. The large caverns that honeycombed the mountain were clearly natural, but the wide passages connecting them often seemed to have been dug through the stone with pure, brutish force. In many spots, the walls showed great gouges like the marks of immense claws.

If it was easy to track something so large, he soon found that it was not always so easy to follow. Some of the steep places that he had to descend must have been only gentle stairs for the ogre but were like cliffs to Morgan, and he was grateful for all the time in the last year that he had spent in trees and clambering over slippery cave-crystals. More than once he found himself hanging by only his fingers, or by one hand and the toe of his boot. The descent was taking him far longer than he had imagined, but he would not let himself be stopped, because each passing moment made him more fearful for Nezeru. Then he came upon an obstacle that no amount of skillful climbing could carry him past.

He stumbled to a halt before a crumbling, arch-shaped passage into more caverns beyond. The vast hole was clearly big enough, even for something the size of an ogre, and the cave floor beneath it was littered with limestone rubble from pieces the monster must have knocked loose while passing through—this was clearly one of the ogre's frequented passageways. The problem was that just on the other side of the wide, low-ceilinged cavern stood yet another hole, nearly as large and similarly strewn with the detritus of the *uro'eni's* passage.

Merciful God and all the saints, help me! It is not just one tunnel under the mountain. The thing has a maze down here. How can I possibly guess which way it went? The dreadful discovery was followed a moment later by a shamed and miserable realization. *Nezeru, I'm so sorry. I've failed you.*

No more than a few moments had passed, yet everything had changed. Tzoja could only stand and stare at the still-trembling branches where Jarnulf and Goh Gam Gar had disappeared.

"Come out," she told Vordis. "The giant is gone. They're both gone."

Vordis appeared, feeling her way out of their hiding place. "Both?"

"Jarnulf is the giant's friend. Or pet." Tzoja was furious, though she knew it was not all his fault. But not only had he and his monster left her in the middle of utterly unfamiliar country, Jarnulf had done so only moments after admitting that it had been him, the man she had saved from torture and death, who had disgraced her daughter Nezeru so that she was forced out of the Order of Sacrifice.

"What will we do?"

Tzoja shook her head, then remembered that was little use to her friend. "I don't know. Follow them, I suppose."

"Follow them? But they were going to kill Hikeda'ya soldiers! I heard the giant say so." Vordis was trembling. "I have never heard a voice like that. For once, I am glad I lost my sight. I cannot imagine having to see such a horrible creature. How could Jarnulf go with it and leave us alone?"

"He said he owed the giant a favor." But she didn't want to apologize for the man—didn't want to let go of her own anger. "Here we are, no matter the reasons. We can try to go back the way we came, but I was following Jarnulf—I don't know that I could find my way back. And find our way back to where? That fortress where we were first kept, Naglimund? It's a ruin now."

"We can find things to eat in the forest," said Vordis, her confident words a little undercut by the quaver in her voice.

"Yes, we can, and we are lucky I spent years living among healers and learned much about plants. But who can guess what else shares these woods? Bears? More giants? Jarnulf may have known one giant, but I doubt he knows them all—the queen has many in her army."

"But if we follow Jarnulf, we will be going toward the very people who were hunting us."

"Yes, but at least we will have a plain track to follow. The giant doesn't go around things, it goes through them. Perhaps they will need to stop. The giant was wounded, suffering . . ." She trailed off. In truth, none of the possibilities seemed like good ones, but they could not simply wait. The Wolf Moon air would be freezing cold at night, and they would certainly miss Jarnulf's hunting skills. He had also found or built their shelters. "I don't know," she admitted. "But I can't think of anything better. I think we have to follow them."

Vordis was crying quietly. She wiped her cheeks. "I am sorry, Tzoja. It is frightening, not being able to see and being far away from anything I know, but I will be brave, like you."

"I'm sorry we've come to this, too, but we must make the best of it. Let's gather up our things and start walking before they get too far ahead. We have a few hours of daylight left."

"You're exhausted, dear," she told Vordis. "You're stumbling."

"I would not mind resting, just for a moment."

"You stay here, then. I'll just walk a little ahead, to see if there's a better place for us to stop."

"Don't go too far, please, Tzoja."

She paused for a moment. "I wonder if I should keep that name."

Vordis raised her head. "I don't understand. Please, don't frighten me. You're Tzoja."

"I didn't mean it that way. Tzoja is the name Lord Viyeki gave me. For most of my life, I had another one—Derra."

"But I know you as Tzoja." Vordis seemed on the verge of tears again. "It would be too strange to start calling you something new."

"You don't have to. You may call me what you wish. It's just something I'm thinking about. Sit and rest."

She could not help wondering at herself as she followed the broken branches and scarred trunks left by the giant's passage. *Why such a thought now? I haven't been Derra for years. I don't even think of myself that way.* She had been renamed by Viyeki, and Viyeki was gone. She had been brought here by Jarnulf, and Jarnulf was gone. *I'm tired of being somebody else's something,* she realized, and the thought was like an unexpected breeze on a hot day. *If I live through this, I'll only do what I want—what Derra used to want, before it was all taken away from her, first by the Skalijar bandits, then by the Hikeda'ya.*

She paused in a clearing. An upthrust wedge of stone offered shelter from the wind, if not the cold, and the marks of the giant's passage were plain to see on the clearing's far side. *We only have a few hours of daylight left,* she thought, *and we're both so weary. If I bring Vordis this far, we can stay here and keep searching in the morning. This will do.*

She had gone back perhaps a couple of dozen steps when a pair of dark shapes slid noiselessly from the shadows and blocked her path. She knew that armor and did not need to see the soldier's bone-white faces to know who had found her.

"A straggler," said one of the Sacrifices. "We haven't caught up to that cursed giant, but if we return this wandering she-goat to the flock, it could be the chieftain will let us off easy."

"I'd rather be whipped than find that giant, anyway," said the other, taking a rough hold on Tzoja's arm. "Have you seen its tracks? It must be one of the biggest we have."

Suddenly, she heard Vordis call out. "Tzoja, is that you?"

"More stragglers," said the first Sacrifice, tightening his grip on her arm. "How many more are you? Any of them armed?"

Tzoja shook her head, hopeless and defeated. Their freedom had lasted less than half a day after Jarnulf's departure. "Just the one. She's blind—don't harm her. We are both Anchoresses—we serve the queen herself—"

"Our chieftain will hear all that," said the second soldier. "You can tell your story to her. If you're lucky, she won't simply have your heads for running off."

"We didn't run off!" Tzoja said. "We . . . we were taken. Against our will. By an escaped prisoner." She hesitated, not wanting even now to give up Jarnulf's identity. "And then the giant came, and the two of them went off together." She pointed up the broken trackway through the forest. "That way."

The soldiers shared a glance, then the first one turned to her. "The giant, you say. Why were you following them if this prisoner forced you to leave the rest of the queen's company?"

She had momentarily forgotten that there were very few stupid Hikeda'ya, even among the lower ranks of the Order of Sacrifice. "Because we thought we would starve without them. The man had been doing the hunting for us."

The first Sacrifice stared at her for a long moment, then nodded to his companion, who vanished into the undergrowth. He returned a short time later with Vordis, who was understandably confused and frightened.

"All is well," Tzoja told her, with an emphasis as subtle as she could manage. "These soldiers will take us back to the others. We're safe now."

Vordis only nodded, but her expression was wretched.

Jarnulf did not soon catch up to the giant, but after running as fast as he could for a long time, he found the great beast waiting there for him in a ring of trees.

"Too slow," said Goh Gam Gar. "I do not wait for you another time."

"Then how can I repay the favors I still owe you?"

The giant bared his fangs in sour amusement, then reached out a massive hand and closed his fingers around Jarnulf's waist. Before he could do more than wonder in sudden apprehension whether the creature had decided to kill him after all, Jarnulf was jerked off his feet. The giant then began to run up the valley once more, this time at an even more fearsome pace, with Jarnulf clutched in his mighty hand, helpless as a kitten.

For the first moments, Jarnulf felt as if he had been lifted by a powerful wind and was being swept along, helpless as a fallen leaf while the forest flashed past him, trees appearing and disappearing as branches swiped at his face. Goh Gam Gar was carrying him as a man might hold a stick or stone or anything else he did not care much about shaking or breaking. Jarnulf wanted to demand that the giant put him down, but at first it was all he could do to keep from being sick.

"Put me down!" he cried when he could speak again. "I cannot travel like this."

The giant slowed, then lifted Jarnulf up and stared at him. It occurred to him, and not for the first time, that Goh Gam Gar could chew off his head as easily as he himself would bite into a boiled turnip. It was staggering how big the creature was, how one hand could fold all the way around a full-grown man's midsection. "Down?" the giant growled. "No. I said, you are too slow."

"Too slow for what? Are we in a hurry?"

The giant's great brow-ridge furrowed, like the beginnings of an avalanche. "It is all ending. I feel it in my bones. The masked *Higdaja* queen makes it so. All ending. If we are slow, we miss it."

It had been hard to think while being waved in the air like a plucked dandelion, but Jarnulf was realizing he might have been hasty in joining Goh Gam Gar's mission. "What does that mean—all ending? And how do you know?"

"Old Gam heard it from others of my kind in the *Higdaja* camp. We can all feel it. The end is coming now, in *Tangaru*, the valley that sings."

"Just put me down. I run very fast. I can keep up."

Goh Gam Gar made a face that clearly expressed his feelings about the self-estimations of mortal men. "No. Not just how fast. Soon we reach the *Higdaja* soldiers. There will be much killing. If you are on foot, you will be lost. Cut to pieces, no help to old Gam. Remember, man-flesh, you owe me many favors."

"Two, I think." Jarnulf was certain now that he'd made a bad choice. "Put me on your shoulders, then. I will ride on your yoke."

The odd, green-yellow eyes narrowed. "You cannot make Goh Gam Gar do what you want. Only the one who holds the rod can burn me."

"I don't want to make you do anything. I simply don't want to be smashed through every tree branch between here and wherever we're going."

Again, the giant examined him. The creature's breath was horrifying, but that was the least of Jarnulf's worries. At last, Goh Gam Gar nodded his huge head, then lifted Jarnulf and set him atop his wide, wide shoulders. After a bit of slipping and sliding, Jarnulf was able to find a somewhat comfortable position atop the witchwood yoke, though the breadth of the giant's neck made his legs feel like he was riding an extremely fat horse. Still, it was better than being beaten to pieces against the forest vegetation. The great beast was clearly not used to going around things instead of simply charging through them.

"Right, then," Jarnulf said when he was in place. "I may have to grab onto your pelt sometimes to keep from falling."

A deep, rumbling laugh made his seat shake. "Try not to hurt old Gam too badly."

As the giant pounded northward along the steep upper slopes of the Narrowdark Valley, bound for the river's headwaters, Jarnulf wondered about himself: was he hurrying toward something or away from something else? He was a little ashamed to have left Tzoja and Vordis by themselves in such a strange, dangerous land, but once he had admitted his role in her daughter Nezeru's being declared a traitor, surely nothing could have been left of their friendship, if it could ever have been called by such a name.

I helped them, they helped me—nothing more. That is how it is in time of war, whether a great war like the one the giant says the Hikeda'ya queen is making, or my own private war against her. There can be no promises. And in any case, my Lord God knows that I have no future. If I am lucky, I will have one last chance at the witch-queen, but I cannot believe I will live through it. Those two are better off without me.

Only moments later, they came upon a Hikeda'ya Sacrifice troop. As the giant crashed out of the trees, the Hikeda'ya soldiers in the clearing looked up in startlement and dawning fear, but the giant did not give either them or Jarnulf time for much consideration. He leaped forward, growling so that the forest echoed, and he was among the Norn soldiers in an instant, his vast, meaty hands seizing and rending armored bodies like a starving Nakkiga slave eating cave shrimps. A flick of the monster's wrist here and a helmeted head flew away and rolled down the hill. Another backhanded strike and a Sacrifice officer and his horse were both smashed into gobbets of bloody bones and flesh and pieces of witchwood armor plate.

There had been at least half a score of armed Sacrifices in the small company, all trained killers, but less than two dozen heartbeats passed before they all died, most of them crushed into disarticulated, nearly unrecognizable shapes. In all his years and all his battles, Jarnulf had never seen anything like it. Much as he hated the Hikeda'ya, and particularly the Order of Sacrifice, he found it hard to look at what had been done to them.

"Hold a moment," he said when he had mastered himself. "Put me down."

"Do you want to piss on them?" the giant asked. "That is not a bad idea."

"No. No! I need a real bow and some arrows. There's bound to be more fighting as we get closer to the queen, and it doesn't seem fair that you kill all the Sacrifices by yourself. I can't be much help on your shoulders with only a sword."

Goh Gam Gar grunted and set him down. Jarnulf rummaged among the bloody remnants until he found a bow whose draw he liked, then he picked up a red-smeared quiver and began collecting arrows. It took a little time, because the giant had swung several of the Hikeda'ya archers by their legs before smashing the life out of them and their arrows had flown everywhere.

"Hurry," rumbled Goh Gam Gar. "*Higdaja* are waiting to be killed."

When he had slipped at least two dozen arrows into his new quiver, Jarnulf let the giant lift him back to his seat atop the witchwood yoke.

"Soon, now," said the giant, licking his clawed, scarlet-smeared fingers. "I spread *Higdaja* blood from here all the way back to Nakkiga. I have waited long for this."

So, this is how my ending begins, O Lord, Jarnulf thought. *But You know best. My life and soul are in Your hands.* Out loud, he said only, "It is time to kill a queen."

From there, the journey became more difficult and even bloodier. As the giant raced toward the end of the valley with Jarnulf perched on the witchwood yoke, they encountered three more Hikeda'ya companies, each larger than the one before. Goh Gam Gar tore his way through the first two troops without much resistance, although not without a few arrows stuck in his shaggy hide. Jarnulf was lucky: although the fighting was fierce, it was over quickly, and none of the shafts loosed by their enemies struck him. But the third troop had its own giant.

Even as Goh Gam Gar tore into the astonished Sacrifices, the other Hunë reared up suddenly, roaring in fury. This new beast's fur was the yellowish white of fresh cream, and it stood almost as tall as Goh Gam Gar himself, who was by far the biggest giant that Jarnulf had ever seen. This new creature also wore leather armor and a massive bronze helmet the size of a cauldron and clutched a war-club as large as Jarnulf himself, which it immediately swung at them as they neared. Goh Gam Gar lurched to one side to avoid the massive club, then stopped so abruptly that Jarnulf was flung from the giant's neck. He struck the ground and rolled another dozen yards downslope, scattering arrows as he went. Doing his best to ignore the pain of his landing, he pulled himself into a crouch, fitted the first arrow that he could reach to his bowstring, pulled back hard, and immediately let it fly, bringing down the nearest of the Hikeda'ya soldiers charging toward him.

The two giants flung themselves together, snarling and barking so loudly that Jarnulf's ears hurt. Most of the panicked Sacrifices were busy trying to get away from the brawling monsters, and others were crushed in the first moments of the struggle. One brave Norn soldier did try to stab Goh Gam Gar as he rolled near, but one of the giant's great paws lashed out and sent him flying.

Jarnulf realized that he was going to be a much less threatening target for the remaining Hikeda'ya than his huge companion. He grabbed up as many fallen arrows as he could and began loosing them swiftly at the recovering Sacrifices as Goh Gam Gar climbed onto the younger giant's back. The giant put his great knee in his enemy's spine and caught the rim of the other's huge helmet in his clawed hands; as Jarnulf watched in astonishment, roaring Goh Gam Gar bent the other giant's head back, farther and farther, until its pale yellow neck snapped and the huge beast went limp.

Jarnulf was hurriedly collecting more arrows when Goh Gam Gar turned, his dead foe's club now gripped in his vast hairy hand, then began to pulp every living thing within his long reach—soldiers, horses, and even the nearest trees. A few of the Sacrifices heeded the desperate shouts of their officer and tried to stab at the giant with spears or swords—half a dozen Norn arrows were already wagging uselessly in Goh Gam Gar's gray fur—but within a matter of moments the Sacrifices and their commander had been smashed into silent wreckage.

Goh Gam Gar reached Jarnulf in two long strides, snatched him up with a huge, bloody hand, and set him back astride the heavy yoke. The giant was breathing hard, but he was also laughing, a deep, satisfied sound that echoed along the slope and made Jarnulf bounce in place.

"Yes! Yes!" The monster's roar must have carried for leagues. "Time now! Kill the *Higdaja* queen!"

All through the long afternoon, as the giant ran through the valley on great, tireless legs, the mist had been thick along the ground and almost as thick in the air above them, clouds of white ooze that flowed like oil on water. But as they approached the end of the valley and heard the growing noise of rushing water, the mists seemed to grow thinner. In fact, for the first time in hours, the sky above them cleared enough that Jarnulf could see the downward dipping sun above the western peaks. As the giant emerged from a grove of pines, leaving more than a few trees broken in his wake, and clambered up onto a spur of rock, Jarnulf could finally see the end of their journey.

His heart went cold. Before him was an immense force of Sacrifices—a thousand or more.

In all his travels, Jarnulf had never seen anything like Tanakirú. The long river valley, which in places had stretched almost a league from side to side, here narrowed to a sliver between steep, rocky slopes and—but for the slopes on the western side—was almost entirely filled by the powerful rush of the Narrowdark. The river was born from water hurrying down from the northern Wealdhelm that flung itself over the Tanakirú cliffs in a series of cataracts. The largest of these, a great white ribbon, fell so far that much of it frayed into swirling vapor, then plunged down at the eastern edge of the valley, churning the river's headwaters into leaping froth. But this eternally crashing water, though it had cut a deep gorge into the valley's floor and carved the path of the river as well, had left an undisturbed shelf of stony ground behind the river gorge, tucked in at the base of the high cliffs at valley's end. Protected by the Narrowdark's angry, impassable waters, this plateau should have been unreachable by any attackers, but although much of the valley floor was filled by the rushing river, a single spur of heavy stone stood out from the western slope—not long enough to reach the plateau by itself, but a clear objective for anyone wishing to cross the gorge; because of that, the Sithi defenders had built a wall across from it at the edge of the plateau. He could see a few of the defenders peering out from the battlements, armored in so many different colors they looked like a garden of blooms. The Hikeda'ya army seemed to have already heaved a siege engine into place at the end of the promontory, a long bridge that reached the defensive wall, and it was the immense force of Sacrifices—a thousand or more—advancing toward the bridge that had turned his innards to ice.

This battle is all but over, he thought. *Unless the Zida'ya are hiding a thousand archers of their own.* But only a few arrows flew from the top of the wall, enough to feather a few Hikeda'ya shields, but not to slow down the Sacrifices advancing toward the bridge. He could not puzzle out why they had not already swept across the span to finish their enemies.

"What do we do now?" he asked the giant.

"Kill more *Higdaja,*" said Goh Gam Gar.

"There are too many of them for us to—" Jarnulf began, then stopped. "Stay—what is that?" A swirl of white shapes was issuing from the caverns at the base of the cliffs. The pale surge moved so swiftly that for a moment Jarnulf thought a new cataract had burst out of the mountain and was foaming out onto the stony plateau. "By God and His Mother," he said when he understood. "Those are Queen's Teeth soldiers—they've got in behind the Zida'ya!"

Even as Jarnulf spoke, Goh Gam Gar suddenly lurched forward again, crashing out of the sheltering trees into the open, then charging downhill like an avalanche on two vast, shaggy legs. Jarnulf could barely cling to the yoke. "What are you doing?" he cried.

"The queen!" growled the giant, his huge strides swallowing the distance in great bites. The nearest of the Hikeda'ya troops heard his thunderous approach and turned, mouths gaping in confusion. "I see the cursed white queen herself on the other side of the water! *She is here!"*

Jarnulf was bouncing so hard and clinging so desperately that he could barely see anything. Goh Gam Gar reached the rearmost of the Sacrifices who swarmed around the base of the bridge in only moments. Hikeda'ya arrows began to snap past them, but the giant paid no heed. As they reached the nearest soldiers, the giant's huge war-club raked from side to side, smashing bodies into fragments, sending corpses flying and helmets bouncing with Hikeda'ya heads still inside. Goh Gam Gar was howling now, a reverberating, deafening cry of bloodthirsty glee that cleared the way before them almost as swiftly as the giant's blood-soaked, bronze-bound club. Whatever else the Sacrifice troops on the southern side of the gorge had believed would follow Queen Utuk'ku's appearance on the plateau, the sudden arrival of a maddened giant twice their size was not it. Though Sacrifice discipline was strong, and many of the Hikeda'ya tried to turn and fight, it was as hopeless as a mischief of rats pitted against a mastiff. Fleeing Sacrifices tumbled over their comrades' broken bodies as Goh Gam Gar waded through them with barking, growling joy, flinging corpses and bits of corpses in all directions.

Jarnulf realized that he could not get off a single arrow, but that was the least of his worries: he hung the bow around his neck so that he could use both hands to grip the giant's witchwood yoke. As they careened toward the gorge, smashing through ranks of doomed Sacrifices, Jarnulf could only press his head down against Goh Gam Gar's bristling, stinking neck to avoid the arrows buzzing past him. He began to murmur the *Mansa sea Cuelossan*—the prayer for the dead.

Though pierced by a dozen arrows or more, Goh Gam Gar swiftly reached the massive engine that supported the siege bridge over the gorge; he leaped onto it without hesitation. As Jarnulf bounced violently and almost lost his grip again, a moment later he felt the sturdy span shaking and bending under the giant's great weight.

His two-legged mount lurched across the swaying bridge and sprang onto the top of the defensive wall. His landing sent stones flying and knocked several Zida'ya defenders to the ground, but the great beast had no interest in them. As if in a dream, Jarnulf looked up from his desperate grip on the giant's yoke and saw a slender figure half a furlong away across the plateau, dressed all in flowing, ghostly white. The pale, upright shape stood upon a stone at the center of a troop of her white-helmeted, white-armored guards.

It is truly her, thought Jarnulf. *The witch herself! Thank you, my Lord, for giving me one more chance to end her wicked life.*

But even as Goh Gam Gar sprang down from the wall and thundered toward the assemblage of gleaming white shapes, as Jarnulf struggled to hold on and simultaneously free his bow again so that he could take advantage of this divine gift, the slender, white-clad figure atop the stone turned toward the giant. Her gleaming mask caught a flare of red sunset, then the queen lifted her hands in the air.

Something seized Jarnulf then, a burning clutch of pain that surged through his hands and seemed to squeeze and shake his entire body in a grip even stronger than the giant's. It burned like fire. His belly felt as if it was boiling inside him, his heart swelling until it must burst.

The yoke, he realized, *the giant's cursed yoke—*

But he could not let go, as if his hands had become part of the witchwood. Then the pain became too much, and though Jarnulf felt himself topple from his perch atop Goh Gam Gar's shoulders, he never felt himself hit the ground.

Even as Viyeki struggled onto his feet, covered with dirt, stone dust, and purpling bruises, feeling like a sack of something breakable that had been thrown off a cliff, rock continued to fall from the ceiling. When a stone the size of a bushel basket crashed down just behind him, followed by a spatter of smaller but still murderous bits of broken rock, Viyeki realized that although he had survived the main collapse of the tunnel, he was still in deadly danger. His ears were still ringing as he limped down the passage toward the valley floor, dodging more falling chunks of tunnel. He could still hear ominous sounds of grinding and cracking stone, so he limped downward as fast as his battered legs would carry him, following the path the queen's company had taken. Here and there he saw piles of rubble with pale limbs protruding from beneath them, and he knew some of them must be his fellow Hikeda'ya nobles and soldiers, but he could not fully grasp what that meant—what he had done. His ears were still ringing painfully and his thoughts felt curiously untethered, as though all that was happening was merely a dream. But somewhere deep inside himself he knew he had brought down the tunnel roof, separating Queen Utuk'ku from most of her army. He had richly earned a traitor's death, and not just for himself, but for his family and likely all the others of his clan.

Nobody has ever done such a thing, he thought, marveling in a dull, dreamlike way that he should be the one to cross such a dreadful boundary. *But I only wanted to be a good magister. I only wanted what was best for my people and for the Mother of All.*

He heard the queen's party ahead of him now, some of them shouting at the others to stay in line, forcing Sacrifice discipline on what must have been a terrified crowd. Viyeki stayed well behind them as they reached the bottom of the rough-hewn passage, and the Queen's Teeth guards herded them along at spearpoint while never breaking their eerie silence. Despite the tunnel collapse, Utuk'ku and her followers were still proceeding with the planned attack. Viyeki heard General Kikiti order his hammer-wielders to knock out the last pieces of stone at the end of the tunnel. The stone cracked, broke, and fell, then the Queen's Teeth flooded out into sudden light. The outside seemed as bright as a revelation to hidden Viyeki, squinting as he watched the queen's and Hakatri's litters borne out behind the guards.

He heard shouts of surprise and alarm from the Zida'ya outside as they saw the white plate of the guards' armor. He waited until they had all passed through, then he continued down the tunnel, through a patter of small ceiling stones, until he reached the place the guards had broken through to reach the plateau. Viyeki crept forward, still confused and oddly detached, and crouched in the shattered rubble to look out at where his fellow Hikeda'ya had gone.

What have I done?

In the middle of the plateau, two of the Queen's Teeth were helping the Mother of All descend from her litter. Utuk'ku seemed slow and infirm, but her back was straight and she held her head high, the marriage veil floating like a cloud around her. The guards helped her onto a great lump of stone so that she stood high above them, then she lifted her hands toward the sky, fingers curling as if she meant to pull down the firmament itself. Viyeki could only stare.

No power can oppose her. What was I thinking?

He heard screams, then a deep roar that he felt more than heard, and for an instant thought that the valley's fearsome *uro'eni* might have come, despite the sun not having set. That idea seemed no stranger than anything else he saw, and although it frightened him, it was only a dim fear, as if wrapped in several layers of linen.

Now a thunderously growling shape bounded over a siege-bridge that had been wheeled into place so the Sacrifice army could reach the plateau. The giant leaped from it onto the wall, and then from the wall down to the stony plateau. It was a giant, but not the ogre: still, it was the biggest and most frightening giant Viyeki had ever seen. It carried something vaguely man-shaped on its shoulders, but before he could make out what that was, the very air of the plateau seemed to bend and move, as if rippling above a fire. Whatever the giant had been carrying fell away from it, but the huge beast only hurried on toward the queen, howling in fury or pain or both. The Mother of All did not move—did not even show a sign of being aware of its approach—but her guards lowered their spears and tightened around her in a defensive ring.

An instant later, Viyeki saw the charging giant catch fire—a fire from nowhere. Flames licked upward through its shaggy gray fur until its neck and head were ablaze, streaming smoke even as it staggered toward the queen. It took half a dozen steps, bellowing in torment, then stumbled, barely staying upright. It batted uselessly at the flames that had now all but obscured its head, and—still roaring—it lurched a few more steps toward the queen, until it had almost reached the outermost ring of guards. Still, Utuk'ku did not move, but only stood with arms upraised. The giant staggered another step, much of the upper part of its body now ablaze, then it finally seemed to lose momentum and halted just a few paces short of Utuk'ku and her Queen's Teeth. For a moment the monstrous thing only stood, long arms dangling, clawed hands twitching, its head and upper body entirely engulfed by fire. Then, with a horrible groan, the giant folded to its knees and fell, to lie in a smoking, motionless heap before the guards.

The queen slowly lowered her arms, then turned to survey the valley. She spoke, and he heard her triumphant thought in his head, painfully loud, as from someone shouting only inches from his ear *You will listen, all who hear me. You will heed my Word of Command.* Then she spoke aloud in her true voice—a single word, a ragged wisp of sound that Viyeki could barely hear at first, but which echoed louder and louder until the very cliffs seemed to tremble. He did not recognize the word—could barely tell that it *was* a word—but it still struck him like a thunderbolt. He wanted desperately to escape, to put as much distance as possible between himself and the overwhelming, shattering word resounding so painfully in his ears and thoughts—but he could not. His body would no longer do what he wanted. He folded helplessly to his knees and then slumped against the edge of the tunnel mouth. He could not make any of his limbs obey him. He could move his eyes, he could still breathe, but all other choice of movement seemed denied to him.

Across the plateau, nothing else moved either, though the queen and her guards still stood upright. All the Zida'ya defenders had folded to the ground at the queen's Word of Command, limp and helpless.

The Mother of the People finally has what she wants, Viyeki thought, despairing. *We are all her helpless slaves.*

28

The Seastone

Ayaminu and Dunao had ordered a halt, not just to water the horses this time, but also to decide what to do next. In a rare moment out of the saddle, Tanahaya walked across the misty grove in search of Ki'ushapo. When she found him, she was surprised to see Brother Etan was seated crouching beside Ki'ushapo, cleaning the Sitha's healing wound with a wet rag.

"I did not expect to find you here, Brother," she said.

"I wanted to see how Ki'ushapo was feeling." He looked a little shamefaced, as if he had been caught doing something wrong.

Ki'ushapo, still weak but finally able to ride by himself, gave her a hand-sign of greeting, but his teeth were clenched in discomfort as the monk probed at the arrow-spite in his back. She knew Ki'ushapo well—he was perhaps Jiriki's closest friend other than his sister Aditu and Tanahaya herself—and could only wonder how much it must hurt if he let it show on his usually imperturbable face.

"If the pain is too distracting," she said, "Lady Ayaminu has a little *kei-vishaa* left."

"Save it for the battlefield," he said, "for the truly wounded. I am almost whole again."

She doubted that—deep discomfort showed in his every movement—but she also knew it was pointless to try to force it on him. Ki'ushapo was like Jiriki that way, determined to take nothing that another might need, uninterested in his own suffering.

The mere thought of her lover seemed to make the life inside her—the life he had fathered—shiver awake. *A female child, Aditu said.* She put a hand on her belly. *A strange and wonderful female child.* She took a deep, uneasy breath. *Please, if there is any sense to this life, any meaning left to this world, let her be born! Let her live her life free and happy!* But there seemed little chance of that coming to pass.

"Mistress Ayaminu and Lord Dunao are speaking of what we should do next," she told Ki'ushapo. "They asked if you are able to join them."

"I am." He pulled down his arming shirt, and then, with help from Tanahaya and the monk, strapped on his armor. Etan showed good sense, helping him rise to his feet without making it obvious. Tanahaya was worried to see how weak Ki'ushapo still was. Like Jiriki, he was known for his skill in war, although—also like Jiriki—he took little pride in it and no joy at all. Tanahaya could not help thinking that he did not seem capable of much fighting at the present.

But we go to join a doomed cause, she thought. *I am not even a warrior, but I will have to fight too. Oh, Jiriki, my love, why was this our time? Why could we not have found each other in an era of peace?*

And what era would that have been? a dark inner voice asked. *Our people have been shrinking and failing almost since the ships brought us to this land.*

"Am I expected to come to this . . . council?" Brother Etan asked her.

"I do not believe so. But you would be welcome, I think."

"And then you would all have to speak my tongue. Even Ki'ushapo, who speaks it so barbarously it makes my ears ache. No, thank you. I will try to find a patch of sunlight to sit in."

"Barbarously?" growled Ki'ushapo. "I should slay you for that insult, mortal dog."

For a moment Tanahaya was stunned. She had never heard Jiriki's kinsman say anything so harsh. Then she realized that the normally stern Ki'ushapo was jesting. Etan's mock frown and headshake showed he knew it too. *By the Garden, have these two become friends?*

If the world wasn't ending, it certainly seemed to be changing. Tanahaya's hand crept again to the still-inconspicuous presence in her belly. *What will we see next? Utuk'ku pleading for Zida'ya and Hikeda'ya to reconcile? The rebuilding of the Nine Cities?*

It was a wistfully amusing thought, but of course she didn't believe it for an instant.

"Why do we waste time in talk?" Dunao complained. "The horses are watered. The sun is climbing the sky. Let us ride!"

"Ride to what?" asked Ayaminu. "We have not heard what the scouts have seen at the site of battle."

Dunao made a hand-sign of frustration—*deafened by wind*, an ancient Landborn gesture Tanahaya had never seen, only read of in books. "The scouts have confirmed what I already told you. Ensume's Hikeda'ya have taken all the valley except the Tanakirú plateau at the northern end, beneath the Ninth Ship. They outnumber our defenders by a dozen to one or more. They have giants, war engines, everything our people do not. It is only a matter of hours—not days—until they force their way across the Narrowdark's headwaters and destroy us. So why are we not riding?"

"Because even if we ride to Tanakirú without stopping, driving our horses to the point of death, and with the wind at our backs as well, we still will not reach them in time to play a part." Ayaminu spoke as if she had already seen it happen.

Tanahaya went cold all over. Jiriki was there—she could feel it as surely as she felt the child that grew inside her. "Surely that can't be true!"

"Utter foolishness," said Dunao. "How can you say such a thing, Ayaminu? Our folk have defended that valley for many years, and even after the Hornet's Nest fell, they have held the Hikeda'ya out of Tanakirú itself since the Fire-Knight Moon. Do you doubt your own people's bravery?"

"Never," said Ayaminu, but her face was stony.

"I know your wisdom, Ayaminu," said Ki'ushapo. "We all do. But your words make my heart heavy. Why do you think this is true?"

"Because this battle is greater than you know," she said, "and it is not being fought only at Tanakirú. I am no Sa'onsera, but I have gifts that the rest of you do not. And those gifts—though they begin to seem more like a curse in these wretched days—tell me that the battle for Tanakirú will be over by the fall of darkness tonight. I would like to say, 'It will be over, win or lose', but Utuk'ku will reach for what she wants, and I feel woefully certain that unless something happens that I simply cannot foresee or even imagine, she will succeed."

"What madness—?" Dunao began.

Ayaminu raised her hand, fingers spread. "Please," she said. "I do not have the strength to argue, Gray Rider, and in one thing you may be correct—we still must hurry there, to help any of our folk who may survive, though we can have no say in whether Hamakho's greedy heiress gains what she seeks. So hold your questions and your angry objections." She stared at him, and for the first time Tanahaya could see the weariness and strain Ayaminu had been carrying. "You know what day it is, do you not?" Ayaminu continued. "Tonight, when the sun sets, the Year-Torch will be in the sky for the last time. Back in Anvi'janya, Aditu will finish the Year-Dancing ceremony. Any adept will tell you that songs of great power are made stronger still by choosing not just the proper words but also the proper hour. Our enemy Utuk'ku knows that, and the end of a Great Year is such a time—one of the most powerful and dangerous of all."

Dunao was still stiff with anger. "Lady Ayaminu, you may spend your time musing on such matters. I will take our fighters and hurry to Tanakirú."

"Do not doubt that we will all ride to Tanakirú together," she said, with more than a suggestion of anger. "The horses are being readied again even now. But even if they had wings, we would not reach the valley's end in time to stop Utuk'ku. I feel that strongly, though it squeezes at my heart until I fear it will stop."

"Then what *is* our task?" demanded Dunao. "To bury the dead? To offer our surrender to the witch of Nakkiga?"

Ayaminu only shook her head. "I wish I could say, Rider. But I have told you all I know."

As they hurried north along the western edge of the valley, the memory that had been tickling the edges of Tanahaya's thoughts finally fluttered close enough for her to grasp. As the horses passed in silent single file down a long, forested slope, she heard the noise of running water in the distance, and it pulled her back to the first time she had entered the Narrowdark Valley, following the mortal prince, Morgan. The strangeness of the place, even during that brief incursion, had struck her. Thinking of it now brought everything back.

"Lady Ayaminu," she said quietly. "Do you know the Hikeda'yasao word *zhin'ju*? Is it the same as our word *shin'iu*?"

"It is, yes—the spirit of a place, the essence which makes it what it is. Why?"

"Because it was something that troubled me in Anvi'janya, and I have been trying to remember why. I first came across it in the Repository, in the records of Sa-Ruyan Mardae's trial."

"Were Utuk'ku and her minions questioning the origins of the Ninth Ship? Speak, child—what have you remembered?"

"That Yedade began to ask the prisoner Mardae about it—harsh, pushing questions—but Utuk'ku herself stopped him. Yedade had demanded of the prisoner, *'Tell me about the* zhin'ju *of the great ship,'* but then the question was withdrawn and there was no more mention of it."

"Yet it troubled you," said Ayaminu. "It stayed in your thoughts."

"It did." She looked at the line of riders stretching before them, journeying without complaint or even outward sadness toward something that no one seemed to think they would survive. "It made no sense to me then and still does not. If *zhin'ju* means the same as *shin'iu*, how can a ship have such a thing? It is not a natural thing, not a grove or a standing stone or a waterfall."

Ayaminu seemed thoughtful. "Perhaps the Hikeda'ya do not use the word in quite the same way as we do."

"There is more." Tanahaya hesitated. "But I am ashamed. I took something from Anvi'janya's repository by accident and did not realize until we were underway. Here. Do you know the poet Fololi Unshoon?"

"Barefoot Fololi? Yes, I know of him. He lived and died a long time ago. He was said to be among the strangest of our folk—an intimate of the infamous Lady Azosha, one of her pet philosophers. Some consider him a wonderful poet, while others judge his extravagant fancies more harshly. Is this something of his?" She accepted the parchment, frowning a little. "It is very creased, scholar. Archivist Dineke will be most unhappy when he sees it."

"Please, Mistress. I feel bad enough already." The chain of Aditu's Seastone had slipped free of Tanahaya's collar and was bumping against her armor as they rode. She absently reached up to hold it so it would not distract her. "Look at the poem, please. It is this part here that stuck in my memory."

Ayaminu nodded and read the words aloud.

And so they set out upon the great Sea, inconstant Mother to all,
Just as the living stars spin dancing through the firmament at the touch of Her hand.
Guided by Her motive forces and carried by the labor of their yoked spirits,
Our ships braved the Great Darkness in search of a new haven for the Garden's castaways.

Ayaminu looked up from the parchment. "I see the word *shin'iue*—'spirits'—that you asked me about."

"Yes, but that is not all. During the Tinukeda'ya leader Mardae's trial, Yedade tried to ask him about the "motive forces" of the Ninth Ship, though he then withdrew the question. And the same words occur in Fololi's poem, written many Great Years earlier."

"Ah." Ayaminu nodded. "Very strange, but I do not see the significance."

"Why was Yedade asking after such an obscure matter?" Tanahaya asked, still clutching the Seastone as though Aditu's heirloom might provide an answer. "And why should Fololi put those particular words into a poem written long before that trial—a poem not about the Ninth Ship, because Fololi could not have known of it, but a celebration of the famed Eight Ships that brought us here from the Garden? And why does he speak of their *shin'iue*? What kind of spirits could unliving ships have?" But even as she spoke, Tanahaya found herself distracted by the sudden, strong odor of something burning. "What is that smell . . . ?"

Ayaminu seemed farther away now. Her mouth also seemed to move very slowly, and her words were faint, as if they had traveled a great distance. "What do you mean, child?"

But the acrid scent became ever stronger, and Tanahaya's fingers, where they touched the Seastone, were suddenly hot—no, not hot, but full of light, of something she could not name—

And then she fell out of the world.

Snenneq recovered quickly from his struggle with the Norn soldier and his fall from the stairs, but Qina would not let him get up until she felt the bloody lump on his head.

"I am well," he said. "We must hurry after Morgan!"

"And do what?" Qina demanded. "You saw the thing that took her. What could we do? Like mice fighting a bear, that is all we would be."

"We cannot desert Morgan." He clambered to his feet. "You said the ogre has taken Nezeru. We both know that Morgan will follow it until it kills him."

"And us, if we follow," she said, but it was an argument she knew she would lose.

"That is not all the tale of this disaster," Kuyu-Kun said in the trolls' Qanuc tongue. The ancient Tinukeda'ya rose from the cabin floor with Tih-Rumi's help and stood on shaking legs. "The Hikeda'ya have stolen the ship's heart."

Snenneq looked at Qina, then back to the old Tinukeda'ya. "I confess, I am puzzled by what you say."

"No time for that." Timid and retiring Kuyu-Kun now seemed transformed, full of desperate intensity. "We need all your ropes and climbing irons. We must hurry!"

Snenneq shook his head, not in negation but in confusion. "But what is the ship's heart?"

"Ropes! Hurry!"

Snenneq stared up at the roof of the dome, now shattered like an eggshell, only shards of crystal and broken witchwood beams remaining. "Did the ogre come because of the Hikeda'ya?" he asked. "It has never troubled us until now."

"Yes, the Great Protector came because of the Hikeda'ya soldiers," said Kuyu-Kun, but he wore an odd expression on his face. "It sensed them searching for the ship's heart."

"Great protector?" said Snenneq. "Ship's heart? Where does that come from? You have not said it before."

Kuyu-Kun paused and looked briefly to Tih-Rumi, then turned back to the trolls with a worried shake of his hairless head. "In truth, I do not know. It came into my thoughts when it all happened. I have not heard either of those things before." He looked frightened. "But it is true—I know it. I *feel* it. The thing you call an ogre protects the great ship. It is part of the ship, somehow—perhaps it *is* the ship."

"Enough," said Qina. "We must hurry. They are far ahead of us. You can see where the giant thing has gone." She pointed to the trail of destruction across the deck; fragile, makeshift shelters kicked into flinders, mats of vines and small forests uprooted and scraped aside.

"I see you counting," someone called to them in Westerling speech. *"If you mean to follow your friend and the Protector, you must count us, too. The Hikeda'ya have stolen something from us, and the Lady of the Ship is unhappy."*

Qina turned to see the man Yek Fisher approaching, followed by nearly a dozen more of the folk who had been sheltering in the cabin when the invaders came. She began to respond in Qanuc, realized the newcomers could not understand it, and cursed inwardly at having to use her awkward flatlander speech. *"Why you fight for us?"* she asked.

"Not just for you—for the ship. Can you not feel it? The old one does, see!" Yek Fisher pointed at Kuyu-Kun. *"He knows the ship has lost its spirit—its heart."*

"You call me the Aedon," said a solemn voice from the crowd behind him. *"But I am also mortal like you. Fear not, for though I die, I will always be with you."*

"It is worse than even the loss of the ship's heart," said Kuyu-Kun, ignoring the strange religious quotation. He had changed to the mortal tongue as easily as he might have exchanged one cloak for another. *"Far, far worse than that."*

"What does that mean?" Snenneq asked him as the others crowded forward. Qina scowled in frustration as even her beloved was now speaking the Westerling tongue.

The Voice of the Dreaming Sea raised a shaking hand. *"I cannot say. It is like . . . a bad dream. But I feel it. Something terrible is happening, and we must recover the ship's heart or all is lost!"* He shook his head as helplessly as a man beset by biting flies. *"Its voice screams in my thoughts—no, her voice, Ruyan Ká's. Can no one else hear it?"*

"No, but I feel it, Master," said Tih-Rumi. *"A terrible emptiness. The ship is dying."*

"Dying?" Qina was almost mad with impatience. *"What you say? Ship is alive?"*

"It does not matter," Little Snenneq declared in their Qanuc tongue. "We must go after Morgan, beloved, and we dare not refuse any help."

She looked at the ragged, wide-eyed folk ranged around Yek Fisher. "So you would chase that huge, terrible beast without any plan, Snenneq? Trusting your life to these folk that we hardly know? And my life too?"

"Nothing is certain anymore, my love." He reached out for her hand. "Morgan is gone, Nezeru is gone, and a giant as big as Mintahoq Mountain has stolen the heart of a ship. Who can know what to trust? But I trust us if we are together."

"Then so it must be," she said, and sighed. "Though I fear how it will end. But I will not let you go without me."

At first Tanahaya could not guess what had happened, and only barely knew who she was. She drifted in a darkness shot through with blurry streaks of light, streaks which were slowly growing brighter.

The Seastone, she remembered. *I was touching the Seastone.* She felt a moment of wild hope. *Aditu said it was part of the stone from which the Mist Lamp Witness was created. Has Utuk'ku fallen, then? Has she lost her grip on the Road of Dreams, so that the Witnesses have come back to life?*

The thought of being able to speak to Jiriki again gave her something to cling to and helped to keep the terror at bay. The darkness around her now dwindled to mere shadow. The streaks of light became the trunks of trees.

Shisae'ron. Home. It was not such a surprise this time to see the place where she had grown appear before her, the place where generations of her people had lived out their lives during the great years of peace between the Parting and the Northmen's overthrow of Asu'a. But if the last Tanahaya had seen of dream-Shisae'ron had been the valley in bloom, as it had been during the happy days before her mother's decline, what was taking shape before her looked bleak and disturbing. Surely her home had never fallen so far into ruination, even after her mother died and the rest of the clan deserted the place. The trees were all naked, the birches bare and white as bleached bones, the leafless willow branches dangling like exhausted serpents. And everywhere she looked, the rich, loamy soil had turned to dried, cracked mud.

As Tanahaya climbed the track toward Willow Hall, she knew she was crossing a landscape of dream, but a part of her could not let go of the hope that even this wretched version of Shisae'ron's most beautiful spot was somehow real—that she could simply walk through it to a time before her father Kaniho died and her mother Siriaya slowly and irreparably lost her joy in living.

As she crested the rise she saw her childhood home spread across the hilltop, blending in with the trees and jutting stones and long grasses so gracefully that, but for the long horizontal line of the roof, a careless glance would not have discerned her family's dwelling.

Someone was waiting for her there.

Tanahaya's heart lifted. Surely that dim shape seated beneath the long, shadowed porch could only be her mother Siriaya in her favorite spot, where she spent hours every day watching the dance of birds across the sky and the slow migration of clouds. But even as Tanahaya sped her steps toward the house, a part of her knew that it was not possible, that her mother was long gone and that their last worldly conversation, in which Siriaya had not even recognized her daughter, would never have a happy sequel. If she dreamed now, where was her living body? Had she been struck by an arrow fired from some Norn ambush? Or had she fallen from her horse and struck her head? She did not want to let a dream of her lost home, however welcome and tempting, sweep her away from the real world.

I have a life inside me beside my own. I cannot afford to let regret make me lose sight of that, no matter how strong those feelings might be. Himano taught me that memory is a needle, as quick to wound as to mend.

But as she drew closer to the shadowed figure, she saw that though everything else about the house was familiar, the waiting shape was not her mother but something far more disquieting—a shrouded, featureless bundle, as pale and complicated as a *srinyedu* tapestry. As Tanahaya approached, two spots of buttery light appeared at the top of the shape like eyes opening, startling her with their intensity.

The Garden is still good to us. I feared I would not have the strength. It was the same voice Tanahaya had heard while trapped beneath the fallen pillars of Da'ai Chikiza.

You spoke to me before, Tanahaya said. *But who are you?*

The eyes gleamed like lanterns in fog. *You know me. I know you. And our need is terrible.*

Our need?

The shape extended two arms as if to embrace her. *My son. My son has fallen.*

Likimeya? Is this you? She felt a sudden clutch of horror. *Are you saying something has happened to Jiriki?*

Thunderbolt has fallen from his hand. I see blood. I hear cries of fear from our people. You must hurry to him. And you must bring them all together—the Keida'ya.

A feverish chill seemed to seize her now. *I don't understand you. Speak plainly, I beg you! What has happened? Does Jiriki still live?*

I do not know. But you must hurry to him. You must bring the children to him. And you must tell his sister to let me go.

Tanahaya wanted to leap onto the porch, to grab the featureless figure and shake it. *We are hurrying to join Jiriki as swiftly as we can, Sa'onsera Likimeya, but we are at least a day's ride from reaching him!*

Tanahaya felt rather than heard a wordless cry of despair. *Then all may be lost! I cannot know for certain, but even now I feel the strands of possibility snapping. Soon there will be none left that lead to anything but disaster—or worse than disaster.*

Tanahaya dropped to her knees on the steps. Movement caught her eye, and she looked up to see the birchwood beams that held up the porch were completely covered with trembling wings—but all the butterflies were black. *If you are the Sa'onsera, you must tell me more clearly what to do. What do I take to Jiriki? What children? Do you mean the child he and I have made—the child in my belly? And we have left Aditu behind in Anvi'janya—how can I tell her anything?*

I do not know, the apparition conveyed. *I cannot touch her, even though she is deep in the sacred ceremony. The song of the Three Who Are One enwraps me, silences me, keeps me apart from those I most need.* There was an edge almost of madness in the apparition's words. *The queen's device threatens everything!* Several of the black butterflies sprang free from the eaves and fluttered aimlessly before settling again.

No, Tanahaya said. *No, we have solved that mystery. The queen's so-called "device" was a trick to lure your son away from Tanakirú, but he must be heading back by now.*

Utuk'ku's true device has not yet been employed—I can feel that. She wants more than just to seize the witchwood crown. The voice was quieter now, as if it floated down a long hallway. *She wants its spirit—its heart. My son has fallen trying to stop her. You must hurry to him! Hurry—!*

Even as these words rang in Tanahaya's thoughts, the voice grew faint and the familiar lines and shadows of the porch began to dim, as though twilight was rushing toward evening. Within moments everything had fallen dark, and the only sound Tanahaya could hear was the feathery, almost silent rustle of black wings.

"Likimeya? Likimeya, don't leave me! What children? What device do you mean? I do not understand."

But even the whispering of the wings had been silenced.

"Likimeya!"

Something touched her—a cool hand on her brow. "No. Peace, young one. It is me—Ayaminu."

Tanahaya opened her eyes to discover the mistress of Anvi'janya leaning over her. "What happened?"

"You fell from your saddle, scholar—but something was already wrong before that."

Tanahaya sat up. Her horse stood a short distance away, watching with an almost woeful gaze, as if to say, "You have no right to frighten me that way." Ayaminu was crouching beside her, and several other Sithi had reined up a short distance away. "It was the Seastone," said Tanahaya. "I was touching it, then . . . then I was back in Shisae'ron once more, and Likimeya spoke to me again."

Ayaminu's narrow, shrewd face showed no great reaction, but her voice was firm. "Tell me everything you remember."

When Tanahaya had finished her explanation, Ayaminu shook her head, then helped her stand. "None of this seems good to me," Ayaminu said. "Jiriki wounded, talk of the queen's device—again—and a message for Aditu."

"We must send to tell her what her mother said—that she must let Likimeya go, whatever that might mean. Then we must hurry to Jiriki."

Ayaminu shook her head slowly. "We will dispatch a messenger to Aditu, of course, but we are already several days out from Anvi'janya. Even a fast rider will not get there until long after Year-Dancing is over and we have reached Tanakirú."

"Is all for naught, then?" Tanahaya asked. "Do we ride with such haste just to witness the end of our people?"

"I do not know," said Ayaminu. "But if there is any use in sending a messenger, we must do it now. And I will tell Dunao we must go faster—if that is possible. Are you well enough to get back into the saddle?"

Tanahaya nodded. She could think of nothing now but reaching Jiriki, her fear for him so great that she found it hard to draw breath. "I am whole, *S'huesa*, and so is the child inside me. Although what kind of world she will see, if she is ever born, I cannot imagine."

Ayaminu gave her a strange look. "I thought you might be carrying a child, but I was not certain."

"I am—she is mine and Jiriki's. Aditu said she will be a Sa'onsera one day. That is the only hope I can still cling to."

"Then cling to it!" said Ayaminu. "Hope can make a light when all others have been extinguished."

The Silver Stags had beaten Eolair's grand-nephew, Aelin, until he could barely stand, let alone walk, but still they dragged him from the place he had been imprisoned and marched him, along with Lord Murdo, Earl of Carn Inbarh, his daughter Isleen, and several other important prisoners, up the high street into Woolyard Square in the gray winter afternoon. The Brynioch Temple dominated the square, a tall, precarious-looking wooden edifice that was said to have stood there since the long-ago days of Prince Sinnach, who fought the first Rimmersman invaders. But looming above the temple and the city stood the Taig on its high mount, the ancient seat of the Hernystiri kings. The Taig had its own walls, and, it was painfully clear to Aelin, its own rules.

Some of the citizens who had gathered early for the day's festivities shouted and hissed at the prisoners, while others threw rubbish or screamed threats. If it had not been for the armed soldiers lining the route, it seemed likely the angry shouters might have tried to take the punishment of the king's declared enemies into their own hands. But even in his battered, dispirited state, Aelin could not help noticing that many in the crowd looked troubled, and although no one dared show any outward support for Hugh's prisoners, Aelin felt certain that some of them felt real sympathy for him and the others.

Not that sympathy would do them any good, Aelin knew. *Guilty or not, sung of as traitors or martyrs, we will be just as dead.*

Every time Aelin's limping progress slowed, one of Hugh's soldiers jabbed him with something sharp. Beside him, Evan walked with eyes closed, his lips moving in silent prayer. Aelin hoped the young man's faith was giving him more comfort at this moment than Aelin's own. Aelin believed in the gods and believed in Heaven, but the Aedonites seemed to believe that their God saw everything that happened, watching over each person like an adoring father. Aelin's own gods were not such sticklers. They might take sides in a war or heed a sufficiency of prayers after a year of poor harvests, but he held no hope they would reach down from their home in the sky and save him from what was to come.

And as he and the rest of the prisoners were prodded along into the square at spearpoint, what was to come became fearsomely obvious. On one side of the square a great viewing platform had been erected. It was hung with banners bearing the White Stag of Hern the Great and was clearly meant for the king and his closest minions. Opposite the viewing stand, in front of the barred and shuttered Brynioch Temple, stood a scaffold of raw new wood, constructed with far less care than had been lavished on the royal platform. On the cobbles beside it a great pyre had been built, layers of straw and wood stacked as high as a man. Atop the pyre stood the empty frame of the Withy Crow, a great cage built of willow staves lashed together into the crude shape of a bird, perched on the pyre as if sitting on a nest. Just seeing it made Aelin feel light-headed and ill. He heard Isleen let out a muffled gasp of horror.

"Courage," he said. "They can only kill us once. Then we will be with the gods." But his heart was struggling inside his chest like a trapped animal.

"The old, evil days have truly returned," she said in an unsteady voice. "But no matter what, I will never beg Hugh for anything—not even death."

Aelin could only admire her courage. He hoped he would be as brave when the time came.

Now the soldiers herded the prisoners, including many likely innocents rounded up from the neighborhood of the farrier's shop, into the center of the square, but did not lead them to the Withy Crow. Instead, they were forced to one end of the square and kept there for what seemed most of an hour as the sun dropped toward the horizon, making the roofs of the tallest houses, guild-halls, and temples all shine with blood-hued light. They waited so long that Aelin's dread turned to something colder and more resigned, and he began to wonder whether Maccus and the others who had not been caught with him had escaped. He prayed that they had. Even if only a few of those who knew the truth survived, Hugh could never be entirely secure on his throne. The people of Hernystir might forgive a monarch many faults, but Aelin did not think that conspiring with the dreaded Norns would be one of them. The white-skinned northern fairies had been objects of superstitious terror since even before the days of King Cormach the Lame.

Trumpets began to blow. The king was here.

Hugh rode into Woolyard Square on a black stallion, surrounded by his Silver Stags. Close behind rode Lady Tylleth, demurely mounted side-saddle. The crowd cheered for Hugh, particularly the wealthy folk watching from high windows around the square, but Aelin thought he detected a sullenness in the people on the ground. Things had not been good in the last years, with Hugh's court favorites reaching out with both hands to seize whatever they wanted. Unrest had taken hold even among those who knew nothing of Hugh's dealings with the Norn Queen.

But none of that matters now, Aelin told himself. *I must make myself right with Heaven.*

As the king and his lady climbed the steps to the viewing stand, Count Curudan, a florid, bearded man with the unearned swagger of a great conqueror, stood to read the bill of attainder. Aelin was surprised to hear that the charges all seemed directed against his great-uncle Count Eolair and the dowager queen Inahwen, though they were nowhere to be seen, while Aelin and the others standing before the king in chains were not mentioned in the long list of supposedly traitorous plottings and incitements.

The lengthy scroll finished, Curudan returned to his chair beside the king and Tylleth. Ax-faced Captain Samreas now moved to the edge of the platform and looked out at the prisoners with a predatory smile. Still so sore from a night of beatings that his trembling legs could barely hold him upright, Aelin did his best to stare back at the Silver Stag captain without showing fear.

"Hear me, Murdo of Carn Inbarh, Aelin of Nad Mullach, and all your liegemen and co-conspirators," Samreas said loudly, so the watching crowd could hear every word. "You also have been brought to stand before the king's justice, accused of many vile crimes against the throne. But because we have not had time to question you properly, the decision on your fates will be put off for a matter of some days."

Aelin was sickened. Hugh was going to force him to watch his great-uncle's execution, then make him wait for his own. "I do not know what you still hope to learn," he shouted at the viewing stand. "But I still have a few bones you have not broken, so do what you will."

Samreas laughed. "Spoken like a brave little traitor—I see Eolair's apprentice has grown as arrogant as his criminal master."

"My great-uncle is innocent, and so is the queen," cried Aelin. "Do what you will. The gods know who stands straight and who is crooked."

"Your Majesty—King Hugh!" Isleen called out from Aelin's side. "Your people do not want to see such . . . such a terrible thing done to our good Queen Inahwen—"

"—who plotted with Count Eolair against the lawful monarch, as Count Curudan has already read out," retorted Samreas. "Enough, Lady Isleen. You and your father were given a chance for clemency, but you threw it back in His Majesty's face, so you will doubtless suffer the same fate as all other traitors when we have learned the full truth. Watch and learn what is in store for you."

Aelin was shocked again—Isleen and Lord Murdo had been offered forgiveness but had turned it down? He took a deep breath. Such bravery demanded that they all die bravely, too. "Can King Hugh not speak for himself?" he called. "His people must wonder why he is silent when his bravest and most loyal subjects are treated like criminals—when he condemns even his own loving stepmother to a terrible death!"

Hugh finally rose from his seat. It was hard to tell at such a distance, but Aelin thought he saw a smile play across the king's handsome features. The king wore dark armor of an unusual design, the plates fluted and finished like the scaly hide of some fabulous sea creature from an old tapestry.

"I see you have your uncle's sharp tongue, Sir Aelin," Hugh declared. "And his self-satisfaction. It is too bad neither of you thought to use them in service to your rightful lord."

"My great-uncle Count Eolair has never done anything *but* serve Hernystir and its throne!" Aelin shouted. "While *you* have made compact with the Norns—with the Norn Queen herself, the Witch of the North! And because my liegemen and I were witnesses to that foul bargain, we are being executed!"

"Your words are as deranged as your plan to murder me and seize the throne," said Hugh. "Let us see whether the gods support you." Now his smile was broad and obvious; Aelin, who had known Hugh for years, thought he looked quite mad. "Bring in the condemned!"

To the muffled beat of drums, Count Eolair and Queen Inahwen were led out of a shop on the edge of the square where they had been held. Their hands were bound behind them, but they were neither gagged nor blindfolded. Both were pale and silent as they were marched up to the scaffold. Then soldiers forced them into the cage in the center of the Withy Crow and chained the door shut.

No priest came to say the Prayer of the White Shield. Instead, Hugh himself stood at the edge of the platform, glaring down at the prisoners. "May you stand before the judgment of Holy Talamh for your foul treachery," the king intoned. "And with the flight of your souls to judgment, we hallow this, her holy day, that comes with the setting sun. Now light the—"

"Tyrant!" someone shouted. "King Hugh is a tyrant!"

"No, you fool—!" cried Aelin, recognizing the voice, but it was too late. Black-bearded Maccus had stepped forward out of the crowd, drawing back the string of the bow that had been hidden under his cloak; the exposed figure of King Hugh stood only thirty paces away. But before Maccus could loose his arrow, half a dozen shafts flew at him and pierced his chest and throat; a few struck others in the crowd behind him. Maccus was thrown back, bleeding from the mouth, dead before he struck the ground, and the people around him cowered and shrieked out their innocence.

"That is all your traitorous rebellion has come to in the end," said Hugh. "And now you will learn what all traitors must learn." He raised his voice to a great shout. "Light the pyre. Let those who hate us burn!"

29

A Last Sunset

A few desperate Sithi defenders on the wall were still trying to dislodge the Norn's siege-bridge as Simon and several others carried Jiriki down to the Tanakirú plateau, but the massive hooks at the end of the heavy structure had dug deep into the piled stones and could not be torn loose.

As they set Jiriki down at the base of the wall, Rukayu came and crouched beside Simon, staring wide-eyed and silent at the gash in Jiriki's armor. Yizashi Grayspear called out—likely for a healer, but Rukayu did not translate. Another Sitha came running to them and, with Yizashi's help, he unbuckled Jiriki's breastplate and carefully lifted it away. When Simon saw the deep, bloody gouge in his friend's chest he could only gasp. He reached down and took Jiriki's hand, but the fingers were cold and limp.

"Can they save him?" he asked Rukayu. His eyes swam with tears as he squeezed Jiriki's hand again, but Rukayu was slow to respond. She seemed barely to have the strength to shake her head. "I do not know. And it likely does not matter. We are caught between two Hikeda'ya armies now."

Simon looked up. Most of the remaining Sithi were hurrying across the plateau to join their fellows beneath the wall, the Hikeda'ya across the gorge momentarily forgotten. The queen of the Norns and her armored guards had marched to the center of the plateau, only a few hundred paces from Simon and the others. He could see Utuk'ku's silver mask gleaming beneath her high, strange headdress and billowing veil—that perfect, horrifyingly imperturbable metal face. He had seen it in dreams, had seen it as an illusion, but never in person, and he could not stop shivering. *I pray it isn't the last thing I ever see.* Nausea nearly made him double up. *I always hoped there would be a way—that somehow we would all come out of this . . .*

But despite the Norns' huge advantage, Utuk'ku and her silent, white-armored soldiers seemed content to stand and watch their enemies flee before them.

Simon turned back to his friend. The Sithi healer had swiftly cleaned away much of the blood on Jiriki's chest and layered fragrant leaves and pads of linen over the wound. Yizashi then held them in place while the white-haired healer wrapped long strips of linen around Jiriki's ribcage to hold the medicaments and bandages in place. As Simon watched, praying, he heard a rising sound, not from the Norn Queen's company, but from her army on the far side of the gorge. For a few terrified moments Simon thought they must be clambering across the bridge to attack, heartened by the queen's arrival. He knew that if they came in force, they would make short work of the few Sithi still guarding the span, so he began to clamber back onto his feet, determined to return to the wall and give what strength he could to the Sithi's last-ditch defense, as the Norn Queen and her troops were now between him and his granddaughter Lillia. But before he could even take a step toward the ladder, he realized that the sound was not the cry of an attacking army but a single deep, reverberating roar, growing louder with each moment until it throbbed in his bones. Now he could hear shrieks of pain and surprise that—Simon realized in astonishment—were coming from the Hikeda'ya soldiers on the far side of the siege-bridge. Then he heard a rapid series of pounding steps and realized that something heavy was rushing across the siege-bridge toward the wall and the last defenders.

But it can't be the ogre, he thought, as the thunderous approach grew louder. *The bridge could never hold it! What new horror has the queen summoned?*

Suddenly the pounding footsteps stopped, then a huge shadow flew from the top of the wall behind him, passed above his head, and crashed to the stony ground of the Tanakirú plateau a dozen paces beyond the wall. Most of the remaining Sithi turned to fight, but the immense, gray-furred monstrosity that had seemed to drop from the sky did not even waste a glance in their direction. Instead, it charged straight toward the center of the plateau, where the Norn Queen stood above the ring of her guards like a white candle on a church altar.

This new beast was not the ogre, Simon saw, but only a giant—though it was a very large giant indeed. Stranger still, as it ran toward Utuk'ku, Simon could see a manlike shape riding behind the giant's broad neck.

Everything happened swiftly now—almost too swiftly for Simon to understand. One moment the shaggy giant was pelting toward the ring of white-armored guards, roaring so loudly that even some of the Sithi had to cover their ears; a moment later it flung its long arms out and stumbled, and the smaller shape that had been clinging onto its neck slipped off and fell away like a discarded sack. The giant somehow kept its feet and continued toward the queen. As the great Hunë neared the first of the queen's guards, Simon experienced a surprising moment of hope. *Yes, kill her,* he thought. *Kill the witch! I'll be content to die if I knew she died first.*

Utuk'ku raised her gloved hands in the air. The giant stumbled again. Smoke was streaming from its fur, and flames began to lick up its body, as if it had been shot with a dozen fiery arrows. The blaze rose around the giant's snarling head, engulfing the upper part of its body, but still it staggered toward the queen, long arms and clawed hands reaching as though to grab Utuk'ku and tear her into pieces. But it did not reach her.

The innermost circle of guards stood braced and waiting when the giant finally lurched to a halt a few paces from them, hairy upper half blazing like a torch, and lowered its huge, twitching arms. For a moment the giant swayed in place, hands tightening convulsively, then it toppled like a great tree to lie, still smoldering, only a short distance from the stone on which the queen stood.

Utuk'ku lowered her arms, then spoke in Simon's head—in everyone's head, from the reactions all around the plateau. Her voice seemed in the first instants as loud as a storm, as if it might tear up the very trees of the valley by their roots and blow them away, but the storm was entirely inside Simon's skull. He slumped to the ground with his head in his hands, shaking all over. He had never felt anything like it.

You will listen, all who hear me, the queen of the Norns thoughts filled his skull, scalding like hot metal. *You will heed my Word of Command.* Then she spoke a single word aloud. Her spoken voice was little more than a breathy murmur, but the sound grew both in his ears and inside his skull until he could hear and think of nothing else. At last the terrible roar faded, but it had changed everything.

I can't move, Simon realized in growing terror. *Can't move!* Numbness spread through him like an icy fever. Utuk'ku had reached into his head and pushed out everything but her own will. He had not imagined that anyone but God could wield such might.

On every side, his Sithi allies slumped to the ground, wide-eyed but helpless, and Simon realized as the world tilted that he had fallen too. He struggled desperately against Utuk'ku's Word of Command, but like all Tanakirú's other defenders, he was utterly unable to make his body obey his will.

As his litter was carried out of the tunnels and into fast-fading daylight, Hakatri experienced a strange inversion. Instead of Tanakirú, the end of a valley hemmed in on three sides by towering cliffs, he instead found himself back on tall Sesuad'ra on that day so long ago, when he had traveled there with his loyal Tinukeda'ya armiger, Pamon Kes, seeking an end to the endless torment of the dragon's burning blood. Even more astonishing, Hakatri once more had his living body: he could feel wind on his skin, smell grass and stony soil. As it had on that long-ago day atop Sesuad'ra, the crumbling structure called the Crossroads stood before him, and something inside it was calling to him, urging him forward. He let himself be pulled toward the ruined building.

Hakatri! The Voice of Three pierced his thoughts like a crow's raucous creak, plunging him suddenly back into Tanakirú. Once more, he was staring out at a world of shadows through the scratched crystal of Ruyan the Navigator's helm. *Your time has come around at last, Hakatri,* the Voice told him. *Do you feel the ship?*

He pushed the distracting, pointless memory of Sesuad'ra from his thoughts. *I do feel it, praise the Garden. I hear its music.* He had waited so long in this between-state, denied the peace of death but without the return of true life. Now he could finally do what had to be done—revenge his family and his people. Then, perhaps, he could return to the blissful unknowing he so desired.

Take command of the ship, Hakatri, the Voice directed him. *Call upon the blood that fouled you, the blood of the thrice-cursed Dreaming Sea, and order the ship to send its protector to me. I can feel that it is close.*

Freedom, Hakatri told himself. *Oblivion. It is coming soon.* He sent his thoughts outward until they touched the music of the ship; but he sensed a strange discord in its harmonies this time. Something had changed. Hakatri let the music surround him, searching for the thing that had been at the heart of it before, but it was strangely absent.

Haste! The Voice of Three was growing impatient. *Our hour is upon us. The boundaries are growing thin. Time grows short. You must master the ship now and send its protector to me.*

Something about the Voice's words made Hakatri uncomfortable—a tone of imperious authority he had never felt even from his own parents, a cold hardness almost as painful in its own way as being drenched in the dragon Hidohebhi's scalding black blood.

No, he told himself. *I must not be distracted. I must not let myself be confused. My parents were murdered, and the mortals are to blame. They must be punished. I must trust the Voice of Three. Revenge, justice—that is how I will finally have peace.*

As he mastered himself once more, he let his thoughts reach out, until he at last sensed the thought at the center of the ship's music. He could feel that it was full of fear and chaotic, fearful impulses, like a hive of agitated bees, and for a moment he could not even approach it. Hakatri carefully, delicately touched that center and the presence that lived there.

Peace, he told it. *I have come to give you peace.*

No peace. The thought was violent—it was all Hakatri could do to preserve the fragile bond between them. *Only Vao. All else deadly. Living spirit has been stolen—stolen from Vao!*

Vao meant the Tinukeda'ya folk, Hakatri knew, though he was not at all certain how he knew that, and *Vao* meant the Dreaming Sea. But somehow, Vao was also the black scourge of the dying dragon's blood, the scalding fountain that had changed everything in a moment. The memory of his pain seized him once more, powerful and agonizing. But Hakatri knew pain—the two were old acquaintances—and he also knew his only hope to return to nothingness was to obey the Voice of Three. *Yes, only help Vao,* he told the ship. *Only listen to Vao. Can you feel me? I am Vao.*

You wear the Navigator's Helm. The ship's thought was cautious. *You wear the Navigator's Armor. And you have the Dreaming Sea in your blood. Are you the Navigator? Are you . . . Father?*

He knew now what voice he had heard. This ship, or whatever inhabited it, was an orphan, just as his own daughter had become when he had left his family behind. Orphaned, deserted, frightened—

The Voice of Three cut through his thoughts. *You hesitate, Hakatri, and by doing so you will doom your own kind! Year's End pulls the fabric of everything so tight that it begins to tear, and even the strength of the Three Who Are One cannot hold the breach open for long. Do what you must to make it obey—whatever you must—but do it now. Our moment is here!*

Ship. He put aside his confusion, his doubts. *Ship. Do you feel me?*

Ruyan Ká. I was . . . I am . . . Ruyan Ká. Is that you, Father?

He felt the ship's central presence hesitate, fearful as a cornered beast. A name came to him, though he knew he had no right to it. It was a terrible treachery, he felt that, but his overwhelming desire for the end of his suffering outweighed all else. *Yes,* he told it. *Do not fear me, daughter. I am your father, Ruyan Vé, and I need you to save the Vao from our enemies.*

The song of the ship was almost entirely muted now, supplanted by the slow, confused thoughts of the thing that called itself Ruyan Ká. *Enemies. All around. Never stop. Tried to take . . . take my heart. Never stop.*

No, they will stop, I promise. We will end them. But you must let me guide you.

Guide me . . . ?

Yes. Trust me. Trust your father. Hakatri could feel the ship yielding, and knew he had won, though he felt shame for his shabby trick. Outside, in the living world beyond the stolen helm, he could see only red-shot darkness and dim shapes as ever, but he could also feel the thinning that the Voice of Three had described as the day's light failed and the new Great Year came on, more implacable than any ogre. The balance of everything had become suddenly tentative. *Follow me, Ruyan Ká,* he said, more urgently now. *The mortals are a curse—they have tried to destroy the Vao, to destroy the Garden and the Dreaming Sea. Heed me and I will show you what to do. The Voice of Three has a task for the ship's protector. Send the protector, obey what the Voice of Three tells you, and together we will destroy our enemies. Then you can rest. Then we can both rest.*

Simon had never felt so helpless. Even when he had been chained in Pasevalles' dungeon or strapped to Inch's water wheel, his body had still been his own. His limbs might have been bound, but he had still been able to clench his fingers into fists and fight against his restraints, useless though such struggle might have been. But now, with a single potent word, the Queen of the Norns had robbed Simon and the rest of her enemies of their freedom. They had become less than worms, which at least could wriggle toward some dark hiding place.

And who's to say she couldn't stop our breath just as easily?

He struggled on against Utuk'ku's control. By a supreme effort he made his limbs twitch a little and his eyes blink, and he could even swallow, but he was otherwise as helpless as a newborn.

Simon cast his eyes down to see that he was still clasping Jiriki's hand, but he could not have released it even if he wanted to. The healer who had been tending Jiriki lay slumped on the ground beside him. Jiriki was so pale that Simon could not tell whether he still lived.

Now Queen Utuk'ku turned away from her enemies and stared out to the hills on the other side of the gorge, where the valley began to widen. Simon followed with his eyes and saw that a crowd of Norns had gathered on a high bluff in a fan-shaped crowd, looking down at the plateau like the choir for some religious ceremony.

Do not fear, my people—my children. Utuk'ku now seemed to speak to the Hikeda'ya watching from across the gorge, but her words echoed loudly in Simon's thoughts, and by their wincing expressions, it was clear the Sithi around him could not escape the queen's voice either. *The wretched Zida'ya have long kept this prize from us,* she said, *but today we have triumphed. Do you see it high on the cliff, agleam with the light of the setting sun?* She turned and spread her white gloved hands, as if she might pluck the great ship from its place and bring it down by herself. *The Ninth Ship! Despite our ties of blood, our treacherous Zida'ya kin tried to keep it from us, as they have tried to cheat us of so many things that were rightfully ours—but they failed. They tried to destroy me, but their treachery has rebounded on them, and now the prize is mine.*

A faint cheer went up from the crowd of Hikeda'ya gathered on the bluff across the river, but Simon thought they did not sound entirely certain themselves about what was happening.

Utuk'ku's silent speech seemed to be gaining strength. *Hakatri, scion of Asu'a, the time is come. Summon the uro'eni. Summon the protector of the Ninth Ship!*

Another voice rolled through Simon's head then—hollow, distant, but powerful, like a gale wind swirling beyond thick walls. *I hear,* the new voice said. Simon saw a strange figure now standing before the base of the stone where the queen stood. Even in the fading afternoon light, its armor glittered and shone like the stained-glass windows of St. Sutrin's cathedral, but it wore a helm like nothing Simon had ever seen before, its visor a grotesque mask with round eyes and mouth, like the idiot expression of a kilpa. *I have called her, Voice of Three.* The hollow voice echoed in Simon's head like a funeral bell. *Ruyan Ká comes. Our time is finally here. Peace awaits.*

So it does, said Utuk'ku.

The Norn Queen is summoning the ogre, Simon realized. *But how can she control something like that? Isn't there any limit to what she can do?* He and the Sithi were still held as helplessly as ants in sticky tree sap. The soldiers of the Queen's Teeth could walk among them if they wished, slaughtering at will. But for the moment, Utuk'ku's white-helmeted guards only held their circle around her.

Simon struggled but still could not make his limbs respond. Whatever terrible spell the witch-queen had spoken was strong enough to imprison him and more than a hundred Sithi. The healer still lay motionless beside Jiriki. Rukayu stared out at the center of the Tanakirú plateau but did not stir; her furrowed brow and ferocious scowl told Simon that she was having no more luck moving than he was.

Will the queen simply stop the blood in our veins? he wondered, close to panic. *Squeeze our hearts until they burst? Why does she wait to end this? Does she simply enjoy our helplessness?*

And even as he thought these wretched thoughts, Simon heard a new noise—felt it, too, a shuddering vibration that seemed to set the whole plateau trembling. He struggled to turn his head, and after a fierce effort managed an inch of movement. He swiveled his eyes until he could see the distant cliffs where the Sithi had been camped.

One of the larger caves at the base of the cliffs seemed to be falling to pieces: a rain of stones and dust tumbled to the ground as something pushed its way out of the cavern, like a horrible, frightening birth.

As a large piece of the cliffside above the cavern slid free, crumbled, and fell to the ground in a billowing cloud of dust and bouncing stone, Simon realized the mists had disappeared, letting the clouded sky show above the valley, now painted in sunset flame. A moment later, the vast shape emerging from the cave straightened to its full height, a vast shadow surrounded by settling dust.

Simon had been told about the creature, had even seen it a few times in the foggy distance, but it was still nearly impossible to believe. His heart threatened to stutter to a halt in sheer terror; his helpless limbs squirmed in a futile attempt to crawl away. The ogre loomed above everything but the cliffs themselves, and its head turned slowly, slowly, like a bear that had just awakened from a winter sleep. But no bear had ever stood as big as a castle tower, nor had any living thing ever worn such a strange shape.

It's made of . . . it's made of . . .

The immense figure had somehow been shaped out of great curved boards and long planks of silvery-gray witchwood, Simon realized in helpless astonishment—the substance of the Ninth Ship itself. This collection of odd and mismatched timbers was bound together by a twisting array of vines and branches, giving it the appearance of a giant, monstrous scarecrow, something made by hasty hands. The planks stuck out at all angles in a chaotic tangle, so that the ogre's silhouette reminded Simon of nothing so much as a spiny porpentine he had seen in one of Doctor Morgenes' books when he was young. It had a vaguely manlike shape, but squat and so bent so that its arms almost reached the ground. Its massive head was the greater horror, a crude summit of timbers and vines. The only semblance of a face came from the gaping, ragged hole of its mouth and the empty, uneven pits that were its eyes.

A dim chorus of terrified voices now washed across the valley. Simon realized that even the Hikeda'ya watching from the safety of the gorge's far side were shouting in fright at the dreadful thing their queen had summoned. Simon would have done the same, would have shrieked in fear, but Utuk'ku's invisible hand was still around his throat, silencing him.

Bid it come to us, Hakatri, the queen commanded, her voice resounding in every head.

The armored shape standing before her stretched out a gleaming, gauntleted hand, which flashed coppery red in the light of the day's ending. The ogre shuddered—Simon could hear its boards and planks rub nosily against each other—and then it began to move toward the queen.

Doom. Doom. Doom. The ogre's footfalls even shook the rocky plateau. *Doom. Doom.* It was so tall that it seemed to blot out the sky. Simon could not look away. He had never seen anything like it, had never even imagined anything like it.

Wait, Hakatri, said Utuk'ku sharply. *It clutches something.* For the first time, there was something other than command in her voice—irritation? Curiosity? *Bid the uro'eni drop its burden here before me.*

The hollow, distant voice answered her. *As you wish, Voice of Three.*

The ogre extended one of its misshapen claws and let a collection of limp, dark shapes fall to the ground beside the stone where Utuk'ku stood. They were bodies in Hikeda'ya armor, Simon saw, but crushed into cruel, bloody shapelessness.

So. Utuk'ku sounded almost amused as she stared down at the terrible mound. Her satisfaction made Simon's thoughts itch and squirm. *Jijibo,* she said, eyes on the body of her mad relative. *Of course, it is you.*

One of the broken shapes was somehow still moving, trying to rise but failing. Simon heard a voice—not in his thoughts this time, but with his ears—but it was too far away for him to make out the words.

No, you did not do me a service, said Utuk'ku contemptuously. *What the Mother of All wants, she takes, and the ship's protector would have brought the* Zhin'ju *to me even if you had never been born. But do not fear, little descendant—you have saved me a wait, and that is good, because time is growing short. The Year-Torch is rising into the sky. Now that I have the heart of the ship, you will indeed be rewarded.* Her thought-voice grew stronger. *But first, it is time for those who conspired against me for so long to pay for their treachery. Hakatri, set the* uro'eni *on the Zida'ya traitors. Destroy the wretched creatures who took arms against me. Let it pull them to pieces and grind them beneath its heel. I want them to suffer before the end comes.*

Simon could not bear to look at the towering, inhuman shape any longer, did not want to witness the moment of his own helpless death. Still clutching Jiriki's cold hand in his own, he shut his eyes. *I am sorry, Lillia—so sorry,* he thought. *I pray your end is swift. I should never have brought you here.*

Morgan had finally chosen one of the two tunnels, and it was now all too clear that he had chosen the wrong one. He lifted Nezeru's *ni'yo* and let its light flare across his surroundings one more time, but the view was still the same.

The high ceiling, studded with limestone knobs, had been getting lower and lower as he descended, while remaining just high enough that something the size of the ogre might be able to crawl through. A few moments earlier he had reached a place where the passage of something huge had scraped the stalactites from the cavern roof, and Morgan had been relieved that he had guessed correctly. Then, a few paces later, he discovered that the tunnel abruptly ended in an expanse of dark water.

He stood at the water's edge looking down in fearful frustration. He had no idea how wide or deep the water was, but from the size of the cataracts he had seen from the ship's deck, he knew he might have to swim for a very long distance, and there might be places where the surface was inaccessible and he would be unable to lift his head above water. *And if that thing went down into the water here, even if Nezeru was alive before that, she may have been drowned.*

The impulse to dive in was still very strong. It seemed impossible that his search for her could simply end this way. His grandfather had told him that nobody knew they were in a story while it was happening to them, or how it was going to end—but how could his own story end so dreadfully? How could everything that had happened to him since he had first been lost in the Aldheorte have led him to this terrible conclusion?

He held the *ni'yo*'s broad light out over the surprisingly placid water but saw no ripples on its surface, no sign of recent passage by the ogre or anything else. The stone floor of the cavern simply sloped down into the water and then vanished in darkness beyond the light's reach.

Nezeru. A pain seized him, so great he felt as if he might burst. Then he remembered. *There was another tunnel. The ogre might use both—it could have taken her that way.*

He stood for a moment in painful indecision. It would take a long time to get back to the place where the tunnels forked, and there was just as much chance the ogre had gone this way, into the water.

I can't wait. I must decide. It didn't matter whether he believed that Heaven watched over him. It didn't matter whether he believed he and Nezeru shared a destiny. None of it mattered now. If life truly was a story, as his grandfather said, no one could know the true ending of their own story, not peasants, or priests, or princes.

No good choices. But I still must choose.

He was laboring up a long, loose slope of scree in a part of the caverns he only dimly remembered—things looked much different climbing up than they did sliding down—when he heard the muffled noise of footsteps above him. It was far too quiet and ordinary to be the thundering tread of the ogre, but only a short time ago, that invading troop of Norns must have made their way through these caverns and onto the great ship, and though the ogre had killed most of them when it smashed the ship's dome, there might still be more Sacrifices roaming through Kushiba's cave-riddled interior.

Morgan found a spot at the side of the passage where he could crouch and wait, steadying himself so he would not send any stones tumbling that might give him away.

There—he heard it again, the sound of more footfalls. He was certain now that someone was in the tunnel ahead of him, and not far distant. He drew Snakesplitter from its scabbard as silently as he could manage, wincing a little as the tip scraped on the stony floor, then slowly shifted his balance so he could get his feet under him without tumbling down the slope he had just climbed.

At the first sounds, Morgan had shrouded Nezeru's glowing sphere in his tattered sleeve, and in the sudden darkness he could see a faint gleam at the far end of the tunnel, dim and inconstant, but unquestionably real. *Torches*. Whoever was moving above him had torches.

More certain than ever that he had stumbled onto a war-band of Norns—or that the war-band was about to stumble onto him—he rose until he was half-standing, feet wide apart for balance on the slippery scree, and waited. A part of him was almost glad at the idea that if he had failed Nezeru, he would at least be able to inflict some damage on the enemies now hunting him.

He heard someone whispering, and at first he felt certain he could detect the harsh Hikeda'ya speech. Snakesplitter's hilt grew slippery in his sweating grip.

"Quiet," someone replied to the first speaker—in Westerling. "This way he go, but maybe other things too."

For a moment Morgan could not believe his ears. Then he took a few slithering steps up the spill of gravel and loose stones. *"Qina?"* he called. "*Is that you?"*

"Morgan Prince? You are there?"

He scrambled up the slope as fast as he could, then onto the uneven floor of the high cavern at the top of the tunnel where he found the trolls and Yek Fisher, with almost a dozen others from the ship's dome, the fluttering flames of their torches making the weird shapes of the cave even weirder. Morgan had to jump across a rivulet of water that coursed down the middle of the chamber before he could embrace the trolls. "Nezeru—have you seen her?"

"Then you have not found her, either," said Little Snenneq.

Morgan's happiness at finding his friends dissolved. "If it took her this way, we can't follow her. This tunnel ends in an underground lake—water fills the whole thing."

"You follow the so-big giant?" Qina asked. "Go wrong way."

"We have been following you, friend Morgan," Snenneq explained. "But the ogre went out through the other tunnel."

"How do you know that?" He was excited, but also furious with himself to think that he had wasted so much time following the wrong path.

"We found a high place at the end of the other tunnel," Snenneq explained. "We could see all the way to the valley below. There is more to say, but the ogre is down there."

Morgan sheathed Snakesplitter. "Then we have to go. Now! That thing has Nezeru."

The two trolls seemed to exchange a look with Kuyu-Kun and Tih-Rumi, but none of them said anything.

"So, then," said Snenneq, "we will go up once more, and you will see. But do not rush blindly. Something very strange is going on out there."

DOOM. DOOM. DOOM. DOOM.

Slowly, almost as if reluctant, the *uro'eni* trudged across the stony plateau toward the place where Simon and the defenders lay helpless in the shadow of the wall. As death approached, Simon kept his eyes tightly shut and prayed.

Haste! ordered Utuk'ku. Her satisfaction felt like salt in an already mortal wound. *Sweep them up, every treacherous one. Crush all who tried to cheat me into nothingness.*

A long moment passed.

Why do you wait? Utuk'ku demanded. *Hakatri, tell the ship's guardian to destroy them. The sun is setting! Our time is short.* The intensity of her thought increased until Simon thought he could feel his wits boiling inside his skull like a pudding. *A curse on you, Zida'ya—why do you hesitate?*

"Perhaps," said a new voice—a thing of air and sound, not just thought—"because your poor slave Hakatri of the Sa'onserei begins to sense that he has been tricked."

Simon knew that rough voice, but it was not the sound of it that made him start in terror and open his eyes, struggling to turn his head against the crushing grip of Utuk'ku's spell. It was what he knew he would see.

A small shape emerged from the caverns at the base of the cliff—a shape that was all too dreadfully familiar to Simon. He tried to call out but could only manage to murmur her name miserably into his own beard: "Lillia."

Hakatri, said the queen, and everyone who heard her thoughts could feel her rage, *crush that thing! That is our greatest enemy.*

I . . . I cannot. Hakatri's thoughts seemed tumbled, confused. *The ship's protector resists me. It says this new thing is Vao.*

"Yes. I am Vao," Geloë declared. "As is the spirit of Ruyan Ká that gives the ogre life and has kept the Ninth Ship safe all these long years. We are the Vao, the race you so despise, but which saved your people, Utuk'ku. We are the Dreaming Sea your kind destroyed, but which still lives. We are the true soul of the Garden."

Arrogant little blot! Insect! You and your verminous, changeling race—it ends for you in this hour, in this place!

"Perhaps—but not by Hakatri's hand, I think." The child's body turned from the looming ogre to the thing in Ruyan Vé's armor, which had fallen into shadow as twilight came. "Scion of Asu'a, did you know that your grandson Jiriki lies dying on this very field? Cut down by one of Utuk'ku's ill-made, sorcerous creatures? And that your daughter Likimeya has long been trapped between life and death, also by Utuk'ku's hand?"

Lies! Utuk'ku raised one white-gloved hand and the air around Lillia's small form began to warp and shift. *Take them with you into darkness, Changeling! Hakatri, these are the creatures who destroyed your family and your home! Make them die.*

The ogre raised its great, ragged hand over the child. Talons of jutting timbers flexed into a fist the size of a hay wain. Simon tried again to cry out, but could only twitch, as tears streamed down his cheeks.

Something was making it hard for Hakatri to think. He dimly sensed voices speaking to him, occasional words that flickered into his thoughts and then vanished—*Vao, grandson, Likimeya*—like the gleam of fireflies, but they were almost nothing. The only thing he could hear clearly were the resounding words of the Three Who Are One, and the overwhelming strength behind them.

Hakatri, these are the creatures who destroyed your family—your home, the Voice of Three declared. *Tell the ship to make them die.*

He was growingly desperate to escape and find peace. The sooner he helped avenge his people and this madness finally ended, the sooner he would be able to fall back into nothingness. He tried to force Ruyan Ká to lift the ogre's great hand and put an end the small thing that so dismayed the Voice of Three, but something prevented him. It was not just his own hesitation alone that held him back, but also resistance from the singing choir of the ship itself, or of Ruyan Ká or whatever animated the witchwood ogre.

Ruyan Ká! Do not resist, Hakatri called into the darkness. *Kill that mortal creature.*

Vao. He felt the swelling musical voices of the ship rather than heard them, sensed Ruyan Ká's voice foremost among them. *There is Vao in it, Father. Vao is ours. Vao is us.*

He could not understand the resistance, did not want to understand. *Now! Do it now.*

Hurry! cried the Voice of the Three, like cold fingers squeezing his thoughts.

No, we cannot destroy Vao. Vao is us.

But we must, he said. *The Voice of the Three commands it.*

Three is only one, and that one is Hikeda'ya. The ship's voice—Ruyan's Ká's voice—had grown stubborn, although he could also feel its fear and uncertainty. *We do not listen to Hikeda'ya, only to you, Father. Hikeda'ya have always tricked and trapped us.*

Hakatri was baffled and exhausted. The anger of the Voice of Three was growing, and its every harsh thought intensified the burning of his tortured blood. He could sense that as long as he wore the armor of Navigator, he had the strength to force Ruyan Ká to do his bidding. The lost soul that was the ship's protector was growing weaker, and its understanding was limited: she could not resist him forever. And whatever happened afterward would no longer be his concern, Hakatri consoled himself: he would have returned to oblivion—to sweet, painless unknowing.

But as he exerted the power of the Navigator's armor, forcing Ruyan Ká to lift the ogre's fist above the child-body, he suddenly remembered his own daughter Likimeya's voice so long, long in the past, and her chilling words as he walked to his ship's gangplank to sail away from his home and family.

"My real father would not leave."

But he *was* Likimeya's real father, just as the Navigator Ruyan Vé had been the father of the poor, frightened spirit that haunted the Ninth Ship and animated the fearsome *uro'eni*. And he had lied to this suffering creature, just as he had lied when he had told his own daughter, *"I promise I will come back to you."*

Save me. Save the Vao. Save us. The music of the ship was fading now and falling into discord: Ruyan Ká's words barely reached him.

I cannot save you, he told Ruyan Ká. *We cannot undo the past, we can only punish those who harmed us.*

The spirit of the Ninth Ship was too diminished by its long, lonely struggle to win out. Slowly, Hakatri's sharper will began to dominate, until Ruyan Ká's resistance slackened, then failed entirely.

Again the ogre's great hand lifted. The last rays of the sun flashed on the valley's eastern peaks, and even inside the coffin of his armor, Hakatri could sense the presence of the Year-Torch high above, a point of burning light now climbing the firmament with a new year in its shimmering train.

May this be the last earthly sunset I ever see, Hakatri prayed. *Let me be done with this world. Let me be done with being.* With the surrender of its guiding presence, he could feel the ogre's massive form as though it was his own body, could sense it yielding to his command. *We must do as we are bid, child of the Navigator,* he consoled broken Ruyan Ká. *Then we can both sleep away the ages in peace. We will punish them, my child, as the Voice has decreed. We will make them suffer, then end them and end our own suffering.*

30

Yedade's Box

"We have to go swiftly now," Ayaminu told her as they returned to their mounts. "You cannot use a Witness like the Seastone and still ride safely—not without much experience. Come, sit on the saddle before me. Do not fear—your horse will stay with us."

Tanahaya climbed into place. "I do not worry over that. I know the quality of Anvi'janya's stables." It was strange, so strange, to feel the older Sitha's arms on either side of her, to lean back against her reassuring solidity. So had her mother held her as a child the first time Tanahaya sat a horse.

Within moments the Sithi steeds began to quicken their pace from trot to gallop, but so smoothly that Tanahaya, eyes closed and Seastone clutched in one hand, scarcely felt it. She even opened her eyes to be certain they were truly moving, but the sentry trees were indeed sweeping by as they followed the ancient track along the hillside above the fog-shrouded Narrowdark.

Shutting her eyes once more, Tanahaya rested her hand against her breast and tried to empty her mind of all other things. Himano had been the first to teach her how to use a Witness; even now, so many years later, she could still hear his voice, saying "*Stones, Scales, Pools, and Pyres—they are not things, Tanahaya. They are places where the fabric of what we think of as the world grows thin. But not weak from misuse or wear—do not think of these places as flaws. Witnesses mark out the points of utter truth, the ties that stitch the cosmos together.*"

She had not understood him at the time and still was not certain she grasped precisely what he meant, but under Himano's patient tutelage she had learned to ignore her own questions and simply feel for the places where the light of what lay beyond everything shone through.

Now, more than ever, she needed to find one of those places, but her task was much harder than usual, because she had no idea whether her friend had a Witness too.

Aditu, can you hear me? I have set out on the Road of Dreams. My need is great. Can you hear me?

Tanahaya let her thoughts roam across her interior darkness. *Himano said that our Witnesses stitch the cosmos together,* she thought, groping, searching for a hint of light. *The thoughts of each one of us float in the dark like islands on an endless, sun-*

less sea. Except for those closest to us, we are scarcely aware that the others even exist. So many islands! Such a broad, dark sea!

She tried to touch Aditu's thoughts for a long time without success. Even if Utuk'ku had been weakened, she decided, or had otherwise slackened her grip on the Road of Dreams, it was still not enough for Tanahaya to achieve her aim. At last, she opened her eyes.

"It is no use," she said. "I try and try, but Aditu is not within my reach. All I find are shadows."

"It is all shadows," said Ayaminu. "Until you discern a distant light. You cannot give up, child. If Sa'onsera Likimeya spoke to you, it was in direst need and with her last strength. Despite all my learning, I cannot find her thoughts—I tried many times before Utuk'ku silenced the Witnesses—but I have felt her light growing steadily dimmer. Now it scarcely gleams."

Helplessness fueled Tanahaya's anger: she spoke more harshly than she meant to. "I know that! I felt her terror and need when she spoke to me. It made my heart shrink within my breast, Ayaminu. Please, do not reproach me—I am doing all that I can!"

"Perhaps that is the problem," said the mistress of Anvi'janya. "You do all that you can, but we are each one of us fallible. Give yourself over to need instead. Ask the Road of Dreams what needs to be done, then do that."

Tanahaya's anger was mixed with confusion. "That makes no sense. You talk as if the Road of Dreams was a thing—a person, even."

"I do not know what makes the Road of Dreams," Ayaminu told her, "I do not know if it is a thing, a place, an idea. We move through it as a fish swims through different currents, warm and cold, fast and slow, but that does not mean the fish understands water. Use your need, not your learning, and if the Road of Dreams will let you, use *its* need as well. After all, the Road is part of the order of all things, and it is greater than any of us—perhaps than all of us. Open yourself to it as you never have. Surrender to your need, but also surrender to the Road."

Tanahaya swallowed a tart reply. Her beloved lay hours away from this place, wounded and perhaps dying. His mother had called out to her in a dream and begged for help. Perhaps Ayaminu was right—perhaps thinking she could accomplish this task with only her own determination was indeed folly.

She closed her eyes again. At first, she was all too aware of the horse's moving smoothly beneath her, of Ayaminu's arms around her waist, of the flashing of late sunlight through leaves and the sound of the horse's hooves drumming on the hillside track.

Darkness. Silence. She clutched the Seastone in her hand once more and sought those things, then pulled them over her like a cloak. She burrowed deeper, like a mole digging a hole and letting the dirt fall back in behind it, until nothingness surrounded her completely.

Darkness. Silence.

Aditu, where are you? Oh, please, dear friend, better-than-sister, I need you!

Still only darkness. But at last, something cracked the deep silence. *Tanahaya?*

Yes! Oh, Rabbit, I am searching for you, but I can't find you. Speak to me! Help me!

She was answered, but the distant presence felt cautious. *How can this be? I have begun the final hymn—the Year-Torch has just climbed into the evening sky. But I do not have a Witness—and the Witnesses have been silenced—!*

Ask no questions, dear friend, please, Tanahaya told her. *Believe in this moment while we have it.* She thought she perceived a faint glow in the emptiness, but no matter how she tried, she could draw no closer to it. *I cannot see you, but I can hear you and you can hear me. May the Garden grant that will be enough.*

But why do you interrupt the ceremony? We are come to an important moment. Soon the last hymn will end, then I must lead the Year-Dance.

Your mother. Your mother Likimeya came to me on the Road of Dreams. She said Jiriki has been badly wounded.

She could feel Aditu's fear like a splash of chilly water. *Was that the terrible thing I felt? A pain in my heart, sharp as any knife.* But her thoughts were suddenly distorted, rippling like waters perturbed by a sudden strong wind. *Why did Likimeya not speak directly to me?*

I do not know. You said you two could not reach each other—that you had tried many times. But she had a message for you—a warning, a plea. She said you must let her go.

What came back to Tanahaya this time, though it had the feeling of Aditu, was soured by something unfamiliar—a hint of suspicion. *My mother? My mother begs for me to let her go? Go where?*

I do not know. I can only tell you what she told me.

Into death. Aditu's presence suddenly grew icy. *That is all your message could mean. And I do not believe you are Tanahaya.*

She had never considered she might reach Aditu but still not be trusted. Despair swept through her. *Never say that!*

Why? Who would benefit most from my mother's death? Only the witch of Nakkiga. Only Utuk'ku. And who has held sway over the Witnesses, so that we of the Zida'ya could not use them? I do not believe you.

Her despair became deeper—became horror. Even surrounded by utter darkness, Tanahaya felt an abyss open beneath her, a hole into something worse than nothingness. *Do not say that! I am your Spark! Rabbit, we have loved each other since we were children. Since we first met in the meadow at Ju'unei.*

And the flowers . . . ?

There were many—the blossom choir, we called it that day. But the bell lilies were blooming for the first time of the season, and it was their smell that you loved. But you also called them funeral shrouds because their berries are full of poison.

Silence. Then: *It truly is you. I am sorry for doubting, dear Spark. I am so full of fear.*

Yes, dear heart, dear friend. It is truly me. And your mother begged me to tell you—

But my thoughts are terribly confused. It is like a storm in my heart and head, like great winds that try to pull everything loose and carry it away. I can barely remember the invocations of the Ceremony. And now, hearing you and speaking to you—I must be standing, dumbfounded, in front of all Anvi'janya.

Let her go—that is all I can say. Let your mother go. That is what she wants—what she pleaded with me to tell you.

That is the request that made me doubt you. It seems like something that she—that vile, hollow-hearted creature—would want. Aditu's presence had retreated a little. *But I cannot do it, Spark! I dare not. I can feel the Great Year teetering on the threshold, waiting for me to open the way. But this is no ordinary Year-Dancing. Utuk'ku's evil song makes everything painful, everything difficult. I need all the strength I can take from my mother to complete the ceremony without losing my wits—or losing my life and the life of the child I carry.*

For the first time, Tanahaya had a true feeling, though only a taste, of what Aditu had taken on. *She carries a child who is near to time. The weight of her people's need is on her. And she must travel to the place where only the Sa'onsera goes . . . but she is not the Sa'onsera.*

I cannot advise you what to do, dear friend, Tanahaya conceded—and she could almost feel her thoughts leap through the Seastone and out into the terrifying world, speeding toward her endangered friend. *I can only tell you what your mother told me.*

Wait. Let me—! For a moment Aditu's presence drew back and was silent, hidden, like the flower of a bell-lily, secret inside its bud. Then, after a frighteningly long absence, Tanahaya felt her again. *When you first spoke, you said something had happened to Jiriki. You said my brother was badly wounded.*

We are hastening to him as fast as we can ride, Rabbit, but I fear we will not reach him today. Tanahaya could feel her friend's thoughts; they were full of barely hidden fear. *May the Garden watch over him—oh, please, may it give him strength and life!* But with that, something in Aditu's presence seemed to change. Her next words were harder, more distant. *Save him if you can, dear one, and comfort him if you cannot.*

Aditu? What is it?

I see now what I must do, and only I can do it.

Now Tanahaya was the one who was frightened. *Let no harm come to you!*

All will be as it must be. I see that now. There are patterns—for me, for my beloved brother, for our mother, even for you, dear one. I think I can trace them now, at least a little. The mistress of Nakkiga has draped her webs over everything to hide her schemes, but that means we can seek what she plans by seeing what she hides. Go to my brother, dear Spark. Go swiftly. I will do what I must.

Tanahaya did not wish to let go. *What you must do? You frighten me.*

We should all be frightened. But I need to leave you now. Our people are waiting and the Ceremony hangs on the brink of failure, and the year-door will not stay open long. Go to my brother! Tell him I love him forever.

I will, said Tanahaya, but she could no longer feel Aditu's presence. The next thing she knew, she was swaying in Ayaminu's arms.

"You almost fell," Ayaminu said. "Something must have startled you. Did you find Aditu on the Dream-Road?"

"I did." Around her, the wooded hillside was a blur of colors sliding past, like something seen through tears. "Like us, she is fighting against time itself."

"Then let us put you back on your own mount while you tell me, so my horse at least can make its greatest pace again," Ayaminu said. "Unless you learned something truly unexpected, we must still hasten on to Tanakirú and pray we are not too late."

Somehow, though she could not begin to understand it, Nezeru had fallen through a hole in time and back into her own childhood in Nakkiga, when she had been tested to discover what order would claim her. Or that, at least, was the only way she could make sense of what had happened: somehow, she was again trapped in Yedade's Box.

Just as it was on that day in her childhood, it was dark around her, as dark could be. Her limbs were pinioned at her sides, and she could smell the familiar scent of worked witchwood. What else could this be but the rite that had determined she would enter the Order of Sacrifice?

Even after many days of preparation, Nezeru had been fearful on that day, as the lid of the box closed and the latches slid into place. But at least she had been warned about what to expect during her childhood ordeal, but not why she was trapped in this current darkness. Her head hurt badly, she realized, though she could not remember why that should be true either. Something dark and dreadful had left a hole in her memory—not just a hole, a gaping wound—and although Nezeru would not admit it, even to herself, she was terrified by what it might be.

A Sacrifice does not think—the Order's maddening, oft-used training phrase. *A Sacrifice does.*

She tried to bring one of her arms up past her chest to touch the surface in front of her: she knew only that it was witchwood. But her best efforts, though they at least revealed she was still wearing her armor, could not force her arm high enough. But knowing that she was wearing armor proved that she had not returned to her childhood, and that was a relief.

But is this still a test? What has happened to me?

No matter how she tried, she could not recall how she had come there, or even what she had last been doing before the empty spot in her memory. She had been on the great ship, the Ninth Ship, but then something terrifying had happened, pulling her into this frightening blackness.

Slow, heart. Slow, breath, Nezeru told herself. She might no longer be a child, but she had survived the Box then—she could survive it now. On that long-ago day, the smells and sounds of the testing chamber had seemed so powerful they had almost attacked her senses. She recalled feeling light-headed and soft-legged when she was called, as though she might collapse, and she had to force herself to remain upright as she was led to the Box. *Do not fall, I told myself. Do not fall. The Queen will be ashamed of you. Your father will be shamed, too. But I did not even think of my mother, Tzoja.* A gust of mourning swept through her. *She was unimportant to me—a mortal slave. The only ones I worried about were the Mother of All and my father.*

How did she *feel, my poor, mortal mother? She must have known, and known for a long time, that I worried about shaming others but that I was shamed by her mere existence.*

As the Celebrants had lowered her into the box, so like a casket, she had heard the voices of the acolytes reciting the Catechism of Selection over her. Her heart had been beating so rapidly she barely heard them, but it had not mattered. She had heard the words recited so many times in the past few days she could have repeated them herself without a single error. The acolytes had sprinkled dried verbena blossoms on her—a tangy scent that she would ever afterward associate with terror and need—then the lid of the Box had been lowered and slid into place and the joints locked, wood against wood, leaving her only enough air for perhaps an hour. If she did not escape by then, she could use the Shameful Knock to call for release. Not all failed candidates had the courage to use that signal: many Hikeda'ya children, more afraid of disgrace than death, struggled until they suffocated. A few were saved by their humiliated parents as the hour elapsed, but many were not, and those who died were even granted a kind of elevated status as Yedade's Martyrs—ironic, since years later Yedade himself would also die gasping for air.

As on that day, Nezeru's arms were pinioned at her side. As a child, she had slid herself down to the bottom of the Box with agonizing slowness until her feet touched the bottom panel. The child Nezeru had spread her knees until she could put her feet flat against the wood, then began to push. At first she had not been able to budge the bottom panel, and she had despaired, but after a long time probing with her toes, she had found a weak spot at one corner—a place where the join was a little less than snug—and at last, with head and lungs pounding and both of her feet bleeding from torn skin and broken nails, she had managed to dislodge the bottom panel and let in the life-giving air.

It had taken her a long time to slide herself out, but that hadn't mattered: she had defeated the Box. The actions of a true Sacrifice, the examining Celebrants had told her, thinking she had forced the bottom through sheer strength instead of the box itself being flawed. It had been, she realized now, the first lie she had accepted, because a Sacrifice was the most honorable thing to become. No Sacrifice who did her duty would ever be shamed, would ever be thought of as less than a true Hikeda'ya. It was untrue, but on that day, the young Nezeru had been willing to believe everything she had been taught. She had fought the Box and she had triumphed. She would join the Order of Sacrifice.

With the memories of that first confinement brought back, Nezeru began the agonizingly difficult slide down to the bottom of the witchwood cage or box or coffin where she found herself. As she did, she struggled again to remember how she got there and to understand why her head hurt as though someone had reached into her skull and yanked out the memory of it happening.

Why am I trapped? It cannot be Yedade's Box, so what holds me? A sudden thought almost stopped her speeding heart. *Could I be in the Cold, Slow Halls?* Sacrifice soldiers had been on the great ship, she suddenly remembered—Sacrifice soldiers, commanded by mad Lord Jijibo. But what had the queen's reckless descendant been doing? Why had he come to the ship? She recalled now that Jijibo and his troop of Sacrifice soldiers had been looking for something . . . and then . . . .

Abruptly, it all came back to her, with as much terror and force as if it was happening again, startling Nezeru into a gasp of shock. That monstrous claw, big as a war wagon! It had smashed through the dome and then began crushing Sacrifice soldiers like insects. Great chunks of crystal had been falling, and people were shouting—Nezeru thought she remembered hearing Morgan's voice—and then something heavy had struck her and after that she could summon nothing until her wits had come back to her here, in this prison, this trap. But what was it that held her? Where was she?

She continued inching downward, and finally reached the end of the confining space so she could feel her booted feet touch the bottom. There was no flat bottom panel, as there had been in the box of her childhood ritual, only a narrowing of the space. Nezeru could find nothing to push against, and her probing feet were in danger of getting stuck at a painful angle, so she inched back upward a short distance.

She was wondering what else she could try when the entire box that held her began to move. The sudden movement was so jarring—up and down, swinging so that she slid from one end to the other and then back. For long moments her thoughts lost all coherence. When she could gather them back again, she realized that the movement of her prison had already begun to change once more, slowing to a gentler sway, and that the box or whatever held her was now upright, so that her feet were down and her head up. Nezeru braced herself to keep from slipping down into the too-narrow angle at the base of the box, and for a distracting moment remembered being stuck in the tree with Morgan, and what had come of it.

No. Morgan is not here. I am alone and must only think of what is around me. But even that realization was painful, as if everything that had happened since she fled her own Order had only been a dream, and would now slowly dissolve, as dreams did.

As Nezeru braced against the sides of her narrow prison to keep herself from being rattled like a dried pea, she realized that she could hear someone talking.

The words sounded as though they came from somewhere nearby, a spew of thoughts as irregular and meandering as a spring stream.

". . . The dreams were right. The old fellow's writings were right, but the time was wrong and now the queen will be angry—so angry!—and I will have to crawl for forgiveness. I will have to crawl. I wish I could make her *crawl, make her see that she should have trusted me but oh! it would have been sweet to possess the ship-spirit for more than that single moment—so sweet! I could feel all its terrible capability! I would have been able to do anything and no one would have dared to look at me except with love and reverence or I would make them all into strips of skin and piles of wet bones . . ."*

Nezeru had heard that voice before—heard it only a short while earlier, beneath the dome of the ship, before the ogre's hand had broken through and turned all into chaos.

Jijibo, she thought. *The Despoiler of the Dead. May the Garden preserve me, am I a prisoner of that dreadful creature?*

In her terror and surprise, she must have made a noise, because the voice abruptly stopped speaking. For long moments Nezeru pitched gently in the moving box, praying that she had not been heard.

"I know you are still there," the voice said. "I can hear you breathing. Does she not know how keen my ears are, how sharp my wits? She cannot be of Nakkiga, or she would know me well. She must tell me who and what she is, so that I may make some plan to deal with her. Perhaps I may offer her to the *uro'eni* in my own place."

Nezeru stayed silent, biting her lip. Wherever she now was, the queen's deranged relative seemed to be there too.

"Why so quiet, child?" Jijibo's voice took on a sweetness so false it made Nezeru feel ill. "You should know that I am of the Hamakha, and we are sworn to protect all our race. Are you one of my Sacrifice guards? Answer me, so I may better know how to help you." A moment later, and just as plainly, he added, "Does she not know I can smell and hear her? How dare she not answer me, the queen's own descendant? I have skinned important nobles for less than that."

Nezeru was terrified to engage with this infamous creature—even the most doughty of the Order of Sacrifice feared Jijibo, whose derangement was so unusual among the Hikeda'ya that it seemed almost a magical power.

But I cannot ignore anything that might help me, because I do not think I can free myself. "I hear you, great lord," she said at last.

"Ah, now she finally speaks." Jijibo sounded pleased. "Rest assured, soldier, we will be safe. I will see to it."

She risked a question. "Where am I?"

"Listen to this foolish she-goat. Without the wit to understand anything." He continued in precisely the same tone. "We are temporarily prisoners of the *uro'eni*, dear child. Can you see any way to free yourself?"

"Prisoners? Of the ogre?"

"I am clutched in the terrible thing's claws, pressed into several of your Sacrifice comrades. Most of them are quite dead, I believe, because there is something dripping over me that feels thicker than water. I am sorely wounded myself. Quite crushed and ruined." His wet laugh was unsettling. "You did not answer my question, child. But perhaps the useless creature did not properly understand me—these days, the ranks of the Sacrifice Order are filled with society's dregs because Great-Grandmother's need is so great. Can you get free, soldier?"

"No, my lord. I have tried, but I am trapped."

"Hmmmm." He sounded disappointed. "Well, then I suppose you must die squealing like the animal you are."

The sea surrounded her. The Dreaming Sea, whatever that meant—that was what the woman who brought her here had called it. But she had also told Lillia not to enter it, yet here she was, waist-deep, tingling not just with cold, but with the feeling of something alive surrounding her.

Fear not, a voice had told her. *We do not come to harm you, but to welcome you back.* But Lillia had no idea what that meant, and she was not inclined to trust anything in this strange, lonely place, least of all a talking ocean.

You are not so afraid now, the voice said, all the voices said as one. *That is good.*

Lillia could not understand how water could have so many tongues to speak—or how it could have any tongue at all. "Who are you? Who's talking?"

There is no who, no person, no name. We are what we are, something that has always been and always will be. We are the Dreaming Sea.

"I don't know what that means!"

Nor do you need to know, child. For the moment, you are safe. Nothing will harm you, although dangerous things are happening, and our shores are threatened in many places. But for now, the Silvermask is gone.

Shrugging, feeling chilly again, Lillia began to wade toward the shore, but it was hard: her legs felt clumsy and she was afraid she might lose her balance and fall into the strange waters.

But do not leave us yet! the voices pleaded. *There is much we do not yet understand. You are of us, but you are not of us. You are separate and individual, as we are not, but the same sea flows through you. How did you come to us?*

"I don't know. A woman brought me." She held up the feather that she had threatened to burn, enraging the floating thing. "She gave me this to call her if I was frightened." She stopped, shivering. "I didn't know it 'til now, but I think I've been frightened for a long time. I'm going to call her."

First, we beg you, let us taste it.

Lillia was startled. "What do you mean?"

Dip it in the waters. Let us feel the one who gave this to you. Help us to make more sense of the confusing things we feel.

Now Lillia was not just frightened, but worried too. The Silvermask, as the waters called it, had wanted the feather, and had tried to take it from her. The woman who had given it to her had said to use it only in great need and had also told her not to go into the ocean. How was she to know these talking waters could be trusted? How could she know anything at all in this senseless place?

"I want my grandfather." A few tears ran down her cheek. She reached up to blot them with her sleeve and felt sudden agitation from the thing or things that called itself the Dreaming Sea. "I miss him! And my mama's dead."

Do not wipe away those drops, please! the voice implored. *Let them fall! Let us learn more about you, we beg you. You have a savor we do not know—mortal and yet also part of us, like those parts of us that left the great whole to take mortal shapes.*

Surprised and uncertain, Lillia lowered her arm and let her tears run down her cheek. One fell from her jaw, another from her chin. She did not see them strike the water, but she felt something as they did—a heightened, fluttering attention, as if a thousand tiny fish had surrounded her and were gently nosing her skin.

Ah, yes—a river-line, the voice that was many voices said. *Part of the Garden's legacy to the new lands, another gift of the* Witchwood Crown.

Lillia did not understand any of that, but she was tired of saying so. "What should I do?"

That we cannot say. We are only another living thing, like you. We all must make choices. We must all follow the glowing line of thought and breath and change. There is no certainty—even in our home, the Garden, there was no certainty. That is not how things are. We create what will happen and it happens. We can create it another way if we choose differently. But we cannot know which choice leads to which happening.

Lillia was shivering in earnest now. "Let me go back to the beach—back to the fire. I'm cold."

Let us taste the feather, young one. We ask only that. But be aware that only while you are with us can we give you protection from the Silvermask. Her reach is long, and she likes to end things.

But Lillia couldn't do it. As much as she wanted to trust the voice of the waters, which had not frightened her and had said nothing wrong, she knew that the silver-faced phantom had also spoken kindly at first. Instead of answering the ocean-voice, she again began wading up the sloping strand toward the beach and her abandoned campfire.

The water was only at her knees now, and the Dreaming Sea had said nothing more—no pleading, no threats, as if it truly were an ocean and knew that eventually everything would return to it—when she saw movement at the edge of her vision. She stopped, heart pounding.

The masked specter had returned to the edge of the water, and was waiting for her there, drifting like a slashed and deserted spiderweb.

"Go away," cried Lillia, almost crying again. "Go away! Leave me alone!"

You are a mere child, the silver mask said in a voice cold and solemn and firm.

You are too full of yourself, as all young creatures are. Only moments ago, I punished another mortal for no greater a crime than distracting me at an inopportune moment. But you—you defy me outright! The voice grew in force but also gained a sort of weird sweetness. *Come, little one. There are great things at work here, things you cannot possibly understand. I am merciful with you because I was a mother once, but do not expect my forbearance to last forever. I have spent many mortal lifetimes planning for this hour, and I am stretched very thin. I will not have those plans endangered by a creature scarcely out of infancy. I must know who brought you here—must know who my enemy truly is. Give me the token and everything you wish will be yours. Resist me and, child or no, I will have to end you and all those that you love.*

Half-truths and outright lies, the voice of the Dreaming Sea told her as the waters lapped around her knees. Lillia did not think that the silver-masked one could hear it speak. *Even if she gives you your heart's desire, you will not have it for long.*

"Can't you make her go away? Can't you drive her off?"

Who do you speak to, child? Is it my enemy?

No, we cannot drive her away, said the voice of the tide tugging gently at her legs. *She has usurped a great power—she burns like a cold white sun. She cannot corrupt or even understand the Dreaming Sea, but as she stirs events elsewhere, she has also made her way to this place by sheer strength and will—a will such as we have never seen in these lands or in our Garden.*

Lillia began crying again. She was caught in the ocean as the far-off sun was sinking into the horizon and the cold winds rose, but a terrifying *something* waited for her on the sand. She knew she did not dare go near enough to the masked shape to risk it capturing her, or even touching her, but she was shivering badly now and knew she could not stay in the sea forever.

At last, she held the token up before her. The owl's feather was such a small, pretty thing, shaped like the leaf of a southern chestnut, with white stripes across it like the bars on a knight's shield. What did it mean? she wondered. Why did the silver mask want it so badly?

Yes, the floating figure said now, and moved even closer, so that its translucent, trailing draperies almost touched the foam where it spread on the sand. Lillia could feel its hunger. *Yes, child. Give it to me and you will have all that you desire. Home? Safety? Your family together once more? Nothing could be easier once I have the feather. Just give it to me.*

Do not trust the Silvermask, Child Lillia, warned the green waters around her legs. *A great fear is on her. She will promise anything but will twist even the most solemn, powerful words afterward to cheat you.*

"I know," she said. "I know what liars sound like."

What? Who is there? The mask turned from side to side, and for a moment the shiny thing reflected the distant sun—a solitary spot of red like the first poppy of spring. *Who speaks to you?*

Lillia held the feather high in the air and thought of the one who had given it to her. "Come to me!" she begged. "You said to call if I needed you, and I do—someone is here, and I need you now. Come help me!"

The floating, masked thing did not speak, but grew as still as a cat waiting for a mouse to venture out of its hole.

Nothing happened—the feather-woman did not come. Lillia called out again, but still had no reply. The wind grew sharper, and darkness began to spread across the waves.

31

Voiceless Laughter

The terrible dream would not end. As Simon struggled against a prisoning force he could not see or touch, his granddaughter stood helpless beneath a vast, impossible creature who could crush her in a heartbeat.

But Geloë promised she wouldn't let Lillia be harmed! Promised!

He wanted to scream himself hoarse, but the very air seemed to press against his throat, squeezing him and silencing him. He could move, but just barely. A blink took several heartbeats; turning his head took even longer, and except for a few useless tremors, he could not make his limbs move at all.

He tried once more to draw in enough air to call out to her, but even as did, Lillia's small, round face turned toward him and picked him out from all the hundreds or thousands watching. Then he heard a faint whisper of Geloë's thought.

Not yet, Simon. Do not let slip my name yet.

Weeping with frustration, he tried desperately to crawl toward her across the rocky plateau, wanting at least to shield Lillia's body with his own, but could only squirm in place, terrified that he might soon watch his grandchild die.

But for some reason the great ogre, so tall that its weird, malformed head was still in late sun while the rest of its malformed body was submerged in twilight shadow, did not complete the downward swing of its arm. Had the Norn Queen's disabling spell affected it too? In fact, everything in the valley seemed weirdly poised, as if the slightest movement or noise might tip things one way or another.

Simon forced his glance down to Jiriki. Utuk'ku's spell might keep her enemies fixed in place, but it did not stop the seeping of the Sitha's blood, which was pooling beneath him.

Please let Jiriki live, he prayed. *His people need him. And please, merciful Usires, I beg you to spare my innocent Lillia, even if the rest of us cannot survive.*

"You have grown strong, Utuk'ku." Geloë's voice spoke again, echoing inside Simon's ears as well as his thoughts. "But that strength does not belong to you."

Hakatri, called Utuk'ku, her thoughts cold and sharp as icicles, *force the* uro'eni *to crush that thing. It is not a child, it is a fearsome enemy disguised in a stolen mortal body. It must be crushed—silenced!*

"Stolen?" Geloë replied in a mocking tone. "You are a shameless creature, Utuk'ku. Even Hamakho in his final madness would have been disgusted by what you have become. You have stolen life from your own people by hoarding the witchwood fruits, stolen the power of the Three Who Are One by trickery and murder, and tried to steal Hakatri i-Sa'onserei from his own tribe—then to make him their destroyer." Her voice grew stronger, and she turned toward the armor that contained Hakatri's essence. "But she has lied to you, Hakatri, again and again! She dragged you back to this world only to use you as a weapon, to control the spirit of the Night Ship, because it would never have trusted her or any Hikeda'ya. And not just to use the Ninth Ship against the mortals, but against my kind and your own kind, too." She pointed across the plateau toward the wall where Simon and the others lay, helpless. "Look, Hakatri! See what she has done here! Your own grandson, Likimeya's child Jiriki, lies mortally wounded there! He fell defending your Zida'ya people from one of Utuk'ku's deadly creations. Do not let the pain you have suffered blind you to the horrors she would make you commit!"

Emotionless as a carved mask, the crude face of the ogre continued to stare down at Lillia's tiny form. Despite Geloë's words, the massive claw slowly folded into a fist.

You are nothing, you changeling vermin! Utuk'ku's thoughts crashed into Simon's skull like a blow, flattening him against the ground once more. *I have lived since long before you were born,* she raged, *waited longer than you can imagine for this moment! Who are you to set yourself against me? What are you? You are nothing!!*

"I may be nothing, but I am enough," Geloë said with Lillia's voice. "Because I have returned from death, I can speak only the truth, and your resurrected slave can feel that." The small shape in the shadow of the ogre now turned back to Hakatri. "Proud son of Amerasu and Iyu'unigato, loving father of Likimeya, heed me! I know the lies Utuk'ku has told you. In truth, your brother Ineluki died because of his own unhappy, violent madness, but she led him to it. Then, even after he died, this arrogant creature dragged your poor, tormented brother back to the living world, just as she did to you, and tried to use him to turn back time itself and erase mortals from the world. Now she means to use you against not just mortals, but your own people as well. She calls herself a queen, and so she is—the queen of lies."

You will die for that! Utuk'ku's voice blazed like lightning in Simon's head, furious, violent. He almost expected to see the white queen clawing at the air like a trapped wildcat, but she still stood unmoving, arms uplifted, silver mask perfect and inscrutable. He felt strange currents all around, as if the ancient queen and her enemy in a child's body strove against each other, though neither of them moved. *Foul changeling!* Utuk'ku's thoughts grew jagged and harder to understand, but she still held him and the others helpless. *I feel your . . . . not be spoken to this way . . . any other living thing!* Simon struggled to hold on to his wits. *Hakatri, curses upon you, why . . . wait? The* uro'eni *. . . yours to command!* Her voice swept through Simon's head like an irresistible wind. His sight grew blurry, and his head was forced down toward the stony ground. *Destroy them, Hakatri!*

"Father Ruyan, why are you angry with me?" The voices were tangled through the ship's music like innumerable slender roots, but still spoke to Hakatri as if it were a single being, and that being was full of despair. Beyond the prison of his armor, the noises and dim sights of the Tanakirú plateau faded away until all he could sense was the presence of Ruyan Ká, the spirit that animated the ship and its guardian ogre.

"The Voice of Three has given us our task," Hakatri told her sternly, "and that is to destroy our enemy. Why do you fight against me?"

"The one you call enemy is Vao, Father—like us! We are forbidden to harm our own kind."

"Vao? Do you mean Tinukeda'ya? No, it is only a mortal child. Do not let the words it speaks confuse you."

"The child also carries the blood of the Dreaming Sea—but one of our own family shelters inside her, too."

Hakatri was more desperate than ever to leave the world behind, to crawl back into oblivion and an end to all the torment of this dragging half-life. "No. The Voice of Three said that is all lies."

"But what is the Voice of Three? Why do we listen to it, Father?"

"Because we must! No more questions! Do as I have told you."

There was a long silence. When the ship spoke again, Hakatri could sense defiance. "To do such a thing would destroy me as well."

Hakatri was consumed by fury that he had seldom known in life or death—fury with more than a whiff of terror. He was suffering every moment, and he would continue suffering as long as he inhabited this earthly shell, the bizarre, foreign armor that held his essence like smoke in a jar. But smoke did not feel pain. "Do it now, child! Remember who I am and do as I say!" And in that moment, he almost forgot that Ruyan Ká was not his true daughter, Likimeya, and that their disagreement was not about the fate of those gathered at Tanakirú, but about Hakatri leaving his family behind. "You cannot even guess at the pain I feel!"

"No, Father, I cannot. But you cannot guess at the pain it would give me to do what you say."

Hakatri knew he had the strength to force her to obey—he could sense it. For all her protests, the spirit of Ruyan Ká had exhausted most of her power and could not much longer resist the authority that the Navigator's armor and Hakatri's own dragon-fouled blood gave him. *Just as Likimeya, for all her childish anger, could not force me to stay. All she could do was speak bitterly to me and poison my leavetaking. And now she does it again—*

In that moment of confusion, Hakatri saw her again, his true child, as she had been on that long ago day. "My real father would not leave us," little Likimeya had said, but her eyes had been wet with weeping. Somehow, he had forgotten that her words were spoken through tears.

She did not seek to thwart me. The realization was sudden and painful. *She could not understand how much the dragon's blood hurt me. She was only a child and wanted her father to stay.*

It was chilly winter in the mountain valley, but beads of sweat ran down Simon's skin as he struggled once more to rise.

Lillia needs me. She's all I have left—!

He narrowed his mind and forced himself to think about just one hand, his right hand, which lay as uselessly in front of him as something that had died and tumbled to earth. He stared at it, so familiar, so far away. *Spread my fingers. I can't stand up if I can't put my hand flat on the ground.* He stared at the hand as though it were a recalcitrant child. *Spread.* The air seemed to tighten against him, gripping him on every surface, pushing down at his hand as though the entire world had been set upon it. At last, agonizingly, slow as a new butterfly emerging into the sun, he moved one of his fingers, then another. *Spread my fingers.* Through the dripping curtain of his own tears and perspiration he watched the fingers move apart. *Now push*, he thought, but could not make any pushing happen. *Lillia!* he thought in shame and anger. *She didn't want to come here. She trusted me.*

"Hakatri!" He heard Geloë's voice again and slowly raised his head to look. Lillia's small body had turned toward the man-sized shape just beneath the Norn Queen, a shape made of a thousand shining scales and a horrible, expressionless helmet. She seemed to be speaking to it and to it alone. "We are here now, Hakatri. The place we have always been and perhaps will always be. Tanakirú is like Sesuad'ra—can you remember the day I spoke to you there? And Sesuad'ra is like Tanakirú, a place where what is real grows thin and permeable. Everything stands in precarious balance—here, now, and all through the corridors of time. Do you recognize the moment yet?"

Silence! thundered Utuk'ku. *Silence!* The force of her wrath—and could that be fear he sensed as well, making the Norn Queen's thoughts so ragged?—held Simon down as easily as the ogre's great hand would have. Defeated, he lay like a fish drowning in air.

"Hakatri of the Year-Dancing, can you remember?" Geloë's words began to echo away, not down the valley, but outward into some inexplicable void. She had not moved, but still lingered beneath the ogre's vast, threatening claw, against all sense. *"I bring you no prophecy, but a memory that has not yet come to be."* Now her voice seemed doubled, then it multiplied again and again until the words

of a thousand Geloës filled Simon's mind. "*There will come a moment when only you, Hakatri of the Year-Dancers, stand between life and darkness. In that moment, you must remember this, and you will have to choose.*"

The winter sun had all but set as they raced through the hills above the Narrowdark. Tanahaya could see the first stars shivering into life in the darkening sky.

Oh, faster, faster, she thought. *We must go faster. Jiriki is hurt and the year is ending and I am so frightened.* Their swift, nearly tireless horses had made astounding time along the steep upper reaches of the valley, but they still had leagues to go. As another patch of evening sky appeared beyond the over-arching trees, Tanahaya saw the white starpoint and misty trail of the Year-Torch hanging just above the horizon. The Hour of Passage was upon them. The new Great Year had arrived, a fearsome guest who would enter whether invited or not.

The hooves of their mounts barely seemed to touch the ground as they passed out of the trees. The darkening sky suddenly leaped out above Tanahaya in all directions, an immense violet blanket glittering with diamonds, but it was the Year-Torch that held her eye, with all it represented and all it threatened.

Utuk'ku means to make Tanakirú hers, to seize the great ship. She must have planned to do it now, as the new year comes in, when the invisible world will be most vulnerable to her dark songs.

But why such an intricate plan, simply to win a battle—or even a war? The question came suddenly, and she could not answer it. What might Utuk'ku want with a ship that was meant only to carry the Tinukeda'ya out of bondage, away from both Zida'ya and Hikeda'ya? What value for someone as powerful as the Hikeda'ya queen in a ship that had traveled only half of the journey it was meant for?

The zhin'ju, she remembered. *That was what Yedade asked about over and over as Geloë's father, Sa-Ruyan Mardae, was tortured.* But why had the Hikeda'ya philosopher dug so purposefully at that one thing about the ship, she wondered, like a hound scraping after an alluring scent? *Even arrogant Yedade would not have dared take up so much time in an important trial unless his queen wished it.*

And as Tanahaya rode, hunched low in the saddle as they re-entered the trees and the Year-Torch vanished from her sight once more, she puzzled over it until a memory suddenly floated up to her and threw everything into frightening disarray. Tanahaya reined up without realizing it, startled and fearful. For a moment, the Sithi around her sped on as if they had not noticed, but the few who rode behind her slowed until they had surrounded her; one of them was Ayaminu.

"What is it, scholar?" she asked. "Why do you halt so suddenly? Is it Likimeya again, or Aditu?"

"No," she said, although the Seastone had begun to feel oddly warm against her breastbone. There was also the hint of a strange scent in her nostrils again, something like the tang that followed a lightning flare . . . but Tanahaya would not let herself be distracted. "Listen, please. I think I have grasped Utuk'ku's scheme. She wants the Ninth Ship's *zhin'ju*—its spirit." She struggled to keep her voice even. "It must contain . . . some great power . . ." Ayaminu's face had become dim and imprecise, as if mist obscured it, and that puzzled Tanahaya. Why had the mist gathered so swiftly? Why was it everywhere?

Then she could see only darkness, an emptiness interrupted by tiny flashes of light. She was falling—falling—!

Spark! Aditu's bodiless voice was full of fear. *Speak to me! By the Garden that gave us all life, I need you now!*

But before she could reach out to her friend, another voice joined her in the blackness, weak but still understandable.

Heart-daughter, can you hear me? Oh, I beg you, say you can!

The two voices were speaking at the same time, as if they could not hear each other, but Tanahaya could hear them both, and it was all she could do not to shriek into the darkness, maddened by the force of their pleas and their terror.

The Year-Torch! said the presence that was Aditu.

The Veil. It is open, but only for a moment, cried Likimeya. *Tell her! Tell her it is time to let me go.*

The Year-Torch—I can feel it hanging over me like a great weight! said Aditu. *The time has come, but I do not have the strength to open the way.* Tanahaya had never heard Aditu so fearful. *The Year-Dance will fail.*

For a mad moment, Tanahaya tried to grasp what it would mean for the ceremony to fail. Would time itself stop? Would its flow swell like a dammed river until it flooded over the banks? Or would the failure of the ceremony only kill her dearest friend?

What do you want me to do? she cried into the darkness. *I hear you both, but how can I help you?*

Tell my mother I cannot succeed without her help. Tell her she must stay with me, or we will lose everything.

Tell my daughter that the moment is slipping. I have been caught between one existence and another too long, held prisoner by the white witch's spells. Tell her to let me go!

Your mother says you must let her go, Aditu. She is speaking to me, even as you are. She says that the moment is slipping.

I cannot, Spark. I am not strong enough. Without her help, I will fail!

Courage, Tanahaya told her. *I do not believe that, and neither should you.*

It is time, said Likimeya. *And that time has all but fled. My children must let me go.*

Your mother says it is time, dearer-than-sister. She says her children must let her go.

But I cannot be the Sa'onsera without her, mourned Aditu. *I cannot bring our people into a new Great Year by myself. I have tried, but I do not have the skill.*

Peace, said Tanahaya. *I think I understand now—at least a little. You say you cannot be the Sa'onsera without her, but I believe you cannot be the Sa'onsera with her—not when she still lingers on this side of the Veil of Death. She wants you to let her go, Aditu. She wants to go.*

Give her up?

No. But let her travel where she must. As long as your need holds her here in the circles of this world, you cannot become what you must. It felt true, but she could only hope she was right.

If she releases me, it will unbind the knot of Utuk'ku's spell, the Three Who Are One. Likimeya's presence seemed calmer now, as though she had seen something ahead that eased her heart. *Utuk'ku's plan draws much of its strength from that terrible song. With its power, the white queen has stretched herself wide but also thin, seeking to assure each part of her scheme. No creature has ever tried to dominate so many at once.*

Tanahaya was afraid to repeat so much to Aditu—she could feel her friend's agitation and fear. *Trust Likimeya,* she said. *Your mother has good reasons.*

Likimeya said, *And somehow, somewhere, I may meet my lost loved ones again. A small hope, but any hope is a good thing.*

A blessing, some would call it, Tanahaya told her. *Aditu, can you still hear? If you love me, if you love your mother, you must trust me—and trust her. You and I carry the future, but to reach those yet-unseen days, we must step into the unknown. Nothing else will save us.*

For a long moment of silence Tanahaya seemed to float alone in a cold, uncaring void—long enough for her to begin to fear she had lost them both in the mystifying fogs of the Dream-Road. Then she felt Aditu once more and heard her speak, her words and thoughts full of aching regret.

I love you, Likimeya of the Sa'onserei—my mother. If I disappointed you, I am sorry for it.

And, somehow, Likimeya could now hear Aditu. *Disappoint me? No, daughter. Only the world disappointed me, never my children. Now set me free, my courageous, laughing child. Kiss me and set me free, then some hope may remain for our people.*

Oh. Oh! Mother, you are there! Aditu's voice was suffused with wonder. *So little after so long, but each bit of it more precious than all the witchwood that ever was. And there is so much more that must be left unsaid! But what must be . . . must—*

They were pulled apart then—all three swiftly receding, each from the others. Moments later, the shock of Likimeya's final departure struck Tanahaya like a phantom knife, a dagger that cut through time and fate and straight to the core of her being. A silent sound bloomed in the emptiness, a rush of possibilities both dire and hopeful now all dispersed into never-ness as something important changed forever.

Tanahaya awoke on the ground. Ki'ushapo, Ayaminu, and several other Sithi stood around her. This time it was the mortal, Brother Etan, who was kneeling at her side.

"You have had a fainting spell," the monk said in his own tongue. *"You should rest—"*

She sat up, ignoring him. "Sa'onsera Likimeya is gone," she told the Sithi. "I felt her finally leave her body." They looked at each other and made hand-signs of mourning and fearful concern. "But there is more to explain," she said, "though there is little we can do about it. I believe I know what Utuk'ku seeks. She never wanted the whole ship—only its deadly heart."

"I bring you no prophecy," the child-thing said to Hakatri, *"but a memory that has not yet come to be."* The words felt chillingly familiar to him. *"There will come a moment when only you, Hakatri of the Year-Dancers, stand between life and darkness. In that moment you must remember this, and you will have to choose."*

A memory was wrapped in those words, buried and, until that moment, all but forgotten. Hakatri did not want to face it. He wanted an end to pain. He wanted the freedom of nothingness. "No," he said. "There is nothing but this moment."

"A moment that never ended, and which began long ago," the child-voice said. "I bid you remember!"

Impossible as it was, Hakatri saw the shadowy blur that was the great cliffs of the Narrowdark turn transparent as air, until it seemed he was no longer in a valley but on a wide, empty plain. Before him loomed a single massive hill, a pillar of upthrust rock. He could not help recognizing it, though he did not want to. "I know this place—!"

"You do. On a long-ago day, you came to Sesuad'ra in search of healing—the Stone of Farewell, as the mortals call it. We spoke across time itself, and I told you that there would be a moment when only you, Hakatri of the Year-Dancers, stood between life and final darkness," she continued. "That moment is here. You must choose."

"I want only an end to suffering. Surely I deserve that."

"Choose."

Another voice came to him then. *Father? What is it? I feel your hesitation, and I am frightened! Tell me what to do!*

But he could tell the ship's spirit nothing. Memories were bursting in on him like light refracted through a gem, scattering awareness everywhere, bringing radiance into corners that had long been dark.

By our shared Garden, what have I done? What have I been part of?

Father?

No. I am not your father, Ruyan Ká, if that was your name. I lied to you, to my great shame. I am not the Navigator. I let my pain and rage rule me—change me. I . . . I am sorry, child.

Not—?

No. I am sorry.

Sesuad'ra now faded and the cliffs of the Narrowdark Valley grew and solidified around him once more. *Tricked,* he thought. *I have been tricked—and in my selfishness, I let it happen.* It seemed almost impossible to order his careening thoughts. *I have lied to a lost and frightened spirit. What have I become? I must . . . I must—.*

But then another voice—a sharp-edged and familiar voice—slashed through his thoughts. *Hakatri, if you do not act, the mortals who destroyed your family will triumph.* It was the Voice of Three, strong, angry, and impossible to ignore. The pain of his burning intensified, agonizingly worse than it had been since he had first been summoned back, as if he had abruptly returned to his tormented living body. *Remember this pain!* the Voice cried. *It is the fault of the mortals who deserted you in the dragon's shadow. They left you to fight alone!* The torment grew worse, until he could barely think at all. *Do what you must do!*

Enough, he told the Voice of Three. *I will obey your command.*

Simon could only watch in frozen horror as the ogre took a step toward Lillia, its vast, misshapen body creaking like a ship's timbers in a storm. But instead of reaching down to crush the tiny, defiant figure, the ogre took another step and passed her, then another, bearing down on its new quarry.

Utuk'ku stared up at the approaching monstrosity, then the Norn Queen flung out her hand and shouted something in her true voice, a single word that Simon could not understand, which struck him like a hammer blow. The sky itself seemed to wobble, and even the Hikeda'ya gathered on the distant hill fell to their knees in pain and terror; only the queen's white-armored Teeth soldiers did not flinch and cower at the terrible sound of that single word. A wind leaped up, swirling around the queen and her attendants, and the sky above her turned dark as tar.

Even as the ogre reached out for Nakkiga's mistress, it swayed and stopped, then its monstrous extended arm splintered and fell to pieces, dropping great spars of witchwood all around the queen without touching her, though its fall crushed several of her guards, who died in silence.

You cannot do it, changeling, cried Utuk'ku. *You cannot turn my own crafting against me!*

"Are you so certain?" asked Geloë in his granddaughter's high, sweet voice. "With the power of the Three Who Are One you sang up a spell to drag Hakatri back from death, and you have also meddled with his reason, but you could not keep him ignorant and confused forever. He understands now who you are and what you have done, Utuk'ku, and he will follow you no more. Nor is that all you have lost. The Three Who Are One is unraveling, too. Because I hold the strand that you meant for Ommu the Whisperer, and now Likimeya, so long prisoned by you in a magical sleep, has let go of hers and left the world. Your great song of power is now silenced."

I have strength enough without it to treat with a nuisance like you, wretched little changeling, declared the queen. *You . . . you are nothing.*

As Simon watched in astonishment, a tiny flame of hope kindling in his breast, the Lillia-figure lifted her arms and drew an incomprehensible design in the air. "It is time for you to learn my name, Utuk'ku seyt-Hamakha, since the knowledge will do you no good now that the three-strand knot has come undone." Her voice grew stronger, louder, until it seemed as powerful as the queen's thought-speech. "I am Sa-Ruyan Ela, called Geloë, the last of the Navigator's line. You drove my grandfather Xaniko out of Nakkiga into exile. You tortured my father, Mardae, over the secrets of this very ship, which you now think to take for your own. But you have grasped at more than you can hold, Eldest."

Enough of your boasts, said Utuk'ku contemptuously. *What do you think you have the power to do? What do you think you have achieved with your meddling?*

"This," said Geloë, and turned to face the unmoving figure wearing the armor made of glinting crystal. "Hakatri i-Sa'onserei, you were pulled unwitting and unwilling from the lands beyond life because Utuk'ku herself could never command one of the Vao. Now you must choose—will you stay in this living world that is no longer your home, or will you be released to find your own way?"

Simon stared, amazed and uncertain. In only a few moments the world had turned upside down, then downside up, then upside down once more, and he had no idea what would happen next.

The creature in the shining armor turned away from Utuk'ku without a backward glance, then began to walk slowly toward the place where Simon sprawled. When it reached him, he could see for the first time the fires that burned in the crystal-clad eye holes of its helm, but Hakatri was not looking at him, but at Jiriki, lying silent, pale, and motionless. The thing in the armor slowly raised one gauntleted hand to its tiled breast, to the place where in life a heart would have been, then the fires behind its crystal eyes guttered and went dark.

Simon sensed a change then, swift and final as a closed door: something important had gone out of the world. An instant later, his granddaughter Lillia's body suddenly went limp and dropped to the stony ground within a few steps of the queen's guards. Horrified, he tried to climb to his feet, but the strange immobility still held him.

"Do not fear for her, Simon," said a strange, buzzing voice, and for a confusing instant he thought it was Utuk'ku speaking inside his head again. But this odd voice, like the hum of a beehive, was in his ears instead, a thing of air and natural vibration. *"Lillia is unharmed."*

The Navigator's crystal-studded armor, which only moments before had been empty as a dry well, now turned from Jiriki to face the center of the plateau where the queen, her remaining Queen's Teeth guards, and the huge, motionless shape of the one-armed ogre still stood. *"And so, we come full circle,"* declared the buzzing voice, and Simon understood that Geloë's spirit had somehow left Lillia to take Hakatri's place inside the Navigator's armor of crystal and golden wire. *"You sought to bring Ommu the Whisperer out of the lands beyond,*

Utuk'ku," Geloë said, "*but instead you brought me, your enemy. You sought to trick Hakatri of the Zida'ya into doing what you could not, but he has escaped your clutches. And without Hakatri, you cannot force the ship's giant protector to obey your will. All your schemes have come apart. Will you still try to force these Hikeda'ya and Zida'ya to fight to the death when your battle is already lost? Will you sacrifice even more of your subjects and kin for your petty jealousies and your ancient hatreds?"*

The sun had vanished behind the western hills and twilight was descending on the valley, the cliffs now little more than looming blocks of shadow. Those who could still move, the Hikeda'ya watching from the far side of the gorge and Utuk'ku's silent honor guard, all turned toward their queen in alarm.

Geloë has done it! Simon thought, exulting. *Against all reason, against all odds, she has beaten the Norn Queen!*

Then something rolled through his head, a terrible, triumphant sensation that felt as if it should have rattled the surrounding cliffs and made the rocks fall. But it resounded only within the confines of his skull, and inside the heads of all others in the valley, so that even those still prisoned by Utuk'ku's power cried out in dismay and shock. It felt so strange, so unprecedented, that for the span of a dozen heartbeats Simon could only clutch the stony ground, wondering what was shaking him so fearfully.

It's the Norn Queen, he realized at last.

Utuk'ku was laughing.

You are all fools. In the darkening evening, the queen of the Hikeda'ya's slender figure shone like a white flame. *Do you think that I would have dallied with you so long if there was still a chance you could thwart me, little Changeling? No, what I came here for is already in my hands, and there is nothing you can do about it. Nothing!*

Interlude

Hakatri

Even as he floated free of his earthly prison, he could sense the anger, terror, and confusion that raged behind him, a storm of possible consequences, most of them dire. He hesitated, suddenly wondering whether he had doomed those he had left behind.

Perhaps, said a voice. *But it is beyond us now. We are finished with it.*

Who are you?

Do you not know me, Father?

Are you the spirit of the ship? Are you Ruyan Ká? Have you too been released?

No, Father. He felt a hint of amusement from the other, but it ended quickly. *The Navigator's children are still within the world—still struggling against the darkness. I am not Ruyan Ká.*

But then . . . It came to him slowly, unfolding until he understood. *Likimeya? My true daughter?*

I rejoice that you remember, because I think we will not keep our names for long. Yes, Father. I too have been freed from my earthly form.

Bodiless, without sight or sound or any other earthly sense, he reached out for her and found her, pulling her to him, reveling in the gift, however long it might last. *I was lost, daughter.*

And so was I.

But even before I died, I was lost. I beg your forgiveness, my child. I left you and your mother when I should not have. I let pain and fear rule me, and I chased something I never found.

I feel your sorrow, Father, and it echoes my own, but the past cannot be mended now.

And what of those we left behind? The cruel she-thing who lied to me and used me still threatens our kind—all kinds.

We can no longer change anything, Father. We are released from both duty and guilt—from all earthly things. Our time there is over. Now we are free.

Free to do what?

I do not know. Again, he sensed amusement. *I have never died before.*

Your mother, he suddenly remembered. *By the sacred Grove, I forgot my beloved! Is Briseyu here somewhere too—here, beyond the living world?*

I do not know that either. I spent a long time between life and death, and I think that is too simple a question, Father. But there is only one way to learn the truth.

And that is—?

To go on to whatever is next. Perhaps nothing—we may only be our own last fleeting thoughts. Or we may find the Garden and be surrounded again by all that we loved.

I knew you only as a child—a stubborn, clever, determined child. How did you grow to be so wise?

Necessity. Now her presence moved a little away. *Come, Father. Let us go together while we still can. Let us find what awaits.*

I . . . I am fearful, Daughter. I fear to lose you again. I have lost so much.

So have I—but I think now that it was never mine. Not in the way I believed. Now, come. Time to go on, and we will seek for answers together—at least for as long as it is given to us.

32

Illumination

The sun had disappeared behind the tower of the Brynioch Temple. Inside its wooden walls, Count Eolair knew, stood the stones that had once topped the hill, erected by his ancestors in the unimaginably distant past.

I will remember those stones, he thought. *I will do my best to stand as silently as they do when the flames reach me.* But the fear of what was to come threatened to overwhelm him, and he sagged back against the willow-staves of the Withy Crow.

At King Hugh's command, Count Curudan stood and called for the torchbearers. Eolair looked down into Woolyard Square where Aelin and Murdo and the rest stood huddled together under strong guard. He did not doubt that Curudan, only a season ago a mere baron, now a count, was looking forward to being awarded Murdo's earldom after its owner had been executed. *When the hawk is felled, the crows hurry to mock him.*

As the torchbearers applied their flaming brands to the cardinal corners of the pyre, and the first wisps of smoke drifted upward, Eolair looked at King Hugh, who had come to the edge of the platform to watch his enemies burn. Eolair tried to reach out to Inahwen with the hands tied behind his back but he could not reach her.

"Courage," he told her softly. "We belong to the gods now."

Inahwen did not reply. Her head was bowed, her eyes closed.

Eolair was smelling the first harsh bloom of smoke when Hugh stepped to the middle of the platform to address the gathered crowd.

"For long," he cried, "these disloyal nobles have had their way, forcing Hernystir into a sickly subservience to the monarchs of Erkynland—Aedonite monarchs, believers in an upstart southern god. But we know better. We know the old gods have never left us, and today we mark our celebration of Talamh of the Land. In ancient days, when our ancestors were free men, not slaves, we called her the Morriga. We carried her on our standards into battle, and our enemies quaked at the sight of her!"

The smell of smoke made Eolair's nostrils itch, but the flames were only now beginning to heat the platform beneath his feet. *Hugh has had them build it of hardwood,* he realized, *the better to make our suffering last.*

"But I have discovered more than simply a forgotten goddess, however mighty," Hugh declared as the flames began to crackle loudly under the Withy Crow. "I have made a pact with her, without the intercession of priest or scryer—yes, I alone! And as we offer these traitors in sacrifice, she will give us the gifts she has promised—power over those who have held us down!"

Most of the crowd seemed confused. Eolair was finding it harder and harder to breathe without coughing. Beside him, Inahwen had slumped against the branches of the cage, though her breast still heaved in the struggle for air. Eolair prayed that the end would come for her before the flames did.

"Now I will summon the Morriga!" Hugh shouted. "You will see the power that your king now wields—a power that will make Hern's holy land the first of all the nations of the world!" He held something up to show to the watching citizens—Eolair could dimly see it gleam as he showed it to the watching citizens. "Now you will hear what only I have heard—the voice of Talamh of the Land, the mighty Morriga!" He struck an exaggerated pose, holding the mirror above him as he stared into it. "I call now for the queen of Heaven! I call for She who is the Mother of All—it is King Hugh of Hernystir who calls her! See what we do! The sacrifice has begun, deaths dedicated to the Crow Mother! Come, Talamh—come, fearsome Morriga! Breathe the ashes of your enemies and shower us with the gifts of your power!"

Eolair was no longer certain any of this was truly happening. His ordered thoughts were being driven away from each other or into each other, like an armada overwhelmed by a raging storm. He could barely draw enough breath to stay awake, though he sucked in air as hard as he could.

Better to stop trying. Better to let my breathing cease. His feet and ankles were now in terrible pain, though it seemed curiously distant. *Because the fire comes next.* He tried to say Inahwen's name, but nothing emerged from his throat but a low rasp of sound. For a moment, he thought he saw something strange beyond the gaping faces of the crowd. The rooftops above Woolyard Square seemed alive with bright shapes.

Are the gods watching? he wondered. *Oh, poor Maegwin, have I fallen into your madness at the end? Because I swear I can see the gods themselves, come to Hernysadharc.* Then he fell back against the bars of the cage once more, choking, fighting for breath, and it seemed his soul was rising with the smoke toward a Heaven he could only imagine.

Despite being hemmed in by armed soldiers, Aelin struggled, but his hands were chained behind his back and the links were far too strong to yield to mere flesh. The smoke that billowed from the pyre had all but obscured the two prisoners, but he could hear them coughing and choking. *That must be why they were tied but not gagged,* he realized. Hugh cared little if they denounced him, but he wanted to hear them scream as they died.

Aelin fought pointlessly against his chains, weeping a little in his frustration. King Hugh was strutting along the edge of the viewing platform, declaiming his mad ideas to the crowd of onlookers. Many of the watchers were talking urgently and even fearfully to each other, but Aelin knew the presence of the Silver Stags and the king's other soldiers would prevent any resistance.

"Come, Morriga, Queen of Heaven!" the king shouted. "Breathe the ashes of your enemies and shower us with wisdom and the gifts of your power!"

Aelin could not bear to look toward the Withy Crow any longer. The flames had climbed halfway up the horrid structure, and the highest tongues were already licking the bird's willow-stave head. He turned his eyes upward instead, searching for a patch of sky beyond the smoke, hoping to see something of Heaven and not this manmade Hell.

"I have called to you, Crow Mother!" shouted Hugh, still holding the glinting object before him. "I offer you the flames of sacrifice. I offer you the old bargain—blood for power!"

But if something had heard his prayer, it did not seem in any hurry to reply.

"I am Hugh! King of all Hernystir! I have done all you asked, Morriga, Dark Sow, Phantom Goddess—now give me what is my due. *Heed me, Queen of Three! I, Hugh, greatest of mortal kings, demand that you honor your pledge!"*

Hugh fell silent then. The crowd, too, was restlessly quiet, everything hushed except for the crackling flames devouring the Withy Crow. King Hugh stared fiercely into the thing he held, which Aelin now realized was a mirror—the mirror the Norns had given to him. Then, without warning, something flashed from its depths like the withering blast of Brynioch's own lightning, a glaring whiteness so complete and all-consuming that it seemed to obliterate Woolyard Square. Even Aelin, far away from the terrible flash, was so dazzled that he turned his head away. In the aftermath of the fierce glare he saw nothing except a blackness pulsing before his eyes.

Then he heard Hugh's voice—a ragged, astonished shriek: *"Aaaaaahh! Blind! I am blinded! She has betrayed me! A curse on all gods!"*

The blackness began to fade from Aelin's eyes then: the torches set around the walls of the square were the first things he could see. He looked up toward the cool sky, half-blind, tears streaming out of his eyes from the astoundingly bright flash of the mirror, and as his sight returned, he saw something astonishing. All around Woolyard Square, the rooftops were suddenly full of swiftly moving shapes, as though the city's tall chimneypots had come to life and deserted their posts.

These startling figures leaped outward to the edges of every roof around the square. They had bows in their hands. They wore colors he could now see even in the smoke-filled twilight—bright reds and yellows, greens of new-mown grass and blues of spring skies. Aelin thought he might have gone mad in his grief; then, the astonishingly bright phantoms loosed their first arrows. Up on the viewing platform Count Curudan, the king's favorite, stumbled forward with an arrow quivering in his thigh and blood spurting from the wound. As he staggered out from the crush of Silver Stags, most of whom were seeking shelter from the sudden hail of arrows, several more shafts found him and Curudan fell face-down on the boards.

The soldiers who had killed Maccus had inadvertently exposed themselves to these attackers; after Curudan, they were the next to fall. But the Silver Stags and the Hernystiri guards were no cowards. Even as the crowd dissolved and people began to flee in all directions, the Stags gathered on the royal platform behind their linked shields, covering their own archers, who began to let fly at these unexpected, swiftly moving attackers. Within moments a deadly storm of darts ripped across the square in all directions, hitting several fleeing spectators and forcing others to throw themselves onto the muddy ground.

Eolair! Aelin struggled against his chains. He struggled, eyes streaming and lungs burning from the hovering smoke, but he could not slip either of his hands loose from its manacle. Then someone seized him, imprisoning his arms behind his back, and he despaired. He tried to turn, but it only made whoever had seized him grasp more firmly, but in that brief instant he looked over his shoulder and saw a topknot of red hair almost as bright as blood.

"Do not make such struggle," Yeja'aro told him. "I might cut one of your hands from your wrist."

"You!" Aelin was utterly astounded. "What are you doing here?"

"Taking back my honor. I do what Jiriki sent me to do."

"Hang your honor. Free me! My uncle and the queen are burning to death!"

"Then stop your squirm. Now, sit down." Before Aelin could entirely understand, Yeja'aro shoved him downward into an uncomfortable squat, then pulled Aelin's arms out straight behind him. The length of chain clanked against a paving stone, then he felt a sharp impact as they parted. Aelin flexed his fingers against the sting of returning blood. "Give me your ax," he said.

Yeja'aro looked at him for a moment, then handed him the ax of silvery-gray, whorled wood.

Aelin paused only long enough to chop through Isleen's chains. He told her to lead her father and the others to safety before trying to remove their bonds, then he dashed across the square, arrows snapping past him and shadowy, smoke-obscured figures reeling in and out of view—a succession of deadly struggles he ignored on his way to the gibbet. It was empty, although a couple of dead Hernystiri soldiers and one dead Sitha lay in a puddle of scarlet at the far end.

Aelin scrambled up the steps toward the Withy Crow. He could see little of what was inside the smoke-filled willow cage, though the flames had not yet overwhelmed the crude sculpture, and he could only pray that Eolair and Inahwen still lived. He hacked away at the latch on the cage gate, wheezing as the smoke seemed to fill every part of him, eyes, nose, mouth, lungs, then he tore off the door. He took a step into the terrible heat, flames licking greedily around his feet, and saw Count Eolair huddled in the far corner, motionless and insensible; though his hands were still tied, Eolair had curled his body protectively around Queen Inahwen, who was equally still.

He knew what Eolair would want him to do. He grabbed Inahwen and dragged her back to the door of the cage. As he pulled her up onto the platform, he saw that the battle had taken over the entire square and had even spilled into some of the surrounding alleys. Isleen had apparently found a way to free her father and Evan and the rest, because he could see Murdo wading into the thickest of the fighting with only his parted chains for a weapon.

"Someone, help!" Aelin cried, though he doubted any could hear him over the sound of shouts, screams, and curses. "Someone help our queen!"

He did not stay to see if anyone heeded him but took a deep breath, then waded back into the fiery furnace of the Withy Crow.

♛

Eolair wandered through an ancient, deserted Sithi city. He recognized the place, its endless labyrinth of shadowy corridors, but could not remember its name. Neither could he remember how he had come there, although he knew that something important must have drawn him so deep into the earth.

What do the gods want of me? How have I failed them?

Down and down he went, ever deeper, through tunnels so close he could scarcely breathe. He was carrying a torch, he realized, and its smoke kept blowing into his face, choking him.

But I must go on. Someone waits for me.

At last, he found himself in a vast chamber—no natural cavern, but a place hollowed and shaped by crafting hands, suffused with directionless light. But the harshness of the air that had plagued him in the upper tunnels still troubled him here, and he had trouble getting a deep breath. At the center of the wide, circular chamber a small, bright glow flickered, and he wondered if this might be what was filling his lungs with smoke. He took a few steps forward, or thought he did, though he did not truly feel himself walking, and just as he saw that the glow came from a trough of smoldering coals set in the stone floor, he saw a figure sitting on the far side of it, head down, fair hair hanging over its face.

Who are you, he asked. *Why have I come here?*

Look around you, the voice said—a strangely familiar voice, light but solemn—but the figure did not look up at him. He turned to the inner surface of the underground dome and saw traces of dim light on every side, streaks and lines and crisscrosses that turned the walls into something like a builder's plans or a scroll covered in scribal runes. *What is all this?* he asked.

You are in the Pattern Hall, the figure on the far side of the brazier told him, and now he knew the voice. *This is the pattern of your life—your life as it touches on many others.*

Maegwin? Is that you?

The figure lifted its head. The hair fell back, revealing the pale but achingly familiar face. *Yes, I am here. Do not ask me why. Ask yourself.*

I am so sorry. He realized he had been waiting to say it—that the unspoken words had poisoned him for so many years he could scarcely remember a time when they had not tormented him. *I am so sorry for all I failed to see—your love for me, and of course my love for you. Can you forgive me?*

Do not ask me—ask yourself. She seemed older than he remembered, not in an earthly way, worn down by time, but as though a part of herself had withered away. *This is not my Pattern Hall. This is yours.*

But why am I here? What do you mean, this is mine?

Again, you ask the wrong question. Are you awake, Eolair of Nad Mullach?

He was caught by surprise. *I . . . I thought so. Now I am not so certain.*

You stand on the edge of something. Now look around you. You have made this place, and you have made me.

But my love for you—my regret—they are both real!

As may be. But they are yours alone now. And you know that.

Are you saying—? The thought suddenly chilled him, and the cavernous chamber became darker. *That you . . .*

Enough. Look what you have made. Is there more to your tale, or does it end here? Where do the lines lead, Eolair? What have you made of them, and what are you called to do?

You are dead.

I am.

And this is not truly you, is it? This is some ghost sent to haunt me. Some ghost meant to task me for the wrong I have done.

If so, then you will know where the blame lies for the haunting. Not with me. The Maegwin-shape shook its head, and for a moment, as its fair hair slowly fluttered in the light of the coals, like kelp waving in a tidal pool, he remembered her as she had been.

But with me?

Perhaps. It is part of your story, though. She raised a hand once more, gesturing toward the encircling walls. *All this is your story—to this hour. To this moment. Is there more? Or does it end here?*

You speak as if I had a choice.

No, you speak as if you had a choice. And if you believe you do, perhaps you do.

But I am weary, so weary. And I have felt that way for so long.

Death is restful, said the specter. *That is true. But nothing changes. Life is beyond your reach then—and life is change. Tell me farewell, then go and seek your pattern. Find its ending if you choose. Or make one.*

And with that, the light dimmed farther, until all he could see was the glare of the coals. The fair-haired figure was gone.

Then the light faded.

As he dragged his great-uncle's limp body from the growing inferno of the Withy Crow, Aelin felt as if the skin of his own hands and face were being burned into charred crackling. Even Eolair's rough homespun garments were brutally hot, and Aelin had no sooner dragged him free and beat out the flames in both their clothes before he fell to his knees. His hands hurt so badly that he might have carried smoking iron out of a forge without gauntlets.

Beside him, several people he did not recognize were tending Queen Inahwen, bathing her face in water, forcing a little between her cracked lips, but she showed no signs of life. Eolair was similarly motionless, his mouth hanging loosely open, his eyes rolled up beneath his lids. Aelin was reaching for the bowl of water when a voice cut loudly through the tumult.

"You at least I will kill before this is ended, Mullachi."

Samreas, captain of the Silver Stags, stood above him gripping a long sword, its blade smeared with blood.

Aelin spat on the wood of the gibbet. "It matters not," he said through fire-chapped lips. "The Fair Folk have come to Hernystir's aid again. Your time is over."

"A blind king is still a king," said Samreas. "Hugh still rules. And you are still a traitor."

"Sir Aelin!" someone shouted. "'Ware!" Something clanged onto the planks of the platform in front of him, and before Samreas could set his boot upon it, Aelin snatched up the sword and was able to block Samreas's sudden hacking blow, which bounced off with a loud ring. He did not dare look back, but he thought the warning voice might have been Evan's.

Bless you, Aedonite, he thought. *Bless all good folk.* Holding the sword before him, he climbed carefully to his feet, keeping Samreas always at the other end of the blade. The unfamiliar weapon had a good heft, though it was lighter than he was used to, and as he stood and made his way along the gibbet platform, trying to edge the Silver Stag captain away from the helpless forms of Eolair and Inahwen, he made a few calculating sweeps with it, finding its balance and also his own, ignoring the protests of his aching sinews, his bruised and burnt flesh.

Aelin knew he could not beat Samreas. In a fair fight, with both men healthy, he might have—but not after the beating he had taken, and the long hours with his arms manacled behind his back, and his burns. But he thought he could hold him off until others could get Inahwen and Eolair to safety.

As the two circled each other, thick smoke billowed in their faces. Samreas must have realized he would lose his advantage over Aelin if he could not see or breathe, so he sprang up onto the higher ground of the royal platform. For a moment Aelin strongly considered not following him, but his allies were still trying to carry away Count Eolair, so he had to keep Samreas distracted. He swiped hard at Samreas's legs, making the other man block downward and take several steps back, then Aelin scrambled up onto the platform. The two men resumed circling each other. Every time they swung around so Aelin could see the market square behind his enemy, all he could make out through the swirling smoke was chaos—vaguely human shapes struggling with each other, shrieks of pain, the screams of terrified children, and lightning-swift swirls of color that he guessed might be Sithi armor.

Samreas might have preferred to take his time killing Aelin, but circumstances dictated otherwise. He began to drive Aelin backward, relying on his own armor to protect him while swiping again and again at Aelin's unprotected legs. Aelin was painfully aware, not least from the heat at his back, that he was being driven toward the edge of the platform, and that the burning Withy Crow and its pyre had begun to collapse and spread, so now hungry flames leaped just beneath the edge of the royal platform. Samreas saw this and increased his efforts, smashing Aelin with blow after blow, forcing him toward the edge. Aelin was barely able to turn or block the heavy attacks, and each time his defense became a little slower. Already he was struggling for air and having trouble holding up the sword.

As the Stag captain pushed him backward, both fighters panting like dogs, Aelin's heel momentarily slipped off the edge of the platform onto nothing. As he swayed at the edge, a dark shape came out of the smoke and stumbled directly between the two fighters, forcing Samreas to hold back a blow that might have finished Aelin. The sudden apparition clutched the Stag captain like a drowning man seizing a floating spar, and almost dragged Samreas to the ground. The face of the newcomer swung toward Aelin but did not see him. It was King Hugh, his skin burned bright, oozing red, his eyes empty white, like boiled eggs.

"Help me!" Hugh cried, but even as he opened his mouth to speak, Samreas shoved him away, fearing a counterattack from Aelin, only realizing what he had done as the king lurched blindly toward the edge of the platform. Aelin leaped out of his way, but even as the king took another step, and his clutching hand scratched Aelin's face, he tottered at the edge of the platform.

"Majesty!" Samreas cried, springing to drag him back, but Hugh had overbalanced. The king's arms waved uselessly in the air, then he plummeted out of sight. Aelin heard an immense *whoomp* as Hugh crashed down into the blazing remains of the pyre with a scream, but it did not last long. Flames and a burst of sparks flew into the air.

Aelin was so tired he could barely stand, but Samreas stood only a step away, staring down into the fire in astonishment. Aelin heaved up his borrowed sword and tried to hack through the Stag captain's neck. At the last moment, Samreas looked up and flinched away, but the blade tore through the side of his neck and into his throat, followed by a great freshet of blood.

Samreas swayed, sword still held before him even as his eyes lost their fixity and began to grow dull. Aelin watched his enemy crumple, then he walked forward and shoved the body off and into the fire. Below, King Hugh had become a silent, charred shape nestled deep in the flames.

Aelin took a step back from the edge, turned toward the center of the platform, took one more step, then the world spun sideways and he tumbled into darkness.

Eolair, Count of Nad Mullach and Hand of the High Throne, woke to discover a figure in flowing white bent over him, laving his brow with cool water. For a moment he could only rejoice in the sensation after unending fire and thick smoke—but after a moment he began to wonder.

"Is this . . . Heaven?" he asked in Hernystiri, since that seemed the likeliest tongue that the gods would speak. His voice was a croak, his throat as sore as if he had swallowed broken pottery.

The white figure jumped a little. "Oh! You are awake!" His caretaker was a handsome woman of middle age, white-aproned, her head in a coif. "Tell them that the count has wakened!" she called to someone, somewhere.

"Then this is not Heaven?" He felt a bit disappointed. "Where have the gods brought me?"

The woman gave him a look that was nearly stern, as a mother might a beloved but misbehaving child. "I cannot tell you about the gods, my lord—it was men who brought you—but you are in the House of Irmeidh. You came to us when the bells rang the first night watch, and there is little else I can tell you."

Someone had brought him to the temple of the healing goddess, he realized. Suddenly he thrust himself up on his elbows. "Inahwen! The queen!"

"Peace, my lord, peace. She is with us too." The woman's tone softened a little. "Poor thing. She still sleeps, but her heart beats more strongly now, and our High Mother thinks she will again be well."

"I will see her."

"You will not." She frowned. "I know who you are, Count Eolair, and I bear you no ill will, but you will not go rampaging in to disturb our poor queen. What she needs is rest and quiet. The gods almost took you both. In any case, there is someone here waiting to see you."

"Inahwen is alive!" That alone seemed more unbelievable news than his own survival. "Who waits?"

"An important fellow you may know. But if you will insist on rousing yourself, and holy Irmeidh has given you back the strength to do it, I will not stand in your way." Her face grew very serious again. "But if I find you mollocking about, disturbing Queen Inahwen—!"

"I understand." Even under the best of conditions he would not have wanted to have this strong, serious woman angry at him, but he felt so weak and old and weary at this moment that he almost laughed at the thought of trying to wrestle his way past her. "Lead on, my lady."

"You may call me Sister Morwen. I have stripped you naked and applied vinegar, herbs, and rose oil salve to all your burns. That, I think, means we can use each other's names."

Eolair laughed, though it hurt his lungs and the skin of his face to do so. It all still felt like a dream. How could this be? The last thing he recalled was the blazing Withy Crow falling to pieces under his feet as he struggled to hold Inahwen upright and keep her safe from the flames as long as possible.

He followed the white-gowned priestess out into the echoing hallway. He still smelled smoke but supposed that the inside of his nose and mouth must have been thoroughly singed. Sister Morwen led him to a courtyard, then stepped aside. "Don't be long out of bed, now. You are not so strong as you think you are. If you make yourself unwell again, you will have only yourself to blame . . . Eolair." At the last moment, as she turned away, he thought he saw the hint of a smile.

The figure waiting in the courtyard garden stood and turned as he approached.

"Murdo!" said Eolair. "Praise all the gods. It is really you, and alive—unless we are all in Heaven. If so, I warn you that the goddesses here are on the strict side."

"We brought you here when Aelin pulled you and the queen from the fire." Earl Murdo was still covered with traces of smoke and smudge and had more than a few hastily bandaged wounds of his own. "The Irmeidhi Sisters are the only ones I trusted to do their duty in these angry, dangerous times."

"You said Aelin—"

"He lives. He has done you proud, my friend. And Hugh is dead."

"Dead!" Eolair listened, astounded, as Murdo told him all that had happened. "The Silver Stags are dead or run away," the earl finished. "We will round up them up as the time permits. But at the moment, we need something else—you."

"Me? How so? And when can I see Aelin?"

Murdo looked up. "Now. We have been waiting for him."

Eolair's young kinsman tottered into the courtyard, filthy with ash and as tattered as a fox saved only at the last possible moment from being torn apart by hounds. He barely had the strength to smile. "Uncle!"

"Ah, may the gods be praised and praised!" Eolair struggled up from the bench, then for long moments they stood silently, both reassuring themselves with the fact of the other's solidity. "It is over, then? Truly? I still do not understand what happened. What of that dog, Count Curudan?"

"Dead with the first Sithi arrows," Aelin replied. "Lady Tylleth still lives, but she has fled the city, and we will catch her soon, do not fear."

"Was that truly the Sithi that came to our aid? Astonishing! I thought I saw them, but—"

"You did, Uncle. And I have brought them with me. Well, two of them are Sithi, the other . . . I'm not certain." Aelin waved toward the doorway and a trio of figures stepped out into the courtyard. The tallest of them looked familiar—angularly handsome, with lambent eyes that seemed even fiercer and more upturned than most of his race, and his hair of a shade so fiery that it almost made Eolair recoil. *It might be some time before I can stand the nearness of actual flame,* Eolair guessed. "This is Yeja'aro of the Forbidden Hills," said Aelin.

"Yeja'aro and I have met," said Eolair. "Some moons ago, in Aldheorte forest, when young Prince Morgan and I were sent as envoys for the High Throne. But I was under the impression that you and your uncle Khendraja'aro didn't like our mortal kind very much, Yeja'aro. I am almost as surprised to see you as I am grateful."

The red-haired Sitha managed to give the impression that he was being somehow imposed upon, but nodded and said, in slightly awkward Westerling, "I recognize you, Eolair the count. My Arrow-Bearer, Jiriki of Year-Dancing, sent me to bring help to you. If I had failed my honor would have been lost." He nodded in tight-lipped satisfaction. "But I did not fail."

"I cannot thank Jiriki enough," Eolair said, meaning every word. "Once again, he has proved himself a true friend to the descendants of Hern. And if you are his captain, then we thank you too, with all our hearts."

"Not captain but messenger, though I sped the first arrow," said Yeja'aro, then gestured to the black-haired female Sitha beside him. "Here stands Yisume of Skyglass Lake. It was her people that I brought to your aid with Jiriki's summons."

She stepped forward and made an elaborate but unfamiliar gesture before saying, in surprisingly good Hernystiri, "Greetings, Count Eolair. On behalf of my father Yizashi Grayspear, who fights with Jiriki far away in the north, I received Jiriki's summons and we came. The ties between your people and ours are old ones, and we have never forgotten your Prince Sinnach standing by our sides at the battle you call Ach Samrath." She beckoned forward the last of the three, a slender, slightly bent figure—not quite Sitha, but not quite a mortal man, either, with a wide, round stare like a night bird. "And here is Kai-Ono, co-ruler of our Skyglass Lake settlement."

This was the first Eolair had heard of such a thing, but he was already stuffed so full with surprises and mysteries that he could only nod and exchange bows with the owl-eyed Kai-Ono. "We are grateful to you all," he said. "You have saved our kingdom from destruction or worse."

"It is not safe yet," said Yisume. "I do not wish to sully what should be glad moments and proper mourning for the dead, but even as we speak, my father and Jiriki are engaged in a great battle in the north against Utuk'ku and her Hikeda'ya armies. Our Witnesses have been smothered and silenced. We do not know what is happening in the distant valley called Tanakirú, but we know it may yet bring down everything we have saved."

With these ominous words, Yisume and Kai-Ono took their leave. When they had gone, Yeja'aro said, "I have no time for talk either, but I do not go to Tanakirú, though I could fight the enemy there. But my woman, Aditu, is about to give birth in far Anvi'janya, and that city is several days ride away, so I too take my leave now." And with just such small ceremony, he bowed to the company and made his way out of the Temple of Irmeidh.

When he had gone, Eolair turned to Aelin. "And you, my boy—no, a man, in truth, and more. You have done well indeed, and our kingdom owes you much. We will have many things to talk about anon." He turned to Murdo. "You said you needed me, old friend. I have a little while still before I will tip over and fall down, but I suspect Sister Morwen will come for me first and drive me back to bed. I can hardly hold all that has happened in my poor, muddled head—the Sithi came to help us! That seems a miracle of the gods to me. And I will want to hear more about everything. But as I said, I think my time today is short."

"What we want from you is simple enough," Murdo said. "You are the best-known man in all the kingdom, Eolair. Inahwen will take the throne again, but times of great confusion lie ahead of us in the wake of Hugh's death. Already rumor must be traveling across the land with the speed of the wind. We need you to take the kingdom in hand."

Eolair surprised even himself with the strength of his response. "Ha!" He laughed, coughed, and laughed again, the second time a little weakly. "No," he said finally. "I think not."

"But why, Uncle?" pleaded Aelin. "Lord Murdo is right—you have the best name in all of Hernystir."

"Best-known, perhaps, but not best loved. I have been long absent, and I do not doubt that King Hugh and his cronies darkened my reputation in every corner of the land. If you want an old man's considerations then I will advise you, and I will always be loyal to Inahwen, but I am far past the day when I want to take on such a task."

"Even for the good of the country you love?" asked Murdo. "The country you have spent so long serving, which is now in an hour of great need?"

Eolair regarded him balefully. Each breath hurt his chest—it felt as if his throat and lungs were full of scratchy sand. He made a noise of disgust. "*Pfah*. I remember you from the old days, Murdo, when we used to play at quoits on the Taig's lawns. You were a cheat then and you are one still. When you set it out like that, what can I say? But I did not lie—I am too old and weary for putting down revolts or thundering across a field to rally troops with banner and sword. Yes, I will help Inahwen, of course—I will be hand of her throne, if any of the Erkynlandish royal line remain alive to release me from my vow to them." He fixed Murdo with an amused look. "But I will not forget this treachery."

"We will leave you to rest, then," said the earl with a smile. "But we will be back soon."

"I have no doubt of it," said Eolair. "Ah, I forgot. Your daughter Isleen—is she well?"

"She is, praise to the gods and thanks to your Aelin."

"I can see there are many stories you still have to tell me," Eolair said to his grand-nephew. "But not today. Tell Sister Morwen I am going back to my bed."

33

Cold Root, Cold Heart

Tzoja had marched through the valley for hours, in the shadow of the tall cliffs, prodded along by Hikeda'ya guards while cursing Jarnulf and his tame giant with almost every step. The afternoon was gone, and evening was growing as dark as her hopes.

How could this have happened? she wondered. *We were free, on our own, away from the Hikeda'ya—it was Jarnulf's own idea!* But now they were prisoners again, being dragged to only God or the gods knew what kind of fate.

Along with a score or so of other stragglers the guards had rounded up, Tzoja and Vordis were driven toward the place where the mountains came together, fast-marched along the valley's windy heights toward the growing noise of falling water.

"It sounds like the Tearfall back in Nakkiga!" Vordis said quietly. "So loud! It must be very large."

Soon Tzoja could see water falling down the high cliffs in torrents but also boiling and surging in a deep gorge at the base of the valley, the Narrowdark's source. But what drew and held her eye was not the stunning sweep of cliffs and cataracts but a monstrous, impossible creature looming over the plateau at the far side of the gorge. Though its shape was thick and heavy, like that of a bear or an ape, it was taller than the steeple of a village church and so unmoving that though Tzoja remembered Jarnulf talking about an ogre, she thought this apparition must be a statue. Others around her had seen it too, many of them stopping short with cries of alarm before the guards forced them on.

Tzoja continued to stare at the massive shape with such amazement that they had marched a long way toward the valley's end before she noticed the strange wedge shape jutting from the cliffside high above the plateau, like an ax blade that had broken off in a thick trunk. She thought from its immense size that it must be a city of some kind, though she could make no sense of who would build one in such a strange place, or how they might accomplish it, since she could see no road or even tracks that led up the sheer cliff face to the sweep of wood.

"Your breath—you sound startled. What do you see?" asked Vordis.

She could think of no reason to frighten her friend with a description of the terrifyingly huge figure; so far, it seemed more manmade idol than living thing.

As for the strange shape embedded in the cliff, she could not be entirely sure it wasn't some natural feature. "I cannot say yet what I see. I will tell you when we are a little closer."

Tzoja was too tired and too hopeless to do more than wonder at it all. Jarnulf had said many times that he did not understand why the Sacrifices were marching the Nakkiga nobles to this spot. It seemed likely now that either the monster or the strange city growing out of the cliff were the object.

Along with the rest of the stragglers, Tzoja and Vordis were shunted off on a side-trail before they reached the valley floor where a sprawling Sacrifice camp had been erected beside the gorge. Tzoja thought there must be at least a thousand soldiers, all waiting near a slender bridge that stretched over the chasm, linking the far plateau with the near side of the valley.

If the Norns seek to capture that place on the other side, why have they stopped? Is it fear of that great shape? But it cannot be real—it does not move. As she and the other captives were driven uphill to a place where they could look down on the whole scene, Tzoja narrowed her eyes, trying to make out what was happening on the plateau below them. A circle of distant white figures stood at the center of the plateau, like a fairy-ring of mushrooms, and she realized that she was looking down at an entire company of the fierce and justly feared Queen's Teeth. Which must mean that the tiny, slender figure dressed all in white, standing on a stone in their midst, was the queen herself. But how was that possible? The Hikeda'ya's Mother of All had marched out with an army not long ago, bound to wage war in southern Erkynland. Why would she be here now? And what was the giant thing?

Tzoja remembered her lover Viyeki returning to their house, shocked and disturbed by the queen's raising of Ommu the Whisperer, the deathless thing that had summoned Tzoja at Naglimund, and by doing so, almost got her killed by the dangerous, unstable Jijibo. Was this gigantic shape another of the queen's summonings?

She and Vordis had been directed to join the crowd, which she realized contained not only slaves but Hikeda'ya nobles as well. Now the distant queen turned toward them, the setting sun's light glinting from her shiny mask so that for a moment her high-crowned figure seemed to have a face of pure fire.

All my life, Utuk'ku declared, *I have given all my strength to my people.* The queen's ringing words resounded in Tzoja's head so powerfully that it made her stomach lurch and her temples throb. Utuk'ku's thoughts were harsh and felt as dangerous as a lightning storm. *Do you understand that?* the queen demanded. *Can you even guess how I have suffered for you?*

Beside her, Vordis let out a cry of pain and sank to her knees, pointlessly covering her ears with her hands. But Tzoja thought she heard something frayed in the queen's voice, something almost desperate. Then Utuk'ku's thought-speech crashed in on her again, and Tzoja found herself struggling to stay on her feet.

All my strength, the queen repeated. *Spent for my people. Sacrifice! I know it better than any creature who has ever lived. But now that strength has been exhausted. The watching eyes, those hateful, watching shapes, rejoice at my weakness.* The Hikeda'ya nobles around Tzoja cried out at this; some of them even wept, so distressed were they by Utuk'ku's words, or perhaps by the sheer force of the queen's thoughts inside their skulls. *The fruit of the witchwood tree kept me alive through the long, long years of our exile. Now that witchwood is gone, the trees all dead, and soon I will end, too.*

Many of the Hikeda'ya cried out in dismay, even some of the Sacrifice warriors. Fear showed on nearly every face, nobles and slaves alike. *But I have never given up hope that we can command our own destinies, and today that hope has produced fruit more valuable than even that of the sacred trees that gave our people a name! Believe me, I know your greatest fear, my subjects. There has never been a time in these lands when you did not have your queen to protect you—and now I can promise you that such a time will* never *come.* The white shape lifted both arms. *Rejoice, my faithful* Keida'ya *subjects, for today we have won!*

The Hikeda'ya nobles around Tzoja seemed uncertain, though many did their best to raise their voices in praise of the queen. Tzoja felt only dread. *If Utuk'ku has won here,* she thought, *then the tide of her Sacrifice soldiers will soon drown all lands. What need will the Hikeda'ya have for despised mortals when they can make even the proud Sithi their slaves? What need for creatures like me?*

I hear your gratitude, said the queen, but anger tainted her thoughts, so that they pricked like burrs in Tzoja's head. *But some of you do not seem to understand that this is our great day of victory. Instead of trusting your queen, you wonder how we have won—and* what *we have won.* Utuk'ku gestured to the strange shape protruding from the cliff-face. *You see before you the Ninth Ship, the last thing ever to escape the ruin of our Garden home, but you cannot understand yet what possessing it means for us.*

It's . . . a ship? Tzoja was stunned. Surely that could not be true—nothing so vast could ever sail upon the sea. And how could it have run aground in the side of a tall peak, so high above the river and the valley floor?

Utuk'ku now lifted something in the air. Tzoja could not make it out—some moments it seemed to gleam like the queen's mask, other times it was all but invisible, and hurt Tzoja's eyes as they tried to fix on it.

The shining thing I hold in my hand is the zhin'ju *of the Ninth Ship,* the queen proclaimed, *the ship's inner genius, the spark that kindles its flame. I know you cannot understand this subtle, terrible tool, but understand this—today we have captured it from the treacherous Zida'ya, so rejoice, Hikeda'ya! Our lives are now in our own hands, and we will finally have peace—but peace on* our *terms! And no Changeling, murdering mortal, or traitor Zida'ya can prevent it! I command you to rejoice, because at last, we have triumphed!*

The queen's thoughts seemed to be growing stranger and more disjointed with every moment, but that did not diminish their strength. Tzoja fell to her knees with tears in her eyes.

Mad! she thought in growing terror. *The Mother of All has gone mad!*

Awareness came back slowly, in fragments. First was the pain. Someone was shouting in Jarnulf's ear—no, in both his ears. No, not in his ears at all, but inside his head.

Our lives are now in our own hands. We will finally have peace—but peace on our own terms! Jarnulf had never heard Queen Utuk'ku's voice before, but he knew instantly whose harsh words battered his thoughts. *And no Changeling, murdering mortal, or traitor Zida'ya can prevent it! At last, we have triumphed!*

What happened? Jarnulf groaned and rolled over. He felt as if someone had tried to pull all his limbs off at the same time and only barely failed. The ride to the plateau came back to him in dreamlike pictures—Goh Gam Gar thundering across the bridge, tossing bloody bodies aside, then the sudden, burning agony that had seized Jarnulf and flung him off the giant's back.

His heart was racing. *I must do something—must get up. The queen's Sacrifices will be on me in a moment!* He managed to raise himself onto his hands and knees so he could see over the motionless figures that lay around him. He saw dead Hikeda'ya, and what looked like the bodies of fallen Zida'ya as well, but no sign of Goh Gam Gar. His own body felt lightning-struck, his head full of sparks and shadows that, as he let his eyes move across the plateau, only slowly resolved themselves into a scene weirdly bereft of motion and life, as if some terrible blizzard had swept through and frozen every living creature. *Every creature,* he realized, *but one.*

Utuk'ku, Queen of the Norns, stood on a stone behind a ring of her royal guard, holding something in the air. Jarnulf could not quite make it out, but it had the look of a strange musical instrument, long and angular and disturbingly translucent. The Mother of All lifted it high above her head as though it were a sword that could destroy all her enemies with a single blow.

This is the zhin'ju*—the spirit, the living heart of the Ninth Ship!* the queen exulted. *Do you see that thread of purest black running through the middle of the crystal shell, my children? It is prisoned—surrounded—by waters of the Dreaming Sea that surrounded the Garden. Those waters are the only thing that can resist that black mote, though even they cannot suppress it forever.* Her glee was so fierce that it felt poisonous in Jarnulf's head. *Do you know yet what this writhing black thread is?* she asked. *It is Unbeing, my children. If it were to shatter on the stones below me, then Unbeing would escape the restraint of the Dreaming Sea's waters and begin to swallow up all that is—land, ocean, and living things. Like a black cloud spreading, like a lightless tide, Unbeing swallows all that is.* The idea of this destruction seemed to bring her a fierce joy—her voiceless voice rose in strength. *Swiftly at first, then slower as it widens its sway, leaving nothing behind—not even memory, for nothing will be left behind that could remember what went before. In my hands is the single most potent object in this world, and it is ours. Yes, rejoice, because we have triumphed! Your queen has saved you from the fate you most fear!*

Utuk'ku lowered her arms, but she still cradled the shimmering object like a beloved child. *I have suffered so long,* she said, *clinging to a life grown increasingly painful and bitter to me, because I could not bear to leave my people without their queen—the only queen you have ever known!*

Abruptly, her voice in Jarnulf's head slid from exultation to self-pity. *I am tired, my children, so tired. You cannot guess all the perils and all the suffering that I have gone through for you! But that is over now. When I smash the* zhin'ju's *casing, Unbeing will escape its crystalline prison. Without the Dreaming Sea to hold it back, it will begin to grow, spreading until it takes us all. But fear not, my children! It will be a swift end for those of us in this place, though it will take longer to spread across the rest of this ruined, unhappy world. It is the best ending we could hope for! I am failing, and there are no more witchwood fruits to sustain me. How could I leave you without your queen in such a corrupted world? So, in my great love for you, my closest kin and my most faithful nobles, I have brought you here to celebrate the end with me—*

"With all respect, great Majesty—" said Akhenabi, who until now had stood silent and still, his sentiments hidden. Jarnulf could hear a quaver of shock in the Lord of Song's voice. "With all respect, my queen, this is not the plan you shared with us, your most loyal servants. You promised us years ago that we must fight for the Ninth Ship so that we could board it together and leave this misbegotten place for another land, to escape the traitors and persecutors."

Utuk'ku's thoughts felt unconcerned. *I told you that in the same way a mother tells her children a soothing fable to shield them from the truth at a difficult time. But I saw long ago that this would be the only way to save our kind from degradation. There is no future for the Hikeda'ya without me. I will not allow my people to be left without their queen in a world that hates them, to be swallowed up by decay while the verminous mortals and their Zida'ya lackeys create history and make villains of us.*

"But, Majesty, this cannot be!" Akhenabi now took a few steps forward, dark eyes wide in his skin-masked face. "No one should destroy everything on a whim! Not even you, great queen!"

A whim? Jarnulf could feel Utuk'ku's anger now barely contained, her thought-words chaotic and increasingly hard to understand. *You badly overreach yourself, Singer Akhenabi. I have considered this both night and day, waking and sleeping since before you were born. Have you traveled beyond the Veil of Death? Seen the eyes that watch and heard the things that scratch and scrape at the walls of what is real? A whim, you say?* The jaggedness of her mood increased. *Why do you try to thwart me, little trickster—try to thwart our triumph? Do you not see the joy that is ours today? Everything finished! All burdens lifted from our shoulders! The watchers silenced and the prophesies fulfilled! All the Hikeda'ya will end together, as did our noble families in the old days, leaping together into a boiling pool with a song on their lips, putting themselves beyond their enemies' reach for eternity! This is the ending all Hikeda'ya want—who would know better than me? We will finally be free from all the glaring, spying eyes that hide in the shadows!*

"I fear this is true madness," said Akhenabi, turning from the queen to address those surrounding her, their spears angled outward like the thorns of a defensive hedge. "Soldiers of the Queen's Teeth, you have heard your mistress. She intends the destruction of all—our homes, our families, even the very history of what you have done for your people. The queen is obviously ill and confused. Will you stand by and let her obliterate not just our own people, but all this world?"

But for all the emotion they showed at his demand, the Queen's Teeth might have been just pieces on a *shent* board, not only mute but deaf as well. Then, as if being silently ignored by the queen's guard had answered a vital question, Akhenabi wheeled again and began to trace symbols in the air with his gloved hands, accompanying each gesture with a low, rasping murmur of song that Jarnulf could barely hear. Much of what Utuk'ku had said—watching eyes, Unbeing, a ninth ship—had been incomprehensible to him, but her talk of death for all and Akhenabi's shocking resistance made it plain that something dreadful was happening. Jarnulf kept his head low and crawled forward until he could reach a witchwood bow and scatter of arrows that had belonged to one of the Zida'ya corpses lying near him.

But many of these Sithi look like they are still alive, just not moving, he thought. *Why do they none of them attack the witch-queen? Why don't they at least die fighting?*

"Her Majesty's madness must be stopped now," Akhenabi declared, then beckoned to someone Jarnulf could not see. "Here, come stand beside me." A moment later a dark-robed figure left the other nobles on the plateau and joined the Lord of Song. To Jarnulf's astonishment, even among so many other surprises, he recognized this newcomer as the half-mortal Singer Saomeji, his nemesis on the journey back from Urmsheim with the captured dragon.

Why should Akhenabi single out the halfblood for protection? he wondered.

As Jarnulf watched, the air began to thicken around Akhenabi, until both Saomeji and the Lord of Song were surrounded by what looked like a faceted jewel made of foggy air. Wordless as ever, several of the Queen's Teeth flung their lances at the shimmering blur that Akhenabi's song had created, but their weapons only bounced off and clattered to the stony ground.

Traitor! howled Utuk'ku. Jarnulf fell onto his elbows, clutching his head in his hands in a useless attempt to keep out the queen's soundless scream of fury. *You will burn for this!*

Still clutching the *zhin'ju* in one gloved hand, she made a flinging gesture with the other; the air between the high place where she stood and Akhenabi's blurry shield twisted and thickened, so that the world beyond it seemed to bulge, shrinking and stretching at the same time. Now blue lightning played across the surface of Akhenabi's spell-sung protection—crackling, spitting flecks of azure light that filled the air with the smell of burning—but somehow the shield held. Jarnulf could see the shapes of Akhenabi and Saomeji standing within it, the Lord of Song with his arms spread wide, as though he held the shelter together by sheer strength of will.

The storm of writhing air between the queen and her chief servant contorted again, wriggling like a dying snake. Eruptions of flame and sparks coiled around Akhenabi's shield and then spiraled up into the air; still, his defensive spell survived.

Is it possible? Jarnulf wondered. *Could Akhenabi truly defeat Utuk'ku?*

Then he saw unusual movement in the shield of solid air, as if the two figures inside it suddenly embraced. Utuk'ku's lightnings died away, and for long moments the huddled figures stood motionless, like carvings on an ancient frieze. Then one of them slumped to the ground. The Lord of Song's defensive shield dissolved like a handful of salt tossed into boiling water.

Akhenabi lay face down at Saomeji's feet, a dagger in the back of his neck. The queen spat out a single spoken word, and the Lord of Song's body huffed into flames. Saomeji stepped away from the blaze, eyes wide, hands clenching and unclenching.

You have killed your own father, little Singer, Utuk'ku said to him. *How like him you are.*

Father? Akhenabi was his father? In the middle of such chaos, Jarnulf felt only dull surprise.

Saomeji dropped to his knees, crying, "I could not let even the one who sired me defy the Mother of All, my queen." Jarnulf thought the half-blood looked as though he was in the grip of a fever, his unexpectedly golden eyes wide, his exulting face shiny with sweat.

I honor your loyalty, the queen said. *Come, Saomeji, and stand within the circle of my guards. When the end comes, you shall be near me.*

Jarnulf felt battered to the point of collapse. His very bones ached—he felt sure he had broken a few of them when he fell—and the only one with the strength to resist the madness of the Norn Queen now lay smoldering on the ground like a lump of burning peat. The world had lost its meaning. He tried to pray but could not summon any words. Was God even watching any longer?

Nezeru decided that if mad Jijibo and several Sacrifices had been caught up by the ogre, and if she could hear them but not see them, she too must be held somehow by the enormous, impossible giant. *Perhaps I am even inside it—swallowed.* Her heart stuttered with fear at the thought. But what hemmed her and held her was only witchwood, its smell and feel told her, so if she was inside the ogre, then the monster was made of the stuff. But it lived! She had seen it trudging along the Narrowdark river course, hunting through the misty valley. How could a living, walking thing be made from wood?

Impossible, she thought, but another oft-repeated phrase from her training came rolling up from her memory: *"As long as you keep your thoughts fixed on duty, nothing can come to you but victory or holy sacrifice."* She might no longer be a soldier—every Hikeda'ya might now reject her and call her traitor—but she was still a Sacrifice, trained, death-sung, and many times blooded. She might have lost both her own people and her mortal friends, but she would not lose herself.

But even as she made this resolution, Nezeru found herself tumbling through the air once more, suddenly weightless, unable to do anything except bounce painfully against the confines of her wooden prison. Then something slammed against her hard, and for long moments she could only wonder if she was finally and utterly broken. She lifted her head and realized she could now glimpse sky at the end of the ruined wooden chamber that had held her. Crawling forward, wincing from the bruises of her latest fall, she found that though she could see outside, escape was blocked—not by more witchwood, but by the mangled bodies of several Sacrifice soldiers.

When the ogre snatched up Jijibo and his men, it must have grabbed me too. I must have fallen into a hollow place in its arm. She began to push her way through the horrifying obstruction, trying not to think about the slippery blood, torn limbs, and sagging, lifeless faces. She knew some of these soldiers might have trained with her in the Sacrifice Order, though all were unrecognizable now, squeezed into new and dreadful shapes as if they had been made of butter, with fragile broom-straws for bones.

My comrades cast me out, she reminded herself. *I did not leave the Order by choice.* But that did not make her crawl any more pleasant.

Now it is time for all this to end—for everything to end, she heard—or felt—Queen Utuk'ku declare. The queen's voice had grown even more intrusive, as if the witchwood of the ogre's body had offered Nezeru some protection from it. *Jijibo, you are fortunate I honor the blood of our ancestors in your veins,* the queen said, *or you would be burning like Akhenabi. But I will let you live until Unbeing takes us all. You may thank me now.*

Then she heard Jijibo's voice. "Thank you, great ancestor. Thank you!" He sounded badly broken, but she wanted only to avoid him. "Why does she not understand?" the queen's descendant Jijibo continued in the same tone. "I am curious—Great-Great-Grandmother knows that is my nature. I only wished to play with the ship's *zhin'ju* for a little while before I brought it to the Mother of All—"

And you did bring it to me, though that was not your intent.

Even inside the ogre's fallen arm, Nezeru was assaulted by Utuk'ku's words: the queen no longer seemed to care who could hear her thought-speech

And though you flouted my command, you are Hamakha and of my blood, the queen told Lord Jijibo, *so I will allow you to see the last moments.*

They had followed the tunnel all the way to its end in the cliff face, and now Morgan could look down onto the plateau. He ached with all his heart to keep following the monster until he could find and rescue Nezeru, but the tunnel opening where they watched was six or seven times his height above the stony ground—an easy climb for the ogre, but too high for him to jump down without killing himself.

"Rope," he cried. "I know you, Snenneq—you always have rope! I need to get down the cliff!"

"Not good," said Qina, pointing. "Not go down. Look to there."

The mist had cleared: he could see down to the plateau, but what he saw made him feel as if he were dreaming. The scene below was like something immortalized in one of the great windows of St. Sutrin's cathedral, but far stranger than any of them. The impossibly huge ogre towered above all, right in the center of things but utterly motionless, and one of its arms seemed to have broken off and fallen to the ground. A silver-masked figure that could only be Utuk'ku, the infamous Norn Queen herself, stood beside it at the center of the plateau, surrounded by her ring of guards and by many motionless dead, but also—Morgan could see them struggling to move—what seemed nearly as many of the helpless living. "Why are the Sithi all so still? Why do they not fight or run away?"

"The silver queen has used a Word of Command, I am supposing," said Snenneq. "A great song of force. How much strength she must have, to hold so many!"

"All the more reason to attack now," said Morgan. "Look! There is the thing that took Nezeru. We need to save her!"

"We have followed you here," said Yek Fisher, one of the people from the great ship. "But we will not go down there—not where the Hikeda'ya are. They live only to kill our kind."

"They will kill you anyway if you don't fight back," declared Morgan angrily. "Do you think they will let you live on the ship in peace? The ship must be why they came here."

"*The Aedon gathers all souls and sees all deeds,*" said the tall, solemn-faced man called the Friar. "*But He does not raise His hand when a man chooses to throw his life away.*"

"He is right," said Yek, and several of the other ship-dwellers nodded emphatically. "Even if your cause is just, the White Foxes are too many. You will be killed, and then what will happen to your Norn friend?"

Morgan did not reply, because he had seen movement beside the pile of bodies that lay not far from Queen Utuk'ku: something alive that was crawling out of the wreckage of the ogre's huge, fallen arm. What was the monster made from—what blasphemous ritual had brought it to life? The parts Morgan could see looked like wood, but he had seen the creature walk, had almost died under its monstrous heel.

Even as he watched, a tiny pale hand appeared at the end of the ogre's broken arm, scrabbling for a hold; then the rest of the arm, shoulders and at last a bloody, white-haired head emerge from the pile of dead Sacrifices. The ogre's mighty limb had fallen in the center of the ring of white-armored guards, behind the Norn Queen, so no one else had yet noticed the moving figure, but Morgan stared at the survivor with growing excitement.

"By our Sacred Redeemer!" he breathed, and his heart sped like a horse in full gallop. He grabbed Snenneq by the elbow. It was all he could do not to shout. "Can you see? There, in the center of the queen's guards!"

"I cannot see anything while you shake me around so!"

"It's Nezeru! And she's alive!"

Nezeru dragged herself free of the sticky tangle of the last dead Sacrifice, then crawled out into the light and onto the stone of the plateau. Exhausted and battered, she remained on hands and knees for a long moment, like a sacrificial goat with its throat slit, not yet aware it was dead. The sky tilted crazily above her so that she almost fell on her face, and she realized for the first time how much her head hurt.

I crawled through the blood and bones and torn meat of my fellow Sacrifices for a reason, she remembered, but could not immediately remember what that was. *I meant to do something.* Then it came back to her.

The queen is going to kill us all. My father, my mother—Morgan too, if he survived the ogre's attack. The madness is not just in the queen's commanders and minions. It comes down from the Mother of All herself, like poisoned air.

She dragged Cold Root out of its scabbard, although it was a struggle to do so. Utuk'ku stood only a few paces away, perched atop a stone like a crow on a roof ridge, but the shining thing that the queen held was so difficult to see that Nezeru wondered if the blow to her head had robbed her of some of her vision. With an agonizing effort, skull throbbing as if it would crack open, she struggled to her feet, but the weight of Cold Root felt overwhelming: she could barely lift its point off the ground. And though Nezeru did not think she had yet made a sound, the queen somehow knew she was there. The cold silver face turned to regard her.

The Mother of All has never seen me before. Nezeru's mind was beginning to wander. *What will she think of me, so covered in blood and filth?*

Utuk'ku's black eyes glared out of the holes in her mask. She lifted one hand and the air around her spread fingers wavered. Nezeru's skin began to grow hotter and hotter, first as though she had taken a fever, then as if she lay on a funeral pyre. She managed to raise Cold Root to waist level, but the pain was so great that she staggered and almost fell. Smoke was rising in wisps from her armor as Nezeru felt herself begin to burn.

Jarnulf had finally managed to sit up, but the effort made his head throb so brutally that he had not heard or understood most of the Norn Queen's words.

He could not understand why her other enemies lay all around him, living but somehow stunned, doing nothing to resist her, but Jarnulf had made a promise to God—a promise still unfulfilled, to his shame. He at least would remain true to his pledge.

He scrabbled an arrow onto the string of the scavenged witchwood bow, then raised it. His enemy stood only a few dozen paces away, surrounded by guards but exposed atop a tall stone. Hands and arms trembling, he took aim. If he somehow struck her, he might not kill her, but she would at least drop that shimmering object that she held, the weapon with which she was threatening everyone. Perhaps then, he thought, with the shining thing out of her hands, the others would decide to fight.

At that moment, something distracted Utuk'ku; she turned to look behind her. Seeing his chance, Jarnulf let his arrow fly. It sped straight and true, but somehow Utuk'ku perceived the danger and spun back around, swift as a striking viper. She did not even raise her hand, but still somehow the shaft began to slow, as if caught in a powerful wind, then stopped altogether, suspended in the air. For an instant the arrow trailed smoke, then it caught fire. As Utuk'ku glared, the arrow blazed until it was only an ashen replica, then it crumbled and even the remains blew away.

Failed again, was all Jarnulf could think, sick and defeated. *The witch cannot be killed.* Utuk'ku turned away from him again, still concerned with something behind her. But her guards had seen the arrow's flight and now hurried toward Jarnulf, who was already nocking another arrow, though he knew it was pointless. Oddly, a wisp of smoke was rising from a spot just behind Utuk'ku—the queen's slender form blocked his view of what was burning—then she raised the strange object over her head once more. The valley had gone silent, with even the roar of the Narrowdark reduced to what seemed a murmur in Jarnulf's ears.

"No! Don't hurt her!" a terrified voice shouted in Westerling from somewhere across the plateau, and the cry echoed from the cliffs. "*Nezeru!*"

Then a very strange thing happened. Queen Utuk'ku began to look around her, darting glances in all directions as if desperate to learn who had cried out.

Nezeru? Utuk'ku's thoughts crashed in on Jarnulf, but they seemed bizarrely confused and fearful. *No! That can't be! The prophecy—*

Then a gleaming, spiky shape burst out of the queen's torso, a gout of blood spattering down her long white gown. A blade had pierced her from behind. But though Utuk'ku had been stabbed through, from back to belly, she did not fall but only staggered atop her stone, still holding the shimmering, ever-changing object over her head, and Jarnulf let his second arrow fly.

The queen's fleeting thought was all anger and astonishment. *How—?*

Jarnulf's second shaft struck her in the forehead, piercing her shining mask just above her right eye. She took one last step, then tumbled from the stone promontory. The shining thing flew out of her hands and spun through the air, with nothing between it and the stony ground.

As all living eyes followed its path, a huge, hairy gray arm reached up from the ground and caught it. With a grunt that might have been pain or satisfaction, Goh Gam Gar curled the object to his charred, blackened chest and then fell back.

Utuk'ku had fallen and lay sprawled on her back at the base of the stone, the middle of her white gown a welter of blood. Jarnulf's arrow was lodged in her forehead. The queen's mask had split and lay on her face in two pieces.

Simon lay near the base of the wall, next to wounded Jiriki. His eyes were blurry with tears of rage, frustration, and fear. He could not see precisely what was happening, but a shape in Hikeda'ya armor seemed to strike at the Norn Queen from behind, was momentarily held off, then something else distracted Utuk'ku and she turned her back on the first attacker. A moment later the queen fell, and with her fall, the restraint that had held him helpless abruptly left him. Simon could not see whether Utuk'ku had fulfilled her threat to break the crystalline thing she had held, but at least the world had not yet ended, as far as he could tell. He turned to see that the Sithi healer with Jiriki had also regained the use of his limbs and had begun once more to try to stanch Jiriki's wound. Simon could do nothing more to help his friend, so he crawled across the plateau, directly past the spot where the queen had fallen and lay surrounded by white-armored guards. If they noticed him, her soldiers could easily kill him, Simon knew, but he did not care.

No one tried to stop him. He crawled until he reached his granddaughter Lillia where she lay not far from the center of the plateau, still insensible. He stretched out on the stone beside her and stroked her cool cheek, oblivious to his own numerous hurts. "Live," he whispered into her ear, then wrapped his arms around her and pulled her against his chest. She still did not wake. "Live, dear child," he said. "Oh, I beg you."

34

The Promise of an Ending

Shapes stirred and sat up around him, frozen figures returning to life. Jarnulf was suffused with weary joy: he had finally done what he had set out to do so long ago. The wretched queen was dead: he could see her body sprawled on the ground in the circle of her guards. No healers had gathered around her, and not even the silent Queen's Teeth had tried to revive their mistress. No, Utuk'ku must be truly dead, though Jarnulf knew that he would soon follow the queen—her Sacrifice slaves would see to that.

I am coming to You, Lord. A weight seemed to have lifted from him after a very long time, leaving him both utterly free and utterly empty. *I hope You will receive me—I have finally accomplished the task You set for me.*

He might still have escaped—nobody seemed to have noticed him yet, all attention fixed on the fallen queen—but he had one more obligation that he could not ignore. He began to crawl between the sprawled bodies, some dead but many recovering, toward the spot where Goh Gam Gar lay.

Jarnulf could smell the charred flesh and burnt hair long before he reached him. He had been astonished to see the giant reach up and catch the queen's weapon when she fell, and now was almost as surprised to discover that the monster still lived, his massive chest lifting and falling, though each breath was harsh and uneven.

He did not dare to touch the giant for fear of causing him more pain, so he crouched beside the heaving arch of his chest. Goh Gam Gar still clutched the queen's mysterious prize in his huge, singed hand. Even from mere inches away it was difficult for Jarnulf to see it clearly: his eyes would not fix on it for more than an instant but kept sliding off onto other things.

The giant's breathing grew more strained, as if the end was approaching. Jarnulf leaned close, for the first time ever careless of the fangs as long as his fingers, though they were bared in a grimace of agony only a handsbreadth from Jarnulf's face.

Let him kill me if that is his choice. When the queen's soldiers find me, they will send me to a worse fate. He looked past the wide-eyed Queen's Teeth gathered around Utuk'ku's corpse to the smoking remains of Akhenabi, the Lord of Song, lying alone and ignored on the rocky ground. *At least* that *torturing monster has gone before me. God is good!*

It seemed Goh Gam Gar was not quite dead but had been searching for enough air to speak. "I . . . can barely smell you," the giant said, startling Jarnulf considerably. "But I think that is you, mortal man. Have you come to . . . pay back the favors you owe me?"

"It seems so," Jarnulf said. "The tally was two, as I remember."

"Yesssss," breathed the giant, and grinned, showing bloody teeth in the charred wreckage of his face. "And I want . . . both."

"Tell me what I must do."

"First—" said the giant, then was wracked with a cough that seemed to run like a tremor though all his huge body. When he had regained his breath, a dribble of red ran down his burned cheek. His words were halting, and he was clearly in terrible pain, though he still had his wits. "First, promise that when I am dead, I will not be thrown in a pit or burned like the carcass of a beast. Make me a cairn of stones, so those who come here will know that old Gam . . . the eldest of his folk . . . died here."

Tears formed in Jarnulf's eyes. "It shall be done. You saved us all."

It was no short time before the giant again found the breath to speak. "I . . . saved my own folk . . . but they will never know it."

"I will make sure the story is told everywhere."

The giant lifted his immense free hand, misshapen by fire, and waved away Jarnulf's words. "Second . . . take your blade and end me."

"End you?"

The giant let out a groan of anger and pain. "I am ruined, dying, and I hurt so that no words can tell. If there is any honor among your kind, do not make me beg!"

Jarnulf rubbed tears from his eyes. "Peace, friend. A moment."

"I . . . hurt."

Jarnulf crawled to the nearby corpse of a Zida'ya fighter. Her gloved hand still clutched her witchwood sword in a death grip, and he had to struggle to extricate it. He looked briefly at the fallen Sitha's face, the golden skin largely drained of color, and wondered who she had been. *So many killed because of the accursed Norn Queen,* he thought, *and not just here but all over the world and all through the centuries. But at last, her evil is ended.* He wondered who else had helped him slay Utuk'ku—he knew someone had stabbed her as she stopped his first arrow, though he had not been able to see who it was. *In any hap, it was not my hand that shot that final arrow,* he chided himself. *It was God's.*

When he had crawled back to Goh Gam Gar's side, still apparently unnoticed by the queen's guards only a few dozen paces away, who were listening to some high-ranking Hikeda'ya official. Jarnulf laid his hand on one of the few unburnt parts of the giant's body. "I have a blade now," he said.

The giant groaned and lifted his free hand to gesture at his belly. "Here. Beneath my ribs. Thrust upward . . . toward the heart."

Jarnulf set the point of the sword just beneath the bottom of the giant's rib-cage, a short distance from the eye-confounding object that Goh Gam Gar still clutched to his breast, but then hesitated. It did not seem right simply to dispatch him this way, like an old horse, even if it was the giant's own wish.

"May I say some words?" Jarnulf asked. "Prayers to my God?"

"No. Say it after. I . . . hurt."

Jarnulf closed his eyes then, praying silently to himself, and set the heel of his other hand against the base of the hilt, prepared to deliver the giant from his suffering. But as he steeled himself, a heavy hand clutched his shoulder.

"Do not do that," said an odd, pinched voice behind him in Hikeda'yasao speech. "Even in mercy. Wait for a moment."

Jarnulf turned to see an astounding shape leaning over him, manlike in form, but with a body made of shining tiles and a head like some idol out of an ancient barrow. Startled, he let go of the sword; it slid down the giant's broad chest and clanged to the stone. Waiting for the pain to end, Goh Gam Gar moaned, a deep rumble that Jarnulf felt in his guts and bones.

Jarnulf shook off the gauntleted hand on his shoulder and snatched up the fallen blade, prepared to fight. "Who are you? Wait, are you not Hakatri, the creature the queen brought back from death?"

"I am not. That one is gone now, and I have taken his place in Ruyan Vé's armor," the bizarre figure said. *"I do not know who you are, either, nor what you seek to do here, though I sense it has pity in it. I will not stop you—but you are trifling with things beyond your understanding."* The glittering hand pointed at the object the giant clutched. *"I must take this—if it even becomes cracked, the world perishes. What is this giant's name?"*

Staring up at the faceless helm, Jarnulf could only shake his head in astonishment. "He is Goh Gam Gar," he said at last, "and he is not just a giant. Today he has proved himself as good as any man."

The voice from the odd helmet was thin and without much depth, but Jarnulf thought he heard amusement: *"Not all would agree that you honor him by saying so."* The crystal-armored figure leaned closer to the giant. *"Goh Gam Gar, do you hear me? I am Geloë—Sa-Ruyan Ela of the Vao, the same immortal tribe from which your kind springs. We are all the heirs of the Dreaming Sea. I must take the* zhin'ju *from you for the safety of all. Will you release it?"*

The giant opened a single eye. Then, a moment later, it fell shut again. "Take," he growled, and his great clawed hand sagged open. The one who called herself Geloë reached down and lifted the object with the care of a priest handling a holy relic. She would have turned to walk away then, but Jarnulf bade her stop.

"Stay a moment longer," he said. "If you are somehow of the giant's tribe, stand with me as he leaves the world. He did a mighty deed today, I think."

"Yes, he did," said the weird voice. *"May he find peace."*

Jarnulf set the tip of the blade back where it had been and said another swift, silent prayer. Then he shoved the sword through the burned pelt and up under the giant's ribs as firmly as he could, leaning against the creature's scorched body to apply all his strength. As the sword entered Goh Gam Gar's chest the giant let out a gasp and his vast body stiffened, then went limp. A long rattle of air escaped his throat.

"Farewell, brother," said Jarnulf.

He was still praying when the one called Geloë said, *"He is truly gone. And now I must return this to the ship."*

"No, you will not," said a hard, commanding voice. "You will learn the secret and terrible ways of the Cold, Slow Hall instead. *Seize them both!"*

Viyeki was still hiding in the rubble of the tunnel exit, trying to understand what was happening in front of him on the plateau. He could see a confusing struggle around the figure of the queen, then he felt a pain in his ears that threatened to force him to his knees. A moment later the shocking pain ended, but in its wake came another groan from the mountain above him, and more stones fell from the tunnel ceiling. Then, with a scraping noise that almost deafened him, two huge limestone slabs came down at the same time just behind him, enough stone to kill several hundred Viyekis, and another rush of small stones followed.

The whole tunnel is going now, he thought. *Min-Senya and his Delvers knew what they were doing.* To stay was likely certain death. Although a part of him wished nothing more than a swift, anonymous ending, he instead staggered out of the tunnel into the dying light of day, even as another thousandweight of stone tumbled down behind him and sent chips flying. Like arrowheads, several chunks scored his skin even through his heavy robes and a billow of rock dust rolled over and past him. He coughed and staggered on blindly, trying to wipe limestone dust from his eyes. Once outside, at the edge of the plateau, he could see again but could make little sense of what he saw.

Where is the queen? She was right there. Has she fallen? He had scraped the worst of the stone-dust from his face, but still could not find her, although the ring of her guards had contracted into a white-armored knot around the stone where she had stood, as if to protect their mistress. Viyeki could also see that the Hikeda'ya and Zida'ya combatants, who had all mysteriously frozen in place across the entire plateau in mid-battle, were now beginning to move again, slow and confused as sleepwalkers.

Viyeki desperately wanted to learn what had happened but knew it would be foolish to rush out into the open, especially if the fighting was about to resume. The decision had already been made for him, however: several Queen's Teeth guards had spotted him and were hurrying toward him across the stony ground, lances in hand, faces expressionless beneath their pointed white helmets. Viyeki tried to flee back into the passage, but it was blocked with tumbled stone. The leader of the guard troop pointed at him and made a forceful hand-sign, forbidding him to move. Viyeki was terrified but he knew he could not escape the queen's fiercest and most dedicated troops over open ground, so he stood numbly and waited for them to surround him.

Whatever had happened during the last strange and fateful hour, Viyeki knew that his own fate had not changed. He had betrayed his queen and the Hikeda'ya people. He was not even certain why he had done it, except that the questions from Min-Senya and the bruised and bloody face of the poor, simple mortal named Cuff continued to revolve in his thoughts. Had he doomed himself and his family out of pity for flawed creatures like the mortals and Tinukeda'ya?

No, he told himself as the Teeth surrounded him and pinioned his arms behind his back. *Not just for those two. I did what I did because there has been enough killing, enough suffering, and more than enough lies.*

A moment later the silent soldiers were marching him toward the center of the plateau. With the sun disappearing behind the western cliffs a cold wind had sprung up, and as he passed through the long, broad shadow of the still utterly motionless one-armed ogre, he shivered, once more wearily trying to prepare himself for execution.

Nezeru found herself sprawled face-down on the stony ground, her skull throbbing like a sounding drum. Whatever fire-magic Utuk'ku had cast at her was gone, though her face and hands felt scorched. She tried to lift her head and look around, but it was easier to consider than to do. None of her muscles would do their work at first but only twitched uselessly until she finally gained some mastery over herself and could roll over.

Cliffs. The first thing she saw were the peaks along the eastern edge of the valley, their pinnacles lightly brushed by the last rays of the sunken sun, the sky now turning a deep violet. Then she saw the crowd of Queen's Teeth clustered around a small, silent form, and suddenly it all came back to her.

Queen Utuk'ku. She was going to destroy us all. And . . . by the Lost Garden . . . did I truly . . . ? I attacked her. I think . . . I think I may have killed her. She remembered how easily the blade had gone into the Mother of All, as if the queen had been no more substantial than the straw figures the Sacrifices had used to practice their sword play.

She was almost gone. Nothing left . . . but hate.

It had all happened so quickly. She had heard Utuk'ku proclaim the death of all living things, then seen a moment of vulnerability—the queen half-turned, distracted by someone's cry—and in that fateful moment Nezeru's years of training had taken hold. *By the Lost Garden, I struck down the Mother of All! How could it have come to this?*

She rolled over, groaning at the pain of her many injuries, obscured until now by the strangeness of the situation—then she saw the monstrous shadow of the ogre looming above her. Nezeru gasped and tried to push herself backward, but then paused. The huge thing seemed utterly lifeless, as if whatever spirit had inhabited it had now fled. Had she really been caught inside that thing? The shattered remnants of the arm lying nearby brought back a tissue of confused memory—striking the ground, struggling into a crouch, seeing the surprisingly small figure of the queen standing atop a stone not three steps away. And the queen's voice—so powerful!—shouting in her head until she thought her skull would crack.

"The assassin is alive!" someone cried in the Hikeda'ya tongue. A few heartbeats later, half a dozen black-armored Sacrifices had crowded around Nezeru, swords and spearheads leveled at her unprotected throat. She was exhausted, her sword was beyond her reach, and her aching body felt as if she had fallen a great distance. She could not have beaten even one of her former comrades, let alone so many.

No matter, she thought, and lifted her hands in surrender. *I have killed the queen. Even if I saved everyone here, there can be only one penalty for that.*

A tall figure in black armor and fur-lined cloak stepped between the Sacrifices to glare down at her. Nezeru recognized her captor's hawkish face. Kikiti carried the High Marshal's rod of office, but she had seen him when he was still only a general, inspecting the new Sacrifices, lofty and fierce as a bird of prey.

"There has been no shame like this in all our history." Kikiti bit off the words as if they had bones in them. Like most high officers, he no doubt prided himself on his imperturbability, but he was so furious that his hand trembled as he pointed at Nezeru. "See! The queen's assassin wears the armor of our order—insult added to the unthinkable! I will not give this wretched creature to the Order of Song, I will cut her to pieces myself right here—"

"I think you will not," said a new and strange voice, part hiss like escaping steam, part buzz like an ill-played lute string.

All eyes turned, including Nezeru's. A short distance away, surrounded by another small company of Sacrifice soldiers, stood a figure Nezeru could not understand, as strange in its way as the unmoving but astounding ogre. It wore a suit of armor that seemed made of glinting, lucid scales, but it was what should have been its face that caught and held Nezeru's gaze—two round, crystal-covered eyes and an equally round, gaping black mouth. Then she realized the grotesque head was a sort of casque, a battle helmet, although she had never seen one so strange. The weird figure held something in its crystal-studded gauntlets, but she could not make sense of the object, either: it was translucent and incomprehensibly intricate, like a musical instrument made for impossible hands to play.

The helmeted creature lifted this strange thing above its head and the thin, droning voice came again.

"I see you signal to your soldiers, Marshal Kikiti, to surround me," it said. *"Bid them all stand down. Queen Utuk'ku lied about many things, but she did not lie about what the* zhin'ju *of the Ninth Ship can do. Look closely, Marshal. This tiny splotch of black*

in its center is Unbeing itself, prisoned in the waters of the Dreaming Sea, and though it looks to be less than a spoonful, be assured that if I drop this and the water leaks out, that black speck will grow quickly, devouring first you and your soldiers, and eventually all the lands of the Hikeda'ya, too. It will grow greater and greater, swallowing all it finds, and eventually will fill the streets and houses of Nakkiga like a great black flood, swallowing everything—even memory. So, consider carefully, Marshal. Do you think it wiser to have your revenge, or to bargain with me?"

"Demon," snarled Kikiti, but his hands dropped to his side. "What are you? What evil magic brought you?"

"Evil magic?" The crystal-armored shape laughed, a loud whir like the wings of angry hornets. It laid a gauntlet against its own chest. *"Your queen stole this, the hallowed armor of my forebear—stole it out of his grave with his bones still inside it, without respect or ceremony. Then she lured one of the greatest of the Zida'ya back from the dead and forced him into this same armor, all to give her power over that pitiable thing—"* she gestured with a broad, glittering hand toward the ogre—*"so she could steal the deadly object I hold out of the Ninth Ship. And why? Because your beloved Queen Utuk'ku meant to murder every living thing in all the lands—including you, Marshal Kikiti, all your Sacrifices, all their families, and all your folk—simply because she did not want to die alone. And you dare talk to me of evil magic?"*

The inhuman voice had reached a painful strength. It was all Nezeru could do not to cover her ears. Kikiti raised a finger, holding back his troops, but he did not look very patient.

"Who do you think this armor belongs to?" the stranger continued, still holding up the inconstantly gleaming *zhin'ju,* and it was impossible for Nezeru not to think of what would happen if it fell. *"Who do you think built that ship back in the Garden, as well as all the other great ships, and put a heart much like this one into each, so they could traverse the Ocean Indefinite and Eternal and bring all the Garden-dwellers to safety in these lands? The Tinukeda'ya did that—the Vao. My people. And your Mother of All wanted to take it from us and use it to murder the world."*

Kikiti was quivering with such rage that Nezeru feared he would do something violent and foolish. And if the creature brandishing the *zhin'ju* was as angry and reckless as Kikiti, Nezeru thought that Unbeing might still be loosed, ending all and everything.

As Viyeki was driven toward the center of the plateau by Queen's Teeth guards, he could not help observing the unprecedented confusion of Sacrifice troops, officers, and silent Teeth. Many of them still lingered near the body of the queen, which someone had covered with a white spider-silk cloak, but there did not seem to be any order or sense to their milling.

I never thought to see such a day, Viyeki thought. *Once I would have believed it meant the end of the world, the end of everything I most love.* An unexpected thought suddenly came to him. *No matter what happens, I will have outlived the Mother of All—who could have dreamed such a thing?*

Viyeki recognized the tallest of the Sacrifices and his heart sank even lower. It was General Kikiti—no, *Marshal* Kikiti now, and perhaps soon to become King Kikiti. There would be no mercy for him there.

May it be quick, he prayed. *Better a traitor's execution than to go to the Order of Song and be tormented for their amusement. It is too bad the queen's death will likely change so little.*

Standing in front of the marshal, Viyeki saw the weird, armored form of Hakatri. It held something in its gauntleted hands, something Viyeki found strangely familiar, though he felt certain he had never seen it before. A moment later, it came to him: the weird, shining object reminded him of the Breathing Harp. But this object was smaller: if the Harp, the Master Witness that floated above the Well deep under Nakkiga was the size of a war shield or a wagon wheel, this thing was no larger than a serving tray but just as unnatural. *What is happening here?* he wondered, but it was hard to make himself care with his death so near.

I begin to long for it, he thought. *Just for the relief it will bring. I have prepared myself so many times.*

"So you would threaten me and all your own kind with destruction," Kikiti said to the armored thing. "I think that is a bluff. In any case, you cannot be allowed to keep this thing—I would never let such a weapon stay in the hands of the Tinukeda'ya!"

"Do not test me, soldier of Nakkiga," said the thing Viyeki thought was Hakatri. *"Not here, not today."* The buzzing voice was almost without inflection, as strange as a raven's. Viyeki was astonished to hear it, and let out a noise of surprise—when had Hakatri learned to do that? And what had Kikiti meant by calling him Tinukeda'ya? Whatever else Hakatri might have become after returning from death, the resurrected Zida'ya was no changeling.

Kikiti heard Viyeki's gasp and turned. When he saw who the Teeth had dragged to him through the crowd of white- and black-armored soldiers, the marshal unfurled a mirthless smile. "Ah, the chief traitor himself," Kikiti said. "I doubt not that the collapse of the tunnel was your work."

"I am no traitor," said Viyeki, determined not to beg or show fear. "I love my people. If I betrayed anything, it was my former allegiance to a cult of death and destruction."

"No one cares what you think, vermin. If Her Majesty had only listened to me, none of this would have happened."

"And you and all of us would be dead!" Viyeki struggled against the grip of his silent captors.

"Better that than committing the greatest act of treason our people have ever known!" Kikiti waved his hand and one of the Queen's Teeth hesitated for a moment, then pushed Viyeki to his knees. "I will give up the pleasure of making you suffer a lengthy torment in favor of ending you now and leaving your traitor's corpse for rats and crows to pick at, Viyeki sey-Enduya."

"Father?"

Viyeki heard the cry but at first could make no sense of it. Nearby, he could see someone struggling in the hands of several Sacrifice soldiers, but several other soldiers blocked his view. "Who calls?" he said.

"Father?" the voice called again, fearful, astonished. "Is that truly you?"

Viyeki craned his neck, both hope and horror bubbling up inside him. "Nezeru? Oh, daughter, why? Why are you here? I do not want you to see this."

"Drag her over and push her down beside him," Kikiti said with a mixture of fury and triumph. "So Viyeki's daughter was one of the assassins? I should have known it would be so. Oh, by the sacred blood of martyred Drukhi, I am torn! Torn between dispatching the dog and his whelp here beside our martyred queen or knowing that their punishment will continue for countless years!"

"*Do not harm them,*" said the buzzing voice of the creature Viyeki was no longer certain was Hakatri, though he could not guess who else might inhabit the Navigator's armor. *"You will regret it."*

Kikiti laughed harshly. "I think not. Would you destroy everything that lives over the fate of two traitors not even of your own race?"

"I did not say that," replied the helmeted thing. *"I said you will regret it. I have died and returned. I know things you do not, and I can only tell the truth."*

"So you say." Kikiti waved to one of his lieutenants. "Do you have your sword? I see no value except enjoyment in keeping these two alive any longer. Take their heads."

As his daughter was pushed down beside him on the stony ground, Viyeki tried to turn toward her, but a Sacrifice soldier grabbed his hair and pulled it straight up, baring his neck. "Do not fear, Nezeru," he said. "Know that the Garden awaits us."

"I am not frightened, Father." Her tone matched her words.

"The Garden?" Kikiti scoffed. "For you? Enough. Kill them."

"Hold!" cried a loud, firm voice. "What do you think you do here, Marshal Kikiti?"

Viyeki recognized that voice and was almost disappointed. He had readied himself for the fatal, ending blow. Now it seemed he would have to wait again for the inevitable.

"This is nothing to do with you, Prince Templar," Kikiti said with more than a touch of distaste. "I would advise you to stay out of things that do not concern you."

"Would you?" Pratiki's voice had an icy tone that Viyeki had not heard from the prince-templar before, and he felt a momentary flush of joy to hear someone at last stand up to Kikiti. "And who do you think I am, exactly?"

"I know who you are, Serenity," said the marshal. "And I respect you as a high Hamakha noble, and our poor, late queen's relative. But this is a battlefield, and—"

"You mistake me, Marshal," said Pratiki, and the pitiless tone was enough to cause the soldier holding Viyeki's hair to ease his grip. Viyeki turned to see Pratiki staring at Kikiti, eye to eye. Pratiki was accompanied by a dozen Queen's Teeth. "I am not just a Hamakha noble," the prince-templar said, "with the queen's death, I am *the* Hamakha noble. I am Utuk'ku's successor, and the magister you are about to execute without permission is not only high magister of my Builder's Order, but my trusted advisor as well. I order you to release him—and his daughter, too."

The two Sacrifices, recognizing the tone of true Hamakha command, let go of Viyeki and sprang back. For a moment he could only wonder if this might be nothing more than some new and heartbreaking strategy. *Am I to spend the rest of my life on the verge of execution?*

Kikiti stared at Pratiki as if he had never seen him before. The marshal's anger, which several times had seemed near to overcoming him, was now rising again. His hands flexed, as if he wished to close them around someone's neck and snap it. "This cannot be."

"I can assure you, Marshal, it can. High Celebrant Zuniyabe, where are you?" He looked around until he saw the masked celebrant and nodded toward him. "Ah, there. Good. Note my words, please. High Magister Viyeki sey-Enduya and his daughter—what is her name? Viyeki, tell me your daughter's name."

"Nezeru seyt-Enduya." he said breathlessly, still not quite daring to be hopeful.

"There, see that it is put down in the records, Zuniyabe. They have both been charged with treason by High Marshal Kikiti. And they have now both been acquitted."

"What?" Kikiti cried in outrage. "This pair conspired to kill the Mother of All! And did! This filth—" he waved a hand at Nezeru, "stabbed our queen in front of all eyes! This is *all* treason!" Kikiti turned to his Sacrifice soldiers, who were looking from him to Pratiki and the inscrutable ranks of the Queen's Teeth in confusion—as well as, Viyeki thought, a little barely hidden terror. "Will you stand there and do nothing, Sacrifices? Arrest the prince-templar. He has lost his wits!"

"You force my hand," said Pratiki. "I hereby strip you of your Marshal's rank. Queen's Teeth, arrest Kikiti."

There was nothing in all the world that a Hikeda'ya Sacrifice hated and feared more than a confusion of orders. Hierarchy was sacred—the queen at the top, everything else in ordered ranks beneath her, all the way down to the individual soldiers. Kikiti's black-armored soldiers muttered and cast glances at each other, but they clearly had no idea what to do. The Queen's Teeth, though, displayed no such hesitation. The queen was dead, but they were ready to follow her heir. The white-armored guards lowered their spears and forced their way through the still hesitating Sacrifices to surround Kikiti.

"What is this?" Kikiti's expression was a mixture of outrage and dawning uncertainty. "I have always faithfully served the queen!"

"And now you will serve her in whatever place she has gone." Pratiki spoke with fearsome solemnity. "If you had come to question me in private about this confusing time, Kikiti, I would have honored you and treated you like the hero you once were. But you have challenged and threatened me in front of the queen's own guards and the Order of Sacrifice. You have sowed dissension and cast doubt on the Hamakha Clan's right to lead." He lifted a hand and said to the nearest Queen's Teeth officer, "The sentence is death."

Kikiti tried to draw his sword, with the clear intent of attacking the prince-templar, but as Viyeki watched in astonishment, several Queen's Teeth soldiers surrounded him with their spears and disarmed him. Two of them grasped the marshal's arms and forced him onto his knees even as he shouted his protests. The third lifted his sword above Kikiti's neck.

"Will you not even hear my last words?" Kikiti cried.

"You have just spoken them." Pratiki flicked his finger. A moment later, Kikiti's head, hair still knotted in precise war-braids, was rolling on the ground as his life's blood sprayed and gurgled onto the stone.

"Does anyone else here wish to contest my right to rule the Hikeda'ya?" asked Pratiki, turning from the headless corpse. "No? I thought not."

In a day already filled with things that had never happened in all of history, Viyeki now looked at his daughter's face. Nezeru was bloodied and ash-smeared but apparently whole. Wordlessly, he opened his arms to her; then, also wordlessly, she crawled to him and was folded in his embrace.

"I will make my camp here on the plateau for now," said Pratiki calmly. "There is much to do and much to decide in the hours ahead. Captain," he said to the nearest of the Queen's Teeth, "you and an honor guard will carry our queen's body to one of the caverns where she may remain in sacred rest until her mortal remains can be returned to Nakkiga. And send a goodly number of your men to that bridge over the gorge, to keep the rest of the Order of Sacrifice on the far side—I do not need any upstart officers hoping to become the next Kikiti. Ah, and send someone to find Lady Miga of the Jinnata Clan, who should be among the crowd of nobles across the gorge and bring her to me." As the white-armored soldiers went off to do his bidding, Pratiki turned to the thing in what Viyeki thought of as Hakatri's armor, though it seemed clear to him now that Hakatri no longer inhabited it. "And by what name do I call you?"

"I was born Sa-Ruyan Ela," it said in a flat hum like a cricket's evening song. "But I was more often known as Geloë."

"I recall the name, I think. Let us speak together now, you and I," said the new lord of the Hikeda'ya. "You hold something dangerous to all of us, and we must resolve that first. Then we will assemble the others. It seems we have a new world to discuss."

"We do, Pratiki," said the strange, armored figure. *"And perhaps not just one."*

Lillia stirred in his arms. Her downy lashes fluttered, then her eyes opened. "Grandfather?"

"I'm here with you, little cub." He gave her a squeeze that was meant to be reassuring, but he could not help worrying he had squeezed her too hard. "How do you feel?"

Her eyes opened wider as she saw Jiriki lying on his makeshift bed nearby, his face so pale that he looked almost like a mortal—or even like one of his Hikeda'ya cousins. A moment later she looked up at the bumpy ceiling. "Am I awake? Who is that over there?"

"Yes, you are awake. And that is Jiriki—my Sitha friend. You met him before."

She frowned. "I think I remember. Where are we?"

At the end of the world, he almost said, but perhaps now it would not be that. "We are safe." His granddaughter seemed well, but Jiriki was very weak, his breathing slow and shallow.

"Your friend looks ill," said Lillia. "What happened to him?"

"He saved us all. He fought against a terrible thing and held the bridge. But he was hurt. I am afraid for him." For a moment his own chest contracted, and he feared he would weep. Simon had cried more than a few times of late, but just now he did not want to frighten his granddaughter.

Outside the healers' cave, he knew, matters of life and death were being discussed. A part of him was just as happy to have one less crushing responsibility, but he had been a king too long to feel entirely comfortable letting anyone—except for Miriamele, his beloved Miri—make decisions for him. *But these are not my decisions,* he told himself. *Though they may affect me and mine.* That thought brought a sharp spike of pain. *Mine. What is mine anymore? This child, yes—mine to protect. But her brother is gone, my wife is dead, and our home, the symbol of our kingdom, has burnt to the ground.* For a moment he was again filled with a caustic hatred for the Queen of the Norns. *I'm glad that witch is dead. I only wish it hadn't been so quick.* Still, it was astonishing that it had happened at all. Who would have guessed that such a powerful sorceress could be killed with a sword and a single arrow?

As if she felt something of his dark thoughts, Lillia squirmed a little. "What happened to the shiny-face lady? She tried to catch me! She scares me."

Simon knew who the shiny-face lady had to be, but otherwise had no idea what his granddaughter meant, since she had been nowhere near the fighting or Utuk'ku's death. A terrible thought came to him: could Lillia have been aware while Geloë had used her body to face down the Norn Queen and Unbeing?

"The bad lady is gone," he told her. "She'll never come back. You don't have to be afraid of her anymore."

"What about the ocean lady?"

Simon could only shake his head. "Ocean lady?"

He heard a slow, muffled tread behind him. *"She means me,"* said a droning, inhuman voice.

Lillia shrank close against his chest. "Is that really you?" she asked. "Why do you look like that?"

"Yes, it is me, child. This . . . armor . . . is a place for me to be now. For a little while."

Simon craned his neck to look at Geloë. The glitter of her crystal-tiled armor was muted here in the cave, but the shadows made the strange, round-mouthed helmet even more unnerving.

"I am glad to see your granddaughter is well."

Simon reminded himself that this was still Geloë, however odd her appearance. "She called you 'ocean lady'. Is that because you are Tinukeda'ya? One of the Ocean Children? But how would she know that?"

"I know about the ocean because I was there!" said Lillia with defiant pride.

"Yes, child, you were."

"It was far away, in another place. And I went into the water! I had to! Because the silver mask lady was after me and you wouldn't come to help me!"

The expressionless mask regarded her. *"I am not certain that is exactly how it happened, Lillia, but we can talk more about it later—all of us,"* she added, nodding to Simon. *"For now, though, I have come to see Jiriki."*

"Can you help him?" Simon heard the desperate hopefulness in his own voice. "Please, Geloë, can you help him?"

"I offer no promises, or even much hope," she said. *"But there are things to be discussed and decided, and he is the Protector of Year-Dancing House, which means he would speak for most of the Zida'ya here."*

Simon lurched awkwardly to his feet with his granddaughter still in his arms and followed Geloë to Jiriki's side. Geloë's gauntlets were also made of crystal tiles, but the palms and fingers were woven in a mesh of gold wires, like those that held the scales of the armor together. She knelt slowly—Simon could not tell if it was ceremony or merely the clumsiness of the tiled garment—then touched one of her gold-threaded fingers to Jiriki's forehead and held it there for a substantial, silent time. Next, she placed her hands on either side of the bulge where the terrible wound in his chest had been packed with linen and herbs, then bandaged by Sithi healers. She knelt over him for no little time, swaying slightly, but always with her gloved hands pressed against his chest.

Simon thought he saw Jiriki move a little, and as she finally lifted her hands he felt a flash of hope, but of course the weird, masklike helmet showed nothing of Geloë's thought.

"Can you help him? Will he heal?"

She was silent for a long, long moment, and his heart sank. Finally, she reached out and placed one of the gold-woven gloves on Simon's arm. He felt a crackle on his skin, like the snap-sting from rubbing a cat's fur. *"I did what I could, but I do not believe he can heal. His wounds are too great. But I have managed to give him a little strength, because he wanted it and he helped me. Because he is not ready."*

"I don't understand," said Simon.

"She means," said Jiriki, his voice as weak and breathy as distant flute-song, "that I will not last much longer, Seoman my friend, but I am not ready to go and seek the Garden until I have said my farewells to those I love."

Weeping again—it seemed he had been shedding tears for days—Simon reached out and took Jiriki's cold hand.

"Do not be sad." He spoke slowly. Each breath before speaking seemed a struggle. "Nothing is given to us when we come to this world but the promise of an ending, Seoman—so we must believe it to be a gift."

35

Widows

It had been a merry night, perhaps the first truly happy time Miriamele experienced since she fled Nabban—certainly the first since she had heard the news about Simon. The trolls' joy at discovering she was alive had been contagious, making her consider for the first time how lucky she had been to survive this last, terrible year. Nothing could ease the crushing daily burden of having to go on without her beloved husband but being reunited with their Qanuc friends gave her a chance to laugh and grieve with people she loved and people who had loved him.

Now it was morning. Miriamele stirred, her head still muzzy with the wine they had all drunk during their middle-of-the-night reunion; she dimly realized that she had fallen asleep in her high-backed chair. Even Binabik, while still maintaining the superiority of the trollish *kangkang* liquor, in its absence had allowed himself to imbibe a quantity—a very healthy quantity—of Perdruinese brandy. After that, he had sung the story of how the hero Chukku was saved from death by the divine snow maiden Qinkipa, acting out all the parts with such intoxicated verve that Miriamele almost choked herself giggling. Tiamak, a little less convivial than he might have been if Thelía were present, had been very happy to see Binabik and Sisqi again although, after a bit of celebrating, he went back to bed. Jesa lasted a little longer, then had been called to soothe little Serasina. But Miri and her two old friends had sat up hours longer.

Now, as she tried to rise from the chair where she had fallen asleep, she discovered that something was clutching her hand. She looked down and saw that it was Sisqi, fast asleep on a stool beside her, leaning against the arm of Miriamele's chair with Miriamele's fingers clutched in her own small hand as though she had been keeping her flatlander friend from vanishing once more.

"So, you are now awake," said Binabik, rising from a pile of blankets in the corner of the royal tent. "Here, let me give help." He gently extricated Miri's hand, and when Sisqi murmured unhappily, bent and kissed his wife on the forehead. She frowned, but it was only mild confusion, not unhappiness, and a moment later she relaxed back into deep slumber.

"We have been many nights traveling," he said. "And days, too, following your army, wondering whose army it was and if they were friends we could trust. If you are not minding the company in your tent, please let her sleep for more time."

"Mind?" Miri laughed. "As if I could feel anything but joy to find you both again." She straightened, arching her back, trying to stretch out the aches. Sleeping in a chair instead of a bed was for young people. *But only two moons ago, you were sleeping on the ground when you and Jesa escaped from that madman's house,* she reminded herself. *And you were glad of it. Usires said, "A hovel will be as good as a palace if you are with Me," and it's also true if you are with people who are close to your heart.*

And there will be hard days ahead, a siege and perhaps deadly fighting, she reminded herself. *Who knows when happiness like last night's will come again? Take nothing as given, Queen Miriamele of Erkynland.*

Before she sent a messenger to Tiamak to begin the day's business, she tottered back to where Sisqi still slept and lifted her—Sisqi mumbled in protest, but acquiesced—into the queen's now-empty chair, then placed a kiss on her Qanuc friend's forehead.

"She is most uncooperative," Pasevalles said. "It begins to irritate me."

"Who?" asked Hulgar. "The Duchess?"

Pasevalles permitted himself a small sigh of frustration. *I suppose I should have guessed that the largest, strongest mercenary from the grasslands might not also be the cleverest.* "I meant Countess Marah, Aglaf's wife. She has given back the map page that shows the tunnel entrance, but even with her husband dead and her son likely dead too, she still will not tell us what we most need to know."

"Where the gold is," said Hulgar.

"Yes, the gold." Pasevalles rose from his chair in the great hall. "I know that shortly before the grasslanders' attack began Aglaf's reeves collected the taxes. Nobody knows better than I do that none of those taxes ever reached the Hayholt. So, we will try once more, because time is growing short. Do you hear the sounds of building outside? The Duchess—or whatever upstart uses that name—is preparing to knock down our castle walls. I would prefer not to be here when that happens."

Hulgar seemed to think this over carefully. "Even if we use the tunnel, where will we go?"

"I sent Fecca the Gemmian to Nabban for a reason, nor is it his first journey there on my behalf. He is preparing our way."

The grasslander snorted. "Preparing himself a way, most likely. If you sent him with any gold or silver, he's already gone."

"That is not for you to worry about," said Pasevalles. "What *is* yours is the task of making certain the tunnel beneath the crypt still leads to the old mine shaft."

Hulgar frowned. "Still leads to . . . ? Of course it does. Tunnels don't change direction—they're not rivers."

"Idiot." Pasevalles no longer needed to hide his contempt—not with the slow Norn poison already flowing in Hulgar's veins. By the time the huge clansman realized the antidote was useless, Pasevalles would no longer need him. "No, tunnels do not change direction, but ceilings can fall, rocks slide. It will do us little good to try to make our way out in a bad moment only to find that we are caught between a collapsed wall and an angry besieging army."

"Huh." Hulgar nodded. "I see. What should I do?"

"Take Broga and at least half dozen strong men and make certain the way is clear. The besiegers have been searching all over the countryside, but they have not yet found the hidden way into the mine. Make certain that is still true, then hurry back to me."

"Why do we not leave now?"

"Without telling your men, hoping they do not notice us going? Or should we take them all with us and then feed them and watch over them while we flee to Nabban? They would sell us out in a heartbeat. They are mercenaries, Hulgar."

"So am I," he said with childlike sullenness.

"Yes, but your life is tied to mine, isn't it? Because I, at least, am no fool."

Hulgar looked at him for a long moment. The Thrithings-man with the mangled mouth had never been good at disguising his feelings, and the look he gave contained such hatred that Pasevalles was more convinced than ever that the huge man's usefulness was nearly at an end.

"I think it is a mistake," Tiamak told her.

"Which mistake do you mean?" Miriamele asked. "You seem to have more than a single objection." She looked out across the grassy meadow, the turf torn and scarred with muddy ruts during the battle in which her husband had died. She could not look at it long.

"It is a mistake to begin the siege before we have finished discovering all the ways they might escape Winstowe Castle," said her counselor. "What if you drive Pasevalles out before we find all the places he can escape? We might never find him again."

The hammering of the builders assembling the siege engines was beginning to make Miri's head ache. Several hundred men were hauling logs down from the wooded slopes on the far side of the Laestfinger to be floated across to the near side, where they were being cut and shaped. "My skull is splitting," she said. "Let us go into the tent where I can hear myself think. Not to mention take off this veil. It feels like I'm wearing a shroud."

Once inside, she threw the veil back and let one of the soldiers waiting attendance pour wine for her and her counselor. Tiamak took his cup in both hands and stared into it like a worried scryer looking for hopeful omens.

"Drink up," she said. "You look like you need it."

He set the wine down untouched on the large wooden chest that the queen was using for a table. "You have not answered my question, Majesty. What if Pasevalles takes flight before we are ready?"

"He doesn't know that we're stopping up all his burrows. And he is too arrogant to abandon the castle simply because some other pretender to the throne—as he likely sees it—has set up shop in front of his bolt hole."

"Assumptions, Majesty, assumptions. We have all underestimated him many times. He is a monster, but he is no fool."

Miri waved her hand. "I never said he was, Tiamak. But neither am I. I say he will not simply flee this stolen fortress of his but will send soldiers first—probably his Thrithings mercenaries—to make certain whatever tunnels he plans to use are open. That will make it even easier to discover which tunnels he prefers, will it not?"

"Unless his sentries atop the walls spot the Erkynguards who are currently spread all through the hills, being led to those places by the local people. Then the game is up."

"If he can't escape, then he will fight," she said with grim relish. "And I will have him."

Tiamak shook his head in frustration. "And many more of our people will die. Why am I here when you clearly have no intention of listening to my advice?"

"A sensible queen—or king—listens to all advice, then chooses what she will do. You know that. I trust you and your sharp wit, Tiamak, or Simon and I would not have given you such an important position. But that does not mean I will always be ruled by your counsel. You know that, too."

He sighed. "Yes, Majesty. But that does not mean I can stand by and watch without sharing my unhappiness. And *you* know *that*."

She smiled a little. "I do. Now, tell me what you hear from Erchester."

"Duke Osric is still weak—and to be truthful, still a little shaky in his understanding of everything that has happened. Which means that in many ways Lord Captain Zakiel is ruling in your stead, whether he wishes to or not."

"There are worse men than Zakiel to have that charge. Unless you think he might be another Pasevalles, or one of the traitor's secret servants. But you assured me he was not."

"A cloud of uncertainty still hangs over everything. The fire destroyed so much. But, no, I do not believe Zakiel had any idea what Pasevalles was doing, or I would have protested against leaving him as Osric's right hand." He frowned. "But we are playing a dangerous game as long as you do not proclaim your true identity. Any noble with a claim to the throne, however tenuous, may decide to test the waters. Do you really want to put down a rebellion of your own barons when they would flock to your banner immediately if you reveal yourself?"

"I take the problems in the order they must be confronted," she said. "And I make my choices by what is most important. Right now, I do not want Pasevalles to know I am alive. Zakiel may be trustworthy, but who can guess what other nobles or military commanders might have taken the criminal's gold? Your best advice cannot save me from a knife in the back or poison in my soup."

He sighed, a longer and deeper sound of resignation this time. "You are the queen, Miriamele. You are *my* queen, and I swore to serve you and Simon faithfully. My shame at helping to harbor a traitor for so long, if only by my own obliviousness, prevents me from arguing this with you."

"Nonsense. Argue away. You were not the only one Pasevalles fooled. Simon and I were just as blind to what he was doing."

"Poor Bishop Boez. We all made mistakes, but he saw what was wrong and tried to tell me . . . then paid for it with his life. The signs were all there if I could only have understood them—"

"Stop," she said. "There is more than enough guilt and shame for all of us, Tiamak. We can wallow in it, or we can do what we must to root out the causes and destroy the source. I have thought long about this too, but what I do not understand is men like Pasevalles. We gave him land, gold, and respect, but all he wanted was to harm us."

"Most people, I think, wish only to live their lives in a little comfort, and free from fear," said Tiamak. "Although to be fair, many want something more of life—I ached to see more of the world than I could from my hut in Village Grove. But there are a number of men in this world—and women, I suppose—who only want to take everything for themselves, or to deny things to others. Aedonites would say they were corrupted by the Devil. Or it could simply be that they have some hole in their spirit that nothing can fill, but still they keep trying to shove more in. Sadly, I think there will always be such creatures among us."

"But how can we keep such folk from having the power to harm others?"

"That, not even the wisest counselor could tell you."

She smiled. "Nor even try, I see." She shook her head. "So, then, bring out your map and tell me what you have learned about the hills around the castle—"

An armored Erkynguard entered the tent and bowed. "There is someone to see you, Majesty."

"Do you forget, Hubart? You must call me 'Duchess'," she told him sternly. "Until we have won here, Queen Miriamele must remain dead. Always remember that. But you should also remember that I can hardly receive visitors if we want to protect that secret."

Guardsman Hubart was clearly uncomfortable. "But that's the problem, Maj . . . Duchess. She says she knows who you are—she named you. She said you know her, too, and she begged to speak to you." He made a face. "Actually, it is wrong to say she begged. It was more like a command. 'Tell your mistress that her aunt wants to speak with her.' That's what she said."

"Aunt?" For a moment, Miriamele was too surprised to understand, then it suddenly came to her. "By our Lady, she has nerve. But she always did. Bring her in."

The guard bowed and went out. He returned in a matter of moments, leading a cloaked figure in ragged, travel-stained clothes. Even before the visitor threw back her hood Miriamele knew she was right, and when the spare, handsome features and short gray hair were revealed, only said, "It has been a very long time since we saw each other last, Lady Vorzheva. Before we were both widowed."

"So. How long has it been?" Miriamele had not yet asked her visitor to sit, and Tiamak wondered if she would. He had seldom heard the queen's voice colder. "More than twenty years, that is certain. You look . . . well."

"I look like an old woman," said Vorzheva flatly. And it was true, Tiamak thought: Vorzheva's handsome, hawkish face was deeply lined, her complexion darkened and weathered by what he guessed had been years living on the sunny grasslands. Still, he thought, she carried herself as though she too, were a queen, Majesty's equal counterpart.

"Neither of us has escaped the insults of time. La! What a shame," said Miriamele. "How did you even know that I still live? Most think me dead."

Vorzheva waved her hand. "Your soldiers buy supplies from many Thrithings-folk out here, especially horses and feed. A man of my Stallion Clan heard rumors from your camp about who this *Duchess* truly was."

"Really?" Miriamele frowned. "Then some of my guards should be punished, it seems—or maybe some of my loose-lipped nobles. But enough of pleasantries, my lady. The greater question is, Why are you here? I know you did not come simply to mend a broken friendship."

"Friendship?" Vorzheva seemed about to fly into a rage, but closed her eyes until she was calm again. "No. No, Your Majesty, I have come to beg for my son's life." For a moment she and Miriamele stared at each other, then—to Tiamak's utter astonishment—Vorzheva got down on her knees. "I have come to beg, Miriamele, to crawl before you. Does that please you?"

Miriamele's laugh was harsh. "Please me? Lady, when did I become your enemy? Because I was never told of it."

"You . . . you are not my enemy," said Vorzheva, but the words seemed to come out against her will.

"Strange." Miriamele was clearly struggling against her own rage. "Because in all the years Simon and I hunted for your husband Prince Josua, I heard nothing from you—but I heard of many unpleasant things you said about us."

Vorzheva lowered her eyes. "I was angry then, Majesty."

"Josua's friends, Count Eolair and Lord Tiamak—do you remember them? Tiamak visited you in your house in Kwanitupul. The two of them searched from the southern islands to Rimmersgard for news of Josua, but all we learned was that after he was gone, you told everyone who would listen that we had turned him against you, that we had taken him away from you. The friends that loved him best in all the world!" The queen did not seem to know what to do with her hands, and at last folded the in her lap. "Before I grant you any further audience, you must answer a question. No one we can find has seen or heard anything of Josua in more than a score of years—we came to fear that he must be dead. The only one we could never ask was you—his wife, the mother of his children. So, do you know anything of what happened to my uncle?"

Vorzheva looked up. Tiamak could not untangle the mixture of emotions he saw on her face. "I do not know. He left us and never came back. No one brought word of him. I did everything I could, but I was angry. I thought he had left me for some city-woman, the sort that you and his other noble friends would approve." Down went the eyes again. "After a time passed, I began to think it was not a woman that had taken him, but some bandit or murderer, that he had been killed on his journey."

"Strange that you only decided that after twenty years," said the queen. "Twenty years when you did not speak to us or ask us for the help we would gladly have given you."

"I wanted no help." The older woman sounded angry, but something painful was in her face. Tiamak thought she looked like a soldier who had survived a terrible losing battle. "It was not only you and your husband that I turned away from."

Miriamele considered this for a short time, then gestured to the chest beside her. One of the soldiers hurried forward to remove the ewer and cups. "Sit, if you wish, and I will listen. I do not care much for you, Lady, but I will hear you out—which is more than you ever did for Simon or for me."

Vorzheva rose slowly and seated herself on the chest. Tiamak was still astounded that the woman he and others had searched for so long had simply walked into Miriamele's tent. A soldier offered her a cup of wine, but Vorzheva shook her head.

"Your son, you said." Miriamele sipped her own wine. "Deornoth. We have heard nothing of him, either—until now."

"He no longer goes by that name," said Vorzheva. "He calls himself Unver now."

Tiamak sat up, wondering if he had heard wrongly, but Miriamele seemed intent on other things. "And where is he, that you would beg for his life?"

Vorzheva took a breath. "Inside the castle you are besieging."

The queen's eyes widened. "Inside Winstowe Castle? With the traitor Pasevalles? I know better now than to expect loyalty or even simple politeness from you, Lady Vorzheva, but your son fights for the man who tried to kill me and take the throne? That seems bad judgment of an entirely different order."

"He does not fight for Pasevalles," said Vorzheva. "He hates him. He has told me many times."

Miriamele waved her hand. "I think this audience is over, my lady. I will not deliberately murder your son, but neither will I put my own soldiers at risk trying to capture him while they are fighting for their lives. If he survives and is taken prisoner—well, we shall see then what happens."

"You do not understand! My son is no mere soldier—his life is worth far more than you can imagine. He holds the clans together. If he dies, there is no telling what might happen."

Tiamak's alarm was growing. "Majesty, I think—"

Miriamele held up a hand to quiet him. "What do you mean, 'he holds the clans together'?"

For a moment Vorzheva's stubborn, vexed expression did not change. Then something like shame made her lower her eyes. "He is the lord of all the grasslands. My son is Unver Shan."

Miriamele's cup fell from her fingers. Wine ran out, puddling in the costly Perdruinese rug. "Your son is Unver Shan? *The man who killed my husband?"*

For a frightening moment, Tiamak thought that the queen might grab the other woman by the throat. The soldiers near the door of the tent watched him, waiting for a signal. Vorzheva lifted her hands to her breast and crossed them, like a bound prisoner. "That is a lie!" she cried. "I swear by the Grass Thunderer and Heaven itself that it is a lie. Ask any who were there—ask any who saw what truly happened. I did."

The queen had gone as white as a Norn. From her labored breathing Tiamak guessed that she could barely contain her fury. "Tiamak?" she said in a strangled voice. "Is it a lie?"

"I was not there, Majesty," he said hurriedly. "You may remember I was not at Winstowe. But I have heard stories, most notably from my helper, Brother Etan, who was on the battlefield and saw it all."

"Then call him. We will hear what this witness has to say about Vorzheva's murdering son."

"We cannot, my queen," Tiamak said. "Etan has gone north, I fear. I sent him on . . . on an errand of my own. A *most important* errand," he quickly added. "But there are others who were with Simon on the field there and saw what happened, although I only learned that in the last few days. I meant to tell you, but the siege, and the reappearance of Binabik and his wife—" He broke off. "I am sorry, Majesty."

"And what do *they* say about Winstowe, these others?" The queen's voice was icy.

"That your husband recognized Unver as Josua's son. That Simon bared his breast to him but Unver refused to strike. It was no sword-blow but an apoplexy that took the king—perhaps because of his great astonishment at learning Unver's identity." He spread his hands. "That is only what I have heard, but I have heard it from several people."

One of the soldiers had picked up Miriamele's fallen cup. She waited until he had refilled it and handed it to her. She took a swallow, then another, before turning back to Vorzheva. "Perhaps your son did not kill my husband, my lady—not precisely. But your people most certainly invaded Erkynland, which was why my husband was there, fighting. Tell me, Vorzheva, even if that terrible, pointless war had not happened, why is your son—this Unver Shan—hiding in a castle with my mortal enemy, the murderer and thief who tried to destroy my family and steal the High Throne? I cannot imagine what answer you will make, but I confess I am interested to hear your excuses for him. Why is this Unver with Pasevalles if he hates him so?"

Vorzheva was staring at the rug again. She remained on her knees, like a criminal awaiting execution. "I . . . I do not know."

"A poor answer for someone seeking clemency. Try again."

Vorzheva finally looked up in helpless fury. "I do not know! When I heard the rumors that my son was gone, I went to the thane he had left to rule in his place. But Odobreg would not tell me why Deor—why Unver had gone to the stone castle of Pasevalles. I told Odobreg I would kill myself in his wagon if he did not answer me. I held a knife to my heart."

"Ah," said Tiamak. "When he came back from the Thrithings, Count Eolair reported that you are a deft hand with a blade."

"Not so deft as to manage to kill herself with one," Miriamele snapped back.

Vorzheva colored but would not be distracted. "Thane Odobreg did not want the Shan's mother dead. I know he was telling me the truth when he said Unver had not explained his decision. Odobreg remembered that my son had said something about being angry at being a stone-dweller's pawn. My son believed Pasevalles had bribed someone to poison the old Thrithings leader Rudur Redbeard and he wanted to see this Pasevalles for himself. That is all Odobreg could tell me." She hung her head again, but her jaw was tight with suppressed anger. "It is all I know."

"That is certainly the strangest story I have heard in a year full of strange stories," said the queen.

Tiamak thought Miriamele might be underestimating the quality and quantity of strangeness that had surrounded the throne for months, but he remained silent.

"But even if what you say is true—that your son has gone to Pasevalles not to help him, but to learn something about him . . ." She waved one hand. "I still sit in the same position. I will not connive at his death, but I will not risk my men's lives for his sake, either. He chose his own path. I do not understand it, and I will not waste time trying. I *will* see Pasevalles on the gibbet. Everything else will be as it will be."

Vorzheva slowly rose, then stood looking down on the queen in a way that made Tiamak look nervously to the guards. "So," she said at last. "I expected no more from you, but I had to try—had to hope. I will go back to my people and tell them what has happened here today."

"You will do nothing of the sort. You will remain here until the battle is over. *Guards!*" the queen called out. "Take this woman and find accomodation suitable for a noblewoman. Treat her with fairness and courtesy or risk my displeasure, but she is not to leave this camp without my permission."

As the soldiers surrounded her, Vorzheva drew herself up, prepared to deliver some threat or curse.

"And cover her mouth until she's away from me or I might change my mind," Miriamele said. "Go, my lady. And thank your luck I am not the monster you have made me out to be."

When the Erkynguards had led out the furious, struggling Vorzheva, Miriamele turned to Tiamak. "I don't want to see that look, old friend. What else could I do?"

"You mistake me, Majesty. I am shocked, but not at you. I am amazed by what has happened here today. Vorzheva herself, after all these years! And her son—Prince Josua's son—is the Shan of all the grasslands."

Miriamele's face was grim. "She expects me to move all Heaven and earth to save her son—a man raised to hate us and too foolish to stay where he belongs." She lifted her wine but stopped before the cup reached her lips. Her hand was shaking. "Is all that was once good destined to end in bitterness, Tiamak? Is this all that's left of the story you and I and Simon tried to make? Old quarrels still plaguing us and young fools who do not remember the past?"

"I hope not," Tiamak said. "But as Simon used to say, no one can see the end of a story when they are in it."

"He was right."

To Tiamak's surprise, tears were running down Miriamele's cheeks. "I will never forgive him for leaving me behind to finish our story alone, but my husband was right, and I can see no good ending before us. Perhaps God believes that if we knew what awaits us, we would never find the strength to finish living our stories."

"Or perhaps even God doesn't know how things will end."

Miriamele looked at him, then tipped back her head and swallowed down her wine in a single gulp. She wiped her lips. "Perhaps not," she said.

Little Serasina had begun to crawl. Now that she had found she could do it, she fought like a wet cat against being held.

"Now you," Jesa said. "Now you. Here, have a sweetmeat." She handed the infant a bit of sugared plum, holding it steady until the tiny, fat fingers curled around it and conducted it to the rosebud mouth.

There were better places for a child to be than in a siege camp, but after the attempted assassination by Aglaf's pitiful son, Queen Miriamele had decided neither of them should be left behind. Jesa had never wanted to leave the queen's side in the first place. She trusted Miriamele—more in some ways than she had trusted even Canthia, who had sometimes forgotten that Jesa was a person and not another child or piece of pretty furniture.

But she could not help that, Jesa thought sadly. *In those last months Canthia was so frightened! And she was right to be so.* The thought of her friend's terrible ending came back to Jesa nearly every day, and when she did not have little Serasina to hold, she found herself looking desperately for something, anything, to distract herself.

"But here you are," she told the baby now. "Here you are." Death ended only one life at a time, after all—other lives had to continue.

Jesa had been raised to believe that when death came, She Who Waits To Take All Back summoned your spirit out of your body, leaving the husk behind, but her people did not speak much about what happened afterward. They simply said, "So-and-so has gone with Her" and that was enough. The corpse was carried to high ground, the *jom mologi* or 'death hill' to be burned, then the ashes were scattered over the waters of the swamp. Soon after, an ancestor stone would be painted for the family, to keep the departed's spirit close to the home they had known in life.

But what will happen to me if I die here? Who will paint my ancestor stone? And what home will it live in? She no longer knew where home was. Red Pig Lagoon was far in the past, the Sancellan Mahistrevis had been taken, and the Hayholt burned.

Serasina belched loudly, then kicked her legs with pleasure at her own cleverness.

Ah, well, Jesa told herself, *living or dead, as long as I can watch over this child, I will be content.*

Even inside the tent, Jesa kept sleeping Serasina bundled close against her body under her cloak. The winter weather was not overly chill, but for someone raised in the Wran, who had then spent years in the warm southern climate of Nabban, even a mild day like this one felt like a freezing assault to her. The queen had told her a few tales of the Storm King's War, and the horrors of the unending, bitter winter had stayed with Jesa and haunted her sleep. People died sitting up, Miriamele had told her, frozen in place like statues, only discovered days after one of the blizzards when neighbors could finally dig through the snow.

The queen's tent was the largest in the camp but warmed by several braziers. Jesa found a place to sit, readjusted sleeping Serasina beneath her cloak, and watched the smoke from the coals entwine toward the gap in the roof to be blown away by the intermittent winds.

It took no little time for the queen's various advisers to assemble, but at last they were all seated on benches. The walls of the tent trembled in the Jonever wind, and Jesa could hear it thrashing the trees outside.

Miriamele stood up. She still wore her dark, mourning clothes, but she had dispensed with her veil. "I have been thinking long and carefully," she began, "in large part because of suggestions that our able counselor Tiamak has made. Many, *many* times." She gave the Wrannaman a fond, mocking look. "When I first decided to keep myself hidden and the truth of my survival secret, it was because I feared the traitor Pasevalles might have secret allies among the nobles, and that we could not hunt for him properly while having to constantly guard against unexpected treachery. Also, I did not know what gifts or weapons he might have had from the Norn Queen. Although there have been attacks on us from his mercenaries, and he tried to use Count Aglaf's poor son to assassinate me, the barons and the rest of the nobles have shown no sign of rising to support Pasevalles and have even been sending inquiries to know if I am truly Duchess Nelda, Osric's wife. In other words, the fears about Pasevalles' reach were properly cautious, but no longer seem necessary. We have surrounded his lair, but still no allies have appeared to help him."

"None that we have seen," said Baron Norvel.

"Our scouts have ranged far and wide," the queen said. "In truth, the local people have already turned against him simply because his grassland mercenaries have been violent in gathering supplies. If Pasevalles has hidden allies, bought with gold stolen from us, then they have cheated him by not coming to his aid—is that not right, Lord Tiamak?"

"We have certainly seen no sign of such allies."

Despite her occasional awkward exchanges with him, Jesa was still thrilled to see a man of her own people in such a position of trust. She thought Baron Norvel and the other important folk seemed to listen to him as attentively as they would a well-regarded Erkynlandish noble. *And why shouldn't they?* she thought. *This man from little Village Grove has proved himself right about so many things.*

"Thus," said Miriamele, "as Lord Tiamak has long suggested, I think it a good time to end the masquerade. Lady Vorzheva, wife of my uncle, Josua, was able to find me and demand my help, so the secret is already fraying at the edges. There seems little value any longer in trying to keep my survival secret, and there may be great advantage. At the very least, it will ensure that any other ambitious nobles reconsider their plans. It is time to let the arch-criminal Pasevalles know that the woman he tried to kill is alive and now sits outside the walls of his hiding-hole. I want him to know, and I want it to frighten him. So we will call for a parley."

"Do you truly think he will come himself?" asked Baron Snell.

"No, but even if he sends someone who does not recognize me, just being told who I am—being told that he failed to murder me—will fill the traitor with anger, worry, and likely even fear. I am certain of that."

"I beg your pardon, Majesty," said Tiamak, "and I am glad we will finally reveal ourselves, but we cannot know for certain yet that Pasevalles has not received some magical help from Utuk'ku and the Hikeda'ya."

"It is possible," the queen allowed. "But there will be risks no matter what I do. The time has come to see if we can end this without risking the death of the innocents trapped in Winstowe with the traitor. Revealing myself will certainly not convince Pasevalles to surrender, but it may convince his paid soldiers that they have a better chance of survival if they hand him over."

Little Serasina had wakened again and was squirming against Jesa's breast. The child would be hungry soon, but Jesa didn't want to leave the gathering. She rocked a little from side to side until Serasina grew quiet again. "How can you be certain you will be safe to talk to that Pasevalles or his generals, my queen?" Jesa asked.

"I cannot be certain. But I trust Baron Norvel, Lord Snell, Captain Kenrick, and the rest of you to come up with the best possible plan. We are not deciding whether I should or should not reveal myself. I have already decided that I will. But I will not go to war against my own people—many of whom are doubtless already suffering from the earlier battles against Unver Shan—when there may be another way."

"May God watch over you, Majesty," said Norvel.

"God will, I am certain, my lord, but I would like to take a few precautions closer to hand as well."

36

Playing the Crown

Simon had assumed that any council between the two tribes of immortals would take place in the Norn military camp, since their superiority of numbers was obvious, so it surprised him when Rukayu told him he was called to attend the parley in the part of the caverns where the Sithi were sheltered.

The young Zida'ya Xila, who had accompanied Rukayu, wanted to apologize. "I tried to look after Lillia, King Seoman, I truly did. But the spirit sheltering inside your granddaughter would not be held back. I tried to restrain her from going out to where the fighting was, but she told me to stay—and I stayed. I did not want to, but I did."

"You don't need to apologize," Simon told her. "We are all part of something bigger than anything we can understand—except perhaps for Geloë herself."

"I do not feel ashamed to say she frightens me," admitted Xila. "She has a fierce, stern essence."

"And so does my granddaughter," Simon said, smiling as he gestured to where Lillia lay nearby like an exhausted puppy, sprawled in sleep upon a Sithi cloak. "As you will discover when she wakes up and wants to find me. They were well-matched, that pair."

After kissing his granddaughter's cheek, he let Rukayu lead him to the chamber where the others were gathered. She then made a sign of farewell and departed.

Simon had been a part of many strange gatherings in his life, but none, he thought, had been half so strange as this. The Sithi were there, of course—Cheka'iso and Red Okajata, both of whom had been so badly wounded that they had to be helped into the cavern, and Yizashi Grayspear, whom he remembered from the Storm King's War, but he did not know the rest of the solemn, golden-eyed faces.

Norn nobles were present as well, including Utuk'ku's apparent successor, tall, stern Prince Pratiki, who Simon watched with almost instinctive mistrust. The prince was surrounded by many of his own people. Pratiki did not wear a mask, but many other Norns did, and Simon wondered how common ground could ever be found between the Sithi and these secretive, hostile creatures. He did see one Norn noblewoman who seemed important and went unmasked. She was dressed in sumptuous but frayed robes, and she sat beside the prince. But if this gathering of immortals around a single fire was not odd enough, there was also Geloë in her ancestor Ruyan the Navigator's crystalline armor. She never moved, seeming more statue than person.

"Here is King Seoman of Erkynland, the ruler over the mortal High Ward," announced Yizashi when he saw Simon in the doorway. "He is Protector Jiriki's *Hikka Staja* and friend."

Pratiki, neither masked nor wearing the runic face tattoos several of his followers had, gave Simon a careful inspection. "Then I will speak the mortal Westerling tongue, at least for now," the prince said. "Any trusted ally of the Sithi is welcome, of course. We Hikeda'ya have not come to dictate terms—or have them dictated to us, either—but to find some solution to this conflict and avoid more bloodshed."

This Norn almost sounded reasonable, Simon thought, which immediately made him cautious. Could an important Hikeda'ya noble, relative of the queen—and thus one of the monsters who had conducted cruel, pointless war against mortals and Sithi—truly be interested in peace?

But Miriamele had taught him to be cautious with both trust and suspicion, whatever his inner thoughts. "Thank you for your gracious words, Prince Pratiki," he said. "I will not have much to say, except when your talk touches on my folk. But I am glad to be included."

Pratiki nodded. "Let us start, then. My first question is about Jiriki of the Year-Dancing Clan. I have heard he was badly wounded. How does he fare?"

Caught by surprise, Simon swallowed hard and for a moment could not speak.

"Not well," Geloë intoned in her nearly expressionless voice. "I have given him what strength I can—he is determined to wait for someone he is expecting—but I fear he is too far gone to survive very long."

Simon started to say something, to protest, but realized there was nothing he could offer except to complain against fate.

"I am sorry to hear that," said Pratiki slowly. "His courageous battle against General Ensume and the thing called Ur-Makho will be long remembered."

Simon's suspicions flared again. This Norn was being entirely too generous—surely the Sithi could see it must be a trick. "Speaking of the battle," Simon asked abruptly, "where is the weapon that Utuk'ku fought so hard to capture?" Perhaps this prince was being so magnanimous because he knew he could destroy them all whenever he wanted.

"*I* have it." Geloë's words sounded like a fingernail scraping down a lute-string, far more noise than music. "Or, rather, Ruyan Ká has it, and will return it to the ship. It belongs there. It is the spirit of the vessel—its motive genius."

"I am no philosopher," said Yizashi Grayspear. "I do not understand what all those words mean, but are you saying you have handed that terrible weapon back to the ogre that killed so many of us, and so many Hikeda'ya as well? That sounds like madness to me."

"I will explain more if I am given the chance," said Geloë—a little sharply, Simon thought. Even victory had not made her patient. "But I assure you, the ship's heart is not meant to be a weapon. It will be safer back in the ship, where it has lain for so long, than in the hands of anyone here—myself included."

"And who *are* you, precisely?" asked Pratiki. "I have asked our Chroniclers and Order of Song and have received many different answers. Why should I . . . why should we trust you with something that was almost used to destroy everything?"

"A fair question," Geloë told him. "Although I remind you that it was your queen who planned that destruction." Simon thought he could detect a trace of amusement in the droning voice. "Who I am is not as important as *what* I am—a Tinukeda'ya of the Navigator's own bloodline—and why I am here at all. As she later did with Jiriki's grandfather Hakatri, Utuk'ku summoned me from beyond the veil of death, though she did not know it—she meant to resurrect her trusted and powerful ally, Ommu the Whisperer. You should be grateful for that mistake, Prince Pratiki, because had it not happened, we would not be here to have this council. Nor would anything else."

Yizashi shook his head wearily. "Much of this talk is beyond me, but unlike my father I have learned to listen to the Tinukeda'ya. We Zida'ya have much to learn from them—and to atone for."

"I do not mean any disrespect, Serene Highness," said the Norn noblewoman beside Prince Pratiki, "but it seems obvious that this Geloë is our only authority on the ship and the weapon that so nearly doomed us all. If she promises us the *zhin'ju* is safe for the moment, perhaps we should talk of other things—important matters, like what becomes of the Hikeda'ya and Zida'ya gathered here in Tanakirú."

"It will never be entirely safe anywhere until the *zhin'ju* is gone from these lands," said Geloë. "But it will be kept secure for now on the Ninth Ship."

"But you might as well say that of a fire," pointed out one of the Sithi nobles, a blue-clad male whose name Simon did not know. "A fire is contained until it is not contained—but not so easily contained again once it escapes."

"It will not escape," said Geloë. "I think Lady Miga is right—we have other things to discuss first. And remember, for once we all have more in common than separates us."

"Yes!" said Lady Miga with surprising passion. "That is an excellent starting point. We are all—saving this mortal king—Children of the Garden."

"A little of the Dreaming Sea also runs in this mortal king's veins, I believe," said Geloë. Several of the gathered immortals turned to look at Simon with gold-flecked or midnight-dark eyes.

"What strange news we have had today," said Yizashi Grayspear with a rueful laugh. "And my guess is that there is more to come."

"Oh, yes," Geloë said. "Much more."

Even with all the rope Little Snenneq and Qina carried, the combined length still came up far short of the stony ground below them.

"We have to find another way down," said Morgan, struggling to remain calm. "We must! They're not fighting anymore down there, but they've taken Nezeru away and who knows what they will do to her?" He hadn't been able to see clearly from such a distance but had witnessed enough to know that something had struck down the Norn Queen, and shortly thereafter, Nezeru and a few others had been surrounded by Norns in white armor and marched off toward one of the caverns that lined the plateau. He was desperate to get to her.

"Then we must find another way down, friend Morgan," said Snenneq. Beside him, Qina nodded.

"But this tunnel and the one that went under the water were the only places big enough for the ogre to pass. How did it get down there?" Morgan paced back and forth, feeling every pulse-beat in his temples. "Let's go back to the ship—there must be more rope or cord there. Or we'll make something out of vines—"

Even as he spoke, he and the others were startled by a strange and extremely loud scraping noise that echoed down the tunnel. "What is that?" asked Tih-Rumi.

"It is Ruyan Ká," said the other Tinukeda'ya, ancient hairless Kuyu-Kun. "Or at least a part of her. She is fading now, but I can still sense her spirit as plainly I would know the sound of my mother's voice."

Morgan had no idea what a part of a dead Tinukeda'ya might be and didn't much care. "Whatever that means," he said, "something is happening up the tunnel behind us, and it might be the Norns. Maybe they've finally won the battle and they're coming after us."

"Or just want ship," Qina said.

"Or that, yes. I'm going to find out."

"Do not go, my friend!" called Snenneq, but Morgan had already begun clambering up the sloping tunnel. "Or at least you must wait for me, too!"

Morgan had already reached the first level area, if an expanse of limestone whorls, runnels, and lumps could be called level. He was about to clamber up the next rise when the scraping noise, loud to begin with, suddenly became much louder. Morgan shrank back against the wall just as Snenneq scrambled up the rise. As Qina caught up, they all pushed themselves back into a crevice in the tunnel wall. A quick look back down the tunnel showed Morgan that old Kuyu-Kun and the others from the ship had also scurried to find cover.

The scraping noise grew louder still, and Morgan spotted something moving ahead of them in the tunnel, on the far side of the long, narrow passage. He started to say something to the trolls, but quickly forgot all about talking, or where he was, and instead simply stared in gape-jawed astonishment.

The wide crack he had just noticed ran much of the way up one wall of the broad passage, but it was not the fault in the stone that had seized his attention. A tangle of what he at first had taken for roots stuck out of the crack, but the tendrils seemed more animal than vegetable, twisting and writhing like snakes even as he watched. As odd protrusions continued to squirm outward, stretching several paces beyond the crevice, he saw that they were neither roots nor serpents, but animated individual planks of wood that only looked small and narrow because of distance. As they emerged, the boards began to wrap around themselves, until they had become a single, massive limb far wider than the narrow opening they had come from.

"Can you see that?" he asked in a shocked whisper.

"Is the big so big giant!" said Qina. "How?"

Within moments, the wood-woven arm was followed by other thick strands that seemed to have separated themselves to fit through the crevice but were now knitting back together. Morgan could not deny his eyes: the monstrous *uro'eni,* the thing that had stalked them up and down the valley, a creature as tall as a cathedral spire, was emerging from a comparatively tiny crevice right before their eyes, like a many-legged devilfish. The ogre's shoulder and its blunt, nearly featureless head now appeared and re-knit itself, the process weirdly silent. Then the rest of its massive body, flattened until it was no thicker than the length of Morgan's arm, forced its way out and unfolded into the unmistakably vast, vaguely manlike shape that had stalked them through the valley. For the first time Morgan could see the immense thing whole.

"It's not even real . . ." he gasped, heart speeding. "I mean, it *is* real, but . . . but it's made of wood!"

"Witchwood," said Snenneq. "There is enough light to see that."

"Why talk?" said Qina urgently. "Wood, flesh—it will smash us."

But Morgan was caught as if under a spell, and although every healthy sense was telling him to turn and run back down the tunnel to the place where the Tinukeda'ya and others were hiding, he could only stare helplessly as the thing straightened up to nearly its full height, crouching a little to avoid scraping the cavern's ceiling.

The crude head slowly turned toward them, regarding them with its vague semblance of a face, with only empty depressions where eyes should be. Then, as though a minor, passing curiosity had been satisfied, the huge thing turned away from them and trudged away up the sloping cavern.

"It only has one arm," Morgan whispered, a detail so strange and so comparatively unimportant that he felt as if he were dreaming. "What is it? What is happening here?"

"That is a question, yes," said Snenneq. "But more importantly, did we not just see that same ogre, down below?"

Morgan was still trying to make any kind of sense out of the wooden monster, a toy for some impossible child—a child the size of a mountain.

"If the valley floor is where the ogre came from," Snenneq said, "then though it may have had to struggle to get through that crack, the opening should easily be wide enough for us, do you not think?"

Morgan turned to him. "Praise God, you're right! You are the wisest troll who ever lived!"

Snenneq turned to look at Qina. "Did you hear what the prince said?"

Their midday meal featured a wide but—to Simon's tastes—unsettling array of Sithi and Norn foods: the Norn contributions looked as though they might have been scraped from the walls of the very caverns where they were gathered. As they ate, Yizashi Grayspear came and crouched next to him. Simon was startled and a little dismayed to see how unchanged Yizashi looked since their first meeting thirty years earlier.

I am gray all over now, Simon thought, *but he looks as if only a day or two has passed since then.*

"I have come to tell you that the Hikeda'ya are complaining," Yizashi said.

"About me? Because I'm a mortal?"

Yizashi shook his head. "No. And that is strange, too, because the Hamakha Clan—Utuk'ku's clan—has always hated your kind, ever since the death of the queen's son Drukhi at mortal hands."

"I have heard the story. But that was many centuries ago."

"It was, but our kind have long memories. However, that is not the reason the Hikeda'ya complain." Yizashi slid a little closer, graceful as an alighting sparrow, and lowered his voice. "They are not used to your mortal tongue, Seoman. Some of them cannot understand Westerling at all, and they fear they will miss important matters. The things that we discuss next are—"

Simon lifted his hands. "Say no more! It was never my wish that everyone should speak so I could understand. Perhaps Rukayu or one of the other Sithi can render things into my tongue—if it is even necessary for me to be here."

Yizashi nodded. He had a sharp, lean face more like that of the Hikeda'ya, Simon thought, but his golden eyes were sympathetic. "Jiriki wished particularly for you to attend. He is concerned that all our peoples should build whatever comes next together."

"Of course." Simon tried to smile, but his heart felt badly bruised. "Of course he would worry about such things even as he's suffering."

Yizashi only nodded, but Simon thought he saw a flicker of deep mournfulness in the Skyglass Lake protector's otherwise imperturbable face. "So we are settled, then? Do you wish me to find someone who can speak your tongue?"

Simon shook his head. "I will ask Rukayu of Peja'ura. If she can't do it, then I may need your help."

"Very well." Yizashi stood. "Do you understand how strange these times are, Seoman King? I think this must be the first time Hikeda'ya and Zida'ya have sat down together to eat and talk since the Parting."

Simon could only hope it would work out better this time. But before he could say anything, he saw that Yizashi had already gone.

"Now that we come to the heart of things," said Pratiki, "I ask you to sit beside me, Magister Viyeki. Many things will happen here. I want you to hear all and then tell me anything you think I need to know."

Viyeki was still stunned, not only by his own reprieve, but by the swift, stunning dispatch of Marshal Kikiti that had followed. He could not help but think that Pratiki had been planning it a long time, and though he was grateful to know his hated enemy was dead, the suddenness of Kikiti's downfall was not reassuring.

"I will of course help in any way I can, Serenity. But I must be honest—I still do not understand what you want of me, or why you chose me at all."

"Do you remember our talk of loyalty—of a day when change might come? That day has now come, Magister. And I did not save you out of pity, I saved you because I need you. Also, you are one of the few besides Lady Miga and myself who can speak the mortal tongue."

"Would it be forward of me to inquire about Lady Miga of the Jinnata and her place in things?" Viyeki asked. "I had thought she was part of the Order of Chroniclers. Is she here as history's witness for this—what did you say, Serenity?—this 'heart of things'?"

"In part, yes. Unless I badly miss my guess, there will be matters discussed today that our descendants—if we have any—will want to know."

Viyeki felt a chill run through him. "'If we have any?' You make me fearful, Prince-Templar."

"Just 'Prince' now. I will find someone else to be the guardian of Nakkiga's temples—it was only a commission meant to keep me under Utuk'ku's eye. Which is also why she brought me here. She did not want any of the high Clan Hamakha bloodline left alone at Nakkiga when she was gone, for fear of an uprising. My ancestor always had schemes within schemes."

Viyeki looked at the Hikeda'ya and Zida'ya who had fought to the death the previous day, but now scattered around the large cavern in full view of each other as if their struggle had meant nothing. In some cases, members of the two clans were even sitting together, although some of those conversations looked strained. High Celebrant Zuniyabe and Lady Miga—both Hikeda'ya—were huddled with Protector Yizashi, the acting leader of the Zida'ya company.

"I confess," began Viyeki, "that I am surprised the queen let you live, Highness." Only a few days ago his remark would have been clear treason, and immediately after he spoke, he was seized by fear and fury at his own careless honesty.

Pratiki only smiled. "The succession, at least while she lived on and on, was mostly for show. But that show was very important to Utuk'ku. She wanted all our people to know that the Hamakha would always lead them."

And the Hamakha still do lead, thought Viyeki. *That is clear. Kikiti learned it in a way he did not like. But does that mean Pratiki will bring better times, or will he just be a more subtle tyrant than his forebear?* "I am confident you will do what is right, Highness," he said, half hopefully, half defensively.

As if Pratiki had surmised Viyeki's thoughts, he smiled again, but the quirk of his lips seemed a little less natural this time. "We both hope for that," he said, no longer looking at Viyeki, but letting his eyes roam over the strange, mixed company. "But whether I will be allowed to—that we shall have to wait see."

Rukayu seemed even more astonished to be joining the unusual gathering than Simon had been. "When I return to the cedar forest," she said, "I shall tell my clan of this day and it will become a famous story. Not one of us has seen or even dreamed of anything like what is happening here."

"Not even your grandfather? He's seen so much."

She made the sinuous motion that among the Sithi passed for a shrug. "I do not think so, but we cannot know. He was killed in the last hour of battle."

Simon was startled. "Shen'de the Bowman is dead? I did not know! Oh, Rukayu, I am very sad to hear that."

Her wide, golden eyes showed no more sorrow than he would have seen in the stare of a hunting hawk. "Do not be, Seoman King. His ending was quick, and it came in battle. He fought only on the side of righteousness, won most of those fights, and lived to a vital old age. He shot the arrow that killed General Ensume, and his skill and keen eye helped keep all our people here alive. Who knows what may come of that? Perhaps a better future. No, Shen'de the Bowman would not want to be celebrated in sadness or sorrow. We will take him back to his beloved Peja'ura and he can rest there until the Garden is made again."

Before Simon could ask any more questions, Prince Pratiki stood and began to speak, this time in his own tongue, which was apparently so close to the Sithi's that the two warring clans could easily understand each other, making it clear to Simon what a sacrifice the immortals had made in using his mortal tongue at all. Rukayu sat by his side and whispered a translation of the Norn Prince's words.

"We have trusted you with the ship's heart, Sa-Ruyan Geloë," Pratiki said, "the *zhin'ju*, the terrible container of Unbeing that threatens us all, although we barely understand it, and we cannot rely on trust alone. How can it be made safe?"

"It never can, I fear," said Geloë's toneless voice. Hearing her speak the Sithi tongue in those inhuman tones as Rukayu translated, Simon thought it sounded more like dissonant music than actual speech. "Unbeing is not a thing, but an absence of things—of matter, air, thought, of *everything.* It leaves behind only a spreading hole in what is."

"We are already suitably fearful," said Yizashi curtly. "That is why we have deferred to you."

"And that was wise of you, Protector," she said. "Very few beyond Utuk'ku's inner circle of Sacrifices and Singers know anything about it at all."

A Singer with runic tattoos on her face spoke up. "Few but Akhenabi and Her Majesty even knew such a thing existed. And perhaps the queen's mad kinsman, Jijibo—."

Prince Pratiki gave her pointed a look. She fell silent.

"It frightens me greatly," said Lady Miga. "You said that all of the famous Eight Ships each had such a thing at their hearts."

"Yes, which enabled them to cross the Ocean Indefinite and Eternal," Geloë replied. "It is no ordinary journey to come here from the Garden. That ocean is not the sort you know of—not merely a thing of water and wind. But I will tell more of that later, for I sense you have a more pressing question."

"I do," said Miga. "When we came here from the Garden, the first arrivals built settlements in the remains of the great ships—Asu'a, Tumet'ai, Kementari, all of them have one of the fabled vessels as their foundations. Does this mean that somewhere beneath them the same terrible Unbeing is waiting, ready to spill out and destroy us all?"

Simon saw a visible tremor of uneasiness travel around the gathered immortals. Lady Miga had been first to see the danger, but the others now understood it and were fearful.

"That, at least, is one thing that need not worry you, Lady," said Geloë. "The *zhin'jui* of those eight ships were only meant to carry the ships to this place—this *plane*, as I might put it. Peace! I promise I will explain that later, too. But the heart of the Ninth Ship, the thing that Utuk'ku wished to use to bring on the world's end, was meant to be used again, for a second journey. Its potency—and danger—remains."

"What other secrets have been kept from us?" demanded Yizashi. "And why have we only learned this now, while you seem to have known much about it?"

"Your anger should be with Utuk'ku and her ministers, not me, Lord Grayspear. My people were forced into learning to keep secrets." Even without much inflection, Geloë's bitterness was clear. "Most of us were slaves, remember? The Ninth Ship was the last to sail. Hoping to escape bondage, we had begun building it long before the terror of Unbeing was released, but before it could be finished and we could escape, that supreme meddler Urudade allowed Unbeing to escape into the Garden . . . and everything changed. My forebear Ruyan Vé convinced his folk that no matter the woes your people had inflicted on us, we could not simply leave you to be destroyed, so we built eight more vessels that would carry all the Gardenfolk away but kept the first one secret. But the Navigator knew your kind would never trust the vessels we made for them if we did not travel with them, so it was agreed we would flee the Garden with you on the Eight Ships and our secret ship would follow us. That vessel and its captain, the Navigator's daughter, Ruyan Ká, were lost somehow in the Ocean Indefinite on the way here, and only arrived many centuries after the others. But Ruyan's plan had been that once your people found refuge in this new land, we would board our secret ship and find a safe haven for ourselves elsewhere. Because it was meant to make another journey, the Ninth Ship carried twice as much Unbeing in its heart as the others."

A fresh round of quiet conversation began among the gathered Sithi and Norns. Yizashi stood. "So the heart of the Ninth Ship, what you call its *zhin'ju,* was only half spent?"

"Near enough," Geloë told him. "As long as the Unbeing inside it remains surrounded and outweighed by the waters of the Dreaming Sea, the ship can travel between the planes of existence. And now I intend to use it for its original purpose."

A murmur of surprise ran through the cavern. "Hold, hold," said Pratiki sharply. "What do you mean? The ship is a wreck, stuck in solid stone. And what exactly are these 'planes' you speak of? That is a philosopher's word, an idea—not a place."

At that moment, one of the white-armored Queen's Teeth—*or Prince's Teeth, now, I suppose,* Simon thought—entered the cavern and made her way past the other guards to Pratiki, then waited patiently as the prince stared at Geloë, waiting for an answer.

"I mean what I said, Prince Pratiki," Geloë told him. "I have thrown off death and fought a hundred battles you know nothing of, then helped unravel Utuk'ku's plans, but always with this intent behind it—if we survived. And we have survived. My original purpose has not changed, and I owe it to my ancestors to accomplish it." The uninflected voice rose, as though to make sure all could hear. "We Vao will take the Ninth Ship and leave the lands of Osten Ard behind. We will find a place to start anew, without either Zida'ya or Hikeda'ya masters. The Dreaming Sea that surrounded the Garden may be no more, but some of its waters still remain, and it also lives in the hearts of all Vao."

"I understand little of this," said Pratiki in frustration. "It sounds like madness. Do you think we will simply let you take such a valuable thing as that ship, as well as the terrible weapon it contains, without you so much as asking?" He finally noticed the white-armored guard and beckoned her closer. She communicated her message in a swift and complex succession of hand signals. "Forgive me," Pratiki said when the guard had finished. "Some news has come, but it will keep for a moment. I still want an answer to my question."

"And you will have one, Prince Pratiki—but not because you can order me to give it to you." Geloë's helmeted head swiveled to survey the gathered immortals. "Many moons ago I began to summon those of my folk who could hear my call to join me here. Many have come, and more are still arriving. The Vao who answered my summons are hidden throughout this valley, in holes in the cliffs and upon the heights—even on the Ninth Ship itself. If it had been the only way to save my race, I might even have sent them against Utuk'ku in the final instance. Few of them are trained fighters, but I would guess they greatly outnumber the remnants of both armies here."

Yizashi Grayspear stood. "Are you threatening us?"

Geloë stood silent for a few moments. "I promise you I have no interest in making threats," she said at last. "I am only telling you how things stand. My people were dragged from the Garden against our will after we had already been turned into beasts of burden by the Keida'ya—your two clans. After we came here, after rescuing you, my ancestor Ruyan the Navigator was imprisoned for keeping secrets from the Hamakha and died in chains. My own father Mardae was tortured for his knowledge about the ship and its *zhin'ju*. Oh, yes, we Vao have ample reasons for vengeance—" she held up a gauntleted hand at the stir of dismay—"but I promise we intend no harm to any of you. Not even the Hikeda'ya. However, do not forget that my people built that ship before your kind knew such a thing was possible. It is *ours*. I now wear the Navigator's armor, forged and spell-sung to command such a ship, just as the Navigator's daughter, Ruyan Ká, captained the vessel that waits in the cliff above us. Only the Garden knows how she suffered in the long journey through the between-places, but in the end, she succeeded—the crown was kept safe and soon she can find her true rest. I know what must be done next, and I will not fail that trust." She again lifted a gold-threaded hand, holding off questions and arguments. "That is all you need to know. The Vao will not otherwise interfere with anything Zida'ya and Hikeda'ya agree here—but make no mistake, the crown is ours and we will take it."

"You keep saying the crown," said Pratiki darkly. "Are you saying you mean to take power here somehow? That sounds very much like a threat."

"No, no," the buzzing voice replied. "I am simply saying that for once—unlike the time of the Parting—the needs of the Vao cannot be overlooked or bargained away. We are present, we are many, and the crown rightly belongs to us. But I said I want no conflict and I meant it." The helmeted head swiveled slowly across the throng. "Ah. Could it be that none of you know what I mean when I speak of 'the crown'? It is simple. All of the fabled Eight Ships had names—Lantern Bearer, Sacred Seed, you know them well. But the one that had been built first, meant to bear my people out of the Garden to freedom, was given its name from the game of *shent*—a small jest by its Tinukeda'ya builders, since in the game it is a move made to succeed by losing—or at least appearing to lose. Utuk'ku seems to have found the name appropriate for her own plan—to end herself, and thereby gain a greater victory than ever before, namely the end of everything." The crystal eyes of the helmet turned back to Pratiki. "The name my ancestors gave our ship was *The Witchwood Crown*."

As a hush fell over the gathering, Simon marveled. It truly had been the *Witchwood Crown* that the Norn Queen had sought, but it was not what any of them had guessed.

Prince Pratiki broke the silence. "This is much to take in. And in any case,

I am told that a company has arrived from Anvi'janya, led by Kuroyi's daughter, Ayaminu. You Zida'ya may want her to be a part of any further discussions, so if Sa-Ruyan Geloë agrees, I suggest we all practice patience until the new arrivals have been settled."

The armored shape made a small gesture which Pratiki took for agreement. He turned to Yizashi. "Dunao the Rider and a company of armed warriors have come with Ayaminu. I have requested that they be kept on the far side of the gorge until you have had a chance to explain to them what has happened here. Mistress Ayaminu is of course welcome to cross over immediately, along with any others you deem appropriate."

Yizashi nodded. "I am a bit overwhelmed myself, Prince Pratiki, by all we have heard today. As you suggested, let us put these matters aside for a little while. I will send for Ayaminu." He left, followed by his guards, and the other immortals began to drift out of the cavern, conversing in murmurs, until the chamber had gone silent.

"Few good things are born from fear," Geloë said then, as if answering someone's question. Simon did not know what she meant and did not want to ask. Instead, he followed Rukayu out, leaving the figure in the Navigator's glittering armor alone in the cavern.

37

Under the Mask

"I beg you—take me with you!" cried Tanahaya as Ayaminu readied herself at the base of the siege-bridge. She had to speak loudly because of the cataracts and the Narrowdark thundering in the gorge below them. The Sacrifice soldiers who had been sent to bring Anvi'janya's mistress across the bridge were being unexpectedly solicitous, and although it made Tanahaya wary, it also gave her a shiver of hope that with Utuk'ku dead, things might be different—better, even—between the two clans that had been struggling against each other for so long.

"Of course," said Ayaminu. "You must go to Jiriki, and you will. Our friend Dunao will boil a bit at being made to wait here, but he is a warrior and thus is being treated like one. Which reminds me—we are asked to leave all arms behind."

"Simple enough." Tanahaya undid her sword belt, then handed it and her scabbarded sword to one of Ayaminu's younger clansfolk. "Please protect it for me," she said. "It was my mother's."

"It will be stored respectfully, Scholar," the Sitha assured her.

Tanahaya half-hoped she would never have to wear it again—that it might someday be only an old family keepsake. It had spilled too much blood already, especially in the last few moons. *The blood of my own kin*, she thought sadly, *though they would have killed me if they could have.*

"Is there truly a chance of peace?" she asked Ayaminu. "It seems almost too much to hope for. What do you know of this Prince Pratiki—and is the mad queen really and truly dead?"

"You can read Yizashi's letter if you wish," said Ayaminu, holding out the rolled parchment.

"For once in my life, I am too apprehensive to read. I am desperate to reach Jiriki. Perhaps I will look at it after we have seen him, if it still matters to me then."

Ayaminu nodded. "I understand. In short, he says that yes, Utuk'ku has died, and that she meant to destroy not just us but her own kind as well. And, as we have already heard, he confirms that Pratiki, highest of the Hamakha bloodline, is now master of the clan. Which means, of course, that he is also master of all the Hikeda'ya, although he still may have some struggle to make that true in fact."

"Struggle?"

"Utuk'ku brought most of her nobles here—to be with her at the ending of all things, which she seemed to think was a great honor, but also, I suspect, to keep them under her eye in case her plans did not work out. But thousands of Hikeda'ya remain in Nakkiga, and it is not necessary to be related to the monarch to harbor ambition. Pratiki may have things in hand here, but his capital is a long way away, and there is no knowing what will happen under the mountain when news of Utuk'ku's passing reaches them."

"Am I wrong to hope things might be different now?" Tanahaya was doing her best to wait patiently, but Ayaminu was taking what seemed an unconscionably long time to get ready, giving out quiet orders and sending dispatches to Dunao and his warriors. *I am coming, Jiriki—my dear Willow-switch, my love,* she thought. *Do not give up on me. Do not surrender yourself.*

"You are never wrong to hope," said Ayaminu. "That is always the best and first thing to do. But even the most fervent hope must look up to see the world and how things are." She called for her horse. "I do not know as much about this Prince Pratiki as I would like. He is said to be popular among his people—but there are many ways to earn the love of the crowd, not all of them good. Utuk'ku made him the master of all the temples, an appropriate position for a high Hamakha noble that does not tell us much useful about him. But Yizashi Grayspear's words seem to suggest that the prince wants the bloodshed between our clans to end, and he apparently makes no secret that he did not approve of Utuk'ku's mad plan. So, yes, we may hope. But that is all we can do, because his troops vastly outnumber ours, and we are far from any possible help from either our own folk or the mortal kingdoms."

"So, we should not give up our vigilance yet. We can hope, but we must also look at the world that is around us."

Ayaminu smiled. "Are you repeating my own words like a trained raven, child? Very impolite. But yes—that is what I am saying." She settled her feet in the stirrups, then looked around. "Here comes Ki'ushapo to join us. It is time." A thought struck her. "You have the box that the mortal Tiamak sent from the Hayholt, do you not? If he is hale enough, Jiriki must see it."

"I do. Of course I do."

"Let us be off," said Ki'ushapo as he rode up. "I ache to see Jiriki, Yizashi, and the rest. But I dread to learn how many did not survive." He still looked pale, Tanahaya thought, but he could sit proudly straight now, as he could not only a few days earlier.

As Tanahaya swung into her own saddle, one of Ayaminu's clansfolk came running toward them. The newcomer was breathing deeply, which for one of the nearly tireless Zida'ya indicated that she had run far and fast. The Sacrifice soldiers around the great siege engine stopped her, but at Ayaminu's calm order they stepped back and allowed the messenger to come forward.

"A mortal soldier has arrived in the valley, *S'huesa*," she announced.

Ayaminu raised an eyebrow. "A mortal? Truly?"

The messenger nodded. "He came up the western bank of the Narrowdark, though I am not certain where from and he would not say. He in turn did not know who should receive this letter, but said perhaps it could go to Protector Jiriki, so I brought it to you at once."

"You did well, Hizuma," said Ayaminu, accepting the sealed parchment. She broke the wax and briefly read over it, then folded it again. "I will see that it reaches Jiriki—or whoever else should see it instead."

"May I look at it?" asked Tanahaya. "Where did a mortal soldier come from? We are almost outside of the world entirely!"

"I will not share it now," said Ayaminu. "In truth, I think this message is meant for someone other than your beloved, but if Jiriki receives it, he will doubtless share it with you."

Tanahaya felt a bit rebuked, but she was also anxious to cross the bridge. "Well, then, let us be off. We can talk of it later."

"Indeed. There is still much talking to be done in the hours and days ahead—negotiation, too, necessary but tedious. But that is always better than spilling blood. Let us cross the gorge. Now that you have crossed our Silken Span, I think you will have no need to fear this bridge, despite its slenderness."

"I was not afraid of the Silken Span," protested Tanahaya, but could not help feeling she sounded a like a child.

"This story is all beyond me." Viyeki held his daughter's hand so tightly that she found it almost painful. "You came here with a mortal, and trolls, and Tinukeda'ya, you say? Well, I must hear the whole tale when you have time to tell it, but there is much to do at this moment. Still, I cannot say how grateful I am to see you alive, my daughter, and I ache for you, for the wounds you have taken."

Nezeru shook her head. "The wounds are nothing, Father. My greatest pain is what I had to do—and the comrades I had to leave behind."

"Do you mean the Order of Sacrifice? *Pfagh.* They turned on you. If Pratiki continues to favor me, I will see that—"

"No, not the order, Father. It is the ones I came with that I mourn for—especially the mortal. I thought I heard his voice when . . . when everything was happening—just when I came back to myself and struck at the queen." She shook her head. "I feel such powerful shame even saying it aloud! But what else could I do? Our queen lied to us all! She would have murdered not just us, but all the world!"

He pulled her close and wrapped her in trembling arms. "You did a brave thing, Nezeru, an impossible thing that no one should ever have to do. I am just grateful that you survived it all—grateful beyond telling. I have had many terrible decisions to make since I left Nakkiga, and because of that, had to prepare myself for death many times." His face was haggard, but she could still see a light of relief in it that she had not seen before. "But somehow we have survived all our trials."

"Do not declare victory quite yet, Father—it worries me. In my order they taught us, 'The last to die often think the battle has already ended.'"

"Good advice, I suppose, but I always wished you had not been chosen for such a gloomy, cruel order."

Now she laughed, but it began with a gasp of pain and sadness. "Oh, Father—you cannot even imagine! Or perhaps you can." She sobered in an instant. "Is that not Prince Pratiki coming toward us? How should I address him?"

"Highness," her father hissed. "Or perhaps Serenity. I do not know—the ground is still shifting. But first, stand and bow."

As she lifted her head, Nezeru had her first proper look at the Hikeda'ya's new ruler. Pratiki was accompanied by a pair of clerics and a half-dozen white-helmeted Teeth, but at Pratiki's signal they all kept a respectful distance as he stepped forward to greet her father.

Well, that at least is something new, she thought. *The Mother of All hardly ever went anywhere outside the Maze Palace except in a company of hundreds.*

As Viyeki straightened from his bow, Nezeru saw that his movements seemed slow and stiff. *Perhaps, if I am truly going to be spared, my task will be to look after my father.* She could think of worse fates.

"I apologize for involving you in so many things so quickly, High Magister, with barely a gesture of explanation," said Pratiki. "But you of all people know that things have been changing very quickly here."

"Of course, Highness."

"And here we have the infamous Sacrifice, Nezeru." The prince's gaze was sharp, but she had expected nothing else. The Hamakha were an unusual clan: to survive so long among them, Prince Pratiki would have had to outlast countless dangers, not least those that would have come from the queen herself.

The prince was tall and thin even by the standards of her people. He wore a templar's long gray tunic over black shirt and boots, with a single silver chain across his breast—a spare ensemble for a high noble, and certainly nothing like the finery worn by the others of his clan that Nezeru had seen during ceremonial inspections. He had the elevated Hamakha brow only ever witnessed on the younger, maskless members of the clan, though presumably it was a family trait.

"I apologize for keeping you waiting," Pratiki said. "I am wrestling for my life with Celebrant Zuniyabe, who would have me lighting candles and listening to singing priests every bell of the day—though we have no proper bells here." He displayed a brief, wintry smile. "But I will not bore you with such small matters. Come with me, Magister. There is something I wish to show you. You too, Sacrifice Nezeru."

"I am not certain it is correct to call me that any longer, Highness."

He gestured in a way that suggested it made little difference to him. "We will make sense of all this later on. We faced utter destruction. You were there and prevented it. That is not the act of a traitor, but a hero—though I cannot promise all of Nakkiga will feel the same way."

He led them from a place near the meeting cavern and into a tunnel so roughly hewn that even Nezeru could tell it had only been recently made. Her father hastened to keep up with the prince. "Do you mean my daughter's life will be in danger if she goes back to Nakkiga?" he asked.

Again, Pratiki made the *small stone bouncing* gesture. "It is far too early to guess at what might happen next. But I think the odds are quite strong that my life will also be in danger from my own people—some of them, in any case—especially when it is learned that I pardoned both of my royal ancestor's assassins."

Nezeru took several more steps before the import of Pratiki's words sank in.

"Both of her assassins? Do you mean my father, or did someone else beside me strike at her?"

He did not answer her question, continuing as if she had not spoken. "Do not worry unduly about your safety. The Mother of All insured that the Queen's Teeth were utterly obedient to her. Unlike those in the Order of Sacrifice, the Teeth have never known their parents or clans, but were given to the Guardhouse at birth, beginning their training before they could even crawl. And because they were loyal to her, they are—I thank the Garden—just as loyal to me. Because what would they be—what would their lives mean—without a Hamakha on the throne? Since I have their loyalty, I can control things here. There is still some unrest among the officers of the Order of Sacrifice, but I believe it will settle once we have rooted out the worst troublemakers."

"There is resistance to you even here?" she asked.

Pratiki made a dismissive gesture. "I have it in hand. However, things may be a touch more complicated when we return to Nakkiga." He led them out of the corridor into a broadly open area with another recently cut entrance in one side. "But now I want to show you something. While you are within this chamber, you must not say a word unless I speak to you first. The celebrants are most fierce, and they are slaves to very old rules." This time his smile was a little less sour. "There is irony in that, of course. We have had only one ruler since we left the Garden—it has always been Utuk'ku—and we never had a ruler like her when we lived in Tzo during the ancient days, so exactly which ancient rules they are protecting seems open to question. But I have learned in my years in the palace that starting fights with underlings is at best impolite and can turn out to be far more dangerous than that." Again, the thin smile. "As High Singer Akhenabi himself learned, though he likely did not have much time to reflect on it. Now, remember—silence, unless I ask you to respond."

"What will happen to Saomeji?" Nezeru asked. "Someone told me that he was Akhenabi's half-blood son."

But Pratiki only shook his head.

Nezeru was so much a creature of her order that she still half-feared she and her father were being led to an execution, the prince's conversation only meant to keep them docile until it was too late to escape. Pratiki guided them to a natural limestone cavern lit by dozens of dimmed *ni'yo* spheres, with Queen's Teeth standing silently on either side of the door and half a dozen celebrants and priests kneeling in front of a bier carved out of a nodule of smooth, natural stone. On it lay the body of Queen Utuk'ku beneath a diaphanous, almost invisible spidersilk shroud.

Nezeru flinched back, wondering whether she had been right to fear a surprise execution. Why would Prince Pratiki bring them here? But the white-armored guards on either side of the door and at either end of the bier did not move or even look in their direction—in this chamber, at least, the queen who was dead was still more important than the prince who lived—and so she let Pratiki lead them toward Utuk'ku's corpse. The celebrants rose and backed away to give the prince room.

Nezeru had never felt such stomach-churning conflict in all her life, not even when caught between her growing feelings for Morgan and her Sacrifice training. This cold, lifeless figure was the Mother of All, revered far beyond all others through all Nezeru's young life. And Nezeru herself had killed her—or at least helped to kill her if she truly had not been the only assassin. The Mother of All had ruled over Nezeru's life and the lives of uncounted generations before hers, as unchanging as the moon, as powerful as the sun, and seemingly more permanent than even the stony roots of Ur-Nakkiga, and Nezeru was struck all over again by the awesome and terrible gravity of what she had done. She suddenly felt light-headed, and slowly lowered herself until she was kneeling before the bier, her guts in a wrangle and her thoughts just as twisted and uncomfortable. As she struggled to regain a grip on the world, she dimly sensed her father kneel beside her.

"No need to remain on your knees," said Pratiki after a little time had passed. "I brought you here to show you something. Prepare yourself—Her Majesty's wound is not pretty."

Nezeru slowly rose to her feet. Was Pratiki going to make her look at the horrible injury left by Cold Root as it passed through the queen's body? The death blow Nezeru herself had struck? She kept her eyes closed, breathing carefully, until she felt she had regained a little control of herself and was ready to look.

Pratiki reached out a long-fingered hand and pulled down the queen's shroud. Utuk'ku had been carefully dressed in one of her white gowns—not the strange wedding garment she had worn in her last hour, but something more like her ordinary daily garb, beautiful and finely made. She had apparently been prepared by accomplished funerary celebrants because there was no sign of the fateful wound Nezeru had given her—no blood spots, no lump of bandaging beneath the silky cloth.

Pratiki saw her staring at the queen's midsection. "Not that." He spoke almost gently. "I wanted you to see this." He gestured to the queen's face.

Utuk'ku wore her silver mask, but it had been split in half: a line ran through it from the top, beginning at the queen's snow-white hairline, then through a hole that must have been punched through it by an arrow, and all the way down to the chin. Carefully, almost reverently, Pratiki lifted both sides of the mask at the same time, revealing Utuk'ku's face, and Nezeru sucked in a sudden breath.

The first surprise was the ragged hole in the queen's white forehead, just above one eye, the wound red-rimmed and unhidden. The second was how ordinary the queen's face looked. Nezeru had heard countless rumors about what was beneath the queen's mask, wild tales and whispered gossip, but what she saw now beneath the queen's thick white skin paint was only a face, Utuk'ku's still firm jawline that of a Hikeda'ya not much beyond middle life: the fabled *kei-t'si* elixir had apparently worked very well indeed. But as Nezeru, feeling queasy, stared at the queen's fine-boned features, looking for any signs of Utuk'ku's impossibly great age, she saw something that surprised her even more.

She looked at her father, whose eyes were closed as if in prayer, then she turned to Prince Pratiki. His inquisitive stare suggested he had been expecting her reaction. "Do you have a question?" he asked.

Having been given permission, she had to decide what she was willing to say. "The queen wears a great deal of paint on her face, Highness," she said. "Is that what is usually done for members of the Hamakha family?"

"Only the oldest. And, yes, there is a great deal of paint," the prince agreed. "But not everywhere." He reached down and tugged gently at the high collar around Utuk'ku's slender neck, revealing a strip of skin that was decidedly darker than that of her face. "Here, for instance. What do you think?"

Nezeru could only stare, uncertain of what to say. The lower part of the queen's neck was clearly a different color than her face, and even by the uncertain light of *ni'yo* and funerary candles, it looked to be the same golden color as that of the Zida'ya. She took another careful breath. "It looks like—"

"It looks like the skin of our kinfolk, the Zida'ya, does it not?" said Pratiki. "And there is good reason for that."

Nezeru's father seemed even more stunned than Nezeru. "Should we be told about such matters, Highness?" he asked, then lifted his hand to his mouth, startled into speaking without being spoken to, but Pratiki ignored his error.

"It was a poorly held secret, at least among the innermost circles of the Hamakha Clan," the prince said. "The Keida'ya were one people when they came to these lands from the Garden—a single clan, though riven by disagreements between those who would eventually become the Zida'ya and our Hikeda'ya. And they all looked much the same then—'Skin like honey, hair like snow' as the poet says. But after the two clans divided their fates, many Hikeda'ya in Nakkiga began to be born with paler skin and darker eyes, and Utuk'ku and the other survivors of the Garden began to hide their golden skin from their own people."

"But why?" asked Nezeru.

"No one living remembers for certain," Pratiki said. "But I think the change to the younger Hikeda'ya may have come about through things done by Yedade in the quest to eliminate those who were deemed unfit, and later by the queen's descendant Jijibo, who is reputed to have practiced unimaginably foul arts in his secret workshops. I cannot tell you more. They might have already begun to breed our folk with other races—perhaps even with the Tinukeda'ya, who change to fit the world and creatures around them. But somehow, as the years rolled past, we Hikeda'ya changed but Utuk'ku and her peers of course did not. Thus, the Mother of All and her closest kin and servitors began to wear masks and paint themselves to hide that difference from the rest of their people."

"And this was known?" said Nezeru. "I have never heard it."

Pratiki gave her a hard look. "Only a few outside the highest circles of the Hamakha know it even now—it was the Mother of All's wish it be kept secret, and thus the law." He saw her look. "Yes, you may speak. What would you say?"

"I only want to know if it will remain secret."

Pratiki made a disinterested hand-sign. "'It is not yet true dawn,' as sublime Shun'y'asu tells us, 'but only the night's blush at having been caught lingering.' Much still remains to be decided, as you can no doubt imagine."

Despite the implied rebuke, Nezeru felt something like hope—an unusual sensation. A need for truth had led her halfway across the world, fighting monsters and even her own kind. Perhaps now there would be more truth for her people to share. Surely that could not be a bad thing.

As if he sensed her thought, the prince said, "Shun'y'asu also wrote, 'The greatest truths—glorious, immutable, and terrifying—cannot be revealed all at once. Thus, it is given to living things to learn them only in singular, small moments.' I do not wish to cripple my own people with too much at once. There will be terror and uncertainty enough in the days ahead as it is."

She bowed her head.

Pratiki led them out. Her father, who had been withdrawn and largely silent since they had entered the makeshift chapel asked, "And what of me, Highness? How may I serve you in these coming days?"

"It is precisely that I am pondering," the prince said. "Much rests on what we—and the Zida'ya, I suppose—agree in the next hours and days."

Nezeru was surprised to hear the Zida'ya were in any way involved with deciding what the prince and people of Nakkiga would do next. "Thank you for sharing this secret, and your time, with us," she said.

He nodded. "I do not fear to trust you," he said, and Nezeru thought she saw another faint smile. "After all, I am the only one who can keep you both alive."

As Morgan and his companions emerged into daylight, the plateau opened before him and the noise of rushing waters filled his ears. He was seeing the cliffs that surrounded the valley and the waterfalls from ground level for the first time, but what immediately seized his attention was the peaceful intermingling of Sithi and Norns he saw all around. He knew that only a few hours earlier they had been killing each other here—wet blood gleamed on the stones, and bodies were still being carried from the battlefield—but the two warring sides now seemed to be working together. Some great, unknown change had clearly swept through Tanakirú. Still, all Morgan truly cared about was discovering what had happened to Nezeru.

Once they left the rocky passage, they were quickly met by Norn guards wearing the fearsome symbols of Sacrifice companies, and for a moment Morgan thought they might be arrested, or worse. Instead, old Kuyu-kun spoke to the soldiers in their own language and the Norns seemed to listen to him without malice, though it was hard to tell with Norn faces at the best of times, as Morgan had learned from many mistakes made with Nezeru.

"They say if we want to know of Nezeru of the Enduya," Kuyu-kun reported, "we must inquire at the High Celebrant's camp, over there." He pointed a long, trembling finger toward a cavern mouth on the far side of the plateau.

"What has happened here?" Morgan asked.

"Mourning," said Kuyu-kun. "I do not know for whom, but I recognize the signs. Even you must see how quiet the Hikeda'ya are, how . . . suppressed."

"Perhaps the queen or one of their important generals has died," said Tih-Rumi.

"Utuk'ku?" Kuyu-kun shook his head. "She has lived since the Garden. It cannot be her."

"Still," offered Little Snenneq, "something strange has surely happened—Norns and Sithi pay so little attention to each other."

"I see too that," said Qina.

"As do I," agreed Morgan. "But we should be finding Nezeru." The last time he had seen her, from the cliff, she had seemed injured, and she had been surrounded by armed Sacrifice soldiers—the very comrades, he supposed, who had turned on her and sentenced her to death. "Come—make haste!" He started off across the plateau, weaving through a crowd of apparently incurious immortals.

"Unless you have now mastered the Hikeda'ya tongue," Kuyu-kun called after him, "you may learn more and faster if you wait for me to come with you."

Morgan stopped while the rest of his company caught up. Trying to discover whether Nezeru still lived was like jumping from a high place, he thought: It was hard enough to nerve himself to do it, but even harder when he kept getting interrupted.

Kuyu-kun translated what the Norn celebrant—a kind of priest or cleric, Morgan guessed—had to say about Nezeru. "He says you must look for her where Prince Pratiki is, because that is who summoned her."

"Summoned her?" He felt a stir of hope. "Then she's alive?"

"It seems so," Kuyu-kun said. "But more than that I cannot tell you. This fellow seems to be a mere functionary, and suggests you wait with him until High Celebrant Zuniyabe returns."

"Wait? How could I wait? Ask him where this Prince Pritiki can be found. Please."

Kuyu-kun frowned but turned back to the Norn.

"Perhaps I should go first, friend Morgan," Snenneq suggested. "I am small and very hard to notice. I can go in and learn what is the truth of things, then come back."

"Not you only," said Qina in an aggrieved tone.

"It's not necessary," Morgan told Snenneq. "But I will be glad of your company, do not doubt it."

Kuyu-kun finished his conversation with the celebrant, who turned away. "He also wanted to know if you were part of the mortal king's company," Kuyu-Kun said. "If you were part of his household and came with him."

"Mortal king?" At first, Morgan couldn't imagine who that might be, then he had an ugly thought: Perhaps it was that sneering Hernystiri fellow, King Hugh. Perhaps he had come here to make a pact with the Norns. Morgan had not liked the pagan monarch at all and would not put it past him, but why would Hugh have come so far himself? Surely all kings, even the heathen kind, had messengers and envoys for such things? "Mysteries up, mysteries down, mysteries all around," he said at last.

"Now you sound like one of the Vao," Tih-Rumi told him solemnly.

Ancient Kuyu-kun led them through a maze of tunnels and open spaces, both natural and carved, but his slow pace was maddening for Morgan. He was just about to demand that the Voice of the Dreaming Sea share the directions with him so he could hurry ahead when he saw the light of several gleaming *ni'yo* spheres. A small procession was approaching from the far end of the passage, led by a tall Norn dressed in garments that looked more suitable for court life than a battlefield. Behind him came another Norn noble, similarly dressed, and they were followed closely by several white-armored guards. It was only when this group turned to make their way down a gradual limestone slope toward Morgan and his company that he saw the third person the guards seemed to be protecting.

He could not be mistaken—he could not! He was moving before Snenneq and the others even had a chance to ask where he was going, and in just a few heartbeats he had run the length of the passage. Nezeru looked up at his swift approach, and her hand reflexively dropped to where her sword should have been, but she was unarmed. The guards suffered no such lack, however, and aggressively lowered their spears toward him, but the noble who led them said something and they set them at rest again. As Morgan neared, Nezeru recognized him. Her black eyes widened.

"Oh, blessings!" Morgan cried. "Praise Usires!" He dashed past the first of the Norn guards and threw his arms around Nezeru, who seemed too startled at first to react. "God is good, so good! You live!" Then, as he lifted her in the air, she grabbed one of his forearms and squeezed, painfully enough to startle him.

"Put me down, Morgan," she said in a low, harsh voice. "Now."

For a moment he only stood, shocked by her reaction, so she tightened her grip. He had forgotten her strength. He set her back down again, confused but still mightily relieved to have found her. "You have no idea how afraid I was—" he began, but Nezeru lifted a hand to silence him.

"Wait, Morgan. No, you must wait. And listen." She reached out and clutched one of his arms, more gently this time, then gestured to the tall Norn who had been leading them through the cavern. "This is Prince Pratiki sey-Hamakha. He now rules our people. And this is my father, Viyeki sey-Enduya," she said, nodding toward the other, a compact, handsome noble of indeterminate age. "Please forgive him, my lords," she said to the two Norns. "He is a mortal with whom I traveled, and he has been frightened for my safety."

"That I could see," said the prince in perfectly good Westerling—good enough to suggest a hint of irony in his words. Morgan suddenly realized he had forgotten all sense of what was proper and bent his knee to this new Norn ruler. *What happened here?* he wondered. Were the Norns still at war with the Sithi—and thus with his own people, too? But even more importantly, after all they'd been through, why was Nezeru treating him as little better than a stranger—a mere companion, met during her travels? Was she truly so ashamed of him?

"I beg pardon, Your Highness," he said.

"Granted," said the prince. "Rise. It seems that Nezeru's story is even stranger than what I have been told so far. I look forward to hearing the whole of it. But now, I fear, I have other duties. Magister Viyeki, I need you to accompany me."

"And I will go where my father goes, Prince Pratiki, if you will allow me," Nezeru announced.

Morgan suddenly felt a crushing weight in his middle, as if his lungs had turned to stone and were pressing down on his innards.

"But, Nezeru . . ." he began, then could not think of how to finish.

"We will talk, Morgan, I promise." But her face was empty of any feeling, as if some tidy servant had come and wiped it clean. "I want to hear from you about what happened as much as you want to hear from me. But it must be later. I have only just found my father again, and the prince still has much to tell us. Grant me this freedom now."

He realized he had already made a fool of himself in front of the most important personage among the Norns, and protesting would only make it worse. With a swiftly beating pulse and a heart full of dread and longing, he stepped aside and let her go, wondering if he was making a mistake he would regret forever.

As his companions, the trolls and Tinukeda'ya, whispered among themselves,

Morgan followed a few steps after Nezeru, wistfully watching as she moved gracefully down the passage and out of sight. He turned back, but walked past his companions and continued a distance up the cavern slope, unable to shake off his unhappiness. He had been so joyful to see her alive and well, only to be treated like an annoying younger sibling. But the humiliation of it was far less than the pain of seeing not even a fraction of his own longing reflected in her dark, cold eyes.

The cavern above opened into a place where several swiftly carved passages came together, and this too was lit by an arrangement of glowing *ni'yo*s, but at the far end Morgan could see a shaft of pure sunlight arrow down from a hidden opening to the sky, making the limestone nodules on the walls glow like the finest alabaster. Just as he was about to return to his companions, he saw movement in a corridor mouth just beyond the point where the sunlight fell—likely more Sithi or Norns who would look at him as though he was some cleverly trained animal. But just before he turned away, he caught a glimpse of golden hair.

He stared. The shape that had wandered out into the column of sunshine, hair glinting so brightly, had the look of a child—a very familiar child, though Morgan knew it could not possibly be her. Still, he took a few clumsy steps forward, and with each step became more certain that he was either right or had gone utterly mad.

"Lillia?" he called. "That can't be you—can it? Lillia?"

The child turned toward him, and for a long moment he was certain he had been mistaken—for one thing, this girl was a full head taller than his young sister. But then a wide smile stretched across her face. She let out a shriek and ran toward him, arms open wide.

"Morgan, Morgan, *Morgan*!" she shouted. "Is it really you? Why are you here? Did you come for me?" She had not even reached him but was gushing words like water out of a crumbling dike. "Did you see the really giant giant? And I was in the ocean and it talked to me."

She flew into his arms, striking him like a tiny, dirty thunderbolt. He let himself sink down until he was sitting on the stony floor. His sister climbed onto him, squealing in excitement. At last, she calmed and took his face in both her hands. "Oh! You have a beard now," she said, staring. "It makes you look silly."

"But, by our sacred Lady and all the angels, how can this be? What are you *doing* here, Lil? And what do you mean, the ocean talked to you?"

"Oh, so many things have happened. I was lost a long time down in the underneath. Then I got saved. Then we went on horses with the Sithers, and I was dreaming, but I was also in the ocean too." She was flushed and he half worried her wild words might be fueled by a bad fever. "Oh, I was so angry at you because you didn't come back!"

Suddenly Morgan began to weep. He gasped out a ragged breath, then wrapped his arms tightly around his sister and squeezed until she let out a squeak. "I was so frightened, Lil," he said. "Frightened I wouldn't see you again."

"Silly. I knew we'd find you someday. I told Grandfather."

He laughed through the tears. "I'm sure you did." His friends had drifted up from the other cavern but stood a respectful distance away, watching the reunion. But now he became aware of another presence, someone closer, and tried to look up, but Lillia had climbed higher on his chest, blocking his eyes and almost smothering him.

"Look, Grandfather," she cried. "I told you. I told you!"

"What is this?" said a voice Morgan recognized, although it hardly seemed possible. But neither, he realized, should Lillia. He managed to detach her and lower her into his lap, then turned to find an immensely shaggy gray and red beard hovering over him, with his grandfather Simon's face peering out from behind it.

"Blessed Saint Rhiap," the king breathed. Tears pooled in his eyes then brimmed over and ran down into his whiskers. "It really is you, Morgan. Ah, Merciful God, this is a true miracle! If only your grandmother could have lived to see it."

38

Lifeblood

Jiriki's voice was as insubstantial as thistledown. "Morgan," he said slowly, breathlessly. "What strange chances must have guided you, that we meet again here."

Simon had told his grandson as much as he could on their way to the healers' cavern. He prayed that Morgan, who despite his increased size and sun-darkened skin, was still only a very young man, would understand the importance of the meeting—the memory of Isgrimnur's sickbed was still deeply painful for Simon. To his relief, Morgan seemed to grasp the moment: he knelt beside Jiriki's pallet and took the Sitha's hand in his own. "I am so sorry to see you this way, Lord Jiriki," he said, and kissed Jiriki's fingertips, once honey-golden, now pale as powdered sulfur. "This is my sister, Lillia."

"We have met." Jiriki gathered his breath. "She accompanied us here, to Tanakirú."

Lillia looked on, wide-eyed but oddly composed. "Are you going to die?" she asked.

"Lillia!" Simon was aghast, but Jiriki only showed a weary smile.

"It seems very likely," he said. "I am badly hurt, little one. But I am waiting for someone, and she is very close now."

"Where will you go when you die?" Lillia asked, and this time Simon did not bother to reprimand her, since her impertinent questions did not seem to bother Jiriki and might even have amused him, though his weariness was obvious.

"That, no one knows." Jiriki reached out an unsteady hand. The child hesitated for a moment, then let him fold her fingers in his. "Some of my people believe we go to a peaceful garden—a place where we all once lived, but which we lost."

"My mama and my grandmother died." said Lillia. Morgan let out a gasp of grief. Simon had only just given him the news, and was very glad he had, since Lillia was indiscreet even for a child her age. "Did they go to that garden?" she asked.

Jiriki closed his eyes. The moment stretched long enough that Simon's heart climbed into his throat, but then Jiriki's amber eyes opened again and regarded the child with calm amusement. "Again, Lillia, no one knows. But whatever happens, I do not think the troubles of life go with them especially if they have lived a full life. Not if they have been surrounded . . . by those who love them, and whom they loved in return."

"He is tired now," Simon said. "Morgan, will you take your sister out to walk for a little while? I'm sure you have many things to tell her about what you have seen and done."

"I have even more to tell him!" said Lillia indignantly. "I fought a red devil—a real one who tried to catch me. I hit it and kicked it and then I ran away! And then the silver mask lady tried to catch me too, but I tricked her and went into the talking ocean!"

Morgan laughed a little. "It does sound very astounding and exciting, all of it. Come, Pigling. Let's walk a while and you can tell me all. A red devil!"

Simon leaned toward his grandson. "Be careful of her, Morgan," he said quietly. "This is a dangerous place, and I still do not trust the Norns, however peaceable they are acting."

"I promise I will watch her closely." Morgan looked over his shoulder. "Lillia, wait. You cannot go without me."

Simon beckoned him back. "She has many stories, some strange beyond belief," he said quietly. "But she was asleep most of the time she was with me, so I think she must have dreamed much of it."

Now Morgan had a true laugh. "Ah, I have missed her stories. But after what I have seen and done, I will not quickly doubt other people's tales—not even my sister's, impossible as they may sound." He paused. "And no more unlikely than us all finding each other here."

"At the end of the world." Simon nodded, then turned back to Jiriki, who had drifted into sleep. "True enough."

Brother Etan had been carried along by the Sithi to this utterly confusing place, a narrow valley ending in a plateau beneath stark cliffs pockmarked at the base with caves, and threaded with tumbling, foaming cataracts. Then they had almost immediately deserted him. Tanahaya had not even said farewell before she vanished over the bridge toward the caves. She had also taken the box Tiamak had entrusted to Etan, which left him feeling like the dangling end of something left outside a door when it closed, unwanted and forgotten. He also could not forget that the legions of Norn soldiers surrounding him were of the same folk who had captured and tormented him only days before.

He found one of the Sithi who had come with Tanahaya and the rest, a female with the same raptor's stare as the rest of her kind. He knew she spoke at least a little of the mortal tongue, so he asked if she could help him. She silently assented, then led him to the Norn soldiers guarding the bridge. Despite Etan's trepidation, the Norns seemed curiously listless, as though something vital had been cut out of them. Their faces remained expressionless as they talked quietly but intensely with his Sitha interpreter, but Etan could not help sensing resentment, if not outright hatred, in the glitter of their dark eyes when they looked at him. Because of this, he was surprised when his interpreter said, "The guards tell that if you be also one of Protector Jiriki's friends, then are you permitted to cross. But no weapons may you take. By their prince's order, all war-tools must be this side left." She pointed to a collection of spears, swords, and bows stacked near the siege-engine that anchored the bridge.

"I have no weapons," he said, and held up his arms, conscious for the first time in days how long it had been since he had washed. "They may search me if they wish."

Another brief exchange, then a frozen-faced Norn guard patted his robe in a perfunctory manner before gesturing toward the bridge. Etan thanked his Sitha helper and climbed onto the huge siege engine—no easy task for a man in a monk's cassock.

The bridge over the chasm was barely twice Etan's own width, and it was also disturbingly limber, as if made of willow laths instead of the heavy planks he saw beneath his feet. It swayed and jounced as he made his way across, but even as he looked down at mid-span into the swirling, icy waters beneath him and the thunderous noise rolled over him, he was not as frightened as he had thought he would be.

If God means to take me, He has had many chances. I will wait to see what He wants of me.

As he crossed the midway point and began down its gently sloping far side, he dared to look up at the great panorama of cliffs looming above him. He was so dizzied by what he saw that he had to stop and make certain his feet were firmly planted on the bridge. The strange shape protruding from the mountain slope above him, he now saw, was no mere outcropping, but something quite different, the long edge of an object distinctly separate in color and texture from the stone cliff face.

What is that? he wondered. *Has someone built a city hanging from the mountainside, almost in mid-air? Is that why there was fighting here?* He knew the Sithi were great builders—he had seen drawings and tapestries of the imposingly tall Green Angel Tower, which had collapsed in the Storm King's War before Etan was born—but it was not the *how* of the thing that puzzled him most, but the *why*.

Abruptly aware of the danger of stumbling over into the gorge, he lowered his gaze from the strange shape embedded in the cliff and continued more cautiously until he was off the too-supple bridge and back on solid stone once more. None of the dozens of folk he saw, Sithi or Norn, seemed at all interested in him, and no one questioned his presence. Bewildered, he wandered across the plateau into the shadow of the cliffs, heading for the most obvious entrance, the widest of the caverns lining the base of the cliffs like mouseholes in an ancient hall.

"Along strange paths I will guide you into strange lands," someone said.

Etan turned to see a man dressed in a hooded robe much like his own—clearly a mortal, the skin of his ascetic face as tanned as old leather. He was a good deal older than Etan, and had a gentle smile, but something about him seemed a little strange and the monk watched him carefully.

"I beg your pardon?"

"I will bring light to dark places. I will smooth the roughest road."

Etan recognized the sacred words of Usires Aedon and made the Sign of the Tree. The stranger did likewise. Etan wondered if he was being challenged somehow but detected no malice or even contention. As if shy or frightened, the stranger would not meet Etan's gaze. "Who are you, Brother?" Etan asked him. "Are you one of the Granisians, or some other mendicant order?"

"You might as well ask if he's a milk cow, sir," said a new voice.

Etan turned, surprised again, and found himself face to face with several more men and one woman, all seemingly as mortal as Etan himself. "And who are you?" he asked, startled out of his usual courtesy. "Or perhaps I should ask, What are you doing here?"

"We could ask the same, sir, but won't. Most of us are here because we were bid by the Lady. Was you too?" The speaker was small and bandy-legged, with a round, friendly face and wide-set eyes.

"I'm not sure what you mean."

The small man bobbed his head. "The Lady that comes in dreams. She called for all of us. That is our friar you were talking to. He only speaks in words from the Aedon-book."

Etan turned to look again at the hooded man. "Is he truly a mendicant friar? I am of the Sutrinians myself. My name is Brother Etan, and I came here with the Sithi."

The small man nodded as though this confirmed something he had guessed, but he only said, "We know nothing of them, Brother. We've nothing against them Fair Folk, but the ogre did not much like them—nor, I think, did the Lady, though she never said it so plain."

Etan could only shake his head: the conversation was getting more and more odd. "I do not know of this Lady, unless you mean the queen of the Norns, but they tell me she is dead now."

The other shook his head. "No, not that one. Not that one! No, the Lady is the one who called to us—and we came." He smiled. "But here I am, prattling away like a net-mender on a stormy day, without sharing names. Yek Fisher, I am, out of the southern lands, and these are the others who have come here like me. We are the Ship-Called, or so we say of ourselves. We are looking for some of our companions to make certain they are safe and to share our news. Because these are great days for us! Our dreams have returned, do you see? The Lady has begun to speak again, after long silence. She tells us the day we have waited for is almost here! It is a mighty blessing for us."

"Ah." Having exhausted his supply of useful responses, Etan bobbed his head, half acknowledgment, half bow. "Then I am glad to meet you and wish you—and your Lady—all luck. I am looking for my Sithi friends. Do you know where they might be?"

"The Sithi-folk be there, mostly," said Fisher, pointing to one of the other cavern openings. "But go not in there without a guide—it be powerful twisty and easy to lose y'self there."

"Thank you for that." Etan considered for a moment, then made the Sign of the Tree again, this time not on his own breast but over all assembled. "May God watch over you and keep you safe."

"Aye, p'raps, but it is the Lady we look to just now," said Fisher, and the others nodded solemnly, all except the friar.

"She sees all that happens by night," he intoned. *"Her wings spread over all."*

Etan backed away, smiling, and thanked them again, but in truth the entire meeting was confusing and fretsome. Not looking to God, but to a Lady? Not even the most dogmatic of Elysians would set the mother of Usires above God Himself. *Still,* he reasoned, *what else can be expected at the edge of the world? Who knows how many strange creeds have sprung up here, so far from the rest of Aedondom?* Which led to another question, which he considered as he made his way across the plateau, past more than a few seemingly oblivious immortals, toward the cave that Yek Fisher had indicated: *How did those human folk come here? Is this their home? That Fisher fellow looked to have Niskie blood. Why should they be in such a strange place at all?*

Several unfamiliar Sithi turned to him as he entered the cavern. "Ki'ushapo?" Etan asked slowly and loudly. "Tanahaya? Where are they?"

One of the Sithi, a slight-figured male, stepped forward and took Etan's hand, startling him a little, then led him into the shadowed cavern.

Despite the heartwarmingly familiar sound of his little sister's voice, Morgan was finding it hard to pay attention to the tales of confusing adventures that rushed out of her like a snowmelt brook. Many of them—as the king had warned—could have only happened in dreams. Only a short time had passed since his grandfather had given him the terrible news about his mother and grandmother, and much as Morgan loved Lillia, it was hard to keep his attention on what seemed like imaginary details.

He felt curiously blank, like a sanded parchment yet to be written on, an emptiness that might be filled with almost anything—choking sorrow, rage, or even a surprising and painful indifference. Why couldn't he feel anything? His mother was dead. His grandmother, the queen, was dead, too. And Nezeru had made it plain she did not care much about him, which enfolded everything, even news that was clearly much more devastating, in a blanket of cold emptiness as thick as a Frostmarch snowfall.

". . . but when they talked to me, they didn't have out-loud voices, not like people do, but kind of inside-my-head voices. And they said they had been waiting for me."

Pulled back to the moment, Morgan looked down at his sister. She was bigger, or at least taller, but she seemed no less fanciful. "Who is this now? Who talked to you in your head?"

"The ocean! The waves, I think. They said they wanted to taste the feather, but I was scared of that because the silver mask lady wanted it too."

Morgan could only shake his head, though the child's mention of a 'silver mask lady' brought a chill. What could little Lillia know of horrid Queen Utuk'ku? As he looked at her, half disturbed, half amused, but happy to push his other, dire thoughts away to resume listening, a pair of figures entered the tunnel at the far end. The smaller of the two bowed, then turned and left the passage, leaving the other alone. He wore a hooded robe and had a shape more akin to another mortal than to one of the Sithi or Norns. He slowly began to approach, then abruptly threw back his hood, revealing the shaven head of what looked like a monk, and hurried forward. When he reached them, he got down onto his knees in front of Lillia.

"Oh, praise God," the newcomer said. "They told me, but I did not know how it could be true. Princess Lillia, I thank Heaven to find you safe!"

"I know you," she said. "You're the gardener."

The monk laughed, but he seemed on the verge of tears. "I am—of sorts. I am Brother Etan." He turned to Morgan for the first time. "Your pardon, sir, but there has been much fear about—" He broke off, staring. "It cannot be. Can this be? How—?" Etan stared at him so fixedly that Morgan felt embarrassed. "Is it truly you, Highness? You are changed—grown! But surely you can only be Prince Morgan. Oh, God is great! How come you here?" He shook his head violently. "Forgive me. I have no right to question you, Highness, but I am so surprised—"

Morgan smiled, though he still felt empty. "And I know you, Brother Etan. You are Lord Tiamak's friend."

Lillia looked up. "Uncle Timo? Is he here? He's not dead too, is he?"

Etan, who had gone quite pale, shook his head. "When I last saw him, he was hurt, but not beyond mending, Princess. He is at the Hayholt."

"With Auntie Tia-Lia?"

Etan nodded. "Yes. And I'm sure she is taking good care of him." He turned back to the prince. "Again, forgive me, Highness, but this place has given me one surprise after another."

"And me, Brother," said Morgan. "Walk with us, and we will share our news. I am sure my story is no stranger than yours." He considered. "Well, perhaps a bit more. We will see. Then we will take you to our grandfather the king."

Etan stared, dumbfounded. "Did you say the king? Is Duke Osric now the king, then?"

"I hope not," said Morgan with a pang of worry. What else had happened during his long absence? "It would be rude of him—and premature. No, I speak of our other grandfather, King Simon. You will see him shortly, have no doubt."

"It cannot be," was all the monk said.

Morgan was not certain what Etan meant, but he recognized the other's look of exhausted astonishment. "Oh, but it can. Many things can. Especially here, it seems."

"I talked to the ocean!" announced Lillia. "And it talked to me."

Simon had scarcely settled in again beside Jiriki's pallet when he heard a clatter outside the healers' cavern. A slender Sitha appeared in the entrance and darted looks from side to side until she saw Jiriki. She rushed toward him then, speaking the Sithi language, and Simon saw that her eyes were streaming with tears. He rose and stepped back to give her room to kneel beside Jiriki, then watched as she buried her face in his neck and covered his cheek with kisses. Simon was surprised; he had never seen any of the Fair Folk make such shows of either affection or misery, let alone both, and he decided the newcomer must be Tanahaya.

Jiriki lay silent as she whispered in his ear, but Simon thought he could see a little warming in the color of his friend's cheeks, and for a foolish instant even let himself feel a sliver of hope. As Simon watched, Jiriki reached out to touch Tanahaya's belly and murmured something to her, and her tears poured out afresh. Simon stood and went to the cavern entrance, all too aware that he must be intruding on a lover's reunion but not wanting to stray too far away. He saw several more Sithi approaching, picking their way through the uneven tunnel with their accustomed grace, like deer going swiftly over a perilous track. The first was female, a face he did not recognize, solemn and dignified, though her clothes were travel stained. She held a wooden box against her breast, and Simon was utterly astonished to see that it was John Josua's gift from Miriamele, the same decorated chest he had last seen back in the Hayholt, so many moons ago. The sight of it so confounded him that he could not even ask the obvious question. The female Sitha gave him a nod of greeting as she strode past him to join Tanahaya at Jiriki's side, but the last Sitha, a male, stopped in front of Simon and, to his growing bewilderment, bowed to him.

"Seoman King," he said. "It is good to see you again, even at a sad time."

"I must beg your pardon—" Simon began.

"I am Ki'ushapo," the Sitha said. "You and I met first in the snows at the edge of the Oldheart Forest, half a Great Year ago—thirty winters and more in your reckoning."

"Ki'ushapo! Jiriki's kinsman. Yes, I remember you now. Jiriki said you were lost back at the Hayholt."

"And so I would have been, but one of your people found me where I was trapped. He came with me—it was he who had the box that Mistress Ayaminu is so carefully holding—but I fear we left him behind in our haste to come to Jiriki. Brother Etan, he is named."

"Brother Etan!" Simon could only shake his head. "Truly? Is he well?"

"When last I saw him," Ki'ushapo said. "But we crossed the bridge over the river gorge in haste and I have not seen him since. Now, if you will forgive me, I must go to my kinsman—"

"Of course. Your pardon." Simon began to move toward the entrance, thinking he would go find Morgan and Lillia. He still did not entirely believe his luck in having them both with him and safe, and he did not want them long out of his sight. But before he reached the tunnel a calm voice called to him.

"Do not leave, Seoman King."

He turned to see the older female Sitha, the one holding John Josua's box, beckoning him back. He stopped, puzzled.

"Jiriki insists that you stay," she said. "I ask your pardon for not introducing myself. I am Ayaminu of Anvi'janya. And this is Tanahaya, but you will forgive her not rising to greet you."

"Of course," he said. The one called Tanahaya hardly seemed to realize anyone else was in the cavern.

"Come back and join us," Ayaminu bade him. "I promise you, it is Jiriki's wish. And though you know it not, you are in part responsible for the things we have brought to him."

Simon returned, if a shade reluctantly. Whatever relief or happiness that had rallied his Sitha friend's spirits seemed to have dwindled. Breathing with obvious difficulty, Jiriki had let his head fall back once more against the rolled cloak that was his makeshift cushion. Still, he managed to turn and extend a shaking hand, summoning Simon closer. "All is change," said Jiriki. "But life persists."

Simon was again puzzled. He watched as Ayaminu gave the box to Tanahaya, whose cheeks were wet with weeping, something he had scarcely ever seen on Sithi faces, even after Amerasu's murder in Jao é-Tinukai'i.

Tanahaya opened the faintly rattling box and took out three objects. Simon had seen them before, when Tiamak had shown the box to him back in the Hayholt, but the way all four Sithi looked at them made him wonder what he had failed to notice. He had believed the silver and black spheres to be jewelry of some kind, intricately carved wooden beads from a necklace perhaps, each one with a smaller pearlescent sphere inside it, protected by the silvery-gray lattice of the outer sphere. Tanahaya carefully placed them in Jiriki's hands and helped him raise them until they were close to his face so he could see them.

"Kei-in," Jiriki breathed in the Zida'ya tongue, almost reverently, his voice so soft Simon could barely hear him. *"Kei-in dho Keida'ya."*

"I don't understand," said Simon. "What are they?"

"Witchwood seeds," said Ayaminu. "It seems that Utuk'ku's false story that Hamakho's witchwood crown was lost beneath the Hayholt was not so false after all, though she surely believed it to be a lie. Your son must have found them during his explorations of the ruins of old Asu'a under the castle." She saw the look of puzzlement on his face. "Someone called Lord Tiamak sent them with Brother Etan, and that was his guess."

Jiriki could no longer hold up the witchwood seeds. His hands dropped to his bandaged chest; after a moment, Tanahaya carefully took the seeds back. Jiriki said something in his own tongue, a middling-long speech, then reached out and touched Ki'ushapo's hand and his kinsman bent his head. Jiriki spoke again and the other three Sithi turned to stare at Simon, as if he had just done something astonishing.

"Why are you all looking at me?" he finally asked.

"Because Jiriki says it is his wish that you decide what is to be done with the witchwood seeds," Ayaminu said, "—if they can still quicken. If they will grow. It is his last office as Protector before he gives the calling over to Ki'ushapo."

"Decide . . . ? But why me?" Simon was astounded. "Why would he choose me? I do not know anything about witchwood seeds! And I don't know any of your Sithi laws or rules!"

"Why you? Because Jiriki wishes it," said Ayaminu calmly. "You are his *Hikka Staja*, as great an honor as there is among our folk. And at such a complicated time, he thinks it is best that one who is neither Zida'ya nor Hikeda'ya decides what to do with them."

As Simon struggled with this profoundly unexpected idea, Tanahaya, who had been leaning over Jiriki and whispering into his ear, sat back and turned to hand the witchwood seeds to Ayaminu, then abruptly stopped, staring wide-eyed at the silvery things.

"By the Lost Garden and our dear, failed Grove," Tanahaya said in a voice so full of awe it almost sounded like fear. "Look!" She held out the seeds. During the handling, all three spheres had been smeared with blood from Jiriki's wound, and each seed now revealed a tiny tendril of silvery gray-green emerging from its innermost kernel.

For a long moment, Simon and the three Sithi stared at these astonishing signs of life. Then Tanahaya turned back to Jiriki, but when she saw the great and final calm that now suffused his face, she let out a muffled cry of grief and threw herself upon his breast once more.

Ayaminu carefully put the seeds back into John Josua's wooden shaving box, then passed it to Simon without a word. She nodded to Ki'ushapo, then folded her hands across her chest and said a few words in the Zida'ya tongue before turning to leave the healers' chamber.

Ki'ushapo crouched beside his kinsman's body, eyes downcast. Simon took Jiriki's cold hand and wept, shaking with helpless grief.

39

A Halo of Fire

"I'm sorry you're sad, Grandfather," Lillia said. "And I'm sorry that Morgan is sad, too."

"I'm not," Morgan said, but he knew he did not sound convincing.

"Is it because Mama died?" she asked him. "I was sad about that too. I still am, I think, but then sometimes I'm not because it already happened a long time ago. Before I was under the castle. Did I tell you about the spiderwebs and the glowing ball, Morgan?"

"Lillia, please," pleaded the king. "Not so much talk. My heart is very heavy."

"Of course I'm sad because Mama died," Morgan told her. "And Grandmother Miriamele, and everyone else. Can't you go find that Sithi child and play with her?"

"Xila?" Lillia shook her head. "She doesn't know how to play—not the right way. She's like a grown person. I'd rather stay with you."

Her grandfather frowned. "I'm trying to think about something, little cub, and all these questions are not helping."

"Why? I'm doing my best to help. And why do you have that box? It looks old."

"That is what I'm trying to think about," the king said. He and Morgan shared a look.

Morgan's sister was not done asking questions. "What's in it?"

"Several things. Seeds. Seeds are the most important things. And I'm trying to decide what to do with them."

"Give them to me and I'll plant them. I know just where they could go in the Hedge Garden—"

"Please, Lillia." It was Morgan's turn to try. "Just be quiet for a little while."

She showed him a fiercely outthrust lower lip. "That's what everyone always says."

The king looked up; a moment later, so did Morgan. A figure stood in the entrance to the cavern, still and straight as the image of a saint.

"Lady . . . Ayaminu, is it?"

"It is, King Seoman," she said. "And I have greetings for you from Jiriki's sister, Aditu."

"Aditu is here?" asked Simon.

"No, no, she is still in Anvi'janya. But with Utuk'ku dead, the spell that silenced the Witnesses is no more and we can share our thoughts again. Aditu has been part of our preparations to bury Jiriki at Jao é-Tinukai'i."

"Jao é-Tinukai'i?" The king was obviously surprised. "I thought that your people had left that place. That it was empty."

"It is empty of the living," Ayaminu said. "But many were returned to earth there and still remain, and one of those was Jiriki's great-grandmother, Amerasu."

"I would like to go there with you, if I may," Simon said.

"And you may—but first you have another duty, as you know, a duty your friend Jiriki gave to you, *Hikka Staja*."

Morgan did not know what those words meant but his grandfather acknowledged them with a heavy nod of his head. "Shall I come with you now?" Simon asked.

Ayaminu inclined her head. "When you will. But I believe first there is something you will want to see—a message from some fellow mortals. I ask only that you refrain from acting on it until you speak to Protector Ki'ushapo." The king took the parchment from her and unfolded it. His eyes widened as he read, and something almost like a smile began to play across his face. He asked Ayaminu, "Do you know if there is a way down from the peaks at this end of the valley? Likely not, I suppose, or the Norns would have attacked from there instead of coming down through all these caverns and tunnels."

"In truth there is such a way," said Ayaminu. "A narrow and perilous hidden track that only our folk here knew. They did not fear the Norns would use it even if they discovered it, because any enemy would have to come down it in file and be exposed to arrows from below."

"Good!" Watching, Morgan thought his grandfather had regained a little of his old vigor. "I would ask that someone could go to the top and find the one who sent this, then guide him back down. But they should make the descent slowly and carefully—the one who wrote this is no longer young and is a little gone to fat." He turned to Morgan. "I know not how long I will have to wait here. Perhaps you could take Lillia for a while." He gave Morgan a pleading look.

Morgan stood. "Come on, Lilly-lizard. Our grandfather wants a little time to himself."

"But I could help him," his sister protested. "Truly, I could."

"I do not doubt it," said the king. "But later, please. Things may get a bit delicate here in the next hours, and you might accidentally be helpful at the wrong time, Granddaughter."

What is that parchment about? wondered Morgan. *And why must I always be sent away? Have I still not proved myself to him? Because God knows I could use a distraction.*

Troubled by that thought, as well as the despair that two days without word from Nezeru had brought him, he led his pouting sister out of the cavern.

Simon had thought he would slip quietly into the cavern as he had before, but he was wrong. As soon as he entered, all the dozen or more immortals gathered there turned to look at him with unblinking eyes, like a room full of cats.

To his immense relief, he saw Rukayu beckoning him to join her on the far side of the fire. The many amber eyes never left him, though, even after he sat, until Geloë lifted her gold-woven, gauntleted hand. The immortals now turned to watch her instead, with expressions ranging from restrained concern to outright distrust.

"We are all here," she said in the Sithi tongue as Rukayu quietly rendered her words into Westerling. "Prince Pratiki, you will speak for the Hikeda'ya. Protector Ki'ushapo, you will speak for the Zida'ya."

"Remember, Ki'ushapo may speak for us," said Yizashi Grayspear, "but he cannot compel us. Our clans are linked by blood and history, but even the much respected House of Year-Dancing cannot force their fellows to act against their will. Not even Jenjiyana or Amerasu Ship-born could do that."

Ki'ushapo nodded in agreement. "I speak only for my own clan, as Yizashi does for his, and Okajata for hers."

"The distinction is noted," said Geloë's dry voice.

"I must point out that the situation of the Hikeda'ya is not so different from that of the Zida'ya," said Prince Pratiki in a stern voice. Simon wondered whether his coldness came from anger or was simply the way of Norn folk. "I may be the leader of Clan Hamakha and thus Utuk'ku's heir, but there is no telling what will happen when news reaches Nakkiga that the queen—the only ruler we have ever known—is dead. Still, I am grateful to all those who helped me prepare for this fateful day, especially Lady Ayaminu of the Zida'ya. We may all hope for less fearful days ahead."

Geloë spoke up again. "I will not restate what I plan to do, and I certainly will not ask permission. Without malice, I say that the twin tribes of the Keida'ya have no rights over the ship called *The Witchwood Crown*, and no rights over the Vao. We will take the ship, and that is that. All with Tinukeda'ya blood who wish to leave these lands will do so with me. Will any here dispute our right to do so?"

"How will you 'take' a ship that is stuck halfway into a mountainside?" demanded Okajata. "I do not think even if you gathered a thousand times a thousand Tinukeda'ya that they could chisel it out of its stony tomb."

Pratiki stood once more. "Enough of such questions—we have more pressing matters to talk about today. I think it likely that all gathered here know what the mortal king Seoman of Erchester has in that wooden box. Are any of you still unaware of this great and strange discovery?" He looked around but all remained silent. "Then let us continue."

"But what right does a mortal have to make such an awesome, terrible decision?" demanded one of the Norn nobles. "The witchwood trees and their seeds belong to those who brought them here from the Garden!"

A few of those gathered began to argue this question among themselves, quietly and calmly at first, but Simon could see that such restraint would not last long, even among the usually patient immortals.

"Listen to me!" Simon said in a loud voice. "I was given these from the dying hand of Jiriki i-Sa'onserei." He surprised himself by losing control of his voice, ending his words with a catch in his throat, almost sobbing. As Rukayu shaped his words into their own tongue, the gathered immortals stared at him, some with pity, others as if they had never seen tears of any kind. "Forgive me," Simon continued. "The wound of his death is very fresh. As to who has the right, these seeds were left tens of centuries ago—that is in mortal years, I don't know how to do the sums for your Great Years—in the ruins underneath the Hayholt, my castle."

"The seeds from Hamakho the Great's own memorial crown," said a Norn.

"And your castle was built atop the ruins of Asu'a," one of the Sithi pointed out. "*Our* castle, destroyed by mortals."

"*Overrun* by mortals," said Geloë. "But it was destroyed in large part by Ineluki, with help from Utuk'ku's Red Hand in their desperate and reckless attempt to stop the invading Northmen."

"It is a mistake to try to untangle first grievances," declared Ki'ushapo. "That we are here today is proof of that. Utuk'ku's fury began ages before any of us were born, yet it nearly killed us all."

The room once more fell into silence, but now Simon could sense the strained tension of the gathered immortals. He took a breath to steady his voice, then began again. "These long-lost seeds were found by a mortal—by my son, as it happens—and recognized for what they were by another mortal, then carried by his mortal messenger until they finally reached Jiriki. You will see them." He stared around the cavern and put his sorrow and frustration into his words. "Jiriki's blood is on them, and at his touch, they sprouted. To me, that seems a miracle . . . but I am only a mortal. Still, since it was Jiriki's family who held Asu'a last, I think it is clear he had a right to decide what to do with them, and he asked me to take up that task on his behalf . . . just before . . ." He had to pause for a moment. "Just before he died."

"May he find the Garden," said Ki'ushapo, and several of his folk echoed him as Rukayu translated it for Simon, but the party of Norns only listened silently.

"I will not take much of your time," Simon went on. "But I want you to know that I spent a sleepless night wondering what would be the right thing to do. I did not want this responsibility, but Jiriki was my friend. And I have come to a decision. But I have a question for you," he looked to Prince Pratiki, "and you," he turned to Ki'ushapo, "before I tell you what I decided, and it is this: Will your people abide by what I say? Because otherwise, I will simply take the seeds back to Erkynland, unless you kill me and steal them from the one Jiriki chose to watch over them and decide their fate. Well? What say you all?"

Ki'ushapo was the first to speak. "There was none among us more honorable or brave than my kinsman Jiriki. He cared only for what was just. And I know this mortal king too and have fought beside him. I trust his good will. Speaking for the Sa'onserei, I say I will abide by his decision." He turned to the other Zida'ya seated around the fire. "What say the rest of you?"

One by one, the representatives of the other clans present nodded their acceptance, although it was clear even to Simon that many of them had misgivings.

"The subject has a sharper edge for the Hikeda'ya," said Pratiki. "If the seeds truly came from the memorial crown of Hamakho, it could be claimed they are ours by right." He raised his hand to forestall any response. "And neither is it certain that I will continue to speak for my people. But for this moment I do, and I say that I will trust the judgment of Jiriki i-Sa'onserei and abide by the mortal's choice."

A palpable stir of unhappiness passed through the gathered Norns, and though it would have been nothing from a mortal crowd, it clearly angered Prince Pratiki. "Enough!" he cried in a commanding tone. "We will not start the war again. Either the Hikeda'ya accept my decisions as master of the Hamakha Clan or I will step down and open the gates to new chaos. Is that what you wish, my kinfolk?"

For a moment the balance seemed to sway, and although Simon could not begin to know exactly what went on among the Norns, he saw looks and hand-signals flashing back and forth between them. At last, though, they all turned back to Pratiki and, one by one, lowered their heads in fealty.

"So," the prince said, his voice still harsh. "It seems we Hikeda'ya also abide by Jiriki's choice."

Simon nodded in relief and took a deep breath. "Then I will tell you what I have decided." He opened the box and took out the first of the three seeds. Already a slender, green-gray root tendril was curling its way out of the silvery tangle that protected the kernel. "There are three seeds. I give this one to Valada Geloë. All of you owe her more than you probably know. Without her, it is likely we would all be dead. If she is to take her people and start again in some other land—begin again, this time in freedom—they should have some of the witchwood that came from the Garden."

It was clear that his decision did not please all present, especially among the Hikeda'ya, but Prince Pratiki only nodded, his pale, narrow face empty of expression. Simon got up and handed Geloë the seed. She folded the fingers of her gauntlet around it with surprising delicacy.

"I had hoped for this," she said. "Thank you, Simon."

He turned back to the fire. "And now there are two. It doesn't take a great wit, or even the sort of wit that I have, to see that both clans, Norns and Sithi—your pardon, *Hikeda'ya* and *Zida'ya*—should each have one." He held up his hand. "But I have another demand. If the two clans cannot agree to it, then I will give these two to Geloë and her people as well." Even Ki'ushapo looked distressed by this pronouncement. This was the moment Simon had feared. "Hear me out," he said. "Because these will be the last two seeds in this land until they grow and can make more seeds, I give one to Pratiki's people and one to the Zida'ya—but only if they plant them and tend them together."

"But where would we do such a thing?" asked Pratiki slowly. He did not sound unhappy, just curious. "They came from the ruins of Asu'a, but that is a mortal place now."

"That mortal place was also burned to the ground at your queen's orders," Simon pointed out. "But that is not where they should be planted."

"Then where?"

"I thought about this, too," said Simon. "I think the new grove, if that is what it's called, should be started in the same place that Jiriki will be laid in the earth—in Jao é-Tinukai'i."

"But that is far from Nakkiga," said Celebrant Zuniyabe. "Surrounded by the lands of the Zida'ya. How is that fair?"

"I never said it was fair. But Jao é-Tinukai'i was deserted because of Utuk'ku's monstrous attack on Amerasu, and Amerasu's body lies there, too. I say that both peoples should make a common grove, starting with these two seeds, and tend them together. Let only those who tend the witchwood trees live there, and no more Zida'ya than Hikeda'ya. You will grow the witchwood again together." He felt stubbornly certain he was right, although there could be no precedent for such a strange thing, and no way for Simon himself to force the two tribes of immortals to obey after the seeds were surrendered. "That is my choice. What do you say?"

And then, to his utter shock, someone laughed. The tall Hikeda'ya noble sitting on Prince Pratiki's left clapped her long, graceful hands together. "I cannot imagine anything better!" she said.

Pratiki looked at her, bemused. "Do you truly think so, Lady Miga?"

"Our two tribes came to this land together, Highness," she said. "We have let Utuk'ku's living malice, and the hatreds that belonged to many who are long long dead, keep us apart for too long. This mortal king has told us that Hikeda'ya and Zida'ya must tend the trees together or we will both lose them. How right! How fitting!"

Then the whole company fell into active conversation and dispute, none of it loud, some of it entirely silent and conducted in hand gestures, but Rukayu did not bother to translate any more, as if the arguments meant little.

For you, Jiriki, Simon thought. Because what had finally swayed him to this solution in the night's last hours was the thought that this was what Jiriki himself would have done.

"Why does everyone always tell different stories?" Lillia asked as they made their way out of the caverns and into the cold daylight.

"About what?" Morgan asked.

"About what people do when they die. Where they go."

Morgan felt so heavy-hearted that it took a while to work up the strength to reply. "Because . . . well, because nobody really knows."

"But what about Heaven? Father Nulles at the Hayholt said we go to Heaven. And that's what Grandfather King Simon said, too, when Mama died. But then why does everybody cry? That isn't right."

"They cry—we cry—because we're going to miss them, I suppose. Even if we know we're going to see them again someday. You're just a little girl, Lil. I hope it will be a long, long time before you see Mama again in Heaven, because I want you to be here with us."

"But Grandfather said the lady—can I say her name now? I can say her name now, can't I? The lady Geloë was dead, but then she came back alive. Will Mama or Grandmother Queen Miriamele come back alive?"

"I don't know, Lil. But I think what happened with Geloë"—the name was still strange to him, and his infrequent glimpses of the weird, armored figure were not particularly reassuring about life after death—"is not like what happens when ordinary people die."

"But Grandmother Miriamele was the queen!"

"I don't mean ordinary that way." He shook his head. "I don't know what I mean, Lil. Can we talk about something else?"

She made a noise of irritation. "*Mmmf.* Nobody ever wants to talk about it. But the Dreaming Sea told me that everyone can live forever and never die. So why did the voices say that?"

"Who told you that—?" But Morgan had already lost the thread of his sister's burble of conversation, because he had seen someone that he realized he had been looking for since he and his sister had left their grandfather's side. She was sitting by herself on a ridge of stone a short distance away, staring out at the gorge and the icy rainbows picked out in the mist by the winter sun. "Lillia, can you sit here for a moment? Just here, where I can see you?"

She gave him a look of suspicion. "Why?" She let her gaze travel in the direction Morgan had been looking. "Do you want to talk to that lady? Is she your sweetheart? Why is she so white?"

"Will you just stay here for a moment?"

"You are a terrible brother. What if the Norns try to get me?"

"That lady *is* a Norn. And she is perfectly nice and wouldn't try to 'get' you. Unless she had to listen to you when you never stop talking."

Lillia gave him a hurt look. "I do so. Sometimes. But my thoughts are all piled up right now."

"Then I'm sorry. Don't go away, Pigling. Just stay where I can see you when I look over." And before she could think of more questions to ask, he walked toward the place where Nezeru sat watching the nearly invisible winter rainbows.

She knew his scent so well that she sensed his presence before he even stepped out of the cave. When he appeared, though, with a small child at his side, she quickly looked away, not wanting him to get the wrong idea about anything.

"Nezeru. It is good to see you."

She looked up, not quite willing to feign surprise, but also not wanting to let him know how much a part of her—a foolish, dangerous part—had hoped he would come toward her. "Morgan," she said as plainly as she could. Why did she have this congested feeling in her chest, as though she could not get a full breath? It was extremely annoying. "It is good to see you well. Is that truly your sister? How did she come to this place?"

She was pleased with herself, because now he had a reason to spend some time telling her a version of how his grandfather and sister came to be here at Tanakirú, which meant she could get a good, deep breath and begin feeling the way she knew she ought to feel before she had to speak again.

". . . But I'm not the only one who's had a reunion," he said at last. "You found your father."

"Yes. The Mother of A . . . the queen brought him here. He had to build a tunnel down through the mountain because she wanted to bring Sacrifice troops from there"—she pointed to the broad western flank of Kushiba—"so they could attack the Zida'ya from behind. The tunnel was very long and very steep, and he had only a very short time to dig it."

"And he did it all by himself. His hands must have hurt."

For a moment she thought he must not even be listening to her, to ask a question so idiotic, but then she realized he was making what he must have thought was a jest. "No, he did not dig it himself," she said with a certain emphasized dignity. "He had his Builders to do it—and slaves from the mortal fortress."

"From Naglimund?" Morgan's tone changed. "He used slaves to do the work here?"

"Slaves that were going to be killed by General Kikiti," she said. "My father saved them by telling the queen and everyone else that he could not do the work without them. And he made certain they were fed and didn't freeze to death, too."

"Ah. So he is one of the *good* Hikeda'ya."

She bit back an angry reply. Her stomach was sour. "Is this why you wanted to see me, Morgan? To insult my father?"

He too seemed to struggle with the urge to say something unpleasant. "No," he said at last. "No, it's not. And I believe you when you say he saved lives. I'm sorry. I just . . ." He trailed off. "I don't know what to say, to tell truth. I . . . I miss you, Nezeru. I can't believe that we're not going to see each other anymore."

She was mollified, but only a little. "Are you certain it's not just that you wish you could couple with me again?"

"A little," he admitted. "But it's more. I just don't have the words for what I feel."

"Then don't look for them," she said. "I tried to warn you. I tried!"

"Warned me of what? That you didn't care about me? But you admitted that you did, Nezeru. The last night on the ship, before that . . . thing snatched you up and went off with you. You said, 'I care for you, Morgan.'"

"And I do. But that is not enough."

"Enough for what?"

"Enough to try to change the world. Enough to pretend that what happened between us was anything but . . . but . . ."

"A meaningless dalliance during a time of war," he finished for her.

"I do not know that word, 'dalliance', but if it means what I think—yes!"

He stared at her for a long time. She tried to meet his angry gaze, but at last had to look down. "Even when I thought you were my enemy," he said, "I never thought you were a coward."

"What?"

"You heard me, Nezeru. A coward. Afraid of things that you don't know. Afraid of doing something that would shame you in front of the same Sacrifice soldiers that threw you out of your order and tried to kill you. Or is it your father that you're afraid of shaming?"

She laughed bitterly. "You don't know anything. My father sired me with a mortal woman! Shamed? My mother is a mortal just like you!" She felt a sudden clutch at her heart. "Oh, by the White Prince, my mother! What has happened to her? My stepmother hated her so much . . ."

Silence fell between them. They were both consumed with worry and fear, but for the moment, neither of them could find words.

"I am Lady Miga seyt-Jinnata," the Hikeda'ya noblewoman said. "You are Jarnulf, a Queen's Huntsman, yes?"

"Not precisely," he said. "But if you come to me with bad news, I suppose it doesn't really matter. Has the prince decided I need to die after all?"

Her look of amusement should have made him feel better, but some Hikeda'ya nobles had very strange ideas about what was humorous. "May I enter?" she asked. "What did you mean, 'not precisely'?"

"It doesn't matter." He gestured for her to enter his current residence, a cave that was little more than a dimple in a tunnel wall close to the place where the

Queen's Teeth guards had their temporary barracks. "I have no furniture except my cloak to sit on," he said. "Apologies."

"No need. I will not be here long—and neither will you."

"I do not find that reassuring, Lady Miga."

She nodded. "I will make things clearer. Prince Pratiki has decided that it is too difficult to keep you safe."

He did his best to ignore the sudden, swift beating of his heart. "Then I am going to be executed after all?"

"No, no. But as you can imagine, there are many here among our people who would happily see you dead. I am not one of them, just so you know." Perhaps out of old habit, she looked around as if someone might be listening. "I have hoped for many years that this day of freedom would come. I feared the queen more than I feared any of our people's enemies."

"So, Pratiki won't kill me. Then what?"

"He is going to send you to the Zida'ya and their mortal ally, King Seoman. You will be safer with them—you may even be a hero of sorts—whereas here, among our folk, there is a strong chance that even with the Queen's Teeth watching over you, someone might decide to take revenge on behalf of Utuk'ku's angriest mourners."

"Ah." He thought about it for a moment. "It sounds a reasonable plan. When do I go?"

"Now," she said. "I—along with a few of the prince's guards—will escort you."

"Please give me time to gather up all my many possessions." He bent for his wrinkled and weather-stained cloak. "Done," he said. "Lead the way. But it will be strange to live among my own kind again—mortals, I mean. I am not quite certain how they behave."

"Nor am I," she said. "But I am beginning to believe that I should learn."

Jarnulf could not help wondering who these mortals were, and if this could really be the King Seoman he had heard of who, with his queen, were the rulers of the High Ward. It seemed odd and unlikely though: in his short time of freedom before Prince Pratiki had more or less imprisoned him for his own protection, he had seen no mortals here in Tanakirú, and certainly nothing like the retinue that should accompany such an important king. He could not help thinking of the risk he had taken to send a message to the royal company on his way to Urmsheim, and the treasured object he had sent with it to show his sincerity, now almost certainly lost forever. As he remembered the night he had spent on the hilltop, trapped by mortal soldiers with Makho and Nezeru and the rest, he also remembered his first bargain with Goh Gam Gar, and was surprised by the surge of sadness that came with the memory.

Perhaps the only friend I have made since Father vanished, he thought. *And I ended his life.* The fact that the giant had begged him to do so did little to drive the hurt away. *I owed him more than just a merciful death, but that was all I could give him, and I could do nothing about seeing him properly buried, despite my other promise. I pray God will look after him.*

"Lady Miga," he began, "I owe a debt to the giant Goh Gam Gar, who was struck down by the queen. I promised him I would see that he had a proper cairn—that his body would not be dragged away and left for scavengers."

"It is strange you should ask that," she said as she led him across the broad stone plateau that had become something like the commons-yard of Tanakirú. The space was splashed with pale afternoon sun and full of Hikeda'ya and Zida'ya who all seemed—if he didn't examine their faces and postures too closely—to have abruptly put aside their hatred of each other. "Has someone given you news of it?"

"News of what?"

"High Magister Viyeki, the prince's factor, decreed that the giant should be buried with due honor, like the other fallen of the battle—except for Utuk'ku, of course, who will be returned to Nakkiga to rest in the Clan Hamakha vault."

"Truly?" The name Viyeki was familiar, but Jarnulf could not immediately recognize it. *I cannot even be sure what my own name is any longer,* he thought, *so why do I recognize his?* "I am glad, then—though I do not quite understand it. I thought I alone had made a promise to honor him."

"*Much is done, little of it spoken first, none of it admitted afterward,* as the poet writes," said Lady Miga as they walked. "Do you know the poems of Shun'y'asu of Blue Spirit Peak? He is a favorite of Prince Pratiki's."

"No, I fear I do not, Lady." His enslaved childhood had not left him much time for poetry, and Father had quoted nothing but the Book of Aedon.

Near the entrance to one of the caverns in the cliff face, he saw two people talking in an urgent, unhappy way. At first he thought that he had merely tricked himself into seeing someone he recognized, but as Lady Miga led him past the pair, he decided that he had not tricked himself at all.

"My Lady, will you pardon me for a moment?" he asked. "I think I see someone with whom I should speak." He had never known much about how to address a Hikeda'ya superior: in his youth, he had been taught to call any of them he encountered 'master' unless corrected.

Lady Miga gave him a look that did not entirely hide surprise. Was it his imagination, or was this noble less hidden in her thoughts than those he had met in the past? "Very well," she said. "But do not take too long. The prince expects me back shortly and I promised I would deliver you to the mortal king myself."

As he approached, the person he felt certain was Nezeru finished speaking with a young male mortal, who turned abruptly and walked away.

"Nezeru?" he asked as he approached, though he now felt certain. "Is that truly you?"

She turned. A very odd series of expressions crossed her face as she recognized him. He could not help thinking that she, too, seemed to have lost some of her Sacrifice-instilled reserve. "Jarnulf. What are you doing here? I should kill you for what you did to me."

"Perhaps. But there are several others of your folk who are also waiting for that privilege," he said. "You must settle precedence among yourselves."

"What are you doing here?" she asked again. "And why would you think I would wish to speak to you?"

"I didn't," he said. "I want to speak to you, though, and tell you I am sorry for what happened, but not sorry that I did it."

"So, you admit you ruined me as a Sacrifice. And you think an apology—"

"I do not apologize for that, but for stealing your senses with the *kei-vishaa* and tying you to my horse. I later breathed that wretched dust myself, so I know how unpleasant it must have been."

She stared at him, clearly struggling with a desire to gut him on the spot. "And you came all the way to this end-of-the-world place just to tell me that?"

"No. I came to this place to kill Queen Utuk'ku. And I succeeded. You may do what you want to me now that you know." He lifted his hands to show that he carried no weapon. "As I said, most of your people would like me dead, so this is your chance to outdo them and prove your loyalty."

She seemed to have suddenly remembered her heritage: her face went cold and expressionless. "What do you mean, you killed the queen?"

"I shot her in the head with an arrow. I had tried many times and failed, and thought I had failed this time, too, but someone stabbed her even as I aimed my second dart, and it caught her unaware."

"That was you?" She stared as though she thought he was lying. "And you do not know who stabbed her?"

"No. I could not see. I was blocked by the Queen's Teeth." He suddenly touched his forehead. "Ah! I remember now why I knew that name! Viyeki is your father—a high nobleman. Is that why the giant Goh Gam Gar is getting a proper burial? Was it you who arranged it?"

Her stiff facade softened a little. "The giant was more of an ally to me than my own people. He saved us all. Yes, I asked my father to make certain he would be treated with respect."

"I thank you for it. And I have something to tell you that may also come as a surprise," he began, but saw that Nezeru's attention had been drawn elsewhere. He turned to follow her gaze and saw that the mortal youth with whom she had been arguing was now striding back toward them, face set in hard, bitter lines.

"No," said this newcomer loudly before he was even within a half-dozen paces. "No, Nezeru, I cannot let it rest so. I have thought about everything you said and the more I consider, the more stupid it seems to me."

"Morgan, no." She gestured toward Jarnulf. "I am speaking with someone."

Jarnulf was about to excuse himself. After all, he had made the apology he needed to make, and she had not tried to kill him. Surely it would do no good to press his luck any further—they were never going to be friends. But he found himself suddenly distracted: as the one she called Morgan drew closer, he passed through a beam of afternoon sun that lanced down through a gap in the clouds and his golden-brown hair suddenly became a fiery halo around his head. Though the young man's comely face was stiff with anger, there was something about him that made Jarnulf stare, something that made his breath catch in his throat.

"Who is this?" Jarnulf asked in an unsteady voice. He had never seen this youth before, but he felt as though he had been waiting for him as long as he could remember.

"What?" Nezeru turned toward him, distracted. "By the White Prince, what a spot this Tanakirú is—as busy as a marketplace. Morgan, this is Jarnulf. We traveled to Urmsheim together. I told you about him."

The youth slowed, finally looking at Jarnulf. "The one who kidnapped you?"

Saved her, I would put it, was what Jarnulf intended to say, but found he could not make the proper words. After a moment of strangled hesitation, he said, "I was Gilhedur before I was Jarnulf. Before Nezeru knew me. I think I might become Gilhedur again." He could not take his eyes off the youth, but neither could he put a name to his feelings. He almost felt dizzy.

Nezeru made a noise of frustration. "Another name? Will you run away then, and start over? Is that what you do, Jarnulf?"

"Introduce me," he managed to say to Nezeru. "I beg you."

Her eyes widened, but she could not seem to think of a reason to object. "This is Prince Morgan of Erkynland," she said. "King Simon is his grandfather. Prince Morgan is the heir to the High Throne."

"That is a great deal to put on a first meeting," complained Morgan. "And you are . . . Gil . . . Gilharnulf, did you say? Or was it Jarn-something?" Now his eyes widened. "Hold a moment—was it Jarnulf? Are you the one who sent the message to my grandfather—a letter tied to an arrow?"

But Jarnulf had already taken a step toward the young man, who still stood unknowingly bathed in a shaft of Godly sunlight. He dropped to one knee. "When you come into your kingdom, Prince Morgan," he said in a shamefully unsteady voice, "then I pray that you will make me your knight and let me serve you. I promise to faithfully do your will, in God's name."

Surprised and confused, the golden youth looked down at him. "I beg your pardon?"

"It seems," said Nezeru, in a tone that suggested she was only slightly less puzzled by Jarnulf's action than the prince was, "that we all have things to talk about."

"I will return, then," said Jarnulf, rising. "I ask your pardons. I hope we will speak soon, Prince Morgan, but Lady Miga is waiting there to make me your grandfather's prisoner, and I have kept her waiting long enough."

Morgan did not bother to hide his bewilderment and irritation. "If you say so, Sir Whatever Your Name May Be. I bid you good day."

My purpose—my new purpose, thought Jarnulf as he walked back to waiting Lady Miga. *To serve a prince—a king someday! And I will be his finest knight.* His heart was beating as swiftly as a dove's wings. A look back revealed the two of them staring after him. *You have revealed my destiny to me once again, my Lord God. Thank You, Heavenly Father, for always looking after your humble servant.*

40

News from the North

At first Simon thought Lady Ayaminu had brought him another Sithi visitor, because the silhouette in the cavern entrance was so slender.

"There is a messenger here to see you," was all she said. "I will leave you alone to talk." She slipped away, silent as smoke.

"King Simon?" the stranger said in a voice that he at first thought must be female.

"Yes, that is me."

The newcomer stepped into the light of the glowing sphere, revealing himself to be a mortal boy not quite into manhood, long of leg, with pale hair as disarrayed as the pelt of a wet cat, and wearing an expression that might have belonged on a knight entering a dragon's den. "Jarl Sludig is my father, Your Majesty. I am Hinrig, the third-born."

"I take it that your father, bless him, did not want to follow the Sithi trail down from the peak."

"He took one look, your Majesty, and called for me. 'You are half goat, child,' was what he said. 'Go and see what this person wants, and whether it really is King Simon, which I doubt.'" The boy's jaw worked nervously for a moment. "He told me to ask you something so I would know if it was truly you."

Simon smiled. "Ask away, lad."

"He said, 'King Simon has a dragon mark. Have him show you.' But I don't know what that is."

Simon beckoned the youth forward. "Here it is, on my cheek. You can see it in my hair, too, although it is not so plain as it once was, so much gray having crept in." He leaned into better light. "See the streak of white? That was where dragon's blood splashed me. Your father was there."

The boy nodded, clearly relieved. "I see it."

"Come and sit, then," said Simon. "Tell me what brought my friend Sludig out here, so far from his farm."

Hinrig dropped down beside the small fire with the unthinking ease of youth, then peered at Simon, still a little shy. "Father received a message from Lord Tikamak in Erchester."

"Tiamak, but close enough. I am glad to hear my councilor is still looking after the kingdom, though he must have sent the letter out some time ago. What did it say?"

"I do not know all of it, Majesty, but my father said that Lord Tik . . . that the lord wrote to say a great battle of Norns and Sithi was taking place at the northern end of the Wealdhelm, and that Prince Jiriki, friend to the mortal kingdoms, was fighting desperately against the White Foxes and their mistress, the Norn Queen." As soon as he uttered the name he stopped and looked around, as though the dread queen might suddenly appear in a puff of smoke. Then he made the Sign of the Tree.

"I am happy to tell you that the witch is dead," said Simon. "Go on."

"Duke Grimbrand gave my father permission to bring a company to help this Jiriki but told him to make certain of the situation first. We crossed the White Waste and when we got here, we found traces of the Norns—a road leading into the heights. Then we climbed high up the mountain, where my father waits now."

"The mountain you just climbed down. I suppose I was a bit ambitious thinking Sludig could manage it."

"It is rather steep, Majesty," Hinrig admitted. "The Sitha-fairy who led me down had to stop and wait for me many times."

The melancholy that had struck Simon at the mention of Jiriki's name now widened into something more complicated, an entire trove of memories. "I have followed more than a few Sithi in my time, lad, over mountains and through forests, and I know exactly what you mean. They do not seek to make you feel bad about it, but you can sense their polite impatience."

"That is just it, Majesty," said Hinrig, nodding vigorously. "And the way they leap! I half expected my guide to simply keep going and never land, to fly like a white-faced goose!"

"Yes, I know. But I want to hear what happened on the mountainside, before Sludig sent his letter."

"Oh! It was very odd, Majesty. We went up the mountain road, scouts going first because we did not know what we would find. My father kept me near him even when I wanted to go with them." A shadow of frustration passed over his face at the memory; in that moment, Simon saw his old friend revealed, a hint of Sludig's scowl when he had been balked by something. "When the scouts finally came back, they told a strange story."

"You can hurry past the scouts' reports and onto what you actually found there," Simon said, but kindly.

"Oh. Oh! Very well, Majesty. When we were about halfway up, we found the Norns' camp—but the Norns did not rule there."

Simon raised an eyebrow. "Explain."

"Do you know the creatures we call Dvernings in Rimmersgard?" Hinrig asked. "Thin, with big eyes, and hands like hayforks?"

"Dwarrows, we say in Erkynland, or sometimes they are called Delvers. They are of the Tinukeda'ya. Stoneworkers and builders. Why do you ask?"

"Because we found only a few dozen Norns left in the camp, all prisoners. The camp was held by Dvernings instead—perhaps a hundred of them or more! It was a strange sight, Your Majesty, but it was better than the bloody fight we were expecting."

Simon knew nothing of this Hikeda'ya mountain camp. He guessed it must be the place where Queen Utuk'ku entered the tunnels with her soldiers, seeking to ambush the Sithi from behind. "So, these Tinukeda'ya—these Dvernings—had captured the Norns? Were they slaves who rebelled?"

Hinrig nodded. "That's what they said. But the Norns they had prisoned in a paddock were not the only ones—many, many more Norn soldiers were trapped inside a cavern there. The Dvernings said one end of the tunnel had collapsed, and then they had blocked the near end before the Norn soldiers could get out."

Simon laughed in sheer pleasure. "Clever! The Dwarrows are not fighters, but they are magicians with stone and earth." He stood, ignoring the crackle and pop of his joints, which was almost as loud as the sounds of the fire. "And will you be able to make your way back up to your father, bearing a letter from me?"

Young Hinrig was not yet much good at hiding his feelings. "Of . . . of course, Majesty."

"Is something wrong, lad?"

"I am tired, sir. And I did not get much to eat before I left this morning—"

"Blessed Saint Rhiap, I did not mean for you to go this moment! We will feed you, and you will sleep here tonight and go up again in the morning. But will your father worry?"

"The Sitha told him I would not be able to get down and come back under a single sun. I remember that because I thought it was funny—'a single sun'. As if there might be more than one."

"You have done well, young Hinrig," Simon told him. "Your sire will be proud. Come and let us find you something good to fill your belly. I will warn you to stick to what you can get from the Sithi. The Norns are currently peaceful here, but the food they eat is terrifying."

"We cannot stay here any longer," Tzoja told her friend Vordis. "I have just seen Viyeki's wife Khimabu again with several other nobles—complaining to the guards, as usual. I do not think she saw me, but it is only a matter of time before our luck runs out."

Vordis straightened. "I do not like it here much," she said, "but where else can we go? Do you think we could escape the valley and all these Hikeda'ya soldiers? That frightens me, Tzoja, but I will try to be brave if you say we must."

Tzoja looked around at the camp, which although still nominally maintained by guards from the Order of Sacrifice, had become less ordered and more anarchic every day. "Leave the valley? No, not that. At least here we are being fed. I mean to cross the bridge over the gorge—to the other side, where everything important seems to be happening."

The siege-bridge over the Narrowdark's violent headwaters had finally been replaced with a stronger, more permanent structure. The building of the new bridge had taken two full days, and Tzoja had watched the construction avidly, praying for a glimpse of Viyeki, but although it was his Order of Builders who had put up the new span, he had never made an appearance.

"I beg you, though, do not leave me!" Vordis was doing her best to keep her voice steady. "I know only what you have told me about this strange place, and I have never hated my blindness so much. I would be terrified to be alone here."

"I did not intend to leave you behind." She reached out and squeezed her friend's hand. "I would never leave you in danger. Khimabu is a vengeful creature and I feel sure she would take out at least some of her anger on you if she couldn't find me. No, let us gather up our things and try to cross."

"But how? You said they hardly let anyone onto the bridge."

"Which is why I want to cross to the other side. So far, the Hikeda'ya nobles like Lady Khimabu are being kept here in the camp. As to how—well, I will think of something."

Vordis looked doubtful but began feeling around for her few belongings. "I do not want to be a burden to you, Tzoja."

"Oh! Never! Never, dear one. You have saved me just by being with me. I would have given in to despair long ago, otherwise."

"And Jarnulf. Don't forget him. He helped keep us alive too."

And helped get my daughter driven from the Order of Sacrifice as a traitor, Tzoja thought but didn't say. *Before deserting us to run off with a mad giant.* "No, don't worry. I haven't forgotten him."

"Lady Miga, it is good to see you as always." Viyeki bowed. "And Lady Ayaminu, I have heard much about you over the years. Even in the Maze Palace, your name was spoken with respect. It is an honor finally to meet you."

Ayaminu did not hide her skepticism. Viyeki had been surprised several times by how much less guarded and formal than his own folk the present-day Zida'ya seemed to be. "I cannot believe you heard much good about me at the Nakkiga court, High Magister," she said, "but I will believe you for the sake of courtesy."

"How can I help you?" he asked. "Is there a question I can put before Prince Pratiki?"

"Pratiki already knows the worst of the day's news—but you may not," said Lady Miga. "Saomeji has escaped."

"The rogue Singer? Akhenabi's son?" He shook his head. "It is still hard to believe that . . ." He hesitated, then threw away caution. "That such a monster ever spawned a child." The import of what Miga had said suddenly struck him. "Escaped? How?"

She shook her head. "We do not know. For myself, I suspect a sympathetic Sacrifice guard or two may have helped him."

"This is grave news. He will likely bolt for Nakkiga where he will have many allies." Viyeki had a plunging feeling in his gut. "He will do his best to turn people against Pratiki."

"The prince is already aware, as I said," Miga told him. "And the Order of Echoes has passed on Pratiki's warnings to their counterparts in the Maze Palace. The Hamakha Guard will be on the watch for Saomeji, never fear."

"But how many others like him are out there?" Viyeki knitted his fingers together to keep from drumming them on his leg in an unseemly display of worry. "More importantly, what can I do?"

"About Saomeji? Nothing. But since Pratiki shows such trust in you, we thought it was time we all spoke together."

Viyeki felt the hackles stir on his neck. Why was Lady Miga, a member of the Order of Chroniclers, suddenly such an important personage? And she and Ayaminu seemed almost like old friends—or old confederates. But how could that be? Queen Utuk'ku had very strictly prohibited Nakkiga's nobles from communicating with any of the Zida'ya houses; some Hikeda'ya had even been put to death over breaches of that rule. "I welcome your confidence," he said now, "but confess I am still not certain what you want of me if His Highness Pratiki already knows about the escape."

"Saomeji is not what brought us here," said Lady Miga. "But we are waiting for one more. Then you will know all."

"One more?" said Viyeki. This was beginning to feel more like an ambush than a conversation.

One of Viyeki's guards stepped into the cavern. "High Celebrant Zuniyabe has come," he announced.

"Welcome, High Celebrant," said Ayaminu, beckoning him in.

For long moments Viyeki could only stare at the new arrival in amazement, even after he realized how obvious his surprise must be. The High Celebrant, for the first time in Viyeki's memory, was unmasked. More than that, he had apparently also foresworn the white face paint that all the older Hikeda'ya had been forced to wear to mimic their white-skinned descendants: his lean, sharp-eyed face was the same golden color as the Zida'ya Ayaminu's. Confused about how to react, Viyeki only stood and bowed to the venerable court official.

"So, then, we are all here," Zuniyabe said. "What have you told the high magister, Lady Miga?"

"He knows about Saomeji."

Zuniyabe shook his head sadly. The marks of his age were plain, the bone around his eyes prominent, the skin a shade thin. Still, he seemed calm and in better spirits than Viyeki could remember seeing him. "Our prince made a mistake, I fear. He should have dealt with Akhenabi's whelp at the same time as he ended Kikiti. Mark me, that one will make trouble for us one day."

It had been startling enough to hear people talk openly about the faults of the late Queen Utuk'ku, but somehow, it was even more unsettling to hear Hikeda'ya nobles openly criticize Pratiki's decisions.

It truly is a new world, Viyeki thought. *I wonder if there is a place in it for me? Or perhaps that is why they have all come here—to tell me there is not. I could live with that . . . if they let me live. I have found my daughter again. I serve in this confusing way, without definition or rules, only because Pratiki asked me to. I would gladly go back to directing my order again, or even something less exalted.* It came to him then. *I simply want to live a while without fear. What freedom that would be!*

"It is not so much that we want anything from you, High Magister," said Lady Miga. "We want to assure you that things are not quite as chaotic as they seem."

This was such a confounding statement that Viyeki could only shake his head. "The queen who has always ruled us is dead—killed by my own daughter, whom the prince pardoned, because he knows the queen would have killed us all. We have found living witchwood seeds once more, but the Hikeda'ya may only have them if we make compact with Lady Ayaminu's people, after years of hostility and war between us. And apparently the Tinukeda'ya, led by a dead woman, are going to somehow sail away on the last of the great ships that came from the Garden." He made the sign for *hands too full.* "Things *seem* chaotic? Surely things *are* chaotic—and have never been more so. By all means, though, reassure me."

To Viyeki's surprise, Zuniyabe smiled. Viyeki had never known the High Celebrant as anything other than a distant, careful upholder of the old virtues and it was startling. "You are right, Magister. It *is* chaos. But I think what Lady Miga means is that we wish to let you know that things are not as . . . aimless as they must seem. We have been planning for some time in case this day should come."

"We? You mean you three? Your pardon, but how did Hikeda'ya nobles of Nakkiga and—" he gestured respectfully toward Ayaminu—"one of the best known of the Zida'ya, plan anything without being discovered and executed by the queen?"

"It was not easy," Zuniyabe said. "But we have your old master to thank for beginning it."

"My old . . . Yaarike? The former high magister of the Builders?"

Zuniyabe nodded. "He came to me many years ago, before the Storm King's War. He was fearful of what Utuk'ku's hatred of mortals would bring, and disturbed, as I was, that she planned to use such a dangerous weapon as Ineluki against them. And as you know, that plan ended in horror and destruction—for us even more than for the mortals. So Yaarike sounded me out. We were both extremely cautious at first, of course. I'm sure you can understand that, Magister."

Thinking of the complicated dance of poems and puzzles that Prince Pratiki had led him through during their time together, Viyeki could only agree. "I am amazed you ever trusted each other."

"It took a while," said Zuniyabe. "But I already suspected that many among the Zida'ya were concerned about Utuk'ku, her power and her plans. Yaarike, who was wise and surprisingly well informed for someone who avoided the queen's court as much as possible, pointed us to other like-minded folk among the nobles of Nakkiga. Each approach we made was slow and cautious, of course, for fear of betrayal. Yaarike suggested Lady Miga here, and more importantly—I mean no disrespect, my lady—"

Miga nodded and made the sign for "*unnecessary.*"

"More importantly, your former master provided us with the most necessary conspirator of all—His Serene Highness, Prince Pratiki. Even had we wished to make ourselves martyrs to our cause, we could not have killed Utuk'ku. The Queen's Teeth were far too careful, guarding her day and night with fanatical zeal. But if we are to succeed—and it is still by no means certain—that zeal, now bent toward defending Prince Pratiki, will be what brings us ultimate victory."

Viyeki sat back. "And all this was happening around me—under my nose, as it were—and I never saw or suspected a thing."

"If *anyone* not part of our cabal had suspected anything, we might not be here today," said Lady Miga.

"But why did Yaarike not tell me?" Viyeki asked. "Did he doubt my loyalty?"

"You may think of it that way," said Zuniyabe. "But perhaps he trusted your heart and good sense enough to know you would do what was right when the time came, even if you were not told ahead of time. He did not want to chance compromising you, since he hoped to make you the next high magister. And he did accomplish that."

Viyeki turned to Ayaminu. "And, your pardon, Lady. Forgive me for blunt questions, but how did you come into all this?"

Ayaminu, with her austere face and white hair, could quite easily have been an effigy on one of the older Nakkiga tombs. "Your old master, again," she said. "You see, I once lived in Hikehikayo when Zida'ya and Hikeda'ya could still live together. In those long-ago days I met Yaarike, and we became friends, of sorts. When the time finally came, he brought me into his circle of conspirators because my father Kuroyi was one of the most respected of the Zida'ya protectors. Do you remember the Siege of Nakkiga at the end of the Storm King's War?"

"Remember? How could I forget? How could anyone who was there ever forget?"

"Precisely. Then you remember how Akhenabi, Lord of Song, raised the mortal dead on that night of madness and confusion. The gates of Nakkiga were opened and General Suno'ku rode out, hoping to destroy the invaders' great battering ram."

"I recall, yes, of course."

"In the chaos of that night, with the gates briefly open, Zuniyabe and Yaarike were able to meet with me—the first time I had seen Yaarike in many Great Years. Face to face, we agreed on what would have to happen for the Hikeda'ya and Zida'ya to be at peace with each other. We knew that Utuk'ku could not simply be killed or overthrown, but we hoped she might not return from the *keta-yi'indra*—the long, healing sleep she undertook after the Storm King was defeated. But she woke this time with an even more fearsome idea, though we did not know at the time. But we could see another war was coming. We had to trust that the Garden would lead us to a moment when we could make our plans real."

"I am quite overwhelmed by all this," Viyeki said at last. "But I am still not certain what you all want from me."

"Only for you to continue being the person you are," Ayaminu told him. "To help us and help Prince Pratiki during this fateful time, and to trust in what we are trying to do."

"I do, of course," said Viyeki, although he felt as if his mind was stuffed too full of new things, and it would take a while to let them all settle. "So Pratiki was part of this plan?"

"We could not have done it without one of the high Hamakha," said Lady Miga. "However . . ." She suddenly stopped.

"However, what?" Viyeki sensed they had finally come to the matter which had brought them in the first place. "Please, after all this, do not fall silent now."

Zuniyabe finally spoke. "We wish you also to keep a careful eye on Prince Pratiki."

"What? You said he was part of your planning—that he has known of your preparations for a long time!"

"And so he has," Zuniyabe assured him. "And we have trusted him with our lives since before you became the magister of your order. But the Hamakha have never given up their advantages willingly. We worry—though Pratiki has given us no reason to do so—that the very weight of the Hamakha Crown might shade his judgment. For his entire life, his forebear's every whim was absolute law. Now he sits in her place. We rely on you to let us know if . . ." Zuniyabe made a vague gesture.

"To let you know if he begins to enjoy his power too much," Viyeki finished for him, once more feeling a little sick at the stomach. "To let you know if Pratiki himself becomes a danger." Viyeki could not entirely keep the unhappiness out of his voice.

"Yes," said Ayaminu. "He trusts you, High Magister, perhaps more than he trusts any of us."

"And I should repay that trust by spying on him?"

"Not spying—watching," said Zuniyabe. "Because peace—and the future of both our peoples—still balances on a knife's edge."

"Sadly, that is the world we have inherited from our queen, Magister Viyeki," said Lady Miga. "It will be a long, long time before real trust can bloom, and many of our people have been raised only to fear and hate. We must be careful." She seemed about to say something else, but only repeated, *"We must be careful."*

"I am sorry for your loss," Brother Etan told Tanahaya. "And yours, Majesty," he added for the benefit of King Simon, then shook his head. "It will be a long time, I think, before I understand everything that has happened here."

Tanahaya nodded. Her mood had been lifted a little to see Etan's unfeigned joy at discovering that the king and his grandchildren still lived, but being in the presence of her beloved's cold, unmoving body had quickly pressed down on her again, and she had almost turned and walked out of the grotto where Jiriki lay. She had quickly harnessed her emotions once more, but she still wanted, more than anything, to be alone with her dead lover and her thoughts. Even though he was gone, she still had many things she wanted to tell him, but it was not possible in the company of these near-strangers.

She looked down at her beloved in his willow-weave coffin, wrapped in a shroud of nearly invisible silk, and pressed her hands against the place in her belly where their child was growing. *She will have everything that your sister and I can give her,* Tanahaya promised silently. *She will miss you, my love, but she will hear much of you. She will know you as if you were still here.*

"Would it be inappropriate for me to say some Aedonite words for him?" Etan asked, breaking her reverie. "I do not wish to offend."

She turned toward him, blinking away the sudden tears. "He would have known it for what it is," she said. "And so do I. No kindness can go amiss, Brother. Jiriki was the kindest person I have ever known."

Now King Simon got down on his knees and made the Sign of the Tree as the monk began the *Mansa sea Cuelossan.* When Tanahaya had prepared to become the envoy to the Hayholt she had learned many of the strange customs of the mortal Sudhoda'ya, but she had never imagined that the first time she heard their death-ritual performed might be for her beloved. It was an irony that she thought might have amused Jiriki, but it did not much please her.

When Etan had finished, drawing the Tree one last time over Jiriki's body, he knelt silently for a long moment, then stood.

"I thank you for letting me pay my respects," he told her. "I never knew him, but from all that Ki'ushapo and you have told me, I feel as if I did, and I am truly, truly sorry that you and your people have lost him."

"I thank the Garden that I had my last moments with him," she said, "that we had our farewells—and that I could tell him the things he needed to know."

Etan could not help letting his gaze stray to her belly, which still showed little of what was to come. "May Heaven bless you and your issue," he said.

King Simon climbed wearily to his feet. "Come, Brother Etan. Let us leave Tanahaya to her thoughts. I still have much to ask you about the Hayholt and how things fare there. Just knowing that Tiamak and Lady Thelía survived has heartened me."

"I will come with you," Tanahaya said, surprising them both. "I will say my final words to Jiriki later. I am exhausted with sorrow and would welcome some other talk."

"I fear any tales I can tell of the Hayholt will not bring you or King Simon much happiness," Etan said. "But in truth, things began to go wrong the day that Pasevalles brought you into the castle, Lady Tanahaya, near dead from poison." He stopped just outside the entrance to the grotto where Jiriki's body lay. "By our good Lord, I have just seen what I should have seen long ago. That devil Pasevalles *knew.* He knew you had been attacked by his own killers—likely Thrithings mercenaries. I have wondered why he brought you back and seemed to work so hard to see your life saved. It must have been because he was afraid what you might reveal, and he wanted to be the first to hear what you remembered!" He reached out as if to touch her arm, then thought better of it. "I do not doubt you had a lucky escape, my lady. If you could have named your attackers, he likely would have killed you and tried to make it look as though you had succumbed to the Norn poison on the arrowheads."

"That seems likely," she said. "But I would never have guessed it from my memories of him. He is clearly a man of many layers and schemes—and one whose lies are not revealed by his face or voice or even his scent."

"Yes, many layers, but every single one corrupt and rotten," said the king. "When we find him—and I *will* find him if I have to do it myself—he will pay a terrible reckoning, for my Miri, and Morgan's and Lillia's mother, and all his crimes. He is no man, but a monster—a demon."

"And yet even Pasevalles must have a soul, and so be capable of redemption," Etan said. "Otherwise, our faith in Heaven and the Aedon would be false."

"*Pfah*," snorted the king. "If a poisonous snake seeks to bite you, it is all well and good to wonder if the serpent is to blame or if it is simply the beast's nature, but the first thing to do is pick up a hoe and cut off its head. You and the rest of God's closest servants can discuss what our Lord intended afterward."

Etan smiled sadly. "I have no doubt of our God's good intent, Majesty, and that in conception, all souls can be saved—but I also agree with you that Pasevalles deserves to die. And may God forgive me, but even if I were the last Aedonite in holy orders remaining in Erkynland, I would not say a *mansa* over his grave."

In a strange way, the openness of the plateau in the shadow of the tall cliffs, as well as the jumble of different kinds of people milling about on it, reminded Tzoja more than a little of the Animal Market outside Nakkiga's gates. The weather here was cold, too, as it was even on a summer day in the high Nornfells: a few flakes of snow drifted down as she led Vordis across the wide space.

But it was impossible to forget that a deadly battle had just been fought here. In many places great smears of dried blood still stained the rock, and she was glad Vordis could not see them.

Tzoja's inquiries in nearly flawless Hikeda'yasao confused the guards a little, but she and Vordis were directed to the wide cavern opening at the base of the cliffs that was apparently the camp of Prince Pratiki, Utuk'ku's successor. It took even more courage than Tzoja had expected to approach the place. The far side of the bridge had been in confusion, hierarchies compromised, the Sacrifice guards uncertain of what to do and of how far their authority extended, and so they were more than usually cautious. But here on this side the prince had a firm grip on power, as Tzoja could tell by a glance at the white-armored Teeth standing rigidly beside the cavern's entrance. She had no doubt that if she were seen as a problem, she would be immediately imprisoned or even executed.

She found the place where Viyeki seemed to be working, but the clerics and guards there would not let her in. At last, she convinced one of the clerics to announce her to the high magister. She told the other Hikeda'ya, in her most authoritative voice, to watch over the safety of Vordis, then followed the first cleric through a drapery used as a makeshift door and into Viyeki's chamber.

She paused for a moment just inside, suspecting that at any moment the guards might burst in to stop her. She immediately saw Viyeki talking to the cleric, but when he saw her, for a long, disturbing moment he did not seem to recognize her. Then his expression changed. He hurried toward her and enfolded her in his strong arms, lifting her from the ground in a fearfully tight embrace.

"What are you doing here?" he asked, turning in a circle, her feet still not touching the ground. "No, wait—let me send the others away." He set her down and dismissed most of his underlings, then beckoned for her to sit on a bench beside him. It was a strange scene, the narrow cavern dressed up with a table and a few tapestries, but still very obviously a cave. *Only the Hikeda'ya could truly be comfortable in a place like this,* she thought, and it felt like a warning.

"I still cannot believe it!" said Viyeki. "Tell me all. Tell me how you came here. I have dreamed of holding you in my arms so many times, little Tzoja! It is all I can do not to take you to bed immediately."

She was not certain what was stopping him, since he seemed to hold an important enough place to order cleric-priests and guards about without a backward glance; but although she had longed for this moment, she was also aware that something felt different than she had expected.

She gave him an abbreviated but thorough summation of her adventures, not forgetting to make certain he knew his wife Khimabu had tried several times to kill her. Viyeki then told her something of his own travails, and how close he had come to execution for disappointing the queen. But when she questioned him about Utuk'ku's death and what would happen next for him and the rest of the Hikeda'ya, he seemed reticent.

"It is hard to know—hard to say," he told her. "We will follow Prince

Pratiki. As for Khimabu, do not fear her. I will end the marriage. I joined myself to her out of loyalty to my clan, who wished it, and for my own ambition, because her Daesa Clan is an important one. But we never cared greatly for each other. Now I have you back and I want no other! You can come and live with me—the prince has given me a fine tent not far from his own in the main cavern."

She was surprised by her own hesitancy. For so long she had thought of this moment, of being reunited with the only one of his race who had treated her with real kindness, but now she was suddenly unsure—disturbed, perhaps, to be under stone once more, after so long in the sun and open air. "My friend Vordis waits outside. She has no one else. I could not leave her alone."

"No matter," said Viyeki with good cheer. "She can join our household."

"Our household? Do you mean you would marry me?"

His look suddenly changed. "I cannot do that, dear Tzoja. You understand—you must. At such a time, with so many things uncertain . . ." He trailed off. "But you will still be mistress of the house. No Hikeda'ya woman will ever be raised above you ever again."

She nodded, but it felt as though the ground beneath her was less solid than it had seemed an hour earlier. "I suppose it would be no worse for your reputation than the halfblood daughter we have already made. But before I can do anything, think of anything, we must find Nezeru. I will never have a moment's true rest until I know she is safe."

Viyeki came as close as she had ever seen to displaying real surprise, a subtle drawing-upward of both eyebrows, a rounding of his dark, dark eyes. "But do you mean you do not know?"

Her heart sank. "Know what? Oh, please, do not—"

"She is safe. Nezeru is safe. She is here in Tanakirú."

"What? I cannot believe it. Where? Tell me!"

He told her. She leaped to her feet, kissed him in honest, heart-swelling gratitude, then hurried out of the cavern despite his protests. She stopped outside to lean down and squeeze Vordis's hand between hers. "Stay here, dear one," she told her startled friend. "I must go find someone, but I promise I will come back for you soon."

Nezeru watched Morgan go. It had taken all her strength to listen to him, to hear all his arguments about why she was being unfair, not just to him but to herself, without losing her temper. The problem was, of course, that he was at least partly right. She did miss him, she did long for him in a way she dared not admit, and she suspected she would never find anyone who made her feel quite the way Morgan did, amused and protective by turns, yet constantly surprised.

But he does not understand—he cannot understand. The difference between us is too great and always will be. He has the innocence of his upbringing—the idea that everything bad can be solved if a good person with power only wills it so. But I know better.

The last person she wanted to see at this moment was Jarnulf, but there he was, again making his way toward her as she sat brooding in front of King Simon's cave-camp, drinking in the last of the afternoon sun.

"Ho, Nezeru," he called as he approached.

"What do you want?"

"There are a few more things I believe you should know, and we had little time to talk before." He seemed in an uncommonly good mood. "Will you give me some moments of your time?"

She would rather have not, but in a short time the sun would be gone. She had grown to enjoy its warmth—something she would never have thought possible—and was loath to be driven into back into the caverns. "If I must."

But even as Jarnulf started to speak, she lost track of what he was saying, because she saw an impossibly familiar figure hurrying toward them from Prince Pratiki's side of the plateau—a small, clearly mortal figure. She stared until she was certain, and Jarnulf's words floated past her as unremarked upon as the snow that had fluttered earlier, then she leaped to her feet and left Jarnulf to sputter into silence as she ran toward her mother.

For long moments neither she nor Tzoja could speak, and only held each other's hands, turning in a slow circle, mountains and river gorge revolving around them, then they fell into each other's arms. Nezeru was a little surprised to realize that tears were running down her cheeks, less surprised to see they were streaming down her mother's as well.

They both tried to tell each other a dozen things at once while simultaneously asking questions, and only succeeded in making a complete and incomprehensible muddle. They laughed, then embraced again. Finally, Nezeru remembered Jarnulf, and though she would have preferred to forget him, she had come to believe that whatever other crimes he had committed against her, he truly had meant to remove her from the danger of his own plans against the queen. She took her mother's hand and led her toward the place where Jarnulf waited, somewhat chastened now, and introduced him, but only as someone with whom she had traveled.

"She underestimates us both, I fear," Jarnulf said. "Your daughter is famous. Infamous, too. She killed the queen of the Norns. Well, in truth, we both did."

Nezeru was furious that he should so brazenly insert himself into the story of the queen's death. But even as her mother stared at them both in shock and something like fear, Jarnulf seemed to lose interest. He took a few steps backward, as if something had surprised him, then walked directly past Nezeru toward a small company of mortals who had come out of King Simon's camp and were headed toward the bridge over the river.

"It cannot be," she heard him say. "But it is. *It is!*" He hurried to the group of men, ignoring all but one of them, a mortal man, thin and tall but slightly bent, who wore a hooded robe and seemed to be lost in his own thoughts. Jarnulf reached him and leaned in to stare at the man's spare, whiskery face.

"By all that is holy! God is indeed great!" Jarnulf shouted, then turned to

Nezeru, gesturing wildly. "It is him! The one I told you about—the priest, the man I call Father! I thought him lost forever!" He threw his arms around the stranger, who did not resist, but did not seem much moved, either. "Nezeru, come here!" Jarnulf called. "This is the one who saved my life when I was young!" He turned to the man, who still had not spoken, but only stared at him as though at an unexpected obstacle. "How did you come here, Father? What happened to you? You vanished that night, and I could never find you again!"

Nezeru turned back to her mother, planning to lead Tzoja away so Jarnulf could continue his odd reunion with his stiff and apparently somewhat dull-witted mentor. But now her mother was walking toward the group as if she felt she had to introduce herself, and Nezeru was furious with Jarnulf for once again yanking something important away from her with his endless self-involvement.

But to her astonishment, her mother walked right up to the strangers, who watched her with varying degrees of unease or surprise, pushing past Jarnulf as if she scarcely saw him. She went straight to the tall thin man in the robe and threw back his hood, revealing a close-cropped head of gray hair and a passive but slightly bewildered expression on his mild, thin face. *"For behold, I am a new thing,"* the man said.

Tzoja turned on Jarnulf, and for some reason she seemed angry. "*Your* father? You don't know—you cannot know. He cannot be your father—he is *mine*!" She looked at Nezeru, her face wilder than Nezeru had ever seen it, almost feverish. "Look, child, by all the gods—look!" Tzoja cried. "This is your grandfather, though I know not how he came here out of all the world. I thought . . . I thought he was dead." And suddenly she was weeping, though she was laughing, too. "It is my own father, my lost father—Prince Josua of Erkynland."

41

Parley

"Ah, yes—Sir Rawlie." Tiamak beckoned Winstowe's envoy into the tent that had been prepared for the parley. "I promise you courtesy and safety, though it is strange to see you here. Did you know the man you speak for is a traitor and a murderer?"

"I beg your pardon?" Already fidgeting, and with a slight dew of perspiration on his upper lip, the Winstowe castellan did not at first seem to have heard, then he abruptly turned. "Stay a moment—what did you say?"

"I believe you meant, 'What did you say, Lord Tiamak?' Because although it is no doubt galling to be exceeded by a small and limping fellow from the marshy south, you would never forget that I am chief councilor to the High Throne, would you?"

"No, of course not . . . my lord." Rawlie's gaze darted around the otherwise empty tent. "But do you claim that the High Throne still exists? Truly? With the king and queen dead, no living heirs, and the Hayholt itself burned to its foundations?"

"Yes, the High Throne still exists, both in material form—dragon bones are not easy to burn—and in its full power of authority. But I am willing to believe you did not know those things, or you might not have been so quick to accept employment with Erkynland's most infamous criminal, Pasevalles."

Now the emissary finally realized that he had stumbled into some kind of ambush. "I did not c-come here to insult you, my lord," he stammered, "but I did not come to be insulted either. Lord Pasevalles sent me to meet the one who has so cruelly and unnecessarily declared war on him. In fact, I have a letter he has written—"

"Oh, save it for the duchess, I beg you," said Tiamak. "She will want to see it. I am sure she will find much to entertain her in the murderer's excuses, lies, and—no doubt—ludicrous demands. Unless it is an instrument of immediate surrender . . . ? That might placate the duchess enough to save at least a few of Pasevalles's accomplices, people like yourself, from the headsman's block."

Sir Rawlie had gone a shade paler but did his best to cover it. "This is pure bluster, my lord. Who is the duchess? If she is some legitimate heir of the royal family, why does she go nameless and secret across the countryside, offering destruction to those who only seek to preserve the peace in Erkynland? Lord Pasevalles demands that this military encampment and the army assembled here—unlawfully assembled by our own ancient laws, I should add—should immediately be disbanded, and—"

"No, no, I told you, you must save all this." Tiamak silenced him with a harsh gesture. "The one who has been waiting for you has had scant time for entertainment and will be disappointed to miss out on such amusing tales." He gestured to a bench facing a single tall chair at the center of the tent. "Please, Sir Knight, seat yourself and be a little patient. She will be with you soon."

Reluctantly, Rawlie lowered himself onto the bench. His fine clothes were a little threadbare in places, as though Winstowe might have a dearth of seamstresses at the moment, but he was clearly doing his best to appear to be the envoy of a side that held the advantage.

Tiamak said nothing more, allowing the man to digest what he had heard; after all, Tiamak reminded himself, *digest*, in alchemical terms, meant to allow something to steep at high temperatures.

Tiamak did not know this Rawlie well, but what little he knew was not favorable. The knight-castellan was a relative of Countess Marah, Aglaf's wife, and he was known for flattering the powerful and ignoring the untitled—exactly the sort of person Tiamak had always disliked. But because most powerful people enjoyed flattery, he was also the sort of person who often rose to a position of power serving those he aggressively praised.

Time trudged on, and Sir Rawlie became ever more restless, but each time he looked to Tiamak, the Wrannaman only stared blankly back, killing any questions before they were uttered. Hunched and unhappy on his hard seat, Rawlie wove his fingers together and stared at them. Tiamak had chosen the bench precisely for its inhospitability.

At last, a pair of Erkynguard swept open the doorway of the tent and stepped smartly to either side of it. They were followed by a herald, who stopped, pounded his staff upon the carpeted ground, and said, "Her Majesty, Mistress of Erkynland and the High Throne, Queen Miriamele."

Tiamak had already begun kneeling as the guards entered, so now he could watch as Winstowe's envoy half-stood, mouth slack and eyes bulging, like a dead fish in a dockside market. When Miriamele swept in behind the herald, Rawlie took a stumbling backward step.

"Your greeting does not quite seem what a queen should expect." The lightness of the queen's tone was like a slim but flexible blade. "Are you not the envoy from Winstowe, sir? Which, I seem to recall, has many times sworn loyalty to our house and line? Were you not Count Aglaf's chief factor? Is he aware of your change of allegiance?"

Rawlie swayed, then dropped clumsily to his knees. "M-M-Majesty?" the envoy stuttered. "You . . . live?"

"It does seem that way." Her voice became harsher. "Alive, but heartsick to see how swiftly some of our subjects have thrown over their responsibilities at the first sign of trouble. It is a lucky thing for you that you are here in a lawful parley, otherwise I would be tempted to have a few bits of you chopped off, just to make certain you never forget your own cowardice." She looked at him with distaste. "In truth, I might do it anyway. A hand, perhaps. Or both hands, such as once was done to thieves. Because your queen is not pleased, and I—"

She did not have a chance to finish, because the Winstowe emissary had fallen into a dead faint.

"And thus the duchess now stands revealed," the queen said to Tiamak after Rawlie had been helped onto his horse and sent back to Winstowe. "The question is, what will Pasevalles do?"

"If he had enough men to do anything meaningful, he would have done it already," declared Captain Kenrick, who had joined them. "The traitor has had every chance to come out and fight, but we have ten times his number. He knows it would be hopeless."

"But what of the raids we have already suffered?" Miriamele asked. "If it were not for our Qanuc friends, the last one might have taken many lives."

"I think Kenrick is right," Tiamak offered. "From the few mercenaries who survived to be made prisoners, we know that the raids on our camp were not planned but came when some of the enemy's foraging parties returned to find they could not get back into Winstowe. There are likely other Thrithings foragers who simply melted away when they saw what was happening."

"Or are still hiding and waiting to attack us, perhaps at some signal from Pasevalles," the queen said. "Which would be the time he would pick to attempt escape, coward that he is." She turned to Kenrick. "Have we found all the ways out of Winstowe?"

"I think so, Majesty. With the help of the valley-folk we have found and stopped up several of the old shafts, and we are guarding the ones that are not so easily sealed."

Tiamak saw that Sisqi was whispering in her husband's ear. When she finished, Binabik raised his hand for the queen's attention.

"I would like to ask that we go back again to the place where Vaqana was being excited yesterday," the troll said.

"Vaqana is his wolf," Sir Porto explained to Baron Norvel. "He rides it."

"But there was nothing there," said Kenrick. "We did as you asked. The engineers looked carefully all along that hillside. It is a great stony cliff that a thousand men together could not shift."

"There is no engineer—or any person—who has more cleverness than Vaqana's nose," Binabik asserted. "But if soldiers cannot be spared, Sisqi and I will go to look at it ourselves." He paused as Sisqi whispered something else. She spoke Westerling fairly well, but Tiamak guessed she was reluctant to speak it in front of relative strangers like Norvel and Captain Kenrick.

"I will go with them," said Porto. "If Her Majesty allows it, of course. I would have been glad for the wolf's nose when we were hunting Norns along the slopes of Nakkiga in the last war."

"If anyone knows to trust Binabik and his animal companions, I do," Miriamele said. "Simon and I owed our lives to them many times over." She paused, and Tiamak could sense her pain and the discomfort it caused in all those around her; it was hard for the queen to talk about her husband. "But go carefully, staying out of bowshot from the walls. I do not want to lose one of you to a chance arrow." She stood. "We must all be even more alert now. Pasevalles knew he was surrounded, but now he knows who has done it. Now go, all of you, with God's blessing. It is time to take back our Erkynland."

As the others followed Miriamele out, Tiamak waited. When the tent was empty he rose from his seat. His leg was hurting, and he did not want the others to see how hard it is for him to stand.

Ah, vanity, he thought. *One of the few things I still have left to enjoy.* He folded his parchments and slipped them back into the wooden case, which reminded him about Etan and John Josua's wooden box. He said a silent prayer for the monk's safety to He Who Always Steps on Sand, then went out to join the others.

"Don't let him get behind you," Fremur said quietly. "He might stab you in the back. Do not accept food or drink from him either—they might be poisoned. Be suspicious of *everything*—this Pasevalles is a trickster."

Unver shot him a look. "Do I seem as though I need another mother, Fremur?"

"Be angry at me if you wish but remember my words."

"I cannot forget them. You have said the same thing to me more times than I can count."

They were waiting outside the main hall of Winstowe Castle. Pasevalles could be heard shouting on the other side of the doors. The castellan Rawlie had returned only a short time ago, and it seemed that the news he brought had displeased the castle's current master.

"I do not doubt your cleverness," Fremur whispered. "But sometimes you are too willing to trust in the spirits."

"The spirits raised me to become the Shan, did they not?" Unver made one of the dismissive gestures that Fremur hated. "If they wanted me dead, what could I do to change that?"

"You would not let a man stab you in the heart, would you? Does that not thwart the will of Heaven?"

"Enough, Fremur. If the spirits want my time to end, it will—"

The doors of the hall slammed open, propelled by a single shove of Hulgar's massive arm, then Rawlie stumbled out. His lip was bleeding, and he had a broad, red mark on his cheek that looked like it might soon close his left eye. Hulgar watched him scurry out, then withdrew into the hall.

Pasevalles's anger had not cooled. Fremur could hear him clearly, even with the doors closed.

"—Whorseson castellan is a coward, Hulgar, but I do not doubt that he saw what he saw. Still, how could it have happened? Curse that treacherous beast, Fecca! He was told to make certain of the deaths of a few unarmed women and children. If he were here, I would have his eyes."

Hulgar said something too quiet for Fremur to hear.

"Yes, God curse it. Let us look to our other choices. Take that fat fool Broomstraw and half a dozen men and do what I told you." A moment of silence followed. "Go on! Why do you wait?"

Again, Hulgar's words were unintelligible.

"Because you will need several men when the time comes. It has likely not been forced in years."

After a bit more inaudible conversation, Hulgar emerged, his ruined face a mask of poorly hidden fury. "Sanver," he growled, staring at the Shan with what Fremur thought was obvious dislike. "Inside." He glared at Fremur, who had not moved or made a sound. "You, stay outside."

Fremur nodded, but as soon as Hulgar left, he sidled up to the closed doors and leaned as close as he dared. Pasevalles's growing distrust of those around him meant that he kept no other guards close to him but Hulgar, which meant Fremur could eavesdrop in relative safety. He held his breath, listening.

"So, Sanver," he heard Pasevalles say. "Here. Drink up. It is nearly the last of this very good harvest, and we will not have such excellent wine again for many days. Not until we reach our destination."

He would not be such a fool as to drink it, would he? Fremur prayed. *Sky-Piercer, spirit of our clan, do not let it happen!*

"I said we are going somewhere, but you do not ask me where." Now Pasevalles sounded annoyed.

"I foresee that you will tell me," said Unver. "Or did you call me in simply to help you finish off the count's wine?"

"You are a clever one, aren't you? That is why I called for you—your eyes see farther and clearer than your fellows do. No, do not pretend. I know you are not like the rest of my Thrithings-men."

He knows! He knows who Unver is! Fremur looked around, but the antechamber was deserted, the only guards a pair of mercenaries outside the far door. Fremur loosened his sword in its sheath, but the next thing Pasevalles said caught him by surprise.

"I had a dream last night. Shall I tell you?"

Fremur heard Unver grunt. It was not particularly a noise of assent, but Pasevalles continued.

"I dreamed of a falcon, held aloft on a gloved fist, which took to the air and brought down one bird after another. Have you ever flown a falcon? I thought not. My uncle was a great man for hawking. He told me once, 'If a bird can be taught to rely on you, he will never fail you. But they are still wild in their souls. They have no pity and no kindness.' I think you are such a creature, Sanver. The others here, Hulgar and Broga and the rest, are mere brutes, only wishing to be left alone to feed and rut. Fierce enough when disturbed—or when paid to be so—but otherwise ignorant and uncaring. But you see farther, always looking for your next prey. Am I right?"

"If you say so, my lord."

"Aha! Carefully spoken. It is a sign of the slow wits of my other men that they have not marked you as something different."

He must know. Fremur was squeezing the hilt of his sword so hard that his hand trembled, but he forced himself to relax his grip and breathe more slowly. *Unver knows I am here. He will call for me if he needs me.* A panicky thought came to him. *But will it matter? Has he already swallowed poison?*

Unver had not replied, or Fremur had not heard him, but Pasevalles went on as if they were having a merry conversation. "The time is coming when we will have to leave this place. I have made plans—that is all you need to know. But I know that at some point, those I have trusted so far will fail me."

Unver finally spoke so Fremur could hear. "Fail you, my lord?"

"Yes. Believe me, there is no one who knows the look of a man about to betray his trust better than I do. I have seen Hulgar and Broga whispering when they thought I was elsewhere. And I have seen Broga talking to his underlings. They think we are trapped here. Given a chance, they will bargain with the besiegers."

"Then we are *not* trapped, my lord?"

"Here, have another cup—I see you have finished the first. It is good, is it not? It has been one of the few pleasures of this backwater castle, drinking up Aglaf's cellars. No, there is a way out for us, through . . . well, you must trust me, Sanver of the Kestrels, since I would be a fool to show all my strategy."

"And what can I do, Lord Pasevalles?" Unver's tone was flat. "What do you want of me?"

"I have a bolt hole prepared for when I leave this place," Pasevalles said, "one where my enemies cannot touch me and I will be protected by powerful friends. When I ruled Erkynland in everything but name, I sent much gold to wait for me there, because I knew that things might change. And the man who serves me well will share in that treasure. In short, Sanver, if you are what I think you are, fierce but also far-sighted, you can live like a king."

"Like a king, my lord?"

"Land, women, gold, all will be yours. I will give with open hands. What more could you ask for?"

"Some surety, my lord."

Now Fremur could hear Pasevalles move nearer to the door; he tensed, prepared to fall back. The man's voice had anger in it, but also what sounded like amusement. "You would bargain with me, Sanver?"

"You want something of me, Lord Pasevalles, or you would not have called for me. When else should a man bargain, but when he has something to sell?"

"I see I was right about you. But you have mistaken which of us holds the high ground. Because, you see, I have just poisoned you." Pasevalles's voice rose. "Ah! Stay where you are, grasslander—hear me out if you want to live!"

No! Unver could not have been so careless! Fremur had gone cold all over.

"I can cure you," Pasevalles continued. "But only if you understand that you belong to me now. Only I have the cure—no one else can save you."

"So, this is how you repay your underlings," said Unver.

"I make certain that my underlings know where their interests lie. And I swear that if you will be my falcon and fly only where and against whom I send you, you will live a long time and you will prosper. But turn on me and you will die in terrible agony. Do we understand each other?"

A long silence. "We do, my lord."

"Good. Then return to me after the evening meal, and I will give you the first drops of your cure."

Fremur retreated from the door, heartsick and terrified, as Unver emerged. The Shan's face was expressionless, but his eyes were mere slits, as though a demon peered out at the world through the mask of a person. For the first time, Fremur felt truly frightened of the man he had known so long.

"What will we do?" Fremur whispered after they had left the antechamber. "I told you not to trust him!"

"I did not drink any wine," said Unver. "Do you think me such a fool? I threw it into the ashes of the fire when his back was turned."

"Oh, thank the Sky-Piercer." Fremur's heart was still beating too swiftly. "But we must leave this place. You see that now, Unver."

"We will leave when I say it is time. Not before. I am to be Pasevalles's falcon, he said. I wonder what prey he thinks I will bring him."

It has become a contest between the two of them now, Fremur realized, *with the rest of us caught between*. For the first time, he wondered what fate his loyalty to Unver would earn him. *Trapped between poison and pride. Not a good place.*

Porto watched the wolf as she slipped in and out through the trees like a white rag tossed in a swirling wind. He couldn't tell if she was following a scent or simply excited to run free where she would. When he asked Binabik, the troll only shook his head.

"Too early to tell, it is still." He smiled like a proud parent. "She smells so many things, all of them of interest!"

"I only ask because we are near the same spot she marked before."

"I know. And see, she is running to it again. You and I and Sisqi must climb after her."

Porto descended from his horse and tied the reins to a low branch. "When

I was young, scrambling up and down the slopes of Nakkiga for Duke Isgrimnur, I often wished I could go on four legs like a dog or cat. We men are not built to climb hills. We are too upright."

"Ha!" chortled Binabik. "Speak for yourself, good Sir Porto. We Qanuc are made much closer to the ground and are not so likely for tipping over as you tall folk."

"Quiet. No jokes," said Sisqi. "Listen."

Porto heard nothing and said so.

"That is what," she told him. "Vaqana stops running."

He realized she was right: the sound of the wolf rustling through the undergrowth had ceased. "Does it mean she has found something?"

"Or she is making water on something," Binabik said. "My first wolf, Qantaqa, was a great one for the making of noises, barks and whines and yip-yip-yips. Vaqana is not so much talkative, but her sense of smelling has just as much skill."

The trolls emerged from the trees before Porto did. The old knight was winded, and when he caught up, he stopped to catch his breath while looking at stony face of the cliff. Vaqana was walking around its base, sniffing at the place where the unbroken sheet of stone vanished into the surrounding vegetation. "The same one as before."

Binabik got down on his knees and crawled into the undergrowth, at one point having to shove past Vaqana, who wanted to sniff in the spot where he was crawling.

The troll emerged a little time later. "It is planted well into the earth, this great piece of rock, and I see no sign of crevice or crack where anyone could slip in or out. I do not know what is making her so interested."

"Is she smelling other wolf?" Sisqi asked.

Binabik shook his head. "I have seen her once or twice near others of her kind. She is not like this behaving, but more cautious. This has the feeling of when she is hunting voles or other ground-living creatures. Excitement."

"But you don't see a tunnel or any digging?" Porto asked.

"No. I crawled far around, but I was not seeing any tunnel or sign of one."

But the troll looked unhappy, Porto thought. "Should we go on, then? Search somewhere else?"

"It is seeming so. Still, something has caught at Vaqana's attention here. Perhaps it is only a now-empty nest of rabbits or something like, but I cannot help to feel it is more." He got to his feet. "As was said by Queen Miriamele, I have learned to trust the noses of wolves."

The evening meal was over. The news of the apparent survival of the Erkynlandish queen had run through Winstowe like a fire, and the clansmen in the main hall were drinking heavily. It felt like the hours before a storm, Fremur thought, the air heavy with dire possibility.

"I am going to be given the first of my 'cure,'" Unver told him quietly. "You will come with me."

"He will try to make me drink poison too," Fremur protested.

"I will make sure he does not. But I will need you in case Pasevalles must be distracted. I did not take his poison and I will not take his cure, either."

Fremur's doomful mood only worsened. "A distraction, is it?"

"Nothing obvious. But if I touch my eye, like so—" he demonstrated, "—then you must make a noise, or knock something over."

"Pasevalles is no fool. He will know."

"Pasevalles is not as clever as he thinks he is, or I would have swallowed the wine and be begging him for his so-called cure already. Poisoners always think they are smarter than everyone else—as the shaman Volfrag did. And Volfrag is nothing but bones now."

The current lord of Winstowe looked coldly at the two of them as they stood before him in the count's retiring room. "Why is he here?" he asked, staring at Fremur. "You test my patience, Sanver."

"This man is like a brother to me," Unver said. "His family raised me after my own died. He goes where I go and does what I do. But he will not drink your wine."

Pasevalles raised one eyebrow. "What did you say?"

"His health was frail when he was young. It is one reason I have kept him with me. Do not fear, he can fight as well as any man, but I will not have his life put at risk. I am surety enough for you, am I not? I owe you my life—as we both know."

Pasevalles frowned, then shook his head as if such squabbles were beneath his dignity. "Well enough, then. But you are responsible for him. If you betray me, he will die too, just not by poison. Understood?"

"It is. Now, you told me to come for my cure. I am here."

Pasevalles produced a stoppered jar. "Do not bother to look at it too carefully," he said as he twisted out the cork. "I have many such and they all look alike, both poisons and cures. No one but me can guess which is which."

Fremur was breathlessly poised to provide some diversion but Unver's hand never strayed anywhere near his face. Instead, in front of Fremur's horrified eyes, Unver let Pasevalles discharge the contents of a slender glass pipe into his mouth, then even appeared to swallow. A moment later Unver bent, coughing and covering his mouth with his hand.

"It is foul!" he said when he straightened up.

"Strong physic for strong poison," said Pasevalles, grinning wolfishly. "Still, I did not think you so cream-livered, Sanver. I have seen children take the apothecary's drops with less protest."

"Think what you want, my lord. May I go now? Or do you have orders for me?" Unver did not bother to disguise his anger.

"I will tell you what you must do when the time comes," said Pasevalles, still grinning. He seemed pleased by Unver's compliance and just as pleased with his unhappiness. "Go and make merry with the rest of your fellow barbarians. Enjoy the count's wine. You will seldom have better, especially for free."

"I have had more wine than I want today," Unver said shortly. "I bid you good night, my lord."

Outside, Fremur was desperate to question him, but Unver only shook his head and led him away, across the main hall and out into the nearest courtyard. He looked around to make certain they were alone, then nodded.

"You let him pour it in your mouth!"

"He was watching too closely. He was looking for some trick."

"So you swallowed it instead? Are you mad? What if it was more poison?"

Unver shook his head. "I spit it into my hand and wiped it on my tunic. It was foul, but it was not poison."

"How could you know that?"

"Because he thinks he already has me. Why would he poison me twice? Pasevalles only sees two kinds of men, fools and mercenaries. He lies to the fools and buys off the mercenaries—one way or another. But I am neither."

"And what if you are wrong?"

Unver smiled, his face half in shadow, half illuminated by torchlight from the hall. "Then I will complain to the spirits when I stand before them. And since Pasevalles will never let you live after I am dead, my friend, you will be there to remind me."

42

Unwanted Wisdom

I have decided I will not go with you to Jao é-Tinukai'i to bury him, Protector Ki'ushapo," said Tanahaya. "I am dry as dust—I have not wept so much in all my life before this, even when my mother died, and I have no more tears left."

He nodded. "I would not compel you to come even if I could. That would be a poor tribute to Jiriki and a poor start to my new responsibilities. I already fear I cannot be even half of what he was."

"Such modesty! You certainly sound like he always did, Protector," she said, laughing a little, though there was pain, too.

"Please, Tanahaya," he said. "To my friends and family, I will always be simply Ki'ushapo, as Jiriki named me."

"Ki'ushapo, then, and I will treasure the privilege."

"Jiriki will be laid in the earth with proper ceremony, I promise."

She shook her head. "It matters less to me than I thought it would. What I keep of him is more important, and that will not be found in a grave, however dignified, but here, here, and here." She touched her head, her heart, and then gently stretched one hand over her belly. "It will be a girl child. Aditu told me."

Ki'ushapo made the sign for *a good life.* "So, now that the Witnesses can be used once more, have you spoken to her?"

Tanahaya nodded. "I have. Her time is near—she thinks her child will come in the Dove Moon—and she is mourning her mother as well as her brother. I will go to her, and we will mourn together, and also welcome a new life to the Zida'ya."

"Then I pray you journey well, Tanahaya of Shisae'ron. Assure Aditu of my love and my promise to bear her brother's legacy with all my strength."

"I will, Protector Onion Skin." She smiled, then rose, and they embraced. "Our new Sa'onsera has as much confidence in you as I do," she told him, "and that is a great amount."

As she prepared herself to depart, she sensed someone standing outside the cavern chamber—not one of her own folk. She was not so confident of peace between Zida'ya and Hikeda'ya that she had lost her protective instincts. Her sheathed sword was propped against a stone, so before she turned, she felt to make sure her knife was on her belt.

"Tanahaya?"

Her eyes widened. "Morgan! Come in. I did not know it was you. Your scent is very different."

He frowned. "That's a troubling thought. It is true, though, that I have bathed since you last saw me—or smelled me."

"No, no. Before you smelled strongly of pine sap from climbing in trees. It is how I followed you through Da'ai Chikiza after the ceiling fell." She beckoned. "Come and sit. When I heard you were here, I was delighted. To speak truthfully, I did not think any of us would survive Tanakirú. But I have been caught up with other things."

"I am so very sorry," he said, bowing his head. "I hardly knew Jiriki, but he was kind to me—kinder than I realized at the time. I do not want to interrupt your mourning."

"Nor I yours," she said. "We have all lost people we loved because of this mad war. I think it is a 'miracle', as your people call it, that so many of us survived. But we will be mourning those who are gone for a long time, so let that not stand in our way now. Come. Sit."

Tanahaya thought that Morgan seemed quite different. Certainly, he had grown—he was half a hand taller than when she had seen him last—but that was not surprising in a mortal of his age. He also seemed both more and less sure of himself, as though some of his boyish impatience and distraction had burned away, but what was left behind was a streak of sadness.

But sometimes sadness is only another name for unwanted wisdom, she told herself. *Sorrow is not in and of itself a bad thing.*

"I'm mourning too," he said when he had settled on a rock near her. "Not just for my mother and grandmother—those things are still not quite real to me, I suppose—but for another lost love. And I haven't even lost her yet."

As Tanahaya listened, more than a little surprised, he told her how he had met Nezeru in Da'ai Chikiza, how he had been her prisoner first, then her reluctant ally, and how their alliance had slowly become something else. Tanahaya felt more than a little pity for him, but also was not quite certain why he was telling her.

"You have set yourself a very hard problem indeed," she said when his story had meandered to its melancholy end. "But if she refuses your love, there seems little to be done but to accept it."

"But I don't believe her!" he said. "Her feelings for me were real. I may only be a mortal—only young—but she admitted it."

"That does not mean she is being false. There are many reasons she might think there is no future in your love. The two of you being *Hikeda'ya* and *Sudhoda'ya* is likely only one of them, but it is a reason many would find compelling by itself."

"I know. I only wanted to ask you . . ." He struggled to find the words. "Can immortals like you and Nezeru change? Do you ever change? About anything?"

The prince was a handsome young man, she recognized, but now she saw something of the impatient boy he had been—the boy she had at times found more than a little annoying. She decided letting him feel sorry for himself would be a poor parting gift.

"Certainly, we can—and often do," she said. "The story of my people is full of such things. But we change much more slowly than your people do because our lives are longer. In any case, Morgan, it is not a good idea to wait for someone to fall in love with you. It is even more foolish, I fear, for a mortal to wait for one of my kind to change her mind."

"But Nezeru is half mortal!"

"But she might live as long as a pureblood Hikeda'ya. We still know little of what will happen to Nakkiga's breeding of their people with mortals—it has only been happening for half a Great Year."

They talked for a while longer, sharing news of the many strange and surprising things that had happened since they had parted in Da'ai Chikiza, but she could tell that Morgan had not received the answers from her that he had hoped for. At last, he rose to go.

"We will meet again, Morgan," she told him. "I have learned much about your people since this all began—enough to realize how little I knew before. It could be that when Aditu's child has come and my heart has healed somewhat, I will even come to the Hayholt as an envoy again, if Protector Ki'ushapo thinks it a good idea."

He shook his head. "But the Hayholt has burned to its foundations, my grandfather tells me, though I can hardly believe it."

She smiled. "Your people will build again—if not there, then elsewhere. One of the things our people always marvel at is how your folk never mourn for long. It is a lesson we could learn from you, I think." She opened her arms. "Come and bid me farewell, Morgan. You and I traveled a long way together and survived many dangers, and I learned more about mortals from you than I did in the rest of my life until now. You will always be important to me. Never despair."

"You are important to me too, Tanahaya," he said as he returned her embrace. He kissed her on the cheek, chaste as a child, which amused her. "You saved my life many times."

"Travel well," she told him. "Cherish those you love every day, every hour. That is the greatest lesson of all. We must make our Garden here on earth."

"I can scarcely believe it is Josua," said Simon. "He is so changed."

"But it is him!" the woman named Tzoja told him, her voice tight with anger. It had taken Simon no little while to understand that she was, or had been, Derra, one of Josua's and Vorzheva's children and the twin of Unver, who he had faced at Winstowe. "I would know my father anywhere."

"I do not doubt you." But as he watched the mild, slightly distracted face of the man who stood before him, Simon still could not quite force himself to believe. So many years had passed since he had last seen Prince Josua. This man was missing his right hand, just like Josua, and the fine-boned face certainly could be his, though aged through several seemingly harsh decades. The man's disarranged gray hair was mostly gone in front, but that too was only in keeping with the amount of time since Simon had last seen his hero and friend, the man who had knighted him during the Storm King's War. But what Simon could not reconcile was the empty, incurious stare. "The traitor, Pasevalles—he bragged to me that he killed your father."

"Oh, to the devil with this Pasevalles! Did you not see the back of my father's head? It is plain he took a cruel blow there once. It has healed but can still be felt." She was near weeping again.

Simon had indeed seen and felt the dint in the man's skull, and all the time he had been studying it, this presumed Josua Lackhand had stood as serenely as an old dog being patted. He had no fire, no curiosity, and only seemed to speak in occasional phrases from the Book of Aedon. He certainly looked like Miri's beloved uncle, but if this was all that was left of him, then Simon almost regretted that he still lived.

"When the Lord hid His face from me, I was sore afraid," murmured Josua, as if hearing Simon's thoughts.

"He studied with the Usirean Brothers," Simon said. "He once told me that if he had not been a prince, he might have been a monk."

"When we met him," said Tzoja's white-faced daughter, Nezeru, "the others on the ship thought he was—they called him 'the Friar.' And Jarnulf, who traveled with him in Erkynland long ago, thought he must have been a priest."

Josua's appearance was not the only surprise. As they were waiting for Nezeru to join them, Tzoja had revealed that her half-Norn daughter was the object of Morgan's misery—that the king's grandson had traveled with her for months and had come to love her. As far as Simon could tell, though, Nezeru did not feel the same way about Morgan.

Which is a kindness, I suppose, he thought. *Already we are returning to a home that has been destroyed by Utuk'ku's army. We have all lost so much in this terrible year. How could we tell the survivors of the Hayholt that the heir to the throne loves a Norn?*

He turned his attention back to Tzoja, who had gone to Josua's side. He thought he could see elements of both Josua and Vorzheva in her, as he had with the enemy leader Unver, but told himself he might be letting the strange circumstances sway his opinion. But she had the same high forehead and narrow nose, the same clear-eyed gaze. She seemed too young to have a daughter the age of the half-Norn Nezeru, but everyone had begun to seem young to Simon, and being surrounded here by ageless Sithi and Norns had not helped.

Is it really him? Could his own daughter be mistaken? It's a pity Vorzheva isn't here.

He realized with sour amusement that this must be the first time he had ever wished to have the spiky, difficult Thrithings-woman around.

It must be Josua. It is *Josua. Why am I reluctant to admit it?*

But the answer was obvious. This might be the long-lost prince, but he was a damaged shadow of himself, not the beloved mentor Simon and Josua's other friends had sought for so long. *Perhaps it is just as well Miri isn't here to see him,* he thought, but his heart immediately rebuked him: *No, anything and everything would be better with Miri here beside me.*

"What should we do?" he asked out loud. "Josua's old castle at Naglimund is a ruin now, they tell me. And the Norns have all but destroyed the Hayholt. Still, I feel I should bring him home to Erkynland." He looked at Tzoja almost shyly—she was part of his family, and yet she was utterly a stranger. How odd the world had become! "Or would you rather take him back to . . . to Nakkiga, I suppose? That is where you live, isn't it? No, that wouldn't be right."

"It certainly would not," Tzoja said, as if he had proposed leaving Josua in a field somewhere. "I do not think I will ever go back there. We will go with you, King Simon. At least for now."

Simon could only nod. "Of course, if that's your wish. Prince Josua—and his family—will always have a home with us. But you will have to forgive the confusion you will find back in Erkynland."

Her laugh had a grim sound. "I have been a slave, both the queen's favored anchoress and the ordinary sort, Your Majesty. I have been living in the forest with my friend Vordis, eating the slop that the Order of Sacrifice deigned to ladle out for us, because Utuk'ku wanted us with her to see her triumph, as she must have thought of it. But out of all this horror, I have found both my daughter and my father alive. That outweighs any small amount of suffering I've endured or will endure. We will take the shelter you offer with thanks."

Simon nodded. *She is a clever woman,* he thought, *this Derra who is also Tzoja, to stay alive as a Norn slave so long. Her father's wit and her mother's fierceness.* It also gave him a better idea of how this woman's daughter could have so fascinated his own grandson. "We will discuss Josua's future—and yours, I suppose—as we travel to Jao é-Tinukai'i," he told her. "But until we reach Erchester and see how things stand there, I cannot tell you yet where you will live."

"It doesn't matter," she said, patting Josua's arm as if to reassure him, though he seemed quite unaware of their conversation. "If I can bring my poor father some comfort after he has been wandering the world so long without his family, I will be happy to live in the meanest hovel."

"Is the man I called 'Father' truly your grandsire, Nezeru? If so, what greater proof do you need of God's plan?" Jarnulf set another stone atop the small mountain he was constructing over Goh Gam Gar's enormous grave. Viyeki had sent a Builders Order wagon to carry the giant's body back across the gorge, because the plateau was all stone. Jarnulf had chosen a spot ringed by currently leafless birch trees on a hill on one side of the valley, and he had helped as the Builders dug the grave.

"I do not believe in your 'god's plans,' but my mother says that man is truly her father." Nezeru had appeared a short while earlier, as if she had just stumbled onto the spot where the giant had been laid to rest, but Jarnulf thought he knew better. In her own way, she was paying respect. "I have never seen either of my mortal grandparents, so I have to rely on my mother's word." She bent and picked up a stone half as big as her head and tossed it onto the cairn. "Will the giant have a gravestone, too?"

Jarnulf shrugged. "I do not know if it can be done in time. Most of those here will be leaving tomorrow." He gave her a sidelong glance. He was still conscious of a debt owed to her, although he had no idea of how it might be requited. "And you? Will you be one of them? Will you go back to Nakkiga now that Pratiki is going to usher in A Great Age of Peace?"

"You sound sour," she said. "Do you think he will be only another Hamakha tyrant? If that's the case, then you and I have accomplished nothing with our regicide."

He grinned. "I have accomplished exactly what I promised my God I would do. I feel no regret. God will decide what happens next."

"That sounds very pleasant," she said. "Letting God decide."

"You should try it, Nezeru."

She gave him a sharp look at his easy use of her name. "I cannot make myself believe in divine guidance, as you do. Least of all now, after seeing the truth behind all the things I believed for so long. And you, Gilhedur who used to be Jarnulf, what will you do?"

"I have already said. I will follow Prince Morgan. God has told me that is my fate, to become his knight."

She laughed, but it sounded a little shrill. "Oh! Again, I would love to live in such certainty. And has Morgan said he accepts your fealty? I must have missed that."

"There is always time for God to do His work. I will go to Erkynland with the prince, and he will see that no one else can do the things I can."

"You sound like Morgan's troll friend, Snenneq."

"Who is that?"

Her laugh this time was easier. "Oh, you will find out. But if you truly seek to become Morgan's paramount knight, you already have some fierce competition." She stood. "There is a last gathering today, I was told, and it must be starting now. I am going back over the bridge." She hesitated. "What of you?"

"I will stay a little while," he said as he carefully placed another stone on the pile. "I made a promise, and your father has helped me fulfill it. I did not think I would so soon owe gratitude to one of the Hikeda'ya, but I am grateful to him. I will stay a little longer and say my farewells."

She nodded, then looked at the cairn for a long, silent moment. "He was not what I thought he was," she said. "The giant, I mean."

"Few of us are what others think we are," he replied. "Only God knows who we truly are."

She nodded again, then turned and began to make her way down the hill toward the valley and the bridge. Jarnulf watched her for a little while, then turned back to the cairn.

43

Old Grudges

Tzoja was still unnerved by how utterly disinterested her father was in the world around him. Josua scarcely did anything but sit and stare at nothing, occasionally quoting from the Book of Aedon, and hardly seemed to notice he had exchanged a group of strangers on the Ninth Ship for his true family. *Does he have any idea who I am?* she wondered. *Does he understand that I am his daughter?* But Tzoja—Derra, then—had still been young when he disappeared, and now had lived thirty summers and more.

She was distracted by the arrival of a Builder's Order clerk bearing a folded letter. She recognized the seal immediately, but barely had a moment to glance at it before the messenger turned to leave.

"Hold," she said. "Didn't your master tell you to wait in case there was a reply?"

The Hikeda'ya functionary wore a look she could not quite unravel. Poorly hidden fear? Was he somehow afraid of her—a mere mortal? "The High Magister's secretary Nonao gave it to me, Mistress," he said, eyes downcast, "and directed me to take it to you. He said nothing about a reply."

Which made sense if Nonao was only passing along a message from Viyeki. "Very well, then." When she saw he still hesitated, she had a momentary sense of unreality: a member of the ruling race—albeit a low-level functionary—was waiting for her to dismiss him! "You may go."

He left quickly, with the merest scrape of a bow, but even that was unexpected. *Has Viyeki told them what I am to him?* she wondered. *Or is it simply that the world they knew has turned downside-up?*

Both the seal and the hand, she saw as she unwrapped the letter, were Viyeki's.

I am caught up in Order business on the far side of the bridge, it read, *near the Hikeda'ya camp, but I need to speak to you. Please come to me as soon as you can.*

He had signed it with just the first "V" rune of his name, something he did when he was in a hurry. Tzoja told herself it was as likely to be happy news as bad, but she was not entirely convinced.

"It seems I must find someone to stay with you, Father," she said to Josua. "I have to go out for a little while. Perhaps your granddaughter would like the chance to get to know you better."

"Pain and woe are visited, generation after generation, upon those who do not accept the living God and His gift to us, Usires the Aedon," he replied with what Tzoja thought was a certain morbid satisfaction.

"We've had enough pain and more than enough woe," she told him, though she doubted he understood. "Now, you stay put while I find Nezeru."

The afternoon sun had ranged far into the west, so the hills on the valley's near side were draped in shade while everything else still basked in cold, slanting sunlight. The new bridge over the foaming gorge was now in constant use, mostly by Hikeda'ya soldiers and nobles, but a few colorful Zida'ya livened the view and lifted Tzoja's heart. She had forgotten how much the Hikeda'ya's cousin-race liked to dress in bold hues and put color in their hair; after so long among Viyeki's people, who either dyed their hair a somber black or left it deathly white, it was like seeing spring flowers emerge through the snow.

A guard in the livery of Viyeki's Enduya Clan, with a Stone Frog brooch on the shoulder of his cape, was waiting for her at the base of the bridge. "You are Mistress Tzoja?" he asked, examining her carefully. She agreed that she was. "The High Magister has sent me to escort you to him. Come with me, please."

Assuming that what had brought Viyeki across to this side of the gorge was political rather than professional—digging earth or setting stone on stone—Tzoja expected to be led into the heart of the Hikeda'ya camp. Instead, to her mild surprise, the Enduya guard led her toward the valley's western slopes, which were still badly scarred from the battle—pitted, muddy earth, toppled trees, and the gouges of countless boot prints, many fresh.

Burial crews, she thought, and shuddered. *How many died here? What a waste it was. All at a madwoman's whim.*

It was not as hard an ascent as she had first feared: Sacrifice Order engineers had constructed a winding road into the heights, crude but sturdy, to allow war engines and wagons to be hauled up and down. Within moments they had reached the road's first great turning, and she could look back to see the camp.

It was a strange sight. When she and Vordis had been marched into Tanakirú, it had been exactly the sort of closely ordered Sacrifice outpost she would have expected, the fires set out in careful geometric order and each fifty-troop dutifully confined to their own areas. Now it had taken on the appearance of a sprawling marketplace, with Hikeda'ya soldiers and nobles milling everywhere and no obvious delineation between one troop and another. As on the bridge, a few Zida'ya wandered among them, apparently allowed to go where they would. Many of the Sacrifice soldiers had even shed their armor, or at least parts of it, and none of them seemed to have much to do.

Maybe things really will change now, she thought. *And not just for me and the other slaves.* As she knew only too well because of Nezeru, even the Sacrifices themselves, proud as they might be, were little better than thralls who could be tortured or executed for the smallest infractions.

The road turned again, and the camp fell away out of sight behind a stand of spruces that had somehow survived the fighting. In fact, this part of the slope was becoming more and more forested, and Tzoja couldn't help wondering what sort of duty, either for his order or for Prince Pratiki, had brought Viyeki out here.

Only a little way farther on and the road became something less formal, a cleared track with a thin covering of packed earth that wound upward through more spruces, this time a thick grove that crowded in on either side of the track and cut off most of the afternoon sunlight.

"How far is it?" she asked the guard who followed close behind her.

He was silent for some moments, as though mulling a complicated response, but when he spoke it was only to say, "The High Magister has sent me to escort you to him"—the same words he had used before, as if he had been forced to learn them by heart. But they were both speaking the Hikeda'ya tongue. Tzoja took a dozen more steps, puzzled by the man's flat response, his almost sullen repetition of his own words, then she turned back to ask him again, only to see two more Enduya guards abruptly emerge from the trees and fall in behind the first guard. A sudden chill swept over her, and it was nothing to do with the tree-blocked sun.

As she turned back to the road, Tzoja saw that a cloaked, white-faced figure now stood in the center of the trackway before her, barely visible in the gloom, and for a happy moment she thought it must be Viyeki. Then the moment ended.

"Tzoja the husband stealer," said Khimabu, spreading her slender, pale hands in a parody of welcome. "Tzoja the brood cow. So, here you are. And without your mortal barbarian this time."

Tzoja stopped, her heart speeding but her blood turning cold in her veins. "Where is Viyeki?" she demanded.

"Do you still think *he* sent that message?" said Khimabu with icy satisfaction. "I learned to imitate my husband's writing long ago."

She was caught between three armed Hikeda'ya soldiers and her enemy, far from any help. Tzoja suddenly found it very hard to breathe. "You cannot do this," she said. "If you kill me, you will be caught and punished. Viyeki is going to end your marriage."

"And I know whose idea that was." Khimabu's words dripped with honeyed venom. "But I care little. If I want him back, I will have him back—especially with you gone. Or I will find a better mate. Viyeki was never bold enough. He always let others have what should have been his."

Now anger began to surge through her, driving out a little of the numbing chill. If she was to die here, she would not do so silently or humbly. "And I gave him what you could not—a child to carry his legacy. No wonder you hate me."

"Hate you?" Khimabu began to move down the track toward her, one hand concealed behind her back. "Because you gave birth to a traitor? To the wretched creature who murdered our queen?"

Tzoja took a step back, then felt something sharp against the small of her back. The Enduya guards had continued to move forward, and one prodded her with the tip of an unsheathed sword. "She saved us all," Tzoja said. "My daughter saved us all!"

"So many problems created by an overreaching mortal and her treacherous, bastard child." Khimabu made a finger-sign she didn't recognize. "But the halfblood will be dealt with, too. I will not even have to dirty my hands—others will see to her death, and very soon."

Tzoja could not retreat, not with three swords behind her, but she could sense Khimabu working herself up to a murderous pitch. With a scream that was equal parts fury and terror, she threw herself at her tormentor, hoping to knock Khimabu down and then escape the armored soldiers in the heavily wooded hills. She had forgotten that even a female of the Hikeda'ya was still stronger than she was. She managed to knock Khimabu back a stumbling step, but even as she tried to force her way past, Khimabu reached out and caught her by the hair, tearing some loose so painfully that Tzoja screamed before her enemy yanked her off her feet and onto her knees.

"You dare attack me?" A tiny flush had risen on both of Khimabu's angled cheeks.

"Ha! I would kill you if I could," said Tzoja through tears of pain.

"Enough of this—" Khimabu began, then something dropped out of the trees beside the road.

It was Nezeru, holding a long witchwood sword in her hand. "Let go of my mother," she said.

Tzoja was so startled, confused, and surprised that she almost asked her daughter who was watching Josua, but then several things happened all at once. Khimabu yanked Tzoja backward. An instant later, her head still prisoned by Khimabu's broad handful of her hair, she felt a slim blade push against her throat.

"Kill the halfblood," Khimabu spat. The three guards leaped toward Nezeru. Blades rang. Tzoja, stumbling in her enemy's grip, could not see what was happening, but she did not think Khimabu would wait until the fight was over before slitting her throat. She struggled, but Khimabu managed to pin one of her arms while still holding onto her hair, and then the blade was against her throat again.

"I would prefer to make you watch your daughter die, but I have waited too long to be finished with you," she murmured in Tzoja's ear.

She strained to lean away from the blade, but Khimabu's grasp was surprisingly firm, and despite Tzoja's struggles to avoid it, Khimabu began to push the dagger home. As it pierced deeper, Tzoja let out a panicked cry.

"Mother!" shouted Nezeru. "Here! Hold out your hand!"

One arm was pinioned by Khimabu's grip, but she managed to extend her other hand, though she had no idea why. Nezeru seemed to have downed one of her opponents, but she was caught between the other two guards, blocking and slipping their attacks, the clack of witchwood against bronze as rapid as woodpecker's hammering. Then Nezeru pivoted, reached behind her back, and flung something toward the place where her mother and Khimabu struggled. It flew, end over blurry end, and smacked against Tzoja's outstretched hand, but she could not hold onto it and it tumbled to the ground. Still trying to lean away from Khimabu's blade, she saw that what her daughter had thrown was a witchwood dagger, so deftly aimed that only the hilt had struck her hand. Desperate, Tzoja suddenly let her knees buckle so that she sagged toward the ground, then managed to wrap her fingers around the knife-hilt even as she felt a burning pain scrape across the back of her head. Without thinking, she turned and stabbed at the hand that still clutched her hair. Khimabu's grip loosened and Tzoja spun all the way around to drive the witchwood knife into her enemy's side even as Khimabu tried again to stab at her throat. Khimabu only managed to slice the edge of Tzoja's neck, but Tzoja's blow slid home beneath her enemy's ribs.

Still clutching the now-bloodied blade, Tzoja fought free, prepared to run, but Khimabu was not even looking at her. A blossom of red had appeared at the waist of her gown. Eyes wide with surprise, Khimabu dropped her own knife and grabbed at the wound, white fingers suddenly dyed scarlet. Tzoja was beyond all reason now: with a cry of disgust and terrified anger, she leaped to her feet and drove the knife into her enemy's chest. It made a sound she could both hear and feel as the blade punched through meat and gristle into the hollow beneath.

Khimabu took a few stumbling steps backward, then turned as if to run off in that direction, but after another step she slumped to the hard winter ground.

Nezeru was standing over the bodies of three Enduya guards, watching her mother as she absently wiped her sword clean with one of the guards' cloaks. "Are you well, Mother? Did she hurt you badly? You are bleeding."

Tzoja honestly had no idea. As she felt herself for injuries, wincing at the deep cut on her scalp and the bloody place where a hank of her hair had been torn loose, she looked back. Khimabu still lay where she had fallen.

Nezeru came forward and took the witchwood knife from Tzoja's shaking grasp. "General Suno'ku would be proud, I think, even though it was a mortal hand that wielded Cold Leaf today."

Tzoja could only stare at her enemy's body. "Who? Cold what?"

"Never mind. Let us leave these corpses for the ravens. You are bleeding all over yourself."

As they made their way down the hill, Tzoja leaning heavily on Nezeru's arm, she finally asked, "Who is watching over your father?"

"Vordis."

"But she can't—!"

"Can't see? Mother, Vordis is a grown woman who survived for years as a blind mortal in the Hamakha court. You worry about her as though she was your child."

Tzoja laughed. Once she started, it was hard to stop, and it hurt. With every uncontrollable rush of laughter, her torn scalp hurt as if it was on fire.

Nezeru halted. "What is wrong?"

"Nothing." The helpless laugh had run its course. They began to walk again. "Truly. It's just this talk of treating Vordis like my child." Nezeru was staring at her as though she feared Tzoja had lost her wits. "Don't you see? You didn't call me 'Tzoja' today, like you always did. That used to make me so sad. You called me 'Mother'. I never knew until now how much it would mean to me." She staggered a little but caught herself. "Tell me how this happened. Did you follow us out here?"

"Of course I followed you. I didn't like the sound of any of it. My father would have sent an armed escort for you."

"I suppose so," Tzoja said. "But it's hard for me to think just now."

"Let's get you back, then. If you need me to carry you, I can."

"You are quite amazing," said Tzoja proudly. "Carry *me*, after you outfought three armed guards! *And* you called me 'Mother.'"

"Hush, now." But her voice was gentle.

They met in the place Simon had begun to think of as the council chamber, the large cavern with a firepit at its center. Many had gathered, several dozen each of the Sithi and Norns, as well as Simon, his family, and Brother Etan.

Ki'ushapo was the first to speak.

Even after so many years, and more time spent among them than perhaps any other mortal could boast, Simon still had trouble understanding the subtleties of the Zida'ya, although he thought that Ki'ushapo would make a good protector. He seemed more stolid and cautious than Jiriki, but Simon thought that might be a good thing in a time of fearfully sudden change for his people. Like almost all present, the Sitha still wore his battle-gear, though without his weapons.

"Tomorrow, we set out for Jao é-Tinukai'i, the refuge that sheltered the Zida'ya from the fall of Asu'a until the death of Amerasu Ship-born." Ki'ushapo glanced conspicuously toward Prince Pratiki. "I say this not to reopen old wounds but to remind myself and my comrades how much has changed in so short a time. I have never hated our Hikeda'ya kinfolk, though I hated the things they did under Utuk'ku's rule. But we go to Jao é-Tinukai'i not only to mourn what we have lost, but also to begin what we hope will be a new and better theme in the ancient song of our people. We hope it will be the first of many for all the Keida'ya folk."

As Rukayu rendered the Protector's careful words into Westerling, Simon only half-listened. He was working away at a thought—not a new one, but one that had come back to him powerfully in the last days. He looked at his grandson Morgan, who was listening to Rukayu's explanation, and felt a mixture of pride and worry. If there was a lesson to be taken from the fall of Utuk'ku, Simon thought, it was not from her death but from her life. She had been the only source of authority among the Norn people, and as her wisdom and ambition had soured over the centuries, she had carried all her folk with her into a kind of murderous madness. Simon hoped Prince Pratiki truly meant to change that. Would the Norns' habit of obedience help him? That was the problem living under an all-powerful ruler: with no one to gainsay her, Utuk'ku's anger had, like a corrupted, miasmic air, eventually infected her whole society.

And what if Pasevalles succeeded? *He still might. God only knows what he has done while I have been here in the north.* Despite having been king for decades, Simon had never thought in anything but practical terms about what power truly meant and how it was wielded, but the past year had shoved the question into his face, forcing him to consider it. When he looked at those who held sway over the lives of others, he could find few happy instances. The Sithi seemed to rule themselves with grace, although he knew that even the Zida'ya had disagreements—Amerasu's last speech on the night she died had been a condemnation of her people's behavior—but none of them seemed to have ultimate authority. Even a Sa'onsera like Amerasu or the fabled Jenjiyana seemed to rule mostly because their wisdom inspired trust.

The mortal monarchs he knew were far less inspiring. He and Miriamele had honestly tried to do what seemed best for their people, but the trust that the High Throne had inspired had made it easy for a corrupt servant like Pasevalles to do tremendous harm. And Hugh of Hernystir? It was not Hugh's illegitimacy that made him untrustworthy. He was an untrustworthy man who had gained the power of a throne.

And, of course, the greatest and most threatening example of all was the dead queen of the Hikeda'ya. Utuk'ku had been her people's all and everything, and she had come to believe it herself—so much so that she would have dragged every living thing down to death with her when her time had come.

So, is there an answer? he wondered. *Can men rule themselves, or must they always set someone higher, as God rules above us? But no mere ruler, mortal or immortal, can ever be as loving as God, or as far-seeing . . .*

He realized with a start that he had missed much of Ki'ushapo's address. He sat a little straighter and did his best to fix his attention as the protector gave way to Pratiki.

"As Protector Ki'ushapo said," the Norn prince began, "we may hope that what we have spoken about and done here will someday be seen as the beginning of a great and hopeful change for our two clans. Those of you gathered here have helped to lay the foundations for what will be called the Treaty of Tanakirú, though it will be formalized on another day in another place—an agreement as important as the Parting itself. We may even dare to hope it might be the first step toward one day undoing that great division."

Simon looked around the cavern, trying to gauge the reactions of the immortal. All their eyes, black or honey-golden, were watching Pratiki.

"Do not mistake intention for success, though," warned the prince. "We have not yet sent the news of change to our own folk back in Nakkiga, although I suspect some word of what happened here has already reached them. I have told and is making its way to the rest of our people, just as the name 'Witchwood Crown' escaped even the fierce grip of Utuk'ku's inner circle."

"And we will not be finished here until that selfsame Witchwood Crown has been discussed," Geloë broke in, her less-than-human voice a harsh surprise after Ki'ushapo's and Pratiki's liquid tones. "You speak of the Keida'ya as though your two clans are the only ones who have suffered from the evils of the past."

"That is not my intended meaning." Pratiki did not sound pleased at the interruption.

"I do not doubt your intentions, Prince," she said, "but history teaches me that Keida'ya intentions, however fair-minded, usually fail to account for *my* people. When we Vao joined you in the Garden, nobody ever told us, 'We will make you into slaves'—but that is what happened. And when your folk came to my ancestor Ruyan the Navigator seeking his help, many promises were made that if we would help your kind escape from the horrifying results of your own mistake, we would all find happiness together in a new land. But those were lies—!"

"Peace, lady, peace!" said Pratiki, and for the first time Simon could see anger on the prince's pale face and hear it in his words. "We have heard all this before, but we cannot solve centuries of injustice in the space of a few days."

"I know. Which is one reason why I will take those of my people who came here and depart these lands entirely. But you are returning to Nakkiga soon, Pratiki. What of the Tinukeda'ya who did not come here to Tanakirú?"

"What of them? Do you expect me to round them up and send them to you?"

"Do not say such a thing even in jest. No, I ask you what you will do with your slaves—Tinukeda'ya and mortal alike—when you have taken power in Nakkiga. When you sit enthroned in the Maze Palace, will you free them? Or will you prove your noble words a lie by keeping them in chains?"

"Do not speak that way to me." Pratiki was clearly struggling to keep his patience. "Despite all the good you have done here, you have not the right. The Hamakha—the Hikeda'ya people—are not to be instructed by anyone in what they should do."

The massive helmet did not move, but Simon could almost imagine Geloë nodding in grim satisfaction. "I see that after only a few pokes," she said, "the snake coils and prepares to bite."

As soon as Simon heard Rukayu's translation, he clambered to his feet. "Valada Geloë," he said, "I have known you since I was more or less a child. I have always respected your wisdom, but I do not think this is the right way."

The helmet swiveled toward him. "So. And what have I done wrong, King Simon?" demanded the harsh, inflectionless voice.

"Nothing wrong. The right is on your side. But I think you have mistaken who your enemies are."

"Simon, do you truly mean to explain history to me? My people have been on the wrong end of it even before we came to this land."

"No, I cannot explain or defend it," He struggled to find the proper words. "Such evil can never be completely undone."

"Just so," she said. "I have often heard arguments like this from the Zida'ya—even Jiriki. 'Things will change,' we were told. 'Only be patient.' But if I had been patient, your world would be black nothingness now, devoured by Unbeing."

"Because Utuk'ku believed in all or nothing, too," Simon said, and the words finally came to him. "She wanted things only her own way or, like a child, she would throw down the toy and break it."

"Are you saying I am a child, King Simon?" Her strange voice had grown dangerously soft. "Or that I am like Utuk'ku?"

"Neither, Geloë. I am saying that I know you are better than your anger with Pratiki—wiser, too. You would not have worked so hard to save this world unless you felt it was worth saving."

The roomful of eyes, golden and night-dark, watched them intently.

"I did not work for the world. I worked to save my own people. Do you think that after centuries of cruelty and enslavement toward my people, I should trust the Hikeda'ya to do better once I am gone and I no longer have any hold over them?"

"Yes!" Simon realized he had spoken too loudly. "Yes. Because what else can you do?" He turned to the sea of golden and white faces. "What else can anyone do? You say you are leaving, Geloë—though I don't understand how, not really. Prince Pratiki could promise you anything here today and break those promises later, after you have gone. What else can you do but trust that things will get better, that the rest of us will remember and care? And what will you do if you do not get the promises you seek? Threaten us with the power of the ship's heart, as Utuk'ku did? But you are not her. I know that much."

As Ruykayu's long translation of his words ended, the armored figure regarded Simon for a long moment. "So you beg me to exchange power—something we Vao have not often had—for trust," said Geloë. "But we have seen what trust brought my people—and they are your people, too, Simon, as I told you, whether you believe it or not. So, consider carefully and then tell me—what would your advice be?"

Simon took a long breath. "Trust," he said finally. "We all must trust something. If evil deeds are only met with more evil deeds—well, what could come from that but another sort of Unbeing? Nothing else would survive."

"And justice?" asked Geloë. "If evil is only met with kindness, what about justice?"

"There must be justice, too," he admitted. "I am not God, I am only a mortal man. I do not have all the answers."

No one spoke for a moment, and the silence seemed as though it might last forever. Then Ki'ushapo rose and came to Geloë. He knelt in front of her and bowed his head. "I cannot promise your people their long-overdue justice, Sa-Ruyan Ela," he said, "but I can promise you that I will work to make the lot of all your folk who remain in this land better than it was. I swear that by the honor of House Sa'onserei."

Now the grotesque, helmeted head swiveled toward Pratiki. A moment later, he too came forward and, to Simon's surprise—as well as the evident surprise of many others in the cavern—lowered himself to one knee.

"I cannot promise anything," he said. "I do not even know if I will be able to hold my people together. But I am sorry for the many wrongs done to the Tinukeda'ya, and if I live, I promise I will work to make things better between your folk and mine. I swear that not simply on the word of Clan Hamakha, but on my own honor."

Geloë contemplated the two kneeling leaders for a moment, then turned away from them to address the others watching. "You have heard those who speak for Zida'ya and Hikeda'ya. You are all witnesses. And now I say to you, go! Your time here is done, and it is our time now—time to prepare our leavetaking. Carry Jiriki to his place of rest and celebrate him. Shut the so-called queen's body away in a Nakkiga vault, where I pray that she will be forgotten. But before you leave this place, follow me, and I will show you something you will never forget."

She turned and walked slowly out of the cavern. After a moment, the others got up and followed her in a nearly silent throng. She led them through the tunnels and out onto the plateau, then stopped and raised her gauntleted hands, the crystalline tiles of her armor glinting in the afternoon sun.

"See!" she cried. "They are coming now. All those I summoned."

And Simon saw that she was right. Down the sides of the forested valley in straggling lines, and out of many hidden places in the tumbled cliffs, hundreds of Tinukeda'ya were streaming toward the plateau. He could see more tiny figures standing atop the great ship where it loomed on the cliffside high above him. The Tinukeda'ya seemed to have almost as many shapes as there were individuals, tall and short, straight and bent; Simon saw Dwarrows, Niskies, and many others whose forms he could not recognize.

"Do not fear," said Geloë, though most of the Hikeda'ya and Ziday'a looked more stunned than fearful. "My people come not to make war, but to make the great ship ready. The skill to do it is in our blood and in our dreaming minds. Oh, we have waited so long for this day! Go now and remember what you have promised! And if the rest of you would see the *Witchwood Crown* depart this land to take my people to a new life, you need only return to this place on Midsummer's Day."

PART THREE

Witchwood Crown

Some speak of better days;
Others weep for what is gone.
What use? The river never ceases to flow,
And to mark a moment or a life is to try to seize a ripple,
A wave, a fleck of foam. Listen to the voice of the river,
Lady, for you will have no other answer.

—FROM THE DAYBOOK OF
LADY MIGA SEYT-JINNATA

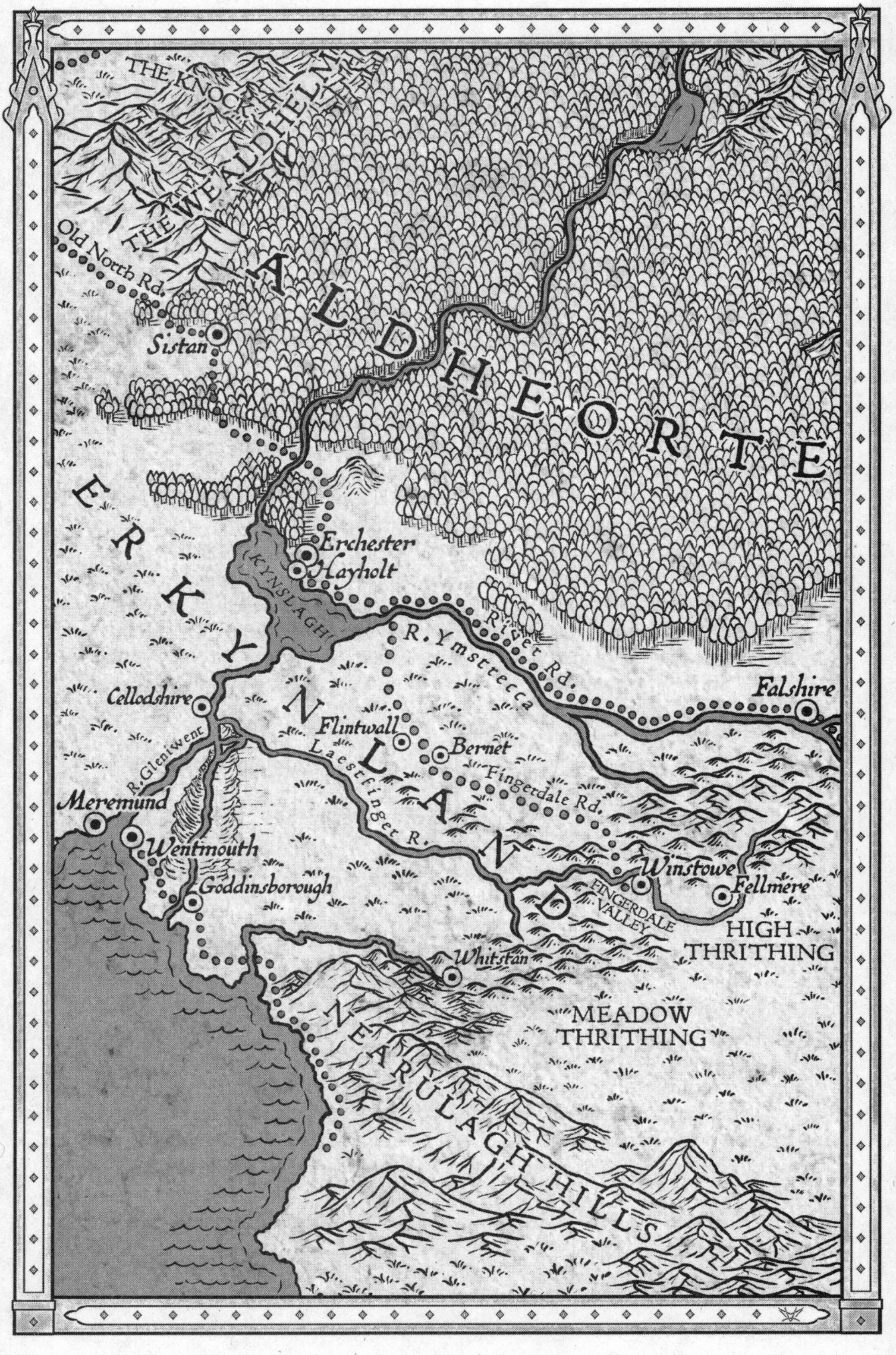
THE KNOCK
THE WEALDHELM
Old North Rd.
ALDHEORTE
Sistan
ERKYNLAND
Erchester
Hayholt
KYNSLAGH
R. Ymstrecca
Rivet Rd.
Falshire
Cellodshire
R. Gleniwent
Flintwall
Bernet
Laestfinger R.
Fingerdale Rd.
Meremund
Wentmouth
Goddinsborough
Winstowe
Fellmere
FINGERDALE VALLEY
HIGH THRITHING
Whitstan
MEADOW THRITHING
NEARULAGH HILLS

44

The Nearer Wolf

"Oh!" Inahwen said, surprised. "Eolair, look at your poor hands!"

"It is nothing much. The burns are not as bad as they seem. In any case, Sister Morwen ordered me to heal quickly, so I am doing my best not to make her angry." He carefully lowered himself to one knee before her. "I will be honest, my queen. That Morwen woman frightens me."

She laughed. "Get up, you silly old fool. Come and sit beside me."

Eolair examined the throne beside the queen's. Light streamed in through the Taig's high windows, making the drifting dust sparkle. "Since I am looking at what used to be her seat, I should ask what happened to Lady Tylleth."

"Caught trying to sneak out of Hernysadharc dressed as one of her own servants. She has been returned in shame to her father, who is not particularly pleased to have her back."

"And the baby that she hinted at?"

"There never was one." She sighed. "No one is going to lift this burden from my shoulders, I fear."

"Don't say that, even in jest. Hugh, the last bastard heir, turned out badly. But tell me instead, how are you, Majesty?"

"Shaken, of course. My own burns are healing—it is mostly my legs." Inahwen shook her head. "We should both be dead."

"We were fortunate—more fortunate than I, at least, deserved," he said. "I badly underestimated Hugh's madness."

"None of us thought it would go so far. Do not take the blame on yourself."

Eolair had not yet risen from his bow, in part because he was not certain whether he wanted to mount the daïs beside her. The Taig's throne room was full of the usual courtiers, perhaps even a bit more crowded than usual, and he was hesitant about giving tongues any new excuse to wag. He looked to the ancient clan carvings hanging from the roof beams and wondered at all that the wooden birds and beasts must have seen as they dangled there, year after year, century after century. "It does not feel right that I should sit beside you," he finally admitted.

"Do not be so cautious." Inahwen extended a hand still red and raw with healing burns. "It is my wish that you join me, and you must honor it. Or have you already forgotten the loving words you wrote?"

"Never, my lady." Giving in, he climbed the steps and lowered himself into the high-backed chair. "But I would hate to have anyone think I wooed you with the hope of sitting here."

"Hang what people think," she said. "Is that not the sort of thing you would say yourself?"

"I like to think I would be a bit more judicious, Majesty."

"And hang 'judicious,' too. I am an old woman who has given her whole life to Hernystir, and for that sacrifice I was mocked, imprisoned, and then set on fire. Do you think I care what gossips may say?"

He smiled despite himself. "And what might gossips say, my dear woman?"

"That you are going to marry me and be my consort. Unless you really do regret what you wrote to me."

"Not for a moment. And if that is your royal command—"

"It is."

For a moment, Eolair hesitated. His feelings for her were deep and real, but he could not so easily shake off the habits of a lifetime; his nature was to consider every possibility first, good and bad. He lowered his voice. "But what about the succession, my dear? It seems unlikely that our union will produce any children."

"You never know until you try," she said, laughing again.

He could not help admiring her, and for the moment was content to follow her lead. "Your escape from death seems to have made you a great deal more certain of what you want."

"How could it not? And even if I had not been through that . . . ordeal . . . I would be all too aware of how close we are to the end of our lives. We are beyond ripe, you and I, my dear Eolair. We are all but used up, and I wish to save a little of what remains for happiness. You and I can find that happiness together, or so I think. What do you think?"

He looked at her face and could see the brave but unready child who had become King Lluth's third wife, as well as the woman who had lived through so much. "I think we do deserve some happiness, yes. But I still worry about the succession."

She waved her hand. "Easy enough. Aelin is already your heir. When we marry, I will make him mine as well. The people think a great deal of him already, and that will only grow as the news of what happened in Hugh's last hours continues to spread."

Eolair nodded. "You seem to have everything planned. Is this how it will be in our marriage as well?"

"That is what happens when you marry a queen, Count Eolair." She frowned. "I wonder if I shall have to elevate you. It wouldn't do to have people think I am marrying below my station." She gave him a sidelong glance. "What would you think of being a prince-consort?"

"Hmmmm," he said. "I am not certain I would like it. It sounds a bit tamed."

"Well, we shall talk about it another time. Shall I call for Aelin to tell him?"

"You make me quite breathless, Inahwen! But I think my nephew is busy bidding our Fair Folk saviors farewell just now."

"In truth, I should have remembered that, because I already gave Yisume and her Skyglass Lake people my royal gratitude this morning, before you arrived. I dearly hope that we can keep some ties of friendship with the Sithi, especially those at Skyglass Lake. Perhaps that can be your official task, dear Eolair—ambassador to the immortals. The Fair Folk have always liked you."

"Do you know, I would find that a very fitting occupation for my declining years," he said. "Truly, I would. But I cannot simply leave the High Ward without any word of warning when so many dire problems still threaten."

"You have reminded me. When he has quite recovered, I wish to send young Aelin with a force of men to the border, both to see what Hugh did there—there may be mischief of his to undo, and a few of his treacherous minions still to be rooted out—and also to support any legitimate claimant to the High Throne of Erkynland, now that Simon and Miriamele are gone. Do you think Duke Osric will take the crown?"

"I have not given up on Prince Morgan yet. He is a resilient youth and may have managed to survive on his own. He is the true heir, after all. I would support Osric continuing as regent, of course, in the hope that we can find Morgan."

"I suppose we can only wait. Have you heard these rumors of Duchess Nelda besieging Winstowe under her own banner? They say she has Pasevalles mewed up there. But why would Nelda do such a thing? I would not imagine it of her."

"The first thing to do after hearing a rumor is to forget it," he said, "because soon you will hear another that will fly in the face of the first. It may all be Osric, not wanting Pasevalles or whoever holds Winstowe to know whether he is in Erchester or outside their walls."

She looked at him fondly. "You were born to do this sort of thing, my beloved—no wonder Lluth recognized your quality when you were but young. Your mind is as intricate as the explanations of a misbehaving priest."

He laughed. "Is it truly possible that this is how our story ends, my dear? In peace and better times?"

"And in love," she said. "Never forget that. It will be the foundation of our stewardship, until we pass it all on to Aelin. But who will he marry?"

"It seems a bit too early to worry about that, Inahwen."

"Nonsense. You of all people should know better. It is never too early to start planning important things, and we need a healthy succession. What do you think of Isleen, Lord Murdo's daughter? She strikes me as a young woman who will speak her mind. Any king needs that in a wife."

"And any queen needs that in a husband, too?"

"Of course." She reached over and patted his knee. "Of course, dear."

He shook his head. "But should we not let Aelin decide who he wants to marry? We do not even know that he cares for this Isleen."

"Nonsense," she said for the second time. "Young people never know what they truly want. That is why old people are not merely useful but necessary. We will make certain he sees where his best course lies."

"Well, it seems that all the important things are settled," Eolair said, smiling again. His chair was indeed comfortable and well-padded, and he had to admit he enjoyed the elevated view of the throne room and the famous cloud of wooden carvings that hung from its ceiling. "And we will pray to all the gods for a peaceful result to the unrest in Erkynland."

"And the gods willing, for good news from the north as well," said Inahwen. "The Sithi seemed quite fearful about what was happening there."

"By Mircha's tears, I forgot about the cursed Norns and their cursed queen! Now that you have reminded me, I am fearful too. We will never be safe while the real Crow Mother lives and schemes."

"But we will face the future side by side, dear Eolair," she said, "however fearful it may be, and whatever it brings. That is something hopeful, is it not?"

"Yes, my queen." He reached out for her hand, carefully avoiding her burns. "It is."

Sir Porto, Binabik, and Sisqi were on their hands and knees, searching in the undergrowth at the base of the crag on which Winstowe Castle stood—a spot that continued to fascinate Binabik's wolf, Vaqana. The castle itself loomed high above them, a blocky shadow against the night. They had spent an hour on this latest search at the base of the prominence; and again they had found nothing unusual. Meanwhile, the white wolf kept digging small scrapes in different spots around the bottom of the crag, then abandoning each one after a short while and beginning another

Binabik sat up. "Vaqana, what is consuming you so?" Despite his annoyance, he kept his voice low, since the castle parapets were only a long bowshot above them. Vaqana had just given up on another abortive dig. She sat, tongue lolling, and watched Binabik with what Porto could have sworn was frustration. "I do not understand," the troll told her. "Show me! *Mamiq-iq*!"

Vaqana lurched forward to scratch at the sandy earth, but again surrendered after a short while digging and gave a whimper that Porto thought might be a complaint about the stupidity of humans.

Binabik leaned down and began digging in the same spot. "The soil is loose. It slides back on top of itself," he said after a little time—then, in a tone of growing surprise, "*Very* loose. Has there been digging here before?"

Sisqi moved in beside him to help dig. The wolf came and leaned over Binabik's shoulder, as if pleased that her master had finally done something right.

"Be careful of your fingers, beloved," Binabik told Sisqi. "There is rock under here." He leaned in and dug faster. Vaqana danced back as the troll began actively tossing dirt behind him, and it was all Porto could do to stay out of the way of flying soil.

"Daughter of the Mountains!" Binabik leaned close to the growing hole, then turned to Porto. "Can you see what I am seeing?"

The old knight crouched down beside the troll. "What have you found? A tunnel?"

"It is being the opposite," said Binabik. "See? Deep underneath the dirt, the ground is all stone."

"So that's why your wolf kept starting scrapes and then giving up. Bedrock, is it?"

"Not at all. Quick, Sisqi, help me clear a little more." They dug furiously, and Vaqana dashed back and forth behind them, excited. After no little time, the trolls stopped and moved back from the broad area they had excavated. "Can you see now, Sir Porto?" Binabik asked.

He squinted and saw a flat expanse of stone at the bottom of the hole. "Bedrock," he said.

"Look closer," the troll whispered. "No, it is too dark. Give me your hand." He took Porto's fingers in his small, callused grip and guided the knight's hand. At first all Porto could feel at the bottom of the hole was the smooth surface of the stone, like weather-polished granite. Binabik then gently slid Porto's hand across the flat face of the stone until it touched a distinct crack in the surface. "Run your fingers carefully on that," said the troll. "It is being very straight, is it not?"

"I . . . I suppose." Porto continued to trace the crevice. "Yes. Very straight."

"Continue and you will find where it runs into another stone—also with a straight edge."

Porto felt it then and sat up. "Something made by men."

Binabik nodded. "It is. A floor of stone flags is built here all around the base of the stony cliff. That is why Vaqana kept returning to this place—it had the smell of something that did not belong. And who knows what is beneath it? A tunnel for escaping Winstowe Castle? To me, that seems most likely."

"What should we do?" asked Porto. "Should we keep digging and see if we can find out what's beneath it?"

"Dig, yes," said Binabik. "Also, we must swiftly tell Captain Kenrick and Queen Miriamele what we have found. But we cannot leave it unwatched now that we know something is here." Porto could almost hear the small man frowning in indecision. "I do not like to send you, though, Sir Porto. It will take you a long while to get back to where your horse is tied."

"I will go," said Sisqi. "Ooki will carry me safely back to Miriamele's camp. I will tell them, and bring back with captain and soldiers."

Binabik climbed to his feet and embraced her. "Go quickly, my love," he said. "This has not been used for many years, I am thinking, but if Vaqana is so taken by it, there may now be men beneath us, preparing to open it up."

"I will go fast as the icy Namyet Mountain wind," she said, clambering onto Ooki's back. "Do nothing foolish, husband! I fear already for our daughter and Snenneq, and ache to see them again. I could not bear to lose you too."

"I promise to do nothing you would not approve, Sisqinanamook my beloved." He touched her cheek. "But the longer we are speaking, the longer until proper soldiers can come and watch this place."

"I hear you." She turned Ooki around and thumped her heels lightly against his sides, sending the ram off through the trees at a swift trot.

Binabik went back to digging dirt out of the hole, and soon had revealed most of a large, flat paving stone only a couple of fingers wide. Porto experimentally slid the tip of his sword into the crack along the edge of the stone, wondering if he could pry it up. Not only did he fail to lift it, but when he applied a little force, his sword blade bent and then abruptly snapped .

"What? May God blast it!" he hissed, then felt a rush of shame at cursing in the Lord's name—his friend Sergeant Levias would not approve. He stared mournfully at the sword, which had less than half blade left beyond the hilt. "Cursed thing."

Binabik managed to free the orphaned end of the sword from the crack. Porto lifted it stared mournfully before tossing it into the underbrush. The troll had just begun digging with his hands again when they heard a sound rise into the night from the direction of the not-too-distant Thrithings—weird, wailing cries like the voices of lost souls. The hairs on Porto's neck rose in animal alarm.

"Wolves," he said. "It sounds like many of them."

"They are far away," said Binabik. "Too far away to worry us."

Vaqana, who had been watching them dig as if scornful of their slow human scraping, suddenly tilted her long muzzle toward the moon and howled, her much louder voice rising to join the distant chorus.

"She tells those others not to think of coming here." Binabik laughed and went back to digging.

"Are you certain?" Porto asked, a little shaken by the reminder that they were far from the comparative safety of either castle walls or an army camp.

Vaqana howled again, and even after her distant fellows finished, she continued to sing on by herself, making the hillside echo.

Fremur had waited all through the long evening for a chance to talk to Unver alone.

Several scuffles had broken out among the mercenaries in the wake of the news about the Erkynlandish queen and her army at their gates—one scuffle serious enough to lead to a stabbing. Hulgar returned from his errand in the castle's undercroft in time to lay the knife-wielder out with a single blow of his huge fist. The other grasslander was not badly wounded, but it was clear that the men were dangerously unsettled, and the few remaining members of Count Aglaf's household were doing their best to make themselves scarce.

Pasevalles had called for Unver hours earlier, and only sent him away sometime near midnight, at which point Fremur saw the Shan cross the great hall and make his way out of the hall. After a discreet amount of time had passed, Fremur followed him.

As he came out of the doors, he saw Unver's tall frame on the stairs leading up to the walls. Fremur hurried after and caught him at the top of the first turning.

"I want to talk to you."

Unver barely glanced back. "Farther up," was all he said.

They climbed until they reached the top of the guard tower and could step out onto the walls. A pair of mercenaries on sentry duty looked up hopefully, as if Fremur and Unver might have come to replace them, but Unver only strode past them and out onto the battlements.

When they were many paces away from the guard tower, with nothing on either side of them and only the cloud-wreathed moon to overhear them, Unver stopped and leaned on the parapet, staring out into the darkness and the mass of tents and fires that was the enemy camp, set up just beyond bowshot.

Fremur moved in beside him. "What are we doing?" he asked quietly.

"Taking the air," said Unver. "It is ungodly hot and smoky in that hall, and smells of sweat and beards."

"I don't mean that. I mean what are we doing *here*? In this cursed castle?"

"We are here because I wanted to see something of this Pasevalles, and you chose to come with me."

"Do not play at words with me, Unver Shan. You know I would follow you even into the Gray Lands. I followed you before anyone else did—believed in you before any others."

Something like a smile curled the edge of Unver's lips. "You did, yes. But now you are troubled."

"Troubled is not the word. Am I less of a clansman if I admit I am terrified? I am not afraid to die at your side, but this feels like pure folly. Why did we not leave this place while we still could? Now we are trapped here, surrounded by angry stone-dwellers and a queen bent on revenge."

"The spirits of our people made me Shan. The spirits also wanted me here. It is not for me to dispute them."

It was all Fremur could do not to shout with frustration. Unver had always been maddeningly hard to get useful words from, and he could not imagine ever winning an argument with him, but this went beyond anything. Desperate, he reached into his shirt and pulled out the locket he wore. "Look," he said. "Do you see this?"

"A nice piece of gold, as best I can make it out in this light," said Unver. "Did you win it from one of Broomstraw's men?"

"I bought it from a trader at Blood Lake, before the stone-dwellers attacked the bison camp." He took it and held it under the Shan's nose. "Open it."

Unver flicked the locket open with his thumbnail. "A lock of hair," he said.

"A lock of Hyara's hair," said Fremur. "When I told her you said we could marry, and she accepted me, I cut it from her head myself."

Unver handed it back. "I do not think you need to worry. It is a small tress only—she will look none the worse for its lack."

"You mock me. That is your right, but it feels cruel. Why will you not tell me what you plan, Unver?" He fought to keep his voice even. "Is there a plan at all? Or are we simply going to die here, fighting for a man you do not like, against people who hate him but who hate you too? Do not forget, you almost killed their king on this very spot."

"It was a fair fight. And I spared him."

"Please, Unver. Please, my Shan," he pleaded. "Was I a fool to tell Hyara that I would come back and marry her? Did you truly have a reason to come here?"

Unver finally turned to look at him. "You must trust the spirits, Fremur," he said quietly. "You were the first to believe that they had chosen me. Have you lost your faith?"

"In you? No. Although it has been tested these last days. We are locked in a besieged stone-dweller castle with a poisoner!"

"A place to which the spirits called me," Unver said.

"And what do the spirits want us to do here?" The locket had not seemed to have any effect on Unver's reticence. Fremur slid the thong back over his neck and dropped it into his shirt. "To fight? Die? Can you ask them why they did not bid us escape while we still could have?"

"The spirits do not seem to answer questions," said Unver. "Except from old Burtan. But that is no reason to think they are unconcerned with our fate."

"So that is all you will tell me?" He let out a ragged breath. "I thought we were friends."

Now Unver turned to look at him again. A strange expression had hardened Unver's face: he seemed something carved in stone at an ancient fain. "We have been friends, Fremur. And if we live beyond this place and time, we will doubtless be friends again. But the great spirits of the grassland care little for friendship, or clan loyalties, or blood ties. They demand loyalty only to themselves. I have heard them in my dreams, Fremur, and some of what they have promised me—or threatened me with—is terrifying. But once I accepted what they intended for me, I gave over my right to question or bargain. I was told to come here, told to learn who Pasevalles is and what his attack on the stone-dweller crown meant for our people. When the spirits are done with me, they will let me know. And if you would open your heart to them perhaps you would learn what they want for you, too."

Fremur shook his head. "I am a simple man, Unver. I am not fit to listen to the voices of the Sky-Piercer and the rest."

"Then you must wait to see what they will ask of me."

"So that is your only plan? To wait for the spirits of the grassland to send you a sign? Pasevalles will make certain that we are all killed defending him—"

Even as he spoke, a weird sound rose in the east, low and wavering at first, but lifting to an unignorable pitch and echoing along the river valley—the howling of wolves in the distant hills. Fremur's hackles rose, remembering the night the pack had come to Unver on the plain, gathering around him as though he were their king.

And even as the original howls began to die down, another howl came—much closer, this time, as though its source was just outside the castle walls. It was a throaty, mournful sound, like the lament of a lonely and forgotten ghost.

In the silence that followed, Fremur could not speak for a long moment. "Was that a sign for you, Unver Shan?" he said at last. "Were those the voices of the spirits? The last one was just outside the castle."

"It was certainly a sign for someone." Unver grinned, showing his teeth, but he did not look cheerful. "A warning, perhaps. When you hear the wolves singing, there is always one wolf nearer than you knew."

45

Two Horses in a Meadow

This was certainly not Nezeru's first funeral procession. In her Sacrifice days, a dead acolyte from the Order house had been consigned either to a family vault or the Fields of the Nameless (depending on how honorable their deaths had been) at least once or twice in every moon. At the time such deaths had meant little to her, even when it was someone she had known as more than a face or a cruel nickname. But this procession felt different.

The Zida'ya sincerely mourned their fallen protector, Jiriki é-Sa'onserei. That was plain on every face, from the eight solemn bearers of the willow-wood coffin to the new protector, Ki'ushapo, who led the procession with stern solemnity. But Nezeru had heard laughter from them, too, sudden and surprising, and occasionally members of the funeral party would even break into joyful song, which only confused her more. She knew little of Jiriki's life, but she knew that Morgan thought well of him, and that he had been a good friend to Morgan's grandfather, King Simon.

And how did that come to be? she wondered. What unlikely circumstances had conspired to bring a mortal and an immortal together and create a friendship?

She could have asked Morgan, but she was carefully staying away from him. She had not wanted to come on this journey, where they might be thrown together, over and over. She would even have preferred to return to Nakkiga, despite all the danger that entailed, but Viyeki had been told by Prince Pratiki to go south with the Zida'ya. Unless she wanted to lose her father again after they had been so newly reunited, she had no choice but to accompany him.

She was still trying to get to know the father she had seen so little of, for so much of her life. The four dead bodies she and her mother had left on the hillside could not be ignored, and it had taken her most of an evening to work up the courage to tell him about the ambush. But once he was certain that she and Tzoja were both largely unharmed, Viyeki seemed unmoved hearing of Khimabu's death, which only confirmed what Nezeru had supposed about their marriage.

"Like the queen," he said, "she let her grudges rule her. I am sorry it happened, but you had to defend your mother, so I cannot mourn Khimabu."

Although her mother Tzoja was still recovering from several superficial but painful wounds, she had made it clear she would also be part of the company heading south, though where the journey would end for her was still uncertain. Tzoja said she was too busy nursing the man she called her father to decide yet, but Nezeru thought that after the attempt on her life, even with Khimabu now gone, her mother might choose to return to her own mortal kind.

So, after I survived so many hazards and found my family again, it may come apart once more, scattered like the shards of a fallen jar. Nezeru could not help feeling sour. And catching an occasional look from Morgan as the procession marched south—looks that spoke eloquently of his longing and confusion—did not make anything easier.

Why does he not understand that we cannot be together? Is there something wrong with mortals, that they cannot see what is obvious? Or is it only Morgan?

"I have been watching you, daughter," her father Viyeki told her as the company made camp that night on a slope high above the misty and suspect Narrowdark River. "You have been through a very hard time, I know. And what you and poor Tzoja just survived was terrible—Khimabu's murderous trick shames me, and despite our years together, I cannot regret her death. But even given all these happenings, you still seem unduly troubled."

"It is not for you to worry about me, Father. You have important matters to consider. You are the prince's high envoy now."

He shook his head regretfully. "And the prince is now on his way to Nakkiga with the queen's body and many troubles of his own, so here the decisions are mine. I cannot ignore seeing my own child in mourning, even if I do not understand precisely why she is so unhappy."

It was strange to see her father in this new way, not as the star that lit her sky when she was small, or as the symbol of all those she might disappoint as she struggled through her training in the Order of Sacrifice, but as a living, breathing person with fears and frailties of his own. She took up Cold Root, which for reasons she could not understand, Pratiki had left in her possession, then laid it across her knees before taking out her whetstone.

"I feel I have seen that sword before," her father said.

"You have," she said. "The blade that killed the queen is the famous Cold Root."

"General Suno'ku's sword—truly?" he said, eyes suddenly wide. "By my clan, another story I have not heard! Sometimes it seems there is no escaping the past."

"Not for us Hikeda'ya." She oiled and sharpened the blade while her father directed his secretary and others in setting up camp. When Viyeki returned, she had finished and sheathed it again. The relentless sounds of the river had often accompanied her and Morgan on their journey, and it was intruding into her thoughts now, sending them places she did not wish them to go.

"Was Khimabu as mad as the queen?" she asked after a long silence. "Why did she harbor such hatred against my mother?"

"I promise it was not for love of me," said Viyeki. "Beyond that, I can only guess what led her down that deep and dark passage. But the favor that Utuk'ku showed you by making you a Queen's Talon—you, the child of her husband's mortal concubine—certainly galled her." He signaled to one of his servitors for a cup of wine. He made a face as he tasted it. "We have obviously run through all the acceptable jars Nonao brought. Still, it is better than nothing. Will you have some?"

She shook her head. "The memory of the queen's favor, as you called it, only adds to my puzzlement." She hesitated. "Here is another question—one that has long troubled me. Do you know why was I chosen to be part of a Queen's Talon, Father? Were you informed of the reason I was given such an honor? Because I cannot make sense of it."

"Well, it may have troubled you, but it troubled the Mother of All too, at the end." He laughed, then shook his head. "Look at me. Jesting about what happened while the rest of our people mourn! And to think I once loved our queen more than my own family! But as to your place in her Talon, I always supposed it was because you were one of the best of your file among all the young Sacrifices."

"I was—but that was an insufficient reason, I now see. The other Talons were all trusted veterans—except Saomeji, who turned out to be Akhenabi's halfblood bastard."

"Then I cannot answer your question, daughter. Why are you still so bothered by it when the queen herself is no more?"

"Because I was chosen to join an important Talon for reasons I don't understand. That seems to me to be worth questioning."

He did not respond immediately but sipped at his wine. "I think I grasp your unease. I was troubled too when the Tinukeda'ya singled me out on Kushiba. I could not guess why they thought I might be sympathetic to them, why they thought I would do anything but denounce them."

"Did you? Denounce them?"

"No. And that is precisely why it troubled me. What did they recognize in me? And if mere changelings could tell that I was insufficiently loyal, I wondered what my peers must think. And, as I so often did, I wondered if it would end in my execution." Viyeki then told her all that had happened in the tunnels of Kushiba, and how, at last, he had swung the maul and thus closed the passage to the rest of Utuk'ku's Sacrifice troops, who would otherwise have swept out of the tunnel and crushed Tanakirú's defenders. Nezeru was astonished; in their previous conversations, her father had only told her that he had been in a difficult position and had feared the queen's anger.

"By the Lost Garden," she told him, "you are as much a traitor as I am!"

Reflexively, he looked around. "Don't say such things, Nezeru—even now."

"Still, I am impressed." She moved over to sit on the log beside him so they could keep their voices low. "But do not punish yourself, Father. We both reached an hour where we could no longer live with untruth."

"It was not just untruth," he said. "It was the pure, savage cruelty shown to helpless creatures—a wickedness which I could no longer ignore. I understand war, I think, but I could never truly understand cruelty, though most of our folk would not call it such. I used to think of my aversion as a failing in myself—as an indulgent sentimentality. It was only in the last moons that I came to understand that this failing was too much a part of me to be ignored any longer."

She nodded. "It seems you have become a revolutionary."

This time he didn't look around. "Not at all. Just one who reached his limit." The campfire had been lit; it cast active shadows among the surrounding trees. "But now I have a question for you, daughter—or rather the same question again. What are you mourning?"

"Mourning? Me?" But she could not quite look him in the eyes.

"I hope your time as a Sacrifice has not convinced you that all outside that order are fools—especially your own sire. Yes, mourning. I see it in your every expression. I see it in your posture as you ride." He reached out and took her hand, which surprised her, though he did not hold it long. "I have scarcely been a father to you, Nezeru, I know. The order became your parent, as is the way for our children, and I have seen you only infrequently since they took you away. I have no right to ask you to treat me as anything other than an acquaintance—"

"You have every right!" she said and was surprised by her own vehemence. "Who do you think I reported to every night when training was done and we were sent to our barracks?"

"What? Who?"

"You, of course. Each night I told you what I had done as if you were there, hoping that somehow you knew and would be proud."

"I would have been, I think." He smiled. "Ah, I missed so much! But that does not mean I am content to continue that way." He rose and waved to his secretary on the far side of the clearing. "My daughter and I are going to walk before we eat," he announced. "Will you call me when the food is prepared?"

Nonao, who had instantly presented himself for duty when it had become clear that Viyeki was going to survive the death of the queen and even prosper in its wake, nodded briskly. "Of course, High Magister."

They followed a deer track along the hillside above the Narrowdark until the fires of the camp had vanished behind them. After a few clear days, the mists of Tanakirú had once more begun to collect in the valley: Nezeru could not see the stars, but she still felt a curious sense of freedom as she told her father about what had happened between herself and the mortal youth, Morgan. He listened without asking questions or making any show of his feelings, which seemed to mark a change in their relationship. In her early childhood, her father had been stern with her failings but also swift to compliment her for doing something well. She had missed that bitterly while in the Order, where success was expected, and failure was unthinkable and often fatal.

When she had finished, Viyeki stopped and stood silently beside her for a long moment, looking up into the overcast sky as though searching for an answer there. "Do you care for this mortal prince?" he asked at last.

"I don't know. I suppose I do—I still think of him—but he makes me angry because he will not accept that any connection between us is impossible. He will not forget me."

"Whereas you have forgotten him entirely."

"No, of course not." She gave him a narrow-eyed look. "You are making fun of me."

"You have just spent a great deal of time telling me that you cannot stop thinking about this mortal youth because he will not stop thinking about you. Do you see the contradiction, my daughter?"

"It is not my fault he will not leave me alone."

"We have been riding three days. He looks at you, it's true—"

"You have seen?"

"It is hard not to notice the two of you casting glances back and forth, measuring out your dance of pride and sorrow." He shook his head. "Do you know, your mother Tzoja once told me that her kind and my kind could not care for each other because we are too different. But when I saw her again at Tanakirú, I realized how much I did care for her. I asked her to live with me—almost as a wife, though even in Pratiki's new Nakkiga, I doubt we would be allowed to marry. But," he said, grave now, "she told me she cannot, or will not, until she decides what she will do about this long-lost father of hers."

Nezeru sighed. "A part of me wishes I could wake up and discover that all that happened in the moons since I left Nakkiga was but a strange dream."

"You would have the queen alive again?"

She made the hand sign against bad luck. "No, no, but there are times I would have certainty back—although I imagine that, as soon as I did, I would begin to chafe against it once more." She tried to smile. "Some of us just cannot be satisfied, it seems."

"Some things one should not be satisfied with," he said. "And even a people as terrified by change as ours cannot resist it forever. Our queen was a monster, it can no longer be denied—or at least she became one. You, my daughter, did a brave, heroic thing, and if there is any justice, future generations will hail you and that Jarnulf fellow for the deed."

"Good God!" she said, unwittingly using one of Morgan's favorite expressions, "please don't yoke me to Jarnulf for all time, Father!"

"Let us forget about him for a moment, then. So, what will you do, child? I will go to Jao é-Tinukai'i at Prince Pratiki's bidding, to plant and nurture the new witchwood seeds. You are welcome to remain there with me, of course."

"I do not know what I will do afterward. But at least Morgan and his family are bound to return to their own country. It will be easier for me to decide after he is gone."

He looked at her keenly. "It is a new world, Nezeru, and you have helped to bring it about." He shrugged. "I suppose I have, as well. But do not be too quick to return to the old ways of thinking."

"You are not taking Morgan's side, I hope."

"I am taking no side. I scarcely know my own name just now, so many things are different. I have learned things I never dreamed were true, seen things I never imagined were possible. I did not even know why we were fighting in this valley until the queen was dead, and I still can hardly believe it—a ship! A ninth Great Ship! No, do not doubt it. This is a new world, my daughter, but we will not know what kind of world it is until we finish building it."

"I am glad you are not going back to Nakkiga, Father," she said, and squeezed his hand, suddenly afraid she might lose him again. "Such a philosophy is likely to get you killed there. Not everyone wants a new world."

"No," he said. "I fear you are right about that."

Nearly eight hundred Rimmersmen were camped in Wormscale Gorge beside the lake. Simon could only marvel as he held his arms outstretched. "By our merciful Lord, Sludig, did my stout old friend and his men run all the way from Tanakirú? How did you get here before us?"

The Rimmersman embraced him, squeezing until the king almost lost his breath. "I doubt we could have outsped even a Sithi funeral procession if it had not been stopping so often to accommodate frail old mortals like yourself, Majesty."

"Ah! A sharp hit! I am wounded." Simon laughed and took a step back. "In all honesty, I have seen few sights in a long time better than you, my friend."

Sludig nodded. "And I am glad to see you as well. We heard all kinds of terrible rumors."

"Some of them are true. The traitor Pasevalles caused Miri's death—and many others'. Having your stout Rimmersmen with me when we get to Erkynland will help me make certain he pays for his crimes. Please give Duke Grimbrand my gratitude for sending you, when you see him next."

"I will. And my wife Alva sends her best regards. She wanted me to tell you particularly how sorry she is to hear about Queen Miriamele. She was very taken with her when they met."

Simon shook his head. "We have so much to talk about. But I am reminded—tell your lady when you see her next that her dreams about the White Foxes were again true ones."

"They were, were they?"

"I cannot forget what she said, since it was the same night I realized I had stopped dreaming myself—the night of Isgrimnur's funeral, do you remember?"

"How could I forget that night, Majesty? It was sad and joyful, both."

"Enough of the 'Majesty,' you old dog. It is one thing when we are in front of others, but you and I go back too far for that." Simon pulled Sludig a little to one side. "I remember that your wife told us that a saint came to her in a dream and said, 'They march to a city that never was. They seek to win the everything that is nothing.' And when you hear the story that I have to tell you, you will see that she was right about both!"

"I am not surprised—she is well-known for it in Engby. But I am aching to know what happened. The Norn Queen is dead, you said in your message. Is that blessed news true?"

"Yes, praise God, Utuk'ku is dead at last, and I pray she stays that way, though after fighting Ineluki the Storm King—and seeing the Storm King's brother Hakatri brought back to life—I trust no certainty."

"Hakatri? This is another new and strange tale," Sludig said.

"And the sooner we sit by a fire with a flagon for each of us, the sooner I can prove to you that the true stories are often stranger than any made-up ones you have heard." He saw Henrig lurking a few yards away, watching his father and the king with greedy interest. "Bring your son along to the fire. He earned it by climbing down the cliff you would not even attempt."

"Did you look at that path? I saw it and felt certain you were trying to kill me."

"I confess I had not seen it. And I think, in any case, I was remembering the Sludig that was, instead of the much stouter Sludig who now is."

"And so I am paid back for my earlier words!"

Simon laughed and beckoned to young Henrig. "Come along, lad. Let us get warm and find something to eat and drink, because your father and I have much to talk about."

After leaving the gorge, the funeral company and Sludig's mounted troop followed the Coolblood River south through the great forest until they had nearly reached Jao é-Tinukai'i, which was empty now of all but memories and graves. After a long day's ride, they reached the edge of the settlement's old boundaries in the late evening, and in deference to the weariness of the mortal travelers, the Sithi decided to make camp there and continue into Jao the next morning.

That night, as campfires flickered and mortals and immortals gathered in fragile comradeship, Morgan sat and nursed a cup of wine that Sludig's warriors had provided from their own store. The Sithi at Tanakirú had used up nearly all their supplies during the siege, holding back their strong drink to clean wounds, so this was the first wine Morgan had drunk in so long he could not remember the last time. Though the taste and feel of it on his tongue was instantly familiar, and the warmth it created in his stomach equally resonant, he found himself reluctant to do more than sip at it.

Nezeru and her father, along with a contingent of Builders, had made their camp on the other side of the Sithi encampment, and Morgan was wondering if that might have been at Nezeru's request, to keep her as far from Morgan as possible. He more than half wished that she had gone west to Nakkiga as she had wanted to do, so he would not have to look at her every day. But a desperate and desperately sad part of him still wanted to see her, wanted to feel every morsel of pain, because that was something real, and everything else about this time and place felt utterly unreal. The deep part of the forest they had reached, with its air of age and its thick, almost choking greenery, added to his feeling of being adrift in an unfamiliar world.

I suppose things could be worse, he told himself. *I seem to have lost Jarnulf, at least for the moment, though he will find me again soon enough.* The man from the north, though always respectful to his chosen prince, had proved utterly immune to Morgan's indifference and as hard to dislodge as a thorny briar. Jarnulf was determined to prove himself trustworthy, but Morgan wanted only to be left alone to wade in his misery.

Morgan saw his grandfather and Jarl Sludig once again deep in talk by the fire. Young Henrig watched them with wide, shining eyes, thrilled simply to listen to the grown men's conversation, as Morgan himself had once sat proudly at his father's knee. Morgan had resolved to be a better grandson to Simon—since Tanakirú, he had been trying hard to pay attention to all the things the king said and did—but his heart was not in this night's gathering. He knew it was hard for his grandfather to have lost his friend Jiriki so soon after the death of Grandmother Miriamele, but surely real death was better than the living death of seeing Nezeru without being able to touch her or even talk to her.

"And here he is, wine cup in hand!" said someone behind him. "So much time passed, and yet nothing has changed even a jot!"

Startled by the familiar voice, he turned to see the slyly grinning face of Sir Astrian at his shoulder, and behind him, the morose features of Sir Olveris. Morgan jumped to his feet and embraced them both.

"What are you doing here?" he cried. "What brings you to this middle-of-nowhere spot?"

"You, Highness," said Astrian. "We have been tracking you at your grandfather's request since Octander-month, following every whisper or rumor of you we could find. It almost felt as though you hid from us!"

"My grandfather?"

"Duke Osric, of course. But now we have learned that your other grandfather still lives, may God be thanked!" And so saying, Astrian went and knelt before the king, who gave him a sharp look.

"I know you," said Simon. "Both of you. But what are you doing here?"

"Trekking up hill and down dale in search of your grandson, Your Majesty."

The king gave him a grim look. "And you found us in the middle of the Aldheorte? How?"

Astrian and Olveris shared a quick look.

"Hard work, Your Majesty," said Astrian. "We learned that many folk, both mortals and immortals, had been seen riding north through Erkynland, headed toward the far end of the Wealdhelm. But as we followed the river, we came upon your camp here, saving us much riding!"

The king did not seem convinced. "What a lucky turn of events. And who gave you this quest?"

"We were sent out to search for Prince Morgan by his other grandfather, His Grace, Duke Osric," said Astrian. "But we are utterly delighted to find that God has spared not only our friend the prince, but your royal self as well, Majesty. The prayers of all the High Ward are answered!"

"Binabik used to have a saying about oily tongues," Simon said from beneath an arched eyebrow. "And snowshoes. Nevertheless, it is good to see you both alive."

Astrian turned to Morgan. "I have lifted a jar of good red wine from some of the Rimmersmen," he said in a not-particularly-subtle whisper.

The king certainly heard, and his expression hardened a little, but to Morgan's relief, instead of shaming him, his grandfather only said, "I do not doubt the prince would rather spend time with you two than with old folk like Sludig and myself. Go on, Morgan. You have my permission to go."

Morgan was not certain whether he was being freed or dismissed, but it did not take much coaxing from Astrian for him to get up, cup still in hand, and follow the Nabbanai knights across the camp.

Sir Astrian had drunk quite a bit of wine. He was walking in broad, disordered circles, talking and talking as they made their way along the hillside. The camp was now so far behind them that during the infrequent intervals of silence, the murmuring of the Narrowdark was all Morgan could hear.

". . . It was most amusing. You would have thought from your grandfather's royal expression we had just emerged from the ground like moles! 'Where did you come from?' He did not seem amused, but I can promise that I was." Astrian thrust the jar at Morgan. "Here, drink up. You are too quiet."

"Because you have not stopped talking."

"It is the duty of the most interesting person in any gathering to delight and educate the others."

Morgan lifted the jug to his lips. He had rediscovered the knack of wine, he decided: You drank it until you could not remember when you had last drunk any. He wiped his lips and handed the jar to Sir Olveris.

"By that measure, Astrian," said tall Olveris, "you would have to be the only one present. But I could swear that Prince Morgan and I are here too."

"Oh, la and ho-ho—a jest! The great stone statue has made a jest." Astrian sat down heavily on a log and reached out his hand.

Morgan didn't think Olveris had even taken a drink yet, but, he handed the jug back.

"We are lacking only Porto," Astrian declared, "then the numbers of overly tall and overly boring folk would match the number of well-shaped conversationalists."

"Let's keep moving," said Olveris.

"No need," Astrian replied. "Everything is spinning already."

★ ★ ★

"Where am I going, Olveris?" Astrian said sometime later. "I fear I have quite forgotten."

"We were following you, little man."

"That is why I am asking you. I have already asked the leader of the expedition—who is myself—and discovered that I did not know."

"I should get back." Morgan was not enjoying this return to drunken irresponsibility as much as he had anticipated. "My grandfather will be unhappy if I am gone too long."

"Grandfathers are always angry," said Astrian. "Like bulls and wasps. Besides, it is good for a man the king's age to be angry occasionally. It strengthens the heart by warming the blood."

Morgan frowned. "You just say things and hope they make sense."

"No, I say things and hope someone sensible is listening," said Astrian between quiet hiccoughs.

"This way," said Olveris, and steered them along the slope.

"What adventures you must have had, my prince!" Astrian stopped so suddenly that Morgan almost ran into him. "I hear you befriended a Norn girl. Are they cold to the touch? Like ice?"

"Where did you hear that?" Morgan's head felt heavy, and his thoughts were clouded. Had he truly drunk that much?

"It was the talk of the camp! As we made our way among the Northmen, we heard all kinds of tales. Isn't that right, Olveris?"

But Olveris had changed direction again and was leading them higher up the slope. A few moments later they emerged onto a wide meadow open to the stars. A pair of saddled horses stood at the near end, cropping at the waist-high grass.

Astrian stopped abruptly once more. "Whose horses are those? Olveris, are they ours?"

"They are now. I made sure their owners would not miss them."

"What are you talking about?" Astrian was puzzled. "I don't need another horse. I have a perfectly good one back at the camp."

"We're not going back to the camp," said Olveris, and grabbed one of Morgan's arms. At first Morgan thought he was being helped when he did not need it—he had been drunker than this and had managed—so he tried to pull loose, but Olveris would not let him go.

"What are you doing?" Morgan demanded. "I can't go anywhere. My grandfather will be furious."

Then something crashed against his head and blackness swallowed him.

Morgan did not immediately remember where he was or what he had been doing. He was lying on the wet ground, that much was certain, and he could hear the voices of two people arguing.

"Have you lost your wits, you great lout? Why did you hit him?"

"So that it will be easier to get him onto the back of that horse. Seems obvious enough."

"The back of a horse?" Astrian was clearly struggling to understand. "Why? What have you done?"

"It is not what I've done, it's what will be done to us," Morgan heard Olveris say. "King Simon is on his way with those northman soldiers to run down Pasevalles. And if Pasevalles is captured alive, do you think he will be silent about the ones who helped him—who took his gold? Like you and I?"

Still bemused by the blow to his head and only half-understanding, Morgan thought it was rare to hear Olveris say so much in one mouthful.

"Pasevalles is doomed to a traitor's death. But we committed no treason, you long-legged fool." Astrian had sobered a little but still had trouble making his words come out correctly. "We can easily say we only worked for him before we realized the debts . . . the depths . . . of his guilt."

"Perhaps you would rather take your chances with the king's forgiveness—the king whose wife was burned to charcoal by Pasevalles' mercenaries. I would rather have something to bargain with."

Astrian's astonishment was unmistakable. "You would kidnap the prince of Erkynland, then try to bargain with the High Throne?"

"No, idiot. You should have drunk less and listened more to the talk around the camp. King Simon is on his way to Winstowe, where Pasevalles is. When they find out that the king's alive, the people will rally around him, and Pasevalles will eventually be taken, either by force or starvation. But if we get there first with Morgan, then Pasevalles will have something valuable to bargain with—you know that the king will do anything to get his heir back. But, whatever happens, the king and Pasevalles will keep each other occupied while you and I slip away. We will be safely across the border and back in Nabban by the time it's all finished."

Morgan was finally able to order his thoughts enough to lift his head. Olveris and Astrian stood a few paces away, facing each other, though with the moon gone down they were little more than silhouettes, one compact, the other much taller.

"This is madness, Olveris," said the small shadow. "I am the last man to speak of honor, but even I have my limit. I cannot let you do this. Pasevalles may see no escape and simply kill Morgan."

"Making it even less likely anyone will bother looking for us."

"No." Astrian's hand dropped to his sword hilt. "I will not be a party to this. Take one of the horses and go. I will say I do not know where you went."

"A shame," said Olveris, drawing his sword. "We were good partners."

Crawl away! Morgan told himself, doing his addled best to suit action to thought, but Olveris, who seemed accursedly sober, took a quick step toward him while blocking a thrust from Astrian's slender blade. Morgan could hear the swish and clank of their struggle, but his head seemed one great, throbbing bruise and he could not bear to lift it. He tried to crawl again but found that he had somehow tipped over and was lying on his back as the stars of the night sky stared incuriously down at him.

Neither of the two swordsmen were talking anymore. He could see them only dimly and upside down. The clank of blade on blade was loud and made his head hurt even more, but a strange lassitude had enveloped him. When he heard Astrian gasp, and saw one of the two figures stumble and fall, he could only slowly make sense of what had happened.

First, a scrape as Olveris sheathed his sword. Then Morgan felt the sharp point of a dagger against his throat. "Come along, Your Highness," he said. "I had to kill my only friend. Do not test me." After Morgan struggled to his feet, the tall man pulled his arms behind his back, then wrapped a cord around his wrists as quickly and efficiently as a shearer readying a sheep for fleecing. Then he lifted Morgan up and dropped him head-down across the back of one of the waiting horses, so that the air was driven out of his chest. For a moment the world spun, and the stars seemed to wheel from the sky down to the earth.

Recovering himself a little, Morgan tried to slide back off the horse, but Olveris reached up and gave him a stinging slap on the back of the head, not enough to knock him senseless again, but hard enough of rattle his teeth.

"I said, do not test me." Olveris waded around through the thick grass and lifted a foot into the nearest stirrup, but before he could vault into the saddle, he let out a sudden cry and stumbled backward, cursing. Morgan, still befuddled by the blow to the head and his upside-down position, saw Olveris draw his sword once more and prayed that the man he had thought his friend had been bitten by a venomous snake.

"Who is there?" the tall man snarled. "I can hear you, and that is all I need to cut you to pieces." But an instant later he reeled back with another cry of pain, slapping his neck as though trying to kill a wasp.

Morgan had seen many strange battles in the last year: men against giants, Jijibo and his Norns against the monstrous ogre, and the fight against the malformed kilpa of the crystal caverns, but he had never seen anything quite like this. Olveris swung his sword like a reaper, mowing the high grass so that it flew up in great tufts, but Morgan could see no opponent, and for a moment he thought the knight might simply have lost his mind. Olveris let out another loud cry and bent to grab at his knee, then something swished through the grass and sent Morgan's captor reeling back toward the horse where the prince still hung over the saddle, arse-up and struggling to tip himself onto the ground.

Olveris now seemed to have decided that discretion was better than valor. He clambered into the saddle, dragged Morgan back into place with a horribly painful yank on his tied arms, then kicked the horse's ribs and set it bounding through the grass, away from his invisible foe.

Morgan lifted his head to see the tall grass ahead of them bowing and rippling, then an incomprehensible shape burst out into an open space a few paces before them, causing Olveris' mount to rear in surprise before leaping away at an angle. The shape was a shaggy, horned ram, Morgan dimly realized, and a moment later he saw that the small person riding it was one of the trolls—Qina—and she was twirling a loop of rope in her hand as she whooped and shouted.

Morgan felt the rope fall over him, and it must have fallen over Olveris as well, because a moment later it pulled taut, nearly breaking the prince's neck, and he and his captor were yanked out of the saddle as Qina's ram dug its hooves into the ground. They both toppled to the ground, Morgan on top of his captor, but his hands were still bound, and he had no leverage. Olveris seemed unhurt, and quickly slid out from under him before dragging Morgan to his feet. The horse continued running, riderless, and disappeared into the trees surrounding the grassy clearing. "You!" Olveris snarled at Qina, "not an inch farther!" As Morgan felt the heavy touch of a sword blade on his throat, a shocking wave of sobriety rolled over him.

Qina reined up, staring at the Nabbanai knight with cold hatred. "Let go him," she said.

"Don't be stupid. Where is your friend, the other troll? Tell him to step out where I can see him, or I swear I will kill the prince where he stands."

"If you do, it is you who are the fool," called Little Snenneq as he crawled out of the grass and stood up, his long stick in hand. "Because I would kill you myself. It is a pity that I had none of my poisoned darts left."

"I have seen you fight, little fellow," said Olveris. "And while it is tempting to learn how you would fare against someone who is not a fat, drunk Rimmersman, I do not have the time to waste." He flicked a glance to Qina. "I do not like it that you are still holding that rope, troll. Do you see this blade? Do you wish to see what it will do to the prince's gorge? Let the rope go and fetch me the other horse. No, get off your sheep and walk. No tricks." As he spoke, Olveris shrugged off the coil dangling around his shoulders, keeping his blade pressed firmly against Morgan's throat. The prince tried to think of what he could do, but he was still dizzy from the blow to his head and the tumble from the horse, and both Qina and Snenneq were too far away to be of any help even if he managed to slip free for a moment.

As Qina led the remaining horse toward them, Olveris carefully watched both trolls.

Even dazed, Morgan could see that Snenneq was furious; he prayed that the troll wouldn't do anything foolish while the blade was pressed against Morgan's neck.

Olveris reached out and took the horse's reins then, with a violent wave of his free hand, ordered Qina to move back. "You, get onto the saddle," he told Morgan. "Head first. And do it swiftly. I need you alive, but I can take an ear off without marring your value."

Morgan could not understand how he was supposed to get on the back of a horse with his hands tied, so he only stood. Olveris cursed and grabbed Morgan's waist to lift him, but a moment later he let go again to clutch at the back of his own neck. Morgan lost his balance and tumbled against the horse before sliding to the ground.

"God curse you, troll!" Olveris shouted as he stood over Morgan. "I warned you all! I will have your prince's eye out!"

Then a stripe of shadow appeared on his neck, and for a long instant Olveris only stood, goggle-eyed, before he sagged to his knees and crumpled into the long grass, revealing the arrow that had gone through his throat and out the back of his neck. He was still alive, choking on his own blood, and Morgan, half in mercy, half in loathing, pressed his boot down hard on his would-be kidnapper's neck until Olveris stopped moving.

"Morgan Prince!" said Qina, running toward him. "You are well alive?"

Little Snenneq hurried toward him as well. "If I had only had my poison darts! Never would it have gone so far!"

"What . . . ?" Morgan was still struggling to understand what had happened.

"I beg your pardon, Highness," said a new voice. A figure stepped from the trees at the clearing's edge—the pale-haired mortal, Jarnulf. "I had to wait until I had a clear sight of him, for fear of hitting you."

"I told you that we could do without your help." Snenneq did not sound happy. "What if you had hit Prince Morgan with your arrow?"

"But I did not," Jarnulf pointed out.

The troll was not mollified. "It was a risk we did not need. I still had a few tricks to play."

"Do you think you two could stop arguing?" Morgan asked. "Because I do not feel very well." A moment later the sky began to spin, then the ground sprang up and flung darkness into his face.

46

A Quiet Place

"Grandfather is very angry with Morgan," Lillia told Brother Etan in an unnecessarily loud conspiratorial whisper.

"I'm certain there is some good reason your brother is not back, Princess," Etan told her.

"P'raps." But the child did not look like she believed it.

"No, I am not angry, Lillia," said the king through clenched teeth. "I am disappointed. More than that, I am worried, because Jiriki's funeral ceremony begins at sunrise. I cannot believe your brother would simply wander off and forget it."

"Sludig's men and Morgan's friends are searching for him all through the woods, Majesty. I can only suggest we pray for guidance," said Etan. "Our blessed Elysia, the Lord's mother, is known to be sympathetic to the fears of parents . . . and grandparents."

"I should never have let him go off with those drunkard ne'er-do-wells." Instead of joining Etan in prayer, the king stood and began to pace. "Old habits, old tricks."

Torches were kindling across the Sithi camp. Etan knew that the immortals did not need them to find their way around in darkness—they seemed to be able to see at night like cats—so it meant the procession must be forming to carry Jiriki to the place they called the Little Garden, where a place had been prepared for him.

Etan saw rather than heard the first signs of the prince's return—a ripple of sudden movement through the torchlit Sithi camp. Moments later, he heard Morgan calling.

"Grandfather, I am here!"

"By Blessed Rhiap!" Simon rose from the log on which he sat. "We have all been worrying! Where have you been?"

"They tried to take me!" Morgan told him. "I mean, Sir Olveris did—he would have handed me over to Pasevalles. And Astrian, poor Astrian, he died because he would not go along with it." Morgan reached the king, followed closely by the two trolls and the quiet, darkly tanned northern man who always seemed near the prince these days. "But Jarnulf here killed Olveris and saved me."

"It was nothing," Jarnulf said.

"It was nothing so simple, at least," countered Little Snenneq.

"Oh, yes, and Snenneq and Qina helped save me too," Morgan added.

Simon seemed quite stunned. "Those fellows truly tried to take you?" He clutched Morgan's hand, then pulled him close, and for a moment Etan thought the king looked like a much older man. "I suppose I am grateful not to have known, because the worry would have killed me. Tell me all that happened. Quickly, because the Sithi are about to set out."

As Morgan explained, with occasional and slightly confusing elaborations from Qina in her halting Westerling, Snenneq only stood and glowered. Jarnulf had found a spot to kneel by himself at the far side of the camp and appeared to be praying.

"That damnable Pasevalles again, that cursed, cursed traitor!" King Simon cried. "Even here, we must fear his hand. Even here, many leagues away, he strikes at my family. God's Bloody Tree, he will pay for this. But at least those false knights are dead."

"But Sir Astrian didn't know what Olveris planned—he tried to save me, Grandfather." Morgan seemed almost giddy, and Etan could not help wondering if the prince was not still a bit muddled from being hit on the head. "I feel bad for him. He was never as wicked as you thought him."

"If he was partners with the other criminal, and they took our stolen gold in payment from Pasevalles, that is wickedness enough for me." The king eyed Morgan carefully. "Still, if he fought to save you, we must at least give this Astrian fellow a decent Aedonite burial, but I will be damned if we do anything for the other. Let the wolves and crows have him." Simon sent one of Sludig's Rimmersmen to ask the jarl for men to dig the knight a grave. "Now, brush off some of that dirt, lad. Remember, we are burying my friend today, and he is deserving of all the honor we can show him."

It was hard for Morgan to believe that this part of the great wood had ever been what his grandfather had described—an entire city of Sithi people, with roads and houses and meeting-places. In the thirty or so years since his grandfather had been a captive here, the forest had grown back over the settlement so completely that he could see no trace of former habitation except the wide, roughly circular dell that Simon said had once been Jao é-Tinukai'i's witchwood grove.

After his brush with captivity and being dragged off to Pasevalles, Morgan's heart was still beating hard. It was difficult to walk slowly behind the crowd of singing, torch-bearing Sithi, but he matched his steps to his grandfather's as best he could.

If I was able to wait for hours in a tree in the hopes of catching something to eat, I can get through this, he told himself. It was not the funeral ritual itself that made him restless and unhappy, but rather knowing that the following day he would leave Nezeru behind forever.

The small party of Norns were not part of Jiriki's procession, but they stood respectfully as the Sithi walked past carrying Jiriki's willow-reed coffin. Morgan could not help looking as he passed, and quickly spotted Nezeru and her father Viyeki among the dark-clad Hikeda'ya, but Nezeru was carefully looking at anything other than Morgan. He looked away again, his face hot with embarrassment. *So that is how it will be*, he thought bitterly. *Our time together never happened—it was all a dream.*

The parade of silent Sithi stopped at last on a sloping hillside not far from the place where the witchwood grove would grow again someday if all went well. Morgan tried to pay attention, but Protector Ki'ushapo was speaking the liquid, rolling tongue of the Sithi, and Morgan could not understand a word of it. He could see the deep pain on his grandfather's face, but he, himself, could think only of how Nezeru had turned away from him.

"It is a good place for Jiriki," the king whispered as Ki'ushapo paused his eulogy and he and the other Sithi began to sing. "A quiet place next to Amerasu's mound. I have told you about her many times, the wisest person I ever met—even more than Morgenes or Geloë, and that is saying much."

Morgan nodded. "I remember. First Grandmother, you said Jiriki called her."

"She was killed very near here. At the Norn Queen's order, when the two clans were supposed to be at peace." He shook his head. "It was a terrible night."

"Will they truly make peace now?" Morgan asked as the gentle music floated through the glen. "The Sithi and the Norns? Is that possible?"

"Anything is possible," said Simon. "There is at least a chance now that the witch of the north is finally dead. We must pray for them—pray they can find forgiveness for each other."

Morgan was caught by his grandfather's words. Forgiveness? Yes, the Aedon demanded it of his followers, but how could forgiveness cure the ills of the world? Pain was not easily forgotten. *How could I forgive Nezeru,* he wondered, *after what she has done to my heart? Impossible!*

A small, warm hand took his and gently squeezed. Morgan had forgotten his little sister, who stood at his side. He looked down, worried that he had ignored her when she might be overwhelmed by the sadness of Jiriki's funeral ceremony.

Lillia looked up at him, her little face solemn. "Forgive her," she said in a whisper. "She is frightened just like you are, Morgan."

He was so stunned by his sister's words that he did not even realize the ceremony had ended until Jiriki's slender coffin was lowered into the ground. The Sithi mourners sang again as they began to leave the glen, an oddly twining melody that Morgan thought seemed to speak more of a life sadly lost than a Garden regained.

He left his grandfather kneeling at the graveside with Lillia standing beside him, one small pink hand on the king's trembling shoulder. Morgan knew he should probably stay, but he very badly needed to walk and think.

Nezeru was proud to see her father Viyeki take charge of both his own Builders and the group of Harvesters that High Gatherer Luk'kaya had sent to oversee the planting and nurturing of the witchwood, but another part of her felt as if she had been left in the center of a battlefield to face the enemy alone. Just as she had feared, as her father busied himself directing his underlings to clear the overgrowth from the abandoned grove where the witchwood trees had once stood, she saw Morgan coming toward her. In a betrayal of all her years of training in the Order of Sacrifice, she immediately retreated.

She did not get far before the mortal youth caught up with her. To her surprise, though, he did not try to slow her or grab at her arm, but only walked beside her in silence.

At last, she stopped. "What do you want, Prince Morgan?"

"Well, not to get too far from the others, for one thing. My grandfather is already quite unhappy with me for almost getting killed last night."

Nezeru listened as he explained. *If they had tried such a trick while Morgan traveled with me,* she told herself, *I would have carved them into ribbons.* But he had his own friends to protect him now, as was right. The fact that one of them was Jarnulf was merely incidental, because she knew the trolls were trustworthy, and would keep the young prince from harm until he was back home.

When he finished, they stood for a long moment in silence. "I am sorry to hear what you went through," she said, "but I still don't know what you want. Morgan. I am keeping my father waiting."

"Then we are both disappointing our elders. But fear not—I won't keep you long. I know we are parting here. I know you must stay with your father. I came only to ask you to forgive me."

For a long moment she thought she had misheard him. "To forgive you?" she said at last.

"Yes. Forgive me, please, Nezeru, for my angry words. I do not want us to part that way, not after all we have been through. I owe you my life many times over, and I still care for you deeply. It is not your fault that you cannot . . . that you do not feel the same for me."

She stared at him, looking for any hint of mockery. After days of his furious arguments, clumsy attempts at persuasion, and everything short of outright begging for her affection, it was the last thing she had expected. "Of course," she said, still not quite trusting. "Of course, Prince Morgan. You saved my life a few times, too."

"Yes, I suppose I might have." He attempted to smile, but his brave air finally faltered and he turned away. "That was all I wanted to say. I hope that things go well for you and your father, that your people and the Sithi can keep the peace, and that the witchwood grows."

A weight seemed to lift from her. "I . . . I am glad we can part as friends, Morgan. We had . . . we did many things together. Things that no others of our folk have ever done."

"We did," he said. "And I will never forget any of it. Not if I live to be a hundred years old." He reached out with one hand. She did not understand. "It is how friends say farewell among my people," he explained. "With a handclasp."

"Friends . . . ?" she said slowly, then nodded. "Friends. Yes. Travel well, Morgan. Good luck to you and your grandfather, the king. May he return to his throne safely, and may you find happiness."

Morgan struggled with his expression once more, but this time Nezeru felt no superiority over his mortal transparency because she was having trouble keeping her own face set in the stolid Sacrifice mask. "And may you find the same, Nezeru." He turned abruptly and began to walk away, then hesitated. "If you ever wish to meet me again—to talk of old times, perhaps—I would always welcome seeing you."

She nodded, silently cursing her treacherous face, which seemed to think it should make its own decisions. To her horror, she even felt as if she might weep. She was furious with herself—and with Morgan, for witnessing her weakness. *Now that he has said his piece, however generous, why will he not go? Does he want to humiliate me completely by making me shed tears as if I was one of his mortal girls?*

Morgan seemed to understand. He smiled sadly, bowed, then turned and walked away, this time without turning back.

"We are leaving, Father," Tzoja told Josua. "We are taking you back to Erkynland."

"Fallen, fallen is great Khand," he said.

"No, not Khand—your old home, Erkynland. Can you not remember? You were the prince there, King John Presbyter's son. And your brother Elias ruled after him, but he was led astray by the Storm King. You fought your brother and won."

"*He who says he loves Me but hates his brother is a liar.*" Josua seemed content to be helped to his feet, offering no resistance as Tzoja and blind Vordis made certain his cloak was fastened and the hood pulled over his poor, wounded head.

"You should have had a crown to wear," said Tzoja, remembering. "That's what our mother always used to say. Of course, she said many things. I suppose I'm glad I can't remember them all." She realized she was prattling and leaned in to look at her father's face. "Can you remember my mother, Vorzheva?" He stared back as though he had not understood a word. Tzoja could not help wondering if her mother still lived. She had no great urge to see her again—well, perhaps a tug of complicated affection, an acknowledgment that her most bruised feelings had largely healed, but Vorzheva had been a very difficult mother.

Tzoja felt a sudden twinge of shame. *And how much of a mother have I been to Nezeru? I let the Sacrifice Order take her away. I have scarcely seen her for years, and even now that we are together, I spend my time tending my poor father. Perhaps a mother is not always to blame for everything that happens to a child.*

"Come now," she told Josua. "Help me by climbing up into the saddle. We have a long ride to Erkynland—days and days." It had become clear the first day out of Tanakirú that her father could not ride by himself—his attention wandered, then his horse did too—so she had carried him on her own mount all the way here to the deserted site of Jao é-Tinukai'i. With her father sitting on the saddle behind her, and Vordis's horse tied to hers, she knew they must make a strange little procession, but she was grateful simply to have the two of them safe and under her watchful eye. She wished Nezeru was with her too, but her daughter, after their initial reunion, had remained painfully distant.

Even now, she would rather be with her father than with me. But was that surprising? What life could Tzoja offer her—what had she ever been able to offer her halfblood child, except the gift of a mother's helpless love and the shame of mortal heritage? Small wonder Nezeru preferred Viyeki's company.

But knowing this did not make the hurt any less, of course.

Parting from the Sithi proved more painful than Simon had expected. Ki'ushapo made a point of promising that things would be different in the years ahead, that this time the Zida'ya would maintain their ties with the mortal kingdoms, but Simon had shared a similar agreement with his good friend Jiriki which had come to nothing. He did not doubt the new protector's sincerity, but as they said their farewells, it was easy to feel that instead of a new era beginning, an old era was ending with no assurance that anything better would follow.

Now that the Sithi and Norns had been left behind in Jao é-Tinukai'i to begin their uneasy alliance, tending what all hoped would be a new witchwood grove, it was an almost entirely mortal caravan that continued south through the Aldheorte, led to the forest's edge down ancient, hidden tracks by a pair of Sithi guides, who then bade them farewell and vanished into the trees so swiftly that within moments it was hard to believe the immortals had been there at all.

As Simon stared out across the expanse of grassy hills stretching away southward, the pain of all he had lost swept over him.

Just a year ago we had everything, though we did not know it. We had our home, and the High Ward was strong—or at least we thought it was—and Miri and I had each other. Now Nabban had overthrown its duke and murdered him, King Hugh of Hernystir had proved himself an enemy, the Hayholt had burned, and Miri . . . Miri . . .

The pain was startlingly strong.

But all is not lost, he told himself. He looked to Morgan and did his best to ignore the bleak, lost expression on the young man's face. *I have my heir back, and he has grown in important ways, it seems.* Lillia rode on the saddle before him, and Simon was reassured by the way the young prince kept a protective arm around her. *And my little cub Lillia is back too. I must never let what I've lost make me forget what I have.*

"Shall we camp here tonight, at the forest's edge?" Sludig asked.

Simon nodded. "We are not far from Stanshire now, a good-sized town. Send in a few of your men under the guise of traders, have them see what tales are being told. I know nothing of what has happened here since I was first struck down at Winstowe, except for the little Brother Etan has been able to tell me. I am particularly keen to have some news of the traitor. If we are lucky, Osric has caught him already and we can ride straight to Erchester."

"Will the local people be honest with foreigners?" Sludig asked. "I know in Engby any strangers asking questions are always looked at with suspicion."

"I could do it, Grandfather," Morgan said. "I have never been to Stanshire. No one would know me."

"And I would go with him to protect him," declared Jarnulf.

Simon shook his head. "You have done us good service, Jarnulf, so do not take my refusal amiss. I have not forgotten that you tried to warn us about the Witchwood Crown, though we never did puzzle out what it was until Geloë told us—who would have guessed it was a ship? Anyway, for that alone we would honor you. But you do not sound like an Erkynlander, young man. If they would be suspicious of Sludig's men asking questions, they would be just as chary of you." He turned toward Little Snenneq, who had already opened his mouth to speak. "And while you and Qina are both very brave, you Qanuc would also attract attention, and that is not what we want."

"But neither of those things are true of me," said Morgan. "Let me go and find out what the mood of the people is, Your Majesty."

"No." Simon saw the look of anger on his grandson's face and had to dampen a spark of irritation. Would he rather that his heir did not offer himself in service? Had he liked it better in days past when his grandson preferred drinking and dicing to princely duties? "It is not lack of trust, Morgan, I swear that on my crown and my honor. No, the truth is that I am a coward. After so many losses, I could not bear to have either you or Lillia out of my sight again until we are safe back in Erchester. I nearly lost my wits last night when you did not come back."

Morgan held his gaze for a long moment, then nodded, though not without a touch of youthful disappointment. "I think I understand, Majesty," he said, and sounded as though he meant it. "But if not me, then I believe it will have to be poor old Brother Etan who must go sound out the Stanshire-folk."

* * *

The monk did not look any happier to learn he was being sent out than Morgan had at being told he was not, but Etan did his admirable best to show a brave face when the king spoke to him. "Of course, Majesty. I will be discreet, but I will learn everything I can. Many people will talk to a man of the cloth who would be close-mouthed with another traveler."

"Excellent. Tiamak chose his helper well, I can see that."

"Your Majesty is too kind." But the monk seemed buoyed by Simon's words and went to prepare himself for his spying mission with a determined air.

Sludig had been watching Simon. "I see you are down to just a few followers now, old friend, but they are your usual strange assortment—trolls, a renegade Black Rimmersman, a monk—"

"—And a brave cattle farmer as well, although he is a bit old and a trifle out of shape. Do you even have room in your belt for a pair of axes anymore?"

"Ha." Sludig spat on the ground. "Wait until I find this Pasevalles on the field of battle. You will see and remember Sludig Two-Axes then, I promise you."

"No, old friend." Simon made the Sign of the Tree. "I only jested. I do not doubt you are just as formidable as ever. But the traitor is mine and I want him alive."

"I only mean to hack a few bits off him first."

"He arranged Miriamele's death and murdered my son's widow with his own hands—he boasted about it to me. And he tried to kill Josua too, although he failed. I want Pasevalles captured alive. He kept me chained and then tormented me with all he had done. I do not want him to have a clean, easy death in battle."

Sludig had grinned as if he meant to make another jest, but as he heard Simon's tone, his look grew serious. "I hear you, Simon. If it is given to me, I will drag him to you alive."

"Good. Perhaps I will let you hack off a piece or two afterward, when I'm done with him."

"Not much joy there, but I suppose an old farmer like me must take his pleasure where he can," said Sludig.

Night had fallen and the meager evening meal had been finished by the time Brother Etan returned. Morgan, who had wanted to be by himself, was sharpening Snakesplitter—his time with Nezeru had confirmed him in that discipline, at least—when one of Sludig's men told him that the king wanted him.

The informal royal council had already assembled around the main fire on either side of the king—Sludig and his second-in-command, named Thane Breki, Morgan's two Qanuc friends, and Jarnulf. The monk, clearly just returned, was drinking deeply from a wine cup, a piece of salted fish in his other hand.

"There you are," Simon said to Morgan. "Now we can begin. Brother Etan, tell us what you have learned."

"Much, Your Majesty, although many questions still remain unanswered. I spent the day in the marketplace and bought a few drinks in the taverns. The first thing I learned is that people are worried."

"Surely that's not surprising," said Morgan. "Their king gone, the Hayholt burned by Norns, the queen . . ." He looked at his grandfather and fell silent.

"Who do they say is ruling?" Simon asked. "Is it Morgan's other grandfather, the duke?"

"There seems to be a struggle for the throne, from what people were saying, though they are not entirely certain of it. There are many rumors. But Pasevalles is part of it."

"Damn that traitor to Hell forever!" cried Simon.

Etan was startled, and it took him a moment to find his thread again. "But here is the strange part, Majesty. It seems that Pasevalles has gone to ground at Winstowe Castle where you fought Unver, and he is besieged there by the duchess."

"The *duchess?"* growled Simon. "What duchess is that? Nelda, Osric's wife? By Heaven, I pray that does not mean that the duke has died."

"Nobody knows, Majesty, although it seems it must be her."

Morgan could not in any shape or form imagine his fretful, pious grandmother leading soldiers into war. The king did not seem to believe it either. "Nelda is an old woman, not some female Sitha warrior," he said. "Someone else must be commanding the siege."

"That seems likely," Etan agreed. "But if so, no one in Stanshire seems to know who that is. The talk is more about how long Winstowe can hold out. It seems that Count Aglaf had prepared against siege only a short while ago, when the grasslanders attacked, so the castle is well fortified and well supplied. If Pasevalles is truly there, he might hold out for a very long time."

"A long time?" Simon could barely hold back his rage. "I will drag him out by his neck before the next moon is in the sky. How did Aglaf let this happen? Was he in league with Pasevalles all along?"

"The folk I spoke with seemed to believe Count Aglaf is dead, just from the ways that Pasevalles' mercenaries spoke about him as they were plundering the local villages and farms. And they say that Pasevalles is still holding the count's family as hostages."

Simon glowered. "And what is this duchess—Nelda or whoever uses her name—doing about it? What kind of siege can it be, if the enemy only needs to sit in his castle and laugh at us?"

"I cannot tell you, Majesty," said Etan. "But you have not heard my choicest piece of news."

Simon was still scowling. "Well, don't swallow your tongue, monk. Out with it!"

"I met a fellow whose brother had sold wood to the besieging army—the

Duchess's soldiers. He loaned them wagons to take what they had cut back to their camp along the Laestfinger, and he went with them to retrieve his wagons when they had done. He said the men who felled the trees were all Erkynlandish soldiers—"

"That means little," the king interjected. "It might be Osric in command, but it might also be some other noble. Any would-be usurper will be commanding Erkynlandish soldiers. God curse it, we may have to fight both sides!"

Etan was smiling. "I beg pardon, but you did not let me finish, Majesty. This man told me that his brother, when he returned, told him a strange thing. In the siege camp in the valley below Winstowe, he saw two very strange folk among the soldiers—two very small folk." The others around the campfire leaned forward at this. "The man said that his brother swore they were trolls," Etan went on, "and that he swore one of them was followed everywhere by a white wolf."

"Glory!" cried Simon. "Glory to God! Oh, Etan, you are the best of men—the prince of monkish spies! That can only be Binabik and Sisqi!"

Little Snenneq had wrapped his burly arms around Qina, who seemed still to be working through the Westerling speech. "Did you hear, beloved?" he said. "Did you hear? Your parents! It is your parents!"

"True?" she asked, then turned to the king, eyes wide. "For true?"

"Ah, I feel a hundred times better," the king said. "Binabik and your mother would never ally themselves with some usurper, Qina. Never! It must be Osric or Nelda or someone else they would trust. Oh, this is excellent news." He sprang to his feet. "We must ride to Winstowe at once!"

Morgan raised his hand. "Perhaps we should wait until morning, Grandfather. If we mean to travel swiftly, it will be safer for our horses."

"What?" For a moment King Simon looked as though he did in truth plan to jump into his saddle right that moment. "Ah, of course. And we will have to go at least a little carefully—we do not want to arrive unlooked-for and unknown. In the dark, we might end up fighting against our own people." The king was pacing now, so full of excitement that Morgan almost laughed. "Yes! We ride at first light, Sludig."

"As you wish," said the Rimmersman. "I will go and see if I can squeeze both my axes under my belt."

"But remember—and not just Sludig, but all of you!" Simon said. "No matter what happens, Pasevalles must be taken alive. He has much to answer for."

"He does. He killed my mother." Morgan was beginning to catch his grandfather's vengeful mood. "You said he killed her with his own hands."

"He told me so," said the king. "Bragged of it! But never fear, Morgan—Hell is waiting for Pasevalles, that is certain."

47

The Door Beneath the Stone

"Are you awake, Sir Porto?" someone whispered.

It took him a moment to remember that he was, in fact, Sir Porto, that it was the troll Binabik talking to him, and that he was slouched awkwardly against the trunk of a tree and all his bones were aching. "Yes. Yes, certainly! Just closed my eyes to think."

"That is good. Because Vaqana is showing much restlessness, and I think I hear noises from beneath the flat stone where we were digging."

"What do you mean?" Porto sat up, heart beating fast. "Beneath the stone?"

"I think it is so. Listen."

Even the night seemed to hold its breath as Porto cocked his head. They were camped—if it could be called a camp, with no fire and no proper flat place to stretch out—at the base of the slope beneath the tall crag that had fascinated the wolf for two days. Porto shook his head. "I don't hear anything."

"It is a very quiet sound of voices, I am thinking. Do you truly not hear it?"

"I am old, and my ears are just as old as the rest of me." He grunted as he clambered to his knees, then onto his feet. "You might just be hearing the sentries on the walls above."

The stars were hidden behind overcast skies; Porto could only barely see the troll shake his head. "I have heard those, too. This comes from closer, but very muffled. There is something here—that floor of stone shows it—and I fear the castle defenders may be trying to escape now. I wish my Sisqi would hurry back with Captain Kenrick and his archers."

"How long has your lady been gone?" Porto was definitely awake now and trying to work the kinks out of his neck, which crackled like a fistful of straw.

"Not long. Watching the moon, I would say we are not yet at middle-night." As the troll spoke, the great white wolf, who was lying beside him, stirred and let out a low growl. Binabik put his hand on her back. "*Shummuk, Vaqana,*" he whispered. "Listen again, Sir Porto. Do you hear it now?"

And he did, although just barely—a sound like the beating of a muffled drum, but less regular. "What is it?"

"It is perhaps someone beneath the ground, trying to force open a door or gate long closed," said the troll. "They are beneath the very stones we found, I am guessing. It appears that Vaqana's nose was as trustworthy as ever."

"But by God, man, what will we do? There are only two of us and my sword is broken."

"There are three of us. Vaqana is not to be underestimated if it comes to a fight. But with some luck, we may avoid that. You have a bow, do you not?"

"Yes, but I have shot precious few arrows since my days on Nakkiga hunting the Norns."

"These are not such clever, fast-moving folk as those, but mortal Thrithings mercenaries," said the troll. "We will hide and then do what damage we can from concealment, and hope that way to keep them at bay until help comes from Kenrick."

Porto's skin had gone colder than the brisk winter night. "Let us pray your wife brings him back quickly."

"That she will try to do. I hope he takes her at her word—"

Binabik was interrupted by a louder but still muffled noise, a heavy thump of impact Porto could feel through his feet, followed by a long moment of silence. "That sounds like they've opened it."

"Then let us retreat a short way," said the troll. "How far can you send an arrow?"

"With good aim? Twenty or thirty paces, unless I have forgotten all my skill."

"I cannot send my poison darts so far." Binabik had split his walking stick into two sections. "But perhaps that is well. We will give them more confusion if we attack from different places—they will not know how many we are. In fact, I have a plan. Take your place a safe distance back, where you may safely let your arrows fly, and do not be alarmed by anything you see."

With this piece of unsettling advice, Binabik curled his fingers in Vaqana's hackles and led the wolf into a thick tangle of vegetation less than a dozen paces to the side of the exposed stones. Porto snatched up his bow, heart racing, and retreated downslope to a vantage point behind a fallen tree, praying silently as he bent the yew around his leg and slipped the waxed bowstring into place. *Peace,* he told himself. *Then pull. Breathe out. Loose.* As he laid an arrow on the string, he could hear Binabik and the wolf moving from place to place.

Now Porto heard the scraping again, and even what sounded like voices. The ground was rising over the slab, crumbling and falling away as the stone was shoved upward from below. At last, hands appeared in the opening, but in the dim night Porto could not see whose hands they were. He remembered childhood tales of Dwarrows and goblins, and had a moment of superstitious fear, but two sets of arms shoved the stone slab upright until it fell over backward; then the arms began pushing up the slab beside it as well—human arms, hairy and a-jangle with bracelets.

Porto lifted his bow and sighted down the shaft, waiting for one of the enemy to emerge, but after the second slab rose out of the way the arms disappeared again, and for long moments the dark, rectangular hole remained empty and silent. Then a heavy-set, bearded figure pulled itself out and squatted by the opening, reaching back to help a second shadowy form.

Grasslanders, indeed, Porto thought. Two bulky silhouettes now crouched beside the hole, both looking from side to side while a third figure, considerably larger than the first two, began to clamber up from below. Seeing the greater size of the third man, Porto was about to let his arrow fly, hoping that if he killed this one his size alone might block those below him. He re-sighted on the imposingly broad chest, now exposed, and was about to loose his shaft when a fizzing sound startled him. An instant later, the night suddenly filled with glaring light.

A gash of fire had sprung up on one side of the opening, where Binabik had first vanished; in the next instant, another burst into life a few paces away. As Porto watched, almost as surprised as the mercenaries must have been, more fires blazed up in a ragged semi-circle among the surrounding trees, some of the blazes as far as twenty or thirty paces away.

Porto, realizing that this must be the trollish trick Binabik had warned him about, turned his feverish attention back to the hole, ready to skewer the biggest of the grasslanders, but that one was gone. He cursed himself at the missed chance, aimed at the nearer of the two remaining shapes and let fly. He thought he saw his arrow strike, but he could not be certain until the man he had targeted crawled awkwardly away from the hole and then collapsed. Voices began shouting from inside the hole; Porto could not help wondering how many mercenaries might be crowding up toward the surface, perhaps with Pasevalles himself among them. Several more fires sprang to life around the clearing, painting the cliff face above with reddish light. Porto had just got his second arrow onto the string and was taking aim at the other figure when it jumped to its feet, perhaps dazzled by the fires, and bolted away along the hillside, vanishing quickly in the darkness. A bellow of rage erupted from the hole in the earth, then the huge figure came scrambling out once more, moving with surprising speed. Before Porto could even take aim the great, shadowy shape was running down the slope toward him. He let the arrow fly but missed, and as he tried to fumble another shaft from his quiver, the arrows slipped from his fingers and tumbled into the undergrowth like a child's game of jackstraws.

The gigantic mercenary hurtled down the slope toward him, sword raised. Porto lifted his bow to use it as a club but already knowing it would shatter uselessly against such a huge opponent, and that would be the end. He commended his soul to God.

Fremur had spent enough time with Unver to know that he would hear nothing more useful than that strange remark about wolves until the Shan was ready, so he left Unver dicing with several drunken mercenaries in the hall and went to walk off some of the fearful agitation that gripped him. Outside the high-ceilinged hall, the castle had a haunted aspect, the corridors empty, the defenders either up on the walls or—Fremur guessed—drunk and asleep in some dark corner. The few mercenaries he saw had the wild, wide eyes of cornered animals, and Fremur kept his distance from even the ones he recognized. Despite Unver and the handful of men gambling in the great hall, this was not a night for fellowship.

To avoid a trio of extremely drunk mercenaries arguing and shoving each other as they came toward him down a passage, Fremur slipped into the castle's chapel, where only a few candles burned on the altar, leaving the rest of the chamber in deep shadow. He stood silently as the drunken men lurched past the doorway, still cursing each other. The chapel had likely been rich and well-appointed before Pasevalles and his sell-swords had arrived, but it was hard to tell that now: the costly wall hangings had been torn down with so little care that tattered remnants still hung high on the walls, and the altar had been denuded of its candlesticks and Holy Tree. Even the Pelippan font, painstakingly carved from Harcha marble, had been pushed over and lay in pieces on the stone flags.

He was making his way back toward the chapel doorway when he heard more voices, so he ducked back into the shadows again. This time the speakers did not pass the entrance but stopped just outside it, and Fremur had to retreat behind the battered trow screen that divided the chapel's chancel from its nave. To Fremur's dismay, the men now moved into the chapel proper, and he had to crouch low to keep from being seen. Several of them walked past, the shadows thrown by their torches striping the walls and chapel ceiling.

"Behind the altar," said a rasping voice, and Fremur felt a chill across his heart. Those deep-chested tones, he realized, could only come from Hulgar, Pasevalles' bearlike lieutenant, as tall as Unver but twice the Shan's weight—a brute whom Fremur had seen break a servant's neck with a squeeze of one vast hand. He dared not reveal himself now; the jagged-toothed mercenary had made it clear that he hated Unver, guessing that Pasevalles was grooming the Shan as a potential replacement for Hulgar himself. Fremur had no doubt that if his presence was revealed, he would be accused of being Unver's spy. He held his breath as the mercenaries tramped past, then he heard gasps and cursing and the tortured scrape of stone on stone as something large—the altar, he guessed—was laboriously shoved to one side.

The sound of echoing footsteps followed, and the voices grew more faint. Fremur listened until silence fell again, then cautiously slipped out from behind the trow screen.

The altar had indeed been pushed to one side to reveal descending steps built into the chapel floor. Fremur peered down the winding stairwell, but the light of the men's torches had disappeared. His first impulse was to get out of the chapel as quickly as possible before Hulgar and his bravos returned, but he could not help wondering what they were doing under the chapel. *Is there a way out down there? Is Hulgar about to leave the rest of us behind and save himself?*

Spurred by this idea, he crept into the stairwell. He could make out a little light at the bottom, so he stopped a few steps above the lower doorway and peered through it. He saw quickly that the stone-walled chamber below was empty except for a single torch burning in a wall-bracket—empty of living men, at least, although half a dozen carved figures lay in niches in the walls, each one a funeral effigy atop a heavy coffin.

This must be where the lords of Winstowe buried their dead, he realized, and the thought made him even more uncomfortable. He did not fear the shades of these long-dead men—not with Hulgar and the rest talking loudly somewhere just out of sight—but the thought of being sealed inside a stone vault inside a stone castle for all eternity filled him with a deep and almost sickening unease. *What kind of place for the dead is this? Only stone-dwellers would want to be shut up in stone this way.* Fremur's people burned their dead or, if the departed were important enough to be remembered, laid them to rest beneath grassy mounds on the open plain, under the sky and the eternal stars. But this place was like some terrible underground nest, a burrow for rats, an abode of spiders and bats.

O, Sky-Piercer, please do not let me die and be entombed in this castle, he prayed. *Please let my ashes lie in clean earth.*

He could see a door had been forced at the far side of the crypt, and light beyond the doorway, so he stole cautiously past the slumbering effigies until he could hear the voices again. They had a strange echo, so he risked a swift look past the door frame and saw that a stone tunnel led out from there, he presumed through the rocky hill itself, and that Hulgar and the others were crowded together on a staircase at the far end, this one leading upward. He shrank back into the doorway.

The first words he could make out were Broga Broomstraw's—complaints, as usual. "If the stone-dweller thinks this door can be forced, why does he not come down and see to it himself?"

"Because he is the one paying," growled Hulgar. It was easy to recognize his voice, not just by its deep sound, but because his broken teeth shaped his speech, fraying the edges of many of his words.

"He *was* paying," Broga spat back. "But I have not had a single copper since the first Red Moon. We were promised gold. We were promised neck-rings and arm-rings and gold coins by the sack. What have we had instead? Only more promises."

"I promise you that you will have my knife in your guts if you do not bend to that bar and open that door," said Hulgar, and for a while nobody spoke, and Fremur heard only grunts of effort and the pounding of what sounded like a heavy blacksmith's hammer. At last, the clatter of hammering ended.

"The bolt is loose now," said one of the other men.

"Then open it, fool," said Hulgar. "And you two go first."

"What if the stone-dwellers are waiting?" asked the man who had spoken.

"You'd had better hope they are not, because I will be right behind you," said Hulgar. "And if you try to climb over me in cowardly flight, I will break your back. Now shift those stones."

Fremur heard the door being forced open, rusty hinges screeching in protest, and then more grunting and cursing as what sounded like heavy stones were shifted. Then Hulgar gave a quiet order Fremur could not hear, and he could only assume that they were climbing out of the hole they had made. To freedom? To escape? Fremur felt a moment of real hope, the first he had felt in several days. If Hulgar, Broga and the rest got away, he would run back and find Unver. The two of them could slip out of this death trap and be back in the grasslands again by the next day. He touched the locket beneath his tunic. Hyara would be waiting for him.

Light suddenly glared in the tunnel, as if several torches had been lit at once, and as the men at the far end gasped and a few shouted in dismay, Fremur ducked back into the stairwell once more. He heard more shouting, then someone said "They killed Colmunt! Run!"

"If you run," Fremur heard Hulgar snarl, "I will catch you and kill you with my own hands. Be men, curse you! I am going back up. Follow me!"

For a long moment Fremur heard nothing more, then someone shouted in alarm, "They have set the hill on fire!" He heard Hulgar's voice, distant now, bellowing a war cry.

"The fool is a dead man," he heard Broga say. "They were waiting! Shut the door and ram the bolt!"

"But Hulgar is—" protested one of the other men.

"Hulgar Horse-Slayer is as good as dead," Broga snarled. "Do you want to die for the stone-dweller Pasevalles too?"

Their answer was obvious: Fremur heard the loud crash as the door was closed, then the metallic clamor of the bolt being shot and hammered into place. He retreated up the stairs and made it back into the crypt only moments ahead of the fleeing mercenaries. All the niches were occupied by coffins, and Fremur could see no place to hide, so he crouched just behind the door to the tunnel and threw his cloak over his head, hoping that in their hurried retreat none of them would notice another clump of shadow.

To his immense relief, Broga and the others rushed past him as if pursued by demons, but as he heard them climbing the stairs back up to the chapel, arguing and cursing once more, he realized that if he stayed where he was he might be closed in with the stone-dweller dead, so Fremur threw back his cloak and followed them up the steps.

He was fortunate. The fleeing men did not pause to shove the altar back into place in their rush to leave the chapel. Fremur followed a little behind them and at last reached the top, then—after making certain he was not observed—he slipped out into the hallway and hurried off to find the Shan.

His remaining arrows lost in the bracken, Porto staggered to his feet and gripped his bow in both hands, though he knew it would offer no defense against the huge grasslander charging toward him. In the fitful light of the troll's fires, the roaring Thrithings-man with the mouth full of broken teeth looked as much a monster as the mountain giant Porto and his fellow soldiers had fought on the Nakkiga slopes all those years ago.

The mercenary's first blow smashed through the heavy branches of the thicket like a reaper's scythe, and Porto barely managed to stumble backward to avoid it. Another sweep of the long, curved sword whistled just over his head, but he had run out of space to retreat. Then something white rushed through the darkness behind his attacker like a comet fallen to earth and seized the grasslander by the back of his leg. With a choking cry of rage and pain, the big man staggered, then struck at this new opponent with his heavy blade, but the wolf leaped away, muzzle red with the Thrithings-man's blood. Porto swung his bow as hard as he could at his attacker's face and heard something crack. The grasslander roared again, his nose a splotch of dark blood, but he seemed more surprised than badly wounded. When the wolf dove in again, trying to tear at the bearded giant's loins, he managed to knock the beast aside with one knee, then kicked the white wolf so hard that it flew off its feet and skidded away. Porto dropped the shattered remnant of his bow and pulled his broken sword from his belt, though it seemed as pointless a weapon as a thistle-stalk against his much larger opponent.

Another bright streak rushed across the darkness, starting just behind Porto, a flare of brightly glowing red—Binabik, carrying a scoop of bark filled with burning coals. Even as the grasslander saw him, the troll flung the smoldering missiles into his ruined face. This time the mercenary let out a much more savage and primitive cry of pain and rage, but also of desperate frustration, then dropped his sword as he tried to beat away the blazing fragments that clung to his clothes, hair, and beard. He kicked out wildly as he did so, but the troll was already gone.

Knowing he might not have another chance, Porto hurried forward, hoping to drive his half-blade into the taller man's groin. He missed, because his target was writhing as he tried to beat out the flames, but Porto still managed to carve a long slice down the inside of his enemy's leg before a huge, backhand fist caught him on the side of the head and flung him off his feet. Porto landed on his rump, and for a long, swirling moment could only sit, trying to understand where he was and what had just happened. If the grasslander had followed to finish him he would have ended there, but the distraction of the fiery coals had been enough to allow the white wolf to climb back onto her feet. She lunged again and again at the man's legs. But the attacker, though wreathed in tendrils of smoke from his smoldering clothes and hair, bent and snatched up his curved sword again even as the snarling wolf gathered herself for another attack. His wits returned, Porto saw that his sword had fallen several paces away, so he snatched up a stone as big as his fist, then flung it as hard as he could. It struck the center of the grasslander's chest, and though his enemy took only a single backward step, the blow distracted him enough that he failed to split the wolf's skull with his downward stroke, though he still drew blood from her shoulder. Vaqana sank in her teeth and worried at his calf, drawing blood, but after a moment whined and retreated, limping badly. Porto despaired.

But in that moment of distraction, something dropped out of the tree onto the Thrithings-man's back. He grunted in surprise and tried to shake off his attacker, but Binabik had gripped the man's braided hair with one hand and could not be dislodged. The troll pulled himself up until he could wrap his short legs around his enemy's neck, then, still holding on to the grasslander's head, he began to plunge something over and over into the big man's throat.

"Mintahoq!" shouted the troll. *"Mintahoq odo Yiqanuc pikak!"*

Porto had recovered his half blade, and now, sensing an opportunity, lurched toward their attacker. He evaded a crazed swing of the mercenary's curved blade and drove the broken end of his own sword through the man's leather jerkin and into his belly before being knocked to the ground by his flailing enemy. One of the man's booted feet stepped on Porto's back, pinning him against the icy earth, and the old knight could only clamp his hands over his head, knowing that he could not stop the blow that was coming. Then the foot lifted again.

Porto rolled out of from underneath the malformed shadow-shape as it swayed above him, blocking and then revealing and then blocking the stars once more. The reason for the silhouette's odd shape became clear as Binabik, still clinging to the big man's neck, drove his bone-handled knife yet again into the grasslander's throat and blood sprayed out. Porto barely had time to roll away as the mercenary's knees wobbled and bent, then the big man crashed to the ground and lay still. Binabik stepped off his back.

"Are you alive? Are you hurt?" he asked Porto.

"Alive? Yes. Yes, I think so."

Binabik hurried to where Vaqana lay, doing her best to lick herself where the sword had bit at her shoulder. Binabik riffled through her fur until he found the wound but seemed relieved. "Nothing that is mortal," he told Porto. "She has taken a long swipe, but not deep."

"What did you shout?" Porto asked, still dazed. He glanced over at the motionless thing that only moments earlier had been trying very hard to kill them. "You shouted something."

"I have no idea," admitted the troll. "Something of desperation. We were losing, was my thought."

"My thought, too." Porto rolled onto his back and felt the wind scouring his hot cheeks, still damp with perspiration. He opened his eyes and felt he had seldom been so grateful to see the sky. *God has spared me again,* he thought, *against all likelihood. And I am truly grateful, my Lord.*

Then a clatter in the bushes on the slope below startled both troll and knight. Porto rolled over and struggled painfully to his feet while Binabik crouched, knife at the ready.

"Sir Porto? Troll?" said a quiet voice. "Are you there?"

"Kenrick!" exclaimed Porto. "Thank God. Yes, we are here!"

The captain and half a dozen archers came out of the trees and hurried toward them. They stopped inside the clearing, staring at the dead man with obvious surprise.

"Please all keep quiet," Binabik said, finger to his lips. "There is a tunnel just there, though I think the other Thrithings-men have been retreating to the castle."

Kenrick had to pull hard with both hands to roll the large corpse over onto its back. "I know this brute," he said. "I have seen him often enough on the walls, shouting down at us. This was Hulgar, Pasevalles' main henchman, big as a house and strong as an ox. How did you kill him?"

"Binabik did it," said Porto. "He jumped on him out of the tree and nearly cut the bastard's head off."

"It was by no means just me," the troll protested. "Porto also was fighting him." He reached down and patted the white wolf, who had returned to licking her wound. "And noble Vaqana."

"The wolf saved me, it's true," said Porto.

Kenrick shook his head. "It sounds like a fireside tale—one of the less likely ones—but I cannot doubt what I see before me. Come, our archers will stay behind and keep watch on this place, and we will send reinforcements, too, though I doubt they will try the spot again. Meanwhile, let me take you all—yes, the wolf as well—back to camp, where your wounds can be tended."

48

A Long Night

If things had been less desperate, Fremur thought, it would have been amusing to watch Broga Broomstraw being scolded. He was crouched at Pasevalles's feet like a strapping grandson cringing in front of a heartless family patriarch.

"You *left* him there? Our best fighter, my right-hand man? You left him to die while you and the rest fled like cowards?"

"It was an ambush, Lord Pasevalles. There were dozens of them." Broga held up thick, tattooed fingers. "Archers, waiting for us. Two of my men were killed right off, then Hulgar ran at the attackers. There were torches everywhere, and arrows as thick as flies. If we had followed him, we would have been dead too, and the crypt gate would have been left open."

"Idiot. No, you are worse than an idiot." Pasevalles turned to Unver Shan, who was watching with barely concealed amusement. "And you—do you think this is something to smile at? We are surrounded by Erkynlandish troops, our one path to escape has been discovered, and now Hulgar is dead. You are trapped here with me, you barbarian fool. What is there to grin about?"

Unver considered for a moment before answering. "It depends, my lord."

"On what?"

"On whether death is something to be feared or not."

Pasevalles stared at him so hard that Fremur wondered if he was trying to kill Unver with thought alone. "I am not entertained by your rustic philosophy. You may feel different about death when it comes for you."

"The spirits will do what they will do," said Unver.

Pasevalles turned and picked up his goblet, took a long swallow, then threw the metal cup so that it clanged across the floor of the throne hall and rolled almost to the door. He pointed at Broga. "So then, Sanver, what if I told you to cut off this useless creature's head?" he demanded.

Broga Broomstraw reared up in shock, but Unver barely moved. "Do you want me to?" he asked.

"No," Pasevalles snarled. "Not this time. But I am angry—very angry. Do you fools not understand that I am the only one who can keep you alive? The Norn poison is the most terrible way to die, I promise you—your blood burns in your veins!—and only I can prevent that. Why do I need to explain any of this? I have never trusted the stories my people tell about the slow wits of Thrithings-men, but I am beginning to think they were right."

"I am sorry, Lord Pasevalles," said Broga, looking sidelong at Unver as though he wished he could throttle him. "You know what Hulgar Horse-Slayer was like. I have never feared any man, but I feared him. I could not have stopped him without killing him."

"But the Erkynlanders took care of that, so you did not even have to exert yourself." Pasevalles sank back into Aglaf's tall chair, which was decorated with a gilded carving of the family's Lionfish crest, and held out his hand, flexing his fingers in a demand for more wine. A servant hurried forward.

Pasevalles stared into this new cup as though he might find another way out of the castle among the lees at the bottom. "We shall have to break out," he finally said. "The only good thing to come from your failure, Broga, is that now the queen and her soldiers will be watching the tunnels and mineshafts even more closely, which means they will be spread around the whole of Winstowe. A determined charge on a weak spot in the ring may force a way through."

"So that is your plan?" Unver asked.

"Do you have a better one?" Pasevalles seemed to consider throwing his wine at the Shan's head, but instead drank again. "Or are you simply in a hurry to meet that death—the one you do not fear."

"I never said that I didn't fear death," said Unver. "But no matter. I wonder if you will be able to convince the men to ride out against an army many times our size. Surely many of them will surrender instead."

"I will give them a little something to warm them up, first," said Pasevalles. "And Broga will convince them that it is in their best interest to fight and break free. Yes, Broga—not you, Sanver. None of men trust you, with your silences and your air of being above everyone else."

Unver lifted his eyebrows but said nothing.

"I do not know if the men will fight, my lord," said Broga. "They have not been paid since the First Red Moon, and they were full of complaints even before they learned of the Erkynlandish queen."

"All you have to do is tell them what they must do," Pasevalles said. "I will make certain that they are in the right spirit. But we must decide who will lead them."

"Lead them?" Broga was confused. "Will it not be you, Lord Pasevalles?"

"Good God, no," he said. "Nor you, nor even Sanver and his catamite there. I need you all to stay with me, and you need me to stay alive. No, while the men break out and attack the queen's soldiers tonight, we will be on our own way. I have both treasure and allies waiting for me. With the Erkynlanders distracted, we will have an easy time escaping. And if I must kill their so-called queen again before my victory is secure . . . well, so be it."

Dawn was only just warming the eastern sky, but the company had set out an hour before. Sludig and his Rimmersmen had already made a long and very swift journey south from the Aldheorte, but King Simon was impatient and had been forcing them to an even faster pace as they closed in on the Fingerdale.

Tzoja, who had already suffered being carted by wagon out of distant Nakkiga, then herded on foot from the conquered mortal fortress into the Narrowdark Valley, only wanted to settle somewhere so she could rest and to nurse her father. She could not guess where things would end—had they escaped destruction in Tanakirú only to find it in the unknown south?

Long days of travel had passed since they had left the Hikeda'ya and their Zida'ya cousins in the abandoned refuge of Jao é-Tinukai'i. Parting from Viyeki had been painful enough, though something had changed between the high magister and herself during the long moons of their separation. But leaving Nezeru had shaken Tzoja to her depths.

What did I think? That she would desert her father and follow me into mortal lands? What has she ever known of my people except the poison that the Sacrifice Order filled her with? Even the mortal youth who loved her couldn't overcome that.

It had come down to a choice, though, a dreadful choice, and Tzoja had forced herself to make it. She had regretted it through all the hours since but would not have changed it even if she could have. *I will live among my own people. I will try to find a life beyond slavery, under the light of the sky.* This was her determination—her prayer, although it did not always soothe the hurt or even help very much.

The young Rimmersgard boy Henrig, son of the northmen's leader, had elected himself Vordis's caretaker, and appeared now to tell her it was time to mount up once more.

"Good morrow, Mistress Tzoja," he said in Westerling. *"The king wants us to make haste. I am sorry, but we must ride now."*

Tzoja had feared traveling with the northerners, because the night the Skalijar bandits had taken her out of the Astaline convent and into misery still burned in her memory, but meeting this kind, earnest child, Henrig, had reminded her that not all his people were red-handed monsters.

Tzoja translated for her friend; Vordis nodded and let Henrig help her onto the back of his saddle, then he swung himself up so she could wrap her arms around his slender waist. *And it is not enough I must see to my poor, muddled father,* Tzoja thought. *I am taking Vordis into a new world. I will have to teach her Westerling, or she will never be able to leave me.*

Even the thought of losing Vordis struck her like a blow. *Gods, may she never leave me! Already I have given up my kind lover and my beloved child for this suffering man I scarcely know.* It was a lonely feeling, one that threatened to overwhelm her. She looked at Josua, who was waiting calmly and seemingly without interest for her to direct him, as he always did. What sort of life lay ahead of her?

It does not matter, she told herself as she gathered up her few possessions. *This pair are my family now. My duty is to them.*

Still, the shape of the days ahead seemed as misty and uncertain as the road that stretched before her.

Pasevalles looked down from the gallery at the grasslanders drinking and dicing in the great hall. "I detect a certain sullenness among your countrymen," he said.

"They know the siege will only get worse, sire," said Broga, and wiped his lips. He had been drinking with just as much dedication as his fellow mercenaries below.

"They will be more bitter still when they learn we have to break out," said Unver in a flat voice.

Pasevalles laughed. "Let them! They are ungrateful animals who have feasted at my table for a long time." But though his words were harsh, he seemed in good cheer, which only made Fremur more uneasy. "It is a mystery why I still treat them so well." He signaled to his Erkynlandish minion, Sir Rawlie, who waited in the doorway, and Rawlie disappeared; a few moments later, servants began to carry barrels into the hall. The mercenaries nearest the door shouted in pleasure, and soon the casks were surrounded by bearded Thrithings-men.

Pasevalles leaned over the railing. "The last of the late count's supply," he called down. "Where Aglaf has gone, he will not need it, so I give it to you." He raised his own cup. "And I will also toast the impostor who claims to be the Erkynlandish queen. For that crime, I will hand her over to you when we capture her."

Some of the men shouted out their approval, but the others were already busy breaching the casks. "Ale!" shouted one tattooed warrior as he scooped it into his cup. He downed it and belched loudly. "And it is good!"

The rest crowded forward, shoving for a place near the barrels, and soon almost as much of the frothing beer was being spilled onto the rushes of the floor as was making its way into mugs.

"Where was that hidden?" asked Broga in surprise. "The men looked all over!" Pasevalles gave him a hard stare. "Or so I heard, at least."

"Did you think I would share everything I have from the very first?" Pasevalles wore a crooked grin. "Keep nothing to myself? I would be a poor planner, then. I have saved this brew carefully, and they will never have tasted anything like it."

Fremur felt a sudden clutch in his belly and stared at the cup in his own hand.

Pasevalles was amused. "Ah, look—Sanver's little friend is fearful. Worry not. Neither the wine you drink nor the ale the men are so happily guzzling is poisoned. I need to keep our soldiers content if we are to escape this annoying situation."

The master of the castle spoke the Thrithings tongue very well, but Fremur thought that, considering they were surrounded by a force of trained soldiers many times the size of their own, 'annoying' was not the word he should have chosen.

Not even an hour had passed, Fremur felt sure, but the interior of the great hall had become a much different place. The ale casks had all been emptied. A few of the men were fighting among themselves, but it did not seem like the usual drunken brawling. One former member of the Goat Clan had been stabbed through the eye by a man he had not even been arguing with, and several other grasslanders had been beaten to the point of insensibility without apparent reason, each swarmed by three or four of their fellows. Even those not fighting had a strange air, Fremur thought, red-eyed and unduly quiet; he heard none of the usual boasts or crack-voiced singing. At first it reminded him of nothing so much as a crowd of grassland scavengers, buzzards, or wild dogs, gathered to watch something die. But as he saw the hired warriors milling about without apparent purpose, staring distrustfully at each other, or in some cases merely gazing into empty space, he realized something else was going on.

"I do not like this," said Fremur quietly. "They have been given poison."

Pasevalles heard him. "No, it is not poison. There was a pinch of something I had from the Norns in each of those barrels. The White Foxes give it to their own soldiers to make them even fiercer. Never fear, these men will do what I need them to. In a little while they will fear nothing, feel nothing, and will fight like madmen."

"Men of the Thrithings already know how to fight," said Unver. "They do not need to be maddened by fairy powders."

"We shall see if you still believe that when we are free and on our way to sanctuary," Pasevalles replied. "You have not seen what the *saya-vishaa* can do." He did not seem offended by Unver's resistance, but Fremur wondered how long that would last.

Pasevalles strode to the railing of the gallery, cup in hand, and raised it high in the air. "Men of the Thrithings!" he called. "The stone-dwellers think they have you trapped. They believe you will surrender now and march out of this castle into slavery with your heads bowed and eyes downcast."

In the hall below, heads turned toward him, and dozens of red-rimmed eyes watched, but for the moment, none of them spoke.

"Even now," Pasevalles said, "most of the stone-dwellers are asleep in their cloaks, certain that they have won. Even their sentries nod on watch. The one who claims to be their queen sleeps in her tent, certain that we will give up without a fight." He leaned outward, looking down on them. "The stone-dwellers believe all grasslanders are cowards. You raid, then run away again. Faced with the greater strength of the castle-men, you will flee, as you always do. Do not growl at me, clansmen—that is what they think! They do not fear you."

Pasevalles' words were having an effect. The men gathered in the hall below, who had seemed distracted or simply dazed a short while earlier, had now all turned toward the gallery, watching him carefully; some had open mouths, as if they expected to have meat thrown down to them. They no longer looked like wild dogs, Fremur thought, but like the wolves that had come to surround Unver on the open plain. The Norn magic was beginning to do its work.

"They will fear us soon!" one of the mercenaries cried, shaking his fist. "We will beat them down. We will eat their livers!"

"Take their women and kill all their children!" bellowed another, and a deep growl of approval rose around him. Some of the men began to beat their cups against the benches and walls. Fremur watched uneasily as Pasevalles walked back and forth from one end of the gallery to the other, insulting and then cajoling the mercenaries. Some of the things he said were outright lies—he claimed to know that the Erkynlanders would ride on after winning the siege and roll into the Thrithings to burn wagons and slaughter any who resisted, dragging grasslander captives off to slavery in Nabban. As he spoke, the men responded as though the truth of his every world shone like a bright star. They grew louder and angrier, until Fremur began to worry they would turn on each other in a frenzy of bloodlust.

"Take up your long, sharp spears!" cried Pasevalles. "They think you are humbled! Will you show them the truth? Will you show them what their own blood looks like?"

Roaring like a cage full of hungry beasts, the men sprang to pick up their weapons and shields, while several of them hurried to the armory to fetch the long pikes kept in racks on the walls.

"Why does Pasevalles keep us with him?" Fremur whispered. "Why show us his trick?"

Unver leaned close. "It is only another and more subtle trick. He marks us out to make us grateful that we are not part of the herd."

"I would rather not be either sort," said Fremur, but Pasevalles was approaching and he fell silent.

"Go to the chest behind my chair, you," Pasevalles told Fremur. "Bring four of the cloaks you find in it."

He looked to Unver, but his friend gave him no sign, so he turned and made his way down the stairs onto the floor of the hall. The men there did not merely look different, many of them wild-eyed and laughing, they smelled different as well; a strange, subtle reek hung in the hall, like the metallic tang of a working forge. They moved strangely, too, he thought, stabbing at things with their hands instead of merely reaching, heads twitching, sometimes talking to themselves.

If he had not told us, Fremur thought, *I would swear he had enchanted them.*

He found the chest and opened it, then counted out four of the heavy, hooded wool cloaks. They were a uniform dark green, he saw when he lifted them to the light, and there was something familiar about them. It was only as he carried them hurriedly back up the stairs, dodging several heedless, pop-eyed grasslanders, that he realized why he recognized the color.

These are the same as the stone-dwellers' royal soldiers wear. Does he think the besiegers will not kill us if we dress this way? He could not make sense of that.

"By all the saints, you are slow," said Pasevalles, taking three of the cloaks and handing one to Unver and one to Broga. "Put these on."

Unver held his up, frowning. "These are Erkynguard cloaks."

"They most certainly are. The officers here during the first siege were members of that guard. The ones who were killed left these behind, and I have kept them for just such a moment."

"And do you think these will allow us to slip away from the battle, unnoticed?" demanded Unver. "More likely they will get us killed by our own men in the fighting."

"Slip away?" Pasevalles laughed. He almost looked as though he had tasted a little of his own physic, the stuff that had so enflamed the mercenaries. "No, there is only one way that we can win here tonight and escape, and that is to sow chaos among our enemies. These garments will allow us to slip into the enemy camp and get close enough to kill a queen."

My dearest Thelía,

It is late and I am very weary, but if I finish this tonight it can go out with the post rider in the morning and you will have it all the sooner. I beg pardon for taking so long to reply, but our lady has kept me very busy. The effects of the Hayholt's burning reach a long way, and I think our army has given out as much food to the people here as we have consumed ourselves. When this siege is over, and I pray it will be soon, we will still have much work to do. And of course it is not only the immortals who are to blame. Pasevalles dripped his poison into so many parts of the High Throne's affairs that I fear we may never find and heal all the wounds.

I do not mean to sound despairing, my good wife, and I am very aware that you must be exhausted with your own

Tiamak looked up. He had been aware of the noise for a few moments, but had thought it only the wind, which sometimes coursed down the valley like a crowd of mournful voices. But this howling, distant as it was, sounded less mournful than enraged; even more worrisome, he could now hear some of the sentries shouting in obvious alarm.

He dropped his pen and set the board down, then rose and limped to the door of the tent. The noise was rising, and his skin crawled as he realized he was hearing men shouting with what sounded like battle-madness. Closer to hand, Erkynguards were tumbling out of the surrounding tents like apples from a tipped basket.

Captain Kenrick appeared, half-armored and trailed by two pages who were still struggling to do up the last laces of his armor. "The grasslanders are trying to break out of Winstowe," he called to Tiamak. "Where is the bloody herald? Why is the alarm not given yet?"

At that moment a ragged trumpet call arose from the southeastern edge of the camp; another horn replied from the camp's far side.

"An attack! You must look to the queen, Kenrick!" Tiamak cried.

"I left her well-guarded," he called back. "Look to yourself, my lord. Stay safe!" Then he turned and hurried away toward the edge of camp, trailed by his pages, who were still carrying the captain's greaves and gauntlets.

Despite Kenrick's reassurance, Tiamak headed toward the queen's tent. The confusion had become general now, soldiers and others rushing in all directions, some trying to find the rest of their company, others merely trying to find safety. For once, Tiamak was almost grateful for his small stature and his game leg: none of these excited, armed men were likely to mistake him for a threat.

As he reached Miriamele's tent at the center of camp, marked out from the rest by its size and the Tree and Dragons banner hanging above it, he heard a deep animal growl that he could feel in his middle. He stumbled to a sudden halt, the hairs on his head, neck, and arms all standing up, and his imagination leaped into nightmare. Could Pasevalles have been given giants by the Norn Queen?

The tent flap opened, revealing a compact shadow in the doorway silhouetted by lamplight. *"Aia ummu, Vaqana! Ummu!"* it called. A moment later, it spoke in Westerling: "Who is there?"

"It's me, Binabik—Tiamak!"

"Hurry, then. Come inside."

As Tiamak entered, the huge white wolf came forward to sniff at him, as if not entirely confident of its master's choice of friends. Tiamak saw Miriamele standing behind the troll—the queen had pulled on a mail shirt—and Jesa clutching little Serasina.

"The queen sent her guards away," said Binabik. "I need you to stay, Tiamak, or Sisqi will ride without me."

"I didn't send them away," she said, "I sent them to fight. And once I find a helmet, I can fight, too. Tell him, Tiamak. You know I can defend myself."

"As do I, but you are to be doing nothing of that sort," countered Binabik, sounding unusually angry. "We know nothing of this attack. It could be desperation only, the last few castle defenders. What if you are arrow-pierced and killed in a fight without meaning?"

The queen made the Sign of the Tree. "Am I just to wait here to learn what happens, then?"

Binabik turned to Tiamak. "The Thrithings-men have kept their swift horses fed during the siege, it seems. There is much that Vaqana and I can do that is useful on the field. Stay with Miriamele. Speak sense to her, I beg you."

"He's right, Majesty," said Jesa. "You must stay here with me and the child."

The queen scowled but nodded. "Go, then, Binabik. Good luck to you and Sisqi."

"If she did not already ride off without me," he said, climbing onto Vaqana's broad, furry back. "She is fierce, my wife."

We seem to have no lack of fierce women, Tiamak thought as the troll and his tongue-lolling mount bounded out of the tent and disappeared into the darkness. *I only hope they do not have to prove themselves against fierce, desperate men.* "Is there a weapon I can use?" he asked.

Jesa lifted a long dagger and held it out to him. "Take this," she said. "I would rather have both hands to hold the baby."

Miriamele was scrabbling through one of the several chests, flinging clothes behind her like a dog digging a hole. "It is here somewhere. I swear that it is!"

Tiamak stared at the dagger and regretted his unfinished letter to his wife.

When the sally port opened, the riders swarmed down the slope with hoarse screams of battle-rage, but Pasevalles held Fremur, Broga, and Unver back. Fremur's blood was pounding at the sensation of riding a proper grassland horse once more, and he almost missed the lord of Winstowe's upraised hand.

"You would send them forward without us?" Unver asked in disbelief. "We are the best fighters you have left."

"You are almost the only fighters I have left," said Pasevalles. "I have little faith in the rest of that rabble." Already the mass of riders had galloped far down the grassy slope. "No, we will wait and see where our attack causes the most concern and thus learn where the encirclement is weakest. Then we can make our way to where the one who calls herself queen is hiding."

"She is not hiding," said Unver. "She revealed herself to you on purpose."

And perhaps she was hoping for just such a desperate response, Fremur thought. He stole a quick glance at the Shan, but it was impossible to tell from Unver's expression what he was thinking.

They watched in silence from in front of the sally port as the first wave of grasslanders reached the outskirts of the Erkynlandish camp. Fremur had followed the Shan through many raids and battles, as well as the campaigns along the Fingerlast, and knew Unver would never have commanded such a slipshod attack. Also, any attack he ordered, the Shan led himself. Unver had been right about Pasevalles—the stone-dweller used gold and lies to get what he wanted, waiting for other men to do his bidding.

But now we are those other men. A wave of hopelessness threatened to pull him down. *No,* Fremur told himself, *I must hang onto my courage. When there is nothing else to believe, I must trust Unver Shan.*

* * *

He could almost feel Unver's anger and impatience. They still lingered in the shadow of Winstowe's great outwall, all but invisible in their dark green cloaks, as the fighting raged at the bottom of the hill. The Shan demanded over and over that they be freed to help their fellows, but each time Pasevalles refused him. At last, as sudden fires broke out at different spots in the besieging camp, tents being set ablaze by the attacking grasslanders, Pasevalles seemed satisfied.

"Forward now," he said. "And remember, as long as the Norn poison runs in your veins, I hold your lives in my hands. Stay with me until we find the queen. But you must keep me alive if you wish to live too."

They spurred forward, heading down the slope toward the center of the camp, where the shouts and shadows were thickest.

Kenrick had sent two more men-at-arms to guard the queen's tent, but Jesa did not feel at all safe. Shouts and cries of pain echoed through the night, and several times she heard the clang of blade on blade fearfully close to where she sat at Miriamele's side. Serasina was awake and struggling, and it was all Jesa could do to keep the child somewhat quiet. The little girl's first tooth was coming in, and Serasina was so tired of being placated with Jesa's finger in her mouth that she was learning how to bite.

"What will we do if they get here?" Jesa asked.

"Run," said Tiamak. "Try to get away. Miriamele must live or all is lost."

"Do not frighten her," the queen said. "We have faced worse and lived. You and I survived the ghant's nest, did we not? Have you forgotten that?"

"I have certainly tried."

"You were in a ghant's nest?" Jesa had not heard this story. "How could that be?"

"Now is not the time for old tales," Miriamele said. "But I promise I will tell you about it when we are safe."

"The queen and our other companions came back for me," Tiamak said. "That at least I will never forget. And I will not desert you now, Miriamele."

"I never thought you would."

As the two of them exchanged a look, Jesa wondered at the bonds of unusual friendship Miriamele had forged, not just with Jesa herself and this other Wrannaman, but also with the trolls. She was startled out of the thought moments later by loud voices and the sound of fighting, very close to the tent. As they listened in wide-eyed silence, the noises moved slowly around the tent, from behind them toward the entry flap at the front. The ring of steel on steel stopped, cut off sharply by a cry of terrible pain, then silence fell.

After long moments without any further sounds from outside, Miriamele stood. "I will go see what has happened," she said in a whisper.

"Are you mad?" Jesa was shaking all over, her knees trembling and even the arms that held little Serasina so tightly feeling weak. "You cannot go!"

"I will do it," said Tiamak quietly. He held the small dagger out before him, but Jesa did not wait for him to reach the door. She turned and put the baby in the queen's arms, then pushed past Tiamak and toward the tent flap.

"No!" the queen whispered, but Jesa did not heed her. She pulled the flap just a little way open and peered out. She saw no movement outside the tent, so she nerved herself to slip through the opening.

A torch lay on the wet grass, still burning. Several vague and shadowy forms were sprawled beside it, and as Jesa crouched for a better look, she saw that they were three dead men. Two of them wore the livery of the queen's Erkynguard.

Frightened, she opened her mouth to call to Miriamele about what had happened, then a shadow fell over her as something stepped between her and the fallen torch. A hand curled in Jesa's hair and yanked her onto her feet so suddenly and powerfully that she did not cry out but only gasped in surprise.

A grinning face, the cheeks crisscrossed with deep scars, leaned in like something from a fever dream. The clansman growled something Jesa could not understand, then a great hand came up and struck her so hard she was flung to one side. For long moments she could make no sense of up or down.

"Soon," the grasslander said, then headed toward the queen's tent. In one hand he had an ax, in the other a long knife. Jesa tried to call out, to warn her companions inside, but her head has been so badly rattled that she could only make a croaking noise.

Not little Serasina! she thought helplessly. *He Who Always Steps on Sand, spare her!*

The Thrithings-man paused for a moment just outside the flap, listening. Satisfied, he shoved his way into the tent. In her numbed, helpless state Jesa expected to hear Miriamele or Tiamak cry out, but nothing came, only silence. Then something fell against the tent flap, which billowed outward as though it had suddenly come to life. A shape then untangled itself from the heavy canvas, took an unsteady step backward, and fell to the ground only a few paces from where Jesa lay. It was the scar-cheeked clansman, an arrow now jutting from his broad chest.

Then Jesa lost herself for a little while: the next thing she knew, she was back inside the tent with Tiamak crouching over her. "She is awake, Majesty," he announced. "She has a knot the size of a goose's egg on her head, but she is back with us." He returned his attention to Jesa. "How do you feel?"

She groaned, then abruptly struggled to sit up, although it made her head hurt so badly that she thought it would roll right off her shoulders. "The baby—!"

"She is here," said Miriamele. "Safe in my arms. I gave her to Tiamak, and he held her while I found my hunting bow." She shook her head. "I knew I had brought it with me, but it was down at the bottom of one of the chests." The queen smiled, but Jesa could see how pale she was. "And here I was afraid I wouldn't get to use it."

"That man—" said Jesa.

"Is quite dead," Tiamak told her. "I looked."

"And I still have several more arrows," said the queen. "Tiamak can take little Serasina again if I need to use them, so just lie there until you feel better. The night may be a long one."

And even as she spoke, a long, trembling call rose, echoing along the valley. Tiamak jumped. Then, as they all looked at each other in surprise, it sounded again.

"They are coming from the west," said Tiamak. "And they are coming on quickly. Who is it?"

"Let us hope it is not Unver Shan and a thousand more grasslanders, come to finish what he started," said Miriamele, her face grim. "I think we should move to a less conspicuous hiding-place, don't you? Jesa, take the baby in case I need both hands free to put an arrow in someone."

Fremur knew only a little of battle tactics, but he had followed Unver long enough to see that Pasevalles' breakout was a sloppy and ill-coordinated affair. The knot of enraged, *saya-vishaa*-addled mercenaries had begun to fray quickly, and instead of driving through the attenuated lines of the queen's besieging army, had broken apart to attack in several different spots along the riverbank. They had found success in a few places—a dozen tents or more were being consumed by flames, and fighting had spread widely around those yet unfired—but the advantage of surprise had dissipated.

"Let us keep riding," Fremur said to Unver as they sped down the slope, their horses' hooves muffled thunder on the wet grass. "He has no hold over you but the false threat of poison."

Unver was crouched low, the better to avoid stray arrows. "I have made promises," he called. "But you can ride on if you want."

"Promises?" Fremur almost pulled up, but with the Erkynlandish lines nearing fast, he knew he would not have another chance to speak before the Shan would reach the fighting. "Do you mean to kill the queen? Haven't we done enough to make the stone-dwellers angry?"

"'Ware!" cried Unver, and rode his horse against Fremur's, sending his mount stumbling to one side even as an invisible something sang past with a sound like an angry wasp.

"By the Piercer, how did you see that?"

"I saw the bowman."

The sound of a war-horn cracked the darkness, distant and wavering but very urgent. "What is that?" Fremur asked. "*Who* is that?"

"Pull up, pull up," cried Unver, staring into the darkness beyond the fires and the knots of struggling men. "There are riders coming down the valley. See the torches?"

And Fremur did, though he had missed them until now because of the nearer fires. A line of lights was winding rapidly down between two hills on the far side of the river, like a snake made of smoldering coals. Those battling in the camp and along the river had heard the horn too; the sound seemed to have draped the field in a fog of hesitation and confusion. Some of the struggling knots of men broke apart, but others fought with added urgency, wanting to finish their work before the horn-blowers arrived.

"Who is it? Who is coming?" Fremur asked, fighting to keep his voice even. The night sky seemed to have dropped down on them like a smothering blanket, and for a moment he felt certain he had reached the place where he was going to die. *Beneath the sky, at least—thank the spirits! But still unmarried,* was his next thought. *I am sorry, Hyara. My loyalty was greater than my sense.*

"I can see them now." Unver yanked back on the reins until his horse reared, kicking at air. "They are Rimmersmen, and I doubt they have come to help us. Turn!" he shouted. "Back to the castle, or we will be caught between the queen's anvil and this hammer." But to Fremur's astonishment, Unver did not pull his own horse around and head for the sally port. Instead, he rode at speed along the edges of the siege camp, shouting in the Thrithings tongue as loud as he could, *"It is a trap! Back to the castle! Turn and ride back, men, or die here!"*

It said much that even in the red haze of war, and with their blood boiling with Norn magicks, the sound and quality of Unver's voice did what he wanted it to do. Whether it was just his tone or the words themselves, the mercenaries began to fall back even as the first of the Rimmersmen swept through the camp and along the slope above the river; even Fremur could see that they hoped to catch the clansmen between themselves and the Erkynlanders. But the enemy had announced themselves too soon, and Unver's words had turned most of the mercenaries like jerking a string. Within moments the Shan had completed his circuit and was riding back up the slope with a hundred or more grasslanders following him.

Fremur joined the retreat. He had lost track of Unver, whom he prayed was somewhere in the crowd of men and straining horses rushing for the sally port. The queen's soldiers were pursuing them up the slope, shouting and loosing arrows, but the Erkynlanders did not have the grasslanders' long history of shooting from horseback, and though a few Thrithings-men fell beneath this near-invisible hail of iron-headed darts, the rest of the mercenaries reached the top of the slope and Winstowe's sally port, Fremur saw with almost as much foreboding as gratitude, still stood open.

I did not want to die surrounded by stone, he thought. *Ah, well. Where Unver goes, I follow. For a short while, though, I hoped I had found a happier end.*

49

Legacy

They could not hurry south fast enough for Simon, and though they set out even before first light touched the sky, they had a long way yet to travel, and the previous day's sun had set while the river valley was still far away. But now that they could use the roads of northern Erkynland—which, though not always in perfect repair, were much less dangerous than the Sithi's almost invisible forest tracks—Sludig's Rimmersmen and their companions could ride through darkness. At Simon's insistence, they did so.

Morning came, then a gray afternoon, but Simon would let them pause only briefly to water the horses before starting again. The sun set, but still they rode on, and it was past midnight when they entered the grassy meadowlands at the edge of the Fingerdale and saw the distant fires. At first Simon hoped they were celebratory bonfires, heralds of a victorious siege, but the noises of conflict quickly made it obvious that they had an unhappier tale to tell.

"What do you think has happened?" Sludig called to Simon. "Have the Shan and his Thrithings-men come to the traitor's aid?"

"Who knows? But they can't have reckoned with us. If we hurry, we can catch them by surprise," the king called back. "Send Breki along the slope at the base of the castle hill—you and I will follow the river to the camp. That way, if it is an attack by the grasslanders, we can keep Pasevalles' men from helping them."

Sludig conferred briefly with his lieutenant, Thane Breki, then the company split into two, with Simon's and Sludig's troop following the south bank of the river as it wound through the valley, while Breki led the others along the north bank. Simon fell back to where Morgan rode with Lillia on the saddle before him, accompanied by the odd, would-be knight, Jarnulf. The trolls, he could see, were some way behind on their rams, but the last thing Simon wanted was for Morgan and his followers to be in the fighting.

"You will not forgive me," he told his grandson when he was close enough to be heard, "but I leave you to watch over your sister. You have seen the fires in the camp. Those are tents on fire."

Morgan nodded. Despite their headlong pace, Lillia had fallen asleep behind the shield of her brother's arm. "And you, Grandfather? Pray tell me you will not do anything foolish, after we all thought we'd lost you."

"Not if I can help it, but I can scarcely ask Sludig's men to risk their lives for Erkynlanders if I hang back." He saw the look on Morgan's face. "I know, lad, I know—it is hard to be held out, but your time will come. And if this is another attack from out of the Thrithings, that time may come before the night is over. If that happens, send Lillia to Erchester with the trolls. But until then, keep her safe!" He turned to Jarnulf. "These are my precious heirs. Protect them and find a place in my heart. Fail and—"

"I will not fail, Majesty!" he cried. "I have pledged my life to your grandson!"

"I don't want your life," Simon called as he spurred away. "I want his life—and my granddaughter's—preserved."

To his frustration and unhappiness, even as he caught up with Sludig, Simon heard the horns of Breki's riders echoing through the hills.

"What is he doing?" he demanded. "Why make our approach known so early?"

"If you wanted him to creep up, you should have told him." Sludig looked almost pleased at the prospect of sword-blows and bloodshed. "But I guess he means to give heart to those under attack."

"Still," said Simon, but fell silent. The damage was done. Better to fix his mind on what was ahead. "You and your men continue along the edge of the camp," he told Sludig, "try to catch the bulk of the attackers between yourself and Breki. But give me a dozen riders and I will scour the camp. Someone is starting those fires, and we do not want them behind us when the real fighting starts."

As they reached the first lines of the siege-town, a shabby, close-packed assortment of wagons and campsites, Simon took his small troop and peeled off from the main company. Almost immediately upon entering the sprawling camp, they met a handful of grasslanders whose arms were weighted down with plunder. With the advantage of surprise, the mounted Rimmersmen cut them down without mercy. The mercenaries put up a poor fight: Simon thought they might even be drunk.

Simon was wearing Sludig's spare mail-shirt, which was much too large, and a helmet given to him by Ki'ushapo, which had belonged to a Sitha who had died at Tanakirú. The helm did not quite fit him right—his head did not have the fairy-shape—but at least it was snug across the cheeks and temples, so it did not swing and jounce as Sludig's coat of armor did. But it pressed so closely on the thick beard that now covered his chops that Simon could scarcely open his mouth without tasting his own whiskers.

As they neared the center of the camp where the fires were thickest, the haphazard aisles between the tents became increasingly full of smoke; before he knew it, Simon had inadvertently separated himself from the Rimmersmen accompanying him. Realizing that he was now alone, he pulled back on the reins and tilted his helmet back on his forehead to see better. A few score of paces ahead of him, a pair of large, armored figures were chasing a trio of smaller shapes through the forest of tents, pursuers and pursued all on foot. None of the camp's defenders were in sight, so Simon turned his horse to follow them.

As he caught up to the armored men, the people they were chasing abruptly turned and disappeared into the smoky vagueness between a row of tents, so Simon shouted to distract the pursuers. When one of the armored men turned to look back, Simon could see his telltale braided beard and tattoos. His dislike of the barbarians was still strong from the previous fight at Winstowe: he spurred his horse and pounded down on the man even as the clansman turned and raised his ax to defend himself. Simon drove his spear into the grasslander's chest even as the bearded man opened his mouth to shout a curse or a challenge.

The second grasslander had a spear of his own, and crouched low as Simon rode down on him, clearly hoping to drive the long weapon into the chest of Simon's mount. Instead of trying to pierce the man's body as he had the first grasslander, Simon seized his spear with both hands by the butt-end and swung it like a thresher's flail. The iron spearhead struck the man's helmet with a crash that could be heard even over the ruckus of nearby battle. The grasslander's legs flew out from under him and he went down like a straw doll, to lie unmoving in the muddy, torn grass, but the pike shivered and broke in Simon's hands with the blow. He cast it aside.

Now he gave the horse his heels, spurring after the grasslanders' would-be victims. As his mount dug around a collection of camp wagons, Simon saw them again a short distance ahead. They were still running, although not making very good time across the wetly treacherous ground.

"Hoy!" he cried after them, but they did not slow or even look back. All three of them were cloaked and hooded, and they all seemed small—were they women? For a moment he considered simply letting them go so he could turn and find Sludig's northmen once more. "Hoy!" he shouted again.

This time one the rearmost of the trio stopped and turned in the middle of the makeshift roadway. Simon saw a hint of face and a flash of pale hair in the hood, but before he could call out that he was an ally, the person he had been trying to save raised a bow and loosed an arrow at his face with commendable accuracy.

In truth, he did not realize that it was an arrow until it struck him a great buffet to the head, almost knocking him out of his saddle. Stunned and dizzy, he watched the three figures hurrying away. He pulled off the Sithi helm and saw that it now had a profound dint in the left cheek guard; he was suddenly very glad Ki'ushapo had insisted he wear it. Simon was about to turn away and let the ungrateful trio find their own way to safety when he heard a shriek of mixed anger and fear from the spot they had disappeared—a woman's voice, he was certain. He cursed to himself and headed his horse toward the cry.

As the smoke and night-mist cleared before him, he saw the same fleeing threesome, but this time they had encountered not a single mercenary, but four of them, all armed, but also quite drunk, by the staggering look of them. Even as he watched, one of the pursued stumbled and fell, hood flown back to reveal dark hair and feminine features. Simon saw that the woman on the ground held an infant in her arms and was desperately and pointlessly trying to shield the child with her own body from the bearded grasslander who was about to smash an ax down on them. Simon bellowed in rage and spurred forward, swinging his sword as he came. But instead of standing and fighting, the ax-wielding clansman looked up in shock at the armored and shouting horseman bearing down on him, then turned and ran.

The other three, though, were not so cowardly, or they might have been less sober: they all turned to face him. Simon did not want to give up his mounted position, but he did not want them to surround him and pull him down, either; for a moment, he hesitated. Then one of the fleeing trio that he seemed to have been, willy-nilly, elected to defend turned toward him, face twisted in a mixture of fear and pleading in the glare of a burning tent, and Simon experienced a moment of perfect astonishment.

"Tiamak?" he cried. "Merciful Rhiap, man, is that *you*?"

The small, dark-skinned man only stared back at him, and Simon remembered he was wearing a helmet that hid his face. The remaining grasslanders now began to move toward him, fanning out just as he had feared. His horse whirled in a tight semicircle, rearing and kicking each time one of the bearded men got too near.

The hooded archer who had tried to skewer Simon through the face seemed to have run out of arrows, because he dashed forward to help Tiamak, swinging his bow at the nearest clansman. The bow broke and flew apart against an armored shoulder; the clansman staggered back a couple of steps but seemed otherwise unharmed. While Simon was distracted by this foolish bravery, one of the other grasslanders managed to dive in and catch Simon's horse by its harness. The other two saw their chance and hurried toward him, crouching low as Simon tried to keep them at bay with his sword, which was beginning to seem a woefully inadequate weapon under the circumstances.

"Run!" he called to Tiamak and the other two, then turned just in time to swipe through the traces of his bridle, freeing his horse, which reared again, muddy hooves glinting wetly in the firelight. Simon only kept from falling by clinging to the horse's mane. The nearest mercenary abruptly straightened with a shout of surprise, then pitched forward onto his face, an arrow in his back.

Several more horsemen rode toward them through the tents, but Simon saw with relief that it was Sludig and young Henrig, along with at least one very capable archer.

"You grasslanders," Sludig shouted to the Thrithings-men as he approached. "Surrender if you want to live!"

The surviving mercenaries saw that they were now outnumbered, and that several of the newcomers had arrows nocked and aimed at their chests, so they dropped their weapons and knelt in the muddy grass. Several of Sludig's men slid from their saddles and bound the prisoners, then led them away. Another Rimmersmen went to help the woman with the baby as Simon dismounted and ran toward Tiamak.

"My friend, you live!" he cried. "Praise the Highest! Etan told me he thought it was so, but I could only hope it was true!"

Tiamak was staring at him with an expression Simon had never seen, a mixture of utter confusion and something else—fear? Could it be the helmet? Did they still not know he was a friend? He pulled it off and tossed it aside as he quick-stepped over the muddy ground.

"See! It is me!" he said. "Simon! The king! I cannot believe the good luck of finding you here." He laughed—a little wildly, he realized—and added, "although your friend here damned near put a shaft in my eye!"

Simon seized the little man in a fierce embrace—a one-sided embrace, because Tiamak was as limp as a raw sausage. Simon let go of him and took a step back in dismay. "What's wrong? Are you not happy to see me? Did you think me lost for good? Wait until I tell you—"

But the Wrannaman was not even looking at him. Instead, he had turned to his hooded comrade, the one still holding the broken bow, who let the pieces drop to the ground, seemingly as dumbfounded as Tiamak himself. Then, slowly, hands rose to the hood and pulled it back, and Simon saw a face he thought he would never see again in life. In the first moments his heart leaped so hard in his breast and pounded so fast that he thought he might quit the world again. "What is this?" he asked, staring, mouth dry. "What madness . . . ? Am I still alive?"

"Simon?" She looked at him, her beloved face full of a thousand things all at once—hope, despair, disbelief, confusion. "But you . . . they told me you—"

"You died," Simon said. "God in Heaven, is this another Norn trick?" His vision swam as tears filled his eyes. "I saw your poor, burned body."

"Oh," she said, pale as parchment but for the dirt on her cheek. "Blessed Usires, Blessed Ransomer—can this be true? That was not me. Oh, my love, I don't know how you still live when they said you were dead and gone. But it was not me you buried."

And then she ran to him, because he could not make his legs do what they were told. When she reached him, they grabbed at each other like drowning swimmers and held tightly, talking and weeping and laughing into each other's faces as the world spun on around them, unremembered and unmissed.

Pasevalles was as pale as what Fremur imagined one of the northern witch-fairies must look like, his face a stretched mask of rage as he cursed the grassland mercenaries who had made it back to Winstowe. Many of them were wounded, but their spites went untended as they huddled together in the courtyard behind the sally port, all staring at each other with the exhausted look of death in their eyes.

"Once the northmen came," Unver said, "there was nothing to be done."

"I am not interested in your mewling excuses." Pasevalles was like ice. "Broga! Round up the Count's household and bring them up onto the curtain wall by the west tower—and make certain you get all the women and children. I will meet you there. And you two—" he pointed at a pair of weary clansmen, "—go and hang a white parley flag from the battlements."

"Our bargaining position does not seem very strong," Unver pointed out. "We have just lost a battle and we are still surrounded."

"I want no advice from you," spat Pasevalles. "It was a mistake to put faith in even paid grasslanders. I can do nothing about that now, but I have still a few cards left to play. We will see how much stomach the queen has for the true fortunes of war."

The mood of the royal camp had swung from terror to celebration so swiftly that Jesa felt it almost like a flush of fever, a kind of sudden, hot madness. Only a short time earlier she had been awakened by the blood-freezing shouts of an attack and had feared for her life, and even more for the life of little Serasina. Now it felt like a Midsummer's Night fête, or her own people's Wind Festival. All the dead had now been hauled away, and thanks to the timely arrival of the Rimmersmen, only a few of the queen's Erkynlanders had been killed. Already some of the surviving soldiers had brought out a fife, a tabor-drum, and a stringed instrument called a Devan rebec, and had begun making loud and mostly tuneful music by the largest fire. Men were dancing with each other, deep-bearded Rimmersmen and Erkynlanders together; it was clear that someone had breached the liquor casks.

Jesa had only just managed to settle the baby back into a sort of half-sleep, so she stayed well away from the dancing for fear of waking her again. Serasina had grown plump under Jesa's careful stewardship, and even when asleep she was a heavy burden to carry, however beloved; when she woke and struggled to be set down, it was all Jesa could do to hang onto her.

It was King Simon whose return was most important, of course, especially to Queen Miriamele. The reunited pair wandered through the camp hand in hand like young lovers, weeping more than they talked, beaming and nodding at well-wishers, but Simon was not the only one thought lost who had appeared with the Rimmersmen. She saw Tiamak deep in excited conversation with a monk, and she had also witnessed Miriamele embracing a young man and a girl that someone said were her grandchildren. The queen's eyes had been full of glad tears, and the tall youth had also wept, but the little girl smiled so calmly at seeing her grandmother again that if someone had told Jesa that the child already knew of the queen's survival, she would have believed it.

"Serasina," she whispered, her face close to the child's, "this is a rare and magical night. You will not remember it, but I will tell you about it when you are older. I think it will be famous."

A small and petty part of her wondered what the return of all these folks thought lost or even dead would mean for her—surely the queen would not need the advice of a Wran-girl now that her husband and their lost heir had returned—but she pushed away the unworthy thought. More important, it seemed, was the fact that the castle called Winstowe still had not fallen, and that most of the traitor's hirelings had managed to survive the Rimmersmen's charge and retreat behind the castle walls. It was plain to see by the delirious faces and the exaltation of the Erkynlanders that the return of their king and young prince had heartened everyone here, but the siege had not been won yet, and Jesa felt certain that neither of them had brought any weapons to knock down stone walls. The criminal Pasevalles was still free.

The sound of furious merriment increased. Queen Miriamele and her husband had vanished, and though Jesa longed to return to the queen's tent and try to get Serasina back to sleep, she did not want to disturb the reunited couple she thought might have stolen off to its comparative privacy, so she wandered away from the music and shouting. The receding music put her in mind of a Wind Festival song, and she swayed as she walked and sang it softly into Serasina's ear.

Pretty Dawn is weeping—why is she weeping?
Oh, so sad! Just hear her cry!
She sits by a sky tree deep in the grove
The sky tree is wet and its trunk is so slippery
She cannot reach the top where the sunfruits grow
Oh, so sad! Just hear her cry!

Kirala, kirala, *how I hunger for* kirala*!*
Oh, she cries! So sad, she cries!
That is what Dawn cries, pretty, shy Dawn
My cruel stepmother, she will not let me eat them
She says if I climb then I will fall down
Oh, she cries! So sad, she cries!

Weep not, Dawn, for I will help you!
See my wings! Yes, wings have I!
So sings Fantail, many-colored Fantail
I will fly to the top and bring them down
Then you will feast on the bright, sweet sunfruit
See my wings! Yes, wings have I!

Even as Jesa sang, the sable sky began to lighten, warming at the eastern horizon as if Fantail had truly carried Dawn away to his nest in the top of the tree.

Behind her, the noises of revelry had begun to diminish a little, as when the first traces of morning in the Wran sent the spirits flying back to their daylight niches in trees and rocks and deep in hidden green pools.

When I was a child, I never imagined I would see the dawn arrive anywhere but Red Pig Lagoon, she thought. *But instead, I have flown across the world like my namesake, Green Honeybird herself.* The baby had finally sunk into true sleep, so Jesa began to retrace her steps toward the center of the camp. A few soldiers building up their fire nodded to her as she passed. She had walked often through the camp with the child during the long days of the siege, and many of the men now recognized her as the queen's helper.

She turned one last time to look back toward the castle at the top of the hill, wondering how even the king and queen of the High Throne would breach those great stone walls, and saw something moving on the ramparts, barely visible in the first unshuttering of morning. She stared as something slid down the wall just beneath the battlements, then spread, and was caught in a breeze that made it twist and flap. At first she could make no sense of it—it looked like someone had hung out their washing to dry, though the size of the immense white expanse of cloth would not have fit even in one of the monstrous linen chests of the Sancellan Mahistrevis itself. Then she realized what she was seeing and clutched Serasina close so she could hurry back across the camp.

But Jesa was not the only one to see it, and even before she reached the place where the people were gathering, she could hear them shouting to each other.

"A white flag—it's surrender!" a soldier cried.

"Don't be a fool," another said sharply. "But they are asking for parley—that's sure enough."

"Have we won, then?" someone else asked. "Is it over?"

They Who Watch and Shape, Jesa prayed as she hurried toward the queen's tent, *if you can hear me in this strange, cold country, please let it be so!*

Fremur could not help admiring the apparent iron resolve of Countess Marah, wife of the late Aglaf. Even as she and her young daughter and several ladies-in-waiting were driven up the stairs by Broga's men, she kept her composure and reassured the other women.

"They are surrounded, and their attack failed," the countess told them in a voice lowered so that only Fremur, at the back of the group, could hear. "Their only hope is surrender and mercy."

Her daughter Atara, scarcely out of childhood, could not manage such a brave face. "Will they hurt us, Mama?"

"Hush, darling," her mother said. "They would not dare. Here, dry your eyes. Do not give them the satisfaction of seeing those tears."

Fremur could not help but wonder how things had gone so wrong. Unver had beaten the stone-dwellers several times before the waxing of the Third Red

Moon and had all but killed the king of Erkynland in single combat. But he had thrown it all aside to come here—this dreadful stone tomb—simply to take the measure of the man Pasevalles.

Who has proved worse than any kinslaying clansman. Why, Unver? Why?

But as they emerged from the tower onto the open battlement, Unver was standing next to Pasevalles, so that question could not be asked.

"Ah," said the castle's current master. "The ladies are here. What of the children?"

"They are harder to move," said Broga, shamefaced. "They cry and throw themselves down. And you said we could not harm them—"

"Because we are bargaining here, you lout of a grasslander. If you are trading one of your horses for gold, would you whip the horse until it was bloody before reaching the market? Go and hurry them, Broomstraw, or you will be sorry." Pasevalles looked down at the grassy slope below the outwall. "Ah. And here she comes—Miriamele, the Queen of Arrogance herself."

"I thought you said this queen was an impostor," said Unver.

"I say many things. At other times, I keep my mouth shut and say nothing. You might learn from that example, barbarian." Pasevalles watched as a good-sized company, the leaders on horseback, proceeded from the camp beside the river toward the base of the slope. "And so our game continues."

Game? Fremur felt a sickened fury. *Dozens of our clansmen dead in the night's fighting and you call it a game?*

The besiegers stopped well before base of the buttressed outer wall. A dozen archers with longbows moved up from the company and stood in a line, arrows nocked. The queen and several others took up places behind this line of archers. The queen was bareheaded except for a circlet of silver, but she was wearing a mail coat, and a sword hung at her side, giving her a warlike look. She seemed able to pick Pasevalles out from the others crowding the battlement, because she fixed her eyes on him before calling up to him in a surprisingly loud voice.

"We have given you an honor with this parley that you in no wise deserve, traitor," she said. "But we know you hold subjects of ours prisoner in Winstowe. Speak, if you have something to say."

Fremur had never seen the queen before. Her flat tone and stern face reminded him a little of Unver's mother, but she had an air of calm self-possession that Vorzheva did not.

"I will not bandy words," Pasevalles called down. "I want safe passage for myself and my men into the High Thrithings. In return for that, I will surrender the castle and all the hostages to you."

Fremur expected the queen to turn and confer with the men who surrounded her, but instead she only shook her head. "Pasevalles, you disappoint me," she called. "Safe passage? After you murdered my daughter-in-law, and killed Bishop Boez, and only God knows how many others?" She raised her voice. "If you men surrender Pasevalles to me now, without conditions, I will let you go free—as long as you leave Erkynland."

"I feared you would take an overly sentimental approach to this negotiation, Your Majesty," answered Pasevalles. "I admire your attempt to turn these men against me, but I have already ensured their loyalty, and no bribe from you will change that. But you do not bargain well. You forgot to ask me what my surety is that you will meet my original price."

"You have little with which to bargain, Pasevalles. We have stopped up all your burrows. You will run out of food soon. You are surrounded."

"Bring the girl up here—the count's daughter," Pasevalles told Broga. When she had been dragged to his side, he turned back to the queen and her company. "Do you know Lady Atara, daughter of Count Aglaf and Countess Marah? I can arrange for you to meet her face-to-face if you like." And he shoved the trembling girl close to the parapet. Atara let out a cry of fear.

"Please, let her be," the countess implored him. "She is but a child! Take me instead!"

Pasevalles shook his head. "Does no one here understand commerce? You are an aging widow, my lady, though still reasonably comely. But this pure vessel—" he had Atara by the neck now and pushed her until she was leaning forward over the parapet, "will, I think, bring a better price. Why offer mutton when the market is better for spring lamb?"

Fremur looked at Unver. The Shan, who stood with folded arms next to Pasevalles and the crying girl, had an unreadable expression on his scarred face.

"What do you say, Your Majesty?" Pasevalles called down to the watching crowd. "I have more than a few of Winstowe's ladies here with me—ah, and several children as well, all noble-born! I would not insult you by offering to trade mere servants for my freedom."

Even from such a distance, Fremur could see that the queen's face had gone deathly pale. "You threaten to throw an innocent to her death? Hell will be too good for you, Pasevalles."

"Oh, without a doubt, but I will make do—when I get there." He looked around at Broga and the other clansmen as if he expected them to be enjoying the give and take, but they were all as bleakly expressionless as Unver. "But I am never hasty, Miriamele. Before I start throwing down these prisoners, I will let my men toy with them a bit, and let you listen to their play. And afterward I might even send Atara here and these other captives down not whole, but piecemeal."

"You murdering dog!" This angry cry came from a tall, bearded man standing beside the queen. "You will pay for everything you've done!"

"By the Tree, is that the old king I see?" Pasevalles sounded truly surprised. "King Simon—among the living? Hah! I should have left someone with better sense than Zhadu Split-Jaw to hand you over to the Norn Queen. Welladay, live to learn." He spread his arms. "So. We have had a merry morning, and in truth it is a pleasure to find you both still live, Miriamele, Simon. It would have been much less entertaining to have this conversation with confused old Duchess Nelda. But the time has come to seal our bargain. And to show you that I am in earnest, I will throw you down a token." He turned to the mercenaries. "Broga, come here and cut the girl's hand off. But then we must straightly bind up her wrist—I do not want her dying without earning her full value in trade."

Atara began to scream and struggle, but Pasevalles had a tight grip on the back of her neck and held her in place. "Broga?" he said. "I am waiting—!"

"You will wait longer still," said Unver abruptly, then turned and smashed his scarred fist into the side of Pasevalles' head. Caught utterly by surprise, Pasevalles lost his grip on the girl and sagged onto one knee. Unver caught Atara's arm and pulled her away from the battlement, then shoved her toward her mother; the girl ran into the countess's arms.

Pasevalles looked up, a crooked grin stretching his face. Blood showed between his teeth. "So," he said. "I thought from your frequent disapproving looks that you had the smell of a moralist, Sanver. Hurting girl-children a bit much for your primitive code, is it? Tell that to all the little ones slaughtered by your raids along the borders of Nabban." Rubbing his jaw, he got unsteadily to his feet just beyond Unver's reach. "But though your hypocrisy does not bother me, striking me does. Broomstraw and the rest of you men, kill this fool."

A long moment went by, even as Fremur's hand dropped to his hilt, ready to defend his Shan—but nothing happened.

"Broga!" Pasevalles snarled. "Step up, you coward. There are a dozen of you and only one of him."

"Broga is mine," said Unver calmly. "After my warning, he avoided your poison. He serves me, not you. In truth, Broomstraw and I recognized each other when I first came to Winstowe. Long ago, we carried out some of those raids you spoke of together."

Pasevalles spat blood onto the stone. "What nonsense are you talking?"

"He is the Shan," said Broga in a hoarse voice. "The spirits chose him to lead us. He is Unver, the Shan of all the grasslands."

On the last word, Unver moved with astonishing swiftness, lunging forward to seize Pasevalles before he could move and locking an arm around his neck. An instant later, his forearm still squeezing his enemy's throat, the Shan pushed Pasevalles belly-first against the top of the parapet. "I am Unver, Shan of the Thrithings," he bellowed at the gaping faces below. "You bargain with me now."

"Let go of me, traitor!" Pasevalles squirmed desperately but could not escape the taller man's iron grasp.

Fremur saw the prisoner's hands reach up behind Unver's head, and at first thought Pasevalles was going to scratch at the Shan or strike him, but then one hand went to the other sleeve and closed on something hidden there.

"A knife!" Fremur cried, leaping forward. He caught Pasevalles' wrist just as he withdrew the dagger from his cuff, then twisted until he heard something pop. Pasevalles uttered a sharp cry of pain and let the blade fall.

Unver, still holding his captive in a throttling grip, looked down at the short, slim knife. "Poisoned, too, or I miss my guess. Do not touch it." He shoved Pasevalles back against the parapet so hard that Fremur heard the man gasp out air, and perhaps even the crack of a rib breaking. "Speak to me," Unver called down to the besiegers. "What is your enemy worth to you? I want the same thing he did, but I do not threaten women and children. If you let my men return with me to our lands, I will give you your traitor. What say you, Queen Miriamele and King Simon?"

"There is no need for this," the king shouted. "I know you are an honorable man, whether you go by Deornoth or Unver. You could have killed me on this very field when I bared my breast to you, but you did not. Your enemy is Pasevalles, not us."

"He is *your* enemy. You want revenge," said Unver. "I only want freedom for my clansmen. They have been trapped here and many have died because of Pasevalles' lies."

"I will kill you!" hissed his prisoner, squirming against the parapet. "All of you!"

"Pasevalles is more your enemy than you even know," called Miriamele. "Look! Do you see this man?" She gestured and a cloaked figure was urged forward. The queen lifted away his hood. "Do you recognize him?"

Unver shook his head. "No. What is the point of this?"

Pasevalles struggled and cursed with new energy. The Shan gave him another brutal shove against the battlement to silence him.

"The point is that this is your father, Prince Josua of Erkynland," the king cried. "Pasevalles tried to kill him, and thought he had. He bragged about it to me when I was his captive. Twenty years ago, he met Josua on the way to the Hayholt and clubbed him with a stone, then left him for dead—but your father did not die. His wits are confused, but I swear this is Josua himself. We found him wandering in the north."

"I can barely see him," cried Unver, but his voice sounded strange. "How can I trust that it is him?"

"It is him," said a new voice. "It is our father, Deor. I swear it is so."

A woman had stepped up to stand beside the muddled-looking older man.

"Derra?" Fremur had never seen Unver looking so off-balance. "You too?"

"This is our father, Deor. And I think you know it is true. Hand the traitor over to the king and queen and come down."

Unver turned Pasevalles around, remorseless as a slowly grinding wheel, until he could stare into his wide, frightened eyes. "You are worse than I ever guessed," the Shan said, and spat in the prisoner's face. "Your wretched life is mine now." He wrapped one hand around Pasevalles' neck and grabbed his sword belt with the other; then, with a crack of straining muscles, Unver heaved him up above his head. Pasevalles let out a thin shriek of terror and scratched desperately at Unver's hands, but Unver held him high in the air, though his strong arms trembled. "You want him in chains!" Unver shouted down to the king and queen. "But I want him dead. I came here because this man and his poison killed Rudur, making me Shan of all the grasslands. I had to know who it was who had done the spirits' work. And I learned."

"Bring him down, Unver Shan," cried King Simon. "I promise he will get the justice he deserves!"

"You want him in chains," Unver repeated. "But I want him dead. So we will let the spirits decide." And with that, he flung his struggling prisoner out into the empty air beyond the battlement. Screeching and flailing, Pasevalles plummeted out of sight, and Fremur was too far from the edge to see where he fell, but the dwindling cry ended suddenly.

At the base of the wall, everyone stared in stunned silence until Miriamele waved to the king and their royal guards and started up the slope. "Follow me."

"What do you mean?" Simon said. "We must work something out with Unver. The siege is not ended."

"I don't care about the siege," said Miriamele. "I want to see if Pasevalles still lives."

"He can't be alive after such a fall."

"We'll find out." She continued up the slope. Several startled Erkynguards and Simon hurried to catch up.

"Miri, what are you going to do?" he asked.

But his wife did not answer, and Simon could only climb after her through the wet grass.

Pasevalles lay broken, limbs sprawled at angles that were painful even to contemplate. His eyes were open. As Miriamele reached him and stood over him, his gaze slowly turned toward her.

"Not gone yet?" she said. "Good. You tried to destroy my family, after we had taken you in and given you trust and kindness and gold. You stole from us and plotted against us. But you failed. Failed, do you hear?"

The broken shape on the ground tried to speak, but though his lips moved, only a red froth emerged.

"You tried to kill me, but instead only murdered blameless Duchess Canthia of Nabban—but her child still lives. The duke's line survives." She leaned a little closer. "And you tried to kill my husband, the king—but here he stands. And both our grandchildren are alive, too. Even Prince Josua survived your cowardly attack all those years ago, and Josua's son is the one who flung you down, like the Adversary himself cast from the firmament. Do you hear me, Pasevalles, you wretched snake? You have failed at everything you tried to do. Most of your evil is already undone."

The dying man was having trouble fixing his eyes on her, but the queen was not satisfied. She got down on her knees. Simon put his hand on her shoulder. "He's going, my love. Don't waste any more breath on this beast."

"And you will be no more than a beast after death, either, traitor," she said, close enough to the dying man's face that he could see only her. "Do you think people will whisper of you afterward? Of the dangerous traitor Pasevalles, who nearly brought down the High Throne? No. No, we will bury you in the forest here at Winstowe, and the hole will have no marker—no holy Tree, not even a stone, nothing to preserve your name. Then we will scratch your marks and your records from every ledger. No one will remember you—not even as a failure. Do you hear me, Pasevalles? You are nothing now. It will be as if your miserable life never happened."

The dying man's eyes stopped following her. At last, she sat up, breathing hard, as though she had run a distance. "By God, he went too easily after all his crimes," she said. "I wish I could have given him back the pain he has given us."

"Still," said Simon as he helped her to stand. "I believe you made your feelings plain to him at the end." He shook his head. "I would not want you for an enemy, wife."

"Then never leave me again," she said.

He guided her back down the slope, leaving the broken thing behind them. "I swear it on all that is holy. And I would say the same to you." He was suddenly teary-eyed. "Never leave me again, Miri."

The queen was crying too, even as their friends and family and a bounding white she-wolf surged forward to surround them. She held his hand tightly, and he squeezed back. "With God's blessing, dear Simon," she promised, "I never will."

50

In Moderation

"I don't know how I can start over, Miri."

"Start over? What do you mean, my love?"

"I thought the worst thing that could ever happen had happened. I thought you were dead. I *saw* you dead—and it was . . ."

"I know. Don't talk about it. When I think of poor Canthia—"

"But now I have to start again. To be afraid all over again. Because, what if I lose you . . . again?"

"Hah! Would you be happier if you still thought I was dead, husband?"

"No! God's Mercy, no! My damnable words are all muddled—and you are being difficult on purpose. Do you truly not know what I mean?"

"I am teasing you a bit, yes, but only because it all hurts so much. I thought I had lost you too, remember. *My* worst fear. But I am a queen. I did what I had to, day after horrible day, but I was empty inside. And now here you are, with your arms around me, breathing wine fumes on my cheek. No, don't let go. Here I am, and here you are, and this is what we have. And I know as well as you do that it could be taken away from us again."

"We are mortal. It *will* be taken away from us again someday."

"But we have already survived that terrible loss once, Simon. We know we are strong enough. And perhaps we will be lucky. Perhaps we will both be killed at the same moment."

"That is not much of a jest, Miri."

"It was not meant to be one. Oh, Simon, only God can decide what happens. And we are promised to be with each other again even after we leave this life and this world."

"I thought I believed that. Now I am not so certain."

"Don't you dare! Look at what we have been given—another chance! Both alive! And after everything that's happened, surely you can't doubt that Heaven is real."

"I was dead, you know. More or less. I told you, after I fought Deor . . . Unver at Winstowe. I was certain he'd killed me. And then I met Likimeya on the Dream-Road, and . . . well, I had never imagined it would be like that. It shook me, Miri. And Geloë, who simply decided not to die . . . I do not know what I believe now."

"Believe in this. Believe in us."

"When I can hold you this way, I can believe."

"Then don't let go. Don't ever let go. Now kiss me again. Of all the things I mourned, I should have mourned losing this most of all—just being held. Just kissing you. Because in some ways, this is the best of all—better than thrones, better than anything."

"Oh, my love. How did a kitchen-boy like me ever happen to end up with someone like you?"

"Some kitchen-boys are just lucky, it seems. Now be quiet and do that again."

By royal decree, the rest of the grassland mercenaries remained under guard in Winstowe Castle until negotiations were completed. After all the hostages from Aglaf's household had been set free, Unver Shan had been allowed out to meet with the king and queen in their great tent, accompanied only by his trusted lieutenant, a youthful-looking thane named Fremur. From what Tiamak could tell, though, the other Thrithings-men would likely be allowed to return to the grasslands under Unver's promise that they would never again take up arms against Erkynland. Then, after the treaty was completed, the Shan's sister and father would be brought to him. Simon had wanted to bring them all together immediately, but Queen Miriamele—practical as always—had insisted that the formal surrender be agreed first.

But as the principals bargained, Tiamak suddenly remembered that Vorzheva was being held under house arrest here in the encampment. He left Etan to write down what the High Throne and the Shan of the Thrithings agreed, then hastened off to where she was being held, fast as his game leg could carry him.

Tiamak had gained enough trust from Captain Kenrick's men during the siege that Vorzheva's guards quickly released her to him. As he led her back across the sprawling camp, he did his best to explain everything that had happened. Vorzheva remained silent, showing barely a hint of her feelings, but he could tell by how she began to walk faster that she was not unmoved by his words.

When they reached the royal tent, they found Prince Josua sitting on a stool and Unver kneeling before him, holding his father's hand in both of his. His sister Derra stood silently behind him. Derra had been the first to recognize Josua, Tiamak had been told, and he could not guess what she must be feeling.

As Tiamak announced Lady Vorzheva, a look passed between mother and daughter, but it was too subtle for him to unpuzzle. Then Vorzheva moved swiftly to stand beside Unver. She put a hand on his shoulder—the Shan looked up in surprise—but it was Josua's weathered face and mild gray eyes that held her stare. Vorzheva's hard, careful expression lost its foundation; she suddenly leaned forward and gently put her hands on Josua's head, feeling the place where his skull had been broken and then had knit again.

"You," she said. "It truly is you." Tears ran down her cheeks and she did not wipe them away. "And you did not leave me of your own choice? Is that true?"

Josua stared up at her, then gently took her hands. "I . . . know you, I think," he said slowly. "You were my beloved. You were . . . Vorzheva?"

Now tears came to her eyes and spilled down her face. "I thought you were dead or had left me!" she cried. "You should not have gone away so long! Why is your God so cruel?"

"*There is no answer greater than to keep faith,*" Josua said as if by rote, then looked at her again with a near-smile. "That is what the prophet tells us."

"A curse on your prophets!" Vorzheva fell to her knees, still weeping helplessly, and laid her head in his lap. Josua looked down as he stroked her hair.

"Vorzheva," he said again. It sounded like a benediction.

Their daughter now took Unver Shan by the hand and led him out of the tent. The one called Fremur quickly followed but stayed a respectful distance behind them as brother and sister, born in the same hour but so long separated, walked and talked together.

Tiamak and Kenrick made certain that the heralds were sent out well before the royal company as they left the Fingerdales and began to make their way back to Erchester. With every league they traveled, more people came out to see them, some wondering fearfully who their new masters would be, and others, who had better understood the heralds, wanting to be certain the declarations were true. Simon and Miriamele had traveled the country often in their younger years, so they were well known and quickly recognized. The crowds gathering along the great road soon became a sort of walking fairground, and many who came to cheer followed the company all the way home, camping in a great throng around the royal party at each halt. When the king and queen finally marched up Main Row into Market Square, it was at the head of a roaring, almost delirious throng, and the city descended into festival madness.

Morgan stood atop Erchester's eastern wall, gazing out at the ruined sprawl of the Hayholt, its stones scorched and tumbled. Only a few of the castle's best-known features had survived. Holy Tree Tower remained, though its base was blackened and its guardhouse had collapsed. The Nearulagh Gate and its famous carvings had also survived the burning, though not entirely unscathed. And to Morgan's dismay, Hjeldin's Tower, the Red Priest's former lair, still squatted near the castle's center, streaked with black soot but otherwise unharmed. *God save us,* Morgan thought, *can nothing destroy that lump of horror?* Tiamak had told him of their struggle beneath the tower with the horrid thing that claimed to be Pryrates' mother, so Morgan now knew what had been lurking there the night he and Snenneq had climbed to its roof.

He briefly considered exploring the Hayholt's grounds to see what else might remain, but he did not have the heart for it. His home, at least the home that had been, was gone forever. Something else might rise here—Morgan half-hoped it would—but it could not be the same.

Nothing ever lasts, he thought. *Every day is new. Each sunset pushes another day into the past, out of reach except in memory.*

The thought did not ease the sudden ache of loneliness, so he climbed down from the wall and went to look for Qina and Little Snenneq.

Porto found his friend in the makeshift barracks set up in a warehouse near Market Square. Levias struggled to sit up on his pallet, arms spread wide.

"You!" Levias cried. "Oh, my friend, I cannot tell you how I worried about you!"

"Not half so much as I worried about me," said Porto, laughing.

"God is good, so good!" said Levias. "Come, kneel with me and together we will thank our Lord for your safe return."

"Is your wound healed enough to be crawling around on a cold floor?" asked Porto, but Levias had already struggled out of bed, so the tall old knight gingerly lowered himself to kneel beside him.

When Levias had finished his prayer of thanksgiving, he climbed carefully back onto his straw-stuffed pallet. "I do not know where we will put you, good Porto, but I am certain we can find a spare bed. It is a shame we have nothing better for one who has served so long—"

"But that is what I came to tell you," Porto said. "The king and queen have very kindly rewarded me for my service. I have been given a little gold, a comfortable house, lands in Hewenshire, and a herd of fine Thrithings horses that belonged to the traitor Pasevalles." He grinned. "Queen Miriamele told me, 'It is not the animals' fault that their master was a villain,' and commended them to my care. I expect they will be just the sort of crop whose by-blows I can sell to the Erkynguard in years to come, providing an income for my declining years."

Levias was clearly caught by surprise. "Oh! Well, that is splendid news, Porto, and I am most happy for you!" He hesitated. "But Hewenshire—that is a long way from here. I will miss talking with you about theology and other things. I hope you will continue to say your prayers—"

"You are a fool, my friend," said Porto. "A dear fool, but a fool. I did not come to tell you that I am leaving you behind, I came to ask you if you will go with me. I am certain that you have honors coming to you too for all you did on behalf of the High Throne, so if you say yes, we will be bachelor knights together. What say you?"

Levias sat up straight. "Truly?"

"Of course," said Porto, laughing. "Long ago, as you know, I lost a friend I had sworn to protect. I would not let that happen again. We will be rustic esquires, raising our herds."

"But I cannot do much—my wounds—" Levias began.

"I have gold, remember? We will hire help. Herders and grooms, a cook, and certainly a butler, because if I must live in the country, away from the excitement of the town, I must at least have wine."

"God does not want you to be a drunkard, Porto."

"No, but I think God will not mind if I begin drinking a better quality of spirits—still in moderation, of course."

"Still in moderation," Levias agreed, smiling now.

"Speaking of which," said Porto, "I have a flask here that Prince Morgan gave me—a present from his trollish friends. It contains a Qanuc liquor called *kangkang,* which Morgan says he no longer drinks, but we might enjoy. Shall we raise a toast to our future in the countryside?" He held up the flask and took a swallow. When he had finished wheezing, he passed it to Levias.

"To rustic gentlemen!" his friend said. "Long may we live!"

"Long may we live," Porto echoed. "Or if not long, at least happily."

This cathedral has seen many things, Simon thought. *But I'd wager it never saw anything quite like this.*

"*This*" was the spectacle of the accolades of knighthood being bestowed on Prince Morgan's protectors, attended by most of Erchester's remaining nobles and leading citizens. Jarnulf and the two younger trolls knelt before the altar, and as Miriamele stood by—*probably worrying I'll cut myself with the sword,* Simon thought—he asked, "Who comes before me?"

Morgan stepped forward. "One who would be made a knight, Majesty—your servant and God's. He is Gilhedur of White Snail Castle, and he has—"

"Your pardon, Prince Morgan."

Morgan turned to the kneeling man, a little startled. "Yes?"

"Forgive me, Highness, but I have decided to keep the name Jarnulf." He shrugged. "I'll explain if you wish—"

"No need," said Morgan quickly. "Jarnulf it is." He lifted his voice once more. "He is Jarnulf of White Snail Castle, and he has done the High Throne great service."

Simon was amused. "Who speaks for him and swears that this is true?"

"I am Morgan, prince of Erkynland and heir to the High Throne, and I swear that this is true."

"And has Jarnulf kept his vigil, and been shriven?"

"He has."

More ritual questions and answers followed; when they were finished,

Simon touched the flat of his sword to each of the kneeling man's shoulders. "I dub thee Sir Jarnulf, now a knight of Erkynland." Jarnulf remained on his knees—Simon could see that he was trembling—as Miriamele took the sword from her husband and moved to stand before Little Snenneq. The same questions were asked, with Morgan responding for his friend, until the queen asked if the troll was shriven. Before Morgan could reply, Snenneq spoke up. "I have a concern, Majesties, that I must share. We Qanuc do not follow the same faith as you here, and it seems to me that to be shriven would mean—"

Simon groaned quietly and heard Binabik do the same. "Peace," Simon said. "Did a priest bless you?"

"One of your Aedonite priests, yes, but—" Little Snenneq began, ignoring Qina as she vigorously applied her elbow to his side.

"If he splashed you with enough holy water, then I'd say you're shriven," the king decided. "Go on, please, Queen Miriamele. And swiftly, before he thinks of something else to wonder about."

When an abashed Snenneq had received his accolade, Simon took the sword back and stood over Qina.

"Who comes before me?" he asked.

Morgan stood once more. "One who would be made a knight, Majesty—your servant and God's. She is Qina of Mintahoq, daughter of Sisqinanamook and Binbinaqegabenik, and she has done the High Throne great service."

This last candidate did not seem interested in quibbling about religious details, so Simon gratefully completed the ceremony. "Then I dub thee Lady Qina, a knight of Erkynland."

"*Sir* Lady Qina," she piped up. "Please same as men."

"I dub thee Sir Lady Qina," Simon corrected himself. "And may our Ransomer, Usires Aedon, watch over all of you. God save Erkynland!"

The celebration that followed the granting of accolades was undoubtedly less joyful than it might have been, since the Hayholt's ruins were in plain sight atop the hill just beyond the city walls, but Morgan did not have much stomach for festivities in any case.

All four floors of the city's largest guild hall were filled with merrymakers, but the king and queen had set up court in the main hall on the second floor, and that was where Morgan wandered, at loose ends. A part of him missed the days when he would have been half-drunk already, with no greater concern than to finish the job, but he had learned that his current worries could not be assuaged or even forgotten for long merely by the application of strong drink.

Binabik and Sisqi were in one corner of the broad room, allowing the children of the merchants and city officials to pet and stroke Vaqana, albeit under strict trollish supervision. The wolf seemed to enjoy it, and lay on her side with tongue lolling, though Morgan suspected the great beast might have been even happier out in the Kynswood, killing squirrels. *We all have our duty to do, wolf,* he told her silently. *You, me, all of us.*

Unable to settle, he made his way at last to where the king and queen sat on their high-backed chairs, holding hands as they watched the proceedings. Morgan had no one's hand to hold except Lillia's, and his little sister was currently part of the crowd around the white wolf. And though the tale of his grandmother's death had turned out to be untrue, that of his own mother's death had not, and that was another heaviness on his heart. His mother Idela had not always been the most demonstrative or dutiful parent, but Morgan had never doubted that she loved him, and he had particularly clung to that certainty after the terrible things his father John Josua had said about Lillia during his last month of life.

He wanted my sister to be born dead. Morgan watched Lillia laughing as she buried her face in Vaqana's snowy belly-fur. *How could I mourn him, knowing that? Did he hate my mother too? And me?*

These thoughts felt poisonous, and Morgan again considered the idea of getting very drunk. Without Nezeru, everything seemed foolish, even pointless. How had this happened to him? Several young women had wept in his presence over the years because he did not love them, and several more had likely done it in his absence. Yet here he was, crippled in the heart and consumed by thoughts of the one woman—not even a true woman, but a half-fairy—who had made it very clear she would do splendidly without him.

Unable to find peace, and with the companions of earlier festivities either dead or, like Porto, more or less reformed, Morgan sighed and retreated to where the king and queen sat. His other grandfather, Duke Osric, had been seated at the king's right hand, but was making his farewells.

"Not quite back to my old self yet, curse this hole in my chest, but it's better every day." Osric bent slowly and carefully to kiss the queen's hand. "It is nothing but a miracle that you are with us again, Majesty."

"And I am happier than I can tell to find you alive too, Your Grace," she said. "Please tell dear Nelda that I send my love and regard."

"You know how her feet give her problems. 'If I can't dance, I'm not going,' she told me. 'Ask Queen Miriamele to come see me, if she'll be so good.' That's what she said, and I hope no offense given, Majesty."

The queen smiled. "Never, my lord duke. Tell her I will come to visit her within the sennight."

As Osric departed, Morgan sat down in the spot he had just vacated. "Majesties," he said.

"You don't look like someone who has just had his first three knights made," said the king.

"I don't feel very festive, I suppose."

"Still pining over the Hikeda'ya girl?"

Morgan did not answer: it seemed obvious and also pointless.

"Look around, dear," his grandmother told him. "Here is a hall full of lovely young women, many of whom are almost suitable for you. For instance, there goes Abigal, the Count of Torickshire's daughter, just for the sake of discussion. She has a beautiful singing voice—I have heard it—and can ride as well as any man, too, they say."

He nodded. Lady Abigal was certainly pretty, and he was willing to believe she was accomplished, but she could have been her father for all Morgan cared. "I fear I am not much in the mind for romance, Majesty. In truth, I would like to ask you two a question of statecraft instead."

"Go ahead, lad," said his grandfather. "I am glad to see you taking an interest."

Morgan took a breath, suddenly worried about questioning his grandparents' judgement. "Why did you let Unver go? He and his men killed many Erkynlanders during those battles. And yet you let him take his mercenaries—little better than bandits—and ride back to the Thrithings as if nothing had happened."

"They may have been mercenaries," said the king, "but Unver did not hire them—Pasevalles did, with the gold he stole from us. Beside, what else could we do? Unver is the son of Miri's uncle, Prince Josua—one of my oldest friends—and since we have now found Josua alive although injured, someone must take care of him. In the Thrithings, he will have his wife, daughter, and son. He will be part of a family, safe and protected. We could have insisted they bring him here to Erchester, but neither your grandmother nor I believed that was the right thing to do."

"But Unver killed people! Your subjects!"

"It is not so simple, Morgan," his grandmother said. "The things that a monarch must decide seldom are."

"Unver felt he had a legitimate reason to go to war," the king explained. "He believed he had been lied to and cheated by the High Throne. As it turned out, it was likely more of Pasevalles' work, and meant to cause the trouble it did—God help us, that man was a blight on all he touched!—but Unver could not know that. And there is also the hard fact that Unver is a king in his own right."

"King of the grasslands. Of barbarian tribesmen."

"They are still people, Morgan," said the queen. "And they are *his* people." She leaned over and took her grandson's hand. "Josua's son could have done far more damage when he invaded Erkynland. We know that he held his men back when they would have razed the whole countryside, burning towns and castles alike."

"And those barbarians, as you call them, will be important in the years to come," Simon added. "They are a rising nation—split into squabbling tribes now, but Unver is a very clever fellow, and I suspect he will make them more than they have been. You will want to deal very carefully with him—fairly and honorably, but without any illusions, either. His father Josua never wanted power and hated the idea of having to rule others. But Unver is not like his father. I do not think he wants power for its own sake, but he will do what he thinks best to protect his people. You will have to be careful—"

"You keep saying *I* will have to deal with him, *I* will have to be careful."

"Because someday, God willing, you will be the king of Erkynland, and the responsibility will be yours."

Morgan fell silent. Musicians struck up a spritely tune on the far side of the hall, and many in the crowded room began to move toward them, cheering and spinning around even before they had joined the dance.

"Ah," said Simon, "but it is good to see happy people again!"

"I do not think I am wise enough ever to be king," Morgan said. "I do not know enough. I do not understand the world."

"What do you mean?" the queen asked. "You have just returned from seeing quite a bit of it."

"I was a young fool before the mission to seek out the Sithi, as you told me many times, Grandmother. And you were right—I know that now. Merciful God, do I know it! I have seen a little bit of the world since then, mostly trees, and fairy-folk who wanted to murder me, but it opened my eyes as often as it almost killed me. The world is so much bigger and more confounding than I ever guessed. How can any single person hope to know enough to rule justly?"

The queen nodded. "Asking that question is the first step in your true apprenticeship."

"But this is not learning how to make a glove, Majesty," Morgan said. "If that craft is learned poorly, only some leather is spoiled. But these are the lives of our people at risk. I am not ready to be a king. I may not ever be ready." A sudden memory struck him, making his skin tingle: Was this what Little Snenneq's casting of the knuckle bones had meant to tell him, all those months ago, on that moonlit peak in Rimmersgard? *"Something you have long expected will not come to you,"* the troll said, puzzling over how the bones had fallen. *"Or will come, perhaps, but in much different form than you had been thinking."*

Is that what God or fate has always had in store for me? Morgan wondered. *To be a prince but not a monarch?* He had a sudden vision of himself leaving his family behind and striking out into the wilderness to find Nezeru, then following her wherever she went, even to Nakkiga itself.

Hjeldin's Tower still stands, he thought. *The poison still lurks in the ground. If we rebuild, we build on top of old sins. My mother is dead. My father grew to despise his family even before the sickness took him—why else would he have said that about Lillia, innocent and unborn?*

So many contradictory thoughts ranged through Morgan's head that he could no longer sit and make civil talk with his grandparents. He stood up, made his excuses, and left them looking at each other in concern.

"Are the fortunes you tell with the knuckle bones always right?" he asked Little Snenneq.

Snenneq watched as the children of nobles and servants alike made free with

Vaqana's snowy pelt and marveled at the wolf's great, grinning jaws. "Friend Morgan, it is not a matter of right against wrong." Snenneq shook his head. "You might as well ask, 'Is the sky always right?' Because just like clouds in the sky and the feel and smell of the wind, sometimes the bones show things that are coming and cannot be avoided. Other times they serve only as a warning of what might be." He gave the prince a quizzical look. "Something troubles you, that I can see. I am your knight, my friend, sworn to your service. Tell me and I will do my best to help."

"Also me," said Qina, who had been listening. "Knight too."

But Morgan could not make sense out of his own confused ideas. "It's not important," he said. "What will you two do now? Will you stay or go back to Yiqanuc?"

"We are sworn to your knighthood!" said Snenneq, offended. "But we must return to Mintahoq Mountain, or else our nuptial journey will remain unfinished, and we cannot marry. We would be forever *nukapik* and never *nukapo*."

"Of course," Morgan said. "But after that?"

"We will never go long without seeing you, my friend," Snenneq assured him. "I have told you that I knew from the first that we were destined to be famous friends. But do not worry—Qina and I will not complete our journey home for some while. Her parents will remain in this city of Erchester until it is time to go north to the launching of the *Witchwood Crown* in Tanakirú. Then we will continue onward to meet our fellow Qanuc at Blue Mud Lake, and at the end of summer we will continue to Mintahoq." He smiled broadly. "You should come with us, Morgan. It will be a rare homecoming. We will feast! Ptarmigan will be thawed and prepared, ice-thistles boiled to a delectable savor, and you shall be given the finest delicacies, such as the livers of snow-bears."

"Eat only bears that try us to kill," said Qina hurriedly. "Not all bears."

"It sounds . . . lovely," said Morgan, trying hard to sound convincing. "But I don't know what I'm doing yet. I might be gone."

"Gone?" said Qina. "Gone means go away?"

"I'm not certain. My head is full of thoughts." Morgan sighed. "It's hard to explain."

"You will not leave your family," said Snenneq with invincible certainty. "They need you. You are to be king one day!"

"There's always Lillia," he said, and felt a tap on his back. He was startled to find that his sister had appeared behind him—she must have come up very quietly.

"You were talking about me," she said. "I heard you."

He wasn't certain he wanted to share his thoughts with his sister. She was so young; she should be protected from the worries of her elders. "I just said that I am not the only heir to the High Throne. You're here too."

"But you will be the last king of Osten Ard, Morgan," she said, her face serious and solemn. Then she laughed. "You look so surprised!"

Before he could ask Lillia what she meant by this strange pronouncement, one of the other children called her to come join a game, and she turned without another word and skipped off across the hall.

"The last king?" He shook his head. "What on earth could that mean?"

"She seems thoughtful beyond her years," said Little Snenneq. "The other day, she told me she believed Qina and I would have two children, born together."

"Swans," said Qina proudly.

"I think the word is 'twins,' my heart," Snenneq advised her gently.

"Twins, swans, same," she said with a shrug. "Means two babies."

51

In Badger Street

As winter courteously began to make way for spring, and with the Marris-month change in weather, Sludig announced that he and his Rimmersmen would ride back north.

"You and Miriamele seem to have things in hand," he told Simon as they said their farewells. "And we have been away from our homes too long. Time for planting, and for calves to be born."

Simon smiled. "I forgot you are a cattle-breeder now. Go with our blessing, my friend, and give all thanks to Duke Grimbrand for sending you to us. Things might have gone much worse without you, especially at Winstowe."

Sludig waved away this claim. "I suspect you would have managed without our help, O King. You and your wife seem to have the hand of Heaven over you."

Simon traced the Tree against his breast. "I hope that is true. Certainly, we have been through much."

"And do not forget to give our love and regards to your wife Alva as well," said the queen. "In fact, take her this, from me." She stood on tiptoe to place a kiss on Sludig's whiskery cheek.

"I shall indeed, Majesty," he said. "I hope it will not be long until we all see each other again. Now, where is my boy Henrig? He was meant to find that damned troll and his troll-wife, because I will not depart without their blessing."

"Here, you *croohok* scoundrel!" called Binabik. As he and Sisqi said their goodbyes to the Rimmersmen, Simon thought he saw a tear in Binabik's eye. Soon enough, Sludig's company set off across Market Square, waving their farewells, hooves clopping on the cobbles as they headed for Erchester's northern gate. Many who had gathered to watch them ride shouted good wishes to the northerners as they passed.

"I see those tears," Simon teased. "You grow sentimental in your old age."

"In a world of such wideness and wildness," Binabik replied, "it is only a fool who has no feelings of sentiment when saying goodbye to a treasured companion. I never thought a Rimmersman would be so dear to me, but that one is."

"We will miss him," Miriamele agreed. "But I'm sure Lady Alva has been missing him too—and missing her youngest child as well."

"I told Sludig to send Henrig back to us when he is old enough to be a knight," Simon said. "I liked the boy. He has wit and self-possession."

"Not a mooncalf, then, as some folks were at that age?"

Simon grinned. "No, my dear. True mooncalves are rare creatures. You do not come across them every day."

The Inner Council had gathered in the Archbishop's Dining Hall of St. Sutrin's cathedral, temporary seat of government for the High Throne. Tiamak was there as acting Hand of the Throne, along with Brother Etan, Countess Rhona, Lord Constable Zakiel, and Guard Captain Kenrick. The newly knighted Sir Jarnulf also had a seat, joined by all four trolls and several more nobles and functionaries. Even Tiamak's friend Lord Aengas was present, his huge, unwieldy chair carried into the hall by a half-dozen servitors.

"It is good to see you, Lord Aengas," the queen said when he had settled into place. "We have not had the pleasure of your company enough lately."

"Your flattery is much appreciated, dearest Majesty," he told her. "But this wretched little man, Lord Tiamak, has kept me horridly busy with all kinds of foolishness—reading unnecessarily wordy reports, judging scribbled plans, a constant flood of tasks. It has been almost like having a profession, and I have to say I don't like it at all."

"But you *do* have a profession," said Tiamak. "You are a Scrollbearer now, remember?"

"Whatever that means," Aengas said. "It certainly meant that I had to give up working for the Northern Alliance. In truth, my darlings, 'Scrollbearer' seems to be a word that signifies nothing much beyond 'You are now the Wrannaman's slave.'"

Simon could not help laughing. He did not always understand everything Aengas said, but he enjoyed the large fellow's reckless informality, which less confident monarchs might have considered disrespect. "Then how goes the Scroll League, Lord Aengas?"

"You must ask Tiamak. As I said, I am but a miserable minion, kept slaving and starving in the dark."

"Yes, our poor Aengas," said Tiamak. "You can see before you the tragic results of all that starvation." He gave his friend a wry look. "But to answer your question, King Simon, the League is still but a shadow of its former self. Aengas and Etan have both joined Binabik, myself, and Lady Thelía, but we are still short. The knight, Sir Porto, insists that he encountered an excellent candidate in the Thrithings—a fellow named Ruzhvang, shaman of the Snake Clan, who I will endeavor to find . . . somehow. Still, I wish we had a few more members. The traditional strength of the League was seven, so we remain short-handed."

"What about the woman Faiera in Perdruin?" asked Miriamele. "I was very moved when I read your letter about meeting her, Brother Etan."

"Yes, I confess to feeling sorry for the lady," he said.

Tiamak shook his head. "I wrote to Lady Faiera to tell her what has happened since then, especially the news of Josua surviving. But I have not heard anything from her—and to be honest, we may never do so."

"For myself, I hope she does not stay silent forever," Etan said. "I liked her and pitied her, both."

"I too hope we hear from her," said Tiamak. "We need more female voices in the councils of the wise, and at the moment we have only one female Scrollbearer, my good wife. Would you consider joining us, Queen Miriamele?"

The queen said, "Oh, Tiamak, how? When? No, it is not possible. I barely have enough time between dawn and dusk to deal with the things Simon and I must do every day. You would be forever waiting on me."

"Too bad," he said. "If there is any other woman who has seen as much of the good and bad the world has to offer, my queen, it is you."

"What about you, Rhona?" the queen asked her friend. "You are one of the most thoroughly educated women I know."

"Ah," said Tiamak. "I have already asked her, but the countess has not yet given me an answer."

"I told you," said Rhona, "I will decide after I speak to my husband and learn how things are back home in Nad Glehs."

"I will be patient, then."

At that moment, Tiamak's countrywoman Jesa appeared in the doorway of the hall. "I beg your Majesties' pardon," she said, making a courtesy. "I was only now able to get Serasina to lie down and sleep for a while. She is dreadful unless she has a nap at this time of the day."

"No need to apologize," the queen told her. "In any case, we have many other things to discuss today. First among them is the state of the High Ward."

"And its state is dire, I fear," said Tiamak. "No worse than it was when we first returned from Winstowe, I am glad to say but certainly no better. Rimmersgard is still steadfast in its allegiance, but they suffered in many skirmishes with the Norns before the peace was declared. And though Count Eolair's good news from Hernystir has cheered me mightily, Nabban is still lost to us."

"Has anything changed there?" Simon asked.

"Sallin Ingadaris has the strongest position, but he faces open resistance from the Dominiate. The Forty Families see no virtue in losing a duke without increasing their own power."

"What of his cousin, that little witch Turia, who was married to Drusis?" asked Miri. Simon thought she sounded unusually cold.

"Hard to say, since we have no informants in the Ingadarine household. There is a rumor Sallin keeps her as a sort of prisoner, since her marriage to Drusis is his only real link to the previous duke, and thus to legitimacy."

"Mark my words," said Miri, "if Turia is not holding the reins of power yet, someday she will. That child made my blood freeze."

"Certainly, things are confused there," Tiamak added. "There are even rumors of uprisings against Nabbanai rule across the southern islands."

"But for the moment there is nothing we can do about any of it," declared Simon. "We all know that. Erkynland has lost too many men and too much gold to try to remake the High Ward by force." He hesitated. "And I begin to wonder whether it is even worth it."

"What do you mean, Majesty?" asked Countess Rhona. "Surely that is the greatest legacy of the queen's grandfather, King John."

Simon and Miriamele exchanged looks. "That is a conversation for another day," said the queen. "For now, we must keep our eyes fixed closer to home. We have not yet decided whether to rebuild the Hayholt or make a new capital elsewhere. I am still fond of Meremund," she said, a touch wistfully.

"But what would happen to Erchester if we moved?" asked Simon. "I fear that our city here would wither away without the High Throne to keep it vital."

Many members of the Inner Council had ideas of their own about this, and the conversation went on for no little while, though without resolution. At last, Miriamele raised her hand to end it.

"We will not solve this today," she said. "And we need not decide what to do next until the land where the old castle stood has been cleared of wreckage and we can see what remains. What else needs our attention?"

Several possibilities were expressed, but before any of them could be settled on, Aengas coughed in an apologetic way. "If I may, Majesties?"

"Of course," said the queen.

"I wished to inform you—or warn you, perhaps—that I have decided to accompany you on your trip back to the north for Midsummer."

"Did we invite him?" the queen whispered to her husband.

"I'm not certain," Simon said. "Maybe Tiamak did."

"But Tiamak's not even going!"

Aengas was still explaining. "Why? I hear you ask, Majesties. Because after hearing handsome young Etan's tales of changelings and ogres and a magical ship stuck in a mountainside like a fly in amber . . . well, by sweet Mircha's healing rain, I cannot imagine missing such a spectacle! But do not fear—!" he said quickly. "I know my traveling arrangements will be costly." He gestured to his immense, heavy chair. "Fortunately, I am not a poor man. I will send for my own people out of my household in Ban Farrig to carry me across the many leagues stretching between Erchester and this mystical place, Tanakirú. If it meets with your majesties' approval, that is."

"It will be a strange errand," said the king. "That is sure. But I am aching to know what Geloë thinks she can do with that monstrous ship hanging so far above the water, and I would like to see again the place that my dear friend Jiriki fought and died to protect. As far as I'm concerned, Lord Aengas, you are most welcome."

"He is welcome, yes, but fie on such early planning!" said the queen, frowning. "I will not throw everything into an uproar yet. We have fully two months before we can even think of leaving to be there for Midsummer. Let us return to more pressing business."

Tiamak had seldom visited this quarter of Erchester and was not entirely comfortable. The establishment he sought was on Badger Street—at the bad end, a neighborhood of encroaching balconies that leaned close overhead and blocked the spring sun, with streets awash in mud and filth of all descriptions. The men he saw loitering in doorways seemed to have little to do except watch him as he passed, and he guessed that at least a few of them were wondering whether this small, dark-skinned man might have something worth stealing. He clutched his parcel more carefully.

This is one part of the city where I might go utterly unrecognized as an important councilor to the High Throne, he thought. *If all I wanted was to be anonymous, that would be a good thing, but I am more concerned with being attacked. I should have brought guards, or at least Brother Etan.*

He hurried along as best he could, scanning the fronts of the ramshackle buildings for any hint of his destination, and to his relief, spotted it at last: a hanging sign with a crude painting of a woman and an equally crude legend beneath it that read, "The Quarely Maid." Tiamak stepped through the doorway and was immediately entangled in a group of drunken men arguing over a wager. They paid no attention to Tiamak, and as the dispute ebbed back and forth, he found himself being forced back out the door.

"Here, now," shouted a thickset man with impressively large forearms, shoving his way through the crowd. "Bad enough, your yammering, without you keep out them as might be paying customers. Away, you lot. You have not bought a drop in an hour. Take your quarrel outside."

The men at last dispersed with much grumbling and a few threats. The man who had broken up their discussion helped Tiamak to his feet—the little man had tripped over the doorsill—and brushed him off with swift but considerate strokes.

"There, lordship, there," he said. "A shame, that is. They are louts, sire. Pay no mind. There—right as rain."

Tiamak was grateful he had decided to wear one of his less shabby robes: evidently its quality had alerted this man he might be worth rescuing. "Are you the owner, good sir?" he asked.

"That I am, your lordship. Named Hatcher, and the Maid is all mine, for my sins. And you're one of the castle-folk, I can see that. We've had more than a few in here, I can tell you. Do not let the humble crowd you see today give you a wrong idea of our quality. Why, even this very hour, His Royal Highness is here in this very establishment. Yes, the prince himself! He is an old friend and one of my best customers!" His look changed, the forced cheer giving way to something more like sadness. "At least he used to be—"

"You are speaking of Prince Morgan," said Tiamak. "And that is who I've come to see. Take me to him, please." He reached into his robe and produced a two silver pieces, then held them before Hatcher's wide-eyed face. "Take these and see that we have a little privacy, will you?"

"Of course, Lordship! His Highness is on the upper floor—what I like to call the gallery. I'll take you right to him."

I can only pray the prince is not yet too drunk to talk sense, thought Tiamak as he followed the publican across the tavern to the stairs.

Morgan was sitting by himself at a table, the only resident of the gallery, or at least the only conscious one: a pair of men sat at one of the tables at the far end, both slumped across the table, sleeping on their folded arms. The prince looked up as Tiamak approached and raised an eyebrow in mild surprise.

"What are you doing here, my lord?" he asked. "This does not seem like your sort of place." To Tiamak's surprise, Morgan seemed entirely sober, though a cup of wine sat by his elbow.

"What will you have, my lord?" Hatcher was hovering.

"Do you have fern beer?"

Hatcher frowned, his face folding like dough being kneaded. "Fern beer? Can't say as I've heard of it, master. No, nothing like that. Would you like me to see if I can get it for your next visit?"

Which will be never, thought Tiamak, looking around at the sopping, blood-spattered sawdust strewn across the earthen floor. "Ordinary ale will do," he said. "But please, make it your best." At least that might not sicken him outright.

"Gladly, my lord! I knew you were quality, sir. Spotted it as soon as you walked in. I'll have it back to you directly."

Tiamak turned to the prince, who did not seem in a great hurry to find out why the Wrannaman was here.

"It is strange," Morgan said. "I have tried sitting here until I was so drunk that I could barely stand. Then I tried sitting here without drinking more than a few swallows. Today is one of those." He shrugged. "Strangely, I find very little difference between the two."

"I am sorry that you are troubled, Prince Morgan."

"If it was something extraordinary, at least, I would not feel so shamed," the prince said. "After all, I escaped from the Norns, I met the monstrous *uro'eni*—that is what the Sithi call an ogre—and talked to the fairy queen in dreams. I lived in the trees with changelings! Many incredible and fearful things happened to me, but I survived them all. Yet here I sit, brought low by the oldest sadness of all." He slowly, mournfully shook his head. "She doesn't love me, Tiamak."

Now that he had been with him a short time, Tiamak was no longer certain of the prince's absolute sobriety. Something was wrong with Morgan, something almost broken. Tiamak had watched how hard the youth had worked since his return to Erkynland, how carefully he had done what his grandparents wanted him to do, but Tiamak had also seen a hollowness behind the prince's dutiful behavior that worried him, even frightened him. "Is all your unhappiness about the Norn woman, Morgan?"

Morgan was interested by Tiamak's omission of his title. "What else would it be, my lord? I am a prince! I can have anything I want! I could choose any woman here—!" He spread his arms in an inclusive gesture, but after a moment he noticed what Tiamak had already seen: in the Quarely Maid at midday, they were surrounded entirely by men, and not the comeliest of the sex, either.

Hatcher bustled up with a foaming mug for Tiamak and set it on the trestle before him with a flourish. "If you two would like to move downstairs where we have a real table, I'll clear some of the rabble out . . ."

"No, thank you," said Tiamak. "We are well here."

Hatcher finally left after swiping the trestle top several times with the same dirty rag he had used to mop his brow. Not entirely without trepidation, Tiamak took a sip of his ale and discovered that, in drink at least, Hatcher had given him good value.

"You still have not said what brings you here, Lord Tiamak," said Morgan. "Did my grandparents send you to fetch me back?" He shrugged. "I am no longer disgracing the family, as you can see. Astrian and Olveris are no more, and with them gone I have lost the taste for my old pastimes. But my tragedy is that I have found nothing else that I care about."

Tiamak felt awkward now. "In truth, Highness, I have been looking for you almost a sennight, but you are seldom in the residence."

The prince shrugged again. "I walk. I think. Sometimes I go down to the docks and watch the waves roll in. Like a lovesick poet in an old song." He laughed. Tiamak thought it did not sound good. "But why have you been searching for me, my lord?"

"To give you something." Tiamak lifted out the bound volume. "I found it when I was moving books from the Hayholt to St. Sutrin's. It belonged to your father, Prince John Josua."

Morgan's expression, which had grown lighter for a moment, suddenly hardened into something forbiddingly distant. "I don't want it. Give it to my grandparents."

"I offered it to them, Highness. First your grandfather, then the queen. Both said the same thing. 'Not yet—the pain is still too great.'"

Morgan still looked defiant. "And what makes you think I would feel any differently?"

"Because I have read it, and I have brought it to say you should read it too. I think it makes it clear that Pasevalles connived at your father's death."

"And I don't care. I am tired of hearing the traitor's name, and whatever he may have done, he is not the cause of my unhappiness with my noble sire."

Tiamak was caught by surprise. "Unhappiness? What do you mean?"

After a long silence, the prince told him of the day, impossible to forget, when his mother had announced that she carried a second child—the child that would be Lillia—and of the terrible thing that his father had said. "If you can convince me that I misheard, Sir Wrannaman," he finished, "then there might be some reason to read my father's words. Can you? Tell me, can you?" Beneath the angry stare, Tiamak thought he saw something almost like pleading.

"No, you did not mishear," Tiamak admitted. "But I say you cannot understand those days, that time, until you read your father's words."

"Grandmother always said you were the second stubbornest man she knew—after my grandfather." The prince shook his head. "Go back to the cathedral, Lord Tiamak. Leave me to my miserable sobriety."

Tiamak finished his cup of ale, then stood up, but left the book lying on the pitted trestle. "I will go, Highness, but I will also leave you your father's words. They are the last record of what he did in the world, what he thought and who he was. Your grandparents are not ready to see them—perhaps never will be. But I think you would benefit from them."

"Benefit?" Morgan was angry now. "By hearing how he lost all interest in us? And do not tell me he was ill—he stopped caring about my mother and me long before the disease struck him."

"It is your choice to read your father's journal or not," said Tiamak. "I cannot compel you, nor would I even if I could. But I leave it with you for the moment, and I wish you good afternoon. If you do not wish to look at your father's book, I ask that you please bring it back with you, Highness, and I will keep it for the day your grandparents may be ready to learn more about his last days."

And with that, Tiamak limped to the stairs, then made his way across the crowded ground floor, through the lazily quarreling customers, and back out into deep-shadowed Badger Street.

Morgan stared at the leather-bound book for a long time after Tiamak left. It was not that he feared to learn some new terrible thing about his father if he opened it. John Josua had never purposefully frightened Morgan or harmed him in any way. In truth, the prince had scarcely even raised his voice in anger to his young son. But during much of the last year of his life, he had simply drifted away from his wife and Morgan like a rudderless boat being pushed by the wind.

At first it had been John Josua returning to the residence later and later each night, usually long after Morgan had gone to sleep. Then he had set up a pallet in his working chamber in the Granary Tower and began to sleep there as well, apparently too consumed by his studies to return to his family. He also forbade Idela and Morgan from visiting his tower chambers. "There are too many expensive and dangerous instruments there, and I dare not take the time to prepare for your visits," he told them, and would answer no further questions on the matter.

Morgan's mother had seemed to take this in stride, but Morgan had felt the denial deeply: his father no longer needed or even wanted to be around him, that was clear, and the knowledge hurt him deeply.

He flipped open the cover of the book and idly perused the first page, on which were only his father's name—he had not bothered with his royal title—and a quote from Plesinnen of Myrme, "*If you are afraid of appearing foolish, then foolish you will certainly remain.*"

The second page was dated several years before John Josua's death. It seemed to be a record of some sort of alchemical assay, full of symbols Morgan could not decipher. The following pages looked much the same, careful rows of symbols and runes and numbers, all incomprehensible. Morgan flipped a few more pages. What did Tiamak think he would learn from this mess of arcana? How little he knew? Did the little Wrannaman, who loved learning so much, think his father's writings would somehow tempt Morgan into scholarship?

Other than the pages of cyphers, the first half of the book also contained more than a few illustrations that his father had clearly made himself, pictures of alchemical tools in various configurations and drawings of natural things, odd stones and swirls of clouds and the composition of leaves and branches, their smallest structures drawn in impressive detail, if not with overwhelming skill. Morgan turned to a sketch of a butterfly and instantly remembered the spring day it had been drawn. He had been looking over his father's shoulder as John Josua knelt beside a lilac bush in the Hedge Garden, trying to capture the insect's essence on paper before it flew away. John Josua had not discouraged Morgan's presence—had even seemed to welcome it—and had pointed out the butterfly's long, curly tongue as it sipped nectar from a purple blossom.

The dates on the following pages leaped forward at irregular intervals, and soon Morgan found that he had reached the time when his father began to separate himself from his family. It seemed to coincide with a gift from Pasevalles of a book that the chancellor claimed to have found, a work John Josua called *'the Aetheric Whispers,'* which had once belonged to the infamous red priest Pryrates. Seeing that name written out in his father's hand, Morgan almost shut the journal.

By God, why would he even accept such a thing? John Josua had known of no reason to distrust Pasevalles—no one had, back in those days—but he should have known that anything which had once belonged to Pryrates must be cursed. Morgan was angry with his father. *He should have burned it.*

Almost without being aware, Morgan read on, page by page, as his father described with growing excitement the new and fascinating directions Pryrates' book was leading him—and not just in his thinking. John Josua came to realize that the castle itself was a repository of ancient knowledge—especially the deepest parts below the foundations of the present buildings. And when he found a passage below the Granary Tower that could lead him into those depths, he began to explore.

For Morgan, it was like watching someone stumble closer and closer to mortal danger and not being able to warn them. His father was years dead, but as his careful, precise hand flowed from one page to the next, it felt to his son as though he still lived, as though he could somehow still be warned of what lay in store for him.

But what did lie in store for him? Morgan thought. *A terrible illness. A deadly fever. What could anyone have done to prevent that?*

Most of the rest of the pages were full of lists and drawings of the things his father had found while exploring the castle's underbelly—explorations that seemed to have become ever more important to him as the months passed. Then Morgan's attention was suddenly caught by a rough sketch of three objects—the witchwood seeds that he had seen in Tanakirú before his grandfather divided them up among the immortals. John Josua had not known what they were, and had labeled them as "little bells, or part of a Sithi necklace." *You found living witchwood,* Morgan thought. *You found something that the Sithi and Norns were searching for all over the world, and you didn't even know it.*

But John Josua only marked down a few more of his finds, then the date jumped forward to the next year—the year of his death. And John Josua's writing, so careful before, looked quite different in this last section, crooked and sprawling, as if written in a great hurry or with failing control over his hands and fingers. Morgan felt dread creep through him, but he forced himself to continue reading.

As much as I despise my own foolishness for having meddled in things that everyone I trust, especially my great-uncle and namesake Josua, strongly advised me should be left alone, it is the effect of my mistakes on others that brings me the most grief. Why did I not leave the red priest's cursed book unopened? Poor Lord Pasevalles, who brought it to me, could never have guessed what a curse he was handing me, but a curse it was, and in my heedless pursuit of knowledge at any cost, I have cursed myself.

But so much of what has fascinated me since I learned the history of this place, my home—both the story of its ancient days and happenings much more recent—were touched on in that book. I guess that it might even have led Pryrates down his own doomed path, though I suspect he would have found his way to perdition one way or another. But how proud I was, how arrogant, to think I could study the same secrets and remain untouched! Now God or Fate has shown me my error, and I fear my fleshly body is lost, but I still hope my soul can be saved.

In the days when I first began to explore beneath the castle, finding and collecting such oddments as caught my fancy, I was protected by my ignorance. I had no particular goal, but I was excited by any evidence of the Fair Folk who had lived on this hilltop and built their great castle here long before there was an Erkynland.

What I found were but novelties to me, because I knew so little. Thus, my first mistake was not ignorance, but a little knowledge—just enough to stoke my curiosity, but not enough to make me cautious.

Pryrates's copy of Aetheric Whispers *led me to wonder what else might be hidden beneath the Hayholt—not only remnants of the Sithi who had lived here so long ago, but things that Pryrates himself might have found or made. My parents had long ago closed off the red priest's tower, filling it with stones and sealing all its doors as far down as the castle cellars, but out of fear or—as it now seems to me—good sense, they had not explored it to see if Pryrates had dug down into the old Sithi ruins. But when I read the priest's notes in the margins of his book, certain cryptic phrases made me believe he had done just that. I pray my God may forgive me, because when I found a way down into those greater depths, I could only think of the chance I now had to search those dark, dark places for secrets Pryrates might have left behind. In my lack of humility, I thought my parents' caution was laughable. Pryrates was twenty years dead! What was there still to fear?*

Usires Aedon, protect Your mortal children from arrogance and lead them to the right path! It is too late for me, but not for mankind. There are some things that are meant to stay hidden.

One of the first times I journeyed down into the most hidden depths, I caught my sleeve on something sharp and it wounded my arm. I thought little of it until I held my lamp near the thing that had pierced my skin and saw that it was a metal spike, like a carpenter's nail with no head, which had been forced into a crack in the wall. It seemed meant to do just what it had done to me, snag and puncture the skin of anyone who should unwittingly come against it. As I examined it, wondering if it was something Pryrates himself had set out to discourage those who might come looking for entry into his tower, I saw that the end of the metal barb was covered with a dark, sticky substance, and that whatever it was had eaten away at the barb's sharp tip.

Suddenly terrified that the needle might have been poisoned, I took my knife and deepened the puncture in my arm, then put my lips to it and tried to suck out the venom. In the first moment I could taste the stuff—strange and foul—but quickly my lips and tongue lost all feeling. Nevertheless, I sucked and spat out until feeling came back to my mouth and I tasted nothing but salty blood. I wrapped my sleeve around the spike and plucked it from its crevice, thinking to examine it in better light, then I turned and hurried back to the castle above, where I washed my wound with brandy and poulticed it with goldenseal, comfrey, and honey. I considered calling on Tiamak, our best educated healer, but feared telling him of how I had been injured, since the ruins of the fairy castle had long been forbidden to all.

For the first few months afterward, I felt no ill effects, and I was certain I had physicked myself correctly. But a terrible thing happened that made me see myself as an unwitting monster.

One day I returned to the chambers I kept in the Granary Tower and discovered one of the maids there, a young woman named Bethil. Despite my warnings that

I did not want anyone in those chambers without me, she had taken it upon herself to clear them. She was fond of me, and as women do, regarded my strictures against entering my rooms as a sort of excuse for me to live in squalor. When I found her, she was embarrassed to be caught, and said she had wanted to surprise me, but I could not stop looking at the cloth she had wrapped around her hand. She told me it was nothing, that she had been ordering things on my table and had picked up a sharp piece of metal and pricked herself.

In growing horror, I went to the table and saw that after studying it late at night, I had neglected to put away the spike that had wounded me.

"Tell me that you did not hurt yourself on this," I said, hurriedly putting the spike back in a box and hiding it away, but the damage was done. Bethil admitted she had, then apologized for having upset me. I asked her how long ago she had pricked herself, and she said it had happened an hour before, when she was first cleaning, and that it had already stopped bleeding. She unwrapped her hand to show me, and I stared at the wound with a heart suddenly gone as cold as ice.

Of course I cleaned her wound as best I could, with all the methods I had used on my own injury, and I insisted that she come back to me if it did not heal immediately. She promised she would, and with reluctance I let her go.

May God forgive me, I curse myself for this, for my carelessness and my foolish secrecy, but now it has all gone too far, and I can think of nothing that will make it right. Not only did I doom myself with my careless exploration, but I killed an innocent serving girl as well.

I do not know whether poor Bethil was wounded more deeply than I was, or whether it was the time before cleaning the puncture that doomed her. Within a week she began to sicken, and although Lord Tiamak and his wife Lady Thelía labored to save her, they could not. And as she was dying in terrible pain, each of her cries of suffering another stab in my shamed heart, I began to feel the illness growing stronger in my own blood as well. I had not cured it, I realized, but had only slowed the onset of the deathly poisoning.

On the day Bethil died, I wandered the castle as if I were already dead myself—a ghost, the weight of my sins so heavy that I could barely talk. When at last I made my way back to my wife's chambers, she told me, with a face full of barely hidden delight, that she had a secret to share. I wanted to tell her what had happened and what would happen to me, but I could not do it while she seemed so joyful, and while our son Morgan watched. Instead, I could only stand and listen as she told me that she was carrying another child.

Even here, writing only for myself, I cannot find the words to describe my horror at her news. This second child was conceived after the illness was already in my body, so my sullied, envenomed blood would doubtless find its way into this child as well. I did my best to pretend pleasure in front of Idela, but it was too difficult, and I had to excuse myself. I prayed to God in His infinite mercy to let the child be born dead, rather than bring them into the world only to suffer the way Bethil had.

And now I feel it in me every day, this corruption of my blood, the thing that is killing me only a little more slowly than it killed the poor servant girl.

That was the last of what his father had written. Morgan leafed through the final pages, but they were empty.

He dried his eyes, put the book down, and stared at the wine cup before him, then lifted it and drained it in a single draught. He nearly called Hatcher to bring him another, or even several, but instead picked up the cursed book and left the Quarely Maid.

52

The Late King and Queen

Nezeru had tried her hardest, but she had decided she could never be truly comfortable living in Jao é-Tinukai'i. She had been away from Nakkiga's bleak, dark corridors long enough that she at least appreciated this place's airy beauty, but the aimlessness of the untamed forest and the ephemeral nature of the Sithi dwellings made her long for the security of stone walls and stone ceilings.

The Jao é-Tinukai'i settlement had been abandoned since Amerasu's death half a Great Year before, but even when many hundreds or even thousands of Zida'ya had lived there, it had never been a proper dwelling place by Nezeru's Hikeda'ya standards. After their escape from the fall of Asu'a, the Sithi had mostly given up building in stone, preferring to make their homes in cloth and supple wood, structures that could be taken apart and moved swiftly. And the Zida'ya who had accompanied Nezeru, her father, his Builders, and a small company of Gatherers to Jao é-Tinukai'i, had put up the new settlement in the same style. The Hikeda'ya of course preferred safer, more secure structures made from stone or dug into the earth, but because the end of winter had been stormy and wet, most of these were still not finished. Thus, Nezeru had been living with her father in a collection of silken tents, and such wispy surroundings made her feel as if she had discovered, during a deadly fight, that she had forgotten to don her armor.

She was waiting to talk to her father, who was with the Order of Echoes, using their Witness to converse with Prince Pratiki back in Nakkiga. Midsummer was coming, and that was another cause of her unrest: she felt certain that Morgan and his family would return to Tanakirú to see the fulfillment of the changeling woman Geloë's plan, and she feared that they might visit Jao é-Tinukai'i on their way.

Nonao, her father's secretary, looked in to tell her that Viyeki was on his way back from meeting with the Echoes, and that he wanted to speak to her when he returned.

"I thank you," she told him. "I am waiting for him. Do you mind if I ask you a question while you are here?"

"Of course not, Sacrifice," he said after a moment. Nonao was apparently still trying to decide where she belonged in his hierarchical calculations. She was not of the Builder's Order, but she was his master's halfblood child, and apparently blessed with Prince Pratiki's favor. "How can I help you?"

"You heard, of course, about the attempt on my mother Tzoja's life by the High Magister's wife, Khimabu."

Surprise was plain even on the secretary's well-trained features, but he only nodded. "Of course. I was horrified. I never would have imagined the lady to be capable of such a thing."

Nezeru gave him a long look. "My question is, how did you come by the forged letter purporting to be from my father—the message that led my mother into that ambush?"

She thought she saw an almost imperceptible flinch, but that proved little: any veteran of the Nakkiga court and its noble households knew that even baseless rumors could result in fatal conclusions. "It was left for her and seemed to be from your father," he said. "I did not know it was Lady Khimabu's hand that had addressed it. I swear it, Sacrifice."

"Did it not occur to you to wonder that such a message had arrived at all? My father was deep in the Kushiba tunnels that day, helping to assess the work to be done there." The problem was, she reflected, that constant terror had been a part of Hikeda'ya life for so long that the secretary's obvious fear proved nothing.

"I thought he had sent it from the tunnels with another messenger," Nonao said. "I had been out doing your father's bidding at various sites, and I returned to find the letter on my table. That is all I can tell you. Please believe me, Sacrifice Nezeru. I know your mother is important to the high magister. I would never have helped anyone hurt her."

"Do not fear, Secretary," she told him. "The old days are gone—so our Prince Pratiki has declared. No one is to be condemned on mere suspicions anymore. You may go now, and I will tell my father that you passed along his message." But even as she saw his fear begin to ebb, she added, "But know this—if I ever find that anything you have told me is not true, Secretary Nonao, or that you conspired in any way with Lady Khimabu to murder my mother, I will kill you with my own hands. And during the moons and years to come, I will be watching you carefully. Do we understand each other?"

Nonao closed his eyes for a long moment; when he opened them, he had once more donned a good servant's impenetrable, masklike expression. "We do, Sacrifice Nezeru, and I thank you for your forbearance and wisdom. These are indeed different days for our folk." He bowed carefully, then left the room.

Not long after he departed, her father came in, shedding his heavy, rain-sodden cloak and hanging it to dry. "My daughter, I am glad you are here."

"Where else would I be?" She tried not to sound too resentful, but it was a painful fact that she had little to do here in Jao—she was trained as a warrior, not as a builder or as a gardener, and so far there had been no threats more dangerous than an occasional bobcat wandering through the settlement, and once a bear who blundered into the newly planted garden, but was driven out again quickly by the songs of the Gatherers.

Viyeki looked sad, but the fact that he showed his feelings at all was heartening. Dedicated to a courtier's life, her father had always kept his emotions hidden and had taught Nezeru to do the same even before the Order of Sacrifice had begun to drum the lesson into her even more strongly, with beatings and punishments. But it seemed that she was not the only one who had changed in the last, tumultuous year. "I know it has been hard for you," he said. "I hope my news will bring you some cheer."

She felt a sudden tightening in her middle. "Are we commanded back to Nakkiga?" In some ways it felt like a relief, but she knew it would be much harder for both of them back at home. Her late stepmother's family would poison the air against her father, and that meant people would certainly be talking about his halfblood daughter, too—the rogue Sacrifice who had killed their godlike queen.

"No, do not fear," he said, and it was clear that he could see her thoughts as clearly as she could see his.

What have we become? she wondered. *Transparent as mortals?*

"Prince Pratiki has met the expected resistance of the old guard," Viyeki continued, "but as he predicted, his complete command over the Queen's Teeth has kept him safe. But even so, he says the time is not right for us to return."

She was both relieved and disappointed. "Then what is your news, Father?"

"His Serene Highness is sending Lady Luk'kaya's most experienced factor from Nakkiga to improve the nurturing of the sacred witchwood. And I have been given a new task."

She was surprised. "Prince Pratiki is not disappointed, is he? You have done heroic work, especially with so little time to prepare."

"I do not think the prince is disappointed. Rather, he is looking to the future. He sends me as the very first Hikeda'ya envoy to the mortal High Throne. I am commanded to go to Erchester in Erkynland—the place where Great Asu'a once stood."

She was astonished, and more than a little horrified. "To the court of Morgan's grandfather, King Simon? But Queen Utuk'ku burned down their castle!"

"A castle is not a kingdom," said her father. "But here is what I most wanted to say, my daughter—I hope you will go with me. I cannot imagine living among mortals without your experience to help me."

Nezeru was all but struck dumb. She could see that her father was quite aware he was asking her to join him in a place where she might have to encounter the mortal prince every day. A part of her wanted never to think of Morgan again; another held more complicated feelings, but she was not yet ready to contemplate that particular sliver of her innermost being.

"What choice do I have?" she said.

"All the choice in the world," her father told her. "I would not compel you, daughter—I know that there will be pain for you if you go there. You can stay here in Jao é-Tinukai'i—"

"—And protect the witchwood from rabbits and deer." She knew she sounded bitter. "A suitable chore for a disgraced soldier." She shook her head. "I shall have to think carefully, Father. I truly do not know what I should do."

"As I said, I cannot and will not compel you. But I would find your company a very reassuring thing if I must go and live among a people so strange to us, so foreign."

"I cannot answer you now. When are you to leave?"

"Not right away. First the prince wants me to travel back to Tanakirú, to be the eyes and ears of our people when this odd event surrounding the Ninth Ship takes place." He hesitated. "I hope you will go there with me, too."

"Tanakirú?" Nezeru closed her eyes and fought a sudden swirl of dizziness. It felt as though the world was squeezing her too tightly.

Many of the same people who had greeted them so enthusiastically when they marched into Erchester only months before had come out today to watch their monarchs ride out again, but this time the spectators were quieter. The largest reason was that, though there were many rumors, nobody outside the circle of royal intimates knew exactly why or where the king and queen were going. Some rumors claimed they had made a promise to the King of Fairies, but others scoffed that there was no such person. Others worried that the infamous Norn Queen might not have been as thoroughly killed as everyone had hoped. But the heralds who announced the royal mission proclaimed the trip to be nothing more than a courtesy to the allies that had helped them overcome the traitor Pasevalles and the dreadful Utuk'ku. Most of the citizens of Erchester and the surrounding country were willing to believe that, but it would have been strange if the folk of Erkynland were not anxious at having both of their rulers leave again so soon after the attack on the Hayholt and Simon and Miriamele's almost miraculous return.

Thus, it was no surprise that the crowds waiting on either side of Main Row looked a bit uncertain. But watching their king and queen wave and smile, clearly in good health despite having been thought dead only half a year earlier, did much to reassure them.

"I am not complaining, husband," Lady Thelía said as they watched the procession from atop St. Sutrin's ceremonial balcony, "but I am still surprised that you are not going with them."

"I am surprised too," Tiamak said. "What happened there sounds astonishing, and what will happen next—well, no one except Geloë can say, but it is also likely to be highly unusual. And ten years ago, I would have done or promised almost anything to accompany them, if only to see for myself the site of what will be one of the most famous battles in history. Instead, I will rely on Lord Aengas to tell me all that happens."

"But you are a historian!"

"Of sorts, my dear. In truth, until I finish my book about the Hayholt and its antecedents, I cannot truly claim the profession."

"Nonsense. You wrote a wonderful book on Wran healers."

Tiamak smiled. "Treatises on swamp herbs do not qualify as history for most scholars."

"If you truly wanted to go with the king and queen, I would not have objected. I might even have thrown my responsibilities aside and gone with you."

He turned to look at her. "I know that, my splendid wife. The fire of learning burns as hot in you as it does in me. But I discovered last winter that I am no longer young."

"Only then?"

"You are teasing me. But still, I suppose there is truth in that. Until I found myself on the Frostmarch last year, far from home and comfort, I never realized how much I could yearn for those things. You know my leg and how it pains me—there are days when it is hard to get out of bed. A fortnight on a horse, or even riding in a great chair like Aengas, would be hard on me. And there is much to do here. Duke Osric relies on us in Simon and Miriamele's absence, and the kingdom is still far from recovered."

She frowned. "I wish Osric would stop calling you 'Wrannaman,' as if that were your name."

Tiamak shook his head. "I fight only the battles I must. The duke can be convinced to do the right thing, but it is not always easy, and I prefer to conserve my remaining strength and choose my fights carefully."

"Your remaining strength? Oh, my poor, ancient husband, you frighten me."

This time he only gave her a sideways glance. "Mocking me again. You are a very bad wife. I should have sent you back to the convent."

"If you tried, I would have sent you back to your banyan tree."

"I did not live in a tree, as I have told you many times. I lived in a perfectly adequate hut—although I confess it was not quite as large as our current accommodations in the archbishop's palace."

The royal company had all but vanished from sight now, trailed by a ragtag of well-wishers, and the rest of the crowd along Main Row was slowly dispersing, pursued by the peddlers who had not managed to sell all their wares.

"Then let us retire to our large and commodious hut," Thelía said. "Early this morning, I found a lemon snail living among our lettuce leaves and I would like you to see it, because instead of yellow it is quite pink!"

"Then lead on, my lady. Take me to this prodigy of Nature."

As they left the cathedral, they spotted Princess Lillia accompanied by Lady Jesa, who was carrying little Serasina. "Uncle Timo! Aunt Tia-Lia!" the princess called. "We just watched Morgan and Grandfather and Grandmother ride out. My brother looked awfully grown—did you see?"

"We did," said Lady Thelía. "I confess I am a little surprised that you did not insist on going with them, young mistress."

"Don't need to," Lillia said with airy certainty. "I know what's going to happen."

"Do you now?" Tiamak smiled. "But how about tonight? Do you know what is going to happen tonight?"

Suddenly unsure, she looked sideways at him. "No. What?"

"You, Highness, as well as Lady Jesa and little Serasina, are going to join us for supper. At least that is what I hope will happen. We all have many tales to share, and I particularly want to hear the rest of yours."

"I was very, very brave," Lillia admitted.

"I do not doubt it," said Tiamak gravely. "And you, Jesa, can you and the baby—or just you—join us at our humble table?"

"Lady Shulamit told me she would love to take the baby for a time," said Jesa. "If Serasina isn't the one you want to see, then perhaps I could leave her behind for one evening."

"Splendid," said Thelía. "Then it's settled."

"Do you mind if we talk as we ride?" his grandfather asked.

Morgan, who had sensed the king's discomfort all day, was ready to be told he was no longer the heir to the throne. "Of course, Majesty."

"Miri, is it well with you if we do?"

The queen had brought up her chestnut palfrey and was now pacing them. Morgan thought his grandmother rode with admirable form, and he was momentarily prickly with pride about his family. "As long as you do not intend to leave me out of your conversation," Miriamele said.

"Never! It is about the same thing you and I were up half the night discussing."

"Ah," she said, but nothing more.

Now Morgan felt even more anxious, certain that they had taken him at his word about being unfit to be their heir. Not that he felt very different today but reading his father's journal had lifted some of the doomful weight from his heart, and he wished he had not been so quick to point up his own shortcomings. He suddenly realized that he wanted his grandparents to be proud of him. "I'm listening, Majesty," he said.

"Hmmm." Simon suddenly seemed to have lost his momentum. "So, then. What we have been talking about . . . what we have been thinking . . ." Astonishingly, the king's cheeks flushed above his beard. "God's Bloody Tree, I'm no good with this sort of thing, Miri. You tell him what we're thinking."

She gave him a look of annoyance mixed with unshakeable love that Morgan could only hope to inspire in someone someday. "Your grandfather and I have been through a great deal in the last year," she said. "You know that, Morgan."

It did not need a response, so he only nodded.

"And because of that, we both—quite separately—began to think about some of the same things. It's a question of power—how it is given, how it is wielded, and how to protect our subjects from its being used wrongly."

Morgan had no idea where this was going, and it must have shown on his face, because the queen hurried on. "This is not about you or your capabilities, Morgan. Your grandfather and I are impressed with how much you've grown, how you've changed—."

"But you don't think I'm up to the responsibility," he finished for her. "You're going to pass me by. Does that mean you'll make Lillia the heir-apparent?"

"What?" Simon was obviously confused. "No. No, your grandmother already said our concerns were nothing to do with you. It's the High Ward, you see. It's the monstrous Norn Queen. It's Hugh. It's . . . oh, hang it, I've muddled things again. Tell him, Miri."

She gently shook her head, as if to disperse her husband's fog of words. "We are thinking of letting the High Ward lapse, Morgan. Of returning sovereignty back to Hernystir, Rimmersgard, Nabban, and all the others. Part of it is mere cost, of course—the treasury has been picked clean, and we can no longer afford the kind of close rule we have tried to employ across the whole of the Ward. But more importantly, the king and I have both seen what too much power in one pair of hands can do. Yes, we trust you, Morgan—wipe away that frown, young man. We also trusted King Lluth, and he reigned long and well, but after his death his throne went to the madman Hugh who nearly plunged Hernystir into darkness. We have seen what a despot with a throne can do. Pasevalles tried to overthrow the High Ward from inside and all but succeeded. Utuk'ku would have destroyed her own people on a cowardly whim." She looked Morgan in the eyes. "Power over so many nations in one person's hands no longer seems good to the king and myself. So we think we must divide that power and hand much of it back. In any case, the High Ward has become unwieldy and hard to govern. We would prefer that you only had the welfare of Erkynland to concern you."

"I don't understand," said Morgan. "You're going to end the High Ward?"

"Not immediately," said his grandmother. "And not without your agreement. But yes, we think it would be best. My grandfather King John had a dream of the whole world united under his throne. And for many years, it worked, mainly because John had defeated all the other rulers on the battlefield. But victories like that seldom last. You've heard what has happened in Nabban. That horrible child Turia told me, 'You don't understand Nabban,'—and I fear she was right. We no longer believe that any one person—or even two, like your grandfather and I—can know enough to rule an entire world wisely. Kings and queens must always rely on others, and the wider the kingdom, the more difficult it becomes to know that the ones you've chosen are doing what is best for the people they are ruling. I saw Duke Saluceris make terrible mistakes in Nabban and could not stop him, even though I was there. And the lesson of the Norn Queen's subjects, who were little more than slaves, is even more fearful."

"Please," said Morgan. "Just tell me the truth. I told you once, I don't think I'm clever enough to be a king, not ever. I need to know what you want from me."

"We want you to be what you are," said Simon with surprising gentleness. "A good man. A young man who has learned many lessons. Who has made mistakes but then tried to learn from them."

"If mistakes are the measure of a king," said Morgan ruefully, "then I could be one of the old Nabbanai Imperators and rule all the world."

"To be honest," his grandfather said, "if you were anxious to rule others, I would be concerned. Not that I preferred it when you didn't give a damn," he added, grinning sourly. "But too much desire for power is a worrisome trait. No, we do not plan to pass over you as heir, Morgan. Not at all! But we wish to begin a process that will give more . . . responsibility is the word, I suppose. That's right, isn't it, Miri? We want to give more responsibility back to the nations of the High Ward. And when the day comes—"

"Hopefully many long years in the future, since we have just found each other again," said his grandmother, giving the king such a look of affection that Morgan almost felt embarrassed to see it. "But when your day to rule comes, we will have prepared the ground for you to finish the work."

"So, you are leaving me an empire only to give it away." He did not mean his words to sound bitter but realized they might. "I want to hear more about how such a thing would work."

"Of course you do," said Miriamele. "And we will tell you everything. We envision a Council of the Ward made up of all the countries John united. Something like the Dominiate in Nabban, where the nations can come together and solve their problems and settle trade and such—and, hopefully, avoid war."

"But we're not going to force you against your will," said the king. "That needs to be clear."

Morgan shook his head, still confused. "Are you ending the High Ward or not?"

"We will not complete the dismantling of it during our reign, but only prepare the foundations of what might replace it," the queen told him. "We will leave it to you, when you become king, to finish the task . . . if that is what you think best. Your grandfather and I will be gone then, remember, not looking over your shoulder—at least not in our earthly forms. But we think that if you are part of the plan from the first, you will understand your choices better when the time comes."

They talked for a while longer, but Morgan could only absorb a little of what was said—the future was far away, after all, while his heartaches were of the moment and seemed far more real than mere politics. He thanked the king and queen for being honest with him, then rode ahead so he could be on his own for a bit, his thoughts turning over and over to a hilltop on a full-moon night that seemed a lifetime ago, and a prophecy read from a scatter of knucklebones.

They were crossing the rolling grasslands of northwestern Erkynland, with the Wealdhelm in sight, when they were overtaken by a company of riders out of the southwest. Miriamele had an anxious moment—things were still unsettled across much of the land, authority only now being restored, and these newcomers were armed.

Simon lifted a hand to bring the approaching riders to a halt.

"Hail!" cried the leading horseman as he reined up. "Hail and well met, Your Majesties! I bring you greetings from Queen Inahwen!"

"Hernystiri," said Miriamele in relief.

"Yes, and I know their leader," her husband said. "That's Count Eolair's whatever-he-is—grand-nephew, I think. Aelin, yes, that's his name. A good lad. He came to us on our way back from Rimmersgard, remember?" He raised his voice. "Hail, Sir Aelin! You are welcome!"

Aelin and his troop, who had been riding swiftly for days, were quite content to adopt the royal company's slower speed, and Aelin joined the king and queen and Morgan. Miriamele thought he seemed an admirable young man, a few years older than Morgan and thus a bit more self-assured. She saw glimpses of Eolair's familiar features in Aelin's windburned face, and it filled her with a sudden sadness at the way Time plodded remorselessly on, aging those she knew and bringing forward their replacements without regard for the feelings of those who knew and loved the originals.

But Eolair was a descendant of others, just as I am—just as Simon is, she thought. She recalled the strange things Geloë had told Simon about his changeling blood, however small a part of him it likely was. Could it be true—her own husband with the blood of the Garden? It seemed odd and unlikely. The Tinukeda'ya she knew best were the Niskies, and it was very hard for her to reconcile those strange, seafaring people with her husband—her dear and all too human Simon.

But there was that strange thing the court astrologer said when I was in Nabban, she remembered—then was distracted by her husband.

"Isn't that right, Miri?"

"I beg pardon, I didn't hear."

"I was just telling Aelin how gladdened we have been by Eolair's letters. We have a powerful fondness for Queen Inahwen."

"Yes," Miri said. "We were horrified to hear what almost happened. We knew Hugh had become difficult, even dangerous, but we never guessed that it would come to that. We are so grateful that you were able to save Eolair's and Inahwen's lives, Sir Aelin."

"I thank you, but it was by no means just me, Your Majesty. In truth, that is one reason I am here. The greatest authors of our salvation were the Sithi from Skyglass Lake. Without their intervention, I think we would all be dead. Sadly, we know from your letters, Majesties, that Prince Jiriki, the one who asked them to help us, died in the fighting up north. But I intend to thank his family and his clan on behalf of our queen." He looked at Miriamele, blushed, and smiled. "Our *Hernystiri* queen, I mean. Queen Inahwen."

"I understand that you knew Jiriki," said Simon. "Will you stop at Jao é-Tinukai'i to pay your respects at his grave? I fear our party cannot go so far out of the way this trip."

"I may do so on the way back—but only if I can find a Sithi guide to take me there." Aelin shrugged. "I would not try to find anything in the middle of that endless forest without help, especially a place as famously hard to discover as the Sithi's old settlement."

"That's probably wise," said Simon. "You may not know it, Sir Aelin, but when I was a young man—younger than you—I wandered in that same forest for days and days and days. It was snowing, too! I had nothing to eat, and was almost dead from cold and hunger . . ."

Miriamele thought from the young Hernystirman's face that he might have already heard some version of this well-known story, but she also knew once Simon began, nothing short of an armed attack was going to stop him. She sighed—quietly, discreetly—and let him tell it.

Nobody was more relieved than Morgan to learn that they would not be returning to Jao é-Tinukai'i on this journey. He knew enough about his grandfather's whims that he had been half-certain the king would abruptly decide that they must all go to visit Jiriki's grave, and that would have forced him to see Nezeru again.

Morgan had struggled with his hurt all spring, doing his best to distract himself—not in the old ways, with wine, women, and dubious behavior, but by helping to set Erkynland back on its feet again. The country's problems were many, exacerbated by the fact that few people in all the land understood what had happened, why the Norns had attacked the Hayholt, or why the king and queen had been thought dead and then discovered to be alive. And, naturally, for every true story that made its way among the Erkynlandish people, half a dozen more tales that ranged from merely wrong to utterly fantastical were passed around as well, so that any three people asked to explain the events of the last year would likely give three quite different answers.

But as Grandfather says, we are stubborn creatures, we mortals. You cannot force people to think what you want them to think, you can only tell them what you think and why, then hope they see the same things that you do.

Still, despite the good company, the long ride north left Morgan with more time to think than he would have liked. It was not only memories of Nezeru that haunted him, either: he was only beginning to realize how close to death he had come, and how many times it had happened. He could not help wondering if his having survived meant that God had indeed been watching over him.

But if so, why? Why did I live but Jiriki did not? He looked at Jarnulf who, as usual, was watching him carefully, likely hoping for a reason to be of service. *Why did Sir Jarnulf survive so many things—was it just so that he could recognize Prince Josua? Why did so many die at Tanakirú but others like me live to return half a year later, on this strange pilgrimage?*

Sometimes it seemed that the world made no sense at all.

The royal company followed the line of the forest until they reached the southernmost foothills, then turned north along the Wealdhelm Road. The Nartha River, flush with the spring rains, was running high on its banks, joyously noisy as a child let out to play after a long confinement. During their first days traveling beside it, Morgan was buoyed by its cheerful song, and by the fact that this route promised they would not go near Jao é-Tinukai'i. His life was more than good, he told himself. He had been reunited with his sister and grandparents after he had thought that impossible. He had survived an adventure as wild and dangerous as anything the king or queen had experienced. Even the future seemed less shadowed. If the throne of Erkynland did come to him, or even the whole of the High Ward, then he would simply do his best. If things somehow turned out differently, he would live with that too.

As the days passed on the northward trek, Morgan also found himself warming to Sir Aelin. The Hernystiri knight had at first seemed almost fearfully serious, and Morgan's first impression was that Aelin was an honorable man who had no sense of fun. But as they talked after the royal party camped in the evenings, he began to see a little of the sly humor he had often seen in Aelin's great-uncle Eolair, and he realized he had underestimated the young Hernystirman.

One night, as they talked beside a healthy, crackling fire, Aelin confessed that Queen Inahwen wanted to make him the heir to the throne, but that he felt unready for such a burden to be placed on him. Morgan's heart opened immediately, and he admitted that he was in much the same situation. Aelin seemed quite surprised.

"But you have always known you were the heir."

"You would not say so if you heard my grandparents before I got lost in the woods. They were always telling me that I was disgracing the crown, that I was a fool, and that my friends were bad for me." His smile was rueful. "One of them did try to kill me later, so I can't say they were entirely wrong."

Aelin laughed, then told of the struggles he had experienced trying to hold his very small party together while sneaking past Norn troops, and his countrymen's open resistance to traveling with the Sitha Yeja'aro. "Maccus is dead, sadly," he said. "Killed by Hugh's men. I had known him since we were boys.

But Evan the Aedonite is with me still." He pointed out one of the other Hernystiri, a young rider who Morgan thought looked even more serious than his first impressions of Aelin.

"I would like to meet this fellow Aedonite," he said. "Especially since he is important to someone who will be my brother monarch—if Fate insists on us both accepting our burdens. It is not common for your folk to be Aedonites, is it? Yes, it would be interesting to talk with him. To be honest, my own faith could use some bolstering. Will you introduce us?"

"I would be glad to do so, Highness," said Aelin. "But I warn you, Evan drinks only water."

Morgan laughed. "I'm more careful myself these days—though not quite *that* careful. Still, I won't judge him harshly for being abstemious."

"Then you will find him a good and thoughtful man, Highness."

"You should probably just call me 'Morgan' if you're going to be a king someday too."

Aelin blew out his breath. "King. *Pfffff.* And I thought almost galloping into an angry giant was the most frightening thing that would ever happen to me."

No question, Morgan thought. *I am warming to this pagan fellow.*

"You explained why we were riding up the western side of the Wealdhelm, Majesty," Morgan said to his grandfather one night in camp. "But I confess I was tired and did not take it all in. Explain to me again why we are not going through the forest and up the Narrowdark Valley."

"Geloë told me before we left that she would have her Tinukeda'ya people clear the tunnel down from the Norn camp on Kushiba Mountain, because some of her people were still making their way to Tanakirú, and she could not wait for them to go the long way through the forest and up the valley." The king gestured vaguely. "Apparently the choice of Midsummer for her plan to be finished was not merely a day we could all remember, but important in itself."

"Something magical?" Morgan suggested.

"I do not even know what that means anymore," Simon confessed. "I have seen so many wonders and so many appalling, impossible things that I no longer know what is natural and what is magical. It cannot mean the same thing to you, Morgan, but the woman we are going to meet died thirty years ago."

"I know."

"Yes, but you did not know her as I did. It is just a story to you but it was part of my life! She was alive, then she died. Then she came back." He shuddered a little. "It makes it hard to believe anything is certain."

Morgan nodded. "I know just what you mean, Grandfather. Remember, you always used to say that nobody knew they were in a story when it was happening? Well, I have been in one now too, but I still find it all hard to believe."

Simon smiled, the lines around his eyes crinkling. "Did I say that? Hah. Then I am not such an old dodderer as you thought me, am I?"

"Please, sire. I am ashamed of my own ignorance."

The king laughed. "Don't be. We all start out ignorant, lad. A baby like Miri's little pet Serasina must learn to crawl before she can walk. A young man must think he is invincible and all-knowing until he learns otherwise, then hope the lessons that reveal his shortcomings are not fatal. And a king—or a queen, like your grandmother—must think they are not wise enough to rule by their own knowledge, so that they will listen to what truly wise people say, then make the best choice they can." The king squinted at Morgan. "Why are you looking at me like that?"

"Because you have just said several more wise things, Majesty, all at once. Should I write them down, or can you repeat them for me later?"

"Bah! Now you are teasing me, you wretched youth."

"Only a little, Grandfather. But in truth, what you say strikes home."

Finally, after many days, they reached the northern reaches of the Wealdhelm, where the modest hills gave way to an ever-rising series of peaks, as if the range was a jaw full of teeth and they had left the grinding molars behind and now approached the fangs. One tall, sharp dogtooth seemed to stand above the rest—the peak Erkynlanders called "The Watchtower" and the Norns and Sithi called Kushiba. King Simon explained that they would be climbing to what had been a Sithi camp before the Norns took it in a dreadful battle.

"And are any Norns still there?" Sir Jarnulf wanted to know. He looked, Morgan thought, as if he hoped they would be, and that they would want to start trouble.

"I think not," said Simon. "Geloë and her workers have been using the tunnels since we left."

At the base of the mountain, Lord Aengas' heavy chair was lifted from the wagon that had carried it out of Erchester and onto the shoulders of eight burly men Aengas had brought from his home in Ban Farrig. Then the company began to make their winding way up the mountain.

It grew colder as they climbed. Morgan was glad they were making the ascent in summer, but there were times when the wind blew hard enough that he almost wished he was back in the sheltering tunnels of the valley's far side, rogue kilpa or no. But eventually they reached the spot where the immortals had fought each other, and where the Norns had afterward been trapped by a collapsing tunnel so that they could not aid their queen, and there royal party found two of Geloë's company waiting to guide them.

Morgan was happily surprised to recognize both Tih-Rumi, the Voice of the Dreaming Sea's companion, and Yek Fisher. "It is good to see you again," he told them. "Who would have believed all this when we first met?"

"We did," said Yek Fisher. "We knew we had been called. And our Lady told only the truth."

"Where is the old fellow, Kuyu-Kun?" Morgan asked. "I hope he is still well?"

"Well? He is more than well, he is inspired," said Tih-Rumi. "After thinking he had foreseen the death of all our people, my master has decided that he will go with Geloë to the new land, to be certain that our history will be carried to the Tinukeda'ya's new home. And to his delight, he has discovered that many of the folk Geloë summoned brought their old books and carved tablets and treasured old tales with them. Even as we speak, the story of our people is growing." Now he laughed ruefully. "I shall be up late for several nights catching up on all he has learned since I left him to come meet you."

"So, you are still his acolyte?" asked Morgan. "Will you go with him or stay?"

"Stay, I think," said Tih-Rumi, with a touch of uncertainty. "Though the decision is Kuyu-Kun's. I am his trained successor, after all—I do not think he would want his people here to lose his knowledge when he goes." He shook his head. "But as I said, he is quite busy and distracted. I do not know precisely what he will want me to do, so I must wait and see how things unfold."

Morgan nodded. "Then you are in good company, my friend—you are not the only one waiting to learn what his future will be. Come, I will introduce you to Sir Aelin of Hernystir, and we can all wait on the future together."

So it was that early the next morning Tih-Rumi led them into the tunnels that Nezeru's father, Viyeki, and his Builders hewed out of the mountain's network of caverns. Their arduous journey down to the valley was made more difficult by having to squeeze Lord Aengas's massive chair through some of the tighter spots. Finally, at the suggestion of the troll Binabik, they partially dismantled the chair, leaving behind some of its bulkiest bits—and a great amount of his riding comfort as well, Aengas complained—to be retrieved on their return journey.

The Hernystirmen marveled at the great limestone caverns full of strange formations, and at the long, twisting tunnels Nezeru's father and his workers had dug to link the natural caves into a single descending passage.

"I would never have believed it," said Aelin. "This mountain must be almost as hollow as a drinking horn!"

"And few things are sadder than an empty drinking horn," Morgan suggested with a wry smile.

"I will confess, it frightens me," said Evan, hurriedly making the Sign of the Tree on his breast. "Our land of Hernystir is full of these fairy-scapes. The whole of the Grianspog is riddled with their burrows."

"They are not burrows, and the Sithi are not animals," said Aelin sternly. "My uncle Eolair has been inside the Silverhome, their ancient city. He said it was greater and grander than anything built by men."

"Fairy magic," said Evan.

Aelin caught Morgan's eye and made a weary face. Morgan had to suppress a laugh.

The journey down to the plateau took half a day, and by the time they reached the end of the tunnels and stepped out onto the stony ground, the sun was in the west and the Narrowdark Valley was bathed in slanting light. Morgan took a deep breath as he experienced his first view of Tanakirú since the days after the fighting, and was surprised that it seemed smaller than in his memory. As he waited for the king and queen and the rest to emerge, he felt once more the terror that had overwhelmed him when he thought they had lost, that the Norn Queen would have her way, and this steep valley, so far from the world he had known, was the last place he would ever see. And he thought about Nezeru and the panic that had overwhelmed him when he thought she would be killed. He looked up, wondering if the ship had somehow been taken from the cliff and brought down to a place where it could be moved into water, but it was still in place high above him, like a wasp's nest tucked under the eaves of a house.

And at that moment, as he stared up at the shadowed underside of the great ship and the rest of the royal company began spilling out into the daylight around him, he heard someone call his name.

"So," said Nezeru. "You are here as well."

53
The Voyage of a Booklouse

"I hope I have not transgressed, Your Majesties," said the Norn noble, Viyeki. "The request should have come from Prince Pratiki, and doubtless his formal request for you to accept me as ambassador soon will, but since you and the king are here, and I am here . . ."

"No, not at all," said Miriamele, although in truth she had been caught by surprise. "We are gratified by your prince's desire to craft better ties with us, and of course you will be welcome in Erkynland. It is just . . . it such a short time since—"

"Since our two people were so recently at war," Viyeki finished, nodding. "Of course. And please forgive me for speaking without asking permission. I have no idea what protocol is in your court."

Simon laughed, although he sounded a little uncomfortable. "If you come to understand it, please inform me. I am widely known for never getting it right. Just speak what you think, Lord Viyeki."

"High Magister, I think is his title," Miriamele said. "And I am certain the high magister will have no problems learning our ways—whatever he may decide he thinks of them." But inside she was still surprised. An envoy from Nakkiga to the High Throne? And not only that, but by all appearances a permanent embassy?

Blessed Elysia, she wondered, *where should we put him?*

"One more thing, Majesties." Viyeki's appearance of complete, calm control now slipped just a little. "I believe I will be bringing my daughter Nezeru with me."

"Nezeru?" said Simon. "The one that Morgan was—?"

Miriamele gave him a meaningful nudge. "Of course, Nezeru, the soldier who so bravely attacked the mad queen." She realized she might have gone too far—she had no idea what this Viyeki's attachment to his dead monarch might have been. "Your daughter risked her life to save us all," she elaborated. "We are very impressed by her bravery, High Magister. She is certainly welcome in our country and in our royal court, though we are not completely certain yet where that court will be. Several scattered parts of the city of Erchester comprise our home at the moment."

Viyeki was looking out across the plateau toward the spot where his daughter and Morgan seemed to be in very earnest conversation.

"You are generous, Majesties," he said, but Miriamele thought she could see the look of a worried father, even on a Norn. As she looked at Morgan's pale face, and Nezeru's, which of course was even paler, she could not guess what was passing between them. She could only hope she and Simon were not ruining their grandson's happiness by agreeing to this unexpected embassy.

"These are strange days for all of us," said Simon. "We will all have to learn how to live in this new world from day to day."

Her husband had a knack for saying simple things that were nevertheless exactly true. *Yes, we will have to learn,* Miriamele thought. *And may Heaven help us all.*

♛

Relieved and surprised, Viyeki finished his audience with the mortal king and queen. He was grateful they had not insisted on waiting for an official request from Pratiki, but he knew they would—and should—remain at least a bit suspicious until it arrived. Only a few moons earlier and he would have been deemed not an envoy but a likely spy. Viyeki knew the request was real and would arrive, by and by, but he had been surprised by how ordinary the monarchs of Erkynland and the High Ward seemed to be. Part of it was simply that they were mortal and had not lived through the treacherous, always dangerous court life of Utuk'ku's Maze Palace, but there was something else about them that he had not yet grasped, something that puzzled him. Of course, mortals wore their feelings very openly, but that was true of all their kind as far as Viyeki knew. No, there was something else about the king and queen that he had not yet grasped, and it interested him.

Shun'y'asu said, "Wisdom never comes as a flood, but as drips upon drips until it dissolves even stone." I will have time to understand these mortals better, he told himself. *If my daughter does not kill their grandson first, that is.* He had thought it to amuse himself, but he still did not feel he knew Nezeru well enough to be completely certain such a thing would never happen.

As Viyeki talked with the mortal monarchs, the plateau had filled with folk of all kinds, shapes, and sizes, to the extent that he could not easily find Nezeru in the growing crowd.

"*It is almost time,*" an odd, buzzing voice announced, and Viyeki recognized the unmusical tones of Geloë, the changeling woman who now wore the Navigator's armor. He turned and saw not only her, but also the mortals and Zida'ya who had returned to Tanakirú, as well as Geloë's own Tinukeda'ya helpers. All had gathered around her in the center of the plateau. He gave in to the pull of the crowd and went along to see what would happen next, deciding he would find Nezeru afterward.

Geloë stood in the middle of a throng of Tinukeda'ya, but mortals and Zida'ya now moved in around her as well. She raised her gauntleted hands to the sky; the eye holes of the helmet, round as if in permanent surprise, surveyed the expectant crowd.

"Tomorrow the *Witchwood Crown* will leave this place," she declared, "as it was meant to do when it first set out from the garden in the ancient past. As I will try to explain, the way that the Great Ships travel is largely unknowable."

"Even to you, Valada Geloë?" asked Ki'ushapo.

The helmet swiveled toward him. "Even to me, Protector. I am part of the Dreaming Sea—all my people are—but the wisdom of that sea is beyond my merely mortal understanding. That wisdom brought all our peoples out of the Garden to these lands, so I do not doubt that it will suffice to take us to some new and better place. But first I have things I need to tell you all." She pointed southward. "Tomorrow morning, Midsummer's Day, you must assemble over there, on the far side of the gorge, where the Hikeda'ya armies camped while they besieged Tanakirú, because it is possible there will be falling stones and other dangers here on the plateau when the ship departs. When the *Witchwood Crown* first landed here, five mortal centuries ago, so many pieces of the cliffs fell that they blocked the source of the Coolblood River. It would not be good for any of you to be too near the cliffs tomorrow."

"How will you get the ship down to the water?" asked King Simon. Viyeki had been wondering much the same thing.

"You cannot understand what will happen here if you rely on what you know of this world's ships and oceans," said Geloë. "That is not how *Witchwood Crown* or any of the Great Ships travel."

"Then tell us how," said the mortal king. "Or is it a secret only for the Tinukeda'ya?"

Geloë let out a single sharp sound that Viyeki thought might be a laugh. "Kingship and almost dying have not made you any more patient, Simon. I was planning to explain, but you are hurrying me."

"Sorry, sorry," he said. Viyeki could see that there was an old connection between them, maybe even friendship, though it was hard to believe anyone could be friends with the weird, armored thing at the center of the plateau.

Geloë spoke again. "Before I tell you more of the journey to come, there is still something I must do—a sacred duty. And I wish to discharge it here before you. Ruyan Ká, come forth!"

Then, with a rasp and creak of timbers, a massive shape appeared over the side of the gorge, climbing up from some tunnel below the spectators' view. Viyeki had seen the immense thing before, but it still shocked him. The mortal queen and a many others who had never encountered the *uro'eni* fell back in alarm, but even those who had seen it before were startled and frightened by its coming.

Slowly, ponderously, the huge witchwood figure pulled itself up onto the plateau and trudged forward, each step an impact that Viyeki could feel in his stomach. The spectators hurried to get out of its way, opening a broad path to the place where Geloë stood, and when it reached her, the ogre kneeled.

"No, Navigator's Daughter!" Geloë said. "You should not kneel to me, even though I wear your revered father's armor. Rather, all your people should kneel to you." And so saying, she slowly sank to one knee before the looming figure. "Your father gave you the most important role of all—that of guiding his people to a better place once the rest of the Gardenborn had been settled here. And although your voyage went astray for reasons none here can know, you never gave over your responsibility, and your loyalty never wavered. Long after your body had wasted away, your spirit kept the ship vital, and protected it and all this valley. You have spent the last moons helping to make the *Witchwood Crown* ready to sail again. But now the work is all but finished, and it is time to return the last pieces of the ship to their places. Thus, you are now released from your oath, Ruyan Ká, and from the bondage of this world and this life. You have the undying gratitude of all your people. Your ship is safe now, and I will bring it to a better place—a new home for our kind."

Silence followed. For long moments the kneeling *uro'eni* remained motionless, as though in deep thought or even prayer. Then it raised its massive, almost faceless head toward the sky—or perhaps toward the *Witchwood Crown,* still lodged in the cliff face above—and the ogre slowly began to fall apart.

As Viyeki and the others watched in open-mouthed astonishment, its witchwood spars began to fall to the ground—slowly at first, like a tree shedding leaves in autumn, but then the unbinding began to hasten. The occasional sound of wood striking stone rose to a constant clatter as pieces of witchwood rained down. Within a surprisingly short time, nothing was left of the ogre's original form but a great pile of boards and beams and tangled roots, all jumbled on the ground at the center of the plateau—a pile that towered high above kneeling Geloë.

"Go where you will, faithful Ruyan Ká," she cried, her unnatural voice carrying above the murmurs of the watching crowd. "Go where you are called to go and find your deserved rest. Know that you have helped to save your people. We will never forget you."

Even as the last upright section of witchwood teetered and fell to the ground, a parade of Geloë's Tinukeda'ya workers came forward to carry away the remains. Each one took up a piece, and then, like ants, bore them in a line toward the caverns at the base of the great cliff.

"Now the last parts of the ship will be remade," Geloë said. "And tomorrow, when the sun rises, we will depart."

"But you still haven't told us how you will make the ship sail," said King Simon. "How you're going to get it down from there. Does it fly like an eagle? Or float like a feather?" Viyeki was amused despite himself at the mortal monarch's single-mindedness.

"Very well, Simon. One last lesson for old time's sake," said the armored figure, and this time Viyeki was certain he could hear exasperated amusement in the buzzing voice. "I will do my best to explain. Do not blame me if none of you understands—I do not wholly understand it myself. Though I am of the Dreaming Sea, as are all my folk, that Sea is greater, older, and deeper than any of us who wear bodies can understand.

"After what all of you have experienced here, you will not be surprised when I tell you that what we see is not all that exists of truth. And what I will tell you today is only the truth as I understand it—a very small truth, at that—but it is what brought all the great ships here from the Garden, and that is all I need know. King Simon asks whether the *Witchwood Crown* will fly like an eagle or sail on the water like an ordinary ship. The answer is, neither—that is not how the great ships travel. But to explain their voyaging, I must tell of the other worlds that surround us."

"Other worlds?" said Simon. "Do you mean the lands that lie beyond the sea or across the eastern mountains?"

"No, that is not what I mean," Geloë told him. "We are utterly surrounded by other worlds, but we cannot see them." She held up a gauntleted hand. "Please. If what I say makes you uneasy, you need not listen. The ship will do what it was made to do, understood or not."

"Say on," said the mortal king. "I want to hear."

"Then do not interrupt me. It is hard enough to find words that can be understood. Hear me, then—there are countless worlds, separate from ours, but as close to us as our thoughts. We are surrounded by them, though we cannot see them or discern them, and each is a semblance of our own world, each slightly different. The Garden itself was such a semblance—or perhaps Osten Ard, the land in which we stand now, is but a semblance of the Garden. Either way, these phantoms surround us, one pressed close upon the other, like onion skins."

"Hah," said Ki'ushapo, the Protector of Year-Dancing House, just loud enough for those around him to hear. "Our Jiriki was wiser than anyone knew."

Viyeki had no idea what that meant.

The helmeted head swiveled. "Kuyu-Kun, where are you?" Geloë called.

The old Tinukeda'ya rose, swaying, to his feet. "Here, Sa-Ruyan."

"Do you have the book Tih-Rumi brought you this morning?"

"In my hands, Sa-Ruyan."

"Give it to me, please." She accepted the leather-bound volume and held it out for the watching crowd to see, its covers closed, the parchment pages tight-packed. "Imagine that each page of this book is a world," she said. "Pressed close together, but each separate from the next. Now imagine that instead of a few score of parchment pages, this book contained more pages than you could count in your lifetime." She held it up, the spine lying on her hands, and let its covers fall open so that the pages spread like a fan. "Now let us imagine two small creatures, an ant and a booklouse, both of them wanting to journey from the first page of this great book to the last. The ant must travel across each page to the next, up one side, down the other, walking, walking, walking." She slid a woven-wire finger up one page, over the edge, and down the next, then repeated. "Even an ant with a life as long as one of the Keida'ya would be hard-pressed to reach the end. But that is how an ordinary ship sails—or how any movement from place to place occurs in this world. Now consider a booklouse, a tiny creature that eats through the substance of the parchments themselves. The voyage of a booklouse covers the smallest possible distance through the book, because our louse does not march across each page in turn, but burrows through them in a line." She swiped her finger across the ends of the pages to show a direct path straight through the volume. "That is how all of the Dreaming Sea's great ships traveled to Osten Ard, and how the *Witchwood Crown* will make its journey at tomorrow's sunrise. In truth, it is even stranger than that, because the ships do not move like a booklouse, but stay in one place and allow the worlds to pass through them, until they choose one and the ship stops there."

There was a long silence, broken only by a little quiet talk among the listeners.

"I still don't understand," said the mortal king at last.

"Simon, it doesn't matter," his wife told him. "Geloë knows what to do."

"Just so, Queen Miriamele," said the armored figure. "In any case, I do not want to try to explain too much. Urudade using the power of the Dreaming Sea unwisely is the reason that Unbeing came into existence—but that is not a story for this hopeful day. Let it suffice to say that our ship will have no need for water, nor will it fly.

"But the departure of something so large will cause disruption," she continued, "as it did when the ship first came here. That is why you must all be well away from the cliffs when we depart."

Those gathered began actively to call out questions, and after listening for some moments, Geloë raised her hand again. "I cannot answer you, and not just to protect this world from unearned wisdom. We Vao still have much to do to prepare our departure. Tih-Rumi of the Tinukeda'ya, acolyte of the Sa'Vao, will remain here to become the next Sa-Vao of our people, and he has heard all that Kuyu-Kun and I discussed of the ship. When we are gone, you may ask him what you will, and he will choose what to tell you. Now I must go to watch over the final preparations and make certain the last of my people are safely boarded."

With that, she lowered her gauntleted hand and headed back toward the caverns. Several of the Zida'ya followed her, asking questions, but as far as Viyeki could tell she did not answer any of them.

Miriamele was still reeling. Geloë's survival—if it could be called that—had been a shocking piece of news when Simon told her, but hearing Geloë's distorted but undeniable voice coming out of the strange, inhuman armor she now wore had been more upsetting than Miriamele expected. Still, nothing could have prepared her for the sight of the massive Ninth Ship or the terrifying ogre, and as she and Simon made their way back across the plateau toward the caverns, she found she was trembling all over, but her fretful thoughts were interrupted by the appearance of two Sithi, one her own size, the other not much taller than her granddaughter.

"Rukayu!" said Simon. "And Xila! It is good to see you both. Miri, these are the two who helped watch over our granddaughter . . . and over me."

"We are well met again, King Seoman," said Rukayu. "I had to come back and see the end. My grandfather Shen'de gave his life so that tomorrow might happen."

"That is the truth," Simon said. "I hope the Tinukeda'ya will remember and honor him and the others who fought here."

"He never wanted to be honored," Rukayu said with a shrug, then bowed to Miriamele. "It is good to discover that your husband's deep mourning for you was premature."

"We each thought the other was dead," said Miri. "I thank you from the bottom of my heart for the help and kindness you gave to Simon and my granddaughter."

"Xila spent more time with young Lillia than I did," said Rukayu.

But Xila was scarcely paying attention, instead staring up at the cliff face and the shadow of the great ship. "They would not let me go with them," she said sadly.

"What do you mean?" Simon asked.

"I asked to go with them on the *Witchwood Crown*," Xila said. "My family is dead. I would rather go to some new place, see new things. But Sa-Ruyan Geloë said that only Tinukeda'ya could go." She gave an angry little shake of her head. "So I must stay behind, alone."

"We all stay behind," said Miriamele. "But not alone. You have friends here in this world, though you may not know it. Simon will agree with me—because of your kindness to my husband and granddaughter, you are always welcome in our home, and any favor we can do, you have only to ask. You too, Rukayu."

Rukayu bowed, but Xila looked at the queen in a speculating manner. "Hmm. Then it could be that I will come to you then one day. I have never seen how mortals live."

"As long as our family holds the throne, you will be received with honor," Miriamele promised.

"Our troll friends are beckoning to us," said Simon. "Will you come and meet them?"

Rukayu smiled. "Perhaps later. I have matters I must discuss with Protector Ki'ushapo now, and then take the news back to my people in Peja'ura. The world is changing, and I think we must change too."

"As my husband said only a short while ago," Miriamele agreed, "we will all have to learn to live in this new world."

Morgan and Nezeru had been too enwrapped in their own talk to join the others listening to Geloë. Even after her bulky, armored figure had retreated and the crowd began to scatter, they were still arguing, although Morgan was no longer certain what they were arguing about.

"You keep saying you have something to tell me," he protested, "but then you do not tell me. This is painful, Nezeru."

"Perhaps it is painful for me, too, Morgan."

He sighed. "Then speak to me. Just speak! Tell me what these thoughts are, because all I can imagine is that you are searching for words to explain how much you despise me—something you have already made clear."

"No! That is not what I am trying to tell you."

"Then simply say what is on your mind. You are as maddening as your old friend Jarnulf, who follows me around like a spy. I cannot even guess at what either of you want of me."

To his astonishment, Nezeru laughed. "Do you really not understand Jarnulf? It is as plain as a single cloud in an otherwise empty sky. He is in love with you, Morgan."

Morgan stared, his thoughts suddenly flung in many directions. "What?" he said at last. "How can that be? He is a man, I am a man . . ."

"Do men never love men among you mortals? Do women never love other women?"

"Yes, but it is called shameful."

"And who calls it that? Other mortals?" She made a gesture Morgan did not recognize. "In any case, such things matter little, because Jarnulf's feelings are obviously real, whether you like the idea or not. Have you truly not noticed, Morgan? It is there to be seen in his every movement, every glance. He may not even know himself why he is so fascinated with you—he is a strange man, full of his religious faith but also full of painful doubts, I think. But I tell you this without fear of being wrong—your new knight Jarnulf is in love with you."

For a long moment Morgan was disturbed by the idea. *How can I have a knight in my service who loves me that way? What will people think?* But a moment later he realized that, in truth, it mattered little to him. "Whatever the case, I am not made that way. I will never love him in return. Not as I love . . . as I have loved women."

"People have lived out their lives before without the object of their desire returning it," said Nezeru. "I see several possibilities for Jarnulf, or Gilhedur, or whatever name he has settled on. He may pine for you all his life but learn to live with it. He may also find other men to love if he is truly made that way.

Or he may bury his desire so deep within himself that he never understands the true cause of his loyalty to you."

"But I don't care about him." Morgan was growing frustrated. "I wanted to hear what you said you would tell me, but if this is it, I am finished. Jarnulf has been knighted and is sworn to my service. Leave it at that. But you—you! You have tormented my thoughts for months, Nezeru. I did not want to see you—I can imagine you didn't want to see me, either—and yet here you are. But instead of us leaving each other alone, you made a point of finding me, and of threatening to tell me some important thing, but will not do so. Well, tell me now or let me go. My heart is too sore to let you keep hurting me."

He fully expected her next words to be angry, but instead he was astonished to see her eyes grow bright with tears. "Oh, Morgan," she said. "I never wanted to give you pain. I thought I was sparing you. I thought I was sparing myself. But I have suffered too, as the moons waxed and waned."

"Are you . . . crying?"

She wiped angrily at her eyes. "My cursed mortal side." She blinked. "No. That is wrong and unfair. It is my mortal side that lets me experience something more of the world than simply what I was raised to understand in the Sacrifice Order. And it is my mortal half that will help me survive in my new life."

He shook his head. "I don't understand you."

Her words came in a rush. "My father has been made ambassador to your court, Morgan. Yes, he has been ordered to Erchester City or whatever you call it, to live among your people. And he has asked me to go with him."

For an instant Morgan was filled with hope, but then the likelihood of what he was about to hear came crashing in on him. "He will be made welcome, of course," he said stiffly. "My grandparents are wise, kind people."

"So I have heard—and seen, at least a little. That is why I have decided to accompany him."

Morgan could not entirely trust his ears. "You are coming . . . to Erchester?"

"That is what I have decided, yes." She gave him a long, unflinching look, and he thought her eyes had never looked so dark, so deep. "Because what happened between you and I was rare—very rare—but I have run from it since the first moment. I thought that was only the practicality of my Sacrifice training, and in part it was. But it was also my mortal side as well, which recognized something very mortal in me—very human." She lowered her head and was silent for a long moment, then looked up again to meet his eyes. "I do have deep feelings for you, Morgan, and those feelings have never gone away—if anything, our separation has only made them stronger. I knew real happiness in your company, the first time I think I have felt that since I was a small child in my parents' arms."

Hearing that, he felt as if a painful weight had lifted from his heart. He reached out to pull her to him, but she set her hand against his chest.

"Please," she said. "You must hear me first. We must agree. I care for you,

Morgan. It may even be what you call love, but I do not trust the word, since I have never felt love before for anyone but my parents—and this is quite a different feeling."

"Which is how it should be!" he said, but he let her keep her distance.

"Perhaps. But many pitfalls lie before me—before both of us—so I need you to understand me first. I care deeply for you, Morgan. I will no longer lie to myself about that. I wish to be with you, to spend time with you, to do lovemaking with you—"

"God be praised!"

She could not help laughing a little. "But you must honor my fears. I will not belong to you. I will not be known as 'the prince's fairy-woman.' In truth, I do not think we can ever marry—the problems it would make for you are terrible to imagine—but beyond that I will set no limits . . . for now. We will live under the same roof, and we will trust time to show us what comes next."

"Agreed. Oh, yes, praise the Aedon, agreed! But we cannot stop people from talking, either my people or yours—."

"I know. But I am not ready to be seen as an ornament on your arm, like a war trophy, and in truth I may never be ready. Can you understand that? Can you let our bond be enough without much outward show? Because that may be all we can have."

"Of course. Of course! I would have given an arm or a leg—or both!—to have you come back with me. How much better that you also admit you love me!"

She frowned. "I did not quite say that. But I take it you agree to my terms?"

"I do."

She smiled with relief, as though she had shed a painful burden. "Then come to me after the evening meal and we will seal our bargain properly."

"Properly? In a tent with your father?"

"Foolish youth," she said sternly. "I was a Sacrifice. I do not need a magister's luxuries. I have my own tent." She pointed. "There, at the outer edge of the plateau."

He grinned. His heart was beating so rapidly it was all he could do not to shout out his answer. "I will, Nezeru. Joyfully."

"Then you may kiss me, Morgan. Yes, even here and now, amid all these Zida'ya. I do not care what the Zida'ya think."

Nezeru carefully slipped out from beneath Morgan's enfolding arm and sat up. He slept in that odd, deadened way that mortals had—like brute beasts. When she had first experienced it with him, it had faintly disturbed her: were his people never threatened in their sleep? Did they simply trust that they would wake again each morning, alive and safe, after shutting out the world and its dangers so completely? But now it seemed only another example of Morgan-ness. He had trusted her almost from the first, against all likelihood and, certainly, all good sense. But instead of filling her with contempt, as it once would have, it made her long to be the same, to trust in the world even when she was insensible to it, as if it were an old friend who meant only good things for her.

But I cannot. Perhaps someday things will change, but not yet. She rose and reached for her armor.

When she was dressed, she stood over Morgan for a long time, watching his fitful movements, the tiny changes in his face and breathing as he slumbered. *He agreed to everything I asked. But will that still be true now that the lovemaking is over?* Still, Nezeru had more pressing questions just now. She slipped out of the tent without waking him.

Though it was still hours before dawn, the train of connected caverns that Utuk'ku had used to descend to the plateau with her Queen's Teeth was now crowded with Tinukeda'ya. They seemed to be the final stragglers, as they carried no pieces of the *Witchwood Crown*, but instead bundles of personal belongings. As she joined the throng making its way up the tunnel toward the ship she saw entire families of Tinukeda'ya, Niskies and half-Niskies, as well as many of the big-eyed Delvers of the same kind as Kuyu-Kun. Other creatures were boarding too, many of whom she would never have known were intelligent beings if she had encountered them in any other setting.

By the time she had climbed with them for a time, she realized that she was troubled by the nearness of so many of the Ocean Children. Her own reaction puzzled her. She had never been frightened of them before. The Tinukeda'ya seldom resorted to violence of any sort, either in Nakkiga where fear kept them down, or elsewhere—at least from what she knew.

She turned to the long-fingered creature walking beside her. "What is your name?" she asked. "My mother named me Nezeru. I am the daughter of Magister Viyeki."

To her surprise, the look on the Tinukeda'ya's face was of ill-hidden fear. "I am called Dor-Sinno, Mistress."

"I am no one's master or mistress," she said. "Your kind of speech sounds familiar, though. Do you come from Nakkiga?"

He nodded, still watching as though he feared a sudden blow. "I did," he said, with a hint of quiet defiance. "Now I am part of our new world. Or I will be." He hesitated now. "Unless you mean to prevent me."

Nezeru was astounded. "Why would I try to do such a thing?"

He made a gesture of resignation, but she thought she saw anger behind his wide-eyed stare. "You are of the Hikeda'ya, Mistress—and of a high Nakkiga family, from the way you make your words. We were your slaves. We know what you think of us."

"Forget what you think you know. I have no power over you, nor do I want any. Just tell me—how did you come here?"

"I was part of the amnesty." He still did not entirely trust her; he had moved a little way back, though the ascending corridor was narrow. "The prince of

Nakkiga allowed us to leave. I have been traveling since the Wind-Child's Moon." For a moment his stiff facade showed a few cracks. "I did . . . I did not think I would arrive in time. My brother died on the journey."

"I am sorry, Dor-Sinno," she said. "So, Prince Pratiki set you free?"

"Not all of us. Many who were part of important work in Nakkiga were forbidden. Some of us left anyway." The glowing stones of the corridor revealed his sudden loss of color. "I should not have said that."

"It is nothing to me. I intend you no harm."

"That is hard to believe," he said, "after all I have seen in my life. But the world is changing."

"It is." For the first time the weight of what her people had done to the Tinukeda'ya truly fell on her. All these people—thinking, feeling creatures like her—had possessed less freedom to live their lives than the lowest Sacrifice cast-off. And she had never noticed, any more than she had noticed the love her mother Tzoja had so desperately tried to give her. "Perhaps this world is not beyond hope," she said. "I pray that is so. And I wish you a good journey, Dor-Sinno, and a happy life in your new home."

He stared, then shook his head in surprise. His thin neck made him look like a poppy wagging in the wind. "That is a kind wish," he said.

Nezeru had to climb a good deal farther to find the one she sought, and several times she wondered whether she was on a foolish errand. What did the lies and madness of the old queen's reign matter now? Utuk'ku was dead, and Prince Pratiki was their new monarch, for good or ill. What happened before had no more sway over her life.

But I came to Tanakirú in the first place for answers, she thought, *risking my life and the lives of my companions. And tomorrow, some of those answers will be gone forever.*

She found Geloë outside the *Witchwood Crown*'s monstrous hull, or at least the part of it visible behind Kushiba's encroaching stone. The armored figure was watching the last arrivals. It must have been a frantic time for those hurrying to get on board, and not much less so for Geloë herself, but the expressionless helmet gave nothing away.

"I know the hour is late," Nezeru said. "Can you find a moment to speak to me?"

The masklike face swiveled toward her. "I can. This world owes you much, Nezeru of the Enduya."

"Soon to be Nezeru of Erchester," she said, though it felt incredibly strange.

The eye holes of the mask fixed on her. She could see something yellow and inconstant glimmering in the depths behind the crystal. "Ah. Interesting," said the buzzing voice. "But you have climbed a long way. All the others who have made the climb will join me on our voyage—but that is not your purpose, is it?"

"No. I have a question. I do not think anyone can answer it . . . except, perhaps, you. Because of what you have seen and what you have learned." She suddenly found it hard to explain. "I . . . I felt you, felt your thoughts, as you strove with the queen. I think you know many things I do not."

Geloë's strange voice was brisk, almost harsh. "Dawn is coming soon, Nezeru. My people owe you much, but nothing will keep me from this ship's timely departure. If we miss the Midsummer of a Great Year, we will have a long wait before things are right again. Ask me what you wish to know."

"In the last moments before Utuk'ku died—before I helped to kill her—she heard Morgan call my name, and it startled her. I was almost mad from pain and fear, but I could not have mistaken that. The queen knew my name and was surprised to hear it. That makes no sense to me. But you understand so many things about what Utuk'ku wanted and what she planned."

"Out of necessity," said the dry, buzzing voice. "Not out of any desire to explore her dark, angry thoughts."

"Understood. But do you have any idea why she seemed to know me, and why it should startle her to know I was there? She picked me for one of her Talons, but I never met her face to face, and I was the least important part of that company."

Geloë was quiet for no little time as the last of the Tinukeda'ya continued to eddy past them at a respectful distance. "Are you certain you want to know, child?" she said after long moments. "Sometimes, ignorance is preferable."

"I cannot agree. I came to this place precisely because I wanted to know why my life has been as it has been." Nezeru stepped back a little as a throng of small, hairy creatures pushed their way past her and headed for the ship's opening. "I have not changed."

Something bumped against her leg. Nezeru looked down to discover a creature not much larger than a rabbit nuzzling her ankle—no, sniffing it. She was about to push it away when she remembered that these creatures, even this little, hairy thing, were all Tinukeda'ya—Geloë's fellow Vao. A small, bright-eyed face was gazing up at her. It was not a rabbit, not a squirrel, but something slightly more person-like than either.

"I ask you one last time, child," said Geloë. "Do you truly wish to know the secrets of the dead?"

The small, furry creature now climbed up Nezeru's leg, swift as a rock-roach, startling her. It was all she could do not to pluck it loose and send it away, but something in the trusting manner with which it settled itself into her arms made her pause, shocked by such unwarranted affection and trust. She did not want more distractions before Geloë could answer, so she simply held it. The little creature seemed in no hurry to continue into the ship, though its fellows had stopped just inside the hole in the hull and were watching with anxious expressions on their rodent-like faces. "Yes, I wish to know. Why do you say, 'secrets of the dead'"?

"Because I learned it—and many other things—beyond the Veil. My body had died, and I was trapped there a long time. Do you know anything of that place?"

"No, thank the Garden. But I am not afraid to hear."

"It is a place where the dead, the near-dead, and the never-quite-alive mingle, some knowing where and what they are, as I did, while others drift like sleepwalkers. And everywhere in that shadowy place, ancient songs of power, old, puzzling stories, and forgotten prophecies drift on the wind like stray feathers. Many of these tales are shared over and over among the presences gathered there. But those who stray beyond the Veil but are still alive, as Utuk'ku was when she was in her healing sleep, place great value on the prophesies of time to come, because it is known that the dead cannot lie. One such prophecy came to Utuk'ku when she was in that land of spirits and shadows.

"The prophecy said, *The Clan of Frogs will bring the Great Serpent what she most desires.*"

"The clan of frogs? My father's clan, the Enduya, hold the stone frog as their totem."

"Yes, and it is clear enough who the great serpent must be. Or rather, was." Geloë finally seemed to notice the furry living thing in Nezeru's arms. "Ah. You have made a friend, it appears." Her words seemed incongruous, spoken in the humming, inhuman voice. "This little thing seems to know your scent, or at least to find it pleasant."

Nezeru carefully set the creature down. It reached out a stubby paw to pat her booted foot, then turned and scampered away to join the rest of its kind inside the ship. "Perhaps it is one of the creatures Morgan met," she said. "Chikri, he called them. Perhaps it smelled his scent on me."

"Perhaps," said Geloë.

"Do you think that prophecy is what the queen believed of me? That my clan would somehow bring her everything that she desired?"

"Prophecies from beyond the Veil are always true," Geloë said "—although sometimes in ways not immediately obvious. It does not pay to think one can understand the dead, even less to think that their terrible knowledge can easily be put to use by the living."

"But did Utuk'ku truly get what she most desired?"

"If what she wanted was an escape from her wretched, endless life, then yes. Everything else came from her selfish unwillingness to die alone."

And so, a prophecy explains why I was advanced above my fellows to join a Queen's Talon. Nezeru felt both relieved and shamed. *Jarnulf was right—there was a secret reason I was favored beyond what I deserved. I must tell him.* She took a deep breath. *Some day.* "I thank you, Ruyan's Own. I have much to think on now."

The armored figure was silent for a long moment before speaking again. "And do you really mean to live among the mortals in Erchester? With the king and queen of the High Throne?"

"I will—or at least I will try. Why do you ask?"

"Because there was another piece to that prophecy, one that Utuk'ku must have thought only a blow-by-blow of her plans to end everything. When I was masking as Ommu the Whisperer, I was curious that so much should seemingly revolve around your family's clan—not the most important of Hikeda'ya noble houses, after all. The rest of the prophecy said, *And the youngest of the frog-clan will end the reign of mortal kings in Osten Ard.*"

Nezeru's hackles lifted. "'End the reign . . .' What does that mean? And why should there be prophesies about my family in the lands of the dead?"

"I do not pretend to know. Remember, child, it is folly for the living to try to understand what is said beyond the Veil, let alone to act upon it. That kind of foolishness and pride is what helped destroy the queen of the Hikeda'ya."

"I understand. But it will be impossible not to remember." She did her best to calm her rapidly beating heart. "Still, I thank you for giving me answers, Sa-Ruyan. You have eased my mind—at least about some things." She bowed. "Travel well, you and all your folk."

"It is not the journey itself I look forward to," said Geloë, "but a rest from my labors, which I most desire, and that will come at the end."

Nezeru bowed. "Then I hope you find that peace."

"And I wish the same for you, child—though I hope you find yours here in this world."

54

Family Matters

"It is nearly time," Fremur said.

"Time for what?" asked Hyara. "You broke your fast hours ago—are you hungry again? Ha, you still have butter on your chin."

He wiped at his beard. He had not realized that he had spoken his thought aloud. "Time to return to the Lakelands, I meant. After the thanemoot, I must go back to the Clan Kragni lands. I have been too long away from them."

Hyara did not seem worried. "The Crane Clan are on their way here to Blood Lake for that very thanemoot, so you will be with them soon. If they have forgotten you already, they will quickly remember."

"I do not fear being forgotten!" He spoke with a little more heat than he intended. "But there are still some among the Cranes who think I am too young to shepherd the clan—that I have nothing to commend me but my friendship with Unver Shan."

"Your friendship with the Shan is nothing to be ashamed of, Fremur."

He felt an upwelling of frustration. *But this is why I chose her,* he reminded himself. *Because she is not easily silenced. Because she speaks her mind always, even to Unver. But not like Vorzheva, whose tongue is as sharp as a fox's tooth.*

He turned and gestured to the spot next to him on the steps. "Come, please, wife. Sit with me."

She came out of the wagon and settled herself beside him. They sat for a time in silence, watching the grassy hills glowing with late morning light. Horses and cattle grazed on the slopes, lifting their heads when a breeze touched them.

"We are lucky," said Hyara.

"We are."

"I was so fearful while you and Unver were gone, husband. Every night as I tried to sleep, I had terrible visions of what might happen to you. I could not make myself believe that you would truly come back, and that even if you did, that you would still want me."

"I was afraid too. I confess that I thought Unver Shan had lost his wits. I believed we would die in that dreadful stone tomb of a castle."

"Don't say it! It chills me even now."

Fremur took her hand. "I was wrong, of course. I had forgotten the most important thing about your sister's son—he never stops watching and thinking. He saw the shape of things from the first moment he entered the place and began to consider what he should do, and I think he had begun planning Pasevalles's destruction before he even met the man. Yes, several times I thought the stone-dweller had gulled him or trapped him—trapped us both—but each time I was wrong. I was a fool to doubt him."

Hyara was silent for a long time. The call of a quail leading hatchlings—*peet-tee-weet*—sounded from the grass nearby. "You should not worship him," she finally said. "My nephew is a good man, but he is still only a man."

"He is a man the spirits have chosen."

"Even so. I fear what might happen if you follow him too readily, without ever questioning."

This made him uneasy again. "I do nothing without questioning, Hyara. But you forget, I have seen the power of the spirits upon him—I saw the wild wolves of the grasslands bow down and obey him! You yourself saw crows come to his aid when he fought for his life, and even cast themselves into fire for Unver's sake. If I cannot trust such a man, who in this world *can* be trusted?"

"You are angry with me now," she said. "But it is not Unver I fear for, it is you, husband. Great warriors draw others to them. Great leaders, the same. But it is not the great warriors and leaders who pay the price of making an empire, but their followers. I feared for you while you were gone. Now that we are married, I fear even more, because you have brought me happiness, and I do not want to lose it."

"I am Unver's man," he said, but his annoyance had softened. "I too would like to live only this life we have here. But if the Shan needs me to fight, I will fight. I could do nothing else."

"I know. You would not be the man I care for if you did otherwise." She clasped his hand tightly. "And I know there will be fighting again—someday. But remember that even if the spirits have chosen him, Unver has chosen *you*, my husband. You owe him not just your fealty, but also your best counsel, and he should listen to you."

Fremur was amused. "Do you think I am undervalued by our Shan, then?"

"No. But you have a family now. You have me. What you do touches more than just yourself. You must never forget that."

"Unver is not your rival, Hyara," he told her as gently as he could. "You have no rival in my heart."

"Do not think I am my sister, Fremur. I do not let jealousy rule me. But Unver does not have a family of his own, and he is a man who sees great wrongs in the world and means to right them. That frightens me, because I know that where he goes, you will go."

"Unver does not have a family?" He shook his head in amazement. "By the Sky-Piercer, woman, he has more family now than he knows what to do with—his mother, his crippled father, and now a long-lost sister as well!"

"You do not understand me. He cares for all of them, yes, but until his heart is tied to another with the strongest cords of all, tied to a wife or a child or both, he will never think twice about the *cost* of justice, only about justice itself."

"I think Unver is more cautious than you understand, Hyara. But I truly must go now. The man we discuss is expecting me by noon."

She gave him a long look. "He is a little taken with the blind woman, his sister's friend, I think. Perhaps that will become something."

Fremur laughed. "Are you trying to marry him off? I will never understand how women think."

"Spend all day in a wagon, day after day, waiting for your man to come back and wondering why you have so little say over your own life. Then you may understand us a little better."

He looked at her flushed face and despite the unhappiness with which she had spoken, he suddenly loved her more desperately than he could have imagined. "Are we having a fight?" he asked. "Truly? We should celebrate. It is our first."

She gave him a hard look but could not keep it long before she smiled a little, though there was pain in it. "I suppose we are. I suppose we should."

"I am happy that someone in the world cares enough for me to worry over me, Hyara. I thank the Sky-Piercer every day for bringing you to me."

She leaned toward him then and kissed him. "Then remember what I say, I beg you, my young, brave husband. When the Nabbanai next raid the lakelands and you are sent off to punish them, remember that someone at home is fearful for you."

"I will never, ever forget it," he said. "That I promise on my heart and my honor."

"Give it to me," Vorzheva demanded. "He eats better when I feed him."

"He does not need to be fed like a child," said Tzoja, but she surrendered the wooden spoon to her mother.

"Not need to be fed," her father muttered, but Tzoja could not tell if he meant it or was simply repeating her words.

"Nonsense, Josua. You are too thin," Vorzheva told him. "And if you are to keep getting better, you must be strong. Open your mouth now. You still have half the bowl left!"

It troubled Tzoja to be pushed away from her father so abruptly, but her bond with her mother, such as it was, was still new and very fragile. Each day contained many such moments, and each had to be carefully negotiated to maintain harmony. She thanked God—or the gods—that she had a wagon of her own to retreat to, with no one to please but sweet-tempered Vordis. For a moment, as she looked around her brother's wagon—a fine and very big one that had once belonged to Thane Rudur, but still only a wagon—she wondered if she had made a mistake accompanying her father back to the Thrithings.

Even if it is only for a short time, I left my daughter behind to take care of my father. And I had found her only a brief time before I found my father, then let her go with Viyeki. And it hurt.

Though she believed Josua could get better physic among his own people, Erchester was a place Vorzheva would not go without a dreadful struggle. She could not bear pulling her father away from her mother, so she had compromised, trying to do what was best for her father and even for her difficult, spiky mother.

And for me? Where do I go? Where do I belong? I could have been with Viyeki, living in a palace with him and Nezeru—or at least somewhere my mother didn't scold me as though I were still a child. Vorzheva did not know how to talk without scolding, and though it made their struggles no more pleasant, it gave Tzoja at least a little peace to understand her mother's wounded nature. *See how she cannot rest, even with Father returned to her. She cannot simply be happy.* Tzoja knew very well from her own childhood experiences with her cruel grandfather Fikolmij what Vorzheva's childhood in the Stallion Clan must have been like. But understanding alone could not make her love her mother more.

I do not know how long I can stay here. Nezeru, oh, my fierce daughter, I miss you so! And Viyeki too, who was kind to me when he did not need to be—

"Where is your friend?" Unver abruptly asked.

It took a moment to pull her thoughts back. "Vordis?" she said. "Still in our wagon. Why do you ask?"

"No reason. I only wondered." As usual when the family was together, Unver had been brooding in his tall chair for most of the last hour. When someone knocked on the wagon's door, he looked up expectantly, then turned to her and said, "The door, Derra."

"Yes, I heard it," Tzoja told him. "So did you. Or did I come back to the grasslands only to wait upon you as I once waited on my charming grandfather?"

He grinned, surprising her. "You have his *and* our mother's sweet nature."

Tzoja darted a quick look at Vorzheva, but her mother was not listening, busy murmuring encouragement to Josua even as the spoon hovered in front of his clenched teeth.

"Not need to be fed," her father said once more. Tzoja wondered if she should intervene.

The knock came again. "Come in!" Unver bellowed. "Our womenfolk are too good to open doors!"

Fremur poked his head carefully around the doorframe, as if prepared to dodge a thrown object. "Your pardon, Shan. I come at your summons."

"By the Anvil-Smasher, is it already noon?" Unver rose and stretched, tall enough that he could not stand without bumping his head against the wagon's ceiling. "I have been thinking all morning."

"'Thinking' is my brother's way of saying 'Making others do all the work,'" Tzoja explained.

Fremur ducked his head, perhaps to hide a smile. "And it is good to see you, Derra. Is it allowed for me to call you that? That is how your brother always called you."

"I have been telling you since the First Blue Moon that you can call me either. Or, who knows?—perhaps I will pick a new name entirely. If so, I welcome your suggestions."

"Now you are jesting," the young thane said. "But such clever jokes are wasted on simple folks like ourselves."

Without preamble, Unver announced, "We have had more trouble in the Lakelands, Fremur. The Nabbanai do not seem to understand what we proved in Erkynland. It might be time to teach them a lesson."

"I have heard already from my clansfolk that they are building new settlements at the edge of the Varn," Fremur said. "They must think we are still weak from our battles against the other stone-dwellers. Either that or they have lost their wits entirely."

"I do not think they are using much wit at all," Unver said. "The head of the Ingadarine House, Sallin is his name—he is a fool. I hear he has already lost the support of many of the rich families in Nabban's Dominiate. Perhaps he thinks to provoke us barbarians into something so he can prove his fitness to rule."

"Your people are finally enjoying a little peace after a bloody year, Deor," said Tzoja. "And if you fight this Sallin fellow by attacking Nabbanai settlements, will you not be doing what he wants?"

Her brother gave her an annoyed look. "Not if we burn a few of those settlements to the ground. None of those rich stone-dwellers will think that is a good thing."

Tzoja shrugged. She was not going to argue with Unver in front of the family. Her brother had inherited a little of their mother's stubborn pride, and it was never a good idea to poke him hard enough to bring it out.

"But for now," Unver told Fremur, "it might be better simply to harry their supply lines. Those settlements when they are first built cannot support themselves. If we prevent Nabban from sending them soldiers, as well as grain and gold to *keep* the soldiers, it will be like starving a caged animal. These are our lands. We can outwait them, as long as we can convince our own people to be patient a little longer."

Another knock came. This time it was Vordis, who stopped in the doorway. "Is Tzoja here?" she asked.

"I am, dear one. Over here."

"I have killed a chicken for dinner, Tzoja. They are so fat here! Will you be eating with me?"

Unver stood again. "Come in, Vordis. Sit down, you are welcome. Here, sit in my chair."

The young woman colored. "I could not, Unver Shan. You are too generous."

"Nonsense. As I said, you are welcome."

As Unver squeezed his long frame into one corner of the wagon so Vordis could have his chair, Fremur sidled over to stand beside Tzoja. "The Shan likes her," he whispered.

"She is pretty and she is kind," she whispered back. "I have met only one man who did not like Vordis, and he was a man I don't think cares for women at all."

"No, it is more than that," Fremur said, keeping his voice low, though the whole width of the wagon separated them from where Unver was guiding Vordis into his tall chair. "Your friend looks more than a little like my sister, Kulva. Unver was . . . fond of her."

"Truly? He has never said anything about it."

"That is because Kulva was killed by our brother, and then Unver killed him because of it. He has never spoken her name to me since."

Tzoja felt a chill. Every time she thought she had come to understand her brother after so many years apart, she realized she knew almost nothing. "Well, if he still pines for your sister, there are worse women he could take a liking to than Vordis."

"And you?" Fremur asked. "Hyara told me that a great Norn lord wanted to marry you."

"Hyara should not repeat things I told her," she said. "And if she must, she should get the story right. No, he did not ask me to marry him. But he is a good man—if I can say that of a Norn and a Nakkiga noble—and I still have not decided." *But it becomes ever clearer that I do not belong here*, she realized. *Glad as I am to know my brother again, this present situation can only be for a little time. Then I must bring my poor father to the stone-dweller city for help—he is uncle to the queen of Erkynland, after all, and she must have skillful healers.* But the thought was daunting. *I owe it to him, whether my mother will have it or not. Better she follows him to a place she fears and hates than he languishes here among the wagons.*

Fremur nodded slowly, considering what she had said. "I have never seen any Norns, Derra. It seems strange to me to think of marrying one of them, but if you do go to him in the north, we will miss you. Your brother is much changed since you came to live with us—almost happy, sometimes."

"Almost happy? That has a grim sound."

"Unver is a grim man. He has been so as long as I've known him. I scarcely ever saw him smile before we walked out of Winstowe Castle—only the kind of smile you see on a hungry wolf. But now I have seen it several times!"

She laughed a little. "Do not fear, Fremur—I will not go anywhere soon. I want to spend time among my family after all these years. And I have Vordis to worry about, too."

"Hmmm. Perhaps not for long," he said, and she turned to look where he was looking. Unver was crouching beside her friend, talking in quiet tones, and though of course he knew that Vordis could not see him, the Shan's eyes were downcast, as though he feared to watch her too closely.

As she was wondering whether Unver's interest in her friend was in truth more than the attention he might pay to any pretty young woman, yet another knock sounded at the door of the wagon.

"By Tasdar's Hammer," said Unver, standing up so suddenly that he struck his head on the ceiling. "Is this a home or a market-field?"

This time it was Odobreg. The Badger Clan thane took one look at the crowded interior and said, "I will not come in, great Shan, but I would like to speak with you. I have just heard that the Adder Clan raided one of the Nabbanai towns near the Varn and it did not go well. Somehow, they were expected. Nabbanai soldiers were waiting in great numbers. Only three of the Adder raiding party made it back to camp."

"Those fools," said Unver. "Now we will have to strike back, whether we want to or not, or the clans will think I let the Nabbanai do as they please." He shook his head, then walked heavily toward the door. "Come, Fremur. Let you and I and Odobreg go outside and talk where we will have a little room. We will do our best to punish them without starting another war. This time."

They went outside, and although Tzoja was mildly resentful that she, like all Thrithings womenfolk, had been left out of an important conversation, she also had to admit that she was tired of conflict. She could stay, she could go to Viyeki, or to the Hayholt in Erkynland, but it seemed there was nowhere in the world she could escape men wanting to kill and dominate other men.

"Marry a Norn?" she said, half to herself. "If I could be sure of a little peace in this world, I would marry a frog and live in a pond."

"Careful," said her father around a spoonful of soup. "God listens and God grants."

Her cousin stood in the doorway. Sallin's look of self-satisfaction would have been insufferable if she had not long ago decided that she would kill him as soon as it was practical, which allowed her to ignore the petty, day-to-day annoyances he caused her. "You look pleased," she said.

"I am, Turia, I am. I have been elected Aucteris by the Dominiate. Something my father never managed."

"There was no Aucteris while Uncle Dallo was alive," she pointed out. "Did you come here to seek my congratulations?"

"What benefits me benefits all of House Ingadaris," he said, scowling. "And even if the title has only been revived since Duke Saluceris died, it still makes me first citizen of Nabban."

"Congratulations, then," she said in the same tone with which she would have informed someone they had dropped something on the floor.

"Why are you so spiteful, Turia? You have everything you could want, servants, fine clothes—"

"And I cannot leave the house! What difference does any of the rest make when I am a prisoner in my own home?" She softened her voice. "But let's not argue. I am impressed, Sallin, of course I am. You have been given a great honor, one that will be written not just in the family annals but in the history of Nabban."

"It's true," he said. "But of course, I am more interested in the well-being of our family than any mere personal glory. It has been a long time since the Ingadarines stood so high."

"Of course," she said, fighting hard not to let hatred creep back into her words. "But now that you have been named Aucteris, surely there is no need to keep me mewed up this way. My husband is almost a year dead. There is no child. What sort of threat could I be to you?"

"Threat?" He waved his hand. "Who ever said you were a threat? You are still a child yourself, Turia. And that means I am your guardian and must protect your interests."

"My interest would be to let me move into my husband's house, which is mine by marriage."

"Not until your minority is ended." He smiled. "What sort of relative would I be if I took no care to protect you and your reputation?"

She shut her eyes for a moment, calming herself. "I am grateful, Cousin Sallin, but I would be more grateful still to have a little more freedom. I am a countess, but I might as well be a servant."

"You are such a child, Turia—a servant! You, with all your luxuries! In any case, I only came to tell you that you must accompany me to the investiture, which will be on St. Ambrosis' Day. House Ingadaris must present a dignified and united front."

"Of course, I will come with you." After all, it would mean several hours out of the family compound, and perhaps a chance to meet with some of her secret vassals—her real servants, not the dull country girls that Sallin had delegated to wait on her. "But I must have a new gown. Something suitable for such an important occasion." Her dressmaker was one of those who would carry messages for her, which was why she had so many gowns.

"Another?" He shook his head. "But I suppose you are right. We must put on a bold show at the Hall of the Dominiate! My rivals would seize on any opportunity to belittle us. Very well, a new gown. But it must be fittingly chaste for a widow."

"Thank you, Cousin Sallin." She showed him a sad but grateful smile. *And for lording it over me in this way*, she thought, *when I was the one who brought down the High Ward in Nabban, opening your way to power. Oh, have no doubt, I will make certain your ending is neither swift nor merciful.*

Several days later, with her cousin gone out to discuss the many details of his investiture ceremony, Turia looked up to a knock on the door of her chambers.

"Come," she said.

As usual, the guard looked at everything but Turia herself. Sallin had made it clear that any guards showing too much interest in his young cousin would be punished, and since none of them knew what qualified as "too much interest," they tended to act like she was invisible. "The fortune teller is here to see you, Lady Turia."

"Fortune teller? I did—" She silenced herself. "Of course. Send the fortune teller in."

"At once, Excellency." Still watching only the floor, he bowed and went out.

Turia had not asked for any fortune teller. She wondered if her cousin had finally decided keeping her alive was no longer advantageous. Perhaps his new title had convinced him he no longer needed her connection to the Benidrivine House, the previous rulers of Nabban. She took the slender knife she always kept beneath her pillow, then returned to her chair and hid it under the book she had been reading.

The fortune teller swept in, skirts swirling, matted gray hair hanging in her face. She bowed low.

"If you are a woman, surely you should offer a courtesy instead," Turia said.

"How could anyone be near your magnificence and not bow down," the gray-haired figure said in an impressively deep voice.

"Fecca, you are the ugliest woman I have seen in a long time," she said. "And I have recently had a visit from Iulia Preves and her two ghastly daughters."

He came forward, brushing the strands of his gray wig off his face. He was grinning. "I never claimed to be beautiful, Lady Turia. Only useful."

"You took a risk," she said. "If Sallin knew you were here, you would never leave the house alive."

"If Lord Sallin were here, then I would not be," he replied. "But we have not spoken for a long time, and I have news for you."

"Say on, then. I don't know how long until my cousin returns."

"Not until the evening meal," Fecca said. "One of the door guards at the hall received some tips from me about upcoming horse races, and in return he told me that Count Sallin and his cronies would be in discussion all afternoon. Much planning to be done for his big day!" He gave her a bright-eyed look. "It is not too late for me to arrange for a madman or some other useful fool to kill your cousin at the ceremony, my lady. Or perhaps just after, to make the crime more shocking—nobody has killed an Aucteris in a very long time."

"No." She shook her head. "It would be satisfying, but it is not yet time. He still has allies, and I still cannot get to the gold Pasevalles put aside for me."

Fecca shook his head in feigned sadness. "Poor Pasevalles. He planned for everything except his own mistakes. I fear I have nothing to hearten you on that account. The gold remains in a merchant bank in Perdruin, and only Pasevalles himself—or you, my lady—can touch it. And you . . ."

"Cannot cross the road by myself without Sallin's guards, let alone take a ship to Perdruin. But if my cousin dies now, I will become the ward of one of his cronies, and whoever it was would not only keep me a prisoner, but likely force me into marriage as well." She glowered. "Still, I must marry someone. That is the only way I will get out of Sallin's grasp."

"I at least will serve you, Excellency." Fecca grinned. "And you will remember me when you have the gold—and House Ingadaris, too."

"You have met many of those who are loyal to me, and you know why they are loyal. I do not forget those who have helped me, and I never forget those who betray me."

"As Sallin has."

"As Sallin has," she agreed. "If only Pasevalles had not been quite so careful with his ill-gotten gold or turned so ambitious at the end. Instead of failing to grab power in Erkynland, he and I could have controlled all of Nabban."

"You would not have been able to trust him, though, my lady."

"I trust no one, Fecca. You know that. Allies must build on a foundation of mutual desperation. Without you, I cannot keep in touch with my friends and supporters. And without me—"

"I would be a criminal under sentence of death here as well as back in Erkynland." He nodded, grinning. "Well-a-day, we must cling to each other, eh, my lady?"

"I cling to no one," she said. "Don't get above yourself, Fecca.".

"Never, my lady."

They spoke in low voices for another hour, fearful of being overheard by the servants. Fecca related all his meetings with Ingadarines who were either jealous of Sallin or simply distrusted him; and with her secret allies in other houses among the Fifty Families. Nabban was still reeling from the overthrow and killing of Duke Saluceris, and very few of the richest households did not have some ambition to improve their lot. Also, the name of Drusis, the duke's murdered brother and Turia's late husband, still carried much weight. He had been a popular military hero, and many Nabbanai, especially in the lands that border the Thrithings, held him in memory as though he were a saint. And Turia, young as she was, was Drusis's widow, and thus the object of much sympathy and even admiration among Nabban's common people.

At last, Fecca rose. "I should go now."

"There will be talk about a fortune teller coming to the house," she said. "I shall have to prepare a story for Sallin when he asks me. Do not come again without a summons from me. I will send for you in the usual way."

"As you say, Excellency." Fecca brushed the coarse gray hair back into his face and again assumed the bent posture of an old woman. Then he straightened. "A question, my lady."

She was tired. Fecca's news had all been useful, but having to work so hard to overcome her own current helplessness was exhausting. "Yes? Quickly."

"Did you ever come to understand the gift Pasevalles sent you in the last days of the siege? The one I brought?"

"The mirror?" She shook her head. "It is an old Sithi thing, or at least that is what the astrologer told me, though he could not tell me what value it had, if any. It was a strange thing for Pasevalles to send."

"There was a letter, too, but as I told you, it was lost while I was avoiding guards at the Erkynland border. I was lucky to be able to hang onto the mirror."

"I suppose we will never know."

"Ah. I suppose not. I thank you for your time, Lady Turia." He bowed again, then remained in that hunched position as he made his way out past the guards waiting on either side of the door.

I will tell Sallin I had the fortune teller in to ask about the day of the ceremony, she thought. *To make certain that the omens were good for House Ingadaris. He has probably been to the scryers himself hoping for good auguries, so he will think nothing odd of it.*

But Fecca's words had set her thinking. She went to the secretary where she kept her correspondence and writing tools. She knew her cousin had a key of his own, and checked through her letters carefully on the few occasions she was allowed out of her chambers, but he did not know about the false panel in the back, because the hair stretched almost invisibly across it had never been disturbed. She went to the door and listened, and when satisfied no one was nearby, returned and carefully removed the panel and took out the cloth-wrapped object.

It was strangely heavy for something not much larger than her palm and which looked to be made of nothing more solid than wood and polished mother-of-pearl. She held it up to the light, watching the colors glint in the reflective surface, and wondered why Pasevalles had sent it to her. The astrologer had called it a Sithi Witness, but had not known much more than that, except to say that old stories claimed the Sithi had used such things to talk to each other over great distances. But when Fecca had first brought it she had held it as she was holding it now for a very long time, staring at her own face until she almost grew dizzy, and nothing had come of it.

Pasevalles had dabbled with various Sithi and Norn magicks, or so she had heard, and she could not help wondering if handling this thing might be dangerous, but she also knew that Pasevalles had died a most ordinary death, fallen from the battlements of a castle in Erkynland, rather than anything to do with sorcery. Was it some kind of weapon? Could it be used to, say, wish a hideous wasting disease on her wretched cousin Sallin?

As she stared into her dim reflection, contemplating the satisfaction she would feel if she learned that Sallin had pitched over in a fit on his way home from the Dominiate, she felt something stirring in the air around her, a bite of cold that made her skin pimple and raised the hairs on her arms and neck. Turia had never in her young life felt true fear, despite having survived a childhood in the nest of serpents that was House Ingadaris, and so she did not immediately recognize the sensation, except that it felt like someone was watching her—someone close, someone hidden.

She looked around but saw nothing unusual. These were still her same chambers, the well-appointed dungeon in which she had been immured for most of the last year under the not-so-benign care of Sallin and his sycophants. She turned back to the Sithi mirror and saw that her reflection had become foggy and vague. She was about to try to wipe off whatever was clouding her view when her reflection faded into blackness, and she found herself falling into that dark emptiness—an emptiness that grew to swallow all the world.

Nothing, was her first desperate, panicky thought. *There is nothing around me. Am I dead? I should never have touched the cursed thing. Was Pasevalles trying to kill me?*

But then she heard a sound—a breathy voice chanting words she did not recognize. The nothingness around her was freezing cold, and though she felt as though she could look around in all directions, nothing changed when she did. All remained in darkness.

Turia Ingadaris. The soft voice spoke her name and her heart stuttered in her breast. *Turia Ingadaris. Future queen of Nabban. Mistress of the world.*

"Who . . . who is there?" Even her own words sounded distant.

One who will teach you everything you need to know. One who will help you to make your dreams real, bring you everything you wish, and bend the necks of your enemies.

"But who are you?"

After a long moment, the quiet, scratchy voice spoke again. *Those who still remember me call me the Whisperer.*

55

An Angel Made of Stars

Simon was deep in a pleasant dream of sailing on a calm ocean when someone began to shake him.

"Not now, Miri," he said. "After we make land."

"Wake up. I am not your wife. It is me, Binabik."

Simon thrashed his way up into wakefulness. He was alone in the bedroll, with his small friend standing over him. "Where's Miri?"

"No worry is needed," the troll said, grinning. "She asked me to come back for you."

"Come back?" He sat up, trying to make sense of things. "Come back where?"

His friend chuckled. "She woke you once already, she said—do you not remember? You said you were coming with her, but then your appearing did not happen."

"I'm confused. Why are you here, Binabik? Are we still in the what's-it-called place—Tanakirú? No, of course we are. I was dreaming I was at sea."

"And I am glad you can dream again, friend Simon. But your wife is waiting for you. Several more folk have just arrived from the Sithi city of Anvi'janya and Aditu has asked for you."

"Aditu? Very well, I'm getting up. You don't have to wait for me."

"Yes, my friend, I fear I do. I was given strict ordering by your wife."

Simon grunted and reached for his boots.

A few of the Erkynlandish contingent were awake, but most still slept. The Zida'ya folk, however, were all up as Simon made his way to the center of their camp. *But they hardly ever sleep anyway*, he thought sourly. *Not very fair, showing up this time of night.*

His bad temper did not last long after seeing Aditu and the rest of her company beside a large and welcoming campfire, surrounded by fellow Sithi.

"Seoman!" Aditu cried—the name Jiriki had always called him. "It has been far, far too long. Come and see what I have done."

He made his way through the throng of well-wishers with his family and the trolls following behind him. Aditu smiled up at Simon from a circle of Sithi and offered her golden cheek to be kissed. As he leaned down, Simon finally saw what she was holding in her arms.

"Oh, by the sacred Aedon, you truly have done it!" he said. "I heard you were expecting a child, but—" He crouched so he could better see the small face peering from its blanket, but all he could make out were the infant's solemn golden eyes reflecting the firelight. "He? She?"

"I named him Sujati," Aditu said. "It means, 'a small truth', and that is what he is."

"A thousand congratulations." Simon knew enough of the immortals to know how rare and exciting it was for them to have a new birth.

"I fathered him," declared the stern-faced Sitha standing over her, and for the first time Simon realized who this was—Yeja'aro, the Sitha who had left him to die in his cell beneath the Hayholt, though the immortal's once flame-red hair had now returned to an undyed white. Simon did his best to let the anger flow through him without sharing any of it, but because he remembered very plainly what it felt like to be deserted and left in chains, it was not easy. He nodded toward Yeja'aro before turning his attention back to Aditu. With her glossy black hair, those bright, mischievous eyes and flawless skin, Jiriki's sister looked no different than the last time he had seen her, years and years ago, when he had still thought of himself as a young man. This unhappiness too he pushed away—it was not possible to be friends with Sithi without confronting their much longer lifespans.

"I am happy for you—both," he said. "I am glad to see something good after all the evil that happened here."

Aditu's smile turned wistful. "In truth, much good happened here as well, not least because of you and Prince Morgan." For the first time Simon noticed his grandson, who stood a short distance away talking animatedly with another female Sitha, who Simon did not immediately recognize. *Good God,* Simon thought, *he's not romancing two different immortals, is he?* But if he was, Nezeru, who stood beside Morgan, did not seem to object much.

"That must be Tanahaya, who almost died when she came to the Hayholt," Miriamele whispered in his ear. "The one who was poisoned."

"Ah," said Simon. "Yes, of course. She and Morgan traveled together. I only met her when Jiriki was . . ." He turned back to Aditu. "Your brother," he began, "he—"

"He loved you, Seoman," Aditu said. "And I know you loved him also. Later, when the *Witchwood Crown* has set out, you and I will talk of him. I hope you are not taking the blame on yourself for his passing."

Simon shrugged uncomfortably. "It hurts," was all he said.

Another figure stepped forward, another female Sitha, but one who looked older than either Aditu or Tanahaya—she might have been a mortal woman in the prime of life, but Simon guessed she was much, much older. "King Simon and I spoke only a few months ago, but Queen Miriamele will not remember me, though we met once at the end of the Storm King's War. I am Ayaminu of Anvi'janya. With your permission, I accompanied Duke Isgrimnur to Nakkiga."

"I had forgotten that!" said Simon.

"As had I," said Miriamele. "We were so very young then."

Ayaminu smiled. "To my mind, you still are. I also know you have ruled wisely and well over your people for many years, but what you did that day that must seem so long ago, when you permitted me to accompany Isgrimnur, was part of the good things that happened here, and all that we still hope may come from Utuk'ku's fall."

Simon was feeling the pull of slumber again, but he waited patiently as Miriamele and the trolls admired little Sujati, asking Aditu what seemed like countless questions about the birth. At last, his wife noticed that he was having trouble staying upright and made their excuses before leading him away.

"We will have a chance to spend time with Aditu before we go," she said. "But it is good to see her again, is it not?"

Groggy and only half-listening, Simon grunted a reply.

"You do not think I am still jealous of her, do you?" Miri asked. "Because I am not, even though she still looks young and beautiful. That was so long ago. I was just a child then."

Simon's very slow thoughts were clumping together to tell him that he should say something appropriate—and fairly soon—when they were interrupted by the sudden and silent appearance of a tall, slender shape.

"King Seoman," said Yeja'aro. "I wish to speak to you." He turned to Miriamele. "I do not know what is proper. I know you are his partner and a queen. You may stay or go as you wish."

Miriamele stared at him, half-amused, half-appalled. "I may, may I?"

Simon summoned his weary strength. "We are listening, Yeja'aro."

But the Sitha seemed suddenly uncertain of what he wanted to say. "Aditu has spoken with me," he said. "Several times. Very precisely and with some force."

"I'm sorry," Simon said. "I really don't understand—"

"She explained to me that I was foolish and cruel. That it was unreasonable of me to take such care to fulfill Jiriki's exact words to me—to find you, his friend, and give you his message about your grandson—and not heed the spirit behind them." He let a sinuous ripple pass through him that among the Sithi passed for a shrug. "I am not the cleverest of my people, and sometimes I do not understand what is expected of me. Also, I was raised to fight for the Forbidden Hills, and Aditu tells me that I hold fighting and honor too highly." He shook his head. "I still do not understand how that could be true, but even Mistress Ayaminu agreed with her, and Ayaminu is known to be very wise." He stopped and fell silent, as though he had said all that needed saying.

"Yeja'aro, I am glad you have Aditu and the others to help you find your way through life," Simon said at last, wondering if this would ever end. He was desperate for sleep now, and they would have to be up again in a short time. "Is there anything else you wanted to say to me?"

The Sitha took a deep breath. "Yes. I am sorry. Jiriki would have been ashamed of me if he had known, and that is a wound that will not heal. I ask for your forgiveness."

Simon stared, surprised by the pain he saw on Yeja'aro's face. "You have it, of course. I feel better knowing that it was a matter of you not understanding. I hope our peoples can be closer. That is what Jiriki would have wanted."

The Sitha bowed. "Thank you, King Seoman and Queen Miriamele. My heart can rest a little now."

As he turned to go, Miri called after him, "You and Aditu have a beautiful son."

He turned and smiled, something Simon felt sure was not a common expression for him. "It is true," he said. "We do." Then he slipped back into the dark and headed toward the Sithi camp.

"Was that the one who—?" Miri asked her husband.

"It was. I wanted to murder him at the time. It still seems strange Aditu would choose him."

"It only shows that you never know who you are going to fall into love with."

"I heard that, but I am too tired to be snippy."

"Come, let me hold you while you fall back to sleep."

"For a little while, then we'll have to get up again."

"For a little while," she agreed.

Viyeki had been restless all night and had not even considered trying to sleep. He did not recognize the young Tinukeda'ya who approached him in the predawn hour before the *Witchwood Crown*'s departure. The newcomer was a Delver, or at least had the same slender frame, wide eyes, and huge hands Viyeki had seen on others of that kind.

"High Magister?"

"Yes?"

"Greetings. My name is Tih-Rumi, chief acolyte of the Sa-Vao, Kuyu-Kun. I have brought a message for you."

Viyeki was puzzled. He knew nothing of any Kuyu-Kun. "Why does your master send me a message?"

"It is not from him, but from someone else. I have just come from the *Witchwood Crown*, where I was saying farewell to my master, who will take ship with Sa-Ruyan Geloë and the others." He bobbed his head. "And one of our people named Min-Senya asked if I was returning to Tanakirú, and if so whether I would give you something that had been entrusted to him."

Min-Senya—the changeling who had left Viyeki the heavy, long-handled maul and the terrible decision about what to do with it. "I am listening."

Tih-Rumi drew a curl of parchment from the sleeve of his robe. "Min-Senya said to tell you this was made by one you may remember." He proffered the piece of parchment.

Viyeki unrolled it, but his confusion only deepened. It was a picture of a crude, manlike figure drawn with charcoal, but he could make little sense of it other than legs, arms, a smiling head, and jagged lines surrounding the figure.

He looked up in confusion. "What is this?"

Tih-Rumi smiled. "The one who wished it given to you is a mortal youth named Cuff the Scaler. Min-Senya said that this Cuff wanted to tell you these words. *'This is for the white-faced Father. It is the Angel Made of Stars and she is real. She is taking me with her. I love you.'* I told Min-Senya I would pass it and the boy's words along to you." Tih-Rumi bowed. "That done, I must go now and join those of my people who are staying behind—as many of us are, for many different reasons. It is a day of strong feelings for us."

"Thank you," said Viyeki. "I . . . thank you." When he at last looked up from the picture, the young Tinukeda'ya had gone.

Miriamele could not help thinking of the ecstatic, cheering crowd that had surrounded them on their return to Erchester. This far more reserved throng stood together on a slope overlooking the Tanakirú gorge, where Simon said that thousands of Hikeda'ya Sacrifices had camped the previous winter. The current group of watchers numbered less than a hundred altogether, mostly mortals and Sithi, but it included two Norns, Lord Viyeki and his daughter Nezeru, and the mood of the crowd was unlike anything Miriamele had experienced. *It feels as if we're gathered in a church,* she thought. *But as if we're not certain what we're here to worship.* Her husband's ill-tempered grumbling at being re-awakened had also been reminiscent of early mornings in the Hayholt chapel.

The first rays of the rising sun had turned the eastern sky fiery yellow, but the eastern cliffs were still mostly dark, even as sunlight began to creep down the valley's western walls. From their vantage point on the south side of the gorge, Miriamele saw for the first time how truly strange the place was, as if Tanakirú had been created solely for a day like this one, a vast open-air chapel constructed solely to host an unprecedented ritual. She could see movement on the cliff face where the last of the Tinukeda'ya workers were finishing their labors on the upper deck of the ship, tiny as insects and almost impossible to make out at such a distance except by their movement. The rest of the valley seemed to come to a point around the southern face of Mount Kushiba, out of whose rocky slope the *Witchwood Crown* protruded like a huge thorn.

"Is that Geloë?" asked Binabik, shielding his eyes. "There, on the top of the ship. I see a figure waving."

"I can see nothing at all with these old eyes of mine except the ship itself," said Simon. "Because that at least is as big as Perdruin and easy to spot. But waving doesn't sound like Geloë, does it?"

"I can't make it out either," said Miriamele. "But I will pretend it is Geloë saying farewell."

"It is her," Nezeru assured them. "I could not mistake Ruyan's armor. But I do not think she is waving. I think she is summoning something or singing to something. To me, her gestures have the look of ritual."

Miriamele watched the young Norn and wondered what things would be like in the days ahead. Did this Nezeru truly love her grandson, or did Morgan have heartache ahead of him? And even if their bond was strong, Miriamele knew it would be an uphill struggle to win over the citizens of Erkynland—of all the High Ward, in truth—to accept one of the pale race who had burned the Hayholt to the ground, and whose queen had been an object of terrifying stories for generations.

Simon squeezed her hand and said quietly, "They forgave you for your father's madness and they forgave me for being a commoner."

She looked at him, surprised at how precisely he had guessed her mood, then stood on her tiptoes to kiss his whiskered cheek. "Do they forgive?" she asked. "Or do they simply forget?"

"I will take either," her husband said. "Beside, there are worse things than the unexpected—"

He did not finish, because at that moment a great, somber tone rang through the whole of the north end of the valley, so deep it was more feeling than sound, like the chiming of some monstrous bell as big as the mountains themselves. Miriamele felt it through her feet and in her bones and teeth.

"It begins!" said Binabik. The white wolf Vaqana lay panting beside him, looking quite unbothered by the noise. "Look, Sisqi! The mists are vanishing, too. We will be able to see everything!"

Not far away from where Miriamele stood with her mortal family and friends, Protector Ki'ushapo began to sing—not loudly but sweetly. Several other Sithi joined him, their voices climbing, falling, twisting around each other like invisible strands on a loom made of melody. Miriamele stared up at the ship, still below the descending curtain of stark morning light, and felt oddly soothed by the Zida'ya song. *This has been a long time coming,* she thought. *That is what I hear in their voices, I think. Not quite joy, but something like relief.*

When it finally happened, it was so swift and so unexpected that many who had looked away for only a few moments missed it entirely. As the leading edge of sunlight slid down the crag and finally touched the ship, the vast hull seemed to catch fire as it was bathed by the rosy dawn glow, then the deep tolling rang again through the stones of the valley, shaking Miriamele to her core. Simon clutched her hand, and for a moment she held her breath, not certain what would happen next. The glow became brighter, then a bright gleam lanced upward from the center of the *Witchwood Crown* and spread over it, a great expanse of pulsing radiance above the ship. *Like a sail,* Miriamele marveled. *A sail made of light.* Then the glow began to fade, though the sun's rays still fell fixedly on the cliff face, and Miriamele realized in astonishment that the great vessel had become as transparent as chapel glass, like a cloud of smoke suddenly dispersed by a breeze. Then the ship was gone, simply gone.

As she stared, dumbfounded, the empty crevice where the ship had stood began to deepen from mere shadow into utter blackness, as though they could look through the mountain into a starless night, though the true, dawn-yellow sky could be seen all around the peak.

"I can see stars in there," said Morgan in a choked voice. "Inside the mountain!"

"So can I," said Simon.

In the crevice where the ship had been imprisoned, the blackness had begun to bloom with individual points of hanging light that twinkled like suspended diamonds. Then both stars and blackness faded into ordinary shadow, and it was only a cliff once more, with a great, empty gash in the limestone where the ship had been. A few chunks of the limestone cliff broke and fell away from the top of the crevice, then caromed down the cliffs to the plateau far below; it was only when they struck the ground and shattered that Miriamele realized some of the fragments were as large as houses. "Geloë was wise to have us assemble so far away," she said.

"It just . . . went away," Simon said in wonder. "That whole ship, big as a city. As if it had never been there at all. Like a conjuring trick."

"It was no trick, King Seoman," called Ki'ushapo, turning toward them. "Not in the way you mean. Geloë and the Tinukeda'ya have let go of this world. They let the *Witchwood Crown* drift out into the Ocean Indefinite and Eternal."

"Trick or drift, call it what you want." Simon laughed, but his wife could hear that he was shaken. "I have never seen anything like it—and I've seen quite a few mad things."

"Sail on!" Ki'ushapo cried loudly to the air. "Travel well, Ruyan's Own! May you and your people find safe harbor!" Miriamele echoed him in a whisper. Her heart was pounding, and she was as astonished as Simon, though she also felt something she had not expected, a strange joy, an exhilaration that it took a moment for her to understand.

She bowed her head. *I pray they find the freedom they have sought so long.*

"I am sorry we did not have more time with you here," said Little Snenneq, "but we had to go to rescue our rams from the place we left them. But look! They are in fine health, both my so-handsome Falku and Qina's Tipalak."

Morgan dutifully admired the rams, who did in fact seem to have weathered their exile very well.

"In the morning, we Qanuc must be traveling north," Little Snenneq continued. "But as I told you, have no fear—we will see you again soon. Remember, as I told you, we have destiny!"

Morgan smiled. "I never doubted it." He laughed. "Well, perhaps I did, at first. It took me a while to realize I had made such good friends when I hadn't expected it." He paused and looked at Nezeru, who was on one knee, talking quietly to Qina. "Perhaps one day soon, even before you return to us, I will come to visit you—*we* will come to visit you."

"That would be a very good thing," said Snenneq. "I would enjoy showing you both the beauties of our mountains—and Mintahoq, I must humbly but honestly confess, is the most beautiful of all of them."

Qina had finished embracing Nezeru. Qina had tears in her eyes, and although Nezeru's eyes were dry, Morgan was impressed to see how little his Hikeda'ya lover was trying to hide her sadness at the parting.

"Oh, Morgan Prince," said Qina. "We will mix you."

"She is right," said Little Snenneq. "We will miss you. But the world will seem smaller to us all now."

Nezeru stood. "If you and Qina's parents are going to leave by morning light, we can have one last night together. Come to the fire and I will teach you some good war-songs. I do not miss my old order—not very much, at least—but I do miss singing songs about how brave I am."

"That sounds exactly like the song I should learn," Snenneq said.

"Sound like all songs you already sing," said Qina.

Simon and Miriamele stood at the edge of the camp, watching as their mortal companions mixed with the Sithi and even the two Norns, spreading their time among several campfires.

"Is that Nezeru . . . singing?" Miri asked her husband. "It looks like her, but surely it must be a trick of the light."

"It should be your turn next," said Simon. "It has been too long since I heard you sing, my love—my wife."

"But we have so much to talk about! What will come next, how we will deal with Nabban, whether to rebuild the Hayholt—"

"We will have plenty of time to do that on the ride home."

"Home? But that's just it—where *is* home now? Our old home is just ashes."

Simon shook his head. "No. Our home is right where it's always been."

She gave him a sideways look. "Very mysterious, Your Majesty."

The singing had grown louder, mellifluous Sithi voices blending with the less tuneful voices of Morgan and the Erkynlanders. Nezeru was watching, amused, as Morgan tried to sing along with a Sithi tune whose words he clearly did not know.

"By our Lady," said Miriamele. "The Norn girl is smiling. I never thought I would see such a thing."

"Do we know she's still a girl?" Simon asked. "She could be a hundred or more."

Miri shook her head. "A hundred? How? She is Derra's daughter!"

Simon nodded. "And that's why you are the sensible one and I am the . . . well, I do not need to say it."

"No, you don't. But you need to say what you meant about home. 'Right where it's always been,' you said."

"Ah, yes." He put his arm around her, drew her close. "Doctor Morgenes once told me something very wise—'Make your home in your head, Simon,' he said. But I came to see in the last year that there's even more to it than that. Making a home in your head is a good start, but you must also make a home in your heart for the people you love." He looked out at the milling throng of mortals and immortals. Ki'ushapo was trying to teach Morgan the words to the song he had been so enthusiastically butchering, and now Nezeru was laughing out loud. "And, my dear one," Simon went on, "we have certainly done that. And though I despaired for a while—I will not lie, I truly did—in the end we have recovered what was most important. The Hayholt was only a building made of stone. Morgan, Lillia, Tiamak, Binabik and Sisqi, Aditu—we have them in our hearts forever. And Jiriki, too, of course, and our dear John Josua. Even death cannot end it."

"What you are telling me," said Miriamele, smiling, "is that we do in fact have a home."

"Yes, my clever and queenly wife. Wherever you are, that is home for this once-upon-a-time kitchen boy. I learned that in the most painful way I could have imagined, so I will never forget it. Home is where our family and friends are, even if they only live in our hearts and memories."

She laid her head against his shoulder as the sounds of merriment echoed from the valley's walls, rising above even the rush and tumble of the Narrowdark cataracts. Firelight flickered and leaped. "Husband, you are perhaps the wisest mooncalf I have ever met."

"Perhaps?" said Simon. "Only perhaps?"

Appendix

PEOPLE

ERKYNLANDERS

Abigal—a noblewoman; daughter of the Count of Torickshire
Aglaf, Count—the ruler of Winstowe
Atara, Lady—daughter of Countess Marah and Count Aglaf of Winstowe
Averel, Lord—son of Countess Marah and Count Aglaf of Winstowe
Bethil—a maid in the Hayholt
Boez, Bishop –Chief Almoner of the Hayholt
Cuff the Scaler—a Naglimunder made slave by the Norns
Dorret, Lady—Earl Durward's older daughter
Eahlstan Fiskerne, King—former king of the Hayholt
Ebbe, Saint—an Aedonite saint, martyred by drowning in a barrel
Elyweld—younger sister of Lillia's friend Aedonita
Etan, Brother—an Aedonite monk of the Sutrinian Order
Fincher, Captain—master of the *Elysiamansa*
Gar Cockerel—a castellan of Winstowe
Gervis, Archbishop—Erkynland's leading religious authority and Escritor-elect, though not yet invested
Hatcher—owner of The Quarely Maid tavern in Erchester
Hubart—one of Queen Miriamele's royal guards
Idela, Princess—deceased; widow of Prince John Josua, mother of Morgan and Lillia
Jeremias, Lord—Lord Chamberlain of the Hayholt, King Simon's boyhood friend
John Josua, Prince—dead son of King Simon and Queen Miriamele; father of Prince Morgan and Princess Lillia
John Presbyter, King—former High King; Queen Miriamele's grandfather
Josua, Prince—Queen Miriamele's uncle, current whereabouts unknown
Kenrick, Sir—guard captain, Zakiel's second in command
Levias, Sergeant—an officer of the Erkynguard, friend of Sir Porto
Lillia, Princess—granddaughter of King Simon and Queen Miriamele, sister of Morgan
Marah, Countess—wife of Count Aglaf of Winstowe
Miriamele, Queen—High Queen of Osten Ard; wife of King Simon
Morgan, Prince—heir to the High Throne; grandson of King Simon and Queen Miriamele, brother of Lillia
Morgenes, Doctor –Scrollbearer; young Simon's friend and mentor, killed by Pryrates

Nelda, Duchess—wife of Duke Osric; Princess Idela's mother
Nulles, Father—Aedonite chaplain of the Hayholt
Osric, Duke—Lord Constable, Duke of Falshire and Wentmouth; grandfather of Morgan and Lillia
Rawlie, Sir—a castellan of Winstowe
Shulamit—a noblewoman
Simon, King—High King of Osten Ard and husband of Queen Miriamele; also known by his birth name, "Seoman"; sometimes called "Snowlock"
Snell, Baron—lord of Brockfordshire
Tzoja—mistress of Lord Viyeki; mother of Nezeru; Unver's twin sister, named "Derra" by her parents, Prince Josua and Lady Vorzheva
Zakiel of Garwynswold, Sir—Captain of the Erkynguard; Sir Kenrick's commander

HERNYSTIRI

Aelin, Sir—a knight, grand-nephew of Count Eolair
Aengas ec-Carpilbin of Ban Farrig—a noble, merchant factor, and scholar
Brannan—former monk, Aengas' cook
Brygit—shepherdess of the sun, sister of Mircha the rain goddess
Brynioch of the Skies—sky god, called "Skyfather"
Colum, Viscount—nobleman of Dor Drumm
Cormach, King—former king of Hernystir, called "the lame"
Cuamh—earth deity, called "Earth-dog"
Curudan, Count—Commander of the Silver Stags
Dunn—God of the underworld, death
Eolair, Count—Count of Nad Mullach and Hand of the High Throne
Ethna, Lady—powerful noblewoman, wife of Baron Gilmor
Evan—an Aedonite soldier, one of Sir Aelin's companions
Fintan—an Aedonite soldier of the Silver Stags
Fionola, Lady—noblewoman, wife of Tace Odhran
Flann Coilleoir—Flann the Woodsman, legendary hero; also known as "Jack Mundwode" in Erkynland
Gilmor, Baron—nobleman, husband of Lady Ethna
Glinn—soldier of Silver Stags, from Shanross
Gwythinn, Prince—King Hugh's father, Maegwin's brother, killed in the Storm King's War
Hern, King—legendary founder of Hernystir
Hugh ubh-Gwythinn, King—bastard son of Gwythinn, ruler of Hernystir
Inahwen—Dowager Queen of Hernystir; widow of Hugh's grandfather, King Lluth
Irmeidh—Hernystiri goddess of healing

Isleen, Lady—daughter of Earl Murdo
Lluth, King—former ruler of Hernystir; father of Maegwin and Gwythinn; killed at the Battle of the Inniscrich
Maccus—a soldier; Sir Aelin's companion, called "Blackbeard"
Maegwin—daughter of King Lluth, died in the Storm King's War
Morriga—an ancient goddess of war and death, called "Maker of Orphans," "Crow Mother"
Morwen, Sister—priestess of Irmeidh
Murdo, Earl of Carn Inbarh—a powerful noble; ally of Count Eolair and Sir Aelin
Murhagh—god of battle, called "One-Arm"
Nial, Count—a nobleman of Nad Glehs; Countess Rhona's husband
Odhran, Tace—nobleman of Carn Buic
Orin—son of Odhran and Fionola
Rhona, Countess—noblewoman of Nad Glehs and close friend to Queen Miriamele
Rhynn—a storm god, called "Rhynn of the Cauldron"
Samreas, Sir—Baron Curudan's lieutenant; chieftain of the Silver Stags
Sinnach, Prince—famous prince of Hernystir, Sithi ally, also known as "The Red Fox"
Silver Stags—an elite warrior troop loyal to King Hugh
Talamh of the Land—goddess, an aspect of the Morriga
Tethtain, King—fifth king of the Hayholt; called the "Holly King" and "Tethtain the Usurper"
Torin of the Meadows—nobleman and warrior
Tylleth, Lady—betrothed of King Hugh

RIMMERSGARDERS

Aerling Surefoot—one of Duke Isgrimnur's soldiers at Nakkiga
Alva, Lady—wife of Sludig
Black Rimmersmen—Far-northern Rimmersmen enslaved by the Norns
Breki, Thane—Sludig's second-in-command
Dror—old thunder-god in pagan times
Fingil, King—called "the conqueror"; first mortal ruler of the Hayholt
Gilhedur—Jarnulf's given name
Grimbrand of Elvritshalla, Duke—ruler of Rimmersgard
Hjeldin, King—second ruler of the Hayholt, called the "Mad King"
Hoderund—an Aedonite martyr
Isgrimnur of Elvritshalla, Duke—Duke Grimbrand's late father
Jarnulf Godtru—a former Norn slave, sworn to kill Utuk'ku
Skali Sharp-nose—Rimmersgard traitor during the Storm King's War

Skalijar—a troop of brigands in northern Rimmersgard
Sludig—Jarl of Engby, one of King Simon's companions during the Storm King's War
Vordis—Tzoja's companion, born as a slave in Nakkiga

QANUC

Binabik (Binbiniqegabenik)—Scrollbearer; Singing Man of the Qanuc; dear friend to King Simon and Queen Miriamele
Chukku—legendary troll hero saved from death
Little Snenneq—Qina's betrothed
Qina (Qinananamookta)—daughter of Binabik and Sisqi
Qinkipa—divine snow-maiden; savior of Chukku
Sisqi (Sisqinanamook)—Binabik's wife, daughter of the Herder and Huntress (rulers of Mintahoq Mountain)

THRITHINGS-FOLK

Broga—mercenary, called "Broomstraw"; formerly of the Great-horn Bull Clan
Burtan—a shaman of the Crane Clan
Colmunt—a mercenary
Fikolmij—deceased; former March-thane of the Stallion Clan and High Thrithings; Vorzheva's and Hyara's father
Fremur, Thane—leader of the Crane Clan; Unver's first follower and closest friend
Hulgar—a mercenary serving Pasevalles
Hurvalt—father of Fremur; also used as a false name
Hyara—Vorzheva's sister; Unver's aunt
Kulva—sister of Fremur, killed on her wedding day
Odobreg, Thane—leader of the Badger Clan, Unver's supporter
Rudur Redbeard, Thane—leader of Black Bear Clan; March-thane of the Meadow Thrithings; killed by poison
Ruzhvang—shaman of the Serpent Clan
Sanver—Unver's original Crane-clan name, also used as a false name
Sky-Piercer—title for the Crane of the Crane Clan
Tasdar of the Iron Arm—a Thrithings tutelary spirit; a metal-working deity worshiped by all the grassland clans, also called Tasdar the Anvil Smasher
Unver—"Nobody," the Thane of the Stallion Clan and Shan of all the Thrithings; Tzoja's twin brother, named "Deornoth" by his parents, Prince Josua and Lady Vorzheva
Volfrag—Rudur Redbeard's former chief shaman
Vorzheva—Unver's mother; Prince Josua's wife; daughter of Fikolmij; sister of Hyara

Zhadu,—a clansman in Erchester, Hulgar's brother in league with Pasevalles, called "Split Jaw," "Split-Face," and "Two-Faces"

NABBANAI

Ambrosis—Nabbanai saint, celebrated in Anitul-month
Astrian, Sir—swordsman, drinking companion of Prince Morgan, now part of Duke Osric's host
Benedrivine House—the ruling family of Nabban
Camaris-sá-Vinitta, Sir—King John's greatest knight, also known as "Camaris Benidrivis"; disappeared at the end of the Storm King's War
Canthia, Duchess—wife of Duke Saluceris and mother of Blasis and Serasina; killed while fleeing Nabban
Crexis the Goat—historic Imperator who executed Usires Aedon
Dallo Ingadaris—Queen Miriamele's late cousin
Dominiate, the—ruling council of Nabban, consisting primarily of the highest noble families
Drusis, Earl—Earl of Trevinta and Eadne; Duke Saluceris' late brother and rival
Elysia—mother of Usires Aedon; called "Mother of God"
Iulia Preves—a noblewoman
Pasevalles, Lord—Lord Chancellor to the High Throne
Pelippan Sisters—an order of Aedonite nuns
Plesinnen of Myrme—a famous scholar
Pryrates—priest, alchemist, and wizard; apparently killed during the fall of Green Angel Tower at the end of the Storm King's War
Rhiappa, Saint—Aedonite saint, called "Rhiap" in Erkynland
Sallin Ingadaris—currently most powerful man in Nabban
Saluceris, Duke—late ruler of Nabban
Serasina—infant daughter of Duchess Canthia and Duke Saluceris
Thelía, Lady—a scholar and herbalist; Lord Tiamak's wife
Turia Ingadaris, Lady—cousin to Sallin Ingadaris, wife of late Earl Drusis; rumored to be pregnant with the heir to Nabban
Usires Aedon—Aedonite Son of God; also called "the Ransomer" and "the Redeemer"
Vilderivis, Saint—founder of Vilderivan Order
Zinovia—wife of Imperator Crexis

PERDRUINESE

Faiera, Lady—a noblewoman and former Scrollbearer
Gen-Suru—a Niskie
Je-Suru—a Niskie

Porto, Sir—a hero of the Battles of Nakkiga; one of Prince Morgan's companions, now member of Duke Osric's host
Shim-Suru—a Niskie
Tallistro, Sir—a legendary knight and member of Prester John's famous court

WRANNA-FOLK

He Who Always Steps on Sand—a god or spirit
Jesa—nurse to Duke Saluceris' and Duchess Canthia's infant daughter Serasina; named "Green Honeybird" by her elders
Green Honeybird—mythical Wranna spirit; Jesa's namesake
She Who Waits to Take All Back—death goddess
They Who Watch and Shape—gods
Tiamak, Lord—Scrollbearer and scholar; close friend and counselor to King Simon and Queen Miriamele

SITHI (ZIDA'YA)

Aditu no'e-Sa'onserei—daughter of Likimeya; Jiriki's sister
Amerasu y-Senditu no'e-Sa'onserei—mother of Ineluki and Hakatri; called "First Grandmother," also known as "Amerasu Ship-Born," killed during the Storm King's War
Ayaminu—mistress of Anvi'janya, daughter of Kuroyi and Minasennu
Benhaya—a poet
Cheka'iso—called "Amber-Locks," member of Sunrise House clan
Dineke—archive-master of Anvi'janya
Dunao the Gray Rider—a supporter of Protector Khendraja'aro
Enazashi Blackspear—former master of Mezutu'a, the "Silverhome"
Fololi Unshoon—called "Barefoot Fololi"; poet from Hikehikayo
Hakatri i-Sa'onserei—resurrected son of Amerasu Ship-born, father of Likimeya
Heart-Seed Clan—Tanahaya's clan
Himano of the Flowering Hills—a scholar; Tanahaya's former teacher
Hizuma—an Anvi'janyan Sitha
Ineluki—brother of Hakatri, resurrected by Utuk'ku and named the "Storm King"
Izuka—warrior of the Snowdrop Clan
Jakoya the Gatherer—near-mythical figure from the Lost Garden
Jenjiyana of the Nightingales—historic figure; mother of Nenais'u
Jiriki i-Sa'onserei—son of Likimeya; brother of Aditu, Simon's friend
Kaniho –father of Tanahaya
Ki'ushapo—Jiriki's kinsman and friend, real name "Kisha'atu"

Kuroyi—former ruler of Anvi'janya, killed in the Storm King's War; Ayaminu's father
Khendraja'aro—Likimeya's half-brother; uncle of Jiriki and Aditu; Protector of House of Year-Dancing
Likimeya y-Briseyu no'e-Sa'onserei—the Sa'onsera; mother of Jiriki and Aditu, badly wounded by mortals
Minasennu—mother of Ayaminu, known for her wisdom; called "Minasennu of the Pool"
Mushroom Circle—group of clan protectors and leaders
Okajata—called "Red"; protector of the Firethorn Clan
Rabbit—family nickname for Aditu
Rukayu—warrior of the Redstart Clan from Peja'ura, nicknamed "Crow's-Claw"
Sa'onsera the Preserver—historic figure; wife of Hamakho Wormslayer; founding-mother of House of Year-Dancing
Sa'onserei—clan name of Jiriki and Aditu; also called "House of Year-Dancing"
Selusana—warrior, called "Moonhouse"; mother of Xila
Shen'de the Bowman—warrior from Peja'ura
Shima'onari—father of Jiriki and Aditu; killed during the Storm King's War
Siriaya—mother of Tanahaya
Spark—Jiriki and Aditu's nickname for Tanahaya
Sujati—a young Zida'ya
Shun'y'asu—famed poet; called "of the Blue Peak"
Tanahaya of Shisae'ron—a Sithi scholar; companion of Morgan in Aldheorte
Tululiko the Herald—Ayaminu's ancestor, husband of Virayu
Virayu—Ayaminu's ancestor, wife of Tululiko
Willow-switch—family nickname for Jiriki
Xila—a young Zida'ya; daughter of Selusana
Yeja'aro of the Forbidden Hills—Khendraja'aro's nephew, father of Aditu's unborn child
Yisume—daughter of Yizashi Grayspear
Yizashi Grayspear—son of Enazashi Blackspear, Protector of Skyglass Lake
Zinya of the River—a clan protector and member of the Mushroom Circle

NORNS (HIKEDA'YA)

Akhenabi, Lord—High Mage of the Order of Song, also called "Lord of Song"
Anchoresses—Queen Utuk'ku's female body-slaves
Drukhi—long-dead son of Queen Utuk'ku and Ekimeniso; killed by mortals
Ekimeniso—Queen Utuk'ku's dead husband
Ekisuno, Marshal—Sacrifice military leader, killed during the Storm King's War
Enduya—Viyeki's clan, a middling noble family

Ensume—Sacrifice general of the northeastern host, leader of Spider Legion
Gan'ua, Lady—noblewoman, wife of the lieutenant commander of Owl Legion
Hamakha—clan of Queen Utuk'ku
Hamakho Wormslayer—historic figure; founder of Queen Utuk'ku's Clan Hamakha and a famous warrior of the Garden
Jijibo—a close descendant of Queen Utuk'ku, called "the Dreamer"
Khimabu, Lady—Lord Viyeki's wife
Kikiti é-Sanga, General—General of the host accompanying Viyeki's builders; elevated to High Marshal
Lord of Dreaming—nickname for Lord Jijibo of Nakkiga
Makho—gravely wounded Hand Chieftain turned into a weapon by Akhenabi
Miga seyt-Jinnata, Lady—a Chronicler
Muyare sey-Iyora—High Marshal of the Hikeda'ya
Nerudade—philosopher, responsible for escape of Unbeing, father of Yedade
Nezeru seyt-Enduya—Daughter of Lord Viyeki and his mistress Tzoja; travels with Morgan through Aldheorte
Nonao—Lord Viyeki's secretary
Ommu the Whisperer—Singer; former member of the Red Hand; resurrected by Queen Utuk'ku
Pratiki—Prince-Templar, member of the Hamakha Clan; close descendant of Queen Utuk'ku
Queen's Teeth—Queen Utuk'ku's silent personal guard
Saomeji—Singer; a half-mortal member of Makho's Talon
Sogeyu—Singer, one of Akhenabi's trusted underlings
Suno'ku—a famous general, killed in the aftermath of the Storm King's War, wielder of Cold Root and Cold Leaf
Utuk'ku seyt-Hamakha—Norn Queen, Mistress of Nakkiga; last survivor of the Lost Garden
Viyeki sey-Enduya, Lord—High Magister of the Order of Builders, father of Nezeru
White Foxes—mortal name for Norns
Xaniko—Hikeda'ya dragonslayer exiled from Nakkiga
Xoka—weapons-master at White Snail Castle
Yaarike sey-Kijana, Lord—Viyeki's predecessor as High Magister of the Order of Builders
Yedade—Hikeda'ya philosopher
Zuniyabe—High Celebrant of Nakkiga

TINUKEDA'YA

Chikri—tree-dweller creatures in Aldheorte Forest
Conn—a Hernystiri from Crannhyr
Daffn—a Hernystiri from Crannhyr

Delver—a mortal name for a type of Tinukeda'ya skilled at shaping stone: also called "Dwarrow" or "Dverning" or "Domhaini"
Dor-Sinno—a Tinukeda'ya from Nakkiga
Geloë—a wise woman, called "Valada Geloë"; killed during the Storm King's War; also known as "Sa-Ruyan Geloë" and "Sa-Ruyan Ela"
Ghants—chitinous Wran-dwelling creatures
Giants—large, shaggy, manlike creatures, sometimes called "Hunën"
Goh Gam Gar—a large, old giant who helped Makho's Talon catch a dragon
Hidden, the—Tinukeda'ya hiding from their masters in Nakkiga
Kai-Ono—co-ruler of Skyglass Lake
Kilpa—manlike aquatic creatures
Kuyu-kun Sa'Vao—current voice of the Dreaming Sea; Tinukeda'ya racial memory
Mardae, Sa-Ruyan—father of Geloë, son of Xaniko and Lady (Sa-Ruyan) Ona
Min-Senya—a Delver
Mother, The—described by the Tinukeda'ya as the "angel made of lights"
Niskies—a type of Tinukeda'ya who serve aboard ships; they "sing the kilpa down"
Pamon Kes—Hakatri's most loyal servant
Ruyan Ká—the last navigator
Ruyan Vé—fabled patriarch of the Tinukeda'ya; called "The Navigator"
Tih-Rumi—acolyte to Kuyu-Kun
Vao—Tinukeda'ya name for their people
Yek Fisher—a half-mortal summoned to Tanakirú
Zin-Seyvu—leader of a Tinukeda'ya group traveling through Aldheorte Forest

OTHERS

Adversary, the—the Aedonite devil
Fecca the Gemmian—a man from Warinsten Island, henchman of Pasevalles
Fortis the Recluse—a 6th century bishop on Warinsten Island; writer of an infamous book
Friar, the—a religious man summoned to Tanakirú
Halwende—a northerner summoned to Tanakirú
Munshazou—a woman of the Southern Islands, Pryrates' housekeeper
Qo'sei—one of the first mortal peoples in Osten Ard

CREATURES

Cloudfoot—Ayaminu's horse, given to Jiriki
Falku—Snenneq's ram

Fantail—a bird in a Wran legend
Keeva—Tace Odhran's goat
Mite—a cat in the Hayholt
Ooki—Sisqi's ram
Scand—a donkey, usually ridden by Tiamak
Shadowswift—Ki'ushapo's black mare
Snowdrake—dragon killed by Kuroyi of Anvi'janya
Uro'eni—Sithi name for the ogre of Misty Vale
Vaqana—Binabik's wolf companion

PLACES

Aelfwent—a great river in Aldheorte Forest; called *T'si Suhyasei* in Sithi
Aldheorte—also known as Oldheart; a large forest to the north and east of Erkynland
Ansis Pelippé—capital of Perdruin
Anvi'janya—a famous Sithi settlement in Aldheorte forest
Asu'a—Sithi name of the Hayholt, their most important city before it fell to mortals
Ban Farrig—Aengas's family home
Bayun Risa—"Risa City," largest settlement on Risa Island
Blue Cavern—Nakkiga home of weaving spiders
Blue Mud Lake—a body of water south of the mountains of Yiqanuc
Carn Buic—seat of Tace Odhran, a few leagues from Hernysadharc
Carn Inbarh—a castle in Hernystir; home of Earl Murdo, Eolair's ally
Cold, Slow Halls—a place of torture in Nakkiga
Coolblood—a river and valley in Aldheorte Forest
Crannhyr—ancient Hernystiri town on the coast
Crossroads—a crumbling ruin on Sesuad'ra
Da'ai Chikiza—ruined Sithi city in Aldheorte Forest; called "Tree of the Singing Wind," one of the nine Gardenborn cities
Eastern Wastes—the eastern lands beyond the grasslands
Elvritshalla—capital of Rimmersgard
Engby—Sludig's earldom In Rimmersgard
Enki-e-Shao'saye—one of the Nine Sithi Cities
Erchester—capital of Erkynland and seat of the High Throne
Ereb Irigú—a site of battle between Sithi and Rimmersmen centuries ago
Erkynland—a kingdom in central Osten Ard
Fellmere Castle—first refuge of Osric's army after retreating to Fingerdale
Fingerdale—valley around Winstowe Castle in eastern Erkynland
Flowering Hills—a region in Aldheorte Forest; home of Himano
Forbidden Hills—Sithi stronghold, home of Khendraja'aro

Frostmarch, the—a wintry region in northern Hernystir and southern Rimmersgard
Gemmia—old name for Warinsten from the time of the Nabbanai Imperium
Go-jao'e—Little Boats; name for small Sithi settlements in Aldheorte forest
Granary Tower—a tower in the Hayholt, once Prince John Josua's chambers and study
Grianspog, the—largest mountain range in Hernystir
Hayholt, the—seat of the High Throne of Osten Ard, located above Erchester
Heartwood Road—old Sithi road through Aldheorte Forest
Hernysadharc—the capital of Hernystir
Hernystir—a kingdom in the west of Osten Ard
Hewenshire—town and county in Erkynland
Hikehikayo—one of the nine Gardenborn cities, located in the far northwest; called Cloud Castle and long abandoned
Hjeldin's Tower—a sealed tower of ominous repute in the Hayholt
H'ran Go-jao—the most easterly of the Go-jao'e (Little Boats)
Holy Tree Tower—tower in the Hayholt
House of Dunn—mythical home of Hernystiri god of death
Inner Bailey—the innermost portion of Hayholt Castle
Jao é-Tinukai'i—former settlement of Sithi in Aldheorte Forest, now deserted
Kementari—one of the nine Gardenborn cities, now lost
Khand—a lost and fabled mortal kingdom; also known as Khandia
Kushiba—the Beak, a mountain in Aldheorte Forest
Kwanitupul—the biggest city in the Wran
Kynslagh—a lake in central Erkynland
Laestfinger—a river on Erkynland's eastern border, called "Fingerlast" by Thrithings-folk
Little Erkyn—district of Hernysadharc
Main Row—major thoroughfare in the city of Erchester
Market Square—a marketplace in Erchester
Meremund—Erkynlandish town on the rivers Greenwade and Gleniwent; birthplace of Queen Miriamele
Middle Bailey—the court between the Inner and Outer Baileys of Hayholt Castle
Mintahoq—a mountain of Yiqanuc; Binabik's home
Naarved—a city in the west of Rimmersgard
Nabban—a duchy in the southern part of Osten Ard; former seat of empire
Nad Glehs—home of Countess Rhona and Count Nial in Hernystir
Nad Mullach—Count Eolair's home in eastern Hernystir
Naglimund—a fortress in northern Erkynland; place of battles during the Storm King's War, captured by Utuk'ku's armies; also called "Ujin" or "Ujin-do"—"the Trap"
Nakkiga—Gardenborn city beneath Stormspike Mountain, meaning "Mask of Tears"; home of the Hikeda'ya (Norns)

Nartha—a river that runs north/south along the base of the Wealdhelm
Narrowdark, the—also known as *Dekusao*, a river near Misty Vale
Nascadu—desert lands south of the Wran
Nearulagh Gate—main entrance to the Hayholt
Ocean Indefinite and Eternal—crossed by Keida'ya and Tinukeda'ya on their way to Osten Ard
Osten Ard—the land, home of mortals and immortals alike (Rimmerspakk for "Eastern Land")
Outer Bailey—the outermost of Hayholt Castle's enclosures
Peja'ura—a Sithi settlement in Aldheorte
Perdruin—an island in the Bay of Emettin
Quarely Maid, The—an inn in Erchester
Red Pig Lagoon—Jesa's home village in the Wran
Redenturine Hill—one of the hills of Nabban, seat of the Sancellan Aedonitis
Repository—the archive at Anvi'janya
Rimmersgard—duchy in the north of Osten Ard
St. Sutrin's—the cathedral in Erchester
St. Tankred's—the cathedral in Meremund
Sesuad'ra—the Stone of Farewell
Silken Span, the—bridge leading to Anvi'janya, connecting two mountain peaks
Snakeskin Pass—long canyon between Coolblood River valley and Narrowdark River valley
Shisae'ron—a valley in the southwestern part of Aldheorte Forest; birthplace of Tanahaya
Storm Cove—a sheltered bay on the Kynslaugh
Swertclif—the heights just outside Hayholt; site of the royal cemetery
Taig, the—a wooden castle in Hernysadharc, home to Hernystir's ruling family
Tanakirú—a valley in Aldheorte Forest, also known as "Misty Vale" or "the Valley of Mists"; specifically, the far northern end of the valley
Tethtain's Way—a main street through Hernysadharc
Thrithings—plain of grassland in the southeast of Osten Ard, divided into High Thrithings, Meadow Thrithings, and Lake Thrithings
Torickshire—an Erkynlandish county
Tumet'ai—one of the Nine Cities of the Sithi
Tzo—greatest city of the Lost Garden
Ujin—fortress, place of Ruyan Vé's confinement: means "The Trap"
Urmsheim—a fabled mountain in the far north, home of dragons
Venyha Do'sae—also known as the Lost Garden, the fabled place from whose destruction the Keida'ya fled
Village Grove—Tiamak's original home in the Wran
Wealdhelm—a range of hills in Erkynland, called Yi'ire Highlands by the Zida'ya

White Snail Castle—a Hikeda'ya castle on the shoulder of Nakkiga Mountain
Winstowe Castle—a fortress in the Fingerdale, site of sieges and battles
Winwood—forest surrounding Winstowe
Willow Hall—the place in Shisae'ron where Tanahaya grew up
Wran, the—vast marshland in southern Osten Ard, called "Varn" by Thrithings-folk
Wormscale Gorge—location of a Zida'ya fortress in Aldheorte, mouth of Snakeskin Pass
Wormscale Lake—a lake in Aldheorte Forest, in Snakeskin Pass
Yiqanuc—home of the Qanuc people; also known as the Trollfells

THINGS

Aedonites—followers of the faith of Usires Aedon
Aetheric Whispers, The—a banned and dangerous book
Aucteris—a leadership position appointed by the Dominiate of Nabban
Book of the Aedon—the Aedonite holy book
Breathing Harp—Master Witness in Nakkiga, stolen from Kementari
Catechism of Selection—Norn celebrants' chant over Yedade's Box
Changeling—another name for the Tinukeda'ya
Cold Leaf—witchwood dagger
Cold Root—Makho's witchwood sword, now in Nezeru's possession
Devan rebec—a stringed instrument, originally from Deva
Dragonbone Chair—the seat of the High Throne, made from the bones of Shurakai
Dream-road—place where dreams, life, and death connect and mingle
Drukhi's Day—Hikeda'ya holiday commemorating Queen Utuk'ku's dead son, celebrated during Stone-Listener's Moon
Edicts of Cormac—Hernystiri governing principles
Elysiamansa, The—ship that brings Miriamele and Jesa from Meremund to Hayholt
Elysians—followers of Elysia, the mother of Usires Aedon
Erkynguard—the royal guard of the Hayholt
Fatwood—resinous heartwood dug from pine stumps
Fern beer—a Wran beverage
First Wave—a sigil of the Navigator
Fulaich—the ancient festival of the Morriga
Gardenborn—all who came to Osten Ard from Venyha Do'sae (the Garden)
Granisian Order—Aedonite order of monks
Great Year—a Gardenborn time span, around 60 human years
Hall of Flowers—a cavern underneath Kushiba
Hall of the Dominiate—gathering-place of the the ruling council of Nabban

Hikeda'yasao—the language of Nakkiga
Holy Tree Tower—replaced fallen Green Angel Tower at the Hayholt
Hour of Passage—part of the Years-End ceremony
Jingizu—Ineluki's terrible sword: "Sorrow"
Keida'ya—common name of Zida'ya and Hikeda'ya: "Children of the Witchwood"
Kei-t'si—"witchwood blood," an elixir made from witchwood fruit
Kei-vishaa—witchwood pollen used by the Gardenborn with hallucinatory and poisonous effects
Landborn—those Sithi and Norns born after the Gardenborn's arrival in Osten Ard
Mother Church—the Aedonite church
Ni'yo—a glowing sphere
Parting, the—the separation of the Sithi and Norns, solemnized at Sesuad'ra
Pauh Morriga—"the Morriga's cook-pot," a torture by fire
Puju—bread made from the white barley grown in the cold valleys below Stormspike
Queen's device, the—Utuk'ku's signature rune
Queen's Huntsman—an honorific given by Queen Utuk'ku to a skilled mortal servant
Sacrifice—a Zida'ya of the soldiers' order
Saya-vishaa—a medicinal drug made from cave mushrooms, used to increase fighting spirit
Seastone—a Sa'onserei family heirloom, made from a shard of stone that formed the Mist Lamp
Shameful Knock—surrender-gesture by those who fail Yedade's Box
Shent—a strategic board game played by the Keida'ya
Snakesplitter—Prince Morgan's sword
Stone Frog—symbol of Viyeki's Clan Enduya
Sunfruit—called "kraile" by Sithi, "kerala" by Wran-folk
Sunrise House—Sithi clan of Cheka'iso Amber-Locks
Talon—a squad of five elite, specially-trained Hikeda'ya warriors and assassins
Tace—an old Hernystiri word for chieftain
Three Who Are One—a terrible, powerful spell, unused since the Lost Garden
Thanemoot—a yearly gathering of all Thrithings clans at Blood Lake
Tree, the—"Holy Tree" or "Execution Tree"; symbol of Usires Aedon's execution and the Aedonite faith
Trow screen—a partition of carved wood or stone separating nave and chancel in an Aedonite church; named for the old Erkynlandish word for "tree"
Unbeing—an ancient threat which utterly destroyed the Garden
Westerling—language originating from Waristen Island; now the common tongue of humans in Osten Ard
Witchwood—rare wood from trees brought from the Garden; can be worked until as hard as metal

Witchwood Crown, the—Sithi: "kei-jáyha." A circlet for heroes; a group of witchwood trees; a move in Shaynat/Shent
Witness—a Sithi object used to talk over long distances and enter the Road of Dreams, oftentimes made from a dragon scale
Yedade's Box—a Hikeda'ya device for separating children into orders

STARS AND CONSTELLATIONS

Bend of the River—one of the stars of Venyha Do'sae, the Lost Garden
Blade—a star of Venyha Do'sae
Dancer—a star of Venyha Do'sae
Dásaku, the Winter-Lantern—a Sithi constellation
Horned Owl—Erkynlandish
Lamp—Erkynlandish
Lantern—Hikeda'ya
Pool—a star of Venyha Do'sae
Staff—Erkynlandish
Swallower—a star of Venyha Do'sae

HOLIDAYS

Jonever 31—Saint Asak's Day
Feyever 2—Candlemansa
Marris 25—Elysiamansa
Marris 31—Fool's Night
Avrel 1—All Fool's Day
Avrel 3—St. Vultinia's Day
Avrel 24—St. Dinan's Day
Avrel 30—Stoning Night
Maia 1—Belthainn Day
Yuven 23—Midsummer's Eve
Tiyagar 15—Saint Sutrin's Day
Anitul 1—Hlafmansa
Septander 29—Saint Granis' Day
Octander 30—Harrows Eve
Novander 1—Soul's Day
Decander 21—Saint Tunath's Day
Decander 24—Aedonmansa
Asak's Eve—year-end holiday in the Wran city of Kwanitupul
Embolg—Hernystiri holiday
Queen's Rule Festival—equivalent to Year-Dancing Festival, celebrated by the Hikeda'ya

DAYS OF THE WEEK

Sunday, Moonday, Tiasday, Udunsday, Drorsday, Frayday, Satrinsday

MONTHS OF THE YEAR

AEDONITE	SITHI	HIKEDA'YA	THRITHING
Jonever	Raven	Ice-Mother	Second Blue Moon
Feyever	Serpent	Serpent	Third Blue Moon
Marris	Hare	Wind-Child	First Green Moon
Avrel	Grieving Sister	Dove	Second Green Moon
Maia	Nightingale	Cloud-Song	Third Green Moon
Yuven	Lantern Bearer	Otter	First Yellow Moon
Tiyagar	Fox	Stone-Listener	Second Yellow Moon
Anitul	Lynx	Lynx	Third Yellow Moon
Septander	Crane	Sky-Singer	First Red Moon
Octander	Tortoise	Tortoise	Second Red Moon
Novander	Rooster	Fire-Knight	Third Red Moon
Decander	Moon-Herald	Wolf	First Blue Moon

KNUCKLEBONES

Qanuc auguring tools
Patterns include:

- Wingless Bird
- Fish-Spear
- The Shadowed Path
- Torch at the Cave-Mouth
- Balking Ram
- Clouds in the Pass
- The Black Crevice
- Unwrapped Dart
- Circle of Stones
- Mountain Dancing
- Masterless Ram
- Slippery Snow
- Unexpected Visitor
- Unnatural Birth
- No Shadow

THE EIGHT SHIPS

Lantern Bearer, Singing Fire, Time of Gathering, Jakoya's Dream, Dance of Sacrifice, Sacred Seed, Gate Opener, Cloud of Birds

HIKEDA'YA ORDERS

Order, Ordination, Ordinal
Order House—actual location of Order's school, offices
Orders mentioned: Sacrifices; Whisperers; Echoes; Singers; Builders; Chroniclers; Tillers; Celebrants; Gatherers

THRITHINGS CLANS AND THEIR THRITHINGS

Adder—Lake
Antelope—Meadow
Bison—High
Black Bear—Meadow
Crane or "Kragni"—Lake
Fitch—Lake
Fox—High
Grouse—High
Kestrel—Lake
Lynx—Lake
Polecat—Lake
Sparrow—High
Stallion or "Mehrdon"—High
White Spot Deer—Lake
Wood Duck—Lake
Other clans include:

Badger, Boar, Bustard, Great-horn Bull, Otter, Pheasant, Roebuck, Snake, Sparrowhawk, Vulture, Whipsnake, and Wild Horse

WORDS AND PHRASES

QANUC

Croohok—"Rimmersgarder"
Da muqang—"Enough, now!"

Hinik aia—"Get back"
Mamiq-iq!—"Show me!"
Mintahoq odo Yiqanuc pikak! —"Mintahoq fights for Yiqanuc!"
Ninit—"Come"
Nukapik—"betrothed"
Nukapo—"spouse"
Shummuk—"wait"

SITHI (KEIDA'YASO)

Hageloi—an unclean or evil creation
Hikka Staja—"Arrow bearer"
Kei-in dho Keida'ya—"Witchwood seeds for the Witchwood Children"
srinyedu—"string art"
Staja ame—"white arrow"
Shin'iu—the spirit of a place, the essence which makes it what it is; Hikeda'ya: "Zhinju"
Uro'eni—"ogre"
Zida'ya—"Dawn Children"

NORN (HIKEDA'YASO)

Enduya, s'a-e!—"My Enduya! (clan)"
Hikeda'ya—"Cloud Children"
Uro'ye—giant
Zhin'ju—the spirit of a place, the essence which makes it what it is

OTHER

Jom mologi—Wran term meaning "death hill"
Higdaja—Giants' name for Hikeda'ya
Tangaru—Giants' name for Tanakirú, also called "the valley that sings"